EVERYMAN,
I WILL GO WITH THEE,
AND BE THY GUIDE,
IN THY MOST NEED
TO GO BY THY SIDE

JAMES ELLROY

THE UNDERWORLD U.S.A. TRILOGY

VOLUME I
AMERICAN TABLOID
THE COLD SIX THOUSAND

WITH AN INTRODUCTION
BY THOMAS MALLON

EVERYMAN'S LIBRARY
Alfred A. Knopf   New York   London   Toronto

389

THIS IS A BORZOI BOOK
PUBLISHED BY ALFRED A. KNOPF

First included in Everyman's Library, 2019

American Tabloid
Copyright © 1995 by James Ellroy
First published in the United States by Alfred A. Knopf, a division of
Random House, Inc., New York, and in Great Britain by Century,
London, in 1995.

The Cold Six Thousand
Copyright © 2001 by James Ellroy
First published in the United States by Alfred A. Knopf, a division of
Random House, Inc., New York, and in Great Britain by Century,
London, in 2001.

Introduction copyright © 2019 by Thomas Mallon
Select Bibliography and Chronology copyright © 2019
by Everyman's Library

www.randomhouse/everymans
www.everymanslibrary.co.uk

ISBN 978-1-101-90804-4 (US)
978-1-84159-389-0 (UK)

A CIP catalogue reference for this book is available from
the British Library

Typography by Peter B. Willberg

Book design by Barbara de Wilde and Carol Devine Carson

Typeset in the UK by Input Data Services, Isle Abbotts, Somerset

Printed and bound in Germany by GGP Media GmbH, Pössneck

CONTENTS

———

INTRODUCTION

In a review of *American Tabloid* (1995), William T. Vollmann made the extraordinary and correct observation that "every sentence advances the plot" in James Ellroy's 576-page novel. The two subsequent books of Ellroy's "Underworld U.S.A. Trilogy" are even longer, even more densely sequenced, so I won't make a fool's attempt to describe their narrative action. Nor will I even try to expound upon their themes—no matter that they show Ellroy long ago embracing what everyone now calls the Deep State, whose extreme-high and extreme-low hidden forces squeeze history out of the vast citizenry caught in the middle. What I can only hope to suggest is the *intimacy* of these novels, how they remain wondrously suffused, even in moments of spectacular mayhem, with the inner torments of those inflicting violence on others. These relentlessly plotted books are finally not about events; they're about characters.

Some are tormented by crude certainties and brutal secrets. The most important of these is Pete Bondurant, Ellroy's "big Caucasian madman," forty years old in 1960, who began piling up a vertiginous body count in the battle of Saipan ("He killed them and killed them and killed them"). Those deaths, along with the subsequent murder of his own brother back home, become the first reel of Bondurant's "*standard* nightmares." Later, he is at the bone-breaking beck and call of Jimmy Hoffa and Howard Hughes and a rogue CIA officer named John Stanton. Though he rampages freely, Pete has the wild sentimentality of a convict: he is able to strangle Betty McDonald, an inconvenient witness, before becoming helplessly devoted to her cat. For years he has the love of Barb Jahelka—dedicated, damaged, implicated—but he has to worry he'll lose her over his involvement in Jack Kennedy's death and then Bobby's. It is an absurd triumph of Ellroy's artistry, a testament to his own depths of feeling, that Bondurant remains believable.

But it is the characters tormented by ambivalence, the ones sickened more by doubt than gore, who compel the reader's own disturbed devotion. In *American Tabloid* and *The Cold Six Thousand* (2001), we are ensnared by the existence of Ward Littell, a lifelong weathervane in an unending electrical storm. This orphan "raised in Jesuit foster homes," an ex-seminarian and trained lawyer turned disillusioned FBI agent, continually divides into "Angry Ward" and "Cautious Ward." He is flooded with guilt, drink, paranoia and masochism; Hoover sees him as "the world's most dangerous wimp." Drifting left, he gives his heart to the young rackets-busting Robert Kennedy, even while he's supposed to be undermining him for Hoover. Littell embarks on a Grail quest for the Teamsters' secret pension-fund books, a potential offering to RFK, but ends up being pulled into the servitude of the Mafia and of Hoffa himself. Five months of sobriety teaches Littell one essential fact: "You're capable of anything."

"Anything" runs from maudlin tenderness to multiple murders; even to "an ugly wave of love" for Hoover. He'll imagine he's protecting Martin Luther King's movement even as he's duped into a white-supremacist plot. After the decade's trinity of King and Kennedy assassinations, he'll be able to cry: "Their blood's on me." And he will be left with no alternative to the self-erasure he's been seeking all along. As he exits the trilogy, the reader is left terrified of his own suppressions and contradictions.

The novels are driven by men whose longings and impulses cannot suppress *or* resolve themselves. Wayne Tedrow, Jr., lives through the last two volumes in the same kind of polarized pain that Littell endures for the first two. A young officer "considered incorruptible by Las Vegas Police standards," Wayne is sent to Dallas by his father, a friend of Hoover's, just prior to the Kennedy assassination. ("You never know when you might rub shoulders with history.") He experiences incestuous flirtation, revenge-fucking and finally a tender, intense connection with his stepmother, Janice. Wayne Jr. despises his own race hatred and spends his psychological energy trying to control and atone for it, even as he keeps killing blacks. Sonny Liston, the onetime heavyweight champion and occasional goon-savant of the trilogy, puts it this way: "That boy just didn't have no hate for anybody, but shit kept finding him. He kept trying to find niggers to kill and niggers to save, and this woman of his thought it was all the same goddamn thing."

Wayne Sr. explains his son to Ward Littell, who ought to know: "Junior was a hider. Junior was a watcher. Junior lit flames. Junior torched. Junior lived in his head." By the spring of '68 he'll be "muscling" Sirhan Sirhan toward RFK at the Ambassador Hotel, and when he watches the riots that follow the killing of Martin Luther King, he thinks: "*I Did That.*" When the Nixon years begin, he abets the Mob's scheme to recreate its old Cuba-style action in the Dominican Republic—until he flips again and literally cuts the shackles from the slaves building the casinos.

The greatest of Ellroy's doomed ambivalents, and the biggest stretch of his imagination, is Marshall E. Bowen—"Anomaly. Incongruity. Anti-white hate-tract subscriber, potential L.A. cop"—who doesn't come along until the last volume, *Blood's a Rover* (2009). This African-American who infiltrates left-wing and black militant groups appears cool and pacific but actually "lives for the game." On the downlow sexually and in every other way possible, Bowen keeps a journal about the mental vise he lives inside: "As always, I abut that maddening disjuncture: the viable construction of black identity and the dubious construction of revolution, as implemented by criminal scum seeking to cash in on legitimate social grievance and cultural trend." (He can't live authentically even in the diary; it ends up being doctored by those who need to frame him.) Bowen finds romantic escape in his obsession—shared by a number of characters, including the white-racist cop Scotty Bennett—with the years-old unsolved heist of an armored car full of emeralds. But like Littell and Tedrow he can reach only death, not fulfillment.

It's the same with Dwight Holly, another rogue FBI agent who figures largely in the last two volumes, a man Hoover calls "my obedient Yalie thug." Holly shoulders the guilt of some long-ago drunk-driving murders; heads up the racist Operation Black Rabbit; becomes enthralled with two different women of the far left and is nearly, but not quite, persuaded to take out Hoover. In Ellroy's political-psychological calculus, he too has to die, unresolved and unredeemed.

Which leaves a transfiguring space for the most unlikely character of them all, the real-life Don Crutchfield, a twenty-three-year-old wheelman for an L.A. private investigator, universally regarded as a "dipshit," who stumbles into the last volume of the trilogy. Crutch seems at first to be a throwaway, a goofball version of the author's feckless youth: his résumé includes Ellroy's legendary phase of peeping, B&E and panty-sniffing, as well as a mother who's been missing, if not actually dead, since he was ten. Crutch could have remained a harmless bit of authorial self-indulgence, Ellroy's comic riff on his own over-interpreted personal mythology, but the character gradually becomes the most important figure in the whole three-volume epic of violence and longing. It is this dipshit who finally pulls Excalibur from its bloody stone; it is this boy-man who hatches out of his own obsessions to receive anointing.

Crutch begins as an emulator, an overgrown Robin to dirty Batman-like cop Scotty Bennett and the political mass-killer Jean-Philippe Mesplede. He will decide he wants a piece of the mayhem he overhears and initially fears, and will be swept into anti-Castro scalpings; the Mob's Dominican scheme; the ramifying mystery of the emeralds. But his real fixation remains "the knife-scar woman," the peerlessly rendered Joan Rosen Klein, Ellroy's avatar of twentieth-century American radicalism and a compulsive passion for Dwight Holly as well. Crutch's crusade for connection with her turns him into "the nexus of great and startling events," a position that truly, in a different way from what we expected, makes him the analog of Ellroy, who has this whole fictional world in his hands. He explains to Joan the motive for everything he's done: "So women will love me." For women, read Joan, who contains multitudes.

Ellroy himself has said that his books "are all about one thing and one thing only, a man meets a woman." But in the next breath of the same interview, the author stated: "I'm a Christian: the books are about redemption." Crutch has that covered, too, more fully than any other character in the trilogy. He is not, even early on, just a peeper. He is learning to see not only through the window but also to see himself in the glass. His action becomes bolder; his vision keener. But one never supplants the other. When he finally makes love to Joan, he watches himself doing it.

Crutch will devote his whole life to avenging her and destroying Hoover, who has called so many tunes in the trilogy, and whose files are themselves a paper castle of voyeurism. Ellroy may be a man of the right, but his fictional alter ego is the one who completes a leftwards political transformation that the ambivalents only begin and then abort. A conservative might say that Ellroy, like Milton, is of the devil's party without knowing it, but the author rejects any notion of apostasy. *Blood's a Rover* is what it is because a real-life Joan entered *Ellroy's* real life. He wrote it for her.

After Hoover and his files meet their fate, the transcendent Crutch, like Ishmael, becomes the only one left to tell the tale. "God gave me a restless temperament and a searcher's discipline." Ellroy, who could so easily have remained a dipshit instead of becoming a front-rank artist, allows Crutchfield something he can't allow Littell or Wayne Jr., or Holly or Bowen. He lets him live.

*

SHE LIVES!

Thus, on September 21, 1996, did Ellroy inscribe to me an advance copy of *My Dark Places*. We were in Toledo, Ohio, at a regional convention of the American Booksellers Association, where I was pushing my novel *Dewey Defeats Truman* and James was drumming up business for *My Dark Places*, the story of his unsuccessful but liberating search for the man who had murdered Geneva Hilliker Ellroy in 1958. If the case stayed unsolved, the author's childhood trauma bloomed into a new self-awareness. Ellroy is now conscious that *Blood's a Rover*, more than ten years in the future, would never have been written without the maternal reckoning he experienced in the mid-1990s.

James had published "My Mother's Killer," the dry run for *My Dark Places*, in *Gentlemen's Quarterly*, where I was the books columnist and we developed a friendly acquaintance. In Toledo we ran into each other in the hotel elevator and went off for a drink. No, *I* had a drink; James had coffee. I describe him in my diary on that day as "militantly sober"—"for nineteen years," he told me, before diagnosing a number of our publishing colleagues as people ruining themselves with alcohol and cigarettes. "His conversation is as jazzy and juju-ridden as ever," I noted. We talked about the Kennedy assassination, he from the Grassy Knoll and I from the lone-nutter's sniper perch. But what I most took away from the encounter was a sense of James' discipline, his pride in being a man of letters. He has said that he would like to give younger writers, along with an impulse toward "moral fiction and Romanticism," a belief in "meticulous and assiduous planning." The mapping out of his novels is a matter of Homeric, painstaking rigor. It's his outlines, hundreds of pages per book, that allow him "to live improvisationally within the text." No matter how violent and entropic the action on the page may seem, the novels require his obedience to their own laws and consistencies. Freedom follows form. As an artist, Ellroy is closer to Petrarch than to Kerouac.

But he is also a breaker of forms. He has, in fact, reversed the polarity of most historical fiction. Instead of inventing previously nonexistent characters to function as narrative conveniences, means of access to the famous real-life figures in whom the reader is truly interested, Ellroy makes *his* creations the focus of reader attention. In the underworld trilogy, Robert F. Kennedy is of no importance except for how he acts upon the psychology of Ward Littell. Ellroy's Howard Hughes and especially J. Edgar Hoover—reptilian, slightly camp, brilliantly bent and ultimately demented—provide over-the-top entertainment, but *they* are the foils, the vehicles to plunge us into the churning inner lives of Ellroy's own newborns, such as Pete Bondurant and Dwight Holly. However brilliantly drawn, the major-but-finally-minor historical figures never provide the viewpoint and never lead us to the truth.

The invented characters and the reincarnations share an extended opus that is brought to life from an astonishing arsenal of techniques. Start with Ellroy's parodic skills: they derive from an avid and incomparable ear. *Hush-Hush* magazine, the scandal sheet beloved by readers of the L.A. Quartet, alliterates its way to new political life in *American Tabloid*, thanks to Lenny Sands, lounge singer, snitch and now stringer: CANCEROUS CASTRO COMMUNISTICALLY CALCIFIES CUBA WHILE HEROIC HERMANOS HUNGER FOR HOMELAND! FBI wiretap transcripts and memoranda scarcely need the typewriter font they're given in the text; their illusion of authenticity is accomplished by the exactness of their diction. Ellroy is not the first writer to deliver hilarious Mob dialogue ("It's Mount Ararat, Jimmy. Mount Vesuvius is in fucking Yellowstone Park"), but unlike most practitioners of *noir* he knows the limits of cleverness. "Repartee is one thing," says Joe Kennedy's supposed illegitimate daughter, "and the truth is another."

Slang, in both the narration and dialogue, is always operating on two levels, the literal and the ironic; it may be amusing, but it's to be respected, sifted for meaning. When *The Cold Six Thousand* takes us to Vietnam, the French-Viet patois—all "diphthongs and shouts"—proves a fresh aural bonanza. It'll be the same when *Blood's a Rover* gets to Haiti: "Tinted windows shaded all the *pauvre* shit outside." If the right language, the right words, don't exist, Ellroy makes them up—letting compound adjectives take life from a verb: it's "smack-your-head hot," and the little Dominican houses have "boing-your-eyes paint jobs."

Every one of those sentences advancing the plot still has to have peripheral vision, a strobe-lit descriptive capacity to capture the world we're marauding through. The economy of Ellroy's representations consistently stuns. During the FBI raid of a Cuban exiles' camp, "a big bilingual roar went up." That's all you require. JFK's marriage vows are "expedient and whimsical"; his funeral will give rise to "epidemic boo-hoo." A woman widowed by Teamster violence "smelled like Vicks VapoRub and cigarettes." She lives.

Ellroy regards participles with about the same contempt he does drink. Why would he let them slow him down, take the edge off his pacing and perceptions? "Shoes went thunk." Period. The action typically feels both immediate and habitual; it's lyric *and* refrain. "Time slogged. Wayne yawned. Wayne stretched. Wayne picked his nose." The author goes beyond keeping his verbs active. Again and again he gives agency to theoretically inanimate objects: "Wood chips sliced his face . . . mulch slammed up against his goggles"; "Blood-soaked feathers billowed." *Everything* lives. And every tableau is *vivant*:

They killed time. The jumbo pad let them kill it separately.
  Chucky watched spic TV. King Carlos buzzed his serfs long-distance. Pete fantasized ninety-nine ways to murder Ward Littell.

Success depends not just on perfect pitch, but also on superb period detail—Wayne Jr. goes through someone's kitchen drawers on January 12, 1964, finding "flatware and Green Stamps"—and the knowledge, before you describe something like a wiretap, of how it actually works: "House-to-car bug feeds always ran rough."

When it's just gossip about celebrities, sex in Ellroy is good, guffawing, *Hush-Hush* fun: "Bing Crosby knocked up Dinah Shore. Dinah got twin Binglets scraped at a clap clinic in Cleveland." When it's between the major characters he's created himself, it's a holy, serious business—rarely seen with any explicitness or at any length. It's desperate, intense sex for desperate, intense people. Barb's "big veins and big freckles looked like nothing [Pete had] ever seen. He kissed them and bit them and pushed her into the wall with his mouth." The most moving of the sex scenes occurs at the end of *The Cold Six Thousand*, when Wayne Jr. sleeps with his cancer-ridden stepmother, Janice: "She tasted sick. It stunned him. The taste settled in. He tasted her inside. He kissed her new scars. Her breath fluttered thin." Sex is collusive, deep need reaching to deep need, each drowning the other. Surface sex bores Ellroy as much as the "small lives" he sees as the *cuisine-minceur* subject matter of most American literary fiction.

His great invented characters, those ambivalents, may be the blood and bone of the saga, but even as we inhabit them, follow what they have at stake, dodge their dangers and nauseate on their guilts, Ellroy never makes them "point-of-view" characters in the ways conventional to fiction. We do not come to them via the "close third person"—that narrative staple in which echoes of a character's diction and thought processes nearly, but never quite, turn third person into first. At regular intervals the characters are called—pulled up short—by their proper names instead of pronouns. No matter how deep inside them Ellroy goes, the narrative voice always remains the narrator's. Except for brief stretches—in those "collage" elements of memoranda and transcript and private diaries—the narrator will not surrender it, not even to Crutchfield, except for three italicized pages at the beginning and the very end of *Blood's a Rover*: Ellroy's highest vocal honor. Otherwise, like God or a woman, the author remains free to bug out on these characters anytime he wants to.

For all his certainties of craft, the style of the trilogy morphs from book to book. It shrinks; it grows; it explodes. *American Tabloid* will not feel too alien to those who know the L.A. Quartet. But then, in *The Cold Six Thousand*, the syntax becomes so abbreviated and staccato that noun phrases sometimes go without predicates: "Scotch and wet tobacco. Old barroom smells." After that, according to Ellroy himself, *Blood's a Rover* is more "explicated," easier on the reader sentence for sentence if not chapter by chapter. Its plot is the trilogy's most intricate and interconnected; its impact the deepest and most chastening of the three books.

In the trilogy's sixth paragraph, published more than twenty years ago, Ellroy said it was "time to demythologize" the sixties "and build a new myth from the gutter to the stars." Two thousand pages on, under a rain of emeralds, the reader will find himself, like the author, very much bigger than when he began.

Thomas Mallon

THOMAS MALLON is the author of ten novels, including *Henry and Clara, Dewey Defeats Truman, Fellow Travelers*, and *Watergate*. He is a frequent contributor to *The New Yorker, The New York Times Book Review*, and *The Atlantic*.

SELECT BIBLIOGRAPHY

GRAY, PAUL, "James Ellroy: The Real Pulp Fiction" in *Time Magazine*, 4/10/1995. Review of *American Tabloid*.

MANCALL, JIM, *James Ellroy: A Companion to the Mystery Fiction*, McFarland Companions to Mystery Fiction (series editor Elizabeth Foxwell), McFarland & Company, Inc., Jefferson NC, 2014.

POWELL, STEVEN (ed.), *Conversations with James Ellroy* (Literary Conversations Series), University Press of Mississippi, Jackson MS, revised edition 2012.

POWELL, STEVEN, *James Ellroy: Demon Dog of Crime Fiction*, Palgrave Macmillan UK, Basingstoke, 2016.

VOLLMAN, WILLIAM T., "En Route to the Grassy Knoll" in *The New York Times*, 2/26/1995. Review of *American Tabloid*.

WOLFE, PETER, *Like Hot Knives to the Brain: James Ellroy's Search for Himself*, Lexington Books, Lanham MD, 2006.

DATE	AUTHOR'S LIFE	LITERARY CONTEXT
1948	Born March 4, in Los Angeles, California.	Capote: *Other Voices, Other Rooms*. Carr: *The Skeleton in the Clock*. Faulkner: *Intruder in the Dust*. Mailer: *The Naked and the Dead*.
1949		Algren: *The Man with the Golden Arm*. Miller: *Death of a Salesman*. Orwell: *Nineteen Eighty-Four*. Stout: *The Second Confession*.
1950		Hemingway: *Across the River and Into the Trees*. Highsmith: *Strangers on a Train*. Welch: *A Voice Through a Cloud*.
1951		Jones: *From Here to Eternity*. Salinger: *The Catcher in the Rye*. Williams: *The Rose Tattoo*. Wouk: *The Caine Mutiny*.
1952		Ellison: *Invisible Man*. Hemingway: *The Old Man and the Sea*. O'Connor: *Wise Blood*. Steinbeck: *East of Eden*.
1953		Baldwin: *Go Tell It on the Mountain*. Bellow: *The Adventures of Augie March*. Burroughs: *Junkie*. Chandler: *The Long Goodbye*. Grubb: *The Night of the Hunter*. Levin: *A Kiss Before Dying*. Thompson: *Savage Night*.
1954		Huxley: *The Doors of Perception*. Réage: *Story of O*. Thompson: *Not as a Stranger*.
1955	Late November: parents separate and acrimoniously divorce.	Highsmith: *The Talented Mr. Ripley*. Mailer: *The Deer Park*. Miller: *A View from the Bridge*. Nabokov: *Lolita*.

President Harry Truman signs the Marshall Plan, authorizing $13 billion in aid to Western Europe in the aftermath of World War II. State of Israel established. Soviet blockade of Berlin and Allied airlift. Communist coup in Czechoslovakia. *Apartheid* becomes official policy in South Africa. Assassination of Gandhi.

North Atlantic Treaty signed, creating NATO, involving United States, Canada, and several Western European nations in collective security pact against the Soviet Union. Communists seize power in China after Civil War.

U.S. Senator McCarthy begins investigating alleged Communist infiltration of federal government. Korean War breaks out.

Great flood in U.S. Midwest. First oral contraceptive invented by Luis E. Miramontes.

Eisenhower elected U.S. President. U.S. explodes first thermonuclear bomb at Enewetak Atoll. Richard Nixon's "Checkers speech" on TV attracts audience of 56 million.

Stalin dies. Korean War ends.

Vietnam War begins. Nasser comes to power in Egypt.

Soviet Union and Eastern Bloc allies sign Warsaw Pact as response to NATO. U.S. begins involvement in Vietnam War. Rosa Parks arrested in bus protest in Montgomery, Alabama.

DATE	AUTHOR'S LIFE	LITERARY CONTEXT
1955 *cont.*		O'Connor: *A Good Man Is Hard to Find.*
		Stout: *Before Midnight.*
1956		Algren: *A Walk on the Wild Side.*
		Bellow: *Seize the Day.*
		Ginsberg: *Howl.*
		McBain: *Cop Hater.*
		O'Neill: *Long Day's Journey Into Night.*
1957		Cheever: *The Wapshot Chronicle.*
		Kerouac: *On the Road.*
		Rand: *Atlas Shrugged.*
		Williams: *Baby Doll.*
1958	June 22: mother, Jean Hilliker, murdered in Los Angeles County suburb. The crime remains unsolved.	Carr: *The Dead Man's Knock.*
		MacDonald: *The Executioners.*
		Williams: *Suddenly, Last Summer.*
1959		Bloch: *Psycho.*
		Burroughs: *Naked Lunch.*
		Jackson: *The Haunting of Hill House.*
		Roth: *Goodbye, Columbus.*
1960		Lee: *To Kill a Mockingbird.*
		O'Connor: *The Violent Bear It Away.*
		Updike: *Rabbit* tetralogy (to 1981).
1961		Fanon: *The Wretched of the Earth.*
		Heller: *Catch-22.*
		Highsmith: *This Sweet Sickness.*
		Yates: *Revolutionary Road.*
1962		Albee: *Who's Afraid of Virginia Woolf?*
		Baldwin: *Another Country.*
		Carson: *Silent Spring.*
		Jackson: *We Have Always Lived in the Castle.*
		Kesey: *One Flew Over the Cuckoo's Nest.*
		Nabokov: *Pale Fire.*
1963		Baldwin: *The Fire Next Time.*
		McCarthy: *The Group.*
		Pynchon: *V.*
		Thompson: *The Grifters.*

HISTORICAL EVENTS

Soviet invasion of Hungary. Suez Crisis. Elvis Presley performs "Hound Dog" on U.S. television, scandalizing the nation.

Civil Rights Commission established in U.S. to safeguard voting rights. The U.S. military sustains its first combat fatality in Vietnam.

U.S. launches first satellite, Explorer 1. Integrated circuit created by Jack Kilby. Khrushchev becomes Premier of Soviet Union.

Fidel Castro seizes power in Cuba, forms Socialist government.

Kennedy elected U.S. President.

Attempted U.S. invasion of Cuba, Bay of Pigs. Berlin Wall erected. Yuri Gagarin first man in space.

Cuban Missile Crisis. Telstar, world's first commercial communications satellite, launched and activated.

Kennedy assassinated in Dallas, Lyndon Johnson becomes President. Civil rights leader Martin Luther King Jr. arrested.

DATE	AUTHOR'S LIFE	LITERARY CONTEXT
1964		Bellow: *Herzog*. Berne: *Games People Play*. Cheever: *The Wapshot Scandal*. Selby: *Last Exit to Brooklyn*.
1965	Expelled from high school for truancy and disruptive behavior. Numerous arrests and short county-jail terms for misdemeanor offenses (until 1975).	Herlihy: *Midnight Cowboy*. Mailer: *An American Dream*. Wolfe: *The Kandy-Kolored Tangerine-Flake Streamline Baby*.
1966		Capote: *In Cold Blood*. Pynchon: *The Crying of Lot 49*. Stout: *Death of a Doxy*. Styron: *The Confessions of Nat Turner*. Susann: *Valley of the Dolls*. Thompson: *Hell's Angels*.
1967		Levin: *Rosemary's Baby*. Manchester: *The Death of a President*. Thomas: *Down These Mean Streets*.
1968		Cleaver: *Soul on Ice*. Derleth: *Wisconsin Murders*. Mailer: *Armies of the Night*. Updike: *Couples*. Vidal: *Myra Breckinridge*.
1969		Greenlee: *The Spook Who Sat by the Door*. Leonard: *The Big Bounce*. Oates: *Them*. Puzo: *The Godfather*. Roth: *Portnoy's Complaint*.
1970		Dickey: *Deliverance*. Fo: *Accidental Death of an Anarchist*. Morrison: *The Bluest Eye*.
1971		Blatty: *The Exorcist*. McCarthy: *Birds of America*. O'Connor: *The Complete Stories*. Selby: *The Room*. Stegner: *Angle of Repose*. Wolfe: *The Electric Kool-Aid Acid Test*.

CHRONOLOGY

DATE	AUTHOR'S LIFE	LITERARY CONTEXT
1972		Higgins: *The Friends of Eddie Coyle*. Levin: *The Stepford Wives*. Thompson: *Fear and Loathing in Las Vegas*.
1973		Algren: *The Last Carousel*. Pynchon: *Gravity's Rainbow*. Schumacher: *Small Is Beautiful*. Thompson: *Fear and Loathing on the Campaign Trail '72*.
1974		Benchley: *Jaws*. Heller: *Something Happened*. Jong: *Fear of Flying*. King: *Carrie*. Roth: *My Life as a Man*.
1975		Agee: *Inside the Company*. Bellow: *Humboldt's Gift*. Doctorow: *Ragtime*. Stout: *A Family Affair*.
1976		Selby: *The Demon*. Woodward & Bernstein: *The Final Days*.
1977		Cheever: *Falconer*. Coover: *The Public Burning*. King: *The Shining*. Morrison: *Song of Solomon*.
1978		Levin: *Deathtrap*. Said: *Orientalism*. Selby: *Requiem for a Dream*. Yates: *A Good School*.
1979		Mailer: *The Executioner's Song*. Roth: *The Ghost Writer*. Straub: *Ghost Story*. Styron: *Sophie's Choice*. Wolfe: *The Right Stuff*.
1980		King: *Firestarter*. Ludlum: *The Bourne Identity*. Toole: *A Confederacy of Dunces*.
1981	First novel, *Brown's Requiem*, published.	Carver: *What We Talk About When We Talk About Love*. Irving: *The Hotel New Hampshire*.
1982	Second novel, *Clandestine*, published.	Galeano: *Memory of Fire*. McCullough: *An Indecent Obsession*. Walker: *The Color Purple*.

HISTORICAL EVENTS

U.S. and U.S.S.R. sign Strategic Arms Limitation Treaty (SALT I). Eleven Israeli athletes killed by Arab guerrillas at Olympic Village, Munich.

U.S. Supreme Court suspends capital punishment (until 1976).
Chile: Allende and over 2,500 others killed in coup led by Pinochet.

Nixon resigns after Watergate scandal, Ford becomes U.S. President.

Vietnam War ends. Oil price tops $13.00 a barrel.

Carter becomes U.S. President. China: Chairman Mao dies.

Elvis Presley dies. Egyptian President Sadat recognizes Israel.

Camp David Agreement signed by Carter, Sadat and Israeli prime minister Begin.

Iran: Shah forced into exile, Ayatollah Khomeini establishes Islamic state. U.K.: Thatcher becomes country's first female prime minister. Carter and Brezhnev sign SALT II. Soviet troops occupy Afghanistan.

Reagan elected U.S. President. Iran–Iraq War begins (to 1988). Lech Walesa, shipyard worker, leads strikes in Poland.

Assassination attempt on Reagan, Washington. Egypt: Sadat killed by Islamic fundamentalists.

Beginning of 1980s stock market boom in U.S. Lebanese Civil War: multinational force lands in Beirut to oversee the P.L.O. withdrawal from Lebanon.

DATE	AUTHOR'S LIFE	LITERARY CONTEXT
1983		Mailer: *Ancient Evenings.*
		Vidal: *Duluth.*
1984	Third novel, *Blood on the Moon,* published.	Amis: *Money.*
		King & Straub: *The Talisman.*
		Updike: *The Witches of Eastwick.*
1985	Fourth novel, *Because the Night,* published.	DeLillo: *White Noise.*
		Ellis: *Less than Zero.*
		McCarthy: *Blood Meridian.*
1986	Fifth and sixth novels, *Suicide Hill* and *Silent Terror,* published.	Amis: *The Moronic Inferno.*
		Ford: *The Sportswriter.*
		Hiaasen: *Tourist Season.*
1987	First novel of *The L.A. Quartet, The Black Dahlia,* published.	Auster: *The New York Trilogy.*
		Morrison: *Beloved.*
		Turow: *Presumed Innocent.*
		Wolfe: *The Bonfire of the Vanities.*
1988	Second novel of *The L.A. Quartet, The Big Nowhere,* published.	Chabon: *The Mysteries of Pittsburgh.*
		DeLillo: *Libra.*
		Harris: *The Silence of the Lambs.*
		Rushdie: *The Satanic Verses.*
		Tyler: *Breathing Lessons.*
1989		Irving: *A Prayer for Owen Meany.*
		King: *The Dark Half.*
1990	Third novel of *The L.A. Quartet, L.A. Confidential,* published.	Crichton: *Jurassic Park.*
		Leonard: *Get Shorty.*
		Pynchon: *Vineland.*
1991		Ellis: *American Psycho.*
		Grisham: *The Firm.*
		Madonna: *Sex.*
		Smiley: *A Thousand Acres.*
1992	Concluding novel of *The L.A. Quartet, White Jazz,* published.	Algren: *America Eats.*
		Grisham: *The Pelican Brief.*
		Morrison: *Jazz.*
		Tartt: *The Secret History.*
1993		Proulx: *The Shipping News.*
		Welsh: *Trainspotting.*
1994	Unsuccessfully investigates unsolved murder of Jean Hilliker (until 1995).	Grisham: *The Chamber.*
		King: *Insomniac.*
1995	First novel of *The Underworld U.S.A. Trilogy, American Tabloid,* published, named *Time Magazine*'s Novel of the Year.	Baudrillard: *The Gulf War Did Not Take Place.*
		Ford: *Independence Day.*
		Kane: *Blasted.*
		Roth: *Sabbath's Theater.*

CHRONOLOGY

HISTORICAL EVENTS

U.S. troops invade Granada after government overthrown.

Reagan re-elected in landslide. India: Indira Gandhi assassinated. Famine in Ethiopia.

U.S.S.R.: reform begun under new General Secretary of the Communist Party, Gorbachev.

U.S. bombs Libya. Gorbachev–Reagan summit. Nuclear explosion in Chernobyl, U.S.S.R.

Reagan makes Berlin Wall speech. World population reaches 5 billion.

George Bush elected U.S. President. Soviet troops withdrawn in large numbers from Afghanistan.

Berlin Wall dismantled, Communism collapses in Eastern Europe. U.S.S.R. holds first democratic elections. China: Tiananmen Square masssacre.

Hubble Space Telescope launched during Space Shuttle Discovery mission. South Africa: Nelson Mandela released. Yeltsin elected first leader of Russian Federation after end of Communist rule.
Gulf War begins. War breaks out in former Yugoslavia. South Africa: *Apartheid* ends. Bush and Gorbachev sign START arms reduction treaty.

Clinton elected U.S. President. Riots in Los Angeles.

World Trade Center bombed. Palestinian leader Arafat signs peace agreement with Israeli prime minister Rabin.
South Africa: Mandela's A.N.C. takes power after elections. Rwanda: civil war. Russia takes military action in Chechen Republic.

Oklahoma City bombing: 168 people, including eight Federal Marshals and nineteen children, killed. Israel: Rabin assassinated.

DATE	AUTHOR'S LIFE	LITERARY CONTEXT
1996	*My Dark Places*, memoir of the Jean Hilliker murder investigation, published.	Atwood: *Alias Grace.* Huntington: *The Clash of Civilizations and the Remaking of World Order.* Palahniuk: *Fight Club.* Wallace: *Infinite Jest.*
1997	Much-heralded film version of *L.A. Confidential* released.	Bellow: *The Actual.* DeLillo: *Underworld.* Pynchon: *Mason & Dixon.* Roth: *American Pastoral.*
1998		Bolaño: *The Savage Detectives.* Roth: *I Married a Communist.*
1999		Coatzee: *Disgrace.* Hiaasen: *Sick Puppy.* Southwell: *Conspiracy Theories.* Stephenson: *Cryptonomicon.*
2000		Brown: *Angels & Demons.* Kingsolver: *Prodigal Summer.* Roth: *The Human Stain.*
2001	*The Cold Six Thousand*, second novel of *The Underworld U.S.A. Trilogy*, published.	Frantzen: *The Corrections.* Moore: *Stupid White Men.*
2002		Auster: *The Book of Illusions.* Patchett: *Bel Canto.* Tartt: *The Little Friend.*
2003		Brown: *The Da Vinci Code.* DeLillo: *Cosmopolis.* Gibson: *Pattern Recognition.* Moore: *Dude, Where's My Country?*
2004		Robinson: *Gilead.* Roth: *The Plot Against America.* Stephenson: *Baroque Trilogy* (concludes).
2005		Didion: *The Year of Magical Thinking.* Ellis: *Lunar Park.* Koontz: *Velocity.* Larsson: *The Girl with the Dragon Tattoo.*
2006	Much-scorned film version of *The Black Dahlia* released.	Dawkins: *The God Delusion.* Ford: *Lay of the Land.* McCarthy: *The Road.* Pynchon: *Against the Day.* Updike: *Terrorist.*

CHRONOLOGY

DATE	AUTHOR'S LIFE	LITERARY CONTEXT
2007		Klein: *The Shock Doctrine*.
2008		Bolaño: *2666*.
		Robinson: *Home*.
		Roth: *Indignation*.
2009	*Blood's a Rover*, concluding volume of *The Underworld U.S.A. Trilogy*, published.	Foer: *Eating Animals*.
		Larsson: *The Girl Who Played with Fire*.
		Moore: *The Gate at the Stairs*.
		Prebble: *ENRON*.
		Roth: *The Humbling*.
2010	*The Hilliker Curse*, companion volume to *My Dark Places*, published.	Coover: *Noir*.
		Egan: *A Visit from the Goon Squad*.
		Ferris: *The Unnamed*.
		Larsson: *The Girl Who Kicked the Hornets' Nest*.
		Roth: *Nemesis*.
2011		Child: *The Affair*.
		Patchett: *State of Wonder*.
		Wallace: *The Pale King*.
2012		Ford: *Canada*.
		Leonard: *Raylan*.
		Robinson: *2312*.
2013		Kimmel: *Angry White Men*.
		Tartt: *The Goldfinch*.
2014	*Perfidia*, first novel of *The Second L.A. Quartet*, published.	Grossman: *A Horse Walks into a Bar*.
		Klein: *This Changes Everything*.
2015		Beatty: *The Sellout*.
		Franzen: *Purity*.
		Lee: *Go Set a Watchman*.
		Stephenson: *Seveneves*.
2016		Alderman: *The Power*.
		Smith: *Swing Time*.
2017		Auster: *4 3 2 1*.
		Saunders: *Lincoln in the Bardo*.
		Strout: *Anything Is Possible*.
2018	*This Storm*, second novel of *The Second L.A. Quartet*, in preparation for publication 2019.	Burns: *Milkman*.
		Wolff: *Fire and Fury*.

CHRONOLOGY

HISTORICAL EVENTS

Bush reduces U.S. forces in Iraq; 853 military deaths. Al Gore and U.N. climate scientists win Nobel Peace Prize. Russia: Yeltsin dies.
Barack Obama, Democratic Senator from Illinois, becomes first black presidential nominee.

Ongoing world financial crisis. H1N1 ("swine flu") global pandemic.

Healthcare Reform Bill passed by President Obama. Deepwater Horizon (B.P. rig) oilspill in Gulf of Mexico.

"Arab Spring": uprisings against repressive regimes across Middle East; civil war in Syria. Osama Bin Laden killed by U.S. Navy Seals.

Obama re-elected U.S. President. Mars Science Laboratory ("Curiosity Rover") lands on Mars.

Nelson Mandela and Margaret Thatcher die. Pope Benedict XVI resigns.

Russia annexes Crimea. ISIS declares Islamic Caliphate.

Black Lives Matter protests begin in U.S. Greek debt crisis. France: Islamic terrorists attack offices of satirical magazine *Charlie Hebdo*.

Donald Trump elected U.S. President.

Trump takes up office of President, promising to "make America great again" and fueling rise of populism worldwide.

Trump announces his intention to withdraw the United States from the Iranian nuclear agreement, but negotiates with North Korea's Kim Jong-un over denuclearization. Populism continues to proliferate worldwide.

AMERICAN TABLOID

To
NAT SOBEL

America was never innocent. We popped our cherry on the boat over and looked back with no regrets. You can't ascribe our fall from grace to any single event or set of circumstances. You can't lose what you lacked at conception.

Mass-market nostalgia gets you hopped up for a past that never existed. Hagiography sanctifies shuck-and-jive politicians and reinvents their expedient gestures as moments of great moral weight. Our continuing narrative line is blurred past truth and hindsight. Only a reckless verisimilitude can set that line straight.

The real Trinity of Camelot was Look Good, Kick Ass, Get Laid. Jack Kennedy was the mythological front man for a particularly juicy slice of our history. He talked a slick line and wore a world-class haircut. He was Bill Clinton minus pervasive media scrutiny and a few rolls of flab.

Jack got whacked at the optimum moment to assure his sainthood. Lies continue to swirl around his eternal flame. It's time to dislodge his urn and cast light on a few men who attended his ascent and facilitated his fall.

They were rogue cops and shakedown artists. They were wiretappers and soldiers of fortune and faggot lounge entertainers. Had one second of their lives deviated off course, American History would not exist as we know it.

It's time to demythologize an era and build a new myth from the gutter to the stars. It's time to embrace bad men and the price they paid to secretly define their time.

Here's to them.

PART ONE

SHAKEDOWNS

November–December 1958

I

PETE BONDURANT

(Beverly Hills, 11/22/58)

HE ALWAYS SHOT up by TV light.

Some spics waved guns. The head spic plucked bugs from his beard and fomented. Black & white footage; CBS geeks in jungle fatigues. A newsman said, Cuba, bad juju—Fidel Castro's rebels vs. Fulgencio Batista's standing army.

Howard Hughes found a vein and mainlined codeine. Pete watched on the sly—Hughes left his bedroom door ajar.

The dope hit home. Big Howard went slack-faced.

Room service carts clattered outside. Hughes wiped off his spike and flipped channels. The "Howdy Doody" show replaced the news—standard Beverly Hills Hotel business.

Pete walked out to the patio—pool view, a good bird-dog spot. Crappy weather today: no starlet types in bikinis.

He checked his watch, antsy.

He had a divorce gig at noon—the husband drank lunch alone and dug young cooze. Get *quality* flashbulbs: blurry photos looked like spiders fucking. On Hughes' timecard: find out who's hawking subpoenas for the TWA antitrust divestment case and bribe them into reporting that Big Howard blasted off for Mars.

Crafty Howard put it this way: "I'm not going to fight this divestment, Pete. I'm simply going to stay incommunicado indefinitely and force the price up until I *have* to sell. I'm tired of TWA anyway, and I'm not going to sell until I can realize *at least* five hundred million dollars."

He'd said it pouty: Lord Fauntleroy, aging junkie.

Ava Gardner cruised by the pool. Pete waved; Ava flipped him the bird. They went back: he got her an abortion in exchange for a weekend with Hughes. Renaissance Man Pete: pimp, dope procurer, licensed PI goon.

Hughes and him went *waaay* back.

June '52. L.A. County Deputy Sheriff Pete Bondurant—night watch commander at the San Dimas Substation. That one shitty night: a nigger rape-o at large, the drunk tank packed with howling juiceheads.

This wino gave him grief. "I know you, tough guy. You kill innocent women and your own—"

He beat the man to death barefisted.

The Sheriff's hushed it up. An eyeball witness squealed to the Feds. The L.A. agent-in-charge tagged Joe Wino "Joe Civil Rights Victim."

Two agents leaned on him: Kemper Boyd and Ward J. Littell. Howard Hughes saw his picture in the paper and sensed strong-arm potential. Hughes got the beef quashed and offered him a job: fixer, pimp, dope conduit.

Howard married Jean Peters and installed her in a mansion by herself. Add "watchdog" to his duties; add the world's greatest rent-free doghouse: the mansion next door.

Howard Hughes on marriage: "I find it a delightful institution, Pete, but I also find cohabitation stressful. Explain that to Jean periodically, won't you? And if she gets lonely, tell her that she's in my thoughts, even though I'm very busy."

Pete lit a cigarette. Clouds passed over—pool loungers shivered. The intercom crackled—Hughes was beckoning.

He walked into the bedroom. "Captain Kangaroo" was on TV, the volume down low.

Dim black & white lighting—and Big Howard in deep-focus shadows.

"Sir?"

"It's 'Howard' when we're alone. You know that."

"I'm feeling subservient today."

"You mean you're feeling your oats with your paramour, Miss Gail Hendee. Tell me, is she enjoying the surveillance house?"

"She likes it. She's as hinky of shack jobs as you are, and she says twenty-four rooms for two people smooths things out."

"I like independent women."

"No you don't."

Hughes plumped up his pillows. "You're correct. But I do like the *idea* of independent women, which I have always tried to exploit in my movies. And I'm sure Miss Hendee is both a wonderful extortion partner *and* mistress. Now, Pete, about the TWA divestment . . ."

Pete pulled a chair up. "The process servers won't get to you. I've got every employee at this hotel bribed, and I've got an actor set up in a bungalow two rows over. He looks like you and dresses like you, and I've got call girls going in at all hours, to perpetuate the myth that you still fuck women. I check every man and woman who applies for work here, to make sure the Justice Department doesn't slip a ringer in. All the shift bosses here play the stock market, and for every month you go unfucking-subpoenaed I give them twenty shares of Hughes Tool Company stock apiece. As long as you stay in this bungalow, you won't be served and you won't have to appear in court."

Hughes plucked at his robe—little palsied fidgets. "You're a very cruel man."

"No, I'm *your* very cruel man, which is why you let me talk back to you."

"You're 'my man,' but you still retain your somewhat tawdry private investigator sideline."

"That's because you crowd me. That's because I'm not so good at cohabitation either."

"Despite what I pay you?"

"No, *because* of it."

"For instance?"

"For instance, I've got a mansion in Holmby Hills, but you've got the deed. I've got a '58 Pontiac coupe, but you've got the pink slip. I've got a—"

"This is getting us nowhere."

"Howard, you want something. Tell me what it is and I'll do it."

Hughes tapped his remote-control gizmo. "Captain Kangaroo" blipped off. "I've purchased *Hush-Hush* magazine. My reasons for acquiring a scurrilous scandal rag are twofold. One, I've been corresponding with J. Edgar Hoover, and I want to solidify my friendship with him. We both love the type of Hollywood gossip that *Hush-Hush* purveys, so owning the magazine would be both pleasurable and a smart political move. Second, there's politics itself. To be blunt, I want to be able to smear politicians that I dislike, especially profligate playboys like Senator John Kennedy, who might be running for President against my good friend Dick Nixon in 1960. As you undoubtedly know, Kennedy's father and I were business rivals back in the '20s, and frankly, I hate the entire family."

Pete said, "And?"

"And I know that you've worked for *Hush-Hush* as a 'story verifier,' so I know you understand that aspect of the business. It's a quasi-extortion aspect, so I know it's something you'll be good at."

Pete popped his knuckles. "'Story verification' means 'Don't sue the magazine or I'll hurt you.' If you want me to help out that way, fine."

"Good. That's a start."

"Wrap it up, Howard. I know the people there, so tell me who's going and who's staying."

Hughes flinched—just a tad. "The receptionist was a Negro woman with dandruff, so I fired her. The stringer and so-called 'dirt digger' quit, and I want you to find me a new one. I'm keeping Sol Maltzman on. He's been writing all the articles, under a pseudonym, for years, so I'm prone to retaining him, even though he's a blacklisted Commie known to belong to no less than twenty-nine left-wing organizations, and—"

"And that's all the staff you need. Sol does a good job, and if worse comes to worse, Gail can fill in for him—she's written for *Hush-Hush* on and off for a couple of years. You've got your lawyer Dick Steisel for the legal stuff, and I can get you Fred Turentine for bug work. I'll find you a good dirt digger. I'll keep my nose down and ask around, but it might take a while."

"I trust you. You'll do your usual superb job."

Pete worked his knuckles. The joints ached—a sure sign that rain was coming. Hughes said, "Is that necessary?"

"These hands of mine brought us together, Boss. I'm just letting you know they're still here."

The watchdog house living room was 84′ by 80′.

The foyer walls were gold-flecked marble.

Nine bedrooms. Walk-in freezers thirty feet deep. Hughes had the carpets cleaned monthly—a jigaboo walked across them once.

Surveillance cameras were mounted on the roof and the upstairs landings—aimed at Mrs. Hughes' bedroom next door.

Pete found Gail in the kitchen. She had these great curves and long brown hair—her looks still got to him.

She said, "You usually hear people walk into houses, but our front door's a half-mile away."

"We've been here a year, and you're still cracking jokes."

"I live in the Taj Mahal. That takes some getting used to."

Pete straddled a chair. "You're nervous."

Gail slid her chair away from him. "Well . . . as extortionists go, I'm the nervous type. What's the man's name today?"

"Walter P. Kinnard. He's forty-seven years old, and he's been cheating on his wife since their honeymoon. He's got kids he dotes on, and the wife says he'll fold if I squeeze him with pictures and threaten to show them to the kids. He's a juicer, and he always gets a load on at lunchtime."

Gail crossed herself—half shtick, half for real. "Where?"

"You meet him at Dale's Secret Harbor. He's got a fuck pad a few blocks away where he bangs his secretary, but you insist on the Ambassador. You're in town for a convention, and you've got a snazzy room with a wet bar."

Gail shivered. Early a.m. chills—a sure sign that she had the yips.

Pete slipped her a key. "I rented the room next door to yours, so you can lock up and make it look good. I picked the lock on the connecting door, so I don't think this one will be noisy."

Gail lit a cigarette. Steady hands—good. "Distract me. Tell me what Howard the Recluse wanted."

"He bought *Hush-Hush*. He wants me to find him a stringer, so he can pull his pud over Hollywood gossip and share it with his pal J. Edgar Hoover. He wants to smear his political enemies, like your old boyfriend Jack Kennedy."

Gail smiled toasty warm. "A few weekends didn't make him my boyfriend."

"That fucking smile made him something."

"He flew me down to Acapulco once. That's a Howard the Recluse kind of gesture, so it makes you jealous."

"He flew you down on his honeymoon."

"So? He got married for political reasons, and politics makes for strange bedfellows. And my God, you are *suuuch* a voyeur."

Pete unholstered his piece and checked the clip—so fast that he didn't know why. Gail said, "Don't you think our lives are strange?"

* * *

They took separate cars downtown. Gail sat at the bar; Pete grabbed a booth close by and nursed a highball.

The restaurant was crowded—Dale's did a solid lunch biz. Pete got choice seating—he broke up a fag squeeze on the owner once.

Lots of women circulating: mid-Wilshire office stuff mostly. Gail stuck out: beaucoup more je ne sais quoi. Pete wolfed cocktail nuts—he forgot to eat breakfast.

Kinnard was late. Pete scanned the room, X-ray-eye-style.

There's Jack Whalen by the pay phones—L.A.'s #1 bookie collector. There's some LAPD brass two booths down. They're fucking whispering: "Bondurant" . . . "Right, that Cressmeyer woman."

There's Ruth Mildred Cressmeyer's ghost at the bar: this sad old girl with the shakes.

Pete slid down Memory Lane.

Late '49. He had some good sidelines going: card-game guard and abortion procurer. The scrape doctor was his kid brother, Frank.

Pete joined the U.S. Marines to bag a green card. Frank stayed with the family in Quebec and went to medical school.

Pete got hip early. Frank got hip late.

Don't speak French, speak English. Lose your accent and go to America.

Frank hit L.A. with a hard-on for money. He passed his medical boards and hung out his shingle: abortions and morphine for sale.

Frank loved showgirls and cards. Frank loved hoodlums. Frank loved Mickey Cohen's Thursday-night poker game.

Frank made friends with a stickup guy named Huey Cressmeyer. Huey's mom ran a Niggertown scrape clinic. Huey got his girlfriend pregnant and asked Mom and Frank for help. Huey got stupid and heisted the Thursday-night game—Pete was off guard duty with the flu.

Mickey gave Pete the contract.

Pete got a tip: Huey was holed up at a pad in El Segundo. The house belonged to a Jack Dragna trigger.

Mickey hated Jack Dragna. Mickey doubled the price and told him to kill everyone in the house.

December 14, 1949—overcast and chilly.

Pete torched the hideout with a Molotov cocktail. Four shapes ran out the back door swatting at flames. Pete shot them and left them to burn.

The papers ID'd them:

Hubert John Cressmeyer, 24.

Ruth Mildred Cressmeyer, 56.

Linda Jane Camrose, 20, four months pregnant.

François Bondurant, 27, a physician and French-Canadian émigré.

The snuffs stayed officially unsolved. The story filtered out to insiders.

Somebody called his father in Quebec and ratted him. The old man called him and begged him to deny it.

He must have faltered or oozed guilt. The old man and old lady sucked down monoxide fumes the same day.

That old babe at the bar was fucking Ruth Mildred's twin.

Time dragged. He sent the old girl an on-the-house refill. Walter P. Kinnard walked in and sat down next to Gail.

The poetry commenced.

Gail signaled the bartender. Attentive Walter caught the gesture and whistled. Joe Barman zoomed over with his martini shaker—regular boozer Walt packed some weight here.

Helpless Gail searched her purse for matches. Helpful Walt flicked his lighter and smiled. Sexy Walt was dripping scalp flakes all over the back of his jacket.

Gail smiled. Sexy Walt smiled. Well-dressed Walt wore white socks with a three-piece chalk-stripe suit.

The lovebirds settled in for martinis and small talk. Pete eyeballed the pre-bed warmup. Gail guzzled her drink for courage—her jaggedy nerves showed through plain.

She touched Walt's arm. Her guilty heart showed plain—except for the money, she hates it.

Pete walked over to the Ambassador and went up to his room. The setup was perfect: his room, Gail's room, one connecting door for a slick covert entrance.

He loaded his camera and attached a flashbulb strip. He greased the connecting doorjamb. He framed angles for some face shots.

Ten minutes crawled by. Pete listened for next-door sounds. There, Gail's signal—"Damn, where's my key?" a beat too loud.

Pete pressed up to the wall. He heard Lonely Walt pitch some boohoo: my wife and kids don't know a man has certain needs.

Gail said, Why'd you have *seven* kids then? Walt said, It keeps my wife at home, where a woman belongs.

Their voices faded out bed-bound. Shoes went thunk. Gail kicked a high-heeled pump at the wall—her three-minutes-to-blastoff signal.

Pete laughed—thirty-dollar-a-night rooms with goddamn wafer-thin walls.

Zippers snagged. Bedsprings creaked. Seconds tick-tick-ticked. Walter P. Kinnard started groaning—Pete clocked him saddled in at 2:44.

He waited for 3:00 even. He eeeeased the door open—that doorjamb grease lubed out every little scriiich.

There: Gail and Walter P. Kinnard fucking.

In the missionary style, with their heads close together—courtroom adultery evidence. Walt was loving it. Gail was feigning ecstasy and picking at a hangnail.

Pete got closeup close and let fly.

One, two, three—flashbulb blips Tommy-gun fast. The whole goddamn room went glare bright.

Kinnard shrieked and pulled out dishrag limp. Gail tumbled off the bed and ran for the bathroom.

Sexy buck-naked Walt: 5′9″, 210, pudgy.

Pete dropped his camera and picked him up by the neck. Pete laid his pitch out nice and slow.

"Your wife wants a divorce. She wants eight hundred a month, the house, the '56 Buick and orthodontic treatments for your son Timmy. You give her everything she wants, or I'll find you and kill you."

Kinnard popped spit bubbles. Pete admired his color: half shock-blue, half cardiac-red.

Steam whooshed out the bathroom door—Gail's standard postfuck shower always went down quick.

Pete dropped Walt on the floor. His arm fluttered from the lift: two hundred pounds plus, not bad.

Kinnard grabbed his clothes and stumbled out the door. Pete saw him tripping down the hallway, trying to get his trousers on right.

Gail walked out of a steam cloud. Her "I can't take much more of this" was no big surprise.

Walter P. Kinnard settled non-litigiously. Pete's shutout string jumped to Wives 23, Husbands 0. Mrs. Kinnard paid off: five grand up front, with 25% of her alimony promised in perpetuity.

Next: three days on Howard Hughes' time clock.

The TWA suit was spooking Big Howard. Pete stepped up his diversions.

He paid hookers to spiel to the papers: Hughes was holed up in numerous fuck pads. He bombarded process servers with phone tips: Hughes was in Bangkok, Maracaibo, Seoul. He set up a second Hughes double at the Biltmore: an old stag-movie vet, beaucoup hung. Pops was priapic for real—he sent Barbara Payton over to service him. Booze-addled Babs thought the old geek really *was* Hughes. She dished far and wide: Little Howard grew six inches.

J. Edgar Hoover could stall the suit easy. Hughes refused to ask him for help.

"Not yet, Pete. I need to cement my friendship with Mr. Hoover first. I see my ownership of *Hush-Hush* as the key, but I need you to find me a new scandal man first. You *know* how much Mr. Hoover loves to accrue titillating information. . . ."

Pete put the word out on the grapevine:

New *Hush-Hush* dirt digger needed. Interested bottom-feeders—call Pete B.

Pete stuck by the watchdog house phone. Geeks called. Pete said, Give me a hot dirt tidbit to prove your credibility.

The geeks complied. Dig the sampling:

Pat Nixon just hatched Nat "King" Cole's baby. Lawrence Welk ran male prosties. A hot duo: Patti Page and Francis the Talking Mule.

Eisenhower had certified spook blood. Rin Tin Tin got Lassie pregnant. Jesus Christ ran a coon whorehouse in Watts.

It got worse. Pete logged in nineteen applicants—all fucking strange-o's.

The phone rang—Strange-O #20 loomed. Pete heard crackle on the line—the call was probably long distance.

"Who's this?"

"Pete? It's Jimmy."

HOFFA.

"Jimmy, how are you?"

"Right now I'm cold. It's cold in Chicago. I'm calling from a pal's house, and the heater's on the blink. Are you sure *your* phone's not tapped?"

"I'm sure. Freddy Turentine runs tap checks on all of Mr. Hughes' phones once a month."

"I can talk then?"

"You can talk."

Hoffa cut loose. Pete held the phone at arm's length and heard him juuuust fine.

"The McClellan Committee's on me like flies on shit. That little weasel cocksucker Bobby Kennedy's got half the country convinced the Teamsters are worse than the goddamn Commies, and he's fucking hounding me and my people with subpoenas, and he's got investigators crawling all over my union like—"

"Jimmy—"

"—fleas on a dog. First he chases Dave Beck out, and now he wants *me*. Bobby Kennedy is a fucking avalanche of dogshit. I'm building this resort in Florida called Sun Valley, and Bobby's trying to trace the three million that bankrolled it. He figures I took it from the Central States Pension Fund—"

"Jimmy—"

"—and he thinks he can use me to get his pussy-hound brother elected President. He thinks James Riddle Hoffa's a fucking political steppingstone. He thinks I'm gonna bend over and take it in the keester like some goddamn homosexual queer. He thinks—"

"Jimmy—"

"—I'm some pansy like him and his brother. He thinks I'm gonna roll over like Dave Beck. As if all this ain't enough, I own this cabstand in Miami. I've got these hothead Cuban refugees working there, and all they do is debate fucking Castro versus fucking Batista like like like . . ."

Hoffa gasped out hoarse. Pete said, "What do you want?"

Jimmy caught some breath. "I've got a job for you in Miami."

"How much?"

"Ten thousand."

Pete said, "I'll take it."

He booked a midnight flight. He used a fake passenger name and charged a first-class seat to Hughes Aircraft. The plane landed at 8:00 A.M., on time.

Miami was balmy working on hot.

Pete cabbed over to a Teamster-owned U-Drive and picked

up a new Caddy Eldo. Jimmy pulled strings: no deposit or ID was required.

A note was taped under the dashboard.

"Go by cabstand: Flagler at N.W. 46th. Talk to Fulo Machado." Directions followed: causeways to surface streets marked on a little map.

Pete drove over. The scenery evaporated quick.

Big houses got smaller and smaller. White squares went to white trash, jigs and spics. Flagler was wall-to-wall low-rent storefronts.

The cabstand was tiger-striped stucco. The cabs in the lot had tiger-stripe paint jobs. Dig those tiger-shirted spics on the curb—snarfing doughnuts and T-Bird wine.

A sign above the door read: Tiger Kab. Se Habla Español.

Pete parked directly in front. Tiger men scoped him out and jabbered. He stretched to six-five-plus and let his shirttail hike. The spics saw his piece and jabbered on overdrive.

He walked in to the dispatch hut. Nice wallpaper: tiger photos taped floor to ceiling. *National Geographic* stock—Pete almost howled.

The dispatcher waved him over. Dig his face: scarred by tic-tac-toe knife cuts.

Pete pulled a chair up. Butt-Ugly said, "I'm Fulo Machado. Batista's secret police did this to me, so take your free introductory look now and forget about it, all right?"

"You speak English pretty well."

"I used to work at the Nacional Hotel in Havana. An American croupier guy taught me. It turned out he was a *maricón* trying to corrupt me."

"What did you do to him?"

"The *maricón* had a shack on a pork farm outside of Havana, where he brought little Cuban boys to corrupt them. I found him there with another *maricón* and murdered them with my machete. I stole all the pigs' food from their troughs and left the door of the shack open. You see, I had read in the *National Geographic* that starving pigs found decomposing human flesh irresistible."

Pete said, "Fulo, I like you."

"Please reserve judgment. I can be volatile where the enemies of Jesus Christ and Fidel Castro are concerned."

Pete stifled a yuk. "Did one of Jimmy's guys leave an envelope for me?"

Fulo forked it over. Pete ripped it open, itchy to roll.

Nice—a simple note and a photo.

"Anton Gretzler, 114 Hibiscus, Lake Weir, Fla. (near Sun Valley). OL4-8812." The pic showed a tall guy almost too fat to live.

Pete said, "Jimmy must trust you."

"He does. He sponsored my green card, so he knows that I will remain loyal."

"What's this Sun Valley place?"

"It is what I think is called a 'sub-division.' Jimmy is selling lots to Teamster members."

Pete said, "So who do you think's got more juice these days—Jesus or Castro?"

"I would say it is currently a toss-up."

Pete checked in at the Eden Roc and buzzed Anton Gretzler from a pay phone. The fat man agreed to a meet: 3:00, outside Sun Valley.

Pete took a snooze and drove out early. Sun Valley was the shits: three dirt roads gouged from swampland forty yards off the Interstate.

It was "sub-divided"—into matchbook-size lots piled with junk siding. Marshland formed the perimeter—Pete saw gators out sunning.

It was hot and humid. A wicked sun cooked greenery dry brown.

Pete leaned against the car and stretched some kinks out. A truck crawled down the highway belching steam; the man in the passenger seat waved for help. Pete turned his back and let the geeks pass by.

A breeze kicked dust clouds up. The access road hazed over. A big sedan turned off the Interstate and barreled in blind.

Pete stood aside. The car brodied to a stop. Fat Anton Gretzler got out.

Pete walked over to him. Gretzler said, "Mr. Peterson?"

"That's me. Mr. Gretzler?"

Fats stuck his hand out. Pete ignored it.

"Is something wrong? You said you wanted to see a lot."

Pete steered Fat Boy down to a marsh glade. Gretzler caught on quick: Don't resist. Gator eyes poked out of the water.

Pete said, "Look at my car. Do I look like some union schmuck in the market for a do-it-yourself house?"

"Well . . . no."

"Then don't you think you're doing Jimmy raw by showing me these piece-of-shit pads?"

"Well . . ."

"Jimmy told me he's got a nice block of houses around here just about ready to go. You're supposed to wait and show *them* to the Teamsters."

"Well . . . I thought I—"

"Jimmy says you're an impetuous guy. He says he shouldn't have made you a partner in this thing. He says you've told people he borrowed money from the Teamsters' Pension Fund and skimmed some off the top. He's says you've been talking up the Fund like you're a made guy."

Gretzler squirmed. Pete grabbed his wrist and snapped it— bones sheared and poked out through his skin. Gretzler tried to scream and choked up mute.

"Has the McClellan Committee subpoenaed you?"

Gretzler made "yes" nods, frantic.

"Have you talked to Robert Kennedy or his investigators?"

Gretzler made "no" nods, shit-your-pants scared.

Pete checked the highway. No cars in view, no witnesses— Gretzler said, "PLEASE."

Pete blew his brains out halfway through a rosary.

2

KEMPER BOYD

(Philadelphia, 11/27/58)

THE CAR: A Jaguar XK-140, British racing green/tan leather. The garage: subterranean and dead quiet. The job: steal the Jag for the FBI and entrap the fool who paid you to do it.

The man pried the driver's-side door open and hot-wired the ignition. The upholstery smelled rich: full leather boosted the "resale" price into the stratosphere.

He eased the car up to the street and waited for traffic to pass. Cold air fogged the windshield.

His buyer was standing at the corner. He was a Walter Mitty crime-voyeur type who had to get close.

The man pulled out. A squad car cut him off. His buyer saw what was happening—and ran.

Philly cops packing shotguns swooped down. They shouted standard auto-theft commands: "Get out of the car with your hands up!"/"Out—now!"/"Down on the ground!"

He obeyed them. The cops threw on full armor: cuffs, manacles and drag chains.

They frisked him and jerked him to his feet. His head hit a prowl car cherry light—

The cell looked familiar. He swung his legs off the bunk and got his identity straight.

I'm Special Agent Kemper C. Boyd, FBI, interstate car theft infiltrator.

I'm *not* Bob Aiken, freelance car thief.

I'm forty-two years old. I'm a Yale Law School grad. I'm a seventeen-year Bureau veteran, divorced, with a daughter in college—and a longtime FBI-sanctioned car booster.

He placed his cell: tier B at the Philly Fed Building.

His head throbbed. His wrists and ankles ached. He tamped down his identity a last notch.

I've rigged auto-job evidence and skimmed money off of it for years. IS THIS AN INTERNAL BUREAU ROUST?

He saw empty cells down both sides of the catwalk. He spotted some papers on his sink: newspaper mock-ups topped by banner headlines:

"Car Thief Suffers Heart Attack in Federal Custody"/"Car Thief Expires in Federal Building Cell."

The text was typed out below.

This afternoon, Philadelphia Police enacted a daring arrest in the shadow of picturesque Rittenhouse Square.

Acting on information supplied by an unnamed informant, Sergeant Gerald P. Griffen and four other officers captured Robert Henry Aiken, 42, in the act of stealing an expensive Jaguar automobile. Aiken meekly let the officers restrain him and—

Someone coughed and said, "Sir?"

Kemper looked up. A clerk type unlocked the cell and held the door open for him.

"You can go out the back way, sir. There's a car waiting for you."

Kemper brushed off his clothes and combed his hair. He walked out the freight exit and saw a government limo blocking the alley.

His limo.

Kemper got in the back. J. Edgar Hoover said, "Hello, Mr. Boyd."

"Good afternoon, Sir."

A partition slid up and closed the backseat off. The driver pulled out.

Hoover coughed. "Your infiltration assignment was terminated rather precipitously. The Philadelphia Police were somewhat rough, but they have a reputation for that, and anything less would have lacked verisimilitude."

"I've learned to stay in character in situations like that. I'm sure the arrest was believable."

"Did you affect an East Coast accent for your role?"

"No, a midwestern drawl. I learned the accent and speech patterns when I worked the St. Louis office, and I thought they'd complement my physical appearance more effectively."

"You're correct, of course. And personally, I would not want to second-guess you on anything pertaining to criminal role-playing. That sports jacket you're wearing, for instance. I would not appreciate it as standard Bureau attire, but it's quite appropriate for a Philadelphia car thief."

Get to it, you officious little—

"In fact, you've always dressed distinctly. Perhaps 'expensively' is more apt. To be blunt, there have been times when I wondered how your salary could sustain your wardrobe."

"Sir, you should see my apartment. What my wardrobe possesses, it lacks."

Hoover chuckled. "Be that as it may, I doubt if I've seen you in the same suit twice. I'm sure the women you're so fond of appreciate your sartorial flair."

"Sir, I hope so."

"You endure my amenities with considerable flair, Mr. Boyd. Most men squirm. You express both your inimitable personal panache and a concurrent respect for me that is quite alluring. Do you know what this means?"

"No, Sir. I don't."

"It means that I like you and am prone to forgive indiscretions that I would crucify other agents for. You're a dangerous and ruthless man, but you possess a certain beguiling charm. This balance of attributes outweighs your profligate tendencies and allows me to be fond of you."

DON'T SAY "WHAT INDISCRETIONS?"— HE'LL TELL YOU AND MAIM YOU.

"Sir, I greatly appreciate your respect, and I reciprocate it fully."

"You didn't include 'fondness' in your reciprocity, but I won't press the point. Now, business. I have an opportunity for you to earn two regular paychecks, which should delight you no end."

Hoover leaned back coax-me style. Kemper said, "Sir?"

The limo accelerated. Hoover flexed his hands and straightened his necktie. "The Kennedy brothers' recent actions have distressed me. Bobby seems to be using the McClellan Committee's labor racketeering mandate as a means to upstage the Bureau and advance his brother's presidential aspirations. This displeases me. I've been running the Bureau since before Bobby was born. Jack Kennedy is a desiccated liberal playboy with the moral convictions of a crotch-sniffing hound dog. He's playing crimefighter on the McClellan Committee, and the very existence of the committee is an implicit slap in the Bureau's face. Old Joe Kennedy is determined to buy his son the White House, and I want to possess information to help mitigate the boy's more degenerately egalitarian policies, should he succeed."

Kemper caught his cue. "Sir?"

"I want you to infiltrate the Kennedy organization. The McClellan Committee's labor-racketeering mandate ends next spring, but Bobby Kennedy is still hiring lawyer-investigators. As of now you are retired from the FBI, although you will continue to draw full pay until July 1961, the date you reach twenty years of Bureau service. You are to prepare a convincing FBI retirement story and secure an attorney's job with the McClellan Committee. I know that both you and Jack Kennedy have been intimate with a Senate aide named Sally Lefferts. Miss Lefferts is a talkative woman, so I'm sure young Jack has heard about you. Young Jack is on the McClellan Committee, and young Jack loves sexual gossip and dangerous friends. Mr. Boyd, I am sure that you will fit in with the Kennedys. I'm sure that this will be both a salutary opportunity for you to practice your skills of dissembling and duplicity, *and* the chance to exercise your more promiscuous tastes."

Kemper felt weightless. The limo cruised on thin air.

Hoover said, "Your reaction delights me. Rest now. We'll arrive in Washington in an hour, and I'll drop you at your apartment."

Hoover supplied up-to-date study notes—in a leather binder stamped "CONFIDENTIAL." Kemper mixed a pitcher of extra-dry martinis and pulled up his favorite chair to read through them.

The notes boiled down to one thing: Bobby Kennedy vs. Jimmy Hoffa.

Senator John McClellan chaired the U.S. Senate's Select Committee on Improper Activities in the Labor and Management Field, established in January 1957. Its subsidiary members: Senators Ives, Kennedy, McNamara, McCarthy, Ervin, Mundt, Goldwater. Its chief counsel and investigative boss: Robert F. Kennedy.

Current personnel: thirty-five investigators, forty-five accountants, twenty-five stenographers and clerks. Its current housing: the Senate Office Building, suite 101.

The Committee's stated goals:

To expose corrupt labor practices; to expose labor unions collusively linked to organized crime. The Committee's methods: witness subpoenas, document subpoenas, and the charting of union funds diverted and misused in organized crime activities.

The Committee's de facto target: the International Brotherhood of Teamsters, the most powerful transportation union on earth, arguably the most corrupt and powerful labor union ever.

Its president: James Riddle Hoffa, age 45.

Hoffa: mob bought-and-paid-for. The suborner of: extortion, wholesale bribery, beatings, bombings, management side deals and epic abuse of union funds.

Hoffa's suspected holdings, in violation of fourteen antitrust statutes:

Trucking firms, used car lots, a dog track, a car-rental chain, a Miami cabstand staffed by Cuban refugees with extensive criminal records.

Hoffa's close friends:

Mr. Sam Giancana, the Mafia boss of Chicago; Mr. Santo

Trafficante Jr., the Mafia boss of Tampa, Florida; Mr. Carlos Marcello, the Mafia boss of New Orleans.

Jimmy Hoffa:

Who lends his "friends" millions of dollars, put to use illegally.

Who owns percentages of mob-run casinos in Havana, Cuba.

Who illegally funnels cash to Cuban strongman Fulgencio Batista *and* rebel firebrand Fidel Castro.

Who rapes the Teamsters' Central States Pension Fund, a cash-rich watering hole rumored to be administered by Sam Giancana's Chicago mob—a loan-shark scheme wherein gangsters and crooked entrepreneurs borrow large sums at usurious interest rates, with nonpayment penalties up to and including torture and death.

Kemper caught the gist: Hoover's jealous. He always said the Mob didn't exist—because he knew he couldn't prosecute it successfully. Now Bobby Kennedy begs to differ. . . .

A chronology followed.

Early '57: the Committee targets Teamster president Dave Beck. Beck testifies five times; Bobby Kennedy's relentless goading breaks the man. A Seattle grand jury indicts him for larceny and income tax evasion.

Spring '57: Jimmy Hoffa assumes complete control of the Teamsters.

August '57: Hoffa vows to rid his union of gangster influence—a large lie.

September '57: Hoffa goes to trial in Detroit. The charge: tapping the phones of Teamster subordinates. A hung jury—Hoffa escapes sentencing.

October '57: Hoffa is elected International Teamster president. A persistent rumor: 70% of his delegates were illegally selected.

July '58: the Committee begins to investigate direct links between the Teamsters and organized crime. Closely scrutinized: the November '57 Apalachin Conclave.

Fifty-nine high-ranking mobsters meet at the upstate New York home of a "civilian" friend. A state trooper named *Edgar* Croswell runs their license plates. A raid ensues—and Mr. Hoover's longstanding "there is no Mafia" stance becomes untenable.

July '58: Bobby Kennedy proves that Hoffa resolves strikes through management bribes—this practice dating back to '49.

August '58: Hoffa appears before the Committee. Bobby Kennedy goes at him—and traps him in numerous lies.

The notes concluded.

The Committee was currently probing Hoffa's Sun Valley resort outside Lake Weir, Florida. Bobby Kennedy subpoenaed the Central States Pension Fund books and saw that three million dollars went into the project—much more than reasonable building costs. Kennedy's theory: Hoffa skimmed at least a million dollars off the top and was selling his union brothers defective prefab material and alligator-infested swampland.

Ergo: felony land fraud.

A closing addendum:

"Hoffa has a Sun Valley front man: Anton William Gretzler, 46, a Florida resident with three previous bunco convictions. Gretzler was subpoenaed 10/29/58, but now appears to be missing."

Kemper checked the Hoffa "Known Associates" list. One name sizzled:

Pete Bondurant, W.M., 6'5", 230, DOB 7/16/20, Montreal, Canada.

No criminal convictions. Licensed private investigator/ former Los Angeles County deputy sheriff.

Big Pete: shakedown man and Howard Hughes' pet goon. He and Ward Littell arrested him once—he beat a Sheriff's inmate to death. Littell's comment: "Perhaps the most fearsome and competent rogue cop of our era."

Kemper poured a fresh drink and let his mind drift. The impersonation took shape: heroic aristocrats form a common bond.

He liked women, and cheated on his wife throughout their marriage. Jack Kennedy liked women—and held his marriage vows expedient and whimsical. Bobby liked his wife and kept her pregnant—insider talk tagged him faithful.

Yale for him; Harvard for the Kennedys. Filthy-rich Irish Catholics; filthy-rich Tennessee Anglicans gone bankrupt. Their family was large and photogenic; his family was broke and dead. Someday he might tell Jack and Bobby how his father shot himself and took a month to die.

Southerners and Boston Irish: both afflicted with incongruous accents. He'd resurrect the drawl it took so long to lose.

Kemper prowled his clothes closet. Impersonation details clicked in.

The charcoal worsted for the interview. A holstered .38 to impress tough guy Bobby. No Yale cuff links—Bobby might possess a proletarian streak.

His closet was twelve feet deep. The back wall was offset by framed photographs.

His ex-wife, Katherine—the best-looking woman who ever breathed. They debuted at the Nashville Cotillion—a society scribe called them "southern grace personified." He married her for sex and her father's money. She divorced him when the Boyd fortune evaporated and Hoover addressed his law school class and *personally* invited him to join the FBI.

Katherine, in November 1940:

"You watch out for that prissy little fussbudget, do you hear me, Kemper? I think he has carnal designs on you."

She didn't know that Mr. Hoover only fucked power.

In matching frames: his daughter, Claire, Susan Littell and Helen Agee—three FBI daughters hell-bent on law careers.

The girls were best friends split up by studies at Tulane and Notre Dame. Helen was disfigured—he kept the pictures in his closet to quash pitying comments.

Tom Agee was sitting in his car—working a routine stakeout for some bank heisters outside a whorehouse. His wife had just left him—Tom couldn't find a sitter for nine-year-old Helen. She was sleeping in the backseat when the heisters came up shooting.

Tom was killed. Helen was muzzle-burned and left for dead. Help arrived—six hours later. Flash particles had scorched Helen's cheeks and scarred her for life.

Kemper laid out his interview clothes. He got some lies straight and called Sally Lefferts.

The phone rang twice. "Uh, hello?"—Sally's little boy picked up.

"Son, get your mother. Tell her it's a friend from the office."

"Uh . . . yessir."

Sally came on the line. "Who's this from the U.S. Senate clerical pool bothering this poor overworked aide?"

"It's me. Kemper."

"Kemper, what are you doing calling me with my husband in the backyard right now as we speak!"

"Ssssh. I'm calling you for a job referral."

"What are you saying? Are you saying Mr. Hoover got wise to your evil ways with women and showed you the gate?"

"I retired, Sally. I utilized a dangerous-duty dispensation clause and retired three years early."

"Well, my heavens, Kemper Cathcart Boyd!"

"Are you still seeing Jack Kennedy, Sally?"

"Occasionally, dear heart, since *you* gave *me* the gate. Is this about trading little black books and evil tales out of school, or—?"

"I'm thinking of applying for a job with the McClellan Committee."

Sally whooped. "Well, I think you *should*! I think I should put a note on Robert Kennedy's desk recommending you, and you should send me a dozen long-stemmed Southern Beauty roses for the effort!"

"You're the southern beauty, Sally."

"I was too much woman for De Ridder, Louisiana, and that is a fact!"

Kemper hung up with kisses. Sally would spread the word: ex-FBI car thief now seeking work.

He'd tell Bobby how he crashed the Corvette theft ring. He wouldn't mention the Vettes he stripped for parts.

He moved the next day. He walked right in to the Senate Office Building and suite 101.

The receptionist heard him out and tapped her intercom. "Mr. Kennedy, there's a man here who wants to apply for an investigator's position. He has FBI retirement credentials."

The office spread out unpartitioned behind her—all cabinet rows, cubicles and conference rooms. Men worked elbow-to-elbow tight—the place hummed.

The woman smiled. "Mr. Kennedy will see you. Take this first little aisle straight back."

Kemper walked into the hum. The office had a scavenged look: mismatched desks and filing bins, and corkboards top-heavy with paper.

"Mr. Boyd?"

Robert Kennedy stepped out of his cubicle. It was the standard size, the standard desk and two chairs.

He offered the standard too-hard handshake—totally predictable.

Kemper sat down. Kennedy pointed to his holster bulge. "I didn't know that retired FBI men were allowed to carry guns."

"I've incurred enemies through the years. My retirement won't stop them from hating me."

"Senate investigators don't wear sidearms."

"If you hire me, I'll put mine in a drawer."

Kennedy smiled and leaned against his desk. "You're from the South?"

"Nashville, Tennessee."

"Sally Lefferts said you were with the FBI for what, fifteen years?"

"Seventeen."

"Why did you retire early?"

"I worked auto-theft infiltration assignments for the past nine years, and it had gotten to the point where I was too well known to car thieves to go undercover convincingly. The Bureau bylaws contain an early-retirement clause for agents who have engaged in prolonged stints of hazardous duty, and I utilized it."

"'Utilized'? Did those assignments debilitate you in some way?"

"I applied for a position with the Top Hoodlum Program first. Mr. Hoover rejected my application personally, although he knew full well that I had desired organized crime work for some time. No, I wasn't debilitated. I was frustrated."

Kennedy brushed hair from his forehead. "So you quit."

"Is that an accusation?"

"No, it's an observation. And frankly, I'm surprised. The FBI is a tight-knit organization that inspires great loyalty, and agents do not tend to retire out of pique."

Kemper raised his voice—just barely. "A great many agents realize that organized crime, not domestic Communism, poses the greatest threat to America. The Apalachin revelations forced Mr. Hoover to form the Top Hoodlum Program, which of course he did with some reluctance. The program is accruing antimob intelligence, but not seeking hard evidence to build toward Federal prosecution, but at least that's something, and I wanted to be part of it."

Kennedy smiled. "I understand your frustration, and I agree with your critique of Mr. Hoover's priorities. But I'm still surprised that you quit."

Kemper smiled. "Before I 'quit,' I snuck a look at Mr.

Hoover's private file on the McClellan Committee. I'm up-to-date on the Committee's work, up to and including Sun Valley and your missing witness Anton Gretzler. I 'quit' because Mr. Hoover has the Bureau neurotically focused on harmless leftists, while the McClellan Committee is going after the real bad guys. I 'quit' because given my choice of monomaniacs, I'd rather work for you."

Kennedy grinned. "Our mandate ends in five months. You'll be out of work."

"I have an FBI pension, and you'll have forwarded so much evidence to municipal grand juries that they'll be begging your investigators to work for them ad hoc."

Kennedy tapped a stack of papers. "We work hard here. We plod. We subpoena and trace money and litigate. We don't risk our lives stealing sports cars or dawdle over lunch or take women to the Willard Hotel for quickies. Our idea of a good time is to talk about how much we hate Jimmy Hoffa and the Mob."

Kemper stood up. "I hate Hoffa and the Mob like Mr. Hoover hates you and your brother."

Bobby laughed. "I'll let you know within a few days."

Kemper strolled by Sally Lefferts' office. It was 2:30—Sally might be up for a quickie at the Willard.

Her door was open. Sally was at her desk fretting tissues—with a man straddling a chair up close to her.

She said, "Oh, hello, Kemper."

Her color was up: rosy verging on flushed. She had that too-bright I've-lost-at-love-again glow on.

"Are you busy? I can come back."

The man swiveled his chair around. Kemper said, "Hello, Senator."

John Kennedy smiled. Sally dabbed at her eyes. "Jack, this is my friend Kemper Boyd."

They shook hands. Kennedy did a little half-bow.

"Mr. Boyd, a pleasure."

"My pleasure entirely, sir."

Sally forced a smile. Her rouge was streaked—she'd been crying.

"Kemper, how did your interview go?"

"It went well, I think. Sally, I have to go. I just wanted to thank you for the referral."

Little nods went around. Nobody's eyes met. Kennedy handed Sally a fresh tissue.

Kemper walked downstairs and outside. A storm had fired up—he ducked under a statue ledge and let the rain graze him.

The Kennedy coincidence felt strange. He walked straight from an interview with Bobby into a chance meeting with Jack. It felt like he was gently pushed in that direction.

Kemper thought it through.

Mr. Hoover mentioned Sally—as his most specific link to Jack Kennedy. Mr. Hoover knew that he and Jack shared a fondness for women. Mr. Hoover sensed that he'd visit Sally after his interview with Bobby.

Mr. Hoover *sensed* that he'd call Sally for an interview referral immediately. Mr. Hoover knew that Bobby needed investigators and interviewed walk-in prospects at whim.

Kemper took the logical leap—

Mr. Hoover has Capitol Hill hot-wired. He knew that you broke up with Sally at her office—to forestall a big public scene. He picked up a tip that Jack Kennedy was planning the same thing—and took a stab at maneuvering you into a position to witness it.

It felt logically sound. It felt quintessentially Hoover.

Mr. Hoover doesn't entirely trust you to forge a bond with Bobby. He took a shot at placing you in a symbiotic context with Jack.

The rain felt good. Lightning crackled down and backlit the Capitol dome. It felt like he could stand here and let the whole world come to him.

Kemper heard foot scrapes behind him. He knew who it was instantly.

"Mr. Boyd?"

He turned around. John Kennedy was cinching up his overcoat.

"Senator."

"Call me Jack."

"All right, Jack."

Kennedy shivered. "Why the hell are we standing here?"

"We can run for the Mayflower bar when this lets up a bit."

"We can, and I think we should. You know, Sally's told me about you. She told me I should work on losing my accent the way you lost yours, so I was surprised to hear you speak."

Kemper dropped his drawl. "Southerners make the best cops. You lay on the cornpone and people tend to underestimate you and let their secrets slip. I thought your brother might know that, so I acted accordingly. You're on the McClellan Committee, so I figured I should go for uniformity."

Kennedy laughed. "Your secret's safe with me."

"Thanks. And don't worry about Sally. She likes men the way we like women, and she gets over the attendant heartaches pretty fast."

"I knew you figured it out. Sally told me you cut her off in a similar fashion."

Kemper smiled. "You can always go back occasionally. Sally appreciates an occasional afternoon at a good hotel."

"I'll remember that. A man with my aspirations has to be conscious of his entanglements."

Kemper stepped closer to "Jack." He could almost see Mr. Hoover grinning.

"I know a fair number of women who know how to keep things unentangled."

Kennedy smiled and steered him into the rain. "Let's go get a drink and talk about it. I've got an hour to kill before I meet my wife."

3

WARD J. LITTELL

(Chicago, 11/30/58)

BLACK BAG WORK—a classic FBI Commie crib prowl.

Littell snapped the lock with a ruler. His hands dripped sweat—apartment-house break-ins always played risky.

Neighbors heard B&E noise. Hallway sounds muffled incoming footsteps.

He closed the door behind him. The living room took shape: ratty furniture, bookshelves, labor protest posters. It was a typical CPUSA member's dwelling—he'd find documents in the dinette cupboard.

He did. Ditto the standard wall photos: Sad old "Free the Rosenbergs" shots.

Pathos.

He'd surveilled Morton Katzenbach for months. He'd heard scads of leftist invective. He knew one thing: Morty posed no threat to America.

A Commie cell met at Morty's doughnut stand. Their big-time "treason": feeding bear claws to striking auto workers.

Littell got out his Minox and snapped "documents." He blew three rolls of film on donation tallies—all short of fifty dollars a month.

It was boring, shitty work. His old refrain kicked in automatically.

You're forty-five years old. You're an expert bug/wire man. You're an ex-Jesuit seminarian with a law degree, two years and two months shy of retirement. You've got an alimony-fat ex-wife and a daughter at Notre Dame, and if you pass the Illinois Bar exam and quit the FBI, your gross earnings over the next X-number of years will more than compensate for your forfeited pension.

He shot two lists of "political expenses." Morty annotated his doughnut handouts: "Plain," "Chocolate," "Glazed."

He heard key-in-the-lock noise. He saw the door open ten feet in front of him.

Faye Katzenbach lugged groceries in. She saw him and shook her head like he was the saddest thing on earth.

"So you people are common thieves now?"

Littell knocked over a lamp running past her.

The squadroom was noontime quiet—just a few agents standing around clipping teletypes. Littell found a note on his desk.

K. Boyd called. In town en route to Florida. Pump Room, 7:00?

Kemper—yes!

Chick Leahy walked up, waving file carbons. "I'll need the complete Katzenbach folder, with photo attachments, by December 11th. Mr. Tolson's coming in for an inspection tour, and he wants a CPUSA presentation."

"You'll have it."

"Good. Complete with documents?"

"Some. Mrs. Katzenbach caught me before I finished."

"Jesus. Did she—?"

"She did *not* call the Chicago PD, because she knew who I was and what I was doing. Mr. Leahy, half the Commies on earth know the term 'black bag job.'"

Leahy sighed. "Say it, Ward. I'm going to turn you down, but you'll feel better if you say it."

"All right. I want a Mob assignment. I want a transfer to the Top Hoodlum Program."

Leahy said, "No. Our THP roster is full. And as special agent-in-charge my assessment of you is that you're best suited for political surveillance, which I consider important work. Mr. Hoover considers domestic Communists more dangerous than the Mafia, and I have to say that I agree with him."

They stared at each other. Littell broke it off—Leahy would stand there all day if he didn't.

Leahy walked back to his office. Littell shut his cubicle door and got out his bar texts. Civic statutes went unmemorized—Kemper Boyd memories cut them adrift.

Late '53: they corner a kidnapper in L.A. The man pulls a gun; *he* shakes so hard he drops his. Some LAPD men laugh at him. Kemper doctors the report to make *him* the hero.

They protest the disposition of Tom Agee's pension—Mr. Hoover wants to award it to Tom's floozy wife. Kemper talks him into a surviving-daughter disbursement; Helen now has a handsome sinecure.

They arrest Big Pete Bondurant. *He* makes a gaffe: ribbing Pete in Québecois French. Bondurant snaps his handcuff chain and goes for his throat.

He runs. Big Pete laughs. Kemper bribes Bondurant into silence on the matter—catered cell food does the trick.

Kemper never judged his fearful side. Kemper said, "We both joined the Bureau to avoid the war, so who's to judge?" Kemper taught him how to burglarize—a good fear tamper-downer.

Kemper said, "You're my priest-cop confessor. I'll reciprocate and hear your confessions, but since my secrets are worse than yours, I'll always get the better end of the deal."

Littell closed his textbook. Civil statutes were dead boring.

The Pump Room was packed. A gale blew off the lake—people seemed to whoosh inside.

Littell secured a back booth. The maître d' took his drink order: two martinis, straight up. The restaurant was beautiful: colored waiters and a pre-symphony crowd had the place sparkling.

The drinks arrived. Littell arranged them for a quick toast. Boyd walked in, via the hotel lobby.

Littell laughed. "Don't tell me you're staying here."

"My plane doesn't leave until two A.M., and I needed a place to stretch my legs. Hello, Ward."

"Hello, Kemper. A valedictory?"

Boyd raised his glass. "To my daughter Claire, your daughter Susan and Helen Agee. May they do well in school and become better attorneys than their fathers."

They clicked goblets. "Neither of whom ever practiced law."

"You clerked, though. And I heard you wrote deportation writs that saw litigation."

"We're not doing so badly. At least you're not. So who's putting you up here?"

"My new temporary employer booked me a room out by Midway, but I decided to splurge and make up the difference out of my pocket. And the difference between the Skyliner Motel and the Ambassador-East is pretty steep."

Littell smiled. "What new temporary employer? Are you working Cointelpro?"

"No, it's something a good deal more interesting. I'll tell you a few drinks down the line, when you're more likely to get blasphemous and say, 'Jesus Fucking Christ.'"

"I'll say it now. You've just effectively killed small talk, so I will say it *fucking* now."

Boyd sipped his martini. "Not yet. You just hit the jackpot on the wayward-daughter front, though. That should cheer you up."

"Let me guess. Claire's transferring from Tulane to Notre Dame."

"No. Helen graduated Tulane a semester early. She's been accepted at the University of Chicago law school, and she'll be moving here next month."

"Jesus!"

"I knew you'd be pleased."

"Helen's a courageous girl. She'll make a damn fine lawyer."

"She will. And she'll make some man a damn fine consort, if we haven't ruined her for young men her own age."

"It would take a—"

"Special young man to get by her affliction?"

"Yes."

Boyd winked. "Well, she's twenty-one. Think of how the two of you would upset Margaret."

Littell killed his drink. "And upset my own daughter. Susan, by the way, says Margaret is spending weekends with a man in Charlevoix. But she'll never marry him as long as she has my paycheck attached."

"You're her devil. You're the seminarian boy who got her pregnant. And in the religious terms you're so fond of, your marriage was purgatory."

"No, my job is. I black-bagged a Commie's apartment today and photographed an entire ledger page devoted to doughnuts. I honestly don't know how much longer I can do this kind of thing."

Fresh drinks arrived. The waiter bowed—Kemper inspired subservience. Littell said, "I figured something out in the process, right between the chocolate and the glazed."

"What?"

"That Mr. Hoover hates left-wingers because their philosophy is based on human frailty, while his own is based on an excruciating rectitude that denies such things."

Boyd held his glass up. "You never disappoint me."

"Kemper—"

Waiters swooped past. Candlelight bounced off gold flatware. Crêpe suzettes ignited—an old woman squealed.

"*Kemper*—"

"Mr. Hoover had me infiltrate the McClellan Committee. He hates Bobby Kennedy and his brother Jack, and he's afraid their father will buy Jack the White House in '60. I'm now a fake FBI retiree on an indefinite assignment to cozy up to both brothers. I applied for a job as a temporary Committee investigator, and I got the word today that Bobby hired me. I'm flying to Miami in a few hours to look for a missing witness."

Littell said, "Jesus Fucking Christ."

Boyd said, "You never disappoint me."

"I suppose you're drawing two salaries?"

"You know I love money."

"Yes, but do you like the brothers?"

"Yes, I do. Bobby's a vindictive little bulldog, and Jack's charming and not as smart as he thinks he is. Bobby's the stronger man, and he hates organized crime like you do."

Littell shook his head. "You don't hate anything."

"I can't afford to."

"I've never understood your loyalties."

"Let's just say they're ambiguous."

DOCUMENT INSERT: 12/2/58.
Official FBI telephone call transcript: ''Recorded
at the Director's Request''/''Classified Confidential
1-A: Director's Eyes Only.'' Speaking: Director
Hoover, Special Agent Kemper Boyd.

JEH: Mr. Boyd?

KB: Sir, good morning.

JEH: Yes, it is a good morning. Are you calling from
a secure phone?

KB: Yes. I'm at a coin phone. If the connection
seems weak, it's because I'm calling from Miami.

JEH: Little Brother has put you to work already?

KB: Little Brother doesn't waste time.

JEH: Interpret your rapid hiring. Use names if you
must.

KB: Little Brother was initially suspicious of me,
and I think it will take time to win him over. I ran
into Big Brother at Sally Lefferts' office, and
circumstances forced us into a private conversation.
We went out for a drink and developed a rapport. Like
many charming men, Big Brother is also easily
charmed. We hit it off quite well, and I'm certain he
told Little Brother to hire me.

JEH: Describe the ''circumstances'' you mentioned.

KB: We discovered that we shared an interest in
sophisticated and provocative women, and we went to
the Mayflower bar to discuss related matters. Big
Brother confirmed that he is going to run in 1960, and
that Little Brother will begin the campaign
groundwork when the McClellan Committee mandate ends
this coming April.

JEH: Continue.

KB: Big Brother and I discussed politics. I
portrayed myself as incongruously liberal by Bureau
standards, which Big Brother—

JEH: You have no political convictions, which adds
to your efficacy in situations like this. Continue.

KB: Big Brother found my feigned political
convictions interesting and opened up. He said that
he considers Little Brother's hatred of Mr. H.

somewhat untoward, although justified. Both Big
Brother and their father have urged Little Brother to
strategically retreat and offer Mr. H. a deal if he
cleans up his organization, but Little Brother has
refused. My personal opinion is that Mr. H. is legally
inviolate at this time. Big Brother shares that
opinion, as do a number of Committee investigators.
Sir, I think Little Brother is ferociously dedicated
and competent. My feeling is that he will take Mr. H.
down, but not in the foreseeable future. I think it
will take years and most likely many indictments, and
that it certainly won't happen within the Committee
mandate time frame.

JEH: You're saying the Committee will hand the ball
to municipal grand juries once their mandate expires?

KB: Yes. I think it will take years for the Brothers
to reap real political benefit from Mr. H. And I think
a backlash might set in and hurt Big Brother.
Democratic candidates can't afford to be viewed as
antiunion.

JEH: Your assessments seem quite astute.

KB: Thank you, Sir.

JEH: Did Big Brother bring my name up?

KB: Yes. He knows about your extensive files on
politicians and movie stars you deem subversive, and
he's afraid you have a file on him. I told him your file
on his family ran to a thousand pages.

JEH: Good. You would have lost credibility had you
been less candid. What else did you and Big Brother
discuss?

KB: Chiefly women. Big Brother mentioned a trip to
Los Angeles on December 9th. I gave him the phone
number of a promiscuous woman named Darleen Shoftel
and urged him to call her.

JEH: Do you think he has called her?

KB: No, Sir. But I think he will.

JEH: Describe your duties for the Committee thus
far.

KB: I've been looking for a subpoenaed witness
named Anton Gretzler here in Florida. Little Brother
wanted me to serve him a backup summons. There's an

aspect of this we should discuss, since Gretzler's
disappearance may tie in to a friend of yours.

JEH: Continue.

KB: Gretzler was Mr. H.'s partner in the alleged
Sun Valley land fraud. He—

JEH: You said ''was.'' You're assuming Gretzler is
dead?

KB: I'm certain he's dead.

JEH: Continue.

KB: He disappeared on the afternoon of November
26th. He told his secretary he was going to meet a
''sales prospect'' at Sun Valley and never returned.
The Lake Weir Police found his car in a swamp marsh
nearby, but they haven't been able to locate a body.
They canvassed for witnesses and turned up a man who
was driving by Sun Valley on the Interstate at the
same time the ''sales prospect'' was to meet
Gretzler. The man said he saw a man parked on the Sun
Valley access road. He said the man averted his face
when he drove by, so it's doubtful he could identify
him. He did describe him, however. Six foot four or
five, ''huge,'' two hundred and forty pounds. Dark
hair, thirty-five to forty. I'm thinking it—

JEH: Your old friend Peter Bondurant. He's
singularly outsized, and he's on that list of Mr. H.'s
known associates that I gave you.

KB: Yes, Sir. I checked airline and car rental
records in Los Angeles and Miami and turned up a
Hughes Aircraft charge that I'm certain Bondurant
made. I know he was in Florida on November 26th, and
I'm circumstantially certain that Mr. H. hired him to
kill Gretzler. I know that you and Howard Hughes are
friends, so I thought I'd inform you of this before
I told Little Brother.

JEH: Do not inform Little Brother under any
circumstances. The status of your investigation
should remain thus: Gretzler is missing, perhaps
dead. There are no leads and no suspects. Pete
Bondurant is invaluable to Howard Hughes, who is a
valuable friend of the Bureau. Mr. Hughes recently
purchased a scandal magazine to help disseminate

political information favorable to the Bureau, and
I do not want his feathers ruffled. Do you understand?

KB: Yes, Sir.

JEH: I want you to fly to Los Angeles on a Bureau
charge and tweak Pete Bondurant with your suspicions.
Get a favor from him, and cloak your friendly
overtures with the knowledge that you can hurt him.
And when your Committee duties permit, go back to
Florida and clean up potential loose ends on the
Gretzler front.

KB: I'll wrap up here and fly to L.A. late tomorrow.

JEH: Good. And while you're in Los Angeles, I want
you to bug and wire Miss Darleen Shoftel's home. If
Big Brother contacts her, I want to know.

KB: She won't voluntarily assent, so I'll have to
rig her apartment sub rosa. Can I bring in Ward
Littell? He's a great wire man.

JEH: Yes, bring him in. This reminds me that
Littell has been coveting a Top Hoodlum Squad spot for
some time. Do you think he'd like a transfer as a
reward for this job?

KB: He'd love it.

JEH: Good, but let me be the one to inform him.
Goodbye, Mr. Boyd. I commend you for work well done.

KB: Thank you, Sir. Goodbye.

4

(Beverly Hills, 12/4/58)

HOWARD HUGHES CRANKED his bed up a notch. "I can't tell
you how lackluster the last two issues have been. *Hush-Hush* is a
weekly now, which increases the need for interesting gossip
incrementally. *We need a new dirt digger.* We've got you for story
verification, Dick Steisel for legal vetting and Sol Maltzman to
write the pieces, but we're only as good as our scandals, and our
scandals have been chaste and ridiculously dull."

Pete slouched in a chair and thumbed last week's issue. On
the cover: "Migrant Workers Carry VD Plague!" A co-feature:
"Hollywood Ranch Market—Homo Heaven!"

"I'll keep at it. We're looking for a guy with unique fucking qualifications, and that takes time."

Hughes said, "You do it. And tell Sol Maltzman that I want a piece entitled 'Negroes: Overbreeding Creates TB Epidemic' on next week's cover."

"That sounds pretty far-fetched."

"Facts can be bent to conform to any thesis."

"I'll tell him, Boss."

"Good. And while you're out . . ."

"Will I get you some more dope and disposable hypos? *Yes, sir!*"

Hughes flinched and turned the TV on. "Sheriff John's Lunch Brigade" hit the bedroom—squealing tots and cartoon mice the size of Lassie.

Pete strolled out to the parking lot. Lounging upside his car like he owned it: Special Agent Kemper Fucking Boyd.

Six years older and still too handsome to live. That dark gray suit had to run four hundred clams easy.

"What is this?"

Boyd folded his arms over his chest. "This is a friendly errand for Mr. Hoover. He's concerned about your extracurricular work for Jimmy Hoffa."

"What are you talking about?"

"I've got an 'in' on the McClellan Committee. They've got some pay phones near Hoffa's house in Virginia rigged to register slug calls. That cheap fuck Hoffa makes his business calls from public booths and uses slugs."

"Keep going. Your slug call pitch is bullshit, but let's see where you're taking it."

Boyd winked—brass-balled motherfucker.

"One, Hoffa called you twice late last month. Two, you bought a round-trip L.A.-to-Miami ticket under an assumed name and charged it to Hughes Aircraft. Three, you rented a car at a Teamster-owned rent-a-car outlet and were *maybe* seen waiting for a man named Anton Gretzler. I think Gretzler's dead, and I think Hoffa hired you to clip him."

They'd never find a corpse: he tossed Gretzler in a swamp and watched gators eat him.

"So arrest me."

"No. Mr. Hoover doesn't like Bobby Kennedy, and I'm sure he wouldn't want to upset Mr. Hughes. He can live with you and Jimmy on the loose, and so can I."

"So?"

"So let's do something nice for Mr. Hoover."

"Give me a hint. I'm just dying to roll over."

Boyd smiled. "The head writer at *Hush-Hush* is a Commie. I know Mr. Hughes appreciates cheap help, but I still think you should fire him immediately."

Pete said, "I'll do that. And you tell Mr. Hoover that I'm a patriotic guy who knows how friendship works."

Boyd waltzed off—no nod, no wink, suspect dismissed. He walked two car rows over and bagged a blue Ford with a Hertz bumper sticker.

The car pulled out. Boyd fucking waved.

Pete ran to the hotel phone bank and called information. An operator shot him the main Hertz number.

He dialed it. A woman answered: "Good morning, Hertz Rent-a-Car."

"Good morning. This is Officer Peterson, LAPD. I need a current customer listing on one of your cars."

"Has there been an accident?"

"No, it's just routine. The car is a blue '56 Ford Fairlane, license V as in 'Victor,' D as in 'dog,' H as in 'Henry,' four-nine-zero."

"One minute, Officer."

Pete held the line. Boyd's McClellan pitch danced around in his head.

"I have your listing, Officer."

"Shoot."

"The car was rented to a Mr. Kemper C. Boyd, whose current Los Angeles address is the Miramar Hotel in Santa Monica. The invoice says the charge is to be billed to the U.S. Senate Select Committee on Investigations. Does that help?—"

Pete hung up. His head dance went stereophonic.

Strange: Boyd in a Committee-rented car. Strange because: Hoover and Bobby Kennedy were rivals. Boyd as FBI man *and* Committee cop?—Hoover would never allow him to moonlight.

Boyd was stylish working on slick—and a good man to front friendly warnings.

A good man to spy on Bobby?—"Maybe" working on "Yes."

* * *

Sol Maltzman lived in Silverlake—a dive above a tux rental joint.

Pete knocked. Sol opened up, pissed—this knock-kneed geek in Bermuda shorts and a T-shirt.

"What is it, Bondurant? I'm very busy."

"Bohn-dew-rahn"—the little Commie prick said it French-style.

The pad reeked of cigarettes and cat litter. Manila folders dripped off every stick of furniture; a wooden cabinet blocked the one window.

He's got Hollywood dirt files. He's just the type to hoard scandal skank.

"Bohn-dew-rahn, what *is* it?"

Pete grabbed a folder off a lamp stand. Press clippings on Ike and Dick Nixon—snoresville.

"Put that down and tell me what you want!"

Pete grabbed his neck. "You're fired from *Hush-Hush*. I'm sure you've got some dirt files we can use, and if you point them out and save me trouble, I'll tell Mr. Hughes to shoot you some severance pay."

Sol flipped him off—the double bird, twirling at eye level.

Pete let him go. Dig his neck: 360'd by a jumbo hand print.

"I'll bet you keep the good stuff in that cabinet."

"No! There's nothing in there you'd want!"

"Open it for me, then."

"No! It's locked, and I'm not giving you the combination!"

Pete kneed him in the balls. Maltzman hit the floor gasping. Pete tore his shirt off and stuffed a wad of fabric in his mouth.

Check that TV by the couch—gooood audial cover.

Pete turned it on full blast. A car huckster hit the screen, screaming shit about the new Buick line. Pete pulled his piece and shot the padlock off the cabinet—wood chips sprayed out craaaazy.

Three files fell out—maybe thirty skank pages total.

Sol Maltzman shrieked through his gag. Pete kicked him unconscious and turned the TV down.

He had three files and a bad case of the post-strongarm hungries. The ticket was Mike Lyman's and the Steak Lunch De-Luxe.

Dirt De-Luxe pending: Sol wouldn't hoard bum information.

Pete took a back booth and noshed a T-bone and hash browns. He laid the folders out for easy perusal.

The first file featured document photos and typed notes. No Hollywood gossip; no *Hush-Hush* feature ammo.

The pix detailed bankbook tallies and an income tax return. The tax filer's name came off familiar: Mr. Hughes' pal George Killebrew, some Tricky Dick Nixon flunky.

The name on the bankbook was "George Kill*ington*." The 1957 deposit total was $87,416.04. George Kill*ebrew*'s reported income for the year: $16,850.00.

A two-syllable name change—hiding over seventy grand.

Sol Maltzman wrote: "Bank employees confirm that Killebrew deposited the entire $87,000 in five to ten thousand dollar cash increments. They also confirm that the tax identification number that he gave was false. He withdrew the entire amount in cash, along with six thousand odd dollars in interest, closing out the account before the bank sent out its standard notification of interest income to the Federal tax authorities."

Unreported income and unreported bank interest. Bingo: felony tax fraud.

Pete made a late snap-connection.

The House Committee on Un-American Activists fucked Sol Maltzman. Dick Nixon was a HUAC member; George Killebrew worked for him.

File #2 featured blow-job pix galore. The suckee: a teenage pansy. The sucker, Sol Maltzman identified: "HUAC counsel Leonard Hosney, 43, of Grand Rapids, Michigan. My soul-debilitating work for *Hush-Hush* finally paid off in the form of a tip proffered by a bouncer at a male brothel in Hermosa Beach. He took the photos and assured me that the boy is a minor. He will be supplying additional documentation photos in the near future."

Pete chained a cigarette butt to tip. The Big Picture came into focus.

The files were Sol's revenge against HUAC. It was some kind of fucked-up penance: Sol wrote right-wing-slanted smears and stashed this shit for belated payback.

File #3 packed more photos: of canceled checks, deposit slips and bank notes. Pete shoved his food aside—*this* was smear bait supreme.

Sol Maltzman wrote: "The political implications of Howard Hughes' 1956 loan of $200,000 to Richard Nixon's brother Donald are staggering, especially since Nixon is expected to be the 1960 Republican Presidential nominee. This is a clear-cut case of an immensely wealthy industrialist buying political influence. It can be circumstantially supported by serving up many verifiable examples of Nixon-initiated policy directly beneficial to Hughes."

Pete rechecked the evidence pix. The verification was solid—straight down the line.

His food was cold. He'd sweated his shirt starched to wilted.

Insider knowledge was a big fucking blast.

His day was all aces and 8's—some dead man's hand he couldn't play or fold.

He could hold onto the Hughes/Nixon dirt. He could let Gail take Sol's job at *Hush-Hush*—she'd done magazine work before—she was tired of divorce shakedowns anyway.

The HUAC staff was aces flush, but MONEY angles eluded him. Kemper Boyd's walk-on had his antenna feelers perk-perk-perking.

Pete drove to the Miramar Hotel and staked out the parking lot. Boyd's car was stashed back by the pool. Lots of women in swimsuits were out sunning—surveillance conditions could be worse.

Hours dragged by. The women came and went. Dusk hampered and shut down the view.

Miami crossed his mind—tiger-striped cabs and hungry gators.

6:00 P.M., 6:30, 7:00. 7:22: Boyd and Ward Fucking Littell walking by the pool.

They got into Boyd's rent-a-car. They pulled out onto Wilshire eastbound.

Littell was Joe Scaredy Cat to Boyd's Cool Cat. Memory Lane: those Feds and him shared a history.

Pete eased into traffic behind them. They did a two-car roll-out: east on Wilshire, Barrington north to Sunset. Pete dawdled back and leapfrogged lanes—mobile bird-dog jobs jazzed him.

He was good. Boyd was unhip to the tail—he could tell.

They cruised east on Sunset: Beverly Hills, the Strip, Hollywood. Boyd turned north on Alta Vista and parked—midway down a block of small stucco houses.

Pete slid to the curb three doors up. Boyd and Littell got out; a streetlamp lit their moves.

They put on gloves. They grabbed flashlights. Littell unlocked the trunk and picked up a tool box.

They walked up to a pink stucco house, picked the lock and entered.

Flashlight beams crisscrossed the windows. Pete U-turned and spotted the curb plate: 1541 North.

It had to be a bug/wire job. FBI men called B&E's "black baggers."

The living-room lights snapped on. The fuckers were going at it brazen.

Pete grabbed his reverse book off the backseat. He skimmed it by the dashboard light.

1541 North Alta Vista matched to: Darleen Shoftel, HO3-6811.

Bug jobs took about an hour—he could run her through R&I. He saw a phone booth back at the corner—he could call and watch the house simultaneous.

He walked down and buzzed the County line. Karen Hiltscher picked up—he recognized her voice immediately.

"Records and Information."

"Karen, it's Pete Bondurant."

"You knew it was me after all this time?"

"I guess it's just one of those voices. Look, can you run somebody for me?"

"I suppose, even though you're not a deputy sheriff anymore, and I really shouldn't."

"You're a pal."

"I sure am, especially after the way you—"

"The name's Darleen Shoftel. That's D-A-R-L-E-E-N, S-H-O-F-T-E-L. The last known address I have is 1541 North Alta Vista, Los Angeles. Check all—"

"I know what to do, Pete. You just hold the line."

Pete held. House lights blinked up the block—covert Feds at work.

Karen came back on. "Darleen Shoftel, white female, DOB 3/9/32. No wants, no warrants, no criminal record. She's clean with the DMV, but West Hollywood Vice has a blue sheet on her. There's one notation, dated 8/14/57. It says that a complaint was filed against her by the management at Dino's Lodge. She was soliciting for acts of prostitution at the bar. She was questioned and released, and the investigating detective described her as a 'high-class call girl.'"

"That's all?"

"That's not bad for one phone call."

Pete hung up. He saw the house lights blip off and checked his watch.

Boyd and Littell walked out and loaded their car. Sixteen minutes flat—a black-bag world record.

They drove away. Pete leaned against the booth and worked up a scenario.

Sol Maltzman was working up his own scheme, unknown to the Feds. Boyd was in town to warn him on the Gretzler hit and hot-wire a call girl's pad. Boyd was a glib liar: "I've got an 'in' on the McClellan Committee."

Boyd knew he clipped Gretzler—a McClellan Committee witness. Boyd told Hoover he clipped Gretzler. Hoover said, That's no skin off my ass.

Boyd's car: McClellan Committee-vouchered. Hoover: well-known Bobby Kennedy hater and subterfuge king. Boyd, smooth and educated: probably a good infiltration man.

Question #1: Did the infiltration tie in to the wire job? Question #2: If this turns into money, who signs *my* paycheck?

Maybe Jimmy Hoffa—the McClellan Committee's chief target. Fred Turentine could piggyback the Fed wiring and pick up every word the Feds did.

Pete saw $$$'s—like a 3-across slot-machine jackpot.

He drove home to the watchdog pad. Gail was on the portico— her cigarette tip bobbed and dipped, like she was pacing.

He parked and walked up. He kicked an overflowing ashtray and spilled butts on some prize rosebushes.

Gail backed away from him. Pete kept his voice soft and low.

"How long have you been out here?"

"For hours. Sol was calling every ten minutes, begging for his files. He said you stole some files of his and pushed him around."

"It was business."

"He was frantic. I couldn't listen."

Pete reached for her arms. "It's cold out. Let's go inside."

"No. I don't want to."

"Gail—"

She pulled away. "No! I don't want to go back in that big awful house!"

Pete cracked some knuckles. "I'll take care of Sol. He won't bother you anymore."

Gail laughed—shrill and weird and something else. "I know he won't."

"What do you mean?"

"I mean he's dead. I called him back to try to calm him down, and a policeman answered the phone. He said Sol shot himself."

Pete shrugged. He didn't know what to do with his hands.

Gail ran to her car. She stripped gears pulling out of the driveway—and almost plowed a woman pushing a baby carriage.

5

(Washington, D.C., 12/7/58)

WARD WAS SCARED. Kemper knew why: Mr. Hoover's private briefings spawned legends.

They waited in his outer office. Ward sat hold-your-breath still. Kemper knew: he'll be twenty minutes late exactly.

He wants Ward cowed. He wants *me* here to buttress the effect.

He'd already phoned in his report: The Shoftel job went perfectly. A Los Angeles-based agent was assigned to monitor the bug and wiretap recordings from a listening post and forward the salient tapes to Littell in Chicago. Ace wire man Ward would cull them—and send the best excerpts to Mr. Hoover.

Jack wasn't due in L.A. until December 9th. Darleen Shoftel was servicing four tricks a night—the listening-post man praised her stamina. The L.A. *Times* ran a brief mention of Sol Maltzman's suicide. Mr. Hoover said Pete Bondurant probably "fired him" rather harshly.

Ward crossed his legs and straightened his necktie. Don't: Mr. Hoover hates fidgeters. He ordered us here to reward you—so please do not fidget.

Hoover walked in. Kemper and Littell stood up.

"Gentlemen, good morning."

They said, "Good morning, Sir"—in unison, with no overlap.

"I'm afraid this will have to be brief. I'm meeting Vice-President Nixon shortly."

Littell said, "I'm very pleased to be here, Sir."

Kemper almost winced: Do not interject comments, however servile.

"My schedule forces me to effect brevity. Mr. Littell, I appreciate the job you and Mr. Boyd did in Los Angeles. I'm rewarding you with a position on the Chicago Top Hoodlum Squad. I'm doing this at the displeasure of SAC Leahy, who considers you best suited for political surveillance work. I realize, Mr. Littell, that you consider the CPUSA ineffectual, if not moribund. I deem this attitude dangerously fatuous, and sincerely hope you'll outgrow it. You're a personal colleague of mine now, but I warn you not to be seduced by the dangerous life. You can't possibly be as good at it as Kemper Boyd is."

6

(Washington, D.C., 12/8/58)

LITTELL DID PAPERWORK in his bathrobe.

He did it exultantly hung over: they celebrated with Cordon Rouge and Glenlivet. The damage showed: empty bottles and room-service carts piled with untouched food.

Kemper showed restraint. He didn't. Hoover's "brevity" stung; champagne and scotch let him make fun of it. Coffee and aspirin hardly dented his hangover.

A snowstorm closed the airport—he was stuck in his hotel room. Hoover sent up a mimeo file for him to study.

CHICAGO TOP HOODLUM SQUAD CONFIDENTIAL: CRIME FIGURES, LOCATIONS, METHODS OF OPERATION AND RELATED OBSERVATIONS.

It ran sixty detail-padded pages. Littell popped two more aspirin and underlined salient facts.

The current stated goal of the Top Hoodlum Program (outlined in Bureau Directive #3401, 12/19/57) is the gathering of organized crime intelligence. At this date, and until direct notice of a superseding policy, any and all criminal intelligence gathered is to be retained solely for future use. The Top Hoodlum Program is not mandated to gather intelligence to be employed in the process of directly building cases for Federal prosecution. Criminal intelligence obtained through electronic surveillance methods may be, at the discretion of the Regional SAC, transmitted to municipal police agencies and prosecuting bodies.

The elliptical gist: Hoover knows you can't prosecute the Mob and consistently win. He won't sacrifice Bureau prestige for occasional convictions.

Top Hoodlum Program squads may employ electronic surveillance methods on their own autonomy. Verbatim tape and transcription logs are to be rigorously kept and transmitted to the Regional SAC for periodic review.

Bug-and-tap carte blanche—good.

The Chicago THP Squad has effected an electronic surveillance penetration (microphone placements only) at Celano's Custom Tailors, 620 North Michigan Avenue. Both the U.S. Attorney's Office (Northern Illinois Region) and the Cook County Sheriff's Intelligence Division consider this location to be the informal headquarters of ranking Chicago mobsters, their chief lieutenants and selected underlings. A comprehensive tape and stenographer-transcribed intelligence library has been established on the listening post premises.

The suborning of informants should be considered a priority of all THP agents. As of this (12/19/57) date, no informants with intimate knowledge of the Chicago Crime Syndicate have been activated. Note: All transactions involving the exchange of informant intelligence for Bureau-vouchered monies must first be approved by the Regional SAC.

Translation: FIND YOUR OWN SNITCH.

The Top Hoodlum Program mandate currently allows for the assignment of six agents and one secretary/stenographer per regional office. Yearly budgets are not to exceed the guidelines established in Bureau directive #3403, 12/19/57.

Budget stats droned on. Littell flipped to CRIME FIGURES.

Sam Giancana, born 1908. AKA "Mo," "Momo," "Mooney." Giancana is the Chicago Mob "Boss of Bosses." He follows Al Capone, Paul "The Waiter" Ricca and Anthony "Joe Batters"/"Big Tuna" Accardo as the Chicago overlord of all gambling, loan-sharking, numbers, vending machine, prostitution and labor rackets. Giancana has been personally involved in numerous Mob-related killings. He was rejected for World War II service as a "constitutional psychopath." Giancana lives in suburban Oak Park. He is frequently seen in the company of his personal bodyguard Dominic Michael Montalvo, AKA "Butch Montrose," born 1919. Giancana is a close personal associate of International Brotherhood of Teamsters President James Riddle Hoffa. He is rumored to have a voice in the loan selection process of the Teamsters' Central States Pension Fund, an exceedingly rich and dubiously administered union trust believed to have financed many illegal ventures.

Gus Alex, born 1916. (Numerous AKA's.) Alex is the former North Side rackets boss now deployed as the Chicago Mob's political "fixer" and liaison to corrupt elements within the Chicago Police Department and the Cook County Sheriff's Office. He is a closely allied associate of Murray Llewellyn Humphreys, AKA "Hump" and "The Camel," born 1899. Humphreys is the Chicago Mob's "elder statesman." He is semi-retired, but is sometimes consulted on Chicago Mob policy decisions.

John "Johnny" Rosselli, born 1905. Rosselli is a closely allied associate of Sam Giancana and serves as the front man of the Chicago Mob-owned Stardust Hotel and Casino in Las Vegas. Rosselli is rumored to have substantial casino-hotel holdings in Havana, Cuba, along with Cuban gambling magnates Santo Trafficante Jr. and Carlos Marcello, the Mob bosses of Tampa, Florida, and New Orleans, Louisiana, respectively.

Known-associate and investment lists followed. Staggering:

Giancana/Hoffa/Rosselli/Trafficante/Marcello et al. knew every major hoodlum in every major U.S. city and owned legitimate interests in trucking firms, nightclubs, factories, race horses, banks, movie theaters, amusement parks and over three hundred Italian restaurants. Their collective indictment-to-conviction ratio: 308 to 14.

Littell skimmed an appendix: MINOR CRIME FIGURES. Mob bosses wouldn't snitch—but the little fish might.

> Jacob Rubenstein, born 1911. AKA "Jack Ruby." This man operates a striptease club in Dallas, Texas, and is known to dabble in small-time loansharking. He is rumored to occasionally transmit Chicago Mob money to Cuban politicians, including President Fulgencio Batista and rebel leader Fidel Castro. Rubenstein/Ruby is Chicago-born and has maintained extensive ties within the Chicago Mob. He is a frequent Chicago visitor.
>
> Herschel Meyer Ryskind, born 1901. AKA "Hersh," "Hesh," "Heshie." This man is a former (circa 1930s) member of the Detroit-based "Purple Gang." He resides in Arizona and Texas, but maintains strong Chicago Mob ties. He is rumored to be active in the Gulf Coast heroin trade. He is alleged to be a close friend of Sam Giancana and James Riddle Hoffa and is said to have mediated labor disputes for the Chicago Mob.

"Alleged to be"/"rumored to have"/"believed to be." Key phrases revealing a key truth: the file read noncommittal and equivocal. Hoover didn't really hate the Mob—the THP was his response to Apalachin.

> Lenny Sands, born 1924. (Formerly Leonard Joseph Seidelwitz), AKA "Jewboy Lenny." This man is considered to be a mascot to the Chicago Mob. His nominal occupation is lounge entertainer. He frequently entertains at Chicago Mob and Cook County Teamster gatherings. Sands is said to have occasionally delivered Chicago Mob funds to Cuban police officials as part of the Chicago Mob's efforts to maintain a friendly political climate in Cuba and insure the continued success of their Havana casinos. Sands

has a vending machine pick-up route and is a salaried employee of the Chicago Mob's quasi-legitimate "Vendo-King" business front. (Note: <u>Sands</u> is a well-established Las Vegas/Los Angeles entertainment business "fringe character." He is also rumored to have given U.S. Senator John Kennedy (D–Massachusetts) speech lessons during his 1946 Congressional campaign.)

A Mob flunky knew Jack Kennedy. And *he* wired a whore's pad to entrap him.

Littell jumped back and forth: MINOR CRIME FIGURES to RELATED OBSERVATIONS.

Chicago Mob territories are geographically divided. The North Side, Near North Side, West Side, South Side, Loop, Lakefront and northern suburb areas are run by underbosses who report directly to <u>Sam Giancana</u>.

<u>Mario Salvatore D'Onofrio</u>, born 1912. <u>AKA "Mad Sal."</u> This man is an independent loan shark and bookmaker. He is allowed to operate because he pays <u>Sam Giancana</u> a large operating tribute. <u>D'Onofrio</u> was convicted of 2nd Degree Manslaughter in 1951 and served a five-year sentence at the Illinois State Penitentiary at Joliet. A prison psychiatrist described him as a "Psychopathically-derived criminal sadist with uncontrollable psycho-sexual urges to inflict pain." He was recently a suspect in the torture-murders of two Bob O'Link Country Club golf professionals rumored to owe him money.

Independent bookmaker-loansharks flourish in Chicago. This is due to <u>Sam Giancana</u>'s policy of extracting high-percentage operating tributes. One of Giancana's most fearsome underbosses, <u>Anthony "Icepick Tony" Iannone</u> (born 1917), serves as the Chicago Mob's liaison to independent bookmaker-loanshark factions. <u>Iannone</u> is strongly believed to be responsible for the mutilation murders of no less than nine heavily indebted loanshark customers.

Names jumped out. Odd appellations made him laugh.

Tony "the Ant" Spilotro, Felix "Milwaukee Phil" Alderisio, Frank "Franky Strongy" Ferraro.

Joe Amato, Joseph Cesar Di Varco, Jackie "Jackie the Lackey" Cerone.

The Teamsters' Central States Pension Fund remains a source of constant law enforcement speculation. Does <u>Sam Giancana</u> have final Fund loan approval? What is the established protocol for granting loans to criminals, quasi-legitimate businessmen and labor racketeers seeking capital?

Jimmy "Turk" Torello, Louie "the Mooch" Eboli.

The Miami PD Intelligence Squad believes that <u>Sam Giancana</u> is a silent partner in the <u>Tiger Kab Kompany</u>, a Teamster-owned taxi service run by Cuban refugees believed to possess extensive criminal records.

Daniel "Donkey Dan" Versace, "Fat Bob" Paolucci—
The phone rang. Littell fumbled for it—eyestrain had him seeing double.

"Hello?"

"It's me."

"Kemper, hi."

"What have you been doing? When I left you were two sheets to the wind."

Littell laughed. "I've been reading the THP file. And so far, I'm not too impressed with Mr. Hoover's anti-Mob mandate."

"Watch your mouth, he might have bugged your room."

"That's a cruel thought."

"Yes, if not far-fetched. Ward, look, it's still snowing, and you'll never be able to fly out today. Why don't you meet me at the Committee office? Bobby and I are grilling a witness. He's a Chicago man, and you might learn something."

"I could use some air. You're at the old Senate Office Building?"

"Right, suite 101. I'll be in interview room A. It's got an observation corridor, so you'll be able to watch. And remember my cover. I'm retired from the FBI."

"You're a glib dissembler, Kemper. It's rather sad."

"Don't get lost in the snow."

* * *

The setup was perfect: a closed hallway with one-way glass access and wall-mounted speakers. Partitioned off in cubicle A: the Kennedy brothers, Kemper, and a blond man.

Cubicles B, C and D were vacant. He had the watching gallery to himself—the snowstorm must have scared people home.

Littell hit the speaker switch. Voices crackled out with minimum static.

The men sat around a desk. Robert Kennedy played host and worked the tape recorder.

"Take your time, Mr. Kirpaski. You're a voluntary witness, and we're here at your disposal."

The blond man said, "Call me Roland. Nobody calls me Mr. Kirpaski."

Kemper grinned. "Any man who rolls over on Jimmy Hoffa deserves that formality."

Brilliant Kemper—reviving his Tennessee drawl.

Roland Kirpaski said, "That's nice, I guess. But you know, Jimmy Hoffa's Jimmy Hoffa. What I mean is, it's like they say about the elephant. He don't forget."

Robert Kennedy laced his hands behind his head. "Hoffa will have plenty of time in prison to remember everything that put him there."

Kirpaski coughed. "I'd like to say something. And I'd . . . uh . . . like to read it off when I testify in front of the Committee."

Kemper said, "Go ahead."

Kirpaski leaned his chair back. "I'm a union guy. *I'm a Teamster.* Now, I told you all them stories about Jimmy doing this and doing that, you know, telling his guys to lean on these other guys that wouldn't play ball and so forth. I guess maybe all that stuff is illegal, but you know what? That don't bother me so much. The only reason I'm so-called rolling over on Jimmy is because I can add up two and two and get four, and I heard enough at fucking Chicago Local 2109 to figure out that Jimmy Fucking Hoffa is cutting side deals with management, which means that he is a scab piece of shit, pardon my French, and I want to go on the record as saying that that is my motive for ratting him off."

John Kennedy laughed. Littell flashed on the Shoftel job and winced.

Robert Kennedy said, "Duly noted, Roland. You'll be able to read any statement you like before you testify. And remember, we're saving your testimony for a televised session. Millions of people will see you."

Kemper said, "The more publicity you get, the more unlikely it is that Hoffa will attempt reprisals."

Kirpaski said, "Jimmy don't forget. He's like an elephant that way. You know those gangster pictures you showed me? Those guys I saw Jimmy with?"

Robert Kennedy held up some photos. "Santo Trafficante Jr. and Carlos Marcello."

Kirpaski nodded. "Right. I also want to go on the record as saying that I've heard good things about those guys. I heard they hire union men exclusively. No Mafia guy ever said, 'Roland, you're a dumb Southside Polack' to me. Like I said, they visited Jimmy at his suite at the Drake, and all they talked about was the weather, the Cubs and politics in Cuba. I want to go on the record as saying I got no gripe against the fucking Mafia."

Kemper winked at the one-way. "Neither does J. Edgar Hoover."

Littell laughed. Kirpaski said, "What?"

Robert Kennedy drummed the table. "Mr. Boyd is performing for some unseen colleague of his. Now, Roland, let's get back to Miami and Sun Valley."

Kirpaski said, "I'd like to. Jesus, this snow."

Kemper stood up and stretched his legs. "Walk us through your observations again."

Kirpaski sighed. "I was a Chicago delegate to the convention last year. We stayed at the Deauville in Miami. I was still friendly with Jimmy then, because I hadn't figured out he was a scab cocksucker cutting side deals with—"

Robert Kennedy cut in. "Stick to the point, please."

"The point is I ran some errands for Jimmy. I went by the Tiger Kab stand, which is spelled with a goddamn K, and picked up some cash so Jimmy could take some guys from the Miami locals out on a boat to shoot sharks with Tommy guns, which is one of Jimmy's favorite Florida things to do. I must have picked up three grand easy. The cabstand was like the planet Mars. All these crazy Cuban guys wearing tiger-colored shirts. The boss Cuban was this guy Fulo. He was selling these hot TVs out of the parking lot. The Tiger Kab business is strictly cash-operated. If you want my considered opinion, it's a tax evasion bounce looking to happen."

Static rattled the speaker—Littell tapped the squelch button and smoothed the volume out. John Kennedy looked bored and restless.

Robert Kennedy doodled on a notepad. "Tell us about Anton Gretzler again."

Kirpaski said, "We all went out shark shooting. Gretzler came along. Him and Jimmy were talking by themselves over on one end of the boat away from the shark shooters. I was down in the can, being seasick. I guess they thought they had privacy, because they were talking up this not-too-legal-sounding stuff, which I want to go on the record as stating was no skin off my ass, because it didn't involve collusion with management."

John Kennedy tapped his watch. Kemper prompted Kirpaski. "What exactly did they discuss?"

"Sun Valley. Gretzler said he had land surveys done, and his surveyor said the land wouldn't fall into the swamp for five years or so, which would let them off the hook, legally speaking. Jimmy said he could tap the Pension Fund for three million dollars to purchase the land and prefab material, and maybe they could pocket some cash up front."

Robert Kennedy jumped up. His chair crashed—the one-way glass shimmied. "That is very strong testimony! That is a virtual admission of conspiracy to commit land fraud and intent to defraud the Pension Fund!"

Kemper picked the chair up. "It's only courtroom valid if Gretzler corroborates it or perjures himself denying it. Without Gretzler, it's Roland's word versus Hoffa's. It comes down to credibility, and Roland has two drunk-driving convictions while Hoffa's record is technically clean."

Bobby fumed. Kemper said, "Bob, Gretzler has to be dead. His car was dumped in a swamp, and the man himself can't be found. I've put a lot of hours in trying to find him, and I haven't turned up one viable lead."

"He could have faked his own death to avoid appearing before the Committee."

"I think that's unlikely."

Bobby straddled his chair and gripped down on the slats. "You may be right. But I may still send you down to Florida to make sure."

Kirpaski said, "I'm hungry."

Jack rolled his eyes. Kemper winked at him.

Kirpaski sighed. "I said I'm hungry."

Kemper checked his watch. "Wrap it up for the senator, Roland. Tell us how Gretzler got drunk and shot his mouth off."

"I get the picture. Sing for your supper."

Bobby said, "Goddamnit—"

"All right, all right. It was after the shark shoot. Gretzler was pissed because Jimmy ridiculed him for holding his Tommy gun like a sissy. Gretzler started talking up these rumors he'd heard about the Pension Fund. He said he heard the Fund is a lot fucking richer than people knew, and nobody could subpoena the books, because the books weren't real. See, Gretzler said there were these 'real' Teamster Fund books, probably in code, with fucking tens of millions of dollars accounted for in them. This money gets loaned out at these exorbitant rates. There's supposed to be some retired Chicago gangster—a real brain—who's the bookkeeper for the 'real' books and the 'real' money, and if you're thinking about corroboration, forget it—I'm the only one Gretzler was talking to."

Bobby Kennedy pushed his hair back. His voice went high, like an excited child's.

"It's our big wedge, Jack. First we subpoena the front books again and determine their solvency. We trace the loaned-out money the Teamsters admit to and try to determine the existence of hidden assets within the Fund and the probability that those 'real' books exist."

Littell pressed up to the glass. He felt magnetized: tousle-haired, passionate Bobby—

Jack Kennedy coughed. "It's strong stuff. *If* you can produce verifiable testimony on those books before the Committee's mandate ends."

Kirpaski applauded. "Hey, he speaks. Hey, Senator, glad you could join us."

Jack Kennedy cringed, mock-wounded. Bobby said, "My investigators will be forwarding our evidence along to other agencies. Whatever we dig up will be acted on."

Jack said, "Eventually?" Littell translated: "Too late to bolster *my* career."

The brothers locked eyes. Kemper leaned across the table between them. "Hoffa's got a block of houses set up at Sun Valley. He's down there himself, giving PR tours. Roland's going down to look around. He runs a Chicago local, so it won't look suspicious. He'll be calling in to report what he sees."

Kirpaski said, "Yeah, and I'm also gonna 'see' this cocktail waitress I met when I went down for the convention. But you know what? I'm not gonna tell my wife she's on the menu."

Jack motioned Kemper in close. Littell caught static-laced whispers:

"I'm flying to L.A. when this snow lets up."/"Call Darleen Shoftel—I'm sure she'd love to meet you."

Kirpaski said, "I'm hungry."

Robert Kennedy packed his briefcase. "Come on, Roland. You can join the family for supper at my house. Try not to say 'fuck' around my children, though. They'll learn the concept soon enough."

The men filed out a back door. Littell hugged the glass for one last look at Bobby.

7

(Los Angeles, 12/9/58)

DARLEEN SHOFTEL FAKED a mean climax. Darleen Shoftel had whore pals over for shop talk.

Darleen was a bigggg name dropper.

She said Franchot Tone dug bondage. She called Dick Contino a champion muff diver. She dubbed B-movie man Steve Cochran "Mr. King Size."

Phone calls came in and went out. Darleen talked to tricks, hooker chums and Mom in Vincennes, Indiana.

Darleen loved to talk. Darleen said nothing to explain why two Feds wired her crib.

They attached the Fed apparatus four days ago. 1541 North Alta Vista was miked up floor to rafters.

Fred Turentine piggybacked the Boyd/Littell setup. He heard everything the FBI heard. The Feds rented a listening-post house down the block; Freddy monitored *his* hookups from a van parked next door and kept Pete supplied with tape copies.

And Pete smelled money and called Jimmy Hoffa—maybe a bit premature.

Jimmy said, "You got a good sense of smell. Come down to

Miami on Thursday and tell me what you got. If you got nothing, we can go out on my boat and shoot sharks."

Thursday was tomorrow. Shark shooting was strictly for geeks. Freddy's pay was two hundred a day—steep for a crash course in extraneous sex jive.

Pete moped around the watchdog house. Pete savored the hints he dropped on Mr. Hughes: I know you lent Dick Nixon's brother some coin. Pete kept playing the piggyback tapes out of sheer boredom.

He hit Play. Darleen moaned and groaned. Bedsprings creaked; something headboard-like slammed something wall-like. Dig it: Darleen with a big fat porker in the saddle.

The phone rang—Pete grabbed it fast.

"Who's this?"

"It's Fred. Get over here now—we just hit paydirt."

The van was crammed with contraptions and gadgets. Pete banged his knees climbing in.

Freddy looked all hopped up. His zipper was down, like he'd been choking the chicken.

He said, "I recognized that Boston accent immediately, and I called you the second they started screwing. Listen, this is live."

Pete put on headphones. Darleen Shoftel spoke, loud and clear.

". . . you're a bigger hero than your brother. I read about you in *Time* magazine. Your PT boat got rammed by the Japs or something."

"I'm a better swimmer than Bobby, that's certainly true."

3-cherry jackpot: Gail Hendee's old squeeze, Jack the K.

Darleen: "I saw your brother's picture in *Newsweek* magazine. Doesn't he have like four thousand kids?"

Jack: "At least three thousand, with new ones popping up all the time. When you visit his house the little shits attach themselves to your ankles. My wife finds Bobby's need to breed vulgar."

Darleen: " 'Need to breed'—that's cute."

Jack: "Bobby's a true Catholic. He needs to have children and punish the men that he hates. If his hate instincts weren't so unerring, he'd be a colossal pain in the ass."

Pete clamped his headset down. Jack Kennedy talked, postfuck languid:

"I don't hate like Bobby does. Bobby hates with a fury. Bobby hates Jimmy Hoffa very powerfully and simply, which is why he'll win in the end. I was in Washington with him yesterday. He was taking a deposition from a Teamster man who'd become disgusted with Hoffa and had decided to inform on him. Here's this dumb brave Polack, Roland something from Chicago, and Bobby takes him home for dinner with his family. You see, uh . . ."

"Darleen."

"Right, Darleen. You see, Darleen, Bobby's more heroic than I am because he's truly passionate and generous."

Gadgets blinked. Tape spun. They hit the royal flush/Irish Sweepstakes jackpot—Jimmy Hoffa would SHIT when he heard it.

Darleen: "I still think that PT boat thing was pretty swell."

Jack: "You know, you're a good listener, Arlene."

Fred looked ready to DROOL. His fucking eyes were dollar-sign dilated.

Pete made fists. "This is mine. You just sit tight and do what I tell you to."

Freddy cringed. Pete smiled—his hands put the fear out every time.

A Tiger Kab met his plane. The driver talked Cuban politics non-stop: *El grande* Castro advancing! *El puto* Batista in retreat!

Pancho dropped him off at the cabstand. Jimmy had the dispatch shack commandeered—goons were packing up life jackets and Tommy guns.

Hoffa shooed them out. Pete said, "Jimmy, how are you?"

Hoffa picked up a nail-studded baseball bat. "I'm all right. You like this? Sometimes the sharks get up close to the boat and you can give them a few whacks."

Pete opened up his tape rig and plugged it into a floor outlet. The tiger-stripe wallpaper made his head swim.

"It's cute, but I brought something better."

"You said you smelled money. That's gotta mean my money for your trouble."

"There's a story behind it."

"I don't like stories, unless I'm the hero. And you know I'm a busy—"

Pete put a hand on his arm. "An FBI man braced me. He said

he had an 'in' on the McClellan Committee. He said he made me for the Gretzler job, and he said Mr. Hoover didn't care. You know Hoover, Jimmy. He's always left you and the Outfit alone."

Hoffa pulled his arm loose. "So? You think they've got evidence? Is that what that tape's all about?"

"No. I think the Fed's spying on Bobby Kennedy and the Committee for Hoover, or something like that, and I think Hoover's on our side. I tailed the guy and his partner up to a fuck pad in Hollywood. They bugged and wired it, and my guy Freddy Turentine hooked up a piggyback. Now, listen."

Hoffa tapped his foot like he was bored. Hoffa brushed tiger-striped lint off his shirt.

Pete tapped Play. Tape hissed. Sex groans and mattress squeaks escalated.

Pete timed the fuck. Senator John F. Kennedy: 2.4-minute man.

Darleen Shoftel faked a climax. There, that Boston bray: "My goddamn back gave out."

Darleen said, "It was goooood. Short and sweet's the best."

Jimmy twirled his baseball bat. Goosebumps bristled up his arms.

Pete pushed buttons and cut to the good stuff. Two-Minute Jack rhapsodized:

". . . a Teamster man who'd become disgusted with Hoffa . . . this dumb brave Polack, Roland something from Chicago."

Hoffa popped goosebumps. Hoffa choked up a grip on his bat.

"This Roland something has working-class panache. . . . Bobby's got his teeth in Hoffa. When Bobby bites down he doesn't let go."

Hoffa popped double goosebumps. Hoffa went bug-eyed like a fright-wig nigger.

Pete stood back.

Hoffa let fly—watch that nail-topped Louisville Slugger GO—

Chairs got smashed to kindling. Desks got knocked legless. Walls got spike-gouged down to the baseboard.

Pete stood *way* back. A glowing plastic Jesus doorstop got shattered into eight million pieces.

Paper stacks flew. Wood chips ricocheted. Drivers watched

from the sidewalk—Jimmy roundhoused the window and glass-blasted them.

James Riddle Hoffa: heaving and voodoo-eyed stuporous.

His bat snagged on a doorjamb. Jimmy stared at it—say what?

Pete grabbed him in a bear hug. Jimmy's eyes rolled back, catatonic-style.

Hoffa flailed and squirmed. Pete squeezed him close to breathless and baby-talked him.

"I can keep Freddy on the piggyback for two hundred a day. Sooner or later we might get something you can fuck the Kennedys with. I've got some political dirt files, too. They might do us some good someday."

Hoffa focused in half-lucid. His voice came out laughing-gas squeaky.

"What . . . do . . . you . . . want?"

"Mr. Hughes is going nuts. I was thinking I'd get next to you and cover my bets."

Hoffa squirmed free. Pete almost choked on his smell: sweat and bargain-basement cologne.

His color receded. He caught his breath. His voice went down a few octaves.

"I'll give you 5% of this cabstand. You keep the piggyback going in L.A. and show up here once in a while to keep these Cubans in line. Don't try to Jew me up to 10%, or I'll say 'fuck you' and send you back to L.A. on the bus."

Pete said, "It's a deal."

Jimmy said, "I've got a job in Sun Valley. I want you to come with me."

They took a Tiger Kab out. Shark-shoot goodies bulged up the trunk: nail bats, Tommy guns and suntan oil.

Fulo Machado drove. Jimmy wore fresh threads. Pete forgot to bring spare clothes—Hoffa's stink stuck to him.

Nobody talked—Jimmy Hoffa sulking killed chitchat. They passed buses filled with Teamster chumps headed for the sucker-bait tract pads.

Pete did mental arithmetic.

Twelve cab drivers working around-the-clock. Twelve men with Jimmy Hoffa-sponsored green cards—taking short-end taxi-fare splits to stay in America. Twelve moonlighters: stickup men, strikebreakers, pimps. 5% of the top-end money and whatever else he could scrounge—this gig packed potential.

Fulo pulled off the highway. Pete saw the spot where he whacked Anton Gretzler. They followed a bus convoy to the bait cribs—three miles from the Interstate easy.

Movie spotlights gave off this huge glow—extra-bright, like a premiere at Grauman's Chinese. The cosmetic Sun Valley looked good: tidy little houses in a blacktop-paved clearing.

Teamsters were boozing at card tables—at least two hundred men squeezed into the walkways between houses. A gravel parking lot was crammed with cars and buses. A bar-b-que pit stood adjacent—check that spike-impaled steer twirling and basting.

Fulo parked close to the action. Jimmy said, "You two wait here."

Pete got out and stretched. Hoffa zoomed into the crowd—toadies swarmed him right off the bat.

Fulo sharpened his machete on a pumice stone. He packed it in a scabbard strapped to the backseat.

Pete watched Jimmy work the crowd.

He showed off the pads. He gave little speeches and wolfed bar-b-que. He seized up and flushed around a blond Polack type.

Pete chain-smoked. Fulo played the cab radio: some Spanish-language pray-for-Jesus show.

A few buses took off. Two carloads of hookers pulled in—trashy Cuban babes chaperoned by off-duty state troopers.

Jimmy huckstered and hawked Sun Valley applications. Some Teamsters grabbed their cars and fishtailed off drunk and rowdy.

The Polack bagged a U-drive Chevy and burned gravel like he had a hot date somewhere.

Jimmy walked up fast—stubby legs chugging on overdrive. You didn't need a fucking road map: the Polack was Roland Kirpaski.

They piled in to the tiger sled. Fulo gunned it. The radio geek cranked up a donation plea.

Lead-foot Fulo got the picture. Lead-foot Fulo went 0 to 60 inside six seconds.

Pete saw the Chevy's taillights. Fulo floored the gas and rammed them. The car swerved off the road, clipped some trees and stalled dead.

Fulo brodied in close. His headlights strafed Kirpaski—stumbling through a clearing thick with marsh grass.

Jimmy got out and chased him. Jimmy waved Fulo's machete. Kirpaski tripped and stood up flashing two fuck-you fingers.

Hoffa came in swinging. Kirpaski went down flailing wrist stumps gouting blood. Jimmy swung two-handed—scalp flaps flew.

The radio clown jabbered. Kirpaski convulsed head to toe. Jimmy wiped blood from his eyes and kept swinging.

8

(Miami, 12/11/58)

KEMPER CALLED THE car game Devil's Advocate. It helped him keep his loyalties straight and honed his ability to project the right persona at the right time.

Bobby Kennedy's distrust inspired the game. His southern accent slipped once—Bobby caught it instantly.

Kemper cruised South Miami. He began the game by marking who knew what.

Mr. Hoover knew *everything*. SA Boyd's "retirement" was cloaked in FBI paperwork: if Bobby sought corroboration, he'd find it.

Claire knew everything. She'd never judge his motives or betray him.

Ward Littell knew of the Kennedy incursion. He most likely disapproved of it—Bobby's crimebuster fervor deeply impressed him. Ward was also an ad hoc infiltration partner, compromised by the Darleen Shoftel wire job. The job shamed him—but gratitude for his THP transfer outweighed his guilt pangs. Ward did not know that Pete Bondurant killed Anton Gretzler; Ward did not know that Mr. Hoover condoned the murder. Bondurant terrified Ward—a sane response to Big Pete and the legend he inspired. The Bondurant matter should be kept from Ward at all cost.

Bobby knew that he was pimping for Jack—supplying him with the numbers of especially susceptible old flames.

Questions and answers next: practice for deflecting skepticism.

Kemper braked for a woman lugging groceries. His game snapped to the present tense.

Bobby thinks I'm chasing leads on Anton Gretzler. I'm really protecting Howard Hughes' pet thug.

Q: You seem bent on crashing the Kennedy inner circle.

A: I can spot comers a mile off. Cozying up to Democrats doesn't make me a Communist. Old Joe Kennedy's as far right as Mr. Hoover.

Q: You "cozied up" to Jack rather fast.

A: If circumstances had been different, I could have been Jack.

Kemper checked his notebook.

He had to go by Tiger Kab. He had to go to Sun Valley and show mug shots to the witness who saw the "big man" avert his face off the Interstate.

He'd show him *old* mug shots—bad current Bondurant likenesses. He'd discourage a confirmation: you didn't really see *this* man, did you?

A tiger-striped taxi swerved in front of him. He saw a tiger-striped hut down the block.

Kemper pulled up and parked across the street. Some curbside loungers smelled COP and dispersed.

He walked into the hut. He laughed—the wallpaper was fresh-flocked tiger-striped velveteen.

Four tiger-shirted Cubans stood up and circled him. They wore their shirttails out to cover waistband bulges.

Kemper pulled his mug shots out. The tiger men circled in tighter. A man pulled out a stiletto and scratched his neck with the blade.

The other tiger men laughed. Kemper braced the closest one. "Have you seen him?"

The man passed the mug strip around. Every man flashed recognition and said "No."

Kemper grabbed the strip. He saw a white man on the sidewalk checking his car out.

The knife man sidled up close. The other tiger men giggled. The knife man twirled his blade right upside the gringo's eyes.

Kemper judo-chopped him. Kemper snapped his knees with a sidekick. The man hit the floor prone and dropped his shiv.

Kemper picked it up. The tiger men backed off en masse. Kemper stepped on the knife man's knife hand and slammed the blade through it.

The knife man screamed. The other tiger men gasped and tittered. Kemper exited with a tight little bow.

* * *

He drove out I-95 to Sun Valley. A gray sedan stuck close behind him. He changed lanes, dawdled and accelerated—the car followed from a classic tail distance.

Kemper eased down an off-ramp. A hicktown main street ran perpendicular to it—just four gas stations and a church. He pulled into a Texaco and parked.

He walked to the men's room. He saw the tail car idle up to the pumps. The white man dawdling by Tiger Kab got out and looked around.

Kemper shut the door and pulled his piece. The room was smelly and filthy.

He counted seconds off his watch. He heard foot scuffs at fifty-one.

The man nudged the door open. Kemper yanked him in and pinned him to the wall.

He was fortyish, sandy-haired, and slender. Kemper pat-searched him from the ankles up.

No badge, no gun, no leatherette ID holder.

The man didn't blink. The man ignored the revolver in his face.

The man said, "My name is John Stanton. I'm a representative of a U.S. Government agency, and I want to talk to you."

"About what?"

Stanton said, "Cuba."

9

(Chicago, 12/11/58)

SNITCH CANDIDATE AT work: "Jewboy Lenny" Sands collecting jukebox cash.

Littell tailed him. They hit six Hyde Park taverns in an hour—Lenny worked fast.

Lenny kibitzed. Lenny cracked jokes. Lenny passed out Johnnie Walker Red Label miniatures. Lenny told the story of Come-San-Chin, the Chinese cocksucker—and bagged his coin receipts inside seven minutes.

Lenny was a deficient tail-spotter. Lenny had unique THP stats: lounge entertainer/Cuban bagman/Mob mascot.

Lenny pulled up to the Tillerman's Lounge. Littell parked and walked in thirty seconds behind him.

The place was overheated. A bar mirror tossed his reflection back: lumberjack coat, chinos, work boots.

He still looked like a college professor.

Teamster regalia lined the walls. A framed glossy stood out: Jimmy Hoffa and Frank Sinatra holding up trophy fish.

Workingmen walked through a hot buffet line. Lenny sat at a back table, with a stocky man wolfing corned beef.

Littell ID'd him: Jacob Rubenstein/AKA Jack Ruby.

Lenny brought his coin sacks. Ruby brought a suitcase. It was a probable vending cash transfer.

There were no empty tables adjoining them.

Men stood at the bar drinking lunch: rye shots and beer chasers. Littell signaled for the same—nobody laughed or snickered.

The barman served him and took his money. He downed his lunch quick—just like his Teamster brothers.

The rye made him sweat; the beer gave him goosebumps. The combination tamped down his nerves.

He'd had one THP Squad meeting. The men seemed to resent him—Mr. Hoover slotted him in personally. An agent named Court Meade came on friendly; the others welcomed him with nods and perfunctory handshakes.

He had three days in as a THP agent. Including three shifts at the bug post, studying Chi-mob voices.

The barman cruised by. Littell raised two fingers—the same way his Teamster brothers called for refills.

Sands and Ruby kept talking. There was no table space near them—he couldn't get close enough to listen.

He drank and paid up. The rye went straight to his head.

Drinking on duty was a Bureau infraction. Not *strictly* illegal—like wiring fuck pads to entrap politicians.

The agent working the Shoftel post was probably swamped—he hadn't sent a single tape out yet. Mr. Hoover's Kennedy hate seemed insanely misguided.

Robert Kennedy seemed heroic. Bobby's kindness to Roland Kirpaski seemed pure and genuine.

A table opened up. Littell walked through the lunch line and grabbed it. Lenny and Rubenstein/Ruby were less than three feet away.

Ruby was talking. Food dribbled down his bib.

"Heshie always thinks he's got cancer or some farkakte disease. With Hesh a pimple's always a malignant tumor."

Lenny picked at a sandwich. "Heshie's a class guy. When I played the Stardust Lounge in '54 he came every night. Heshie always preferred lounge acts to the main-room guys. Jesus Christ and the Apostles could be playing the big room at the Dunes, and Heshie'd be over at some slot palace checking out some guinea crooner 'cause his cousin's a made guy."

Ruby said, "Heshie loves blow jobs. He gets blow jobs exclusively, 'cause he says it's good for his prostrate. He told me he hasn't dipped the schnitzel since he was with the Purples back in the '30s and some shiksa tried to schlam him with a paternity suit. Heshie told me he's had over ten thousand blow jobs. He likes to watch 'The Lawrence Welk Show' while he gets blown. He's got nine doctors for all these diseases he thinks he's got, and all the nurses blow him. That's how he knows it's good for his prostrate."

"Heshie" was most likely Herschel Meyer Ryskind: "active in the Gulf Coast heroin trade."

Lenny said, "Jack, I hate to stiff you with all these coins, but I didn't have time to go to the bank. Sam was very specific. He said you were making rounds and only had limited time. I'm glad we had time to nosh, though, 'cause I always enjoy watching you eat."

Ruby wiped his bib. "I'm worse when the food's better. There's a deli in Big D that's to die for. Here, my shirt's just spritzed. At that deli it's spray-painted."

"Who's the money for?"

"Batista and the Beard. Santo and Sam are hedging their bets political-wise. I'm flying down next week."

Lenny pushed his plate aside. "I've got this new routine where Castro comes to the States and gets a job as a beatnik poet. He's smoking maryjane and talking like a shvartze."

"You're big-room talent, Lenny. I've always said so."

"Keep saying it, Jack. If you keep saying it, somebody might hear you."

Ruby stood up. "Hey, you never know."

"That's right, you never do. Shalom, Jack. It's always a pleasure watching you eat."

Ruby walked out with his suitcase. Jewboy Lenny lit a cigarette and rolled his eyes up to God.

Lounge acts. Blow jobs. Rye and beer for lunch.

Littell walked back to his car lightheaded.

Lenny left twenty minutes later. Littell tailed him to Lake Shore Drive northbound.

Whitecap spray hit the windshield—booming wind had the lake churning. Littell cranked up his heater—too hot replaced too cold.

The liquor left him cotton-mouthed and just a tad woozy. The road kept dipping—just a little.

Lenny signaled to exit. Littell leaped lanes and eased up behind him. They swung down into the Gold Coast—too upscale to be Vendo-King turf.

Lenny turned west on Rush Street. Littell saw high-toned cocktail spots up ahead: brownstone fronts and low-key neon signs.

Lenny parked and walked into Hernando's Hideaway. Littell cruised by extra-slow.

The door swung back. He saw two men kissing—a little half-second teaser blip.

Littell double-parked and switched jackets: lumberjack to blue blazer. The chinos and boots had to stay.

He walked in bucking wind. The place was dark and mid-afternoon quiet. The decor was discreet: all polished wood and forest-green leather.

A banquette section was roped off. Two duos sat at opposite ends of the bar: older men, Lenny and a college boy.

Littell took a seat between them. The bartender ignored him.

Lenny was talking. His inflections were polished now—devoid of growl and Yiddish patter.

"Larry, you should have seen this wretched man eat."

The bartender came over. Littell said, "Rye and beer." Heads turned his way.

The barman poured a shot. Littell downed it and coughed. The barman said, "My, aren't we thirsty!"

Littell reached for his wallet. His ID holder popped out and landed on the bar badge-up.

He grabbed it and threw some change down. The barman said, "Don't we want our beer?"

* * *

Littell drove to the office and typed up a tail report. He chewed a roll of Clorets to kill his liquor breath.

He omitted mention of his beverage intake and his blunder at Hernando's Hideaway. He stressed the basic gist: that Lenny Sands might have a secret homosexual life. This might prove to be a recruitment wedge: he was obviously hiding that life from his Mob associates.

Lenny never noticed him. So far, his tail stood uncompromised.

Court Meade rapped on his cubicle screen. "You've got a long-distance call, Ward. A man named Boyd in Miami on line 2."

Littell picked up. "Kemper, hi. What are you doing back in Florida?"

"Working at cross-purposes for Bobby and Mr. Hoover, but don't tell anyone."

"Are you getting results?"

"Well, people keep approaching me, and Bobby's witnesses keep disappearing, so I'd have to call it a toss-up. Ward . . ."

"You need a favor."

"Actually, two."

Littell leaned his chair back. "I'm listening."

Boyd said, "Helen's flying into Chicago tonight. United flight 84, New Orleans to Midway. She gets in at 5:10. Will you pick her up and take her to her hotel?"

"Of course. And I'll take her to dinner, too. Jesus, that's last-minute but great."

Boyd laughed. "That's our Helen, an impetuous traveler. Ward, do you remember that man Roland Kirpaski?"

"Kemper, I saw him three days ago."

"Yes, you did. In any event, he's allegedly down in Florida, but I can't seem to find him. He was supposed to call Bobby and report on Hoffa's Sun Valley scheme, but he hasn't called, and he left his hotel last night and hasn't returned."

"Do you want me to go by his house and talk to his wife?"

"Yes, if you wouldn't mind. If you get anything pertinent, leave a coded message with Communications in D.C. I haven't found a hotel here yet, but I'll check in with them to see if you've called."

"What's the address?"

"It's 818 South Wabash. Roland's probably off on a toot with some bimbo, but it can't hurt to see if he's called home. And Ward?"

"I know. I'll remember who you're working for and play it close to the vest."

"Thanks."

"You're welcome. And by the way, I saw a man today who's as good a role player as you are."

Boyd said, "That's impossible."

Mary Kirpaski rushed him inside. The house was overfurnished and way overheated.

Littell took off his overcoat. The woman almost pushed him into the kitchen.

"Roland always calls home every night. He said if he didn't call on this trip, I should cooperate with the authorities and show them his notebook."

Littell smelled cabbage and boiled meat. "I'm not with the McClellan Committee, Mrs. Kirpaski. I haven't really worked with your husband."

"But you know Mr. Boyd and Mr. Kennedy."

"I know Mr. Boyd. He's the one who asked me to check on you."

She'd chewed her nails bloody. Her lipstick was applied way off-center.

"Roland didn't call last night. He kept this notebook on Mr. Hoffa's doings, and he didn't take it to Washington because he wanted to talk to Mr. Kennedy before he agreed to testify."

"What notebook?"

"It's a list of Mr. Hoffa's Chicago phone calls, with dates and everything like that. Roland said he stole the phone bills of some of Mr. Hoffa's friends because Mr. Hoffa was afraid to call long distance from his hotel, because he thought his phone might be tapped."

"Mrs. Kirpaski . . ."

She grabbed a binder off the breakfast table. "Roland would be so mad if I didn't show it to the authorities."

Littell opened the binder. Page 1 listed names and phone numbers, neatly arranged in columns.

Mary Kirpaski crowded up to him. "Roland called up the phone companies in all the different cities and found out who the numbers belonged to. I think he impersonated policemen or something like that."

Littell flipped pages front to back. Roland Kirpaski printed legibly and neatly.

Several "calls received" names were familiar: Sam Giancana, Carlos Marcello, Anthony Iannone, Santo Trafficante Jr. One name was familiar and scary: Peter Bondurant, 949 Mapleton Drive, Los Angeles.

Hoffa called Big Pete three times recently: 11/25/58, 12/1/58, 12/2/58.

Bondurant snapped manacles bare-handed. He allegedly killed people for ten thousand dollars and plane fare.

Mary Kirpaski was fondling rosary beads. She smelled like Vicks VapoRub and cigarettes.

"Ma'am, could I use the phone?"

She pointed to a wall extension. Littell pulled the cord to the far end of the kitchen.

She left him alone. Littell heard a radio snap on one room over.

He dialed the long-distance operator. She put him through to the security desk at L.A. International Airport.

A man answered. "Sergeant Donaldson, may I help you?"

"This is Special Agent Littell, Chicago FBI. I need an expedite on some reservation information."

"Yes, sir. Tell me what you need."

"I need you to query the airlines that fly Los Angeles to Miami round-trip. I'm looking for reservations going out on either December the eighth, ninth or tenth, and returning any time after that. I'm looking for a reservation under the name Peter Bondurant, spelled B-O-N-D-U-R-A-N-T, or reservations charged to the Hughes Tool Company or Hughes Aircraft. If you turn up positive on any of that, and the reservation is in a man's name, I need a physical description of the man either picking up his ticket or boarding the airplane."

"Sir, that last part is needle-in-a-haystack stuff."

"I don't think so. My suspect is a male Caucasian in his late thirties, and he's about six-foot-five and very powerfully built. If you see him, you don't forget him."

"I copy. Do you want me to call you back?"

"I'll hold. If you don't get me anything in ten minutes, come back on the line and take my number."

"Yes, sir. You hold now. I'll get right on this."

Littell held the line. An image held him: Big Pete Bondurant crucified. The kitchen cut through it: cramped, hot, saints' days marked on a parish calendar—

Eight minutes crawled by. The sergeant came back on the line, excited.

"Mr. Littell?"

"Yes."

"Sir, we hit. I didn't think we would, but we did."

Littell got out his notebook. "Tell me."

"American Airlines flight 104, Los Angeles to Miami. It left L.A. at 8:00 A.M. yesterday, December 10th, and arrived in Miami at 4:10 P.M. The reservation was made under the name Thomas Peterson and was charged to Hughes Aircraft. I talked to the agent who issued the ticket, and she remembered that man you described. You were right, you don't forget—"

"Is there a return reservation?"

"Yes, sir. American flight 55. It arrives in Los Angeles at 7:00 A.M. tomorrow morning."

Littell felt dizzy. He cracked a window for some air.

"Sir, are you there?"

Littell cut the man off and dialed 0. A cold breeze flooded the kitchen.

"Operator."

"I need Washington, D.C. The number is KL4-8801."

"Yes, sir, just one minute."

The call went through fast. A man said, "Communications, Special Agent Reynolds."

"This is Special Agent Littell in Chicago. I need to transmit a message to SA Kemper Boyd in Miami."

"Is he with the Miami office?"

"No, he's on a detached assignment. I need you to transmit the message to the Miami SAC and have him locate SA Boyd. I think it's a matter of a hotel check, and if it wasn't so urgent, I'd do it myself."

"This is irregular, but I don't see why we can't do it. What's your message?"

Littell spoke slowly. "Have circumstantial and suppositional— underline those two words—evidence that J.H. hired our old oversized French confrere to eliminate Committee witness R.K. Our confrere leaves Miami late tonight, American flight 55. Call me in Chicago for details. Urge that you inform Robert K. immediately. Sign it W.J.L."

The agent repeated the message. Littell heard Mary Kirpaski sobbing just outside the kitchen door.

Helen's flight was late. Littell waited in a cocktail lounge near the gate.

He rechecked the phone call list. His instinct held firm: Pete Bondurant killed Roland Kirpaski.

Kemper mentioned a dead witness named Gretzler. If he could connect the man to Bondurant, TWO murder charges might fly.

Littell sipped rye and beer. He kept checking the back wall mirror to gauge his appearance.

His work clothes looked wrong. His glasses and thinning hair didn't jibe with them.

The rye burned; the beer tickled. Two men walked up to his table and grabbed him.

They jerked him upright. They clamped down on his elbows. They steered him back to an enclosed phone bank.

It was swift and sure—no civilian patrons caught it.

The men pinned his arms back. Chick Leahy stepped out of a shadow and got right up in his face.

Littell felt his knees go. The men propped him up on his toes.

Leahy said, "Your message to Kemper Boyd was intercepted. You could have violated his cover on the incursion. Mr. Hoover does not want to see Robert Kennedy aided, and Peter Bondurant is a valued colleague of Howard Hughes, who is a great friend of Mr. Hoover and the Bureau. Do you know what *fully* coded messages are, Mr. Littell?"

Littell blinked. His glasses fell off. Everything went blurry.

Leahy jabbed his chest, hard. "You're off the THP and back on the Red Squad as of now. And I strongly urge you not to protest."

One man grabbed his notebook. The other man said, "You reek of liquor."

They elbowed him aside and walked out. The whole thing took thirty seconds.

His arms hurt. His glasses were scratched and dented. He couldn't quite breathe or stay balanced on his feet.

He swerved back to his table. He choked down rye and beer and leveled his shakes out.

His glasses fit crooked. He checked out his new mirror image: the world's most ineffectual workingman.

An intercom boomed, "United flight 84 from New Orleans is now arriving."

Littell finished his drinks and chased them with two Clorets. He walked over to the gate and bucked passengers up to the jetway.

Helen saw him and dropped her bags. Her hug almost knocked him down.

People stepped around them. Littell said, "Hey, let me see you."

Helen looked up. Her head grazed his chin—she'd grown tall.

"You look wonderful."

"It's Max Factor number-four blush. It does wonders for my scars."

"What scars?"

"Very funny. And what are *you* now, a lumberjack?"

"I was. For a few days, at least."

"Susan says Mr. Hoover's finally letting you chase gangsters."

A man kicked Helen's garment bag and glared at them. Littell said, "Come on, I'll buy you dinner."

They had steaks at the Stockyard Inn. Helen talked a blue streak and got tipsy on red wine.

She'd gone from coltish to rangy; her face had settled in strong. She'd quit smoking—she said she knew it was fake sophistication.

She always wore her hair in a bun to flaunt her scars. She wore it down now—it rendered her disfigurement matter-of-fact.

A waiter pushed the dessert cart by. Helen ordered pecan pie; Littell ordered brandy.

"Ward, you're letting me do all the talking."

"I was waiting to summarize."

"Summarize what?"

"You at age twenty-one."

Helen groaned. "I was starting to feel mature."

Littell smiled. "I was going to say that you've become poised, but not at the expense of your exuberance. You used to trip over your words when you wanted to make a point, but now you think before you talk."

"Now people just trip over my luggage when I'm excited about meeting a man."

"A man? You mean a friend twenty-four years your senior who watched you grow up?"

She touched his hands. "A man. I had a professor at Tulane who said that things change with old friends and students and teachers, so what's a quarter of a century here and there?"

"You're saying he was twenty-five years older than you?"

Helen laughed. "Twenty-six. He was trying to minimize things to make them seem less embarrassing."

"You're saying you had an affair with him?"

"Yes. And I'm saying it wasn't lurid and pathetic, but going out with undergrad boys who thought I'd be easy because I was scarred up was."

Littell said, "Jesus Christ."

Helen waved her fork at him. "Now I know you're upset, because some part of you is still a Jesuit seminarian, and you only invoke our Savior's name when you're flustered."

Littell sipped brandy. "I was going to say, 'Jesus Christ, have Kemper and I ruined you for young men your own age?' Are you going to spend your youth chasing middle-aged men?"

"You should hear Susan and Claire and I talk."

"You mean my daughter and her best friends swear like longshoremen?"

"No, but we've been discussing men in general and you and Kemper in specific for years, in case you've felt your ears burning."

"I can understand Kemper. He's handsome and dangerous."

"Yes, and he's heroic. But he's a tomcat, and even Claire knows it."

Helen squeezed his hands. He felt his pulse racing. He got this Jesus Fucking Christ crazy idea.

Littell took off his glasses. "I'm not so sure Kemper's heroic. I think heroes are truly passionate and generous."

"That sounds like an epigram."

"It is. Senator John F. Kennedy said it."

"Are you enamored of him? Isn't he some terrible liberal?"

"I'm enamored of his brother Robert, who is truly heroic."

Helen pinched herself. "This is the strangest conversation to be having with an old family friend who's known me since before my father died."

That Idea—Jesus Christ.

Littell said, "I'll be heroic for you."

Helen said, "We can't let this be pathetic."

He drove her to her hotel and carried her bags upstairs. Helen kissed him goodbye on the lips. His glasses snagged in her hair and fell to the floor.

Littell drove back to Midway and caught a 2:00 A.M. flight to Los Angeles. A stewardess gawked at his ticket: his return flight left an hour after they landed.

One last brandy let him sleep. He woke up woozy just as the plane touched down.

He made it with fourteen minutes to spare. Flight 55 from Miami was landing at gate 9, on time.

Littell badged a guard and got permission to walk out on the tarmac. A wicked hangover headache started kicking in.

Baggage men cruised by and checked him out. He looked like a middle-aged bum who'd slept in his clothes.

The airplane landed. A ground crew pushed passenger steps out.

Bondurant exited up front. Jimmy Hoffa flew his killers first-class.

Littell walked up to him. His chest hammered and his legs went numb. His voice fluttered and broke.

"Someday I'm going to punish you. For Kirpaski and everything else."

10

(Los Angeles, 12/14/58)

FREDDY LEFT A note under the wiper blades:

"I'm getting some lunch. Wait for me."

Pete climbed in the back of the van. Freddy had a cooling system rigged: a fan aimed at a big bowl of ice cubes.

Tape spun. Lights flashed. Graph needles twitched. The place was like the cockpit of a low-rent spaceship.

Pete cracked a side window for some air. A Fed type walked by—probably listening-post personnel.

Air blew in—Santa Ana hot.

Pete dropped an ice cube down his pants and laughed falsetto. He sounded just like SA Ward J. Littell.

Littell squeaked his warning. Littell smelled like stale booze and sweat. Littell had jackshit for evidence.

He could have told him:

I whacked Anton Gretzler, but Hoffa killed Kirpaski. I stuffed shotgun shells in his mouth and glued his lips shut. We torched Roland and his car at a refuse dump. Double-aught buckshot blew his head up—you'll never get a dental-work ID.

Littell doesn't know that Jack's big mouth killed Roland Kirpaski. The listening-post Fed might be sending him tapes—but Littell hasn't put the scenario together.

Freddy climbed in the van. He adjusted some graph gizmo and spritzed grief straight off.

"That Fed that just walked by keeps checking out the van. I'm parked here at all fucking hours, and all he needs to do is sweep me with a fucking Geiger counter to figure out I'm doing the same fucking thing he is. I can't park around the fucking block 'cause I'll lose the fucking signal. I need a fucking house around here to work from, 'cause then I can set up some equipment that's fucking powerful enough to pick up from the Shoftel babe's pad, but that fucking Fed bagged the last fucking For Rent sign in the fucking neighborhood, and the fucking two hundred a day you and Jimmy are paying me ain't enough to make up for the fucking risks I'm taking."

Pete snagged an ice cube and squeezed it into shards. "Are you finished?"

"No. I've also got a fucking boil on my fucking ass from sleeping on the fucking floor here."

Pete popped a few knuckles. "Wrap it up."

"I need some *good* money. I need it for fucking hazardous-duty pay, and to upgrade this operation with. Get me some good money and I'll kick a nice piece of it back to you."

"I'll talk to Mr. Hughes and see what I can do."

Howard Hughes got his dope from a nigger drag queen named Peaches. Pete found the drop pad cleaned out—the queen next door said Peaches went up on a sodomy bounce.

Pete improvised.

He drove to a supermarket, bought a box of Rice Krispies and pinned the toy badge inside to his shirt front. He called Karen

Hiltscher at R&I and glommed some prime information: the fry cook at Scrivner's Drive-In sold goofballs and might be extortable. She described him: white, skinny, acne scars and Nazi tattoos.

Pete drove to Scrivner's. The kitchen door was open; the geek was at the deep fryer, dipping spuds.

The geek saw him.

The geek said, "That badge is a fake."

The geek looked at the freezer—a sure sign that he stored his shit there.

Pete said, "How do you want to do this?"

The geek pulled a knife. Pete kicked him in the balls and deep-fried his knife hand. Six seconds only—pill heists didn't rate total mayhem.

The geek screamed. Street noise leveled out the sound. Pete shoved a sandwich in his mouth to muzzle him.

His dope stash was in the freezer next to the ice cream.

The hotel manager gave Mr. Hughes a Christmas tree. It was fully flocked and decorated—a bellboy left it outside the bungalow.

Pete carried it into the bedroom and plugged it in. Sparkly lights blinked and twinkled.

Hughes blipped off a Webster Webfoot cartoon. "What is this? And why are you carrying a tape recorder?"

Pete dug through his pockets and tossed pill vials under the tree. "Ho, ho, fucking ho. It's Christmas ten days early. Codeine and Dilaudid, ho, ho."

Hughes scrunched himself up on his pillows. "Well . . . I'm delighted. But aren't you supposed to be auditioning stringers for *Hush-Hush*?"

Pete yanked the tree cord and plugged in the tape rig. "Do you still hate Senator John F. Kennedy, Boss?"

"I certainly do. His father screwed me on business deals going back to 1927."

Pete brushed pine needles off his shirt. "I think we've got the means to juke him pretty good in *Hush-Hush*, if you've got the money to keep a certain operation going."

"I've got the money to buy the North American continent, and if you don't quit leading me on I'll put you on a slow boat to the Belgian Congo!"

Pete pressed the Play button. Senator Jack and Darleen Shoftel boned and groaned. Howard Hughes clutched his bedsheets, dead ecstatic.

The fuck crescendoed and diminuendoed. Jack K. said, "My goddamn back gave out."

Darleen said, "It was goooood. Short and sweet's the best."

Pete pressed Stop. Howard Hughes twitched and trembled.

"We can have *Hush-Hush* print this up if we're careful, Boss. But we've got to watch the wording real close."

"Where . . . did . . . you . . . get that?"

"The girl's a prostitute. The FBI had her place wired, and Freddy Turentine hooked up on top of it. So we can't print anything that would tip the Feds off. We can't print anything that only could have come from the bug."

Hughes plucked at his sheets. "Yes, I'll finance your 'operation.' Have Gail Hendee write the story up—something like 'Priapic Senator Dallies with Hollywood Playgirl.' We've got an issue coming out the day after tomorrow, so if Gail writes it today and gets it to the office by this evening, it can make that next issue. Have Gail write it today. The Kennedy family will ignore it, but the legitimate newspapers and wire services might come to us asking for details to enlarge the story, which of course we will give them."

Big Howard beamed kid-at-Christmas-like. Pete plugged his tree back in.

Gail needed convincing. Pete sat her down on the watchdog-house veranda and laid out a line of sweet talk.

"Kennedy's a geek. He had you meet him on his goddamned honeymoon. He dropped you two weeks later, and kissed you off with a goddamn mink coat."

Gail smiled. "He was nice, though. He never said, 'Honey, let's get a divorce racket going.' "

"When your old man's worth a hundred million dollars, you don't have to do things like that."

Gail sighed. "You win, like always. And you know why I haven't been wearing that mink lately?"

"No."

"I gave it to Mrs. Walter P. Kinnard. You took a big cut of her alimony, and I figured she could use some cheering up."

Twenty-four hours zipped by.

Hughes kicked loose thirty grand. Pete pocketed fifteen. If the *Hush-Hush* smear exposed the bug, he'd be covered financially.

Freddy bought a long-range transceiver and started looking for a house.

That Fed kept eyeballing his van. Jack K. didn't call or drop by. Freddy figured Darleen was only worth one poke.

Pete stuck by the watchdog-house phone. Geeks kept interrupting his daydreams.

Two *Hush-Hush* stringer prospects called: ex-vice cops hipped on Hollywood lowdown. They flunked his impromptu pop quiz: Who's Ava Gardner fucking?

He made some calls out—and planted a new Hughes double at the Beverly Hilton. Karen Hiltscher recommended the man: her scabby wino father-in-law. Pops said he'd work for three hots and a cot. Pete booked the Presidential Suite and placed a standing room-service order: T-bird and cheeseburgers for breakfast, lunch and dinner.

Jimmy Hoffa called. He said, The *Hush-Hush* thing sounds good, but I want MORE! Pete neglected to share his basic opinion: Jack and Darleen were just a two-minute mattress ride.

He kept thinking about Miami. The cabstand, colorful spics, tropical sunshine.

Miami felt like adventure. Miami felt like money.

He woke up early publication morning. Gail was gone—she'd taken to avoiding him with aimless drives to the beach.

Pete walked outside. His first-press-run copy was stuffed in the mailbox, per instructions.

Dig the cover lines: "Tomcat Senator Likes Catnip! Ask Nipped-At L.A. Kittens!" Dig the illustration: John Kennedy's face on a cartoon cat's body, the tail wrapped around a blonde in a bikini.

He flipped to the piece. Gail used the pen name Peerless Politicopundit.

U.S. Senate cloakroom wags say he's far from being the most dedicatedly demonic Democrat dallier. No, Senator L.B. (Lover Boy?) Johnson probably tops political polls in that department, with Florida's George F. 'Pass the Smackeroos' Smathers coming in second. No, Senator John F. Kennedy is rather a tenuously tumescent tomcat, with a tantalizingly trenchant taste for those finely-furred and felicitous felines who find him fantastically fetching themselves!

Pete skimmed the rest. Gail played it half-assed—the smear wasn't vicious enough. Jack Kennedy ogled women and "bewitched, bothered and bewildered" them with "baubles, bangles, beads" and "brilliant Boston beatitudes." No heavy-duty skank; no implied fucking; no snide jabs at Two-Minute-Man Jack.

Perk, perk, perk—his all-star feelers started twitching—

Pete drove downtown and cruised by the *Hush-Hush* warehouse. Things looked absolutely first-glance SOP.

Men were wheeling bound stacks out on dollies. Men were loading pallets. A line of newsstand trucks were backed up to the dock.

SOP, but:

Two unmarked prowl cars were parked down the street. That ice cream wagon idling by looked dicey—the driver was talking into a hand mike.

Pete circled the block. The fuzz multiplied: four unmarkeds at the curb and two black-and-whites around the corner.

He circled again. The shit hit the fan and sprayed out in all directions.

Four units were jammed up to the loading dock—running full lights and siren.

Plainclothesmen piled out. A bluesuit cordon hit the warehouse with cargo hooks.

An LAPD van blocked the distribution trucks off. Swampers dropped their loads and threw their hands up.

It was fucking scandal-rag chaos. It was fucking skank-sheet Armaggedon—

Pete drove to the Beverly Hills Hotel. A Big Ugly Picture formed: somebody ratted off the Kennedy issue.

He parked and ran by the pool. He saw a big crowd outside the Hughes bungalow.

They were peeping in Big Howard's bedroom window. They looked like fucking ghouls at an accident scene.

He ran up and pushed to the front. Billy Eckstine nudged him. "Hey, check this out."

The window was open. Two men were jacking up Mr. Hughes—double-teaming him with Big Verbal Grief.

Robert Kennedy and Joseph P. Kennedy Sr.

Hughes was swaddled in bed quilts. Bobby was waving a hypo. Old Joe was raging.

". . . You're a pathetic lecher and a narcotics addict. I am two seconds away from exposing you to the whole wide world, and if you think I'm bluffing please note that I opened the window to let your hotel neighbors have a sneak preview of what the whole world will know if you ever allow your filthy scandal rag to write another word about my family."

Hughes cringed. His head banged the wall and sent a picture frame toppling.

Some all-star voyeurs dug the show: Billy, Mickey Cohen, some faggot Mouseketeer sporting a jumbo mouse-ear beanie.

Howard Hughes whimpered. Howard Hughes said, "Please don't hurt me."

Pete drove to the Shoftel pad. The Big Ugly Picture expanded: either Gail snitched or the Feds exposed the piggyback.

He pulled up behind Freddy's van. Freddy was down on his knees in the street—cuffed to the front-bumper housing.

Pete ran over. Freddy yanked at his shackle chain and tried to stand up.

He'd scraped his wrist bloody. He'd ripped his knees raw crawling on the pavement.

Pete knelt down in front of him. "What happened? Quit grabbing at that and look at me."

Freddy did some wrist contortions. Pete slapped him. Freddy snapped to and focused in half-alert.

He said, "The listening-post guy sent his transcripts to some Fed in Chicago and told him he was hinked on my van. Pete, this thing plays wrong to me. There's just one FBI guy working single-o, like he went off half-cocked or some—"

Pete ran across the lawn and bolted the porch. Darleen Shoftel ducked out of his way, snapped a high heel and fell on her ass.

The Big and Ugly Final Picture:

Spackle-coated mikes on the floor. Two tap-gutted phones belly-up on an end table.

And SA Ward J. Littell, standing there in an off-the-rack blue suit.

It was a stalemate. You don't whack FBI men impromptu.

Pete walked up to him. He said, "This is a bullshit roust, or you wouldn't be here alone."

Littell just stood there. His glasses slipped down his nose.

"You keep flying out here to bother me. Next time's the last time."

Littell said, "I've put it together." The words came out all quivery.

"I'm listening."

"Kemper Boyd told me he had an errand at the Beverly Hills Hotel. He talked to you there, and you got suspicious and tailed him. You saw us black-bag this place and got your friend to put in auxiliary wires. Senator Kennedy told Miss Shoftel about Roland Kirpaski testifying, and you heard it and talked Jimmy Hoffa into giving you the contract."

Booze guts. This skinny stringbean cop with 8:00 A.M. liquor breath.

"You've got no proof, and Mr. Hoover doesn't care."

"You're right. I can't arrest you and Turentine."

Pete smiled. "I'll bet Mr. Hoover liked the tapes. I'll bet he won't be too pleased that you blew this operation."

Littell slapped his face. Littell said, "That's for the blood on John Kennedy's hands."

The slap was weak. Most women slapped harder.

He knew she'd leave a note. He found it on their bed, next to her house keys.

> I know you figured out I soft-soaped the article. When the editor didn't question it I realized it wasn't enough and called Bob Kennedy. He said he would probably be able to pull strings and get the issue pulled. Jack is sort of callous in some ways, but he doesn't deserve what you planned. I don't want to be with you any more. Please don't try to find me.

She left the clothes he bought her. Pete dumped them out in the street and watched cars drive over them.

II
(Washington, D.C., 12/18/58)

"TO SAY THAT I am furious belittles the concept of fury. To say that I consider your actions outrageous demeans the notion of outrage."

Mr. Hoover paused. The pillow on his chair made him tower over two tall men.

Kemper looked at Littell. They sat flush in front of Hoover's desk.

Littell said, "I understand your position, Sir."

Hoover patted his lips with a handkerchief. "I do not believe you. And I do not rate the value of objective awareness nearly as high as I rate the virtue of loyalty."

Littell said, "I acted impetuously, Sir. I apologize for that."

" 'Impetuous' describes your attempt to contact Mr. Boyd and foist your preposterous Bondurant suspicions on him and Robert Kennedy. 'Duplicitous' and 'treacherous' describe your unauthorized flight to Los Angeles to uproot an official Bureau operation."

"I considered Bondurant a murder suspect, Sir. I thought that he had implemented a piggyback on the surveillance equipment that Mr. Boyd and I had installed, and I was correct."

Hoover said nothing. Kemper knew he'd let the silence build.

The operation blew from two flanks. Bondurant's girlfriend tipped Bobby to a smear piece; Ward logicked out the Kirpaski hit himself. That logic held a certain validity: Pete was in Miami concurrent with Roland.

Hoover fondled a paperweight. "Is murder a Federal offense, Mr. Littell?"

"No, Sir."

"Are Robert Kennedy and the McClellan Committee direct rivals of the Bureau?"

"I don't consider them that, Sir."

"Then you are a confused and naive man, which your recent actions more than confirm."

Littell sat perfectly still. Kemper saw his pulse hammer his shirt front.

Hoover folded his hands. "January 16, 1961, marks the twentieth anniversary of your Bureau appointment. You are to retire on that day. You are to work at the Chicago office until then. You are to remain on the CPUSA Surveillance Squad until the day you retire."

Littell said, "Yes, Sir."

Hoover stood up. Kemper stood a beat later, per protocol. Littell stood up too fast—his chair teetered.

"You owe your continued career and pension to Mr. Boyd, who was most persuasive in convincing me to be lenient. I expect you to repay my generosity by promising to maintain absolute silence regarding Mr. Boyd's McClellan Committee and Kennedy family incursion. *Do you* promise that, Mr. Littell?"

"Yes, Sir. I do."

Hoover walked out.

Kemper put his drawl on. "You can breathe now, son."

The Mayflower bar featured wraparound banquettes. Kemper sat Littell down and thawed him out with a double scotch-on-the-rocks.

They bucked sleet walking over—there was no chance to talk. Ward took the thrashing better than he expected.

Kemper said, "Any regrets?"

"Not really. I was going to retire at twenty years, and the THP is a half-measure at best."

"Are you rationalizing?"

"I don't think so. I've had a . . ."

"Finish the thought. Don't let me explicate for you."

"Well . . . I've had a . . . taste of something very dangerous and good."

"And you like it."

"Yes. It's almost as if I've touched a new world."

Kemper stirred his martini. "Do you know why Mr. Hoover allowed you to remain with the Bureau?"

"Not exactly."

"I convinced him that you were volatile, irrational and addicted to taking heedless risks. The element of truth in that convinced him that you were better off inside the barn pissing out than outside the barn pissing in. He wanted me there to buttress the intimidation, and if he had signaled me I would have laced into you myself."

Littell smiled. "Kemper, you're leading me. You're like an attorney drawing out a witness."

"Yes, and you're a provocative witness. Now, let me ask you a question. What do you think Pete Bondurant has planned for you?"

"My death?"

"Your postretirement death, more likely. He murdered his own brother, Ward. And his parents killed themselves when they found out. It's a Bondurant rumor that I've chosen to believe."

Littell said, "Jesus Christ."

He was awed. It was a perfectly lucid response.

Kemper speared the olive in his glass. "Are you going to continue the work you started without Bureau sanction?"

"Yes. I've got a good informant prospect now, and—"

"I don't want to know specifics just yet. I just want you to convince me that you understand the risks from both within and outside the Bureau, and that you won't behave foolishly."

Littell smiled—and *almost* looked bold. "Hoover would crucify me. If the Chicago Mob knew I was investigating them without sanction, they'd torture and kill me. Kemper, I've got a wild notion about where you're leading me."

"Tell me."

"You're thinking of working for Robert Kennedy for real. He's gotten to you, and you respect the work he's doing. You're going to turn things over a notch and start feeding Hoover a minimum of information and selected misinformation."

Lyndon Johnson waltzed a redhead by the back booths. He'd seen her before—Jack said he could arrange an introduction.

"You're right, but it's the senator I want to work for. Bobby's more your type. He's as Catholic as you are, and the Mob is just as much his raison d'être."

"And you'll feed Hoover as much information as you deem fit."

"Yes."

"The inherent duplicities won't bother you?"

"Don't judge me, Ward."

Littell laughed. "You enjoy my judgments. You enjoy it that someone besides Mr. Hoover has your number. So *I'll* warn *you*. Be careful with the Kennedys."

Kemper raised his glass. "I will be. And you should know that Jack might damn well be elected President two years from now. If he is, Bobby will have carte blanche to fight organized crime. A

Kennedy administration might mean considerable opportunities for both of us."

Littell raised his glass. "An opportunist like you would know."

"*Salud*. Can I tell Bobby that you'll share your intelligence with the Committee? Anonymously?"

"Yes. And it just hit me that I retire four days before the next presidential inauguration. Should your profligate friend Jack be the one taking office, you might mention a worthy lawyer-cop who needs a job."

Kemper pulled out an envelope. "You were always a quick study. And you forget that Claire has both our numbers."

"You're smirking, Kemper. Read me what you've got there."

Kemper unrolled a sheet of notebook paper. "Quote, 'And Dad, you wouldn't believe this one A.M. phone call I got from Helen. Are you sitting down? She had a hot date with Uncle Ward (date of birth March 8, 1913, to Helen's October 29, 1937) and necked with him in her room. Wait until Susan finds out! Helen's always sideswiped older men, but this is like Snow White attacking Walt Disney! And I always thought you were the one she had eyes for,' unquote."

Littell stood up, blushing. "She's meeting me later, at my hotel. I told her men liked women who traveled for them. And she's been the pursuer so far."

"Helen Agee is a college girl in the guise of a Mack truck. Remember that if things get complicated."

Littell laughed, and walked off primping. His posture was good, but those dented glasses had to go.

Idealists disdained appearances. Ward had no flair for nice things.

Kemper ordered a second martini and watched the back booths. Echoes drifted his way—congressmen were talking up Cuba.

John Stanton called Cuba a potential Agency hotspot. He said, I might have work for you.

Jack Kennedy walked in. Lyndon Johnson's redhead passed him a napkin note.

Jack saw Kemper and winked.

PART TWO

COLLUSION

January 1959–January 1961

1 2

(Chicago, 1/1/59)

UNIDENTIFIED Male #1: "Beard, schmeard. All I know is Mo's real fuckin' nervous."

Unidentified Male #2: "The Outfit's always covered its bets Cuba-wise. Santo T. is Batista's best fuckin' friend. I talked to Mo maybe an hour ago. He goes out for the paper and comes back to watch the fuckin' Rose Bowl on TV. The paper says Happy fuckin' New Year, Castro has just taken over Cuba and who knows if he's pro-U.S., pro-Russian or pro-Man-from-Mars."

Littell tilted his seat back and adjusted his headphones. It was 4:00 P.M. and snowing—but the Celano's Tailor Shop talkfest talked on.

He was alone at the THP bug post. He was violating Bureau regs and Mr. Hoover's direct orders.

Man #1: "Santo and Sam got to be sweating the casinos down there. The gross profit's supposed to run half a million a day."

Man #2: "Mo told me Santo called him right before the kick-off. The crazy fuckin' Cubans down in Miami are pitching a fit. Mo's got a piece of that cabstand, you know the one?"

Man #1: "Yeah, the Tiger Kabs. I went down there for the Teamster convention last year and rode in one of those cabs, and I was picking orange and black fuzz out of my ass for the next six fuckin' months."

Man #2: "Half those Cuban humps are pro-Beard, and half of them are pro-Batista. Santo told Sam it's nuts at the stand, like niggers when their welfare checks don't arrive."

Laughter hit the feed box—static-laced and overamplified. Littell unhooked his headset and stretched.

He had two hours left on his shift. He'd gleaned no salient intelligence so far: Cuban politics didn't interest him. He'd logged in ten days of covert listening—and accrued no hard evidence.

He cut a deal with SA Court Meade—a surreptitious work trade. Meade's mistress lived in Rogers Park; some Commie cell leaders lived nearby. They worked out an agreement: I take your job, you take mine.

They spent cosmetic time working their real assignments and flip-flopped all report writing. Meade chased Reds and an insurance-rich widow. He listened to hoodlums colloquialize.

Court was lazy and pension-secure. Court had twenty-seven years with the Bureau.

He was careful. *He* hoarded insider knowledge of Kemper Boyd's Kennedy incursion. *He* filed detailed Red Squad reports and forged Meade's signature on all THP memoranda.

He always watched the street for approaching agents. He always entered and exited the bug post surreptitiously.

The plan would work—for a while. The lackluster bug talk was vexing—he needed to recruit an informant.

He'd tailed Lenny Sands for ten consecutive nights. Sands did not habituate homosexual meeting spots. His sexual bent might not prove exploitable—Sands might belittle the threat of exposure.

Snow swirled up Michigan Avenue. Littell studied his one wallet photo.

It was a laminated snapshot of Helen. Her hairdo made her burn scars stand out.

The first time he kissed her scars she wept. Kemper called her "the Mack Truck Girl." He gave her a Mack truck bulldog hood hanger for Christmas.

Claire Boyd told Susan they were lovers. Susan said, "When the shock wears off, I'll tell Dad what I think."

She still hadn't called him.

Littell put on his headset. He heard the tailor shop door slam.

Unknown Man #1: "Sal, Sal D. Sal, do you believe this weather? Don't you wish you were down in Havana shooting dice with the Beard?"

"Sal D.": most likely Mario Salvatore D'Onofrio, AKA "Mad Sal." Key THP stats:

Independent bookmaker/loan shark. One manslaughter conviction in 1951. Labeled "a psychopathically-derived criminal sadist with uncontrollable psycho-sexual urges to inflict pain."

Unknown Man #2: "*Che se dice*, Salvatore? Tell us what's new and unusual."

Sal D.: "The news is I lost a bundle on the Colts over the Giants, and I had to tap Sam for a fucking loan."

Unknown Man #1: "You still got the church thing, Sal? Where you take the paisan groups out to Tahoe and Vegas?"

Static hit the line. Littell slapped the feed box and cleared the air flow.

Sal D.: ". . . and Gardena and L.A. We catch Sinatra and Dino, and the casinos set us up in these private slot rooms and kick back a percentage. It's what you call a junket—you know, entertainment and gambling and shit. Hey, Lou, you know Lenny the Jew?"

Lou/Man #1: "Yeah, Sands. Lenny Sands."

Man #2: "Jewboy Lenny. Sam G.'s fuckin' court jester."

Squelch noise drowned out the incoming voices. Littell slapped the console and untangled some feeder cords.

Sal D.: ". . . So I said, 'Lenny, I need a guy to travel with me. I need a guy to keep my junketeers lubed up and laughing, so they'll lose more money and juke up my kickbacks.' He said, 'Sal, I don't audition, but catch me at the North Side Elks on January 1st. I'm doing a Teamster smoker, and if you don't dig—' "

The heat needle started twitching. Littell hit the kill switch and felt the feed box go cool to the touch.

The D'Onofrio/Sands connection was interesting.

He checked Sal D.'s on-post file. The agent's summary read horrific.

D'Onofrio lives in a South Side Italian enclave surrounded by Negro-inhabited housing projects. The majority of his bettors and loan customers live within that enclave and D'Onofrio makes his collection rounds on foot, rarely missing a day. D'Onofrio considers himself to be a guiding light within his community, and the Cook County Sheriff's Gangster Squad believes that he plays the role of "protector"—i.e., protecting Italian-Americans against Negro criminal elements, and that this role and his strong-arm collection and intimidation tactics have helped to insure his long bookmaker/loanshark reign. It should also be noted that D'Onofrio was a suspect in the unsolved 12/19/57 torture-murder of Maurice Theodore Wilkins, a

Negro youth suspected of burglarizing a church rectory in
his neighborhood.

A mug shot was clipped to the folder. Mad Sal was cyst-scarred
and gargoyle ugly.

Littell drove to the South Side and circled D'Onofrio's loan turf.
He spotted him on 59th and Prairie.

The man was walking. Littell ditched his car and foot-tailed
him from thirty yards back.

Mad Sal entered apartment buildings and exited counting
money. Mad Sal tabulated transactions in a prayer book. Mad Sal
picked his nose compulsively and wore low-top tennis shoes in
a blizzard.

Littell stuck close behind him. Wind claps covered his
footsteps.

Mad Sal peeped in windows. Mad Sal took a beat cop's
money: $5 on the Moore/Durelle rematch.

The streets were near-deserted. The tail felt like a sustained
hallucination.

A deli clerk tried to stiff Mad Sal. Mad Sal plugged in a portable stapler and riveted his hands to the counter.

Mad Sal entered a church rectory. Littell stopped at the pay
phone outside and called Helen.

She picked up on the second ring. "Hello?"

"It's me, Helen."

"What's that noise?"

"It's the wind. I'm calling from a phone booth."

"You're outside in this?"

"Yes. Are you studying?"

"I'm studying torts and welcoming this distraction. Susan
called, by the way."

"Oh, shit. And?"

"And she said I'm of age, and you're free, white and forty-five.
She said, 'I'm going to wait and see if you two last before I tell
my mother.' Ward, are you coming over tonight?"

Mad Sal walked out and slipped on the rectory steps. A priest
helped him up and waved goodbye.

Littell took his gloves off and blew on his hands. "I'll be by
late. There's a lounge act I have to catch."

"You're being cryptic. You act like Mr. Hoover's looking over your shoulder every second. Kemper tells *his* daughter everything about his work."

Littell laughed. "I want you to analyze the Freudian slip you just made."

Helen whooped. "Oh, God, you're right!"

A Negro boy walked by. Mad Sal bolted after him.

Littell said, "I have to go."

"Come by later."

"I will."

Mad Sal chased the kid. Snowdrifts and low-cut sneakers slowed him down.

The Elks Hall steps were jammed. Non-Teamster admittance looked dicey: goons were running an ID checkpoint at the door.

Men filed in with bottle bags and six-packs. They had union badges pinned to their topcoats—about the same size as Bureau shields.

A fresh swarm hit the steps. Littell held up his FBI badge and pushed to the middle. The stampede jostled him inside.

A blonde in G-string and pasties ran the coat-check concession. The foyer walls were lined with bootleg slot machines. Every pull hit a jackpot—Teamsters scooped up coins and yelled.

Littell pocketed his badge. The crowd whooshed him into a big rec hall.

Card tables faced a raised bandstand. Every table was set up with whisky bottles, paper cups and ice.

Strippers dispensed cigars. Tips bought unlimited fondling.

Littell grabbed a ringside seat. A redhead dodged hands, naked—cash wads had popped her G-string.

The lights went down. A baby spot hit the bandstand. Littell built a quick scotch-on-the-rocks.

Three other men sat at his table. Total strangers pounded his back.

Lenny Sands walked on stage, twirling a mike cord à la Sinatra. Lenny mimicked Sinatra—straight down to his spitcurl and voice:

"Fly me to the moon in my souped-up Teamster rig! I'll put skidmarks on management's ass, 'cause my union contract's big! In other words, Teamsters are kings!!"

The audience hooted and yelled. A man grabbed a stripper and forced her into some dirty-dog dance steps.

Lenny Sands bowed. "Thank you thank you thank you! And ring-a-ding, men of the Northern Illinois Council of the International Brotherhood of Teamsters!"

The crowd applauded. A stripper brought ice refills by—Littell caught a breast in the face.

Lenny said, "It sure is hot up here!"

The stripper hopped on stage and dropped ice cubes down his pants. The audience howled; the man beside Littell squealed and spat bourbon.

Lenny made ecstatic faces. Lenny shook his trouser legs until the ice dropped out.

The crowd wolf-whistled and shrieked and thumped their tables—

The stripper ducked behind a curtain. Lenny put on a Boston accent—Bobby Kennedy's voice pushed into soprano range.

"Now you listen to me, Mr. Hoffa! You quit associating with those nasty gangsters and nasty truck drivers and snitch off all your friends or I'll tell my daddy on you!"

The room rocked. The room rolled. Foot stomps had the floor shaking.

"Mr. Hoffa, you're a no-goodnik and a nasty man! You quit trying to unionize my six children or I'll tell my daddy and my big brother Jack on you! You be nice or I'll tell my daddy to buy your union and make all your nasty truck drivers servants at our family compound in Hyannis Port!"

The room roared. Littell felt queasy-hot and lightheaded.

Lenny minced. Lenny preened. Lenny DID Robert F. Kennedy, faggot crusader.

"Mr. Hoffa, you stop that nasty forced bargaining this instant!"

"Mr. Hoffa, stop yelling, you're wilting my hairdo!"

"Mr. Hoffa, be NIIICE!"

Lenny squeezed the room dry. Lenny wrung it out from the basement to the roof.

"Mr. Hoffa, you're just SOOOOO butch!"

"Mr. Hoffa, quit scratching—you'll ruin my nylons!"

"Mr. Hoffa, your Teamsters are just TOOOOO sexy! They've got the McClellan Committee and me in such a TIZZY!"

Lenny kept it cranking. Littell caught something three drinks in: he never ridiculed *John* Kennedy. Kemper called it the Bobby/

Jack dichotomy: if you liked one man, you disliked the other.

"Mr. Hoffa, stop confusing me with facts!"

"Mr. Hoffa, stop berating me, or I won't share my hairdressing secrets with your wife!"

The Elks Hall broiled. Open windows laced in freezing air. The drink ice ran out—strippers filled bowls with fresh snow.

Mob men table-hopped. Littell spotted file-photo faces.

Sam "Mo"/"Momo"/"Mooney" Giancana. Icepick Tony Iannone, Chi-mob underboss. Donkey Dan Versace, Fat Bob Paolucci, Mad Sal D'Onofrio himself.

Lenny wrapped it up. The strippers shimmied on stage and took bows.

"So fly me to the stars, union paycheck fat! Jimmy Hoffa is our tiger now—Bobby's just a scrawny rat! In other words, Teamsters are kings!!!!"

Table thumps, claps, cheers, yells, whistles, howls—

Littell ran out a back exit and sucked air in. His sweat froze; his legs fluttered; his scotch dinner stayed down.

He checked the door. A conga line snaked through the rec hall—strippers and Teamsters linked up hands-to-hips. Mad Sal joined them—his tennis shoes squished and leaked snow.

Littell caught his breath and slow-walked around to the parking lot. Lenny Sands was cooling off by his car, scooping ice packs from a snow drift.

Mad Sal walked up and hugged him. Lenny made a face and pulled free.

Littell crouched behind a limousine. Their voices carried his way.

"Lenny, what can I say? You were stupendous."

"Insider crowds are easy, Sal. You just gotta know what switches to flip."

"Lenny, a crowd's a crowd. These Teamsters are working Joes, just like my junket guys. You lay off the politics and pour on the Italian stuff. I fuckin' guarantee, every time you lay on the paisan stuff you'll have a roomful of hyenas on your hands."

"I don't know, Sal. I might have a Vegas gig coming up."

"I am fuckin' begging you, Lenny. And my fuckin' junketeers are well known as the biggest casino losers in fuckin' captivity. Va-va-voom, Lenny. The more they lose, the more we make."

"I don't know, Sal. I might have a chance to open for Tony Bennett at the Dunes."

"Lenny, I am begging. On all fours like a fuckin' dog I am begging."

Lenny laughed. "Before you start barking, go to fifteen percent."

"Fifteen? ... fuck ... You Jew me up, you fuckin' Jew hump."

"Twenty percent, then. I only associate with Jew haters for a price."

"Fuck you, Lenny. You said fifteen."

"Fuck *you*, Sal. I changed my mind."

Silence stretched—Littell visualized a long staredown.

"Okay okay okay. Okay for fuckin' twenty, you fuckin' Jew bandit."

"Sal, I like you. Just don't shake my hand, you're too greasy to touch."

Car doors slammed. Littell saw Mad Sal snag his Caddy and slalom out to the street.

Lenny turned on his headlights and idled the engine. Cigarette smoke blew out the driver's-side window.

Littell walked to his car. Lenny was parked two rows over— he'd spot his departure.

Lenny just sat there. Drunks careened in front of his beams and took pratfalls on ice.

Littell wiped ice off his windshield. The car sat in snow up to its bumpers.

Lenny pulled out. Littell cut him a full minute's slack and followed his tracks in the slush.

They led straight to Lake Shore Drive northbound. Littell caught up with him just short of the ramp.

Lenny swung on. Littell stayed four car lengths behind him.

It was a crawl tail—tire chains on crusted blacktop—two cars and one deserted expressway.

Lenny passed the Gold Coast off-ramps. Littell dawdled back and fixed on his taillights.

They crawled past Chicago proper. They crawled past Glencoe, Evanston and Wilmette.

Signs marked the Winnetka town limits. Lenny spun right and pulled off the highway at the very last second.

There was no way to follow him—he'd spin out or clip a guardrail.

Littell took the next off-ramp down. Winnetka was 1:00 A.M.

quiet and beautiful—all Tudor mansions and freshly plowed streets.

He grid-cruised and hit a business thoroughfare. A stretch of cars were parked outside a cocktail lounge: Perry's Little Log Cabin.

Lenny's Packard Caribbean was nosed up to the curb.

Littell parked and walked in. A ceiling banner brushed his face: "Welcome 1959!" in silver spangles.

The place was cold-weather cozy. The decor was rustic: mock-timber walls, hardwood bar, Naugahyde lounging sofas.

The clientele was all male. The bar was standing room only. Two men sat on a lounge sofa, fondling—Littell looked away.

He stared straight ahead. He felt eyes strafe him. He spotted phone booths near the rear exit—enclosed and safe.

He walked back. Nobody approached him. His holster rig had rubbed his shoulders raw—he'd spent the whole night sweating and fidgeting.

He sat down in the first booth. He cracked the door and caught a full view of the bar.

There's Lenny, drinking Pernod. There's Lenny and a blond man rubbing legs.

Littell watched them. The blond man slipped Lenny a note and waltzed off. A Platters medley hit the jukebox.

The room thinned out a few couples at a time. The sofa couple stood up, unzipped. The bartender announced last call.

Lenny ordered Cointreau. The front door opened. Icepick Tony Iannone walked in.

"One of Giancana's most feared underbosses" started French-kissing the barman. The Chicago Mob killer suspected of nine mutilation murders was sucking and biting on the barman's ear.

Littell went dizzy. Littell went dry-mouthed. Littell felt his pulse go crazy.

Tony/Lenny/Lenny/Tony—who knows who's QUEER?

Tony saw Lenny. Lenny saw Tony. Lenny ran out the rear exit.

Tony chased Lenny. Littell froze. The phone booth went airless and sucked all the breath out of him.

He got the door open. He stumbled outside. Cold air slammed him.

An alley ran behind the bar. He heard noise down and left, by the back of the adjoining building.

Tony had Lenny pinned down on a snowdrift. Lenny was biting and kicking and gouging.

Tony pulled out two switchblades. Littell pulled his gun, fumbled it and dropped it. His warning scream choked out mute.

Lenny kneed Tony. Tony pitched sideways. Lenny bit his nose off.

Littell slid on ice and fell. Soft-packed snow muffled the sound. Fifteen yards between him and them—they couldn't see him or hear him.

Tony tried to scream. Lenny spat his nose out and jammed snow in his mouth. Tony dropped his knives; Lenny grabbed them.

They couldn't see him. He slid on his knees and crawled for his gun.

Tony pawed at the snow. Lenny stabbed him two-handed—in his eyes, in his cheeks, in his throat.

Littell crawled for his gun.

Lenny ran.

Tony died coughing up bloody snow.

Music drifted outside: a soft last-call ballad.

The exit door never opened. Jukebox noise covered the whole—

Littell crawled over to Tony. Littell picked the corpse clean: watch, wallet, key ring. Print-sustaining switchblades shoved in hilt-deep—yes, do it.

He pulled them free. He got his legs. He ran down the alley until his lungs gave out.

13

(Miami, 1/3/59)

PETE PULLED UP to the cabstand. A mango splattered on his windshield.

The street was void of tiger cars and tiger riffraff. Placard wavers prowled the sidewalk, armed with bags full of too-ripe fruit.

Jimmy called him in L.A. yesterday. He said, "Earn your five fucking percent. The Kennedy bug went down, but you still owe me. My Cubans have been batshit since Castro took over. You go to Miami and restore fucking order and you can keep your five fucking—"

Somebody yelled, *"Viva Fidel!"* Somebody yelled, *"Castro, el grande puto communisto!"* A garbage war erupted two doors down: kids tossing fat red pomegranates.

Pete locked his car and ran into the hut. A redneck type was working the switchboard, solo.

Pete said, "Where's Fulo?"

The geek yuk-yuk-yukked. "The trouble with this operation is half the guys are pro-Batista and half the guys are pro-Castro. You just can't get guys like that to show up for work when there's a nifty riot in progress, so here I am all by myself."

"I said, 'Where's Fulo?' "

"Working this switchboard is an education. I've been getting these calls asking me where the action is and 'What should I bring?' I like Cubans, but I think they're prone to untoward displays of violence."

The geek was cadaver thin. He had a bad Texas drawl and the world's worst set of teeth.

Pete cracked his knuckles. "Why don't you tell me where Fulo is."

"Fulo went looking for action, and my guess is he brought his machete. And you're Pete Bondurant, and I'm Chuck Rogers. I'm a good friend of Jimmy and some boys in the Outfit, and I am a *dedicated* opponent of the worldwide Communist conspiracy."

A garbage bomb wobbled the front window. Two lines of placard wavers squared off outside.

The phone rang. Rogers plugged the call in. Pete wiped pomegranate seeds off his shirt.

Rogers unhooked his headset. "That was Fulo. He said if '*el jefe* Big Pete' got in, he should go by his place and give him a hand with something. I think it's 917 Northwest 49th. That's three blocks to the left, two to the right."

Pete dropped his suitcase. Rogers said, "So who do you like, the Beard or Batista?"

The address was a peach stucco shack. A Tiger Kab with four slashed tires blocked the porch.

Pete climbed over it and knocked. Fulo cracked the door and slid a chain off.

Pete shoved his way in. He saw the damage straight off: two

spics wearing party hats, *muerto* on the living-room floor.

Fulo locked up. "We were celebrating, Pedro. They called my beloved Fidel a true Marxist, and I took offense at this slander."

He shot them in the back at point-blank range. Small-bore exit wounds—the cleanup wouldn't be that big a deal.

Pete said, "Let's get going on this."

Fulo smashed their teeth to powder. Pete burned their fingerprints off on a hot plate.

Fulo dug the spent rounds out of the wall and flushed them down the toilet. Pete quick-scorched the floor stains—spectograph tests would read negative.

Fulo pulled down the living-room drapes and wrapped them around the bodies. The exit wounds had congealed—no blood seeped through.

Chuck Rogers showed up. Fulo said he was competent and trustworthy. They dumped the stiffs into the trunk of his car.

Pete said, "Who are you?"

Chuck said, "I'm a petroleum geologist. I'm also a licensed pilot and a professional anti-Communist."

"So who foots the bill?"

Chuck said, "The United States of America."

Chuck felt like cruising. Pete co-signed the notion—Miami grabbed his gonads like L.A. used to.

They cruised. Fulo tossed the bodies off a deserted stretch of the Bal Harbor Causeway. Pete chain-smoked and dug the scenery.

He liked the big white houses and the big white sky—Miami as one big shiny bleach job. He liked the breathing room between swank districts and slums. He liked the shitkicker cops out prowling—they looked like they'd be hell on rambunctious niggers.

Chuck said, "Castro's ideological beliefs are up in the air. He's made statements that can be construed as very pro-U.S. and very pro-Red. My friends in the intelligence community are working on plans to cornhole him if he goes Commie."

They drove back to Flagler. Armed men were guarding the cabstand—off-duty fuzz with that fat-and-sassy look.

Chuck waved to them. "Jimmy takes good care of the police contingent around here. He's got this phantom union set up, and half the cops working this sector have got nice no-show jobs and nice paychecks."

A kid slammed a leaflet on their windshield. Fulo translated odd slogans—Commie-type platitudes all.

Rocks hit the car. Pete said, "This is too crazy. Let's go stash Fulo someplace."

Rogers leased a room in an all-spic boardinghouse. Radio gear and hate leaflets covered every spare inch of floor space.

Fulo and Chuck relaxed with beers. Pete skimmed pamphlet titles and got a good laugh mojo going.

"Kikes Kontrol Kremlin!" "Fluoridation: Vatican Plot?" "Red Stormclouds Brewing—One Patriot's Response." "Why Non-Caucasians Overbreed: A Scientist Explains." "Pro-American Checklist: Do You Score RED or Red, White and Blue?"

Fulo said, "Chuck, it is rather crowded in here."

Rogers futzed with a short-wave receiver. A hate tirade kicked in: Jew bankers, blah blah.

Pete hit a few switches. The rant sputtered out cold.

Chuck smiled. "Politics is something you come around to slow. You can't expect to understand the world situation immediately."

"I should introduce you to Howard Hughes. He's as crazy as you are."

"You think anticommunism is crazy?"

"I think it's good for business, and anything that's good for business is okay with me."

"I don't think that's a very enlightened attitude."

"Think what you like."

"I will. And I know you're thinking, 'Holy Hannah, who is this guy that's my fellow murder-one accessory, because we sure have shared some unusual experiences in our short acquaintance.'"

Pete leaned against the window. He caught a little blip of a prowl car half a block down.

"My guess is you're a CIA contract hand. You're supposed to get next to the Cubans at the stand while everybody waits to see how Castro jumps."

Fulo came on indignant. "Fidel will jump toward the United States of America."

Chuck laughed. "Immigrants make the best Americans. You should know, huh, Pete? Aren't you some kind of frog?"

Pete popped his thumbs. Rogers flinched.

"You just make like I'm a 100% American who knows what's good for business."

"Whoa now. I never doubted your patriotism."

Pete heard whispers outside the door. Looks circulated— Chuck and Fulo caught the gist quick. Pete heard shotgun announcement noise: three loud and clear breach-to-barrel pumps.

He dropped his piece behind some pamphlets. Fulo and Chuck put their hands up.

Plainclothesmen kicked the door down. They ran in with shotgun butts at high port arms.

Pete went down behind a powder-puff shot. Fulo and Chuck played it rugged and got beaten skull-cracking senseless.

A cop said, "The big guy's faking." A cop said, "We can fix that."

Rubber-padded gun butts slammed him. Pete curled up his tongue so he wouldn't bite it off.

He came to cuffed and shackled. Chair slats gouged his back; percussion bopped him upside his brain.

Light hit his eyes. One eye only—tissue flaps cut his sight in half. He made out three cops sitting around a bolted-down table.

Snare drums popped behind his ears. A-bombs ignited up and down his spine.

Pete flexed his arms and snapped his handcuff chain.

Two cops whistled. One cop applauded.

They'd *double*-manacled his ankles—he couldn't give them an encore.

The senior cop crossed his legs. "We got an anonymous tip, Mr. Bondurant. One of Mr. Machado's neighbors saw Mr. Adolfo Herendon and Mr. Armando Cruz-Martín enter Mr. Machado's house, and he heard what might have been shots several hours later. Now, a few hours after that, you and Mr. Rogers arrive separately. The two of you and Mr. Machado leave carrying two large bundles wrapped in window curtains, and the neighbor gets Mr. Rogers' license number. We checked Mr. Rogers' car, and we noticed some debris that looks like skin fragments, and we certainly would like to hear your comments on all of this."

Pete stuck his eyebrow back in place. "Charge me or release me. You know who I am and who I know."

"We know you know Jimmy Hoffa. We know you're pals with Mr. Rogers, Mr. Machado and some other Tiger Kab drivers."

Pete said, "Charge me or release me." The cop tossed cigarettes and matches on his lap.

Cop #2 leaned in close. "You probably think Jimmy Hoffa's bought off every policeman in this town, but son, I'm here to tell you that simply ain't the case."

"Charge me or release me."

"Son, you are trying my patience."

"I'm not your son, you cracker faggot."

"Boy, that kind of talk will get your face slapped."

"If you slap me, I'll go for your eyes. Don't make me prove it."

Cop #3 came on soft. "Whoa, now, whoa. Mr. Bondurant, you know we can hold you for seventy-two hours without charging you. You know you've probably got a concussion and could use some medical attention. Now, why don't you—"

"Give me my phone call, then charge me or release me."

The senior cop laced his hands behind his head. "We let your friend Rogers make a call. He fed the jailer some cock-and-bull story about having government connections and called a Mr. Stanton. Now, who are you gonna call—Jimmy Hoffa? You think Uncle Jimmy's gonna go your bail on a double-homicide charge and maybe engender all kinds of bad publicity that he doesn't need?"

An A-bomb blast hit his neck. Pete almost blacked out.

Cop #2 sighed. "This boy's too woozy to cooperate. Let's let him rest up a bit."

He passed out, woke up, passed out. His headache subsided from A-bomb to nitroglycerine.

He read wall scratchings. He swiveled his neck to stay limber. He broke the world's record for holding a piss.

He broke down the situation.

Fulo cracks or Fulo doesn't crack. Chuck cracks or Chuck doesn't. Jimmy buys them bail or lets them swing. Maybe the DA gets smart: spic-on-spic homicides rate bupkis.

He could call Mr. Hughes. Mr. Hughes could nudge Mr. Hoover—which meant case fucking closed.

He told Hughes he'd be gone three days. Hughes agreed to the trip, no questions asked. Hughes agreed because the Kennedy shakedown backfired. Joe and Bobby shrunk his balls down to peanut size.

And Ward J. Littell slapped *him*.

Which decreed the cocksucker's death sentence.

Gail was gone. The Jack K. gig went pfffft. Hoffa's Kennedy hate sizzled—hot, hot, hot. Hughes was still gossip/smear crazed and hot to find a new *Hush-Hush* stringer.

Pete read wall musings. The Academy Award winner: "Miami PD Sucks Rhino Dick."

Two men walked in and pulled chairs up. A jailer unshackled his legs and walked out fast.

Pete stood up and stretched. The interrogation room dipped and swayed.

The younger man said, "I'm John Stanton, and this is Guy Banister. Mr. Banister is retired FBI, and he was assistant superintendent of the New Orleans Police for a spell."

Stanton was slight and sandy-haired. Banister was big and booze-flushed.

Pete lit a cigarette. Inhaling torqued his headache. "I'm listening."

Banister grinned. "I remember that civil rights trouble of yours. Kemper Boyd and Ward Littell arrested you, didn't they?"

"You know they did."

"I used to be the Chicago SAC, and I always thought Littell was a weak sister."

Stanton straddled his chair. "But Kemper Boyd's another matter. You know, Pete, he went by the Tiger stand and showed your mug shot around. One of the men pulled a knife, and Boyd disarmed him in a rather spectacular fashion."

Pete said, "Boyd's a stylish guy. And this is starting to play like some kind of audition, so I'll tell you that I'd recommend him for just about any kind of law-enforcement work."

Stanton smiled. "You're not a bad audition prospect yourself."

Banister smiled. "You're a licensed private investigator. You're a former deputy sheriff. You're Howard Hughes' man, and you know Jimmy Hoffa, Fulo Machado and Chuck Rogers. Those are stylish credentials."

Pete stubbed his cigarette out on the wall. "The CIA's not so bad, as credentials go. That's who you are, right?"

Stanton stood up. "You're free to go. No charges will be filed on you, Rogers or Machado."

"But you'll be keeping in touch?"

"Not exactly. But I may ask a favor of you one day. And of course, you'll be well paid for it."

14
(New York City, 1/5/59)

THE SUITE WAS magnificent. Joe Kennedy bought it from the hotel outright.

A hundred people left the main room only half-filled. The picture window gave you the breadth of Central Park in a snowstorm.

Jack invited him. He said his father's Carlyle bashes were not to be missed—and besides, Bobby needs to talk to you.

Jack said there might be women. Jack said Lyndon Johnson's redhead might appear.

Kemper watched cliques constellate and dissolve. The party swirled all around him.

Old Joe stood with his horsy daughters. Peter Lawford ruled an all-male group. Jack speared cocktail shrimp with Nelson Rockefeller.

Lawford prophesied the Kennedy cabinet. Frank Sinatra was considered a shoo-in for Prime Minister of Pussy.

Bobby was late. The redhead hadn't arrived—Jack would have signaled him if he saw her first.

Kemper sipped eggnog. His tuxedo jacket fit loose—he'd had it cut to cover a shoulder holster. Bobby enforced a strict no-sidearms policy—*his* men were lawyers, not cops.

He was *twice* a cop—double-salaried and double-dutied.

He told Mr. Hoover that Anton Gretzler and Roland Kirpaski were dead—but their "presumed dead" status had not demoralized Bobby Kennedy. Bobby was determined to chase Hoffa, the Teamsters and the Mob WAY past the McClellan Committee's expiration date. Municipal PD racket squads and grand jury investigators armed with Committee-gathered evidence would then become the Get Hoffa spearhead. Bobby would soon be preparing the groundwork for Jack's 1960 campaign—but Jimmy Hoffa would remain his personal target.

Hoover demanded investigatory specifics. He told him that Bobby wanted to trace the "spooky" three million dollars that financed Hoffa's Sun Valley development—Bobby was convinced that Hoffa skimmed cash off the top and that Sun Valley itself constituted land fraud. Bobby instinctively believed in the existence of separate, perhaps coded, Teamster Central States Pension Fund books—ledgers detailing tens of millions of dollars in hidden assets—money lent to gangsters and crooked businessmen at gargantuan interest rates. An elusive rumor: A retired Chicago hoodlum managed the Fund. Bobby's personal instinct: The total Fund package was his most viable Get Hoffa wedge.

He had two salaries now. He had two sets of conflicting duties. He had John Stanton hinting at offers—if the CIA's Cuban plans stabilized.

It would give him a third salary. It would give him enough income to sustain his own pied-à-terre.

Peter Lawford cornered Leonard Bernstein. Mayor Wagner chatted up Maria Callas.

A waiter refilled Kemper's tankard. Joe Kennedy walked an old man up.

"Kemper, this is Jules Schiffrin. Jules, Kemper Boyd. You two should talk. The two of you are rascals from way back."

They shook hands. Joe slid off to talk to Bennett Cerf.

"How are you, Mr. Schiffrin?"

"I'm fine, thank you. And I know why I'm a rascal. But you? You're too young."

"I'm a year older than Jack Kennedy."

"And I'm four years younger than Joe, so things even out. Is that your occupation, rascal?"

"I'm retired from the FBI. Right now, I'm working for the McClellan Committee."

"You're an ex-G-man? And retired so young?"

Kemper winked. "I got tired of FBI-sanctioned car theft."

Schiffrin mimicked the wink. "Tired, schmired. How bad could it be if it bought you custom mohair tuxedos like you're wearing? I should own such a tux."

Kemper smiled. "What do you do?"

"'Did do' is more like it. And what I did do was serve as a

financier and a labor consultant. Those are euphemisms, in case you're wondering. What I *didn't* do was have lots of lovely children to enjoy in my old age. Such lovely children Joe has. Look at them."

Kemper said, "You're from Chicago?"

Schiffrin beamed. "How did you know that?"

"I've studied regional accents. It's something I'm good at."

"Good doesn't describe it. And that drawl of yours, is that Alabama?"

"Tennessee."

"Aah, the Volunteer State. It's too bad my friend Heshie isn't here. He's a Detroit-born gonif who's lived in the Southwest for years. He's got an accent that would baffle you."

Bobby walked into the foyer. Schiffrin saw him and rolled his eyes. "There's your boss. Pardon my French, but don't you think he's a bit of a shitheel?"

"In his way, yes."

"Now *you're* euphemizing. I remember Joe and I were yakking once, about how we fucked Howard Hughes on a deal thirty years ago. Bobby objected to the word 'fuck' because his kids were in the next room. They couldn't even hear, but—"

Bobby signaled. Kemper caught the gesture and nodded.

"Excuse me, Mr. Schiffrin."

"Go. Your boss beckons. Nine kids Joe had, so one shitbird isn't such a bad average."

Kemper walked over. Bobby steered him straight into the cloakroom. Fur coats and evening capes brushed up against them.

"Jack said you wanted to see me."

"I did. I need you to collate some evidence briefs and write out a summary of everything the Committee's done, so that we can send out a standardized report to all the grand juries who'll be taking over for us. I realize that paperwork isn't your style, but this is imperative."

"I'll start in the morning."

"Good."

Kemper cleared his throat. "Bob, there's something I wanted to run by you."

"What?"

"I have a close friend. He's an agent in the Chicago office. I can't tell you his name just yet, but he's a very capable and intelligent man."

Bobby wiped snow off his topcoat. "Kemper, you're leading me. I realize that you're used to having your way with people, but please get to the point."

"The point is he was transferred off the Top Hoodlum Program against his will. He hates Mr. Hoover and Mr. Hoover's 'There is no Mob' stance, and he wants to conduit anti-Mob intelligence through me to you. He understands the risks, and he's willing to take them. And for what it's worth, he's an ex-Jesuit seminarian."

Bobby hung his coat up. "Can we trust him?"

"Absolutely."

"He wouldn't be a conduit to Hoover?"

Kemper laughed. "Hardly."

Bobby looked at him. Bobby gave him his witness-intimidation stare.

"All right. But I want you to tell the man not to do anything illegal. I don't want a zealot out there wiretapping and God knows what else because he thinks I'll back him up on it."

"I'll tell him. Now, what areas do you—?"

"Tell him I'm interested in the possibility that secret Pension Fund books exist. Tell him that if they do, it's likely that the Chicago Mob administers them. Have him work off that supposition, and see if he can come up with any general Hoffa intelligence while he's at it."

Guests filed past the cloakroom. A woman trailed her mink coat on the floor. Dean Acheson almost tripped over it.

Bobby winced. Kemper saw his eyes slip out of focus.

"What is it?"

"It's nothing."

"Is there anything else you'd—?"

"No, there isn't. Now, if you'll excuse me . . ."

Kemper smiled and walked back to the party. The main room was crowded now—maneuvering was a chore.

The mink woman had heads turning.

She made a butler pet her coat. She insisted that Leonard Bernstein try it on. She mambo-stepped through the crowd and snatched Joe Kennedy's drink.

Joe gave her a small, gift-wrapped box. The woman tucked it in her purse. Three Kennedy sisters walked off in a huff.

Peter Lawford ogled the woman. Bennett Cerf slid by and

peeked down her dress. Vladimir Horowitz waved her over to the piano.

Kemper took a private elevator down to the lobby. He picked up a courtesy phone and badged the switchboard girl for a straight patch to Chicago.

She put him through. Helen answered on the second ring.

"Hello?"

"It's me, sweetheart. The one you used to have a crush on."

"Kemper! What are you doing with that syrupy southern accent!"

"I'm engaged in subterfuge."

"Well, *I'm* engaged in law school and looking for an apartment, and it is *so* difficult!"

"All good things are. Ask your middle-aged boyfriend, he'll tell you."

Helen whispered. "Ward's been moody and secretive lately. Will you try to—?"

Littell came on the line. "Kemper, hi."

Helen blew kisses and put her extension down. Kemper said, "Hello, son."

"Hello yourself. I hate to be abrupt, but have you—?"

"Yes, I have."

"And?"

"And Bobby said yes. He said he wants you to work for us sub rosa, and he wants you to follow up on that lead Roland Kirpaski gave us, and try to determine if there really are secret Pension Fund books hiding untold zillions of dollars."

"Good. This is . . . very good."

Kemper lowered his voice. "Bobby reiterated what I told you. Don't take unnecessary risks. You remember that. Bobby's more of a stickler for legalities than I am, so you just remember to be careful, and remember who you have to look out for."

Littell said, "I'll be careful. I may have a Mob man compromised on a homicide, and I think I might be able to turn him as an informant."

The mink woman walked through the lobby. A slew of bell-boys rushed to get the door for her.

"Ward, I have to go."

"God bless you for this, Kemper. And tell Mr. Kennedy that I won't disappoint him."

Kemper hung up and walked outside. Wind roared down 76th Street and toppled trashcans set out on the curb.

The mink woman was standing under the hotel canopy. She was unwrapping Joe Kennedy's gift.

Kemper stood a few feet away from her. The gift was a diamond broach tucked inside a roll of thousand-dollar bills.

A wino stumbled by. The mink woman gave him the broach. Wind fanned the roll and showed off at least fifty grand.

The wino giggled and looked at his broach. Kemper laughed out loud.

A cab pulled up. The mink woman leaned in and said, "881 Fifth Avenue."

Kemper opened the door for her.

She said, "Aren't the Kennedys vulgar?"

Her eyes were drop-dead translucent green.

15

(Chicago, 1/6/59)

ONE JIGGLE SNAPPED the lock. Littell pulled his pick out and closed the door behind him.

Passing headlights strafed the windows. The front room was small and filled with antiques and art deco gewgaws.

His eyes adjusted to the dark. There was good outside light—he didn't need to risk turning lamps on.

Lenny Sands' apartment was tidy and midwinter stuffy.

The Icepick Tony killing was five days old and unsolved. The TV and papers omitted one fact: that Iannone died outside a queer tryst spot. Court Meade said Giancana put the fix in: he didn't want Tony slandered as a homo, and refused to believe it himself. Meade quoted some scary bug-post talk: "Sam's got scouts out rousting known fruit rollers"; "Mo said Tony's killer is gonna get castrated."

Giancana couldn't believe a self-evident fact. Giancana thought Tony walked into Perry's Little Log Cabin by mistake.

Littell got out his pen flash and Minox. Lenny's recent schedule included Vendo-King pickups until midnight. It was 9:20 now—he had time to work.

Lenny's address book was tucked under the living-room

phone. Littell skimmed through it and noted auspicious names.

Eclectic Lenny knew Rock Hudson and Carlos Marcello. Hollywood Lenny knew Gail Russell and Johnnie Ray. Gangland Lenny knew Giancana, Butch Montrose and Rocco Malvaso.

One strange thing: His Mob address/numbers didn't match the on-file THP listings.

Littell flipped pages. Odd names hit him.

Senator John Kennedy, Hyannis Port, Mass.; Spike Knode, 114 Gardenia, Mobile, Alabama; Laura Hughes, 881 5th Ave., New York City; Paul Bogaards, 1489 Fountain, Milwaukee.

He shot through the book alphabetically. He held the pen flash in his teeth and snapped one photograph per page. He notched thirty-two exposures up to the M's.

His legs ached from squatting down to shoot. The flash kept slipping out of his mouth.

He heard key/lock noise. He heard door rattles—NINETY MINUTES AHEAD OF SCHED—

Littell hugged the wall by the door. He replayed every judo move Kemper taught him.

Lenny Sands walked in. Littell grabbed him from behind and cupped his mouth shut. Remember—"Jam one thumb to the suspect's carotid and take him down supine."

He did it Kemper-pure. Lenny went prone with no resistance. Littell pulled his muzzle hand free and kicked the door shut.

Lenny didn't scream or yell. His face was jammed into a wad of scrunched-up carpet.

Littell eased off the carotid. Lenny coughed and retched.

Littell knelt beside him. Littell pulled out his revolver and cocked it.

"I'm with the Chicago FBI. I've got you for the Tony Iannone killing, and if you don't work for me I'll hand you up to Giancana and the Chicago PD. I'm not asking you to inform on your friends. What I'm interested in is the Teamsters' Pension Fund."

Lenny heaved for breath. Littell stood up and hit a wall switch—the room went bright with glare.

He saw a liquor tray by the couch. Cut-glass decanters full of scotch, bourbon and brandy.

Lenny pulled his knees up and hugged them. Littell tucked his gun in his waistband and pulled out a glassine bag.

It held two blood-crusted switchblades.

He showed them to Lenny. He said, "I dusted them for prints and got four latents that matched your DMV set."

It was a bluff. All he got were smears.

"You've got no choice in this, Lenny. You know what Sam would do to you."

Lenny broke a sweat. Littell poured him a scotch—the smell made him salivate.

Lenny sipped his drink two-handed. His tough-guy voice didn't quite work.

"I know bupkis about the Fund. What I know is that connected guys and certain businessman types apply for these large-interest loans and get pushed up some kind of loan ladder."

"To Sam Giancana?"

"That's one theory."

"Then elaborate on it."

"The theory is that Giancana consults with Jimmy Hoffa on all the big-money loan applications. Then they get accepted or refused."

"Are there alternative Pension Fund books? What I'm thinking of is coded books hiding secret assets."

"I don't know."

Kemper Boyd always said COW YOUR INFORMANTS.

Lenny hauled himself into a chair. Schizophrenic Lenny knew that tough Jewboys don't cringe on the floor.

Littell poured himself a double scotch. Lounge-Act Lenny said, "Make yourself at home."

Littell tucked the switchblades in his pocket. "I checked your address book, and I noticed that your addresses don't match the addresses that the Top Hoodlum Program has on file."

"What addresses?"

"The addresses of members of the Chicago Crime Cartel."

"Oh, *those* addresses."

"Why don't they match?"

Lenny said, "Because they're fuck pads. They're pads where guys go to cheat on their wives. I've got keys to some of the pads, because I drop off jukebox receipts to them. In fact, I was bagging receipts at that fucking queer bar when that fucking faggot Iannone came on to me."

Littell downed his drink. "I *saw* you kill Iannone. I *know* why you were at Perry's Little Log Cabin, and *why* you frequent Hernando's Hideaway. I *know* you've got two lives and two voices and two sets of God knows what else. I *know* that Iannone went after you because he didn't want you knowing that he did, too."

Lenny SQUEEEZED his glass, two-handed. Thick-cut crystal snapped and shattered—

Whisky sprayed out. Blood mixed with it. Lenny did not yelp or flinch or move.

Littell tossed his glass on the couch. "I know you made a deal with Sal D'Onofrio."

No response.

"I know you're going to travel with his gambling junkets."

No response.

"Sal's a loan shark. Could he refer prospects up the Pension Fund ladder?"

No response.

Littell said, "Come on, talk to me. I'm not going to leave until I have what I came for."

Lenny wiped blood off his hands. "I don't know. Maybe, maybe not. As sharks go, Sal's small fry."

"What about Jack Ruby? He sharks part-time down in Dallas."

"Jack's a clown. He knows people, but he's a clown."

Littell lowered his voice. "Do the Chicago boys know you're a homosexual?"

Lenny choked sobs back. Littell said, "Answer the question and admit what you are."

Lenny shut his eyes and nodded, no no no.

"Then answer this question. *Will you be my informant?*"

Lenny shut his eyes and nodded, yes yes yes.

"The papers said Iannone was married."

No response.

"Lenny . . ."

"Yes. He was married."

"Did he have a fuck pad?"

"He must have."

Littell buttoned up his overcoat. "I might do you a solid, Lenny."

No response.

"I'll be in touch. You know what I'm interested in, so get on it."

Lenny ignored him. Lenny started picking glass out of his hands.

* * *

He took a key ring off Iannone's body. It contained four keys on a fob marked "Di Giorgio's Locksmith's, 947 Hudnut Drive, Evanston."

Two car keys and one assumed house key. The remaining key might be for a fuck-pad door.

Littell drove up to Evanston. He hit on some dumb late-night luck: the locksmith lived in back of his shop.

The unexpected FBI roust scared the man. He identified the keys as his work. He said he installed all of Iannone's door locks—at two addresses.

2409 Kenilworth in Oak Park. 84 Wolverton in Evanston.

Iannone lived in Oak Park—that fact made the papers. The Evanston address was a strong fuck-pad possibility.

The locksmith supplied easy-to-follow directions. Littell found the address in just a few minutes.

It was a garage apartment behind a Northwestern U frat house. The neighborhood was dark and dead quiet.

The key fit the door. Littell let himself in, gun first. The place was uninhabited and musty.

He turned on the lights in both rooms. He tossed every cupboard, drawer, shelf, cubbyhole and crawl space. He found dildoes, whips, spiked dog collars, amyl nitrite ampules, twelve jars of K-Y Jelly, a bag of marijuana, a brass-studded motorcycle jacket, a sawed-off shotgun, nine rolls of Benzedrine, a Nazi armband, oil paintings depicting all-male sodomy and soixante-neuf and a snapshot of Icepick Tony Iannone and a college boy nude cheek-to-cheek.

Kemper Boyd always said PROTECT YOUR INFORMANTS.

Littell called Celano's Tailor Shop. A man answered— "Yeah?"—unmistakably Butch Montrose.

Littell disguised his voice. "Don't worry about Tony Iannone. He was a fucking faggot. Go to 84 Wolverton in Evanston and see for yourself."

"Hey, what are you say—?"

Littell hung up. He nailed the snapshot to the wall for the whole world to see.

16

(Los Angeles, 1/11/59)

HUSH-HUSH WAS cramming toward deadline. The office staff was buzzing on Benzedrine-spiked coffee.

"Artists" were pasting up a cover: "Paul Robeson—Royal Red Recidivist." A "correspondent" was typing copy: "Wife Beater Spade Cooley—Will the Country Stomper Stomp Too Far?" A "researcher" was browsing pamphlets, trying to link nigger hygiene to cancer.

Pete watched.

Pete was bored.

MIAMI bopped through his head. *Hush-Hush* felt like a giant cactus shoved up his ass.

Sol Maltzman was dead. Gail Hendee was long gone. The new *Hush-Hush* staff was 100% geek. Howard Hughes was frantic to find a dirt digger.

His prospects all said NO. Everybody knew the L.A. fuzz seized the Kennedy smear issue. *Hush-Hush* was the leper colony of scandal-sheet journalism.

Hughes CRAVED dirt. Hughes CRAVED slander skank to share with Mr. Hoover. What Hughes CRAVED, Hughes BOUGHT.

Pete bought an issue's worth of dirt. His cop contacts supplied him with a one-week load of lackluster skank.

"Spade Cooley, Boozefried Misogynist!" "Marijuana Shack Raid Nets Sal Mineo!" "Beatnik Arrests Shock Hermosa Beach!"

It was pure bullshit. It was very un-Miami.

Miami was goood. Miami was this drug he got withdrawals from. He left Miami with a mild concussion—not bad for the pounding he took.

Jimmy Hoffa called him in to restore order. He got out of jail and did it.

The cabstand demanded order—political rifts had business fucked six ways from Sunday. The riots sputtered out, but Tiger Kab still simmered with factional jive. He had pro-Batista and pro-Castro guys to deal with—left- and right-wing ideologue thugs who needed to be toilet-trained and broken in to the White Man's Rule of Order.

He laid down laws.

No drinking and placard waving on the job. No guns or knives—check your weapons with the dispatcher. No political fraternizing—rival factions must remain segregated.

One Batistaite challenged the rules. Pete beat him half-dead.

He laid down more laws.

No pimping on duty—leave your whores at home. No B&Es or stickups on duty.

He made Chuck Rogers the new day dispatcher. He considered it a political appointment.

Rogers was a CIA contract goon. Co-dispatcher Fulo Machado was CIA-linked.

John Stanton was a mid-level CIA agent—and a new cabstand habitué. He got Fulo's murder-one beef squelched with a snap of his fingers.

Stanton's pal Guy Banister hated Ward Littell. Banister and Stanton were hipped on Kemper Boyd.

Jimmy Hoffa owned Tiger Kab. Jimmy Hoffa had points in two Havana casinos.

Littell and Boyd made *him* for two killings. Stanton and Banister probably didn't know that. Stanton fed him that little teaser: "I may ask a favor of you one day."

Things were dovetailing tight and cozy. His feelers started perk-perk-perking.

Pete buzzed the receptionist. "Donna, get me long distance person-to-person. I want to talk to a man named Kemper Boyd at the McClellan Committee office in Washington, D.C. Tell the operator to try the Senate Office Building, and if you get through, say I'm the caller."

"Yes, sir."

Pete hung up and waited. The call was a longshot—Boyd was probably out somewhere, conniving.

His intercom light flashed. Pete picked up the phone.

"Boyd?"

"Speaking. And surprised."

"Well, I owe you one, so I thought I'd deliver."

"Keep going."

"I was in Miami last week. I ran into two men named John Stanton and Guy Banister, and they seemed real interested in you."

"Mr. Stanton and I have already spoken. But thanks. It's nice to know they're still interested."

"I gave you a good reference."

"You're a sport. Is there anything I can do for you?"

"You can find me a new dirt digger for *Hush-Hush*."

Boyd hung up, laughing.

17
(Miami, 1/13/59)

THE COMMITTEE BOOKED him into a Howard Johnson's. Kemper upgraded to a two-room suite at the Fontainebleau.

He made up the difference out of his own pocket. He was closing in on three salaries—it wasn't that big an extravagance.

Bobby sent him back to Miami. He instigated the trip himself—and promised to return with some key Sun Valley depositions. He didn't tell Bobby that the CIA was thinking about recruiting him.

The trip was a little vacation. If Stanton was good, they'd connect.

Kemper carried a chair out to the balcony. Ward Littell had mailed him a report—he needed to edit it before sending it on to Bobby.

The report was twelve typed pages. Ward included a longhand preface.

> K.B.,
>
> Since we're partners in this gentle subterfuge, I'm giving you a verbatim account of my activities. Of course, you'll want to omit mention of my more flagrant illegalities, given Mr. Kennedy's proviso. As you'll note, I have made substantial progress. And believe me, given the extreme circumstances, I have been very careful.

Kemper read the report. "Extreme circumstances" didn't quite cover it.

Littell witnessed a homosexual murder. The victim was a Chicago Mob underboss. The killer was a Mob fringe dweller named Lenny Sands.

Sands was now Littell's snitch. Sands had recently partnered up with a bookie/loanshark named "Mad Sal" D'Onofrio. D'Onofrio shepherded gambling junkets to Las Vegas and Lake Tahoe—Sands was to accompany the groups as their "traveling lounge act." Sands had keys to mobster "fuck pads." Littell coerced him into making duplicates and surreptitiously entered three fuck pads to look for evidence. Littell observed and left untouched: weapons, narcotics, and $14,000 in cash—hidden in a golf bag at the fuck pad of one Butch Montrose.

Littell located Tony Iannone's fuck pad: a garage apartment littered with homosexual paraphernalia. Littell was determined to protect his informant from potential reprisals. Littell disclosed the fuck pad's location to Chicago Mob members and staked it out to see if they followed up on his anonymous tip. They did: Sam Giancana and two other men broke down the fuck pad door an hour later. They undoubtedly saw Iannone's homosexual contraband.

Amazing. Fully emblematic of the Ward Littell Trinity: luck, instinct, naive courage.

Littell concluded:

My ultimate goal is to facilitate a loan seeker "up the ladder" to the Teamsters' Central States Pension Fund. This loan seeker will be, ideally, my own legally compromised informant. Lenny Sands (and potentially "Mad Sal" D'Onofrio) may prove to be valuable allies in recruiting such an informant. My ideal loan seeker would be a crooked businessman with Organized Crime connections, a man susceptible to physical intimidation and threats of Federal prosecution. Such an informant could help us determine the existence of alternative Pension Fund books containing hidden, thus illegal, assets. This avenue of approach presents Robert Kennedy with unlimited opportunities at prosecution. If such books do exist, the administrators of the hidden assets will be indictable on numerous counts of Grand Larceny and Federal Tax Fraud. I agree with Mr. Kennedy: this may prove to be the way to link Jimmy Hoffa and the Teamsters to the Chicago Mob and break their collective power. If monetary collusion on such a rich and pervasive scale can be proven, heads will roll.

The plan was ambitious and stratospherically risky. Kemper snapped to a possible glitch straight off.

Littell exposed Icepick Tony's sexual bent. Did he consider *all* the potential ramifications?

Kemper called the Miami airport and altered his D.C. flight for a Chicago stopover. The move felt sound: if his hunch proved right, he'd need to give Ward a good thrashing.

Dusk came on. Room service brought his standing order up— punctual to the minute.

He sipped Beefeater's and picked at smoked salmon. Collins Avenue glowed; twinkling lights bracketed the beachfront.

Kemper got a mild glow on. He reprised his moments with the mink woman and thought of a dozen lines he could have used.

Chimes rang. Kemper ran a comb through his hair and opened the door.

John Stanton said, "Hello, Mr. Boyd."

Kemper ushered him in. Stanton walked around and admired the suite.

"Robert Kennedy treats you well."

"You're being disingenuous, Mr. Stanton."

"I'll be blunt, then. You grew up wealthy and lost your family. Now you've adopted the Kennedys. You're in the practice of reclaiming your wealth in small increments, and this really is quite a handsome room."

Kemper smiled. "Would you like a martini?"

"Martinis taste like lighter fluid. I've always judged hotels by their wine list."

"I can send down for whatever you like."

"I won't be here long enough."

"What's on your mind?"

Stanton pointed to the balcony. "Cuba's out there."

"I know that."

"We think Castro will go Communist. He's set to come to America in April and offer his friendship, but we think he'll behave badly and force an official rejection. He's going to deport some 'politically undesirable' Cubans soon, and they'll be granted asylum here in Florida. We need men to train them and form them into an anti-Castro resistance. The pay is two thou- sand dollars a month, in cash, plus the chance to purchase discount-priced stock in Agency-backed front companies. This is a firm offer, and you have my personal assurance that we won't let your Agency work interfere with your other affiliations."

"'Affiliations'? Plural?"

Stanton stepped out on the balcony. Kemper followed him up to the railing.

"You 'retired' from the FBI rather precipitously. You were close to Mr. Hoover, who hates and fears the Kennedy brothers. *Post hoc, ergo propter hoc.* You were an FBI agent on Tuesday, a prospective pimp for Jack Kennedy on Wednesday, and a McClellan Committee investigator on Thursday. I can follow logical—"

"What's the standard pay rate for CIA contract recruits?"

"Eight-fifty a month."

"But my 'affiliations' make me a special case?"

"Yes. We know you're getting close to the Kennedys, and we think Jack Kennedy might be elected President next year. If the Castro problem extends, we'll need someone to help influence his Cuban policy."

"As a lobbyist?"

"No. As a very subtle agent provocateur."

Kemper checked the view. Lights seemed to shimmer way past Cuba.

"I'll consider your offer."

18

(Chicago, 1/14/59)

LITTELL RAN INTO the morgue. Kemper called him from the airport and said MEET ME THERE NOW.

He called half an hour ago. He didn't elaborate. He said just those four words and slammed the phone down.

A row of autopsy rooms extended off the foyer. Sheet-covered gurneys blocked the hallway.

Littell pushed through them. Kemper stood by the far wall, next to a row of freezer slabs.

Littell caught his breath. "What the fuck is—?"

Kemper pulled a slab out. The tray held a male Caucasian dead body.

The boy was torture slashed and cigarette burned. His penis was severed and stuffed in his mouth.

Littell recognized him: the kid in Icepick Tony's nude snapshot.

Kemper grabbed his neck and forced him down close. "This is on you, Ward. You should have destroyed every bit of evidence pointing to Iannone's known associates *before* you tipped off those Mob guys. Guilty or not, they had to kill someone, so they decided to kill the boy in the picture *you* left for them to see."

Littell jerked backward. He smelled stomach bile and blood and forensic dental abrasive.

Kemper shoved him down closer.

"You're working for Bobby Kennedy, and *I* set it up, and Mr. Hoover will destroy me if he finds out. You're damn lucky I decided to check some missing-persons reports, and you had damn well better convince me you won't fuck up like this again."

Littell closed his eyes. Tears spilled out. Kemper shoved him in cheek to cheek with the dead boy.

"Meet me at Lenny Sands' apartment at ten. We'll shore things up."

Work didn't help.

He tailed Commies and wrote out a surveillance log. His hands shook; his printing was near-illegible.

Helen didn't help.

He called her just to hear her voice. Her law school chitchat brought him close to screaming.

Court Meade didn't help.

They met for coffee and exchanged reports. Court told him he looked lousy. Court said his report looked threadbare—like he wasn't spending much time at the listening post.

He couldn't say, I'm slacking off because I found a snitch. He couldn't say, I fucked up and got a boy killed.

Church helped a little.

He lit a candle for the dead boy. He prayed for competence and courage. He cleaned up in the bathroom and remembered something Lenny said: Sal D. was recruiting junketeers at Saint Vibiana's this evening.

A tavern stop helped.

Soup and crackers settled his stomach. Three rye-and-beers cleared his head.

* * *

Sal and Lenny had the Saint Vib's rec hall all to themselves. A dozen K of C men took in their pitch.

The group sat at a clump of bingo tables near the stage. The Knights looked like drunks and wife beaters.

Littell loitered outside a fire exit. He cracked the door to watch and listen.

Sal said, "We leave in two days. Lots of my regulars couldn't get away from their jobs, so I'm lowering my price to nine-fifty, airfare included. First we go to Lake Tahoe, then Vegas and Gardena, outside L.A. Sinatra's playing the Cal-Neva Lodge in Tahoe, and you'll be front row center to catch his show. Now, Lenny Sands, formerly Lenny Sanducci, and a Vegas star in his own right, will give you a Sinatra that out-Sinatras Sinatra. Go, Lenny! Go, paisan!"

Lenny blew smoke rings Sinatra-style. The K of C men clapped. Lenny flicked his cigarette above their heads and glared at them.

"Don't applaud until I finish! What kind of Rat Pack Auxiliary are you! Dino, go get me a couple of blondes! Sammy, go get me a case of gin and ten cartons of cigarettes or I'll put your other eye out! Hop to it, Sammy! When the Chicago Knights of Columbus Chapter 384 snaps its fingers, Frank Sinatra jumps!"

The Knights haw-haw-hawed. A nun pushed a broom by the group and never looked up. Lenny sang, "Fly me to the Coast with Big Sal's junket tour! He's the swingin' gambling junket king, so dig his sweet allure! In other words, Vegas beware!"

The Knights applauded. Sal dumped a paper bag out on a table in front of them.

They sifted through the clutter and grabbed knickknacks. Littell saw poker chips, French ticklers, and Playboy rabbit key chains.

Lenny held up a novelty pen shaped like a penis. "Which one of you big-dick gavones wants to be the first one to sign up?"

A line formed. Littell felt his stomach turn over.

He walked to the curb and vomited. The rye and beer burned his throat. He hunched over and puked himself dry.

Some junket men walked past him twirling key chains. A few laughed at him.

Littell braced himself against a lamppost. He saw Sal and Lenny in the rec hall doorway.

Sal backed Lenny into the wall and jabbed at his chest. Lenny mimed a single word: "Okay."

The door stood ajar. Littell pushed it all the way open.

Kemper was going through Lenny's address book. He'd turned on all the living-room lights.

"Easy, son."

Littell shut the door. "Who let you in?"

"I taught you how to B&E, remember?"

Littell shook his head. "I want him to trust me. Another man showing up like this might frighten him."

Kemper said, "You need to frighten him. Don't underestimate him just because he's queer."

"I saw what he did to Iannone."

"He panicked, Ward. If he panics again, we could get hurt. I want to establish a certain tone tonight."

Littell heard footsteps outside the door. There was no time to kill the lights for surprise.

Lenny walked in. He did a broad stage actor's double-take.

"Who's he?"

"This is Mr. Boyd. He's a friend of mine."

"And you were in the neighborhood, so you thought you'd break in and ask me a few questions."

"Let's not go at things this way."

"*What* way? You said we'd talk on the phone, and you told me you were in this by yourself."

"Lenny—"

Kemper said, "I did have a question."

Lenny hooked his thumbs through his belt loops. "Then ask it. And help yourself to a drink. Mr. Littell always does."

Kemper looked amused. "I glanced through your address book, Lenny."

"I'm not surprised. Mr. Littell always does that, too."

"You know Jack Kennedy and a lot of Hollywood people."

"Yes. And I know you and Mr. Littell, which proves I'm not immune to slumming."

"Who's this woman Laura Hughes? This address of hers—881 Fifth Avenue—interests me."

"Laura interests lots of men."

"You're trembling, Lenny. Your whole manner just changed."

Littell said, "What are you talk—?"

Kemper cut him off. "Is she in her early thirties? Tall, brunette, freckles?"

"That sounds like Laura, yes."

"I saw Joe Kennedy give her a diamond broach and at least fifty thousand dollars. That looks to me like he's sleeping with her."

Lenny laughed. His smile said, Oh, you heathen.

Kemper said, "Tell me about her."

"No. She's got nothing to do with the Teamsters' Pension Fund or anything illegal."

"You're reverting, Lenny. You're not coming off like the hard boy that took out Tony Iannone. You're starting to sound like a little fairy with a squeaky voice."

Lenny went instant baritone. "Is this better, Mr. Boyd?"

"Save the wit for your lounge engagements. Who is she?"

"I don't have to tell you that."

Kemper smiled. "You're a homosexual and a murderer. You have no rights. You're a Federal informant, and the Chicago FBI owns you."

Littell felt queasy. His heartbeat did funny little things.

Kemper said, *"Who is she?"*

Lenny came on hard butch. "This is not FBI-approved. If it was there'd be stenographers and paperwork. This is some sort of private thing with you two. And I won't say a goddamned thing that might hurt Jack Kennedy."

Kemper pulled out a morgue glossy and forced it on Lenny. Littell saw the dead boy with his mouth stuffed full.

Lenny shuddered. Lenny put on an instant rough-trade face.

"So? So this is supposed to scare me?"

"Giancana did this, Lenny. He thought this man killed Tony Iannone. One word from us, and this will be you."

Littell grabbed the snapshot. "Let's hold back a second. You've made your point."

Kemper steered him into the dining room. Kemper pressed him into a cabinet with his fingertips.

"Don't ever contradict me in front of a suspect."

"Kemper . . ."

"Hit him."

"Kemper—"

"*Hit him*. Make him afraid of you."

Littell said, "I can't. Goddamnit, don't do this to me."

"Hit him, or I'll call Giancana and rat him off right now."

"No. Come on . . . please."

Kemper handed him brass knuckles. Kemper made him lace his fingers in.

"Hit him, Ward. Hit him, or I'll let Giancana kill him."

Littell trembled. Kemper slapped him. Littell stumbled over to Lenny and weaved in front of him.

Lenny smiled this preposterous pseudo-tough-guy smile. Littell balled his fist and hit him.

Lenny clipped an end table and went down spitting teeth. Kemper threw a sofa cushion at him.

"Who's Laura Hughes? Tell me in detail."

Littell dropped the knucks. His hand throbbed and went numb.

"I said, 'Who's Laura Hughes?' "

Lenny nuzzled the cushion. Lenny spat out a chunk of gold bridgework.

"I said, 'Who's Laura Hughes?' "

Lenny coughed and cleared his throat. Lenny took a big let's-get-this-over-with breath.

He said, "She's Joe Kennedy's daughter. Her mother's Gloria Swanson."

Littell shut his eyes. The Q&A made absolutely no—

Kemper said, "Keep going."

"How far? I'm the only one outside the family who knows."

Kemper said, "Keep going."

Lenny took another breath. His lip was split up to his nostrils.

"Mr. Kennedy supports Laura. Laura loves him and hates him. Gloria Swanson hates Mr. Kennedy because he cheated her out of lots of money when he was a movie producer. She disowned Laura years ago, and that's all the 'keep going' I've got, goddamn you."

Littell opened his eyes. Lenny picked up the end table and flopped into a chair.

Kemper twirled the knucks on one finger. "Where did she get the name Hughes?"

"From Howard Hughes. Mr. Kennedy hates Hughes, so Laura took the name to annoy him."

Littell closed his eyes. He started seeing things he wasn't conjuring up.

"Ask Mr. Sands a question, Ward."

An image flickered out—Lenny with his phallus-shaped pen.

"Ward, open your eyes and ask Mr. Sands a—"

Littell opened his eyes and took his glasses off. The room went soft and blurry.

"I saw you arguing with Mad Sal outside the church. What was that about?"

Lenny worked a tooth loose. "I tried to quit the junket gig."

"Why?"

"Because Sal's poison. Because he's poison like you are."

He sounded I'm-a-snitch-now resigned.

"But he didn't let you quit?"

"No. I told him I'd work with him for six months tops, if he's still . . ."

Kemper twirled his knucks. "If he's still what?"

"Still fucking alive."

He sounded calm. He sounded like an actor who just figured out his role.

"Why wouldn't he be?"

"Because he's a degenerate gambler. Because he owes Sam G. twelve grand, and a contract's going out if he doesn't pay it back."

Littell put his glasses on. "I want you to stick with Sal, and let me worry about his debts."

Lenny wiped his mouth on the cushion. That one knuck shot cut him a brand-new harelip.

Kemper said, "Answer Mr. Littell."

Lenny said, "Oh yes, yes, Mr. Littell, sir"—arch-ugly-faggot inflected.

Kemper slipped the knucks into his waistband. "Don't tell Laura Hughes about this. And don't tell anybody about our arrangement."

Lenny stood up, knock-kneed. "I wouldn't dream of it."

Kemper winked. "You've got panache, son. And I know a magazine man in L.A. who could use an insider like you."

Lenny pushed his lip flaps together. Littell sent up a prayer: Please let me sleep through this night with no dreams.

DOCUMENT INSERT: 1/16/59.
Official FBI telephone call transcript: ``Recorded at the Director's Request''/``Classified Confidential

1-A: Director's Eyes Only.'' Speaking: Director
Hoover, Special Agent Kemper Boyd.

    JEH: Good morning, Mr. Boyd.

    KB: Sir, good morning.

    JEH: We have an excellent connection. Are you
nearby?

    KB: I'm at a restaurant on Northeast ''I'' Street.

    JEH: I see. The Committee offices are close by, so
I imagine you're hard at work for Little Brother.

    KB: I am, Sir. At least cosmetically.

    JEH: Update me, please.

    KB: I convinced Little Brother to send me back to
Miami. I told him that I could depose some Sun Valley
land fraud witnesses, and in fact I did bring back
some inconclusive depositions.

    JEH: Continue.

    KB: My real motive in traveling to Florida was to
accrue information for you on the Gretzler and
Kirpaski matters. You'll be pleased to know that
I checked in with both the Miami and Lake Weir
Police Departments and learned that both cases have
been moved to open file status. I consider that a
tacit admission that both homicides will remain
unsolved.

    JEH: Excellent. Now update me on the brothers.

    KB: The Committee's labor racketeering mandate
expires in ninety days. The paperwork forwarding
process is now in the compilation stage, and I'll be
sending you carbons of every piece of salient
memoranda sent to our target grand juries. And,
again, Sir, my opinion is that Jimmy Hoffa is legally
inviolate at this time.

    JEH: Continue.

    KB: Big Brother has been calling legitimate labor
leaders allied with the Democratic Party, to assure
them that the trouble that Little Brother has stirred
up with Hoffa does not mean that he is anti-labor
overall. My understanding is that he will announce
his candidacy in early January of next year.

    JEH: And you remain certain that the brothers do

not suspect the Bureau of collusion in the Darleen
Shoftel matter?

KB: I'm certain, Sir. Pete Bondurant's girlfriend
informed Little Brother of the Hush-Hush piece, and
Ward Littell exposed both our primary bug and
Bondurant's secondary bug independent of her.

JEH: I heard the Brothers' father made Howard
Hughes eat crow.

KB: That's true, Sir.

JEH: Hush-Hush has been lackluster lately. The
advance peeks that Mr. Hughes has been sending me have
been quite tame.

KB: I've been staying in touch with Pete Bondurant
on general principles, and I think I've found him a
Hollywood-connected man he could use as a stringer.

JEH: If my bedtime reading improves, I'll know
you've succeeded.

KB: Yes, Sir.

JEH: We have Ward Littell to thank for that entire
Big Brother snafu.

KB: I passed through Chicago and saw Littell two
days ago, Sir.

JEH: Continue.

KB: I had initially thought that his THP expulsion
might push him toward taking anti-Mob actions on his
own, so I decided to check up on him.

JEH: And?

KB: And my concerns were groundless. Littell seems
to be suffering his Red Squad work in silence, and the
only change of habit that I could detect was that he's
begun an affair with Tom Agee's daughter Helen.

JEH: An affair of a sexual nature?

KB: Yes, Sir.

JEH: Is the girl of age?

KB: She's twenty-one, Sir.

JEH: I want you to keep an eye on Littell.

KB: I will, Sir. And while I have you, could I bring
up a tangential matter?

JEH: Certainly.

KB: It involves the Cuban political situation.

JEH: Continue.

KB: In the course of my Florida visits I've met several pro-Batista and pro-Castro Cuban refugees. Now, apparently Castro is going Communist. I've learned that undesirables of varying political stripes will be expelled from Cuba and granted asylum in the U.S., with most of them settling in Miami. Would you like information on them?

JEH: Do you have an information source?

KB: Yes, Sir.

JEH: But you'd rather not reveal it?

KB: Yes, Sir.

JEH: I hope they're paying you.

KB: It's an ambiguous situation, Sir.

JEH: You're an ambiguous man. And yes, any and all Cuban emigre intelligence would be appreciated. Have you anything to add? I'm due at a meeting.

KB: One last thing, Sir. Did you know that the brothers' father had an illegitimate daughter with Gloria Swanson?

JEH: No, I did not know that. You're certain?

KB: Reasonably. Should I follow up on it?

JEH: Yes. But avoid any personal entanglements that might upset your incursion.

KB: Yes, Sir.

JEH: Forewarned is forearmed. You have a tendency to adopt people, such as the morally-impaired Ward Littell. Don't extend that tendency toward the Kennedys. I suspect that their powers of seduction exceed even your own.

KB: I'll be careful, Sir.

JEH: Good day, Mr. Boyd.

KB: Good day, Sir.

19

(Los Angeles, 1/18/59)

DICK STEISEL SAID, "If Mr. Hughes is so tight with J. Edgar Hoover, have *him* call off the goddamn process servers."

Pete scoped out his office. The client photos were boffo

—Hughes shared a wall with some South American dictators and bongo player Preston Epps.

"He won't ask Hoover for favors. He figures he hasn't kissed his ass enough yet."

"He can't keep dodging subpoenas forever. He should simply divest TWA, earn his three or four hundred million and get on to his next conquest."

Pete rocked his chair and put his feet up on Steisel's desk. "He doesn't see things that way."

"And how do you see things?"

"The way he pays me to."

"Which means, in this instance?"

"Which means I'm going to call Central Casting, bag a half-dozen actors and have them made up as Mr. Hughes, then send them out in Hughes Aircraft limos. I'm going to tell them to hit some night spots, throw some cash around and talk up their travel plans. Timbuktu, Nairobi—who gives a shit? It'll buy us some time."

Steisel sifted through desk clutter. "TWA aside, you should know that most of the *Hush-Hush* articles you've sent over for vetting are libelous. Here's an example from that Spade Cooley piece. 'Does Ella Mae Cooley have "Everlast" stamped across her chest? She should, because Spade's been bopping bluegrass ballads on her already dangerously dented decolletage! It seems that Ella Mae told Spade she wanted to join a free love cult! Spade responded with fiddle-honed fisticuffs, and now Ella Mae has been sporting brutally black-and-blue blistered bosomage.' You see, Pete, there's no loophole rhetoric or—"

Steisel moaned and droned. Pete shut him out and daydreamed.

Kemper Boyd called him yesterday. He said, "I've got you a lead on a magazine stringer. His name's Lenny Sands, and he's playing a junket engagement at the Cal-Neva Lodge in Lake Tahoe. Go talk to him—I think he'd be perfect for *Hush-Hush*. *But*—he's tight with Ward Littell, and I know you'll figure out he's FBI-connected. And you should also know that Littell has an eyeball witness on the Gretzler job. Mr. Hoover told him to forget about it, but Littell's the volatile type. I don't want you to even mention Littell to Lenny."

Lenny Sands sounded good. The "eyeball witness" line was horseshit.

Pete said, "I'll go see Sands. But let's talk turkey about something else, too."

"Cuba?"

"Yeah, Cuba. I'm starting to think it's a gravy train for us law-enforcement retirees."

"You're right. And I'm thinking of buying in myself."

"I want in. Howard Hughes is driving me nuts."

"Do something nice, then. Do something John Stanton would like."

"For instance?"

"Look me up in the Washington, D.C. white pages, and send me some goodies."

Steisel jerked him out of his daydream. "Get these college kids to insert 'alleged' and 'supposed,' and make the pieces more hypothetical. Pete, are you listening to me?"

Pete said, "Dick, I'll see you. I've got things to do."

He drove to a pay phone and dialed favors. He called a cop buddy, Mickey Cohen, and Fred Otash, "Private Eye to the Stars." They said they could glom some "goodies," with D.C. delivery guaranteed pronto.

Pete called Spade Cooley. He said, I just kiboshed a new smear on you. Grateful Spade said, "What can *I* do for *you*?"

Pete said, I need six girls from your band. Have them meet me at Central Casting in an hour.

Spade said, Yes, Big-Daddy-O!

Pete called Central Casting and Hughes Aircraft. Two clerks promised satisfaction: six Howard Hughes look-alikes and six limousines would be waiting at Central in one hour.

Pete rendezvoused with his shills and paired them off: six Howards, six women, six limos. The Howards got specific instructions: Live it up through to dawn and spread the word that you're blasting off for Rio!

The limos hauled ass. Spade dropped Pete off at the Burbank airport.

He caught a puddle jumper to Tahoe. The pilot started his downswing right over the Cal-Neva Lodge.

Be good, Lenny.

The casino featured slots, craps, roulette, blackjack, poker, keno, and the world's thickest deep-pile carpets. The lobby featured a panoply of jumbo cardboard Frank Sinatras.

Dig that one by the door—somebody drew a dick in Frankie's mouth.

Dig that tiny cardboard cutout by the bar: "Lenny Sands at the Swingeroo Lounge!"

Somebody yelled, "Pete! Pete the Frenchman!" It had to be somebody Outfit—or somebody suicide prone.

Pete looked around. He saw Johnny Rosselli, waving from a booth just inside the bar enclosure.

He walked over. The booth was all-star: Rosselli, Sam G., Heshie Ryskind, Carlos Marcello.

Rosselli winked. "Frenchman Pete, *che se dice?*"

"Good, Johnny. You?"

"*Ça va*, Pete, *ça va*. You know the boys here? Carlos, Mo and Heshie?"

"Just by reputation."

Handshakes went around. Pete stayed standing—per Outfit protocol.

Rosselli said, "Pete's French-Canadian, but he don't like to be reminded of it."

Giancana said, "Everybody's gotta come from somewhere."

Marcello said, "Except me. I got no fucking birth certificate. I was either born in fucking Tunis, North Africa, or fucking Guatemala. My parents were Sicilian greenhorns with no fucking passports. I shoulda asked them, 'Hey, where was I born?' when I had the chance."

Ryskind said, "Yeah, but I'm a Jew with a finicky prostate. My people came from Russia. And if you don't think that's a handicap in this crowd . . ."

Marcello said, "Pete's been helping Jimmy out in Miami lately. You know, at the cabstand."

Rosselli said, "And don't think we don't appreciate it."

Giancana said, "Cuba has to get worse before it gets better. Now the fucking Beard has 'nationalized' our fucking casinos. He's got Santo T. in custody down there, and he's costing us hundreds of thousands a day."

Rosselli said, "It's like Castro just shoved an atom bomb up the ass of every made guy in America."

Nobody said, "Sit down."

Sam G. pointed out a lowlife walking by counting nickels. "D'Onofrio brings these chumps here. They stink up my room and don't lose enough to compensate. Me and Frank have got forty percent of the Lodge between us. This is a top-line room, not a resort for the lunchpail crowd."

Rosselli laughed. "Your boy Lenny's working with Sal now."

Giancana took a bead on the lowlife and pulled a make-believe trigger. "Somebody's gonna put a new part in Mad Sal D'Onofrio's hair. Bookies that owe more than they take in are like fucking Communists sucking the welfare tit."

Rosselli sipped his highball. "So, Pete, what brings you to the Cal-Neva?"

"I'm interviewing Lenny Sands for a job. I thought he might make a good stringer for *Hush-Hush*."

Sam G. passed him some play chips. "Here, Frenchman, lose a grand on me. But don't move Lenny out of Chicago, all right? I like having him around."

Pete smiled. The "boys" smiled. Get the picture? They've tossed you all the crumbs they think you're worth.

Pete walked. He got caught up in the tail end of a stampede—low rollers heading for the low-rent lounge.

He followed them in. The room was SRO: every table full, latecomers holding up the walls.

Lenny Sands was on stage, backed by a piano and drums.

The keyboard man tickled some blues. Lenny bopped him on the head with his microphone.

"Lew, Lew, Lew. What are we, a bunch of moolies? What are you playing? 'Pass me the Watermelon, Mama, 'Cause My Spareribs are Double-Parked'?"

The audience yukked. Lenny said, "Lew, give me some Frankie."

Lew Piano laid down an intro. Lenny sang, half Sinatra/half fag falsetto:

"I've got you under my skin. I've got you, keestered deep inside of me. So deep, my hemorrhoids are riding me. I've got you—WHOA!—under my skin."

The junket chumps howled. Lenny cranked up his lisp:

"I've got you, chained to my bed. I've got you, and extra K-Y now! So deep, you can't really say why now! I've got you under my skin!"

The geeks yuk-yuk-yukked and tee-hee-heed. Peter Lawford walked in and checked the action—Frank Sinatra's #1 toady.

The drummer popped a rim shot. Lenny stroked his mike at crotch level.

"You gorgeous he-men from the Chicago Knights of Columbus, I just adore you!"

The audience cheered—

"And I want you to know that all my womanizing and chasing ring-a-ding cooze is just subterfuge to hide my overweening lust for YOU, the men of K of C Chapter 384, you gorgeous hunks of manicotti with your king-sized braciolas that I just can't wait to sautee and fricassee and take deep into my tantalizing Tetrazzini!"

Lawford looked hot to trot. It was common insider knowledge that he'd kill to suck up to Sinatra.

The junketeers roared. Some clown waved a K of C flag.

"I just love you love you love you! I can't wait to dress up in drag and invite all of you to sleep over at my Rat Pack slumber party!"

Lawford bolted toward the stage.

Pete tripped him.

Dig the toady's pratfall—an instant all-time classic.

Frank Sinatra shoved his way into the lounge. The junketeers went stone fucking nuts.

Sam G. intercepted him. Sam G. whispered to him, nice and gentle and FIRM.

Pete caught the gist.

Lenny's with the Outfit. Lenny's not a guy you rough up for sport.

Sam was smiling. Sam dug Lenny's act.

Sinatra about-faced. Ass-kissers surrounded him.

Lenny cranked his lisp waaaaay up. "Frankie, come back! Peter, get up off the floor, you gorgeous nincompoop!"

Lenny Sands was one cute shitbird.

He slipped the head blackjack dealer a note to forward to Sands. Lenny showed up at the coffee shop, on-the-dot punctual.

Pete said, "Thanks for coming."

Lenny sat down. "Your note mentioned money. That's something that always gets my attention."

A waitress brought them coffee. Jackpot gongs went off—baby slots were bolted to every table.

"Kemper Boyd recommended you. He said you'd be perfect for the job."

"Are you working for him?"

"No. He's just an acquaintance."

Lenny rubbed a scar above his lips. "What is the job exactly?"

"You'd be the stringer for *Hush-Hush*. You'd be digging up the stories and scandal bits and feeding them to the writers."

"So I'd be a snitch."

"Sort of. You keep your nose down in L.A., Chicago and Nevada, and report back."

"For how much?"

"A grand a month, cash."

"Movie-star dirt, that's what you want. You want the skank on entertainment people."

"Right. And liberal-type politicians."

Lenny poured cream in his coffee. "I've got no beef with that, except for the Kennedys. Bobby I can do without, but Jack I like."

"You were pretty tough on Sinatra. He's pals with Jack, isn't he?"

"He pimps for Jack and brown-noses the whole family. Peter Lawford's married to one of Jack's sisters, and he's Frank's brown-nose contact. Jack thinks Frank's good for chuckles and not much else, and you didn't hear any of this from me."

Pete sipped coffee. "Tell me more."

"No, you ask."

"Okay. I'm on the Sunset Strip and I want to get laid for a C-note. What do I do?"

"You see Mel, the parking-lot man at Dino's Lodge. For a dime, he'll send you to a pad on Havenhurst and Fountain."

"Suppose I want nigger stuff?"

"Go to the drive-in at Washington and La Brea and talk to the colored carhops."

"Suppose I dig boys?"

Lenny flinched. Pete said, "I know you hate fags, but answer the question."

"Shit, I don't ... wait ... the doorman at the Largo runs a string of male prosties."

"Good. Now, what's the story on Mickey Cohen's sex life?"

Lenny smiled. "It's cosmetic. He doesn't really dig cooze, but he likes to be seen with beautiful women. His current quasi-girlfriend is named Sandy Hashhagen. Sometimes he goes out with Candy Barr and Liz Renay."

"Who clipped Tony Trombino and Tony Brancato?"

"Either Jimmy Frattiano or a cop named Dave Klein."

"Who's got the biggest dick in Hollywood?"

"Steve Cochran or John Ireland."

"What's Spade Cooley do for kicks?"

"Pop bennies and beat up his wife."

"Who'd Ava Gardner cheat on Sinatra with?"

"Everybody."

"Who do you see for a quick abortion?"

"I'd go see Freddy Otash."

"Jayne Mansfield?"

"Nympho."

"Dick Contino?"

"Muff diver supreme."

"Gail Russell?"

"Drinking herself to death at a cheap pad in West L.A."

"Lex Barker?"

"Pussy hound with jailbait tendencies."

"Johnnie Ray?"

"Homo."

"Art Pepper?"

"Junkie."

"Lizabeth Scott?"

"Dyke."

"Billy Eckstine?"

"Cunt man."

"Tom Neal?"

"On the skids in Palm Springs."

"Anita O'Day?"

"Hophead."

"Cary Grant?"

"Homo."

"Randolph Scott?"

"Homo."

"Senator William F. Knowland?"

"Drunk."

"Chief Parker?"

"Drunk."

"Bing Crosby?"

"Drunk wife-beater."

"Sergeant John O'Grady?"

"LAPD guy known for planting dope on jazz musicians."

"Desi Arnaz?"

"Whore chaser."

"Scott Brady?"

"Grasshopper."

"Grace Kelly?"

"Frigid. I popped her once myself, and I almost froze my shvantze off."

Pete laughed. "Me?"

Lenny grinned. "Shakedown king. Pimp. Killer. And in case you're wondering, I'm much too smart to ever fuck with you."

Pete said, "You've got the job."

They shook hands.

Mad Sal D. walked in the door, waving two cups spilling nickels.

20

(Washington, D.C., 1/20/59)

UNITED PARCEL DROPPED off three big boxes. Kemper carried them into his kitchen and opened them.

Bondurant wrapped the stuff in oilcloth. Bondurant understood the concept of "goodies."

Bondurant sent him two submachine guns, two hand grenades and nine silencer-fitted .45 automatics.

Bondurant included a succinct, unsigned note:

"Your move and Stanton's."

The machine guns came with fully loaded drums and a maintenance manual. The .45s fit his shoulder rig perfectly.

Kemper strapped one on and drove to the airport. He caught the 1:00 P.M. New York shuttle with time to spare.

881 Fifth Avenue was a high-line Tudor fortress. Kemper ducked past the doorman and pushed the "L. Hughes" lobby buzzer.

A woman's voice came on the intercom. "Take the second lift on the left, please. You can leave the groceries in the foyer."

He elevatored up twelve floors. The doors opened straight into an apartment vestibule.

The vestibule was the size of his living room. The mink woman was leaning against a full-sized Greek column, wearing a tartan robe and slippers.

Her hair was tied back. She was juuust starting to smile.

"I remember you from the Kennedys' party. Jack said you're one of Bobby's policemen."

"My name's Kemper Boyd, Miss Hughes."

"From Lexington, Kentucky?"

"You're close. Nashville, Tennessee."

She folded her arms. "You heard me give the cab driver my address, and you described me to the doorman downstairs. He told you my name, and you rang my bell."

"You're close."

"You saw me give that vulgar diamond broach away. Any man as elegantly dressed as you are would appreciate a gesture like that."

"Only a well-taken-care-of woman would make that kind of gesture."

She shook her head. "That's not a very sharp perception."

Kemper stepped toward her. "Then let's try this. You did it because you knew you had an audience. It was a Kennedy kind of thing to do, and I'm not criticizing you for it."

Laura cinched her robe. "Don't get presumptuous with the Kennedys. Don't even talk presumptuously about them, because when you least expect it they'll cut you off at the knees."

"You've seen it happen?"

"Yes, I have."

"Did it happen to you?"

"No."

"Because you can't expel what you haven't admitted?"

Laura pulled out a cigarette case. "I started smoking because most of the sisters did. They had cases like this, so Mr. Kennedy gave me one."

"Mr. Kennedy?"

"Or Joe. Or Uncle Joe."

Kemper smiled. "My father went broke and killed himself. He willed me ninety-one dollars and the gun he did it with."

"Uncle Joe will leave me a good deal more than that."

"What's the current stipend?"

"A hundred thousand dollars a year and expenses."

"Did you decorate this apartment to resemble the Kennedys' suite at the Carlyle?"

"Yes."

"It's beautiful. Sometimes I think I could live in hotel suites forever."

She walked away from him. She turned on her heels and disappeared down a museum-width hallway.

Kemper let five minutes pass. The apartment was huge and quiet—he couldn't get his bearings.

He worked his way left and got lost. Three corridors led him back to the same pantry; the four entrances to the dining room had him spinning in circles. He hit intersecting hallways, a library, *wings*—

Traffic sounds straightened him out. He heard foot scuffs on the terrace behind the grand piano.

He walked over. The terrace would swallow up his kitchen at least twice.

Laura was leaning against the railing. A breeze ruffled her robe.

She said, "Did Jack tell you?"

"No. I figured it out myself."

"You're lying. The Kennedys and a friend of mine in Chicago are the only ones who know. Did Mr. Hoover tell you? Bobby says he doesn't know, but I've never believed him."

Kemper shook his head. "Mr. Hoover doesn't know. Lenny Sands told a Chicago FBI man who's a friend of mine."

Laura lit a cigarette. Kemper cupped his hands around the match.

"I never thought Lenny would tell a soul."

"He didn't have much choice. If it's any consol—"

"*No*, I don't want to know. Lenny knows bad people, and bad people can make you say things you don't want to."

Kemper touched her arm. "Please don't tell Lenny you met me."

"Why, Mr. Boyd?"

"Because he's embarrassingly well connected."

"No, you don't understand. I'm asking you what you're doing here."

"I saw you at Joe Kennedy's party. I'm sure you can fill in the rest yourself."

"That's not an answer."

"I couldn't very well ask Jack or Bobby for your number."

"Why not?"

"Because Uncle Joe wouldn't approve, and Bobby doesn't entirely trust me."

"Why?"

"Because I'm embarrassingly well connected."

Laura shivered. Kemper draped his suitcoat around her shoulders.

She pointed to his holster. "Bobby told me the McClellan people don't carry guns."

"I'm off duty."

"Did you think I'd be so bored and indolent that you could just ring my bell and seduce me?"

"No, I thought I'd buy you dinner first."

Laura laughed and coughed smoke. "Is Kemper your mother's maiden name?"

"Yes."

"Is she alive?"

"She died in a nursing home in '49."

"What did you do with the gun your father left you?"

"I sold it to a classmate in law school."

"Does he carry it?"

"He died on Iwo Jima."

Laura dropped her cigarette in a coffee cup. "I know so many orphans."

"So do I. You're sort of one your—"

"*No.* That's not true. You're just saying it to make points with me."

"I don't think it's much of a stretch."

She snuggled into his suitcoat. The sleeves flopped in the wind.

"Repartee is one thing, Mr. Boyd, and the truth is another. The truth is my robber-baron father fucked my movie-star mother and got her pregnant. My movie-star mother had already had three abortions and didn't want to risk a fourth. My movie-star mom disowned me, but my father enjoys flaunting me in front of his legitimate family once a year. The boys like me because I'm provocative, and they think I'm nifty because they can't fuck me, because I'm their half-sister. The girls hate me because I'm a coded message from their father that says men can fuck around, but women can't. Do you get the picture, Mr. Boyd? I have a family. My father put me through boarding school and several colleges. My father supports me. My father informed his family of my existence when Jack brought me home from a Harvard alumni mixer as the unwitting pawn in a rather vicious ploy I had initiated to assert myself into the family. Imagine his surprise when Father said, 'Jack, you can't fuck her, she's your half-sister.' Little Bobby, twenty and Calvinistic, overheard the conversation and spread the word. My father figured what the hell, the word's out, and invited me to stay for dinner. Mrs. Kennedy had a rather traumatic reaction to all of this. Our 'embarrassingly well connected' friend Lenny Sands was giving Jack speech lessons for his first congressional campaign, and was at the house for dinner. He stopped Rose from making a scene, and we've been sharing secrets ever since. *I have a family*, Mr. Boyd. My father is evil and grasping and ruthless and willing to destroy anybody who so much as looks the wrong way at the children he publicly acknowledges. And I hate everything about him except the money he gives me and the fact that he would probably destroy anybody who tried to hurt me as well."

Car horns bleeped long and shrill. Laura pointed down at a line of taxis. "They perch there like vultures. They always make the most noise when I'm playing Rachmaninoff."

Kemper unholstered his piece. He homed in on a sign marked Yellow Cabs Only.

He braced his arm on the railing and fired. Two shots sheared the sign off the signpost. The silencer went *thwack*—Pete was a good ordnance supplier.

Laura whooped. Cabbies gestured up, spooked and bewildered.

Kemper said, "I like your hair."

Laura untied it. The wind made it dance.

They talked.

He told her how the Boyd fortune evaporated. She told him how she flunked out of Juilliard and flopped as a socialite.

She called herself a musical dilettante. He called himself an ambitious cop. She recorded Chopin on a vanity label. He sent Christmas cards to car thieves he arrested.

He said he loved Jack but couldn't stand Bobby. She called Bobby deep Beethoven and Jack Mozart most glib. She called Lenny Sands her one true friend and didn't mention his betrayal. He said his daughter, Claire, shared all his secrets.

Devil's Advocate snapped on automatically. He knew exactly what to say and what to omit.

He called Mr. Hoover a vindictive old queen. He portrayed himself as a liberal pragmatist hitched to the Kennedy star.

She revived the orphanhood theme. He described the three-daughter combine.

Susan Littell was judgmental and shrill. Helen Agee was courageous and impetuous. His Claire was too close to know just yet.

He told her about his friendship with Ward. He said he wanted a younger brother for keeps—and the Bureau gave him one. He said Ward worshiped Bobby. She said Bobby sensed that Uncle Joe was evil and chased gangsters to compensate for his patrimony.

He hinted at his own lost brother. He said the loss made him push Ward in odd ways.

They talked themselves exhausted. Laura called "21" and had dinner sent up. The chateaubriand and wine made her drowsy.

They left it unspoken.

Not tonight—next time.

Laura fell asleep. Kemper walked through the apartment.

Two circuits taught him the layout. Laura told him the maid needed a map. The dining room could feed a small army.

He called the Agency's Miami Ops number. John Stanton picked up immediately.

"Yes?"

"It's Kemper Boyd. I'm calling to accept your offer."

"I'm very pleased to hear that. I'll be in touch, Mr. Boyd. We'll have lots to discuss."

"Good night, then."

"Good night."

Kemper walked back to the drawing room. He left the terrace curtains open—skyscrapers across the park threw light on Laura.

He watched her sleep.

21

(Chicago, 1/22/59)

LENNY'S SPARE FUCK-PAD key unlocked the door. Littell hacked the jamb down to the bolt to fake a forensically valid burglar entry.

He broke the blade off his pen knife. The B&E shakes had him hacking too hard.

His trial break-in taught him the floor plan. He knew where everything was.

Littell shut the door and went straight for the golf bag. The $14,000 was still tucked inside the ball pocket.

He put his gloves on. He allotted seven minutes for cosmetic thievery.

He unplugged the hi-fi.

He emptied drawers and ransacked the medicine cabinet.

He dumped a TV, a toaster and the golf bag by the door.

It looked like a classic junkie-pad boost. Butch Montrose would never suspect anything else.

Kemper Boyd always said PROTECT YOUR INFORMANTS.

He pocketed the money. He carried the swag to his car, drove it to the lake and dumped it in a garbage-strewn tide pool.

Littell got home late. Helen was asleep on his side of the bed.

Her side was cold. Sleep wouldn't come—he kept replaying the break-in for errors.

He drifted off around dawn. He dreamed he was choking on a dildo.

He woke up late. Helen left him a note.

> School bodes. What time did you get home? For a (dismayingly) liberal FBI man you certainly are a zealous Communist chaser. What do Communists do at midnight?
> Love, love, love,
> H

Littell forced down coffee and toast. He wrote his note on plain bond paper.

Mr. D'Onofrio,

    Sam Giancana has issued a contract on you. You will be killed unless you repay the $12,000 you owe him. I have a way for you to avoid this. Meet me this afternoon at 4:00. The Kollege Klub, 1281 58th, Hyde Park.

Littell put the note in an envelope and added five hundred dollars. Lenny said the junket tour had concluded—Sal should be back at home.

Kemper Boyd always said SEDUCE YOUR INFORM-ANTS WITH MONEY.

Littell called the Speedy-King Messenger Service. The dispatcher said he'd send a courier right over.

Mad Sal was prompt. Littell pushed his rye and beer aside.

They had the whole row of tables to themselves. The college kids at the bar wouldn't be able to hear them.

Sal sat down across from him. His flab rolls jiggled and hiked his shirt up over his belly button.

He said, "So?"

Littell pulled his gun and held it in his lap. The table covered him.

"So what did you do with that five hundred?"

Sal picked his nose. "I got down on the Blackhawks versus the Canadiens. Ten o'clock tonight that five hundred is a thousand."

"You owe Giancana eleven thousand more than that."

"So who the fuck told you?"

"A reliable source."

"You mean some Fed snitch cocksucker. You're a Fed, right? You're too candy-ass looking to be anything else, and if you was CPD or the Cook County Sheriff's, I'd've bought you off by now, and I'd be fucking your wife and cornholing your snotnose little boy while you was off at work."

"You owe Giancana twelve thousand dollars that you don't have. He's going to kill you."

"Tell me something I don't know."

"You killed a colored boy named Maurice Theodore Wilkins."

"That accusation is stale bread. It is fucking rebop you got out of some file."

"I just turned an eyeball witness."

Sal dug into his ears with a paper clip. "That is horse pucky. Feds don't investigate nigger homicides, and a little birdie told me that that kid was killed by an unknown assailant in the basement of the church rectory he stole from. The birdie said the assailant waited for the priests to go to a ball game, and then he cut the nigger boy up with a chainsaw after he made the nigger boy blow him. The birdie said there was lots of blood, and the assailant took care of the stink with altar wine."

Kemper Boyd always said NEVER SHOW FEAR OR DISGUST.

Littell laid a thousand dollars on the table. "I'm prepared to pay off your debt. In two or three installments, so Giancana won't suspect anything."

Sal grabbed the money. "So I take it, so I don't take it. For all I know, Mo might decide to whack me 'cause he's jealous of my good looks."

Littell cocked his gun. "Put the money down."

Sal did it. "So?"

"So are you interested?"

"So if I'm not?"

"So Giancana clips you. So I put out the word that you killed Tony Iannone. You've heard the rumors—Tony got whacked outside a homo joint. Sal, you're an open book. Jesus, 'blow' and 'cornhole.' I think you developed a few habits in Joliet."

Sal ogled the cash. Sal smelled like tobacco sweat and Aqua Velva lotion.

"You're a loan shark, Sal. What I'm asking for won't be too far out of line."

"S-s-so?"

"So I want to get at the Teamsters' Pension Fund. I want you to help me push somebody up the ladder. I'll find a man with a pedigree looking for a loan, and you help me set him up with Sam and the Fund. It's that simple. And I'm not asking you to snitch anybody."

Sal ogled the money.

Sal popped sweat.

Littell dropped three thousand dollars on the pile.

Sal said, "Okay."

Littell said, "Take it to Giancana. Don't gamble with it."

Sal gave him the bah-fungoo sign. "Stow the lecture. And remember I fucked your mother, which makes me your daddy."

Littell stood up and roundhoused his revolver. Mad Sal caught the barrel square in the teeth.

Kemper Boyd always said COW YOUR INFORMANTS.

Sal coughed up blood and gold fillings. Some kids at the bar watched the whole thing, bug-eyed.

Littell stared them down.

22

(Miami, 2/4/59)

THE BOAT WAS late.

U.S. Customs agents crowded the dock. The U.S. Health Service had a tent pitched in the parking lot behind it.

The refugees would be X-rayed and blood-tested. The contagious ones would be shipped to a state hospital outside Pensacola.

Stanton checked his passenger manifest. "One of our on-island contacts leaked us a list. All the deportees are male."

Waves hit the pilings. Guy Banister flicked a cigarette butt at them.

"Which implies that they're criminals. Castro's getting rid of plain old 'undesirables' under the 'politically undesirable' blanket."

Debriefing huts flanked the dock. U.S. Border Patrol marksmen crouched behind them. They had first-hint-of-trouble/ shoot-to-kill orders.

Kemper stood above the front pilings. Waves smashed up and sprayed his trouser legs.

His specific job was to interview Teofilio Paez, the ex-security boss for the United Fruit Company. A CIA briefing pouch defined UF: "America's largest, most long-established and profitable in-Cuba corporation and the largest on-island employer of unskilled and semi-skilled Cuban National workers. A long-standing bastion of Cuban anti-Communism. Cuban National security aides, working for the company, have long been effective in recruiting anti-Communist youth eager to infiltrate left-wing workers' groups and Cuban educational institutions."

Banister and Stanton watched the skyline. Kemper stepped into a breeze and let it ruffle his hair.

He had ten days in as a contract agent—two briefings at Langley and this. He had ten days in with Laura Hughes—the La Guardia shuttle made trysting easy.

Laura felt legitimate. Laura went crazy when he touched her. Laura said brilliant things and played Chopin *con brio*.

Laura was a Kennedy. Laura spun Kennedy tales with great verve.

He hid those stories from Mr. Hoover.

It felt like near-loyalty. It felt near-poignant—and Hoover-compromised.

He needed Mr. Hoover. He continued to feed him phone reports, but limited them to McClellan Committee intelligence.

He rented a suite at the St. Regis Hotel, not far from Laura's apartment. The monthly rate was brutal.

Manhattan got in your blood. His three paychecks totaled fifty-nine thousand a year—nowhere near enough to sustain the life he wanted.

Bobby kept him busy with boring Committee paperwork. Jack had dropped hints that the family might have post-Committee work for him. His most likely position would be campaign security boss.

Jack enjoyed having him around. Bobby continued to vaguely distrust him.

Bobby wasn't up for grabs—and Ward Littell knew it.

He talked to Ward twice a week. Ward was ballyhooing his new snitch—a bookie/loan shark named Sal D'Onofrio.

Cautious Ward said he had Mad Sal cowed. Angry Ward said Lenny Sands was now working for Pete Bondurant.

Angry Ward knew that *he* set it up.

Ward sent him intelligence reports. He edited out the illegalities and forwarded them to Bobby Kennedy. Bobby knew Littell solely as "The Phantom." Bobby prayed for him and marveled at his courage.

Hopefully, that courage was tinged with circumspection. Hopefully, that boy on the morgue slab taught Ward a few things.

Ward was adaptable and willing to listen. Ward was another orphan—raised in Jesuit foster homes.

Ward had good instincts. Ward believed that "alternative" Pension Fund books existed.

Lenny Sands thought the books were administered by a Mob elder statesman. He'd heard that cash was paid for loan referrals that resulted in large profits.

Littell might be stalking *big* money. It was potential knowledge to hide from Bobby.

He did hide it. He cut every Fund reference from the Phantom's reports.

Littell was malleable for a zealot. The Big Question was this: Could his covert work be hidden from Mr. Hoover?

A dark speck bobbed on the water. Banister held up binoculars. "They don't look wholesome. There's a crap game going on at the back of the barge."

Customs men hit the dock. They packed revolvers, billy clubs and shackle chains.

Stanton showed Kemper a photograph. "This is Paez. We'll grab him right off, so Customs can't requisition him."

Paez looked like a skinny Xavier Cugat. Banister said, "I can see him now. He's up front, and he's cut and bruised."

Stanton winced. "Castro hates United Fruit. Our propaganda section picked up a polemic he wrote on it nine months ago. It was an early indication that he might go Commie."

Whitecaps pushed the barge in close. The men were kicking and clawing to be first off.

Kemper flicked the safety off his piece. "Where are we detaining them?"

Banister pointed north. "The Agency owns a motel in Boynton Beach. They concocted a cover story about fumigation and evicted all the tenants. We'll pack these beaners in six to a room and see who we can use."

The refugees yelled and waved little flags on sticks. Teo Paez was crouched to sprint.

The Customs boss yelled, "On ready!"

The barge tapped the dock. Paez jumped off. Kemper and Stanton grabbed him and bear-hugged him.

They picked him up and ran with him. Banister ran interference—"CIA custody! He's ours!"

The riflemen fired warning shots. The refugees ducked and covered. Customs men grappled the barge in and cinched it to the pilings.

Kemper hustled Paez through the crowd. Stanton ran ahead and unlocked a debriefing hut.

Somebody yelled, "There's a body on the boat!"

They got their man inside. Banister locked the door. Paez hit the floor and smothered it with kisses.

Cigars fell out of his pockets. Banister picked one up and sniffed the wrapper.

Stanton caught his breath. "Welcome to America, Mr. Paez. We've heard very good things about you, and we're very glad you're here."

Kemper cracked a window. The dead man passed by on a gurney—blade-punctured from head to toe. Customs agents lined up the exiles—maybe fifty men total.

Banister set up his tape recorder on a table. Stanton said, "You had a death on the boat?"

Paez slumped into a chair. "No. It was a political execution. We surmised that the man had been deported to serve as an anti-American spy. Under interrogation he revealed that this was true. We acted accordingly."

Kemper sat down. "You speak excellent English, Teo."

"I speak the slow and exaggeratedly formal English of the laboriously self-taught. Native speakers tell me that I sometimes lapse into hilarious malapropisms and mutilations of their language."

Stanton pulled a chair up. "Would you mind talking with us now? We've got a nice apartment ready for you, and Mr. Boyd will drive you there in a little while."

Paez bowed. "I am at your disposable."

"Excellent. I'm John Stanton, by the way. And these are my colleagues, Kemper Boyd and Guy Banister."

Paez shook hands all around. Banister pocketed the rest of the cigars and turned on the tape machine.

"Can we get you anything before we start?"

"No. I would like my first American meal to be a sandwich at Wolfie's Delicatessen in Miami Beach."

Kemper smiled. Banister laughed outright. Stanton said, "Teo, is Fidel Castro a Communist?"

Paez nodded. "Yes. Indubitably so. He is a Communist in both thought and practice, and my old network of student informants have told me that airplanes carrying Russian diplomats have flown in to Havana late at night on several occasions recently. My friend Wilfredo Olmos Delsol, who was on the boat with me, has the flight numbers memorized."

Banister lit a cigarette. "Che Guevara's been Red since way back."

"Yes. And Fidel's brother Raúl is a Communisto pig himself. Moreover, he is a hypocriticize. My friend Tomás Obregón says that Raúl is selling confiscated heroin to rich drug addicts and hypocriticizingly spewing Communist rhetoric at the same time."

Kemper checked his custody list. "Tomás Obregón was on the boat with you."

"Yes."

"How would he have information on the Cuban heroin trade?"

"Because, Mr. Boyd, he was involved in the heroin trade himself. You see, my fellow boat passengers are mostly criminal scum. Fidel wanted to be rid of them and foisted them on America in hopes that they would practice their trades on your shores. What he failed to realize was that Communism is a bigger crime than dope peddling or robbery or murder, and that even criminals might possess the patriotic desire to reclaim their homeland."

Stanton rocked his chair back. "We've heard that Castro has taken over the Mafia-owned hotels and casinos."

"It is true. Fidel calls it 'nationalization.' He has stolen the casinos and millions of dollars from the Mafia. Tomás Obregón told me that the illustrious American gangster Santo Trafficante Jr. is currently in custody at the Nacional Hotel."

Banister sighed. "That cocksucker Castro has a death wish. He is fucking with both the United States of America *and* the Mafia."

"There is no Mafia, Guy. At least Mr. Hoover has always said so."

"Kemper, even God can make mistakes."

Stanton said, "Enough of that. Teo, what's the status of the American citizens remaining inside Cuba?"

Paez scratched and stretched. "Fidel wants to appear humane. He is coddling the influential Americans still in Cuba and allowing them to see only the alleged good his revolution has done. He is going to release them slowly, to return to America as duped tools to dispense communistic propaganda. And in the meantime, Fidel has burned many of the cane fields of my beloved United Fruit, and has tortured and killed many of my student informants under the indictment that they are spies for the '*imperialisto y fascisto*' La United.''

Stanton checked his watch. ''Guy, take Teo over for his medical. Teo, go with Mr. Banister. Mr. Boyd will drive you into Miami in a little while.''

Banister hustled Paez out. Kemper watched them walk to the X-ray shack.

Stanton shut the door. ''Dump the dead man somewhere, Kemper. I'll debrief all the personnel who've seen him. And don't rattle Guy's cage, he can be volatile.''

''I've heard. Rumor has it that he was assistant superintendent of the New Orleans Police for about ten minutes, until he got drunk and shot off his gun in a crowded restaurant.''

Stanton smiled. ''And rumor has it that you've fenced a few hot Corvettes in your day.''

''Touché. And parenthetically, what did you think of Pete Bondurant's gun donation?''

''I was impressed. We're thinking of making Pete an offer, and I'll be bringing it up the next time I talk to the deputy director.''

Kemper said, ''Pete's a good man. He's good at keeping rowdies in line.''

''Yes, he is. Jimmy Hoffa uses him to good effect at that Tiger Kab place. Keep going, Kemper. I can tell that you've got your thinking cap on.''

Kemper turned off the tape recorder. ''John, you're going to find that a sizable percentage of those men out there are uncontrollably psychopathic. Your notion of indoctrinating them and training them as potential anti-Castro guerrillas may not work. If you house them with stable Cuban immigrant families and find them work, per your existing plan, you'll find them reverting to their former criminal predilections as soon as the novelty of being in this country wears off.''

''You're saying we should screen them more thoroughly.''

''No, I'm saying *I* should. I'm saying we should extend the detention period at the Agency's motel, and I should be the one with final authority as to who we recruit.''

Stanton laughed. ''May I ask what qualifies you for this?''

Kemper ticked off points on his fingers. ''I worked undercover for nine years. I know criminals, and I like them. I infiltrated car theft rings, arrested the members and worked with the U.S. Attorney's Office in building their cases for prosecution. I understand the need certain criminals have to acquiesce to authority. John, I got so close to some of those car thieves that they insisted on deposing their confessions to me only—the agent who betrayed them and arrested them."

Stanton whistled—out-of-character for him. "Are you suggesting that you expand your duties and remain with the men you select as their field officer? That seems unrealistic to me, given your other entanglements."

Kemper slapped the table. "*No*. I'm strongly proposing Pete Bondurant for that job. What I'm saying is this: A hardcore criminal contingent, properly indoctrinated and supervised, could be very effective. Let's assume that the Castro problem extends. I think that even at this early date, it's safe to assume that the Agency will have a large pool of future deportees and legally emigrated Cubans to choose from. Let's make this first cadre an elite one. It's *ours*, John. Let's make it the best."

Stanton tapped his chin. "Mr. Dulles was ready to request green cards for all the men. He'd be pleased to know that we're being so selective early on. He hates begging the INS for favors."

Kemper put a hand up. "Don't deport the men we reject. Banister knows some Cubans in New Orleans, doesn't he?"

"Yes. There's a large Batistaite community there."

"Then let Guy have the men we reject. Let them find jobs or not find jobs, and have them file for visas on their own in Louisiana."

"How many men do you think will meet your qualifications?"

"I have no idea."

Stanton looked eager. "Mr. Dulles has approved the purchase of some cheap south Florida land for our initial training site. I think I could convince him to keep our permanent cadre there small and contained, if you think the men you select can also train future arrivals before we disperse them to the other camps that I'm certain will be springing up."

Kemper nodded. "I'll make training skills one of my criteria. Where is this land?"

"It's on the coast, outside a small town named Blessington."

"Is it accessible to Miami?"

"Yes. Why?"

"I was thinking of the Tiger Kab stand as a recruiting hub."

Stanton looked almost hot and bothered. "Gangster connotations aside, I think the Tiger Kab place could be utilized. Chuck Rogers is working there already, so we've already got an in."

Kemper said, "John"—very slowly.

Stanton looked dead ecstatic. "The answer to all your suggestions is yes, pending the deputy director's approval. And bravo, Kemper. You're more than fulfilling my expectations."

Kemper stood up and bowed. "Thanks. And I think we'll make Castro rue the day he sent that boat off."

"From your mouth to God's ears. And by the way, what do you think your friend Jack would say about our little freedom barge?"

Kemper laughed. "Jack would say, 'Where's the women?' "

Paez talked a blue streak. Kemper rolled down his window for relief.

They hit Miami at rush hour. Paez kept jabbering. Kemper drummed the dashboard and tried to replay his talk with Stanton.

". . . and Mr. Thomas Gordean was my *patrón* at La United. He loved pussy until his fondness for I. W. Harper bonded bourbon inappropriated him. Most of the executives at La United got out after Castro took over, but Mr. Gordean has remained behind. Now, he is drinking even more heavily. He has several thousand shares of United Fruit stock with him, and refuses to leave. He has bought off militiamen to be his private bodyguards and is beginning to spout the Communist line himself. My great fear is that Mr. Gordean will go Communisto like the Fidel I loved long ago. I fear that he will become a propaganda tool par eccentricity and . . ."

"Stock shares"—

"Thomas Gordean"—

A light bulb popped on and nearly blinded him. Kemper almost ran his car off the road.

DOCUMENT INSERT: 2/10/59.
Hush-Hush stringer report: Lenny Sands to Pete Bondurant.

Pete,

Here's a lead I've picked up. 1.—Mickey Cohen's diving for crumbs. He's got two goons (George

Piscatelli & Sam Lo Cigno) set to maybe work a sex shakedown racket. I got this from Dick Contino, in Chicago for some accordion soiree. Mickey got the idea when he read Lana Turner's love letters to Johnny Stompanato after Lana's daughter shanked Johnny. Johnny used to screw rich widows and had some out-of-work cameraman film it. Mickey's got some choice film clips. Tell Mr. Hughes he'll sell them for 3 grand.

Cheers, Lenny

DOCUMENT INSERT: 2/24/59.
Hush-Hush stringer report: Lenny Sands to Pete Bondurant.

Pete,

I've been on the road with Sal D'Onofrio's junket gig. Here's some tidbits. 1.—All the midnight shift cocktail waitresses at the Dunes Hotel in Vegas are hookers. They serviced President Eisenhower's Secret Service crew when Ike addressed the Nevada State Legislature. 2.—Rock Hudson's banging the maitre d' at the Cal-Neva restaurant. 3.—Lenny Bruce is hooked on dilaudid. There's a whole squad of L.A. County Sheriffs set to entrap him the next time he appears on the Strip. 4.—Freddy Otash got Jayne Mansfield an abortion. The daddy was a shvartze dishwasher with a 16″ schlong. Peter Lawford's got pictures of the guy stroking it. I bought one off Freddy O. I'll send it to you to forward to Mr. Hughes. 5.—Bing Crosby's drying out at a Catholic Church retreat for alcoholic priests and nuns outside 29 Palms. Cardinal Spellman visited him there. They went on a bender and drove to L.A. blotto. Spellman sideswiped a car filled with wetbacks and sent 3 of them to the hospital. Bing bought them off with autographed pictures and a few hundred dollars. Spellman flew back to New York with the DT's. Bing stayed in L.A. long enough to beat up his wife and then went back to the dry-out farm.

Cheers, Lenny

DOCUMENT INSERT: 3/4/59.
Personal note: J. Edgar Hoover to Howard Hughes.

Dear Howard,

   I thought I would drop you a line to tell you how
much I think Hush-Hush has improved since Mr.
Bondurant hired your new stringer. Now there's a man
who would make an excellent FBI agent! I so look
forward to the verbatim reports that you send me!
Should you wish to expedite their delivery, have Mr.
Bondurant contact Special Agent Rice at the Los
Angeles Office. Many thanks also for the Stompanato
home movie and the snapshot of the prodigiously
endowed negro. Forewarned is forearmed: you have to
know your enemy before you can combat him.

                                        All best, Edgar

DOCUMENT INSERT: 3/19/59.
Personal letter: Kemper Boyd to J. Edgar Hoover.
Marked: EXTREMELY CONFIDENTIAL.

Sir:

   Per our previous conversation, I'm passing on
salient Kennedy family information gleaned from
Laura (Swanson) Hughes.
   I've gained a degree of Miss Hughes' confidence in
the course of establishing a casual friendship with
her. My relationship with the Kennedys gives me
credibility, and Miss Hughes was impressed with the
fact that I determined the secret of her parentage
without actually broaching the topic to Kennedy
family members or her other knowledgeable friends.
   Miss Hughes loves to talk about the family, but she
only discusses John, Robert, Edward, Rose and the
sisters in bland terms. She reserves considerable
wrath for Joseph P. Kennedy Sr., cites his ties to
Boston mobster Raymond L.S. Patriarca and a retired
Chicago ''bootlegger-financier'' named Jules
Schiffrin, and delights in telling stories of Mr.

Kennedy's business rivalry with Howard Hughes. (Miss
Hughes adopted the name ''Hughes'' on her eighteenth
birthday, replacing the Kennedy-Swanson proffered
''Johnson'' in an effort to somehow fluster her
father, one of Howard Hughes' most auspicious
enemies.)

Miss Hughes contends that Joseph P. Kennedy's
gangster ties run considerably deeper than the ''he
was a bootlegger'' tag foisted upon him by the press
in reference to his highly successful scotch whisky
import business pre-prohibition. She cannot cite
specific gangster intimates or recall incidents that
she has witnessed or heard of second-hand;
nevertheless, her sense of Joseph P. Kennedy as
''deeply gangster connected'' remains inchoately
strong.

I will continue my friendship with Miss Hughes and
report all salient Kennedy family intelligence to
you.

Respectfully, Kemper Boyd

DOCUMENT INSERT: 4/21/59.
Summary report: SA Ward J. Littell to Kemper Boyd.
''For editing and forwarding to Robert F. Kennedy.''

Dear Kemper,

Things continue apace here in Chicago. I'm
continuing to pursue domestic Communists per my
regular Bureau assignment, although they impress me
as more pathetic and less dangerous by the day. That
said, I'll move to our real concerns.

Sal D'Onofrio and Lenny Sands continue, unknown to
each other, to serve as my informants. Sal, of course,
paid back the $12,000 he owed Sam Giancana; Giancana
let him off with a beating. Apparently, my theft of
Butch Montrose's $14,000 was never connected to Sal's
$12,000 windfall. I ordered Sal to repay Giancana, in
three increments and he followed that order. My
initial violence directed at Sal proved to be farsighted: I seem to have the man thoroughly cowed. In

the course of casual conversation I told him that
I had been a Jesuit seminarian. D'Onofrio, a self-
described ''Devout Catholic,'' was impressed by this
and now considers me something of a father-confessor.
He has confessed to six torture-murders, and of
course I now have those (gruesomely detailed)
confessions to hold over him. Aside from the
occasional nightmares the confessions have induced,
Sal and I seem to be proceeding on an even keel. I told
him I would appreciate it if he would refrain from
killing and self-destructive gambling while under my
stewardship, and so far he seems to be doing that. Sal
has provided me with rather tame pieces of anti-Mob
intelligence (not worth forwarding to you or Mr.
Kennedy) but has not been of help in steering me
toward a loan seeker to hoist up the Teamster Pension
Fund ladder. This was the sole reason I suborned him
as my informant, and he has failed me in that
capacity. I suspect that proving the existence of
''alternative'' Pension Fund books will be a
gruesomely attenuated process.

Lenny Sands continues to wear almost as many hats
as you. He's the Hush-Hush stringer (God, what ugly
work that must be!), Sal's junket partner and a
general Chicago Mob drone. He says he's actively
engaged in attempting to accrue information on the
workings of the Pension Fund and says that he believes
the rumor that Sam Giancana pays bonuses for Fund loan
referrals is true. He also believes that
''alternative,'' perhaps coded, Pension Fund books
detailing hidden assets do exist. In conclusion, I've
yet to glean hard information from either Sands or
D'Onofrio.

On another front, Mr. Hoover seems to be dodging a
potential opportunity to impede Chicago Mob members.
Court Meade picked up an (elliptically worded)
mention of a robbery on the tailor shop bug. Chicago
Mob soldiers Rocco Malvaso and Dewey Di Pasquale
apparently clouted $80,000 from a (non-Chicago Mob)
high-stakes crap game in Kenilworth. THP agents
airteled this information to Mr. Hoover, who told

them not to forward it to the applicable agencies for follow-up investigation. My God, that man's twisted priorities!

I'll close now. By way of farewell: you continue to amaze me, Kemper. God, you as a CIA man! And with the McClellan Committee disbanded, what will you be doing for the Kennedys?

Godspeed, WJL

DOCUMENT INSERT: 4/26/59.
Personal note: Kemper Boyd to J. Edgar Hoover.
Marked: EXTREMELY CONFIDENTIAL.

Sir:

I thought I would drop you a line and update you on the Ward Littell front. Littell and I continue to speak regularly on the telephone, and I remain convinced that he is not undertaking overt or covert anti-Mob actions on his own authority.

You mentioned that Littell was spotted near Celano's Tailor Shop and the Top Hoodlum Program listening post. I subtly queried Littell on this and am satisfied with his answer: that he was meeting SA Court Meade for lunch.

Littell's personal life seems to revolve around his affair with Helen Agee. This affair has put a strain on his relationship with his daughter, Susan, who disapproves of the liaison. Normally, Helen is in close contact with my daughter Claire, but now that they attend different colleges the frequency of that contact has been curtailed. The Littell-Agee romance seems to be comprised of three or four nights a week of domestic get-togethers. Both retain separate residences, and I think they will continue to do so. I'll continue to keep an eye on Littell.

Respectfully,
Kemper Boyd

DOCUMENT INSERT: 4/30/59.
Personal note: Kemper Boyd to Ward J. Littell.

Ward:

I strongly urge that you stay away from Celano's
Tailor Shop and the listening post area, and avoid
being seen with Court Meade. I think I've eased some
mild suspicions Mr. Hoover might have had, but you
cannot be too careful. I strongly advise you to stop
your assignment trade with Meade. Destroy this letter
immediately.

KB

DOCUMENT INSERT: 5/4/59.
Summary report: Kemper Boyd to John Stanton.
Marked: CONFIDENTIAL/HAND POUCH DELIVER.

John:

Here's the update you requested in your last pouch.
I apologize for the delay, but as you've pointed out,
I'm ''multiply-employed.''
    1.—Yes, the McClellan Committee's labor
racketeering mandate has terminated. No, the
Kennedys haven't offered me a permanent job yet.
I think they will soon. There are numerous
possibilities, since I'm both an attorney and a cop.
Yes, I have discussed Cuba with Jack. He has no
opinion on its viability as a 1960 campaign issue yet.
He is strongly anti-Communist, despite his
reputation as a liberal. I'm optimistic.
    2.—I've concluded my ''auditions'' at the Boynton
Beach Motel. Today marks the end of the 90-day
sequestering period prescribed by Deputy Director
Bissell, and tomorrow the bulk of our men will be sent
to Louisiana. Guy Banister has a network of legally
emigrated Cubans ready to receive them. They will be
providing housing, employment and references aimed
at procuring them visas. Guy will funnel the men into
his own indoctrination/training program.

I have selected four men to form the nucleus of our Blessington Cadre. I consider them to be the best of the fifty-three men on the 2/4/59 ''Banana Boat.'' Since I am ''multiply-employed,'' I was not present for much of the sequestering, but capable case officers followed the indoctrination and psychological testing guidelines I set down.

Those guidelines were exceedingly rigorous. I personally supervised polygraph tests to determine the presence of Castro-planted informants. All fifty-three men passed (I think the man they killed on the boat was the ringer). Backup Sodium Pentothal tests were administered. Again, all the men passed.

Interrogations followed. As I suspected, all fifty-three men possessed extensive criminal records inside Cuba. Their offenses included armed robbery, burglary, arson, rape, heroin smuggling, murder and various ''political crimes.'' One man was revealed to be a deviate who had molested and decapitated six small children in Havana. Another man was a homosexual procurer despised by the other exiles. I deemed both men to be dangerously unstable and terminated them under the indoctrination guidelines set down by the Deputy Director.

All the men were subjected to hard interrogation verging on torture. Most resisted with great courage. All the men were physically drilled and verbally abused in the manner of Marine Corps boot camp. Most responded with the perfect mixture of anger and subservience. The four men I selected are intelligent, violent in a controlled manner, physically skilled, garrulous (they'll be good Miami recruiters), acquiescent to authority and resoundingly pro-American, anti-Communist and anti-Castro. The men are:

A)—TEOFILIO PAEZ himself. DOB 8/6/21. Former Security Chief for United Fruit. Skilled in weaponry and interrogation techniques. Former Cuban Navy frogman. Adept at political recruitment.

B)—TOMAS OBREGON. DOB 1/17/30. Former Castro guerrilla. Former Havana dope courier and bank robber. Skilled in Jujitsu and the manufacture of explosives.

C)—WILFREDO OLMOS DELSOL. DOB 4/9/27. OBREGON's cousin. Former leftist firebrand turned rightist zealot when his bank accounts were ''Nationalized.'' Former Cuban Army drill instructor. Small arms weaponry expert.

D)—RAMON GUTIERREZ. DOB 10/24/19. Pilot. Skilled propaganda pamphleteer. Former torturer for Batista's Secret Police. Expert in counterinsurgency techniques.

3.—I've toured the area surrounding the land the Agency purchased for the Blessington campsite. It is impoverished and inhabited by poor white trash, a fair number of them Ku Klux Klan members. I think we need an impressive white man to run the campsite, a man capable of instilling fear in any local rednecks who become perturbed at the notion of Cuban emigres squatting in their bailiwick. I recommend Pete Bondurant. I checked his World War II Marine Corps record and was impressed: he survived fourteen hand-to-hand combat charges on Saipan, won the Navy Cross and rose from buck private to captain via field commission. I strongly urge you to hire Bondurant on an Agency contract basis.

That's all for now. I'll be at the St. Regis in New York if you need me.

Yours, KB

PS: You were right about Castro's U.S. trip. He refused to register in a hotel that didn't admit Negroes, then went up to Harlem and began issuing anti-U.S. statements. His behavior at the U.N. was deplorable. I salute your prescience: the man was ''forcing a rejection.''

DOCUMENT INSERT: 5/12/59.
Memo: John Stanton to Kemper Boyd.

Kemper,

The Deputy Director has approved the hiring of Pete
Bondurant. I have minor qualms, and I want you to send
him on a trial run of some sort before we approach
him. Use your own discretion.

JS

23
(Chicago, 5/18/59)

HELEN BUTTERED A slice of toast. "Susan's slow burn is getting
to me. I don't think we've spoken more than three or four times
since she heard about us."

Mad Sal was due to call. Littell pushed his breakfast aside—he
had absolutely no appetite.

"I've spoken to her exactly twice. Sometimes I think it's a pure
tradeoff—I gained a girlfriend and lost a daughter."

"You don't seem too bothered by the loss."

"Susan feeds on resentment. She's like her mother that way."

"Claire told me Kemper's having an affair with some rich
New York City woman, but she won't divulge details."

Laura Hughes was one-half Kennedy. Kemper's Kennedy
incursion was now a two-front campaign.

"Ward, you're very remote this morning."

"It's work. It preoccupies me."

"I'm not so sure."

It was almost 9:00—7:00 A.M. Gardena time. Sal was an invet-
erate early-bird gambler.

Helen waved her napkin at him. "Yoo-hoo, Ward! Are you
listening to—?"

"What are you saying? What do you mean, 'I'm not so sure'?"

"I mean your Red Squad work bores and vexes you. You
always describe it with contempt, but for months you've been
engrossed in it."

"And?"

"And you've been having nightmares and mumbling in Latin in your sleep."

"And?"

"And you're starting to hide out from me when we're in the same room. You're starting to act like you're forty-six and I'm twenty-one, and there's things you can't tell me, because I just wouldn't understand."

Littell took her hands. Helen pulled them away and knocked a napkin holder off the table.

"Kemper tells Claire everything. I would think that you'd try to emulate him that way."

"Kemper is Claire's father. I'm not yours."

Helen stood up and grabbed her purse. "I'll think about that on my way home."

"What happened to your 9:30 class?"

"It's Saturday, Ward. You're so 'preoccupied' that you don't know what day it is."

Sal called at 9:35. He sounded agitated.

Littell made nice to calm him down. Sal enjoyed sweet talk.

"How's the tour going?"

"A junket's a junket. Gardena's good 'cause it's close to L.A., but fuckin' Jewboy Lenny keeps taking off to dig up shit for *Hush-Hush* and keeps showing up late for his gigs. You think I should slice him like I did that guy who—"

"Don't confess over the phone, Sal."

"Forgive me, Father, for I have sinned."

"Stop it. You know what I'm interested in, so if you have anything, tell me."

"Okay, okay. I was in Vegas and heard Heshie Ryskind talking. Hesh said the boys are worried on the Cuban front. He said the Outfit paid the Beard a shitload of money in exchange for his word the fuckin' casinos could keep operating if he took over the fuckin' country. But now he's gone Commie and fuckin' nationalized the casinos. Hesh said the Beard's got Santo T. in jail in Havana. The boys don't like the Beard so much these days. Hesh said the Beard's like the low man in a Mongolian cluster fuck. You know, sooner or later he'll get *really* fucked."

Littell said, "And?"

"And before I left Chicago I talked on the phone to Jack Ruby. Jack had a case of the shorts, so I lent him a wad to unload this one strip club and buy himself another one, the Carousel or something. Jack's always good on the payback, 'cause he sharks on the side himself down in Dallas, and—"

"Sal, you're building up to something. Tell me what it is."

"Whoa whoa whoa—I thought cops liked that corroboration stuff."

"Sal—"

"Whoa, listen now. Jack corroborated what Heshie said. He said he'd talked to Carlos Marcello and Johnny Rosselli, and they both said the Beard is costing the Outfit seventy-five thousand a day in bank interest on top of their daily fucking casino profit nut. Think about it, Padre. Think of what the Church could do with seventy-five grand a day."

Littell sighed. "Cuba doesn't interest me. Did Ruby give you anything on the Pension Fund?"

Mad Sal said, "Weeeeel . . ."

"Sal, goddamnit—"

"Naughty, naughty, Padre. Now say ten Hail Marys and check this. Jack told me he forwarded this Texas oil guy straight to Sam G. for a Pension Fund loan, like maybe a year ago. Now this is a class-A tip, and I deserve a reward for it, and I need some fuckin' money to cover bets with, because bookies and shylocks with no bankroll get hurt and can't snitch to candy-ass Fed cocksuckers like you."

Ruby's THP designation: bagman/small-time loan shark.

"Padre Padre Padre. Forgive me because I have bet. Forgive me because—"

"I'll try to get you some money, Sal. *If* I can find a borrower for you to introduce to Giancana. I'm talking about a direct referral, from you to Sam."

"Padre . . . Jesus."

"Sal . . ."

"Padre, you're fucking me so hard it hurts."

"I saved your life, Sal. And this is the only way you'll ever get another dime out of me."

"Okay okay okay. Forgive me, Father, for I have taken it up the dirt road from this ex-seminarian Fed who—"

Littell hung up.

The squadroom was weekend quiet. The agent manning the phone lines ignored him.

Littell cadged the teletype machine and queried the Dallas office.

The reply would take at least ten minutes. He called Midway for flight information—and hit lucky.

A Pan-Am connector departed for Dallas at noon. A return flight would have him home shortly after midnight.

The kickback rolled off the wire: Jacob Rubenstein/AKA Jack Ruby, DOB 3/25/11.

The man had three extortion arrests and no convictions: in '47, '49 and '53.

The man was a suspected pimp and Dallas PD informant.

The man was the subject of a 1956 ASPCA investigation. The man was strongly suspected of sexually molesting dogs. The man was known to occasionally shylock to businessmen and desperate oil wildcatters.

Littell ripped up the teletype. Jack Ruby was worth the trip.

Airplane hum and three scotches lulled him to sleep. Mad Sal's confessions merged like a Hit Parade medley.

Sal makes the Negro boy beg. Sal feeds the bet welcher Drano. Sal decapitates two kids who wolf-whistle at a nun.

He'd verified those deaths. All four stood "Unsolved." All four victims were rectal-raped postmortem.

Littell woke up sweaty. The stewardess handed him a drink unsolicited.

The Carousel Club was a striptease-row dive. The sign out front featured zaftig girls in bikinis.

Another sign said, Open 6:00 P.M.

Littell parked behind the building and waited. His rental car reeked of recent sex and hair pomade.

A few cops cruised by. One man waved. Littell caught on: They think you're a brother cop with your hand in Jack's pocket.

Ruby drove up at 5:15, alone.

He was a dog fucker and a pimp. This would have to be ugly.

Ruby got out and unlocked the back door. Littell ran up and intercepted him.

He said, "FBI. Let's see your hands." He said it in the classic Kemper Boyd style.

Ruby looked skeptical. He was wearing a ridiculous porkpie hat.

Littell said, "Empty your pockets." Ruby obeyed him. A cash roll, dog biscuits, and a .38 snub-nose hit the ground.

Ruby spat on them. "I know out-of-town shakedowns on an intimate level. I know how to deal with cops in cheap blue suits with liquor breath. Now take what you want and leave me the fuck alone."

Littell picked up a dog biscuit. "Eat it, Jack."

Ruby got up on his toes—some kind of lighter-weight boxer's stance. Littell flashed his gun and handcuffs.

"I want you to eat that dog biscuit."

"Now look . . ."

" 'Now look, *sir.*' "

"Now look, *sir,* who the fuck do you—?"

Littell jammed the biscuit in his mouth. Ruby chewed on it to keep from gagging.

"I'm going to make demands of you, Jack. If you don't comply, the IRS will audit you, Federal agents will pat-search your customers every night and the Dallas *Morning News* will expose your sexual bent for dogs."

Ruby chewed. Ruby sprayed crumbs. Littell kicked his legs out from under him.

Ruby went down on his knees. Littell kicked the door open and kicked him inside.

Ruby tried to stand up. Littell kicked him back down. The room was ten-by-ten and littered with piles of striptease gowns.

Littell kicked a pile in Ruby's face. Littell dropped a fresh dog biscuit in his lap.

Ruby put it in his mouth. Ruby made horrible choking sounds.

Littell said, "Answer this question. *Have you ever referred borrowers to higher-end loan sharks than yourself?*"

Ruby nodded—yes yes yes yes yes.

"Sal D'Onofrio lent you the money to buy this place. Nod if that's true."

Ruby nodded. His feet were snagged up in soiled brassieres.

"Sal kills people routinely. Did you know that?"

Ruby nodded. Dogs started barking one room over.

"He tortures people, Jack. He enjoys inflicting pain."

Ruby thrashed his head. His cheeks bulged like that dead boy on the morgue slab.

"Sal burned a man to death with a blowtorch. The man's wife

came home unexpectedly. Sal shoved a gasoline-soaked rag in her mouth and ignited it. He said she died shooting flames like a dragon."

Ruby pissed in his pants. Littell saw the lap stain spread.

"Sal wants you to know a few things. One, your debt to him is erased. Two, if you don't cooperate with me or you rat me to the Outfit or any of your cop friends, he'll come to Dallas and rape you and kill you. Do you understand?"

Ruby nodded—yes yes yes. Biscuit crumbs shot out of his nostrils.

Kemper Boyd always said DON'T FALTER.

"You're not to contact Sal. You're not to know my name. You're not to tell anyone about this. You're to contact me every Tuesday at 11:00 A.M. at a pay phone in Chicago. I'll call you and give you the number. Do you understand?"

Ruby nodded—yes yes yes yes yes yes. The dogs keened and clawed at a door just a few feet in front of him.

"I want you to find a high-end borrower for Sal. Somebody Sal can send up to Giancana and the Pension Fund. Nod if you agree to do it, and nod twice if you understand the whole situation."

Ruby nodded three times.

Littell walked out.

The dog noise went cacophonous.

His return flight landed at midnight. He drove home, keyed up and exhausted.

Helen's car was parked out front. She'd be up; she'd be earnest; she'd be eager to reconcile.

Littell drove to a liquor store and bought a half-pint. A wino panhandled him. He gave him a dollar—the poor shit looked sort of like Jack Ruby.

It was 1:00 A.M. Sunday morning. Court Meade might be working the listening post.

He called. No one answered. Some THP man was ditching his shift.

Kemper urged him to avoid the post. Kemper might not consider one last visit too risky.

Littell drove over and let himself in. The bug transmitter was unplugged; the room was freshly cleaned and tidied up. A note taped to the main console box explained why.

Memo:

Celano's Tailor Shop is undergoing fumigation 5/17–5/20/59. All on-premises shifts will be suspended during that time.

Littell cracked his bottle. A few drinks revitalized him and sent his thoughts scattergunning out in a million directions.

Some brain wires crackled and crossed.

Sal needed money. Court Meade was talking up a dice-game heist. Mr. Hoover said to let the matter rest.

Littell checked the bug transcript logs. He found a colloquy on the job, filed by SA Russ Davis last month.

4/18/59. 2200 hrs. Alone at tailor shop: Rocco Malvaso & Dewey "The Duck" Di Pasquale. What sounded like drinking toasts was obscured by jackhammer and general construction noise outside on Michigan Ave. Two minutes passed while both men apparently used the bathroom. Then this conversation occurred.

Malvaso: Te salud, Duck.

Di Pasquale: Quack, quack. The nice thing is, you know, they can't report it.

Malvaso: The Kenilworth cops would shit. That is the squarejohn town to end all squarejohn towns. The last time two handsome big dick guys like us took down eighty grand in a crap game there was the twelfth of fucking never.

Di Pasquale: Quack, quack. I say they're independent guys who had it coming. I say if you're not mobbed-up with Momo you're duck shit. Hey, we wore masks and disguised our voices. To boot, those Indy cocksuckers don't know we're connected. I felt like Super Duck. I'm thinking I should get a Super Duck costume and wear it the next time I take my kids to Disneyland.

Malvaso: Quack, fucking quack, you web-footed cocksucker. You had to shoot your gun off, though. Like no fucking getaway is fucking complete without some duck-billed cocksucker shooting off his gun.

(Note: the Kenilworth Police report unexplained shots fired on the 2600 block of Westmoreland Ave., 2340 hrs., 4/16/59).

Di Pasquale: Hey, quack, quack. It worked. We've got it stashed nice and safe and—

Malvaso: And too fucking public for my taste.

Di Pasquale: Quack, quack. Sixty days ain't too long to wait for the split. Donald's been waiting fucking twenty years to bang Daisy, 'cause Walt Disney won't let him. Hey, remember last year? Jewboy Lenny did my birthday party? He did that routine where Daisy's sucking Donald off with her beak, what a fucking roar.

Malvaso: Quack, quack, you cocksucker.

(Note: construction noise obscured the rest of this conversation. Door slam sounds at 2310 hrs.)

Littell checked the THP ID file. Malvaso and Di Pasquale lived in Evanston.

He played the 4/18/59 tape and compared it to the typed transcript. Russ Davis forgot to include departing shtick.

The Duck hummed "Chattanooga Choo Choo."

Malvaso sang, "I got the key to your heart."

"Too public," "key" and "choo choo." Two *suburban-situated* robbers waiting sixty days for their split.

There were forty-odd *suburban* train stations linked to Chicago.

With forty-odd waiting rooms lined with storage lockers.

The lockers were rented by the month. For cash only, with no records kept, with no-name receipts issued.

Two robbers. Two *separate* key locks per locker door.

The locks were changed every ninety days—per Illinois TA law.

Thousands of lockers. Unmarked keys. Sixty days until the split—with thirty-three already elapsed.

The lockers were steel-plated. The waiting rooms were guarded 24 hours.

Littell spent two full days thinking it through. It came down to this:

He could tail them. But when they picked up the money, he'd be helpless.

He could only tail them one at a time. It came down to this: pre-existing bad odds doubled against him.

He decided to try anyway. He decided to pad his Red Squad

reports and tail the men on alternate days for one week.

Day one: He tails Rocco Malvaso from 8:00 A.M. to midnight. Rocco drives to his numbers dens, his union shops and his girl-friend's place in Glencoe.

Rocco goes nowhere near a train station.

Day two: He tails Dewey the Duck from 8:00 A.M. to mid-night. Dewey drives to numerous prostitution collections.

Dewey goes nowhere near a train station.

Day three: He tails Rocco Malvaso from 8:00 A.M. to mid-night. Rocco drives to Milwaukee and pistol-whips recalcitrant pimps.

Rocco goes nowhere near a train station.

Day four: He tails Dewey the Duck from 8:00 A.M. to mid-night. Dewey entertains at Dewey Junior's outdoor birthday party, dressed up as Donald Duck.

Dewey goes nowhere near a train station.

Day five: He tails Rocco Malvaso from 8:00 A.M. to midnight. Rocco spends said time with a call girl at the Blackhawk Hotel in Chicago. Rocco goes nowhere near a train station.

Day six, 8:00 A.M.: He picks up his tail on Dewey the Duck. 9:40 A.M.: Dewey's car won't start. Mrs. Duck drives Dewey to the Evanston train station.

Dewey loiters in the waiting room.

Dewey eyes the lockers.

Locker #19 is affixed with a Donald Duck decal.

Littell almost swoons.

Nights six, seven and eight: He stakes out the station. He learns that the watchman leaves for his coffee break at 3:10 A.M.

The man walks down the street to an all-night diner. The waiting room is left unguarded for at least eighteen minutes.

Night nine: He hits the station. He's armed with a crowbar, tin snips, a mallet and a chisel. He snaps the door off locker 19 and steals the four grocery bags full of money inside.

It totals $81,492.

He now has an informant fund. The bills are old and well circulated.

He gives Mad Sal ten thousand dollars for starters.

He finds the Jack Ruby look-alike wino and gives him five hundred.

The Cook County Morgue supplies him with a name. Icepick Tony Iannone's lover was one Bruce William Sifakis.

He sends the boy's parents ten thousand dollars anonymously.

He drops five thousand in the poor box at Saint Anatole's and stays to pray.

He asks forgiveness for his hubris. He tells God that he has gained his selfhood at great cost to other people. He tells God that he loves danger now, and it thrills him much more than it frightens him.

24

(Havana, 5/28/59)

THE PLANE TAXIED in. Pete got out his passport and a fat roll of ten-spots.

The passport was Canadian, and CIA-forged.

Militiamen hit the runway. The Cuban fuzz tapped all the Key West flights for handouts.

Boyd called him two days ago. He said John Stanton and Guy Banister dug that old Big Pete panache. Boyd had just signed on with the Agency. He said he had a tailor-made Big Pete job, which might prove to be a CIA audition run.

He said, "You fly from Key West to Havana under a Canadian passport. You speak French-accented English. You find out where Santo Trafficante is and take delivery of a note from him. The note should be addressed to Carlos Marcello, Johnny Rosselli and Sam Giancana, et al. It should state that Trafficante advises no Mob retaliation against Castro for nationalizing the casinos. You're also to locate a very frightened United Fruit executive named Thomas Gordean and bring him back with you for debriefing. This has to be accomplished very soon—Castro and Ike are set to permanently cancel all commercial flights running from the U.S. to Cuba."

Pete said, "Why me?"

Boyd said, "Because you can handle yourself. Because the cabstand gave you a crash course in Cubans. Because you're not a known Mob man that Castro's secret police might have a file on."

Pete said, "What's the pay?"

Boyd said, "Five thousand dollars. And if you're detained, the same diplomatic courier who's trying to get Trafficante and some other Americans out will arrange for your release. It's just a matter of time before Castro releases all foreign nationals."

Pete wavered. Boyd said, "You'll also receive my personal promise that Ward Littell—a very disturbed and dangerous man—will never touch you. In fact, I set you up with Lenny Sands to buffer the two of you."

Pete laughed.

Boyd said, "If the Cuban cops roust you, tell the truth."

The doors opened. Pete stuck a ten-dollar bill inside his passport. Militiamen climbed into the plane.

They wore mismatched gun belts and carried odd pistols. Their shirt-front regalia was straight out of some Kellogg's Corn Flakes box.

Pete squeezed up toward the cockpit. Arc lights strafed the doorways and windows. He walked down the ramp ducking blinding goddamn glare.

A guard snatched his passport. The ten-spot disappeared. The guard bowed and handed him a beer.

The other passengers filed out. Militia geeks checked their passports for tips and came up empty.

The boss guard shook his head. His minions confiscated purses and wallets. A man protested and tried to hold on to his billfold.

The spics laid him out prone on the runway. They cut his trousers off with razor blades and picked his pockets clean.

The other passengers quit squawking. The boss guard rifled through their stuff.

Pete sipped beer. Some guards walked up with their hands out.

He greased them, one ten-spot per hand. He goofed on their uniforms: lots of frayed khaki and epaulets like the ushers at Grauman's Chinese.

A little spic waved a camera. "You play futbol, hombre? Hey, big man, you play futbol?"

Somebody lobbed a football. Pete caught it one-handed. A flashbulb popped right upside his face.

Get the picture? They want you to pose.

He crouched low and waved the ball like Johnny Unitas. He went deep for a pass, blocked an invisible lineman and bounced the ball off his head like a nigger soccer ace he saw on TV once.

The spics clapped. The spics cheered. Flashbulbs pop-pop-popped.

Somebody yelled, "Hey, eees Robert Mitchum!"

Peasant types ran out on the runway, waving autograph books. Pete ran for a taxi stand by the gate.

Little kids urged him on. Cab doors opened, presto chango.

Pete dodged an oxcart and piled into an old Chevy. The driver said, "Joo are not Robert Mitchum."

They cruised Havana. Animals and street riffraff clogged traffic. They never got above ten miles an hour.

It was 92 degrees at 10:00 P.M. Half the geeks out on the stroll wore fatigues and full Jesus Christ beards.

Dig those whitewashed Spanish-style buildings. Dig the posters on every facade: Fidel Castro smiling, Fidel Castro shouting, Fidel Castro waving a cigar.

Pete flashed the snapshot Boyd gave him. "Do you know this man?"

The driver said, "*Sí.* It is Mr. Santo Junior. He is in custody at the Nacional Hotel."

"Why don't you take me there."

Pancho hung a U-turn. Pete saw hotel row up ahead—a line of half-assed skyscrapers facing the beach.

Lights sparkled down on the water. A big stretch of glow lit the waves up turquoise blue.

The cab pulled up to the Nacional. Bellboys swooped down—clowns in threadbare tuxedos. Pete whipped a ten-spot on the driver—the fuck almost wept.

The bellboys stuck their hands out. Pete lubed them at the rate of ten scoots per. A cordon pushed him into the casino.

The joint was packed. Commies dug capitalisto-style gambling.

The croupiers wore shoulder holsters. Militia geeks ran the blackjack table. The clientele was 100% beaner.

Goats roamed free. Dogs splashed in a crap table filled with water. Dig the floorshow back by the slot machines: an Airedale and a Chihuahua fucking.

Pete grabbed a bellboy and yelled in his ear. "Santo Trafficante. You know him?"

Three hands appeared. Three tens went out. Somebody pushed him into an elevator.

Fidel Castro's Cuba should be renamed Nigger Heaven.

The elevator zoomed up. A militiaman opened the door gun first.

Dollar bills dripped out of his pockets. Pete added a ten-spot. The gun disappeared, *rápidamente*.

'Did you wish to enter custody, *señor*? The fee is fifty dollars a day.'

"What does that include?"

"It includes a room with a television, gourmet food, gambling and women. You see, American passport holders are being temporarily detained here in Cuba, and Havana itself is momentarily unsafe. Why not enjoy your detention in luxury?"

Pete flashed his passport. "I'm Canadian."

"Yes. And of French distraction, I can tell."

Steam trays lined the hallway. Bellboys pushed cocktail carts by. A goat was taking a shit on the carpet two doors down.

Pete laughed. "Your guy Castro's some innkeeper."

"Yes. Even Mr. Santo Trafficante Jr. concedes that there are no four-star jails in America."

"I'd like to see Mr. Trafficante."

"Please follow me, then."

Pete fell in step. Boozed-out gringo fat cats careened down the hallway. The guard pointed out custody high spots.

Suite 2314 featured stag films screened on a bedsheet. Suite 2319 featured roulette, craps and baccarat. Suite 2329 featured naked hookers on call. Suite 2333 featured a live lesbian peep show. Suite 2341 featured suckling pigs broiled on a spit. Suites 2350 through 2390 comprised a full-size golf driving range.

A spic caddy squeezed by them schlepping clubs. The guard clicked his heels outside 2394.

"Mr. Santo, you have a visitor!"

Santo Trafficante Jr. opened the door.

He was fortyish and pudgy. He wore nubby-silk Bermuda shorts and glasses.

The guard scooted off. Trafficante said, "The two things I hate most are Communists and chaos."

"Mr. Trafficante, I'm—"

"I've got eyes. Four, in fact. You're Pete Bondurant, who clips guys for Jimmy. Some six-foot-six gorilla knocks on my door and acts servile, I put two and two together."

Pete walked into the room. Trafficante smiled.

"Did you come to bring me back?"

"No."

"Jimmy sent you, right?"

"No."

"Mo? Carlos? I'm so fucking bored I'm playing guessing games with a six-foot-six gorilla. Hey, what's the difference between a gorilla and a nigger?"

Pete said, "Nothing?"

Trafficante sighed. "You heard it already, you hump. My father killed a guy once who spoiled one of his punch lines. Maybe you've heard of my father?"

"Santo Trafficante *Senior*?"

"*Salud*, Frenchman. Jesus, I'm so fucking bored I'm playing one-up with a gorilla."

Pig grease spattered out a cooling vent. The pad was furnished modern-ugly—lots of fucked-up color combos.

Trafficante scratched his balls. "So who sent you?"

"A CIA man named Boyd."

"The only CIA guy I know is a redneck named Chuck Rogers."

"I know Rogers."

Trafficante shut the door. "I know you know him. I know the whole story of you and the cabstand, and you and Fulo and Rogers, and I know stories about you that I bet you wished I didn't know. You know *how* I know? I know because everybody in this life of ours likes to talk. And the only fucking saving grace is that none of us talks to people outside the life."

Pete looked out the window. The ocean glowed turquoise blue way past the buoy line.

"Boyd wants you to write a note to Carlos Marcello, Sam Giancana and Johnny Rosselli. The note's supposed to say that you recommend no reprisals against Castro for nationalizing the casinos. I think the Agency's afraid the Outfit will go off half-cocked and screw up their own Cuban plans."

Trafficante grabbed a scratch pad and pen off the TV. He wrote fast and enunciated clearly.

"Dear Premier Castro, you Commie dog turd. Your revolution is a crock of Commie shit. We paid you good money to let us keep our casinos running if you took over, but you took our money and fucked us up the brown trail until we bled. You are a bigger piece of shit than that faggot Bobby Kennedy and his faggot McClellan Committee. May you personally get syphilis of the brain and the dick, you Commie cocksucker, for fucking up our beautiful Nacional Hotel."

Golf balls ricocheted down the hallway. Trafficante flinched and held the note up.

Pete read it. Santo Junior delivered—nice, neat, grammatical.

Pete tucked the note in his pocket. "Thanks, Mr. Trafficante."

"You're fucking welcome, and I can tell you're surprised that I can write and say two different things at the same time. Now, you tell your Mr. Boyd that that promise is good for one year and no more. Tell him we're all swimming in the same stream as far as Cuba goes, so it's in our best interest not to piss in his face."

"He'll appreciate it."

"Appreciate, shit. If you appreciated, you'd take me back with you."

Pete checked his watch. "I've only got two Canadian passports, and I'm supposed to bring back a United Fruit man."

Trafficante picked up a golf club. "Then I can't complain. Money's money, and United Fruit's tapped more out of Cuba than the Outfit ever did."

"You'll get out soon. Some courier's working on getting all the Americans out."

Trafficante lined up a make-believe putt. "Good. And I'll set you up with a guide. He'll drive you around and take you and the UF man to the airport. He'll rob you before he drops you off, but that's as good as the help gets with these fucking Reds in power."

A croupier supplied directions to the house—Tom Gordean threw a torch party there just last week. Jesús the guide said Mr. Tom burned a mean cane field—he was hot to revamp his *fascisto* image.

Jesús wore jungle fatigues and a baseball cap. He drove a Volkswagen with a hood-mounted machine gun.

They took dirt roads out of Havana. Jesús steered with one hand and blasted palm trees simultaneous. Sizzling cane fields lit the sky up orange-pink—torch parties were a big deal in post-Batista Cuba.

Phone poles blipped by. Fidel Castro's face adorned every one.

Pete saw house lights in the distance—two hundred yards or so up. Jesús pulled into a clearing dotted with palm stumps.

He eased in like he knew where he was going. He didn't gesture or say one fucking word.

It felt wrong. It felt *prearranged*.

Jesús braked and doused his headlights. A torch whooshed the second they snapped off.

Light spread out over the clearing. Pete saw a Cadillac ragtop, six spics, and a white man reeling drunk.

Jesús said, "That is Señor Tom."

The spics had sawed-off shotguns. The Caddy was stuffed with luggage and mink coats.

Jesús jumped out and jabbered spic to the spics. The spics waved to the gringo in the Volkswagen.

The minks were piled above the door line. U.S. currency was bulging out of a suitcase.

Pete caught on, dead solid perfect.

Thomas Gordean was weaving. He was waving a bottle of Demerara rum. He was putting out a line of pro-Commie jive talk.

He was slurring his words. He was dead drunk working on dead.

Pete saw torches ready to light. Pete saw a gas can sitting on a tree stump.

Gordean kept spritzing. He got up a fucking A-#1 Commie cliché head of steam.

Jesús huddled with the spics. They waved at the gringo again. Gordean puked on the hood of the Caddy.

Pete slid next to the machine gun. The spics turned away and went for their waistbands.

Pete fired. One tight swivel at their backs cut them down. The *ack-ack* sent a flock of birds up squawking.

Gordean hit the ground and curled himself up fetal-tight. The bullet spread missed him by inches.

The spics died screaming. Pete strafed their bodies into pulp. Cordite and muzzle-scorched entrails formed one putrid smell combination.

Pete poured gas on the stiffs and the Volkswagen and torched them. A box of .50-caliber ammo exploded.

Señor Tom Gordean was passed out cold.

Pete tossed him in the backseat of the Caddy. The mink coats made a cozy little bed.

He checked the luggage. He saw a shitload of money and stock certificates.

Their flight left at dawn. Pete found a road map in the glove compartment and marked a route back to Havana.

He got in the Caddy and punched it. French-fried palm trees provided a glow to drive by.

He made the airport before first light. Friendly militiamen swamped El Señor Mitchum.

Tom Gordean woke up with the shakes. Pete fed him rum-and-Cokes to keep him docile. The spics nationalized the money and furs—no big surprise.

Pete signed Robert Mitchum autographs. Some Commie commissar escorted them to the plane.

The pilot said, "You're not Robert Mitchum."

Pete said, "No shit, Sherlock."

Gordean dozed off. The other passengers eyeballed them—they reeked of gasoline and liquor.

The plane landed at 7:00 A.M. Kemper Boyd met them. He handed Pete an envelope containing five thousand dollars.

Boyd was juuuuust a tad nervous. Boyd was more than just a tad dismissive.

He said, "Thanks, Pete. Take that jitney into town with the other people, all right? I'll call you in L.A. in a few days."

He got five grand. Boyd got Gordean and a suitcase full of stock shares. Gordean looked bewildered. Boyd looked quintessentially un-Boyd.

Pete hopped on the jitney. He saw Boyd steer Gordean to a storage hut.

Here's this deserted hick-town airfield. Here's this CIA man and this drunk, alone.

His feelers started twitching in high fucking gear.

25

(Key West, 5/29/59)

THE HUT WAS matchbook-size. He had to cram the table and two chairs in.

Kemper handled Gordean with kid gloves. The interrogation dragged—his subject had the DTs.

"Does your family know that you possess this United Fruit stock?"

"What 'family'? I've been married and divorced more than

Artie Shaw *and* Mickey Rooney. I've got a few cousins in Seattle, but all they know is the way to the bar at the Woodhaven Country Club."

"Who else in Cuba knows that you own this stock?"

"My bodyguards know. But one minute we're drinking and getting ready to expunge a few imperialist cane fields, and the next thing I know I'm in the backseat of my car with that buddy of yours at the wheel. I'm not ashamed to admit that I've been on a toot, and things are pretty dim. That buddy of yours, does he carry a machine gun?"

"I don't think so."

"What about a Volkswagen?"

"Mr. Gordean . . ."

"Mr. Boyce, or whatever your name is, what's going on? You sit me down in this shack and ransack my suitcase. You ask me these questions. You think because I'm a rich American businessman that I'm on your side. You think I don't know how you CIA fuckers rigged the elections in Guatemala? I was on my way to cocktails with Premier Castro when your buddy shanghaied me. That's *Fidel Castro*. He's the liberator of Cuba. He's a nice man and a wonderful basketball player."

Kemper laid down his stock release forms. They were superbly forged—a counterfeiter friend did the job.

"Sign these please, Mr. Gordean. They're reimbursement vouchers for your airfare."

Gordean signed in triplicate. Kemper signed the notary statement and seal-stamped all three signatures.

His friend rigged the seal, at no extra charge.

Gordean laughed. "CIA man/notary public. What a combo."

Kemper pulled his .45 and shot him in the head.

Gordean flew off his chair. Blood sprayed out one ear. Kemper stepped on his head to stanch the spritz.

Something rustled outside. Kemper pushed the door open with his gun.

It was Pete Bondurant, standing there with his hands in his pockets.

They both smiled.

Pete drew "50/50" in the air.

DOCUMENT INSERT: 6/11/59.
Summary Report: Kemper Boyd to John Stanton.
Marked: CONFIDENTIAL/HAND POUCH DELIVER.

John:

   I delayed the writing of this communique for two
reasons. One, I wanted to see a botched incident
through to its conclusion before contacting you. Two,
this note details a mission that I (quite frankly)
blew.

   You had asked me to use my own discretion and send
Pete Bondurant on a trial run to help determine his
suitability for Agency contract employment. I did
this, and sent Bondurant into Cuba to pull out a
United Fruit executive named Thomas Gordean, a man
whom Teofilio Paez described as ''volatile'' and
''espousing the Communist line.'' Bondurant
succeeded in the first part of his mission. We
installed Mr. Gordean at the Rusty Scupper Motel in
Key West for de-briefing, and made the mistake of
leaving him alone to rest. Gordean committed suicide
with a .45 automatic he had secreted on his person.
I summoned the Key West Police, and Bondurant and
I de-briefed them. A coroner's jury ruled Gordean's
death a suicide. Bondurant testified as to Gordean's
apparent alcoholism and depressive behavior. An
autopsy confirmed that Gordean showed signs of
advanced liver damage. His body was shipped to a
distant cousin in Seattle (Gordean had no immediate
family).

   Should you require verification, please contact
Captain Hildreth of the Key West Police. Of course,
I apologize for this boondoggle. And I assure you that
nothing like this will happen again.

                              Sincerely, Kemper Boyd

DOCUMENT INSERT: 6/19/59.
Personal note: John Stanton to Kemper Boyd.

Dear Kemper,

Of course, I am furious. And of course you should
have informed me of this snafu immediately. Thank God
Gordean had no immediate family capable of causing
trouble for the Agency. That expressed, I'll state
that most likely you were to some degree a victim of
mitigating circumstances. After all, as you once
said, you are an attorney and a cop, not a spy.

You'll be pleased to know that Deputy Director
Bissell is quite taken with your idea of creating an
elite cadre to run the Blessington campsite. The
campsite is currently under construction; your four
personally selected recruits (Paez, Obregon, Delsol,
Gutierrez) are undergoing further training at
Langley and doing quite well. As previously stated,
the Deputy Director has approved the hiring of Pete
Bondurant to run the campsite. That, of course, was
before the Gordean snafu. Right now, I want to wait
and reconsider Bondurant.

In conclusion, the Gordean incident sits poorly
with me, but my enthusiasm for you as a contract agent
remains strong. Until I tell you otherwise, undertake
no more missions on your own authority.

                                    John Stanton

DOCUMENT INSERT: 6/28/59.
Personal note: Ward J. Littell to Kemper Boyd. ''For
editing and forwarding to Robert F. Kennedy.''

Kemper,

My anti-Mob intelligence gathering continues
apace. I now have several independently gleaned
indications that alternative (most likely coded)
Teamster Pension Fund books do exist. Lenny Sands
believes they exist. Sal D'Onofrio has heard rumors
to that effect. Other sources have supplied rumors: a

retired Chicago Mob man administers the books; Sam
Giancana serves as the Pension Fund's ''Chief Loan
Approval Officer.'' As pervasive as these rumors are,
I have nothing resembling corroboration. And of
course I won't, until I can suborn a cosmetic borrower
and gain some kind of literal access to the Fund
itself.

And (on May 18th) I coerced a third informant into
my stable. This man (a Dallas-based strip club
operator/loanshark) is searching for a borrower to
refer to Sal D'Onofrio and thence to Sam Giancana.
I consider this man to be a major informant, because
he previously referred a loan seeker to Giancana and
the Pension Fund. He calls me at a pay phone near my
apartment every Tuesday morning; I have given him
money on several occasions. He fears me and respects
me to just the right degree. Like Sal D'Onofrio, he
has perpetual money troubles. I believe that, sooner
or later, he will supply me with a potentially
subornable borrower.

I also now have a fund of my own, i.e., an informant
fund. In late May I secured an $81,000 robbery stash,
one unreported to any police agency. I have paid Sal
D'Onofrio $32,000 from this fund, strengthening my
hold over him. Strange, but I had originally thought
that Lenny Sands would be my most valued informant,
but both Sal and the Dallas man have proven themselves
more competent (or is it more desperate for money)?
I blame you, Kemper. Setting Lenny up with Pete
Bondurant and Hush-Hush was detrimental to my
purposes. Lenny has seemed abstracted lately. He
travels with Sal's junket tours and moonlights for
Hush-Hush, and seems to have forgotten what I hold
over him. Does he talk to your friend Miss Hughes? I'd
be curious to know.

Per your instructions, I'm avoiding Court Meade and
the listening post. Court and I have also formally
ceased our assignment trade. I'm being careful, but
I can't help dreaming utopian dreams. My essential
dream? A John F. Kennedy Presidential
Administration, with Robert Kennedy fulfilling his

brother's anti-Mob mandate. God, Kemper, wouldn't
that be heaven? Tell Mr. Kennedy he's in my prayers.

Yours, WJL

DOCUMENT INSERT: 7/3/59.
Personal note: Kemper Boyd to Robert F. Kennedy.

Dear Bob,

   Just a short note to update you on the work of your
anonymous colleague the ''Chicago Phantom.''
   He's working hard, and I hope you find it gratifying
that there's at least one human being on earth who
hates Organized Crime as much as you do. But, as hard
as he is working—and always within the legal
guidelines you set down to me—he's getting scant
results pursuing the possibility that alternative
Pension Fund books exist. The Chicago Mob is a closed
circle, and he hasn't been able to gain the inside
information he hoped he would.
   Moving along. Aren't you and Jack going to offer me
some post-McClellan Committee employment?

Yours, Kemper

DOCUMENT INSERT: 7/9/59.
Personal Letter: Robert F. Kennedy to Kemper Boyd.

Dear Kemper,

   Thanks for your note on the Phantom. It is good to
know that an ex-seminarian FBI man shares my anti-Mob
fervor, and what most impresses me about him is that
he doesn't seem to want anything. (Jesuit sem boys are
schooled in self-denial.) You, however, want
everything. So, yes, Jack and I have an offer for you.
(We'll discuss details and money later.)
   We want you to stay with our organization and fill
two positions. The first: traffic manager for the
McClellan Committee's legal paperwork. We've
disbanded, but like the Phantom, I'm still afire.
Let's keep our anti-Mob and anti-Hoffa momentum

going. You could be very helpful in seeing that our
evidence gets into the proper investigatory hands.
Secondly, Jack's going to announce his candidacy in
January. He wants you to manage security for his
primary campaigns and hopefully through to November.
How about it?

Bob

DOCUMENT INSERT: 7/13/59.
Personal note: Kemper Boyd to Robert F. Kennedy.

Dear Bob,

I accept. Yes, unlike the Phantom I want
everything. Let's nail Jimmy Hoffa and elect Jack
President.

Kemper

DOCUMENT INSERT: 7/27/59.
Official FBI telephone call transcript: ''Recorded
at the Director's Request''/''Classified Confidential
1-A: Director's Eyes Only.'' Speaking: Director
Hoover, Special Agent Kemper Boyd.

JEH: Good morning, Mr. Boyd.
KB: Good morning, Sir.
JEH: Your message mentioned good news.
KB: Excellent news, Sir. The brothers have hired me
on a more or less permanent basis.
JEH: In what capacity?
KB: I'm to supervise the routing of McClellan
Committee evidence to various grand juries and
investigative agencies, and run security for Big
Brother's campaign.
JEH: Little Brother remains persistent on the Hoffa
front, then.
KB: He'll crucify the man sooner or later.
JEH: Catholics have been known to go overboard with
the concept of crucifixion.
KB: Yes, Sir.
JEH: Let's continue on the Catholic recidivist

front. Is Mr. Littell continuing to walk the straight
and narrow?

KB: Yes, Sir.

JEH: SAC Leahy has airtelled me his Red Squad
reports. He appears to be doing a satisfactory job.

KB: You frightened him last year, Sir. He just
wants to make it through to his retirement. As I've
told you, he's drinking quite a bit and is quite
caught up in his affair with Helen Agee.

JEH: Allow me to use ''affair'' as a segue point.
How is your liaison with Miss Laura Hughes
progressing?

KB: I'd hardly call it a liaison, Sir.

JEH: Mr. Boyd, you are talking to the world's
nonpareil bullshit artist and master of subterfuge.
As good as you are at it, and you are brilliantly
good, I am better. You are fucking Laura Hughes, and
I'm sure you would fuck all the acknowledged Kennedy
sisters and old Rose Kennedy herself if you thought it
would ingratiate you with Jack. There. That said,
what does Miss Hughes have to say about the family?

KB: She limits her anecdotes to her father, Sir.
She's quite vitriolic on the topic of her father and
his friends.

JEH: Continue.

KB: Apparently Joe and his old friend Jules
Schiffrin secreted Mexican illegals across the
border during the '20s. They used the men as set
construction help when Joe owned the RKO Studio. Joe
and Schiffrin used the women sexually, hired them out
as domestics, took half their pay for room-and-board,
then turned them over to the Border Patrol and had
them deported. Schiffrin took a number of the women
back to Chicago with him and opened up a whorehouse
that catered to mobsters and politicians
exclusively. Laura says Joe made a movie
surreptitiously at the whorehouse. It's Huey Long and
two Mexican midgets with oversized breasts.

JEH: Miss Hughes is a vivid anecdotist. What does
she say about the brothers?

KB: She's guarded about them.

JEH: As you yourself are.

KB: I'm fond of them, yes.

JEH: I think you've set limits to your betrayal.
I think you're unaware of how deeply enthralled you
are with that family.

KB: I keep things compartmentalized, Sir.

JEH: Yes, I'll credit you with that. Now, let's
move to your Cuban emigre compartment. Do you recall
telling me that you had access to Cuban exile
intelligence?

KB: Of course, Sir. I'll be sending a detailed
summary report along soon.

JEH: Laura Hughes must be quite expensive.

KB: Sir?

JEH: Don't act disingenuous, Kemper. It's quite
obvious the CIA has recruited you. Three paychecks,
my lord.

KB: Sir, I keep things compartmentalized.

JEH: You certainly do, and far be it from me to
upset those compartments. Good day, Mr. Boyd.

KB: Good day, Sir.

DOCUMENT INSERT: 8/4/59.
Hush-Hush stringer report: Lenny Sands to Pete
Bondurant.

Pete,

It's strange, but every homo in captivity seems to
want to bite my tush these days, which is unusual
because I've been playing some pretty square rooms.
As you know, I've been working my wop gig with Sal
D'Onofrio. We've been playing Reno, Vegas, Tahoe,
Gardena and some Lake Michigan cruise boats that
feature gambling. I've been running into fruits
galore, a regular Layfayette Escad (butt) drill of
fruitness. 1)—Delores' Drive-In on Wilshire & La
Cienega in L.A. employs all fruit carhops
moonlighting as male prosties. A frequent customer:
Adlai (Lay?) Stevenson, 2-time prez'l candidate with
pinko (Lavender?) leanings Mr. Hughes probably

disapproves of. 2)—Dave Garroway of TV's Today Show
was recently popped for honking young boys in NYC's
Times Square. It was (hush?) hushed up, but ''Dave the
Slave'' as he's known on the fag circuit was recently
spotted at an all-male tomcat house outside Vegas.
3)—I ran into an off-duty Marine Corps lance-corporal
in Tahoe. He said he knows a gunnery-sergeant running
a fruit roller ring out of Camp Pendleton. It works
this way: handsome young jarheads prowl Silverlake
(The Swish Alps?) & the Sunset Strip & entrap homos.
They don't put out & shake the fruits down for $.
I called the gunnery sgt & wired him a C-note. He
spilled on some celebrity fruitcakes the fruit roller
ring glommed onto. Dig this: Walter Pidgeon (12" wang)
bangs boys at a plushly-furnished fag crib in the Los
Feliz district. Also, British matinee idol Larry (the
Fairy?) Olivier recently took the law into his own
hands when he groped a Marine MP at the Wiltern
Theatre. Other homos ID'd by the Fruit Roller Corps
include Danny Kaye, Liberace (big surprise), Monty
Clift & conductor Leonard Bernstein. Hey, have you
noticed I'm starting to write in the Hush-Hush style?
More later.

                                        Cheers, Lenny

DOCUMENT INSERT: 8/12/59.
Personal memorandum: Kemper Boyd to John Stanton.
Marked: CONFIDENTIAL/HAND POUCH DELIVER.

John:

   Some further thoughts on Pete Bondurant, the Tiger
Kab stand and our elite Cadre.
   The more I think about it, the more I see Tiger Kab
as the potential hub for our Miami activities.
I broached this thought to Fulo Machado (a former
Castroite now bristlingly anti-Castro), the cabstand
co-dispatcher and a close friend of contract agent
Chuck Rogers. Machado shared my enthusiasm. He agreed
to let Rogers take over as permanent cabstand
dispatcher-boss. Fulo got approval from Jimmy Hoffa,

who frankly prefers white men in supervisory
positions. Fulo is now recruiting for us, on the
cabstand payroll. Hoffa knows that cooperating with
the Agency is smart business. He sees Cuba as our
common cause, farsighted for such a brutal and
single-minded man.

I would like to propose Fulo Machado as the fifth
member of our cadre. I would also like you to allow
Rogers to hire Tomas Obregon, Wilfredo Olmos Delsol,
Teofilio Paez and Ramon Gutierrez as full-time
drivers. Although construction of the Blessington
campsite is almost complete, we do not have exile
recruits to train there. Until more deportees arrive,
I think our men can be best utilized recruiting in
Miami's Cuban community.

Per Bondurant. Yes, he (and I) screwed up on the
Thomas Gordean matter. But, Bondurant is already
employed as Jimmy Hoffa's ad hoc cabstand enforcer.
He also secured a note from Santo Trafficante
personally requesting that no Mafia reprisals be
launched against Castro for nationalizing the Havana
casinos. Bondurant forwarded this note to S.
Giancana, C. Marcello and J. Rosselli. All three
agree with Trafficante's reasoning. Again, brutal,
short-sighted men are cooperating with the Agency out
of a sense of common cause.

Bondurant is also the de-facto editor of a scandal
magazine we can use as a counterintelligence organ.
And, finally, I think he's the best man alive to run
the campsite. They don't come any tougher, as I think
any local rednecks who toy with him will discover.

What do you think of my proposals?

                                        Kemper Boyd

DOCUMENT INSERT: 8/19/59.
Personal memo: John Stanton to Kemper Boyd.

Kemper,

You batted 1000%. Yes, Machado can join the Cadre.
Yes, Rogers can hire Delsol, Obregon, Paez and

Gutierrez as drivers. Yes, have them recruit in
Miami. Yes, hire Pete Bondurant to run Blessington,
but have him retain his job with Howard Hughes as
well. Hughes is a potentially valuable ally, and we
don't want him estranged from the Agency.

 Good work, Kemper.

                                                     John

DOCUMENT INSERT: 8/21/59.
Teletype report: Intelligence Division, Los Angeles
Police Department, to SA Ward J. Littell, Chicago
FBI. Sent ''Private Mail Closure'' to SA Littell's
home address.

Mr. Littell,

 Per your: telephone query on Salvatore D'Onofrio's
recent Los Angeles activities. Be advised that:
 The subject was spot-surveilled as a known
underworld figure.
 He was seen borrowing money from independent
shylocks. Subsequent questioning of said shylocks
revealed that the subject told them he would give them
''big kickbacks'' for referring ''high-ticket''
loan-seekers to him. The subject was also seen
betting heavily at Santa Anita Racetrack.
Surveilling officers heard the subject tell a just-
met acquaintance: ''I've blown half the wad my sugar
daddy-o gave me already.''
 The subject was observed behaving in an erratic
fashion during his gambling junket engagement at the
Lucky Nugget Casino in Gardena. His junket companion,
Leonard Joseph Seidelwitz (AKA Lenny Sands), also a
known underworld figure, was seen entering various
homosexual cocktail lounges. It should be noted that
Seidelwitz's junket skits have become increasingly
obscene and violently anti-homosexual.
 Should you require further information, please let
me know.

                          James E. Hamilton, Captain,
                              Intelligence Division,
                        Los Angeles Police Department

26

(Chicago, 8/23/59)

THE AMP MADE small talk boom. Littell picked up mobster amenities.

He wire-linked Mad Sal's parlor to his back bedroom closet. He overmiked the walls and got excessive voice vibrato.

The closet was hot and cramped. Littell sweated up his headset.

Talking: Mad Sal and "movie producer" Sid Kabikoff.

Sal went on a gambling binge. Littell confronted him with an LAPD teletype describing his actions. Sal said he blew the fifty-odd grand Littell gave him.

The train-locker heist stood unsolved—Sal didn't know where the cash came from. The tailor-shop bug blasted scuttlebutt on the topic— but Malvaso and the Duck remained clueless.

Then Jack Ruby called him.

And said, "I finally got a guy for Sal D. to goose up to the Pension Fund."

His informants were in sync—except for Lenny Sands.

Littell wiped off his headset. Kabikoff spoke, overamp loud: ". . . and Heshie says his blow-job tally's closing in on twenty thousand."

Mad Sal: "Sid, Sid the Yid. You didn't fly up from bumfuck Texas to schmooze the grapevine with me."

Kabikoff: "You're right, Sal. I was passing through Dallas and had a schmooze with Jack Ruby. Jack said, 'See Sal D. In Chicago. Sal's the man to see for a big vigorish loan from the Pension Fund.' Jack said, 'Sal's the middleman. He can fix you up with Momo and above. Sal's the man with access to the money.'"

Mad Sal: "You say 'Momo' like you think you're some kind of made guy."

Kabikoff: "It's like you talking Yiddish. Everybody wants to think they're connected. Everybody wants to be in the loop."

Mad Sal: "The Loop's downtown, you fat bagel bender."

Kabikoff: "Sal, Sal."

Mad Sal: "Sal, my big fat braciola, you lox jockey. Now you tell me the scheme, 'cause there's gotta be a scheme, 'cause you ain't tapping the Fund for your little bagel biter's bar mitzvah."

Kabikoff: "The scheme is smut movies, Sal. I've been shooting smut down in Mexico for a year now. T.J., Juarez, you can get talent cheap down there."

Mad Sal: "Get to it. Cut the fucking travelogue."

Kabikoff: "Hey, I'm setting a mood."

Mad Sal: "I'll mood you, you mameluke."

Kabikoff: "Sal, Sal. I've been shooting smut. I'm good at it. In fact, I'm shooting a picture down in Mexico in a couple of days. I'm using some strippers from Jack's club. It's going to be great—Jack's got some gorgeous gash working for him. Sal, Sal, don't look at me that way. What I want to do is this. I want to make legit horror and action pictures with smut-movie casts. I want to book the legit pictures into the bottom half of double features and film the pornographic shit to help defer costs. Sal, Sal, don't frown like that. It's a moneymaker. I'll cut Sam and the Pension Fund in for 50% of my profits *plus* my payback and vigorish. Sal, listen to me. This deal has got 'Moneymaker' scrawled across the fucking stars in fucking neon."

Silence—twenty-six seconds worth.

Kabikoff: "Sal, quit giving me the evil eye and listen. This deal is a moneymaker, and I want to keep it in the loop. You know, in a way, the Fund and me go way back. See, I heard Jules Schiffrin's the bookkeeper for the Fund. You know, for the real books that people outside the loop don't know about. See, I knew Jules way back when. Like feature back in the '20s even, when he was selling dope and using the profits to finance movies with RKO back when Joe Kennedy owned it. Tell Sam to remember me to Jules, okay? Just to remind him that I'm a trustworthy guy and I'm still in the loop."

Littell clamped down on his headphones. Jesus Fucking—

"Jules Schiffrin"/"Fund bookkeeper"/"real books."

Sweat seeped into the phones—voices fizzed out incoherent. Littell wrote the quotes down verbatim on the closet wall.

Kabikoff: ". . . so I'm flying back to Texas in a few days. Take my card, Sal. No, take two and give one to Momo. Business cards always make a good impression."

Littell heard goodbyes and a door slamming. He took off his headset and stared at the words on the wall.

Mad Sal walked up. Fat jiggled under his T-shirt.

"How'd I do? I had to give him some shit or he wouldn't've believed it was the real me."

"You were good. Now just watch your money. You won't get another dime from me until I've tapped into the Fund."

"What do I do about Kabikoff?"

"I'll call you inside a week and tell you whether or not to refer him to Giancana."

Sal belched. "Call me in L.A. I'm taking another junket out to Gardena."

Littell stared at the wall. He memorized each and every word and copied them over into his notebook.

27

(Gardena, 8/25/59)

LENNY PREENED AND smacked kisses. The junketeers ate it up—go Lenny, go, go, go.

Lenny hated fags. Lenny ate fags like Godzilla ate Tokyo. Lenny ate up the Lucky Nugget lounge.

Pete watched. Lenny spritzed shtick—fag Castro gropes fag Ike at the All-Fag Summit!!!!

"Fidel! Get your beard out of my crotch this instant! Fidel! What a biiiig Havana cigar you have!"

The junketeers loved it. The junketeers thought it was high-tone political satire.

Pete was bored. Stale shtick and stale beer—the Lucky Nugget was an armpit.

Dick Steisel sent him down. Dick had a grievance: Lenny's recent shit was too coarse to print. Hughes and Hoover loved it—but random homo slurs could deep-six *Hush-Hush*.

"Fidel! Pass me the K-Y, and we'll renew diplomatic relations! Fidel! My hemorrhoids are burning up like a United Fruit cane field!"

Kemper Boyd thought Lenny had talent. Kemper had a brainstorm: Let's dispense anti-Castro rage through *Hush-Hush*!

Lenny could write the stuff up. Lenny used to run bag to Batista—he knew the turf and the style, and Cuban Commies couldn't sue.

Lenny cranked shtick. Pete screened 10:00 P.M. daydreams. THAT MOMENT flashed by in Technicolor.

There's Tom Gordean, dead. There's Boyd, smiling. There's the suitcase full of UF stock.

They cut their deal right there beside the body. They rented a motel room, popped a shot off and rigged Gordean in a suicide pose. The stupid Key West cops bought the charade.

Boyd sold the stock. They made $131,000 apiece.

They met in D.C. for the split. Boyd said, "I can get you in on the Cuban thing, but it will probably take months. I'll have to explain the Gordean mission as a fuck-up."

Pete said, "Tell me more."

Boyd said, "Go back to L.A., do your *Hush-Hush* work and baby-sit Howard Hughes. I think Cuba and our combined connections can make us both rich."

He flew back and did it. He told Hughes he might have to go on leave soon.

Hughes was pissed. He unpissed him with a shitload of codeine.

The Cuban Cause had him drooling. He wanted in wicked bad. Santo Trafficante got booted out of Cuba last month, and spread the word that Castro should get butt-fucked for his Crimes Against Casino Profiteering.

Boyd called the cabstand a "potential launching pad." Boyd had this big throbbing wet dream: Jimmy Hoffa sells Tiger Kab to the Agency.

Chuck Rogers called him once a week. He said the cabstand was running trouble-free. Jimmy Hoffa sent him his monthly 5%—and he wasn't doing jackshit to earn it.

Boyd had Rogers hire his pet Cubans: Obregón, Delsol, Paez and Gutiérrez. Chuck fired the six *pro*-Castro geeks on the payroll—the fucks drove off hurling death threats.

Tiger Kab was now 100% anti-Castro.

Lenny ended his routine—with a riff on Ad*lay* Stevenson, King of the Turd Burglars. Pete ducked out behind a standing ovation.

The junketeers loved their Lenny. Lenny brushed through them like a prima diva slumming.

Perk-perk-perk—his feelers kicked in strong. He got this feeler-verified idea: Let's tail the little hump.

They drove north, with three cars between them. Lenny's Packard had a big whip antenna—Pete used it as a tracking device.

They took Western Avenue up to L.A. proper. Lenny swung west on Wilshire and north on Doheny. Traffic had thinned out—Pete hung back and cut the boy some slack.

Lenny turned east on Santa Monica. Pete grooved on the string of fruit bars—the 4-Star, the Klondike, some new ones. It was Memory Lane turf—he extorted every joint on the row back in his Sheriff's days.

Lenny hugged the curb, slooow cruising. He passed the Tropics, the Orchid and Larry's Lasso Room.

Lenny, don't wear your hate so fucking outré and naked.

Pete dawdled two car lengths back. Lenny pulled into the parking lot behind Nat's Nest.

Big Pete's got X-ray eyes. Big Pete's like Superman and the Green Hornet.

Pete circled the block and cruised through the lot. Lenny's car was parked by the back door.

Pete wrote out a note.

If you get lucky, send him home. Meet me at Stan's Drive-In at Sunset & Highland. I'll stay there until after bar closing time.

Pete B.

He stuck the note to Lenny's windshield. A fruit swished by and checked him out head-to-toe.

Pete ate in his car. He had two chili burgers, French fries and coffee.

Carhops skated by. They wore leotards, push-up bras and tights.

Gail Hendee used to call him a voyeur. It always jazzed him when women nailed his shit.

The carhops looked good. Hauling trays on skates kept them trim. The blonde lugging hot fudge sundaes looked like good shakedown bait.

Pete ordered peach pie à la mode. The blonde brought it to him. He saw Lenny walking up to the car.

He opened the passenger door and slid in.

He looked stoic. The prima diva was one tough little fruitfly.

Pete lit a cigarette. "You told me you were too smart to fuck with me. Does that still hold?"

"Yes."

"Is this what Kemper Boyd and Ward Littell have on you?"

"'This'? Yeah, 'this' is."

"I don't buy it, Lenny, and I don't think Sam Giancana would care in the long run. I think I could call Sam right now and say, 'Lenny Sands fucks boys,' and he'd be shocked for a couple of minutes, then sit on the information. If Boyd and Littell tried to bluff you with that, I think you'd have the brains and the stones to call them on it."

Lenny shrugged. "Littell said he'd spill to Sam *and* the cops."

Pete dropped his cigarette in his water glass. "I'm not buying. Now, you see that brunette on skates over there?"

"I see her."

"I want you to tell me what Boyd and Littell squeezed you with by the time she gets over to that blue Chevy."

"Suppose I can't remember?"

"Then figure everything you've heard about me is true, and take it from there."

Lenny smiled, prima-diva-style. "I killed Tony Iannone, and Littell made me for it."

Pete whistled. "I'm impressed. Tony was a rough boy."

"Don't string me along, Pete. Just tell me what you're going to do about it."

"The answer's nothing. All this secret shit of yours goes no further."

"I'll try to believe it."

"You can believe that Littell and I go back awhile, and I don't like him. Boyd and me are friendly, but Littell's something else. I can't lean on him without pissing off Boyd, but if he ever gets too rowdy with you, let me know."

Lenny bristled and clenched up. "I don't need a protector. I'm not that kind of ..."

Carhops zigzagged by. Pete rolled down his back window for some air.

"You've got credentials, Lenny. What you do in your spare time is your business."

"You're an enlightened guy."

"Thanks. Now, do you feel like telling me who or what you're snitching for Littell?"

"No."

"Just plain 'No'?"

"I want to keep working for you. Let me out of here with something, all right?"

Pete popped the passenger door latch. "No more fag stuff for *Hush-Hush*. From now on you write anti-Castro, anti-Commie stuff exclusively. I want you to write the pieces directly for the magazine. I'll get you some information, and you can make the rest of the shit up. You've been to Cuba, and you know Mr. Hughes' politics. Take it from there."

"Is that all?"

"Unless you want pie and coffee."

Lenny Sands fucks boys. Howard Hughes lends Dick Nixon's brother money.

Secret shit.

Big Pete wants a woman. Extortion experience preferred, but not mandatory.

The phone rang too fucking early.

Pete picked up. "Yeah?"

"It's Kemper."

"Kemper, shit, what time is it?"

"You're hired, Pete. Stanton's putting you on immediate contract status. You're going to be running the Blessington campsite."

Pete rubbed his eyes. "That's the official gig, but what's ours?"

"We're going to facilitate a collaboration between the CIA and organized crime."

28

(New York City, 8/26/59)

JOE KENNEDY HANDED out presidential-sealed tie pins. The Carlyle suite took on a fake-presidential glow.

Bobby looked bored. Jack looked amused. Kemper pinned his necktie to his shirt.

Jack said, "Kemper's a thief."

Bobby said, "We came here to discuss the campaign, remember?"

Kemper brushed lint off his trousers. He wore a seersucker suit and white bucks—Joe called him an ice-cream jockey out of work.

Laura loved the outfit. He bought it with his stock-theft money. It was good summertime wedding attire.

Joe said, "FDR gave me those pins. I kept them because I knew I'd host a meeting like this one day."

Joe wanted an event. The butler had arranged hors d'oeuvres on a sideboard near their chairs.

Bobby pulled off his necktie. "My book will be published in hardback in February, about a month after Jack announces. The paperback edition will come out in July, right around the time of the convention. I'm hoping it will put the whole Hoffa crusade in perspective. We don't want Jack's association with the McClellan Committee to hurt him with labor."

Jack laughed. "That goddamn book's eating up all your time. You should get a ghost writer. I did, and I won the Pulitzer Prize."

Joe smeared caviar on a cracker. "I heard Kemper wanted his name deleted from the text. That's too bad, because then you could have titled it *The Ice Cream Jockey Within*."

Kemper toyed with his tie pin. "There's a million car thieves out there who hate me, Mr. Kennedy. I'd prefer that they not know what I'm doing."

Jack said, "Kemper's the furtive type."

Joe said, "Yes, and Bobby could learn from him. I've said it a thousand times before, and I'll say it a thousand times again. This hard-on for Jimmy Hoffa and the Mafia is horseshit. You may need those people to help you get out the vote one day, and now you're adding insult to injury by writing a book on top of chasing them via the goddamn Committee. Kemper plays his cards close to the vest, Bobby. You could learn from him."

Bobby chuckled. "Enjoy the moment, Kemper. Dad sides against his kids with outsiders present once in a decade."

Jack lit a cigar. "Sinatra's pals with those gangster guys. If we need them, we could use him as a go-between."

Bobby punched a chair cushion. "Frank Sinatra is a cowardly, finger-popping lowlife, and I will never make deals with gangster scum."

Jack rolled his eyes. Kemper took it as a cue to play middleman.

"I think the book has possibilities. I think we can distribute copies to union members during the primaries and notch some points that way. I've made a lot of law-enforcement connections working for the Committee, and I think we can forge an alliance of nominally Republican DAs by pushing Jack's anticrime credentials."

Jack blew smoke rings. "Bobby's the gangbuster, not me."

Kemper said, "You were on the Committee."

Bobby smiled. "I'll portray you heroically, Jack. I won't say that you and Dad were soft on Hoffa from the gate."

They all laughed. Bobby grabbed a handful of canapes.

Joe cleared his throat. "Kemper, we invited you to this session chiefly to discuss J. Edgar Hoover. We should discuss the situation now, because I'm hosting a dinner at Pavillon tonight, and I need to get ready."

"Do you mean the files that Hoover has on all of you?"

Jack nodded. "I was thinking specifically of a romance I had during the war. I've heard that Hoover's convinced himself that the woman was a Nazi spy."

"Do you mean Inga Arvad?"

"That's right."

Kemper snatched one of Bobby's canapes. "Mr. Hoover has that documented, yes. He bragged about it to me years ago. May I make a suggestion and clear the air about something?"

Joe nodded. Jack and Bobby pushed up to the edge of their chairs.

Kemper leaned toward them. "I'm sure Mr. Hoover knows that I went to work for the Committee. I'm sure he's disappointed that I haven't been in touch with him. Let me reestablish contact and tell him that I'm working for you. Let me assure him that Jack won't replace him as FBI director if he's elected."

Joe nodded. Jack and Bobby nodded.

"I think it's a smart, cautious move. And while I've got the floor, I'd like to bring up the Cuban issue. Eisenhower and Nixon have declared themselves anti-Castro, and I've been thinking that Jack should establish some anti-Fidel credentials."

Joe fiddled with his tie pin. "Everybody's starting to hate Castro. I don't see Cuba as a partisan issue."

Jack said, "Dad's right. But I've been thinking that I might send some Marines down if I'm elected."

Joe said, "*When* you're elected."

"Right. I'll send some Marines down to liberate the whorehouses. Kemper can lead the troops. I'll have him establish a spearhead in Havana."

Joe winked. "Don't forget your spear, Kemper."

"I won't. And seriously, I'll keep you posted on the Cuban front. I know some ex-FBI men with good anti-Castro intelligence."

Bobby brushed hair off his forehead. "Speaking of FBI men, how's the Phantom?"

"In a word, he's persistent. He's chasing those Pension Fund books, but he's not making much headway."

"He's starting to impress me as pathetic."

"Believe me, he's not."

"Can I meet him?"

"Not until he retires. He's afraid of Mr. Hoover."

Joe said, "We all are."

Everybody laughed.

The St. Regis was a slightly downscale Carlyle. Kemper's suite was a third the size of the Kennedys'. He kept a room at a modest hotel in the West 40s—Jack and Bobby contacted him there.

It was stifling hot outside. The suite was a perfect 68 degrees.

Kemper wrote a note to Mr. Hoover. He said, It's confirmed—if elected, Jack Kennedy won't fire you. He played a game of Devil's Advocate next—his standard post-Kennedy-conference ritual.

Doubters questioned his travels. Doubters questioned his complex allegiances.

He sprang logical traps on himself and evaded them brilliantly.

He was seeing Laura tonight—for dinner and a recital at Carnegie Hall. She'd ridicule the pianist's style and practice his showstopper piece endlessly. It was the Kennedy quintessence: Compete, but don't go public unless you can win. Laura was half-Kennedy and a woman— she possessed competitive spirit but no family sanction. Her half-sisters married skirt chasers and stayed faithful; Laura had affairs. Laura said Joe loved his girls but deep down considered them niggers.

He'd been with Laura for seven months now. The Kennedys had no inkling of the liaison. When an engagement was formalized, he'd tell them.

They would be shocked, then relieved. They considered him

trustworthy and knew that he kept things compartmentalized.

Laura loved ballsy men and the arts. She was a solitary woman—with no real friends except Lenny Sands. She exemplified the pervasive Kennedy orbit: A mobbed-up lounge lizard gave Jack speech lessons and forged a bond with his half-sister.

That bond was borderline scary. Lenny might tell Laura things. Lenny might tell her grisly stories.

Laura never mentioned Lenny—despite the fact that he facilitated their meeting.

She probably talked to Lenny long-distance.

Lenny was volatile. An angry or frightened Lenny might say:

Mr. Boyd made Mr. Littell hit me. Mr. Boyd and Mr. Littell are nasty extortionists. Mr. Boyd got me my *Hush-Hush* job—which is very nasty employment.

His Lenny fears peaked in late April.

The Boynton Beach auditions revealed two security risks: a child molester and a homosexual pimp. CIA guidelines mandated termination. He took them out to the Everglades and shot them.

The pimp saw it coming and begged. He shot him in the mouth to cut his squeals off.

He told Claire he killed two men in cold blood. She responded with anti-Communist platitudes.

The pimp reminded him of Lenny. The pimp sparked Devil's Advocate impromptus that he couldn't lie his way out of.

Lenny could ruin him with Laura. Further coercion might backfire—Lenny was volatile.

There was no cut-and-dried Lenny solution. Easing Laura's loneliness might help—she'd be less inclined to contact Lenny.

He brought Claire up from Tulane and introduced her to Laura in mid-May. She was wowed by Laura—a big-city sophisticate ten years her senior. A friendship clicked—the two became great phone chums. Claire joined Laura for occasional weekends, full of concerts and museum tours.

He traveled to earn his three paychecks. His daughter kept his future fiancée company.

Laura told Claire her whole story. Claire inspired full disclosure. Claire was wowed—My Dad might be the President's secret brother-in-law someday.

He pimped for the maybe future President. Jack went through his little black book and sideswiped a hundred women inside six months. Sally Lefferts called Jack a de facto rapist. "He backs you into a corner and charms you until you're plain bushed. He convinces you that turning him down would make you just about the most worthless female who ever lived."

His little black book was near-depleted. Mr. Hoover might tell him to fix Jack up with FBI-plant call girls.

It might happen. If Jack's campaign flourished, Mr. Hoover might simply say, "DO IT."

The phone rang. Kemper caught it on the second ring.

"Yes?"

A long-distance line crackled. "Kemper? It's Chuck Rogers. I'm at the stand, and something happened I figured you should know about."

"What?"

"Those pro-Castro guys I fired cruised by last night and shot up the parking lot. We were damn lucky nobody got hurt. Fulo says he thinks they've got a hole-up someplace close."

Kemper stretched out on the couch. "I'll be down in a few days. We'll fix things up."

"Fix things how?"

"I want to convince Jimmy to sell the stand to the Agency. You'll see. We'll work something out with him."

"I say let's be decisive. I say we can't lose face in the Cuban community by letting Commie shitheads shoot at us."

"We'll send them a message, Chuck. You won't be disappointed."

Kemper let himself in with his key. Laura left the terrace doors open—concert lights had Central Park sparkling.

It was too simple and too pretty. He'd seen some Cuban reconnaissance shots that put it to shame.

They showed United Fruit buildings torched against a night sky. The pictures were pure raw spellbinding—

Something said:

Check Laura's phone bills.

He rifled her study drawers and found them. She'd called Lenny Sands eleven times within the past three months.

Something said, *Convince yourself decisively.*

It was most likely nothing. Laura never mentioned Lenny or acted in any way suspicious.

Something said, *Make her tell you.*

* * *

They sat down to martinis. Laura was sunburned from a long day shopping.

She said, "How long were you waiting?"

Kemper said, "About an hour."

"I called you at the St. Regis, but the switchboard man said you'd left already."

"I felt like a walk."

"When it's so grisly hot out?"

"I had to check my messages at the other hotel."

"You could have called the desk and asked for them."

"I like to show myself every so often."

Laura laughed. "My lover's a spy."

"Not really."

"What would my ersatz family think if they knew you had a suite at the St. Regis?"

Kemper laughed. "They'd consider it imitative, and wonder how I could afford it."

"I've wondered myself. Your FBI pension and salary from the family aren't that generous."

Kemper put a hand on her knees. "I've been lucky in the stock market. I've said it before, Laura. If you're curious, ask."

"All right, I will. You've never mentioned taking walks before, so why did you take a walk on the hottest day of the year?"

Kemper made his eyes mist over. "I was thinking of my friend Ward, and these walks we'd take along the lakefront in Chicago. I've been missing him lately, and I think I confused the Chicago lakefront climate with Manhattan's. What's the matter, you look sad."

"Oh, nothing."

She took the bait. His Chicago/friend talk nailed her.

"Horseshit, 'Oh, nothing.' Laura ..."

"No, really, it's nothing."

"Laura ..."

She pulled away from him. "Kemper, *it's nothing*."

Kemper sighed. Kemper feigned perfect chagrined exasperation.

"No, it's not, it's Lenny Sands. Something I said reminded you of him."

She relaxed. She was buying the whole verbal package.

"Well, when you said you knew Lenny you were evasive, and I haven't brought him up because I thought it might bother you."

"Did Lenny tell you that he knew me?"

"Yes, and some other nameless FBI man. He wouldn't give me any details, but I could tell that he was afraid of you both."

"We helped him out of trouble, Laura. There was a price. Do you want me to tell you what that price was?"

"No. I don't want to know. It's an ugly world that Lenny lives in . . . and . . . well, it's just that *you* live in hotel suites and work for my quasi-family and God knows who else. I just wish we could be more open somehow."

Her eyes convinced him to do it. It was dead risky but the stuff of legends.

Kemper said, "Put on that green dress I gave you."

Pavillon was all silk brocade and candlelight. A pre-theater crowd came dressed to the nines.

Kemper slipped the maître d' a hundred dollars. A waiter led them back to the family's private room.

Time stood still. Kemper posed Laura beside him and opened the door.

Joe and Bobby looked up and froze. Ava Gardner put her glass down in slow motion.

Jack smiled.

Joe dropped his fork. His soufflé exploded. Ava Gardner caught chocolate sauce on the bodice.

Bobby stood up and balled his fists. Jack grabbed his cummerbund and pulled him back into his chair.

Jack laughed.

Jack said something like, "More balls than brains."

Joe and Bobby glowed—radioactively pissed.

Time stood still. Ava Gardner looked smaller than life.

29

(Dallas, 8/27/59)

HE RENTED A suite at the Adolphus Hotel. His bedroom faced the south side of Commerce Street and Jack Ruby's Carousel Club.

Kemper Boyd always said DON'T SCRIMP ON SURVEILLANCE LODGING.

Littell watched the door with binoculars. It was 4:00 P.M. now, with no Live Striptease Girls until 6:00.

He'd checked Chicago-to-Dallas flight reservations. Sid Kabikoff flew in to Big D yesterday. His itinerary included a rent-a-car pickup.

His final destination was McAllen, Texas—smack on the Mexican border.

He flew down to make a smut film. He told Mad Sal that he was shooting it with Jack Ruby strippers.

Littell called in some sick time. He coughed when he talked to SAC Leahy. He purchased his airplane ticket under a pseudonym—Kemper Boyd always said COVER YOUR TRACKS.

Kabikoff told Mad Sal that "real" Fund books existed. Kabikoff told Mad Sal that Jules Schiffrin kept them. Kabikoff told Mad Sal that Jules Schiffrin knew Joe Kennedy.

It had to be a benign business acquaintance. Joe Kennedy cut a wide business swath.

Littell watched the door. An eyestrain headache slammed him. A crowd formed outside the Carousel Club.

Three muscular young men and three cheap-looking women. Sid Kabikoff himself—fat and sweaty.

They said hellos and lit cigarettes. Kabikoff waved his hands, effusive.

Jack Ruby opened the door. A dachshund ran out and took a shit on the sidewalk. Ruby kicked turds into the gutter.

The crowd moved inside. Littell visualized a rear-entry reconnaissance.

The back door was hook-and-eye latched, with slack at the door-doorjamb juncture. A dressing room connected to the club proper.

He walked across the street and hooked around to the parking lot. He saw one car only: a '56 Ford convertible with the top down.

The registration was strapped to the steering column. The owner was one Jefferson Davis Tippit.

Dogs yapped. Ruby should rename his dive the Carousel Kennel Club. Littell walked up to the door and popped the latch with his penknife.

It was dark. A crack of light cut through the dressing room.

He tiptoed up to the source. He smelled perfume and dog effluvia. The crack was a connecting door left ajar.

He heard overlapping voices. He made out Ruby, Kabikoff and a man with a deep Texas twang.

He squinted into the light. He saw Ruby, Kabikoff and a uniformed Dallas cop—standing by a striptease runway.

Littell craned his neck. His view expanded.

The runway was packed. He saw four girls and four boys, all buck naked.

Ruby said, "J.D., are they not gorgeous?"

The cop said, "I'm partial to women exclusively, but all in all I got to agree."

The boys stroked erections. The girls oohed and aahed. Three dachshunds cavorted on the runway.

Kabikoff giggled. "Jack, you're a better talent scout than Major Bowes and Ted Mack combined. 100%, Jack. I'm talking no rejections for these lovelies."

J.D. said, "When do we meet?"

Kabikoff said, "Tomorrow afternoon, say 2:00. We'll meet at the coffee shop at the Sagebrush Motel in McAllen, and drive across to the shoot from there. What an audition! All auditions should go so smooth!"

One boy had a tattooed penis. Two girls were knife-scarred and bruised. A dogfight erupted—Ruby yelled, "No, children, no!"

Littell ordered a room-service dinner: steak, Caesar salad and Glenlivet. It was a robbery-stash splurge—and more Kemper's style than his.

Three drinks honed his instincts. A fourth made him certain. A nightcap made him call Mad Sal in L.A.

Sal pitched a tantrum: I need money, money, money.

Littell said, I'll try to get you some.

Sal said, Try hard.

Littell said, It's on. I want you to refer Kabikoff for a Fund loan. Call Giancana and set up a meeting. Call Sid in thirty-six hours and confirm it.

Sal gulped. Sal oozed fear. Littell said, I'll try to get you some money.

Sal agreed to do it. Littell hung up before he started begging again.

He didn't tell Sal that his robbery stash was down to eight hundred dollars.

Littell left a 2:00 A.M. wake-up call. His prayers ran long—
Bobby Kennedy had a large family.

The drive took eleven hours. He hit McAllen with sixteen
minutes to spare.

South Texas was pure hot and humid. Littell pulled off the
highway and inventoried his backseat.

He had one blank-paged scrapbook, twelve rolls of Scotch
tape and a Polaroid Land Camera with a long-range Rolliflex
zoom lens. He had forty rolls of color film, a ski mask and a contraband FBI flashing roof light.

It was a complete mobile evidence kit.

Littell eased back into traffic. He spotted the Sagebrush Motel:
a horseshoe-shaped bungalow court right on the main drag.

He pulled in and parked in front of the coffee shop. He put
the car in neutral and idled with the air conditioner on.

J.D. Tippit pulled in at 2:06. His convertible was overloaded:
six smut kids up front and camera gear bulging out of the trunk.

They entered the coffee shop. Littell snapped a zoom-lens shot
to capture the moment.

The camera whirred. A picture popped out and developed in
his hand in less than a minute.

Amazing—

Kabikoff pulled up and beeped his horn. Littell snapped a shot
of his rear license plate.

Tippit and the kids walked out with soft drinks. They divided
up between the cars and headed out southbound.

Littell counted to twenty and followed them. Traffic was
light—they drove surface streets for five minutes and hit the border crossing one-two-three.

A guard waved them through. Littell popped a location-
setting snapshot: two cars en route to Federal violations.

Mexico was a dusty extension of Texas. They drove through
a long string of tin-shack villages.

A car squeezed in behind Tippit. Littell used it for protective
cover.

They drove up into scrub hills. Littell fixed on J.D.'s foxtail-
tipped antenna. The road was half dirt and half blacktop—gravel
chunks snapped under his tires.

Kabikoff turned right at a sign: Domicilio de Estado Policía.
"State Police Barracks"—an easy translation.

Tippit followed Kabikoff. The road was all dirt—the cars sent dust clouds swirling. They fishtailed up a little rock-clustered mountain.

Littell stayed on the main road and kept going. He saw some tree cover fifty yards up the mountainside—a thick clump of scrub pines to shoot from.

He pulled over and parked off the road. He packed his gear into a duffel bag and covered his car with scrub branches and tumbleweeds.

Echoes bounced his way. The "shoot" was just over the top of the hill.

He followed the sounds. He lugged his gear up a 90-degree grade.

The crest looked down on a dirt-packed clearing. His vantage point was goddamn superb.

The "barracks" was a tin-roofed shack. State Police cars were parked beside it—Chevys and old Hudson Hornets.

Tippit was lugging film cans. Fat Sid was bribing Mexican cops. The smut kids were checking out some handcuffed women.

Littell crouched behind a bush and laid out his gear. His zoom lens brought him into close-up range.

He saw wide-open barracks windows and mattresses set up inside. He saw black shirts and armbands on the cops.

The cop cars had leopard-skin seat covers. The women wore prison ID bracelets.

The crowd dispersed. The blackshirts uncuffed the women. Kabikoff hauled equipment inside the barracks.

Littell went to work. The heat had him weaving on his knees. His zoom lens got him in very close.

He snapped pictures and watched them develop. He placed them in neat rows inside his duffel bag.

He snapped smut girls entwined on a mattress. He snapped Sid Kabikoff coercing lesbian action.

He snapped obscene insertions. He snapped dildo gang bangs. He snapped smut boys whipping Mexican women bloody.

The Polaroid cranked out instant closeups. Fat Sid was color-glossy indicted:

For Suborning Lewd Conduct. For Felony Assault. For Filming Pornography for Interstate Sales, in violation of nine Federal statutes.

Littell shot his way through forty rolls of film. Sweat soaked the ground all around him.

Sid Kabikoff was evidence-snapped:

White slaving. Violating the Mann Act. Serving as an accessory to kidnapping and sexual battery.

Snap!—a snack break—cops baking tortillas on a prowl-car roof.

Snap!—a prisoner tries to escape. Snap!/snap!/snap!—two cops catch her and rape her.

Littell walked back to his car. He started sobbing just over the border.

He taped the pictures into his scrapbook and calmed down with prayers and a half-pint. He found a good spot to perch: the access-road curb, a half-mile north of the border.

The road ran one way. It was the only route to the Interstate. It was nicely lit—you could almost read license plate numbers.

Littell waited. Air-conditioner blasts kept him from dozing. Midnight came and went.

Cars drove by law-abidingly slow—the Border Patrol gave tickets all the way to McAllen.

Headlights swept by. Littell kept scanning rear plates. The air-conditioner freeze was making him sick.

Kabikoff's Cadillac passed—

Littell slid out behind him. He slapped the cherry light to his roof and pulled on his ski mask.

The light swirled bright red. Littell hit his high beams and tapped the horn.

Kabikoff pulled over. Littell boxed him in and walked up to his door.

Kabikoff screamed—the mask was bright red with white devil's horns.

Littell remembered making threats.

Littell remembered his final pitch: YOU'RE GOING TO TALK TO GIANCANA WIRED UP.

He remembered a tire iron.

He remembered blood on the dashboard.

He remembered begging God PLEASE DON'T LET ME KILL HIM.

30

(Miami, 8/29/59)

"COCKSUCKING COMMIE FUCKERS shoot up my cabstand! First it's Bobby Kennedy, now it's these Red Cuban shitheels!"

Heads turned their way—Jimmy Hoffa talked loud. Lunch with Jimmy was risky—the hump sprayed food and coffee routinely.

Pete had a headache. The Tiger Kab hut stood catty-corner from the diner—the fucking tiger stripes were giving him eyestrain.

He turned away from the window. "Jimmy, let's talk—"

Hoffa cut him off. "Bobby Kennedy's got every shithead grand jury in America chasing me. Every shithead prosecutor in creation wants to go the rump route with James Riddle Hoffa."

Pete yawned. The red-eye from L.A. was brutal.

Boyd gave him marching orders. Boyd said, Make a deal for the cabstand—I want an intelligence/recruiting hub in Miami. More banana boats are due. When the Blessington campsite flies, we'll need more driver spots for our boys.

A waitress brought fresh coffee—Hoffa had spritzed his cup empty. Pete said, "Jimmy, let's talk business."

Hoffa dumped in cream and sugar. "I didn't think you flew in for that roast-beef sandwich."

Pete lit a cigarette. "The Agency wants to lease a half-interest in the cabstand. There's lots of Agency and Outfit guys that are starting to feel pretty strongly about Cuba, and the Agency thinks the stand would be a good place to recruit out of. And there'll be shitloads of Cuban exiles coming into Miami, which means big business if the stand goes anti-Castro in a big way."

Hoffa belched. "What do you mean, 'lease'?"

"I mean you get a guaranteed $5,000 a month, in cash, plus half the gross profits, plus an Agency freeze with the IRS, just in case. My 5% comes off the top, you'll still have Chuck Rogers and Fulo running the stand, and I'll be coming by to check in regularly, once I start my contract job down in Blessington."

Jimmy's eyes flashed—$$$$$. "I like it. But Fulo said Kemper Boyd's tight with the Kennedys, which I do not like one iota."

Pete shrugged. "Fulo's right."

"Could Boyd get me off the hook with Bobby?"

"I'd say his loyalties are stretched too thin to try it. With Boyd, you take the bitter with the sweet."

Hoffa dabbed a stain off his necktie. "The bitter is those Commie humps who shot up my cabstand. The sweet is that if you took care of them, I'd be inclined to accept that offer."

Pete huddled up a crew at the dispatch hut. Solid guys: Chuck, Fulo, Boyd's man Teo Paez.

They pulled chairs up in front of the air conditioner. Chuck passed a bottle around.

Fulo sharpened his machete on a rock. "I understand that all six of the traitors have vacated their apartments. I have been told that they have moved into a place called a 'safe house.' It is near here, and I believe it is Communisto-financed."

Chuck wiped spit off the bottle. "I saw Rolando Cruz checking out the stand yesterday, so I think it's safe to say we're under surveillance. A cop friend of mine got me their license numbers, so if you say we go trawling, that'll help."

Paez said, "Death to traitors."

Pete ripped the air conditioner off the wall. Steam billowed out.

Chuck said, "I get it. You want to give them a target."

Pete closed down the stand—in full public view. Fulo called an air-conditioner repairman. Chuck radioed his drivers and told them to return their cabs *now*.

The repairman came and removed the wall unit. The drivers dropped off their taxis and went home. Fulo put a sign on the door: Tiger Kab Temporarily Closed.

Teo, Chuck and Fulo went trawling. They drove their radio-rigged off-duty cars, devoid of tiger stripes and Tiger Kab regalia.

Pete snuck back to the hut. He kept the lights off and the windows locked. The dump was brutal hot.

A four-way link hooked in: the three cars to the Tiger Kab switchboard. Fulo prowled Coral Gables; Chuck and Teo prowled Miami. Pete connected in to them via headset and hand microphone.

It was ass-scratching, sit-still duty. Chuck hogged the airwaves with a long rant on the Jew-Nigger Pantheon.

Three hours slogged by. The trawl cars kept a line of chatter up. They did not see hide-nor-fucking-hair of the pro-Castro guys.

Pete dozed with his headset on. The thick air had him wheezing. Crosstalk gibberish sparked these little two-second nightmares.

His *standard* nightmares: charging Jap infantry and Ruth Mildred Cressmeyer's face.

Pete dozed to radio fuzz and wah-wah feedback. He thought he heard Fulo's voice: "Two Car to base, urgent, over."

He jerked awake and snapped his mike on. "Yeah, Fulo."

Fulo clicked on. Traffic noise filtered in behind his voice.

"I have Rolando Cruz and César Salcido in sight. They stopped at a Texaco station and filled up two Coca-Cola bottles with gasoline. They are driving toward the stand rapidly."

"Flagler or 46th?"

"46th Street. Pete, I think they—"

"*They're going to torch the cabs.* Fulo, you stay behind them, and when they turn into the lot, you box them in. *And no shooting, do you understand?*"

"*Sí,* I comprende. Ten-four, over."

Pete dumped his headset. He saw Jimmy's nail-topped baseball bat on a shelf above the switchboard.

He grabbed it and ran out to the parking lot. The sky was pitch black and the air ooooozed moisture.

Pete swung the bat and worked out some kinks. Headlights bounced down 46th—low, like your classic Cubano hot rod.

Pete crouched by a tiger-striped Merc.

The taco wagon swung into the lot.

Fulo's Chevy glided in sans lights and engine, right behind it.

Rolando Cruz got out. He was packing a Molotov cocktail and matches. He didn't notice Fulo's car—

Pete came up behind him. Fulo flashed his brights and backlit Cruz plain as day.

Pete swung the bat full-force. It ripped into Cruz and snagged on his ribs.

Cruz screamed.

Fulo piled out of his car. His high beams strafed Cruz, spitting blood and bone chips. César Salcido piled out of the spicmobile, wet-your-pants scared.

Pete yanked the bat free. The Molotov hit the pavement AND DID NOT SHATTER.

Fulo charged Salcido. The taco wagon idled at a high pitch—good cover noise.

Pete pulled his piece and shot Cruz in the back. The high beams caught Fulo's part of the show.

He's duct-taping Salcido upside the face. He's got the taco-wagon trunk wide open. There's dervish-quick Fulo, uncoiling the parking-lot hose.

Pete dumped Cruz in the trunk. Fulo nozzle-sprayed his entrails down a sewer hole.

It was dark. Cars cruised up and down Flagler, oblivious to the whole fucking thing.

Pete grabbed the Molotov. Fulo parked his Chevy. He was lip-syncing numbers over and over—Salcido probably spilled the safe-house address.

The taco wagon was metal-flake purple and fur-upholstered—a cherry '58 Impala niggered up.

Fulo took the wheel. Pete got in back. Salcido tried to scream through his gag.

They hauled down Flagler. Fulo yelled an address: 1809 Northwest 53rd. Pete turned on the radio full-blast.

Bobby Darin sang "Dream Lover," earsplitting loud. Pete shot Salcido in the back of the head—exploding teeth ripped the tape off his mouth.

Fulo drove VERY VERY SLOW. Blood dripped off the dashboard and seats.

They gagged on muzzle smoke. They kept the windows up to seal the smell in.

Fulo made left turns and right turns. Fulo made nice directional signals. They drove their coffin wagon out to the Coral Gables Causeway—VERY VERY SLOW.

They found an abandoned mooring dock. It ran thirty yards out into the bay.

It was deserted. No winos, no lovebirds, no late-night fly casters.

They got out. Fulo put the car in neutral and pushed it up on the planks. Pete lit the Molotov and tossed it inside.

They ran.

Flames hit the tank. The Impala exploded. The planking ignited kindling-quick.

The dock whooooshed into one long fireball. Waves lapped up and fizzed against it.

Pete coughed his lungs out. He tasted gunsmoke and swallowed blood off the dead men.

The dock caved in. The Impala sunk down on some reef rocks. Steam hissed off the water for a solid minute.

Fulo caught his breath. "Chuck lives nearby. I have a key to his room, and I know he has equipment we can use."

They found suppressor-rigged revolvers and bulletproof vests. They found Chuck's Tiger Kab parked at the curb.

They grabbed the guns and vested up. Pete hot-wired the cab.

Fulo drove a hair too fast. Pete thought of old Ruth Mildred all the way.

The house looked decrepit. The door looked un-break-downable. The place was bracketed by palm groves—the only crib on the block.

The front room lights were on. Gauze curtains covered the window. Shadows stood out well defined.

They crouched beside the porch, just below the windowsill. Pete made out four shadow shapes and four voices. He pictured four men boozing on a couch FACING THE WINDOW.

Fulo seemed to pick up on his brainwaves. They checked their vests and their guns—four revolvers and twenty-four rounds total.

Pete counted off. They stood up and fired on "three"— straight through the window.

Glass exploded. Silencer thunks faded into screams.

The window went down. The curtains went down. They had *real* targets now—Commie spics up against a blood-spattered wall.

The spics were flailing for guns. The spics were wearing shoulder holsters and cross-draw hip rigs.

Pete vaulted the sill. Return fire hit his vest and spun him backward.

Fulo charged. The Commies fired wide; the Commies fired near-death erratic. They got off un-suppressed big-bore pistol shots—tremendously goddamn loud.

A vest deflection sent Fulo spinning. Pete stumbled up to the couch and emptied both his guns at ultraclose range. He notched head hits and neck hits and chest hits, and took in a big gasping breath of gray viscous something—

A diamond ring rolled across the floor. Fulo grabbed it and kissed it.

Pete wiped blood from his eyes. He saw a stack of plastic-wrapped bricks by the TV set.

White powder was leaking out. He knew it was heroin.

3 1
(Miami, 8/30/59)

KEMPER READ BY the Eden Roc pool. A waiter freshened his coffee every few minutes.

The *Herald* ran it in banner print: "Four Dead in Cuban Dope War."

The paper reported no witnesses and no leads. The assumed perpetrators were "Rival Cuban Gangs."

Kemper linked events.

John Stanton sends him a report three days ago. It states that President Eisenhower's Cuban-Ops budget has come in way below the requested amount. It states that Raúl Castro is funding a Miami propaganda drive through heroin sales. It states that a distribution shack/safe house has already been established. It states that the heroin gang includes two ex-Tiger Kab men: César Salcido and Rolando Cruz.

He tells Pete to clear an Agency/cabstand lease deal. He assumes that Jimmy Hoffa will stipulate vengeance on the men who shot up the stand. He knows that Pete will wreak that vengeance with considerable flair.

He has dinner with John Stanton. They discuss his report at length.

John says, Heroin-pushing Commies are tough competition. Ike will kick loose more money later on, but now is now.

More banana boats are due. Anti-Castro zealots will swarm Florida. Hothead ideologues will join the Cause and demand action.

Rampant factionalism might reign. The Blessington campsite is still short of operational and their Elite Cadre is still untested. The dope clique might usurp their strategic edge and financial hegemony.

Kemper said, Heroin-pushing Commies *are* tough. You can't compete with men who'll go that far.

He made Stanton say it himself. He made Stanton say, Unless we exceed their limits.

Talk went ambiguous. Abstractions passed as facts. A euphemistic language asserted itself.

"Self-budgeted," "autonomous" and "compartmentalized." "Need-to-know basis" and "Ad hoc utilization of Agency resources."

"Co-opting of Agency-aligned pharmacological sources on a cash-and-carry basis."

"Without divulging the destination of the merchandise."

They sealed the deal with elliptical rhetoric. He let Stanton think he devised most of the plan.

Kemper skimmed his newspaper. He noticed a page-four banner: "Grisly Causeway Discovery."

An arsoned Chevy collapses a rickety wooden dock. Rolando Cruz and César Salcido are along for the dip.

"Authorities believe the killings of Cruz and Salcido may be connected to the slayings of four other Cubans in Coral Gables late last night."

Kemper flipped back to page one. A single paragraph stood out.

"Although the dead men were rumored to be heroin traffickers, no narcotics were found on the premises."

Be prompt, Pete. And be as smart and farsighted as I think you are.

Pete showed up early, carrying a large paper bag. He didn't check out the women by the pool or walk up with his usual swagger.

Kemper slid a chair out. Pete saw the *Herald* on the table, folded to the page-one headline.

Kemper said, "You?"

Pete put the bag on the table. "Fulo and me."

"Both jobs?"

"That's right."

"What's in the bag?"

"Fourteen point six pounds of uncut heroin and a diamond ring."

Kemper fished the ring out. The stones and gold setting were beautiful.

Pete poured a cup of coffee. "Keep it. To consecrate my marriage to the Agency."

"Thanks. I may be popping a question with it soon."

"I hope she says yes."

"Did Hoffa?"

"Yeah, he did. He put a condition on the deal, which I fucking fulfilled, as I'm sure you already know."

Kemper nudged the bag. "You could have unloaded it yourself. I wouldn't have said anything."

"I'm along for the ride. And for now, I'm enjoying it too much to fuck with your agenda."

"Which is?"

"Compartmentalization."

Kemper smiled. "That's the biggest word I've ever heard you use."

"I read books to teach myself English. I must have read the Webster's Unabridged Dictionary at least ten times."

"You're an immigrant success story."

"Go fuck yourself. But before you do it, tell me my official CIA duties."

Kemper twirled the ring. Sunlight made the diamonds twinkle.

"You'll be nominally running the Blessington campsite. There's some additional buildings and a landing strip going up, and you'll be supervising the construction. Your assignment is to train Cuban refugees for amphibious sabotage runs into Cuba, and to funnel them to other training sites, the cabstand and Miami for general gainful employment."

Pete said, "It sounds too legal."

Pool water splashed at their feet. His suite upstairs was almost Kennedy-sized.

"Boyd—"

"Eisenhower has given the Agency a tacit mandate to covertly undermine Castro. The Outfit wants their casinos back. Nobody wants a Communist dictatorship ninety miles off the Florida coast."

"Tell me something I don't know."

"Ike's budget allocation came in a little low."

"Tell me something interesting."

Kemper poked the bag. A tiny trace of white powder puffed out.

"I have a plan to refinance our part of the Cuban Cause. It's *implicitly* Agency-vetted, and I think it will work."

"I'm getting the picture, but I want to hear you say it."

Kemper lowered his voice. "We link up with Santo Trafficante. We utilize his narcotics connections and my Cadre as pushers, and sell this dope, Santo's dope and all the other dope we can get our hands on in Miami. The Agency has access to a poppy farm in Mexico, and we can buy some fresh-processed stuff there and have Chuck Rogers fly it in. We finance the Cause with the bulk of the money, give Trafficante a percentage as operating tribute and send a small percentage of the dope into Cuba with our Blessington men. They'll distribute it to our on-island contacts, who will sell it and use the money to purchase weapons. Your specific job is to supervise my Cadre and make sure they sell only to Negroes. You make sure my men don't use the dope themselves, and keep their profit skim at a minimum."

Pete said, "What's our percentage?" Pete's response was utterly predictable.

"We don't take one. If Trafficante approves my plan, we'll get something much sweeter."

"Which you're not going to talk about now."

"I'm meeting Trafficante in Tampa this afternoon. I'll let you know what he says."

"And in the meantime?"

"If Trafficante says yes, we'll get going in a week or so. In the meantime, you drive down to Blessington and check things out, meet the Cadre and tell Mr. Hughes that you'll be taking some prolonged Florida vacations."

Pete smiled. "He'll be pissed."

"You know how to get around that."

"If I'm working up in Miami, who's going to run the campsite?"

Kemper got out his address book. "Go see Guy Banister in New Orleans. Tell him we need a tough white man to run the camp, a shitkicker type who can handle the crackers around Blessington. Guy knows every right-wing hardcase on the Gulf Coast. Tell him we need a man who's not too insane and willing to move to South Florida."

Pete wrote Banister's number on a napkin. "You're convinced all this is going to work?"

"I'm certain. Just pray that Castro doesn't go pro-U.S."

"That's a nice sentiment from a Kennedy man."

"Jack would appreciate the irony."

Pete cracked his knuckles. "Jimmy thinks you should tell Jack to put a leash on Bobby."

"Never. And I want to see Jack elected President, and I will not intercede with the Kennedys to help Hoffa. I keep—"

"—things compartmentalized, I know."

Kemper held the ring up. "Stanton wants me to help influence Jack's Cuban policy. We want the Cuban problem to extend, Pete. Hopefully into a Kennedy administration."

Pete cracked his thumbs. "Jack's got a nice head of hair, but I don't see him as President of the United States."

"Qualifications don't count. All Ike did was invade Europe and look like your uncle."

Pete stretched. His shirttail slid up over two revolvers.

"Whatever happens, I'm in. This is too fucking big to pass up."

His rent-a-car came with a discreet dashboard Jesus. Kemper slipped the ring over its head.

The air conditioner died outside Miami. A radio concert kept his mind off the heat.

A virtuoso played Chopin. Kemper replayed the scene at Pavillon.

Jack played peacemaker and smoothed things out. Old Joe's freeze thawed out nicely. They stayed for one awkward drink.

Bobby sulked. Ava Gardner was plain flummoxed. She had no idea what the scene meant.

Joe sent him a note the next day. It closed with, "Laura deserves a man with balls."

Laura said "I love you" that night. He made up his mind to propose to her at Christmas.

He could afford Laura now. He had three paychecks and two full-time hotel suites. He had a low six-figure bank-account balance.

And if Trafficante says yes . . .

Trafficante understood abstract concepts.

"Self-budgeted," "autonomous" and "compartmentalized" amused him.

"Agency-aligned pharmacological sources" made him laugh outright.

He wore a nubby-weave silk suit. His office was turned out in blond-wood Danish modern.

He loved Kemper's plan. He grasped its political thrust immediately.

The meeting extended. A yes-man served anisette and pastry.

Their conversation veered in odd directions. Trafficante critiqued the Big Pete Bondurant myth. The paper bag by Kemper's feet went unmentioned.

The yes-man served espresso and Courvoisier VSOP. Kemper marked the moment with a bow.

"Raúl Castro sent this in, Mr. Trafficante. Pete and I want you to have it, as a symbol of our good faith."

Trafficante picked up the bag. He smiled at the weight and gave it a few little squeezes.

Kemper swirled his brandy. "If Castro is eliminated as a direct or indirect result of our efforts, Pete and I will insure that your contribution is recognized. More importantly, we'll try to convince the new Cuban ruler to allow you, Mr. Giancana, Mr. Marcello and Mr. Rosselli to regain control of your casinos and build new ones."

"And if he refuses?"

"We'll kill him."

"And what do you and Pete want for all your hard work?"

"If Cuba is liberated, we want to split 5% of the profits from the Capri and Nacional Hotel casinos in perpetuity."

"Suppose Cuba stays Communist?"

"Then we get nothing."

Trafficante bowed. "I'll talk to the other boys, and of course, my vote is 'Yes.'"

32

(Chicago, 9/4/59)

LITTELL PICKED UP static interference. House-to-car bug feeds always ran rough.

The signal fed in from fifty yards out. Sid Kabikoff wore the microphone taped to his chest.

Mad Sal had arranged the meet. Sam G. insisted on his apartment—take it or leave it. Butch Montrose met Sid on the stoop and walked him up to the left-rear unit.

The car was broiling. Littell kept his windows up as a sound filter.

Kabikoff: "You've got a nice place, Sam. Really, what a choice pad-à-terre."

Littell heard scratching noise—flush on the mike. He visualized the at-the-source cause.

Sid's stretching the tape. He's rubbing those bruises I inflicted down in Texas.

Giancana's voice came in garbled. Littell thought he heard Mad Sal mentioned.

He tried to find Sal this morning. He cruised his collection turf and couldn't locate him.

Montrose: "We know you knew Jules Schiffrin back in the old days. We know you know some of the boys, so it's like you're recommended from the gate."

Kabikoff: "It's like a loop. If you're in the loop you're in the loop."

Cars boomed by. Windowpanes rattled close to the feed-in.

Kabikoff: "Everybody in the loop knows I'm the best smut man in the West. Everybody knows Sid the Yid's got the best-looking cunt and the boys with the putzes down to their knees."

Giancana: "Did Sal tell you to ask for a Pension Fund loan specific?"

Kabikoff: "Yeah, he did."

Montrose: "Is Sal in some kind of money trouble, Sid?"

Traffic noise covered the signal. Littell timed it at six seconds even.

Montrose: "I know Sal's in the loop, and I know the loop's the loop, but I'm also saying my own little love shack got burglarized in January, and I got rammed for fourteen Gs out of my fucking golf bag."

Giancana: "And in April some friends of ours got clouted for eighty grand they had stashed in a locker. You see, right after these hits Sal started spending new money. Butch and me just put it together, sort of circumstantially."

Littell went lightheaded. His pulse went haywire.

Kabikoff: "No. Sal wouldn't do something like that. No ... he wouldn't. ..."

Montrose: "The loop's the loop and the Fund's the Fund, but the two ain't necessarily the same thing. Jules Schiffrin's with the Fund, but that don't mean he'd roll over for a loan for you, just because you shared spit way back when."

Giancana: "We sort of think somebody's trying to get at Jimmy Hoffa and the Fund through a goddamn fake loan referral. We talked to Sal about it, but he didn't have nothing to say."

Littell hyperventilated. Spots blipped in front of his eyes.

Montrose: "So, did somebody approach you? Like the Feds or the Cook County Sheriff's?"

Thumps hit the mike. It had to be Sid's pulse racing. Fizzing noise overlapped the thumps—Sid's sweat was clogging up the feeder ducts.

The feed sputtered and died. Littell hit his volume switch and got nothing but a static-fuzzed void.

He rolled down the windows and counted off forty-six seconds. Fresh air cleared his head.

He can't rat me. I wore that ski mask both times that we talked.

Kabikoff stumbled out to the sidewalk. Wires dangled from the back of his shirt. He got his car and punched it straight through a red light.

Littell hit the ignition. The car wouldn't start—his bug feed ran down the battery.

He knew what he'd find at Sal's house. Four rye-and-beers prepared him to break in and see it.

They tortured Sal in his basement. They stripped him and tied him to a ceiling pipe. They hosed him and scorched him with jumper cables.

Sal didn't talk. Giancana didn't know the name Littell. Fat Sid didn't know his name or what he looked like.

They might let Sid go back to Texas. They might or might not kill him somewhere down the line.

They left a cable clamped to Sal's tongue. Voltage burned his face shiny black.

Littell called Fat Sid's hotel. The desk clerk said Mr. Kabikoff was in—he had two visitors just an hour ago.

Littell said, "Don't ring his room." He stopped for two more rye-and-beers and drove over to see for himself.

They left the door unlocked. They left Sid in an overflowing bathtub. They tossed a plugged-in TV set on top of him.

The water was still bubbling. Electric shock had burned
Kabikoff bald.

Littell tried to weep. The rye-and-beers left him too
anesthetized.

Kemper Boyd always said DON'T LOOK BACK.

33

(New Orleans, 9/20/59)

BANISTER SUPPLIED FILES and pedigree notes. Pete narrowed
his prospects down to three men.

His hotel room was file-inundated. He was deluged with rap
sheets and FBI reports—the far-right South captured on paper.

He got the scoop on Ku Klux Klan klowns and neo-Nazis. He
learned about the National States Rights Party. He marveled at
the pointy-heads on the FBI payroll—half the Klans in Dixie
were Fed-saturated.

Fed snitches were out castrating and lynching. Hoover's only
real concern was KKK mail-fraud minutiae.

A fan ruffled loose file papers. Pete stretched out on the bed
and blew smoke rings.

Memo to Kemper Boyd:

The Agency should bankroll a Blessington KKK Klavern.
Dirt-poor crackers surrounded the campsite—spic haters all.
Klan hijinks would help keep them diverted.

Pete skimmed rap sheets. His instinct held—his prospects
were the least rabid of the bunch.

Said prospects:

The Reverend Wilton Tompkins Evans, ex-con radio mes-
siah. Pastor of the "Anti-Communist Crusade of the Air," a
weekly short-wave tirade. Spanish-fluent; ex-paratrooper; three
convictions for statutory rape. Banister's assessment: "Capable
and tough, but perhaps too anti-papist to work with Cubans.
He'd be a great training officer and I'm sure he'd relocate, because
he can broadcast his radio program from anywhere. Close friend
of Chuck Rogers."

Douglas Frank Lockhart, FBI informant/Klansman. Ex-Tank
Corps sergeant; ex-Dallas cop; ex-gun runner to rightist dictator
Rafael Trujillo. Banister's assessment: "Probably the premier

Klan informant in the South and a true Klan zealot in his own right. Tough and brave, but easily led and somewhat volatile. Seems to bear no grudge against Latins, especially if they are strongly anti-Communist."

Henry Davis Hudspeth, the South's #1 purveyor of hate propaganda. Spanish fluent; expert in Hapkido jujitsu. World War II fighter ace, with thirteen Pacific Theater kills. Banister's assessment: "I like Hank, but he can be stubborn and untowardedly vitriolic. He's currently working for me as liaison between my exile camp near Lake Pontchartrain and Dougie Frank Lockhart's nearby Klan Klavern. (I own the property both are situated on.) Hank's a good man, but maybe not suited for second banana status."

All three men were close by. All three had party plans tonight—the Klan was torching a cross out by Guy's camp.

Pete tried to notch a pre-cross-burn nap. He was running on a sleep deficit—his past three weeks were hectic and exhausting.

Boyd glommed some morphine from that CIA-friendly dope ranch. He flew it out to L.A. and gave it to Mr. Hughes.

Mr. Hughes appreciated the gift. Mr. Hughes said, Go back to Miami with my best wishes.

He didn't tell him, I'm an anti-Red crusader now. With 5% of two casinos forever—if Cuba trades Red for Red, White and Blue.

Boyd sold the deal to Trafficante. Marcello, Giancana and Rosselli agreed to it. Boyd figured they'd make at least fifteen million dollars per year per man.

He told Lenny to swamp *Hush-Hush* with anti-Castro propaganda. He told him to shitcan the sex jive that Hughes and Hoover drooled for. He told him to make up some skank to keep them happy.

L.A. was prison camp. Florida was summer camp.

He flew back to Miami quicksville. Boyd had signed on the Mexican dope farm as the Cadre's chief supplier. Chuck flew the initial fourteen pounds down for cutting and brought it back at six times the weight. Trafficante kicked loose bonuses for all Cadre personnel.

He gave them sawed-offs and magnums. He gave them bulletproof vests and cherry-new dopemobiles.

Fulo chose a '59 Eldo. Chuck picked out a sweet Ford Vicky. Delsol, Obregón, Paez and Gutiérrez were all Chevy men. Spics will be spics—they tacoized their sleds from stem to stern.

He met the men and got to know them.

Gutiérrez was solid and quiet. Delsol was calculating and smart. His cousin Obregón seemed borderline dicey—Boyd was starting to think he might run light on balls.

Santo Junior retooled his Miami dope biz. The Cadre took over the nigger trade exclusively.

Boyd decreed free tastes for all local junkies. The Cadre dispensed a shitload of shit totally gratis. Chuck renamed Nigger-town Cloud Nine.

They segued from philanthropy to business. They prowled and sold their shit in two-man cars—with shotguns in plain sight. A junkie tried to rob Ramón Gutiérrez. Teo Paez cut him down with rat-poison-laced buckshot.

Santo Junior was pleased so far. Santo proffered the #1 Cadre Commandment: You may not sample the merchandise. Pete proffered Commandment #2: If you use Big "H," I will kill you.

Miami was Crime Heaven. Blessington was the Pearly Gates To.

The campsite took up fourteen acres. The installation included two bunkhouses, a weapons shed, an operations hut, a drill field and a landing strip. A dock and speedboat launch site were still in construction.

Cadre recruiters jumped the gun and sent some training prospects down. Local crackers took offense at the spic squatters on their turf. Pete hired some unemployed Klansmen to work on the dock. The move facilitated a temporary peace—Klavernites and exiles were toiling together.

Fourteen squatters were now in residence. More exiles were fleeing Cuba every day. There were more CIA campsites pending—with forty-odd projected by mid-1960.

Castro would survive—just long enough to make Boyd and him rich.

The cross burned high and wide. Pete caught the glow from half a mile out.

A dirt road veered off the highway. Signs pointed the way: "Nigger stay out!" "KKK—White Man Unite!"

Bugs popped in through his air vents. Pete swatted them off. He saw a barbed-wire fence and Klansmen at parade rest.

They wore white robes and hoods with purple piping. Dig

their kanine kompanions: sheet-swaddled Doberman pinschers.

Pete flashed Banister's gate pass. The pointy-heads checked him out and waved him in.

He parked beside some trucks and went strolling. The cross lit up a segregated pine-forest clearing.

Cubans milled around on one side. Whites boogie-woogied on the other. A row of sign-plastered trailers divided them.

On his left: Klan bake sale, Klan rifle range, vendors hawking Klan regalia. On his right: the Blessington campsite duplicated.

Pete strolled the redneck side. Pointy-hoods bobbed his way—Hey, man, where's your sheet?

Bugs buzz-bombed the cross. Rifle shots and target pings overlapped. The humidity was close to 100%.

Nazi armbands went for $2.99. Jew rabbi voodoo dolls—a steal at 3 for $5.00.

Pete walked by the trailers. He saw a sandwich board propped up against an old Airstream: "WKKK—Rev. Evans Anti-Communist Crusade."

A hi-fi speaker was bolted to the axle. Sound sputtered out—pure crackpot gibberish.

He looked in the window. He saw twenty-odd cats pissing, shitting and fucking. A tall geek was screaming into a microphone. A cat was clawing some short-wave wires, about to get French-fried to kingdom come.

Pete scratched one prospect and kept walking. All the Caucasoids wore hoods—he couldn't match Hudspeth or Lockhart to their mug shots.

"Bondurant! Down here!"

It was Guy Banister's voice, booming up from below ground level.

A hatch snapped out of the dirt. A periscope thingamajig popped up and wiggled.

Guy had rigged himself a fucking bomb shelter.

Pete dropped down into it. Banister pulled the hatch shut behind him.

The space was twelve-by-twelve square. *Playboy* pinups covered the walls. Guy had socked in a shitload of Van Camp's pork & beans and bourbon.

Banister retracted the telescope. "You looked lonesome all by yourself with no sheet."

Pete stretched. His head grazed the ceiling.

"It's sweet, Guy."

"I thought you might like it."

"Who's paying for it?"

"Everybody."

"Which means?"

"Which means I own the land, and the Agency put up the buildings. Carlos Marcello donated three hundred thousand for guns, and Sam Giancana put up some money to buy off the State Police. The Klan folks pay to enter and sell their wares, and the exiles work four hours a day on a road crew and kick back half their pay to the Cause."

An air cooler hummed full-blast. The shelter was a goddamn igloo.

Pete shivered. "You said Hudspeth and Lockhart would be here."

"Hudspeth was arrested for grand theft auto this morning. It's his third offense, so there's no bail. Evans is here, though. And he's not a bad fellow, if you stay off the topic of religion."

Pete said, "He's got to be psycho. And Boyd and I don't want psychos working for us."

"But you'll employ more presentable psychos."

"Have it your way. And if it's Lockhart by default, I want a few minutes alone with him."

"Why?"

"Any man who parades around in a sheet has got to be able to convince me he can keep things compartmentalized."

Banister laughed. "That's a big word for a guy like you, Pete."

"People keep telling me that."

"That's because you're dealing with a higher type of person now that you're Agency."

"Like Evans?"

"Point taken. But offhand, I'd say that that man has stronger anti-Communist credentials than you do."

"Communism's bad for business. Don't pretend it's anything more than that."

Banister hooked his thumbs in his belt. "If you think that makes you sound worldly, you're sadly mistaken."

"Yeah?"

Banister smiled, too smug to live. "Accepting Communism is synonymous with promoting Communism. Your old nemesis Ward Littell accepts Communism, and a friend of mine in

Chicago told me that Mr. Hoover is building a pro-Communist profile on him, based on his inactions more than his actions. You see where being worldly and accepting gets you when the chips are down?"

Pete cracked some knuckles. "Go get Lockhart. You know what Boyd wants, so explain it to him. And from here on in, shit-can the lectures."

Banister flinched. Banister started to open his mouth.

Pete went "Boo!"

Banister scurried out the hatch, double-time quick.

The silence and cold air felt sweet. The canned goods and liquor looked tasty. The wallpaper looked sweet—Miss July, especially.

Say the Russians drop the A-bomb. Say you hole up here. Cabin fever might set in and convince you the women were real.

Lockhart dropped down the hatch. He wore a soot-flecked sheet, cinched by a gunbelt and two revolvers.

He had bright red hair and freckles. His drawl was deep Mississippi.

"The money I like, and the move to Florida don't bother me. But that no-lynching rule has gotta go."

Pete backhanded him. Dougie Frank stayed upright—give him an A-plus for balance.

"Man, I have killed oversized white trash for less than what you just did!"

Punk bravura: Give him a C-minus.

Pete slapped him again. Lockhart pulled his right-hand piece—but didn't aim it.

Nerves: A-plus. Sense of caution: B-minus.

Lockhart wiped blood off his chin. "I like Cubans. I might stretch my racial-exclusion policy and let your guys into my Klavern."

Sense of humor: A-plus.

Lockhart spit a tooth out. "Give *me* something. Let me know that I'm more than just some punching bag."

Pete winked. "Mr. Boyd and I might put you on a bonus plan. And the Agency just might give you your own Ku Klux Klan."

Lockhart did a Stepin Fetchit shuffle. "Thank you, massah! If you was pro-Klan like a real white man, I'd kiss the hem of your sheet!"

Pete kicked him in the balls.

He went down—but didn't yelp or whimper. He cocked his gun—but didn't fire.

The man got passing marks overall.

34

(New York City, 9/29/59)

THE CAB CRAWLED uptown. Kemper balanced paperwork on his briefcase.

A graph showed primary-election states divided by county. Intersecting columns listed his law-enforcement contacts.

He checkmarked the presumed Democrats. He crossed out the presumed GOP hardcases.

It was boring work. Joe should simply buy Jack the White House.

Traffic slogged. The cabbie rode his horn. Kemper played a game of Devil's Advocate—dissembling practice never hurt.

Bobby questioned his constant Florida sojourns. His response verged on indignation.

"I'm in charge of forwarding McClellan Committee evidence, aren't I? Well, the Sun Valley case sticks in my craw, and Florida's a state that Jack needs to carry in the general election. I've been down there talking to some disaffected Teamsters."

The cab passed through slums. Ward Littell crashed his thoughts.

They hadn't talked or corresponded in a month. The D'Onofrio killing made a brief news splash and stayed unsolved. Ward didn't call or write to comment.

He should contact Ward. He should find out if Mad Sal's death derived from his work as Ward's informant.

The driver stopped at the St. Regis. Kemper paid him and quick-walked to the desk.

A clerk hovered. Kemper said, "Would you buzz my suite and ask Miss Hughes to come down?"

The clerk slipped on a headset and punched his switchboard. Kemper checked his watch—they were running way late for dinner.

"She's on the phone, Mr. Boyd. There's a conversation in progress."

Kemper smiled. "It's probably Miss Hughes and my daughter. They talk for hours at hotel rates."

"It's Miss Hughes and a man, actually."

Kemper caught himself clenching. "Let me have your headset, would you?"

"Wellllll . . ."

Kemper slipped him ten dollars.

"Wellllll . . ."

Kemper went to fifty. The clerk palmed it and handed him his earphones.

Kemper slipped them on. Lenny Sands was talking, very high-pitched and fey.

". . . As terrible as he was he's dead, and he worked for the drunk just like me. There's the drunk and the brute, and now the brute has me writing these preposterous articles about Cuba. I can't name names, but Laura, my God . . ."

"You don't mean my friend Kemper Boyd?"

"He's not the one I'm afraid of. It's the brute and the drunk. You never know what the drunk will do, and I haven't heard from him since Sal was killed, which is driving me absolutely stark raving . . ."

It was compartmental turbulence. It would have to be contained.

35

(Chicago, 10/1/59)

WAVES PUSHED LITTER up on the shore. Paper cups and cruise-boat programs shredded at his feet.

Littell kicked them out of his way. He passed the spot where he dumped the Montrose B&E swag.

Garbage then, garbage now.

He had three dead men to light candles for. Jack Ruby seemed to be safe—he called the Carousel Club once a week to hear his voice.

Sal resisted torture. Sal never said "Littell" or "Ruby." Kabikoff knew him only as a cop in a ski mask.

"Mad Sal" and "Sid the Yid"—the nomenclature used to amuse him. Bobby Kennedy allegedly loved Mob nicknames.

He was sloughing off his Phantom reports. He was sloughing off his Red Squad work. He told SAC Leahy that God and Jesus Christ were leftists.

He cut Helen down to one night a week. He quit calling Lenny Sands. He had two constant companions: Old Overholt and Pabst Blue Ribbon.

A sodden magazine washed in. He saw a picture of Jack Kennedy and Jackie.

Kemper said the senator had hound blood. Kemper said Bobby held his marriage vows sacred.

Fat Sid said their dad knew Jules Schiffrin. Schiffrin kept the real Pension Fund books—liquor couldn't numb that one fact.

Littell cut over to Lake Shore Drive. His feet ached and his trouser cuffs spilled sand.

It was dusk. He'd been walking due south for hours.

His bearings clicked in. He saw that he was three blocks away from a real live destination.

He walked over and knocked on Lenny Sands' door. Lenny opened up and just stood there.

Littell said, "It's over. I won't ask anything else of you."

Lenny stepped closer. Words roared out in one long string.

Littell heard "stupid" and "worthless" and "coward." He looked Lenny in the eyes and stood there while he roared himself breathless.

36

(Chicago, 10/2/59)

KEMPER SNAPPED THE lock with his Diners Club card. Lenny didn't learn that it takes deadbolts to keep rogue cops out.

Littell never learned that INFORMANTS DON'T RETIRE. He observed the retirement gala from the street—and saw Ward soak up abuse like a true flagellant.

Kemper closed the door and stood in the dark. Lenny walked to the A&P ten minutes ago, and should return within half an hour.

Laura learned not to press embarrassing topics. She never mentioned that call at the St. Regis.

Kemper heard footsteps and key sounds. He moved toward the light switch and screwed the silencer to his piece.

Lenny walked in. Kemper said, "It's not over."

A shopping bag fell. Glass broke.

"You don't talk to Laura or Littell again. You work *Hush-Hush* for Pete. You find out everything you can about the Pension Fund books and report exclusively to me."

Lenny said, "No."

Kemper hit the switch. The living room lit up—antique-over-furnished and *très, très* effete.

Lenny blinked. Kemper shot the legs off an armoire. The crash shattered bone china and crystal.

He shot up a bookcase. He shot a Louis Fourteen couch into stuffing wads and wood chips. He shot up a hand-painted Chippendale wardrobe.

Sawdust and muzzle smoke swirled. Kemper got out a fresh clip.

Lenny said, "Yes."

DOCUMENT INSERT: 10/5/59.
Hush-Hush magazine article. Written by Lenny Sands, under the pseudonym Peerless Politicopundit.

CANCEROUS CASTRO COMMUNISTICALLY CALCIFIES CUBA
WHILE HEROIC HERMANOS HUNGER FOR HOMELAND!

He's been in power a scant ten months, but the Free World already has the number of that slogan-slamming, stogie-stinking strongman Fidel Castro!

Castro ousted the democratically-elected anti-Communist Cuban Premier Fulgencio Batista last New Year's day. The bombastic bushy-bearded beatnik bard promised land reforms, social justice and pickled plantains on every plate—the standard stipends of welfare-waffled Commie commissars. He took over a small bastion of freedom 90 miles off U.S. shores, pathologically picked the pockets of patriotic patriarchs, nauseously ''nationalized'' U.S.-owned hotel-casinos, fried the friendly fragrant fields of the United Fruit Company and generally absconded with

astronomical amounts of America's most peon-
protecting, Commie-constraining export: money!!!

Yes, kats and kittens, it all comes down to
divinely-deigned dollops of dollars U.S., of course,
those gorgeously garlanded greenbacks replete with
pulsatingly powerful Presidential portraits,
caricatures captivating in their corrosive
condemnation of Communism!!!

Item: the beatnik bard bamboozled beleaguered
bellhops at the formerly swank Nacional and Capri
hotels in Havana, nastily nationalized their tips and
rapidly replaced them with a regiment of rowdy Red
regulators—bandy-legged bantamweight bandidos who
also serve as crucifyingly-corrupt craps croupiers!

Item: fruit fields frantically french-fried! Peons
passionately protected by America's altruistically-
altered egalitarian economy are now welfare-wilted,
pauper-periled Red Recidivists grubbing for Commie
compensation!

Item: Raul ''The Tool'' Castro has flamboyantly
flooded Florida with hellishly horrific, hophead-
hazarding amounts of the demonically deadly ''Big
H'': Heroin!!! He's bent on needle-notching vast
legions of Cuban immigrant slaves: zorched-out
zombies to spread the cancerous Castro gospel between
bouts of Heroin-hiatused, junkie-junketeered
euphoria!

Item: there's a growing number of Cuban exiles and
homegrown American patriots who take egregious
exception to the beatnik brothers' broadside of
bamboozlement. Right now they're recruiting in Miami
and South Florida. These men are tantalizingly tough
tigers who have earned their orange-and-black—not
Red—stripes in the jungles of Castro's jam-packed,
jerry-rigged jails. Every day, more and more men like
them are arriving on America's shores, anxious to
sing the mellifluous melodies of ''My Country 'Tis of
Thee.''

This reporter talked to an American named ''Big
Pete,'' a dedicated anti-Communist currently
training anti-Castro guerrillas. ''It all comes down

to patriotism,'' Big Pete said. ''Do you want a
Communist dictatorship 90 miles off our shores or
not? I don't, so I've joined the Cuban Freedom Cause.
And I'd like to extend an invitation to all Cuban
exiles and native-born men of Cuban descent. Join us.
If you're in Miami, ask around. Local Cubans will tell
you we mean business.''

   Item: with men like Big Pete on the job, Castro
should be considering a new career. Hey! I know a few
coffeehouses in L.A.'s way-out Venice West who could
use a gone beatnik poet like Fidel! Hey, Fidel! Can
you dig it, Daddy-O?

   Remember, dear reader, you heard it first here: off
the record, on the Q.T. and <u>very</u> Hush-Hush.

<u>DOCUMENT INSERT</u>: 10/19/59.
Personal Note: J. Edgar Hoover to Howard Hughes.

Dear Howard,

   I greatly enjoyed Peerless Politicopundit's piece
in the October 5th issue of Hush-Hush. It was, of
course, far-fetched, but subtract the purple prose
and what remains is politically substantive.

   Lenny Sands has certainly adapted to the Hush-Hush
style. And as a fledgling propagandist he shows
promise. I found the subliminally-planted plugs for
the Tiger Kab Kompany to be a nice little aside to the
cognoscenti, and especially enjoyed the lofty
sentiments expressed by our pragmatist friend Pierre
Bondurant.

   All in all, a most salutary issue.

                              Warmest regards, Edgar

<u>DOCUMENT INSERT</u>: 10/30/59.
Summary Report: John Stanton to Kemper Boyd.
Marked: <u>CONFIDENTIAL/HAND POUCH DELIVER</u>.

Dear Kemper,

   A short note to keep you advised of some recent

policy decisions. You remain hard to reach, so I'm
sending this to you via courier.

First off, our superiors are now more than ever
convinced that the Castro problem will extend.
Although the President's latest allocation came in
low, we have every hope that Castro's powers of
persistence will loosen up the White House
pursestrings. To paraphrase our friend Peerless
Politicopundit: ''Nobody wants a Communist
dictatorship ninety miles from our shores.'' (I wish
I could write reports like he writes yellow journalism.)

Mr. Dulles, Deputy Director Bissell and selected
Cuban-expert case officers are beginning to plan for
an exile invasion in late 1960 or early 1961. It is
assumed that by that date the Agency will have a pool
of at least ten thousand well-trained U.S.-based
exile troops to draw from, and that public opinion
will be strongly on our side. The general idea is to
launch an amphibious assault force, backed by air
cover, from Gulf Coast campsite-launch sites. I'll
keep you abreast as plans develop further. And you
keep at our friend Jack. If this plan stays on hold
until after January 20, 1961, there's a chance he'll
be the man to approve it or scrap it.

Since we last spoke, eleven more ''Banana Barges''
have landed in Florida and Louisiana. Regional case
officers have been assigned immigrant caseloads and
are dispersing the men to various campsites. Many who
decline regular Agency assistance will be heading to
Miami. I'll be curious to see if our Cadre latches on
to any of them. As I'm sure you know, the Blessington
site is now ready to house troops formally. I have
approved the hiring of Douglas Frank Lockhart to run
the camp, and I think it is time to rotate our Cadre on
a Miami-business, Blessington-training axis. Put
Pete Bondurant and Chuck Rogers on this immediately,
and have Bondurant pouch deliver a report to me inside
six weeks.

Per our Cadre's Miami ''business,'' and in keeping
with our elliptical way of discussing it, I'll state
that I'm glad profits seem to be growing and that the

agreement you reached with our Agency-friendly source in Mexico seems to be flourishing. I envision a time when our superiors will vet this ''business'' as good common sense, but until anti-Castro rancor or whatever reaches that point I must stress absolute compartmentalization and secrecy. Mr. Trafficante's participation must remain secret, and I would not want it generally known that Mr. S. Giancana and Mr. C. Marcello have also contributed to the Cause.

Keep me posted, and burn this communique.

All best, John

DOCUMENT INSERT: 11/1/59.
Summary Report: Kemper Boyd to Robert F. Kennedy.

Dear Bob,

I had a talk with James Dowd, the head of the Organized Crime Section at the Department of Justice. (I knew him when he was with the U.S. Attorney's Office.) As a courtesy, I had sent Mr. Dowd carbons of the paperwork I forwarded to various grand juries seeking Hoffa evidence, and now that courtesy seems to be bringing results.

As you know, the Landrum-Griffin Labor Reform Bill passed Congress, so now the Republican-dominated Justice Department has a clear ''Get Hoffa'' mandate. Dowd has deployed investigators and assistant-counsels to grand jury investigatory bodies in Ohio, Louisiana and Florida. The McClellan Committee spawned Landrum-Griffin; everyone knows it. Dowd has seen the political light and has decided to concentrate his energy on our Sun Valley evidence. (He thinks the two missing witnesses—Gretzler and Kirpaski—give it a moral weight.) As of 10/25/59, he had assigned six men to serve with three south Florida grand juries. They are actively seeking disgruntled Teamsters who had purchased Sun Valley property. Dowd thinks the ''Get Hoffa'' process will be grindingly attenuated, which suits our political purposes to a degree.

My strongest sense is that <u>we do not want ''Get
Hoffa'' rancor to go too bi-partisan</u>, and we <u>do</u> want
Jack to stand out as <u>the</u> anti-labor corruption
candidate. Dowd told me that he expects Hoffa to
barnstorm primary election states and deluge voters
with anti-Kennedy sentiment, and I think this may
play into our hands. As hard as he sometimes tries to
hide it, under duress Hoffa always comes off as a
psychopathic thug. We want the Teamsters to endorse
the Republican candidate. We want Richard Nixon to
take Hoffa's money and sidestep labor corruption as
an issue in the general election. That said, I think
it is imperative that Jack redouble his efforts to woo
legitimate labor leaders and convince them that he
differentiates them from Hoffaites.

I'm shifting my emphasis now to the primaries. The
Kennedy crime fighter image has impressed many of my
normally-Republican law enforcement acquaintances,
and I'm working my way through Wisconsin, New
Hampshire and West Virginia county by county. Your
local organizations seem sound, and I've told each
and every volunteer I've met to keep their ears down
for Hoffa barnstorming scuttlebutt.

More later. Write your book; I think it could be a
valuable campaign tool.

                                    Yours, Kemper

DOCUMENT INSERT: 11/9/59.
Memorandum: Robert F. Kennedy to Kemper Boyd.

Kemper,

Thanks for the note. You're starting to think
politically, and I think your Hoffa-Republican
observations were quite astute. I'm glad the Justice
Department has focused on Sun Valley, which I have
always considered our strongest Hoffa case.

I've always believed that illegally-procured
Pension Fund money (the ''Spooky'' 3 million) financed
Hoffa's Sun Valley investment, and that Hoffa skimmed
a large amount off the top. Some Pension Fund leads

and/or intelligence on the possibility of ''Real''
Pension Fund books would do us a lot of good now.
What's the Chicago Phantom been doing? You've always
portrayed this anonymous Jesuit crusader as quite a
worker, but you haven't forwarded a Phantom report to
me in months.

Bob

DOCUMENT INSERT: 11/17/59.
Note: Kemper Boyd to Robert F. Kennedy.

Dear Bob,

I agree. We certainly could use some Pension Fund
leads now. The Phantom is working hard, but he's run
up against one brick wall after another. And keep in
mind, he's an FBI agent with a full load of regular
duties. He's persisting, but as I've said before,
it's very slow going.

Kemper

DOCUMENT INSERT: 12/4/59.
FBI Field Surveillance Report: Chicago Special
Agent-in-Charge Charles Leahy to J. Edgar Hoover.
Marked: EXTREMELY CONFIDENTIAL/DIRECTOR'S EYES
ONLY.

Sir,

Per your request, agents co-opted from the Sioux
City Office have kept SA Ward J. Littell under spot
surveillance since 9/15/59. He has not been observed
in the vicinity of Celano's Tailor Shop, and he has
apparently refrained from covert anti-Organized
Crime activity. He has not been seen with SA Kemper
Boyd, and the (11/20/59 initiated) tap on his home
telephone indicates that he speaks only to Helen
Agee, with occasional calls to his ex-wife Margaret.
He does not call or receive calls from his daughter
Susan, and since the 11/20/59 tap initiation date SA
Boyd has not called him.

Littell's work performance has steadily

deteriorated. This decline was in effect before the
spot tails were initiated. Assigned to surveil CPUSA
members in Hyde Park and Rogers Park, Littell
frequently abandons his surveillance positions to
drink in taverns or visit various Catholic churches.

Littell's Red Squad reports have been slipshod. He
regularly misrepresents the hours he spends on his
assignments and his comments on CPUSA members can
only be considered overly charitable.

On 11/26/59, SA W.R. Hinckle observed CPUSA cell
leader Malcolm Chamales accost Littell outside his
apartment building. Chamales accused Littell of
''FBI black bag chicanery'' and challenged him to
respond. Littell invited Chamales to a tavern. SA
Hinckle observed them engaged in a political discussion. They met again on 11/29 and 12/1. SA Hinckle
observed both meetings and believes the two men are
becoming friends or at least drinking companions.

Bureau-friendly University of Chicago sources have
reported that SA Littell and Helen Agee have been seen
on campus arguing heatedly. Their affair appears to
be strained and Miss Agee was overheard urging
Littell to seek help for his drinking problem. On 11/
3/59, SA J.S. Burtler observed Littell and Miss Agee
engage in a political discussion. Miss Agee expressed
admiration for Vice-President Richard Nixon. Littell
referred to Mr. Nixon as ''Tricky Dick'' and called
him a ''Red-baiting, slush-fund financed crypto-
fascist.''

In conclusion: a pro-Communist profile of Littell is
now being compiled. I believe that his subversive
statements, treasonous Red Squad omissions and
friendship with Malcolm Chamales will continue and
comprise a damaging security risk portrait.

Respectfully, Charles Leahy
SAC, Chicago Office

DOCUMENT INSERT: 12/21/59.
Field Report: Pete Bondurant to Kemper Boyd, ``For
Forwarding to John Stanton.''
Marked: <u>KB—BE CAREFUL HOW YOU TRANSMIT THIS</u>.

KB,

   Sorry this report Stanton wanted is late. I don't
like writing things down, so cross out what you want
and get it to him. Make sure Stanton destroys it.
I know he thinks the Agency will go along with what
we're doing 100% somewhere down the line, but that
might be a long time.
   1.—My Klan workers finished up the dock and the
speedboat launch-site. Blessington's now 100%
operational.
   2.—Dougie Frank Lockhart is solid. He's got the
usual crazy ideas that guys in his line of work have,
but that's just the way things are & I don't think
it's too bad if it doesn't interfere with his job. His
FBI contact was pissed that he won't be snitching
those rival KKK's in Louisiana, but he changed his
tune when Lockhart told him you were heading up the
operation. My guess is that he checked with Hoover,
who told him you have carte blanche. Lockhart has done
a good job so far. I got some $ from Trafficante for
him & he's used it to start up his own Klan outside
Blessington. He handed out signing bonuses and all
the local Klan guys quit their old Klans to sign on
with Dougie Frank. I've told him you want no
lynchings, church bombings or beatings. He's
disappointed, but going along. Lockhart gets along
with Cubans & has told his Klan guys not to stir up any
racial trouble with the Cadre or our trainees. So far,
the guys have gone along with his orders.
   3.—Our Miami business is good and getting better.
Last month's gross at the Booker T. Washington
Housing Project was 14% higher than the Trafficante
organization's best month ever. The October gross at
the George Washington Carver Project was 9% higher
than ST's best. Chuck Rogers says the men at the

Mexican ranch are solid. They set up a deal where he
can fly in & out without filing flight logs with the Mex.
State Police. We've got a landing strip at
Blessington now, so Chuck can make the pick-up runs
that much safer. I've been driving the split money to
ST in Tampa every week. He's pleased with his profits
and has been dishing out bonus $ to the Cadre
regularly. He's been kicking back 15% directly to me
to funnel into the Cause and 5% to a gun fund that Guy
Banister has set up in New Orleans. So far, Fulo,
Chuck, Paez, Obregon, Delsol & Gutierrez have been
completely honest. There have been no shortages of
merchandise or $.

   4.—Stanton wanted fitness reports on the men. My
feeling is that until somebody steals merchandise or
$ or punks out on a job they all deserve A+ ratings.
Obregon's a little gunshy about speedboat runs into
Cuba & his cousin Delsol is a little shifty, but so
far this is just minor stuff. What matters is that
these are pro-U.S., anti-Castro diehards who don't
steal from Trafficante. I say let them bootjack fares
at the cabstand and blow off steam with booze and
whores. I say you can't snap their leashes too hard or
they'll get antsy.

   5.—As recruiters, they're not bad. We've got 44
bunks at Blessington & they've been keeping them
filled up. Chuck, Fulo, Lockhart & me have been
training the men in 15 day cycles. We teach small
arms, riflery, hand-to-hand combat & speedboat
sabotage techniques, then funnel the men to Miami
with job leads. The men recruit there & send their own
prospects to a case officer codenamed HK/Cougar, who
sends them to one of the Agcy-backed resident
training camps according to bunk-availability. If
this invasion you told me about ever comes off we
should have a surplus of well-trained soldiers to
pick from.

   6.—Paez, Obregon, Delsol, Gutierrez, Fulo & me have
all made night speedboat runs into Cuba. We've
dropped off merchandise with our on-island contacts &
gunned down some militia patrol boats. Fulo &

Gutierrez made a run & saw some militiamen sleeping on
the beach. They killed all 30 with Tommy guns. Fulo
scalped the ranking officer & now flies the scalp on
the radio antenna of our lead boat.

7.—Like you wanted, I'm spreading myself between
Blessington, our Miami business & the cabstand. Jimmy
Hoffa is sort of pissed that you're pals with the
Kennedys, but he's pleased with the lease deal, & the
more Cuban immigrants that hit Miami the more $ Tiger
Kab makes. And thanks for the merchandise you gave me
for H.H. Since I'm in Florida all the time I guess
that that stuff is what's keeping me on his payroll.
I'd quit, but I know you want to cultivate some kind
of Agcy. connection with him. I call him once a week
to keep my hand in. H.H. says he's got Mormons looking
after him now. They're helping him dodge the TWA
process servers & doing the work I used to, except for
procuring merchandise. I think that as long as I can
supply that I'll draw an L.A. paycheck.

8.—Lenny Sands is editing Hush-Hush single-
handedly. I thought that Cuban piece he wrote
was pretty good & got some good plugs in for the
Cause.

That's it. I don't like writing things down, so
tell Stanton to destroy this.

Viva La Causa!

                                        PB

37

(Blessington, 12/24/59)

LOCKHART PUT HIS feet up on the dashboard. His fiber-fill Santa
Claus suit had him sweating.

"You won't let me bomb churches or kill niggers. Now, what
about enforcing the Klan Moral Kode?"

Pete played in—Dougie Frank was good for yuks. "What's
that?"

"Well, you get word Joe Redneck's sister Sally has eyes for
Leroy with the rumored 12-inch hog leg, and you catch them at

it. You heat up your KKK branding iron and mark Sally as a race mixer."

"What about Leroy?"

"You ask him where he got his, and do they make them that size in white."

Pete laughed. Dougie Frank blew his nose out the window.

"I'm serious, Pete. I'm the Imperial Wizard of the South Florida Royal Knights of the Ku Klux Klan, and so far all I've done is hand out CIA bonus money and start up a softball team to play your goddamn crypto-jigaboo exiles."

Pete swerved around a stray dog. The truck hit a pothole; the gift-wrapped turkeys in the back bounced and slid.

"Don't tell me your FBI operator let you do lynchings."

"No, he didn't. But he also didn't say, 'Dougie Frank, don't kill no niggers while you're on the U.S. Government payroll, now.' You see the difference? You're *tellin'* me I can't do it, and you mean it."

Pete saw shacks up ahead—good turkey drop-off spots. Santo Junior said to lube the locals—he had excess poultry stock off a hijack and figured free Christmas birds would promote goodwill.

"Do your job. This is big stuff we're involved in, so treat it seriously."

Lockhart said, "I am. I am doing my job and keeping my mouth shut about Chuck Rogers flying white powder airlines into the Fort Blessington airstrip, yessir. What I'm also sayin' is my boys need some recreation."

Pete swung around a turn. "I'll talk to Jimmy Hoffa. Maybe he can take your guys out shark shooting."

"What I had in mind was enforcing Moral Kode Bylaw Number Sixty-nine."

"What's that?"

"That's where you catch Leroy's brothers Tyrone and Rufus knockin' on Sally's door."

"What do you do?"

"Tar and feather Sally."

"What about Tyrone and Rufus?"

"You make them pull down their pants to see if it runs in the family."

Pete laughed. Dougie Frank scratched his snowy-white beard. "How come I'm the one who had to dress up like Santa Claus?"

"I couldn't find a red suit my size."

"You could have dressed up one of the Cubans."

"Come on. A spic Santa Claus?"

"I think this job is degrading."

Pete pulled into a ratty dirt playground. Some colored kids saw Santa and went gaga.

Dougie Frank got out and lobbed turkeys at them. The kids ran up and tugged at his beard.

The local whites got turkeys. The local jigs got turkeys. The Blessington cops got turkeys and hijack Jim Beam.

The trainees got turkey dinners and Trojan prophylactics. Santo Junior sent down a Christmas treat: a busload of Tampa whores. Forty-four men and forty-four hookers made for squeaks off forty-four bunks.

Pete sent the girls home at midnight. Lockhart burned a Yuletide cross out in the boonies. Pete got an urge to hit Cuba and kill Commies.

He called Fulo in Miami. Fulo dug the idea. Fulo said, I'll round up some guys and drive down.

Chuck Rogers flew a load of dope in. Pete gassed up the lead speedboat.

Lockhart cruised by with some moonshine. Pete and Chuck traded chugs. Nobody smoked—the shit might ignite.

They sat on the dock. Floodlights lit up the whole campsite.

A trainee screamed in his sleep. Embers blew down off the cross. Pete remembered Xmas '45: The L.A. Sheriff's signed him on fresh out of the Marine Corps.

Fulo's car dipsy-doodled across the runway. Chuck stacked Tommy guns and ammo by the dock moorings.

Dougie Frank said, "Can I go?"

Pete said, "Sure."

Delsol, Obregón and Fulo piled out of the Chevy. They walked sway-bellied—blitzed by too much beer and turkey.

They waddled over to the dock. Tomás Obregón wore shades—at 2:00 A.M. Shades *and* long sleeves—on a half-assed balmy night.

A dog barked out in the sticks. Chuck Rogers mimicked hound yelps like this late-nite cracker deejay he grooved on. Everybody traded holiday back slaps.

Pete slapped Obregón's shades off. The fuck had dope-pinned eyes—floodlight glare nailed them clean.

Obregón froze. Rogers threw a choke hold on him.

Nobody talked. Nobody had to—the picture spread *rápidamente*.

Obregón squirmed. Fulo jerked his sleeves up. Skin-pop tracks ran down his arms, red and ugly.

Everybody looked at Delsol—Obregón's fucking cousin. The picture spread: Let *him* do it.

Chuck let Obregón go. Pete handed his gun to Delsol.

Obregón trembled and almost teetered off the dock. Delsol shot him six times in the chest.

He spun into the water. Steam hissed out his exit wounds.

Fulo dove in and scalped him.

Delsol looked away.

38

(Hyannis Port, 12/25/59)

A CHRISTMAS TREE grazed the ceiling. Spray-on snowflakes dusted a huge pile of gifts.

Kemper sipped eggnog. Jack said, "Holidays make you sad, I can tell."

"Not exactly."

"My parents overdid having children, but yours should have had the foresight to give you a sibling or two."

"I had a younger brother. He died in a hunting accident."

"I didn't know that."

"My father and I were stalking deer near our summer place. We kept getting glimpses, and kept firing through brush. One of the glimpses was Compton Wickwire Boyd, age eight. He was wearing a tan jacket and a hat with white ear flaps. It was October 19, 1934."

Jack looked away. "Kemper, I'm sorry."

"I shouldn't have mentioned it. You said you wanted to talk, and I have to leave for New York in an hour. That story is a guaranteed conversation-stopper."

The den was overheated. Jack inched his chair away from the fireplace.

"You're meeting Laura?"

"Yes. My daughter's having Christmas dinner with some

friends in South Bend, then going on a ski trip. She'll be joining Laura and I in New York."

Pete's ring was buffed and polished. He was set to pop the question tonight.

"You and Laura were a hell of a shock."

"But you're getting used to it?"

"I think everyone is, to one degree or another."

"You're nervous, Jack."

"I'm announcing in eight days. Obstacles keep popping up in my mind, and I keep wondering how to deal with them."

"For instance?"

"West Virginia. What do I say to a coal miner who says, 'Son, I heard your daddy's one of the richest men in America, and you never had to work a day in your life?'"

Kemper smiled. "You say, 'That's true.' And a grizzled old character actor that we plant in the crowd says, 'And son, you ain't missed a damn thing.'"

Jack roared. Kemper snapped to a connection: Giancana and Trafficante ran big blocks of West Virginia.

"I know some people down there who might be able to help you."

"Then indebt me to them in unconscionable ways, so I can embrace my genetic fate as a corrupt Irish politician."

Kemper laughed. "You're still nervous. And you said you wanted to talk to me, which implied a serious discussion."

Jack rocked his chair back and brushed fake snow off his sweater. "We've been thinking of Mr. Hoover. We were thinking he knows the story of Laura's parentage."

Devil's Advocate clicked in, automatically. "He's known for years. He knows I'm seeing Laura, and he told me the facts of her parentage before she did."

Bobby's kids romped through the room. Jack shooed them out and toed the door shut.

"That voyeuristic little faggot cocksucker."

Kemper ad-libbed. "He also knows about all your paternity buyouts, and most of your sustained affairs. Jack, I'm your best hedge against Hoover. He likes me and trusts me, and all he wants is to keep his job if you're elected."

Jack tapped a humidor on his chin. "Dad's got himself half-convinced that Hoover sent you over to spy on us."

"Your dad's no dummy."

"*What?*"

"Hoover caught me skimming off a car-theft investigation and retired me early. I applied for the McClellan Committee job on my own, and Hoover started keeping tabs on me. He learned I was seeing Laura and asked me for information on you. I said no, and Hoover said, 'You owe me one.' "

Jack nodded. His look said: Yes, I'll buy that.

"Dad had a private detective follow you around Manhattan. The man said you keep a suite at the St. Regis."

Kemper winked. "The way you live rubs off, Jack. I've got a pension, a salary and stock dividends, and I'm courting an expensive woman."

"You're in Florida a good deal."

"Hoover has me spying on pro-Castro groups. It's that 'one' I owe him."

"That's why you're so hipped on Cuba as a campaign issue."

"Right. I think Castro's a goddamned menace, and I think you should take a hard line against him."

Jack lit his cigar. His look said: Thank God this is over.

"I'll tell Dad it's all okay. He wants a promise, though."

"Which is?"

"That you won't marry Laura any time soon. He's afraid reporters might get nosy."

Kemper handed him the ring. "Keep this for me. I was planning to ask Laura tonight, but I guess I'll have to wait until you're elected."

Jack slipped it in his pocket. "Thanks. Does this mean you're out a Christmas gift?"

"I'll pick something up in New York."

"There's an emerald pin under the tree there. Laura looks good in green, and Jackie won't miss it."

39

(South Bend, 12/25/59)

LITTELL GOT OFF the train and checked for tails.

The arrivals and departures looked normal—just Notre Dame kids and anxious parents. Some cheerleaders shivered—short-skirted pompom girls out in ten-degree weather.

The crowd dispersed. No platform loiterers stuck close to him. In a phrase: The Phantom sees phantoms.

Tail sightings were a probable booze by-product. The clicks on his phone line were most likely overactive nerves.

He'd dismantled his two phones. He found no wiretap apparatus. The Mob couldn't rig *outside* taps—only police agencies could. That man watching him and Mal Chamales last week—probably just a barfly tweaked by their left-of-center conversation.

Littell hit the station lounge and knocked back three rye-and-beers. Christmas dinner with Susan mandated fortification.

Amenities dragged. Talk bounced between safe topics.

Susan tensed when he hugged her. Helen steered clear of his hands. Claire had grown into a distaff Kemper—the resemblance had solidified amazingly.

Susan never addressed him by name. Claire called him "Ward baby"—Helen said she was in a Rat Pack phase. Susan smoked like her mother now—straight down to match flicks and exhales.

Her apartment mimicked Margaret's: too many porcelain knickknacks and too much stiff furniture.

Claire played Sinatra records. Susan served diluted eggnog—Helen must have told her that her father drank to excess.

He said he hadn't heard from Kemper in months. Claire smiled—she knew all her father's secrets. Susan laid out dinner: Margaret's boring glazed ham and sweet potatoes.

They sat down. Littell bowed his head and offered a prayer.

"O heavenly Father, we ask thy blessing on all of us, and on our absent friends. I commend to you the souls of three men recently departed, whose deaths were caused by arrogant if heartfelt attempts to facilitate justice. I ask you to bless all of us on this sacred day and in the year to come."

Susan rolled her eyes and said "Amen." Claire carved the ham; Helen poured wine.

The girls got full glasses. He got a splash. It was cheap Cabernet Sauvignon.

Claire said, "My Dad's proposing to his mistress tonight. Let's hear it for my Dad and my nifty new mom, who's only nine and a half years older than me."

Littell almost gagged. Social climber Kemper as secret Kennedy in-law—

Susan said, "Claire, really. 'Mistress' and 'nifty' in the same sentence?"

Claire made cat claws. "You forgot to mention the age difference. How could you? We both know that age gaps are your pet peeve."

Helen groaned. Susan pushed her plate aside and lit a cigarette.

Littell filled his glass. Claire said, "Ward baby, assess the three of us as attorneys."

Littell smiled. "It's not hard. Susan prosecutes misdemeanors, Helen defends wayward FBI men, and Claire goes into corporate law to finance her father's expensive tastes in his old age."

Helen and Claire laughed. Susan said, "I don't appreciate being defined by pettiness."

Littell gulped wine. "You can join the Bureau, Susie. I'll be retiring in a year and twenty-one days, and you can take my place and torment pathetic leftists for Mr. Hoover."

"I wouldn't characterize Communists as pathetic, Father. And I don't think you could support your bar tab on a twenty-year pension."

Claire flinched. Helen said, "Susan, please."

Littell grabbed the bottle. "Maybe I'll go to work for John F. Kennedy. Maybe he'll be elected President. His brother hates organized crime more than Communists, so maybe it runs in the family."

Susan said, "I can't believe you place common hoodlums in the same league as a political system that has enslaved half the world. I can't believe that you could be hoodwinked by a fatuous liberal politician whose father intends to buy him the presidency."

"Kemper Boyd likes him."

"Excuse me, Father, and excuse me, Claire, but Kemper Boyd worships money, and we all know that John F. Kennedy has plenty of that."

Claire ran out of the room. Littell flat-guzzled wine.

"Communists don't castrate innocent men. Communists don't hook up car batteries to people's genitals and electrocute them. Communists don't drop TV sets into bathtubs or—"

Helen ran out. Susan said, "Father, goddamn you for your weakness."

* * *

He called in accumulated sick leave and holed up through New Year's. The A&P delivered food and liquor.

Law school finals kept Helen away. They talked on the phone—mostly petty chitchat and sighs. He heard occasional clicks on the line and wrote them off to nerves.

Kemper didn't call or write. The man was ignoring him.

He read Bobby Kennedy's book about the Hoffa wars. The story thrilled him. Kemper Boyd did not appear in the text.

He watched the Rose Bowl and Cotton Bowl on TV. He eulogized Icepick Tony Iannone—dead one year ago exactly.

Exactly four rye-and-beers induced euphoria. He fantasized an exact form of courage: the will to move on Jules Schiffrin and the Fund books.

More liquor killed the notion. To move meant to sacrifice lives. His courage was weakness pushed into grandiosity.

He watched John Kennedy announce his Presidential candidacy. The Senate Caucus Room was packed with his supporters.

Cameras cut to a picket line outside. Teamsters chanted: "Hey, hey, ho, ho, Kennedy says 'Labor NO!' "

A reporter spoke voice-over: "A Florida grand jury has Teamster president James R. Hoffa under close scrutiny. He is suspected of felony land fraud in matters pertaining to the Teamsters' Sun Valley development."

An insert shot caught Hoffa laughing off Sun Valley.

Littell juxtaposed words:

Pete, kill some men for me, will ya?

Father, goddamn you for your weakness.

40

(Tampa, 2/1/60)

JACK RUBY SAID, "I am desperate. That well-known indigent Sal D. owed me a bundle when he died, and the IRS is climbing up my you-know-what for back payments I ain't got. I'm overextended on my club, Sam already turned me down, and you know I am a great friend to the Cuban Cause. A pal and me brought strippers down to entertain the boys in Blessington, which was strictly voluntary on my part and has nothing to do with the request I just made."

Santo Junior sat at his desk. Ruby stood in front of it. Three fat German shepherds drooped off the couch.

Pete watched Ruby grovel. The office stunk: Santo gave his dogs free run of the furniture.

Ruby said, "I am desperate. I am here before you like a supplicant before his local pontiff."

Trafficante said, "No. You brought some girls down when I was locked up in Havana, but that is not ten grand's worth of collateral. I can let you have a thousand out of my pocket, but that's it."

Ruby stuck his hand out. Santo greased him with C-notes off a flash roll. Pete got up and opened the door.

Ruby walked out fondling the money. Santo spritzed cologne on the spot where he stood groveling.

"That man is rumored to have strange sexual tastes. He could give you diseases that would put cancer to shame. Now, tell me some good things, because I don't like to start my day with beggars."

Pete said, "Profits went up 2% in December and January. I think Wilfredo Delsol's okay on his cousin, and I don't think he'd ever rat off the Cadre. Nobody's stealing from us, and I think the Obregón thing put a good little scare out."

"Somebody's fucking up, or you wouldn't've asked to see me."

"Fulo's been running whores. He's got them turning tricks for five-dollar pops and candy bars. He's turning over all the money, but I still think it's bad business."

Trafficante said, "Make him stop."

Pete sat on the edge of the couch. King Tut put out a cursory growl.

"Lockhart and his Klan buddies built a social club down the road from the campsite, and now they're talking about lynching spooks. On top of that, Lockhart's pals with that Dallas cop guy J.D. that drove down here with Ruby. Chuck Rogers wants to take J.D. up in his plane and drop some hate leaflets. He's talking about saturation-bombing South Florida."

Trafficante slapped his desk blotter. "Make this foolishness stop."

"I will."

"You didn't have to run this by me."

"Kemper thinks all discipline should initiate with you. He

wants the men to think we're labor as opposed to management."

"Kemper's a subtle guy."

Pete stroked King Farouk and King Arthur. Fucking King Tut evil-eyed him.

"He's every bit of subtle."

"Castro turned my casinos into pigsties. He lets goats shit on the carpets my wife picked out personally."

Pete said, "He'll pay."

He drove back to Miami. The cabstand was packed with loafers: Lockhart, Fulo, and the whole fucking Cadre.

Minus Chuck Rogers—up in his airplane dropping hate bombs.

Pete shut down the stand and laid down The Law. He called it the Declaration of Cadre Non-Independence and the New KKK Bill of Non-Rights.

No pimping. No robbery. No flim-flam. No B&E. No extortion. No hijacking.

No lynching. No nigger assaults. No church bombings. No racial shit directed at Cubans.

The Blessington Klan's specific mandate:

Love all Cubans. Leave them alone. Fuck up anybody who fucks with your new Cuban brethren.

Lockhart called the mandate quasi-genocidal. Pete cracked his knuckles. Lockhart shut his mouth.

The huddle broke up. Jack Ruby came by and begged a ride— his carburetor blew, and he needed to run his girls down to Blessington.

Pete said okay. The girls wore capris and halter tops—things could be worse.

Ruby rode up front. J.D. Tippit and the strippers rode in the back of the truck. Rain clouds were brewing—if a storm hit, they were screwed.

Pete took two-lane roadways south. He played the radio to keep Ruby quiet. Chuck Rogers flew down from deep nowhere and spun tree-level backflips.

The girls cheered. Chuck dropped a six-pack; J.D. caught it. Hate leaflets blew down—Pete plucked one out of the air.

"Six Reasons Why Jesus Was Pro-Klan." #1 set the tone: because Commies fluoridated the Red Sea.

Ruby eyeballed the scenery. Tippit and the girls guzzled beer.

Chuck blew off his flight pattern and brick-bombed a nigger church.

The radio signal faded. Ruby started whining.

"Santo don't possess the world's longest memory. Santo stiffs me with one-tenth of what I asked him for 'cause his memory's nine-tenths on the blink. Santo don't understand the tsuris I went through bringing those ladies down to Havana. Sure the Beard was giving him grief. But he didn't have no crazy Fed from Chicago leeching onto him."

Pete snapped to. "What Fed from Chicago?"

"I don't know his name. I only met him in the flesh once, praise Allah."

"Describe him."

"Maybe six foot one, maybe forty-six or -seven years of age. Glasses, thin gray hair, and a boozer in my considered opinion, since the one time I met him face-to-face he had whisky on his breath."

The road dipped. Pete hit the brakes and almost stalled the truck out.

"Tell me how he leeched onto you."

"Why? Give me one good reason why I should share this abuse with you."

"I'll give you a thousand dollars to tell me the story. If I like the story, I'll give you four more."

Ruby counted on his fingers—one to five a half dozen times. Pete tapped a little tune on the wheel. The beat ran 1-2-3-4-5. Ruby lip-synched numbers: 1-2-3-4-5, 1-2-3-4-5. Pete held up five fingers. Ruby counted them out loud.

"Five thousand if you like it?"

"That's right, Jack. And a thousand if I don't."

"I am taking a tremendous risk in telling you this."

"Then don't."

Ruby fretted his Jew-star necklace. Pete splayed five fingers out on the dashboard. Ruby kissed the star and took a bigggg breath.

"Last May this farkakte Fed braces me down in Dallas. He makes every conceivable threat on God's green earth, and I believe him, 'cause I know he's this crazy goyishe zealot with nothing to lose. He knows I've sharked in Big D and up in Chicago, and he knows I've sent people looking for high-end loans to Sam Giancana. That's what he's got this colossal hard one for. He wants to trace the money that gets loaned out from the Teamsters' Pension Fund."

It was vintage Littell: bold *and* stupid.

"He gets me to call him at a pay phone in Chicago once a week. He gives me a few dollars when I tell him I'm running on fumes. He gets me to tell him about this movie guy I know, Sid Kabikoff, who's interested in seeing this loan shark named Sal D'Onofrio, who's gonna shoot him up to Momo for a Pension Fund loan. What happened after that I don't know. But I read in the Chicago papers that both Kabikoff and D'Onofrio have been murdered, so-called 'torture-style,' and that both cases are unsolved. I'm not no Einstein, but 'torture' in Chicago means Sam G. And I also know that Sam don't know I was involved, or I'd have been visited. And it don't take an Einstein to figure out the crazy Fed was at the root of all this pain."

Littell was working outlaw. Littell was Boyd's best friend. Lenny Sands worked with Littell *and* D'Onofrio.

Ruby plucked a dog hair off his lap. "Is that five thousand dollars' worth of story?"

The road blurred. Pete damn near plowed a gator.

"Has the Fed called you since Sal D. and Kabikoff died?"

"No, praise Allah. Now what about my five—?"

"You'll get it. And I'll pay you three thousand extra if he calls you again and you get back to me on it. And if you end up helping me out with him, I'll make it another five."

Ruby went apoplectic. "Why? Why the fuck do you care to the extent of all this money?"

Pete smiled. "Let's keep this between the two of us, all right?"

"You want secret, I'll give you secret. I'm a well-known secret type of guy who knows how to keep his mouth shut."

Pete pulled his magnum and drove with his knees. Ruby smiled—ho, ho—What's this?

Pete popped the cylinder, dumped five rounds and spun it.

Ruby smiled—ho, ho—Kid, you're too much.

Pete shot him in the head. The five-to-one odds held: the hammer hit an empty chamber.

Ruby went Klan-sheet white.

Pete said, "Ask around. See what people say about me."

They hit Blessington at dusk. Ruby and Tippit got their strip show ready.

Pete called Midway Airport and impersonated a police officer. A clerk confirmed Ruby's story: A Ward J. Littell flew to Dallas and back last May 18.

He hung up and called the Eden Roc Hotel. The switchboard girl said Kemper Boyd was "out for the day."

Pete left him a message: "10:00 tonight, the Luau Lounge—urgent."

Boyd took it casual. He said, "I know Ward's been chasing the Fund," like he was too bored to breathe.

Pete blew smoke rings. Boyd's tone pissed him off—he drove eighty miles for a display of fucking ennui.

"It doesn't seem to bother you."

"I'm a bit overextended on Littell, but other than that, I don't think it's anything to be concerned about. Do you feel like divulging your source?"

"No. He doesn't know Littell's name, and I've got him cowed pretty good."

A tiki torch lit their table. Boyd flickered in and out of this weird little glow.

"I don't see how this concerns you, Pete."

"It concerns Jimmy Hoffa. He's tied to us on the Cuban thing, and Jimmy *is* the fucking Pension Fund."

Boyd drummed the table. "Littell is fixated on the Chicago Mob and the Fund. It doesn't touch on our Cuban work, and I don't think we owe Jimmy a warning. And I don't want you to talk to Lenny Sands about this. He's not conversant on the topic, and you don't need to trouble him with it."

It was vintage Boyd: "need-to-know basis" straight down the line.

"We don't have to warn Jimmy, but I'll say this loud and clear. Jimmy hired me to clip Anton Gretzler, and I don't want Littell to burn me for it. He's already made me for the job, and he's just crazy enough to go public with it, Mr. Hoover or no Mr. Hoover."

Boyd twirled his martini stick. "You clipped Roland Kirpaski, too."

"No. Jimmy clipped him himself."

Boyd whistled—très, très casual.

Pete got up in his face. "You cut Littell too much slack. You make fucking allowances for him that you shouldn't."

"We both lost brothers, Pete. Let it go at that."

The line didn't compute. Boyd talked on these weird levels sometimes.

Pete leaned back. "Are you watchdogging Littell? How tight a leash are you keeping on him?"

"I haven't been in touch with him in months. I've been distancing myself from him and Mr. Hoover."

"Why?"

"Just an instinct."

"Like an instinct for survival?"

"More of a homing instinct. You move away from some people, and you move toward the people of the moment."

"Like the Kennedys."

"Yes."

Pete laughed. "I've hardly seen you since Jack hit the trail."

"You won't be seeing me at all until after the election. Stanton knows I can't be dividing my time."

"He *should* know. He hired you to get next to the Kennedys."

"He won't regret it."

"I don't. It means I get to run the Cadre solo."

"Can you handle it?"

"Can niggers dance?"

"They surely can."

Pete sipped his beer. It was flat—he forgot he ordered it.

"You said 'election' like you think the job's going through to November."

"I'm reasonably certain it will. Jack's ahead in New Hampshire and Wisconsin, and if we get past West Virginia I think he'll go all the way."

"Then I hope he's anti-Castro."

"He is. He's not as voluble as Richard Nixon, but then Dick's a Red-baiter from way back."

"President Jack. Jesus Christ."

Boyd signaled a waiter. A fresh martini hit the table quick.

"It's seduction, Pete. He'll back the country into a corner with his charm, like it's a woman. When America sees that it's a choice between Jack and twitchy old Dick Nixon, who do you think they'll get between the sheets with?"

Pete raised his beer. "Viva La Causa. Viva Bad-Back Jack."

They clinked glasses. Boyd said, "He'll get behind the Cause. And if the invasion goes, we want it to be in his administration."

Pete lit a cigarette. "I'm not worried about that. Put Littell aside, and there's only one thing to be worried about."

"You're concerned that the Agency at large will find out about our Cadre business."

"That's right."

Boyd said, "I want them to find out. In fact, I'm going to inform them some time before November. It's inevitable that they will find out, and by the time they do my Kennedy connection will make me too valuable to dismiss. The Cadre will have recruited too many good men and have made too much money, and as far as morality goes, how does selling heroin to Negroes rate when compared to illegally invading an island?"

More vintage Boyd: "self-budgeted," "autonomous"—

"And don't worry about Littell. He's trying to accrue evidence to send to Bobby Kennedy, but I monitor all the information that Bobby sees, and I will not let Littell hurt you at all, or hurt Jimmy for the Kirpaski killing or anything else related to you or the Cause. But sooner or later Bobby *will* take Hoffa down, and I do not want you to meddle in it."

Pete felt his head swim. "I can't argue with any of that. But I've got a pipeline to Littell now, and if I think your boy needs a scare, I'm going to scare him."

"And I can't argue with that. You can do whatever you have to do, as long as you don't kill him."

They shook hands. Boyd said, *"Les gens que l'on comprend—ce sont eux que l'on domine."*

En français, Pierre, souviens-toi:

Those we understand are those we control.

41

(New York City/Hyannis Port/
New Hampshire/Wisconsin/Illinois/West Virginia,
2/4/60–5/4/60)

CHRISTMAS DAY MADE him certain. Every day since built on it.

Jack kept Laura's ring. Kemper took Jackie's emerald pin. His car wouldn't start—a Kennedy chauffeur checked it out for him. Kemper strolled the compound and caught Jack in mid-transformation.

He was standing on the beach, alone. He was rehearsing his public persona in full voice.

Kemper stood out of sight and watched him.

Jack went from tallish to tall. He brayed less and rumbled more. His stabbing gestures hit some mark he'd always missed before.

Jack laughed. Jack cocked his head to listen. Jack masterfully summarized Russia, civil rights, the race for space, Cuba, Catholicism, his perceived youth and Richard Nixon as a duplicitous, do-nothing reactionary unfit to lead the greatest country on earth into perilous times.

He looked heroic. Claiming the moment drained all the boy out of him.

The self-possession was always there. He'd postponed the claim until it could give him the world.

Jack knew he'd win. Kemper knew he'd impersonate greatness with the force of an enigma granted form. This new freedom would make people love him.

Laura loved the pin.

Jack took New Hampshire and Wisconsin.

Jimmy Hoffa barnstormed both states. Jimmy mobilized Teamsters and ranted on national TV. Jimmy betrayed his essential lunacy every time he opened his mouth.

Kemper mobilized the backlash. Pro-Jack pickets scuffled with Teamster pickets. The pro-Jack boys were good shouters and good placard swingers.

Bobby's book hit the best-seller lists. Kemper distributed free copies at union halls. The consensus four months in: Jimmy Hoffa was nullified.

Jack was spellbindingly handsome. Hoffa was bloated and harried. All his anti-Kennedy broadsides carried a footnote: "Currently under investigation for land fraud."

People loved Jack. People wanted to touch him. Kemper let the people get non-security close.

Kemper let photographers get close. He wanted people to think Jack's amusement was really love beaming back.

They were running unopposed in Nebraska. The West Virginia primary was six days off—Jack should knock Hubert Humphrey out of the race.

Frank Sinatra was wowing hillbilly voters. A Rat Pack stooge composed a ring-a-ding Jack Anthem. Payola got it constant airplay.

Laura called Sinatra a small penis with a big voice.

Jack's ascent enraged her. She was blood kin and an outcast. Kemper Boyd was a stranger granted insider status.

He called her from the road every night. Laura considered the contact pro forma.

He knew that she missed Lenny Sands. She didn't know that he'd banished him.

Lenny changed his Chicago number—there was no way that Laura could call him. Kemper put a trace on his phone bills and confirmed that he hadn't called her.

Bobby remembered "voice coach" Lenny. Some staffers decreed a brush-up course and invited Lenny to New Hampshire.

Jack "introduced" Lenny to Kemper. Lenny played along and did not display an ounce of rancor or fear.

Lenny worked Jack's speaking voice into top shape. Bobby put him on the Wisconsin payroll—as a crowd-building front man. Lenny built up big crowds on a small budget—Bobby was thrilled.

Claire spent most weekends with Laura. She said Jack's half-sister was a rabid Nixon fan.

Like Mr. Hoover.

They talked in mid-February. Mr. Hoover made the call. He said, "My, it's been a long time!" in a purely disingenuous tone.

Kemper updated his allegiances and detailed Joe Kennedy's old suspicions. Hoover said, "I'll build up a file to buttress your dissemblings. We'll make it appear that all your Florida trips were solely on my behalf. I'll anoint you the Bureau's ace pro-Castro-group monitor."

Kemper supplied key Florida dates. Hoover sent him mock itineraries to memorize.

Hoover never mentioned the campaign. Kemper knew that he sensed a Kennedy victory.

Hoover did not mention Jack and women. Hoover did not suggest hot-wiring prostitutes. Hoover did not nail the reason why Kemper Boyd had stayed distant.

He didn't want to implement another sex shakedown. He wanted to retain one strong loyalty compartment.

Pimp shakedowns?—no. Pimp *service*?—certainly.

He got Jack one call girl per night. He called his local vice squad contacts for referrals—and skin-searched every girl that Jack fucked.

The girls loved Jack.

So did SA Ward Littell.

They hadn't spoken in over six months. Ward showed up at Jack's big Milwaukee rally—the old Chicago Phantom as the new Chicago Wraith.

He looked frail and unkempt. He did not look like anyone's notion of a G-man.

Ward refused to talk Mob scuttlebutt or Pension Fund strategy. Ward refused to discuss the D'Onofrio homicide.

Ward said he was neglecting his Red Squad assignment. He said he'd struck up a friendship with a leftist he was tailing.

The Kennedy campaign thrilled him. He wore Kennedy buttons to work and made a scene when SAC Leahy told him to stop it.

Littell's anti-Mob crusade was dead. Mr. Hoover couldn't touch them now: the Boyd/Littell collusion was null and void.

Kemper told Bobby the Phantom was still plugging. Bobby said, Don't bother me with trifles.

Littell was set to retire in eight months. His drunken dream was a Kennedy appointment.

Ward loves Jack.

New Hampshire loves Jack.

Wisconsin loves Jack.

West Virginia had its heart up for grabs. Greenbrier County was vote-crucial and totally Mob-run.

He decided not to ask the Boys for help. Why indebt Jack to men that Bobby hated?

America loves Jack.

Sinatra put it best:

"That old Jack Magic has me in its spell!"

42

(Blessington/Miami, 2/4/60–5/4/60)

THAT "LOST BROTHERS" line kept zinging him. Pete couldn't get it out of his head.

John Stanton toured the campsite in mid-March. Pete quizzed him on Kemper Boyd's background.

Stanton said the CIA researched the man. The hunting-accident story earned him high marks—Kemper didn't let shit weigh him down.

Boyd spoke French. Boyd made big words come alive. Boyd made his whole world go whoosh—

His last three months: "autonomous," straight from Webster's Unabridged.

Kemper's timecard read strictly KENNEDY. Pete's timecard now read strictly CUBA.

Fulo quit running whores. Lockhart embraced the New Klan Kode. Six two-week cycles worked through Blessington—746 men total.

They learned weaponry, judo, speedboating and demolition fundamentals. Chuck Rogers fed them pro-U.S. doctrine.

The Cadre kept recruiting in Miami. Cuban hotheads kept signing up.

The Agency now had sixty operational campsites. They established an exile "grad school" in Guatemala: a fully equipped military facility.

Ike loosened his pursestrings. Ike approved exile invasion plans. It was a big policy shift—three plots to whack Fidel backfired and scrambled the thinking at Langley.

Shooters couldn't get close. Aides smoked exploding cigars marked for the Beard. Langley figured fuck it—let's invade Cuba.

Maybe early next year. Maybe in Bad-Back Jack's administration.

Boyd said Jack would approve the plan. Boyd was fucking persuasive. Santo Junior spread the word: Kemper Boyd has Jack Kennedy's ear.

The Outfit dropped some coin on Jack's campaign—quietly and anonymously. Big fat compartmentalized donations.

Jimmy Hoffa didn't know. Jack didn't know—and wouldn't be told until the optimum moment to call in the debt.

Sam G. said he could buy Jack Illinois. Lenny Sands said Sam spent a fortune in Wisconsin. West Virginia ditto—Chi-Mob money had the state locked in for Jack.

Pete asked Lenny if Boyd knew about all that finagling. Lenny said, I don't think so. Pete said, Let's keep it that way—Kemper wouldn't like to think that he'd put Jack in hock.

Boyd inspired confidence. Trafficante loved him. Santo passed the Cuban Cause hat—Giancana, Rosselli and Marcello ponied up large.

It was classic compartmentalization.

The CIA high brass condoned the gifts. And they learned about the Cadre dope biz—before Kemper informed them.

They condoned it. They considered it plausibly deniable and told John Stanton to continue. They told Stanton to hide this knowledge from non-CIA personnel.

Like outside police agencies. Like moralistic politicians.

Stanton was relieved. Kemper was amused. He said the issue illustrated the Jack/Bobby dichotomy: dope peddling as divisive moral issue.

Big Brother would wince and try to ignore the alliance. Little Brother would side with God and banish all Mob-CIA contact.

Big Brother was worldly, like his dad. Little Brother was prissy, like a dejuiced Ward Littell with functioning balls.

Bobby had his father's money and his brother's cache. Littell had booze and religion. Jack Ruby had a five-grand pointer's fee—if Littell swerved through his life again, Big Pete would be notified.

Boyd told him not to kill Littell. Boyd co-signed Littell's Pension Fund hard-on—which meant at least an outside chance at co-opting big money.

Littell loved Bad-Back Jack.

Like Darleen Shoftel. Like Gail Hendee.

Like himself.

Hey, Jack—you fucked my old girlfriend. I don't care—Kemper Boyd says you're a white man.

I'm selling dope for you. I'm running cash to a man named Banister—who links YOU to a Jew/papist plot to butt-fuck America.

You'd dig Fort Blessington, Jack. It's a Mob resort now—the Boys come by to catch the anti-Castro floorshow. Santo Junior bought a motel outside town. He'd put you up for free—if you dump your kid brother in the Everglades.

Sam G. drops by. Carlos Marcello visits. Johnny Rosselli brings Dick Contino and his accordion. Lenny Sands puts on shows—his transvestite Fidel shtick brings the house down.

Dope profits were up. Cadre morale was sky-high. Ramón

Gutiérrez kept a tally of speedboat-run scalpees. Heshie Ryskind started up a scalp bonus fund.

Lenny Sands was on smear duty: the Beard as scandal-sheet whipping boy. Mr. Hughes dug the political thrust, but preferred to see *Hush-Hush* exposit sex skank exclusively.

Pete called Hughes once a week. The fucker ranted nonstop.

The TWA gig was dragging on. Dick Steisel kept Hughes look-alikes on retainer. Hughes believed that niggers caused cancer—and kept urging Ike to reinstate slavery.

Germ-obsessed Mormon nuts kept Big Howard company. They kept his bungalow sanitized: A-bomb-strength bug spray worked wonders. Some doofus named Duane Spurgeon bossed the crew. He stretched lubricated rubbers over every doorknob spooks might have touched.

Hughes was on a new kick: getting weekly blood transfusions. He sucked in pure Mormon blood exclusively—purchased from a blood bank outside Salt Lake City.

Hughes always said, Thanks for the dope. Pete always said, Thank the Agency.

He still got a Hughes paycheck. He still got twenty-three alimony cuts. He got 5% of Tiger Kab and his contract agent pay.

He used to pimp and pull shakedowns. Now he rode shotgun to History.

Jimmy Hoffa stopped by the cabstand every few days. His standard M.O. was to rave at non-English-speaking drivers. Wilfredo Delsol was running the switchboard now—whacking his cousin killed his appetite for strongarm.

Wilfredo understood English. He said Jimmy teed off on Cubans, but couldn't sustain it. Whoever took the first few "fuckheads" got a reprieve. Hoffa couldn't scream a sentence that didn't end "Kennedy."

Pete saw Jack and Jimmy on TV back-to-back. Kennedy charmed a heckler speechless. Hoffa wore white socks and an egg-spattered necktie.

Hold the tip sheet—I can spot winners and losers.

Sometimes he just couldn't sleep. That big fucking whoooosh was like a hydrogen bomb inside his head.

43
(Greenbrier, 5/8/60)

FLANKING CORDONS JAMMED up to the rostrum. Pro-Jack and pro-Teamster pickets—hard boys all.

The main drag was blocked off to cars. The pre-rally crowd extended back three blocks: at least six thousand people packed in shoulder-to-shoulder tight.

They jabbered and hummed. Placards bobbed ten feet high.

Jack was set to speak first. Humphrey lost a rigged coin toss and spoke last. Jack regalia outgunned Hubert three to one—the West Virginia campaign in a nutshell.

Teamster goons yelled into bullhorns. Some rednecks hoisted a cartoon banner: Jack with fangs and a papal biretta.

Kemper cupped his ears—the crowd roar was painful. Rocks shredded the banner—he paid some kids to crouch down and let fly.

Jack was due. Bad acoustics and Hoffa invective would drown out his speech.

No great loss—people would still *see* him. The crowd would disperse when Humphrey showed up—free liquor was being served at select downtown taverns.

It was Kemper Boyd liquor. An old pal hijacked a Schenley's truck and sold him the contents.

The street was packed. The sidewalks were packed. Peter Lawford was lobbing tie tacks at a gaggle of nuns.

Kemper mingled and watched the rostrum. He saw non-sequitur faces a few yards apart: Lenny Sands and a prototype Mob guy.

The Mob guy flashed Lenny a thumbs-up. Lenny flashed him two thumbs back.

Lenny was *off* the campaign payroll. Lenny had no *official* duties here.

The Mob man veered right. Lenny pushed his way left and ducked down an alley lined with trash cans.

Kemper followed him. Stray elbows and knees slowed him down.

High-school kids jostled him across the sidewalk. Lenny was midway down the alley, huddled with two cops.

The crowd noise leveled out. Kemper crouched behind a trash can and eavesdropped.

Lenny fanned a cash roll. A cop plucked bills off of it. His buddy said, "For two hundred extra we can stall the Humphrey bus and bring in some boys to shout him down."

Lenny said, "Do it. And this is strictly on Mr. G., so don't mention it to anybody with the campaign."

The cops grabbed the whole roll and squeezed through an alleyway door. Lenny leaned against the wall and lit a cigarette.

Kemper walked up to him. Hipster Lenny said, "So?"

"So, tell me about it."

"What's to tell?"

"Fill in the blanks for me, then."

"What's to fill in? We're both Kennedy guys."

Lenny could maneuver. Lenny could outfrost any cool cat on earth.

"Giancana put money into Wisconsin, too. Is that right? You couldn't have performed the way you did on what Bobby gave you."

Lenny shrugged. "Sam and Hesh Ryskind."

"Who told them to? You?"

"My advice don't rate that high. You know that."

"Spill, Lenny. You're playing coy, and it's starting to annoy me."

Lenny stubbed his cigarette on the wall. "Sinatra was bragging up his influence with Jack. He was saying Jack as President wouldn't be the same Jack that sat on the McClellan Committee, if you catch my meaning."

"And Giancana bought the whole package?"

"No. I think you gave Frank a big fucking assist. Everybody's real impressed with what you've been doing on the Cuba front, so they figured if you like Jack he can't be all bad."

Kemper smiled. "I don't want Bobby and Jack to find out about this."

"Nobody does."

"Until the debt gets called in?"

"Sam don't believe in frivolous reminders. And in case you're thinking of reminding me, I'll tell you now. I haven't come up with bupkis on the Pension Fund."

Kemper heard footscrapes. He saw Teamsters left and Teamsters right—chain swingers crouched at both ends of the alley.

They had their sights on Lenny. Tiny Lenny, Jewish Lenny, Kennedy toady Lenny—

Lenny didn't see them. Pissy Lenny was entrenched in his cool cat/tough guy act.

Kemper said, "I'll be in touch."

Lenny said, "See you in shul."

Kemper backed through the alleyway door and double-locked it behind him. He heard shouts, chain rattles and thuds—the classic labor-goon two-way press.

Lenny never yelled or screamed. Kemper timed the beating at a minute and six seconds.

44

(Chicago, 5/10/60)

THE WORK WAS driving Littell schizophrenic. He had to satisfy the Bureau *and* his conscience.

Chick Leahy hated Mal Chamales. HUAC had linked Mal to sixteen Commie front groups. Leahy's FBI mentor was former Chicago SAC Guy Banister.

Banister hated Mal. Mal's Red Squad sheet was eighty pages long.

He liked Mal. They had coffee every so often. Mal spent '46 to '48 in Lewisburg—Banister built up a sedition profile and talked the U.S. Attorney into an indictment.

Leahy called him this morning. He said, "I want lockstep surveillance on Mal Chamales, Ward. I want you to go to every meeting he goes to and catch him making inflammatory remarks that we can use."

Littell called Chamales and warned him. Mal said, "I'm addressing an SLP group this afternoon. Let's just pretend we don't know each other."

Littell mixed a rye and soda. It was 5:40—he had time to work before the national news.

He padded his report with useless details. He omitted Mal's anti-Bureau tirade. He closed with noncommital remarks.

"The subject's Socialist Labor Party speech was tepid and filled with nebulous cliches of a decidedly leftist, but nonseditious nature. His comments during the question and answer period were not inflammatory or in any way provocative."

Mal called Mr. Hoover "a limp-wristed Fascist in jackboots and lavender lederhosen." An inflammatory statement?—hardly.

Littell turned on the TV. John Kennedy filled the screen—he just won the West Virginia primary.

The doorbell rang. Littell hit the entry buzzer and got out some money for the A&P kid.

Lenny Sands walked in. His face was scabbed, bruised and sutured. A bandaged splint held his nose in place.

Lenny swayed. Lenny smirked. Lenny twirled his fingers at the TV—"Hello, Jack, you gorgeous slice of Irish roast lamb!"

Littell stood up. Lenny weaved into a bookcase and stiff-armed himself steady.

"Ward, you look marvelous! Those frayed slacks from J.C. Penney's and that cheap white shirt are so YOU!"

Kennedy was addressing civil rights. Littell hit the off switch in mid-discourse.

Lenny waved goodbye. "Ta, Jack, my brother-in-law in the best of all possible worlds if I liked girls and you had the profile in courage to acknowledge my dear friend Laura that that gorgeously cruel Mr. Boyd drove out of my life."

Littell moved toward him. "Lenny . . ."

"Don't you fucking come any closer or try to touch me or try to assuage your pathetic guilt or in any way mess with my gorgeous Percodan high or I won't spill my lead on the Teamster Pension Fund books that I've had all along, you sad excuse for a policeman."

Littell stiff-armed a chair. His fingers ripped through the fabric. He started weaving on his feet just like Lenny.

The bookcase shimmied. Lenny was weaving on his heels—doped up and punch-drunk.

"Jules Schiffrin keeps the books someplace in Lake Geneva. He's got an estate there, and he's got the books in safes or in safe-deposit boxes at some banks around there. I know because I played a gig there and I heard Jules and Johnny Rosselli talking. Don't ask for details because I don't have any and concentrating makes my head hurt."

His arm slid. The chair slid behind it. Littell stumbled up against the TV console.

"Why are you telling me this?"

"Because you're a tiny smidgen better than Mr. Beast and Mr.

Boyd and in my opinion Mr. Boyd only wants the information for its profit potential, and besides I took a beating for doing some work for Mr. Sam—"

"Lenny—"

"—and Mr. Sam said he'd make a powerful man crawl for it, but I said please don't do that—"

"Lenny—"

"—and Jules Schiffrin was with him, and they were talking about somebody called 'Irish Joe' back in the '20s, and how they made these movie extra girls crawl—"

"Lenny, come on—"

"—and it all felt so ugly that I popped a few more Percs, and here I am, and if I'm lucky I won't remember all this in the morning."

Littell stepped closer. Lenny slapped and scratched and flailed and kicked him away.

The bookcase fell. Lenny tripped and weaved out the door.

Law texts hit the floor. A framed photograph of Helen Agee shattered.

Littell drove to Lake Geneva. He arrived at midnight and checked in at a motel off the Interstate. He paid cash in advance and registered under a fake name.

The phone book in his room listed Jules Schiffrin. His address was marked "Rural Free Delivery." Littell checked a local map and pegged it: a woodland estate near the lake.

He drove out and parked off the road. Binoculars got him in close.

He saw a stonework mansion on a minimum of ten acres. Trees enclosed the property. There were no walls or fences.

No floodlamps. Two hundred yards from the door to the roadway. Alarm tape bracketing the front windows.

No guard hut and no gate. The Wisconsin State Police probably kept watch on an informal basis.

Lenny said "safes or safe-deposit boxes." Lenny said "Mr. Boyd"/"information"/"profit potential."

Lenny was drugged up but lucid. His Mr. Boyd line was easy to decode.

Kemper was chasing Fund leads independently.

Littell drove back to his motel. He checked the Yellow Pages and found listings for nine local banks.

Discreet behavior would cloak his lack of sanction. Kemper Boyd always stressed boldness *and* discretion.

Kemper shook down Lenny on his own. The revelation didn't shock him at all.

He slept until 10:00. He checked a map and saw that the banks were all within walking distance.

The first four managers cooperated. Their replies were direct: Mr. Schiffrin does not rent with us. The next two managers shook their heads. Their replies were direct: Our facilities do not include safe-deposit boxes.

Manager number seven asked to see a bank writ. It was no great loss: the name Schiffrin sailed past him, unrecognized.

Banks number eight and nine: no safe-deposit boxes on the premises.

There were several major cities nearby. There were two dozen small towns spread out in a hundred-mile radius. Safe-deposit box access was a pipe dream.

"Safes" meant on-site placement. Safe-alarm companies retained placement diagrams—and did not release them without suit for legal cause.

Lenny played an on-site engagement. He might have seen the safe or safes firsthand.

Lenny was too combustible to approach now.

But—

Jack Ruby was a probable Schiffrin acquaintance. Jack Ruby was bribable and acquiescent.

Littell found a pay phone. A long-distance operator patched him through to Dallas.

Ruby picked up on the third ring. "This is the Carousel Club, where your entertainment dollar goes—"

"It's me, Jack. Your friend from Chicago."

"Fuck . . . this is grief I don't . . ."

He sounded flummoxed, flabbergasted and dyspeptically peeved.

"How well do you know Jules Schiffrin, Jack?"

"Casual. I know Jules casual at best. Why? Why? Why?"

"I want you to fly up to Wisconsin and drop by his place in Lake Geneva on some pretext. I need to know the interior layout of his house, and I'll give you my life savings if you do it."

"Fuck. You are grief I don't—"

"Four thousand dollars, Jack."

"Fuck. You are grief I don't—"

Dog yaps cut Ruby off.

45

(Blessington, 5/12/60)

JIMMY HOFFA SAID, "I know how Jesus must have felt. The fucking pharaohs rose to power on his coattails like the fucking Kennedy brothers are rising on mine."

Heshie Ryskind said, "Get your history straight. It was Julius Caesar that did Jesus in."

Santo Junior said, "Joe Kennedy is a man you can reason with. It's strictly Bobby that's the bad seed. Joe will explain certain facts of life to Jack if he makes it."

Johnny Rosselli said, "J. Edgar Hoover hates Bobby. And he knows you can't fight the Outfit and win. If the kid is elected, cooler heads than that little cocksucker Bobby's will prevail."

The Boys were sprawled in deck chairs out on the speedboat dock. Pete kept their drinks fresh and let them run off at the mouth.

Hoffa said, "Fucking Jesus turned fish into bread, and that's about the only thing I haven't tried. I've spent six hundred grand on the primaries and bought every fucking cop and alderman and councilman and mayor and fucking grand juror and senator and judge and DA and fucking prosecutorial investigator who'd let me. I'm like Jesus trying to part the Red Fucking Sea and not getting no further than some motel on the beach."

Ryskind said, "Jimmy, calm down. Go get yourself a nice blow job and relax. I've got some reliable local numbers. These are girls who know their trade and would love to satisfy a famous guy like you."

Rosselli said, "If Jack is elected, Bobby will fade into the woodwork. My bet is he'll run for governor of Massachusetts, and Raymond Patriarca and the Boston boys will have to worry about him."

Santo Junior said, "That will never happen. Old Joe and Raymond go too far back. And when push comes to shove, it's Joe who hands down the law—not Jack or Bobby."

Hoffa said, "It's the handing down of grand jury indictments that bothers me. My lawyer said the Sun Valley thing is unlikely to go my way, which means indictments by the end of the year. So don't make Joe Kennedy sound like Jesus handing God the Ten Commandments on Mount Fucking Vesuvius."

Ryskind said, "Santo was just making a point."

Rosselli said, "It's Mount Ararat, Jimmy. Mount Vesuvius is in fucking Yellowstone Park."

Hoffa said, "You guys don't know Jack Kennedy. Fucking Kemper Boyd's got you convinced he's a gung-ho anti-Castro guy when he's really a pinko, Commie-appeasing, nigger-loving fucking homo masquerading as a cunt man."

Wave spray hit the dock. Cadence counts sounded off fifty yards over—Lockhart was running troops through close-order drill.

Ryskind said, "I could go for a blow job."

Rosselli said, "What's the count at, Hesh?"

Ryskind said, "Somewhere in the vicinity of seventeen thousand."

Santo Junior said, "Don't shit a shitter. I'd say eight thousand tops. Anything more than that and you'd be too fucking occupied to make money."

The dock phone rang. Pete tilted his chair back and grabbed the receiver.

"This is Bondurant."

"I'm glad it's you, but don't you soldier types say hello?"

Jack Ruby—un-fucking-mistakable.

Pete cupped the mouthpiece. "What is it? I told you not to call unless it's important."

"What it is is the crazy Fed. He called me yesterday, and I've been stalling him."

"What did he want?"

"He offered me four Gs to fly up to Lake Geneva Goddamn Wisconsin and case the layout of Jules Schiffrin's house up there. It seems to me this is part of that farkakte Pension Fund—"

"Tell him you'll do it. Set up a meet someplace quiet forty-eight hours from now and call me back."

Ruby gulped and stammered. Pete hung up and popped his knuckles ten across.

The goddamn phone rang again—

Pete snagged it. "Jack, what are you doing?"

A man said, "This ain't Jack. This is a certain Mr. Giancana looking for a certain Mr. Hoffa, who a little birdie told me is there with you."

Pete waved the phone. "It's for you, Jimmy. It's Mo."

Hoffa belched. "Hit that loudspeaker doohickey on that post there. Sam and me got nothing to hide from you guys."

Pete tapped the switch. Hoffa yelled straight at the mike stand: "Yeah, Sam."

The speaker kicked in loud:

"Your West Virginia guys fucked up my boy Lenny Sands, Jimmy. Don't let anything like that happen again or I'd be inclined to make you apologize in front of an audience. My advice to you is to leave politics the fuck alone and concentrate on staying out of jail."

Giancana slammed his phone down. The sound made the whole dock shimmy. Heshie, Johnny and Santo shared this green-at-the-gills look.

Hoffa blew verbal. Birds shot up out of trees and covered the sky.

46

(Lake Geneva, 5/14/60)

THE ROAD BISECTED two fenced-off pastures. Clouds covered the moon—visibility was close to nil.

Littell pulled over and stuffed his money in a grocery bag. It was 10:06—Ruby was late.

Littell turned off his headlights. Clouds skittered by. The moon lit up a huge shape walking toward the car.

The windshield exploded. The dashboard fell on his lap. A steel bar cracked the steering wheel and ripped the gearshift out.

Hands jerked him across the hood. Glass ripped through his cheeks and lodged in his mouth.

Hands dumped him in a ditch.

Hands picked him up and pinioned him against a barbed-wire fence.

He was dangling. Steel barbs pierced his clothes and held him upright.

The monster ripped his holster off. The monster hit him and hit him and hit him.

The fence shook. Twisty metal gouged his backside down to the bone. He coughed up blood and chunks of glass and a big piece of a Chevy hood ornament.

He smelled gasoline. His car exploded. A heat blast singed his hair.

The fence collapsed. He looked up and saw clouds ignite.

DOCUMENT INSERT: 5/19/60.
FBI Memorandum: Milwaukee Special Agent-in-Charge
John Campion to Director J. Edgar Hoover.

Sir:

Our investigation into the near-fatal assault on SA Ward Littell is proceeding but making scant headway, primarily due to SA Littell's poor attitude and lack of cooperation.

Agents from both the Milwaukee and Chicago Offices canvassed Lake Geneva for eyewitnesses to the assault and for witnesses to Littell's general presence in the area and were unable to locate any. Chicago SAC Leahy informed me that Littell was under loose surveillance for matters pertaining to internal Bureau security and that on two recent occasions (May 10th and May 14th) the agents mobile-tailing Littell lost him on roadways leading north to the Wisconsin border. The nature of Littell's business in the Lake Geneva area is thus far unknown.

Per investigatory specifics:

1)—The assault occurred on a rural access road four miles southeast of Lake Geneva. 2)—Brush marks in the dirt near the remains of Littell's car indicate that the assailant obliterated all traces of his tire tracks, rendering forensic casting impossible. 3)— Littell's car was burned with a highly-flammable nitrous gas compound of the type used in the manufacture of military explosives. Such compounds burn themselves out very quickly and are used because they minimize the risk of decimating the area

surrounding the target. The assailant obviously has
military experience and/or access to military
ordnance. 4)—Forensic analysis revealed the presence
of charred U.S. currency laced with paper bag
fragments. The aggregate weight of the fragments
indicates that Littell was carrying a large amount of
money in a grocery sack. 5)—Farmers rescued Littell,
who was pinned to a downed section of barbed-wire
fence. He was taken to Overlander Hospital near Lake
Geneva and treated for a massive series of posterior
cuts and lacerations, broken ribs, contusions, a
broken nose, broken collarbone, internal
hemorrhaging and facial gouges caused by contact with
windshield glass. Littell checked out against
medical advice fourteen hours later and engaged a
taxi cab to drive him to Chicago. Chicago Office
agents assigned to loose-tail Littell saw him
entering his apartment building. He collapsed in the
entry hall, and the agents interceded on their own
authority and drove him to Saint Catherine's
Hospital. 8)—Littell remains at the hospital. He is
listed in ''good condition'' and will most likely be
released within a week. A supervising physician told
agents that the scarring on his face and backside will
be permanent and that he should slowly recover from
his other injuries. 7)—Agents have repeatedly
queried Littell on three topics: his presence in Lake
Geneva, the presence of the burned money and enemies
who might want to hurt him. Littell stated that he was
in Lake Geneva scouting retirement property and
denied the presence of the money. He said that he had
no enemies and considered the assault a case of
mistaken identity. When asked about CPUSA members who
might be seeking vengeance on him for his Bureau Red
Squad work, Littell replied, ''Are you kidding? Those
Commies are all nice guys.'' 8)—Agents have surmised
that Littell has made at least two trips to Lake
Geneva. His name has not appeared on any hotel or
motel ledgers, so we are assuming he either
registered under assumed names or stayed with
friends or acquaintances. Littell's response—that

he took catnaps in his car—was not convincing.

   The investigation continues. I respectfully await
orders.

                                      John Campion
             Special Agent-in-Charge, Milwaukee Office

DOCUMENT INSERT: 6/3/60.
FBI Memorandum: Chicago SAC Charles Leahy to Director
J. Edgar Hoover.

Sir,

   Per SA Ward J. Littell, please be informed.
   SA Littell is now back on light duty and has been
assigned to review Federal deportation briefs in
conjunction with the U.S. Attorney's Office, work
which utilizes the writ-analysis expertise he
developed in law school. He refuses to discuss the
assault with other agents, and as SAC Campion may have
told you, we have yet to find witnesses to his Lake
Geneva visits. Helen Agee told agents that Littell
has not discussed the assault with her. I personally
questioned SA Court Meade, Littell's only friend
in the Chicago Office, and have the following to
report.
   A)—Meade states that in late 1958 and early 1959,
following his expulsion from the Top Hoodlum Program,
Littell ''loitered'' near the THP listening post and
expressed interest in the squad's work. That interest
dissipated, Meade stated, and he further surmised
that it is extremely unlikely that Littell engaged in
anti-Mob actions on his own. Meade scoffed at the
notion that the Chicago Mob was responsible for the
assault or that left-wingers surveilled by Littell
were seeking vengeance for his Red Squad efforts.
Meade thinks that Littell's ''marked bent'' for young
women, as evinced by his continuing affair with Helen
Agee, was the motive for the assault. Meade
colorfully stated, ''Go back up to Wisconsin and look
for some idealistically-inclined girl with nasty
brothers who didn't take kindly to sis consorting

with a forty-seven-year-old boozehound, G-man or no G-man.'' I find this theory plausible.

B)—Littell's Bureau arrest record going back to 1950 was checked with an eye toward uncovering recently paroled felons perhaps inclined toward vengeance. A list of twelve men was compiled, and all twelve were alibi-cleared. I recalled Littell's 1952 arrest of one Pierre ''Pete'' Bondurant, and how the man taunted Littell during detainment procedures. Agents checked Bondurant's whereabouts during the assault time frame and confirmed that he was in Florida.

The pro-Communist profile of Littell continues to develop. Littell remains a confirmed friend of long-term subversive Mal Chamales and phone tap logs now pinpoint a total of nine Littell/Chamales telephone conversations, all of which contain lengthy expressions of Littell's sympathy for left-wing causes and expressions of his disdain for FBI ''witch hunting.'' On May 10 I called Littell and ordered him to implement immediate lockstep surveillance on Mal Chamales. Five minutes later Littell called Chamales and warned him. Chamales addressed a Socialist Labor Party meeting that afternoon. Littell and a trusted Bureau informant attended, unknown to each other. The informant presented me with a verbatim transcript of Chamales' seditious, virulently anti-Bureau, anti-Hoover remarks. Littell's May 10th report on the meeting called these remarks non-inflammatory. The report was filled with numerous other outright lies and distortions of a treasonous nature.

Sir, I believe it is now time to confront Littell on both his lack of cooperation in the assault matter and more pertinently on his recent seditious actions. Will you please respond? I think this demands immediate action.

                                    Respectfully, Charles Leahy

DOCUMENT INSERT: 6/11/60.
FBI Memorandum: Director J. Edgar Hoover to Chicago
SAC Charles Leahy.

Mr. Leahy,

Per Ward Littell: do nothing yet. Put Littell back
on CPUSA surveillance duties, relax the surveillance
on him and keep me informed of the assault
investigation.

JEH

DOCUMENT INSERT: 7/9/60.
Official FBI Telephone Call Transcript: ''Recorded
at the Director's Request''/''Classified Confidential
1-A: Director's Eyes Only.'' Speaking: Director
Hoover, Special Agent Kemper Boyd.

KB: Good afternoon, Sir.
JEH: Kemper, I'm peeved at you. You've been
avoiding me for some time.
KB: I wouldn't put it that way, Sir.
JEH: Of course you wouldn't. You'd put it in a *way*
calculated to minimize my rancor. The question is,
would you have contacted me if I hadn't contacted
you?
KB: Yes, Sir. I would have.
JEH: Before or after the coronation of King Jack
the First?
KB: I wouldn't call the coronation a sure thing,
Sir.
JEH: Does he have a delegate majority?
KB: Almost. I think he'll be nominated on the first
ballot.
JEH: And you think he'll win.
KB: Yes, I'm reasonably certain.
JEH: I can't dispute that. Big Brother and America
have all the earmarks of a fatuous love affair.
KB: He is going to retain you, Sir.
JEH: Of course he is. Every President since Calvin
Coolidge has, and you should temper your distancing

process with the knowledge that Prince Jack will
be in office for a maximum of eight years, while I
shall remain in office until the Millennium.

KB: I'll keep that in mind, Sir.

JEH: I would advise you to. You should also be
advised that my interest in Big Brother extends
beyond the confines of wishing to keep my job. Unlike
you, I have altruistic concerns, such as the internal
security of our nation. Unlike you, my primary
concern is not self-preservation and monetary
advancement. Unlike you, I do not credit the ability
to dissemble as my single greatest skill.

KB: Yes, Sir.

JEH: Allow me to interpret your reluctance to
contact me. Were you afraid I would ask you to
introduce Big Brother to Bureau-friendly women?

KB: Yes and no, Sir.

JEH: Meaning?

KB: Meaning Little Brother doesn't entirely trust
me. Meaning the primary campaign schedule was hectic
and only left me time to procure local call girls.
Meaning I might have been able to house Big Brother in
hotel rooms with standing Bureau bugs, but Little
Brother has been around law enforcement for years,
and he just might know that co-opt bugs like that
exist.

JEH: I always reach a certain point with you.

KB: Meaning?

JEH: Meaning I don't know whether or not you're
lying, and to one degree or another I don't care.

KB: Thank you, Sir.

JEH: You're welcome. It was an appalling
compliment, but a sincere one. Now, are you going to
Los Angeles for the convention?

KB: I'm leaving tomorrow. I'll be staying at the
downtown Statler.

JEH: You'll be contacted. King Jack will not want
for female friendship should he find himself bored
between accolades.

KB: Electronically-adorned friends?

JEH: No, just good listeners. We'll talk about some

co-opt work during the fall campaign, if Little
Brother trusts you with travel plans.

KB: Yes, Sir.

JEH: Who assaulted Ward Littell?

KB: I'm not sure, Sir.

JEH: Have you spoken to Littell?

KB: Helen Agee called and told me about the
beating. I called Ward at the hospital, but he refused
to tell me who did it.

JEH: Pete Bondurant comes to mind. He's involved in
your Cuban escapades, isn't he?

KB: Yes, he is.

JEH: Yes, he is, and?

KB: And we talk as Agency business dictates.

JEH: The Chicago Office was satisfied with
Bondurant's alibi. The alibi-giver was a reputed
Heroin trafficker with numerous rape convictions
inside Cuba, but as Al Capone once said, an alibi is
an alibi.

KB: Yes, Sir. And as you once said, anti-Communism
breeds strange bedfellows.

JEH: Goodbye, Kemper. I very much hope that our
next communique is at your instigation.

KB: Goodbye, Sir.

47
(Los Angeles, 7/13/60)

THE CLERK HANDED him a gold-plated key. "We had a reservations glitch, sir. Your room was inadvertently given away, but
we're going to give you a suite at our regular room rate."

Check-ins pushed up to the desk. Kemper said, "Thanks. It's
a glitch I can live with."

The clerk shuffled papers. "May I ask you a question?"

"Let me guess. If my room is being charged to the Kennedy
campaign, why am I staying here instead of at the Biltmore with
the rest of the staff?"

"Yes, sir. That's it exactly."

Kemper winked. "I'm a spy."

The clerk laughed. Some delegate types waved to get his attention.

Kemper brushed past them and elevatored up to the twelfth floor. His suite: the double-doored, gold-sealed, all-antique Presidential.

He walked through it. He savored the appointments and checked out the north-by-northeast view.

Two bedrooms, three TVs and three phones. Complimentary champagne in a pewter ice bucket marked with the U.S. presidential seal.

He deciphered the "glitch" instantly: J. Edgar Hoover at work.

He wants to scare you. He's saying, "I own you." He's satirizing your Kennedy fervor and love of hotel suites.

He wants potential bug/tap intelligence.

Kemper turned on the living-room TV. Convention commentary hit the screen.

He turned on the other sets—and boosted the volume way up.

He grid-searched the suite. He found condensor mikes inside five table lamps and fake panels behind the bathroom mirrors.

He found two auxiliaries spackled into the living-room wainscoting. Tiny perforations served as sound ducts—nonprofessionals would never spot them. He checked out the telephones. All four were tapped.

Kemper thought it through from Hoover's perspective.

We discussed standing bugs a few days ago. He knows I don't want to set Jack up with "Bureau-friendly" women.

He said he thinks Jack is inevitable. He may be dissembling. He may be seeking knowledge of adultery—to aid his good friend Dick Nixon.

He knows you'll see through the "reservations glitch." He thinks you'll make your confidential calls from pay phones. He thinks you'll curtail your in-suite talk or destroy the bug/taps out of pique.

He knows Littell taught you bug/tap fundamentals. He doesn't know Littell taught you some fine points.

He knows you'll uncover the *main bugs.* He thinks you won't uncover the backups—the ones he plans to sucker-punch you with.

Kemper turned off the TVs. Kemper faked a vivid temper tantrum—"Hoover, goddamn you!" and worse expletives.

He ripped out the primary bug/taps.

He grid-searched the suite again—even more diligently.

He found secondary phone taps. He spotted microphone per-forations on two mattress labels and three chair cushions.

He went down to the lobby and rented room 808 under a pseudonym. He called John Stanton's service and left his fake name and room number.

Pete was in L.A., meeting with Howard Hughes. He called the watchdog house and left a message with the pool cleaner.

He had free time now. Bobby didn't need him until 5:00.

He walked to a hardware store. He bought wire cutters, pliers, a Phillips-head screwdriver, three rolls of friction tape and two small magnets. He walked back to the Statler and worked.

He rewired the buzzer housings. He recircuited the feeder wires. He muffled the bells with pillow stuffing. He scraped the rubber off the lead cables—incoming talk would register inco-herently on all the backup-tapped phones.

He laid the pieces out for easy reassembly. He called room ser-vice for Beefeater's and smoked salmon.

Calls came in. His squelch system worked perfectly.

He barely heard the callers. Line crackle would drown out all second-party talk—the taps would only pick up *his* voice.

His LAPD liaison called. As planned: a motorcycle escort would accompany Senator Kennedy to the convention.

Bobby called. Could he get some cabs to shuttle staffers back to the Biltmore?

Kemper called a car service and implemented Bobby's order. He had to strain to hear the dispatcher talk.

Horns blasted down on Wilshire Boulevard. Kemper checked his watch and the living-room window.

His "Protestants for Kennedy" motorcade passed by. On time to the minute—and prepaid at fifty dollars a car.

Kemper turned on the TVs and paced between them. History beamed out in crisp black & white.

CBS called Jack a first ballot shoo-in. ABC flashed panning shots—a big Stevenson demonstration just erupted. NBC fea-tured a prissy Eleanor Roosevelt: "Senator Kennedy is simply too young!"

ABC ballyhooed Jackie Kennedy. NBC showed Frank

Sinatra working the delegate floor. Frankie was vain—Jack said he spray-painted his bald spot to cut down camera glare.

Kemper paced and flipped channels. He caught a late-afternoon potpourri.

Convention analysis and a baseball game. Convention interviews and a Marilyn Monroe movie. Convention shots, convention shots, convention shots.

He caught some nice shots of Jack's HQ suite. He saw Ted Sorensen, Kenny O'Donnell and Pierre Salinger.

He met Salinger and O'Donnell once only. Jack pointed out Sorensen—"the guy who wrote *Profiles in Courage* for me."

It was "compartmentalization" classically defined. Jack and Bobby knew him—but no one else really did. He was just that cop who fixed things and got Jack women.

Kemper wheeled the TVs together. He created a tableau: Jack in closeups and mid-shots.

He turned the room lights off and dimmed the volume. He got three images and one homogeneous whisper.

Wind ruffled Jack's hair. Pete called Jack's head of hair his chief attribute.

Pete refused to discuss the Littell assault. Pete sidestepped the issue to talk money.

Pete called him while Littell was still in the hospital. Pete got right to the point.

"You're jazzed on the Pension Fund books, and so's Littell. You're goosing him to find them, so you can work a money angle on it. I say, after the election we *both* brace Littell. Whatever the angle is, we split the profit."

Pete emasculated Ward. Pete delivered the "scare" that he said he would.

He called Littell at the hospital. Ward compartmentalized his response.

"I don't trust you on this, Kemper. You can get the forensic particulars from the Bureau, but I'm not telling you WHO or WHY."

The WHERE was Lake Geneva, Wisconsin. The location *had to be* Pension Fund pertinent. "I don't trust you on this" could only mean one thing: Lenny Sands was talking trash to Littell.

Pete knew compartmentalization. Ward and Lenny knew it. John Stanton said the CIA coined that particular concept.

John called him in D.C. in mid-April. He said Langley just erected a compartmental wall.

"They're cutting us off, Kemper. They know about our Cadre business, and they approve, but they will not budget us one nickel. We're on salary as Blessington campsite staff, but our actual Cadre business has been excommunicated."

It meant no CIA cryptonyms. No CIA acronyms. No CIA code names and no CIA initial/oblique-sign gobbledegook.

The Cadre was purely compartmentalized.

Kemper flipped channels with the sound off. He got a gorgeous juxtaposition: Jack and Marilyn Monroe on adjoining TV screens.

He laughed. He snapped to the ultimate tweak-Hoover embellishment.

He picked up the phone and dialed the daily weather number. He got a monotone buzz—barely audible.

He said, "Kenny? Hi, it's Kemper Boyd." He waited four seconds. "No, I need to talk to the senator."

He waited fourteen seconds. He said, "How are you, Jack?"— bright and cheerful.

He waited five seconds to allow for a plausible reply. He said, "Yes, everything *is* set up with the escort."

Twenty-two seconds. "Yes. Right. I know you're busy."

Eight seconds. "Yes. Tell Bobby I've got the security people at the house all set up."

Twelve seconds. "Right, the purpose of this call *is* to see if you want to get laid, because if you do, I'm expecting calls from a few girls who'd love to meet you."

Twenty-four seconds. "I don't believe it."

Nine seconds. "Lawford set it up?"

Eight seconds. "Come on, Jack. *Marilyn Monroe?*"

Eight seconds. "I'll believe it if you tell me not to send my girls over."

Six seconds. "Jesus Christ."

Eight seconds. "They'll be disappointed, but I'll extend the raincheck."

Eight seconds. "Right. Naturally, I'll want details. Right. Goodbye, Jack."

Kemper hung up. Jack and Marilyn bumped television heads.

He just created Voyeur/Wiretap Heaven. Hoover would cream his jeans and maybe even spawn some crazy myth.

48

(Beverly Hills, 7/14/60)

WYOMING WENT FOR Bad-Back Jack. The delegates went stone fucking nuts.

Hughes doused the volume and scrunched up on his pillows. "He's nominated. But that's a far cry from being elected."

Pete said, "Yes, sir."

"You're being deliberately obtuse. 'Yes, sir' is not the proper response, and you're sitting there in that chair being deliberately disrespectful."

A commercial blipped on: Yeakel Oldsmobile, the voters' choice!

"How's this? 'Yes, sir, Jack's got a nice head of hair, but your man Nixon will thrash him soundly in the general election.' "

Hughes said, "It's better, but I detect a certain impertinence."

Pete cracked his thumbs. "I flew out because you said you needed to see me. I brought you a three-month supply of shit. You said you wanted to discuss some subpoena dodging strategy, but all you've done so far is rant about the Kennedys."

Hughes said, "That is *gross* impertinence."

Pete sighed. "Get your Mormons to show me the door, then. Get Duane Spurgeon to score you dope in violation of six trillion fucking state and Federal statutes."

Hughes flinched. His IV tubes stretched; his blood bottle wiggled. Vampire Howard: sucking in transfusions to assure his germ-free longevity.

"You're a very cruel man, Pete."

"No. Like I told you once before, I'm *your* very cruel man."

"Your eyes have gotten smaller and crueler. You keep looking at me strangely."

"I'm waiting for you to bite my neck. I've been around the block a few times, but this new Dracula kick of yours is something to see."

Hughes fucking *smiled*. "It's no more amazing than you fighting Fidel Castro."

Pete smiled. "Was there something important you wanted to talk about?"

The convention flashed back on. Bad-Back Jack supporters whooped and swooned.

"I want you to vet the subpoena-avoidance plans my Mormon colleagues have devised. They've come up with some ingenious—"

"We could have done it over the phone. You've been holding the TWA paperwork off since '57, and I don't think the Justice Department gives a shit anymore."

"Be that as it may, I now have a specific reason to avoid divesting TWA until the most opportune moment."

Pete sighed. Pete said, "I'm listening."

Hughes tapped his drip gizmos. A blood bottle drained red to pink.

"When I finally divest, I want to use the money to buy hotel-casinos in Las Vegas. I want to accumulate large, undetectable cash profits and breathe wholesome, germ-free desert air. I'll have my Mormon colleagues administer the hotels, to insure that Negroes who might pollute the environment are politely but firmly discouraged from entering, and I'll create a cash-flow base that will allow me to diversify into various defense-industry areas without paying taxes on my seed money. I'll—"

Pete tuned him out. Hughes kept spritzing numbers: millions, billions, trillions. Jack the K. was on TV—spritzing "Vote for Me!" with the sound down.

Pete ran numbers in his head.

There's Littell in Lake Geneva—chasing the Pension Fund. There's Jules Schiffrin—a well-respected Chi-Mob graybeard. Jules *just might* have the Pension books stashed at his pad.

Hughes said, "Pete, you're not listening to me. Quit looking at that puerile politician and give me your full attention."

Pete hit the off switch. Jack the Haircut faded out.

Hughes coughed. "That's better. You were looking at that boy with something like admiration."

"It's his hair, Boss. I was wondering how he got it to stand up like that."

"You have a short memory. And I have a short fuse where ironic answers are concerned."

"Yeah?"

"Yes. You might recall that two years ago I gave you thirty thousand dollars to try to compromise that boy with a prostitute."

"I remember."

"That's not a complete answer."

"The complete answer is 'Things change.' And you don't think America's going to get between the sheets with Dick Nixon when they can cozy up to Jack, do you?"

Hughes pushed himself upright. His bed rails shook; his IV rig teetered.

"I own Richard Nixon."

Pete said, "I know you do. And I'm sure he's real grateful for that loan you floated his brother."

Dracula got the shakes. Dracula got his dentures snagged up on the roof of his mouth.

Dracula got some words out. "I—I—I'd forgotten that you knew about that."

"A busy guy like you can't remember everything."

Drac reached for a fresh hypo. "Dick Nixon's a good man, and the entire Kennedy family is rotten down to the core. Joe Kennedy's been lending gangsters money since the '20s, and I know for a fact that the infamous Raymond L. S. Patriarca owes him the very shirt off his back."

He had the Nixon loan documented. He could feed the dope to Boyd and curry big-time favor with Jack.

Pete said, "Like I owe you."

Hughes beamed. "I knew you'd see my point."

49

(Chicago, 7/15/60)

LITTELL STUDIED HIS new face.

His weak jawline was rebuilt with pins and bone chips. His weak chin was smashed into a cleft. The nose he always hated was flattened and ridged.

Helen said he looked dangerous. Helen said his scars put hers to shame.

Littell stepped back from the mirror. Shifting light gave him new angles to savor.

He limped now. His jaw clicked. He put on twenty pounds in the hospital.

Pete Bondurant was a cosmetic surgeon.

He had a bold new face. His old pre-Phantom psyche couldn't live up to it.

He was afraid to move on Jules Schiffrin. He was afraid to confront Kemper. He was afraid to talk on the phone—little line clicks popped in his ears.

The clicks could be jaw-pin malfunctions. The clicks could be audial DTs.

He was six months short of retirement. Mal Chamales said the Party needed lawyers.

A TV boomed next door. John Kennedy's acceptance speech faded into applause.

The Bureau discontinued their assault inquiry. Hoover knew that he could sabotage Boyd's Kennedy incursion.

Littell stepped close to the mirror. The scars above his eyebrows furrowed.

He couldn't stop looking.

50

(Miami/Blessington, 7/16/60–10/12/60)

PETE TURNED FORTY on a speedboat run to Cuba. He led a raid on a militia station and took sixteen scalps.

Ramón Gutiérrez sketched up a Cadre mascot: a pit bull with an alligator snout and razor-blade teeth. Ramón's girlfriend sewed up mascot shoulder patches.

A printer fashioned mascot calling cards. "FREE CUBA!" roared out of the Beast's mouth.

Carlos Marcello carried one. Sam G. carried one. Santo Junior handed out dozens to friends and associates.

The Beast craved blood. The Beast craved Castro's beard on a stick.

Training cycles pushed through Blessington. The invasion plan mandated new ordnance. Dougie Frank Lockhart purchased surplus landing craft and "invaded" Alabama once per cycle.

The Gulf Coast simulated Cuba. Trainees hit the beach and scared the shit out of sunbathers.

Dougie Frank trained troops full-time. Pete trained troops part-time. Chuck, Fulo and Wilfredo Delsol ran the cabstand.

Pete led speedboat runs into Cuba. Everybody went along—except Delsol.

The Obregón kill snipped part of his balls. Pete didn't judge him—losing blood kin in a flash was no picnic.

Everybody sold dope.

The Cadre supplied spook junkies exclusively. The Miami PD implicitly approved. Narco Squad payouts served as disapproval insurance.

A redneck gang tried to crash their turf late in August. One geek shot and killed a Dade County deputy.

Pete found the guy—holed up with seventy grand and a case of Wild Turkey. He took him out with Fulo's machete and donated the cash to the deputy's widow.

Profits zoomed. The % system worked slick as shit—fat stipends went to Blessington and Guy Banister. Lenny Sands ran the *Hush-Hush* propaganda war. Purple prose bopped the Beard every week.

Dracula called weekly. He spouted broken-record bullshit: I want to buy up Las Vegas and render it germ-free! Drac was half lucid and half nuts—and only really cagey where coin was concerned.

Boyd called bi-weekly. Boyd was Bad-Back Jack's security boss and head pimp.

Mr. Hoover kept chasing him with phone calls. Kemper kept avoiding them. Hoover wanted him to slip Jack some hot-wired pussy.

Boyd called it a sprint: Avoid The Man until Jack becomes The Man.

Hoover hot-wired Boyd's L.A. hotel suite. Kemper shot him some spicy misinformation: Jack the K is banging Marilyn Monroe!

Hoover bought the lie. An L.A. agent told Boyd that Monroe was now under intense surveillance: bug/taps and six full-time men.

Said agents were baffled. Jack the Haircut and MM have not been in contact.

Pete laughed himself silly. Dracula confirmed the rumor: Marilyn and Jack were one hot item!!!!

Boyd said he skin-searched all Jack's girls.

Boyd said Kennedy and Nixon were running neck-and-neck.

Pete didn't say, *I've* got dirt. I can SELL it to Jimmy Hoffa; I can GIVE it to you to smear Nixon with.

Jimmy's a colleague. Boyd's a partner. Who's more pro-Cause—Jack or Nixon?

Tricky Dick was hotly anti-Beard. Jack was vocal but still short of rabid.

John Stanton called Nixon "Mr. Invasion." Kemper said Jack would green-light all invasion plans.

Boyd's key campaign issue was COMPART-MENTALIZATION.

Ike and Dick knew the Agency and the Mob were Cuba-linked. The Kennedys didn't know—and might or might not be told if Jack bags the White House.

Who decides whether to spill?—Kemper Cathcart Boyd himself. The deciding factor: moralist Bobby's perceived influence on Big Brother.

Bobby could scut all Mob/CIA ties. Bobby could scut the Boyd/Bondurant casino incentive deal.

Jack or Dick—one very tough call.

The smart bet: Don't smear seasoned Red-baiter Nixon. Not so smart, but sexy: Smear him and put Jack in the White House.

Vote Boyd. Vote the Beast. Vote Fidel Castro's beard on a stick.

DOCUMENT INSERT: 10/13/60.
FBI memorandum: Chicago SAC Charles Leahy to Director J. Edgar Hoover.
Marked: CONFIDENTIAL/DIRECTOR'S EYES ONLY.

Sir,

The pro-Communist derogatory profile on SA Ward J. Littell is now complete. This memo supplants all previous confidential reports pertaining to Littell, with itemized evidence documents to follow under separate cover.

To briefly update you on recent developments:

1.—Claire Boyd (daughter of SA Kemper C. Boyd and longtime Littell family friend) was contacted and agreed not to tell her father of the interview. Miss Boyd stated that last Christmas SA Littell made obscenely disparaging anti-Bureau, anti-Hoover remarks and praised the American Communist Party.

2.—There are no leads in the Littell assault

investigation. We still do not know what Littell was
doing in Lake Geneva, Wisconsin.

   3.—SA Littell's mistress, Helen Agee, was spot-
surveilled for a two-week period last month. Several
of Miss Agee's University of Chicago Law School
professors were quizzed about her political
statements. We now have four confirmed reports that
Miss Agee has also been publicly critical of the
Bureau. One professor (Chicago Office informant
#179) stated that Miss Agee railed against the FBI for
their failure to solve a ''simple assault case up in
Wisconsin'' and went on to call the Bureau ''the
American Gestapo that got my father killed and turned
my lover into a cripple.'' (A U of C dean is going to
recommend that Miss Agee's graduate school grant
funding be rescinded under provisions of a student
loyalty statement that all law school enrollees
sign.)

   In conclusion:

   I think it is now time to approach SA Littell.
I await further orders.

               Respectfully, Charles Leahy, Chicago SAC

DOCUMENT INSERT: 10/15/60.
FBI memorandum: Director J. Edgar Hoover to SAC
Charles Leahy.

Mr. Leahy,

   No approach on SA Littell until I so direct.

                                 JEH

51

(Chicago, 10/16/60)

HIS HANGOVER WAS brutal. Bad dreams left him schizy—every
man in the diner looked like a cop.

   Littell stirred his coffee. His hands shook. Mal Chamales toyed
with a sweet roll and shook almost as hard.

"Mal, you're leading up to something."

"I'm in no position to be asking favors."

"If it's an official FBI favor, you should know that I retire exactly three months from today."

Mal laughed. "Like I said, the Party always needs lawyers."

"I'd have to pass the Illinois Bar first. It's either that or move to D.C. and practice Federal law."

"You're not much of a leftist sympathizer."

"Or a Bureau apologist. Mal—"

"I'm up for a teaching job. The word's out that the State Board of Ed's breaking the blacklist. I want to cover my bets, and I was thinking you could edit your reports to show that I quit the Party."

The tall man at the counter looked familiar. The man loitering outside did, too.

"Ward . . ."

"Sure, Mal. I'll write it up in my next report. I'll say you quit the Party to take a job with the Nixon campaign."

Mal dashed some tears back. Mal almost dumped the table trying to hug him.

Littell said, "Get out of here. I don't like embracing Commies in public."

The diner faced his apartment building. Littell hogged a window seat and killed time polling bumper stickers.

Two Nixon cars were parked at the curb. He saw a Nixon-Lodge decal on his landlord's windshield.

Traffic whizzed by. Littell caught glimpses: six Nixons and three Kennedys.

The waitress topped off his coffee. He added two shots from his flask.

Instant straw poll results: Nixon sweeps Chicago!

Sunlight hit the window. Wonderful distortions hit him: his new face and his jagged new hairline.

Helen ran up the steps outside his apartment. She looked harried—no makeup, no overcoat, mismatched skirt and blouse.

She saw his car. She looked across the street and saw him in the window.

She ran over. Notebook paper flew out of her handbag.

Littell walked to the door. Helen *shoved* it open two-handed.

He tried to grab her. She pulled his gun out of his holster and hit him with it.

She hit him in the chest. She hit him in the arms. She tried to pull the trigger with the safety on. She hit him with flailing girl punches—too fast to stop.

Eyeliner ran down her cheeks. Her handbag capsized and spilled books. She shouted odd words: "grant fund rescinding" and "loyalty oath" and "FBI" and "YOU YOU YOU."

Heads bobbed their way. Two men at the counter pulled *their* guns.

Helen stopped hitting him. Helen said, "Goddamnit, this is YOU, I know it is."

He drove to the office. He boxed in Leahy's car and ran up to the squadroom.

Leahy's door was shut. Court Meade saw him and turned away.

Two men walked by in shirtsleeves and shoulder holsters. Littell remembered them: the phone guys rigging lines outside his apartment.

Leahy's door swung open. A man stuck his head out. Littell remembered him: that guy at the post office yesterday.

The door closed. Voices seeped through it: "Littell," "the Agee girl."

He kicked the door off its hinges. He framed the scene à la Mal Chamales.

Four gray-flannel fascists in conference. Four parasitic, exploitative, right-wing—

Littell said, "Remember what I know. Remember how I can hurt the Bureau."

He bought wire cutters, safety goggles, magnetic shielding strips, a glass cutter, rubber gloves, a .10-gauge shotgun, a hundred rounds of double-aught buckshot, a box of industrial dynamite, three hundred yards of acoustical baffling, a hammer, nails and two large duffel bags.

He stored his car in a service garage.

He rented a '57 Ford Victoria—with fake Cointelpro ID.

He bought three quarts of scotch—just enough to wean himself dry.

He drove south to Sioux City, Iowa.

He turned in his rental car and caught a train north to Milwaukee.

DOCUMENT INSERT: 10/17/60.
Confidential memorandum: John Stanton to Kemper Boyd.

Kemper,

I got a disquieting phone call from Guy Banister, so I thought I'd pass the information along to you. You're hard to reach these days, so I hope this gets to you within a reasonable length of time.
Guy's friends with the Miami SAC, who's tight with the CO of the Miami PD Intelligence Squad. The Squad keeps suspected pro-Castro Cubans under loose surveillance, with routine license plate checks on all the male Latins they are spotted with. Our man Wilfredo Olmos Delsol was seen on two occasions with Gaspar Ramon Blanco, age 37, a known pro-Communist member of the Committee for Cuban Understanding, a Raul Castro-financed propaganda front. This troubles me, chiefly because of PB's set-to with Delsol's cousin Tomas Obregon. Have PB check this out, would you? Our compartmentalization procedures preclude my contacting him directly.

All best, John

52

(Miami, 10/20/60)

THE PILOT ANNOUNCED a late arrival. Kemper checked his watch—Pete's allotted time just evaporated.

Pete caught up with him in Omaha this morning. He said, I've got something for you—something you'll want to *see*.

He promised that the stopover would take no more than twenty minutes. He said, I'll put you on the next plane back to Jack.

Miami twinkled below. He had crucial work in Omaha—postponed by this six-hour detour.

The race was too close to call. Nixon *might* have a slight edge—with eighteen days left to go.

He called Laura from the departure lounge. She lit into his Kennedy ties. Claire kept saying that Laura ached for a Nixon victory.

Claire said FBI men questioned her last month. Their sole topic was Ward Littell's politics.

The agents intimidated her. They cautioned her not to mention the interview to her father.

Claire broke the promise and called him three days ago. He called Ward immediately.

His phone rang and rang. The rings had a distinct wiretap pitch.

He called Court Meade to check on Ward's whereabouts. Meade said Ward kicked the SAC's door down and vanished.

Claire called him in Omaha last night. She said the Bureau got Helen's law school grant revoked.

Mr. Hoover stopped calling him two days ago. It all connected somehow. The campaign had him running too fast to be scared.

Crosswinds roughed up their descent. The plane taxied in with a fishtailing whoosh.

Kemper checked his window. He saw Pete standing outside, with the ground crew. The men were palming cash rolls and fawning at the big guy with the money.

Landing stairs locked in. Kemper crowded up to the door.

The co-pilot cranked it open. There's Pete—with a baggage cart parked on the runway, right below them.

Kemper took the steps three at a time. Pete grabbed him and cupped a yell. "Your plane's delayed! We've got half an hour!"

Kemper jumped on the cart. Pete gunned it. They dodged luggage piles and swung around to a janitor's hut.

A baggage handler got the door. Pete slipped him twenty dollars.

A linen tablecloth was draped over a workbench. On it: gin, vermouth, a glass and six sheets of paper.

Pete said, "Read through that."

Kemper skimmed the top page. His hackles jumped immediately.

Howard Hughes lent Dick Nixon's kid brother $200,000. Check photostats, bookkeeping notes and bank slips proved it.

Somebody compiled an itemized list: Nixon-proffered legislation linked to Hughes government contracts.

Kemper mixed a drink. His hands shook. He spilled Beefeater's all over the workbench.

He looked at Pete. "You haven't asked for money."

"If I wanted money, I would have called Jimmy."

"I'll tell Jack he's got a friend in Miami."

"Tell him to let us invade Cuba, and I'll call it even."

The martini was gorgeously dry. The janitor's hut glowed like the Carlyle.

"Keep an eye on Wilfredo Delsol. It's anticlimactic now, but I think he might be screwing up."

Pete said, "Call Bobby. I want to hear you put the little fuck in hock to me."

DOCUMENT INSERT: 10/23/60.
Cleveland Plain Dealer headline:
HUGHES-NIXON LOAN REVELATIONS ROCK CAMPAIGN

DOCUMENT INSERT: 10/24/60.
Chicago Tribune subhead:
KENNEDY BLASTS NIXON-HUGHES ''COLLUSION''

DOCUMENT INSERT: 10/25/60.
Los Angeles Herald-Express headline and subhead:
NIXON DENIES INFLUENCE-PEDDLING ACCUSATIONS
HUGHES LOAN BROUHAHA CUTS VEEP'S LEAD IN POLLS

DOCUMENT INSERT: 10/26/60.
New York Journal-American subhead:
NIXON CALLS LOAN FLAP ''TEMPEST IN TEAPOT''

DOCUMENT INSERT: 10/28/60.
San Francisco Chronicle headline:
NIXON BROTHER CALLS HUGHES LOAN ''NON-POLITICAL''

DOCUMENT INSERT: 10/29/60.
Kansas City Star subhead:
KENNEDY BLASTS NIXON FOR HUGHES LOAN

DOCUMENT INSERT: 11/3/60:
Boston Globe headline:
GALLUP POLL: PREZ'L RACE DEAD HEAT!

53

(Lake Geneva, 11/5/60)

LITTELL RAN THROUGH his checklist.

Goggles, earplugs, wire cutters, glass cutter—check. Magnet strips, gloves, shotgun, ammunition—check.

Waterproof-fuse dynamite—check. Acoustical baffling, hammer, nails—check.

Check: You wiped every print-sustaining surface in this motel room.

Check: You left your check-out cash on the dresser.

Check: You avoided all contact with your fellow motel tenants.

He ran through his three-week precaution list.

You changed motels every other day—in zigzag patterns throughout southern Wisconsin.

You wore fake beards and fake mustaches at all times.

You changed rental cars at odd intervals. You took buses between car-rental pickups. You secured said cars at distant sites: Des Moines, Minneapolis and Green Bay.

You rented said cars with fake ID.

You paid cash.

You parked said cars nowhere near the motels you checked into.

You made no motel-room phone calls. You print-wiped every surface before you checked out.

You employed tail-evasion tactics. You limited your liquor intake: six shots a night to insure steady nerves.

You spotted no tails.

You stared at single men, gauged their reactions and discerned nothing cop- or Mob-like. Most men evinced discomfort: you were rough-looking now.

You cased Jules Schiffrin's estate. You determined that the man had no live-in help or on-site watchmen.

You learned Schiffrin's routine:

Saturday-night dinner and cards at Badger Glen Country Club. Early-Sunday-morning sojourns at the home of one Glenda Rae Mattson.

Jules Schiffrin was gone from 7:05 P.M. to 2:00 A.M. every Saturday into Sunday. His estate was police patrolled every two hours—cursory perimeter road checks.

You secured safe-placement and alarm diagrams. You queried seventeen services to get them. You impersonated a Milwaukee PD lieutenant and buttressed the impersonations with forged documents and credentials purchased from a forger that you arrested years ago.

All your police impersonations were carried out in disguise.

Two steel-plated safes were installed on the premises. They weighed ninety-five pounds apiece. You had their exact location memorized.

Final checks:

Your new motel room outside Beloit: safely rented.

The newspaper piece on Schiffrin's art collection: clipped out to leave at the crime scene.

Littell took a deep breath and downed three quick shots. His nerves fluttered and *almost* leveled out.

He checked his face in the bathroom mirror. One last look for courage—

Low clouds covered the moon. Littell drove to the half-mile-out point.

It was 11:47. He had two hours and thirteen minutes to get clear.

A State Police cruiser passed him eastbound. On time: the standard 11:45 perimeter check.

Littell swung off the pavement. Hard-packed dirt grabbed his tires. He hit his brights and slalomed downhill.

The slope evened out. He brodied his back wheels to obliterate tread marks.

Trees dotted the clearing—his car couldn't be seen from the road.

He killed the lights and grabbed his duffel bag. He saw house lights due west uphill—a faint directional glow to work off of.

He walked toward it. Leaf clumps obscured his footprints. The glow expanded every few seconds.

He hit the driveway adjoining the carport. Schiffrin's Eldorado Brougham was gone.

He ran to the library window and crouched low. An inside lamp provided hazy light to work by.

He got out his tools and snipped two wires taped to a storm drain. An exterior arc light sputtered. He saw alarm tape bracketing the window glass—mounted between two thick panes.

He gauged the circumference.

He cut magnet-tape strips to cover it.

He stuck them to the outside glass in a near-perfect outline.

His legs ached. Cold sweat stung some shaving cuts.

He ran a magnet over the tape. He traced a circle inside the outline with his glass cutter.

The glass was THICK—it took two hands and all his weight to notch a groove.

No alarms went off. No lights flashed.

He gouged circles in the glass. No sirens whirred; no general pursuit noise went down.

His arms burned. His blade went sharp to dull. His sweat froze and made him shiver.

The outside pane broke. He tucked his sleeves inside his gloves and bore down harder.

TWENTY-NINE MINUTES ELAPSED.

Elbow pressure snapped the inside pane. Littell kicked the frame glass out to make a crawl space.

He vaulted inside. The fit was tight—glass shards cut him down to the skin.

The library was oak-paneled and furnished with green leather chairs. The side walls featured artwork: one Matisse, one Cézanne, one van Gogh.

Floor lamps gave him light—just enough to do the job by.

He arranged his tools.

He found the safes: wall-panel-recessed two feet apart.

He covered every inch of wall space with triple-thick acoustical baffling. He hammered it down tight—fivepenny nails into high-varnished oak.

He X-marked the sections covering the safes. He put on his goggles and stuffed in his earplugs. He loaded his shotgun and let fly.

One round, two rounds—huge contained explosions. Three rounds, four rounds—padding chunks and hardwood decomposing.

Littell reloaded and fired, reloaded and fired, reloaded and fired.

Wood chips sliced his face. Muzzle smoke had him retching. Visibility was zero: mulch slammed up against his goggles.

Littell reloaded and fired, reloaded and fired, reloaded and fired. Forty-odd rounds took the wall and rear ceiling beams down.

Wood and plaster crashed. Second-story furniture dropped down and shattered. Two safes fell out of the rubble.

Littell kicked through it—Please, God, let me breathe.

He vomited splinters and scotch. He coughed up gunsmoke and black phlegm. He dug through wood heaps and lugged the safes over to his duffel bag.

SEVENTY-TWO MINUTES ELAPSED.

The library was blasted through to the dining room. Forty-odd explosions toppled the artwork.

The Cézanne was intact. The Matisse bore slight frame damage. The van Gogh was pellet-shredded nothingness.

Littell dropped the newspaper clip.

Littell lashed the duffel to his back with curtain strips.

Littell grabbed the paintings and ran out the front door.

Pure air made him go lightheaded. He gulped it in and ran.

He slid on leaves and bounced off trees. His bladder went— nothing ever felt so good. He stumbled, hunched over double— two hundred pounds of steel kept him plummeting downhill.

He fell. His body went rubber—he couldn't stand up or lift the duffel bag.

He crawled and dragged it the rest of the way. He loaded his car and fishtailed up to the access road, heaving for breath the whole time.

He caught his face in the rearview mirror. The word "heroic" came up short.

He took switchbacks north/northwest. He found his preselected detonation spot: a forest clearing outside Prairie du Chien.

He lit the clearing with three big Coleman lanterns. He burned the paintings and scattered the ashes.

He crimped the butt ends of six sticks of dynamite and slid them up against the safe dial-housings.

He strung fuses a hundred yards out and lit a match.

The safes blew. The doors shot all the way up to the tree line. A breeze scattered scorched piles of currency.

Littell sifted through them. The blast destroyed at least a hundred thousand dollars.

Undamaged:

Three large ledger books wrapped in plastic.

Littell buried the scraps of money and dumped the safe sections in a sewage stream adjoining the clearing. He drove to his new motel and obeyed all speed limits en route.

Three ledgers. Two hundred pages per unit. Cross-column notations on each page, squared off in a standard bookkeeping style.

Huge figures listed left to right.

Littell laid the books out on the bed. His first instinct:

The amounts exceeded all possible compilations of monthly or yearly Pension Fund dues.

The two brown leather ledgers were coded. The number/letter listings in the far left-hand column roughly corresponded in digit length to names.

Thus:

AH795/WZ458YX =

One five-letter first name and one seven-letter last name.

MAYBE.

The black leather ledger was uncoded. It contained similarly large financial tallies—and two- and three-letter listings in the far left-hand column.

The listings *might* be: lender or lendee initials.

The black book was subdivided into vertical columns. They were real-word designated: "Loan %" and "Transfer #."

Littell put the black book aside. His second instinct: code breaking would not be easy.

He went back to the brown books.

He followed symbol names and figures and watched money accrue horizontally. Neatly doubled sums told him the Pension Fund repayment rate: a usurious 50%.

He spotted letter repetitions—in four-to-six-letter increments—most likely a simple date code. A for 1, B for 2—something told him it was just that simple.

He matched letters to numbers and EXTRAPOLATED:

Fund loan profiteering went back thirty years. The letters and numbers ascended left to right—straight up to early 1960.

The average amount lent was $1.6 million. With repayment fees: $2.4 million.

The smallest loan was $425,000. The largest was $8.6 million.

Numbers growing left to right. Multiplications and divisions in the far right-hand columns—odd percentage calculations.

He EXTRAPOLATED:

The odd numbers were loan investment profits, tallied in over and above payback interest.

Eyestrain made him stop. Three quick shots of scotch refueled him.

He got a brainstorm:

Look for Hoffa's Sun Valley skim money.

He scanned columns with a pencil. He linked the dots: mid '56 to mid '57 and ten symbols to spell "Jimmy Hoffa."

He found 1.2 and 1.8—hypothetically Bobby Kennedy's "spooky" three million. He found five symbols, six, and five in a perfectly intersecting column.

5, 6, 5 = James Riddle Hoffa.

Hoffa laughed off the Sun Valley charges. With valid assurance: his chicanery was very well cloaked.

Littell skimmed the books and picked out odd totals. Tiny zeros extended—the Fund was billionaire rich.

Double vision set in. He corrected it with a magnifying glass.

He quick-scanned the books again. Identical numbers kept recurring—in four-figure brackets.

[1408]—over and over.

Littell went through the brown books page by page. He found twenty-one 1408s—including two next to the Spooky Three Million. Quick addition gave him a total: forty-nine million dollars lent out or borrowed. Mr. 1408 was well-heeled either way.

He checked the black book initial column. It was alphabetically arranged and entered in Jules Schiffrin's neat block printing.

It was 9:00 A.M. He had five hours of study in.

The "Loan %" subhead tweaked him. He saw "B–E" straight down the graph—the number/letter code decoded to 25%.

He EXTRAPOLATED:

The initials tagged Pension Fund lenders—*repaid* at a fat but not brutal rate.

He checked the "Transfer #" column. The listings were strictly uniform: initials and six digits, no more.

He EXTRAPOLATED:

The initials were bank account numbers—repaid mobster money laundered clean. Said initials all ended in B—most likely short for the word "branch."

Littell copied over letters on a scratch pad.

BOABHB = Bank of America, Beverly Hills branch.

HSALMBB = Home Savings & Loan, Miami Beach branch.

It worked.

He was able to form known bank names out of every set of letters.

He jumped columns tracing 1408. Right there on the money: JPK, SR/SFNBB/811512404.

SFN meant Security-First National. BB could mean Buffalo branch, Boston branch, or other B-city branches.

The SR probably denoted a "Senior." Why the added designation?

Just above JPK, SR: JPK [1693] BOADB. The man was a piker compared to 1408: he lent the Fund a paltry $6.4 million.

The added SR was simply to distinguish the lender from someone with the same initials.

JPK, SR [1408] SFNBB/811512404. One filthy-rich money-lending—

Stop.

Stop right there.

JPK, SR.

Joseph P. Kennedy, Senior.

BB for Boston branch.

August '59—Sid Kabikoff talking to Mad Sal:

"I knew Jules way back when"/"when he was SELLING DOPE and USING THE PROFITS to finance movies with RKO back when JOE KENNEDY owned it."

Stop. Make the call. Impersonate a Bureau hard-on and confirm it or refute it.

Littell dialed 0. He dripped sweat all over the telephone.

An operator came on. "What number, please?"

"I want the Security-First National Bank, in Boston, Massachusetts."

"One moment, sir. I'll look the number up and connect you."

Littell held the line. Adrenaline hit: he went dizzy and parched.

A man answered. "Security-First National."

"This is Special Agent Johnson, FBI. Let me speak to the manager, please."

"Please hold. I'll transfer you."

Littell heard connection clicks. A man said, "This is Mr. Carmody. May I help you?"

"Th-this is Special Agent Johnson, FBI. I have an account

number at your bank here, and I need to know who it belongs to."

"Is this an *official* request? It's a Sunday, and I'm here overseeing our monthly inventory—"

"This is an official request. I can get a bank writ, but I'd rather not put you to the trouble of an in-person visit."

"I see. Well . . . I guess. . . ."

Littell came on firm. "The number is 811512404."

The man sighed. "Well, uh, the 404 listings denote safe-deposit-box storage accounts, so if you're interested in balance figures, I'm afraid—"

"How many storage boxes are rented out to that account number?"

"Well, that account is quite familiar to me, because of its size. You see—"

"How many boxes?"

"An entire vault now of ninety."

"Can valuables be transferred directly into that vault from outside sources?"

"Certainly. They could be placed in the boxes sight unseen, by second parties with access to the account holder's password."

Ninety stash boxes. Millions in Mob-laundered CASH—

"Who does that account number belong to?"

"Well . . ."

"Shall I get a writ?"

"Well, I . . ."

Littell almost shouted it. *"Is the account holder Joseph P. Kennedy Sr.?"*

"Well . . . uh . . . yes."

"The senator's father?"

"Yes, the senator's—"

The phone slipped out of his hand. Littell kicked it across the room.

The black book. Mr. 1408, millionaire loan shark.

He went back over the numbers and confirmed it. He triple-checked every digit until his vision blurred.

Yes: Joe Kennedy lent the Fund Sun Valley seed money. Yes: The Fund lent the money out to James Riddle Hoffa.

Sun Valley constituted felony land fraud. Sun Valley spawned two Pete Bondurant killings: Anton Gretzler and Roland Kirpaski.

Littell tracked 1408s across paper. He saw continuous commas—and no cash-out bottom-line one-time profit.

Joe only took interest out. Joe's base loan sums stayed liquid inside the Fund.

Growing.

Laundered, hidden, obfuscated, tax-sheltered and funneled—disbursed to labor thugs, dope pushers, shylocks and mobbed-up fascist dictators.

The all-code books contained specifics. He could crack the code and know exactly where the money went.

My secrets, Bobby—I'll never let you hate your father.

Littell went eight drinks over his limit. He passed out shouting numbers.

54

(Hyannis Port, 11/8/60)

JACK STOOD A million votes up and way ahead in the electoral. Nixon gouged at his lead—the Midwest looked problematic.

Kemper watched three TVs and juggled four phones. His motel room was one big cable socket—the Secret Service demanded multiple lines in and out.

The red phone was his personal line. The two white phones hooked in direct to the Kennedy compound. The blue phone linked the Secret Service to the almost-President-elect.

It was 11:35 P.M.

CBS called Illinois tight. NBC said "Cliffhanger!" ABC said Jack would win, with 51% of the vote.

Kemper checked the window. Secret Service men mingled outside— they'd booked up the entire motel complex.

White phone #2 rang. It was Bobby, with complaints.

A journalist pole-vaulted into the compound. A hot rod sporting Nixon banners plowed the main house lawn.

Kemper called two off-duty cops and sent them over. He told them to beat up all trespassers and impound their vehicles.

The red phone rang. It was Santo Junior, with Mob scuttlebutt.

He said, Illinois looks dicey. He said, Sam G. threw some weight to help Jack.

Lenny Sands was out stuffing ballot boxes. He had a hundred aldermen helping him. Jack should blitz Cook County and eke out a statewide win by a nun's-cunt-hair margin.

Kemper hung up. The red phone rang again. It was Pete, with more secondhand gossip.

He said Mr. Hoover called Mr. Hughes. Mr. Hughes told Pete that Marilyn Monroe was quite naughty.

The Feds had her hot-wired. During the past two weeks she banged disc jockey Allan Freed, Billy Eckstine, Freddy Otash, Rin Tin Tin's trainer, Jon "Ramar of the Jungle" Hall, her pool cleaner, two pizza delivery boys, talk-show man Tom Duggan and her maid's husband—but no Senator John F. Kennedy.

Kemper laughed and hung up. CBS judged the race "too close to call."

ABC retracted its prediction. The race was now "too close to call."

White phone #1 rang.

Kemper picked up. "Bob?"

"It's me. I just called to say we're way ahead in the electoral, and Illinois and Michigan should put us over. The Hughes loan thing helped, Kemper. Your 'unnamed source' should know that it was a factor."

"You don't sound too elated."

"I won't believe it until it's final. And a friend of Dad's just died. He was younger than him, so he's taking it hard."

"Anybody I know?"

"Jules Schiffrin. I think you met him a few years ago. He had a heart attack in Wisconsin. He came home and found his house burglarized, and just keeled over. A friend of Dad's in Lake Geneva called—"

"Lake Geneva?"

"Right. North of Chicago. Kemper . . ."

The Littell assault location. Schiffrin: a Chicago-based gonif type.

"Kemper . . ."

"I'm sorry. I was distracted."

"I was going to say something . . ."

"About Laura?"

"How did you know that?"

"You never come off hesitant unless it's about Laura."

Bobby cleared his throat. "Call her. Tell her we'd appreciate it if she didn't contact the family for a while. I'm sure she'll understand."

Court Meade said Littell vanished. It was circumstantial, but—

"Kemper, are you listening to me?"

"Yes."

"Call Laura. Be kind, but be firm."

"I'll do it."

Bobby hung up. Kemper placed a red phone call through the switchboard: Chicago, BL8-4908.

It went through. He heard two rings and two very faint tap-clicks.

Littell said, "Hello?"

Kemper covered the mouthpiece.

Littell said, "Is that you, Boyd? Are you coming back into my life because you're scared, or because you think I might have something you want?"

Kemper disconnected.

Ward J. Littell—Jesus Fucking Christ.

55

(Miami, 11/9/60)

GUY BANISTER SCREECHED long-distance. Pete felt an earache coming on.

"We're looking at a new papist hegemony. He loves niggers and Jews, and he's been soft-line on Communism since he was a congressman. I can't believe he won. I can't believe the American people bought his line of bull—"

"Get to it, Guy. You said J.D. Tippit picked up something."

Banister de-throttled his spiel. "I forgot I called you for a reason. And I forgot you were soft-line on Kennedy."

Pete said, "I like his hair. It gets my dick hard."

Banister *re*-throttled. Pete cut him off quick.

"It's 8:00 fucking A.M. I've got cab calls backed up and three drivers out sick. Tell me what you want."

"I want Dick Nixon to demand a recount."

"Guy—"

"All right, then. Boyd was supposed to tell you to talk to Wilfredo Delsol."

"He did."

"*Did* you talk to him?"

"No. I've been busy."

"Tippit said he heard Delsol's been seen with some Castro guys. A bunch of us think he should explain."

"I'll go see him."

"You do that. And while you're at it, try to develop some political brains."

Pete laughed. "Jack's a white man. I've got a big hard-on just thinking about his hair."

Pete drove to Wilfredo's pad and knocked on the door. Delsol opened up in his skivvies.

He was bleary-eyed. He was scrawny. He looked too sleepy to stand upright.

He shivered and plucked at his balls. He shook the cobwebs out of his head and caught on fast.

"Somebody told you something bad about me."

"Keep going."

"You only visit people in order to scare them."

"That's right. Or to ask them to explain some things."

"Ask me, then."

"You were seen talking to some pro-Castro guys."

"That's true."

"So?"

"So they heard how my cousin Tomás died. They thought they could get me to betray the Cadre."

"And?"

"And I told them I hated what happened to Tomás, but I hate Fidel Castro more."

Pete leaned against the door. "You don't much like speedboat runs."

"Killing odd militiamen is futile."

"Suppose you get assigned to an invasion group?"

"I'll go."

"Suppose I tell you to whack one of those guys you were seen talking to?"

"I would say Gaspar Blanco lives two blocks from here."

Pete said, "Kill him."

* * *

Pete cruised Niggertown—for the pure time-marking fuck of it. The radio ran election news exclusively.

Nixon conceded. Frau Nixon pitched some boo-hoo. Bad-Back Jack thanked his staff and announced that Frau Bad-Back was pregnant.

Nigger junkies were cliqued up by a shine stand. Fulo and Ramón drove up to service them. Chuck was trading bindles for signed-over welfare checks.

Jack talked up the New Frontier. Fulo dropped off a fat load of shit with the shoeshine man.

A local bulletin flashed on.

Shots fired outside Coral Gables bodega! Police ID dead man as one Gaspar Ramón Blanco!

Pete smiled. November 8, 1960, was an all-time classic day.

He stopped at Tiger Kab after lunch. Teo Paez had a parking-lot sale going: hot TVs for twenty scoots a pop.

The sets were hooked up to a battery pack. Jack the K beamed out of two dozen screens.

Pete mingled with potential buyers. Jimmy Hoffa popped out of the crowd, popping sweat on a nice cool day.

"Hi, Jimmy."

"Don't gloat. I know you and Boyd wanted that cunt-lapping faggot to win."

"Don't worry. He'll put his kid brother on a tight leash."

"As if that's my only worry."

"What do you mean?"

"I mean Jules Schiffrin's dead. His place in Lake Geneva got clouted for some priceless fucking paintings, and some priceless fucking paperwork got lost in the process. Jules had a heart attack, and now our shit has probably been torched in some burglar's fucking basement."

LITTELL. 100% certifiably insane.

Pete started laughing.

Hoffa said, "What's so fucking funny?"

Pete roared.

Hoffa said, "Stop laughing, you frog fuck."

Pete couldn't stop. Hoffa pulled a piece and shot Jack the Haircut six TV screens across.

56

(Washington, D.C., 11/13/60)

THE MAILMAN BROUGHT a special-delivery letter. It was post-marked Chicago and sent without a return address.

Kemper opened the envelope. The one page inside was neatly typed.

I have the books. They are fail-safed against my death or disappearance in a dozen different ways. I will release them only to Robert Kennedy, if I am given a Kennedy Adminis-tration appointment within the next three months. The books are safely hidden. Hidden with them is an 83-page deposition, detailing my knowledge of your McClellan Committee–Kennedy incursion. I will destroy that deposition only if I am given a Kennedy Administration appointment. I remain fond of you, and am grateful for the lessons you taught me. At times, you acted with uncharac-teristic selflessness and risked exposure of your many dupli-citous relationships in an effort to help me achieve what I must fatuously describe as my manhood. That said, I will also state that I do not trust your motives regarding the books. I still consider you a friend, but I do not trust you one iota.

Kemper jotted a note to Pete Bondurant.

Forget about the Teamster books. Littell finessed us, and I'm beginning to rue the day I taught him some things. I made some discreet queries with the Wisconsin State Police, who are frankly baffled. I'll supply forensic details the next time we talk. I think you'll be grudgingly impressed. Enough pissing and moaning. Let's depose Fidel Castro.

57

(Chicago, 12/8/60)

WIND ROCKED THE car. Littell turned up the heat and pushed his seat back to stretch out.

His stakeout was strictly cosmetic. He might join the party himself—Mal would get a huge kick out of it.

It was a Bust the Blacklist bash. The Chicago Board of Ed had hired Mal Chamales to teach remedial math.

Guests walked up to the house. Littell recognized leftists with Red Squad sheets half a mile long.

A few waved to him. Mal said he might send his wife out with coffee and cookies.

Littell watched the house. Mal turned his Christmas lights on—the tree by the porch bloomed all blue and yellow.

He'd stay until 9:30. He'd write the bash up as a routine holiday soiree. Leahy would accept his assessment pro forma—their stalemate precluded direct confrontations.

His door-kicking episode and Lake Geneva time went unquestioned. He had thirty-nine days to go until his retirement. The Bureau's no-confrontation policy would hold and see him through to civilian life.

He had the Fund books stashed in a bank vault in Duluth. He had two dozen cryptography texts at home. He had seventeen days logged in without an ounce of liquor.

He could send the Fund books to Bobby on a moment's notice. He could delete Joe Kennedy's name with a few swipes of a pencil.

Dead leaves strafed the windshield. Littell got out of the car and stretched his legs.

He saw men running up Mal's driveway. He heard metal-on-metal pump-shotgun-slide noise.

He heard footsteps behind him. Hands slammed him across the hood and ripped off his gunbelt.

He gouged his face on a sharp strip of chrome. He saw Chick Leahy and Court Meade kick Mal's door down.

Big men in suits and overcoats swarmed him. His glasses fell off. Everything went claustrophobic and blurry.

Hands dragged him into the street. Hands cuffed and shackled him.

A midnight-blue limo pulled up.

Hands grappled him in. Hands shoved him face-to-face with J. Edgar Hoover.

Hands slapped tape across his mouth.

The limo pulled out. Hoover said, "Mal Chamales is being arrested for sedition and advocating the violent overthrow of the United States of America. Your FBI service is terminated as of this day, your pension has been revoked, and a detailed profile of you as a Communist sympathizer has been sent to the Justice Department, the bar associations of all fifty states and the deans of every university law school in the Continental U.S. Should you go public with information pertaining to Kemper Boyd's clandestine activities, I will guarantee you that your daughter, Susan, and Helen Agee will never practice law, and guarantee that the interesting coincidence of your three-week absence and the destruction of Jules Schiffrin's Lake Geneva estate will be mentioned to key organized-crime figures who might find that co-incidence intriguing. In keeping with your leftist sympathies and bleeding-heart concern for the financially wretched and morally impaired, you will now be deposited into a venue where your instincts for self-abnegation, self-flagellation and pinko vicissitudes will be fully appreciated. Driver, stop the car."

The limo decelerated. Hands uncuffed him and unshackled him. Hands dragged him out the door. Hands dumped him into a South Side gutter.

Colored piss bums walked up and checked him out. Say what, white man?

DOCUMENT INSERT: 12/18/60.
Personal note: Kemper Boyd to Attorney General
Designate Robert F. Kennedy.

Dear Bob,

Congratulations, first of all. You'll make a splendid Attorney General, and I can envision Jimmy Hoffa and certain others swinging from yardarms already.

Hoffa makes for a good segue point. The purpose of this letter is to recommend former Special Agent Ward J. Littell for a Justice Department counselship.

Littell (the Chicago Phantom who has worked for us
sub-rosa since early 1959) is a 1940 Summa Cum Laude
Notre Dame Law grad, Federal-Bar licensed. He is
considered brilliant in the field of Federal
Deportation Statutes and will be bringing with him a
good deal of recently accrued anti-Mob, anti-
Teamster evidence.

I realize that Littell, in his anonymous capacity,
has been out of touch with you for some time, and hope
that that fact will not dampen your enthusiasm for
him. He is a splendid attorney and a dedicated
crimefighter.

Yours, Kemper

DOCUMENT INSERT: 12/21/60.
Personal note: Robert F. Kennedy to Kemper Boyd.

Dear Kemper,

Per Ward Littell, my answer is emphatically ''No.''
I have received a report from Mr. Hoover that, though
perhaps biased, persuasively paints a portrait of
Littell as an alcoholic with ultra left-wing
tendencies. Mr. Hoover also included evidence that
indicates that Littell was receiving bribes from
Chicago Mob members. This, to me, negates the
viability of his alleged anti-Mob, anti-Teamster
evidence.

I realize that Littell is your friend, and that he
did work hard for us at one time. Frankly, though, we
cannot afford even the slightest taint on our new
appointees.

Let's consider the Littell matter closed. The
question of your Kennedy Administration employment
remains, and I think you'll be pleased with what the
President-elect and I have come up with.

Best, Bob

<u>DOCUMENT INSERT</u>: 1/17/61.
Personal letter: J. Edgar Hoover to Kemper Boyd.

Dear Kemper,

   Three-fold congratulations.
   One, your recent evasion tactics were superbly
efficacious. Two, your Marilyn Monroe aside had me
going for quite some time. What a myth you have
created! With luck, it will enter what Hush-Hush
would call the ''Peephole Pantheon!''
   Thirdly, bravo for your appointment as roving
Justice Department counsel. My contacts tell me
you'll be concentrating on voting rights abuse in the
south. How fitting! Now you'll be able to champion
left-inclined negroes with the same tenacity that you
embrace right-wing Cubans!
   I think you've found your metier. I would be hard-
pressed to conceive of work more suitable for a man
with such a lenient code of loyalty.
   I hope we'll get the chance to be colleagues again.

                                    As always, JEH

58

(New York City, 1/20/61)

SHE'D BEEN CRYING. Tear streaks had ruined her makeup.

Kemper stepped into the foyer. Laura cinched her robe and stepped away from him.

He held out a small bouquet. "I'm going down to the Inaugural. I'll be back in a few days."

She ignored the flowers. "I figured that out. I didn't think you put on that tuxedo to impress me."

"Laura ..."

"I wasn't invited. Some neighbors of mine were, though. They donated ten thousand dollars to Jack's campaign."

Her mascara was running. Her whole face looked off-kilter.

"I'll be back in a few days. We'll talk things over then."

Laura pointed to an armoire. "There's a check for three

million dollars in the top drawer. It's mine, if I never contact the family again."

"You could rip it up."

"Would you?"

"I can't answer that question."

Her fingers were cigarette-stained. She'd left overflowing ash-trays out in plain sight.

Laura said, "Them or me?"

Kemper said, "Them."

PART THREE

PIGS

February–November 1961

DOCUMENT INSERT: 2/7/61.
Memorandum: Kemper Boyd to John Stanton.
Marked: CONFIDENTIAL/HAND POUCH DELIVER.

John,

   I've been subtly pressing Little Brother and a few
White House aides for information, and I am sad to
report that as of this date the President is
ambivalent about our invasion plans. The imminent
nature of the plans apparently has him waxing
indecisive. It's obvious that he doesn't want to deal
with something so pressing this early in his
administration.

   The President and Attorney General Kennedy have
been briefed by Director Dulles and Deputy Director
Bissell. Little Brother attends many high-level
presidential briefings; it is obvious that he is
becoming the President's chief advisor on all urgent
matters. Little Brother (to the consternation of some
friends of ours) remains fixated on Organized Crime
and seems to be uninterested in the Cuban issue. My
contacts tell me that the President hasn't updated
him on the ''at-ready'' status of our invasion plans.

   The Blessington campsite stands pre-invasion
ready. Recruit training cycles have been suspended;
as of 1/30/61, the forty-four bunks have been filled
with graduate troops culled from other induction
camps: men specifically trained in amphibious warfare
tactics. These men now stand as the Blessington
Invasion Force. Pete Bondurant and Douglas Frank
Lockhart are putting them through rigorous daily
maneuvers and report that their morale is very high.

   I visited Blessington last week, to assess its at-
ready status prior to Mr. Bissell's 2/10/61
inspection. I'm happy to report that Pete and

Lockhart have whipped things into top-flight shape.

Landing crafts are now docked at camouflaged inlets built by laborers recruited from Lockhart's Klan Klavern. Chuck Rogers gave Ramon Gutierrez a refresher flying course as part of a Bondurant-devised plan to have Gutierrez portray a Castro defector and fly into Blessington on Invasion Day with doctored anti-Castro atrocity photographs to be leaked to the press as genuine. Weapons and ammunition stand inventoried and at-ready. An inlet a half mile from the campsite is being prepared to house the troopship that will carry the Blessington invasion force. It should be at-ready by 2/16/61.

I am now free to spend occasional time in Florida, chiefly because the brothers believe the falsehood that I established over a year ago: that Mr. Hoover has coerced me into spying on anti-Castro groups in the Miami area. My current Justice Department assignment (investigating the accusations of Negroes denied voting rights) should have me sequestered in the south for some time. I specifically requested this assignment because of its proximity to Miami and Blessington. My southern background convinced Little Brother to give me the job, and he has allowed me to choose my initial target districts. I picked the area surrounding Anniston, Alabama. There are eight daily commercial flights to Miami, which should make job hopping just a matter of a ninety-minute plane ride. Should you need me, call my service in D.C. or contact me directly at the Wigwam Motel outside Anniston. (Don't say what you're thinking: I know it's beneath me.)

Again, let me stress the importance of obfuscating all Agency-Outfit links to Little Brother. I was as amazed and dismayed as our Sicilian colleagues when Big Brother tapped him for AG. His anti-Outfit fervor has if anything increased, and we do not want him to learn that Messrs. C.M., S.G. and J.R. have donated money to the Cause, or that our Cadre business even exists.

I'll close now. See you in Blessington 2/10.

KB

DOCUMENT INSERT: 2/9/61.
Memorandum: John Stanton to Kemper Boyd.
Marked: CONFIDENTIAL/HAND POUCH DELIVER.

Kemper,

I received your memo. Things sound excellent,
although I wish Big Brother wasn't waffling. I've
developed some new additions to our basic Blessington
Invasion Plan. Will you tell me what you think when we
meet at the inspection?

1.—I've assigned Pete Bondurant and Chuck Rogers to
coordinate on-site Blessington security and
communications between Blessington and other launch
sites in Nicaragua and Guatemala. Rogers can fly
between sites, and I think Pete will be especially
effective as a rover-peacekeeper.

2.—Teo Paez has brought in a new recruit: Nestor
Javier Chasco, DOB 4/12/23. Teo knew the man in Havana
when he was running a string of informants for United
Fruit. Chasco infiltrated numerous left-wing groups
and once foiled an assassination attempt on a UF
executive.

When Castro took over, Chasco infiltrated Raul
Castro's on-island heroin operation and siphoned
dope to anti-Castro rebels, who of course sold it and
used the money to purchase weapons. Chasco is an
experienced dope trafficker, an expert interrogator,
and a Cuban Army-trained sharpshooter lent out by
President Batista to various South American
government leaders. Teo says that Chasco
assassinated no less than fourteen leftist
insurgents between the years 1951 and 1958.

Chasco, who had been supporting himself by selling
marijuana, escaped Cuba by speedboat last month. He
contacted Paez in Miami and begged him to find him pro-
Cause work. Teo introduced him to Pete Bondurant and
later described the meeting to me as ''Love at first
sight.''

You were unreachable, so Pete contacted me and
recommended Nestor Chasco for immediate Blessington

and Cadre employment. I met Chasco and was very
impressed. I hired the man immediately and had Pete
introduce him to the other Cadre members. Paez told me
that the meetings were amicable. Chasco is learning
the Cadre business ropes and doubling as a
Blessington drill instructor. He'll be shuffling
between Blessington, Miami and our formal facilities
in Guatemala and Nicaragua—a case officer passing
through Blessington noted his training skills and put
in an expedite personnel request directly to Mr.
Bissell.

You'll meet Chasco at the inspection. I think
you'll be impressed, too.

3.—During the actual invasion time frame, I want
you and Chasco to patrol the Cadre's Miami business
sites. Our on-island sources expect some invasion
plan intelligence to leak to Cuba, and I want to make
sure that local pro-Castro groups don't try to hit us
when they think we're focusing solely on invasion
logistics. It should be easy for you to get away.
Miami is Anniston-accessible and you can tell Little
Brother that Mr. H. sent you in to monitor pro-Castro
activity.

I'll close with an embarrassing request.

Carlos M. gave Guy Banister an additional $300,000
gun money. The man is a great friend to the Cause, and
he has some very great (and I think justified) fears
regarding Little Brother. Can you find out what
Bobby's plans are regarding Carlos?

Thanks in advance for considering this. See you
tomorrow in Blessington.

John

59

(Blessington, 2/10/61)

EYES LEFT, EYES RIGHT. Port arms, snap the bolt—let's see those
carbon-free M-1 chambers.

The drill field sparkled. The trainees moved like spic

Rockettes—every turn and slapdown was synchronized.

Lockhart called cadence. Néstor Chasco played flag bearer. The Stars & Stripes and Pit Bull Monster fluttered.

Pete led a white-glove inspection line. Richard Bissell and John Stanton trailed him—civilian squarejohns in worsted wool suits.

The trainees wore starched fatigues and chrome helmets. Fulo, Paez, Delsol, and Gutiérrez stood off in a squad leader flank.

Boyd watched from the dock. He didn't want rank-and-file recruits to know him.

Pete checked weapons and handed them back. Bissell patted shoulders and smiled. Stanton stifled yawns—he knew it was all PR bullshit.

Lockhart yelled, "Shoulderrr arms! Guide-on front and centerrr!"

Forty-four rifles went up. Chasco marched ten paces forward and about-faced.

Chasco saluted. Chasco snapped his flags out at arm's length.

Lockhart yelled, "At ease!" The men hoisted down one by one for a nifty ripple effect.

Bissell gawked. Stanton applauded.

Boyd was eyeballing Chasco. Stanton built the little shitbird up as Jesus Christ sans mercy.

Chasco ate tarantula meat and drank panther piss. Chasco killed Reds from Rangoon to Rio.

Chasco coughed and spat on the pavement. "It is a pleasure to be here with joo in America. It is an honor to be able to fight the tyrant Fidel Castro, and an honor to introduce to joo Señor Richard Bissell."

Locomotive cheers went up—choo-choo-choo fifty voices strong.

Bissell waved the noise down. "Señor Chasco is right. Fidel Castro is a murderous tyrant who needs to be taken down a peg or two. I'm here to tell you that we're going to do it, most likely in the not-too-distant future."

CHOO-CHOO-CHOO-CHOO-CHOO-CHOO—

Bissell stabbed the air Kennedy-style. "Your morale is high, and that's damn good. There's also some pretty damn high morale inside Cuba, and I would have to say that right now that morale is running about three or four brigades' worth. I'm referring to on-island Cubans just waiting for you to establish

a beachhead and show them the way to Fidel Castro's parlor."
CHOO-CHOO-CHOO-CHOO-CHOO—
"You men, and many other men, are going to invade and
recapture your homeland. You are going to link with anti-Castro
forces living on-island and depose Fidel Castro. We have close to
sixteen hundred troops now stationed in Guatemala, Nicaragua
and along the Gulf Coast, ready to be launched from coastal
installations. You are among those troops. You are a crack unit
which will see action. You will be backed by surplus B-26s and
escorted to your homeland by a task force of U.S. Navy supply
boats. You will succeed. You will spend Christmas with your
loved ones in a liberated Cuba."

Pete gave the signal. A forty-four-gun salute shocked Bissell
speechless.

Stanton threw a lunch at the Breakers Motel. The guest list was
White Men Only: Pete, Bissell, Boyd, Chuck Rogers.

Santo Junior owned the place. Blessington men dined and
drank on the cuff. The coffee shop served starchy wop food—
strictly shitsville.

They hogged a choice window table. Bissell hogged the conversation—nobody could squeeze a word in. Pete sat down next
to Boyd and picked at a plate of linguine.

Chuck handed out beers. Boyd passed Pete a note.

I like Chasco. He's got that "Don't underestimate me because
I'm puny" look that I associate with W.J. Littell. Can we send
him in to shoot Fidel?

Pete scribbled up his napkin.

Let's have him shoot Fidel & WJL. Jimmy's scared & pissed
because his Fund books got clouted & we're the only ones who
know who did it. Can't we do something about it?

Boyd wrote *NO* on his menu. Pete laughed out loud.

Bissell took offense. "Did I say something funny, Mr.
Bondurant?"

"No, sir. You didn't."

"I didn't think so. I was saying that President Kennedy has
been briefed several times, but he still won't commit to an invasion date, which I don't find amusing at all."

Pete poured himself a beer. Stanton said, "Mr. Dulles describes the President as 'enthusiastic, but cautious.'"

Bissell smiled. "Our secret weapon is Mr. Boyd here. He's our Kennedy confidant, and I imagine that if push came to shove, he could reveal his covert Agency standing, and then overtly advocate our invasion plan."

Pete froze the moment: Boyd about to lose it six ways from Sunday.

Stanton stepped in. "Mr. Bissell's joking, Kemper."

"I know that. And I know that he understands how complex our alliances have become."

Bissell fingered his napkin. "I do, Mr. Boyd. And I know how generous Mr. Hoffa, Mr. Marcello and a few other Italian gentlemen have been to the Cause, and I know that you possess a certain amount of influence in the Kennedy camp. And as the President's chief Cuban-issue liaison, I also know that Fidel Castro and Communism are a good deal worse than the Mafia, although I wouldn't dream of asking you to intercede on our friends' behalf, because it might cost you credibility with your sacred Kennedys."

Stanton dropped his soup spoon. Pete let a big breath out eeeasy.

Boyd put out a big shit-eating grin. "I'm glad you feel that way, Mr. Bissell. Because if you did ask me, I'd have to tell you to go fuck yourself."

60

(Washington, D.C., 3/6/61)

HE TOOK THREE shots a night—no more, no less.

He switched from whisky to straight gin. The burn compensated for the scant volume.

Three shots tweaked his hatreds. Four shots and up cut those hatreds all the way loose.

Three shots said, You project danger. Four shots or more said, You're ugly and you limp.

He always drank facing his hallway mirror. The glass was chipped and cracked—his new apartment was furnished on the cheap.

Littell knocked the shots back, one-two-three. The glow let him spar with himself.

You're two days shy of forty-eight years old. Helen left you. J. Edgar Hoover fucked you—you fucked him and he fucked you back much more efficaciously.

You risked your life for nothing. Robert F. Kennedy shunned you. You went to hell and back for a form-letter rejection.

You tried to contact Bobby in person. Yes-men showed you out. You sent four notes to Bobby. All four went unanswered.

Kemper tried to get you work at the Justice Department. Bobby nixed it—the alleged Hoover hater kowtowed to Hoover. Hoover put the fix in: No law firm or law school will employ you.

Kemper knows you've got the Fund books. His fear defines your bond now.

You went to a Jesuit retreat in Milwaukee. Newspapers lauded your burglary daring: MYSTERY ART THIEF TEARS LAKE GENEVA ESTATE DOWN! You did odd jobs for the monsignor and imposed your own code of silence.

You boiled the booze out. You put on some muscle. You studied cryptography texts. Prayer told you who to hate and who to forgive.

You read a Chicago *Trib* obit: Court Meade died of a massive heart attack. You toured old haunts. The foster homes you grew up in were still churning out Jesuit robots.

You're licensed to practice in D.C. Hoover left you an escape hatch—in his own backyard.

The move east was invigorating. Washington law firms seeking applicants were shocked by your Commie pedigree.

Kemper comes through. Egalitarian Kemper was still friendly with old car-thief confreres. Car thieves were prone to Federal indictments and always in need of cheap representation.

Car thieves brought you occasional work—enough to sustain an apartment and three shots a night.

Kemper called to chat. He never mentioned the Fund books. You can't hate a man so high up on a ledge. You can't hate a man so immune to hatred himself.

He gave you great gifts. They compensate for his betrayals.

Kemper calls his civil rights work "moving." It's that cheap noblesse oblige the Kennedys evince so condescendingly.

You hate the mass seduction that Joe Kennedy financed. Your

foster fathers bought you one cheap toy per Christmas. Joe
bought his sons the world with cancerous money.

Prayer taught you to hate falsehood. Prayer gave you insight.
Prayer was like a choke hold on mendacity.

You see the President's face and see through it. You see Jimmy
Hoffa skate on Sun Valley charges—a newsman cites insufficient
evidence.

You hold numbers to reverse that injustice. You hold numbers
to indict the Kennedy seduction.

You can break the remaining Fund code. You can expose the
Robber Baron and his son the Priapic Boy Führer.

Littell got out his cryptography books. Three shots a night
taught him this:

You're down, but you're capable of anything.

61

(Washington, D.C., 3/14/61)

BOBBY HELD THE floor. Fourteen lawyers pulled chairs up and
balanced notebooks and ashtrays on their knees.

The briefing room was drafty. Kemper leaned against the back
wall with his topcoat slung over his shoulders.

The AG brayed—there was no need to get close. He had free
time—a storm delayed his flight to Alabama.

Bobby said, "You know why I called you in, and you know
what your basic job is. I've been tied up in red tape since the
Inauguration, so I haven't been able to get to the applicable case
files, and I've decided to let you do that on your own. You're the
Organized Crime Unit, and you know what your mandate is.
And I'll be damned if I'm going to dawdle any longer."

The men got out pens and pencils. Bobby straddled a chair in
front of them.

"We've got lawyers and investigators of our own, and any
attorney worth his salt is also a catch-as-catch-can investigator.
We've got FBI agents we can utilize as needed, if I can convince
Mr. Hoover to shift his priorities a bit. He's still convinced that
domestic Communists are more dangerous than organized crime,
and I think that making the FBI more cooperative is going to be
a major obstacle to overcome."

The men laughed. An ex-McClellan cop said, "We shall overcome."

Bobby loosened his tie. "We shall. And roving counsel Kemper Boyd, who's spying from the peanut gallery, will overcome racial exclusion practices in the South. I won't ask Mr. Boyd to join us, because skulking at the back of the room is very much his modus operandi."

Kemper waved. "I'm a spy."

Bobby waved back. "The President has always contended that."

Kemper laughed. Bobby half-ass liked him now—breaking off with Laura clinched it. Claire and Laura stayed close—he got regular updates from New York.

Bobby said, "Enough bullshit. The McClellan Committee hearings have provided us with a hit list, and at the top we've got Jimmy Hoffa, Sam Giancana, Johnny Rosselli and Carlos Marcello. I want the IRS files on these men pulled, and I want the intelligence files of the Chicago, New York, Los Angeles, Miami, Cleveland and Tampa PDs combed for mention of them. I also want probable-cause briefs written, so that we can subpoena their financial books and personal records."

A man said, "What about Hoffa specifically? He got hung-juried on Sun Valley, but there's got to be other approaches we can use."

Bobby rolled up his sleeves. "A hung jury first time out means an acquittal next time. I've given up hope of tracing the Spooky Three Million, and I'm starting to think that the so-called 'Real' Pension Fund books are nothing but a pipe dream. I think we need to impanel grand juries and deluge them with Hoffa evidence. And while we're at it, I want to pass a Federal law requiring all municipal PDs to obtain Justice Department writs to implement their wiretaps, so that *we* can have access to every bit of wiretap intelligence seized nationwide."

The men cheered. An old McClellanite threw some mock punches.

Bobby stood up. "I found an old deportation order on Carlos Marcello. He was born in Tunis, North Africa, of Italian parents, but he's got a phony Guatemalan birth certificate. I want to deport him to Guatemala, and I want to do it damn soon."

Kemper broke a little lightweight sweat—

62

(Rural Mexico, 3/22/61)

POPPY FIELDS BLITZED the horizon. Stalk bulbs oozing dope covered a valley half the size of Rhode Island.

Prison inmates did the plucking. Mexican cops cracked the whip and did all the conversion work.

Heshie Ryskind led the tour. Pete and Chuck Rogers tagged along and let him play MC.

"This farm has supplied me and Santo for years. They convert 'O' into morphine for the Agency, too, 'cause the Agency's always backing some right-wing insurgents that get shot at and wounded a lot, and they always need the morph as medication. Most of the zombies they got working here stay past the end of their sentence 'cause all they want to do is suck a pipe and nosh a few tortillas on the side. I wish I had such simple needs. I wish I didn't have to keep nine fucking doctors on retainer 'cause I'm such a fucking hypochondriac, and I wish I didn't have the chutz-pah—which is the same as 'audacity' to you goyim—to try to break the world's record for getting blow jobs, 'cause I think I've reached the point where all that suction is doing my prostate more harm than good. And I'm not the blow-job magnet I used to be. I've got to travel with a good cunt man now to see any action at all. Lately, I've had Dick Contino bird-dogging for me. I catch all his lounge gigs, and Dick shoots me all the surplus suction I can handle."

The sun slammed down. They rode out in rickshaws, with junkie inmates at the helm.

Pete said, "We need ten pounds precut for the Cadre. I won't be able to get back here until after the invasion."

Chuck laughed. "If and when your boy Jack approves it."

Pete flicked a bulb—white shit oozed out. "And I want a sub-stantial morphine supply for the medics at Blessington. Let's just figure this is our last visit for a while."

Heshie leaned against his rickshaw. The pilot wore a loincloth and a Dodger baseball cap.

"All this can be arranged. It's a lot simpler than arranging blow jobs for sixty at some farkakte Teamster convention."

Chuck dabbed bulb goo on a shaving cut. "My jaw's going a little numb. It's a nice effect, but I wouldn't ruin my life for it."

Pete laughed. Heshie said, "I'm tired. I'll go back and get your stuff loaded up, then I'm taking a nap."

Chuck hopped in his rickshaw. The pilot looked like fucking Quasimodo.

Pete stood on his tiptoes. The view spread waaay out.

Maybe a thousand stalk rows. Maybe twenty slaves per row. Low worker overhead: cot space, rice and beans came cheap.

Chuck and Heshie took off—dig that crazy rickshaw drag race.

Boyd said Mr. Hoover had a maxim: Anti-Communism breeds strange bedfellows.

They flew from Mexico to Guatemala. The Piper Deuce cruised sluggish—Chucky overstuffed the cargo hold.

With rifles, hate pamphlets, heroin, morphine, tortillas, tequila, Army surplus jump boots, Martin Luther Coon voodoo dolls, back issues of *Hush-Hush*, and five hundred mimeographed copies of a Guy Banister-circulated report culled from the L.A. FBI office, stating that even though Mr. Hoover knew full well that President John F. Kennedy was *not* playing bury-the-brisket with Marilyn Monroe, he kept her under intensive surveillance anyway, and duly noted that during the last six weeks Miss Monroe fucked Louis Prima, two off-duty Marines, Spade Cooley, Franchot Tone, Yves Montand, Stan Kenton, David Seville of David Seville and the Chipmunks, four pizza delivery boys, bantamweight battler Fighting Harada and a disc jockey at an all-spook R&B station.

Chuck called it "essential ordnance."

Pete tried to doze. Air sickness kept him awake. The training camp popped out of a cloud bank, right on schedule.

It loomed biggg. From the air it looked like ten Blessingtons.

Chuck cut his flaps and eased down. Pete puked out his window just shy of the runway.

They taxied in. Pete gargled tequila for a breath rinse. Cuban trainees hit the hold and off-loaded the rifles.

A case officer trotted up with supply forms. Pete got out and itemized them: guns, R&R booze, *Hush-Hush* anti-Beard propaganda.

The guy said, "You can eat now, or wait for Mr. Boyd and Mr. Stanton."

"Let me walk around a little. I've never seen the place."

Chuck pissed on the runway. Pete said, "Any word on a go date?"

The guy shook his head. "Kennedy's waffling. Mr. Bissell's starting to think we'll be lucky to go before summer."

"Jack will come through. He'll see that it's too sweet a deal to pass up."

Pete meandered. The camp was Disneyland for killers.

Six hundred Cubans. Fifty white men running herd. Twelve barracks, a drill field, a rifle range, a pistol range, a landing strip, a mess hall, an infiltration course and a chemical-warfare simulation tunnel.

Three launch inlets gouged out of the Gulf a mile south. Four dozen amphibious crawlers rigged with .50-caliber machine guns.

An ammo dump. A field hospital. A Catholic chapel with a bilingual chaplain.

Pete meandered. Old Blessington grads waved hello. Case officers showed him some good shit.

Dig Néstor Chasco—staging mock-assassination maneuvers.

Dig that anti-Red indoctrination workshop.

Dig the verbal abuse drills—calculated to increase troop subservience.

Dig the corpsman's amphetamine stash—pre-packaged pre-invasion courage.

Dig the action in that barbed-wire enclosure—peons flying on a drug called LSD.

Some of them screamed. Some wept. Some grinned like LSD was a blast. A case officer said John Stanton hatched the idea— let's flood Cuba with this shit before we invade.

Langley co-signed the brainstorm. Langley embellished it: Let's induce mass hallucinations and stage the Second Coming of Christ!!!!!

Langley found some suicidal actors. Langley dolled them up to look like J.C. Langley had them set to pre-invade Cuba, concurrent with the dope saturation.

Pete howled. The case officer said, "It's not funny." A drug-zorched peon whipped out his wang and jacked off.

Pete meandered. Everything sparkled and gleamed.

Dig the bayonet drills. Dig the spit-shined jeeps. Dig that rummy-looking priest dispensing outdoor Holy Communion.

Loudspeakers announced chow call. It was 5:00 and nowhere near dark—military types dined early.

Pete walked over to the lounge hut. A pool table and wet bar ate up two-thirds of the floor space.

Boyd and Stanton walked in. A large fucker blocked the doorway—resplendent in French paratrooper khakis.

Kemper said, *"Entrez, Laurent."*

He was jug-eared and plain huge. He had that frog imperialist swagger down pat.

Pete bowed. *"Salut, capitaine."*

Boyd smiled. "Laurent Guéry, Pete Bondurant."

Froggy clicked his heels. *"Monsieur Bondurant. C'est un grand plaisir de faire votre connaissance. On dit que vous êtes un grand patriote."*

Pete tossed out some Québecois. *"Tout le plaisir est à moi, capitaine. Mais je suis beaucoup plus profiteur que patriote."*

Froggy laughed. Stanton said, "Translate for me, Kemper. I'm starting to feel like a rube."

"You're not missing much."

"You mean it's just Pete trying to be civilized with the only other six-foot-six Frenchman on earth?"

Froggy shrugged—*Quoi? Quoi? Quoi?*

Pete winked. *"Vous êtes quoi donc, capitaine? Etes-vous un* 'right-wing crackpot'? *Etes-vous un* 'mercenary on the Cuban gravy train'*?"*

Froggy shrugged—*Quoi? Quoi? Quoi?*

Boyd steered Pete out to the porch. Spics double-timed through a chow line across from the drill field.

"Be nice, Pete. He's Agency."

"In what fucking capacity?"

"He shoots people."

"Then tell him to clip Fidel and learn English. Tell him to do something impressive, or he's just another frog geek to me."

Boyd laughed. "He killed a man named Lumumba in the Congo last month."

"So what?"

"He's killed quite a few uppity Algerians."

Pete lit a cigarette. "So tell Jack to send him down to Havana. And send Néstor down with him. And tell Jack that he owes me one for the Nixon-Hughes thing, and as far as I'm concerned, history's not moving fast enough. Tell him to give us a go date, or I'll boat on down to Cuba and whack Fidel myself."

Boyd said, "Be patient. Jack's still getting his sea legs, and invading a Communist-held country is a big commitment. Dulles and Bissell are keeping after him, and I'm convinced he'll say yes before too long."

Pete kicked a tin can off the porch. Boyd pulled his piece and unloaded it. The can danced all the way across the drill field.

The chow-line crew applauded. Big-bore reverb had a few guys clutching their ears.

Pete kicked at the shell casings. "*You* talk to Jack. Tell him the invasion's good for business."

Boyd twirled his gun on one finger. "I can't openly proselytize for the invasion without blowing my Agency cover, and I'm damn lucky to have FBI cover to be in Florida in the first place."

"That civil rights gig must be sweet. You just go through the motions and fly to Miami when the niggers start getting on your nerves."

"It's not like that."

"No?"

"No. I like the Negro people I work with just as much as you like our Cubans, and offhand I'd say that their grievances are con- siderably more justified."

Pete tossed his cigarette. "Say what you like. And *I'll* say this again. You cut people too much slack."

"You mean I don't let people get to me."

"That's not what I mean. What I mean is you accept too much weak shit in people, and for my money it's some condescending rich-kid quality you picked up from the Kennedys."

Boyd popped in a fresh clip and slid a round in the chamber. "I'll grant Jack that quality, but not Bobby. Bobby's a true judger and hater."

"He hates some pretty tight friends of ours."

"He does. And he's starting to hate Carlos Marcello more than I'd like him to."

"Did you tell Carlos that?"

"Not yet. But if things escalate a bit more, I might ask you to help him out of a scrape."

Pete cracked a few knuckles. "And I'll say yes, no questions asked. Now, *you* say yes to something."

Boyd aimed at a mound of dirt twenty yards off. "No, you cannot kill Ward Littell."

"Why?"

"He's got the books fail-safed."

"So I torture him for the pertinent information, then kill him."

"It won't work."

"Why?"

Boyd shot a rattlesnake headless.

"I said 'Why?,' Kemper."

"Because he'd die just to prove he could do it."

63

(Washington, D.C., 3/26/61)

HIS CARDS READ:

> Ward J. Littell
> Counselor-At-Law
> Federal Bar Licensed
> OL6-4809

No address—he didn't want clients to know that he worked out of his apartment. No glossy stock or embossed letters—he couldn't really afford them.

Littell cruised the third-floor hallway. Indicted felons took the cards and looked at him like he was crazy.

Shyster. Ambulance chaser. Middle-aged lawyer on the skids.

The Federal courthouse did a brisk business. Six divisions and full arraignment docketing—all unaccompanied lowlifes quali-fied as potential clients.

Littell passed out cards. A man flicked a cigarette butt at him.

Kemper Boyd walked up. Beautiful Kemper—so fit and groomed that he sparkled.

"Can I buy you a drink?"

"I don't drink like I used to."

"Lunch then?"

"Sure."

The Hay-Adams dining room faced the White House. Kemper kept glancing out the window.

". . . And my work entails taking depositions and filing them in Federal District Court. We're trying to insure that Negroes previously barred from voting aren't excluded on the basis of illegally levied poll taxes or constrained by literacy tests that the local registrars want them to fail."

Littell smiled. "And I'm sure the Kennedys will rig binding legal clauses to insure that every Negro in Alabama registers as a Democrat. You have to consider things like that in the early stages of building a dynasty."

Kemper laughed. "The President's civil rights policy isn't that cynically conceived."

"Is your application of it?"

"Hardly. I've always considered suppression ill-advised and futile."

"And you like the people?"

"Yes, I do."

"Your southern accent's back in force."

"It disarms the people I deal with. They appreciate it that a southern white man's on their side. You're grinning, Ward. What is it?"

Littell sipped coffee. "It occurred to me that Alabama is rather close to Florida."

"You were always quick."

"Does the attorney general know that you're moonlighting?"

"No. But I do have a certain sanction on my Florida visits."

"Let me guess. Mr. Hoover's supplying you with cover, and as much as he professes to hate him, Bobby would never do *anything* to upset Mr. Hoover."

Kemper waved a waiter off. "Your hatred's showing, Ward."

"I don't hate Mr. Hoover. You can't hate someone who runs so true to form."

"But Bobby—"

Littell whispered. "You know what I risked for him. And you know what I got back. And what I can't abide is that the Kennedys pretend to be better than that."

Kemper said, "You've got the books." He shot his cuffs and displayed a solid gold Rolex.

Littell pointed to the White House. "Yes, I do. And they're booby-trapped a dozen different ways. I filed instruction contingency briefs with a dozen different lawyers when I was drunk, and even I can't remember them all."

Kemper folded his hands. "With depositions on my Kennedy incursion to go to the Justice Department in the event of your death or prolonged disappearance?"

"No. With depositions on your incursion and depositions on astronomically lucrative Joseph P. Kennedy Mob-linked financial malfeasance to go to municipal PD gangster squads nationwide, and every Republican member of the House and the Senate."

Kemper said, "Bravo."

Littell said, "Thank you."

A waiter placed a phone on their table. Kemper placed a folder next to it.

"Are you broke, Ward?"

"Almost."

"You haven't expressed a word of rancor regarding my recent behavior."

"It wouldn't do any good."

"How do you currently feel about organized crime?"

"My current feelings are relatively charitable."

Kemper tapped the folder. "That's a pilfered INS file. And you're the best deportation-writ lawyer on God's green earth."

Littell's shirt cuffs were soiled and frayed. Kemper wore solid gold cufflinks.

"Ten thousand dollars to start, Ward. I'm certain I can get it for you."

"*For doing what?* For releasing the books to you?"

"Forget the books. All I ask is that you don't release them to anyone else."

"Kemper, what are you talk—?"

"Your client will be Carlos Marcello. And it's Bobby Kennedy who wants to deport him."

The phone rang. Littell dropped his coffee cup.

Kemper said, "That's Carlos. Be obsequious, Ward. He'll expect a certain amount of fawning."

DOCUMENT INSERT: 4/2/61.
Verbatim FBI telephone call transcript:
''TRANSCRIBED AT THE DIRECTOR'S REQUEST''/
''DIRECTOR'S EYES ONLY.'' Speaking: Director J.
Edgar Hoover, Attorney General Robert F. Kennedy.

RFK: It's Bob Kennedy, Mr. Hoover. I was hoping

I could have a few minutes of your time.

JEH: Certainly.

RFK: There were a few matters of protocol I wanted to discuss.

JEH: Yes.

RFK: Communications, to begin with. I sent you a directive requesting carbons of all summary reports submitted by your Top Hoodlum Program squads. That directive was dated February 17th. It's now the 2nd of April, and I've yet to see a single report.

JEH: These directives take time to implement.

RFK: Six weeks seems like ample time to me.

JEH: You perceive an undue delay. I do not.

RFK: Will you expedite the implementation of that directive?

JEH: Certainly. Will you refresh my memory as to why you issued it?

RFK: I want to assess every scrap of anti-Mob intelligence the Bureau acquires and share it where needed with the various regional grand juries that I hope to impanel.

JEH: You may be acting injudiciously. Leaking information that could only have originated from THP sources might jeopardize THP informants and electronic surveillance placements.

RFK: All such information will be evaluated from a security standpoint.

JEH: That function should not be trusted to non-FBI personnel.

RFK: I adamantly disagree. You're going to have to share your information, Mr. Hoover. The simple cultivation of intelligence will not bring Organized Crime to its knees.

JEH: The Top Hoodlum Program mandate does not provide for information-sharing to expedite grand jury indictments.

RFK: Then we're going to have to revise it.

JEH: I would consider that a rash and heedless act.

RFK: Consider it what you like, and consider it done. Consider the Top Hoodlum Program mandate superseded by my direct order.

JEH: May I remind you of this simple fact: you cannot prosecute the Mafia and win.

RFK: May I remind you that for many years you denied that the Mafia existed. May I remind you that the FBI is but one cog in the overall wheel of the Justice Department. May I remind you that the FBI does not dictate Justice Department policy. May I remind you that the President and I consider 99% of the left-wing groups that the FBI routinely monitors to be harmless if not outright moribund, and laughably inoffensive when compared to Organized Crime.

JEH: May I state that I consider that burst of invective to be ill-conceived and fatuous in its historical perspective?

RFK: You may.

JEH: Was there anything of a similar or less offensive nature that you wish to add?

RFK: Yes. You should know that I intend to initiate wiretap accountability legislation. I want the Justice Department to be informed of every single instance of wiretapping undertaken by municipal police departments nationwide.

JEH: Many would consider that undue Federal meddling and a flagrant abuse of States' Rights.

RFK: The concept of States' Rights has been a smokescreen to obscure everything from de facto segregation to outmoded abortion statutes.

JEH: I disagree.

RFK: Duly noted. And I would like you to duly note that from this day on you are to inform me of every electronic surveillance operation that the FBI engages in.

JEH: Yes.

RFK: Duly noted?

JEH: Yes.

RFK: I want you to personally call the New Orleans SAC and have him assign four agents to arrest Carlos Marcello. I want this done within seventy-two hours. Tell the SAC that I'm having Marcello deported to Guatemala. Tell him that the Border Patrol will be contacting him to iron out details.

```
JEH: Yes.
RFK: Duly noted?
JEH: Yes.
RFK: Good day, Mr. Hoover.
JEH: Good day.
```

64

(New Orleans, 4/4/61)

HE WAS TOO late—by seconds.

Four men grappled Carlos Marcello into a Fed sled. Right outside his house—with Mrs. Carlos on the porch, throwing a fit.

Pete pulled up across the street and watched it happen. His rescue mission clocked in half a minute tardy.

Marcello was dressed in BVDs and beach flip-flops. Marcello looked like this low-rent Il Duce on the rag.

Boyd fucked up.

He said, Bobby wants Carlos deported. He said, You and Chuck get to New Orleans and snatch him first. He said, Don't call and warn him—just get there.

Boyd said bureaucratic jive would give them time. Boyd mis-fucking-calculated.

The Feds took off. Frau Carlos stood on the porch, wringing her hands grieving-wife-style.

Pete tailed the Fed car. Early A.M. traffic got between them. He eyeballed the Fed's antenna and rode a purple Lincoln's back bumper.

Chuck was back at Moisant Airport, gassing up the Piper. The Feds were heading that way.

They'd fly Carlos out commercial or dump him on the Border Patrol. He'd be Guatemala-bound—and Guatemala loved the CIA.

The Fed car took surface streets east. Pete saw a bridge up ahead—toll booths and two eastbound lanes across the river.

Both lanes were hemmed in by guardrails. Narrow pedestrian walkways ran flush along the edge of the bridge.

Cars were stacked up in front of the booths—at least twenty per lane.

Pete hopped lanes and swerved in front of the Fed car. He

spotted a squeeze space between the left-hand booth and the guardrail.

He accelerated in. A rail housing snapped off his outside mirror.

Horns blared. His left-side hubcaps went spinning. A toll taker looked over and doused an old lady with coffee.

Pete SQUEEZED past the booths and hit the bridge going forty. The Fed sled was stalled, way way back.

He made it to Moisant fast. His rent-a-car was dinged, chipped and paint-stripped.

He ditched it in an underground lot. He greased a skycap for airport information.

Commercial flights to Guatemala? No, sir, none today. The Border Patrol office? Next to the Trans-Texas counter.

Pete cruised by and loitered behind a newspaper. The office door opened and closed.

Men carried shackles in. Men carried flight logs out. Men stood outside the door and kibitzed.

A guy said, "I heard they popped him in his skivvies."

A guy said, "The pilot really hates wops."

A guy said, "They're flying out at 8:30."

Pete ran to the private-plane hangar. Chucky was perched on the snout of his Piper, reading a hate mag.

Pete caught his breath. "They've got Carlos. We've got to get down to Guatemala City ahead of them and see what we can work out."

Chuck said, "That's a goddamned foreign country. We're only supposed to bring the man back to Blessington. We've barely got the gas to—"

"Let's go. We'll patch some calls in and work something out."

Chuck got clearance to take off and land. Pete called Guy Banister and explained the situation.

Guy said he'd call John Stanton and try to rig a plan. He had shortwave gear out at Lake Pontchartrain and could radio in to Chuck's frequency.

They took off at 8:16. Chuck put on his headphones and cribbed flight calls.

The Border Patrol plane departed late. Their Guatemala City ETA was forty-six minutes behind them.

Chuck flew medium-low and kept his headset on. Pete skimmed hate pamphlets out of sheer boredom.

The titles were a howl. The ultimate: "KKK: Kommunist Krucifixion Krusade!"

He found a skin mag/hate mag combo under his seat. Dig that zaftig blonde with the swastika earrings.

Big Pete wants a woman. Extortion experience preferred, but not mandatory.

Dashboard lights flashed. Chuck bootjacked a plane-to-base message and transcribed it in his log.

> The Border Patrol guys are goofing on Carlos. They radio'd their HQ that they've got no lavatory on board & Carlos refuses to piss in a tin can. (They think he's got a little one.)

Pete laughed. Pete pissed in a cup and doused the Gulf from 6,000 feet.

Time dragged. Stomach flutters came and went. Pete chased a Dramamine with warm beer.

Lights flashed. Chuck rogered a Pontchartrain patch-in and transcribed the message.

> Guy got through to JS. JS pulled strings & got thru to Guat. contacts. We're cleared to land with no passport check & if we can get ahold of CM its set up to register him at G.C. Hilton under name Jose Garcia. JS says KB says to have CM call lawyer in Washington D.C. at OL6-4809 tonight.

Pete pocketed the message. The Dramamine kicked in to his system: good night, sweet prince.

Leg cramps woke him up. Jungle terrain and a big black runway hovered.

Chuck eased the plane down and cut the engines. Some spics rolled out a literal red carpet.

It was a bit frayed, but nice.

The beaners looked like right-wing toady types. The Agency saved Guatemala's ass once—some staged coup expunged a shit-load of Reds.

Pete hopped out and stamped his legs awake. Chuck and the spics talked rapid-fire Spanish.

They were back in Guatemala—too fucking soon.

The talk escalated. Pete felt his ears pop-pop-pop. They had forty-six minutes to rig *something*.

Pete walked over to the Customs shack. He got this little Technicolor brain blip: Carlos Marcello needs to urinate.

The bathroom adjoined the passport counter. Pete checked it out.

It ran about 8 feet by 8 feet square. A flimsy screen covered the back window. The view featured more runways and a line of rattletrap bi-planes.

Carlos was stocky. Chuck was rail thin. He was all-around-huge himself.

Chuck walked in and unzipped by the urinal. "We got a big foul-up. I don't know if it's good news or bad."

"What are you saying?"

"I'm saying the Border Patrol's set to land in seventeen minutes. They've got to refuel here and fly to another airport sixty miles away. *That's* where Customs is set to pick up Carlos. That ETA I got is for the *other* goddamned air—"

"How much money have we got in the plane?"

"Sixteen thousand. Santo said to drop it off with Banister."

Pete shook his head. "We grease the Customs guys with it. We fucking inundate them, so they'll take the risk. All we need is a car and a driver outside that window, and you to push Carlos through."

Chuck said, "I get it."

Pete said, "If he doesn't have to piss, we're fucked."

The spics dug the plan. Chuck greased them at the rate of two grand per man. They said they'd keep the Border Patrol guys busy while Carlos Marcello took the world's longest whiz.

Pete loosened the window screen. Chuck stashed the Piper two hangars over.

The spics supplied a '49 Merc getaway car. The spics supplied a driver—a musclebound fag named Luis.

Pete backed the Merc up to the window. Chuck crouched on the toilet seat with last week's *Hush-Hush*.

The Border Patrol plane landed. A crew hustled out refueling pumps. Pete crouched behind the Customs shack and watched.

The spics zipped out the red carpet. A little geek brushed it off with a whisk broom.

Two Border Patrol clowns deplaned. The pilot said, "Let him go. Where's he gonna run to?"

Carlos tumbled out of the plane. Carlos ran to the shack, knock-kneed in tight BVDs.

Luis idled the engine. Pete heard the bathroom door slam.

Carlos yelled, "ROGERS, WHAT THE FUCK—?"

The window screen popped out. Carlos Marcello squeezed through—and snagged himself bare-assed in the process.

The run to the Hilton took an hour. Marcello blasted Bobby Kennedy nonstop.

In English. In straight Italian. In Sicilian dialect. In New Orleans Cajun French patois—not bad for a wop.

Luis detoured by a men's shop. Chuck took down Marcello's sizes and bought him some threads.

Carlos dressed in the car. Little window-squeeze abrasions bloodied up his shirt.

The hotel manager met them at the freight entrance. They freight-lifted up to the penthouse on the QT.

The manager unlocked the door. One glance said Stanton *delivered*.

The pad featured three bedrooms, three bathrooms and a rec room lined with slot machines. The living room was Kemper Boyd fantasy size.

The bar was fully stocked. A guinea cold-cut buffet was laid out. The envelope by the cheese tray contained twenty grand and a note.

Pete & Chuck,
     I'm betting you were able to get ahold of Mr. Marcello. Take good care of him. He's a valuable friend to the Cause.

                                                        JS

Marcello grabbed the money. The manager genuflected. Pete showed him the door and slipped him a C-note.

Marcello snarfed salami and breadsticks. Chuck built a tall Bloody Mary.

Pete paced off the suite. Forty-two yards lengthwise—whoa!

Chuck curled up with a hate mag. Marcello said, "I really had to piss. When you hold a piss that long it pisses you off."

Pete snagged a beer and some crackers. "Stanton's got you a lawyer in D.C. You're supposed to call him."

"I've talked to him already. I've got the best Jew lawyers money can buy, and now I've got him."

"You should call him now and get it over with."

"You call him. And stay on the line in case I need you to translate. Lawyers talk this language I don't always get the first time around."

Pete grabbed the coffee table extension. The hotel operator placed his call.

Marcello picked up the bar phone. The long-distance rings came through faint.

A man said, "Hello?"

Marcello said, "Who's this? Are you that guy I talked to at the Hay-Adams?"

"Yes, this is Ward Littell. Is this Mr. Marcello?"

Pete almost SHIT—

Carlos slumped into a chair. "This is him, calling from Guatemala City, Guatemala, where he does not want to be. Now, if you want to get my attention, say something bad about the man who put me here."

Pete clenched up wicked bad. He covered his mouthpiece so they wouldn't hear him hyperventilate.

Littell said, "I hate that man. He hurt me once, and there is very little that I wouldn't do to cause him discomfort."

Carlos tee-hee-heed—weird for a bass-baritone. "You got my attention. Now, stow that ass-kiss routine you dropped on me before, and say something to convince me you're good at what you do."

Littell cleared his throat. "I specialize in deportation writ work. I was an FBI agent for close to twenty years. I'm a good friend of Kemper Boyd, and although I distrust his admiration for the Kennedys, I'm convinced that his devotion to the Cuban Cause supersedes it. He wants to see you safely and legally reunited with your loved ones, and I'm here to see that it happens."

Pete felt queasy. BOYD, YOU FUCK—

Marcello snapped breadsticks. "Kemper said you were ten grand's worth of good. Now, if you deliver like you talk, ten grand's just the start of you and me."

Littell came on servile. "It's an honor to work for you. And Kemper apologizes for your inconvenience. He was tipped off on the raid at the last second, and he didn't think they could pull it off as fast as they did."

Marcello scratched his neck with a breadstick. "Kemper always gets the job done. I've got no complaints against him that can't wait until the next time I see that too-handsome face of his face-to-face. And the Kennedys keestered 49.8% of the American voters, including some good friends of mine, so I don't begrudge him that admiration if it don't fuck with my life and limb."

Littell said, "He'll be pleased to hear that. And you should know that I'm writing up a temporary reinstatement brief that will be reviewed by a three-judge Federal panel. I'll be calling your attorney in New York, and we'll begin devising a long-range legal strategy."

Marcello kicked off his shoes. "Do it. Call my wife and tell her I'm okay, and do whatever you need to do to get me the fuck out of here."

"I will. And I'll be bringing some paperwork down for you to sign. You can expect to see me within seventy-two hours."

Marcello said, "I want to go home."

Pete hung up. Steam hissed out of his ears like he was Donald Fucking Duck.

They killed time. The jumbo pad let them kill it separately.

Chucky watched spic TV. King Carlos buzzed his serfs long-distance. Pete fantasized ninety-nine ways to murder Ward Littell.

John Stanton called in. Pete regaled him with the toilet-snatch story. Stanton said the Agency would cover their bribe tab.

Pete said, Boyd fixed Carlos up with a lawyer. Stanton said, I heard he's quite good. Pete almost said, Now I can't kill him. BOYD, YOU FUCK.

Stanton said the fix was in. Ten grand would buy Carlos a temporary visa. The Guatemalan foreign minister was set to publicly state:

Mr. Marcello *was* born in Guatemala. His birth certificate is legitimate. Attorney General Kennedy is wrong. Mr. Marcello's origins are in no way ambiguous.

Mr. Marcello split to America—*legally*. Sadly, we have no

records to corroborate this. The burden of proof now falls upon Mr. Kennedy.

Stanton said the minister hates Jack the K.

Stanton said Jack fucked his wife and both his daughters.

Pete said, Jack fucked my old girlfriend. Stanton said, Wow— and you *still* helped elect him!

Stanton said, Have Chuck grease the minister. And by the way, Jack's still dicking around on a go-date.

Pete hung up and looked out the window. Guatemala City by twilight—strictly the rat's ass.

They all dozed off early. Pete woke up early—a nightmare had him balled up under his sheets, gasping for breath.

Chuck was out on his bribe run. Carlos was on his second cigar.

Pete opened the living-room curtains. He saw a big hubbub down at ground level.

He saw a string of trucks at the curb. He saw men with cameras. He saw cables stretching into the lobby.

He saw people gesturing up.

He saw a big movie camera pointing straight up at them.

Pete said, "We're blown."

Carlos dropped his cigar in his hash browns and ran to the window.

Pete said, "The Agency's got a camp an hour from here. If we can find Chuck and fly out, we'll make it."

Carlos looked down. Carlos saw the ruckus. Carlos pushed his breakfast cart through the window and watched it bullseye down eighteen stories.

65

(Rural Guatemala, 4/8/61)

HEAT SHIMMIED OFF the runway. Blast-oven heat—Kemper should have warned him to dress light.

Kemper warned him that Bondurant would be there. He hustled Marcello out of Guatemala City three days ago and arranged for the CIA to play innkeeper.

Kemper added a postscript: Pete knows you've got the Fund

books. Littell stepped away from the plane. He felt woozy. His connecting flight from Houston was a World War II transport.

Propeller thwack boosted the heat. The campsite was large and dusty—odd buildings plunked down in a red clay jungle clearing.

A jeep skidded up. The driver saluted.

"Mr. Littell?"

"Yes."

"I'll drive you over, sir. Your friends are waiting for you."

Littell got in. The rearview mirror caught his bold new face. He had three shots back in Houston. *Daytime* shots to help him rise to this one-time occasion.

The driver peeled out. Troops marched by in strict formation; cadence counts overlapped.

They pulled into a barrack's quadrangle. The driver stopped in front of a small Quonset hut. Littell grabbed his suitcase and walked in ramrod-straight.

The room was air-conditioned. Bondurant and Carlos Marcello stood by a pool table.

Pete winked. Littell winked back. His whole face contorted.

Pete cracked his knuckles—his old intimidation trademark. Marcello said, "What are you, faggots, winking at each other?"

Littell put his suitcase down. The snaps creaked. His surprise had the damn thing bulging.

"How are you, Mr. Marcello?"

"I'm losing money. Every day Pete and my Agency friends treat me better, so every day I end up pledging more money to the Cause. I figure the nut on this hotel's running me twenty-five grand a day."

Pete chalked up a pool cue. Marcello jammed his hands in his pockets.

Kemper warned him: the man does not shake hands.

"I talked to your attorneys in New York a few hours ago. They want to know if you need anything."

Marcello smiled. "I need to kiss my wife on the cheek and fuck my girlfriend. I need to eat some duck Rochambeau at Galatoire's, and I cannot accomplish any of that here."

Bondurant racked up the table. Littell swung his suitcase up and blocked it off lengthwise.

Marcello chuckled. "I'm starting to detect old grief here."

Pete lit a cigarette. Littell caught the exhale full-on.

"I've got a good deal of paperwork for you to review, Mr. Marcello. We'll need to spend some time together and devise a story that details your immigration history, so that Mr. Wasserman can use it when he files his injunction to get your deportation order rescinded. Some very influential people want to see you repatriated, and I'll be working with them as well. I realize that all this unexpected travel must be exhausting, so Kemper Boyd and I are going to arrange for Chuck Rogers to fly you back to Louisiana in a few days and hide you out."

Marcello did a quick little shuffle. The man was deft and fast on his feet.

Pete said, "What happened to your face, Ward?"

Littell opened the suitcase. Pete picked up the 8-ball and cracked it in half barehanded.

Wood chunks snapped and popped. Marcello said, "I'm not sure I like where this is going."

Littell pulled out the Fund books. A quick prayer tamped down his nerves.

"I'm sure you both know that Jules Schiffrin's estate in Lake Geneva was burglarized last November. Some paintings were stolen, along with some ledgers rumored to contain Teamster Pension Fund notations. The thief was an informant for a Chicago-based Top Hoodlum Program agent named Court Meade, and he gave the books to Meade when he realized that the paintings were too well-known and recognizable to sell. Meade died of a heart attack in January, and he willed the books to me. He told me he never showed them to anyone else, and in my opinion he was waiting to sell them to somebody in the Giancana organization. There's a few pages that have been torn out, but aside from that I think they're intact. I brought them to you because I know how close you are to Mr. Hoffa and the Teamsters."

Marcello went slack-jawed. Pete snapped a pool cue in half.

He tore out fourteen pages back in Houston. He had all the Kennedy entries safely stashed.

Marcello offered his hand. Littell kissed a big diamond ring papal-style.

66

(Anniston, 4/11/61)

VOTING ROLLS AND poll tax reports. Literacy test results and witness statements.

Four corkboard-mounted walls dripping with paper—systematic suppression in typescript black-on-white.

His room was small and drab. The Wigwam Motel was not quite the St. Regis.

Kemper worked up a voting rights obstruction brief. One literacy test and one witness deposition formed his evidentiary basis.

Delmar Herbert Bowen was a male Negro, born 6/14/19 in Anniston, Alabama. He was literate, and a self-described "big reader."

On 6/15/40, Mr. Bowen tried to register to vote. The registrar said, Boy, can you read and write?

Mr. Bowen proved that he could. The registrar asked exclusionary questions, pertaining to advanced calculus.

Mr. Bowen failed to answer them. Mr. Bowen was denied the right to vote.

He subpoenaed Mr. Bowen's literacy test. He determined that the Anniston registrar fabricated the results.

The man said that Mr. Bowen could not spell "dog" and "cat." Mr. Bowen did not know that coitus precipitates childbirth.

Kemper clipped pages. The work bored him. The Kennedy civil rights mandate was not bold enough for his taste.

His mandate was gunboat diplomacy.

He grabbed a sandwich at a lunch counter yesterday. In the colored section—for the pure hell of it.

A cracker called him a "nigger lover." He judo-chopped him into a bowl of grits.

Shots zinged his door last night. A colored man told him the Klan torched a cross down the block.

Kemper finished the Bowen brief. He did it catch-up fast—he had to meet John Stanton in Miami in three hours.

Phone calls blitzed his morning and put him off-schedule. Bobby called for a deposition update; Littell called to drop his latest A-bomb.

Ward delivered the Fund books to Carlos Marcello. Pete Bondurant observed the transaction. Marcello seemed to buy Ward's convoluted cover story.

Ward said, "I made copies, Kemper. And the depositions on your incursion and Joe Kennedy's malfeasance remain fail-safed. And I'd appreciate it if you advised Le Grand Pierre not to kill me."

He called Pete immediately. He said, "Don't kill Littell or tell Carlos his story is bullshit." Pete said, "Credit me with some brains. I've been playing this game as long as you."

Littell finessed them. It was no severe loss—the books were always a moneymaking longshot.

Kemper oiled his .45. Bobby knew he carried it—and laughed it off as pretentious.

He wore it to the Inaugural. He found Bobby on the parade route and told him he cut Laura off clean.

He found Jack at a White House reception. He called him "Mr. President" for the first time. Jack's first presidential decree: "Find me some girls for later tonight."

Kemper rustled up two Georgetown coeds. President Jack told him to stash the girls away for late quickies.

Kemper stashed them in White House guest rooms. Jack caught him yawning and splashing water on his face.

It was 3:00 A.M., with Inaugural galas set to run past dawn.

Jack suggested a pick-me-up. They walked into the Oval Office and saw a doctor preparing vials and hypodermics.

The President rolled up one sleeve. The doctor injected him. John F. Kennedy looked positively orgasmic.

Kemper rolled up one sleeve. The doctor injected him. A rocket payload hit his system.

The ride lasted twenty-four hours. The time and place cohered around it.

Jack's ascent became his. That simple truth felt spellbindingly articulate. The time and place were beholden to one Kemper Cathcart Boyd. In that sense, he and Jack were indistinguishable.

He picked up one of Jack's old flames and made love to her at the Willard. He described the Moment to senators and cab drivers. Judy Garland showed him how to dance the Twist.

The ride sputtered out and left him wanting more. He knew that more would only vulgarize the Moment.

The phone rang. Kemper cinched his overnight bag and picked up.

"This is Boyd."

"It's Bob, Kemper. I've got the President here with me."

"Does he want me to repeat that update I gave you?"

"No. We need you to help us sort out a communications glitch."

"Pertaining to?"

"Cuba. I realize that you're only informally acquainted with some recent developments, but I still think you're the best man for this."

"For what? What are we talking about?"

Bobby came off exasperated. "The projected exile invasion, which you may or may not have heard about. Richard Bissell just dropped by my office and said the CIA's chomping at the bit, and their Cubans are just a bit beyond restless. They've got the key landing site picked out. It's some place called Playa Girón, or the Bay of Pigs."

It was NEW news. Stanton never told him that Langley picked a site.

Kemper faked bewilderment. "I don't see how I can help you. You know I don't know anybody in the CIA."

Jack came on the line. "Bobby didn't know the thing was this far advanced, Kemper. Allen Dulles briefed us on it before I took office, but we haven't discussed it since then. My advisors are split down the middle on the damn thing."

Kemper slipped on his holster. Bobby said, "What we need is an independent assessment of the exiles' readiness."

Kemper laughed. "Because if the invasion fails and it becomes known that you backed the so-called 'rebels,' you'll be fucked in the court of world opinion."

Bobby said, "Vividly put."

Jack said, "And to the point. And I should have taken Bobby into my confidence on this a few weeks ago, but he's been so goddamned busy chasing gangsters. Kemper . . ."

"Yes, Mr. President."

"I've been waffling on a date, and Bissell's been pressing me. I know you've been doing that anti-Castro work for Mr. Hoover, so I know you're at least somewhat . . ."

"I am somewhat conversant on Cuba, at least from a pro-Castro-group standpoint."

Bobby cracked the whip. "Cuba's always been a bit of a fixation for you, so go to Florida and make something positive out of it. Visit the CIA training camps, and take a swing through Miami. Call back and tell us if you think the operation has a chance to succeed, and do it damn fast."

Kemper said, "I'll leave now. I'll report back inside forty-eight hours."

John almost died laughing. Kemper almost called a cardiologist.

They sat on Stanton's private terrace. Langley let him upgrade to the Fontainebleau—hotel-suite living was contagious.

A breeze blew up Collins Avenue. Kemper's throat hurt—he repeated the phone talk replete with Jack's Boston bray.

"John . . ."

Stanton caught his breath. "I'm sorry, but I never thought presidential indecisiveness could be so goddamn funny."

"What do you think I should tell him?"

"How about, 'The invasion will guarantee your re-election.'"

Kemper laughed. "I've got some time to kill in Miami. Any suggestions?"

"Yes, two."

"Tell me, then. And tell me why you wanted to see me when you knew I was swamped in Alabama."

Stanton poured a short scotch-and-water. "That civil rights work must be vexing."

"Not really."

"I think the Negro vote is a mixed blessing. Aren't they easily led?"

"I'd call them slightly less malleable than our Cubans. And considerably less criminally inclined."

Stanton smiled. "Stop it. Don't make me start laughing again."

Kemper put his feet up on the railing. "I think you could use a few laughs. Langley's running you ragged, and you're drinking at 1:00 P.M."

Stanton nodded. "This is true. Everybody from Mr. Dulles on down would like the invasion to go off some time in the next five minutes, and I'm no exception. And to answer your initial question, I want you to spend the next forty-eight hours devising realistic-sounding intelligence on troop readiness to submit to the President, and I want you to pre-patrol our Cadre territory with Fulo and Néstor Chasco. Miami's our best source of street-level intelligence, and I want you to assess just how far and how accurately rumors pertaining to the invasion have spread within the Cuban community."

Kemper mixed a gin and tonic. "I'll get on it right away. Was there anything else?"

"Yes. The Agency wants to set up a Cuban 'government in exile,' to be housed at Blessington during the actual invasion. It's mostly cosmetic, but we've got to have at least a facsimile of a consensus-chosen leadership ready to install if we get Castro out within, say, three or four days of our go date."

"And you want my opinion as to who gets the nod?"

"Right. I know you're not too well versed on exile politics, but I thought you might have picked up some opinions from the Cadre."

Kemper faked deep thought. Steady now, make him wait—

Stanton threw his hands up. "Come on, I didn't tell you to go into a goddamn trance about—"

Kemper snapped out of it—bright-eyed and forceful. "We want far-right-wingers susceptible to working with Santo and our other friends in the Outfit. We want a figurehead leader who can maintain order, and the best way to re-stabilize the Cuban economy is to get the casinos operating on a full profit margin. If Cuba stays volatile or the Reds take over again, we've got to be able to draw on the Outfit for financial assistance."

Stanton laced his hands around one knee. "I was expecting something a bit more enlightened from Kemper Boyd the civil rights reformer. And I'm sure you know that the donations of our Italian friends only account for a tiny percentage of our legit-imately funded government budget."

Kemper shrugged. "Cuba's solvency depends on American tourism. The Outfit can help insure that. United Fruit is out of Cuba now, and only a bribable far-right-winger will be willing to de-nationalize their holdings."

Stanton said, "Keep going. You're close to persuading me."

Kemper stood up. "Carlos is down at the Guatemala camp with my lawyer friend. Chuck's going to fly him to Louisiana in a few days and hide him out, and I've heard that he's getting more pro-exile by the day. I'm betting that the invasion *will* succeed, but that chaos will reign inside Cuba for some time. Whoever we install will fall under intense public scrutiny, which means public

accountability, and we both know that the Agency will be subjected to intense scrutiny that will limit our deniability in all matters pertaining to covert action. We'll need the Cadre then, and
we'll probably need a half-dozen more groups as ruthless and
autonomous as the Cadre, and *we'll need them to be privately funded.*
Our new leader will need a secret police, and the Outfit will provide him with one, and if he falters in his pro-U.S. stance, the
Outfit will assassinate him."

Stanton stood up. He looked bright-eyed verging on
feverish.

"I don't have the final say, but you sold me. Your pitch wasn't
as flowery as your boy's Inaugural address, but it was a good deal
more politically astute."

AND PROFIT-MOTIVATED—

Kemper said, "Thanks. It's an honor to be compared to John
F. Kennedy."

Fulo drove. Néstor talked. Kemper watched.

They cruised Cadre turf in random figure-eights. Slum shacks
and housing projects zipped by.

Néstor said, "Send me back to Cuba. I will shoot Fidel from
a rooftop. I will become the Simón Bolívar of my country."

Fulo's Chevy was packed with dope. Powder puffed out of
plastic bags and dusted the seats.

Néstor said, "Send me back to Cuba as a boxer. I will beat
Fidel to death with bolo punches like Kid Gavilan."

Rheumy eyes popped their way—local junkies knew the car.
Winos pressed up for handouts—Fulo was a well-known soft
touch.

Fulo called it the New Marshall Plan. Fulo said his handouts
inspired subservience.

Kemper watched.

Néstor stopped at drop sites and sold pre-packaged bindles.
Fulo backstopped all transactions with a shotgun.

Kemper watched.

Fulo spotted a *non-Cadre* transaction outside Lucky Time
Liquors. Néstor sprayed the transactors with .12-gauge-
propelled rock salt.

The transactors dispersed every which way. Rock salt tore
through your clothes and made your skin sting like a mother
humper.

Kemper watched.

Néstor said, "Send me back to Cuba as a skin diver. I will shoot Fidel with an underwater spear gun."

Street-corner rummies sucked down T-Bird. Glue fiends sniffed rags. Half the front lawns featured dilapidated jalopies.

Kemper watched. Cab calls squawked up the squawk box. Fulo drove from Darktown to Poquito Habana.

Faces went from black to brown. Incidental colors shifted and went more pastel.

Pastel-fronted churches. Pastel-fronted dance clubs and bodegas. Men in bright pastel guayabera shirts.

Fulo drove. Néstor talked. Kemper watched.

They passed parking-lot crap games. They passed soapbox orations. They passed two kids pummeling a pro-Beard pamphleteer.

Kemper watched.

Fulo glided down Flagler and traded cash for prostitute street talk.

One girl said Castro was queer. One girl said Castro had a 12″ chorizo. All the girls wanted to know one thing: When's this big invasion gonna happen?

A girl said she picked up a rumor down at Blessington. Ain't that big invasion next week?

One girl said Guantánamo was gonna get A-bombed. One girl said, You're wrong—it's Playa Girón. One girl said flying saucers would soon descend on Havana.

Fulo drove. Néstor polled strolling Cubans up and down Flagler.

They'd all heard invasion rumors. They all shared them with gusto.

Kemper shut his eyes and listened. Nouns jumped out of run-on Spanish.

Havana, Playa Girón, Baracoa, Oriente, Playa Girón, Guantánamo, Guantánamo.

Kemper caught the upshot:

People were talking.

On-leave trainees were talking. Agency-front-group men were talking. The talk was innuendo, bullshit, wish fulfillment and truth by default—speculate on enough invasion sites and you'll hit the right one out of sheer luck.

The talk constituted a minor security leak.

Fulo didn't seem worried. Néstor shrugged the talk off. Kemper categorized it as "containable."

They cruised the side streets off Flagler.

Fulo monitored cab calls. Néstor talked up ways to torture Fidel Castro. Kemper looked out his window and savored the view.

Cuban girls blew them kisses. Car radios churned out mambo music. Street loafers gobbled melons soaked in beer.

Fulo clicked off a call. "That was Wilfredo. He said Don Juan knows something about a dope drop, and maybe we should go see him."

Don Juan Pimentel had a TB cough. His front room was littered with customized Barbie and Ken dolls.

They stood just inside the door. Don Juan smelled like mentholated chest rub.

Fulo said, "You can talk in front of Mr. Boyd. He is a wonderful friend of our Cause."

Néstor picked up a nude Barbie. The doll wore a Jackie Kennedy wig and Brillo-pad crotch hair.

Don Juan coughed. "It is twenty-five dollars for the story, and fifty dollars for the story and the address."

Néstor dropped the doll and crossed himself. Fulo handed Don Juan two twenties and a ten.

He tucked the cash in his shirt pocket. "The address is 4980 Balustrol. Four men from the Cuban Intelligence Directorate live there. They are terribly afraid that your invasion will succeed and that their supply from the island will be, how you say, removed. They have at the house a very large supply of single shots packaged to sell in order to make quick money to, how you say, bankroll their resistance to your resistance. They have over a pound of heroin ready to be sold in these small amounts where there is to be the, how you say, most profit."

Kemper smiled. "Is the house guarded?"

"I do not know."

"Who would they sell the stuff to?"

"Certainly not to Cubans. I would say to the negritos and the poor whites."

Kemper nudged Fulo. "Is Mr. Pimentel a reliable informant?"

"Yes. I think so."

"Is he strongly anti-Castro?"

"Yes. I think so."

"Would you trust him not to betray us under any circumstances?"

"Well . . . that is hard to . . ."

Don Juan spat on the floor. "You are a coward not to ask such questions to my face."

Kemper judo-chopped him. Don Juan clipped a doll rack and went down gagging for breath.

Néstor dropped a pillow on his face. Kemper pulled his .45 and fired through it point-blank.

His silencer ate up the noise. Blood-soaked feathers billowed.

Néstor and Fulo looked shocked. Kemper said, "I'll explain later."

REBELS RESCUE CUBA! COMMIES PANDER
POISON DOPE IN RAPACIOUS REVENGE!
HEROIN HOLOCAUST! PUSHER CASTRO
GLOATS! DESPERATE DICTATOR IN EXILE!
DOPE DEATH TOLL MOUNTS!

Kemper printed the headlines on a dispatch sheet. Tiger Kab swirled all around him—the midnight shift was just coming on. He wrote a cover note.

PB,

Have Lenny Sands write up Hush-Hush articles to accompany the enclosed headlines. Tell him to expedite it and to check the Miami papers over the next week or so for background details and call me if necessary. This, of course, pertains to the invasion, and my feeling is that we're very close to a go-date. I can't go into my plan in detail yet, but I think it's something you'd appreciate. If Lenny finds my orders confusing, tell him to extrapolate off the headlines in the inimitable Hush-Hush style.

I know you're somewhere in Nicaragua or Guatemala, and I'm hoping this pouch gets to you. And try to think of WJL as a colleague. Peaceful co-existence doesn't always mean appeasement.

KB

Kemper stamped the envelope: C. ROGERS/NEXT

FLIGHT/URGENT. Fulo and Néstor walked by, looking befuddled—he never explained why he killed Don Juan.

Santo Junior had a pet shark named Batista. They drove to Tampa and dumped Don Juan in his pool.

Kemper pulled a phone into the men's room. He rehearsed his pitch three times, complete with pauses and asides.

He called Bobby's secretary. He told her to turn on her tape recorder.

She jumped to it. She bought his perfectly honed urgency.

He lauded. He gushed. He praised exile morale and combat-readiness. The CIA had a brilliant plan. Their pre-invasion security was water-tight.

He raved like a skeptic newly converted. He inserted New Frontier rhetoric. His Tennessee drawl oozed convert righteousness.

The woman said she'd rush the tape to Bobby. Her voice quivered and broke.

Kemper hung up and walked out to the parking lot. Teo Paez swung by and passed him a note.

> W. Littell called. Said all is well with CM. CM's N.Y. lawyer says Justice Dept. agents are searching Louisiana for CM. W. Littell says CM should stay at Guat. camp or at least out of country for awhile.

Ward Littell in ascent—truly amazing.

A breeze kicked in. Kemper stretched out on a tiger-striped hood and looked at the sky.

The moon hovered close. Batista had bright white teeth the same color.

Kemper dozed. Chants woke him up. He heard GO GO GO GO GO—that one word and nothing else.

The shouts were ecstatic. The dispatch hut boomed like a giant echo chamber.

The invasion date was set. It couldn't be anything less than that.

Santo fed Batista steaks and fried chicken. His pool was an Olympic-sized grease spill.

Batista bit Don Juan's head off. Néstor and Fulo turned away.

He didn't. He was starting to enjoy killing more than he should.

67

(Rural Nicaragua, 4/17/61)

PIGS! PIGS! PIGS! PIGS! PIGS! PIGS! PIGS! PIGS! PIGS!
Six hundred men chanted it.

The staging site shook behind that one word.

The men jumped into trucks. The trucks locked in bumper-to-bumper and headed down to the launch dock.

PIGS PIGS PIGS PIGS PIGS—

Pete watched. John Stanton watched. They jeep-patrolled the site and watched everything click into on-go status.

On-GO at the dock: one insignia-deleted U.S. troop ship. On board: landing craft, mortars, grenades, rifles, machine guns, radio gear, medical gear, mosquito repellent, maps, ammo and six hundred Sheik prophylactics—a Langley shrink foresaw mass rape as a victory by-product.

On-GO: six hundred Benzedrine-blasted Cuban rebels.

On-GO at the air strip: sixteen B-26 bombers, set to hammer Castro's standing air force. Dig their blacked-out U.S. insignia—this gig was non-imperialisto.

PIGS PIGS PIGS PIGS—

The abbreviation fit the destination. John Stanton got the chant going at reveille—that shrink said repetition built up courage.

Pete chased high-octane bennies with coffee. He could see it and feel it and smell it—

The planes neutralize Castro air power. The ships go out—staggered departures from a half-dozen launch sites. A second air strike kills militiamen en masse. Chaos spawns mass desertion.

Freedom fighters hit the beach.

They march. They kill. They defoliate. They link up with on-island dissidents and reclaim Cuba—weakened by dope and propaganda foreplay.

They were waiting for Bad-Back Jack to okay the first air strike. All the orders had to emanate from the Haircut.

PIGS PIGS PIGS PIGS PIGS—

Pete and Stanton jeep-patrolled the site. They had a short-wave set rigged to the dashboard—site-to-site communication made easy.

They had direct feeds to Guatemala, Tiger Kab and

Blessington. They were radio contained at that level—only Langley direct-channeled to the White House.

The order came down: Jack says to send six planes out.

Pete felt his dick go limp. The radio man said Jack wants to move real cautiously.

Six from sixteen was a big fucking reduction.

They kept circuiting the site. Pete chain-smoked. Stanton fretted a Saint Christopher medal.

Boyd pouched a message three days ago—some cryptic *Hush-Hush* orders for Lenny Sands. He forwarded the information. Lenny said he'd write the stuff up quick.

Lenny always delivered. Ward Littell always surprised.

That Teamster book hand-off was superb. Littell's brown-nose job on Carlos was better.

Boyd had them lodged at the Guatemalan campsite. Marcello glommed a private phone line and ran his rackets biz long-distance.

Carlos liked fresh seafood. Carlos liked to throw big dinner parties. Littell had 500 Maine lobsters air-shipped to Guatemala daily.

Carlos turned crack troopers into salivating gluttons. Carlos turned said troopers into coolies—trained exile guerrillas shined his shoes and ran his errands.

Boyd was running the Marcello operation. Boyd gave Pete one direct order: LEAVE LITTELL ALONE.

The Bondurant-Littell truce was Boyd-enforced and *temporary*.

Pete chain-smoked. Cigarettes and bennies had him parched. His hands kept doing things he didn't tell them to.

They kept circuiting. Stanton sweated his clothes wringing wet.

PIGS! PIGS! PIGS! PIGS! PIGS!

They parked by the dock and watched troops climb the boarding plank. Six hundred men hopped on in just under two minutes.

Their short-wave set sputtered. The needle bounced to the Blessington frequency.

Stanton plugged in his headset. Pete lit his zillionth cigarette of the day.

The troop ship creaked and waddled. A fat Cubano puked over the stern.

Stanton said, "Our government-in-exile's in place, and Bissell ended up approving those far-right boys I recommended. That's good, but that fake-defector charade we cooked up backfired. Gutiérrez landed the plane at Blessington, but the reporters that Dougie Lockhart called in recognized Ramón and started booing. It's not a big thing, but a fuck-up's still a fuck-up."

Pete nodded. He smelled vomit and bilge water and oil off six hundred rifles.

Stanton unhooked his headset. His Saint Christopher was fretted shiny to dull.

They kept circuiting. It was gas-guzzling Benzedrine bullshit.

Please, Jack:

Send some more planes in. Give the orders to send the boats out.

Pete got wild-ass itchy. Stanton blathered on and on about his kids.

Hours took decades. Pete ran lists in his head to shut Stanton out.

The men he killed. The women he fucked. The best hamburgers in L.A. and Miami. What he'd be doing if he never left Quebec. What he'd be doing if he never met Kemper Boyd.

Stanton worked the radio. Reports crackled in.

They heard that the air strike fizzled. The bombers nailed less than 10% of Fidel Castro's air force.

Bad-Back Jack took the news hard. He responded in cuntish fashion: no second air strike just yet.

Chuck Rogers squeaked a call in. He said Marcello and Littell were still in Guatemala. He dropped some late-breaking stateside info: the FBI invaded New Orleans in response to fake Carlos sightings!

It was Boyd's doing. He figured erroneous phone tips would keep Bobby diverted and help cover Marcello's tracks.

Chuck signed off. Stanton clamped his headphones down and kept his ears perked for stray calls.

Seconds took years. Minutes took fucking millenniums.

Pete scratched his balls raw. Pete smoked himself hoarse. Pete shot palm fronds off of trees just to shoot *something*.

Stanton rogered a call. "That was Lockhart. He says our government-in-exile's close to rioting. They need you at Blessington, and Rogers is flying in from Guatemala to pick you up."

* * *

They detoured by the Cuban coast. Chuck said it added nil time to their flight plan.

Pete yelled, "Let's get low!"

Chuck throttled down. Pete saw flames from two thousand feet and half a mile out.

They swooped below radar level and belly-rolled along the beach. Pete jammed binoculars out his window.

He saw aircraft wreckage—Cuban and rebel. He saw smoldering palm groves and hose trucks parked on the sand.

Air-raid sirens were blasting full-tilt. Dock-mounted spotlights were pre-dusk operational. Pillboxes had been set up just above the high tide line—fully manned and sandbagged.

Militiamen crowded the dock. Dig those little geeks with Tommy guns and aircraft ID guides.

They were eighty miles south of Playa Girón. *This* stretch of beach was red-alert ready. If the Bay of Pigs was *this* fortified, the entire invasion was fucked.

Pete heard muzzle pops. Little chickenshit pepperings went bip-bip-bip.

Chuck caught on—they're shooting at *us*.

He flipped the Piper belly to backside. Pete spun topsy-turvy.

His head hit the roof. His seatbelt choked him immobile. Chucky rolled and flew upside down all the way to U.S. waters.

Dusk hit. Blessington glowed under high-wattage arc lights.

Pete popped two Dramamines. He saw redneck gawkers and ice cream trucks perched outside the front gates.

Chuck fishtailed down the runway and brought the plane to a dead stall. Pete hopped out woozy—Benzedrine and incipient nausea packed this wicked one-two punch.

A prefab hut stood in the middle of the drill field. Triple-strength barbed wire sequestered it. Unsynchronized shouts boomed out—a far cry from your snappy PIGS PIGS PIGS!

Pete stretched and worked out some muscle kinks. Lockhart ran up to him.

"Goddamnit, get in there and calm those spics down!"

Pete said, "What happened?"

"What happened is Kennedy's stalling. Dick Bissell said he wants a win, but he don't want to go the whole hog and get blamed if the invasion goes bust. I got my rusty old cargo ship all ready to go, but that Pope-worshiping cocksucker in the White House won't—"

Pete slapped him. The little shitbird weaved and stayed upright.

"I said, '*What happened?*'"

Lockhart wiped his nose and giggled. "What happened is my Klan boys sold the provisional government guys some moonshine, and they started arguing politics with some of the regular troops. I whipped up a crew and isolated the troublemakers with that there barbed wire, but that don't alter the fact that you got sixty frustrated and liquored-up Cuban hotheads in there biting at each other like copperheads when they should be concentrating on the problem at hand, which is liberating a Commie-held dictatorship."

"Do they have guns?"

"No sir. I got the weapons shack locked and guarded."

Pete reached into the cockpit. Right upside the dashboard: Chuck's fungo bat and all-purpose tool kit.

He grabbed them. He pulled out the tin snips and tucked the bat into his waistband.

Lockhart said, "What are you doing?"

Chuck said, "I think I know."

Pete pointed to the pump shed. "Let go with the fire hoses in exactly five minutes."

Lockhart hooted. "Them hoses will tear that prefab right down."

"That's what I want."

The sequestered spics laughed and yelled. Lockhart took off and hit the pump shed at a sprint.

Pete ran over to the fence and snipped out a section of coiling. Chuck wrapped his hands in his windbreaker and pulled down a big wall of barbs.

Pete scrunched down and crawled through. He ran up to the hut in a deep fullback crouch. One fungo bat shot took the door down.

His crash-in went unnoticed. The government-in-exile boys were preoccupied.

With arm wrestling, card games and shine-guzzling contests. With a baby-alligator race right there on the floor.

Dig the rooting sections. Dig the blankets covered with bet chits. Dig the bunks weighted down with moonshine jugs.

Pete choked up a bat grip. On-GO: that good old boot-camp pugelstick training.

He waded in. Tight swings clipped chins and ribcages. The government-in-exile boys fought back—odd fists hit him haphazardly.

His bat shattered bunk beams. His bat shattered a fat man's dentures. The gators scurried outside while the getting was good.

The government boys got the picture: Do not resist this big Caucasian madman.

Pete tore through the hut. The spics made like a backdraft and got waaay behind him.

He tore out the rear door and swung at the porch-to-roof stanchions. Five swings left-handed, five swings right—switch-hitting like fucking Mickey Mantle.

The walls shuddered. The roof wiggled. The foundation shimmy-shimmied. The spics evacuated—Earthquake! Earthquake!

The hoses hit. Jet-pressure tore the fence down. Hydraulic force ripped the hut roofless.

Pete caught a spritz and went tumbling. The hut burst into cinderblock shingles.

Dig the government-in-exile:

Running. Stumbling. Doing the jet-spray jigaboo jiggle.

Call it *Hush-Hush* style:

WATER-WHACKED WETBACKS WIGGLE! BOOZE-BLITZED AND BESOAKED BASTION BOOGIE-WOOGIES!

The hoses snapped off. Pete started laughing.

Men stood up soaked and trembling. Pete's laugh went contagious and built to a roar.

The drill field was an instant prefab dump site.

The laughter went locomotive and shaped into a perfect martial cadence. A chant built off of it:

PIGS! PIGS! PIGS! PIGS! PIGS!

Lockhart dispensed blankets. Pete sobered the men up with bennie-laced Kool-Aid.

They loaded the troop ship at midnight. 256 exiles climbed on—hotwired to reclaim their country.

They loaded weapons, landing craft and medical supplies.

Radio channels stayed open: Blessington to Langley and every port-of-departure command post.

The word passed through:

Jack the Haircut says, no second air strike.

Nobody proffered first-strike death stats. Nobody proffered reports on coastal fortifications.

Those spotlights and beach bunkers went unreported. Those militia lookouts went unmentioned.

Pete knew why.

Langley knows it's now or never. Why inform the troops that we're in crap-shoot terrain from here on in?

Pete swigged moonshine to wean himself off the bennies. He passed out on his bunk midway through this weird hallucination.

Japs, Japs, Japs. Saipan, '43—in wide-screen Technicolor.

They swarmed him. He killed them and killed them and killed them. He screamed readiness warnings. Nobody understood his Québecois French.

Dead Japs popped back to life. He rekilled them barehanded. They turned into dead women—Ruth Mildred Cressmeyer clones.

Chuck woke him up at dawn. He said, "Kennedy came halfway through. All the sites launched their troops an hour ago."

Waiting time dragged. Their short-wave set went on the fritz.

Troop ship transmissions came in garbled. Site-to-site feeds registered as static-laced gibberish.

Chuck couldn't nail the malfunction. Pete tried straight telephone contact—calls to Tiger Kab and his Langley drop.

He got two sustained busy signals. Chuck chalked them up to pro-Fidel line jamming.

Lockhart had a hot number memorized: the Agency's Miami Ops office. Boyd called it "Invasion Central"—the sparkplug Cadre guys never got close to.

Pete dialed the number. A busy signal blared extra loud. Chuck nailed the source of the sound: covertly strung phone lines overloaded with incoming calls.

They sat around the barracks. Their radio coughed out strange little sputters.

Time dragged. Seconds took years. Minutes took solar-system eternities.

Pete chained cigarettes. Dougie Frank and Chuck bummed a whole pack off of him.

A Klan guy was hosing off the Piper. Pete and Chuck shared a reeeeealllly long look.

Dougie Frank jammed their wavelength. "Can I go, too?"

Diversionary dips got them close. They caught the Bay of Pigs in tight and ugly.

They saw a supply ship snagged on a reef. They saw dead men flopping out of a hole in the hull. They saw sharks bobbing at body parts twenty yards offshore.

Chuck swung around and made a second pass. Pete bumped the control panel. The extra passenger had them cramped in extra tight.

They saw beached landing craft. They saw live men climbing over dead men. They saw a hundred-yard stretch of bodies in bright-red shallow water.

The invaders kept coming. Flamethrowers nailed them the second they hit the wave break. They got flash-fried and boiled alive.

Fifty-odd rebels were shackled facedown in the sand. A Commie with a chainsaw was running across their backs.

Pete saw the blade drag. Pete saw the blood gout. Pete saw their heads roll into the water.

Flames jumped up at the plane—short by inches.

Chuck pulled off his headset. "I picked up an Ops call! Kennedy says, 'No second air strike,' and he says he won't send in any U.S. troops to help our guys!"

Pete aimed his Magnum out the window. A flame clap spun it out of his hand.

Sharks were churning up the water right below them. This fat Commie fuck waved a severed head.

68

(Rural Guatemala, 4/18/61)

THEIR ROOM ADJOINED the radio hut. Invasion updates seeped through the walls uninvited.

Marcello tried to sleep. Littell tried to study deportation law.

Kennedy refused to order a second air strike. Rebel soldiers were captured and slaughtered on the beach.

Reserve troops were chanting "PIGS! PIGS! PIGS! PIGS! PIGS!" That silly word roared through the barracks quadrangle.

Right-wing dementia: mildly distracting. Mildly gratifying: a detectable rise in contempt for John F. Kennedy.

Littell watched Marcello toss and turn. He was bunking with a Mafia chieftain—mildly amazing.

His charade worked. Carlos scanned ledger columns and recognized his own Fund transactions. His indebtedness increased exponentially.

Carlos was accruing large legal debts. Carlos owed his safety to a reformed FBI crimebuster.

Guy Banister called this morning. He said he picked up some straight dope: Bobby Kennedy knows that Carlos is really hiding out in Guatemala.

Bobby applied diplomatic pressure. The Guatemalan prime minister kowtowed. Carlos would be deported, "but not swiftly."

Banister used to call him a weak sister. His phone manner was near-deferential now.

Marcello started snoring. He was drooping off his army cot in monogrammed silk pajamas.

Littell heard shouts and banging noises next door. He formed a picture: men slapping desks and kicking odd inanimate objects.

"It's a washout"/"That vacillating chickenshit"/"He won't send in planes or ships to shell the beach."

Littell walked outside. The troopers worked up a new chant.

"KEN-NEDY, DON'T SAY NO! KEN-NEDY, LET US GO!"

They bounced around the quad. They swigged straight gin and vodka. They gobbled pills and kicked apothecary jars like soccer balls.

The case officers' lounge had been looted. The dispensary door had been trampled to pulp.

"KEN-NEDY, LET US GO! KEN-NEDY IS A PU-TO!"

Littell stepped inside and grabbed the wall phone. Twelve coded digits got him Tiger Kab direct.

A man said, "*Sí?* Cabstand."

"I'm looking for Kemper Boyd. Tell him it's Ward Littell."

"*Sí.* One second."

Littell unbuttoned his shirt—the humidity was awful. Carlos mumbled through a bad dream.

Kemper picked up. "What is it, Ward?"

"What is it with you? You sound anxious."

"There's riots all over the Cuban section, and the invasion isn't going our way. Ward, what is—?"

"I got word that the Guatemalan government's looking for Carlos. Bobby Kennedy knows he's here, and I think I should move him again."

"Do it. Rent an apartment outside Guatemala City, and call me with the phone number. I'll have Chuck Rogers meet you there and fly you someplace more removed. Ward, I can't talk now. Call me when—"

The line went dead. Overtaxed circuits—mildly annoying. Mildly amusing: Kemper C. Boyd mildly flustered.

Littell walked outside. The chants were a good deal more than mildly pissed-off.

"KEN-NEDY IS A PU-TO! KEN-NEDY FEARS FI-DEL CAS-TRO!"

69

(Miami, 4/18/61)

KEMPER MIXED THE dope. Néstor mixed the poison. They worked on two desks jammed together.

They had the dispatch hut to themselves. Fulo shut down Tiger Kab at 6:00 P.M. and gave the drivers strict orders: Visit riot scenes and maim Fidelistos.

Kemper and Néstor kept working. Their hotshot assembly line moved slowly.

They mixed strychnine and Drano into a heroin-like white powder. They packaged it in single-pop plastic bindles.

They played their short-wave set. Awful death tallies sputtered in.

Hush-Hush went to press yesterday. Lenny called him for details. The piece described a resounding Bay of Pigs victory.

Jack could *still* force a win. The ODs would defame Castro, WIN OR LOSE.

They B&E'd the drop house two days ago—a little safety-first trial run. They found two hundred "H" bindles stashed behind a heating panel.

Don Juan Pimentel fed them straight information. His death eliminated witness testimony.

Néstor cooked up a shot. Kemper loaded a syringe and test-fired it.

A milky liquid squirted out. Néstor said, "It looks believable. I think it will fool the negritos who buy it."

"Let's go by the house. We have to make the switch tonight."

"Yes. And we must pray that President Kennedy acts more boldly."

A rainstorm pushed the riot action indoors. Prowl cars were double-parked outside half the nightclubs on and off Flagler.

They drove to a pay phone. Néstor dialed the drop pad and got an extended dial tone. The house was two blocks away.

They circled by it. The street was middle-class Cubano—small cribs with small front yards and toys on the lawn.

The drop pad was peach-stucco Spanish. It was late-night quiet and nonsecurity dark.

No lights. No cars in the driveway. No TV shadows bouncing out the front window.

Kemper parked at the curb. No doors opened; no window curtains opened or retracted.

Néstor checked their suitcase. "The back door?"

"I don't want to risk it again. The lock mechanism almost splintered last time."

"How do you expect to get in, then?"

Kemper pulled his gloves on. "There's a dog-access door built into the kitchen door. You scoot down, reach in, and pop the inside latch."

"Dog doors mean dogs."

"There was no dog last time."

"Last time does not mean this time."

"Fulo and Teo surveilled the place. They're sure there's no dog."

Néstor slipped gloves on. "Okay, then."

They walked up the driveway. Kemper checked their blind side every few seconds. Low-hanging storm clouds provided extra cover.

The door was perfect for large dogs and small men. Néstor scooted down and pulled himself into the house.

Kemper worked his gloves on extra-snug. Néstor opened the door from the inside.

They locked up. They took off their shoes. They walked through the kitchen to the heat panel. They took three steps straight ahead and four to the right—Kemper paced off exact measurements last time.

Néstor held the flashlight. Kemper removed the panel. The bindles were stashed in the identical position.

Néstor re-counted them. Kemper opened up the suitcase and got out the Polaroid.

Néstor said, "Two hundred exactly." Kemper shot a re-creation closeup.

They waited. The picture popped out of the camera.

Kemper taped it to the wall and held the flashlight on it. Nestor switched bindles. He duplicated the arrangement all the way down to tiny tucks and folds.

They sweated up the floor. Kemper swabbed it dry.

Néstor said, "Let's call Pete and see how things stand."

Kemper said, "It's out of our hands."

Please, Jack—

They agreed on a through-to-dawn car stakeout. Local residents parked on the street—Néstor's Impala wouldn't look out of place.

They slid their seats back and watched the house. Kemper fantasized Jack Saves Face scenarios.

Please come home and get your stash. *Please sell it quick to validate our hot-off-the-press propaganda.*

Néstor dozed. Kemper fantasized Bay of Pigs heroics.

A car pulled into the driveway. Door slams woke Néstor up wild-eyed.

Kemper covered his mouth. "Ssssh, now. Just look."

Two men walked into the house. Interior lights framed the doorway.

Kemper recognized them. They were pro-Castro agitators rumored to dabble in dope.

Néstor pointed to the car. "They left the motor running."

Kemper watched the door. The men locked up and walked out with a large attaché case.

Néstor cracked his window. Kemper caught some Spanish.

Néstor translated. "They're going to an after-hours club to sell the stuff."

The men got back in their car. The inside roof light went on. Kemper saw their faces bright as day.

The driver opened the case. The passenger unwrapped a bindle and snorted it.

And twitched. And spasmed. And convulsed—

GET IT BACK. THEY WON'T SELL IT NOW—

Kemper stumbled out of the car and ran up the driveway. Kemper pulled his piece and charged the dope car head-on.

The OD man spasm-kicked the windshield out.

Kemper aimed at the driver. The OD man lurched and blocked his shot.

The driver pulled a snub-nose and fired. Kemper fired straight back at him. Néstor ran up firing—two shots took out a side window and zinged off the roof of the car.

Kemper caught a slug. Ricochets ripped the convulsing man faceless. Néstor shot the driver in the back and blew him into the horn.

It went off AAAH-OOO-GAAAH, AAAH-OOO-GAAAH—LOUD LOUD LOUD.

Kemper shot the driver in the face. His glasses shattered and tore the pompadour off his toupee.

The horn blared. Néstor blew the steering wheel off the column. The goddamn horn reverberated LOUDER.

Kemper saw his collarbone push through his shirt. He weaved down the driveway wiping somebody's blood out of his eyes. Néstor caught him and piggybacked him to their car.

Kemper heard horn noise. Kemper saw spectators on the sidewalk. Kemper saw Cubano punks by the death car—boosting that attaché case.

Kemper screamed. Néstor popped a real "H" bindle under his nose.

He gagged and sneezed. His heart revved and purred. He coughed up some pretty red blood.

Néstor gunned the car. Spectators ran for cover. That funny-looking bone flopped out at a funny right angle.

DOCUMENT INSERT: 4/19/61.
Des Moines Register headline:
FAILED COUP LINKED TO U.S. SPONSORS

DOCUMENT INSERT: 4/19/61.
Los Angeles Herald-Express headline:
WORLD LEADERS DECRY ''ILLEGAL INTERVENTION''

DOCUMENT INSERT: 4/20/61.
Dallas Morning News headline:
KENNEDY BLASTED FOR ''HEEDLESS PROVOCATIONS''

DOCUMENT INSERT: 4/20/61.
San Francisco Chronicle headline and subhead:
BAY OF PIGS FIASCO REVILED BY U.S. ALLIES
CASTRO GLOATS AS REBEL DEATH TOLL MOUNTS

DOCUMENT INSERT: 4/20/61.
Chicago Tribune headline and subhead:
KENNEDY DEFENDS BAY OF PIGS ACTIONS
WORLDWIDE CENSURE CRIPPLES PRESIDENT'S PRESTIGE

DOCUMENT INSERT: 4/21/61.
Cleveland Plain Dealer headline and subhead:
CIA BLAMED FOR BAY OF PIGS FIASCO
EXILE LEADERS BLAME ''KENNEDY COWARDICE''

DOCUMENT INSERT: 4/22/61.
Miami Herald headline and subhead:
**KENNEDY: ''SECOND AIR STRIKE COULD HAVE SPARKED
WORLD WAR III''**
EXILE COMMUNITY HONORS LOST AND CAPTURED HEROES

DOCUMENT INSERT: 4/23/61.
New York Journal-American headline and subhead:
KENNEDY DEFENDS BAY OF PIGS ACTION
RED LEADERS BLAST ''IMPERIALIST AGGRESSION''

DOCUMENT INSERT: 4/24/61.
Hush-Hush magazine article. Written by Lenny Sands,
under the pseudonym Peerless Politicopundit.
COWARDLY CASTRATO CASTRO OUSTED!
RETREATING REDS WREAK RAT-POISON REVENGE!

   His rancorous Red reign ran for a rotten two years.

Shout it loud, proud and un-kowtowed: Fidel Castro,
the bushy-bearded beatnik bard of bilious
bamboozlement, was determinedly and dramatically
deposed last week by a heroically homeland-hungering
huddle of hopped-up hermanos righteously rankled by
the Red Recidivist's rape of their nation!

Call it D-Day '61, kats & kittens. Call the Bay of
Pigs the Caribbean Carthage; Playa Giron the
Patriotic Parthenon. Call Castro debilitated and
depilatoried—word has it that he shaved off his beard
to dodge the deep and dangerous depths of revenge-
seeker recognition!

Fidel Castro: the shabbily-shorn Samson of 1961!
His deliriously delighted Delilahs: God-fearing,
red, white & blue revering Cuban heroes!!!

Castro and his murderously malignant machinations:
trenchantly terminated, 10-4, over-and-out. The
Monster's maliciously maladroit maneuverings: still
morally mauling Miami!!!!

Item: Fidel Castro craves cornucopias of cash—get
away gelt to felicitously finance future finaglings!

Item: Fidel Castro has cravenly criticized
America's eminently egalitarian and instantly
inclusive racial policies, reproachfully ragging
U.S. leaders for their nauseously niggling neglect of
Negro citizens.

Item: as previously posited, Fidel Castro and
seditious sibling Raul sell homicidally hazardous
Heroin in Miami.

Item: as the Bay of Pigs waggled and waxed as
Castro's Waterloo, the mendacious mastiff's minor
miscreant minions mined Miami's Negro section with
rat-poison-riddled Heroin! Scores of Negro drug
addicts injected these carcinogenic Commie cocktails
and died doomonically draconean deaths!!!

Item: this issue was rushed to press, to insure
that Hush-Hush readers would not be left hungrily
homesick for our properly protectionist parade of
Playa Giron platitudes. Thus we cannot name the
aforementioned Negroes or offer specific details on
their dastardly deaths. That information will appear

in scintillatingly-scheduled subsequent issues, in
courageous conjunction with a new ongoing feature:
''Banana Republic Boxscore: Who's Red? Who's Dead?''

Adios, dear reader—and let's all meet for a tall
Cuba Libre in laceratingly liberated Havana.

DOCUMENT INSERT: 5/1/61.
Personal note: J. Edgar Hoover to Howard Hughes.

Dear Howard,

You must not be concerning yourself with Hush-Hush
these days. If you'll glance at the April 24th issue,
you'll see that it went to press at best precipitously
and at worst with a certain amount of criminal
negligence and/or criminal intent.

Did Mr. L. Sands perhaps possess some spurious
foreknowledge of unforetellable events? His piece
mentioned a number of Negro heroin overdoses in the
Miami area, and my Miami police contacts tell me that
no such overdoses occurred.

Nine Cuban teenagers, however, did die from
injections of poisonous Heroin. My contact told me
that on April 18, two Cuban youths stole an attache
case containing a large quantity of toxic Heroin from
a car involved in an unsolved shootout that left two
Cuban men dead.

My contact mentioned the curiously prophetic (if
historically inaccurate) Hush-Hush piece. I told him
that it was merely one of life's odd coincidences, an
explanation that seemed to satisfy him.

I would advise you to tell Mr. Sands to get his
facts reasonably straight. Hush-Hush should not
publish science fiction, unless it's directly in our
best interest.

All best, Edgar

DOCUMENT INSERT: 5/8/61.
Miami Herald sidebar:
PRESIDENT CONVENES HIGH-LEVEL GROUP TO ASSESS BAY
OF PIGS FAILURE

Calling the aborted Cuban exile invasion at the Bay
of Pigs a ''bitter lesson,'' President Kennedy today
stated that it was also a lesson he intended to learn
from.

The President told an informal gathering of
reporters that he has organized a study group to delve
into precisely why the Bay of Pigs invasion failed and
to also assess U.S.-Cuban policy in the wake of what
he called a ''catastrophically embarrassing
episode.''

The group will interview evacuated Bay of Pigs
survivors, Central Intelligence Agency personnel
involved in high-level invasion planning and Cuban
exile spokesmen from the numerous anti-Castro
organizations currently flourishing in Florida.

The study group will include Admiral Arleigh Burke
and General Maxwell Taylor. The chairman will be
Attorney General Robert F. Kennedy.

DOCUMENT INSERT: 5/10/61.
Personal note: Robert F. Kennedy to Kemper Boyd.

Dear Kemper,

I hate to trouble a wounded man with work, but
I know you're resilient, healing nicely and looking
forward to getting back to your Justice Department
duties. I feel bad about sending you into harm's way,
so thank God you're recovering.

I've got a second assignment for you, one that
geographically suits your work in Anniston and your
occasional Miami excursions for Mr. Hoover. The
President has formed a group to study the Bay of Pigs
mess and the Cuban question in general. We'll be
meeting with CIA administrators, action-level case
officers, Bay of Pigs survivors and representatives
from many CIA-sponsored and non-CIA-sponsored exile
factions. I'm chairing the group, and I want you to
serve as my point man and liaison to the Miami-based
CIA contingent and their Cuban charges.

I think you'll be good at the job, even though your

pre-invasion appraisal of exile readiness turned out
to be quite inaccurate. You should know that the
President and I do not blame you in any way for the
ultimate failure of the invasion. At this stage of
assessment, I think the blame should be leveled at
overzealous CIA men, sloppy pre-invasion security
and an egregious miscalculation of in-Cuba
discontent.

Enjoy another week's rest in Miami. The President
sends his best, and we both think it's ironic that a
forty-five-year-old man who has courted danger all his
adult life should be hit by a stray bullet fired by an
unknown assailant at a riot scene.

Get well and call me next week. Bob

DOCUMENT INSERT: 5/11/61.
Identical airtel memorandums: FBI Director J. Edgar
Hoover to the New York City, Los Angeles, Miami,
Boston, Dallas, Tampa, Chicago and Cleveland Special
Agents-in-Charge. All marked: CONFIDENTIAL 1-A/
DESTROY UPON RECEIPT.

Sir—

Your name has been deleted from this airtel for
security purposes. Consider this communique top
secret and report back to me personally upon
implementation of the following order.

Have your most trustworthy THP agents accelerate
their efforts to install bug/wiretaps in known
Organized Crime meeting places. Consider this your
top priority. Do not communicate information
pertaining to this operation within existing Justice
Department channels. Conduit all oral and written
reports and bug/tap transcripts to me exclusively.
Consider this operation to be self-contained and void
of superseding Justice Department sanction.

JEH

<u>DOCUMENT INSERT</u>: 5/27/61.
Orlando Sentinel ''Crimewatch'' feature.

THE ODD ODYSSEY OF CARLOS MARCELLO

Nobody seems to know where the man was born. It is
generally conceded that (alleged) Mafia Chief Carlos
Marcello was born in either Tunis, North Africa, or
somewhere in Guatemala. Marcello's earliest
recollections are not of either location. They are of
his adopted homeland, the United States of America,
the country that Attorney General Robert F. Kennedy
deported him from on April 4th of this year.

Carlos Marcello: Man Without a Country.

As Marcello tells it, the U.S. Border Patrol
shanghaied him out of New Orleans and deposited him
near Guatemala City, Guatemala. He said that he
daringly escaped from the airport and hid out in
''various Guatemalan hellholes'' with a lawyer
companion frantically seeking to legally return him
to home, hearth, and his (alleged) three hundred
million dollar a year rackets empire. Meanwhile,
Robert F. Kennedy was following up on anonymous tips
that placed the (alleged) Mob boss in numerous
Louisiana locales. The tips did not pan out. Kennedy
realized that Marcello had been hiding out in
Guatemala, with Guatemalan government protection,
since the very moment of his ''daring escape.''

Kennedy exerted diplomatic pressure. The
Guatemalan Prime Minister bowed to it and ordered the
State Police to begin a search for Marcello. The
(alleged) Mafia sultan and his lawyer companion were
discovered living in a rented apartment near
Guatemala City. Both men were immediately deported to
El Salvador.

They walked from village to village, ate in greasy
spoon cantinas and slept in mud huts. The lawyer
attempted to contact a Marcello underling, a pilot
who might fly them to more amenable hideouts. The man
could not be reached, and Marcello and his lawyer
companion, ever fearful of another deportation
action, kept walking.

Robert F. Kennedy and his Justice Department lawyers readied legal briefs. Marcello's lawyer companion wrote briefs and phoned them in to the (alleged) Mafia pasha's formal legal team in New York City. Marcello's pilot friend appeared out of nowhere, and (according to this reporter's confidential source) flew his contraband confreres all the way from El Salvador to Matamoros, Mexico, at treetop level to avoid radar detection.

Marcello and his lawyer companion then walked across the border. The (alleged) Mob maharajah turned himself in at the U.S. Border Patrol Detention Center in McAllen, Texas, confident that a three-judge immigration appeals panel would allow him to be released on bond and remain in America.

His confidence was justified. Marcello walked out of court last week a free man—albeit a man haunted by the awful specter of statelessness.

A Justice Department official told this reporter that the Marcello deportation matter could drag on legally for years. When asked if a suitable compromise might be reached, Attorney General Kennedy said, ''It's possible, if Marcello is willing to give up his U.S. assets and relocate to Russia or Lower Mozambique.''

Carlos Marcello's odd odyssey continues. . . .

DOCUMENT INSERT: 5/30/61.
Personal note: Kemper Boyd to John Stanton.

John,

Thanks for the gin and smoked salmon. It beat the hospital fare hands down and was greatly appreciated.

I've been back in Anniston since the 12th. Little Brother does not respect the concept of convalescence, so I've been bird-dogging freedom riders and collecting statements for his Cuban Study Group. (We can thank N. Chasco for getting me into the hospital sans police notification. Nestor is excellent at bribing bilingual doctors).

The Study Group assignment troubles me. I've been around the Cause since its inception, and one loose word to Little Brother will destroy me with both brothers, get me disbarred as a lawyer and prevent me from ever obtaining any kind of police/intelligence agency work ever again. That said, you should know that I have deliberately sought out exile interviewees that I have not met before and that do not know that I am covertly Agency-employed. I am editing their statements to show the Agency's pre-invasion planning in as positive a light as possible. As you know, Big Brother has become virulently anti-Agency. Little Brother shares his fervor, but is also evincing a true enthusiasm for the Cause. This heartens me, but I must once again stress the absolute necessity of obfuscating all Outfit-exile-Agency links to Little Brother, which now becomes more problematic, given his new proximity to the Cause.

I'm going to absent myself from my Agency contract work and concentrate solely on my two Justice Department assignments. I feel that I can best serve the Agency by working as a direct conduit between them and Little Brother. With the Cuban issue undergoing profound policy reassessment, the closer I remain to the policy shapers the better I can serve the Agency and the Cause.

Our Cadre business remains solidly lucrative. I trust the ability of Fulo and Nestor to keep it that way. Santo tells me that our Italian colleagues will continue to make sizable donations. Playa Giron gave everyone a taste of what could be. Nobody wants to stop now. Wouldn't our lives be a lot easier if Little Brother didn't hate Italians so much?

Yours, Kemper

70

(Miami/Blessington, 6/61–11/61)

TIGER KAB FEATURED a big indoor dartboard. The drivers tacked up Fidel Castro pix and shredded them into confetti.

Pete had his own private targets.

Like Ward Littell. Carlos Marcello's boy now—mobbed-up and untouchable.

Like Howard Hughes—his *ex*-bossman/benefactor.

Hughes fired him. Lenny Sands said the Mormons made him do it. The *Hush-Hush* fiasco helped.

Boyd was in the hospital then, plowed on morphine. He couldn't call Lenny and say, "Pull the issue." Lenny was incommunicado with some bun boy. He didn't know the invasion crapped out.

Dracula loved his Mormons. Boss Mormon Duane Spurgeon glommed some dope contacts. Drac could now fly Narco Airlines without a Pete Bondurant ticket.

The good news: Spurgeon had cancer. The bad news: Hughes scuttled *Hush-Hush*.

The Bay of Pigs/OD piece caught some embarrassing flak. Hughes kept Lenny on the payroll to write a *private* skank sheet.

The sheet would feature skank too skanky for public skank consumption. The sheet would be read by two skank fiends only: Dracula and J. Edgar Hoover.

Drac was paying Lenny five hundred clams a week. Drac was calling Lenny every night. Lenny was fed up with Drac and his "I want Las Vegas!" wet dream.

Hughes and Littell were strictly dartboard prelims. The main event was President John F. Kennedy.

Who:

Waffled, wiggled, weaseled, punked out and pulled out at Pigs.

Who:

Cringed, crawled, crapped his pants, cravenly crybabied and let Cuba stay Commie.

Who:

Shilly-shallied, sashayed, shook and shit his britches while eleven Blessington men got slaughtered.

He handed Jack the Hughes/Nixon loan dirt. *He* co-signed the cocksucker's White House mortgage. The Boyd/Bondurant casino percentage deal—about as au courant as Slippery Dick Nixon.

The Agency kept cloning exile hard-ons. Speedboat crews kept popping the Cuban coast. It was all fart-in-a-hurricane kid stuff.

Jack called a second invasion "quite possible." He wouldn't give a go date or commit beyond nebulous rhetoric.

Jack's chickenshit. Jack's a pouty, panty-waisted, powder puff.

Blessington was still capacity-booked. The Cadre dope biz was still flourishing. Fulo bought off the Boyd shootout witnesses—forty people got fat paydays.

Néstor saved Boyd's life. Néstor knew no fear. Néstor snuck into Havana once a week on the off chance that he might run into the Beard.

Wilfredo Delsol ran the cabstand. The kid was behaving solidly now. His pro-Castro dance was no more than a two-second tango.

Jimmy Hoffa bopped by Tiger Kab occasionally. Jimmy was Kennedy Hater Number One—for good fucking cause.

Bobby K. had Jimmy dancing to his beat: the old Nuisance Roust/Grand Jury Blues. Jimmy got a wild bug up his ass—manifested by nostalgia for the Darleen Shoftel shakedown.

Jimmy said, "We could do it again. I could neutralize Bobby by getting at Jack. You got to believe that Jack still likes cooze."

Jimmy was persistent on the topic. Jimmy echoed the hate that the whole Outfit shared.

Sam G. said, "I rue the day I bought Jack Illinois." Heshie Ryskind said, "Kemper Boyd liked Jack, so we figured he had to be kosher."

Boyd was now some triple or quadruple agent. Boyd was a self-proclaimed insomniac. Boyd said rearranging lies kept him up nights.

Boyd was the Cuban Study Group liaison. Boyd was on Cadre sabbatical—a ploy designed to simplify his life.

Boyd fed Bobby pro-CIA distortions. Boyd fed the CIA Study Group secrets.

Boyd pressed Bobby and Jack. Boyd urged them to assassinate Castro and facilitate a second invasion.

The brothers nixed the notion. Boyd called Bobby more pro-Cause than Jack—but only up to some ambiguous point.

Jack said, No second invasion. Jack refused to grant

whack-the-Beard approval. The Study Group cooked up an alternative called Operation Mongoose.

It was nifty long-range nomenclature. Let's recapture Cuba some time this century. Here's 50 million dollars a year—fetch, CIA, fetch!

Mongoose spawned JM/Wave. JM/Wave was the nifty code name for six buildings on the Miami U campus. JM/Wave featured snazzy graph rooms and the latest in covert study workshops.

JM/Wave was grad school for geeks.

Fetch, CIA, fetch. Monitor your exile groups, but don't act boldly—it might fuck with Jack the Haircut's poll standings.

Boyd still loved Jack. He was in too deep to see through him. Boyd said he loved his civil rights work—because there was no subterfuge involved.

Boyd had trouble sleeping. It's a blessing, Kemper—you don't want my claustrophobic nightmares.

71

(Washington, D.C., 6/61–11/61)

HE LOVED HIS office. Carlos Marcello bought it for him.

It was a spacious three-room suite. The building was very close to the White House.

A professional furnished it. The oak walls and green leather nearly matched Jules Schiffrin's study.

He had no receptionist and no secretary. Carlos did not believe in sharing secrets.

Carlos brought him full circle. The ex-Chicago Phantom was now a Mafia lawyer.

The symmetry felt real. He hitched his star to a man who shared his hatreds. Kemper facilitated the union. He knew that it would jell.

John F. Kennedy took Kemper full circle. They were two charming, shallow men who never grew up. Kennedy sicced thugs on a foreign country and betrayed them when he saw how it looked. Kemper protected certain Negroes and sold heroin to others.

Carlos Marcello played the same rigged game. Carlos used

people and made sure they knew the rules. Carlos knew that he would pay for his life with eternal damnation.

They walked hundreds of miles together. They went to mass in jungle towns and contributed extravagant church tithes.

They walked alone. No bodyguards or back scratchers walked with them.

They ate in cantinas. They bought entire villages lunch. He wrote deportation briefs on tabletops and phoned them in to New York.

Chuck Rogers flew them to Mexico. Carlos said, "I trust you, Ward. If you say 'Turn yourself in,' I'll do it."

He fulfilled that trust. Three judges reviewed the evidence and released Marcello on bond. The Littell writ work was considered audaciously brilliant.

Grateful Carlos set him up with James Riddle Hoffa. Jimmy was predisposed to fondness—Carlos handed the Fund books back to him and described the circumstances behind their return.

Hoffa became his second client. Robert Kennedy remained his sole adversary.

He wrote briefs for Hoffa's formal litigators. The results confirmed his brilliance.

July '61: A second Sun Valley indictment is dismissed. Littell writs prove the grand jury was improperly impaneled.

August '61: A South Florida grand jury is cut off at the knees. A Littell brief proves that evidence was obtained through entrapment.

He'd come full circle.

He quit drinking. He rented a beautiful Georgetown apartment and finally cracked the Fund book code.

Numbers and letters became words. Words became names—to track against police files, city directories and every financial listing in the public domain.

He tracked those names for four months straight. He chased celebrity names, political names, criminal names and anonymous names. He ran obituary checks and criminal record checks. He quadruple-checked names, dates and figures, and cross-referenced all salient data.

He tracked names linked to numbers linked to public stockholder reports. He assessed names and numbers for his own investment portfolio—and amassed a staggering secret history of financial collusion.

Among the Teamster Central States Pension Fund lendees:

Twenty-four U.S. senators, nine governors, 114 congressmen, Allen Dulles, Rafael Trujillo, Fulgencio Batista, Anastasio Somoza, Juan Perón, Nobel Prize researchers, drug-addicted movie stars, loan sharks, labor racketeers, union-busting factory owners, Palm Beach socialites, rogue entrepreneurs, French right-wing crackpots with extensive Algerian holdings, and sixty-seven unsolved homicide victims extrapolatable as Pension Fund deadbeats.

The chief cash conduit/lender was one Joseph P. Kennedy Sr.

Jules Schiffrin died abruptly. He might have sensed uncharted Fund potential—machinations past the grasp of the common mobsters.

He could implement Schiffrin's knowledge. He could put the full force of his will behind that one thing.

Five months stone-cold sober taught him this:

You're capable of anything.

PART FOUR

HEROIN

December 1961–September 1963

72

(Miami, 12/20/61)

AGENCY GUYS CALLED the place "Suntan U." Girls in shorts and halter tops five days before Christmas—no shit.

Big Pete wants a woman. Extortion experience preferred, but not mandat—

Boyd said, "Are you listening to me?"

Pete said, "I'm listening, and I'm observing. It's a nice tour, but the coeds are impressing me more than JM/Wave."

They cut between buildings. The Ops station was cattycorner to the women's gym.

"Pete, are you—?"

"You were saying Fulo and Néstor could run the Cadre business by themselves. You were saying Lockhart went off contract status to start up his own Klan in Mississippi and snitch for the Feds. Chuck's taking his place at Blessington, and *my* new gig is funneling guns to Guy Banister in New Orleans. Lockhart's got some gun connections I can tap into, and Guy's touting some guy named Joe Milteer, who's hooked into some guys in the John Birch Society and the Minutemen. They've got beaucoup fucking gun money, and Milteer will be dropping some off at the cabstand."

They hit a shady walkway and grabbed a bench out of the sun. Pete stretched his legs and eyeballed the gym.

"That's good retention for a bored listener."

Pete yawned. "JM/Wave and Mongoose are boring. Coastal harassment, gun running and monitoring exile groups is one big snore."

Boyd straddled the bench. College kids and Cuban hard-ons fraternized two benches over.

"Describe your ideal course of action."

Pete lit a cigarette. "We should clip Fidel. I'm for it, you're for it, and the only guys that aren't for it are your pals Jack and Bobby."

Boyd smiled. "I'm starting to think we should do it anyway. If we could develop a patsy to take the fall, the hit would probably never be traced back to the Agency or to us."

"Jack and Bobby would just figure they got lucky."

Boyd nodded. "I should run it by Santo."

"I already did."

"Did he like the idea?"

"Yeah, he did. And he ran it by Johnny Rosselli and Sam G., and they both said they wanted to be in on it."

Boyd rubbed his collarbone. "You got a quorum just like that?"

"Not exactly. They all like the idea, but it sounds like they'll need some more convincing."

"Maybe we should hire Ward Littell to whip up a few briefs. He's certainly the chief convincer of the moment."

"You mean you appreciate the way he snowed Carlos and Jimmy."

"Don't you?"

Pete blew smoke rings. "I appreciate a good comeback as much as the next man, but I draw the line at Littell. And you're smiling because your sissy kid brother finally started acting half-ass competent."

College girls walked by. Big Pete wants a—

Boyd said, "He's on our side now, remember?"

"I remember. And I remember that your friend Jack used to be."

"He still is. And he listens to Bobby like he listens to no one else, and Bobby's becoming more pro-Cause by the day."

Pete blew nice concentric rings. "That's good to know. Maybe it means we'll tap into our casino money about the time fucking Bobby himself gets elected President."

Boyd looked distracted. It could be shootout side effects —trauma fucked you up long-range sometimes.

"Kemper, are you listening to—?"

Boyd cut him off. "You were evincing general anti-Kennedy sentiment. You were about to start in on the President, even though he remains our best wedge to get at the casino money, and even though general CIA unpreparedness and *not* Kennedy cowardice was the major contributing cause of the Bay of Pigs disaster."

Pete whooped and slapped the bench. "I should have known better than to rag your boys."

"It's 'boy,' singular."

"I fucking apologize, although I still don't see what's so fucking thrilling about sucking up to the President of the United States."

Boyd grinned. "It's the places he lets you go."

"Like protecting niggers in Meridian, Mississippi?"

"I've got Negro blood now. That transfusion I got at Saint Augustine's came from a colored man."

Pete laughed. "What you've got is a Big White Bwana complex. You've got your spooks and your spics, and you've got this crazy notion that you're their southern aristocrat savior."

Boyd said, "Are you finished?"

Pete clicked his eyes off a tall brunette. "Yeah, I'm finished."

"Do you feel like rationally discussing a Fidel hit?"

Pete flicked his cigarette at a tree. "My one rational comment is 'Let Néstor do it.' "

"I was thinking of Néstor and two expendable backup shooters."

"Where do we find them?"

"We look around. You recruit two two-man teams, I recruit one. Néstor goes with the finalists no matter what."

Pete said, "Let's do it."

Dougie Frank Lockhart had the far-right South wired. Gun seekers knew the man to call: carrot-topped Dougie in Puckett, Mississippi.

Santo and Carlos kicked in fifty Gs apiece. Pete took the coin and went gun shopping.

Dougie Frank brokered the deals for a 5% commission. He procured A-1 hand-me-downs hot off the race hate circuit.

Lockhart knew his job. Lockhart knew the Dixie Right was reassessing its weaponry needs.

The Commie Threat had mandated major ordnance. Tommy guns, mortars and grenades fit the bill. Feisty niggers now eclipsed the Red Menace—and small arms handled them best.

The Deep South was one big loony yard sale.

Pete traded junk pistols for brand-new bazookas. Pete bought operational Thompsons for fifty scoots a pop. Pete supplied six campsites with half a million rounds of ammunition.

The Minutemen, the National States Rights Party, the National Renaissance Party, the Exalted Knights of the Ku Klux Klan, the Royal Knights of the Ku Klux Klan, the Imperial Knights of the Ku Klux Klan and the Klarion Klan Koalition for the New Konfederacy supplied him. He supplied six exile camps, full of expendable backup killers.

Pete spent three weeks gun shopping. He made five Miami–New Orleans circuits.

The fifty grand evaporated. Heshie Ryskind kicked in an additional twenty. Heshie was scared—his doctors diagnosed him with lung cancer.

Heshie whipped up a camp R&R tour to take his mind off his bum health. He brought in Jack Ruby and his strippers, Dick Contino and his accordion.

The strippers stripped and cavorted with exile trainees. Heshie bought entire campsites blow jobs. Dick Contino played "Lady of Spain" six thousand times.

Jimmy Hoffa showed up at the Lake Pontchartrain soiree. Jimmy ranted, railed and raved against the Kennedys nonstop.

Joe Milteer joined the party outside Mobile. He dropped ten grand on the gun fund, unsolicited.

Guy Banister called Old Joe "harmless." Lockhart said the old boy loved to torch nigger churches.

Pete auditioned backup triggers for the Fidel hit. He laid down his criteria with two simple questions.

Are you an expert marksman?

Would you die to set up Néstor Chasco's killshot?

He schmoozed up at least a hundred Cubans. Four men made the cut.

CHINO CROMAJOR:

Bay of Pigs survivor. Willing to detonate Castro with a strip-searchproof enema bomb.

RAFAEL HERNÁNDEZ-BROWN:

Cigar maker/gunman. Willing to slip the Beard a poison panatella and go up in smoke with the man who raped his tobacco fields.

CÉSAR RAMOS:

Former Cuban Army cook. Willing to whip up an exploding suckling pig and die at Castro's Last Supper.

WALTER "JUANITA" CHACON:

Sadistic drag queen. Willing to butt-fuck Fidel and go out orgasmic in exile crossfire.

Memo to Kemper Boyd:

Top my shooters—if you can.

73

(Meridian, 1/11/62)

KEMPER SNORTED A coke-"H" speedball. It was precisely his sixteenth taste of dope.

It was his twelfth since the doctor cut off his medication. It averaged out to 1.3 *nonaddicted* tastes per month.

His head twirled. His brain revved. His shabby room at the Seminole Motel looked almost pretty.

Memo:

Go see that colored preacher. He's rounding up a group of voting rights complainants.

Memo:

See Dougie Frank Lockhart. He's got two would-be triggers lined up for you to audition.

The taste hit *all the way* home.

His collarbone quit throbbing. The pins holding it together meshed clean.

Kemper wiped his nose. The portrait above his desk took on a glow.

It was Jack Kennedy, photographed pre-Pigs. His post-Pigs inscription: "To Kemper Boyd. I guess we both caught a few bullets lately."

Taste #16 felt high-octane. Jack's smile was high-test—Dr. Feelgood shot him up before the photo session.

Jack looked young and invincible. The last nine months knocked a lot of that out of him.

The Bay of Pigs fiasco did it. Jack grew up behind a tidal wave of censure.

Jack blamed himself—and the Agency. Jack fired Allen Dulles and Dick Bissell. Jack said, "I'll smash the CIA into a thousand pieces."

Jack hates the CIA. Bobby doesn't. Bobby now hates Fidel Castro like he hates Hoffa and the Mob.

The Bay of Pigs postmortem was painfully protracted. He double-agented as Kemper Boyd, chaperone. He showed Bobby scores of sanitized exiles—the noncriminal types that Langley wanted him to see.

The Study Group called the invasion:

"Quixotic," "undermanned" and "based on specious intelligence."

He agreed. Langley disagreed.

Langley thought he was a Kennedy apologist. They considered him politically unsound.

John Stanton told him this. He silently agreed with the appraisal.

He vocally agreed: Yes, JM/Wave will prove efficacious.

He silently disagreed. He urged Bobby to assassinate Fidel Castro. Bobby disagreed. He said it was too gangster-like and inimical to Kennedy policy.

Bobby was a bully with strong moral convictions. His guidelines were often hard to gauge.

Bully Bobby set up racket squads in ten major cities. Their one goal was to recruit organized-crime informants. The move enraged Mr. Hoover. Independent Mob-busters might upstage the Top Hoodlum Program.

Bully Bobby hates Bully J. Edgar. Bully J. Edgar reciprocates. It was unprecedented hatred—the Justice Department seethed with it.

Hoover staged protocol slowdowns. Bobby trashed FBI autonomy. Guy Banister said Hoover placed illegal bug/taps in Mob venues coast to coast.

Bobby had no inkling. Mr. Hoover knew how to keep secrets.

So did Ward Littell. Ward's best secret was Joe Kennedy's Teamster Fund "malfeasance."

Joe had a near-fatal stroke late last year. Claire said it "devastated" Laura.

She tried to contact her father. Bobby prevented it. That three-million-dollar buyoff was binding and permanent.

Claire graduated from Tulane magna cum laude. The NYU law school accepted her. She moved to New York City and took an apartment near Laura.

Laura rarely mentioned him. Claire told her he was wounded by a "random gunshot" in Miami. Laura said, "Kemper and 'random'? *Never*."

Claire believed his squeaky-clean version of the shootout. Claire zoomed down to Saint Augustine's the second the doctor called her.

Claire said Laura had a new boyfriend. Claire said he was nice. Claire said she met Laura's "nice friend," Lenny Sands.

Lenny violated his order and resumed contact with Laura. Lenny always played things indirectly—that *Hush-Hush* Bay of Pigs piece was filled with double-edged innuendo.

He didn't care. Lenny was extortable and long gone from his life.

Lenny dug up dirt for Howard Hughes. Lenny tattled certain secrets and quashed others. Lenny possessed circumstantial evidence on how badly Kemper Boyd fucked up in April '61.

Kemper sniffed another speedball.

His heart revved. His collarbone went numb. He remembered how last May compensated for last April.

Bobby ordered him to follow some Freedom Riders. He said, "Just observe, and call for help if Klansmen or whoever get rowdy. Remember, you're still convalescing."

He observed. He got up closer than reporters and camera crews.

He saw civil rights workers board buses. He tailed them. Hymns roared out of wide-open windows.

Shitkickers tailed the buses. Car radios blared "Dixie." He badged a few rock throwers off, with his gun arm still in a sling.

He stopped in Anniston. Some rednecks slashed his tires. A white mob stormed the depot and pelted a Freedom Bus out of town.

He rented an old Chevy and played catch-up. He zoomed out Highway 78 and caught a mob scene.

The bus had been torched. Cops, Freedom Riders and crackers were tangled up off the roadside.

He saw a colored girl batting flames off her pigtails. He saw the torch artist peel rubber. He ran him off the road and pistol-whipped him half-dead.

I take a few tastes now and then. It's just to help me keep things straight.

*   *   *

"... And the best thing about what I'm proposing is that you won't have to testify in open court. Federal judges will read your depositions and my accompanying affidavits and go from there. If any of you are called to testify, it will be in closed session, with no reporters, opposing counsel or local police officials present."

The pretty little church was SRO. The preacher rounded up sixty-odd people.

Kemper said, "Questions?"

A man yelled, "Where you from?" A woman yelled, "What about protection?"

Kemper leaned over the pulpit. "I'm from Nashville, Tennessee. You might recall that we had some boycotts and sit-ins there in 1960, and you might recall that we've made great strides toward integration, with minimum bloodshed. I realize that Mississippi is a whole lot less civilized than my home state, and as far as protection goes, I can only say that when you go to register to vote, you'll have numbers on your side. The more people who offer depositions, the better. The more people who register and vote, the better. I'm not saying that certain elements will take kindly to your voting, but the more of you who vote the better your chance of electing local officials who'll keep those elements in line."

A man said, "We got a nice cemetery outside. It's just that none of us want to move in real soon."

A woman said, "You can't expect the law around here to jump on our side all of a sudden."

Kemper smiled. Two tastes and a two-martini lunch made the church glow.

"As cemeteries go, that one you've got is just about the prettiest I've ever seen, but none of us want to visit it until some time around the year 2000, and as far as protection goes, I can only say that President Kennedy did a pretty good job of protecting those Freedom Riders last year, and if those aforementioned white-trash, peckerwood, redneck-cracker elements turn out in force to suppress your God-given civil rights, then the Federal government will meet that challenge with greater force, because your will to freedom will not be defeated, because it is good and just and true, and you have the strength of kindness, decency and unflinching rectitude on your side."

The congregation rose and applauded.

* * *

"... So it's what you call a sweetheart deal. I got my Royal Knights Klavern, which is basically an FBI franchise, and all I gotta do is keep my ear down and rat off the Exalted Knights and Imperial Knights for mail fraud, which is the only Klan stuff Mr. Hoover really cares about. I got my own informants subcontracted into both them groups, and I pay them out of my Bureau stipend, which helps to consolidate the power of my own group."

The shack reeked of stale socks and stale reefer smoke. Dougie Frank wore a Klan sheet and Levi's.

Kemper smashed a fly perching on his chair. "What about those shooters you mentioned?"

"They're here. They've been bunking with me, 'cause the motels around here don't differentiate between Cubans and niggers. 'Course, you're trying to change all that."

"Where are they now?"

"I got a shooting range down the road. They're there with some of my Royals. You want a beer?"

"How about a dry martini?"

"Ain't none of those in these parts. And any man asks for one's gonna get tagged as a Federal agitator."

Kemper smiled. "I've got a bartender at the Skyline Lounge on my side."

"Must be a Jew or a homo."

Kemper laid on some drawl. "Son, you are trying my patience."

Lockhart flinched. "Well ... shit, then, you should know that I heard Pete found his four boys. Guy Banister said you're still two short, which don't surprise me, given all the integration work you've been doing."

"Tell me about the shooters. Limit your extraneous comments and get to the point."

Lockhart wiggled his chair back. Kemper slid his chair closer to him.

"Well, uh, Banister, he sent them over to me. They stole a speedboat in Cuba and ran it aground off the Alabama coast. They robbed some gas stations and liquor stores and renewed an old acquaintance with that Frenchy guy Laurent Guéry, who told them to call Guy for some anti-Fidel work."

"And?"

"And Guy considered them too goddamn crazy for his taste, which is too crazy for just about anybody's. He sent them to me, but I got about as much use for them as a dog does for fleas."

Kemper moved closer. Lockhart backed his chair into the wall.

"Man, you are crowding me more than I'm used to."

"Tell me about the Cubans."

"Jesus, I thought we were friends."

"We are. Now, tell me about the Cubans."

Lockhart slid his chair sideways. "Their names are Flash Elorde and Juan Canestel. 'Flash' ain't Elorde's real first name. He just took it 'cause there's some famous spic boxer with the same last name as him who uses it as a nickname."

"And?"

"And they're both crack shots and big Fidel haters. Flash ran this prostitution slave trade in Havana, and Juan was this rape-o who got castrated by Castro's secret police, 'cause he raped something like three hundred women between the years 1959 and 1961."

"Are they willing to die for a free Cuba?"

"Shit, yes. Flash says that given the life he's led, every day he wakes up alive is a miracle."

Kemper smiled. "You should adopt that attitude, Dougie."

"Which means?"

"Which means there's a nice colored church outside Meridian. It's called the First Pentecostal Baptist, and it's got a beautiful moss-hung cemetery next door."

Lockhart pinched one nostril and blew snot on the floor. "So fucking what? What are you, some nigger church connosewer?"

Kemper milked his drawl. "Tell your boys not to touch that church."

"Shit, man, how do you expect a self-respecting white man to respond to something like that?"

"Say, 'Yes, sir, Mr. Boyd.' "

Lockhart sputtered. Kemper hummed the "We Shall Overcome" song.

Lockhart said, "Yes, sir, Mr. Boyd."

Flash sported a Mohawk haircut. Juan sported a big testicle bulge—handkerchiefs or wadded-up tissue filled the space where his nuts used to reside.

The range was a vacant lot adjoining a trailer park. Full-dress Klansmen shot tin cans and swigged beer and Jack Daniel's.

They hit one can out of four at thirty yards. Flash and Juan notched all hits from twice that distance.

They shot old M-1s in late-afternoon light. Better rifles and telescopic sights would make them invincible.

Dougie Frank circulated. Kemper watched the Cubans shoot.

Flash and Juan stripped to the waist and used their shirts to swat off mosquitos. Both men were torture-scarred from the hips up. Kemper whistled and signaled Lockhart: Send them over, now.

Dougie Frank rounded them up. Kemper leaned against an old Ford half-ton. The bed was jammed with liquor bottles and guns.

They walked over. Kemper came on courtly and genteel.

Smiles and bows went around. Handshakes went down. Flash and Juan pulled their shirts on—a sign of respect for the Big Bwana white man.

Kemper cut the niceties off. "My name is Boyd. I have a mission to offer you."

Flash said, *"Sí, trabajo. Quién el—"*

Juan shushed him. "What kind of mission?"

Kemper tried Spanish. *"Trabajo muy importante. Para matar el grande puto Fidel Castro."*

Flash jumped up and down. Juan grabbed him and restrained him.

"This is not a joke, Mr. Boyd?"

Kemper pulled out his money clip. "How much would it take to convince you?"

They crowded up to him. Kemper fanned out hundred-dollar bills.

"I hate Fidel Castro just as much as any Cuban patriot. Ask Mr. Banister or your friend Laurent Guéry about me. I'll pay you out of my own pocket until our backers come through, and if we succeed and get Castro, I'll guarantee you large bonuses."

The cash hypnotized them. Kemper went in for the close.

He slipped a hundred to Flash and a hundred to Juan. One to Flash, one to Juan, one to Flash—

Canestel squeezed his hand shut. "We believe you."

Kemper snagged a bottle out of the truck. Flash beat mambo time on the back fender.

A Klansman yelled, "Save some for us white men!"

Kemper took a drink. Flash took a drink. Juan chug-a-lugged half the bottle.

* * *

The cocktail hour segued into get-acquainted time.

Kemper bought Flash and Juan some clothes. They moved their gear out of Lockhart's shack.

Kemper called his broker in New York. He said, Sell some stock and send me five thousand dollars.

The man said, Why? Kemper said, I'm hiring some underlings.

Flash and Juan needed lodging. Kemper braced his friendly desk clerk and asked him to revise his WHITES ONLY policy.

The man agreed. Flash and Juan moved into the Seminole Motel.

Kemper called Pete in New Orleans. He said, Let's arrange a Whack Fidel audition.

They brainstormed.

Kemper set the budget at fifty grand per shooter and two hundred grand for general overhead. Pete suggested severance pay—ten Gs for each rejected shooter.

Kemper agreed. Pete said, Let's do the gig at Blessington. Santo can put Sam G. and Johnny up at the Breakers Motel.

Kemper agreed. Pete said, We need a spic fall guy—non-CIA/non-Cadre-connected. Kemper said, We'll find one.

Pete said, My boys are braver than your boys.

Kemper said, No, they're not.

Flash and Juan felt like drinking. Kemper took them to the Skyline Lounge.

The bartender said, They ain't white. Kemper slipped him twenty dollars. The bartender said, They are now.

Kemper drank martinis. Juan drank I.W. Harper. Flash drank Myers's rum and Coke.

Flash spoke Spanish. Juan translated. Kemper learned the rudiments of slave prostitution.

Flash kidnapped the girls. Laurent Guéry got them hooked on Algerian horse. Juan broke the virgins in and tried to perv them into digging random sex.

Kemper listened. The ugly things drifted away, compartmentalized and non-applicable.

Juan said he missed his balls. He could still get hard and fuck, but he missed the total shoot-your-load experience.

Flash raged against Fidel. Kemper thought: I don't hate the man at all.

* * *

The six wore starched fatigues and camouflage lampblack. It was Pete's idea: Let's turn our shooter candidates out scary.

Néstor built a range behind the Breakers parking lot. Kemper called it a jerry-rig masterpiece.

It featured pulley-mounted targets and chairs scrounged from a demolished cocktail hut. The audition weaponry was CIA-prime: M-1s, assorted pistols, and scope-fitted .30-06's.

Teo Paez fashioned straw-stuffed Castro targets. They were life-size and realistic—replete with beards and cigars.

Laurent Guéry crashed the party. Teo said he blew France *rápidamente*. Néstor said he'd tried to clip Charles de Gaulle.

The judges sat under an awning. S. Trafficante, J. Rosselli and S. Giancana—curled up with highballs and binoculars.

Pete played armorer. Kemper played MC.

"We've got six men for you gentlemen to choose from. You'll be funding this operation, and I know you'll want last say as to who goes in. Pete and I are proposing three-man teams, with Néstor Chasco, who you already know, as the third man in all cases. Before we start, I want to stress that these men are loyal, fearless and fully comprehend the risks involved. If captured, they will commit suicide rather than reveal who set up this operation."

Giancana tapped his watch. "I'm running late. Can we get this show on the road?"

Trafficante tapped his. "Move it, would you, Kemper? I'm due back in Tampa."

Kemper nodded. Pete cranked Fidel #1 fifty feet out. The men loaded their revolvers and assumed the two-handed combat stance.

Pete said, "Fire."

Chino Cromajor blew Castro's hat off. Rafael Hernández-Brown decigared him. César Ramos severed both his ears.

The reverberations faded. Kemper gauged reactions.

Santo looked bored. Sam looked restless. Johnny looked mildly nonplussed.

Juanita Chacón aimed crotch-high and fired. Fidel #1 lost his manhood.

Flash and Juan fired twice. Fidel lost his arms and his legs.

Laurent Guéry clapped. Giancana checked his watch.

Pete cranked Fidel #2 a hundred yards out. The shooters raised their obsolete M-1s.

The judges held up their binoculars. Pete said, "Fire."

Cromajor shot Castro's eyes out. Hernández-Brown lopped off his thumbs.

Ramos nailed his cigar. Juanita castrated him.

Flash blew his legs off at the knees. Juan slammed a cardiac bullseye.

Pete yelled, "Cease fire!" The shooters lowered their weapons and lined up at parade rest.

Giancana said, "It's impressive, but we can't go off half-cocked on something this big."

Trafficante said, "I have to agree with Mo."

Rosselli said, "You need to give us some time to think about it."

Kemper felt queasy. His speedball rush turned ugly.

Pete was trembling.

74

(Washington, D.C., 1/24/62)

LITTELL LOCKED THE money in his desk safe. One month's retainer—$6,000 cash.

Hoffa said, "You didn't count it."

"I trust you."

"I could've made a mistake."

Littell tilted his chair back and looked up at him. "That's unlikely. Especially when you walked it over here yourself."

"You'd've felt better walking over to my shop in this fucking cold?"

"I could have waited until the first."

Hoffa perched on the edge of the desk. His overcoat was soaked with melting snow.

Littell moved some folders. Hoffa picked up his crystal paperweight.

"Did you come for a pep talk, Jimmy?"

"No. But if you got one, I'm all ears."

"How's this. You're going to win and Bobby's going to lose. It's going to be a long and painful war, and you're going to win by sheer attrition."

Jimmy squeezed the paperweight. "I was thinking Kemper

Boyd should leak a copy of my Justice Department file to you."

Littell shook his head. "He won't do it, and I won't ask him to. He's got the Kennedys and Cuba and God knows what else wrapped in tidy little packages that only he knows the logic of. There's lines he won't cross over, and you and Bobby Kennedy are one of them."

Hoffa said, "Lines come and go. And as far as Cuba goes, I think Carlos is the only Outfit guy who still gives a shit. I think Santo, Mo and the others are pissed off and bored with the whole notion of that rinkydink goddamn island."

Littell straightened his necktie. "Good. Because *I'm* bored with everything except keeping you and Carlos one step ahead of Bobby Kennedy."

Hoffa smiled. "You used to like Bobby. I heard you used to really admire him."

"Lines come and go, Jimmy. You said so yourself."

Hoffa dropped the paperweight. "This is true. It is also fucking true that I need an edge on Bobby. And *you* fucking pulled the plug on that Kennedy wire job that Pete Bondurant was working for me back in '58."

Littell forced a wince into a smile. "I didn't know you knew that."

"That is obvious. It should also be fucking obvious that I forgive you."

"And obvious that you want to try it again."

"This is true."

"Call Pete, Jimmy. I don't have much use for him, but he's the best shakedown man alive."

Hoffa leaned across the desk. His trouser legs slid up and showed off cheap white sweat socks.

"I want you in on it, too."

75

(Los Angeles, 2/4/62)

PETE RUBBED HIS neck. It was all kinked and knotted—he flew out in a coach seat made for midgets.

"I jump when you say 'jump,' Jimmy, but coast-to-coast for coffee and pastry is pushing it."

"I think L.A.'s the place to set this up."

"Set what up?"

Hoffa dabbed eclair cream off his necktie. "You'll see soon enough."

Pete heard noise in the kitchen. "Who's that poking around?"

"It's Ward Littell. Sit down, Pete. You're making me nervous."

Pete dropped his garment bag. The house stunk of cigars—Hoffa let visiting Teamsters use it for stag nights.

"Littell, shit. This is grief I don't need."

"Come on. Ancient history's ancient history."

Recent history: *Your* lawyer stole *your* Fund books—

Littell walked in. Hoffa put his hands up, peacemaker-style. "Be nice, you guys. I wouldn't put the two of you in the same room unless it was good."

Pete rubbed his eyes. "I'm a busy guy, and I flew overnight for this little breakfast klatch. Give me one good reason why I should take on additional fucking work, or I'm heading back to the airport."

Hoffa said, "Tell him, Ward."

Littell warmed his hands on a coffee cup. "Bobby Kennedy's coming down unacceptably hard on Jimmy. We want to work up a derogatory tape profile on Jack and use it as a wedge to get him to call off Bobby. If I hadn't interfered, the Shoftel operation might have worked. I think we should do it again, and I think we should recruit a woman that Jack would find interesting enough to sustain an affair with."

Pete rolled his eyes. "You want to shake down the President of the United States?"

"Yes."

"You, me and Jimmy?"

"You, me, Fred Turentine and the woman we bring in."

"And you're going at this like you think we can trust each other."

Littell smiled. "We both hate Jack Kennedy. And I think we've got enough dirt on each other to buttress a non-aggression pact."

Pete popped some prickly little goosebumps. "We can't tell Kemper about this. He'd rat us in a second."

"I agree. Kemper has to stay out of the loop on this one."

Hoffa belched. "I'm watching you two humps stare at each

other, and I'm starting to feel like I'm out of the fucking loop, even though I'm financing the fucking loop."

Littell said, "Lenny Sands."

Hoffa sprayed eclair crumbs. "What the fuck does Jewboy Lenny have to do with fucking anything?"

Pete looked at Littell. Littell looked at Pete. Their brainwaves meshed somewhere over the pastry tray.

Hoffa looked dead flummoxed. His eyes went out of focus somewhere near the planet Mars. Pete steered Littell to the kitchen and shut the door.

"You're thinking Lenny's this big Hollywood insider. You're thinking he might know some women we could use as bait."

"Right. And if he doesn't come through, at least we're here in Los Angeles."

"Which is the best place on earth to find shakedown-type women."

Littell sipped coffee. "Right. And Lenny was my informant once. I've got a hold on him, and if he doesn't cooperate, I'll squeeze him with it."

Pete cracked some knuckles. "He's a homo. He shanked this made guy in an alley behind some fruit bar."

"Lenny told you that?"

"Don't look so hurt. People have this tendency to tell me things they don't want to."

Littell dumped his cup in the sink. Hoffa paced outside the door.

Pete said, "Lenny knows Kemper. And I think he's tight with that Hughes woman that Kemper had a thing with."

"Lenny's safe. If worse comes to worse, we can squeeze him with the Tony Iannone job."

Pete rubbed his neck. "Who else knows we're planning this?"

"Nobody. Why?"

"I was wondering if it was common knowledge all over the Outfit."

Littell shook his head. "You, me and Jimmy. That's the loop."

Pete said, "Let's keep it that way. Lenny's tight with Sam G., and Sam's been known to go apeshit when people get rough with him."

Littell leaned against the stove. "Agreed. And I won't tell Carlos, and you won't tell Trafficante and those other Outfit guys you and Kemper deal with. Let's keep this contained."

"Agreed. A few of those guys hung me and Kemper out to dry on something a couple of weeks ago, so I'm not prone to tell them much of anything."

Littell shrugged. "They'll find out in the end, and they'll be pleased with the results we get. Bobby's been riding them, too, and I think we can safely say that Giancana will find whatever we had to do to Lenny justified."

Pete said, "I like Lenny."

Littell said, "So do I, but business is business."

Pete traced dollar signs on the stove. "What kind of money are we talking about?"

Littell said, "Twenty-five thousand a month, with your expenses and Freddy Turentine's fee worked in. I know you'll need to travel for your CIA job, and that's fine with both Jimmy and me. I've done wire jobs for the Bureau myself, and I think that between you, me and Turentine, we'll be able to cover all our bases."

Hoffa banged on the door. "Why don't you guys come out here and talk to *me*? This tête-à-tête shit is wearing me thin!"

Pete steered Littell back to the laundry room. "It sounds good. We find a woman, wire a few pads and fuck Jack Kennedy where it hurts."

Littell pulled his arm free. "We need to check Lenny's *Hush-Hush* reports. We might get a lead on a woman that way."

"*I'll* do it. I might be able to get a look at the reports Howard Hughes keeps at his office."

"Do it today. I'll be staying at the Ambassador until we get things set up."

The door shook—Jimmy had his tits in a twist.

Littell said, "I want to bring Mr. Hoover in on this."

"Are you insane?"

Littell smiled, kiss-my-ass condescending. "He hates the Kennedys like you and I do. I want to re-establish contact, leak a few tapes to him and have him in my corner as a wedge to help out Jimmy and Carlos."

Not *so* insane—

"You know he's a voyeur, Pete. Do you know what he'd give to have the President of the United States fucking on tape?"

Hoffa barged into the kitchen. His shirt was dotted with doughnut sprinkles—every color of the rainbow.

Pete winked. "I'm starting not to hate you so much, Ward."

* * *

Hughes' business office was marked RESTRICTED ACCESS now. Mormon goons flanked the door and checked IDs with some weird scanner gizmo.

Pete dawdled by the parking lot gate. The guard chewed his ear off.

"Us non-Mormons call this place Castle Dracula. Mr. Hughes we call the Count, and we call Duane Spurgeon—he's the head Mormon—Frankenstein, 'cause he's dying of cancer and looks like he's dead already. I remember when this building wasn't full of religious crackpots, and Mr. Hughes came in in person, and he didn't have this big germ phobia and these crazy plans to buy up Las Vegas, and he didn't get blood transfusions like Bela Lugosi—"

"Larry—"

"—and he actually talked to people, you know? Now the only people he talks to besides the Mormons are Mr. J. Edgar Hoover himself and Lenny the *Hush-Hush* guy. You know why *I'm* talking so much? Because I work the gate all day and pick up scuttlebutt, and the only non-Mormon people I see are the Filipino janitor and this Jap switchboard girl. Mr. Hughes can still wheel and deal, though, I got to say that. I heard he's pushed the TWA divestment price way up, so when he gets the gelt he can funnel it straight into some account he's holding, like some kind of zillion-dollar 'buy up Vegas' fund. . . ."

Larry ran out of breath. Pete whipped out a hundred-dollar bill.

"They keep Lenny's stringer reports in the file room, right?"

"Right."

"There's nine more of these if you get me in there."

Larry shook his head. "That's impossible, Pete. We got virtually an all-Mormon staff here. Some of the guys are Mormon *and* ex-FBI, and Mr. J. Edgar Hoover himself helped pick them."

Pete said, "Lenny's in L.A. full-time now, right?"

"Right. He gave up his place in Chicago. I heard he's writing *Hush-Hush* as some kind of restricted mimeo sheet."

Pete forked over the hundred. "Look up his address for me."

Larry checked his Rolodex and plucked a card. "It's 831 North Kilkea, which isn't that far from here."

A hospital van pulled up. Pete said, "What's that?"

Larry whispered. "Fresh blood for the Count. Certified Mormon-pure."

The new gig felt good, but strictly second-string. The main gig should be WHACK FIDEL.

Santo and Company quashed it. They acted bored, like the Cause meant jackshit.

WHY?

He cut his shooters loose. Kemper took his boys back to Mississippi.

Laurent Guéry went with them. Kemper tapped his own stock fund for Ops cash. Kemper was acting weirdly persistent lately.

Pete turned on to Kilkea. 831 was your standard West Hollywood four-flat.

The standard two-story Spanish-style building. The standard two units per floor. The standard beveled glass doors that your standard B&E guys drooled for.

There was no garage at the back—the tenants had to park at the curb. Lenny's Packard was nowhere in sight.

Pete parked and walked up to the porch. All four doors showed slack at the door-doorjamb juncture.

The street was dead. The porch was dead quiet. The mail slot for the left downstairs unit read "L. Sands."

Pete snapped the lock with his pocketknife. An inside light hit him straight off.

Lenny planned to stay out after dark. He could prowl the pad for four solid hours.

Pete locked himself in. The crib spread out off a hallway— maybe five rooms total.

He checked the kitchen, the dinette and the bedroom. The pad was nice and quiet—Lenny eschewed pets and stay-at-home bun boys.

An office connected to the bedroom. It was cubbyhole size—a desk and a row of file cabinets ate up all the floor space.

Pete checked the top drawer. It was one fat mess—Lenny jammed it full of overstuffed folders.

The folders contained 100% U.S. prime-cut skank.

Published *Hush-Hush* skank and unpublished skank tips. Skank logged in since early '59—the all-time Skank Hit Parade.

Boozer skank, hophead skank, homo skank. Lezbo skank, nympho skank, miscegenation skank. Political skank, incest skank, child molester skank. The one skank problem: the female skankees were too skankily well known.

Pete spotted some non-sequitur skank: a real skankeroo report dated 9/12/60. A *Hush-Hush* editorial memo was attached to the page.

Lenny,

I don't see this one as a feature or anything else. If it went to arrest & trial, great, but it didn't. The whole thing seems skewed to me. Plus, the girl's a nobody.

Pete read the report. Skewed?—no shit.
Lenny "Skank Man" Sands, verbatim:

I learned that gorgeous redhead singer-dancer Barb Jah-elka (the lead attraction in her ex-husband Joey Jahelka's "Swingin' Dance Revue") was arrested on August 26th as part of an extortion scheme levied against Rock Hudson.

It was a photo job. Hudson and Barb were in bed at Rock's house in Beverly Hills when a man snuck in and managed to snap several pictures with infra-red film. A few days later Barb demanded that Hudson pay her 10 thousand dollars or the pictures would be circulated everywhere.

Rock called private detective Fred Otash. Otash called the Beverly Hills PD, and they arrested Barb Jahelka. Hudson then went soft hearted and refused to press charges. I like this for the 9/24/60 issue. Rock's a hot ticket these days, and Barb's a real dish. (I've got bikini pictures of her we can use.) Let me know, so I can formally write the piece up.

Skewed?—no shit, Sherlock.

Rock Hudson was a fruitfly with no yen for cooze. Fred Otash was an ex-cop Hollywood lapdog. Dig the skewed postscript: Freddy's phone number doodled right there on the report.

Pete grabbed the phone and dialed it. A man answered, "Otash."

"It's Pete Bondurant, Freddy."

Otash whistled. "This has to be interesting. The last time you made a sociable phone call was never."

"I'm not starting now."

"This sounds like we're talking about money. If it's your money for my time, I'm listening."

Pete checked the report. "In August of '60 you allegedly helped Rock Hudson out of a jam. I think the whole thing was a setup. I'll give you a thousand dollars to tell me the story."

Otash said, "Go to two thousand and throw in a disclaimer."

Pete said, "Two thousand. And if push comes to shove, I'll say I got the information elsewhere."

Funny noise hit the line. Pete ID'd it: Freddy tapping his teeth with a pencil.

"Okay, Frenchman."

"Okay, and?"

"Okay, and you're right. The setup was Rock was afraid of being exposed as a queer, so he cooked up a deal with Lenny Sands. Lenny brought in this number Barb Jahelka and her ex-husband Joey, and Barb and Rock got between the sheets. Joey faked a break-in and took some pictures, Barb made a fake extortion demand, and Rock fake called me in."

"And you fake called the Beverly Hills PD."

"Right. They popped Barb for extortion one, then Rock got fake sentimental and dropped the charges. Lenny wrote the thing up for *Hush-Hush*, but for some reason it never got published. Lenny tried to leak the story to the legit press, but nobody would touch it, because half the goddamn country knows Rock's a homo."

Pete sighed. "The whole caper went nowhere."

Otash sighed. "That's correct. Rock paid Barb and Joey two Gs apiece, and now you're paying me an extra two just to tell you the whole sorry tale."

Pete laughed. "Tell me about Barb Jahelka while you're at it."

"All right. My take on Barb is that she's slumming, but she doesn't know it. She's smart, she's funny, she looks good and she knows she's not the next Patti Page. I think she's from the Wisconsin boonies, and I think she did six months honor farm for maryjane possession about four or five years ago. She used to have a thing going with Peter Lawford"—

Jack's brother-in-law—

"and she treats her ex-husband Joey, who's a piece of shit, exactly the way he ought to be treated. I'd have to say she likes kicks, and I'll bet she'd tell you she likes danger, but my take is she's never been tested. If you're interested in her whereabouts, try the Reef Club in Ventura. The last I heard, Joey Jahelka was fronting some kind of cut-rate Twist show up there."

Pete said, "You like her, Freddy. You're an open book."

"So are you. And while we're being candid, let me heartily recommend that girl for whatever kind of shakedown you've got in mind."

The Reef Club was all driftwood and fake barnacles. The clientele was mostly college kids and low-rent hipsters.

Pete snagged a table just off the dance floor. Joey's Swingin' Twist Revue went on in ten minutes.

Wall speakers churned out music. Twist geeks flailed and bumped asses. Pete's table vibrated and shook the head off his nice glass of beer.

He called Karen Hiltscher before he left L.A. Sheriff's R&I had a sheet on one Barbara Jane (Lindscott) Jahelka.

She was born 11/18/31, in Tunnel City, Wisconsin. She had a valid California driver's license. She went down on a reefer beef circa 7/57.

She did six months County time. She was suspected of shanking a bull dyke at the Hall of Justice Jail. She was married—8/3/54–1/24/58—to:

Joseph Dominic Jahelka, born 1/16/23, New York City. New York State convictions: statch rape, flimflam, forging Dilaudid prescriptions.

Joey Jahelka was probably a slavering hophead. He'd probably drool for the Dilaudid he just copped back in L.A.

Pete sipped beer. The hi-fi blared jungle-bunny music. A loudspeaker blared, "Ladies and gentlemen, the Reef Club is proud to present for your twisting pleasure—Joey Jahelka and his Swingin' Twist Revue!!!"

Nobody cheered. Nobody applauded. Nobody stopped twisting.

A trio jumped on stage. They wore calypso shirts and mismatched tuxedos. Pawnshop tags dangled off their equipment.

They set up. The twisters and table crowd ignored them. A jukebox tune bled into their opener.

A high-school kid played tenor sax. The drummer was a bantamweight pachuco. The guitar man matched Joey's R&I stats.

The greasy little hump was half on-the-nod. His socks were de-elasticized way below his ankles.

They played loud, shitty music. Pete felt the wax in his ears start to crumble.

Barb Jahelka slinked up to the mike. Barb oozed healthy pulchritude. Barb was no show-biz-subspecies junkie.

Tall Barb. Lanky Barb. That sparkly red bouffant was no fuck-ing dye job.

Dig that tight, low-cut gown. Dig the heels that put her over six feet.

Barb sang. Barb had weak pipes. The combo drowned her out every time she reached for a high note.

Pete watched. Barb sang. Barb DANCED—*Hush-Hush* would tag it HOT, HOT, HOTSVILLE.

Some male twisters stopped twisting to dig on the big rangy redhead. One girl poked her partner—You get your eyes off of her!

Barb sang weak-voiced and monotonous. Barb put out unique gyrations flat-out concurrent.

She kicked her shoes off. She thrust her hips out and popped seams down one leg.

Pete watched her eyes. Pete tapped the envelope in his pocket.

She'd read the note. The money would hook her in. She'd give Joey the dope and urge him to get lost.

Pete chain-smoked. Barb lost a breast and tucked it back before the Twist fiends noticed.

Barb smiled—oops!—dazzling.

Pete passed the envelope to a waitress. Twenty dollars guaran-teed transmittal.

Barb danced. Pete shot her something like a prayer: Please be able to TALK.

He knew she'd be late. He knew she'd close the club and let him sweat for a while. He knew she'd call Freddy O. for a quick run-down of his pedigree.

Pete waited at an all-night coffee shop. His chest hurt—Barb twisted him through two packs of cigarettes.

He called Littell an hour ago. He said, Let's meet at Lenny's at 3:00—I think I might have found our woman.

It was 1:10 now. He might have called Littell just a tad premature.

Pete sipped coffee and checked his watch every few seconds. Barb Jahelka walked in and spotted him.

Her skirt and blouse looked half-assed demure. No-makeup did nice things to her face.

She sat down across from him. Pete said, "I hope you called Freddy."

"I did."

"What did he tell you?"

"That he'd never mess with you. And that your partners always make money."

"Is that all he said?"

"He said you knew Lenny Sands. I called Lenny, but he wasn't home."

Pete pushed his coffee aside. "Did you try to kill that dyke you shivved?"

Barb smiled. "No. I wanted to stop her from touching me, and I didn't want it to cost me the rest of my life."

Pete smiled. "You didn't ask me what this is all about."

"Freddy already gave me his interpretation, and you're paying me five hundred dollars for a chat. And by the way, Joey says, 'Thanks for the taste.' "

A waitress hovered. Pete shooed her away. "Why do you stay with him?"

"Because he wasn't always a drug addict. Because he arranged to have some men who hurt my sister taken care of."

"Those are good reasons."

Barb lit a cigarette. "The best reason is I love Joey's mom. She's senile, and she thinks we're still married. She thinks Joey's sister's kids are our kids."

Pete laughed. "Suppose she dies?"

"Then the day of the funeral is the day I say goodbye to Joey. He'll have to get a new girl singer and a new chauffeur to drive him to his Nalline tests."

"I bet that'll break his heart."

Barb blew smoke rings. "Over's over. That's a concept junkies don't understand."

"You understand it."

"I know. And you're thinking it's a weird thing for a woman to get."

"Not necessarily."

Barb stubbed out her cigarette. "What's this all about?"

"Not yet."

"When?"

"Soon. First, you tell me about you and Peter Lawford."

Barb toyed with her ashtray. "It was brief and ugly, and I broke it off when Peter kept pestering me to go to bed with Frank Sinatra."

"Which you didn't feel like doing."

"Right."

"Did Lawford introduce you to Jack Kennedy?"

"No."

"Do you think he told Kennedy about you?"

"Maybe."

"You've heard about Kennedy and women?"

"Sure. Peter called him 'insatiable,' and a showgirl I knew in Vegas told me some stories."

Pete smelled suntan oil. Redheads and bright stage lights—

Barb said, "Where are we going with this?"

Pete said, "I'll see you at the club tomorrow night and tell you."

Littell met him outside Lenny's building. Night-owl Lenny had his lights on at 3:20 A.M.

Pete said, "The woman's great. All we need is Lenny to front the introduction."

"I want to meet her."

"You will. Is he alone?"

Littell nodded. "He came home with a pickup two hours ago. The boy just left."

Pete yawned—he hadn't slept in twenty-four-plus hours. "Let's take him."

"Good cop-bad cop?"

"Right. Alternating, so we keep him off balance."

They walked up to the porch. Pete rang the bell. Littell screwed a crimped ugly look on his face.

Lenny opened up. "Don't tell me, you forgot—"

Pete pushed him inside. Littell slammed the door and threw the bolt.

Chic Lenny cinched his robe. Fey Lenny threw his head back and laughed.

"I thought we were quits, Ward. And I thought you only crawled around Chicago."

Littell said, "We need some help. And all you have to do is introduce a man to a woman and keep quiet about it."

"Or?"

"Or we hand you up for the Tony Iannone killing."

Pete sighed. "Let's do this civilized."

Littell said, "Why? We're dealing with a sadistic little faggot who killed a man and bit his goddamn nose off."

Lenny sighed. "I've been double-teamed before. This routine is nothing new to me."

Littell said, "We'll try to make it interesting."

Pete said, "Five grand, Lenny. All you have to do is introduce Barb Jahelka to another friend of yours."

Littell popped his knuckles. Lenny said, "Give it up, Ward. Rough-trade mannerisms don't suit you."

Littell slapped him. Lenny slapped him back.

Pete stepped between them. They looked ridiculous—two bloody-nosed pseudo tough guys.

"Come on, you two. Let's do this civilized."

Lenny wiped his nose. "Your face looks different, Ward. Those scars are soooooo you."

Littell wiped his nose. "You didn't seem surprised when Pete mentioned Barb Jahelka."

Lenny laughed. "That's because I was still in shock from the notion of you two as playmates."

Littell said, "That's not a real answer."

Lenny shrugged. "How's this? Barb's in the Life, and everybody in the Life knows everybody else in the Life."

Pete lobbed a change-up. "Name some hotels Jack Kennedy takes his women to."

Lenny twitched. Pete popped his thumbs double-loud.

Littell said, "Name some hotels."

Swishy Lenny squealed, "This is sooooo fun! Hey, let's call Kemper Boyd and make it a foursome!"

Littell slapped him. Lenny popped some tears—fag bravado, adieu.

Pete said, "Name some hotels. Don't make *me* get rough with you."

Lenny put on a lisp. "The El Encanto in Santa Barbara, the Ambassador-East in Chicago, and the Carlyle in New York."

Littell pushed Pete into the hallway—well out of Lenny's earshot. "Hoover's got standing bugs in the El Encanto and Ambassador-East. The managers assign those suites to whoever he tells them to."

Pete whispered. "He's put it together. He knows what we want, so let's close him."

They walked back to the living room. Lenny was guzzling high-test Bacardi.

Littell looked ready to drool. Hoffa said he had ten months off the sauce. Lenny's liquor cart was radioactive—rum and scotch and all kinds of good shit.

Lenny downed the juice two-handed. Pete said, "'Jack, this is Barb. Barb, this is Jack.'"

Lenny wiped his lips. "I have to call him 'Mr. President' now."

Littell said, "When was the last time you saw him?"

Lenny coughed. "A few months ago. At Peter Lawford's beach house."

"Does he always go by Lawford's place when he's in L.A.?"

"Yes. Peter throws wonderful parties."

"Does he invite unattached women?"

Lenny giggled. "Does he *ever*."

"Does he invite you?"

"Usually, dear heart. The President likes to laugh, and what the President likes, the President gets."

Pete stepped in. "Who else goes to the parties? Sinatra and those Rat Pack guys?"

Lenny poured a stiff refill. Littell licked his lips and plugged the bottle.

Pete said, *"Who else goes to those parties?"*

Lenny shrugged. "Amusing people. Frank used to come, but Bobby made Jack drop him."

Littell stepped in. "I read that Kennedy's coming to Los Angeles on February 18th."

"That's true, dear heart. And guess who's throwing a party on the 19th."

"Were you invited, Lenny?"

"Yes, I was."

"Does the Secret Service frisk the guests or run them through a metal detector?"

Lenny reached for the bottle. Pete grabbed it first.

"Answer Mr. Littell's question, goddamnit."

Lenny shook his head. "No. What the Secret Service does is eat, drink and discuss Jack's protean sex drive."

Pete said, "'Barb, this is Jack. Jack, this is Barb.'"

Lenny sighed. "I'm not an imbecile."

Pete smiled. "We're upping your fee to ten thousand, because we know you're way too smart to mention this to anybody."

Littell pushed the liquor cart out of his sight. "That specifically includes Sam Giancana and your Outfit friends, Laura Hughes, Claire Boyd and Kemper Boyd, on the extreme off-chance that you run into them."

Lenny laughed. "Kemper's not in on this? Toooo bad— I wouldn't mind rubbing whatevers with *him* again."

Pete said, "Don't treat this like a joke."

Littell said, "Don't think Sam will let you walk for the Tony job."

Pete said, "Don't think that Sam still likes Jack, or that he'd lift a finger to help him. Sam bought Jack West Virginia and Illinois, but that was a long time ago, and Bobby's been goddamn unfriendly to the Outfit since then."

Lenny weaved into the cart. Littell steadied him.

Lenny pushed him away. "Sam and Bobby must have *something* cooking, 'cause Sam said the Outfit's been doing some work to help Bobby out with Cuba, but Bobby doesn't know about it, and Sam said, 'We sort of think he should be told.' "

Pete caught a quick flash:

The Whack Fidel auditions. Three Outfit biggies, bored and noncommittal.

Littell said, "Lenny, you're drunk. You're not making any—"

Pete cut him off. "What else did Giancana say about Bobby Kennedy and Cuba?"

Lenny leaned against the door. "Nothing. I just heard two seconds of this conversation he was having with Butch Montrose."

"When?"

"Last week. I went to Chicago for a Teamster smoker."

Littell said, "Forget about Cuba." Lenny weaved and flashed the V-for-victory sign.

"Viva Fidel! Down with the U.S. imperialist insect!"

Pete slapped him.

Littell said, " 'Barb, this is Jack.' And remember what we'll do if you betray us."

Lenny spat out some gold bridgework.

The combo played way off-key. Pete figured they were zorched on his Dilaudid.

The Reef Club rocked. Twist nuts had the floor shaking.

Barb danced close to chaste by her standards. Pete figured the potential gig had her distracted.

Littell commandeered a wraparound bar booth. Barb waved when she saw them walk in.

Pete drank beer. Littell drank club soda. Amplifier boom shook their table.

Pete yawned. He got a room at the Statler and slept through the day and half the evening.

Hoffa sent two grand to Fred Otash. Littell wrote a note to Hoover and sent it via Jimmy's FBI contact.

The note said, We want to install bugs and wiretaps. The note said, We want to fuck one of YOUR MAJOR ENEMIES.

Hoffa retained Fred Turentine. Freddy was set to tap phones and plant bugs where needed.

Pete yawned. Lenny's Bobby/Cuba pitch kept twisting through his head.

Littell nudged him. "She's got the looks."

"And the style."

"How smart is she?"

"A lot smarter than my last extortion partner."

Barb worked the "Frisco Twist" into a crescendo. Her junkie backup group kept playing like she wasn't even there.

She walked off stage. Twist clowns jostled her across the dance floor. A horny geek followed her and scoped out her cleavage close up.

Pete waved. Barb slid into the booth next to him.

Pete said, "Miss Lindscott, Mr. Littell."

Barb lit a cigarette. "It's technically 'Jahelka.' When my mother-in-law dies, I'll go back to 'Lindscott.' "

Littell said, "I like 'Lindscott.' "

Barb said, "I know. It fits my face better."

"Have you ever worked as an actress?"

"No."

"What about that charade with Lenny Sands and Rock Hudson?"

"I only had to fool the police and spend a night in jail."

"Was two thousand dollars worth the risk?"

Barb laughed. "Compared to four hundred dollars for three Twist shows a night, six nights a week?"

Pete pushed his beer and pretzels aside. "You'll make a lot more than two thousand dollars with us."

"For doing what? Besides sleeping with some powerful man, I mean."

Littell leaned toward her. "It's high risk, but it's only temporary."

"So? The Twist is temporary and boring."

Littell smiled. "If you met President Kennedy and wanted to impress him, how would you act?"

Barb blew three perfect smoke rings. "I'd act profane and funny."

"What would you wear?"

"Flat heels."

"Why?"

"Men like women they can look down to."

Littell laughed. "What would you do with fifty thousand dollars?"

Barb laughed. "I'd wait out the Twist."

"Suppose you get exposed?"

"Then I'll figure that you're worse than whoever we're shaking down and keep my mouth shut."

Pete said, "It won't come to that."

Barb said, "*What* won't?"

Pete fought this urge to touch her. "You'll be safe. This is one of those high-risk things that gets settled nice and quiet."

Barb leaned close to him. "Tell me what 'it' is. I know what it is, but I want to hear *you* say it."

She brushed his leg. The contact made his whole body flutter.

Pete said, "It's you and Jack Kennedy. You'll meet him at a party at Peter Lawford's house in two weeks. You'll be wearing a microphone, and if you're as good as I think you are, that will just be the start of it."

Barb took their hands and squeezed them. Her look said, Pinch me, am I dreaming?

"Am I some kind of Republican Party shill?"

Pete laughed. Littell laughed harder.

DOCUMENT INSERT: 2/18/62.
Verbatim FBI telephone call transcript: ''TAPED AT
THE DIRECTOR'S REQUEST''/''DIRECTOR'S EYES ONLY.''
Speaking: Director J. Edgar Hoover, Ward J. Littell.

JEH: Mr. Littell?

WJL: Yes, Sir.

JEH: Your communique was quite bold.

WJL: Thank you, Sir.

JEH: I had no idea you were employed by Mr. Hoffa and Mr. Marcello.

WJL: Since last year, Sir.

JEH: I will not comment on the attendant irony.

WJL: I would call it manifest, Sir.

JEH: That is apt. Am I correct in assuming that the ubiquitous and quite overextended Kemper Boyd secured you this employment?

WJL: Yes, Sir. You are correct.

JEH: I bear Mr. Marcello and Mr. Hoffa no ill will. I have viewed the Dark Prince's crusade against them to be ill-conceived from the start.

WJL: They know that, Sir.

JEH: Am I correct in assuming that you have undergone an apostasy concerning the brothers?

WJL: Yes, Sir.

JEH: Am I to assume that the promiscuous King Jack is the target of your operation?

WJL: That is correct, Sir.

JEH: And the fearsome Pete Bondurant is your partner in this endeavor?

WJL: Yes, Sir.

JEH: I will not comment on the attendant irony.

WJL: Sir, do we have your approval?

JEH: You do. And you, personally, have my astonishment.

WJL: Thank you, Sir.

JEH: Is the apparatus in place?

WJL: Yes, Sir. So far we've only been able to wire the Carlyle, and until our plant makes contact with the target and facilitates the affair, we don't really know where they'll be coupling.

JEH: If they couple at all.

WJL: Yes, Sir.

JEH: Your note mentioned certain hotels.

WJL: Yes, Sir, the El Encanto and Ambassador-East. I know that our target likes to take women to those hotels, and I know that the Bureau retains standing bugs at both locations.

JEH: Yes, although the Dark King now likes to cavort in the Presidential Suites.

WJL: I hadn't thought of that, Sir.

JEH: I'll have trustworthy Bureau men install the apparatus and monitor it. And I will share my tapes with you, if you forward copies of your Carlyle tapes to me.

WJL: Of course, Sir.

JEH: Have you considered wiring the first brother-in-law's beach house?

WJL: It's impossible, sir. Fred Turentine can't get in to install the microphones.

JEH: When will your plant meet the Dark King?

WJL: Tomorrow night, Sir. At the beach house you just mentioned.

JEH: Is she attractive?

WJL: Yes, Sir.

JEH: I hope she's wily and resilient and impervious to the boy's charm.

WJL: I think she'll do a fine job, Sir.

JEH: I'm quite anxious to hear her on tape.

WJL: I'll forward only the best transcriptions, Sir.

JEH: You have my admiration. Kemper Boyd taught you well.

WJL: You did, too, Sir.

JEH: I will not comment on the attendant irony.

WJL: Yes, Sir.

JEH: I know that in time you'll ask favors of me. I know that you'll keep me abreast of the transcriptions and ask your favors judiciously.

WJL: I will, Sir.

JEH: I misjudged you and underestimated you, and I'm glad we're colleagues again.

WJL: So am I, Sir.

JEH: Good day, Mr. Littell.

WJL: Good day, Sir.

76
(Meridian, 2/18/62)

SHOTS WOKE HIM up. Rebel yells made him dive for his gun.

Kemper rolled off the bed.

He heard brake squeals down on the highway—non-Lockhart Klansmen or plain old rednecks popping rounds and running.

Word is out.

There's a Fed nigger lover in town. The Seminole Motel is packed with his spic/frog minions.

The shots were scary. The nightmare they cut off was worse.

Jack and Bobby had him under the hot lights. They said, J'accuse—we know you're Mob-CIA linked all the way back to '59.

The nightmare was literal and direct. The origin was Pete's phone call last week.

Pete talked up the Whack Fidel auditions. He said he developed a theory to explain why the Outfit nixed the hit.

Pete said Sam G. might be set to tell Bobby a secret. Hey, Mr. AG—the Outfit's been your Cuban Cause ally for three years now.

Pete picked up a lead that strongly suggested it. Pete thinks Sam might have someone spill the secret soon. Pete thinks Sam wants to embarrass Bobby into a Mob War cease-fire.

Pete said, I'll look into it.

Kemper got up and dry-swallowed three Dexedrine. Pete's theory speedballed and went personal.

Bobby wants *me* to show him JM/Wave some time soon. He thinks my CIA ties date from 5/61 on. JM/Wave is packed with my *pre-Pigs* colleagues—and Cuban exiles well acquainted with organized crime figures.

Kemper shaved and dressed. The Dexedrine kicked in fast. He heard thumps next door—Laurent Guéry pounding early morning push-ups.

John Stanton pulled strings. Laurent, Flash and Juan were granted INS green cards. Néstor Chasco moved to Meridian and joined the group. The Seminole Motel was now "Adjunct" Cadre HQ.

He cashed in twenty thousand dollars' worth of stock. Guy Banister donated matching funds. The Clip Castro Squad was now self-contained and totally autonomous.

He took voting rights reports by day. He staged assassination drills by night.

He won over quite a few local Negroes. First Pentecostal Baptist was now 84% depositioned.

Some crackers roughed up the pastor. He found them and broke their legs with a two-by-four.

Dougie Frank parceled off half his gun range. The Adjunct Cadre practiced seven nights a week.

They shot at standing and moving targets. They took recon tramps through the woods. Cuban infiltration runs would begin soon.

Juan and Flash had him close to Spanish-fluent. He could dye his hair and stain his face and go to Cuba as a covert Latin.

He could get close. He could shoot.

They all loved to talk. They drank post-practice moonshine and gabbed through half the night.

They worked up a three-language patois. They told gory campfire tales and passed around bottles.

Juan described his castration. Chasco talked up his Batista-ordered clip jobs.

Flash saw Playa Girón up close. Laurent saw the hushed-up Paris slaughter—gendarmes beat two hundred Algerians to death and dumped them in the Seine last October.

He could get close. *He* could shoot. The fair-skinned Anglo-Saxon could be Cuban.

The Dexedrine hit full-bore. Cold coffee provided a nice booster.

The date jumped off his Rolex. Happy Birthday—you're forty-six years old and don't look it.

DOCUMENT INSERT: 2/21/62.
Partial microphone to mobile listening post transcript. Transcribed by: Fred Turentine. Tape/ written copies to: P. Bondurant, W. Littell.

9:14 P.M., February 19, 1982. L. Sands & B. Jahelka enter house (target & entourage arrived at 8:03). Traffic noise on Pacific Coast Highway accounts for scrambled signal and large continuity gaps. B. Jahelka's visit clock synchronized & live monitored.

Initial code:

BJ—Barb Jahelka. LS—Lenny Sands. PL—Peter Lawford.
MU 1—Male Unknown #1. MU2—Male Unknown #2. FU 1, 2, 3,
4, 5, 6, 7: Female Unknowns #1–#7. JFK—John F.
Kennedy. RFK—Robert F. Kennedy. (Note: I think MU #1
and #2 are Secret Service agents.)

9:14–9:22: garbled.

9:23–9:26: overlapping voices. BJ's voice comes
through, mostly casual greetings. (I think she was
being introduced to FU #1–#7. Note high-pitched
laughter on tape copies.)

9:27–9:39: BJ & PL.

PL (conversation in progress): You stand out in
this crowd, Barb.

BJ: My beauty or my height?

PL: Both.

BJ: You're so full of shit.

FU3: Hi, Peter.

PL: Hi, doll.

FU6: Peter, I just love the President's hair.

PL: Give it a tug. He won't bite you.

FU3, FU6: laughter.

BJ: Are they showgirls or hookers?

PL: The bleached blonde's a barmaid at the Sip n'
Surf in Malibu. The others work the show line at the
Dunes. You see the brunette with the lungs?

BJ: I see her.

PL: She plays skin flute in Frank Sinatra's all-girl
band.

BJ: Very funny.

PL: Not funny, because Bobby made Jack drop Frank.
Frank put in a heliport at his place in Palm Springs
so Jack could visit him, but that judgmental little
shit Bobby made Jack give him the brush-off, just
because he knows a few gangsters. Look at him. Isn't
he a wicked looking little shit?

BJ: He has buck teeth.

PL: That never touch women.

BJ: Are you saying he's a fag?

PL: I have it on good authority that he only fucks
his wife, doesn't go down, and only gives it to Ethel

for purposes of procreation. Isn't he a wicked
looking little shit?

FU2: Peter! I just met the President out on the
beach!

PL: That's nice. Did you suck his cock?

FU2: You're a pig.

PL: Oink! Oink!

BJ: I think I need a drink.

PL: I think you need a lobotomy. Really, Barb.
I just wanted you to sleep with Frank once.

BJ: He's not my type.

PL: He could have helped you. He would have kicked
that wicked little shit Joey out of your life.

BJ: Joey and I have a history. I'll cut him loose
when the time's right.

PL: You cut me loose too soon. Frank was deeply
smitten with you, doll. He sensed that you were hiding
things, and I have it on good authority that he hired
a private eye to find out what those things were.

BJ: Did he tell you what he found out?

PL: Mum's the word, doll. Mum's the goddamn—

FU1: Oh God, Peter, I just met President Kennedy!

PL: That's nice. Did you suck his cock?

BJ, FU1, FU7: garbled.

PL: Oink! Oink! Oink! I'm a Presidential piglet!

9:40-10:22: garbled. Static quality indicates that
Secret Service men installed and were calling out on
private phone lines.

10:23-10:35: garbled. BJ (standing near hi-fi set)
talking to: FU1, 3, 7. (She should have been told to
avoid noisy appliances & record players.)

10:36-10:41: BJ in bathroom (indicated by sink &
toilet sounds).

10:42-10:49: garbled.

10:50-11:04: BJ & RFK.

BJ (conversation in progress): It's just a craze,
and you have to catch these things before they crest,
and then bail out before they fizzle so you won't look
like a loser.

RFK: Then I guess you could say the Twist is like
politics.

BJ: You could. Opportunism's certainly the common denominator.

RFK: It sounds trite, but you don't talk like an ex-showgirl.

BJ: Have you met a lot of them?

RFK: Quite a few, yes.

BJ: When you were investigating gangsters?

RFK: No, when my brother introduced me to them.

BJ: Did they have a common denominator?

RFK: Yes. Availability.

BJ: I'd have to agree with that.

RFK: Are you going out with Lenny Sands?

BJ: We're not dating. He just brought me to the party.

RFK: How did he bill the gathering?

BJ: He didn't say, 'come join the harem,' if that's what you mean.

RFK: Then you noticed the high woman to man ratio.

BJ: You know I did, Mr. Kennedy.

RFK: Call me Bob.

BJ: All right, Bob.

RFK: I'm just assuming that since you know Peter and Lenny, you know how certain things are.

BJ: I think I follow you.

RFK: I know you do. I'm only mentioning it because I've known Lenny for a long time, and he seems sad and nervous tonight, and I've never seen him that way before. I'd hate to think that Peter put him up to—

BJ: I don't like Peter. I had a fling with him several years ago, and I broke it off when I saw that he was really no better than a toady and a pimp. I came to this party because Lenny needed a date and I thought it would be nice to spend a cool winter evening at the beach and maybe meet the Attorney General and President of the United States—

RFK: Please, I didn't mean to offend you.

BJ: You didn't.

RFK: When I get hornswoggled into evenings like this, I find myself checking out the anomalies from a security standpoint. When the anomaly is a woman, well, you see what I mean.

BJ: Given the other women here, it's good to be an anomaly.

RFK: I'm bored and two drinks over my limit. I don't normally get so personal with people I just met.

BJ: Want to hear a good joke?

RFK: Sure.

BJ: What did Pat Nixon say about her husband?

RFK: I don't know.

BJ: Richard was a strange bedfellow long before he entered politics.

RFK (laughing): Jesus, that's a riot. I'll have to tell that to—

Garbled (airplane flying overhead). Remainder of BJ–RFK conversation lost to static.

11:05–11:12: Hi-fi noise & car noise indicate that BJ is walking thru house & that people are leaving the party.

11:13–11:19: BJ talking directly to microphone. (Tell her not to do this. It's a security risk.)

BJ: I'm out on this deck overlooking the beach. I'm alone, and I'm whispering so people won't hear what I'm saying or think I'm crazy. I haven't met the Big Man yet, but I noticed him notice me and nudge Peter like he was saying, who's the redhead? It's freezing out here, but I dug a mink coat out of a closet, and now I'm nice and warm. Lenny's drunk, but I think he's trying to have a good time. He's schmoozing with Dean Martin now. The Big Man is in Peter's bedroom with two blondes. I saw Bobby a few minutes ago. He was eating out of the fridge like a starving man. The Secret Service men are looking through a stack of Playboy Magazines. You can tell they're thinking, boy, I'm sure glad stodgy old Dick Nixon didn't get elected. Somebody's smoking pot out on the beach, and I'm thinking hard to get's the way to play this. I'm thinking he'll find me. I heard Bobby tell one of the Secret Service men that the Big Man didn't want to leave until 1:00. That gives me some time. Lenny said Peter showed him my infamous Nugget Magazine foldout from November, 1956. He's about 6' or 6'1", so with flats on he'll have a few inches on me. I have to say that

Hollywood trash aside, this is one of those moments
that young girls write about in their diaries. Also,
I declined three invitations to Twist, because
I thought it might rip my microphone loose. Did you
hear that? The bedroom door behind me just shut, and
the two blondes snuck out, giggling. I'm going to shut
up now.

    11:20–11:27: silence. (Wave noise indicates that
BJ has remained on the beach deck.)

    11:28–11:40: BJ & JFK.

    JFK: Hi.

    BJ: Jesus.

    JFK: Hardly, but thanks anyway.

    BJ: How about, hello, Mr. President?

    JFK: How about, hello, Jack?

    BJ: Hello, Jack.

    JFK: What's your name?

    BJ: Barb Jahelka.

    JFK: You don't look like a Jahelka.

    BJ: It's Lindscott, actually. I work with my ex-
husband, so I kept my married name.

    JFK: Is Lindscott Irish?

    BJ: It's an Anglo-German bastardization.

    JFK: The Irish are all bastards. Bastards, cranks
and drunks.

    BJ: Can I quote you?

    JFK: After I'm re-elected. Put it in the portable
John F. Kennedy, next to 'Ask not what your country
can do for you.'

    BJ: Can I ask you a question?

    JFK: Sure.

    BJ: Is being President of the United States the
biggest fucking blast on earth?

    JFK (sustained laughter): It truly is. Your
supporting cast of characters is worth the price of
admission alone.

    BJ: For instance?

    JFK: That rube Lyndon Johnson. Charles de Gaulle,
who's had a poker up his ass since the year 1910. That
closet fairy J. Edgar Hoover. These crazy Cuban
exiles my brother's been dealing with, 80% of whom are

lowlife scum. Harold Macmillan, who defines the word—

MU2: Excuse me, Mr. President.

JFK: Yes?

MU1: You have a call.

JFK: Tell them I'm busy.

MU2: It's Governor Brown.

JFK: Tell him I'll call him back.

MU1: Yes, Sir.

JFK: So, Barb, did you vote for me?

BJ: I was on tour, so I didn't get the chance to vote.

JFK: You could have cast an absentee ballot.

BJ: It slipped my mind.

JFK: What's more important, the Twist or my career?

BJ: The Twist.

JFK (sustained laughter): Excuse my naivete. When you ask a silly question.

BJ: It was more like ask a candid question, get a candid answer.

JFK: That's true. You know, my brother thinks you're overqualified for this party.

BJ: He acts like he's slumming himself.

JFK: That's perceptive.

BJ: Your brother never won a dime at poker.

JFK: Which is one of his strengths. Now, what happens when this silly dance craze of yours wears itself out?

BJ: I'll have saved enough money to set my sister up in a Bob's Big Boy franchise in Tunnel City, Wisconsin.

JFK: I carried Wisconsin.

BJ: I know. My sister voted for you.

JFK: What about your parents?

BJ: My father's dead. My mother hates Catholics, so she voted for Nixon.

JFK: A split vote isn't too bad. That's a lovely mink, by the way.

BJ: I borrowed it from Peter.

JFK: Then it's one of the six thousand furs my father bought my sisters.

BJ: I read about your father's stroke. It made me sad.

JFK: Don't be. He's too evil to die. And by the way, do you travel with that revue Peter told me about?

BJ: Constantly. In fact, I'm leaving for an East Coast swing on the 27th.

JFK: Would you leave your itinerary with the White House switchboard? I thought we might have dinner if our schedules permit.

BJ: I'd like that. And I will call.

JFK: Please. And take the mink with you. You do things for it that my sister never could.

BJ: I couldn't.

JFK: I insist. Really, she won't miss it.

BJ: All right, then.

JFK: I don't normally raid people's closets, but I want you to have it.

BJ: Thank you, Jack.

JFK: My pleasure. And regretfully, I have to make some phone calls.

BJ: Until next time, then.

JFK: Yes. That's the way to look at it.

MU1: Mr. President?

JFK: Hold on, I'm coming.

11:41–12:03: silence. (Wave noise indicates that BJ has remained on the beach deck.)

12:03–12:09: garbled voices and hi-fi noise. (Obvious departures throughout.)

12:10: BJ & LS leave the party. Live tape feed close: 12:11 A.M., February 20, 1962.

DOCUMENT INSERT: 3/4/62.
Carlyle Hotel bedroom microphone transcript. Transcribed by: Fred Turentine. Tape/written copies to: P. Bondurant, W. Littell.

BJ phoned the listening post to say she was meeting the target for ''dinner.'' She was instructed to double open & shut the bedroom door to activate the mike. Active feed from 8:09 P.M. on. Initial log: BJ— Barb Jahelka. JFK—John F. Kennedy.

8:09–8:20: sexual activity. (See tape transcript. High sound quality. Voices discernible.)

8:21–8:33: conversation.

JFK: Oh, God.

BJ: Hmmm.

JFK: Slide over a little. I want to take some pressure off my back.

BJ: How's that?

JFK: Better.

BJ: Want a back rub?

JFK: No. There's nothing you can do that you haven't done already.

BJ: Thanks. And I'm glad you called me.

JFK: What did I get you out of?

BJ: Two shows at the Rumpus Room in Passaic, New Jersey.

JFK: Oh, God.

BJ: Ask me a question.

JFK: All right. Where's that mink coat I gave you?

BJ: My ex-husband sold it.

JFK: You let him do that?

BJ: It's a game we play.

JFK: What do you mean?

BJ: He knows I'm going to leave him soon. I'm in debt to him, so he takes these little advantages whenever he finds them.

JFK: It's a large debt, then?

BJ: Very large.

JFK: You've got my interest. Tell me more.

BJ: It's just grief from Tunnel City, Wisconsin, circa 1948.

JFK: I like Wisconsin.

BJ: I know. You carried it.

JFK (laughing): You're droll. Ask me a question.

BJ: Who's the biggest fuckhead in American politics?

JFK (laughing): That closet queen J. Edgar Hoover, who'll be retiring on January 1, 1965.

BJ: I hadn't heard anything about that.

JFK: You will.

BJ: I get it. You have to be re-elected first.

JFK: You're learning. Now, tell me more about Tunnel City, Wisconsin, in 1948.

BJ: Not now.

JFK: Why?

BJ: I'm tantalizing you, so we can prolong this thing of ours.

JFK (laughing): You know men.

BJ: Yes, I do.

JFK: Who taught you? Initially, I mean.

BJ: The entire adolescent male population of Tunnel City, Wisconsin. Don't look so shocked. The total number of boys was eleven.

JFK: Go on.

BJ: No.

JFK: Why?

BJ: Two seconds after we made love you looked at your watch. I'm thinking that the way to keep you in bed is to string out my autobiography.

JFK (laughing): You can contribute to my memoirs. You can say John F. Kennedy wooed women with room service club sandwiches and quickies.

BJ: It was a great club sandwich.

JFK (laughing): You're droll and cruel.

BJ: Ask me a question.

JFK: No. You ask me one.

BJ: Tell me about Bobby.

JFK: Why?

BJ: He seemed suspicious of me at Peter's party.

JFK: He's suspicious in general, because he's crawling around in the legal gutter with Jimmy Hoffa and the Mafia, and it's starting to get to him. It's some sort of occupational policeman's disease that he's developed. One day it's Jimmy Hoffa and land fraud in Florida. The next day it's deporting Carlos Marcello. Now it's Hoffa and the Test Fleet taxi case in Tennessee, and don't ask me what it means, because I'm not a lawyer and I don't share Bobby's need to pursue and eradicate.

BJ: He's tougher than you, isn't he?

JFK: Yes, he is. And as I told a girl several years ago, he's truly passionate and generous.

BJ: You're looking at your watch again.

JFK: I have to go. I'm due at the U.N.

BJ: Good luck, then.

JFK: I won't need it. The General Assembly is
nothing but fuckheads. Let's do this again, Barb.
I had fun.

BJ: So did I. And thanks for the club sandwich.

JFK (laughing): There's more where that came from.

Single door slam deactivates mike. Transcript
close: 8:34 P.M., March 3rd, 1962.

DOCUMENT INSERT: 4/9/62.
Carlyle Hotel bedroom microphone transcript.
Transcribed by: Fred Turentine. Tape/written copies
to: P. Bondurant, W. Littell.

BJ phoned the listening post at 4:20 P.M. She said she
was meeting the target for ''dinner'' at 5:30. Active
feed from 6:12 P.M. on. Initial log: BJ—Barb Jahelka.
JFK—John F. Kennedy.

6:13-6:25: sexual activity. (See tape transcript.
High sound quality. Voices discernible.)

6:14-6:32: conversation.

BJ: Oh, God.

JFK: Last time I said that.

BJ: This time was better.

JFK (laughing): I thought so, too. But I thought
the club sandwich lacked pizzazz.

BJ: Ask me a question.

JFK: What happened in Tunnel City, Wisconsin, in
1948?

BJ: I'm amazed that you remembered.

JFK: It's only been a month or so.

BJ: I know. But it was just a casual comment that
I made.

JFK: It was a provocative one, though.

BJ: Thanks.

JFK: Barb.

BJ: All right. On May 9, I jilted Billy Kreuger.
Billy got together with Tom McCandless, Fritzie
Schott and Johnny Coates. They decided to teach me a
lesson. I was out of town, though. My parents took me
to a church fellowship convention in Racine. My

sister Margaret stayed at home. She was rebellious, and she hadn't figured out that church conventions were good places to meet boys.

JFK: Keep going.

BJ: To be continued.

JFK: Oh, God. I hate unresolved mysteries.

BJ: Next time.

JFK: How do you know there'll be a next time?

BJ (laughing): I know what kind of interest I'm capable of sustaining.

JFK: You're good, Barb. You're damn good.

BJ: I want to see if it's possible to know a man in one hour, once-a-month increments.

JFK: You'll never make an untoward demand of me, will you?

BJ: No. I will not.

JFK: God bless you.

BJ: Do you believe in God?

JFK: Only for public appearances. Now, ask me a question.

BJ: Do you have somebody who finds women for you?

JFK (laughing): Not really. Kemper Boyd's probably the closest thing, but he makes me a tad uncomfortable, so I haven't really used him since the Inauguration.

BJ: Who's Kemper Boyd?

JFK: He's a Justice Department lawyer. You'd like him. He's wildly good-looking and rather dangerous.

BJ: Are you jealous of him? Is that why he makes you uncomfortable?

JFK: He makes me uncomfortable because his one great regret is that he's not a Kennedy, which is quite a tough regret to respect. He's been dealing with some of those lowlife exiles for Bobby's Study Group, and I think in some ways he's no better than they are. He just went to Yale Law School, latched onto me and proved himself useful.

BJ: Pimps ingratiate themselves with authority. God, look at Peter.

JFK: Kemper's no Peter Lawford, I'll say that for him. Peter's got no soul to sell, and Kemper sold his at a pretty steep price and didn't even know it.

BJ: How so?

JFK: I can't go into details, but he threw over the woman he was engaged to to curry favor with me and my family. You see, he came from money, but his father lost it all and killed himself. He's living out some unsavory fantasy with me, and once you recognize it, the man becomes hard to take.

BJ: Let's talk about something else.

JFK: How about Tunnel City, Wisconsin, in 1948?

BJ: To be continued.

JFK: Shit.

BJ: I like cliffhangers.

JFK: I don't. I hated movie serials when I was a boy.

BJ: You should install a wall clock here. That way, you won't have to sneak looks at your watch.

JFK: You're droll. Hand me my trousers, would you?

BJ: Here.

Single door slam deactivates mike. Transcript close: 6:33 P.M., April 8, 1962.

77

(Miami, 4/15/62)

THE COP WAS late. Pete killed time doodling up dispatch sheets.

He drew little hearts and arrows. He wrote out words Lenny and Barb said and underlined them for emphasis.

The words were strong. Cabstand bustle washed over him like total fucking silence.

Lenny's words spawned a theory. The Outfit wants Bobby K. to know they've been helping out with Cuba. Bobby hasn't been told yet. If he knew, he would have fungooed Kemper Boyd. If he knew, he would have snipped all known Mob-CIA ties.

The Outfit knows that Bobby doesn't want a Fidel hit. They refused to fund the shooter team for just that reason.

His theory simmered for weeks. He ran guns to exile camps and Kemper worked his two gigs in Mississippi. Kemper was out to depilatory the Beard—his lack of Mob sanction did not seem to bother him one bit.

Barb was out to trim Jack the Haircut.

The cop was late. Pete drifted into Barb Overdrive.

Her words were accumulating—on tape and in print. He had the best words memorized.

Fred Turentine was running the Carlyle bug post—an apartment off 76th and Madison. A Barb Fucks Jack tape/print library was now in the works. Littell's Hoover ploy succeeded. Feds wired the Presidential Suites at the El Encanto and Ambassador-East.

Mr. Hoover was their extortion colleague. Feds checked the Carlyle suite once a week—let's keep those bedroom mikes tucked out of sight.

Jack K. was a six-minute bed jockey. Jack K. was a big fucking loudmouth.

Jack called Cuban exiles "lowlifes." Jack called Kemper Boyd a pathetic social climber.

The cop was late. Pete drew more hearts and arrows.

He had a new theory. Dig it: Barb's talking to Jack and to ME.

Barb says she won't leave Joey Jahelka—"because he arranged to have some men who hurt my sister taken care of." Barb won't tell Jack the whole story.

Barb hints that big intrigue went down in May '48.

Barb knows *he'll* play the tapes and read the transcripts. Barb wants *him* to fill in the blanks. Jack won't press too hard for answers—she's just one of his three million steady fucks.

Barb knows *he's* an ex-cop. Barb knows *he* can find out.

He called the Wisconsin State Police. He had Guy Banister initiate Fed queries. The whole thing took forty-eight hours.

5/11/48:

Margaret Lynn Lindscott is gang-raped in Tunnel City, Wisconsin. She IDs her attackers: William Kreuger, Thomas McCandless, Fritz Schott, and John Coates. No charges are filed. All four boys have unshakable alibis.

1/14/52:

William Kreuger is shot and killed in Milwaukee. The "mugging-homicide" remains unsolved.

7/4/52:

Thomas McCandless is shot and killed in Chicago. The "assumed professional hit" remains unsolved.

1/23/54:

Fritz Schott disappears. A decomposed body is found near Des Moines—maybe or maybe not his. Three shell casings are discovered nearby. The "assumed gunshot homicide" remains unsolved.

John Coates is alive and well. He's a cop in Norman, Oklahoma.

Pete unlocked his desk and pulled out the magazine. There's Barb at twenty-five—a pulchritudinous Miss Nugget.

Barb seduced Mob-allied Joey Jahelka. Barb got him to finagle hits on the men who raped her sister.

John Coates was still alive. The Mob did not clip cops without big provocation.

Grateful Barb married Joey. Grateful Barb carried the debt.

The cop was late. Pete studied the foldout for the ten millionth time.

They airbrushed her breasts. They powdered her freckles. The picture didn't nail her smarts and je ne sais quoi.

Pete put the magazine away. Pete doodled up another dispatch sheet.

He called Barb once a week. He tossed out little love checks—You don't *really* dig Jack, do you?

She didn't. She dug the allure—but Jack was just a six-minute erection and some chuckles.

The shakedown was proceeding. Turentine flew out to L.A. and checked up on Lenny Sands. Freddy said Lenny was solid. Freddy said Lenny would never rat off the operation.

He played the Barb tapes over and over. He reran Lenny's blurt almost as much.

Three major Mob contributors abandoned the Cuban Cause. Littell said Carlos Marcello was the only Outfit big who still cared.

Why?

His guess was MONEY.

Pete kept his nose down for two months straight. His theory percolated.

He kept playing theoretical match-ups. He kept linking Cuban Cause and Outfit personnel. Last week he made a big theoretical jump.

November 1960.

Wilfredo Olmos Delsol is seen talking to pro-Castro agents. Wilfredo Olmos Delsol was *recently* seen:

Driving a new car. Wearing new threads. Showing off new women.

He hired a Miami cop to spot-tail Delsol. The man reported back.

Delsol met with hinky Cubans six nights running. Their license plates were fake number/fake tag counterfeits.

The cop tailed the men to their pads. The pads were rented under obvious fake names. The Cubans were pro-Castro agents with no visible means of support.

The cop glommed a phone-company snitch. He paid him five hundred dollars and told him to steal Delsol's recent phone bills.

The cop said his snitch succeeded. The cop was late with the goods.

Pete doodled. He drew little hearts and arrows, ad fucking infinitum.

Sergeant Carl Lennertz showed up a full hour late. Pete waltzed him out to the parking lot.

They exchanged envelopes. The transaction went down in two seconds flat.

Lennertz took off. Pete opened his envelope and pulled out two sheets of paper.

The Florida Bell man delivered. Delsol made four months' worth of suspicious phone calls.

He called Santo and Sam G. at their unlisted numbers. He called six pro-Castro front groups a total of twenty-nine times.

Pete felt his pulse go snap/crackle/pop.

He drove to Delsol's house. The puto's new-money Impala was parked on the front lawn.

He boxed it in with his car. He slashed the tires with his pocket knife. He wedged a porch chair under the front doorknob. He ripped a cord off an outside air cooler and balled it around his right fist.

He heard running water and music inside the house.

Pete walked around to the back. The kitchen door stood ajar.

Delsol was washing dishes. The geek was snapping his dishrag to a mambo beat.

Pete waved. Delsol waved soapy hands—Come on in.

A little radio was perched on the sink ledge. Perez Prado was cranking out "Cherry Pink and Apple Blossom White."

Pete walked in. Delsol said, *"Hola, Pedro."*

Pete sucker-punched him. Delsol jackknifed. Pete dropped the radio in the sink.

Water fizzed. Pete kicked Delsol in the ass and shot him into sink water up to his elbows.

He screamed. He pulled his arms out and cut loose with this godawful shriek.

Steam whooshed through the kitchen—dig that baby mushroom cloud.

Pete shoved the dishrag in his mouth. Delsol's arms were scorched bright red and hairless.

"You've been calling Trafficante, Giancana and some pro-Castro guys. You've been seen with some left-wing Cubans, and you've been spending money."

Delsol flipped him off. Dig that firecracker-red "Fuck You" finger.

"I think most of the Outfit's quits on the Cause, and I want to know why. You put all this together or your face goes into the water."

Delsol spat the rag out. Pete lashed his hands with the air-cooler cord and rabbit-punched him back into the suds.

He spun in sideways. Juiced-up water splashed all over him.

He screamed and pulled his arms out. Pete dragged him to the fridge and buried his hands in ice cubes.

Stabilize, fucker—don't go into shock.

Pete dumped loose cubes into a bowl. Delsol untied the cord with his teeth and wiggled his hands in.

The sink water bubbled and fizzed. Pete lit a cigarette to kill the charred-flesh stink.

Delsol slumped into a chair. His cardiac flush subsided—the puto radiated good resistance.

Pete said, "Well?"

Delsol hugged the bowl with his knees. Ice popped out and hit the floor.

Pete said, "Well?"

"Well, you killed my cousin. Did you think I would always stay loyal?"

His voice stayed just short of a whimper. Spics withstood pain with the best.

"That's not the answer I wanted."

"I thought it was a good answer for a man who killed his own brother by mistake."

Pete picked up a kitchen knife. "Tell me what I want to hear."

Delsol double-flipped him. Dig those two "Fuck You" fingers shedding skin down to the knuckle.

Pete stabbed the chair. The blade ripped a trouser seam half an inch from Delsol's balls.

Delsol pulled the knife loose and dropped it on the floor. Pete said, "Well?"

"Well, I suppose I must tell you."

"Keep going, then. Don't make me work so hard."

Delsol smiled. Delsol was exhibiting fucking epic machismo. "You were right, Pedro. Giancana and Mr. Santo have abandoned La Causa."

"What about Carlos Marcello?"

"No. He is not with them. He is still enthusiastic."

"What about Heshie Ryskind?"

"He is not with them either. I have heard he is very ill."

"Santo is still backing the Cadre."

Delsol smirked. Blisters started bubbling up on his arms.

"I think he will withdraw his support soon. I am certain it will happen."

Pete chained cigarettes. "Who else has betrayed the Cadre?"

"I do not consider what I did betrayal. The man you used to be would not consider it that, either."

Pete flipped his cigarette in the sink. "Just answer my questions. I don't want to hear your extraneous comments."

Delsol said, "All right. I am the only one in this."

" 'This'?"

Delsol shivered. A big blister on his neck popped and spritzed blood.

"Yes. This is what you thought it was."

"Explain it for me, then."

Delsol stared at his hands. "I mean that Mr. Santo and the others have gone over to Fidel. They are just pretending enthusiasm for La Causa, to impress Robert Kennedy and other powerful officials. They are hoping Kennedy will learn about their support and not try to hurt them so hard. Raúl Castro is selling them heroin very cheaply. In exchange, they have given him information on the exile movement."

Heroin was MONEY. His theory was confirmed straight down the line.

"Keep going. I know there's more."

Delsol did a little blank-face number. Pete stared at him. Pete held the stare and held it and held it—

Delsol blinked. "Yes, there is more. Raúl is trying to convince Fidel to let Mr. Santo and the others reopen their casinos in Havana. Mr. Santo and Mr. Sam promised they would inform Raúl on the progress at JM/Wave and try to warn them of any assassination attempts on Fidel."

More confirmation. More potential grief. Santo and Sam could force Boyd to disband his hit squad.

Delsol examined his arms. His tattoos were scorched into odd smudges.

Pete said, "There's more."

"No. There isn't."

Pete sighed. "There's your part. You were recruited because the pro-Castro guys knew the Cadre killed your cousin, and they figured you were vulnerable. You've got a part in this, and it's got something to do with heroin, and if you don't tell me, I'm going to start hurting you again."

"Pedro . . ."

Pete squatted in front of the chair. Pete said, *"Heroin. Tell me about it."*

Delsol crossed himself. The ice-cube bowl slipped to the floor and shattered.

"A Cuban shipment is coming in by speedboat. Two hundred pounds of it, uncut. Some pro-Castro men will be there to guard it. I am supposed to transmit it to Mr. Santo."

"When?"

"The night of May 4th."

"Where?"

"The Gulf Coast in Alabama. A place called Orange Beach."

Pete got the shakes. Delsol caught his fear instantaneously.

"We must pretend this never happened, Pedro. You yourself must pretend that you never really believed in the Cause. We must not interfere with men who are so much more powerful than we are."

Boyd took it cool. Pete steamed up the phone booth yelling.

"We can still make our casino deal happen. We can send in

your team, have them clip Castro and create fucking chaos. Maybe things work out and Santo honors our deal, maybe they don't work out. At the very fucking least, we can snuff Fidel Castro."

Boyd said, "No. The deal is dead and the Cadre is finished, and sending in my men precipitously will only get them killed."

Pete kicked the door off its hinges—

"What do you mean, 'NO'?"

"I mean we should recoup our losses. We should make some money before somebody tells Bobby about the Outfit and the Agency."

The door crashed across the sidewalk. Pedestrians stepped around it. A little kid jumped on it and cracked the glass in half.

"The heroin?"

Boyd was calm. "There's two hundred pounds, Pete. We let it sit for five years and sell it overseas. You, me and Néstor. We'll make at least three million dollars apiece."

Pete went lightheaded. Dig it: that 9.9 earthquake is strictly internal.

DOCUMENT INSERT: 4/25/62.
Carlyle Hotel bedroom microphone transcript.
Transcribed by: Fred Turentine. Tape/written copies
to: P. Bondurant, W. Littell.

BJ phoned the listening post at 3:08 P.M. She said she was meeting the target ''for dinner'' at 5:00. She was instructed to double open & shut the bedroom door to activate the mike. Active feed from 5:23 P.M. on.
Initial log: BJ—Barb Jahelka. JFK— John F. Kennedy.
    5:24-5:33: sexual activity. (See tape transcript. High sound quality. Voices discernible.)
    5:34-5:41: conversation.
JFK: Shit, my back.
BJ: Let me help.
JFK: No, that's all right.
BJ: Stop looking at your watch. We just finished.
JFK (laughing): I really should have that wall clock installed.
BJ: And tell the chef to get with it. That was a lousy club sandwich.

JFK: It was. The turkey was dry and the bacon was soggy.

BJ: You seem distracted, Jack.

JFK: Smart girl.

BJ: The weight of the world?

JFK: No, my brother. He's on the warpath about my friends and the women I see, and he's acting like a colossal pain in the ass.

BJ: For instance?

JFK: He's on a witch hunt. Frank Sinatra knows some gangsters, so Frank had to go. The women Peter sets me up with are gonorrhea carrying tarts, and you're too polished and aware of your effects to be a Twist bunny, so you're suspect on general principles.

BJ (laughing): What's next? Can I expect to see FBI men following me?

JFK (laughing): Hardly. Bobby and Hoover hate each other too much to collaborate on anything that touchy. Bobby's over-worked, so he's touchy, and Hoover's touchy because he's a Nazi faggot who hates all men with normal appetites. Bobby's running Justice, chasing gangsters and running point for my Cuban policy. He's up to his neck in psychopathic lowlife, and Hoover fights him on protocol matters every inch of the way. And I'm the one who takes the brunt of his frustration. Say, why don't we change jobs? You be the President of the United States and I'll Twist at, what's the name of that place you're appearing?

BJ: Del's Den in Stamford, Connecticut.

JFK: Right. What do you say, Barb? Shall we switch jobs?

BJ: It's a deal. And after I take over, I'll fire J. Edgar Hoover and order Bobby to take a vacation.

JFK: You're thinking like a Kennedy now.

BJ: How so?

JFK: I'm going to let Bobby be the one to give Hoover the sack.

BJ: Stop looking at your watch.

JFK: You should hide it from me next time.

BJ: I will.

JFK: I have to go. Hand me my trousers, will you?

BJ: They're wrinkled.

JFK: It's your fault.

Single door slam deactivates mike. Transcript close: 5:42 P.M., April 24, 1962.

DOCUMENT INSERTS: 4/25/62, 4/26/62, 5/1/62. Top Hoodlum Program wiretap outtakes: Los Angeles, Chicago and Newark venues. Marked: CONFIDENTIAL/TOP SECRET/DIRECTOR'S EYES ONLY.

Los Angeles, 4/25/62. Placement: Rick-Rack Restaurant Pay phone. Number dialed: MA2-4691. (Pay phone at Mike Lyman's Restaurant.) Caller: Steven ''Steve the Skeev'' De Santis. (See THP File #814.5, Los Angeles Office.) Person called: unknown male (''Billy''). Six minutes and four seconds of non-applicable conversation precedes the following.

SDS: And Frank shot his big fucking mouth off and Mo believed him. Jack's my boy, blah, blah. Jewboy Lenny told me he stuffed half the fucking ballot boxes in Cook County.

UM: You say Frank like you know the man personal.

SDS: I do, you fuck. I met him backstage at the Dunes Hotel once.

UM: Sinatra's a hump. He walks Outfit and talks Outfit, but he's really just a stupe from Hoboken, New Jersey.

SDS: He's a stupe who should pay, Billy.

UM: He should. Every time that rat prick Bobby comes down on the Outfit, Frankie should take a shot to the nuts. He should pay double for what that cunt Bobby's doing to Jimmy and the Teamsters, and triple for that stroll through Guatemala Uncle Carlos had to take.

SDS: The Kennedys should pay.

UM: In the best of all worlds they would.

SDS: They got no sense of fucking gratitude.

UM: They got no sense, period. I mean, Joe Kennedy and Raymond Patriarca go way back.

SDS: No sense.

UM: No fucking sense.
Non-applicable conversation follows.

Chicago, 4/26/62. Placement: <u>North Side Elks Club pay phone</u>. Number dialed: BL4-0808 (pay phone at <u>Saparito's Trattoria Restaurant</u>). Caller: Dewey ''The Duck'' Di Pasquale. (See THP file #709.9, Chicago Office.) Person called: Pietro ''Pete Sap'' Saparito. Four minutes and twenty-nine seconds of non-applicable conversation precedes the following.

DDP: What's worse than the clap and the syph is the Kennedys. They are trying to grind the Outfit into duck shit. Bobby's got these racket squads set up all over the country. These are cocksuckers who can't be bought for love or money.

PS: Jack Kennedy ate at my restaurant once. I should have poisoned the cocksucker.

DDP: Quack, quack. You should have.

PS: Don't start that duck routine with me, you hump.

DDP: You should invite Jack and Bobby and his racket squad guys to your place and poison them all.

PS: I should. Hey, you know my waitress, Deeleen?

DDP: Sure. I heard she plays skin clarinet with the best.

PS: She does. And she banged Jack Kennedy. She said he had this little piccolo dick.

DDP: The Irish ain't hung for shit. It's a well-known fact.

PS: Italian men have the biggest.

DDP: And the best.

PS: I heard Mo's hung like a mule.

DDP: Who told you?

PS: Mo himself.

Non-applicable conversation follows.

Newark, 5/1/62. Placement: <u>Lou's Lucky Lounge pay phone</u>. Number dialed: MU6-9441 (pay phone at <u>Reuben's Delicatessen</u>, New York City). Caller: Herschel ''Heshie'' Ryskind (See THP file #887.8, Dallas Office). Person called: Morris Milton Weinshank (See

THP file #400.5, New York City Office). Three minutes
and one second of non-applicable conversation
precedes the following.

MMW: We're all sorry you're sick, Hesh. We're all
pulling for you and praying for you.

HR: I want to live long enough to see Sam G. kick
Sinatra's skinny bantamweight tuchus from here to
Palermo. Sinatra and some CIA shitheel convinced
Sam and Santo that Jack the K. was kosher. Use your
noggin and think, Morris. Think about Ike and Harry
Truman and FDR. Did they give us grief like this?

MMW: They did not.

HR: I know it's Bobby and not Jack that's the
instigator. But Jack knows the rules. Jack knows you
can't sic your rabid dogs on people who did you
favors.

MMW: Sam thought Frank had pull with the brothers.
He thought he could get Jack to call Bobby off.

HR: Frank was dreaming. The only pull Frank's got
is with his putz. All Frank and that CIA guy Boyd want
to do is suck the big Kennedy cock.

MMW: Jack and Bobby got nice hair.

HR: Which somebody should part with a forty-five
caliber dum-dum.

MMW: Such hair. I should have such hair.

HR: You want hair? Buy a fucking wig.

Non-applicable conversation follows.

DOCUMENT INSERT: 5/1/62.
Personal note: Howard Hughes to J. Edgar Hoover.

Dear Edgar,

   Duane Spurgeon, my chief aide and legal advisor, is
terminally ill. I need a replacement to go on retainer
immediately. Of course, I would prefer a morally-
sound lawyer with an FBI background. Could you
recommend a man?

                                    All best, Howard

78

(Washington, D.C., 5/2/62)

THEIR BENCH FACED the Lincoln Memorial. Nannies and small children scampered by.

Hoover said, "The woman is quite good."

"Thank you, Sir."

"She lures King Jack into provocative traps."

Littell smiled. "Yes, Sir. She does."

"King Jack has mentioned my forced retirement twice. Did you tell the woman to prod him in that direction?"

"Yes, Sir. I did."

"Why?"

"I wanted to increase your stake in the operation."

Hoover straightened the crease in his trousers. "I see. And I cannot fault your logic."

Littell said, "We want to convince the man to make his brother tone down his assault on my clients and their friends, and if they think you have copies of the tapes, it will go a long way toward convincing them to retain you."

Hoover nodded. "I cannot fault your logic."

"I would rather not go public with the tapes, Sir. I would rather see this resolved behind the scenes."

Hoover patted his briefcase. "Is that why you asked me to return my copies temporarily?"

"Yes, Sir."

"You don't trust me to keep them in cold storage?"

Littell smiled. "I want you to possess absolute deniability should Robert Kennedy bring in outside agency investigators. I want all the tapes kept in a single location, so that they can be destroyed if necessary."

Hoover smiled. "And so that, if worse comes to worse, Pete Bondurant and Fred Turentine can be portrayed as the sole perpetrators of the plot?"

Littell said, "Yes, Sir."

Hoover shooed a perching bird away. "Who's financing this? Is it Mr. Hoffa or Mr. Marcello?"

"I'd rather not say, Sir."

"I see. And I cannot fault your desire for secrecy."

"Thank you, Sir."

"Suppose public exposure becomes necessary?"

"Then I would go forward in late October, right before the congressional elections."

"Yes. That would be the optimum time."

"Yes, Sir. But as I said, I would rather not—"

"You needn't repeat yourself. I'm not senile."

The sun broke out of a cloud bank. Littell broke a slight sweat.

"Yes, Sir."

"You hate them, don't you?"

"Yes, I do."

"You're not alone. The THP has private taps and bugs installed in fourteen critical organized crime locales. We've been picking up a good deal of Kennedy resentment. I haven't informed the Brothers, and I'm not going to."

"I'm not surprised, Sir."

"I've compiled some wonderfully vituperative outtakes. They are hilariously colloquial and profane."

"Yes, Sir."

Hoover smiled. "Tell me what you're thinking."

Littell smiled. "That you trust me. That you trust me because I hate them as much as you do."

Hoover said, "You're correct. And my God, wouldn't Kemper be hurt if he overheard King Jack's assessment of his character?"

"He would be. Thank God he has no idea this operation exists."

A little girl skipped by. Hoover smiled and waved.

"Howard Hughes needs a new right-hand man. He asked me to find him someone with your qualifications, and I've recommended you."

Littell grabbed the bench. "I'm honored, Sir."

"You should be. You should also know that Howard Hughes is a very disturbed man with a rather tenuous hold on reality. He only communicates by telephone and letter, and I think there's a fair chance that you may never meet him face-to-face."

The bench shook. Littell folded his hands over one knee.

"Should I call him?"

"He'll call you, and I would advise you to accept his offer. The man has a silly, if exploitable, plan to purchase Las Vegas hotel-casinos a few years from now, and I think the notion has intelligence-gathering potential. I told Howard the names of your other clients, and he was quite impressed. I think the job is yours for the asking."

Littell said, "I want it."

Hoover said, "Of course you do. You've been hungry all your life, and you've finally reconciled your desires with your conscience."

79

(Orange Beach, 5/4/62)

THEY HAD 3:00 A.M. moonlight to work by. It was half a curse—*total* dark meant SURPRISE.

Pete pulled off the blacktop. He saw sand dunes up ahead—big high ones.

Néstor draped his legs across Wilfredo Delsol. Wilfredo the Mummy was duct-taped head to toe and stuffed between the front and back seats.

Boyd rode shotgun. Delsol wheezed through his nose. They kidnapped him at his pad on their way out of Miami.

Pete shifted to four-wheel drive. The Mummy lurched and banged Néstor's legs.

The jeep bounced between dunes. Boyd examined their track obfuscator—rake prongs attached to metal tubing.

Néstor coughed. "The beach is half a mile. I walked it twice."

Pete braked and cut the engine. Wave noise came on strong. Boyd said, "Listen to that. If we're lucky, they won't hear us."

They got out. Néstor dug a hole and buried Delsol in sand up to his nose.

Pete tossed a tarp over the jeep. It was light tan and sand-dune compatible.

Néstor rigged the rake gizmo. Boyd inventoried hardware.

They had silencer-fitted .45s and machine guns. They had a chainsaw, a clock bomb and two pounds of plastic explosive.

They slapped on lampblack. They loaded up their packs.

They walked. Néstor dragged the rake. Tire tracks and footprints disappeared.

They crossed the blacktop and hiked up to a parallel access road—about a third of a mile. The road-to-waveline sand strip was roughly two hundred yards wide.

Néstor said, "The State Police never patrol here."

Pete held up his infrareds. He spotted clumps 300 yards down the strip.

Boyd said, "Let's get close."

Pete stretched—his bulletproof vest fit tight. "There's nine or ten men just above the west sand. We should come up along the shoreline and hope the goddamn surf noise covers us."

Néstor crossed himself. Boyd filled his hands and his mouth— with two .45s and a Buck knife.

Pete felt earthquake tremors—9.999-fucking-9.

They walked down to the wet sand. They hunkered low and crab-crawled. Pete got this wild-ass notion: I'M THE ONLY ONE WHO KNOWS WHAT THIS MEANS.

Boyd walked point. The shapes took form. Smashing waves supplied audial cover.

The shapes were sleeping men. One insomniac was sitting up—check that glowing cigarette tip.

They got close.

They got closer.

They got very very close.

Pete heard snores. A man moaned in Spanish.

They charged.

Boyd shot the cigarette man. Muzzle flash lit a line of sleeping bags.

Pete fired. Néstor fired. Silencer thuds overlapped.

They had good light now—powder glare off four weapons.

Goose down exploded. Screams kicked in loud and faded into tight little gurgles.

Néstor brought a flashlight in close. Pete saw nine U.S. Army bags, shredded and blood soaked.

Boyd popped in fresh clips and shot the men point-blank in the face. Blood hit Néstor's flashlight and shaded the beam light red.

Pete heaved for breath. Bloody feathers blew into his mouth.

Néstor kept the light steady. Boyd knelt down and slit throats. He went in deep and low—windpipes and spinal cords snapped.

Néstor dragged the bodies out.

Pete turned the sleeping bags over and stuffed them with sand.

Boyd patted them into shape. It was good simulation—the boat men would see dozing men.

Néstor dragged the bodies down to a tide pool. Boyd brought the chainsaw.

Pete yank-started it. Boyd spread the stiffs out for cutting.

The moon passed by low. Néstor supplied extra light.

Pete sawed from a crouch. The teeth caught on a leg bone straight off.

Néstor pulled the man's foot taut. The teeth whirred through easy.

Pete sawed through a string of arms. The saw kept bucking into the sand. Skin and gristle pop-pop-popped in his face.

Pete quartered the men. Boyd severed their heads with his Buck knife. One swipe and one tug at the hair did the job.

Nobody talked.

Pete kept sawing. His arms ached. Bone fragments made the belt-motor skip.

His hands slipped. The teeth jumped and raked a dead man's stomach.

Pete smelled bile. He dropped the saw and puked himself dry.

Boyd took over. Néstor fed body parts to the tide pool. Sharks thrashed in to eat.

Pete walked down to the surf line. His hands shook—lighting a cigarette took forever.

The smoke felt good. The smoke killed the bad smells. DON'T THEY KNOW WHAT THIS MEANS—

The sawing stopped. Dead silence underscored his own crazy heartbeat.

Pete walked back to the tide pool. Sharks flailed and leaped halfway out of the water.

Néstor loaded the machine guns. Boyd twitched and fidgeted—high-pitched by Boyd cool-cat standards.

They crouched behind a shoal bank. Nobody talked. Pete got Barb on the brain wicked good.

Dawn hit just past 5:30. The beach looked plain peaceful. The blood by the sleeping bags looked like plain old wave seepage.

Néstor kept his binoculars up. He got a sighting at 6:12 A.M.

"I see the boat. It's about two hundred yards away."

Boyd coughed and spat. "Delsol said six men would be aboard. We want most of them off before we fire."

Pete heard motor hum. "It's getting close. Néstor, you get down there."

Néstor ran over and crouched by the sleeping bags. The hum

built to a roar. A speedboat bucked waves and fishtailed up on shore.

It was a rat-trap double outboard, with no lower compartment.

Néstor waved. Néstor yelled, *"Bienvenidos! Viva Fidel!"*

Three men hopped off the boat. Three men stayed on. Pete signaled Kemper: ON for you/OFF for me.

Boyd threw a burst at the boat. The windshield exploded and blew the men back against the motors. Pete gunned his men down with one tight strafe.

Néstor walked up to them. He spit in their faces and capped them with shots in the mouth.

Pete ran up and vaulted onto the boat. Boyd circled around to the outboards and finished his three with single head pops.

The heroin was triple-wrapped and stuffed in duffel bags. The sheer weight was astonishing.

Néstor slapped the plastic explosive next to the outboards. The bomb clock was set for 7:15.

Pete off-loaded the dope.

Néstor tossed the sleeping bags and his three dead men on board.

Boyd scalped them. Néstor said, "This is for Playa Girón."

Pete rope-tied the wheel to the helm bracings and turned the boat around. The compass read south-southeast. The boat would stay on course—barring gale winds and tidal waves.

Boyd hit the motors. Both blades caught on his first pull. They jumped off the sides and watched the boat skid off.

It would explode twenty miles out to sea.

Pete shivered. Boyd tucked the scalps into his pack. Orange Beach looked absolutely pristine.

Santo Junior would call. He'd say, Delsol fucked me on a deal. He'd say, Pete, you find that cocksucker.

Santo would omit details. He wouldn't say the deal was Commie-linked and a direct betrayal of the Cadre.

Pete waited for the call at Tiger Kab. He took over the switchboard—Delsol never showed up for work.

Cab calls were backlogged. Drivers kept saying, Where's Wilfredo?

He's at a hideout pad. Néstor's guarding him. There's a pound of Big "H" in plain sight.

Boyd drove the rest of the dope to Mississippi. Boyd was stretched a wee bit thin, like he crossed some line with killing.

Pete felt the real line. DON'T YOU KNOW WHO WE FUCKED?

They'd watchdogged Delsol for two weeks running. He didn't betray them. The dope rendezvous would have been canceled if he did.

He's at his fake hideout. He's an instant junkie—Néstor shot tracks up his arms. He's zorched on horse—waiting for this god-damn phone call.

It was 4:30 P.M. They split Orange Beach nine and a half hours ago.

Cab calls came in. The phones rang every few seconds. They had pickups backlogged and twelve cabs out—Pete felt like screaming or putting a gun to his head.

Teo Paez cupped his desk phone. "Line two, Pete. It's Mr. Santo."

Pete picked up casual slow. "Hi, Boss."

Santo said the words. Santo came through right on cue.

"Wilfredo Delsol fucked me. He's hiding out, and I want you to find him."

"What did he do?"

"Don't ask questions. Just find him and do it right now."

Néstor let him in. He'd turned the living room into an instant junkie pigsty.

Dig the syringe in plain view. Dig the candy bars mashed into the carpet. Dig that white powder residue on every flat cutting surface.

Dig Wilfredo Olmos Delsol: dope-swacked on a plush-velour couch.

Pete shot him in the head. Néstor chopped off three of his fingers and dropped them in an ashtray.

It was 5:20. Santo wouldn't buy a one-hour search-and-find. They had time to reinforce the lie.

Néstor split—Boyd had work for him back in Mississippi. Pete tamped down his nerves with deep breaths and a dozen cigarettes.

He visualized it. He got the details straight in his head. He put his gloves on and did it.

He dumped the icebox.

He slashed the couch down to the springs.

He ripped the living-room walls out in a mock dope-search frenzy.

He burned cooking spoons.

He formed heroin into snort lines on a glass-topped coffee table.

He found a discarded lipstick and smeared it on some filter-tip butts.

He slashed Delsol with a kitchen knife. He scorched his balls with a wood-burning tool he found in the bedroom.

He dipped his hands in Delsol's blood and wrote "Traitor" on the living-room wall.

It was 8:40 P.M.

Pete ran down to a pay phone. Real live fear juked his performance.

Delsol's dead—tortured—I got a tip on his hideout—he was strung-out—dope everywhere—somebody trashed the place—I think he was on a toot with some whores—Santo, tell me, what the fuck is this all about?

80

(Washington, D.C., 5/7/62)

LITTELL MADE BUSINESS calls. Mr. Hoover gave him a tap scrambler to insure that his calls stayed private.

He called Jimmy Hoffa at a pay phone. Jimmy was profoundly tap-phobic.

They discussed the Test Fleet taxi fraud case. Jimmy said, Let's bribe some jurors.

Littell said he'd send him a jury list. He told Hoffa to have front men make the bribe offers.

Jimmy said, What's shaking with the shakedown?

Littell reported, ALL SYSTEMS GO. Baby Jimmy said, Let's squeeze Jack now!!!

Littell said, Be patient. We'll squeeze him at the optimum time.

Jimmy threw a goodbye fit. Littell called Carlos Marcello in New Orleans.

They discussed his deportation case. Littell stressed the need for tactical delays.

"You beat the Federal government by frustrating them. You exhaust them and make them rotate attorneys on and off your case. You try their patience and resources, and stall the hell out of them."

Carlos got the point. Carlos asked a truly silly goodbye question.

"Can I get a tax deduction on my Cuban bag donations?"

Littell said, "Regretfully, no."

Carlos signed off. Littell called Pete in Miami.

He picked up on the first ring. "This is Bondurant."

"It's me, Pete."

"Yeah, Ward. I'm listening."

"Is something wrong? You sound agitated."

"Nothing's wrong. Is something wrong with our deal?"

"Nothing's wrong. I've been thinking of Lenny, though, and I keep thinking he's too close to Sam for my liking."

"You think he'd spill to Sam?"

"Not exactly. What I'm thinking is—"

Pete cut him off. "Don't tell me what you're thinking. You're running this show, so just tell me what you want."

Littell said, "Call Turentine. Have him fly out to L.A. and tap Lenny's phone as an added precaution. Barb's out there, too. She's appearing at a place in Hollywood called the Rabbit's Foot Club. Have Freddy check on her and see how she's holding up."

Pete said, "This sounds good to me. Besides, there's other things I don't want Sam to make Lenny do."

"What are you talking about?"

"Cuban stuff. You wouldn't be interested."

Littell checked his calendar. He saw writ-submission dates running straight into June.

"Call Freddy, Pete. Let's not sit on this."

"Maybe I'll meet him in L.A. I could use a change of scenery."

"Do it. And let me know when the tap's in."

"I will. See you, Ward."

Littell hung up. The scrambler blinked and broke off his line of thought.

Hoover accepted him now. Their courtly moments were over. Hoover reverted to his standard curt behavior.

Hoover expected him to beg.

Please reinstate Helen Agee in law school. Please let my leftist friend out of prison.

He'd never beg.

Pete was nervous. He had a hunch that Kemper Boyd forced Pete into things he couldn't control.

Boyd collected acolytes. Boyd felt at one with Cuban killers and poor Negroes. Kemper's gloss seduced Pete. The Cuban mess pushed them far beyond their ken.

Carlos said they cut a deal with Santo Trafficante. Their potential profit made Carlos laugh. He said Santo would never pay them that much money.

Carlos embraced the Cuban mess. Carlos said Sam and Santo wanted to cut their losses.

Net loss. Net gain. Profit potential.

He had the Fund books. He needed to clear a stretch of time and develop a strategy to exploit them.

Littell turned his chair around and looked out the window. Cherry blossoms brushed the glass—close enough to touch.

The phone rang. Littell tapped the speaker switch. "Yes?"

A man said, "This is Howard Hughes."

Littell almost giggled. Pete told these hilarious Dracula tales—

"This is Ward Littell, Mr. Hughes. And I'm very pleased to talk to you."

Hughes said, "You should be pleased. Mr. Hoover has shared your impeccable credentials with me, and I intend to offer you $200,000 a year for the privilege of entering my employ. I will not require you to move to Los Angeles, and we will communicate solely by letter and telephone. Your specific duties will be to handle the writ work in my painfully protracted TWA divestment suit, and to help me purchase Las Vegas hotel-casinos with the profits I expect to accrue when I finally divest TWA. Your Italian connections will prove invaluable in this regard, and I will expect you to ingratiate yourself with the Nevada State Legislature and help me devise a policy to insure that my hotels remain Negro- and germ-free—"

Littell listened.

Hughes continued.

Littell didn't even try to respond.

81

(Los Angeles, 5/10/62)

PETE HELD THE flashlight. Freddy replaced the dial housing. The work went down bite-your-nails nervous and slow.

Freddy fucked with some loose wires. "I hate Pacific Bell phones. I hate night jobs and working in the dark. I hate bedroom extensions, because the goddamn cords get tangled up behind the goddamn bed."

"Don't complain, just do it."

"My screwdriver keeps jamming. And are you *sure* Littell wants us to tap *both* extensions?"

Pete said, "*Just do it*. Two extensions and a pickup box outside. We'll stash it in those shrubs by the driveway. If you quit complaining, we can be out of here in twenty minutes."

Freddy gouged his thumb. "Fuck. I hate Pacific Bell phones. And Lenny don't have to use his home phones to rat us. He can rat us in person or rat us from a pay phone."

Pete gripped down on the flashlight. The beam wiggled and jumped.

"You fucking stop complaining, or I'll shove this fucking thing up your ass."

Freddy flinched and bumped a shelf. A *Hush-Hush* clipping file went flying.

"All right, all right. You been jumpy since you got off the airplane, so I'll only say it once. *Pacific Bell phones are the shits*. When you tap their lines, half the time the incoming callers can hear clicks. It's fucking unavoidable. And who's going to monitor the pickup box?"

Pete rubbed his eyes. He was nursing an on-and-off migraine since the night he killed Wilfredo Delsol.

"Littell can get some Feds to watch the box. We only need to check it every few days."

Freddy bent a lamp over the phone. "Go watch the door. I can't work with you standing over me."

Pete walked into the living room. His headache popped him right between the eyes.

He popped two aspirin. He washed them down with Lenny's cognac, straight from the bottle.

The stuff went down smooth. Pete knocked back a short refill.

His headache de-torqued. The veins above his eyes stopped pulsing.

Santo bought the charade so far. Santo never said *how* Delsol fucked him.

Santo said Sam G. got fucked, too. He didn't mention hijacked dope or fifteen dead men. He didn't say some big Outfit guys cozied up to Fidel Castro.

He said he had to cut the Cadre loose.

"Just for now, Pete. I've heard there's Federal pressure coming down. I want to extricate out of narcotics for a while."

The man just imported two hundred pounds of Big "H." The man was talking up extrication with a straight face.

Santo showed him a police report. The Miami fuzz bought the charade. They considered it one grisly dope killing—with assumed Cuban exile perpetrators.

Boyd and Néstor went back to Mississippi. The dope was stashed in forty safe-deposit boxes.

They resumed their Whack Castro training. They didn't care that the Outfit dug Fidel now. They didn't seem to know that there were men who could make them stop.

Their fear wasn't screwed on tight.

His was.

They didn't know you don't fuck with the Outfit.

He did.

He always sucked up to men with REAL power. He never broke the rules they set. He had to do what he did—but he didn't know WHY.

Santo swore vengeance. Santo said he'd find the dope thieves—whatever it cost, whatever it took.

Boyd thought they could sell the dope. Boyd was wrong. Boyd said *he'd* snitch the Mob-Agency links. Boyd said he could level out Bobby's rage.

He wouldn't do it. He couldn't do it. He'd never risk losing stature with the Kennedys.

Pete took another drink. His three shots killed a third of the bottle.

Freddy lugged his tools out. "Let's go. I'll drive you back to your hotel."

"You go. I want to take a walk."

"Where to?"

"I don't know."

* * *

The Rabbit's Foot Club was a hotbox—four walls trapping smoke and stale air. Underaged Twisters ruled the dance floor—a big liquor-law infraction.

Joey and the boys played half on-the-nod. Barb was singing some dippy wah-wah tune. A single sad-ass hooker sat at the bar.

Barb spotted him. She smiled and fumbled some lyrics.

The only half-private booth in the room was occupied. Two Marines and two high-school girls—ripe for eviction.

Pete told them to shove off. They caught his size and did it. The girls left their fruity rum drinks on the table.

Pete sat down and sipped at them. His headache leveled off a bit more. Barb closed with a weak "Twilight Time" cover.

A few Twisters clapped. The combo dispersed backstage. Barb walked straight over and joined him.

Pete slid close to her. Barb said, "I'm surprised. Ward said you were in Miami."

"I thought I'd come out and see how things were going."

"You mean you thought you'd check up on me?"

Pete shook his head. "Everybody thinks you're solid. Freddy Turentine and I came out to check on Lenny."

Barb said, "Lenny's in New York. He's visiting a friend."

"A woman named Laura Hughes?"

"I think so. Some rich woman with a place on Fifth Avenue."

Pete toyed with his lighter. "Laura Hughes is Jack Kennedy's half-sister. She used to be engaged to that man Kemper Boyd that Jack told you about. Boyd was Ward Littell's FBI mentor. My old girlfriend Gail Hendee slept with Jack on his honeymoon. Lenny gave Jack speech lessons back in '46."

Barb took one of Pete's cigarettes. "You're saying this is all too cozy for words."

Pete gave her a light. "I don't know what I'm saying."

Barb tossed her hair back. "Did Gail Hendee work gigs with you?"

"Yes."

"Divorce gigs?"

"That's right."

"Was she as good as me?"

"No."

"Were you jealous that she slept with Jack Kennedy?"

"Not until Jack fucked me personally."

"What are you saying?"

"That I had a personal stake in the Bay of Pigs."

Barb smiled. Bar light twinkled off her hair.

"Are you jealous of Jack and me?"

"If I hadn't heard the tapes I might have been."

"What are you saying?"

"That you're not giving him anything real."

Barb laughed. "This nice Secret Service man always drives me back to where I'm staying. We stopped for pizza last time."

"You're saying that's real?"

"Only compared to an hour with Jack."

The jukebox fired up. Pete reached over and pulled the plug.

Barb said, "You blackmailed Lenny into this."

"He's used to getting blackmailed."

"You're nervous. You're tapping your knee against the table, and you don't even know you're doing it."

Pete stopped. His fucking foot started twitching to compensate.

Barb said, "Does our thing scare you?"

Pete jammed his knees down steady. "It's something else."

"Sometimes I think you'll kill me when all this is over."

"We don't kill women."

"You killed a woman once. Lenny told me."

Pete flinched. "And you cozied up to Joey so he'd buy hits on those guys who raped your sister."

She didn't flinch. She didn't move. She didn't show a fucking ounce of fear.

"I should have known you'd be the one to care."

"What are you saying?"

"That I wanted to see if Jack cared enough to do the checking that you did."

Pete shrugged. "Jack's a busy man."

"So are you."

"Does it bug you that Johnny Coates is still alive?"

"Only when I think of Margaret. Only when I think that she'll never let a man touch her."

Pete felt the floor dip.

Barb said, "Tell me what you want."

Pete said, "I want you."

* * *

They took a room at the Hollywood-Roosevelt. The Grauman's Chinese marquee blipped their window.

Pete tripped out of his pants. Barb pulled off her Twist gown. Loose rhinestones hit the floor—Pete gouged his feet on them.

Barb kicked his holster under the bed. Pete pulled the covers down. The stale perfume stuck to the sheets made him sneeze.

She raised her arms and unhooked her necklace. He saw the white-powdered stubble where she shaved.

He pinned her wrists to the wall. She saw what he wanted and let him taste her there.

The taste stung. She flexed her arms so he could have it all.

He felt her nipples. He smelled the sweat dripping off her shoulders.

She pushed her breasts up to him. The big veins and big freckles looked like nothing he'd ever seen. He kissed them and bit them and pushed her into the wall with his mouth.

Her breath went crazy. Her pulse tapped his lips. He slid his hands down her legs and put a finger inside her.

She pushed him off. She stumbled to the bed and lay down crossways. He spread her legs and knelt on the floor between them.

He touched her stomach and her arms and her feet. He felt a pulse every place he touched. She had big veins all over, pulsing out of red hair and freckles.

He jammed his hips into the mattress. The movement got him so hard it hurt.

He tasted her hair. He felt the folds underneath it. He made her pulse go crazy with little bites and nuzzles.

She buckled and thrashed off his mouth. She made crazy funny sounds.

He came without her even touching him. He shook and sobbed and kept tasting her.

She spasmed. She bit through the sheets. She lulled and spasmed, lulled and spasmed, lulled and spasmed. Her back arched and slammed the mattress into the box springs.

He didn't want it to end. He didn't want to lose the taste of her.

82

(Meridian, 5/12/62)

THE AIR CONDITIONER short-circuited and died. Kemper woke up sweaty and congested.

He swallowed four Dexedrine. He started building lies immediately.

I didn't tell you about the links, because:

I didn't know myself. I didn't want Jack to get hurt. I only found out recently, and I thought it best to let sleeping dogs lie.

The Mob and the CIA?—it boggled my mind when I learned.

The lies felt weak. Bobby would investigate and trace his own links back to '59.

Bobby called last night. He said, "Meet me in Miami tomorrow. I want you to show me around JM/Wave."

Pete called from L.A. a few minutes later. He heard a woman humming a Twist tune in the background.

Pete said he just talked to Santo. Santo told him to hunt down the dope heisters.

"He said *find* them, Kemper. He said *don't kill them under any circumstances*. He didn't seem too concerned that I might find out the deal was Castro-financed."

Kemper told him to rig another forensic charade. Pete said, I'll fly to New Orleans and get started. Call me at the Olivier House Hotel or Guy Banister's office.

Kemper mixed a speedball and snorted it. The coke piggy-backed the Dexedrine straight to his head.

He heard cadence counts outside. Laurent pushed the Cubans through calisthenics every morning.

Flash and Juan came up to his chest. Néstor could fit in his knapsack.

Néstor shanked a redneck yesterday. All the man did was nick his fender. Néstor had the post-heist screaming mimis.

Néstor fled. The cracker survived. Flash said Néstor stole a speedboat and headed for Cuba.

Néstor left a note. It said, Save my share of the stuff. I'll be back when Castro's dead.

Kemper showered and shaved. His little pick-me-up had the razor jumping.

Lies wouldn't come.

* * *

Bobby wore dark glasses and a hat. Kemper convinced him to tour JM/Wave incognito.

The AG with shades and a stingy-brim fedora. The AG as Rat Pack reject.

They strolled the facility. Bobby's getup inspired odd looks. Contract men walked by and waved hello.

Lies wouldn't come.

They toured at a leisurely pace. Bobby kept his famous voice to a whisper. A few Cubans recognized him and played along with the ruse.

Kemper showcased the Propaganda Section. A case officer rattled off statistics. Nobody said, Jack Kennedy is a vacillating sob sister.

Nobody dropped Mob names. Nobody dropped hints that they knew Kemper Boyd before the Bay of Pigs invasion.

Bobby liked the air recon plans. The communications room impressed him.

Lies wouldn't come. Details wouldn't mesh with any degree of verisimilitude.

They toured the Map Section. Chuck Rogers walked up, hale-hearty. Kemper steered Bobby away from him.

Bobby used the men's room and stormed out in a huff. Somebody scrawled anti-Kennedy remarks above the urinals.

They walked over to the Miami U cafeteria. Bobby bought them coffee and sweet rolls.

College kids carried trays past their table. Kemper forced himself not to fidget—the Dexedrine was surging especially strong.

Bobby cleared his throat. "Say what you've been thinking."

"What?"

"Say that coastal harassment and intelligence gathering aren't enough. Tell me we need to assassinate Fidel Castro for the three hundredth time and get it out of your system."

Kemper smiled. "We need to assassinate Fidel Castro. And I'll memorize your response, so you won't have to say it again."

Bobby said, "You know my response. I hate redundancy, and I hate this hat. How does Sinatra manage it?"

"He's Italian."

Bobby pointed to some coeds in short shorts. "Don't they have a dress code here?"

"The code is as little as possible."

"I should tell Jack. He could address the student body."

Kemper laughed. "I'm glad to see that you've become more accepting."

"More discerning, maybe."

"And more specifically disapproving?"

"Touché."

Kemper sipped coffee. "Who's the man been seeing?"

"Some fluff. And a Twist performer Lenny Sands introduced him to."

"Who isn't fluff?"

"Let's say she's mentally overqualified for some cheap dance craze."

"You've met her?"

Bobby nodded. "Lenny brought her to Peter Lawford's house in Los Angeles. I got the impression that she thinks a few steps ahead of most people, and Jack always calls me from the Carlyle to say how smart she is, which is not what Jack usually comments on in a woman."

Lenny, the Twist, L.A.—a puzzling little triad.

"What's her name?"

"Barb Jahelka. Jack was on the phone with her this morning. He said he called her at 5:00 A.M. L.A. time, and she still managed to come off smart and funny."

Pete called from L.A. last night. A woman was humming "Let's Twist Again."

"What is it about her that you disapprove of?"

"Probably just the fact that she doesn't behave like most of Jack's quickies."

Pete was a shakedown man. Lenny was an L.A. show-biz reptile.

"Do you think she's dangerous in some way?"

"Not exactly. I'm just suspicious because I'm the attorney general of the United States, and suspiciousness goes with the job. Why do you care? We've given this woman two minutes more than she deserves."

Kemper crumpled his coffee cup. "I was just steering talk away from Fidel."

Bobby laughed. "Good. And no, you and our exile friends cannot assassinate him."

Kemper stood up. "Do you want to look around some more?"

"No. I've got a car picking me up. Do you want a lift to the airport?"

"No. I have to make some phone calls."

Bobby took off his shades. A coed recognized him and squealed.

Kemper commandeered a vacant JM/Wave office. The switchboard put him through to LAPD R&I direct.

A man picked up. "Records and Information. Officer Graham."

"Dennis Payne, please. Tell him it's Kemper Boyd, long distance."

"Hold on, please."

Kemper scribbled up a scratch pad. Payne came on the line posthaste.

"Mr. Boyd, how are you?"

"I'm fine, Sergeant. You?"

"Fair to middling. And I'll bet you have a request to make."

"I do. I need you to check for a rap sheet on a white female named Barbara Jahelka, probable spelling J-A-H-E-L-K-A. She's probably twenty-two to thirty-two, and I think she lives in Los Angeles. I also need you to check for an unlisted number. The name is either Lenny Sands or Leonard J. Seidelwitz, and it's probably a West Hollywood listing."

Payne said, "I copy. You hold, okay? This might take a few minutes."

Kemper held. His pick-me-up was inducing mild palpitations.

Pete didn't state his L.A. business. Lenny was extortable and bribable.

Payne came back on the line. "Mr. Boyd? We've got two positives."

Kemper grabbed a pen. "Keep going."

"The Sands number is OL5-3980, and I got a felony marijuana possession on the girl. She's the only Barbara Jahelka in our files, and her DOB matches up to what you told me."

"Disposition?"

"She was arrested in July '57. She did six months and topped out two years of summary probation."

It was inconclusive information.

"Would you check for something more recent? FI cards or arrests that didn't go to arraignment?"

Payne said, "Will do. I'll check with the Sheriff's and our other local municipals, too. If the girl's been in trouble since '57, we'll know."

"Thanks, Sergeant. I appreciate it."

"Give me an hour, Mr. Boyd. I should have something or nothing by then."

Kemper disconnected. The switchboard patched him in to Lenny's L.A. number.

It rang three times. Kemper heard faint tap clicks and hung up.

Pete was a shakedown man. Pete was a bug/tap man. Pete's bug/tap partner was the celebrated Fred Turentine.

Freddy's brother owned a TV repair shop in L.A. Freddy worked there between wire jobs.

Kemper called Los Angeles information. An operator gave him the number. He fed it to the JM/Wave switchboard and told the girl to put him through.

The line hissed and crackled. A man picked up on the first ring. "Turentine's TV. Good morning."

Kemper faked a lowlife growl. "Is Freddy there? This is Ed. I'm friends with Freddy and Pete Bondurant."

The man coughed. "Freddy's in New York. He was here a few days ago, but he went back."

"Shit. I need to send him something. Did he leave an address?"

"Yeah, he did. Wait ... let's see ... yeah, it's 94 East 76th Street, New York City. The number's MU6-0197."

Kemper said, "Thanks. I appreciate it."

The man coughed. "Tell Freddy hi. Tell him his big brother says to stay out of trouble."

Kemper hung up. The office tilted in and out of focus.

Turentine was lodged near 76th and Madison. The Carlyle Hotel was on the northeast corner.

Kemper dialed the switchboard and gave the girl Lenny's number one more time.

She reconnected him. He heard three rings and three tiny tap clicks.

A woman answered. "Mr. Sands' residence."

"Is this Mr. Sands' service?"

"Yes, sir. And Mr. Sands can be reached in New York City. The number is MU6-2433."

Laura's number.

Kemper disconnected and redialed the switchboard. The girl said, "Yes, Mr. Boyd."

"Get me New York City, please. The number is MU6-0197."

"Please hang up, sir. All my circuits are busy, but I'll put your call through in a second."

Kemper leaned on the cutoff button. The pieces fit—circumstantially, instinctively—

The phone rang. He jerked the receiver up.

"Yes?"

"What do you mean, 'Yes?'? The operator placed *your* call to *me*."

Kemper wiped a line of sweat off his forehead. "That's right, she did. Is this Fred Turentine?"

"That's right."

"This is Kemper Boyd. I work with Pete Bondurant."

Silence stretched a solid beat too long.

"So you're looking for Pete?"

"That's right."

"Well . . . Pete's in New Orleans."

"That's right. I forgot."

"Well . . . why'd you think he'd be here?"

"It was just a hunch."

"Hunch, shit. Pete said he wasn't giving out this number."

"Your brother gave it to me."

"Well . . . shit . . . he wasn't supposed—"

"Thanks, Fred. I'll call Pete in New Orleans."

The line went dead. Turentine hung up dead finessed and dead scared.

Kemper watched the second hand circle his watch. His shirt sleeves were soaked clear through.

Pete would do it. Pete wouldn't do it. Pete was his longtime partner, which constituted proof of—

Nothing.

Business was business. Jack got between them. Call it the Triangle Twist: Jack, Pete and Barb what's-her-name.

Kemper dialed the switchboard. The operator redialed the LAPD.

Payne answered. "Records and Information."

"It's Kemper Boyd, Sergeant."

Payne laughed. "And an hour to the second."

"Did you find out anything else?"

"Yeah, I did. Beverly Hills PD arrested the Jahelka girl for extortion in August 1960."

Jesus God—

"Details?"

"The girl and her ex-husband tried to shake down Rock Hudson with some sex pictures."

"Of Hudson and the girl?"

"That's correct. They demanded some money, but Hudson went to the police. The girl and her ex were arrested, but Hudson retracted the charges."

Kemper said, "It stinks."

Payne said, "To high heaven. A friend of mine on the BHPD said the whole thing was some sort of ploy to establish Hudson as a pussy hound, when he's really some kind of homo. He heard a rumor that *Hush-Hush* was behind the whole thing."

Kemper put the phone down. His little palpitations almost cut his breath off.

LENNY—

He caught a 1:45 connector to La Guardia. He popped four Dexedrine and chased them with two in-flight martinis.

The flight took three and a half hours. Kemper shredded cocktail napkins and checked his watch every few minutes.

They landed on time. Kemper caught a cab outside the terminal. He told the driver to cruise by the Carlyle and drop him at 64th and Fifth.

Rush-hour traffic crawled. The Carlyle run ate up an hour.

94 East 76th Street was fifty yards from the hotel. It was an ideal apartment/listening-post location.

The cabbie swung south and dropped him outside Laura's building. The doorman was busy with a tenant.

Kemper ran into the lobby. An old lady held the elevator for him.

He hit "12." The old lady backed away. He saw his gun in his hand and tried to remember unholstering it.

He tucked it in his waistband. The old lady hid behind a huge handbag. The ride up took forever.

The door opened. Laura had redecorated the foyer—a complete French Provincial makeover.

Kemper walked through it. The elevator zoomed up behind him. He heard laughter on the terrace.

He ran toward the sound. Throw rugs snagged under his feet. He took the last hallway at a sprint and knocked over two lamps and an end table.

They were standing. They were holding drinks and cigarettes. They looked like they weren't quite breathing.

Laura, Lenny and Claire.

They looked funny. They looked like they didn't quite know him.

He saw his gun out. He saw the trigger at half-pull.

He said something about shaking down Jack Kennedy.

Claire said "Dad?" like she wasn't quite sure.

He aimed at Lenny.

Claire said, "Dad, please."

Laura dropped her cigarette. Lenny flicked his cigarette at him and smiled.

The tip burned his face. Ashes singed his suitcoat. He steadied his aim and pulled the trigger.

The gun jammed.

Lenny smiled.

Laura screamed.

Claire's scream made him turn tail and run.

83

(New Orleans, 5/12/62)

BULLSHIT FLOWED BILATERAL. Banister's office was submerged in right-wing rebop.

Guy said the Klan bombed some churches. Pete said Heshie Ryskind had cancer.

Boyd's Clip Castro Team was all-time elite. Dougie Frank Lockhart was one elite gun runner.

Pete said Wilfredo Delsol fucked Santo Junior on a dope deal. The fucker got fucked back by fucker or fuckers unknown.

Banister sipped bourbon. Pete goosed the charade along. Say, Guy, what have *you* heard about this?

Guy said he heard bupkis. No shit, Sherlock—this line of talk is all shuck and jive.

Pete sprawled in a chair and played with a tall Jack Daniel's. He took little medicinal sips for migraine relief.

New Orleans was hot. The office sucked in heat. Guy sat behind his desk and peeled sweat off his forehead with a switchblade.

Pete kept drifting back to Barb. He couldn't hold a non–Barb line of thought for more than six seconds.

The phone rang. Banister dug through desk debris and caught it.

"Yeah? . . . Yeah, he's here. Hold on a second."

Pete stood up and snagged the phone off the desk. "Who's this?"

"It's Fred. And don't you fucking lose your temper for what I'm gonna tell you."

"You just calm down, then."

"You can't calm down when you got a fucking concussion. You can't calm down—"

Pete walked the phone to the far end of the office. The cord stretched taut.

"Calm down, Freddy. Just tell me what happened."

Freddy caught his breath. "Okay. Kemper Boyd called the post this morning. He said he was looking for you, but I knew he was lying. Now, he came by—in person—an hour ago. He knocked on the door looking like a crazy man. I didn't let him in, and I saw him practically knock down an old lady and get into this cab she was getting out of."

The phone cord almost snapped. Pete stepped back and cut it some slack.

"And that's it?"

"Fuck no!"

"Freddy, what are you say—"

"I'm saying Lenny Sands came by a few minutes later. I let him in because I figured he knew what Boyd was up to. He brained me with a chair and sacked the place. He stole all the tapes and written transcripts and took off. I woke up after, shit—I don't know, half an hour. I went by the Carlyle and saw all these police cars out front. Pete, Pete, Pete—"

His legs dipped. The wall caught him.

"Pete, it was Lenny. He kicked the door in and trashed the Kennedy suite. He pulled out the microphones, and fucking escaped out a fire door. Pete, Pete, Pete—

"Pete, we're fucked—

"Pete, it had to be Lenny—

"Pete, I wiped down the post and moved out all my equipment and—"

The connection died—Pete twitched and jerked the cord out of the wall.

Boyd knew he was in New Orleans. Boyd would catch the first available flight down.

The gig was burned. Boyd and Lenny collided and fucked things up somehow.

The Feds knew by now. The Secret Service knew. Boyd couldn't go to Bobby to explain—his Mob ties compromised him.

Boyd would come here. Boyd knew he was staying at the hotel across the street.

Pete sipped bourbon and played every Twist song on the jukebox. A waitress swooped by with regular refills.

A cab would pull up. Boyd would get out. He'd intimidate the desk clerk and gain entrance to room 614.

Boyd would find a note. He'd obey the instructions. He'd carry the tape recorder over here to his booth at Ray Becker's Tropics.

Pete watched the door. Every Twist tune brought Barb back that much stronger.

He called her in L.A. two hours ago. He told her the gig was blown. He told her to drive down to Ensenada and hole up at the Playa Rosada.

She said she'd do it. She said, "*We're* still on, aren't we?"

He said, "Yes."

The bar was hot. New Orleans held the patent on heat. Thunderstorms hit and burned themselves out before you could blink.

Boyd walked in. Pete screwed a silencer to his magnum and placed it on the seat next to him.

Boyd was carrying the tape recorder in a suitcase. He had a .45 automatic pressed to his leg.

He walked up. He sat down across from Pete and put the suitcase on the floor.

Pete pointed to it. "Take the machine out. It's running on batteries, and there's a tape looped in already, so all you have to do is turn it on."

Boyd shook his head. "Put the gun in your lap on the table."

Pete did it. Boyd said, "Now unload it."

Pete did it. Boyd popped the clip out of his piece and wrapped both guns in the tablecloth.

He looked soiled and haggard. The ungroomed Kemper Boyd—a true first.

Pete slipped a .38 snub-nose out of his waistband. "It's compartmentalized, Kemper. It's got nothing to do with our other gigs."

"I don't care."

"You will when you play that tape."

They had a long row of booths to themselves. If it went bad, he could kill him and duck out the back door.

"You crossed the line, Pete. You knew the line was there, and you crossed it."

Pete shrugged. "We didn't hurt Jack, and Bobby's too smart to bring in the law. We can walk out of here and get back to business."

"And trust each other?"

"I don't see why not. Jack's the only thing that ever got between us."

"Do you honestly think it's that simple?"

"I think you can make it that way."

Boyd unlatched the suitcase. Pete laid the machine on the table and hit Play.

His tape splice rolled. Pete turned the volume up to cover the jukebox.

Jack Kennedy said, "Kemper Boyd's probably the closest thing, but he makes me a tad uncomfortable."

Barb Jahelka said, "Who's Kemper Boyd?"

Jack: "He's a Justice Department lawyer."

Jack: "His one great regret is that he's not a Kennedy."

Jack: "He just went to Yale Law School, latched onto me, and—"

Boyd was shaking. Boyd was ungroomed working on unhinged.

Jack: "He threw over the woman he was engaged to to curry favor with me."

Jack: "He's living out some unsavory fantasy—"

Boyd hit the tape rig barefisted. The spools bent and cracked and shattered.

Pete let him beat his hands bloody.

84

(Meridian, 5/13/62)

THE PLANE FISHTAILED in and skidded to a halt. Kemper braced himself against the seat in front of him.

His head throbbed. His hands throbbed. He hadn't slept in thirty-odd hours.

The co-pilot cut the engines and cranked the passenger door open. Sunshine and steamy air blasted in.

Kemper deplaned and walked to his car. His finger wraps seeped blood.

Pete talked him out of reprisals. Pete said Ward Littell built the shakedown from the ground up.

He drove to the motel. The road blurred behind thirty-odd hours of liquor and Dexedrine.

The lot was full. He double-parked beside Flash Elorde's Chevy.

The sun hit twice as hot as it should. Claire kept saying, "Dad, please."

He walked to his room. The door jerked open just as he touched it. A man pulled him inside. A man kicked his legs out. A man threw him prone and cuffed him facedown on the floor.

A man said, "We found narcotics here."

A man said, "And illegal weapons."

A man said, "Lenny Sands killed himself in New York City last night. He rented a cheap hotel room, slashed his wrists and wrote 'I am a homosexual' in blood on the wall above the bed. The sink and toilet were filled with burned-up tape fragments obviously taken off a bug installed in the Kennedy family's suite at the Carlyle Hotel."

Kemper thrashed. A man stepped on his face and held him still.

A man said, "Sands was spotted burglarizing the suite earlier in the day. The NYPD located a listening-post setup a few doors down. It was print-wiped and cleaned out, and obviously rented under a phony name, but the people running it left a large quantity of blank tape behind."

A man said, "You ran the shakedown."

A man said, "We've got your Cubans and that French guy Guéry. They won't talk, but they're going down on weapons charges anyway."

A man said, "Enough."

The Man: Attorney General Robert F. Kennedy.

A man pulled him into a chair. A man uncuffed him and recuffed him to the post at the foot of the bed. The room was packed with Bobby's pet Feds—six or seven men in cheap summer suits.

The men walked out and shut the door behind them. Bobby sat on the edge of the bed.

"Goddamn you, Kemper. Goddamn you for what you tried to do to my brother."

Kemper coughed. His vision shimmied. He saw two beds and two Bobbys.

"I didn't do anything. I tried to break up the operation."

"I don't believe you. I don't believe that your outburst at Laura's apartment was anything but an admission of your guilt."

Kemper flinched. The cuffs gouged his wrists and drew blood.

"Believe what you like, you chaste little piece of dogshit. And tell your brother that nobody ever loved him more and got back less."

Bobby moved closer. "Your daughter Claire informed on you. She told me that you've been a CIA contract agent for over three years. She said the Agency specifically instructed you to disseminate anti-Castro propaganda to my brother. She said that Lenny Sands told her you were instrumental in suborning organized crime figures into participating in covert CIA activities. I've taken all this into consideration and concluded that some initial suspicions of mine were correct. I think Mr. Hoover sent you over to spy on my family, and I'm going to confront him on it the day my brother forces him to resign."

Kemper made fists. Dislocated bones splintered. Bobby got up inside spitting distance.

"I'm going to sever every Mafia-CIA tie. I'm going to prohibit organized crime participation in the Cuban project. I'm going to expel you from the Justice Department and the CIA, I'm going to have you disbarred as a lawyer, and I'm going to prosecute you and your Franco-Cuban friends on weapons possession and narcotics possession charges."

Kemper wet his lips and spoke with a mouthful of spittle.

"If you fuck with my men or try to prosecute me, I'll go public. I'll spill everything I know about your filthy family. I'll smear the Kennedy name with enough verifiable filth to put a taint on it forever."

Bobby slapped him.

Kemper spat in his face.

DOCUMENT INSERT: 5/14/62.
Verbatim FBI telephone call transcript: ''TAPED AT THE DIRECTOR'S REQUEST''/''DIRECTOR'S EYES ONLY.''
Speaking: Director J. Edgar Hoover, Ward J. Littell.

WJL: Good morning, Sir.

JEH: Good morning. And you needn't ask me if I've heard, because I daresay I know more of the story than you do.

WJL: Yes, Sir.

JEH: I hope Kemper has money saved. Disbarment can prove costly, and I doubt that a man of his tastes could live comfortably on an FBI pension.

WJL: I'm certain that Little Brother won't file criminal charges on him.

JEH: Of course he won't.

WJL: Kemper took the fall.

JEH: I will not comment on the attendant irony.

WJL: Yes, Sir.

JEH: Have you spoken to him?

WJL: No, Sir.

JEH: I'd be curious to know what he's doing. The notion of Kemper C. Boyd without police agency sanction is quite startling.

WJL: I think Mr. Marcello will find him work.

JEH: Oh? As a Mafia back scratcher?

WJL: As a Cuban provocateur, Sir. Mr. Marcello has remained committed to the Cause.

JEH: Then he's a fool. Fidel Castro is here to stay. My sources tell me that the Dark King will most likely seek to normalize relations with him.

WJL: The Dark King is an appeaser, Sir.

JEH: Don't try to butter me up. You may have undergone an apostasy regarding the brothers, but your political beliefs are still suspect.

WJL: Be that as it may, Sir, I'm still not giving

up. I'm going to think of something else. I haven't
given up on the King.

   JEH: Bully for you. But please be advised that I do
not wish to be informed of your plans.

   WJL: Yes, Sir.

   JEH: Has Miss Jahelka resumed her normal life?

   WJL: She's going to, Sir. At the moment she's on a
Mexican vacation with a French-Canadian friend of
ours.

   JEH: I hope they don't procreate. They would
produce morally deficient offspring.

   WJL: Yes, Sir.

   JEH: Good day, Mr. Littell.

   WJL: Good day, Sir.

DOCUMENT INSERTS:
Consecutively dated FBI wiretap outtakes.
Marked: ''TOP SECRET/CONFIDENTIAL/DIRECTOR'S
EYES ONLY'' and ''NO DISCLOSURE TO OUTSIDE JUSTICE
DEPARTMENT PERSONNEL.''

Chicago, 6/10/62. BL4-8869 (Celano's Tailor Shop) to
AX8-9600 (home of John Rosselli) (THP File #902.5,
Chicago Office). Speaking: John Rosselli, Sam
''Mo,'' ''Momo,'' ''Mooney'' Giancana (File #480.2).
Conversation nine minutes in progress.

   SG: So fucking Bobby found out on his own.

   JR: Which frankly, did not surprise me.

   SG: We were helping him out, Johnny. Sure, it was
mostly cosmetic. But the basic fucking truth of the
whole thing was that we were helping him and his
brother out.

   JR: We were good to them, Mo. We were nice. And they
kept fucking us and fucking us and fucking us.

   SG: Some sort of fucking shakedown pre-pre-pre—
what's that word that means set up?

   JR: Precipitated, Mo. That's the word you want.

   SG: Right. Some cocksucking shakedown precipitated
Bobby finding out. The word is Jimmy and Frenchman Pete
were in on it. Somebody got careless, and Jewboy Lenny
killed himself.

JR: You can't fault Jimmy and Pete for trying to fuck the Kennedys.

SG: No, you can't.

JR: And it turned out Lenny was a faggot. Can you believe that?

SG: Who would have believed it?

JR: He was Jewish, Mo. The Jewish race has a higher percentage of homos than regular white people.

SG: That's true. Heshie Ryskind's no queer, though. He's had like sixty thousand blow jobs.

JR: Heshie's sick, Mo. He's real sick.

SG: I wish the Kennedys caught his fucking disease. The Kennedys and Sinatra.

JR: Sinatra sold us a bill of goods. He said he had influence with the brothers.

SG: He's useless. The Haircut kicked his guinea ass off the White House guest list. Asking Frank to plead our case with the brothers is useless.

Non-applicable conversation follows.

Cleveland, 8/4/62. BR1-8771 (<u>Sal's River</u> Lounge) to BR4-0811 (<u>Bartolo's Ristorante pay phone</u>). Speaking: John Michael D'Allesio (THP File #180.4, Cleveland Office), Daniel ''Donkey Dan'' Versace (File #206.9, Chicago Office). Conversation sixteen minutes in progress.

DV: Rumors are just rumors. You got to consider the source and take it from there.

JMD: Danny, you like rumors?

DV: You know I do. You know I love a good rumor as much as the next guy, and I don't particularly care if it's true or not.

JMD: Danny, I got a hot rumor.

DV: So tell. Don't be a fucking cock tease.

JMD: The rumor is J. Edgar Hoover and Bobby Kennedy hate each other.

DV: That's your rumor?

JMD: There's more.

DV: I hope so. The Hoover-Bobby feud is stale bread.

JMD: The rumor is Bobby's racket squad guys are

turning snitches. The rumor is Bobby won't let Hoover near his fucking prospects. Furthermore, I heard the fucking McClellan Committee's gearing up to go into session again. They're getting ready to fucking keester the Outfit again. Bobby's working on turning this major informant. When the committee sessions start, this guy's supposed to come on as the starring fucking attraction.

DV: I heard better rumors, Johnny.

JMD: Fuck you.

DV: I prefer sex-type rumors. Haven't you heard any good sex-type shit?

JMD: Fuck you.

Non-applicable conversation follows.

New Orleans, 10/10/62. KL4-0909 (<u>Habana Bar Pay phone</u>) to CR8-8107 (<u>Town & Country Motel pay phone</u>). Note: Carlos Marcello (no THP file extant) owns the <u>Town & Country</u>. Speaking: Leon NMI Broussard (THP File #88.6, New Orleans Office) and unidentified (assumed Cuban) man. Conversation twenty-one minutes in progress.

LB: So you shouldn't give up hope. All is not lost, my friend.

UM: It feels as if it is.

LB: That is simply not true. I know for a fact that Uncle Carlos is still very much a believer.

UM: He is alone, then. A few years ago many of his compatriots were just as generous as he has remained. It is troubling to see powerful friends abandoning the Cause.

LB: Like John F-for-fuckhead Kennedy.

UM: Yes. His betrayal is the worst example. He continues to prohibit a second invasion.

LB: So the fuckhead doesn't care. I'll tell you this, though, my friend. Uncle Carlos does.

UM: I hope you are right.

LB: I know I am. I have it on very good authority that Uncle Carlos is financing an operation that could blow the whole Cuban thing to bits.

UM: I hope you are right.

LB: He's bankrolling some men who want to hit Castro. Three Cuban guys and an ex-French paratrooper. The leader's an ex-FBI/CIA man. Uncle Carlos said he'd die himself just to make the hit.

UM: I hope this is true. You see, the Cause has become scattered. There are hundreds of exile groups now. Some are CIA-financed and some are not. I hate to say it, but many of the groups are filled with crackpots and undesirables. I think direct action is needed, and with so many factions working at cross-purposes, this will be hard to accomplish.

LB: The first thing somebody should accomplish is cutting the Kennedy brothers' balls off. The Outfit was very fucking generous to the Cause until Bobby Kennedy went nuts and cut off all our fucking ties.

UM: It is hard to be optimistic these days. It is hard not to feel impotent.

Non-applicable conversation follows.

Tampa, 10/16/62. OL4-9777 (home of Robert ''Fat Bob'' Paolucci) (THP file #19.3, Miami Office) to GL1-8041 (home of Thomas Richard Scavone) (File #80.0, Miami Office). Speaking: Paolucci and Scavone. Conversation thirty-eight minutes in progress.

RP: I know you know most of the story.

TS: Well, you know how it is. You pick up bits and pieces here and there. What I know specific is that Mo and Santo ain't talked to their Castro contacts since the heist.

RP: It was some heist. Something like fifteen fucking deaths. Santo said the heist guys probably ran the boat out to sea and blew it up. Two hundred pounds, Tommy. Can you estimate the fucking re-sale value?

TS: Off the graph, Bobby. Off the fucking graph.

RP: And it's still out there.

TS: I was just thinking that.

RP: Two hundred pounds. And somebody's got it.

TS: I heard Santo won't give up.

RP: This is true. Pete the Frenchman clipped that Delsol guy, but he was just the tip of the iceberg.

I heard Santo has got Pete out there looking around,
you know, sort of informal. They both figure some crazy
spic exiles were behind the heist, and Pete the Frog's
out there looking for them.

TS: I've met some of them exiles.

RP: So have I. They're all fucking crazy.

TS: You know what I hate about them?

RP: What?

TB: That they think they're as white as Italians.

Non-applicable conversation follows.

New Orleans, 10/19/62. BR8-3408 (home of Leon NMI
Broussard) (THP File #88.6, New Orleans Office) to
Suite 1411 at the Adolphus Hotel in Dallas, Texas.
(Hotel records indicate the suite was rented by
Herschel Meyer Ryskind) (File #887.8, Dallas
Office). Conversation three minutes in progress.

LB: You always had a thing for hotel suites, Hesh. A
hotel suite and a blow job was always your idea of
heaven.

HR: Don't say heaven, Leon. You're giving me a pain
in the prostate.

LB: I get it. You're sick, so you don't want to
think about the thereafter.

HR: It's the hereafter, Leon. And you're right. And
I called you to schmooze because you've always got
your nose in other people's troubles, and I figured you
could dish some gossip on some of the boys with worse
trouble than me and cheer me up.

LB: I'll try, Hesh. And Carlos says hi, by the way.

HR: Let's start with him. What kind of trouble has
that crazy dago hump gotten himself into now?

LB: I gotta say nothing recent. And I also gotta say
the deportation thing is hanging over his head and
making him crazy.

HR: Thank God he's got that lawyer.

LB: Yeah, Littell. The guy's working for Jimmy
Hoffa, too. Uncle Carlos says he hates the Kennedys so
much that he'd probably work for free.

HR: I heard he's a red tape kind of guy. He just
delays and delays and delays.

LB: You're absolutely right. Uncle Carlos said his
INS case probably won't go to trial until late next
year. Littell's got these Justice Department lawyers
fucking exhausted.

HR: Carlos is optimistic, then?

LB: Absolutely. So's Jimmy, from what I've heard.
The trouble with Jimmy's troubles is that he's got
eighty-six-fucking-thousand grand juries chasing
him. My feeling is that sooner or later, somebody gets
a conviction. I don't care how good a lawyer this
Littell guy is.

HR: This makes me happy. Jimmy Hoffa's a guy with
troubles approximating my own. Can you imagine going
to Leavenworth and getting shtupped in the ass by some
shvartze?

LB: That is not a pleasant prospect.

HR: Neither is cancer, you goyisher shitheel.

LB: We're pulling for you, Hesh. You're in our
prayers.

HR: Fuck your prayers. And give me some gossip. You
know that's why I called.

LB: Well.

HR: Well, what? Leon, you owe me money. You know I'm
gonna die before I collect. Give an old dying man the
comfort of some satisfying gossip.

LB: Well, I heard rumors.

HR: Such as?

LB: Such as that lawyer Littell's working for
Howard Hughes. Hughes is supposed to want to buy all
these Las Vegas hotels, and I heard—off the record,
Hesh, really—that Sam G's dying to work some kind of
an angle on the deal.

HR: Which Littell don't know about?

LB: That is correct.

HR: I love this fucking life of ours. It is never
fucking boring.

LB: You are absolutely correct. Think of the
tidbits you pick up in this loop of ours.

HR: I don't want to die, Leon. All this shit is too
good to give up.

Non-applicable conversation follows.

Chicago, 11/19/62. BL4-8869 (<u>Celano's Tailor Shop</u>)
to AX8-9600 (home of <u>John Rosselli</u>) (THP File #902.5,
Chicago Office). Speaking: John Rosselli, Sam
''Mo,'' ''Momo,'' ''Mooney'' Giancana (File #480.2).
Conversation two minutes in progress.

JR: Sinatra's worthless.

SG: He's less than worthless.

JR: The Kennedys won't even take his phone calls.

SG: Nobody hates those Irish cocksuckers more than
I do.

JR: Unless it's Carlos and his lawyer. It's like
Carlos knows that sooner or later he'll get deported
again. It's like he sees himself back in El Salvador
picking cactus thorns out of his ass.

SG: Carlos has his problems, I've got mine. Bobby's
racket squad guys are crawling up my ass like the
regular Feds never did. I would like to take a ball
peen hammer and cave Bobby's fucking head in.

JR: And his brother's.

SG: Especially his brother's. That man is nothing
but a traitor masquerading as a hero. He's nothing but
a Commie-appeaser in wolf's clothing.

JR: He made Khrushchev back down, Mo. I gotta
give him that. Khrushchev moved those goddamn
missiles.

SG: That is horseshit. That is appeasement with a
sugar coating. A CIA guy I know told me Kennedy cut a
side deal with Khrushchev. Okay, he moved the
missiles. But my CIA guy told me Kennedy had to
promise not to invade Cuba ever fucking again. Think
of that, Johnny. Think of our casinos and wave bye-
bye for fucking ever.

JR: Kennedy's supposed to talk to some Bay of Pigs
survivors at the Orange Bowl in December. Think of the
lies he'll tell them.

SG: Some Cuban patriot should pop him. Some Cuban
patriot who don't mind dying.

JR: I heard Kemper Boyd's training some guys like
that to pop Castro.

SG: Kemper Boyd's a faggot. He's got his eyes on the
wrong target. Castro's just some taco eater with a

good line of bullshit. Kennedy's worse for business
than he ever was.

Non-applicable conversation follows.

DOCUMENT INSERT: 11/20/62.
Des Moines Register subhead:
>   HOFFA DENIES BRIBERY ACCUSATIONS

DOCUMENT INSERT: 12/17/62.
Cleveland Plain Dealer headline:
>   **HOFFA ACQUITTED IN TEST FLEET CASE**

DOCUMENT INSERT: 1/12/63.
Los Angeles Times subhead:
>   HOFFA UNDER INVESTIGATION FOR TEST FLEET JURY
>   TAMPERING

DOCUMENT INSERT: 5/10/63.
Dallas Morning News headline and subhead:
>   **HOFFA INDICTED**
>   TEAMSTER BOSS HIT WITH JURY TAMPERING CHARGES

DOCUMENT INSERT: 6/25/63.
Chicago Sun-Times headline and subhead:
>   **HOFFA UNDER SIEGE**
>   TEAMSTER BOSS ARRAIGNED IN CHICAGO ON SEPARATE
>   FRAUD CHARGES

DOCUMENT INSERT: 7/29/63.
FBI wiretap outtake. Marked: TOP SECRET/
CONFIDENTIAL/DIRECTOR'S EYES ONLY and NO
DISCLOSURE TO OUTSIDE JUSTICE DEPARTMENT
PERSONNEL.

Chicago, 7/28/63. BL4-8869 (Celano's Tailor Shop) to
AX8-9600 (home of John Rosselli) (THP File #902.5,
Chicago Office). Speaking: John Rosselli, Sam
''Mo,'' ''Momo,'' Mooney'' Giancana (File #480.2).
Conversation seventeen minutes in progress.

SG: I am woefully fucking tired of this.

JR: Sammy, I hear you.

SG: The FBI's got me under twenty-four-hour
surveillance. Bobby went over Hoover's head to order

it. I'm out on the fucking golf course and I see fucking G-men skulking in the rough and on the fairways, and for all I know, they got the fucking sand traps bugged.

JR: I hear you, Mo.

SG: I'm woefully tired of this. So's Jimmy and so's Carlos. So's every made guy I talk to.

JR: Jimmy's going down. I can see the writing on the wall. I also heard Bobby turned a major snitch. I don't know details, but—

SG: I do. His name's Joe Valachi. He was a button man for Vito Genovese. He was in Atlanta, something like ten to life for narcotics.

JR: I think I met him once.

SG: Everybody in the Life's met everybody else at least once.

JR: That's true.

SG: As I was saying before you interrupted me, Valachi was in Atlanta. He blew his cork and killed another prisoner, because he thought Vito sent him down to clip him. He was wrong, but Vito did put out a contract on him, because the guy he clipped was a good friend of Vito's.

JR: This Valachi is one prime stupe.

SG: He's a scared stupe, too. He begged to go into Federal custody, and Bobby beat Hoover to him. They cut a deal. Valachi gets lifetime protection for ratting the Outfit en fucking masse. The word is Bobby's going to put him in front of the newly fucking revived McClellan Committee, like in September or something.

JR: Oh, fuck. Mo, this is bad.

SG: It's worse than bad. It's probably the worst fucking thing that's ever happened to the Outfit. Valachi's been a made guy for forty years. Do you know what he knows?

JR: Oh, fuck.

SG: Quit saying, oh fuck, you stupid cocksucker. Non-applicable conversation follows.

<u>DOCUMENT INSERT</u>: 9/10/63.
Personal note: Ward J. Littell to Howard Hughes.

Dear Mr. Hughes,

   Please consider this an official business request,
and one tendered only as a last resort. I hope that my
five months in your employ have convinced you that
I would never make an out-of-channels request unless
I deemed it absolutely vital to your interests.

   I need $250,000. This money is to be used to
circumvent official processes and guarantee Mr. J.
Edgar Hoover's continued tenure as FBI Director.

   I deem Mr. Hoover's continued directorship to be
essential to our Las Vegas plans. Please advise me of
your decision as soon as possible, and please keep
this communique in the strictest confidence.

                         Respectfully, Ward J. Littell

<u>DOCUMENT INSERT</u>: 9/12/63.
Personal note: Howard Hughes to Ward J. Littell.

Dear Ward,

   Your plan, however obliquely stated, impressed me
as judicious. The sum you requested will be
forthcoming. Please justify the expense with results
at the earliest possible date.

                                 Yours, HH

PART FIVE

CONTRACT

September–November 1963

DOCUMENT INSERT: 9/13/63.
Justice Department memorandum: Attorney General
Robert F. Kennedy to FBI Director J. Edgar Hoover.

Dear Mr. Hoover,

President Kennedy is seeking to establish a
normalization of relations plan with Communist Cuba
and has become alarmed at the extent of exile-
perpetrated sabotage and harassment aimed at the
Cuban coastline, specifically violent actions
undertaken by non-CIA sponsored exile groups
situated in Florida and along the Gulf Coast.

These non-sanctioned actions must be curtailed.
The President wants this implemented immediately and
has mandated it a top Justice Department-FBI
priority. Florida and Gulf Coast-based agents are to
begin raiding and seizing weapons at all exile camps
not specifically CIA-funded or vetted by established
foreign policy memorandums.

These raids must begin immediately. Please meet me
in my office at 3:00 this afternoon to discuss
particulars and review my list of initial target
sites.

Yours, Robert F. Kennedy

85

(Miami, 9/15/63)

THE DISPATCH HUT was boarded up. The orange-and-black
wallpaper was stripped into souvenir swatches.

Adios, Tiger Kab.

The CIA divested their half-interest. Jimmy Hoffa dumped his half as a tax dodge. He told Pete to sell the cabs and make him some chump change.

Pete ran the parking-lot clearance sale. Buyer-incentive TV sets were perched on every tiger-striped hood.

Pete hooked them up to a portable generator. Two dozen screens blasted news: a spook church in Birmingham got bombed an hour ago.

Four pickaninnies got vaporized. Kemper Boyd, take note.

Browsers jammed the lot. Pete pocketed cash and signed over pink slips.

Goodbye, Tiger Kab. Thanks for the memories.

Agency cutbacks and phaseouts dictated the sale. JM/Wave slogged on, minus mucho personnel.

The Cadre was disbanded. Santo said he was getting out of narcotics—an all-time epic lie.

The formal order came down last December. Merry Xmas—your elite dope squadron is kaput.

Teo Paez was running whores in Pensacola. Fulo Machado was on the bum somewhere. Ramón Gutiérrez was anti-Castroizing outside New Orleans.

Chuck Rogers was phased off contract status. Néstor Chasco was dead or alive in Cuba.

Kemper Boyd was still running his Whack Castro squad.

Mississippi got too hot for him. Civil rights grief was escalating and polarizing the locals.

Boyd moved his squad to Sun Valley, Florida. They took over some abandoned prefab pads. That old Teamster resort finally saw tenants.

They set up a target range and a reconnaissance course. They stayed focused on the KILL FIDEL problem. They infiltrated Cuba nine times—white men Boyd and Guéry included.

They took a hundred Commie scalps. They never saw Néstor. They never got close to Castro.

The dope was still stashed in Mississippi. The "search" for the heist men was still in sporadic progress.

Pete kept chasing fake leads. The fear got bad sometimes. He had Santo and Sam *half*-convinced that the heist men split to Cuba.

Santo and Sam harbored lingering suspicions. They kept

saying, Where's that guy Chasco?—he split the exile scene post-fucking-haste.

He kept chasing fake leads. He synced the chase to Barb's road schedule.

Langley sent him out gun running. His circuits supplied good lead chase cover.

The fear got bad sometimes. The headaches came back. He popped goofballs to insure instant dreamless sleep.

He panicked last March. He was stuck in Tuscaloosa, Alabama—with Barb's local gig stone flat canceled.

Thunderstorms flooded the roads and closed down the airport. He hit an exile-friendly bar and tamped his headache down with bourbon. Two scraggly-assed spics got shit-faced. They started talking heroin, too loud.

He pegged them as skin poppers with a dime-bag clientele. He saw a way to close the fear out once and for all.

He tailed them to a dope den. The place was Hophead Central: spics crapped out on mattresses, spics geezing up, spics scrounging dirty needles off the floor.

He killed them all. He burned his silencer down to the threads shooting junkies in cold blood. He rigged the scene to look like an all-spic dope massacre.

He called Santo with his fear choking him dry.

He said he walked in on a slaughter. He said a dying man confessed to the heist. He said, Read the Tuscaloosa papers—it's got to be big news tomorrow.

He flew to Barb's next gig. The snuffs never hit the papers or TV. Santo said, "Keep looking."

The junkies died on the nod. Chuck said Heshie Ryskind was dying—Big "H" had him phasing out on a painless little cloud.

Bobby Kennedy cleaned house last year. He initiated a shitload of non-painless phaseouts.

Contract guys got fired wholesale. Bobby sacked every contract man suspected of organized crime ties.

He neglected to fire Pete Bondurant.

Memo to Bobby the K.:

Please fire me. Please take me off the exile circuit. Please phase me off this horrible search-and-find mission.

It could happen. Santo might say, Take a rest. Without CIA ties, you're worthless.

Santo might say, Work for me. Santo might say, Look at
Boyd—Carlos has kept him employed.

He could beg off. He could say, I don't hate Castro like I used
to. He could say, I don't hate him like Kemper does—because
I didn't take the fall that he did.

My daughter didn't betray me. The man I worshiped didn't
ridicule me on tape. I didn't transfer my hate for that man to some
loudmouthed spic with a beard.

Boyd's in this deep. I'm treading air. We're like Bobby and
Jack that way.

Bobby says, Go, exiles, go. He means it. Jack refuses to green-
light a second invasion.

Jack cut a side deal with Khrushchev. He's phasing out the
Castro War in not-too-provocative fashion.

He wants to get re-elected. Langley thinks he'll scrap the war
early in his second term.

Jack thinks Fidel is unbeatable. He's not alone. Even Santo and
Sam G. cozied up to the fucker for a while.

Carlos said the dope heist queered their Commie fling. The
Castro brothers, Sam and Santo were now permanently
Splitsville.

Nobody got the dope. Everybody got fucked.

Browsers walked through the lot. An old guy kicked tires.
Teenagers grooved on the spiffy tiger-stripe paint jobs.

Pete pulled a chair into the shade. Some Teamster clowns dispensed free beer and soft drinks. They sold four cars in five
hours—not good, not bad.

Pete tried to doze. A headache started tapping.

Two plainclothesmen crossed the lot and beelined toward
him. Half the crowd sniffed trouble and hotfooted it off down
Flagler.

The TVs were stolen. The sale itself was probably illegal.

Pete stood up. The men boxed him in and flashed FBI ID.

The tall one said, "You're under arrest. This is a non-
sanctioned Cuban-exile meeting place, and you're a known
habitué."

Pete smiled. "This place is defunct. And I'm on CIA contract
status."

The short Fed unhooked his handcuffs. "We're not
unsympathetic. We don't like Communists any more than
you do."

The tall man sighed. "This wasn't Mr. Hoover's idea. Let's just say he had to go along. It's a standard, across-the-board order, and I don't think you'll be in custody that long."

Pete stuck his hands out. The cuffs wouldn't fit around his wrists.

The rest of the browsers vanished. A kid boosted a TV set and high-tailed it.

Pete said, "I'll go peacefully."

The booking tank was triple-capacity packed. Pete shared floor space with a hundred pissed-off Cubans.

They were crammed into a thirty-by-thirty-foot stinkhole. No chairs, no benches—just four cement walls and a wraparound piss gutter.

The Cubans jabbered in English and Spanish. Dig the bilingual gist: Jack the Haircut sicced the Feds on the Cause.

Six campsites were raided yesterday. Weapons were seized. Cuban gunmen were arrested en masse.

It was some sort of first salvo. Jack was out to ram all non-CIA-sanctioned exiles.

He was CIA. *He* got popped anyway. The Feds jerry-rigged a plan and went off half-cocked.

Pete leaned against the wall and shut his eyes. Barb twisted by.

Every time with her was good. Every time was different. Every place was different—two people always moving hooking up in odd locations.

Bobby never harassed her. Barb figured a fix was in. She said she didn't miss Two-Minute Jack.

She gave her sister her shakedown fee. Margaret Lynn Lindscott now owned a Bob's Big Boy franchise.

They met in Seattle, Pittsburgh and Tampa. They met in L.A., Frisco and Portland.

He ran guns. She fronted a cheap dance show. He chased nonexistent dope thieves/killers.

She said the Twist was burning out. He said his Cuban hard-on was, too.

She said, Your fear gets to me. He said, I'll try to tamp it down. She said, Don't—it makes you less frightening.

He said he did something very stupid. He said he didn't know why he did it.

She said, You wanted to force yourself out of the Life.

He couldn't argue.

Barb had a busy autumn pending. She had long club stints in Des Moines and Sioux City and a big Texas run through Thanksgiving.

She added lunch shows to her performance slate. The Twist was phasing out—Joey wanted to wring it dry.

He met Margaret in Milwaukee. She was meek and scared of just about everything.

He offered to kill the cop rape-o. Barb said no.

He said, Why? Barb said, You don't *really* want to.

He couldn't argue.

He had Barb. Boyd had hatred: Jack K. and the Beard as one fucked-up, pervasive thing. Littell had powerful friends.

Like Hoover. Like Hughes. Like Hoffa and Marcello.

Ward hated Jack on a par with Kemper. Bobby fucked them both—but they bypassed him to hate Big Brother.

Littell was Dracula's new Field Marshal. The Count wanted him to buy up Las Vegas and render it germ-free.

You could read Littell's eyes.

I have friends. I have plans. I have the Fund books memorized.

The holding tank smelled. The holding tank boomed with John F. Kennedy hatred.

A guard cranked the door and pulled men out for phone calls. He yelled, "Acosta, Aguilar, Arredondo—"

Pete got ready. A dime would get him Littell in D.C.

Littell could rig a Federal release writ. Littell could hip Kemper to the campsite raids.

The guard yelled, "Bondurant!"

Pete walked up. The guard steered him down the tier to a phone bank.

Guy Banister was waiting there. He was holding a pen and a false-arrest waiver.

The guard walked back to the tank. Pete signed his name in triplicate.

"I'm free to go?"

Banister looked gleeful. "That's right. The SAC didn't know you were Agency, so I informed him."

"Who told you where I was?"

"I was out at Sun Valley. Kemper gave me a note for you, so I went by the stand to deliver it. Some kids were stealing hubcaps. They told me the big gringo got arrested."

Pete rubbed his eyes. A four-aspirin headache started pounding.

Banister pulled out an envelope. "I didn't open it. And Kemper sure seemed anxious for me to make the transmittal."

Pete grabbed it. "I'm glad you're ex-Bureau, Guy. I might've had to stay here awhile."

"Don't fret, big fella. I have a hunch all this Kennedy bullshit is just about to end."

Pete caught a cab back to the stand. Vandals had stripped the tiger cars down to spare parts.

He read the note. Boyd cut straight to the point.

Néstor's here. I got a tip that he was seen begging gun money in Coral Gables. My source says he's holed up at 46th and Collins. (The pink garage apartment on the southwest corner.)

The note meant KILL HIM. Don't let Santo get to him first.

He took bourbon and aspirin for his headache.

He took his magnum and his silencer for the job.

He took some pro-Castro leaflets to plant near the body.

He drove to 46th and Collins. He took this weird revelation with him: You might let Néstor talk you out of it.

The pink garage apartment was right there, as stated. The '58 Chevy at the curb looked like a Néstor-style ride.

Pete parked.

Pete got butterflies.

Go ahead, do it—you've killed at least three hundred men.

He walked up and knocked on the door.

Nobody answered.

He knocked again. He listened for footsteps and whispers.

He couldn't hear a thing. He picked the lock with his penknife and walked in.

Shotgun slides went KA-CHOOK. Some unseen party hit a light switch.

There's Néstor, lashed to a chair. There's two fat henchmen types holding Ithaca pumps.

There's Santo Trafficante with an icepick.

86

(New Orleans, 9/15/63)

LITTELL OPENED HIS briefcase. Stacks of money fell out.

Marcello said, "How much?"

Littell said, "A quarter of a million dollars."

"Where'd you get it?"

"From a client."

Carlos cleared some desk space. His office was top-heavy with Italianate knick-knacks.

"You're saying this is for me?"

"I'm saying it's for you to match."

"What else are you saying?"

Littell dumped the money on the desk. "I'm saying that as an attorney, I can only do so much. With John Kennedy in power, Bobby will get you all sooner or later. I'm also saying that eliminating Bobby would be futile, because Jack would instinctively know who did it and take his vengeance accordingly."

The money smelled. Hughes dredged up old bills.

"But Lyndon Johnson don't like Bobby. He'd put the skids to him just to teach the fucking kid a lesson."

"That's right. Johnson hates Bobby as much as Mr. Hoover does. And like Mr. Hoover, he bears you and our other friends no ill will."

Marcello laughed. "LBJ borrowed some money from the Teamsters once. He is well known as a reasonable guy."

"So is Mr. Hoover. And Mr. Hoover is also very upset about Bobby's plans to put Joe Valachi on TV. He's very much afraid that Valachi's revelations will severely damage his prestige and virtually destroy everything that you and our other friends have built."

Carlos built a little cash skyscraper. Bank stacks rose off his desk blotter.

Littell knocked them over. "I think Mr. Hoover wants it to happen. I think he feels it coming."

"We've all been thinking about it. You can't get a roomful of the boys together without somebody bringing it up."

"It can be made to happen. And it can be made to look like we weren't involved."

"So you're saying . . ."

"I'm saying it's so big and audacious that we'll most likely never be suspected. I'm saying that even if we are, the powers that be will realize that it can never be conclusively proven. I'm saying that a consensus of denial will build off of it. I'm saying that people will want to remember the man as something he wasn't. I'm saying that we'll present them with an explanation, and the powers that be will prefer it to the truth, even though they know better."

Marcello said, "Do it. Make it happen."

87

(Sun Valley, 9/18/63)

THE SQUAD SHARED turf with gators and sand fleas. Kemper called the place "Hoffa's Paradise Lost."

Flash set up targets. Laurent bench-pressed cinderblock siding. Juan Canestel was AWOL—with 8:00 A.M. rifle practice pending.

Nobody heard him drive off. Juan was prone to odd wanderings lately.

Kemper watched Laurent Guéry work out. The man could bench three hundred pounds without breaking a sweat.

Dust swirled up the main road. Teamster Boulevard was now a pistol range.

Flash played his transistor radio. Bad news crackled out.

There were no arrests in the Birmingham church bombing case. The revamped McClellan Committee was set to go to televised sessions.

A woman was found sash-cord strangled outside Lake Weir. The police reported no leads and appealed to the public for assistance.

Juan was one hour AWOL. Pete was missing for three days.

He got the phone tip on Néstor four days ago. The tipster was a freelance exile gunman. He gave Guy Banister a note to relay to Pete.

Guy called and said he delivered it. He said he found Pete at the Federal detention jail. He dropped hints that more FBI raids were coming.

A storm browned out their phone setup two days ago. Pete couldn't call Sun Valley.

Kemper drove to a pay phone off the Interstate last night. He called Pete's apartment six times and got no answer.

Néstor Chasco's death never made the news. Pete would have dumped the body in a newsworthy locale.

Pete would put a pro-Castro spin on the murder. Pete would make sure Trafficante got the word.

His morning Dexedrine surge hit. It took ten pills to kick-start the day—he'd built up a large tolerance.

Juan and Pete were missing. Juan was hanging out with Guy Banister lately—little Lake Weir drinking excursions every other day or so.

The Pete thing felt wrong. The Juan thing felt mildly hinky.

His amphetamine surge said, Do something.

Juan drove a candy-apple-red T-Bird. Flash called it the Rapemobile.

Kemper cruised Lake Weir. The town was small and laid out in a grid pattern—the Rapemobile would be easy to spot.

He checked side streets and the bars near the highway. He checked Karl's Kustom Kar Shop and every parking lot on the main drag.

He didn't spot Juan. He didn't spot Juan's customized T-Bird.

Juan could wait. The Pete thing was more pressing.

Kemper drove to Miami. The pills started to hit counter-productive—he kept yawning and fading out at the wheel.

He stopped at 46th and Collins. That pink garage apartment was right where the tipster said it would be.

A traffic cop walked over. Kemper noticed a No Parking sign on the corner.

He rolled down his window. The cop jammed a smelly rag in his face.

It felt like chemical warfare inside him.

The smell fought his wake-up pills. The smell might be chloroform or embalming fluid. The smell meant he might be dead.

His pulse said, NO—you're alive.

His lips burned. His nose burned. He tasted chloroformed blood.

He tried to spit. His lips wouldn't part. He gagged the blood out through his nose.

He stretched his mouth. Something tugged at his cheeks. It felt like tape coming loose.

He sucked in air. He tried to move his arms and legs.

He tried to stand up. Heavy ballast held him down.

He wiggled. Chair legs scraped wood flooring. He thrashed his arms and got rope burns.

Kemper opened his eyes.

A man laughed. A hand held up Polaroid snapshots glued to cardboard.

He saw Teo Paez, gutted and quartered. He saw Fulo Machado, shivved through the eyes. He saw Ramón Gutiérrez, powder-scorched from big-bore shots to the head.

The photos disappeared. The hand swiveled his neck. Kemper caught a slow 180 view.

He saw a shabby room and two fat men in a doorway. He saw Néstor Chasco—nailed to the far wall with icepicks through his palms and ankles.

Kemper shut his eyes. A hand slapped him. A big heavy ring cut his lips.

Kemper opened his eyes. Hands slid his chair around 360.

They had Pete chained down. They had him double-cuffed and shackled to a chair. They had the chair bolted directly into the floor.

A rag hit his face. Kemper sucked the fumes in voluntarily.

He heard stories filtered through a long echo chamber. He picked out three storytelling voices.

Néstor got close to Castro twice. You got to hand it to him.

A kid that tough—what a shame to put his lights out.

Néstor said he bought off some Castro aide. The aide said Castro was considering a Kennedy hit. The aide said, What's with this Kennedy? First he invades us, then he pulls back—he's like a cunt who can't make up her mind.

Fidel's the cunt. The aide told Chasco he'd never work with the Outfit again. He thinks Santo screwed him on the heroin deal. He didn't know it was Néstor and our boys here.

Bondurant pissed his pants. Look, you can see the stain.

Santo and Mo were not gentle. And I got to say Néstor went out brave.

I'm bored with this. I got to say this waiting around is stretching me thin.

I got to say they'll be back soon. I got to say they'll want to put some hurt on these two.

Kemper felt his bladder go. He took a deep breath and forced himself unconscious.

He dreamed he was moving. He dreamed somebody cleaned him up and changed his clothes. He dreamed he heard fierce Pete Bondurant sobbing.

He dreamed he could breathe. He dreamed he could talk. He kept cursing Jack and Claire for disowning him.

He woke up on a bed. He recognized his old Fontainebleau suite or an exact replica of it.

He was wearing clean clothes. Somebody pulled off his soiled boxer shorts.

He felt rope burns on his wrists. He felt tape fragments stuck to his face.

He heard voices one room over—Pete and Ward Littell.

He tried to stand up. His legs wouldn't function. He sat on the bed and coughed his lungs out.

Littell walked in. He looked commanding—that gabardine suit gave him some bulk.

Kemper said, "There's a price."

Littell nodded. "That's right. It's something I worked out with Carlos and Sam."

"Ward—"

"Santo agreed, too. And you and Pete get to keep what you stole."

Kemper stood up. Ward held him steady.

"What do we have to do?"

Littell said, "Kill John Kennedy."

88

(Miami, 9/23/63)

1933 TO 1963. Thirty years and parallel situations.

Miami, '33. Giuseppe Zangara tries to shoot President-elect Franklin D. Roosevelt. He misses—and kills Chicago Mayor Anton Cermak.

Miami, '63. A Kennedy motorcade is scheduled for November 18.

Littell slow-cruised Biscayne Boulevard. Every inch of ground told him something.

Carlos told him the Zangara story last week.

"Giuseppe was a fucking nut. Some Chicago boys paid him to pop Cermak and take the bounce. He had a fucking death wish, and he got his fucking wish fulfilled. Frank Nitti took care of his family after he got executed."

He met with Carlos, Sam and Santo. He bartered for Pete and Kemper. They discussed the fall-guy issue at length.

Carlos wanted a leftist. He thought a left-wing assassin would galvanize anti-Castro feeling. Trafficante and Giancana overruled him.

They matched Howard Hughes' contribution. They added one stipulation: we want a right-wing patsy.

They still wanted to suck up to Fidel. They wanted to replenish Raúl Castro's dope stash and effect a late-breaking rapprochement. They wanted to say, We financed the hit—now, will you please give us back our casinos?

Their take was too convoluted. Their take was politically naive.

His take was minimalistically downscaled.

The hit can be accomplished. The planners and shooters can walk. Bobby's Mob crusade can be nullified.

Any results beyond that are unforeseeable, and will most likely resolve themselves in a powerfully ambiguous fashion.

Littell drove through downtown Miami. He noted potential motorcade routes—wide streets with high visibility.

He saw tall buildings and rear parking lots. He saw Office for Rent signs.

He saw blighted residential blocks. He saw House for Rent signs and a gun shop.

He could see the motorcade pass. He could see the man's head explode.

They met at the Fontainebleau. Pete ran a wall-to-wall bug sweep before they said one word.

Kemper mixed drinks. They sat around a table by the wet bar.

Littell laid the plan out.

"We bring the fall guy to Miami some time between now and

the first of October. We get him to rent a cheap house on the outskirts of downtown, close to the announced or assumed-to-be-announced motorcade route—*and* an office directly on the route—once that route is determined. I cruised every major airport-to-downtown artery this morning. My educated guess is that we'll have plenty of houses and offices to choose from."

Pete and Kemper stayed quiet. They still looked close to shell-shocked.

"One of us sticks close to the fall guy between the time we bring him here and the morning of the motorcade. There's a gun shop near his office and his house, and one of you burglarizes it and steals several rifles and pistols. Hate literature and other bits of incriminating paraphernalia are planted at the house, and our man handles them to insure latent fingerprints."

Pete said, "Get to the hit." Littell framed the moment: three men at a table and hear-a-pin-drop silence.

He said, "It's the day of the motorcade. We're holding our man hostage at the office on the parade route. There's a rifle from the gun-shop burglary with him, and his fingerprints are all over the stock and barrel housing. Kennedy's car passes. Our two legitimate shooters fire from separate roof perches in the rear and kill him. The man holding our patsy hostage fires at Kennedy's car and misses, drops the rifle and shoots the patsy with a stolen revolver. He flees and drops the revolver down a sewer grate. The police find the guns and compare them to the manifest from the burglary. They'll chalk up the evidence and figure they've got a conspiracy that tenuously succeeded and unraveled at the last second. They'll investigate the dead man and try to build a conspiracy case against his known associates."

Pete lit a cigarette and coughed. "You said 'flee' like you think getting out's a cinch."

Littell spoke slowly. "There are perpendicular side streets off every major thoroughfare that I've designated motorcade-likely. They're all freeway-accessible inside two minutes. Our legitimate shooters will be firing from behind. *They'll fire two shots total*—which will sound at first like car backfires or firecrackers. The Secret Service contingent won't know exactly where the shots came from. They'll still be reacting when *multiple shots*—from our fake shooter and the man guarding him—ring out. They'll storm that building and find a dead man. They'll be distracted, and they'll blow a minute or so.

All our men will have time to get to their cars and drive off."

Kemper said, "It's beautiful."

Pete rubbed his eyes. "I don't like the right-wing-nut part. It's like we came this far and didn't play an angle that could help out the Cause."

Littell slapped the table. "*No*. Trafficante and Giancana want a right-winger. They think they can build a truce with Castro, and if that's what they want, we'll have to go along with it. And remember, they *did* spare your lives."

Kemper freshened his drink. His eyes were still bloodshot from chloroform exposure.

"I want my men to shoot. They've got the hate and they're expert marksmen."

Pete said, "Agreed."

Littell nodded. "We'll pay them $25,000 each, use the rest of the money for expenses and split the difference three ways."

Kemper smiled. "My men are pretty far to the right. We should downplay the fact that we're setting up a fellow right-winger."

Pete mixed a cocktail: two aspirin and Wild Turkey. "We need to get a handle on the parade route."

Littell said, "That's your job. You've got the best Miami PD contacts."

"I'll get on it. And if I find out anything solid, I'll start mapping out the hard logistics."

Kemper coughed. "The key thing is the patsy. Once we get beyond that, we're home free."

Littell shook his head. "No. The key thing is to thwart a full-scale FBI investigation."

Pete and Kemper looked puzzled. They weren't thinking up to his level.

Littell spoke very slowly. "I think Mr. Hoover knows it's coming. He's got private bugs installed in god-knows-how-many Mob meeting places, and he told me he's been picking up a huge amount of Kennedy hatred. He hasn't informed the Secret Service, or they wouldn't be planning motorcades through to the end of the fall."

Kemper nodded. "Hoover wants it to happen. It happens, he's glad it happened, and he still gets assigned to investigate it. What we need is an 'in' to get him to obfuscate or short-shrift the investigation."

Pete nodded. "We need an FBI-linked fall guy."

Kemper said, "Dougie Frank Lockhart."

89

(Miami, 9/27/63)

HE LIKED TO spend time alone with it. Boyd said he was doing the same thing.

Pete laid out bourbon and aspirin. He turned on the window unit and cooled off the living room just right. He leveled off his headache and ran some fresh odds.

The odds they could kill Jack the Haircut. The odds that Santo would kill him and Kemper, deal or no deal.

All the odds hit inconclusive. His living room took on a rather shitty medicinal glow.

Littell loved Dougie Frank's pedigree. The fuck was ultra-right and FBI-filthy.

Littell said, "He's perfect. If Mr. Hoover is forced to investigate, he'll put a blanket on Lockhart and his known associates immediately. If he doesn't, he'll risk exposure of all the Bureau's racist policies."

Lockhart was holed up in Puckett, Mississippi. Littell said, Go there and recruit him.

He strolled through the main MPD squadroom last night. He saw three prospective motorcade maps. They were tacked to a corkboard in plain fucking view.

He memorized them. All three routes ran by their gun shop and For Rent signs.

Boyd said he felt awe more than fear.

Pete said, I know what you mean.

He didn't say, I love this woman. If I die, I came this far and lost her for nothing.

90
(Miami, 9/27/63)

SOMEBODY PLACED A tape recorder on his coffee table. Some-body placed a sealed envelope beside it.

Littell shut the door and thought it through.

Pete and Kemper know you're here. Jimmy and Carlos know you always stay at the Fontainebleau. You went down to the coffee shop for breakfast and were gone less than half an hour.

Littell opened the envelope and pulled out a sheet of paper. Mr. Hoover's block printing explained the surreptitious entry.

> Jules Schiffrin died concurrent with your fall 1960 absence from duty. His estate house was ransacked and cer-tain ledger books were stolen.
>
> Joseph Valachi did extensive Pension Fund forwarding work. He is currently being questioned by a trusted col-league of mine. Robert Kennedy does not know that this interrogation is progressing.
>
> The accompanying tape contains information that Mr. Valachi will refuse to reveal to Mr. Kennedy, the McClellan Committee, and indeed to anyone else. I trust Mr. Valachi to maintain his silence. He has been made aware that the quality and duration of his Federal relocation is predicated on it.
>
> Please destroy this note. Please listen to the tape and keep it in a safe place. I realize that the tape has limitless strategic potential. It should be revealed to Robert Kennedy only as an adjunct to measures of great boldness.

Littell plugged in the machine and prepped the enclosed tape. His hands were butter—the spool kept slipping off the spindle.

He tapped the Play button. The tape splice sputtered and hissed.

> Go over it again, Joe. Like I told you before, slow and easy.
>
> Okay, slow and easy then. Slow and easy for the six-teenth goddamn—

Joe, come on.

Okay. Slow and easy for the stupes in the peanut gallery. Joseph P. Kennedy Sr. was the charter bankroller of the Teamsters' Central States Pension Fund, which loans out money to all kinds of bad people and a few good people at very high interest rates. I did a lot of the forwarding work. Sometimes I delivered cash to people's safe-deposit boxes.

You mean they gave you clearance to enter their boxes?

Right. And I used to visit Joe Kennedy's bank regularly. It's the main Security-First National in Boston. It's account 811512404. It's like ninety or a hundred safe-deposit boxes filled with cash. Raymond Patriarca thinks there's close to a hundred million dollars in there, and Raymond should know, 'cause him and Irish Joe go back a ways. I got to say the notion of Bob Kennedy as a racket buster makes me laugh. I guess the apple does fall pretty far from the tree, 'cause Joe Kennedy money has financed one whole hell of a lot of Outfit deals. I got to say also that old Joe's the only Kennedy that knows about that money. You don't tell people, I got a hundred million in cash put away that my sons the President and Attorney General don't know about. And now Joe's had this stroke, so maybe he's not thinking too clear. You would sort of like to see that money put to use and not just sit there, which it might if old Joe kicks off or goes senile and forgets about it. I should also mention that every big guy in the Outfit knows how dirty Joe is, but they can't shake Bobby down with the knowledge without putting their own tits in the wringer.

The tape ran out. Littell tapped the Stop button and sat perfectly still.

He thought it through. He assumed Hoover's perspective and spoke his thoughts out loud in the first person.

I'm close to Howard Hughes. I set Ward Littell up with him. Littell asked Hughes for money to help assure my FBI directorship.

Jack Kennedy plans to fire me. I've got private taps installed in Mob venues. I've picked up a great deal of Kennedy hatred.

Littell switched back to his own perspective.

Hoover possessed insufficient data. Said data would not lead him to extrapolate a specific hit.

I told Pete and Kemper, Mr. Hoover knows it's coming. I meant it in the metaphorical sense.

The tape and note implied specificity. Hoover called the tape "an adjunct to measures of great boldness."

He was saying, I KNOW.

The tape was a device to humble Bobby. The tape was a device to insure Bobby's silence. The tape should be revealed to Bobby before Jack's death.

Jack's death would explicate the purpose of the humbling. Bobby would thus not seek to establish proof of an assassination conspiracy. Bobby would know that to do so would forever besmirch the Kennedy name.

Bobby would assume that the man who delivered the humbling had foreknowledge of his brother's death. Bobby would be powerless to act upon his assumption.

Littell reassumed Hoover's perspective.

Bobby Kennedy broke Littell's heart. Kennedy hatred binds us. Littell will not resist the urge to maim Bobby. Littell will want Bobby to know that he helped plan his brother's murder.

It was complex and vindictive and psychologically dense Hoover thinking. A single logical thread was missing.

You haven't broken cover. Your financiers presumably haven't.

Kemper and Pete haven't. Kemper hasn't broached the plan to his shooters yet.

Hoover *senses* that you're pushing toward a hit. The tape's your "adjunct"—*if you get there first.*

There's a second plot in the works. Mr. Hoover has specific knowledge of it.

Littell sat perfectly still. Little hotel sounds escalated.

He couldn't lock the conclusion in. He couldn't rate it as much more than a hunch.

Mr. Hoover knew him—as no one else ever had or ever would. He felt an ugly wave of love for the man.

91
(Puckett, 9/28/63)

THE GEEK WORE a monogrammed Klan sheet. Pete fed him bonded bourbon and lies.

"This gig is you, Dougie. It's got 'you' written all over it."

Lockhart burped. "I knew you didn't drive out here at 1:00 A.M. just to share that bottle with me."

The shack smelled like a cat box. Dougie reeked of Wildroot Cream Oil. Pete stood in the doorway—the better to dodge the stink.

"It's three hundred a week. It's an official Agency job, so you won't have to worry about those Fed raids."

Lockhart rocked back in his La–Z–Boy recliner. "Those raids have been pretty indiscriminate. I heard quite a few Agency boys got themselves tangled up in them."

Pete cracked his thumbs. "We need you to ride herd on some Klansmen. The Agency wants to build a string of launch sites in South Florida, and we need a white man to get things going."

Lockhart picked his nose. "Sounds like Blessington all over again. Sounds also like it might be another big fuckin' buildup to another big fuckin' letdown, like a certain invasion we both remember."

Pete took a hit off the bottle. "You can't make history all the time, Dougie. Sometimes the best you can do is make money."

Dougie tapped his chest. "I made history recently."

"Is that right?"

"That's right. It was me that bombed the 16th Street Baptist Church in Birmingham, Alabama. That Communist-inspired hue-and-cry that's going up right now? Well, I got to say I'm the one that inspired it."

The shack was lined with tinfoil. Dig that Martin Luther Coon poster taped to the back wall.

"I'll make it four hundred a week and expenses, through to mid-November. You get your own house and office in Miami. If you leave with me now, I'll throw in a bonus."

Lockhart said, "I'm in."

Pete said, "Clean yourself up. You look like a nigger."

* * *

The ride back went slow. Thunderstorms turned the highway into one long snail trail.

Dougie Frank snored through the deluge. Pete caught newscasts and a Twist show on the radio.

A commentator talked up Joe Valachi's song-and-dance. Valachi dubbed the Mob "La Cosa Nostra."

Valachi was a big TV hit. A newsman called his ratings "boffo." Valachi was snitching East Coast hoodlums up the ying-yang.

A reporter talked to Heshie Ryskind—holed up in some Phoenix cancer ward. Hesh called La Cosa Nostra "a goyishe fantasy."

The Twist program came in scratchy. Barb sang along in Pete's head and out-warbled Chubby Checker.

They talked long-distance right before he left Miami. Barb said, What is it?—you sound frightened again.

He said, I can't tell you. When you hear about it, you'll know.

She said, Will it hurt us?

He said, No.

She said, You're lying. He couldn't argue.

She was flying to Texas in a few days. Joey booked them in for an eight-week statewide run.

He'd fly in for weekends. He'd play stage-door Johnny, straight up to November 18.

They hit Miami at noon. Lockhart dosed his hangover with glazed doughnuts and coffee.

They looped through the downtown area. Dougie pointed out For Rent signs.

Pete drove in circles. The house-and-office search had Dougie yawning.

Pete narrowed his choices down to three offices and three houses. Pete said, Dougie, take your pick.

Dougie picked fast. Dougie wanted to log in some sack time.

He picked a stucco house off Biscayne. He picked an office on Biscayne—dead center on all three parade routes.

Both landlords demanded deposits. Dougie peeled bills off his expense roll and paid them three months' rent in advance.

Pete stayed out of sight. The landlords never saw him.

He watched Dougie lug his gear into the house—this carrot-topped stupe about to be world-famous.

92
(Miami, 9/29/63–10/20/63)

HE MEMORIZED HOOVER'S note. He hid the tape splice. He drove the three routes a dozen times a day for three weeks running. He didn't tell Pete and Kemper that there might be another hit planned.

The press reported the President's fall travel schedule. They emphasized motorcades in New York, Miami and Texas.

Littell sent Bobby a note. It stated his affiliation with James R. Hoffa and asked for ten minutes of his time.

He considered the ramifications for close to a month before acting. His walk to the mailbox felt like his raid on Jules Schiffrin's house—multiplied a thousand times.

Littell drove down Biscayne Boulevard. He timed every signal light with a stopwatch.

Kemper burglarized the gun shop a week ago. He stole three sight-equipped rifles and two revolvers. He wore gloves with distinctive cracked fingertips—filched from Dougie Frank Lockhart.

Kemper surveilled the gun shop the next day. Detectives canvassed the area and technicians dusted for prints. Dougie's cracked-finger gloves were now a matter of forensic record.

The gloves were pressed all over surfaces in Dougie's house and office.

Pete let Dougie fondle the rifles. His fingerprints were pressed to the stocks and barrels.

Kemper stole three cars in South Carolina. He had them repainted and fitted with fake license plates. Two were assigned to the shooters. The third car was for the man assigned to kill Dougie.

Pete brought a fourth man in. Chuck Rogers signed on as their fall-guy impersonator.

Rogers and Lockhart had similar builds and similar features. Dougie's most distinguishing attribute was bright red hair.

Chuck dyed his hair red. Chuck spewed Kennedy hatred all over Miami.

He shot his mouth off at taverns and pool halls. He raged at a skating rink, a gun range and numerous liquor stores. He was paid to rage nonstop until November 15.

Littell drove by Dougie's office. Every circuit gave him a brilliant new embellishment.

He should find some rambunctious kids on the motorcade route. He should give them firecrackers and tell them to let fly.

It would wear the Secret Service escort down. It would inure them to gunshot-like noises.

Kemper was working up some Dougie Frank keepsakes. Lockhart's psychopathology would be summarized in minutiae.

Kemper defaced JFK photographs and carved swastikas on Jack and Jackie dolls. Kemper smeared fecal matter over a dozen Kennedy magazine spreads.

The investigators would find it all in Dougie's bedroom closet.

Currently in progress: Dougie Frank Lockhart's political diary.

It was hunt-and-peck typed, with printed ink corrections. The race-mongering text was truly horrific.

The diary was Pete's idea. Dougie said he bombed the 16th Street Baptist Church—a still-unsolved cause célèbre. Pete wanted to link the Kennedy hit and four dead Negro children.

Dougie told Pete the whole bombing story. Pete typed crucial details into the diary.

They didn't mention the bombing embellishment to Kemper. Kemper had a quirky affection for coloreds.

Pete kept Dougie sequestered at his house. He fed him take-out pizza, marijuana and liquor. Dougie seemed to enjoy the accommodations.

Pete told Dougie that his Agency gig had been postponed. He fed him a cock-and-bull story about the need to stay out of sight.

Kemper moved his men to Blessington. The FBI was raiding non-CIA campsites—housing his team at Sun Valley was risky.

The men bunked at the Breakers Motel. They test-fired .30-06's all day every day. Their rifles were identical to the rifles Kemper stole.

The shooters didn't know about the hit. Kemper would inform them six days before—in time to stage a full-dress Miami rehearsal.

Littell cruised by Dougie's house. Pete said he always came in through the alley and never let the neighbors see him.

They should plant some narcotics at the house. They should expand Dougie's pedigree to assassin/church bomber/dope fiend.

Kemper had a drink with the Miami SAC yesterday. They were old Bureau pals—the meeting wouldn't stand out as anomalous.

The man called the motorcade a "pain in the ass." He called Kennedy "tough to guard." He said the Secret Service let crowds get too close to him.

Kemper said, Any threats? Any loonies coming out of the woodwork?

The man said, No.

Their one risky bluff was holding. No one had reported the loudmouthed pseudo Dougie.

Littell drove back to the Fontainebleau. He wondered how long Pete and Kemper would outlive JFK.

93

(Blessington, 10/21/63)

TRAINING OFFICERS FORMED a cordon just inside the front gate. They wore face shields and packed shotguns filled with rock salt.

Refuge seekers slammed the fence. The entry road was jammed with junk cars and dispossessed Cubans.

Kemper watched the scene escalate. John Stanton called and warned him that the raids went from bad to godawful.

The FBI hit fourteen exile camps yesterday. Half the Cubans on the Gulf Coast were out seeking CIA asylum.

The fence teetered. The training men raised their weapons.

There were twenty men inside and sixty men outside. Only weak chain-links and some barbed wire stood between them.

A Cuban climbed the fence and snagged himself on the barbs at the top. A training man blew him down—one salt round de-snagged him and lacerated his chest.

The Cubans picked up rocks and waved lumber planks. The contract men assumed protective postures. A big bilingual roar went up.

Littell was late. Pete was late, too—the migration probably stalled traffic.

Kemper walked down to the boat dock. His men were shooting buoys floating thirty yards offshore.

They wore earplugs to blot out the gate noise. They looked like high-line, spit-and-polish mercenaries.

He moved them in just under the wire. They had free run of the campsite—John Stanton pulled strings for old times' sake.

Ejected shells hit the dock. Laurent and Flash notched bulls-eyes. Juan fired wide into some waves.

He told them about the hit last night. The pure audacity thrilled them.

He couldn't resist it. He wanted to see their faces ignite.

Laurent and Flash lit up happy. Juan lit up disturbed.

Juan's been acting furtive. Juan's been AWOL three nights running.

The radio reported another dead woman. She was beaten senseless and strangled with a sash cord. The local cops were baffled.

Victim #1 was found near Sun Valley. Victim #2 was found near Blessington.

The gate noise doubled and tripled. Rock-salt rounds exploded.

Kemper popped in earplugs and watched his men shoot. Juan Canestel watched him.

Flash made a buoy jump. Laurent nailed it on the rebound. Juan slammed three straight misses.

Something was wrong.

The State Police cleared the Cubans out. Black-and-whites escorted them to the highway.

Kemper drove behind the convoy. The line was fifty cars long. The rock-salt barrage blew out windshields and stripped convertible tops.

It was a short-sighted solution. John Stanton prophesied exile chaos—and hinted at much worse.

Pete and Ward called to say they'd be late. He said, Good—I have to run an errand. They rescheduled their meet for 2:30 at the Breakers.

He'd tell them Stanton's news. He'd stress that it was strictly speculative.

The car herd crawled—both outbound lanes were jammed up bumper-to-bumper. Two black-and-whites drove point to keep the Cubans boxed in.

Kemper turned onto a switchback. It was the only shortcut to Blessington proper—dirt roads straight in.

Dust kicked up. A light drizzle turned it to mud spray. The Rapemobile passed him, full-throttle on a blind curve.

Kemper hit his wipers. The spray thinned out translucent. He saw exhaust fumes up ahead—and no Rapemobile.

Juan's distracted. He didn't recognize my car.

Kemper hit downtown Blessington. He cruised by the Breakers, Al's Dixie Diner and every exile hangout on both sides of the highway.

No Rapemobile.

He grid-searched side streets. He made systematic circuits— three blocks left, three blocks right. Seven-come-eleven— where's that candy-apple-red T-Bird?

There—

The Rapemobile was parked outside the Larkhaven Motel. Kemper recognized the two cars parked beside it.

Guy Banister's Buick. Carlos Marcello's Lincoln.

The Breakers Motel faced the highway. Kemper's window faced a just-rigged State Police checkpoint.

He saw cops divert cars down an off-ramp. He saw cops force male Latins out at gunpoint.

The cops ran ID checks and INS checks. The cops impounded vehicles and arrested male Latins wholesale.

Kemper watched for one straight hour. The Staties busted thirty-nine male Latins.

They herded the men into jail trucks. They dumped confiscated weapons into one big pile.

He searched Juan's room an hour ago.

He found no sash cords. He found no perverted keepsakes. He saw absolutely nothing incriminating.

Somebody leaned on the doorbell. Kemper opened up quick to stop the noise.

Pete walked in. "Have you seen what's going on out there?"

Kemper nodded. "They were trying to break in to the camp a few hours ago. The head training officer called the Staties."

Pete checked the window. "Those are some pissed-off Cubans."

Kemper pulled the drapes. "Where's Ward?"

"He's coming. And I hope you didn't call us all the way down here to show us some fucking roadblocks."

Kemper walked to the bar and poured Pete a short bourbon. "John Stanton called me. He said Jack Kennedy told Hoover to turn up the heat. The FBI has raided twenty-nine non-Agency campsites within the past forty-eight hours. Every non-Agency exile in captivity is out looking for Agency asylum."

Pete downed his shot. Kemper poured him a refill.

"Stanton said Carlos put up a bail fund. Guy Banister tried to bail out some of his pet exiles, but the INS has put a deportation hold on every Cuban National in custody."

Pete threw his glass at the wall. Kemper plugged the bottle.

"Stanton said the entire exile community is going crazy. He said there's lots of talk about a Kennedy hit. He said there's a good deal of *specific talk* about a motorcade hit in Miami."

Pete punched the wall. His fist smashed through to the baseboard. Kemper stood back and talked slow and easy.

"Nobody on our team has broken cover, so the rumors couldn't have originated from there. And Stanton said he didn't inform the Secret Service, which implies that he wouldn't mind seeing Jack dead."

Pete gouged his knuckles bone-deep. He threw a left hook at the wall—plaster chunks flew.

Kemper stood *way* back. "Ward said Hoover sensed it was coming. He was right, because Hoover would have stalled the raids and sent out warnings to the old-boy network just to screw Bobby—unless he wanted to fuel the hatred against Jack."

Pete grabbed the bottle. Pete doused his hands and wiped them on the drapes.

The fabric seeped beige to red. The wall was half-demolished.

"Pete, listen. There's ways we can—"

Pete shoved him against the window. "No. This is the one we can't get out of. We either kill him or we don't, and they'll probably kill us even if we get him."

Kemper slid free. Pete slid the drapes back.

Exiles were jumping off the highway abutment. Cops were going at them with electric cattle prods.

"Look at that, Kemper. Look at that and tell me we can contain this fucking thing."

Littell walked past the window. Pete opened the door and pulled him in bodily.

He didn't react. He looked glazed and *hurt*.

Kemper shut the door. "Ward, what is it?"

Littell hugged his briefcase. He didn't even blink at the room damage.

"I talked to Sam. He said the Miami hit is out, because his liaison to Castro told him that Castro would never speak to any Outfit man ever again, under any circumstances. They've given up the idea of a rapprochement. I've always considered it far-fetched, and now apparently Sam and Santo agree."

Pete said, "This is all crazy." Kemper read Littell's face: DON'T TAKE THIS AWAY FROM ME.

"Are *we* still on?"

Littell said, "I think so. And I spoke to Guy Banister and figured something out."

Pete looked ready to blow. "So tell us, Ward. We know you're the smartest and the strongest now, so just tell us what you think."

Littell squared his necktie. "Banister saw a copy of a presidential memo. It passed from Jack to Bobby to Mr. Hoover, then through to the New Orleans SAC, who leaked it to Guy. The memo said that the President is sending a personal emissary to talk to Castro in November, and that further JM/Wave cutbacks will be forthcoming."

Pete flicked blood off his hands. "I don't get the Banister connection."

Littell tossed his briefcase on the bed. "It was coincidental. Guy and Carlos are close, and Guy's a frustrated lawyer himself. We talk from time to time, and he just happened to mention the memo. What it all ties in to is my feeling that Mr. Hoover senses there's a hit plan in the works. Since none of us have broken cover, I'm thinking that—*maybe*—there's a second hit in the planning stages. I'm thinking also that Banister might have knowledge of it—and *that's* why Hoover leaked the memo in his direction."

Kemper pointed to the window. "Did you see that checkpoint?"

Littell said, "Yes, of course."

Kemper said, "That's Hoover again. That's him letting the raids happen to keep the hate against Jack peaking. John Stanton called me, Ward. There's supposed to be a half-dozen or six dozen or two dozen more fucking plots in the works, like the fucking assassination metaphysic is just out there too undeniably—"

Pete slapped him.

Kemper pulled his piece.

Pete pulled his.

Littell said, "No," VERY SOFTLY.

Pete dropped his gun on the bed.

Kemper dropped his.

Littell said, "Enough," VERY SOFTLY.

The room crackled and buzzed. Littell unloaded the guns and locked them in his briefcase.

Pete spoke just shy of a whisper. "Banister bailed me out of jail last month. He said, 'This Kennedy bullshit is about to end,' like he had some kind of fucking foreknowledge."

Kemper spoke the same way. "Juan Canestel's been acting strange lately. I tailed him a few hours ago, and spotted his car parked next to Banister's and Carlos Marcello's. It was right down the road here, outside another motel."

Littell said, "The Larkhaven?"

"That's right."

Pete sucked blood off his knuckles. "How'd you know that, Ward? And if Carlos is in on a second hit, are Santo and Mo calling ours off?"

Littell shook his head. "I think we're still on."

"What about this Banister stuff?"

"It's new to me, but it fits. All I know for certain now is that I'm meeting Carlos at the Larkhaven Motel at five. He told me that Santo and Mo have handed the whole thing to him, with two new stipulations."

Kemper rubbed his chin. The slap left his face bright red. "Which are?"

"That we reschedule out of Miami and work up a left-wing patsy. There's no chance at a truce with Castro, so they want to build the killer up as *pro*-Fidel."

Pete kicked the wall. A landscape print hit the floor.

Kemper swallowed a loose tooth. Pete pointed to the highway.

The cops were putting on full riot gear. The cops were running strip searches in broad daylight.

Kemper said, "Look at that. That's all Mr. Hoover's chess game."

Pete said, "You're crazy. He's not *that* fucking good."

Littell laughed in his face.

94

(Blessington, 10/21/63)

CARLOS ARRANGED A liquor tray. The setting was incongru-ous—Hennessy XO and paper-wrapped motel glasses.

Littell took the hard chair. Carlos took the soft one. The tray sat on a coffee table between them.

"Your crew is out, Ward. We're using somebody else. He's been planning his thing all summer, which makes it a better all-around deal."

Littell said, "Guy Banister?"

"How'd you know? Did a little birdie tell you?"

"His car's outside. And there's some things that you just tend to know."

"You're taking it good."

"I don't have a choice."

Carlos toyed with a humidor. "I just learned about it. The thing's been in the works for a while, which to my way of think-ing increases the chance of success."

"Where?"

"Dallas, next month. Guy's got some rich right-wingers back-ing it. He's got a long-term fall guy, one pro shooter and one Cuban."

"Juan Canestel?"

Carlos laughed. "You're a very smart 'tend to know' guy."

Littell crossed his legs. "Kemper figured it out. And in my opinion, you shouldn't trust psychopaths who drive bright red sports cars."

Carlos bit the tip off his cigar. "Guy's a capable guy. He's got a Commie-type patsy with a job on one of the motorcade routes, two real shooters and some cops to kill the patsy. Ward, you can't fault a guy who came up with the same plan as you fucking inde-pendent of you."

He felt calm. Carlos couldn't break him. He still had the chance to maim Bobby.

"I wish it could have been you, Ward. I know you got a per-sonal stake in seeing that man dead."

He felt secure. He felt inimical to Pete and Kemper.

"I wasn't pleased that Mo and Santo cozied up to Castro. Ward, you should have seen me when I found out."

Littell took out his lighter. It was solid gold—a gift from Jimmy Hoffa.

"You're building up to something, Carlos. You're about to say, 'Ward, you're too valuable to risk,' and offer me a drink, even though I haven't touched liquor in over two years."

Marcello leaned in. Littell lit his cigar.

"You're not too valuable to risk, but you're way too valuable to punish. Everybody agrees with me on that, and everybody also agrees that Boyd and Bondurant constitute another fucking matter."

"I still don't want that drink."

"Why should you? You didn't steal two hundred pounds of heroin and shit all over your partners. You took part in a shakedown that you should have told us about, but that's no more than some fucking misdemeanor."

Littell said, "I still don't want that drink. And I'd appreciate it if you told me exactly what you want me to do between now and Dallas."

Carlos brushed ash off his vest. "I want you, Pete and Kemper not to interfere with Guy's plan or try to horn in on it. I want you to cut that Lockhart guy loose and send him back to Mississippi. I want Pete and Kemper to return what they stole."

Littell squeezed his gold lighter. "What happens to them?"

"I don't know. That's not for me to fucking say."

The cigar smelled foul. An air conditioner blew smoke in his face.

"It would have worked, Carlos. We would have made it happen."

Marcello winked. "You always take business on its own terms. You don't do some regret number when things don't go your way."

"I don't get to kill him. That's a regret."

"You'll live with it. And your plan helped Guy set up a diversion."

"What diversion?"

Carlos perched an ashtray on his stomach. "Banister told some nut named Milteer about the Miami job, without naming no personnel. Guy knows Milteer's a loudmouth who's got a Miami PD snitch bird-dogging him. He's hoping Milteer will blab to the snitch, who'll blab to his handler, and somehow the Miami motorcade will get canceled and divert everybody's attention away from Dallas."

Littell smiled. "It's far-fetched. It's something out of 'Terry and the Pirates.' "

Carlos smiled. "So's your story about the Teamster books. So's the whole idea of you thinking I didn't know what really happened from the gate."

A man stepped out of the bathroom. He was holding a cocked revolver.

Littell shut his eyes.

Carlos said, "Everybody but Jimmy knows. We had detectives tailing you from the fucking instant you walked me over the border. They know all about your code books and the research you did at the Library of Congress. I know you got plans for the books, and sonny boy, now you got partners."

Littell opened his eyes. The man wrapped a pillow around his gun.

Carlos poured two drinks. "You're going to set us up with Howard Hughes. We're going to sell him Las Vegas and keester him for most of his profits. You're going to help us turn the Fund books into more legitimate money than Jules Schiffrin ever dreamed of."

He felt weightless. He tried to dredge up a Hail Mary and couldn't remember the words.

Carlos raised his glass. "To Las Vegas and new understandings."

Littell forced the drink down. The exquisite burn made him sob.

95

(Meridian, 11/4/63)

HEROIN BRICKS WEIGHED down the trunk and made the rear wheels drift. A simple traffic shake would net him thirty years in Parchman Prison.

He withdrew his bank-vault stash. Some powder leaked on the floor—enough to sedate rural Mississippi for weeks.

Santo wanted his dope back. Santo reneged on their deal. Santo let certain implications linger.

Santo might have you killed. Santo might let you live. Santo might tease you with some stay of execution.

Kemper pulled up to a stoplight. A colored man waved to him.

Kemper waved back. The man was a Pentecostal deacon—and very skeptical of John F. Kennedy.

The man always said, "I don't trust that boy."

The light changed. Kemper punched the gas.

Be patient, Mr. Deacon. That boy's got eighteen days left to live.

His team was out. Banister's was in. Juan Canestel and Chuck Rogers crossed over to Guy's crew.

The hit was rescheduled for Dallas on November 22. Juan and a Corsican pro would shoot from separate locations. Chuck and two Dallas cops were set to kill the fall guy.

It was Littell's basic plan embellished. It illustrated the ubiquitous Let's Kill Jack metaphysic.

Littell disbanded the team. Lockhart returned to his Klan gig. Pete flew straight to Texas to be with his woman. The Swingin' Twist Revue was scheduled to play Dallas on Hit Day.

Littell cut him loose. Some homing instinct drew him back to Meridian.

Quite a few locals remembered him. Some colored folks greeted him warmly. Some crackers gave him ugly looks and taunted him.

He took a motel room. He half-expected Mob killers to knock on his door. He ate three restaurant meals a day and drove around the countryside.

Dusk hit. Kemper crossed the Puckett town line. He saw a ridiculous sign framed by floodlights: Martin Luther King at a Communist training school.

The photo insert looked doctored. Someone drew devil's horns on the Reverend.

Kemper swung east. He hit the switchback leading out to Dougle Lockhart's old gun range.

Dirt roads took him right up to the edge. Shell casings snapped under his tires.

He killed his lights and got out. It was blessedly quiet—no gunshots and no rebel yells.

Kemper drew his piece. The sky was pitch dark—he couldn't see the target silhouettes.

Shells crunched and skittered. Kemper heard footsteps.

"Who's that? Who's that trespassin' on my property?"

Kemper tapped his headlights. The beams caught Dougie Lockhart head-on.

"It's Kemper Boyd, son."

Lockhart stepped out of the light. "Kemper Boyd, whose accent gets more syrupy the further south he gets. You got a chameleon quality, Kemper. Has anybody ever told you that?"

Kemper hit his brights. The whole range lit up.

Dougie, wash your sheet—you look awful.

Lockhart whooped. "Boss, you got me under the hot lights now! Boss, I gotta confess—it was me that bombed that nigger church in Birmingham!"

He had bad teeth and pimples. His moonshine breath was wafting out a good ten yards.

Kemper said, "Did you really do that?"

"As sure as I'm standing here basking in your light, Boss. As sure as niggers—"

Kemper shot him in the mouth. A full clip took his head off.

96

(Washington, D.C., 11/19/63)

BOBBY MADE HIM wait.

Littell sat outside his office. Bobby's note stressed promptness and closed with a flair: "I'll give any Hoffa lawyer ten minutes of my time."

He was prompt. Bobby was busy. A door separated them.

Littell waited. He felt supremely calm.

Marcello didn't break him. Bobby was a relative child. Marcello bowed when he only took one drink.

The outer office was wood-paneled and spacious. It was very close to Mr. Hoover's office.

The receptionist ignored him. He counted down to the moment.

11/6/63: Kemper gives the dope back. Trafficante rebuffs his handshake.

11/6/63: Carlos Marcello calls. He says, "Santo has a job for you," but will not elaborate further.

11/7/63: Sam Giancana calls. He says, "I think we can find work for Pete. Mr. Hughes hates spooks, and Pete's a good narcotics man."

11/7/63: He conveys this message to Pete. Pete understands that they're letting him live.

If you work for us. *If* you move to Vegas. *If* you sell the local niggers heroin.

11/8/63: Jimmy Hoffa calls, elated. He doesn't seem to care that he's in very deep legal trouble.

Sam told him about the hit. Jimmy tells Heshie Ryskind. Heshie checks into the best hotel in Dallas—to enjoy the event close up.

Heshie brings his entourage: Dick Contino, nurses and hookers. Pete shoots him full of dope twice a day.

Heshie's entourage is baffled. Why uproot to Dallas when you're so close to passing away?

11/8/63: Carlos sends him a news clipping. It reads, "Klan Leader Murdered—Baffling Deep South Riddle!"

The cops suspect rival Klansmen. He suspects a Kemper Boyd gesture.

Carlos includes a note. Carlos says his deportation trial is going quite well.

11/8/63: Mr. Hughes sends him a note. Baby Howard wants Las Vegas like most children want new toys.

He wrote back to him. He promised to visit Nevada and compile research notes before Christmas.

11/9/63: Mr. Hoover calls. He says his private taps have picked up scalding outrage—the Joe Valachi Show is terrifying mobsters coast to coast.

Hoover's inside source says that Bobby is privately interrogating Valachi. Valachi refuses to discuss the Fund books. Bobby is furious.

11/10/63: Kemper calls. He says Guy Banister's "far-fetched" ploy succeeded: the Miami motorcade was canceled.

11/12/63: Pete calls. He reports more campsite raids and hit-plot rumors.

11/15/63: Jack parades through New York City. Teenagers and middle-aged matrons swarm his car.

11/16/63: Dallas newspapers announce the motorcade route. Barb Jahelka has a front-row seat—she's performing a noon show at a club on Commerce Street.

An intercom buzzed. Bobby's voice cut through static: "I'll see Mr. Littell now."

The receptionist got the door. Littell carried his tape recorder in.

Bobby stood behind his desk. He jammed his hands in his pockets and made no forward moves—Mob lawyers received cut-rate civility.

The office was nicely appointed. Bobby's suit was an off-the-rack sack cut.

"Your name seems familiar, Mr. Littell. Have we met before?"

I WAS YOUR PHANTOM. I ACHED TO BE PART OF YOUR VISION.

"No, Mr. Kennedy. We haven't."

"I see you brought a tape recorder."

Littell set it down on the floor. "Yes, I did."

"Has Jimmy owned up to his evil ways? Did you bring me some kind of confession?"

"In a sense. Would you mind listening?"

Bobby checked his watch. "I'm yours for the next nine minutes."

Littell plugged the machine into a wall outlet. Bobby jiggled the coins in his pockets.

Littell tapped Play. Joe Valachi spoke. Bobby leaned against the wall behind his desk.

Littell stood in front of the desk. Bobby stared at him. They stayed absolutely motionless and did not blink or twitch.

Joe Valachi laid down his indictment. Bobby heard the evidence. He did not shut his eyes or in any way discernibly react.

Littell broke a sweat. The silly staring contest continued.

The tape slipped off the spindle. Bobby picked up his desk phone.

"Get Special Agent Conroy in Boston. Have him go to the main Security-First National Bank and find out who account number 811512404 belongs to. Have him examine the safe-deposit boxes and call me back immediately. Tell him to expedite this top-priority, and hold my calls until his comes through."

His voice did not waver. He came on cast-iron/steel-plate/watertight strong.

Bobby put the phone down. The eyeball duel continued. The first one to blink is a coward.

Littell almost giggled. An epigram: Powerful men are children. Time passed. Littell counted minutes off his heartbeat. His glasses started sliding down his nose.

The phone rang. Bobby picked it up and listened.

Littell stood perfectly still and counted forty-one seconds off his pulse. Bobby threw the phone at the wall.

And blinked.

And twitched.

And brushed back tears.

Littell said, "Goddamn you for the pain you caused me."

97

(Dallas, 11/20/63)

SHE'LL KNOW. SHE'LL hear the news and see your face and know you were part of it.

She'll trace it back to the shakedown. You couldn't compromise him, so you killed him.

She'll know it was a Mob hit. She knows how those guys snip dangerous links. She'll blame you for bringing her so close to something so big.

Pete watched Barb sleep. Their bed smelled like suntan oil and sweat.

He was going to Las Vegas. He was going back to Howard "Dracula" Hughes. Ward Littell was their new middleman.

It was strongarm and dope work. It was a boilerplate commuted sentence: death for life imprisonment.

She'd kicked the sheets off. He noticed some new freckles on her legs.

She'd click with Vegas. He'd boot Joey out of her life and fix her up with a permanent lounge gig.

She'd be with him. She'd be close to his work. She'd build a rep as a stand-up woman who knew how to keep secrets.

Barb curled into her pillows. The veins on her breasts stretched out funny.

He woke her up. She snapped awake bright-eyed, like always.

Pete said, "Will you marry me?"

Barb said, "Sure."

* * *

A fifty-dollar bribe waived the blood test. A C-note covered the no-birth-certificate problem.

Pete rented a 52 X-long tuxedo. Barb ran by the Kascade Klub and grabbed her one white Twist gown.

They found a preacher in the phone book. Pete scrounged up two witnesses: Jack Ruby and Dick Contino.

Dick said Uncle Hesh needed a pop. And what's he so excited about? For a dying man, he sure seems keyed up.

Pete ran by the Adolphus Hotel. He shot Heshie full of heroin and slipped him some Hershey bars to nosh on. Heshie thought his tuxedo was the funniest fucking thing he'd ever seen. He laughed so hard he almost ripped his tracheal tube out.

Dick bounced for a wedding gift: the Adolphus bridal suite through the weekend. Pete and Barb moved their things in an hour before the ceremony.

Pete's gun fell out of his suitcase. The bellhop almost shit.

Barb tipped him fifty dollars. The kid genuflected out of the suite. A hotel limo dropped them at the chapel.

The preacher was a juicehead. Ruby brought his yappy dachshunds. Dick banged some wedding numbers on his squeezebox.

They said their vows in a dive off Stemmons Freeway. Barb cried. Pete held her hand so tight that she winced.

The preacher supplied imitation gold rings. Pete's ring wouldn't fit on his ring finger. The preacher said he'd order him a jumbo—he got his stuff from a mail-order house in Des Moines.

Pete dropped the too-small ring in his pocket. The Till Death Do Us Part pitch got him weak in the knees.

They settled in at the hotel. Barb kept up a refrain: Barbara Jane Lindscott Jahelka Bondurant.

Heshie sent them champagne and a giant gift basket. The room-service kid was atwitter—the President's riding by here on Friday!

They made love. The bed was flouncy pink and enormous.

Barb fell asleep. Pete left an 8:00 P.M. call—his bride had a gig at 9:00 sharp.

He couldn't sleep. He didn't touch the bubbly—booze was starting to feel like a weakness.

The phone rang. He got up and grabbed the parlor extension.

"Yeah?"

"It's me, Pete."

"Ward, Jesus. How'd you get this—?"

Littell said, "Banister just called me. He said Juan Canestel's missing in Dallas. I'm sending Kemper in to meet you, and I want the two of you to find him and do what you have to do to make Friday happen."

98

(Dallas, 11/20/63)

THE PLANE TAXIED up to a loading bay. The pilot rode tailwinds all the way from Meridian and made the run in under two hours.

Littell arranged a private charter. He told the pilot to fly balls-to-the-wall. The little two-seater rattled and shook—Kemper couldn't believe it.

It was 11:48 P.M. They were thirty-six hours short of GO.

Car headlights blinked—Pete's signal.

Kemper unhooked his seat belt. The pilot throttled down and cranked the door open for him.

Kemper jumped out. Propeller backspin almost knocked him flat.

The car pulled up. Kemper got in. Pete punched it across a string of small-craft runways.

A jet whooshed overhead. Love Field looked otherworldly.

Pete said, "What did Ward tell you?"

"That Juan's loose. And that Guy's afraid that Carlos and the others will think he fucked up."

"That's what he told me. And I told him that I didn't like the risks involved, unless somebody tells Carlos that we helped him out and saved Banister from blowing the whole fucking hit."

Kemper cracked the window. His goddamn ears kept popping.

"What did Ward say to that?"

"He said he'll tell Carlos after the hit. *If* we find Canestel and save the fucking day."

A 2-way radio sputtered. Pete turned it down.

"This is J.D. Tippit's off-duty car. Him and Rogers are out looking, and if they get a spot on Juan, *we* go in. Tippit can't leave his patrol sector, and Chuck can't do anything that could fuck him out of showing up for the hit."

They dodged baggage carts. Kemper leaned out the window and popped three Dexedrine dry.

"Where's Banister?"

"He's flying in from New Orleans later. He thinks Juan's solid, and if something happens and they lose him, he'll move Rogers into his slot, and go out with him and the pro shooter."

They knew Juan was volatile. They didn't have him tagged as a possible sex killer. The job was fucked up and full of holes and reeked of amateur-night on-the-job training.

"Where are we going?"

"Jack Ruby's place. Rogers said Juan likes to dig on the whores there. You work inside—Ruby doesn't know you."

Kemper laughed. "Ward told Carlos not to trust psychopaths with bright red sports cars."

Pete said, "You did."

"I've had some revelations since then."

"Are you saying there's something I should know about Juan?"

"I'm saying I quit hating Jack. And I don't really care whether they kill him or not."

The Carousel Club was midweek listless.

A stripper was peeling on the runway. Two plainclothes cops and a hooker clique sat at ringside tables.

Kemper sat near a rear exit. He unscrewed the bulb on his table lamp—shadows covered him from the waist up.

He could see the front and back doors. He could see the runway and stage tables. The shadows made him close to invisible.

Pete was out back with the car. He didn't want Jack Ruby to see him.

The stripper stripped to André Kostelanetz. The hi-fi played off-speed. Ruby sat with the cops and spiked their drinks with his flask.

Kemper sipped scotch. It jump-started the Dexedrine. He got cozy with a new revelation: You've got a chance to toy with the hit.

A dog ran across the runway. The stripper shooed it off. Juan Canestel walked in the front door.

He was alone. He was wearing an Ike jacket and blue jeans.

He went straight for the whores' table. A hostess sat him down.

He'd enlarged his prosthetic bulge. Check that shiv in his left hip pocket.

A sash cord was bunched into his waistband.

Juan bought drinks all around. Ruby schmoozed him up. The stripper tossed a few hips his way.

The cops checked him out. They looked mean and full of hate for non-Anglos.

Juan always carries a gun. They might shake him on general principles.

They might book him on a weapons charge. They might rubber-hose him.

He might betray Banister. The Secret Service might cancel the motorcade.

Juan loved to drink. He might show up for the hit hung over. He might jerk the trigger and miss Jack by a country mile.

Juan loved to talk. He might arouse suspicion between now and noon on Friday.

The sash cord leaked out his *front* waistband.

Juan *is* a sex killer. Juan kills with his surrogate balls.

Juan chatted up the whores. The cops kept sizing him up.

The stripper bowed and walked backstage. Ruby announced last call. Juan zeroed in on a zaftig brunette.

They'll walk out the front door. Pete won't see them. Their combustion might affect Juan's hit performance.

Kemper popped the clip out of his piece and dropped it on the floor. He left one round in the chamber—let's toy with the hit a little more.

The brunette stood up. Juan stood up. The cops looked them over.

The cops huddled. One cop shook his head.

The girl walked toward the parking-lot door. Juan followed her.

The lot fed into an alley. The alley was lined with hot-sheet-hotel doorways.

Pete was just outside.

Juan and the girl disappeared. Kemper counted to twenty. A cleanup man started slapping tables with a rag.

Kemper walked outside. A light mist stung his eyes.

Pete was pissing behind a dumpster. Juan and the whore were strolling down the alley. They were moving toward the second doorway on the left-hand side.

Pete saw him. Pete coughed. Pete said, "Kemper, what are you—?"

Pete stopped. Pete said, "Fuck . . . that's Juan. . . ."

Pete ran down the alley. The second door on the left opened and closed.

Kemper ran. They hit the door together at a full sprint.

A center hallway ran back to front. Every door on both sides was closed. There was no elevator—the hotel was one story only.

Kemper counted ten doors. Kemper heard a stifled screech.

Pete started kicking doors in. He threw his weight left, then right—clean pivots and clean flat-heel shots sheared the doors off their hinges.

The floor shook. Lights snapped on. Sad old sleepy winos cringed and cowered.

Six doors went down. Kemper crashed through number seven with a shoulder snap. A bright ceiling light caught the face-off.

Juan had a knife. The whore had a knife. Juan had a dildo strapped to the crotch of his blue jeans.

Kemper aimed at his head. His one round in the chamber went way wide.

Pete pushed him out of the way. Pete aimed low and fired. Two magnum shots blew out Juan's kneecaps.

He spun over the bed rail. His left leg dropped off at the knee.

The whore giggled. The whore looked at Pete. Something passed between them.

Pete held Kemper back.

Pete let the whore slit Juan's throat.

They drove to a doughnut stand and drank coffee. Kemper felt Dallas ooze into slow motion.

They left Juan there. They *walked* to the car. They drove off law-abidingly slow.

They didn't talk. Pete didn't mention his toy-with-fate number.

This weird adrenaline had everything running in slow motion.

Pete walked over to a pay phone. Kemper watched him feed coins into the slots.

He's calling Carlos in New Orleans. He's pleading for your life.

Pete turned his back and hunched over the phone.

He's saying Banister fucked up. He's saying Boyd killed the henchman he never should have trusted.

He's pleading specifics. He's saying, Give Boyd a piece of the hit—you know he's a competent guy.

He's pleading for mercy.

Kemper sipped coffee. Pete hung up and walked back to their table.

"Who'd you call?"

"My wife. I just wanted to tell her I'd be late."

Kemper smiled. "It doesn't cost that much money to call your hotel."

Pete said, "Dallas is pricey. And things are getting more expensive these days."

Kemper laid on some drawl. "They surely are."

Pete crumpled his cup. "Can I drop you somewhere?"

"I'll get a cab to the airport. Littell told that charter man to wait for me."

"Back to Mississippi?"

"Home's home, son."

Pete winked. "Take care, Kemper. And thanks for the ride."

His patio looked out on rolling hillsides. The view was damn nice for a discount motel.

He requested a southern exposure. The clerk rented him a cabin apart from the main building.

The flight back was beautiful. The dawn sky was goddamn lustrous.

He fell asleep and woke up at noon. The radio said Jack arrived in Texas.

He called the White House and the Justice Department. Second-string aides rebuffed him.

His name was on some kind of list. They cut him off midway through his salutations.

He called the Dallas SAC. The man refused to talk to him.

He called the Secret Service. The duty officer hung up.

He quit toying with it. He sat on his patio and replayed the ride start to finish.

Shadows turned the hills dark green. His replay kept expanding in slow motion.

He heard footsteps. Ward Littell walked up. He was carrying a brand-new Burberry raincoat.

Kemper said, "I thought you'd be in Dallas."

Littell shook his head. "I don't need to see it. And there's something in L.A. I do need to see."

"I like your suit, son. It's good to see you dressing so nicely."

Littell dropped the raincoat. Kemper saw the gun and cracked a big shit-eating grin.

Littell shot him. The impact knocked him off his chair.

The second shot felt like HUSH NOW. Kemper died thinking of Jack.

99

(Beverly Hills, 11/22/63)

THE BELLHOP HANDED over his passkey and pointed out the bungalow. Littell handed him a thousand dollars.

The man was astonished. The man kept saying, "You just want to *see* him?"

I WANT TO SEE THE PRICE.

They stood by the housekeeping shed. The bellhop kept checking their blind side. He said, "Make it quick. You've got to be out before those Mormon guys get back from breakfast."

Littell walked away from him. His head raced two hours ahead and locked in to Texas time.

The bungalow was salmon-pink and green. The key unlocked three deadbolts.

Littell walked in. The front room was filled with medical freezers and intravenous drip caddies. The air reeked of witch hazel and bug spray.

He heard children squealing. He identified the noise as a TV kiddie show.

He followed the squeals down a hallway. A wall clock read 8:09–10:09 Dallas time.

The squeals turned into a dog food commercial. Littell pressed up to the wall and looked through the doorway.

An IV bag was feeding the man blood. He was feeding himself with a hypodermic needle. He was lying buck cadaverous naked on a crank-up hospital bed.

He missed a hip vein. He jabbed his penis and hit the plunger.

His hair touched his back. His fingernails curled over halfway to his palms.

The room smelled like urine. Bugs were floating in a bucket filled with piss.

Hughes pulled the needle out. His bed sagged under the weight of a dozen disassembled slot machines.

100

(Dallas, 11/22/63)

THE DOPE HIT home. Heshie unclenched and eked out a smile.

Pete wiped off the needle. "It's happening about six blocks from here. Wheel yourself to the window about 12:15. You'll be able to see the cars go by."

Heshie coughed into a Kleenex. Blood dripped down his chin.

Pete dropped the TV gizmo in his lap. "Turn it on then. They'll interrupt whatever they're showing for a news bulletin."

Heshie tried to talk. Pete fed him some water.

"Don't nod out, Hesh. You don't get a show like this every day."

Crowds packed Commerce Street from curb to storefront. Homemade signs bobbed ten feet high.

Pete walked down to the club. He had to buck entrenched spectators every inch of the way.

Jack's fans held their ground. Cops kept herding avid types out of the street and back onto the sidewalk.

Little kids rode their dads' shoulders. A million tiny flags on sticks fluttered.

He made the club. Barb saved him a table near the bandstand. A lackluster crowd was watching the show—maybe a dozen lunchtime juicers total.

The combo mauled an uptempo number. Barb blew him a kiss. Pete sat down and smiled his "Sing me a soft one" smile.

A roar ripped through the place—HE'S COMING HE'S COMING HE'S COMING!

The combo ripped an off-key crescendo. Joey and the boys looked half-blitzed.

Barb went straight into "Unchained Melody." Every patron and barmaid and kitchen geek ran for the door.

The roar grew. Engine noise built off of it—limousines and full-dress Harley-Davidsons.

They left the door open. He had Barb to himself and couldn't hear a word she was singing.

He watched her. He made up his own words. She held him with her eyes and her mouth.

The roar did a long slow fade. He braced himself for this big fucking scream.

THE COLD
SIX THOUSAND

To
BILL STONER

PART ONE

EXTRADITION

November 22–25, 1963

I

WAYNE TEDROW JR.

(Dallas, 11/22/63)

THEY SENT HIM to Dallas to kill a nigger pimp named Wendell Durfee. He wasn't sure he could do it.

The Casino Operators Council flew him. They supplied first-class fare. They tapped their slush fund. They greased him. They fed him six cold.

Nobody *said* it:

Kill that coon. Do it good. Take our hit fee.

The flight ran smooth. A stew served drinks. She saw his gun. She played up. She asked dumb questions.

He said he worked Vegas PD. He ran the intel squad. He built files and logged information.

She loved it. She swooned.

"Hon, what you doin' in Dallas?"

He told her.

A Negro shivved a twenty-one dealer. The dealer lost an eye. The Negro booked to Big D. She loved it. She brought him highballs. He omitted details.

The dealer provoked the attack. The council issued the contract—death for ADW Two.

The preflight pep talk. Lieutenant Buddy Fritsch:

"I don't have to tell you what we expect, son. And I don't have to add that your father expects it, too."

The stew played geisha girl. The stew fluffed her beehive.

"What's your name?"

"Wayne Tedrow."

She whooped. "You just *have* to be Junior!"

He looked through her. He doodled. He yawned.

She fawned. She just looooooved his daddy. He flew with her

oodles. She knew he was a Mormon wheel. She'd looove to know more.

Wayne laid out Wayne Senior.

He ran a kitchen-help union. He rigged low pay. He had coin. He had pull. He pushed right-wing tracts. He hobnobbed with fat cats. He knew J. Edgar Hoover.

The pilot hit the intercom. Dallas—on time.

The stew fluffed her hair. "I'll bet you're staying at the Adolphus."

Wayne cinched his seat belt. "What makes you say that?"

"Well, your daddy told me he always stays there."

"I'm staying there. Nobody consulted me, but that's where they've got me booked."

The stew hunkered down. Her skirt slid. Her garter belt gapped.

"Your daddy told me they've got a nice little restaurant right there in the hotel, and, well . . ."

The plane hit rough air. Wayne caught it low. He broke a sweat. He shut his eyes. He saw Wendell Durfee.

The stew touched him. Wayne opened his eyes.

He saw her hickeys. He saw her bad teeth. He smelled her shampoo.

"You were looking a little scared there, Wayne Junior."

"Junior" tore it.

"Leave me alone. I'm not what you want, and I don't cheat on my wife."

1:50 P.M.

They touched down. Wayne got off first. Wayne stamped blood back into his legs.

He walked to the terminal. Schoolgirls blocked the gate. One girl cried. One girl fucked with prayer beads.

He stepped around them. He followed baggage signs. People walked past him. They looked sucker-punched.

Red eyes. Boo-hoo. Women with Kleenex.

Wayne stopped at baggage claim. Kids whizzed by. They shot cap pistols. They laughed.

A man walked up—Joe Redneck—tall and fat. He wore a Stetson. He wore big boots. He wore a mother-of-pearl .45.

"If you're Sergeant Tedrow, I'm Officer Maynard D. Moore of the Dallas Police Department."

They shook hands. Moore chewed tobacco. Moore wore cheap cologne. A woman walked by—boo-hoo-hoo—one big red nose.

Wayne said, "What's wrong?"

Moore smiled. "Some kook shot the President."

Most shops closed early. State flags flew low. Some folks flew rebel flags upright.

Moore drove Wayne in. Moore had a plan: Run by the hotel/ get you set in/find us that jigaboo.

John F. Kennedy—dead.

His wife's crush. His stepmom's fixation. JFK got Janice wet. Janice told Wayne Senior. Janice paid. Janice limped. Janice showed off the welts on her thighs.

Dead was dead. He couldn't grab it. He fumbled the rebounds.

Moore chewed Red Man. Moore shot juice out his window. Gunshots overlapped. Joyous shit in the boonies.

Moore said, "Some people ain't so sad."

Wayne shrugged. They passed a billboard—JFK and the UN.

"You sure ain't sayin' much. I got to say that so far, you ain't the most lively extradition partner I ever had."

A gun went off. Close. Wayne grabbed his holster.

"Whoo! You got a case of the yips, boy!"

Wayne futzed with his necktie. "I just want to get this over with."

Moore ran a red light. "In good time. I don't doubt that Mr. Durfee'll be sayin' hi to our fallen hero before too long."

Wayne rolled up his window. Wayne trapped in Moore's cologne.

Moore said, "I been to Lost Wages quite a few times. In fact, I owe a big marker at the Dunes this very moment."

Wayne shrugged. They passed a bus bench. A colored girl sobbed.

"I heard of your daddy, too. I heard he's quite the boy in Nevada."

A truck ran a red. The driver waved a beer and revolver.

"Lots of people know my father. They all tell me they know him, and it gets old pretty quick."

Moore smiled. "Hey, I think I detect a pulse there."

Motorcade confetti. A window sign: *Big D loves Jack & Jackie.*

"I heard about you, too. I heard you got leanings your daddy don't much care for."

"For instance?"

"Let's try nigger lover. Let's try you chauffeur Sonny Liston around when he comes to Vegas, 'cause the PD's afraid he'll get himself in trouble with liquor and white women, and you *like* him, but you *don't* like the nice Italian folks who keep your little town clean."

The car hit a pothole. Wayne hit the dash.

Moore stared at Wayne. Wayne stared back. They held the stare. Moore ran a red. Wayne blinked first.

Moore winked. "We're gonna have big fun this weekend."

The lobby was swank. The carpets ran thick. Men snagged their boot heels.

People pointed outside—look look look—the motorcade passed the hotel. JFK drove by. JFK waved. JFK bought it close by.

People talked. Strangers braced strangers. The men wore western suits. The women dressed faux-Jackie.

Check-ins swamped the desk. Moore ad-libbed. Moore walked Wayne to the bar.

SRO—big barside numbers.

A TV sat on a table. A barman goosed the sound. Moore shoved up to a phone booth. Wayne scoped the TV out.

Folks jabbered. The men wore hats. Everyone wore boots and high heels. Wayne stood on his toes. Wayne popped over hat brims.

The picture jumped and settled in. Sound static and confusion. Cops. A thin punk. Words: "Oswald"/"weapon"/"Red sympath—"

A guy waved a rifle. Newsmen pressed in. A camera panned. There's the punk. He's showing fear and contusions.

The noise was bad. The smoke was thick. Wayne lost his legs.

A man raised a toast. "Oughta give Oswald a—"

Wayne stood down. A woman jostled him—wet cheeks and runny mascara.

Wayne walked to the phone booth. Moore had the door cracked.

He said, "Guy, listen now."

He said, "Wet-nursing some kid on some bullshit extradition—"

"Bullshit" tore it.

Wayne jabbed Moore. Moore swung around. His pant legs hiked up.

Fuck—knives in his boot tops. Brass knucks in one sock.

Wayne said, "Wendell Durfee, remember?"

Moore stood up. Moore got magnetized. Wayne tracked his eyes.

He caught the TV. He caught a caption. He caught a still shot: "Slain Officer J. D. Tippit."

Moore stared. Moore trembled. Moore shook.

Wayne said, "Wendell Durf—"

Moore shoved him. Moore ran outside.

The council booked him a *biggg* suite. A bellboy supplied history. JFK loved the suite. JFK fucked women there. Ava Gardner blew him on the terrace.

Two sitting rooms. Two bedrooms. Three TVs. Slush funds. Six cold. Kill that nigger, boy.

Wayne toured the suite. History lives. JFK loved Dallas quail.

He turned the TVs on. He tuned in three channels. He caught the show three ways. He walked between sets. He nailed the story.

The punk was Lee Harvey Oswald. The punk shot JFK and Tippit. Tippit worked Dallas PD. DPD was tight-knit. Moore probably knew him.

Oswald was pro-Red. Oswald loved Fidel. Oswald worked at a schoolbook plant. Oswald clipped the Prez on his lunch break.

DPD had him. Their HQ teemed. Cops. Reporters. Camera hogs all.

Wayne flopped on a couch. Wayne shut his eyes. Wayne saw Wendell Durfee. Wayne opened his eyes. Wayne saw Lee Oswald.

He killed the sound. He pulled his wallet pix.

There's his mother—back in Peru, Indiana.

She left Wayne Senior. Late '47. Wayne Senior hit her. He broke bones sometimes.

She asked Wayne who he loved most. He said, "My dad." She slapped him. She cried. She apologized.

The slap tore it. He went with Wayne Senior.

He called his mother—May '54—he called en route to the

Army. She said, "Don't fight in silly wars." She said, "Don't hate like Wayne Senior."

He cut her off. Binding/permanent/4-ever.

There's his stepmom.

Wayne Senior ditched Wayne's mom. Wayne Senior wooed Janice. Wayne Senior brought Wayne along. Wayne was thirteen. Wayne was horny. Wayne dug on Janice.

Janice Lukens Tedrow made rooms tilt. She played indolent wife. She played scratch golf. She played A-club tennis.

Wayne Senior feared her spark. She watched Wayne grow up. She torched reciprocal. She left her doors open. She invited looks. Wayne Senior knew it. Wayne Senior didn't care.

There's *his* wife.

Lynette Sproul Tedrow. Perched in his lap. Grad night at Brigham Young.

He's shell-shocked. He got his chem degree—BYU/'59—summa cum laude. He craved action. He joined Vegas PD. Fuck summa cum laude.

He met Lynette in Little Rock. Fall '57. Central High deseg-regates. Rednecks. Colored kids. The Eighty-Second Airborne.

Some white boys prowl. Some white boys snatch a colored boy's sandwich. Lynette hands him hers. The white boys attack. Corporal Wayne Tedrow Jr. counters.

He beats them down. He spears one fuck. The fuck screams, "Mommy!"

Lynette hits on Wayne. She's seventeen. He's twenty-three. He's got some college.

They fucked on a golf course. Sprinklers doused them. He told Janice all.

She said, "You and Lynette peaked early. And you probably liked the fight as much as the sex."

Janice knew him. Janice had the home-court advantage.

Wayne looked out a window. TV crews roamed. News vans double-parked. He walked through the suite. He turned off the TVs. Three Oswalds vanished.

He pulled his file. All carbons: LVPD/Dallas County Sheriff's.

Durfee, Wendell (NMI). Male Negro/DOB 6-6-27/Clark County, Nevada. 6'4"/155.

Pander beefs—3/44 up. "Well-known dice-game habitue." No busts outside Vegas and Dallas.

"Known to drive Cadillacs."

"Known to wear flamboyant attire."

"Known to have fathered 13 children out of wedlock."

"Known to pander Negro women, white women, male homosexuals & Mexican transvestites."

Twenty-two pimp busts. Fourteen convictions. Nine child-support liens. Five bail jumps.

Cop notes: Wendell's smart/Wendell's dumb/Wendell cut that cat at Binion's.

The cat was mobbed up. The cat shanked Wendell first. The council set policy. The LVPD enforced it.

"Known Dallas County Associates":

Marvin Duquesne Settle/male Negro/Texas State custody.

Fenton "Duke" Price/male Negro/Texas State custody.

Alfonzo John Jefferson/male Negro/4219 Wilmington Road, Dallas 8, Tex. "Gambling partner of Wendell Durfee."

County Probation: (Stat. 92.04 Tex. St. Code) 9/14/60–9/14/65. Employed: Dr Pepper Bottling Plant. Note: "Subject to make fine payments for term of probation, i.e.: every 3rd Friday (Dr Pepper payday) County Prob. Off."

Donnell George Lundy/male Negro/Texas State custody.

Manuel "Bobo" Herrara/male Mexican/Texas State cust—

The phone rang. Wayne grabbed it.

"Yeah?"

"It's me, son. Your new best buddy."

Wayne grabbed his holster. "Where are you?"

"Right now I'm noplace worth bein'. But you meet me at eight o'clock."

"Where?"

"The Carousel Club. You be there, and we'll find us that burrhead."

Wayne hung up. Wayne got butterflies.

Wendell, I don't want to kill you.

2

WARD J. LITTELL

(Dallas, 11/22/63)

THERE'S THE LIMO. It's on the runway. It's late-model FBI black.

The plane taxied up. It passed Air Force One. Marines flanked the tailhatch. The pilot cut the engine. The plane fishtailed. The ramp popped and dropped.

Littell got out. His ears popped. His legs uncramped.

They worked fast. They rigged his flight plan. They flew him two-seat non-deluxe.

Mr. Hoover called him—D.C. to L.A.

He said, "The President was shot and killed. I want you to fly to Dallas and monitor the investigation."

The hit occurred at 12:30. It was 4:10 now. Mr. Hoover called at 12:40. Mr. Hoover got the news and called fast.

Littell ran. The limo driver popped the door. The backseat was stuffy. The windows were smoked. Love Field was all monochrome.

Stick figures. Baggage crews. Newsmen and charter planes.

The driver pulled out. Littell saw a box on the seat. He opened it. He emptied it out.

One special agent's shield. One FBI photo ID card. One Bureau-issue .38/holster.

His old photo. *His* old gun.

He gave them up in '60. Mr. Hoover forced him out. He had cover tools now—new and old—he had cosmetic reinstatement.

Mr. Hoover stashed said tools. *In Dallas*. Mr. Hoover predicted the hit.

He knew the locale. He sensed the time frame. He was passively complicit. He sensed Littell's involvement. He sensed Littell's need to quash talk.

Littell looked out his window. The tint made funhouse distortions. Clouds imploded. Buildings weaved. People blipped.

He brought a radio. He played it flying in. He got the basic stats:

One suspect caught—a kid—a sheep-dipped leftist. Guy Banister dipped him. The kid killed a cop. Two cops were set to kill him. Phase Two went bad. The second cop botched his assignment.

Littell holstered up. Littell studied his ID.

Cop/lawyer then. Mob lawyer now. Hoover foe to Hoover ally. A one-man law firm with three clients:

Howard Hughes/Jimmy Hoffa/Carlos Marcello.

He called Carlos. Ten A.M. L.A. time. Carlos was happy. Carlos beat Bobby K.'s deportation bill.

Bobby tried Carlos in New Orleans. Carlos *owned* New Orleans. Carlos was jury-proof there.

Kennedy hubris:

The jury acquits Carlos. Bobby sulks. Jack dies one hour on.

The streets were dead. Windows zipped by. Ten thousand TVs glowed.

It was *his* show.

He developed the plan. Pete Bondurant helped. Carlos okayed it and went with Guy Banister's crew. Guy embellished *his* plan. Guy revised it. Guy botched it.

Pete was in Dallas. Pete just got married. Pete was at the Adolphus Hotel. Guy B. was here. Guy B. was somewhere close.

Littell counted windows. All tint-distorted. Smudges and blurs. His thoughts blew wide. His thoughts cohered:

Talk to Pete. Kill Oswald. Ensure a one-shooter consensus.

The limo hit downtown Dallas. Littell pinned on his shield.

There's Dealey Plaza. The PD building's close. Look for:

The book building/a Hertz sign/Greek columns.

There—

The columns. The sign. Mourners at Houston and Elm. A hot-dog vendor. Nuns sobbing.

Littell shut his eyes. The driver turned right. The driver pulled down a ramp. The driver stopped hard and fast. The back windows slid down.

Somebody coughed. Somebody said, "Mr. Littell?"

Littell opened his eyes. Littell saw a basement garage. There's a kiddy Fed standing there. He's all uptight.

"Sir, I'm Special Agent Burdick, and . . . well, the ASAC said you should come straight up and see the witnesses."

Littell grabbed his briefcase. The gun chafed his hip. He got out. He stretched. He cleaned his glasses.

Burdick stuck close. Burdick rode him tight. They walked to a freight lift. Burdick pushed 3.

"Sir, I have to say it's a madhouse. We've got people saying two shooters, three, four, they can't even agree where the shots—"

"Did you isolate them?"

"Well . . . no."

"Who's interviewing them?"

The boy stuttered. The boy gulped.

"Which *agencies*, son?"

"Well, we've got us, DPD, the Sheriff's, and I—"

The door opened. Noise boomed in. The squadroom was packed.

Littell looked around. Burdick got antsy. Littell ignored him.

The witnesses were antsy. The witnesses wore name tags. The witnesses perched on one bench.

Thirty-odd people: Talking. Fretting. Contaminating facts.

Back-wall cubicles. Cops and civilians—holed up in interview slots. Flustered cops and civilians in shock.

Forty desks. Forty phones. Forty cops talking loud. Odd badges on suitcoats. Wastebaskets dumped. Inter-agency chaos and—

"Sir, can we—"

Littell walked over. Littell checked the bench. The wits squirmed. The wits smoked. Full ashtrays jumped.

I saw this/I saw that/his head went pop! A talkathon—bad work—pure mass-witness slop.

Littell looked for standouts. Solid types/credible wits.

He stood back. He framed the bench. He saw a woman: Dark hair/handsome/thirty-five-plus.

She sat still. She stayed calm. She watched an exit door. She saw Littell. She looked away. She never blinked.

Burdick walked a phone up. Burdick mimed "*Him.*" Littell grabbed the phone. The cord stretched taut.

Mr. Hoover said, "Be concise."

Littell cupped his free ear. The room noise half died.

"The preliminary stage of the investigation has been ineptly executed. That's all I'm certain of at this point."

"I'm not surprised and I'm not disappointed, and I'm thoroughly convinced that Oswald acted without assistance. Your job is to cull the names of potentially embarrassing witnesses who might contradict that thesis."

Littell said, "Yes, sir."

Burdick held up a clipboard. Note slips were clamped in. A witness log/clamped witness statements/drivers' licenses attached.

The phone went dead. Burdick grabbed it. Littell grabbed the clipboard. It bulged. The clip wobbled.

He skimmed the slips.

Two-line statements. Confiscated DLs. Detainment insurance. Ambiguous data: 3/4/5/6 shots/1/2/3 directions.

The stockade fence. The book building. The triple underpass. Head-on shots. Missed shots. Shots from behind.

Littell checked DL pix.

Wit #6: Shots at Houston and Elm. Wit #9: Shots off the freeway. The calm woman: 2 shots/2 directions. Her stats: Arden Smith/West Mockingbird Lane.

The smoke was bad. Littell stepped back. The smoke made him sneeze. He bumped a desk. He dropped the log. He walked to the interview slots.

Burdick tailed him. The room noise doubled. Littell checked the slots.

Shoddy work—no tape machines/no stenos.

He checked slot #1. A thin cop braced a thin kid. The kid laughed. What a gas. My dad voted for Nixon.

Littell checked slot #2. A fat cop braced a fat man.

The cop said, "Mr. Bowers, I'm not disputing what you told me."

Mr. Bowers wore a railroad cap. Mr. Bowers squirmed.

"For the tenth time then, so I can go home. I was up in the tower behind that fence on the knoll. I saw two cars cruising around there about . . . shit . . . a half hour before the shooting, and two men standing right at the edge of the fence, and then just as I heard the shots, I saw a flash of light from that very spot."

The cop doodled. Mr. Bowers tapped a cigarette. Littell studied him. Littell got queasy.

He didn't know the shooter plan. He *did* know credible wits. Bowers was intractably firm. Bowers was *good*.

Burdick tapped Littell. Littell swung around. Littell knocked him back.

"What?"

Burdick stepped back. "Well, I was just thinking that DPD pulled these three guys, bums or something, out of a railroad car behind the fence, about a half hour after the shooting. We've got them in the tank."

Littell went more queasy.

Littell said, "Show me."

Burdick walked point. They passed the slots. They passed a coffee-break room. Hallways crossed. They veered left. They hit a mesh-front pen.

An intercom popped: "Agent Burdick. Front desk, please."

Burdick said, "I should catch that."

Littell nodded. Burdick fidgeted. Burdick took off from a crouch. Littell grabbed the mesh. The light was bad. Littell squinted hard.

He saw two bums. He saw Chuck Rogers.

Chuck was Pete's man. Wet arts/CIA. Chuck was tight with Guy B.

Rogers saw Littell. The bums ignored him. Rogers smiled. Littell touched his shield. Rogers mimed a rifle shot.

He moved his lips. He went "Pow!"

Littell backtracked.

He walked down the hall. He turned right. He hit a bisecting hall. He made the turn. He saw a side door.

He pushed it open. He saw fire steps and rungs. Across the hall: A men's room and a door marked "Jailer."

The men's room door opened. Mr. Bowers walked out. He stretched. He zipped his fly. He settled his nuts.

He saw Littell. He squinted. He keyed on his shield.

"FBI, right?"

"That's right."

"Well, I'm glad I ran into you, 'cause there's something I forgot to tell the other guy."

Littell smiled. "I'll pass it along."

Bowers scratched his neck. "Okay, then. You tell him I saw some cops rousting these hoboes out of a hay car, and one of them looked like one of the guys I saw by the fence."

Littell pulled his notebook.

He scribbled. He smeared some ink. His hand shook. The book shook.

Bowers said, "I sure feel sorry for Jackie."

Littell smiled. Bowers smiled. Bowers tipped his cap. He jiggled some coins. He ambled. He walked away slooooooow.

Littell watched his back.

Bowers ambled. Bowers turned right. Bowers hit the main hall. Littell flexed his hands. Littell caught his breath.

He worked the Jailer door. He jiggled the knob. He forced it. The door popped. Littell stepped in.

A twelve-by-twelve space—dead empty. A desk/a chair/a key rack.

Paperwork—tacked to a corkboard:

Vagrant sheets—"Doyle"/"Paolino"/"Abrahams"—no mug shots attached.

Call it: Rogers packed fake ID. Rogers booked in with it.

One key on the rack—cell-size/thick brass.

Littell grabbed the sheets. Littell pocketed them. Littell grabbed the key. He gulped. He walked out brazen. He walked to the pen.

He unlocked the door. Rogers primed the bums. He pumped them up. He went "Ssshh now." He gave a pep talk.

We got ourselves a savior—just do what I say.

The bums huddled. The bums stepped out. The bums hugged the wall.

Littell walked.

He hit the main hall. He faced the squadroom. He blocked the view. He signaled Rogers. He pointed. The fire door—go.

He heard footsteps. The bums squealed. The bums giggled loud. The fire door creaked. A bum yelled, "Hallelujah!" The fire door slammed.

Littell caught a breeze. His sweat froze. His pulse went haywire.

He walked to the squadroom. His legs fluttered and dipped. He grazed desks. He bumped walls. He bumped into cops.

The wit bench was smoked in. Twenty cigarettes plumed. Arden Smith was gone.

Littell looked around. Littell scanned desks. Littell saw the wit log.

He grabbed it. He checked statements and DLs. Arden Smith's package—gone.

He checked the slots. He checked the halls. He checked the main window.

There's Arden Smith. She's on the street. She's walking fast. She's walking *away*.

She crossed Houston. Cars swerved by her. She made Dealey Plaza.

Littell blinked.

He lost her. Jack's mourners shadowed her up.

3
PETE BONDURANT
(Dallas, 11/22/63)

THE BRIDAL SUITE. The fuck pad supreme.

Gilt wallpaper. Cupids. Pink rugs and chairs. A fake-fur bed-spread—baby-ass pink.

Pete watched Barb sleep.

Her legs slid. She kicked wide. She thrashed the sheets.

Barbara Jane Lindscott Jahelka Bondurant.

He got her back early. He sealed up the suite. He closed out the news. She'll wake up. She'll *get* the news. She'll *know.*

I fucked Jack in '62. It was lackluster and brief. You bugged some rooms. You got his voice. You taped it. The shakedown failed. Your pals regrouped. You killed Jack instead.

Pete moved his chair. Pete got fresh views. Barb tossed. Her hair swirled.

She didn't love Jack. She serviced Jack. She cosigned extortion. She wouldn't cosign death.

6:10 P.M.

Jack should be dead. Guy's boy ditto. Chuck Rogers had a plane stashed. The crew should be out.

Barb twitched. Pete fought a headache. Pete popped aspirin and scotch.

He got *bad* headaches—chronic—they started with the Jack squeeze. The squeeze failed. He stole some Mob heroin. A CIA man helped.

Kemper Cathcart Boyd.

They were *très* tight. They were mobbed up. They shared spit with Sam G. They worked for Carlos M. They worked for Santo Trafficante. They all hated Commies. They all loved Cuba. They all hated the Beard.

Money and turf—dual agendas. Let's pluck the Beard. Let's repluck our casinos.

Santo and Sam played both ends. They sucked up to Castro. They bought "H" off Brother Raúl. Carlos stayed pure. Carlos did not fuck *la Causa.*

Pete and Boyd stole the dope. Sam and Santo nailed them. Pete got the word. They did biz with Fidel.

Carlos stayed neutral. Biz was biz. Outfit laws overruled causes.

They *all* hated Bobby. They *all* hated Jack. Jack fucked them at Pigs. Jack raided Cuban exile camps. Jack nuzzled the Beard.

Bobby deported Carlos. Bobby fucked with the Outfit *très* large. Carlos hated Jack and Bobby—*molto bravissimo*.

Ward Littell hated them. Ward smuggled Carlos back. Ward played factotum. Ward ran his deportation case.

Ward said, Let's clip Jack. Carlos liked it. Carlos talked to Santo and Sam.

They liked it.

Santo and Sam had plans. They said let's clip Pete and Boyd. We want our dope back. We want revenge.

Ward talked to Sam and Carlos. Ward pressed Pete's case. They quashed said clip plan.

The catch:

We let you live. You *owe* us. Now whack Jack the K.

Guy Banister was working up a hit plan. His plan resembled Littell's. Hit plans were running epidemic. Jack pissed off mucho hotheads. The cocksucker was doomed.

Guy had pull. Guy knew Carlos. Guy knew Cuban exiles. Guy knew fat cats with coin. Guy dipped a geek in sheep shit. Guy preempted Ward's plan.

He pitched it to Carlos. Carlos okayed it. Carlos scotched Ward's plan. Shit went sideways. Personnel shifted. Some Pete and Ward guys joined Guy's crew.

Glitches glitched—last-minute—Pete and Boyd unglitched them.

Santo and Sam hated Boyd. They reissued their death decree. Kemper Boyd—*mort sans doute*.

Barb stirred. Pete held his breath. The aspirin hit. His headache fizzled.

Santo and Sam let *him* live. Carlos liked him. He loved *la Causa*. The Boys had plans. He *might* fit in.

He worked for Howard Hughes—'52 to '60. He pimped for him. He scored his dope. He did his strongarm work.

Ward Littell lawyered for Hughes. Hughes wanted to buy up Las Vegas. Hughes craved the Vegas Strip. Hughes craved *all* the hotel-casinos.

Hughes had a buyout plan. Said plan would take years. The Boys had a plan too:

Let's sell Las Vegas. Let's bilk Howard Hughes. We'll keep our work crews. We'll skim Hughes blind. We'll *still* own Las Vegas.

Carlos owned Ward. Ward's job to be: Broker the deal and tailor it *our* way.

The Boys owned Pete. The Boys implied:

Go to Vegas. Work with Ward. Pre-pave the Hughes deal. You know muscle work. You know heroin. We might rescind our no-dope rule. We might let you push to the spooks.

We *might* not kill you. We *might* not kill your Twist queen.

Barb left her gowns out. Blue spangles and green. Two shows tonite. His wife and her ex-hubby's trio.

A sad room. Sad Barb. Let's send one up to Jack.

Hit news preceded the hit. Outfit guys talked. Outfit guys *knew.* Hesh Ryskind checked into the Adolphus. Hesh had cancer. Hesh came to gloat and die.

Hesh watched the motorcade. Hesh died at 1:00 P.M. Hesh kicked with Jack concurrent.

Pete touched the bed. Pink sheets met red hair—one loud color clash.

The doorbell chimed—the B-flat "Eyes of Texas." Barb slept through it. Pete walked over. Pete cracked the door.

Fuck—there's Guy Banister.

Guy popped sweat. Guy was sixty-plus. Guy had heart attacks.

Pete stepped outside. Pete shut the door. Guy waved a high-ball glass.

"Come on. I rented a room down the hall."

Pete followed him over. The floor rugs sent sparks up. Guy unlocked his door and bolted them in.

He grabbed a jug—Old Crow bond—Pete snatched it quick.

"Tell me they're both dead, and this isn't about some fuck-up."

Guy twirled his glass. "King John the First is dead, but my boy killed a cop and got arrested."

The floor dipped. Pete dug his legs in.

"The cop who was supposed to kill him?"

Guy eyeballed the jug. Pete tossed it back.

"That's right, Tippit. My boy pulled a piece and popped him out in Oak Cliff."

"Does *your boy* know your name?"

Guy uncorked the jug. "No, I worked him through a cutout."

Pete slapped the wall. Plaster chips flew. Guy spilled some booze.

"But your boy knows the cutout's name. The cutout knows *your* name, and your boy'll name names sooner or later. Is that a fucking accurate assessment?"

Guy poured a drink. His hand shook. Pete straddled a chair. His headache retorqued. He lit a cigarette. *His* hand shook.

"We have to kill him."

Guy blotted the spill. "Tippit had a backup man, but he wanted to go in alone. It was a two-man job, so we're paying the price now."

Pete squeezed the chairback. The slats shimmied. One slat sheared loose.

"Don't tell me what we should have done. Tell me how we get to your boy."

Guy sat on the bed. Guy stretched out comfy.

"I gave the job to Tippit's backup."

Pete said, "And?"

"And he's got access to the jail, and he's mean enough for the job, and he owes some casino markers, which means he's in hock to the Outfit."

Pete said, "There's more. You're trying to sell me a bill of goods."

"Well . . ."

"Well, shit, *what?*"

"Well, he's a tough nut, and he doesn't want to do it, and he's stuck on a liaison job with some Vegas cop."

Pete cracked his knuckles. "We'll convince him."

"I don't know. He's a tough nut."

Pete flipped his cigarette. It hit Guy clean. He yipped. He snuffed it out. He burned his pillow.

Pete coughed. "You're the first one Carlos will clip if your boy talks."

A TV kicked on—one room down. The walls leeched sound: "Nation mourns"/"valiant first lady."

Guy said, "I'm scared."

"That's your first fucking sensible comment."

"We got him, though. We made the world spin."

The old fuck *glowed*. Sweats and shitty grins.

"Tell me the rest of it."

"What about a toast to the fallen—"

"What about Rogers and the pro shooter?"

Guy coughed. "Okay, first things first. Mr. Hoover flew Littell in as soon as he heard, and I saw him over at DPD. The cops got Rogers on a sweep, but Littell let him out and misplaced the paperwork. He was carrying fake ID, so I think we're clear there."

Glitches/reglitches—

"The pro. Did he get out?"

"Heads up on that. He got down to McAllen and walked across the border. He left a message at my place in New Orleans, and I called him and got the all-clear."

"What about Rog—"

"He's at a motel in Fort Worth. Littell said the witnesses are confused and telling different stories, and Mr. Hoover's hell-bent to prove that it was all my boy. Littell said we've only got one guy to worry about."

Pete said, "Keep going. Don't make me work so hard."

"Okay, then. Littell said a railroad man put a half-ass ID on Rogers, so it's my considered opinion that we should clip him."

Pete shook his head. "It's too close to the hit. You want him to go back to work like nothing happened."

"Then you throw some fear into him."

"No. Let the backup do it. Have him pull a cop number."

That TV blared—"Nation grieves"/"sole killer."

Guy folded his arms. "There's one more thing."

"I'm listening."

"Okay, then. I talked to the pro. He thinks there's a chance that Jack Ruby put it together."

Ruby: Bagman/pimp/Littell's   old   snitch/strip-club entrepre—

"I had the crew at a safe house up in Oklahoma. Rogers called Ruby and arranged for some entertainment. The pro said he showed up with two girls and some flunky, and they saw the rifles out back and—wait now—don't get your tits in a twist—I told the backup to brace Ruby and see what he knows."

The room dipped. Crash dimensions. Pete rode out the drop.

Guy said, "We might have to clip them."

Pete said, "No."

Guy reglowed. Guy previewed Heart Attack 3.

"No? The big man says *no?* The big man says no, like he

doesn't know the Boys are talking, and they're saying he's lost his taste for the Life?"

Pete stood up. Pete cracked his thumbs. Pete flexed his hands. Pete grabbed the chair slats. Pete pulled. Pete ripped the chair to sticks.

Guy pissed his britches. Guy fucking plotzed. The stain spread. His crotch seeped. He doused the sheets.

Pete walked out. The hall dipped. The walls balanced him. He walked back to his suite. He stopped ten feet short. He heard his TV.

He heard Barb sob. He heard Barb throw chairs at a wall.

4

(Dallas, 11/22/63)

A DOG SHIT on the runway. A stripper dodged turds. Welcome to the Carousel Club.

Cops clapped. Cops whooped. Cops ruled the room. The club was closed to the public. The owner loved Jackie. The owner loved JFK.

Let's mourn. Let's ride out this tsuris. Let's show some respect.

You badged in. The owner loved cops. Your host—Jack Ruby.

Wayne walked in. Wayne dropped Maynard Moore's name. Ruby seated him. Dallas cops ran tall. Boot heels did it. Wayne was six-one. The cops dwarfed him.

A bandstand adjoined the runway. A sax and drum worked. Two strippers stripped. The blonde looked like Lynette. The brunette looked like Janice.

Moore was late. The club was loud. The combo played "Night Train." Wayne sipped 7-Up. The music fucked with him. The drum pops set up pix.

Pop—he caps Wendell Durfee. Pop—he plants a throwdown piece.

A stripper swayed by. She wore a pastie-patch. Her crotch stubble showed. A cop snapped her G-string. She swayed his way.

Ruby worked the room.

He dumped ashtrays. He tossed scraps. He lured his dog off the ramp. He poured drinks. He lit cigarettes. He laid out some grief.

A fuck killed his President. The fuck was a beatnik. His book-keeper split. She blew the coop. She blew him off. She wouldn't blow his friends.

He owed the IRS. Arden said she'd help. Arden was skunk cooze. Arden lied and stole. Arden had a fake address. A beatnik shot his hero.

Maynard Moore walked in.

He whooped. He rebel-yelled. He sailed his hat. A stripper snagged it.

Moore walked up to Ruby. Ruby went oh shit. The dog jumped in. Moore grabbed him. Moore kissed him. Moore tweaked his tail.

Ruby yukked. Boychik—you slay me!

Moore dropped the dog. Moore manhandled Ruby. He shoved him. He flicked his mezuzah. He knocked off his hat.

Wayne watched. Moore *squeezed* Ruby.

He jerked his necktie. He snapped his suspenders. He jabbed at his chest. Ruby squirmed. Ruby bumped a rubber machine.

Moore dressed him down. Ruby pulled a handkerchief. Ruby pat-dried his head.

Wayne walked over. Wayne caught Moore in tight.

"Pete's in town. People ain't gonna like what you might know, so you may be owin' some favors."

Wayne coughed. Moore turned around. Ruby squeezed his mezuzah chain.

Moore smiled. "Wayne, this is Jack. Jack's a Yankee, but we like him anyway."

Moore had pressing shit in Plano. Wayne said okay. Fuck it. Let's stall—let's postpone Wendell D.

Traffic was dead. A breeze stirred. Moore drove his off-duty sled. A Chevy 409—lake pipes and slicks—Stemmons Freeway faaaast.

Wayne gripped the dash-bar. Moore sipped Everclear. The fumes stung bad.

The radio howled. A preacher proselytized:

John F-for-Fruitcake Kennedy loved Pope Pinko. He sold his soul to the Jewnited Nations. God bless Lee H-for-Hero Oswald.

Wayne doused the volume. Moore laughed.

"You got a low capacity for the truth, unlike your daddy."

Wayne cracked his wind wing. "Are all the DPD guys like

you, or did they waive the IQ test in your case?"

Moore winked. "DPD runs to the right side of the street. We got some Klan and we got some John Birch. It's like that pamphlet your daddy puts out. 'Do you score red or red, white, and blue?' "

Wayne felt rain. "His pamphlets make money. And you won't see him wearing a sheet in Pigshit, Texas."

"You certainly won't, to his everlasting discredit."

The rain came. The rain went. Wayne fugued on out. The fumes tickled. The car droned. He rehashed recent shit.

West Vegas: Assault One/eight counts. A white man beats up colored whores.

He picked them up. He took them home. He beat them and took snapshots—and LVPD didn't care.

He cared. He told Wayne Senior. Wayne Senior pooh-poohed it.

Moore pulled off the freeway. Moore trawled side streets. He hit his brights. He scanned curb plates. He drove down a tract row.

He grazed curbs. He read mailbox names. He found *the* box. He pulled over and stopped.

Wayne squinted. Wayne saw the name: "Bowers."

Wayne stretched. Moore stretched. Moore grabbed a sandwich bag.

"This won't take no more than two minutes."

Wayne yawned. Moore got out. Wayne got out and leaned on the car.

The house was drab. The lawn was brown. The house had peeled paint and chipped stucco.

Moore walked to the porch. Moore rang the bell. A man opened up. Moore badged him. Moore shoved him inside. Moore kicked the door shut.

Wayne stretched some kinks out. Wayne dug on the car.

He kicked the slicks. He touched the pipes. He popped the hood. He sniffed the fuel valves. He nailed the smell. He broke down the oxide components.

You're a cop now. You're a good one. You're a chemist still.

Somebody screamed. Wayne slammed the hood. It muffled scream #2.

Dogs barked. Curtains jerked. Neighbors scoped the Bowers pad.

Moore walked out.

He grinned. He weaved a tad. He wiped blood off his shirt.

They drove back to Big D. Moore chewed Red Man. He tuned in Wolfman Jack. He mimicked his howl. He lip-synced R&B.

They hit Browntown. They found the guy's shack: Four walls—all plywood and glue.

Moore parked on the lawn. Moore grazed a boss Lincoln. The windows were down. The interior glowed.

Moore spat juice. Moore sprayed the seats good.

"You best believe they'll name a car after Kennedy. And every nigger in captivity'll rob and rape to get one."

Wayne walked up. Moore trailed back. The door stood open. Wayne looked in. Wayne saw a colored guy.

The guy crouched. The guy *worked*. The guy fucked with his TV set. He tapped the dials. He tweaked the cord. He raised static and snow.

Wayne knocked. Moore walked in. Moore scoped this shrine shelf:

A plug-in JFK. Bobby cutouts. A Martin Luther King doll.

The guy saw them. He stood up. He shivered. He double-clutched.

Wayne walked in. "Are you Mr. Jefferson?"

Moore sprayed juice. Moore doused a chair.

"He's the boy. Aka 'Jeff,' aka 'Jeffy,' you think I don't do my homework?"

Jeff said, "That's me. Yessir."

Wayne smiled. "You're in no trouble. We're looking for a friend of—"

"How come you people got all these President names? Half the boys I take down got names more distinguished than mine."

"Yessir, that's true, but I don't know what answer to tell you, so—"

"I popped a boy named Roosevelt D. McKinley, and he didn't even know where his mama stole them names from, which is one sorry-ass state of affairs."

Jeff shrugged. Moore mimicked him. He went slack. He bugged his eyes. He pulled a beavertail sap.

The TV sparked. A picture blipped. There's Lee H. Oswald.

Moore spat on the screen. "There's the boy you should name your pickaninnies after. He killed my friend J. D. Tippit, who was one dickswingin' white man, and it offends me to be in the same room as you on the day he died."

Jeff shrugged. Jeff looked at Wayne. Moore twirled his sap. The TV popped off. Bum tubes crackled.

Jeff twitched. His knees shook. Wayne touched his shoulder. Moore mimicked him. Moore swished.

"You boys are *suuuch* the pair. You'll be holdin' hands any damn second."

That tore—

Wayne shoved Moore. Moore tripped. Moore knocked a lamp down. Jeff shook nelly-style. Wayne shoved him in the kitchen.

They fit tight. The sink cramped them. Wayne toed the door shut.

"Wendell Durfee's running. He always runs to Dallas, so why don't you tell me what you know about that."

"Sir, I don't—"

"Don't call me 'sir,' just tell me what you know."

"Sir, I mean mister, I don't know where Wendell's at. If I'm lyin', I'm flyin'."

"You're shucking me. Stop it, or I'll hand you up to that cracker."

"Mister, I ain't woofin' you. I don't know where Wendell's at."

The walls shook. Shit cracked one room over. Wayne made the sounds:

Sap shots. Hard steel meets plywood and glue.

Jeff shook. Jeff gulped. Jeff picked a hangnail.

Wayne said, "Let's try this. You work at Dr Pepper. You got paid today."

"That's right. If I'm lyin', I'm—"

"And you made your probation payment."

"You ain't woofin' I did."

"Now, you've got some money left. It's burning a hole in your pocket. Wendell's your gambling buddy. There's some kind of payday crap game that you can point me to."

Jeff sucked his hangnail. Jeff gullllped.

"Then how come I ain't at that game right now?"

"Because you lent Wendell most of your money."

Glass broke. Wayne made the sound: One sap shot/one TV screen fucked.

"Wendell Durfee. Give him up, or I tell Tex that you've been porking little white kids."

Jeff lit a cigarette. Jeff choked on it. Jeff coughed smoke out.

"Liddy Baines, she used to go with Wendell. She knowed I owed him money, an' she came by an' said he was lookin' to get down to Mexico. I gave her all but five dollars of my check."

Wood cracked. The walls shook. The floor shook.

"Address?"

"Seventy-first and Dunkirk. The little white house two up from the corner."

"What about the game?"

"Eighty-third and Clifford. The alley by the warehouse."

Wayne opened the door. Jeff stood behind him. Jeff got in a runner's crouch. Moore saw Wayne. Moore bowed. Moore winked.

The TV was dead. The shelf shrine was dust. The walls were pulp and spit.

It got real.

Moore had a throwdown piece. Moore had a pump. A coroner owed him. He'd fudge the wound text.

Wayne went dry. Wayne got pinpricks. Wayne's nuts shriveled up.

They drove. They went Darktown-deep. They went by Liddy Baines' shack. Nobody was home—Liddy, where you at?

They hit a pay phone. Moore called Dispatch. Moore got Liddy Baines' stats: No wants/no warrants/no vehicle extant.

They drove to 83rd and Clifford. They passed junkyards and dumps. Liquor stores and blood banks. Mohammed's Mosque #12.

They passed the alley. They caught a tease: Streetlights/faces/a blanket spread out.

A fat man rolled. A plump man slapped his forehead. A thin man scooped cash.

Moore stopped at 82nd. Moore grabbed his pump. Wayne pulled his piece. Moore popped in earplugs.

"If he's there, we'll arrest him. Then we'll take him out to the sticks and cap him."

Wayne tried to talk. His throat closed. He squeaked. Moore winked. Moore yukked haw-haw.

They walked over. They cleaved to shadows. They crouched.

The air dried up. The ground dropped. Wayne lost his feet.

They hit the alley. Wayne heard jive talk. Wayne saw Wendell Durfee.

His legs went. He stumbled. He toed a beer can. The dice men perked up.

Say *what?*

Who *that?*

Mama, that *you?*

Moore aimed. Moore fired. Moore caught three men low. He sprayed their legs. He diced their blanket. He chopped their money up.

Muzzle boom—twelve-gauge roar—high decibels in tight.

It knocked Wayne flat. Wayne went deaf. Wayne went powder blind. Moore shot a trashcan. The sucker *flew.*

Wayne rubbed his eyes. Wayne got partial sight. Dice men screamed. Dice men scattered. Wendell Durfee ran.

Moore aimed high. Moore sprayed a wall. Pellets bounced and whizzed. They caught Durfee's hat. They sliced the band. They blew the feather up.

Durfee ran. Wayne ran.

He aimed his piece up and out. Durfee backward-aimed his. They fired. Blips lit the alley. Shots cut the walls.

Wayne *saw* it. Wayne *felt* it. Wayne didn't *hear* shit.

He fired. He missed. Durfee fired. Durfee missed. Barrel flames. Sound waves. No *real* sound worth shit.

They ran. They stopped. They fired. They sprinted full-out.

Wayne popped six shots—one full cylinder. Durfee popped eight shots—one full-load clip.

The flares stopped. No light. No directional signs—

Wayne stumbled.

He slid. He fell. He hit gravel. He ate alley grit. He smelled cordite. He licked cigar butts and dirt.

He rolled over. He saw roof lights. He saw cherry lights twirl. Two prowl cars—*behind* him—DPD Fords.

He caught some sounds. He stood up. He caught his breath. He walked back. His feet scraped. He heard it.

Moore stood there. Cops stood there. The dice men lay prone. They were cuffed/shackled/fucked.

Shredded pants. Pellet burns and gouges—cuts to white bone.

They thrashed. Wayne heard partial screams.

Moore walked over. Moore said something. Moore yelled.

Wayne caught "Bowers." His ears popped. He caught whole sounds.

Moore flashed his sandwich bag. Moore spread the flaps. Wayne saw blood and gristle. Wayne saw a man's thumb.

5

(Dallas, 11/23/63)

WINDOW WREATHS/FLAGS/ledge displays. 8:00 A.M.—one day later—the Glenwood Apartments loves Jack.

Two floors. Twelve front windows. Flowers and JFK toys.

Littell leaned on his car. The facade expanded. He got the sun. He got Arden Smith's car. He got her U-Haul.

He borrowed a Bureau car. He ran Arden Smith. She came back clean. He got her vehicle stats. He nailed her Chevy.

She felt dirty. She saw the hit. She ran from the PD. That U-Haul said *RUNNER*.

She lived in 2-D. He'd checked the courtyard. Her windows faced in—no flags/no trinkets/no shrine.

He worked to midnight. He cleared an office space. Floor 3 was bedlam. Cops grilled Oswald. Camera crews roamed.

His bum ploy worked. Rogers walked. The bums escaped clean. He saw Guy B. He told him to brace Lee Bowers.

He read the wit statements. He read the DPD notes. They played ambiguous. Mr. Hoover would issue a mandate. Agents would secure it. Single-shooter evidence would cohere.

Lee Oswald was trouble. Guy said so. Guy called him "nuts."

Lee didn't shoot. The pro shooter did. Said pro shot from Lee's floor perch. Rogers shot from the fence.

Lee knew Guy's cutout. Cops and Feds worked him all night. He named no names. Guy said he knew why.

The kid craved attention. The kid was fucked-up. The kid craved the solo limelight.

Littell checked his watch—8:16 A.M.—sun and low clouds.

He counted flags. He counted wreaths. The Glenwood loved Jack. He knew why. He used to love Jack. He used to love Bobby.

He never met Jack. He met Bobby once.

He tried to join them. Kemper Boyd pushed his case. Bobby

disdained his credentials. Boyd spread his loyalty. Boyd worked for Jack and Bobby. Boyd worked for the CIA.

Boyd got Littell a job. Ward, meet Carlos Marcello.

Carlos hated Jack and Bobby. Jack and Bobby spurned Littell. He built his own hate. He fine-tuned the aesthetic.

He hated Jack. He *knew* Jack. Scrutiny undermined image. Jack was glib. Jack had pizzazz. Jack had no rectitude.

Bobby defined rectitude. Bobby *lived* rectitude. Bobby punished bad men. He hated Bobby now. Bobby dismissed him. Bobby spurned his respect.

Mr. Hoover bugged Mob hangouts. Mr. Hoover picked up hints. He smelled the hit. He never told Jack. He never told Bobby.

Mr. Hoover knew Littell. Mr. Hoover dissected his hatred. Mr. Hoover urged him to hurt Bobby.

Littell had evidence. It indicted Joe Kennedy for long-term Mob collusion. He met Bobby—for one half hour—just five days back.

He stopped by his office. He played him a tape. The tape nailed Joe Kennedy. Bobby was smart. Bobby might link tape to hit. Bobby might gauge the tape as a threat.

Do not talk Mob Hit. Do not stain the name Kennedy. Do not stain sainted Jack. Feel complicitous. Feel guilty. Feel baaaad.

Your Mob Crusade killed your brother. We killed Jack to fuck you.

Littell watched a newscast. Late last night—Air Force One hits D.C. Bobby walks out. Bobby walks calm. Bobby consoles Jackie.

Littell killed Kemper Boyd. Carlos ordered it. Littell shot Boyd on Thursday. It hurt. He owed the Boys. It canceled his debt.

He saw Bobby with Jackie. It hurt more than Boyd.

Arden Smith walked out.

She walked out fast. She lugged a satchel. She carried skirts and sheets. Littell walked over. Arden Smith looked up. Littell flashed his ID.

"Yes?"

"Dealey Plaza, remember? You witnessed the shooting."

She leaned on the U-Haul. She dropped the satchel. She weighed down the skirts.

"I watched you at the squadroom. You measured your chances

and made your move, and I have to say I'm impressed. But you'll
have to explain why you—"

"My information was redundant. Five or six people heard
what I did, and I wanted to put the whole thing behind me."

Littell leaned on the car. "And now you're moving."

"Just temporarily."

"Are you leaving Dallas?"

"Yes, but that has nothing to do—"

"I'm sure it has nothing to do with what you saw in the motorcade, and all I'm interested in is why you stole your preliminary
statement and driver's license from the witness log and left without permission."

She brushed her hair back. "Look, Mr.—"

"Littell."

"Mr. Littell, I tried to do my citizen's duty. I went to the police
department and tried to leave an anonymous statement, but an
officer detained me. Really, I'd had a shock, and I just wanted to
go home and start packing."

Her voice worked. It was firm and southern. It was educated.

Littell smiled. "Can we go inside? I'm uncomfortable talking
out here."

"All right, but you'll have to forgive my apartment."

Littell smiled. She smiled. She walked ahead. Kids ran by.
They shot toy guns. A boy yelled, "Don't shoot me, Lee!"

The door was open. The front room was chaos. The front
room was packed and dollied.

She shut the door. She squared off chairs. She grabbed a coffee
cup. They sat down. She lit a cigarette. She balanced the cup.

Littell pulled his chair back. Smoke bothered him. He pulled
his notebook. He tapped his pen.

"What did you think of John Kennedy?"

"That's an odd question."

"I'm just curious. You don't seem like someone who's easily
charmed, and I can't picture you standing around to watch a man
drive by in a car."

She crossed her legs. "Mr. Littell, you don't know me. I think
your question says more about you and Mr. Kennedy than you
might be willing to admit."

Littell smiled. "Where are you from?"

"Decatur, Georgia."

"Where are you moving to?"

"I thought I'd try Atlanta."

"Your age?"

"You know my age, because you checked me out before you came here."

Littell smiled. She smiled. She dropped ash in her cup.

"I thought FBI men worked in pairs."

"We're short-handed. We weren't planning on an assassination this weekend."

"Where's your gun? All the men in that office had revolvers."

He squeezed his pen. "You saw my identification."

"Yes, but you're taking too much guff from me. Something isn't quite right here."

The pen snapped. Ink dripped. Littell wiped his hands on his coat.

"You're a pro. I knew it yesterday, and you just pushed too hard and confirmed it. You're going to have to convince me—"

The phone rang. She stared at him. The phone rang three times. She got up. She walked to the bedroom. She shut the door.

Littell wiped his hands. Littell smeared his trousers and coat. He looked around. He broke down the room. He quadrant-scanned.

There—

A chest on a dolly. Four drawers all packed.

He got up. He checked the drawers. He brushed socks and underwear. He brushed a slick surface—card-size plastic—he pulled it out.

There—

A Mississippi driver's license—for Arden Elaine *Coates*.

A P.O. box address. Date of birth: 4/15/27. Her *Texas* DL listed 4/15/26.

He put it back. He shut the drawers. He sat down fast. He crossed his legs. He doodled. He made mock notes.

Arden Smith walked out. Arden Smith smiled and *posed*.

Littell coughed. "Why did you watch the motorcade from Dealey Plaza?"

"I heard you had the best view there."

"That's not quite true."

"I'm just saying what I heard."

"Who told you?"

She blinked. "I wasn't told. I read it in the paper when they announced the route."

"When was that?"

"I don't know. A month ago, maybe."

Littell shook his head. "That isn't true. They announced the route ten days ago."

She shrugged. "I'm bad at dates."

"No, you're not. You're good at them, just like you're good at everything you try."

"You don't know that. You don't know *me*."

Littell stared at her. She popped goosebumps.

"You're scared, and you're running."

"*You're* scared, and this isn't a real FBI roust."

He popped goosebumps. "Where do you work?"

"I'm a freelance bookkeeper."

"That's not what I asked you."

"I structure deals to get businessmen out of trouble with the IRS."

"I asked, '*Where do you work?*' "

Her hands jumped. "I work at a place called the Carousel Club."

His hands jumped. The Carousel/Jack Ruby/Mob guy/bent cops.

He looked at her. She looked at him. Their brainwaves crossed.

6

(Dallas, 11/23/63)

SHIT SECURITY. FUCKED-UP/negligent/weak.

Pete toured the PD. Guy scored him a pass. He didn't need it. Some geek sold dupes. Said geek sold weed and pussy pix.

The ground doors stood open. Geeks hobnobbed. Door guards posed for pix. Camera cords snaked up the sidewalk. News vans jammed up the street.

Reporters roamed. Let's bug the DA. Let's bug the cops. *Lots* of cops—Feds/DPD/Sheriff's—all motormouthed.

Oswald's pink. Oswald's Red. Oswald loves Fidel. He loves folk music. He loves dark trim. He loves Martin Lucifer Coon. We know it's him. We got his gun. He did it alone. I think he's queer. He can't piss with men in the room.

Pete roamed. Pete checked hall routes. Pete sketched floor plans. He nursed a headache—a looong one—the fucker had legs.

Barb KNEW.

She said, "You killed him. You and Ward and those Outfit guys you work for."

He lied. He bombed. Barb looked through him.

She said, "Let's leave Dallas." He said, "No." She split to her gig.

He walked to the club. Biz was bad. Barb sang to three drag queens. She looked straight through him. He walked back alone.

He slept alone. Barb slept in the john.

Pete roamed. Pete passed Homicide. Pete stopped at room 317. Geeks cruised for looks. Geeks framed the door. A cop cracked it wide and obliged.

There's Oswald. He looks beat-on. He's cuffed to a chair.

The crowd closed in. The cop shut the door. Talk fired up:

I knew J.D. J.D. was *Klan*. J.D. was *not*. They got to move him soon. They sure will—to the County Jail.

Pete roamed. Pete dodged geeks with carts. Geeks sold poor-boys. Geeks snarfed them. Geeks slurped ketchup.

Pete sketched hall routes. Pete took notes.

One bunco pen. One holding tank adjacent. Basement cells. A press room adjacent. Briefings/newsmen/camera crews.

Pete roamed. Pete saw Jack Ruby. Jack's hawking pens shaped like dicks.

He saw Pete. He seized up. He freaked. He dropped his dick pens. He bent loooow and scooped up.

His pants ripped. Dig those plaid BVDs.

Maynard Moore rubbed him wrong.

His bad breath. His bad teeth. His Klan repartee.

They met at a parking lot. They sat in Guy's car. They faced a nigger church and a blood bank. Moore brought a six-pack. Moore sucked one down. Moore tossed the can out.

Pete said, "Did you brace Ruby?"

Moore said, "Yeah, I did. And I think he knows."

Pete slid his seat back. Moore raised his knees.

"Whoa, now. You're crowdin' me."

Guy dumped his ashtray. "Let's have the details. You can't shut Jack up once he starts talking."

Moore cracked beer #2. "Well, everybody—the crew, I mean—is up at Jack Zangetty's motel in Altus, Oklahoma, where men are men and cows are scared."

Pete cracked his knuckles. "Cut the travelogue."

Moore belched. "Schlitz, breakfast of champions."

Guy said, "Maynard, goddamnit."

Moore giggled. "Okay, so Jack R. gets a call from his old friend Jack Z. It seems that the pilot guy and the French guy want some cooze, so Jack R. says he'll bring some up."

The pilot: Chuck Rogers. The French guy: the pro. Let's observe the no-names policy.

Pete said, "Keep going."

Moore said, "Okay, so Ruby goes up there with his buddy Hank Killiam and these girls Betty McDonald and Arden something. Betty agrees to put out, but Arden don't, which pisses off the French guy something fierce. He slaps her, she burns him with a hot plate, then hightails. Now, Ruby don't know where Arden lives, and he thinks she's got a string of aliases. And the worst part is that everybody saw the rifles and targets, and they might've seen a map of Dealey Plaza layin' around."

Guy smiled. Guy made the finger-throat sign. Pete shook his head. Pete flashed *waaaay* back.

A bomb hits. Flames whoosh. A woman's hair ignites.

Moore belched. "Schlitz, Milwaukee's finest beer."

Pete said, "You're going to clip Oswald."

Moore gagged. Moore sprayed beer suds.

"Uuuh-*uuuuh*. Not this boy. That's a kamikaze mission that you ain't sendin' me on, not when I got an extradition job and a candy-ass partner who won't pull his weight."

Guy dipped his seat. Guy pushed Moore back.

"You and Tippit fucked up. You owe that marker, so you have to pay it off."

Moore cracked beer #3. "Uuuh-*uuuuh*. I'm not flushin' my life down the shitter 'cause I owe some *eye*-talians a few dollars that they won't even miss."

Pete smiled. "It's all right, Maynard. You just find out when they're moving him. We'll do the rest."

Moore burped. "I'll do that. That's a job that won't interfere with the other affairs I got goin'."

Pete reached back. Pete popped the rear hatch. Moore climbed out. Moore stretched. Moore waved bye-bye.

Guy said, "Peckerwood trash."

Moore shagged his 409. Moore laid rubber large.

Pete said, "I'll kill him."

Betty McDonald lived in Oak Cliff—Shitsville, U.S.A.

Pete called DPD. Pete played cop. Pete got her rap sheet: Four prosty beefs/one hot-check caper/one dope bounce.

He tapped out on "Arden." He had no last name.

He went by the Moonbeam Lounge. Carlos owned points. Joe Campisi ran the on-site handbook.

Joe owned the DPD. Cops placed bets. Cops lost. Cops made Joe's collections. Joe shylocked large—vig plus 20%.

Pete schmoozed with Joe. Pete borrowed ten cold. Pete tagged it a margin risk. Nobody said clip them. Nobody said scare them off. Nobody said shit. Guy wasn't Outfit. Guy's wishes meant shit.

Joe supplied a calzone. Pete ate on the freeway. The cheese fucked up his teeth.

He got off. He toured Oak Cliff. He found the address: A shotgun shack/dingy/three small rooms tops.

He parked. He dropped five G's in the calzone box. He schlepped it on up. He knocked on the door. He waited. He checked for eyewits.

Nobody home—zero eyewits.

He got out his comb. He flexed the tines. He picked the lock clean. He walked in and closed the door slow.

The front room smelled—maryjane and cabbage—window light squared him away.

Front room/kitchen/bedroom. Three rooms in a row.

He walked to the kitchen. He opened the fridge. A cat rubbed his legs. He tossed him some fish. The cat scarfed it up. Pete scarfed some Cheez Whiz.

He toured the pad. The cat followed him. He paced the front room. He pulled the drapes. He pulled up a chair and sat by the door.

The cat hopped in his lap. The cat clawed the calzone box. The room was cold. The chair was soft. The walls torqued him back.

Memory Lane. L.A.—12/14/49.

He's a cop. He breaks County strikes. He works *goooood* sidelines. He pulls shakedowns. He extorts queers. He raids the Swish Alps.

He's a card-game guard. He's a scrape procurer. He's Quebecois French. He fought the war. He got green-card Americanized.

Late '48—his brother Frank hits L.A.

Frank was a doctor. Frank had bad habits. Frank made bad friends. Frank whored. Frank gambled. Frank lost money.

Frank did scrapes. Frank scraped Rita Hayworth. Frank was Abortionist to the Stars. Frank played cards. Frank lost money. Frank dug Mickey Cohen's regular game.

Frank partied with scrape folks. Frank met Ruth Mildred Cressmeyer. Ruth did scrapes. Ruth loved her son Huey. Huey did heists.

Huey robbed Mickey's game. Huey's face mask slipped. The players ID'd him. Pete had the flu. Pete took the night off. Mickey told Pete to kill Huey.

Huey laid low. Pete found his pad: An ex-brothel in El Segundo.

Pete torched the pad. Pete stood in the backyard. Pete watched the house flames. Four shapes ran out. Pete shot them. Pete let them scream and burn.

It was dark. Their hair plumed. Smoke blitzed their faces. The papers played it up—FOUR DEAD IN BEACH TORCH—the papers ID'd the vics:

Ruth. Huey. Huey's girlfriend.

And:

One Canuck doctor—François Bondurant.

Someone called their dad. Someone snitched Pete off. His dad called him. His dad begged: Say NO. Say it wasn't YOU.

Pete stammered. Pete tried. Pete failed. His parents grieved. His parents sucked tailpipe fumes. His parents decomped in their car.

The cat fell asleep. Pete stroked him. Time schizzed. He dug on the dark.

He dozed. He stirred. He heard something. The door opened. Light shot straight in.

Pete jumped up. The cat tumbled. The calzone box flew.

There's Betty Mac.

She's got blond hair. She's got curves. She's got harlequin shades.

She saw Pete. She yelled. Pete grabbed her. Pete kicked the door shut.

She scratched. She yelled. She clawed his neck. He covered her mouth. She drew her lips back. She bit him.

He stumbled. He kicked the calzone box. He tripped a wall switch. A light went on. The cash fell out.

Betty looked down. Betty saw the money. Pete let his hand go. Pete rubbed his bite wound.

"There, Jesus Christ. Just get out before someone hurts you."

She eased up. He eased up. She turned around. She saw his face.

Pete hit the wall switch. The room light died. They stood close. They caught their breath. They leaned on the door.

Pete said, "Arden?"

Betty coughed—a smoker's hack—Pete smelled her last reefer.

"I'm not going to hurt her. Come on, you know what we've got—"

She touched his lips. "Don't say it. Don't put a name—"

"Then tell me where—"

"Arden Burke. I think she's at the Glenwood Apartments."

Pete brushed by her. Her hair caught his face. Her perfume stuck to his clothes. He got outside. His hand throbbed. The sun killed his eyes.

Traffic was bad. Pete knew why.

Dealey Plaza was close. Let's take the kids. Let's dig on history and hot dogs.

He split Oak Cliff. He found Arden's building. It ran forty units plus. He parked outside. He checked access routes. The courtyard ruled B&Es out.

He checked the mail slots—no Arden *Burke* listed—Arden *Smith* in 2-D.

Pete toured the courtyard. Pete scanned doorplates: 2-A/B/C—

Stop right—

He made the suit. He made the build. He made the thin hair. He stepped back. He crouched. He *looked*.

Right there—

Ward Littell and a tall woman. Talking close and closing out the world.

DOCUMENT INSERT: 11/23/63.
Verbatim FBI telephone call transcript.
Marked: ''Recorded at the Director's Request''/
''Classified Confidential 1-A: Director's Eyes Only.''
Speaking: Director Hoover, Ward J. Littell.

JEH: Mr. Littell?

WJL: Good afternoon, Sir. How are you?

JEH: Forgo the amenities and tell me about Dallas.
The metaphysical dimensions of this alleged tragedy
do not interest me. Get to the point.

WJL: I would call things encouraging, Sir. There
has been a minimum of talk about a conspiracy, and a
very strong consensus seems to have settled in,
despite some ambiguous statements from the
witnesses. I've spent a good deal of time at the PD,
and I've been told that President Johnson has called
both Chief Curry and the DA personally, and has
expressed his wish that the consensus be confirmed.

JEH: Lyndon Johnson is a blunt and persuasive man,
and he speaks a language those cowpokes understand.
Now, continuing with the witnesses.

WJL: I would say that the contradictory ones could
be intimidated, discredited and successfully
debriefed.

JEH: You've read the witness logs, observed the
interviews and have been through the inevitable glut
of lunatic phone tips. Is that correct?

WJL: Yes, Sir. The phone tips were especially
fanciful and vindictive. John Kennedy had engendered
a good deal of resentment in Dallas.

JEH: Yes, and entirely justified. Continuing with
the witnesses. Have you conducted any interviews
yourself?

WJL: No, Sir.

JEH: You've turned up no witnesses with especially
provocative stories?

WJL: No, Sir. What we have is an alternative
consensus pertaining to the number of shots and their
trajectories. It's a confusing text, Sir. I don't
think it will stand up to the official version.

JEH: How would you rate the investigation to date?

WJL: As incompetent.

JEH: And how would you define it?

WJL: As chaotic.

JEH: How would you assess the efforts to protect Mr. Oswald?

WJL: As shoddy.

JEH: Does that disturb you?

WJL: No.

JEH: The Attorney General has requested periodic updates. What do you suggest that I tell him?

WJL: That a fatuous young psychopath killed his brother, and that he acted alone.

JEH: The Dark Prince is no cretin. He must suspect the factions that most insiders would.

WJL: Yes, Sir. And I'm sure he feels complicitous.

JEH: I hear an unseemly tug of compassion in your voice, Mr. Littell. I will not comment on your protractedly complex relationship with Robert F. Kennedy.

WJL: Yes, Sir.

JEH: I cannot help but think of your blowhard client, James Riddle Hoffa. The Prince is his bête noire.

WJL: Yes, Sir.

JEH: I'm sure Mr. Hoffa would like to know what the Prince really thinks of this gaudy homicide.

WJL: I would like to know myself, Sir.

JEH: I cannot help but think of your brutish client, Carlos Marcello. I suspect that he would enjoy access to Bobby's troubled thoughts.

WJL: Yes, Sir.

JEH: It would be nice to have a source close to the Prince.

WJL: I'll see what I can do.

JEH: Mr. Hoffa gloats in an unseemly manner. He told the New York Times, quote, Bobby Kennedy is just another lawyer now, unquote. It's a felicitous sentiment, but I think there are those in the Italian aggregation who would appreciate more discretion on Mr. Hoffa's part.

WJL: I'll advise him to shut his mouth, Sir.

JEH: On a related topic. Did you know that the Bureau has a file on Jefferson Davis Tippit?

WJL: No, Sir.

JEH: The man belonged to the Ku Klux Klan, National States' Rights Party, National Renaissance Party and a dubious new splinter group called the Thunderbolt Legion. He was a close associate of a Dallas PD officer named Maynard Delbert Moore, a man of similar ideological beliefs and a reportedly puerile demeanor.

WJL: Did you get your information from a DPD source, Sir?

JEH: No. I have a correspondent in Nevada. He's a conservative pamphleteer and mail-order solicitor with very deep and diverse connections on the right flank.

WJL: A Mormon, Sir?

JEH: Yes. All the Nevadan führer manqués are Mormons, and this man is arguably the most gifted.

WJL: He sounds interesting, Sir.

JEH: You're leading me, Mr. Littell. I know full well that Howard Hughes wets his pants for Mormons and has two greedy eyes on Las Vegas. I'll always share a discreet amount of information with you, if you broach the request in a manner that does not insult my intelligence.

WJL: I'm sorry, Sir. You understood my design, and the man does sound interesting.

JEH: He's quite useful and diversified. For example, he runs a hate-tract press covertly. He's planted a number of his subscribers as informants in Klan groups that the Bureau has targeted for mail-fraud indictments. He helps eliminate his hate-mail competition in that manner.

WJL: And he knew the late Officer Tippit.

JEH: Knew or knew of. Judged or did not judge as ideologically unsound and outré. I'm always amusingly surprised by who knows who in which overall contexts. For example, the Dallas SAC told me that a former Bureau man named Guy Williams Banister is in town this weekend. Another agent told me, independently, that he's seen your friend Pierre Bondurant. Imaginative people might point to this confluence and try to link men like that to your mutual chum Carlos Marcello and his hatred of the Royal Family, but I am not disposed to such flights of fancy.

WJL: Yes, Sir.

JEH: Your tone tells me that you wish to ask a favor. For Mr. Hughes, perhaps?

WJL: Yes, Sir. I'd like to see the main Bureau file on the Las Vegas hotel-casino owners, along with the files on the Nevada Gaming Commission, Gaming Control Board, and the Clark County Liquor Board.

JEH: The answer is yes. Quid pro quo?

WJL: Certainly, Sir.

JEH: I would like to forestall potential talk on Mr. Tippit. If the Dallas Office has a separate file on him, I would like it to disappear before my less trusted colleagues get an urge to take the information public.

WJL: I'll take care of it tonight, Sir.

JEH: Do you think the single-gunman consensus will hold?

WJL: I'll do everything I can to insure it.

JEH: Good day, Mr. Littell.

WJL: Good day, Sir.

7

(Dallas, 11/23/63)

GLUT. WASTE. BULLSHIT.

The hotel copped pleas. The hotel blamed Lee Oswald.

The joint bulged—capacity-plus—newsmen shared rooms. They hogged the phone lines. They sapped the hot water. They swamped the room-service crew.

The hotel copped pleas. The hotel blamed Lee Oswald.

Our guests mourn. Our guests weep. Our guests watch TV. They stay in. They call home. They hash out The Show.

Wayne paced his suite. Wayne nursed an earache—that muzzle boom stuck.

Room service called. They said we're sorry—we're running late. Maynard Moore *didn't* call. Durfee escaped. Moore let it ride.

Moore didn't issue warrants. Moore didn't issue holds. Moore wrote up the crap-game snafu. One guy lost a kneecap. One guy lost two pints of blood. One guy lost a toe.

Mr. Bowers lost a thumb. Wayne nursed the picture—all-nite reruns.

He tossed all night. He watched TV. He made phone calls. He called the Border Patrol. He issued crossing holds. Four units grabbed look-alikes and called him.

Wendell Durfee had knife scars—too fucking bad—the look-alikes had none.

He called Lynette. He called Wayne Senior. Lynette mourned JFK. Lynette said trite shit. Wayne Senior cracked jokes.

Jack's last word was "pussy." Jack groped a nurse and a nun.

Janice came on. Janice extolled Jack's style. Janice mourned Jack's hair. Wayne laughed. Wayne Senior was bald. Janice Tedrow—touché!

Room service called. They said we're sorry. We know your supper's late.

Wayne watched TV. Wayne goosed the sound. Wayne caught a press gig.

Newsmen lobbed questions. One cop went wild. Oswald was a "lethal loner!" Wayne saw Jack Ruby. He carried his dog. He passed out dick pens and French ticklers.

The cop calmed down. He said we'll move Oswald tomorrow—late morning looks good.

The phone rang. Wayne killed the sound.

He picked up. "Who's this?"

"It's Buddy Fritsch, and it took me all day to get a call in to you."

"Sorry, Lieutenant. Things are a bit crazy here."

"So I gathered. I also gathered that you had a run-in with Wendell Durfee, and you let him get away."

Wayne made fists. "Who told you?"

"The Border Patrol. They were checking on your fugitive warrant."

"Do you want to hear my version?"

"I don't want to hear excuses. I don't want to know why you're enjoying your luxury hotel suite when you should be out shaking the trees."

Wayne kicked a footrest. It hit the TV.

"Do you know how *big* the border is? Do you know how many crossing posts there are?"

Fritsch coughed. "I know you're sitting on your keester waiting for callbacks that won't come if that nigger went to ground in Dallas, and for all I know you're living it up with that six thousand dollars the casino boys gave you, without doing the job that they paid you for."

Wayne kicked a rug. "I didn't ask for that money."

"No, you sure didn't. And you didn't refuse it, either, 'cause you're the type of boy who likes to have things both ways, so don't—"

"Lieutenant—"

"Don't interrupt me until you outrank me, and let me tell you this now. You can go either way in the Department. There's boys who say Wayne Junior's a white man, and there's boys who say he's a weak sister. Now, if you take care of this, you'll shut the mouths on those latter boys and make everyone *real* proud of you."

His eyes teared up. "Lieutenant . . ."

"That's better. That's the Wayne Junior I like to hear."

Wayne wiped his eyes. "He's down at the border. All my instincts tell me that."

Fritsch laughed. "I think your instincts are telling you lots of things, so I'll tell you this. That file I gave you was Sheriff's, so you see if DPD has a file. That nigger's got to know some other niggers in Dallas, or my name isn't Byron B. Fritsch."

Wayne grabbed his holster. His blocked ear popped.

"I'll give it my best."

"*No.* You find him and kill him."

A door guard let him in. Some Shriners tagged along. The stairs were jammed. The halls were crammed. The lifts were sardine-packed.

People bumped. People chomped hot dogs. People spilled coffee and Cokes. The Shriners pushed through. They wore funny hats. They waved pens and autograph books.

Wayne followed them. They plowed camera guys. They pushed their way upstairs.

They made floor 3. They made the squadroom. It was *double-packed.*

Cops. Newsmen. Misdemeanants cuffed to chairs. Pinned-out ID: shields/stars/press cards.

Wayne pinned his badge on. The noise hurt. His blocked ear repopped. He looked around. He saw the squad bay. He saw cubicles and office doors.

Burglary/Bunco. Auto Theft/Forgery. Homicide/Arson/Theft.

He walked over. He tripped on a wino. A newsman laughed. The wino shook his cuff chain. The wino soliloquized.

Jackie needs the big *braciole.* Widows crave it. *Playboy* magazine says so.

Wayne hit a side hall. Wayne read door plates. Wayne saw Maynard Moore. Moore missed him. Moore stood in a storeroom. Moore cranked a mimeo press.

Wayne ducked by. Wayne passed a break room. Wayne heard a TV blare. A cop watched a press-room feed—live from downstairs.

Wayne checked doorways. Jack Ruby brushed by—leeched to a *very* big cat. He hung on him. He bugged him. He kvetched: "Pete, Pete, *pleeease.*"

Wayne veered by a fish tank. Fish howled within. A perv stuck his dick through the mesh. He stroked it. He wiggled it. He sang "Some Enchanted Evening."

Wayne doubled back. Wayne found the file room. A stand-up space with twelve drawers—two marked "KAs."

He shut the door. He popped the "A to L" drawer. He found a blue sheet:

Durfee, Wendell (NMI).

He skimmed it. He got repeat shit and one new KA:

Rochelle Marie Freelon—DOB 10/3/39. Two kids by Whipout Wendell. 8819 Harvey Street/Dallas.

Two file notes:

12/8/56: Rochelle harbors Wendell/the Sheriff wants him/ he's got nine bench warrants due. 7/5/62: Rochelle violates *her* parole.

She leaves Texas. She drives to Vegas. She visits Wistful Wendell D. No vehicle stats/recent contact/two cubs by Wendell D.

Wayne copied the data. Wayne replaced the file. Wayne drawered loose sheets up. He walked out. He cruised hallways. He passed the break room.

The TV snagged him. He saw *something weird*. He stopped. He leaned in. He looked.

There's a fat man. He's facing a mike. One hand's in a splint. *One* hand—tight gauze—no *thumb*.

A band ID'd him: "Witness Lee Bowers."

Bowers talked. Bowers' voice broke.

"I was in the tower right before he was shot . . . and . . . well . . . I sure didn't see anything."

Bowers blipped off. A cartoon ad blipped on. Bucky Beaver yap-yap-yapped. The fuck hawked Ipana toothpaste.

Wayne went cold—Popsicle chills—ice down his shorts.

A cop said, "You okay, hoss? You look a little green at the gills."

Wayne borrowed a DPD car. Wayne went out alone.

He got directions. Harvey Street was Darktown. Cops called it the Congo and Coonecticut.

Bowers and Moore—reprise that—do it very sloooow.

Wayne tried—it was easy—it was shortbread cake.

Moore was crazy. Moore was bent. Moore drank jar brew. He might push uppers. He might book bets. Bowers might be bent too. They fell out. Moore got pissed. Moore cut hisself a thumb.

Wayne hit Darktown. Wayne found Harvey Street. It was the shits—shacks and hen coops—connected dirt yards.

8819: Dead still and dark.

He parked out front. He hit his brights. He nailed the one window: No window shades/no furniture/no drapes.

Wayne got out. Wayne grabbed a flashlight. Wayne circled the shack. He cut through the backyard. He bumped furniture.

Big piles—yard-sale dimensions. Sofas and chairs—all cheap stuff.

He strafed it. His light roused a hen. She fluffed full. She made claws. She squawked.

Wayne kicked a cushion. A light hit *him*. A man laughed.

"It's my property now. I got a receipt that says so."

Wayne covered his eyes. "Did Wendell Durfee sell it to you?"

"That's right. Him and Rochelle."

"Did he say where they were going?"

The man coughed. "Out of your redneck jurisdiction."

Wayne walked up. The man was fat and high yellow. He twirled his flashlight. The beam jumped.

Wayne said, "I'm not DPD."

The man tapped his badge. "You're that Vegas guy looking for Wendell."

Wayne smiled. Wayne unpinned his coat. Wayne repinned his belt. The man flipped a porch switch. The yard lit up. A pit bull materialized.

Brindle flecks and muscle. Jaw power for two.

Wayne said, "Nice dog."

The man said, "He liked Wendell, so I liked him too."

Wayne walked up. The pit licked his hand. Wayne scratched his ears.

The man said, "I don't always go by that rule, though."

The pit made a fuss. The pit reared and batted his paws.

"Because I'm a policeman?"

"Because Wendell told me how your town works."

"Wendell tried to shoot me, Mr. . . . ."

"It's Willis Beaudine, and Wendell tried to shoot you because you tried to shoot him. Now, tell me that Casino Council didn't give you some recreation money when they put that bounty on Wendell."

Wayne sat on a porch step. The pit nuzzled him.

Beaudine said, "Dogs can be fooled, just like anyone else."

"You're saying Wendell and Rochelle made a run for Mexico."

Beaudine smiled. "Them and their kids. You want my guess? They're decked out in sombreros and having a ball this very second."

Wayne shook his head. "It's bad for coloreds down there. The Mexicans hate them like some people in Vegas do."

Beaudine shook his head. "Like most or all, you mean. Like that dealer guy that Wendell cut. The same guy who won't let coloreds piss in his washroom, the same guy who beat up an old woman for selling *Watchtowers* out of his parking lot."

Wayne looked around. The yard furniture trapped dirt. The yard furniture stunk.

Spilled food. Liquor. Dog fumes. Chipped wood and stuffing exposed.

Wayne stretched. His blocked ear popped. He got This Craaazy Idea.

"Can you place a long-distance call for me?"

Beaudine hiked his belt. "Sure . . . I guess I could."

"The Border Patrol station at Laredo. Make it person-to-person. Ask for the watch commander."

Beaudine hiked his belt. Wayne smiled. Beaudine *snapped* his belt—hard.

Craaazy—

Beaudine walked inside. Beaudine hit some lights. Beaudine dialed a phone. Wayne nuzzled the pit. The pit kissed him. The pit swiped his tongue.

Beaudine pulled the phone out. The cord twanged. Wayne grabbed the receiver.

"Captain?"

"Yes. Who's this?"

"Sergeant Tedrow, Las Vegas PD."

"Oh, shit. I was hoping you'd call when we had some good news."

"Is there *bad* news?"

"Yes. Your fugitive, a woman, and two children tried to cross at McAllen an hour ago, but were turned back. Your boy was intoxicated, and nobody made him in time. Lieutenant Fritsch sent us a teletype with his picture, but we didn't make the connection until—"

Wayne hung up. Beaudine grabbed the phone. Beaudine snapped his belt—*hard*.

"This better be good. That was a two-dollar call."

Wayne pulled out his wallet. Wayne forked up two bucks.

"If he tries to cross again, they'll get him. But if he comes back here, you tell him I'll walk him over myself."

Beaudine hiked his belt. "Why would you take that kind of risk for Wendell?"

"Your dog likes me. Leave it at that."

The Adolphus bar—all male at midnight. The big Jack postmortem.

Pro-Jack stools. Anti-Jack stools adjacent. Youth. Outer space. *Ich bin ein Berliner.*

Wayne sat between factions. Wayne heard hi-fi bullshit in stereo sound.

Cowboy trash—faux tall—big boots don't count. They called Jack "Jack." They took liberties—like they all fucked leprechauns in Hyannis.

Fuck them. *He* slept in Jack's bed. *He* thrashed on Jack's sheets.

Wayne got drunk. Wayne *never* got drunk. Wayne drank small-batch bond.

Shot 1 burned. Shot 2 played a picture: Lee Bowers' thumb. Shot 3 gored his gonads. Dig *these* pix: Janice in halters and shorts.

Jack had hound blood. Wayne Senior said so. Martin Luther King fucked white chicks.

Shot 4—more pix:

Durfee tries to cross. The border cops lose him. Wayne fucked up. Wayne gets called home. Buddy Fritsch recruits a new man. Said man kills Wendell D.

Wayne fucked up. Fritsch fucks him for it. Fritsch fucks him off LVPD. Wayne Senior says don't fuck my boy. The fucking ascends triumphant.

Shot 5:

The thumb/the alley chase/the crap-game snafu.

Jack put a man in orbit. Jack played chicken with Khrushchev. Jack put that shine in Ole Miss.

Maynard Moore walked in. He brought company. That Pete guy—the big guy with Jack Ruby.

Moore saw Wayne. Moore detoured up. Pete tagged along.

Moore said, "Let's go find us that spook. My pal Pete hates spooks, don't you, sahib?"

Pete smiled. Pete rolled his eyes. Pete goofed on dipshit Moore.

Wayne chewed ice cubes. "Fuck off. I'll find him myself."

Moore leaned on the bar. "Your daddy wouldn't like that. It'd let him know the apple falls *real* far from the tree."

Wayne tossed his drink. Moore caught it—hard in the eyes. Bourbon burned him—hi-test sting—triple-digit proof.

The cocksucker rubbed his eyes. The cocksucker squealed.

8

(Dallas, 11/24/63)

PETE WAS LATE. Littell voyeurized.

His room was high up. The window framed a church. A midnight mass convened.

Littell watched. A poster marked the mass—Jack K. in black borders.

Kids defaced it. Littell watched them—late this afternoon. He went to dinner later. He saw the work up close.

Jack had fangs. Jack had devil horns. Jack said, "I'm a homo!"

Mourners filed in. A breeze dumped the poster. A woman picked it up. She saw Jack's picture. She cringed.

A car cruised by. An arm shot out. A stiff finger twirled. The woman sobbed. The woman crossed herself. The woman squeezed rosary beads.

The Statler was low-rent. The Bureau booked cheap rooms. The view compensated.

Pete was late. Pete was with the backup cop. The cop had details. The cop had a map printed up.

Littell watched the church. It diverted him. It subsumed Arden.

They talked for six hours. They skirted IT. He coded a message: I KNOW. I KNOW you KNOW. I don't care how you KNOW. I don't care what you DID.

She coded a message: *I won't probe your stake.* No one said, "Jack Ruby."

They talked. They omitted. They codified.

He said he was a lawyer. He was ex-FBI. He had an ex-wife and an ex-daughter somewhere. She studied his facial scars. He told her flat-out: My best friend put them there.

Le frère Pete—un Frenchman sanglant.

She said she traveled. She said she held jobs. She said she bought and sold stocks and made money. She said she had an ex-husband. She did not state his name.

She impressed him. She knew it. He coded a response: You're a pro. You dissemble. I don't care.

She knew Jack Ruby. She used the word "roust." He skirted it. He offered advice. He told her to find a motel.

She said she would. He gave her *his* hotel number. Please call me. Please do it soon.

He wanted to touch her. He didn't. She touched his arm once. He left her. He drove to the Bureau.

The office was empty—no agents about—Mr. Hoover made sure. He rifled drawers. He found the Tippit file.

Pete was late. Littell skimmed the file. It rambled and digressed.

Dallas PD was far right: Klan kliques and John Birch. Diverse splinter groups: The NSRP/the Minutemen/the Thunderbolt Legion.

Tippit was "klanned up." Tippit joined the Klarion Klan Koalition for the New Konfederacy. The DPD boss was Maynard D. Moore. Moore was an FBI snitch. Moore's handler was Wayne Tedrow Sr.

Tedrow Senior: "Pamphleteer"/"Fund Raiser"/"Entrepreneur"/"Extensive Las Vegas holdings."

Unique stats—familiar—Mr. Hoover's "Führer manqué."

Littell skimmed up. Littell logged stats. Tedrow Senior ran eclectic.

He raised right-wing cash. He might know Guy B. Guy scrounged right-wing funds. Some fat cats greased the hit fund.

Littell skimmed down. Littell logged stats. Littell logged a possible connection.

Guy's backup cop—friend of J. D. Tippit—odds on Maynard D. Moore.

Odds on: Mr. Hoover knew it. Mr. Hoover guessed the connection.

Littell skimmed up. Tedrow Senior's CV expanded.

All-Mormon staff. Ties at Nellis AFB. Tight with the Gaming Control Board. One son: a Vegas policeman.

Senior withheld data from Junior. Junior worked the intel squad. Junior kept board files. Junior withheld data from Senior. Senior "assisted" Mr. Hoover. Senior "dispensed propaganda."

Per: Martin Luther King/the Southern Christian Leadership Conference.

Littell skimmed pages. Littell took notes. Howard Hughes loved Mormons. They had "germ-free" blood. Tedrow Senior was Mormon. Tedrow Senior had Mormon connections.

Littell rubbed his eyes. The doorbell rang. He got up and opened the door.

Pete walked in. Pete grabbed the desk chair. Pete sprawled out tall.

Littell shut the door. "How bad?"

Pete said, "Bad. The map looks good, but he won't pop Oswald. He's crazy, but I can't fault him for brains."

Littell rubbed his eyes. "Maynard Moore, right? That's his name."

Pete yawned. "Guy's slipping. He usually plays his names closer than that."

Littell shook his head. "Mr. Hoover made him. He had a file on Tippit. He assumed that Moore had to be somewhere close."

"That's your interpretation, right? Hoover didn't get that specific."

"He never does."

Pete cracked his knuckles. "How scared are you?"

"It comes and goes, and I wouldn't mind some good news."

Pete lit a cigarette. "Rogers made it down to Juarez. The pro got down, but the Border Patrol detained him and ran a passport check. Guy said he's a French national."

Littell said, "Guy's talking too much."

"He's scared. He knows Carlos is thinking, 'If I went with Pete and Ward's crew, none of this shit would have happened.' "

Littell cleaned his glasses. "Where is he?"

"He drove back to New Orleans. His nerves are shot, and he's popping digitalis like a fucking junkie. All this shit is on him, and he knows it."

Littell said, "And?"

Pete cracked a window. Cold air blew in.

"And what?"

"There's more. Guy wouldn't be going back unless he had an excuse to hand Carlos."

Pete flicked his cigarette out. "Jack Ruby knows. He brought one of his flunkies and some women up to the safe house. They saw the targets and guns. Guy's saying we should clip them. I think he'll tell Carlos that, so he can buy his way out of the shit."

Littell coughed. His pulse zoomed. He held his breath.

"We can't take out four people that close to the hit. It's too obvious."

Pete laughed. "Shit, Ward, say it. I've got no balls for clipping civilians, so why should you?"

Littell smiled. "Ruby aside."

Pete shrugged. "Jack's no skin off my ass either way."

"The women, then. That's what we're talking about."

Pete cracked his thumbs. "I'm not negotiating on that. I already warned one of them off, but I couldn't find the other one."

"Give me their names."

"Betty McDonald and Arden something."

Littell touched his tie. Littell scratched his neck. Littell made his hands quash his nerves.

He twitched. He swallowed. He gulped. The room was cold. He shut the window.

"Oswald."

"Yeah. If he goes, this all disappears."

"When are they moving him?"

"Eleven-thirty. If he hasn't named Guy's cutout by then, we can put the skids to all this."

Littell coughed. "I've arranged for a private interview. The ASAC said he hasn't talked, but I want to make sure."

Pete shook his head. "Bullshit. You want to get close to him. You want to run some kind of fucking absolution number on him, so you can do a number on yourself later."

In nomine patris, et filii et spiritus sancti, Amen.

"It's nice to have someone who knows you."

Pete laughed. "I wasn't doubting you. I just want to work this fucking thing out."

Littell said, "Moore. There's no way he—"

"*No.* He knows too much, drinks too much and talks too much. After Oswald goes, *he* goes, and we draw the line at that."

Littell checked his watch. Shit—1:40 A.M.

"He's a policeman. He could get into the basement."

"*No.* He's too crazy. He's working an extradition gig with a Vegas cop, and he gets in the guy's face in the worst possible way. He's not what we want."

Littell rubbed his eyes. "What was the man's name? The cop, I mean."

"Wayne something. Why?"

"Tedrow?"

Pete said, "Yeah, and why do you care? He's got nothing to do with any of this, and the fucking clock is ticking."

Littell checked his watch. Carlos bought it for him. A gold Rolex/pure ostentat—

"Ward, are you in a fucking trance?"

Littell said, "Jack Ruby."

Pete rocked his chair back. The legs squeaked.

Littell said, "He's insane. He's afraid of us. He's afraid of the Outfit. He's got seven brothers and sisters that we can threaten."

Pete smiled. "The cops know he's crazy. He carries a gun. He's been all over the building all weekend, and he's been saying somebody should shoot that Commie. Ten dozen fucking newsmen have heard him."

Littell said, "He's got tax troubles."

"Who told you that?"

"I don't want to say."

A breeze kicked up. The windowpanes creaked.

Pete said, "And?"

"And what?"

"There's more. I want to know why you'll risk it, with a fucking psycho who knows both our names."

Cherchez la femme, Pierre.

"It's a message. It tells everyone who went to that safe house to run."

9

(Dallas, 11/24/63)

BARB WALKED IN. She wore his raincoat. The sleeves drooped. The shoulders sagged. The hem brushed her feet.

Pete blocked the bathroom. Barb said, "Shit."

Pete checked her ring hand. Pete saw her wedding ring.

She held it up. "I'm not going anywhere. I'm just getting used to it."

Pete carried his ring. It came too small—fucking pygmy-size.

"I'll get used to it when I get mine fitted."

Barb shook her head. "Used to *it*. What *you* did."

Pete snared his ring. Pete tried to squeeze his finger in. Pete jabbed at the hole.

"Say something nice, all right? Tell me how the late show went."

Barb dumped his coat. "It went fine. The Twist is dead, but Dallas doesn't know it."

Pete stretched. His shirt gapped. Barb saw his piece.

"You're going out."

"I won't be that long. I'm just wondering where you'll be when I get back."

"I'm wondering who else knows. I know, so there has to be others."

His headache revived. His headache paved new ground.

"Everyone who knows has a stake. It's what you call an open secret."

Barb said, "I'm scared."

"Don't think about it. I know how these things work."

"You don't know that. There's never been anything *like* this."

Pete said, "It'll be all right."

Barb said, "Bullshit."

Ward was late. Pete watched the Carousel Club.

He stood two doors down. Jack Ruby shooed cops and whores out. They paired off. They piled in cars. The whores jiggled keys.

Jack closed up the club. Jack cleaned his ears with a pencil. Jack kicked a turd in the street.

Jack went back inside. Jack talked to his dogs. Jack talked very loud.

It was cold. It was windy. Motorcade debris swirled: Matchbooks/confetti/Jack & Jackie signs.

Ward was late. Ward might be with "Arden."

He left Ward's room. He heard the phone ring. Ward made him run. He saw Ward and Arden. They didn't see him. He told Ward the safe-house tale.

He said, "Arden." Ward schizzed. He called Ward on Ruby. Ward played it oblique.

Fuck it—for now.

Jack's dogs yapped. Jack baby-talked Yiddish. The noise carried outside. A Fed sled pulled up. Ward got out. His coat pockets bulged.

He walked up. He unloaded his pockets—rogue-cop show-and-tell.

Brass knucks/a sash cord/a pachuco switchblade.

"I went by the property room at the PD. Nobody saw me."

"You thought it through."

Ward restuffed his pockets. "*If* he doesn't agree."

Pete lit a cigarette. "We'll cut him up and make it look like a heist."

A dog yipped. Ward flinched. Pete blew on his cigarette. The tip flared red.

They walked up. Ward knocked on the door. Pete put on a drawl: "Jack! Hey, Jack, I think I left my wallet!"

The dogs barked. The door opened. There's Jack. He saw them. He said, "Oh." His mouth dropped and held.

Pete flicked his butt in. Jack gagged on it. Jack coughed it out wet.

Pete shut the door. Ward grabbed Jack. Pete shoved him. Pete frisked him. Pete pulled a piece off his belt.

Ward hit him. Jack fell down. Jack curled up and sucked air.

The dogs ran. The dogs crouched by the runway. Ward grabbed the gun. Ward dumped five shells.

He knelt down. Jack saw the gun. Jack saw the one shell. Ward shut the drum. Ward spun it. Ward aimed at Jack's head.

He pulled the trigger. The hammer clicked. Jack sobbed and sucked air. Ward twirled the gun. Ward pulled the trigger. Ward dry-shot Jack's head.

Pete said, "You're going to clip Oswald."

Jack sobbed. Jack covered his ears. Jack shook his head. Pete grabbed his belt. Pete dragged him. Jack kicked out at tables and chairs.

Ward walked over. Pete dumped Jack by the runway. The dogs yapped and growled.

Pete walked to the bar. Pete grabbed a fifth of Schenley's. Pete grabbed some dog treats.

He dumped the treats. The dogs tore in. Ward scoped the jug. Ward was a lush. Ward was on the wagon. Booze turned him to mush.

They pulled chairs up. Jack sobbed. Jack wiped his schnoz. The dogs snarfed the treats. The dogs waddled and wheezed. The dogs crapped out cold by the runway.

Jack sat up. Jack hugged his knees. Jack braced his back on the slats. Pete grabbed a stray glass. Pete dumped ice dregs and poured Schenley's.

Jack studied his shoes. Jack squeezed his Jew star on a chain.

Pete said, "*L'chaim*."

Jack looked up. Pete waved the glass. Jack shook his head. Ward twirled the gun. Ward cocked the hammer.

Jack grabbed the glass. His hand shook. Pete clamped it down. Jack imbibed. Jack coughed and gasped. Jack held it down.

Ward said, "You've been saying someone should do it all weekend."

Pete said, "You'll do eighteen months tops. You'll get your own fucking motorcade when you get out."

Ward said, "You'll own this town."

Pete said, "He clipped that Tippit guy. Every cop in Dallas will love you."

Ward said, "Your money worries are over as of this moment."

Pete said, "Think about it. A tax-free pension for life."

Jack said, "No." Jack shook his head.

Ward waved the gun. Ward spun the drum. Ward aimed at Jack's head. He pulled the trigger *two times*. He got two dry clicks.

Jack sobbed. Jack prayed—heavy-duty hebe shit.

Pete poured him a refill—three fingers of Schenley's—Jack shook his head. Pete grabbed his neck. Pete cleared his pipes. Pete force-fed him hard.

Jack kept it down. Jack coughed and gasped.

Pete said, "We'll fix up the club and let your sister Eva run it."

Ward said, "Or we'll kill all your brothers and sisters."

Pete said, "She'll make a mint. This place will be a national monument."

Ward said, "Or we'll torch it to the ground."

Pete said, "Are you getting the picture?"

Ward said, "Do you understand your options?"

Pete said, "If you say no, you die. If you say yes, you'll have the world by the balls. If you blow the job, it's 'Shalom, Jack,' you tried, but we don't appreciate failure, and it's too bad we have to take out your whole fucking family, too."

Jack said, "No."

Pete said, "We'll find a nice home for your dogs. They'll be glad to see you when you get out."

Ward said, "Or we'll kill you."

Pete said, "Your tax troubles will disappear."

Ward said, "Or everyone you love will die."

Jack said, "No." Pete cracked his knuckles. Ward pulled a belt sap—a hose chunk packed with double-aught buck.

Jack stood up. Pete pushed him down. Jack reached for the jug. Pete poured it out. Pete saved a chaser.

Jack said, "No. *No no no no no.*"

Ward sapped him—one rib shot—whap.

Jack balled up. Jack kissed his Jew star. Jack bit his tongue.

Ward grabbed his belt. Ward dragged him. Ward kicked him into his office. Ward kicked the door shut.

Pete laughed. Jack lost a shoe and a tie clip. Ward lost his glasses.

Pete heard thump sounds. Jack screamed. The dogs woke up. Pete popped aspirin and Schenley's. The dogs yapped. The noise got all mixed up.

Pete shut his eyes. Pete rolled his neck. Pete worked his headache—*fuck*.

He smelled smoke. He opened his eyes. Smoke blew out a wall vent. Ash sifted through.

Arden.

Ward got Jack alone. Pete knew why. Do what we want/do what *I* want/don't talk about HER. He torched Jack's files. He torched HER name. He torched Arden WHO?

Jack screamed. The dogs yapped. Smoke blew out the vent. Smoke seeped and pooled.

The door popped open. Smoke whooshed out. Wet ashes flew. Sink sounds. Screams. Loose shot pellets hurled.

Ward walked out. His sap leaked buckshot. The shaft dripped blood. He stumbled. He rubbed his eyes. He stepped on his glasses.

He said, "He'll do it."

10

(Dallas, 11/24/63)

HANGOVER.

The room light hurt. The TV noise hurt. Alka-Seltzer helped. Wayne dosed up and replayed the fight.

He swung. He hit Moore. Moore swung bourbon-blind. Pete got between them. Pete fucking laughed.

Wayne watched TV. Room service was late—SOP for the hotel.

A cop faced a mike. He said we're moving him. Clear a path now.

Willis Beaudine didn't call. Buddy Fritsch did. Buddy had an update. Buddy talked to the border cops.

Wendell Durfee: Still at large.

Wayne dropped *his* plan: I've got a car/I'll drive to McAllen/ I'll liaise with the border cops there.

Fritsch said, "Take Moore with you. If you cap that nigger, you'd better have a Texas cop in your pocket."

Wayne argued. Wayne almost said it: My plan is a shuck. Fritsch said, "Take him out. Earn your fucking keep."

Fritsch won. Wayne lost. He stalled. He watched TV. He never called Moore up.

Wayne sipped Alka-Seltzer. Wayne saw cops with Stetsons. The TV picture jumped.

He slapped the box. He tapped the dials. The picture cohered.

Oswald stepped out. Oswald wore handcuffs. Two cops flanked him. They walked through the basement. They faced some reporters. They cleared a path fast.

A man jumped out. Dark suit/fedora. Right arm outstretched. He stepped up. He aimed a gun. He shot near point-blank.

Wayne blinked. Wayne saw it—oh fuck.

Oswald doubled up. Oswald went "Oooh."

The cops blinked. They saw it—oh fuck.

Commotion. Dogpile. The gunman's down. He's prone. He's disarmed. He's pinned flat.

Rerun that. I think I—

The hat. The bulk. The profile. The dark eyes. The fat.

Wayne grabbed the TV. Wayne shook the sides. Wayne focused in tight.

Jerky shots/camera jumps/a low zoom.

The bulk grew. The profile blossomed. Someone yelled, "Jack!"

No. Asshole Jack Ruby—the dive club/the dogshit/the—

Someone yelled, "Jack!" A man snared his hat. Cops wrestled him. Cops cuffed him. Cops stood him up. Cops went through his pants.

The picture jumped. Wayne slapped the antenna. The picture went flat.

Reruns:

Moore muscles Jack. Jack prowls the PD. Jack knows Pete. Moore knows Pete gooood. Bowers. The thumb. The Kennedy hit—

The picture jumped. The tubes buzzed. The fucking phone rang.

The picture settled. A newsman yelled, "Local nightclub"—

Wayne stood up. Wayne tripped. Wayne grabbed the phone. Wayne snagged the receiver.

"Yeah, this is Tedrow."

"It's Willis Beaudine. Remember, you met me—"

"Yeah, I remember."

"Well, that's good, because Wendell's going for that offer you made. He don't know why you're doing it, but I told him my dog liked you."

The sound died. Jack moved his lips. Cops gave him the big two-cop flank.

Beaudine said, "Man, are you *there?*"

"I'm here."

"Good. Then you be at rest stop number 10, eighty miles south on I-35. Make it three o'clock. Oh, and Wendell wants to know if you've got money."

The cops dwarfed Jack—big men—boots up to six-four.

"Hey, man. Are you *there?*"

"Tell him I've got six thousand dollars."

"Hey, you have to like that!"

Wayne hung up. The TV jumped. Oswald rode a white sheet on a cot.

I I

(Dallas, 11/24/63)

HE SAW IT LIVE.

He'd tuned in Channel 4. He squinted to see. He broke his glasses at Jack's club.

He sat in his room. He watched the show. It capped his inter-view—one hour back.

He sat with Lee Oswald. They talked.

Littell drove I-35. Freeway signs blurred. He hit the slow lane and crawled.

Arden called last night. Oswald died at Parkland. Ruby was under arrest.

Oswald bit his nails. Littell uncuffed him. Oswald rubbed his wrists.

I'm a Marxist. I'm a patsy. I won't elaborate. I'm pro-Fidel. I indict the U.S. I scorn her Cuban misdeeds. I scorn the exiles.

I scorn the CIA. National Fruit is evil. The Bay of Pigs was insane.

Littell agreed. Oswald warmed up. Oswald craved perspect-ive. Oswald craved friends.

Littell faltered then. Oswald craved friends. Guy's cutout knew it. Littell shut down. Oswald caught his tone. Oswald threw it back.

Some sound facts. Some nut talk mixed in. You don't love me—so I'll kill you with The Truth.

Littell walked out then. Littell recuffed Oswald. Littell squeezed his hands.

Freeway signs blurred. Signposts popped. Exit posts slithered. Littell saw "Grandview." Littell pulled right. Littell cut down a ramp.

He saw the Chevron sign. He saw the HoJo's.

There—

The shape between them—motel rooms—one long row.

He crossed an access lane. He parked by the HoJo's. He walked by the rooms. He squinted. He saw the "14."

There—the door's ajar. That's Arden on the bed.

Littell walked in. Littell shut the door. Littell bumped a TV set. The juice was off. The box was warm. He smelled cigarettes.

Arden said, "Sit here."

Littell sat down. The bedsprings sagged. Arden moved her legs.

"You look different without your glasses."

"I broke them."

She had her hair up. She wore a green sweater-dress.

Littell turned a lamp on. Arden blinked. Littell bent the lamp down. It shaded the glare.

"What did you do with your things?"

"I rented a storage garage."

"In your own name?"

"You're being disingenuous. You know I'm better than that."

Littell coughed. "You've been watching television."

"Along with the whole country."

"You know some things they don't."

"We've got our version, they've got theirs. Is that what you're saying?"

"*You're* being disingenuous now."

Arden hugged a pillow. "How did they convince him? How do you make someone do something so crazy on live television?"

"He was crazy to start with. And sometimes the stakes are so high that they play in your favor."

Arden shook her head. "I don't want to get more specific."

Littell shook his head. "We don't have to discuss it."

Arden smiled. "I'm wondering why you're going to so much trouble to help me."

"You know why."

"I may ask you to say it."

"I will. If we go forward on this."

" 'This?' Are we going to define *any* of our terms at all?"

Littell coughed—full ashtrays/stale smoke.

"Confirm something for me. You've been in trouble, you've run before, you know how to do it."

Arden nodded. "It's something I'm good at."

"That's good, because I can get you a completely new identity."

Arden crossed her legs. "Is there a disclosure clause in all '*this*'?"

Littell nodded. "We can hold back some secrets."

"That's important. I don't like to lie unless I have to."

"I'm going to Washington for a few days. Then I'll be setting up a base in Las Vegas. You can meet me there."

Arden grabbed her cigarettes. The pack was empty—she tossed it.

"We both know who's behind this. And *I* know they all pass through Vegas."

"I do work for them. It's one reason why you'll be safe with me."

"I'd feel safer in L.A."

Littell smiled. "Mr. Hughes lives there. I'll need to get a house or apartment."

"I'll meet you, then. I'll trust you that far."

Littell checked his watch—1:24 P.M.—Littell grabbed the phone by the bed.

Arden nodded. He pulled the phone to the bathroom. The cord almost snapped. He shut the door. He dialed the Adolphus. The switchboard patched him through.

Pete picked up. "Yes?"

"It's me."

"Yeah, and you're the white man of the week. I wasn't a hundred percent sure that he'd do it."

"What about Moore?"

"He *goes*. I'll tail him and get him alone."

Littell hung up. Littell walked back. Littell dropped the phone on a chair.

He sat on the bed. Arden slid close.

Arden said, "*Say* it."

He squinted. Her freckles jumped. Her smile blurred.

"I've got nothing but the wrong things, and I want to take something good out of this."

"That's not enough."

Littell said, "I want you." Arden touched his leg.

12

(Dallas, 11/24/63)

RERUNS:

The thumb. Pete and Moore. Killer Jack and Killer Lee.

Wayne drove I-35. The reruns hit. A soundtrack sputtered:

He calls Moore. He says, "Meet me. I've got a lead on Durfee." He lies. He drops details. Static fries the line and blows the connection.

Moore gets the last word. Moore says, ". . . have us big fun."

The freeway was flat. Flat blacktop/flat empty. Flat sand adjacent. Sand flats and scrub. Jackrabbit bones. Sand grit in circulation.

The soundtrack distorted. He'd fucked up the call. The Jack and Lee Show fucked with him.

A rabbit jumped. It hit the road. It cleared his wheels clean. A wind kicked up. It tossed scrub balls and waxed paper.

There's the sign: Rest Stop #10.

Wayne pulled in. Wayne scoped the parking lot slooooow.

Gravel paving. No cars. Tire tracks on sand adjacent. Flat sand. Drift sand. Scrub balls hip-high.

Goooood cover spots.

A men's room. A ladies' room. Two stucco huts and a crawl space between. The huts fronted sand drifts. Said drifts ran way inland. The wind stirred loose sand.

Wayne parked. Beaudine said 3:00. He told Moore to meet him at 4:00. The current time—2:49.

He pulled his piece. He popped the glove box. He pulled out the money—six cold.

He got out. He walked through the men's room. He checked the stalls gun-first. The wind kicked cellophane through.

He walked out. He hit the ladies' room. Empty stalls/dirty sinks/bugs pooled in Lysol.

He walked out. He hugged the walls. He moved around back. Shitfire—there's Wendell Durfee.

He's got pimp threads. He's got a hair net. He's got a jigaboo conk. He's got a piece—it's a quiff automatic.

Durfee stood by the wall. Durfee ducked sand. It messed up his conk good.

He saw Wayne. He said, "Well, now."

Wayne drew down on him. Durfee raised his hands. Wayne walked up slow. Sand filled his shoes.

Durfee said, "Why you doin' this for me?"

Wayne grabbed his piece. Wayne popped the clip. Wayne tucked it down his pants barrel first.

The wind tore a scrub pile. Durfee's sled got exposed. It's a '51 Merc. It's sand-scraped. It's sunk to the hubs.

Wayne said, "Don't talk to me. I don't want to know you."

Durfee said, "I might need me a tow truck."

Wayne heard gravel crunch—back in the lot. Durfee futzed with his hair net. Durfee heard shit.

"Willis said you had money."

Gravel crunch—tire crunch—Durfee missed the sounds dead.

"I'll get it. You wait here."

"Shit. I ain't goin' nowhere without it. You fuckin' Santa Claus, you know that?"

Wayne holstered his piece. Wayne circled back to the lot. Wayne saw Moore's 409.

It's upside his car. It's idling hard. It's throbbing on hi-end shocks. There's Moore. He's at the wheel. He's chomping Red Man.

Wayne stopped. His dick fluttered. Piss leaked out.

He saw something.

A speck—up the freeway—some kind of mirage or a car.

He anchored his legs. He walked up jerky. He leaned on Moore's car.

Moore rolled down his window. "Hey, boy. What's new and noteworthy?"

Wayne leaned in close. Wayne braced on the roof.

"He isn't here. That guy gave me a bad lead."

Moore spat tobacco juice. Moore hit Wayne's shoes.

"Why'd you tell me four o'clock, when you're here before three?"

Wayne shrugged. How should I know? I'm bored with you.

Moore pulled a knife. Moore picked his teeth. Moore sheared pork chop fat. He sprayed juice haphazard. He doused Wayne's shirt.

"He's out back. I reconnoitered a half hour ago. Now, you get your ass back there and kill him."

Wayne saw reruns—in slooooow motion.

"You know Jack Ruby."

Moore picked his teeth. Moore tapped the blade on the dash.

"So what? Everyone knows Jack."

Wayne leaned in the window. "What about Bowers? He saw Kennedy get—"

Moore swung the knife. Moore snagged Wayne's shirt. Moore grabbed Wayne's necktie. They hit heads. Moore swung the knife. His hand hit the door ledge.

Wayne pulled his head back. Wayne pulled his piece. Wayne shot Moore in the head.

Recoil—

It knocked him back. He hit *his* car. He braced and aimed tight. He shot Moore in the head/Moore in the neck/Moore with no face and no chin.

He ripped the seats. He tore up the dash. He blew the windows out. It was loud. It echoed loud. It outblew wind gusts.

Wayne froze. The 409 bounced—reverb off hi-end shocks.

Durfee ran out. Durfee lost his legs. Durfee slid and fell flat. Wayne froze. There's that speck up I-35—it's a car oh fuck.

The car drove up. The car pulled in. The car stopped by Moore's sled. Sand blew. Scrub balls bounced. Gravel scattered.

The speck-car idled. Pete got out. Pete put his hands up.

Wayne aimed at him. Wayne pulled the trigger. The pin clicked—you're empty—you're fucked.

Durfee watched. Durfee tried to run. Durfee stood up and fell flat. Pete walked up to Wayne. Wayne dropped his gun and pulled Durfee's gun. Wayne popped in the clip.

His hand slipped. The gun fell. Pete picked it up.

He said, "Kill him."

Wayne looked at Durfee. Pete said, "Kill him."

Wayne looked at Durfee. Durfee looked at Wayne. Wayne looked at Pete. Pete gave him the gun. Wayne dropped the safety.

Durfee stood up. His legs went. He fell on his ass.

Pete leaned on Moore's car. Pete reached inside. Pete flipped off the key. Wayne leaned in his car. Wayne grabbed the six thousand. Wayne coughed up gravel grit.

Pete said, "Kill him."

Wayne walked up to Durfee. Durfee sobbed. Durfee watched Wayne's hands. He saw a gun. He saw a cash bag. He saw two hands full.

Wayne dropped the bag. Durfee grabbed it. Durfee stood up. Durfee got legs and ran.

Wayne leaned on his knees. Wayne puked his lunch up. Wayne tasted hamburger and sand.

Durfee ran.

He tripped through sand drifts. He got his Merc. He gunned it. He bumped drifts. He plowed them. He made the lot. He made I-35 south.

Pete walked over. Wayne wiped his face. Wayne smeared Maynard Moore's blood.

Pete said, "You picked a good place for it. You picked a good weekend, too."

Wayne leaned on his knees. Wayne dropped the gun. Pete grabbed it up.

"There's an oil dump two miles down. You can ditch the car there."

Wayne straightened up. Pete steadied him. Pete said, "Maybe I'll see you in Vegas."

13

(Dallas, 11/25/63)

JACK'S WAKE BLARED—epidemic boohoo—it cut through the bridal suite walls.

Barb said, "I'm getting the picture. The fix is in."

Pete packed his suitcase. "Some people got Christmas early.

They know how things work, and they know what's best for the country."

Barb folded her gowns. "There's a catch. For us, I mean."

Pete tuned her out. He'd just talked to Guy. Guy just talked to Carlos. Carlos loved the Ruby Show. Carlos wanted to clip Maynard Moore.

Guy told Pete that. Pete ad-libbed. Pete said Moore vanished—kapoof!

Guy spritzed on Moore's Vegas gig. Guy ragged Wayne Junior. Junior knew shit—small fucking world—Wayne Senior greased the hit fund.

Barb said, "The *catch*. Don't tell me there isn't one. And don't tell me those tickets to Vegas aren't part of it."

Pete stashed his piece. "Are you saying that two tickets was being optimistic?"

"No. You know I'll never leave you."

Pete smiled. "There's some fuck-ups I wouldn't have made, if I'd known you better."

Barb smiled. "The catch? *Vegas?* And don't make eyes at me when we have to run for a plane."

Pete shut his suitcase. "The Outfit has plans for Mr. Hughes. Ward's putting some things together."

"It's about staying useful, then."

"Yeah. Stay useful, stay healthy. If I can get them to bend a certain rule, I'd call it a lock."

Barb said, "What rule?"

"Come on, you know what I do."

Barb shook her head. "You're versatile. You run shakedowns and you sell guns and dope. You killed the President of the United States once, but I'd have to call that a one-time opportunity."

Pete laughed. Pete made his sides hurt. Pete leaked some wiiiiiild tears. Barb tossed a towel up. Pete wiped his eyes and de-teared.

"You can't move heroin there. It's a set policy, but it's probably the best way I can make the Boys some real money. They might go for it, if I only sell to the spooks in West Vegas. Mr. Hughes hates jigs. He thinks they should all be doped up, like he is. The Boys might decide to humor him."

Barb got This Look. Pete knew the gestalt. *I* fucked JFK. *You* killed him. *My* craaazy life.

She said, "Useful."

"Yeah, that's it."

Barb grabbed her Twist gowns. Barb dropped them out the window. Pete looked out. A kid looked up. The blue gown hit a ledge.

Barb waved. The kid waved back.

"The Twist is dead, but I'll bet you could get me some lounge gigs."

"We'll be useful."

"I'm still scared."

Pete said, "That's the catch."

PART TWO

EXTORTION

December 1963–October 1964

DOCUMENT INSERT: 12/1/63.
Internally circulated FBI intelligence report.
Marked: ''Classified Confidential 2-A: Restricted
Agent Access''/''Pertinent Facts & Observations on
Major Las Vegas Hotel-Casino Ownerships & Related
Topics.'' Note: Officially logged at Southern Nevada
Office, 2/8/63.

The major Las Vegas hotel-casinos are situated in two
locales: The downtown (Fremont Street/''Glitter
Gulch'') area and ''The Strip'' (Las Vegas Blvd, the
city's main north-south artery). The downtown
establishments are older, less gaudy & cater to local
residents & less affluent tourists who come to
gamble, enjoy low-quality entertainment & engage the
services of prostitutes. Junket groups (Elks,
Kiwanis, Rotary, Shriners, VFW, CYO) are frequent
downtown hotel-casino visitors. The downtown
establishments are largely owned by ''Pioneer''
consortiums (e.g., native Nevadans & general non-
organized crime groups). Some of the owners have been
forced to sell small (5%-8%) interests to organized-
crime groups in exchange for continued
''Preferential Treatment'' (e.g., on-site
''protection,'' a ''service'' to insure the absence
of labor trouble & untoward on-site incidents).
Organized-crime associates frequently serve as
casino ''Pit Bosses'' & thus as enforcers and on-site
informants for their organized-crime patrons.
  The downtown area is jurisdictionally covered by
the Las Vegas Police Department (LVPD). The LVPD's
jurisdiction adjoins that of the Clark County
Sheriff's Department (CCSD). Both agencies work
within the other's jurisdiction by mutual consent.

The Sheriff's Dept patrols the ''Strip'' area south
of the Sahara Hotel. Like the LVPD, it provides
investigatory services for its specific jurisdiction,
with an operational mandate inside LVPD, or ''City''
jurisdiction. The LVPD is similarly allowed to
conduct investigations inside Sheriff's Dept, or
''County'' jurisdiction. It should be noted that both
agencies are widely influenced and corrupted by
factions of organized crime. This corruption is of
the type most identified with ''Company Towns'' (e.g.,
casino revenue forms the financial base of Las Vegas &
thus influences the political base & law-enforcement
policy). Numerous officers within both agencies
benefit from organized-crime bestowed ''Gratuities''
(free hotel stays, free casino gambling chips, the
services of prostitutes, ''police discounts'' at
various businesses owned by organized-crime
associates) & outright bribery. The LVPD and
Sheriff's Dept enforce organized-crime policies with
the implicit consent of the Clark County political
hierarchy & by extension the consent of the Nevada
State Legislature. (E.g., Negroes are strongly
discouraged from entering certain ''Strip'' hotel-
casinos and on-site casino personnel are allowed to
see to their expulsion. E.g., crimes against
organized-crime-connected casino employees are
frequently avenged by LVPD officers, acting on orders
from the Casino Operators Council, an organized-
crime front group. E.g., LVPD officers and Sheriff's
deputies are often used to track down casino card
cheats, ''discourage'' them & run them out of town.)

   The best-known hotel-casinos are situated on the
''Strip.'' Many of them have been infiltrated by
organized crime, with percentage ''Points'' divvied
up among the overlords of organized-crime cartels.
(E.g., the Chicago Crime Cartel controls the Stardust
Hotel-Casino & boss Sam ''Mo,'' ''Momo,'' ''Mooney''
Giancana has an 8% personal interest. Chicago hoodlum
John Rosselli (the Chicago Cartel's Las Vegas
overseer) has a 3% interest & Chicago Mob enforcer
Dominic Michael Montalvo aka ''Butch Montrose'' has a

1% interest.) (See Addendum File #B-2 for complete
list of crime-cartel ownerships & percentage-point
estimates.)

Smaller percentage points are traded between
organized crime factions as part of an ongoing effort
to insure that all factions have a stake in the
expanding Las Vegas casino economy. The profit base is
thus shared & faction-to-faction rivalry is averted.
Thus, organized crime presents a unified face in Las
Vegas. The man responsible for developing &
maintaining this policy is Morris Barney ''Moe''
Dalitz (b. 1899), a former Cleveland mobster &
organized crime's ''Goodwill Ambassador'' & Las
Vegas ''Fix-It Man.'' Dalitz owns points in the
Desert Inn Hotel Casino and is rumored to have points
in several others. Dalitz is known as ''Mr. Las
Vegas,'' because of his numerous philanthropic
endeavors & his convincing non-gangster image.
Dalitz founded the Casino Operators Council,
dictates their enforcement policies & is largely
responsible for the ''Clean Town'' policy that
organized-crime factions believe will help promote
tourism & thus increase hotel-casino revenue.

This ''Policy'' is informally enforced & has the
implicit approval of the Las Vegas political machine
& the LVPD & Sheriff's Dept. One goal is to enforce ad
hoc segregation in the ''Strip'' hotel-casinos
(e.g., admit Negro celebrities or perceived ''High
Class'' Negroes & refuse admittance to all others) &
to isolate Negro housing in the slum area of West Las
Vegas. (Restrictive real-estate covenants are widely
observed by Las Vegas—based realtors.) A key
''Policy'' dictate is the ''No Narcotics'' rule. This
rule applies specifically to heroin. The selling of
heroin is forbidden & is punishable by death. The rule
is enforced to limit the number of narcotics addicts,
specifically those who might support their addiction
by means of robbery, burglary, ''flim-flam'' or other
criminal activities that would sully the reputation
of Las Vegas & thus discourage tourism. Numerous
heroin pushers have been the victims of unsolved

homicides & numerous others have disappeared & are presumed to have been killed per the aforementioned policy (see Addendum File #B-3 for partial list). The last homicide occurred on 4/12/60 & there appears to be no heroin traffic in Las Vegas as of this date. It is fair to conclude that the aforementioned deaths have served as a deterrent.

Dalitz is a close associate of Teamster President James Riddle Hoffa (b. 1914) & has secured large loans from the Teamsters' Central States Pension Fund that have covered the cost of hotel-casino improvements. The Fund (estimated assets 1.6 billion dollars) is a ''Watering Hole'' that organized-crime factions borrow from routinely. Dubious organized-crime-connected ''Businessmen'' also borrow from the Fund at usurious interest rates that often result in the forfeiture of their businesses. It is rumored that a second set of Pension Fund financial books exists (one that is hidden from government subpoena & thus official audit). These books allegedly list a more accurate accounting of Pension Fund assets & detail the illegal & quasi-legal loans & repayment schedules.

Many of the ''Strip'' hotel-casinos routinely hide a large portion of their assets. (See the attached IRS-filed table-by-table profit accountings for all craps, roulette, blackjack, poker, loball, keno, fan-tan & baccarat tables, broken down by hotel.) These reported accountings are generally considered to be only 70–80% accurate. (It is very difficult to detect sustained underestimation of taxable income in large cash-base businesses.) Underestimated table profits are estimated to amount to untaxed revenue of over $105,000,000 per year ('62 fiscal estimate). This practice is called the ''Skim.''

Cash receipts are taken directly from casino counting rooms and dispersed to couriers who messenger the money to prearranged spots. Large-denomination bills are substituted for slot-machine coins & daily accountings are fraudulently tallied inside the counting rooms proper. Casino ''Skim'' is virtually impossible to detect. Most hotel-casino

employees subsist on low wages & untaxed cash
gratuities & would never report irregularities. This
endemic corruption extends to the labor unions who
supply the major hotel-casinos with workers.

The Dealers and Croupiers Local #117 is a Chicago
Crime Cartel front. Its members are paid a low hourly
wage & are given play chips & (presumably stolen)
merchandise as bonuses. All chapters of this union
are rigidly segregated. The Lounge Entertainers
Local #41 is a Detroit Crime Cartel front. Its members
are well-paid, but pay weekly kickbacks to crew
stewards. This union is nominally integrated. Negro
lounge entertainers are ''discouraged'' from
patronizing the hotel-casinos they work in & from
fraternizing with white patrons. The four building &
building-supply locals who service the ''Strip''
hotels are Cleveland Crime Cartel fronts & work
exclusively with organized-crime-connected
contracting firms. The all-female Chambermaids Local
#16 is a Florida Crime Cartel front. Many of its
members have been suborned into prostitution. The
work crews for the above mentioned locals are run by
''Ramrods'' who report to the Casino Operators
Council.

The Kitchen Workers Union (Las Vegas—based only.
There are no other chapters) is not organized-crime-
connected & is allowed to operate as a sop to the Las
Vegas ''Pioneer'' contingent & the largely Mormon
Nevada political machine. The union is run by Wayne
Tedrow Sr. (b. 1905), a conservative pamphleteer,
real-estate investor & the owner of a bottom-rung or
''Grind Joint'' casino, the ''Land o' Gold.'' The
crew chiefs are all Mormons & the workers (mostly
illegal Mexican aliens) are paid substandard wages &
are given ''bonuses'' of dented cans of food & play
chips for the Land o' Gold. The workers live in slum
hotels in a Mexican enclave on the West-North Las
Vegas border. (Note: Tedrow Sr. is rumored to have
hidden points in 14 North Las Vegas ''Grind Joints'' &
6 liquor store/slot machine arcades near Nellis Air
Force Base. If true, these ownerships would

constitute infractions of the Nevada Gaming
Commission charter.)

The Nevada Gaming Commission oversees & regulates
the granting of casino licenses and the hiring of
casino personnel. The Commission is a ''rubber-
stamp'' panel that does the bidding of the Gaming
Control Board and the Clark County Liquor & Control
Board. The same five men (the Clark County Sheriff &
District Attorney & 3 appointed ''Civilian''
members) serve on both boards. Thus, the power to
approve liquor and casino license applicants for the
entire state rests solely in Las Vegas. None of the 5
board members are overtly organized-crime-connected
& it is difficult to assess the level of collusion the
boards engage in, because a majority of the
applications they review cloak hidden organized-
crime backing that is difficult to detect. There are
no dossiers available on members of the above
organizations. The LVPD Intelligence Unit keeps
detailed files on the Gaming Control & Liquor Board
men, but has consistently refused to grant the FBI &
U.S. Attorney's Office access to them. (As previously
stated, the LVPD is strongly organized-crime-
influenced.) The LVPD Intelligence Unit operates city
& countywide & is the sole such unit in Clark County.
It is a 2-man operation. The commanding officer is
Lieutenant Byron B. Fritsch (the adjutant of the LVPD
Detective Bureau & strongly connected to the Casino
Operators Council) & the only assigned officer is
Sergeant Wayne Tedrow Jr. (Sgt. Tedrow is the son of
the aforementioned Wayne Tedrow Sr. He is considered
incorruptible by Las Vegas Police standards.)

Concluding note: Addendum Files #B-1, 2, 3, 4, 5
require duplicate authorization: Southern Nevada SAC
& Deputy Director Tolson.

DOCUMENT INSERT: 12/2/63.
Verbatim FBI telephone call transcript.
Marked: ''Recorded at the Director's Request''/
''Classified Confidential 1-A: Director's Eyes Only.''
Speaking: Director Hoover, Ward J. Littell.

JEH: Good morning, Mr. Littell.

WJL: Good morning, Sir. And thank you for the carbons.

JEH: Las Vegas is a hellhole. It is unfit for sane habitation, which may explain its allure to Howard Hughes.

WJL: Yes, Sir.

JEH: Let's talk about Dallas.

WJL: The consensus feels secure, Sir. And the Oswald killing seems to be a popular denouement.

JEH: Mr. Ruby has gotten four thousand fan letters. He is quite popular with Jews.

WJL: I'll concede him a certain panache, Sir.

JEH: Will you concede his ability to keep his mouth shut?

WJL: Yes, Sir.

JEH: I agree with you on the consensus. And I want you to include your thoughts in a detailed report on the events of that hallowed weekend. I will attribute the report to Dallas agents and submit it directly to President Johnson.

WJL: I'll begin work immediately, Sir.

JEH: The President will announce a commission to investigate King Jack's death. I will hand-pick the field agents. Your report will provide the President with a snappy preview of their findings.

WJL: Has he formed an opinion, Sir?

JEH: He suspects Mr. Castro or unruly Cuban exiles. In his view, the killing stemmed from King Jack's reckless blunders in the Caribbean.

WJL: It's an informed perspective, Sir.

JEH: I'll concede the point and concede that Lyndon Johnson is no dummy. He has a conveniently dead assassin and a citizenry avenged on national television. What more could he ask for?

WJL: Yes, Sir.

JEH: And he's appropriately fed up with the Cuban boondoggle. He's going to drop it as a national-security issue and concentrate on the situation in Vietnam.

WJL: Yes, Sir.

JEH: Your tone did not escape me, Mr. Littell. I know that you disapprove of American colonialism and consider our God-given mandate to contain global communism as ill-conceived.

WJL: That's true, Sir.

JEH: The attendant irony has not escaped me. A closet leftist as front man for Howard Hughes and his colonialist designs.

WJL: Strange bedfellows, Sir.

JEH: And how would you describe his designs?

WJL: He wants to circumvent anti-trust laws and purchase all the hotel-casinos on the Las Vegas Strip. He won't spend a dime until he settles his stock-divestment suit with TWA and accrues at least 500 million dollars. I think the suit will resolve in three or four years.

JEH: And your job is to pre-colonize Las Vegas?

WJL: Yes, Sir.

JEH: I would like a blunt assessment of Mr. Hughes' mental state.

WJL: Mr. Hughes injects codeine in his arms, legs and penis. He eats only pizza pies and ice cream. He receives frequent transfusions of ''germ-free'' Mormon blood. His employees routinely refer to him as ''the Count,'' ''Count Dracula'' and ''Drac.''

JEH: A vivid assessment.

WJL: He's lucid half the time, Sir. And he's single-mindedly fixed on Las Vegas.

JEH: Bobby's anti-Mob crusade may have repercussions there.

WJL: Do you think he'll remain in the cabinet?

JEH: No. He hates Lyndon Johnson, and Lyndon Johnson more than reciprocates. I think he'll resign his appointment. And his successor may have Las Vegas plans that I will be powerless to curtail.

WJL: Specifically, Sir?

JEH: Bobby had been considering skim operations.

WJL: Mr. Marcello and the others have plans for Mr. Hughes' holdings.

JEH: How could they not? They have a drug-addicted vampire to victimize, and you to help them suck his blood.

WJL: They know that you bear them no rancor, Sir. They'll understand that some of Bobby's plans will be implemented by his successor.

JEH: Yes. And if the Count buys into Las Vegas and cleans up its image, those plans might be abandoned.

WJL: Yes, Sir. The thought had occurred to me.

JEH: I would like to know what the Dark Prince thinks about his brother's death.

WJL: So would I.

JEH: Of course you would. Robert F. Kennedy is both your savior and your bête noire, and I'm hardly the one to indict you as a voyeur.

WJL: Yes, Sir.

JEH: Would a bug-and-tap approach work?

WJL: No, Sir. But I'll talk to my other clients and see what they suggest.

JEH: I need someone with a ''fallen liberal'' image. I may ask a favor of you.

WJL: Yes, Sir.

JEH: Good day, Mr. Littell.

WJL: Good day, Sir.

14

(Las Vegas, 12/4/63)

THEY WORKED HIM. Two pros: Buddy Fritsch and Captain Bob Gilstrap.

They used the chief's office. They hemmed Wayne in. They deployed the chief's couch.

He'd stalled the meeting. He'd filed a report and filled lies in. He downplayed Moore's vanishing act.

He drove Moore's car to the dump. He stripped the plates. He pulled out Moore's teeth. He dug out his bullets. He stuffed shotgun shells in his mouth. He gas-soaked a rag. He lit it.

Moore's head blew. He fucked up would-be forensics. He dumped the car in a sludge pit. It sunk fast.

The pit steamed. He knew chemistry. Caustics ate flesh and sheet metal.

He mock-chased Wendell D. He called Buddy Fritsch and lied. He said I can't find him. I can't find Maynard Moore.

He leaned on Willis Beaudine. He told him to split Dallas. Beaudine grabbed his dog and skedaddled. He drove by DPD. He pulled some file sheets. He obscured Wendell Durfee's KAs. He buttonholed cops—you seen Maynard Moore?

Fritsch de-Wendellized him. Fritsch pulled the plug. Fritsch called him back home.

They worked him. They hemmed him in. They cracked JFK jokes. JFK groped a nurse and a nun. JFK's last word was "pussy."

Fritsch said, "We read your report."

Gilstrap said, "You must have had some time. I mean, the Kennedy deal and you trading shots with that spook."

Wayne shrugged. Wayne played it frosty. Fritsch lit a cigarette. Gilstrap bummed one.

Fritsch coughed. "You didn't care much for Officer Moore."

Wayne shrugged. "He was dirty. I didn't respect him as a policeman."

Gilstrap lit up. "Dirty, how?"

"He was drunk half the time. He pressed people too hard."

Fritsch said, "By your standards?"

"By the standards of good police work."

Gilstrap smiled. "Those boys do things their own way."

Fritsch smiled. "You can tell a Texan."

Gilstrap said, "But not much."

Fritsch laughed. Gilstrap slapped his knees.

Wayne said, "What *about* Moore? Did he show up?"

Fritsch shook his head. "That question is unworthy of a smart boy like you."

Gilstrap blew smoke rings. "Try this one on. Moore didn't like you, so he went after Durfee himself. Durfee killed him and stole his car."

Fritsch said, "You got a six-foot-four nigger in an easily identifiable hot rod and a tristate APB out. Tell me it's anything else and you're stupid. And tell me the first cop who spots him won't kill him, just so he can brag about it."

Wayne shrugged. "That's what DPD thinks?"

Fritsch smiled. "Them and us. And we're the only two who count."

Wayne shook his head. "You find the half-dozen Dallas cops who aren't in the Klan and ask them what they think of Moore. They'll tell you how dirty he was, how many people he pissed off, and how many suspects you've got."

Gilstrap picked a hangnail. "That's your pride talking, son. You're blaming yourself because Durfee got away and killed a brother officer."

Fritsch stubbed his cigarette. "DPD's working it hard. They wanted to send one of their IA men up to talk to you, but we said no."

Gilstrap said, "They're talking negligence, son. You scuffled with Moore at the Adolphus, so he went out solo and got himself killed."

Wayne kicked a footrest. An ashtray flew.

"He's trash. If he's dead, he deserved it. You can tell those redneck cops I said that."

Fritsch grabbed the ashtray. "Whoa, now."

Gilstrap scooped up butts. "Nobody's blaming you. You proved yourself to my satisfaction."

Fritsch said, "You showed some poor judgment, *and* you showed some stones. You did your reputation in this man's police department a whole lot of good."

Gilstrap smiled. "Tell your daddy the story. Running fire with one baaaad mother humper."

Fritsch winked. "I feel lucky."

Gilstrap said, "I won't tell."

Fritsch grabbed the chief's desk bandit. Gilstrap pulled the handle. Gears spun. Three cherries clicked. Dimes blew out the chute.

Gilstrap caught them. "There's my lunch money."

Fritsch winked. "You mean there's rank. Captains get to steal from lieutenants."

Gilstrap nudged Wayne. "You'll be a captain one day."

Fritsch said, "Could you have done it? Killed him, I mean."

Wayne smiled. "Durfee or Moore?"

Gilstrap whooped. "Wayne Junior's a fireball today."

Fritsch laughed. "Some folks don't think so, but I say he's his daddy's son after all."

Gilstrap stood up. "Tell true, boy. What did you spend that cold six on?"

Wayne grinned. Wayne said, "Liquor and call girls."

Fritsch stood up. "He's got Wayne Senior's blood in his veins."

Gilstrap winked. "We won't tell Lynette."

Wayne stood up. His legs hurt. He had fucking tension cramps. Gilstrap walked out. Gilstrap whistled and jiggled his dimes.

Fritsch said, "Gil likes you."

"He likes my father."

"Don't sell yourself short."

"Did my father tell you to send me to Dallas?"

"No, but he sure liked the idea."

He worked them back—bait-and-switch—diversion. His heartbeat hit 200. His blood pressure soared. "Lone assassin"—shit. I SAW Dallas.

Wayne drove home. Wayne dawdled. Fremont was packed. Rubes waved bingo sheets. Rubes hopped casinos.

Wayne was brain-fucked. Wayne was brain-fucked off Dallas.

Pete says, "Kill him." He can't. He runs PD checks. He gets Pete's name. He queries three intel squads: L.A./New York/Miami.

Pete Bondurant: Ex-cop/ex-CIA/ex-Howard Hughes goon. Current mobbed-up enforcer.

He runs hotel registrations. 11/25: Pete and Frau Pete hit the Stardust. Their suite is comped. Pete's mobbed up. *Chi*-Mob connections implied.

Car traffic was bad. Foot traffic ditto. Rubes lugged highballs and beers.

Tail Pete. Do it discreet. Hire a patrolman. Pay him in Land o' Gold chips.

Wayne circled back. Wayne recruised Fremont. Wayne dodged Lynette and his dinner.

Lynette was running trite. Lynette ran trite lines verbatim. Jack was young. Jack was brave. Jack *realllly* loved Jackie.

Jack and Jackie lost their baby. Circa '62. Lynette fell for them then. He didn't want kids. Lynette did. She got pregnant in '61.

It froze him up. It shut him down. He froze her out. He told her to get an abortion. She said no. He addressed the Latter-day Saints. He prayed for a dead baby.

Lynette caught the gist. Lynette ran to her folks. Lynette

mailed off chatty letters. She came home bone skinny. She said she miscarried. He went along with the lie.

Daddy Sproul called him. Daddy waxed revisionist. Daddy dropped details. He said Lynette got scraped in Little Rock. He said she hemorrhaged and almost died.

The marriage survived. Trite shit would tear it for real.

Lynette set up TV trays. LBJ crashed their dinner. He announced some Warren probe.

Wayne killed the sound. LBJ moved his lips. Lynette toyed with her food.

"I thought you'd want to follow it more."

"I had too much stuff going on. And it's not like I had a stake in the man."

"Wayne, you were *there*. It's the kind of thing people tell their grand . . ."

"I told you, I didn't see anything. And we're not in the grand-child business."

Lynette balled her napkin. "You've been nothing but sullen since you got back, and don't tell me it's just Wendell Durfee."

"I'm sorry. That crack was ugly."

Lynette wiped her lips. "You know I gave up on that front."

"Tell me what it is, then."

Lynette turned the TV off. "It's the new sullen you, with that patronizing attitude that all the cops have. You know, 'I've seen things that my schoolteacher wife just wouldn't understand.' "

Wayne jabbed his roast beef. Wayne twanged the fork.

Lynette said, "Don't play with your food."

Wayne sipped Kool-Aid. "You're so goddamn smart in your way."

Lynette smiled. "Don't curse at my table."

"You mean your TV tray."

Lynette grabbed the fork. Lynette mock-stabbed him. Blood juice dripped and pooled.

Wayne flinched. Wayne hit the tray. His glass tipped and doused his food.

Lynette said, "Shit."

Wayne walked to the kitchen. Wayne dumped his tray in the sink. He turned around. He saw Lynette by the stove.

She said, "What happened in Dallas?"

* * *

Wayne Senior lived south—Paradise Valley with land and views.

He had fifty acres. He grazed steers. He butchered them for bar-b-que meat. The house was tri-level—redwood and stone—wide decks with wide views.

The carport covered an acre. A runway adjoined it. Wayne Senior flew biplanes. Wayne Senior flew flags: The U.S./the Nevada/the Don't-Tread-on-Me.

Wayne parked. Wayne killed his lights. Wayne skimmed the radio. He caught the McGuire Sisters—three-part harmony.

Janice had a dressing room. It faced the carport. She got bored. She changed clothes. She left her lights on to draw looks.

Wayne settled in. The Sisters crooned. "Sugartime" merged with "Sincerely." Janice walked through the light. Janice wore tennis shorts and a bra.

She posed. She dropped her shorts. She picked up capris. Her panties stretched and slid low.

She put the capris on. She unpinned her hair and combed it back. Her gray streak showed—silver in black—the pink capris clashed.

She pirouetted. Her breasts swayed. The Sisters supplied a soundtrack. The lights dimmed. Wayne blinked. It all went too fast.

He calmed down. He turned the car off. He walked through the house. He went straight back. Wayne Senior always perched outside. The north-deck view magnetized.

It was cold. Leaves strafed the deck. Wayne Senior wore a fat sweater. Wayne leaned on the rail. Wayne killed his view.

"You never get bored with it."

"I appreciate a good vista. I'm like my son that way."

"You never called and asked about Dallas "

"Buddy and Gil briefed me. They were thorough, but I'd still like to hear your version."

Wayne smiled. "In time."

Wayne Senior sipped bourbon. "The crap-game ruckus tickled me. You chasing that colored boy."

"I was brave and stupid. I'm not sure you would have approved."

Wayne Senior twirled his walking stick. "And I'm not sure you want my approval."

Wayne turned around. The Strip beamed. Neon signs pulsed.

"My son rubbed shoulders with history. I wouldn't mind a few details."

Cars left Vegas—the losers' exodus—southbound headlights.

"In time."

"Mr. Hoover saw the autopsy pictures. He said Kennedy had a small pecker."

Wayne heard gunshots north-northeast. Broke gambler blows town. Broke gambler pulls gun. Broke gambler unwinds.

"LBJ told Mr. Hoover a good one. He said, 'Jack was a strange bedfellow long before he entered politics.' "

Wayne turned around. "Don't gloat. It's fucking undignified."

Wayne Senior smiled. "You've got a foul mouth for a Mormon."

"The Mormon Church is a crock of shit, and you know it."

"Then why'd you ask the Saints to kill your baby?"

Wayne grabbed the rail. "I forgot that I told you that."

"You tell me everything—'in time.' "

Wayne dropped his hands. His wedding band slid. He missed meals. He dropped weight. He fretted up Dallas.

"When's your Christmas party?"

Wayne Senior twirled his stick. "Don't divert conversation so abruptly. You tell people what you're afraid of."

"Don't press on Lynette. I know where you're going."

"Then I'll go there. It's a kid marriage that you're bored with, and you know it."

"Like you and my mother?"

"That's right."

"I've heard it before. You're here and you've got what you've got. You're not a cluck selling real estate in Peru, Indiana."

"That's right. Because I knew when to fold my hand with your mother."

Wayne coughed. "You're saying I'll meet my Janice and walk like you did."

Wayne Senior laughed. "Shitfire. Your Janice and my Janice are one and the same."

Wayne blushed. Wayne's ears fucking singed.

"Shitfire. Just when I think I've lost sway with my boy, I light him up like a Christmas tree."

A shotgun blew somewhere. It roused some coyote yells.

Wayne Senior said, "Someone lost money."

Wayne smiled. "He probably lost his stake at one of your joints."

"*One of?* You know I only own one casino."

"The last I heard, you had points in fourteen. And the last time I checked, that was illegal."

Wayne Senior twirled his stick. "There's a trick to lying. Hold to the same line, regardless of who you're with."

"I'll remember that."

"You will. But you'll remember who told you right about the same time."

A flying bug bit Wayne. Wayne swatted it.

"I don't see your point."

"You'll remember that your father told you, and speak some godawful truth out of pure cussedness."

Wayne smiled. Wayne Senior winked. He twirled his stick. He dipped it. He ran his stick repertoire.

"Are you still the only policeman who cares about those beat-up colored whores?"

"That's right."

"Why is that?"

"Pure cussedness."

"That and your spell in Little Rock."

Wayne laughed. "You should have been there. I broke every states' rights law on the books."

Wayne Senior laughed. "Mr. Hoover's going after Martin Luther King. He's got to find himself a 'fallen liberal' first."

"Tell him I'm booked up."

"He told me Vietnam's heating up. I said, 'My son was in the Eighty-Second Airborne. But don't hold your breath for him to re-enlist—he'd rather fight rednecks than Reds.' "

Wayne looked around. Wayne saw a chip bucket. Wayne grabbed some Land o' Gold reds.

"Did you tell Buddy to send me to Dallas?"

"No. But I've always thought a cold money run would do you some good."

Wayne said, "It was enlightening."

"What did you do with the money?"

"Got myself in trouble."

"Was it worth it?"

"I learned a few things."

"Care to tell me?"

Wayne tossed a chip. Wayne Senior pulled his hip piece. He shot the chip. He nailed it. Plastic shards flew.

Wayne walked inside. Wayne detoured by the dressing room. Janice shot him a view.

Bare legs. A dance step. Streaked-hair allure.

15

(Las Vegas, 12/6/63)

DALLAS TWEAKED HIM. He should have killed Junior. Junior should have killed the spook.

Vegas sparkled—fuck death—should-haves meant shit. Nice breeze/nice sun/nice casinos.

Pete cruised the Strip. Pete logged distractions:

The Tropicana course. Cocktail carts abundant. Drive-ins. Carhops on skates. Uplift abundant.

Pete made two circuits. Shit popped out:

Some nuns hit the Sands. They spot Frank Sinatra. They swoon and piss Frank off. They shvitz up his Sy Devore suit.

Grief by the Dunes:

Two cops grab two spics. The spics bleed very large. The scene vibes busboy brouhaha. Juan fucked Ramon's sister. Ramon had first dibs. Shivs by the low-roller buffet.

Nice mountains. Neon signs. Jap-tourist shutterbugs.

Pete made three circuits. The Strip show wore thin. Pete re-tweaked Dallas.

BE USEFUL: Sacred fucking text. The Hughes deal would take years. Ward said so. Carlos agreed. Carlos said Pete *should* push dope in Vegas—but—the other Boys have to agree.

Ward was *très* smart. The Arden move was *très* dumb. Ward tripped on his dick—at a *très* bad time.

Ward was in D.C. and New Orleans. Jimmy H. wanted him. Carlos beckoned. Carlos wants to snip loose ends. Carlos wants Ward's take. Carlos trusts Ward—but Ward always ridicules slaughter.

Arden saw the hit team. Arden knew Betty Mac. Arden knew Hank Killiam. A *très* safe bet: Carlos wants to clip them. A *très* safe bet: Ward calls it rash.

A bug was spreading. Call it the Mercy Flu. Call it the Me-No-Kill Blues.

He should have killed Junior. Junior should have killed the shine.

He watched Junior work. He climbed an adjacent hill. He got a covert view. Junior diced Maynard Moore. Junior cut through his brain pan. Junior pulled slugs. His knife slipped. He ate bone chips. He hacked them out and rocked steady.

He checked Junior out. Three intel squads: L.A./New York/Miami. His guys said Junior checked *him* out.

His contacts hated Junior. They said Wayne Senior was a stud. They said Wayne Junior was a geek.

Junior passed him the mercy bug. Junior let the nigger live. Junior misread his options. The nigger vibed stupe. The nigger vibed homing pigeon. The nigger might home back here.

Pete cruised. Pete checked lounge marquees. Pete got the gestalt.

Name acts. No-name acts. Dick Contino/Art & Dottie Todd/the Girlzapoppin' Revue. Hank Henry/the Vagabonds/Freddy Bell & the Bellboys. The Persian Room/the Sky Room/the Top O' the Strip.

Jack "Jive" Schafer/Gregg Blando/Jody & the Misfits. The Dome of the Sea/the Sultan's Lounge/the Rumpus Room.

Call it: Toilets and carpet joints. Some high-end rooms. Call it for keeps:

Find Barb a spot. Find her some nonunion backup. Scotty & the Scabs or the Happy Horseshitters—a fixed rate and a cut.

Pete parked in the Sands lot. Pete hit some casinos—the Bird/the Riv/the DI. He caught a lull. Shit stood out boldfaced.

He played blackjack. He observed:

A pit boss bops on a card cheat. The fuck wears a card-sleeve prosthesis. The fuck shoots cards out his cuffs.

He saw Johnny Rosselli. They schmoozed. They talked up the Hughes deal. Johnny praised Ward Littell—dig the threat implied.

Ward's crucial to our plans. You're muscle—you're not.

Johnny said *ciao*. Two call girls hovered. It vibed three-way.

Pete walked. Pete hit the Sands/the Dunes/the Flamingo. Pete dug the low lights and thick rugs.

Sparks shot off his feet. His socks bipped and buzzed.

He hit bars. He drank club soda. He honed his cave vision. He watched barmen work. Call girls ducked him. He was 6'5"/230. He vibed strongarm cop.

What's *this:*

A barman pours pills—six in a shot glass—a waitress picks up.

He braced the barman. He flashed a toy badge. He growled very gruff. The barman laughed. His son wore a badge like that. His son ate Cocoa Puffs.

The man oozed style. Pete bought him a drink. The man spritzed on Vegas and dope.

Horse/weed/cocaine—verboten. The fuzz enforced the trifecta. The Mob enforced the No-"H" Law.

They tortured pushers. They killed them. Local hypes copped in L.A. Local hypes rode the Heroin Highway.

Pills were cool: Red devils/yellow jackets/high hoppers. Ditto liquid meth sans spike. Drink it—don't shoot it—fear the spike-phobic fuzz.

The fuzz sanctioned pills. Two Narco units—Sheriff's/ LVPD. Pills got pipelined in: T.J. to L.A./L.A. to Vegas. Local quacks consigned pills. They fed barmen and cabbies. They fed pill fiends Vegaswide.

The West LV coons craved white horse. Said coons itched to ride. The No Horse Rule de-horsed them and kept them desatisfied.

Pete walked. Pete hit the Persian Room. Pete watched Dick Contino rehearse. He knew Dick. Dick played squeeze-box gigs for Sam G. Dick owed the Chicago Cartel. The Boys attached his check. The Boys bought his food. The Boys paid his rent and bought his kids' threads.

Dick pitched a tale of woe—woe is me—lots of woe and no tail. Pete slid him two C's. Dick spritzed the Vegas lounge scene.

The Detroit Boys ran the local. The steward took bribes. He usurped the prime snatch. He suborned them to hook. They worked the Lake Mead cruise boats. Lounge kids kept rough hours. They ate breakfast exclusive. The lounge scene ran on Dexedrine and pancakes.

Pete walked. Pete caught Louis Prima in rehearsal. An old geek chewed his ear off.

Pops booked no-name acts. Pops father-henned the girls if they blew him. Pops told them who to avoid:

Shvartze pimps. "Talent scouts." Cockamamie "producers." Skin-mag men and schmucks with no address.

Pete thanked him. Pops bragged. Pops relived his salad days as a pimp. I ran trim—the best in the west—I scored for the late JFK.

Pete broke three C-notes. Pete glommed sixty five-spots.

He grabbed a scratch pad. He wrote down his phone number sixty fucking times. He hit a liquor store. He bought sixty short dogs. He grabbed his sap and drove to West Vegas.

He cruised in slow. He wore the sap. He held his automatic. He saw:

Dirt streets. Dirt yards. Dirt lots. Shack chateaus abundant.

Tar-paper pads with cinder-block siding. *Beaucoup* churches/ one mosque. ALLAH IS LORD! signs. Allah signs revised to JESUS!

Lots of street activity. Jigs cooking bar-b-que in fifty-gallon drums.

The Wild Goose Bar/the Colony Club/the Sugar Hill Lounge. Streets named for Presidents and letters. Shit cars ubiquitous—ad hoc housing:

Two-tenant Chevys. Bachelor Lincolns. Bring-the-whole-family Fords.

Pete cruised slooooow. Uppity coons flipped him off. They scowled. They chucked beer cans. They dinged his fender skirts.

He stopped at a rib drum. A halfbreed served short ends. A chow line pressed in. They scoped Pete. They snickered. They sneered.

Pete smiled. Pete bowed. Pete bought them lunch.

He tipped the breed fifty. He passed out short dogs and fives. He passed out his phone-number slips.

A silence ensued. Said silence built. Said silence lapsed slooooow.

Say what, big man? Say what, daddy-o?

Pete talked:

Who sells shit? Who's seen Wendell Durfee? Who's hot to buck the No-Horse Law? Shouts overlapped—little gems— some nuggets in rebop & jive.

These busboys sell red devils. They works at the Dunes. Dig on fucking Monarch Cab. Them guys push whites and RDs. Monarch got soul. Monarch work West LV. Monarch go where other cabs won't.

Dig on Curtis and Leroy—they gots plans—they wants to push horse. They baaaaaaaaad. They say fuck the rules. They say fuck them wop motherfuckers.

Shouts overlapped—more rebop/more jive. Pete yelled. Pete displayed charisma. Pete restored calm.

He told the breed to call the Wild Goose. He told the spooks to call HIM.

IF you see Wendell Durfee. *IF* Curtis and Leroy move horse.

He pledged a fat reward. He got an ovation: YOU THE FUCKIN' MAN!

He drove to the Wild Goose. Some spooks jogged along. They capered and waved their short dogs.

The Goose was packed. Pete replayed his act. The coons loved it. Pete cut through jive & rebop.

He got no dish on Curtis and Leroy. He got rumors on Wendell D. Wicked Wendell—worse than his rep—a rape-o/a shitbird/a heel. A homing pigeon—Vegas born-and-bred—a Vegas moth to the flame.

Shouts overlapped. Spooks ad-libbed. A spook defamed Wayne Tedrow Senior.

Slumlord Senior stiffed him. Slumlord Senior fucked him. Slumlord Senior raised his rent. The noise got bad. Pete got a headache. Pete dosed it with pork rinds and scotch.

The Senior talk tweaked him—a gem within jive. Junior worked the Intel squad. Junior had the gaming board files.

The spook gained steam. The spook digressed off Senior. The spook sparked other spooks. They aired the Spook Agenda *wiiiiide*.

Jim Crow. Civil rights. Real-estate sanctions. Praise for Martin Luther King.

The vibe went bad. The spooks vibed lynch mob. Pete caught bum looks:

WE THE MAN! YOU the ofay exploiter!

Pete walked out. Pete moved fast. Pete caught some elbows.

He hit the sidewalk. A kid buffed his car. He tipped him. He pulled out. A Chevy pulled out on cue.

Pete caught the move. Pete checked his rearview. Pete made the driver:

Young/white/cop haircut. Some kind of kid fuzz.

Pete zigzagged. Pete blew a stop sign. The Chevy stuck tail-close. They hit LV proper. Pete stopped at a light. Pete set the emergency brake.

The Chevy idled. Pete walked back. Pete twirled his belt sap. The kid cop played cool. The kid cop twirled a play chip.

Pete reached in. Pete grabbed it. The kid cop guuuulped.

A red chip—$20—scrip for the Land o' Gold. Shit—Wayne Senior's joint.

Pete laughed. Pete said, "Tell Sergeant Tedrow to call me."

16

(Washington, D.C., 12/9/63)

ID WORK—OLD forms and smeared ink.

Littell worked. His kitchen table creaked. He knew paper and smudge art. The FBI taught him.

He smudged a birth-certificate form. He baked it on a hot plate. He sliced pen tubes and rolled smears.

The *old* Arden Smith/Coates—now the *new* Jane Fentress.

The apartment was hot. It helped dry forms. Littell rolled ink on a seal-stamp. He stole it from Dallas PD.

Arden was southern. Arden talked southern. Alabama had a lax driver's-license policy. Applicants sent fees in. Birth certificates ditto. Written test forms went out.

They completed them. They mailed them in. They sent in a snapshot. They got their DL return mail.

Littell flew to Alabama—eight days back. Littell researched births and deaths. Jane Fentress was born in Birmingham. Her DOB was 9/4/26. Her DOD was 8/1/29.

He drove to Bessemer. He rented an apartment. He put "Jane Fentress" on the mailbox. Bessemer to Birmingham—twenty-two miles.

Littell switched pens. Littell spread fresh paper. Littell inked vertical lines.

Arden was a bookkeeper. Arden claimed credentials. Arden went to school in DeKalb, Mississippi. Let's upgrade her—Tulane, '49—let's give her an accounting degree.

He was due in New Orleans. He could visit Tulane. He could skim old catalogs. He could learn the academic terrain. He could forge a transcript. He could solicit Mr. Hoover. Local agents knew Tulane. A man could plant the goods.

Littell lined six sheets—standard college forms. He worked fast. He blotted. He smudged. He smeared.

Arden was safe. He stashed her in Balboa—due south of L.A.

A hotel hideaway—paid for by Hughes Tool. Tool Co. ignored his expenses—per Mr. Hughes' edict.

He swapped notes with Mr. Hughes. They spoke on the phone. They never officially met. He snuck into Drac's lair—one time only—the assassination A.M.

There's Drac:

He's sucking IV blood. He's shooting dope in his dick. He's tall. He's thin. His nails curl back.

Mormons guarded him. Mormons cleaned his spikes. Mormons fed him blood. Mormons swabbed his injection tracks.

Drac stayed in his room. Drac *owned* his room. The hotel endured him—call it squatter's rights—Beverly Hills-style.

Littell spread photos out. Arden—three ways. One passport-DL shot/two keepsakes.

They made love in Balboa. A window blew open. Some kids heard them. The kids laughed. Their dog carried on.

Arden had sharp hips. He was bone-thin. They bumped and scraped and blundered into a fit.

Arden touched up her gray hair. Arden's pulse ran quick. She'd had scarlet fever as a kid. She'd had one abortion.

She was running. He caught her. Her run predated the hit.

Littell studied the photos. Littell studied *her.*

She had one brown eye. She had one hazel eye. Her left breast was smaller than her right. He bought her a cashmere sweater. It stretched snug on one side.

Jimmy Hoffa said, "I'm going *down?* After the fucking coup we just pulled?"

Littell went ssshhh. Hoffa shut up. Littell tossed the room. He checked the lamps. He checked the rugs. He checked under the desk.

"Ward, you worry too much. I got a fucking guard outside my office twenty-four hours a day."

Littell checked the window. Window mounts *worked.* Suction cups could be rigged to glass.

"Ward, Jesus fucking—"

No mounts/no glass plates/no cups.

Hoffa stretched out. Hoffa yawned. Hoffa dipped his chair and dropped his feet on his desk.

Littell sat on the edge. "You'll probably be convicted. The appeal process will buy you at least—"

"That cunt-lapping homo Bobby F-for-Faggot—"

"—but jury tampering is not an offense that falls under Federal sentencing guidelines, which means a discretionary decree, which—"

"—means Bobby F-for-Fuckface Kennedy wins and James R-for-Ridiculous Hoffa goes to the fucking shithouse for five or six fucking years."

Littell smiled. "That's my summary, yes."

Hoffa picked his nose. "There's more. 'That's my summary' is no kind of summary that's worth a fucking shit."

Littell crossed his legs. "You'll stay out on appeals for two or three years. I'm developing a long-range strategy to legitimize Pension Fund money and divert and launder it through foreign sources, which should kick into high gear around the time you get out. I'm meeting the Boys in Vegas next month to discuss it. I can't emphasize how important this may prove to be."

Hoffa picked his teeth. "And in the fucking meantime?"

"In the meantime, we have to worry about those other grand juries that Bobby's impaneled."

Hoffa blew his nose. "That cunt-lapping cocksucker. After what we did to fuck—"

"We need to know what Bobby thinks about the hit. Mr. Hoover wants to know, too."

Hoffa cleaned his ears. Hoffa shined on Littell. He gouged. He went in deep. He jabbed a pen. He prospected for wax.

He said, "Carlos has a lawyer at Justice."

New Orleans was hot. The air hung wet and ripe.

Carlos owned a motel—twelve rooms and one office. Carlos made people wait.

Littell waited. The office smelled—chicory and bug spray. Carlos left a bottle out—Hennessy X.O—Carlos doubted his will to abstain.

He got off the plane. He drove to Tulane. He went through catalogs. He compiled a list of GI Bill classes.

He called Mr. Hoover. He asked his favor. Mr. Hoover agreed. Yes, I'll do it—I'll plant your paper.

The air cooler died. Littell dumped his jacket. Littell undid his tie. Carlos walked in. Carlos slapped the wall unit. Cold air blew high.

"*Come va,* Ward?"

Littell kissed his ring. "*Bene, padrone.*"

Carlos sat on the desk. "You love that shit, and you're not even Italian."

"*Stavo perdiventare un prete, Signor Marcello. Aurei potuto il tuo confessore.*"

Carlos cracked the bottle. "Say the last part in English. Your Italian's better than mine."

Littell smiled. "I could have been your confessor."

Carlos poured two fingers. "You'd be out of a job. I never do anything to piss God off."

Littell smiled. Carlos offered the bottle. Littell shook his head.

Carlos lit a cigar. "So?"

Littell coughed. "We're fine. The commission's a whitewash, and I wrote the narrative brief that they'll work off. It played the way I expected."

"Despite some fuck-ups."

"Guy Banister's. Not Pete's or mine."

Carlos shrugged. "Guy's a capable guy, on the whole."

"I wouldn't say that."

"Of course you wouldn't. You wanted your crew to go in."

Littell coughed. "I don't want to argue the point."

"The fuck you don't. You're a lawyer."

The wall unit died. Carlos slapped it. Cold air blew wide.

Littell said, "The meeting is set for the fourth."

Carlos laughed. "Moe Dalitz is calling it 'the Summit.' "

"That's appropriate. Especially if we still have your vote for Pete's business."

"Pete's *potential* business? Yeah, sure."

"You don't sound too optimistic."

Carlos flicked ash. "Narcotics is a tough sell. Nobody wants to put Vegas in the shitter."

"Vegas *is* the shitter."

"No, Mr. I-Was-Almost-a-Priest, it's your fucking salvation. It's your debt to pay off, and without that debt you'd be in the shitter with your friend Kemper Boyd."

Littell coughed. The smoke was bad. The wall unit swirled it.

Carlos said, "So?"

"So, I have a plan for the Pension Fund books. It's long-range, and it derives from your plans for Mr. Hughes."

"You mean *our* plans."

Littell coughed. "Yes, ours."

Carlos shrugged—I'm bored for now—Carlos held up a file.

"Jimmy said you need a guy next to Bobby."

Littell grabbed the file. Littell skimmed the top page—one Shreveport PD rap sheet/one note.

8/12/54: Doug Eversall drives home. Doug Eversall hits three kids. He's drunk. The kids die. Doug's DA pal buries it.

For *his* pal: Carlos Marcello.

Doug Eversall is a lawyer. Doug Eversall works at Justice. Bobby likes Doug. Bobby hates drunks and loves kids. Bobby doesn't know Doug's a kid-killer.

Carlos said, "You'll like Doug. He's on the wagon, like you."

Littell grabbed his briefcase and stood up. Carlos said, "Not yet."

The smoke was bad. It punched up the booze fumes. Littell almost drooled.

"We got some loose ends, Ward. Ruby bothers me, and I think we should send him a message."

Littell coughed. Here it com—

"Guy said you know the story. You know, all that grief at Jack Zangetty's motel."

Chills now—steam off dry ice.

"I know the story, yes. I know what Guy wants you to do, and I'm against it. It's unnecessary, it's too conspicuous, it's too close to Ruby's arrest."

Carlos shook his head. "They go. Tell Pete to take care of it."

Dizzy—weightless now.

"This is all on Banister. *He* let them go to the safe house. *He* screwed up on Tippit and Oswald. *He's* the drunk who'll be bragging to every right-wing shithead on God's green earth."

Carlos shook his head. Carlos waved four fingers.

"Zangetty, Hank Killiam, that Arden cunt, and Betty McDonald. Tell Pete I don't expect a big delay."

I 7

(Las Vegas, 12/13/63)

THE DALLAS PAPER ran it—page 6 news—NO LEADS ON MISS-ING POLICEMAN.

Wayne sat in Sills' Tip-Top. Wayne hogged a window booth.

He held his gun—locked & cocked—the paper covered it.

The paper loved Maynard Moore. Moore got more ink than Jack Ruby. FAN MAIL FOR ASSASSIN'S SLAYER. CHIEF LAUDS MISSING OFFICER. NEGRO SOUGHT IN BAFFLING DISAPPEARANCE.

Wayne counted down. He had eighteen days in now. The Warren probe/the "Lone Gunman"/no news as good news.

He still worried Dallas. He still skipped meals. He still pissed every six seconds.

Pete walked in. Pete showed up punctual. He saw Wayne. He sat down. He smiled.

He checked Wayne's lap. He peeked and goofed. He saw the paper.

He said, "Aww, come on."

Wayne reholstered. Wayne fumbled his gun. Wayne banged the table. A waitress saw it. Wayne blushed red. Pete cracked his knuckles.

"I watched you clean up. You did a good job, but I wish you'd thought the nigger through."

Wayne felt piss pressure. Wayne clenched up downstairs.

"You're comped at the Stardust. That means the Chicago guys brought you in."

"Keep going."

"You think I owe you for that weekend."

Pete cracked his thumbs. "I want to see your gaming board files."

Wayne said, "No."

Pete grabbed a fork. Pete twirled it. Pete squeezed it and bent it in two. The waitress saw it. The waitress freaked.

She went oooh. She dropped a tray. She made a mess.

"I could go around you. Buddy Fritsch is supposed to be nice."

Wayne looked out the window. Wayne saw a two-car crash.

Pete said, "Fucking tailgaters. I always wrote up guys like—"

"I've got the files stashed, and there's no carbons. It's an old fail-safe policy. If you go to Buddy, I'll have my father intercede. Buddy's afraid of him."

Pete cracked his knuckles. "That's all I get for Dallas?"

"Nothing happened in Dallas. Don't you watch the news?"

Pete walked out. Wayne felt piss pressure. Wayne ran to the can.

18

(Las Vegas, 12/13/63)

ONE MORE HEADACHE/one more headache drink/one more lounge.

The Moon Room at the Stardust—low lights and moon maids in tights.

Pete sipped scotch. A moon maid fed him peanuts. Ward left him a message. A desk clerk relayed it. Wait for a Bible code—I'll Western Union it in.

Wayne Junior said no. Nos hurt. Nos fucked with him.

A moon maid dipped by—a faux redhead—dark roots and dark tan. Fuck faux redheads. Real redheads burned.

He got Barb a gig—three days ago—Sam G. pulled strings. Dig it: Barb & the Bail Bondsmen.

Permanent work—4 shows/6 nites—the Sultan's Lounge at the Sahara. Barb was rehearsing. She said the Twist was out. She said the go-go beat was in.

Nigger music. The Swim/the Fish/the Watusi. White stiffs take note.

He shitcanned Barb's ex. He shitcanned his combo. Dick Contino came through. Dick scored Barb a trio—sax/trumpet/drums—three long-term lounge denizens.

Fags. Beefcake types. USDA-certified swish.

Pete cowed them. Pete warned them. Sam G. spread the word: Barb B. was verboten. Approach once and suffer. Approach twice and die.

Barb dug Vegas. Hotel suites and nightlife. No Presidential motorcades.

West LV looked good. West LV looked contained and vice-ready.

Vice zones worked. He hit Pearl in '42. The SPs shut down some roads and cordoned the clap. White horse would work. The niggers craved it. They'd geez up. They'd stay home. They'd soil their own rug.

A moon maid slid by—a faux blonde—dark roots and Miss Clairol. She fed him some peanuts. She dropped off Ward's note.

Pete killed his drink. Pete went up to the suite. Pete got out the Gideon book. The code spanned the whole text—chapter and verse—Exodus to First John.

He worked off a scratch pad—numbers to letters—letters to words.

There:

"CM's orders. Elim. 4 from motel/safe house. Call tomorrow night, 10:30 EST. Pay phone in Silver Spring, Md.: BL4-9883."

19
(Silver Spring, 12/14/63)

PERFECT:

The off ramp/the road/the train station/the tracks/the platform/the phone.

A freeway adjacent. Off-ramp access. Parking-lot view. Late commuters passing through—milk runs from D.C.

Littell sat in his car. Littell watched the ramp—hold for a powder-blue Ford. Carlos described Eversall. He's a tall guy. He's got one high shoe.

9:26 P.M.

The express blew by. Cars parked and split. The local should stop at 10:00.

Littell studied his script. It stressed Eversall's time in New Orleans. It stressed Lee Oswald's time there. It stressed the '63 racket hearings. It stressed Bobby's star role.

Mob panic ensues. Two months pass. JFK dies. Eversall links the dots. Eversall sees collusion.

Littell checked his watch—9:30 sharp—hold for the man with the high shoe.

A blue Ford pulled in. Littell flashed his lights. Littell strafed the windshield and grille. The Ford braked and stopped. A tall man got out. Said man swayed on a high shoe.

Littell hit his brights. Eversall blinked and tripped. He caught himself. His bad leg buckled. His briefcase balanced him.

Littell killed his brights. Littell popped the passenger door. Eversall limped up—briefcase as ballast—Eversall fell on the seat.

Littell shut the door. Littell hit the rooflight. It haloed Eversall. Littell frisked him.

He grabbed his crotch. He pulled his shirt up. He pulled down his socks. He opened his briefcase. He went through his files. He dropped the script in.

Eversall smelled—sweat and bay rum. His breath reeked of peanuts and gin.

Littell said, "Did Carlos explain?"

Eversall shook his head. His neck muscles bobbed.

"Answer me. I want to hear your voice."

Eversall squirmed. His high shoe hit the dash.

"I never talk to Carlos. I get calls from this Cajun-type guy."

He said it slow. He blinked in time. He blinked and ducked from the light. Littell grabbed his tie. Littell jerked it. Littell pulled him back in the light.

"You're going to wear a wire and talk to Bobby. I want to know what he thinks about the assassination."

Eversall blinked. Eversall st-st-stuttered.

Littell jerked his tie. "I read a piece in the *Post*. Bobby's throwing a Christmas party, and he's inviting some people from Justice."

Eversall blinked. Eversall st-st-stuttered. He tried to talk. He popped *p*'s and *i*'s. He tried to say "Please."

"I've prepared a script. You tell Bobby that you don't like the proximity to the hearings, and you offer to help. If Bobby gets angry, you be that much more persistent."

Eversall blinked. Eversall st-st-stuttered. He tried to talk. He popped *p*'s and *i*'s. He bounced *b*'s for "Bobby."

Littell smelled his piss. Littell saw the stain. Littell rolled the windows down.

He had spare time. The pay phone was close. He cracked all the windows and aired the car out.

Trains rolled in. Women fetched their husbands. A hailstorm hit. It chipped his windshield. He tuned in the radio news.

Mr. Hoover addressed the Boy Scouts. Jack Ruby sulked in his cell. Trouble in Saigon. Bobby Kennedy bereft.

Bobby loved hard. Bobby mourned hard. *He* used to.

Late '58:

He worked the Chicago Office. Bobby worked the McClellan Committee. Kemper Boyd worked *for* Bobby. Kemper Boyd worked *against* him. Mr. Hoover deployed Kemper wide.

Mr. Hoover hated Bobby. Bobby chased the Mob. Mr. Hoover said the Mob did not exist. Bobby humbled Mr. Hoover. Bobby disproved his lie.

Mr. Hoover liked Kemper Boyd. Boyd liked his friend Ward. Boyd got Ward a choice Bureau job:

The Top Hoodlum Program—Mr. Hoover's late retraction—Mr. Hoover's late nod to the Mob. Call it a half-measure. Call it a publicity shuck.

He worked the THP. He fucked up. Mr. Hoover kicked him back to the Red Squad. Boyd stepped up then. Boyd stepped up for Bobby. Boyd offered friend Ward a *real* job.

Covert work—unpaid.

He took the job. He culled anti-Mob data. He leaked it to Boyd. Boyd leaked it to Bobby.

He never met Bobby. Bobby called him the Phantom. Bobby logged a persistent rumor. Bobby passed it on to Kemper Boyd.

The Teamsters kept a *private* set of pension-fund books. The "real" books hid one billion dollars.

He chased the "real" books. He traced them to a man named Jules Schiffrin. He stole the "real" books—late in '60.

Schiffrin discovered the theft. Schiffrin had a heart attack. Schiffrin died that night. Littell hid the books. Said books were coded. Littell decoded one entry fast.

The code rebuked a royal clan. The code proved that Joe Kennedy was mobbed-up tight.

Joe fed the fund. Joe gorged it. Joe invested 49 million dollars. It was laundered. It was lent. It suborned politicians. It financed labor rackets.

The base sum stayed in the fund. The money notched compound interest. The money greeeeeeew.

Joe let it ride. The Teamsters held his assets. Littell did not tell Bobby. Littell did not assault his dad.

He kept the books. He ignored his Red Squad work. He befriended a name leftist. Mr. Hoover found out. Mr. Hoover fired him.

Jack Kennedy was elected. Jack made Bobby his AG. Bobby got Boyd work at Justice.

Boyd interceded. Boyd braced Bobby—employ the Phantom, please.

Mr. Hoover interceded. Mr. Hoover braced Bobby—don't employ Ward J. Littell. He's a drunk. He's a sob sister. He's a Communist.

Bobby kowtowed. Bobby cut the Phantom off. The Phantom kept the "real" books. The Phantom quit booze. The Phantom lawyered freelance. The Phantom cracked the fund-book code.

He tracked a billion dollars. He tracked intakes and transfers. He studied and extrapolated and *knew:*

The funds could be diverted. The funds could be deployed legally.

He hoarded the knowledge. He hid the books. He inked up a duplicate set. He hated Bobby now. He hated Jack K. by extension.

Boyd was fixed on Cuba. Carlos M. ditto. Carlos financed exile groups. The Boys wanted to oust Fidel Castro. The Boys wanted to reclaim their Cuban hotels.

Boyd worked for Bobby. Boyd worked for the CIA. Bobby hated Carlos. Bobby deported Carlos. The Phantom knew deportation law.

Boyd set him up with Carlos. The Phantom became a Mob lawyer. It felt morally and hatefully correct.

Carlos set him up with Jimmy Hoffa. Mr. Hoover reappeared.

Mr. Hoover made nice. Mr. Hoover praised his comeback. Mr. Hoover set him up with Mr. Hughes. Mr. Hoover shared his Bobby-Jack hate.

He worked for Carlos and Jimmy. He planned the Hughes-Vegas deal. Bobby attacked the Mob. Jack dropped the Cuban cause. Jack curtailed the hothead exiles.

Pete and Boyd stole some dope. Things went blooey. The Boys got very mad.

He braced Carlos. He said let's kill Jack. He said let's nullify Bobby. Carlos said yes. Carlos vouched the plan. Carlos brought Pete and Boyd in.

Carlos fucked them. Carlos opted for Guy B. Carlos sent Guy to Dallas.

A late bill came due. Late fees accrued. He had the "real" books. He had the data. He had them unsuspected and clean.

He was wrong. Carlos *knew* he had them. Carlos saw him ascend. Carlos called in the bill due.

Carlos said *you're* going to sell Hughes Las Vegas—and *we're* going to fuck him. *You* know the books. *You* cracked the code. *You* have money plans. *That* money. Plus the *Hughes* money. Equals *our* money—juiced by *your* long-range strategy.

He returned the books. He kept the dupes. His theft was near-open goods. Carlos knew. Carlos told Sam G. Sam told Johnny Rosselli.

Santo knew. Moe Dalitz knew. No one told Jimmy. Jimmy was crazy. Jimmy was shortsighted. Jimmy would kill him.

Littell skimmed newscasts. Littell got crossband blips: LBJ/Kool Menthol/Dr. King and Bobby.

He met Bobby—three days pre-Dallas—he mis-ID'd himself. He said I'm just a lawyer. He said I have a tape. Bobby gave him ten minutes of time.

He played his tape. A hood indicted Joe Kennedy.

For: Pension Fund fraud/collusion/long-term racketeering.

Bobby called his father's bank. The manager confirmed details. Bobby brushed tears back. Bobby raged and grieved. It felt all good then. It felt all hateful now.

The news signed off. A deejay signed on. Mr. Tunes—comin' at ya.

The phone rang.

Littell ran. Littell slid on hailstones. Littell grabbed the receiver.

Pete said, "Junior won't play. The fucking kid stalemated me."

"I'll talk to Sam. We'll make a different app—"

"I'll clip Zangetty and Killiam. That's it. I won't clip the women."

The booth was hot. The windows fogged. The storm produced steam.

"I agree. We'll have to finesse Carlos."

Pete laughed. "Don't shit me. You know it's more than that."

"What are you saying?"

Pete said, "I know about Arden."

DOCUMENT INSERT: 12/19/63.
Verbatim telephone call transcript.
Marked: ''Recorded at Mr. Hughes' request. Copies to: Permanent File/Fiscal '63 File/Security File.''
Speaking: Howard R. Hughes, Ward J. Littell.

HH: Is that you, Ward?

WJL: It's me.

HH: I had a premonition last night. Do you want to hear about it?

WJL: Certainly.

HH: I know that tone. Mollify the boss so he'll get back to business.

(WJL laughs.)

HH: Here's my premonition. You're going to tell me that it will take years to divest my TWA stock, so I should mind my p's and q's and put the whole thing out of mind.

WJL: Your premonition was accurate.

HH: That's all you have to say? You're letting me off that easy?

WJL: I could describe the legal processes involved in divesting half a billion dollars' worth of stock and tell you how much you've impeded the progress by dodging various subpoenas.

HH: You're feeling your oats today. I'm not up to sparring with you.

WJL: I'm not sparring, Mr. Hughes. I'm observing.

HH: And your latest estimate is?

WJL: We're two years away from a judgment. The appeals process will extend for at least nine to fourteen months. You should discuss the details with your other attorneys and move things along by pre-submitting your depositions.

HH: You're my favorite attorney.

WJL: Thank you.

HH: Only Mormons and FBI men have clean blood.

WJL: I'm not much of an expert on blood, Sir.

HH: I am. You know the law, and I know aerodynamics, blood and germs.

WJL: We're expert in our separate fields, Sir.

HH: I know business strategy as well. I have the assets to purchase Las Vegas now, but I prefer to wait and make the purchase with my stock windfall.

WJL: That's a prudent strategy, Sir. But I should point out a few things.

HH: Point, then. I'm listening.

WJL: One, you are not going to purchase the city of Las Vegas or Clark County, Nevada. Two, you are going to attempt to purchase numerous hotel-casinos, the acquisition of which violates numerous state and federal antitrust statutes. Three, you cannot make those purchases now. You would need to deplete the cash flow necessary to operate Hughes Tool to do it,

and you have yet to ingratiate yourself with the
Nevada State Legislature and the right people in
Clark County. Four, that is my job—and it will take
time. Five, I want to wait and follow some other
hotel-chain developments through the court process
and collate the antitrust rulings and precedents.

HH: Jesus, that was some speech. You're a long-
winded guy.

WJL: Yes, Sir.

HH: You didn't mention your Mafia pals.

WJL: Sir?

HH: I talked to Mr. Hoover. He said you've got those
guys in your pocket. What's that guy's name in New
Orleans?

WJL: Carlos Marcello?

HH: Marcello, right. Mr. Hoover said he eats out of
your hand. He said, ''When the time's right, Littell
will jew those dagos down and get you your hotels at
rock-bottom prices.''

WJL: I'll certainly try.

HH: You'll do better than that.

WJL: I'll try, Sir.

HH: We've got to devise a germ policy.

WJL: Sir?

HH: At my hotels. No germs, no Negroes. Negroes are
well-known germ conduits. They'll infect my slot
machines.

WJL: I'll look into it, Sir.

HH: My solution is mass sedation. I've been reading
chemistry books. Certain narcotic substances possess
germ-killing characteristics. We could sedate the
Negroes, lower their white-blood count and keep them
out of my hotels.

WJL: Mass sedation would require certain sanctions
that we might not get.

HH: You're not convinced. I can tell by your voice.

WJL: I'll give it some thought.

HH: Think about this. Lee Oswald was a germ conduit
and a deadly-disease transmitter. He didn't need a
rifle. He could have breathed on Kennedy and killed
him.

WJL: It's an interesting theory, Sir.

HH: Only Mormons and FBI men have clean blood.

WJL: You've got quite a few Mormons in Nevada. There's a man named Wayne Tedrow Senior that I may approach on your behalf.

HH: I've got some good Mormons here. They set me up with Fred Otash.

WJL: I've heard of him.

HH: He's the ''Private Eye to the Stars.'' He's been running a string of Howard Hughes look-alikes all over L.A., like Pete Bondurant used to. Those subpoena servers follow them around like robots.

WJL: Again, Sir. Dodging subpoenas only prolongs the whole process.

HH: Ward, you're a goddamn killjoy.

(WJL laughs.)

HH: Freddy's Lebanese. Those people have high white-cell counts. I like him, but he's no Pete.

WJL: Pete's working with me in Las Vegas.

HH: Good. Frenchmen have low white-cell counts. I read it in the *National Geographic*.

WJL: He'll be pleased to hear it.

HH: Good. Tell him I said hello, and tell him to procure me some medicine. He'll know what I mean. Tell him my Mormons have been bringing me inferior goods.

WJL: I'll tell him.

HH: Let me make one thing clear before I hang up.

WJL: Sir?

HH: I want to buy Las Vegas.

WJL: You've made yourself clear.

HH: The desert air kills germs.

WJL: Yes, Sir.

20

(Las Vegas, 12/23/63)

THE PARTY—a Vegas perennial—Wayne Senior's Christmas bash.

A fag redid the ranch house. He added ice sculptures and

snow-flocked walls. He hired elves and nymphs.

The elves were wetbacks. They slung hors d'oeuvres. They wore mock-rag coats. The nymphs whored at the Dunes. They served cleavage and drinks.

The fag brought a bandstand. The fag added a dance floor. The fag hired a bumfuck quartet.

Barb & the Bail Bondsmen—a singer and three swish ex-cons.

Wayne circulated. The combo bugged him. He popped the trumpet for flim-flam. He popped the sax for stat rape.

The singer compensated—red hair and wild legs.

Lynette circulated. The crowd meshed. Cops and Vegas trash. Mormons and Nellis brass.

Wayne Senior circulated. Janice danced solo. A crowd watched her. Janice shimmied. Janice swayed. Janice dipped looooow.

Wayne Senior walked up. Wayne Senior twirled his walking stick. A Nellis one-star grabbed it.

He cued the combo. Barb tapped a beat. The combo vamped. Barb palmed maracas.

The one-star knelt. The one-star dropped the stick looooow.

Barb ad-libbed. "Vegas limbo mighty good, lady go down like she should."

Janice spread her legs. Janice rolled her hips. Janice popped looooow. The crowd clapped. The crowd stomped. Barb milked the beat.

Janice went looooow. Janice popped sequins and spangles. Janice popped seams. Her high heels snapped. She kicked off her shoes. She went under and up.

The crowd clapped. Janice bowed looooow. She ripped her dress. Her red panties showed.

Wayne Senior passed her a Salem. The lights went low. The combo vamped "Moonglow." A baby spot blinked. It focused on Janice. It swooped and caught Wayne Senior low.

They linked up. Janice held her cigarette. Smoke blew through the light.

Circle dance.

Wayne Senior smiled. Wayne Senior loved it. Janice mugged and mocked this corny shit.

They swayed. Janice dropped sequins. The spotlight jumped. Wayne saw Lynette. Lynette saw Wayne. Lynette saw Wayne ogle Janice.

He dodged her eyes. He walked outside. He paced the front deck. He smelled marijuana—pot alert below.

Janice toked up for parties. Janice shared with the help. You had zorched valets. You had a hundred cars—now check the runway:

One airplane valet-parked—one guest's Piper Deuce.

Wayne paced. Wayne walked the deck. Wayne fretted Dallas up.

Jack Ruby observed Hanukkah. The paper ran x-clusive pix. Two pages in: HOPE FADES FOR MISSING POLICEMAN.

Wayne watched the party. A glass door killed the noise. Check the wino elves—they're digging on Barb.

Wayne watched her.

Barb moves her lips. Barb bumps her hips. Barb hits the mike stand. Barb scans the room. Barb sees a face and melts.

Wayne hugged the glass. Wayne got an angle. Wayne tracked her eyes.

To Mr. Meltman—Pete Bondurant.

Barb melts. Fucking snowdrifts in August. Big Pete reciprocates.

Wayne cracked the door. Wayne caught the vocal: "I Only Have Eyes for You."

Wayne shut the door. His stomach dropped. He leaned on the glass. He caught a chill and saved his dinner.

Barb blew a kiss. Pete blew one back. Pete stretched and bumped his head on the ceiling.

Pete grinned. Pete went ooops! A man joined him—sunburned and thin—some shitkicker runt.

Wayne grabbed a chair. Wayne kicked up his feet. Wayne rocked off the rail. A match flared below him. Reefer smoke plumed its way up.

It smelled good. It sent him back. He toked once himself. Jump School at Fort Bragg. Let's jump stoned and watch clouds change colors.

The door slid open. Noise spilled out. Wayne smelled Janice—cigarettes and Chanel No. 5.

She walked up. She leaned on him. She pressed his shoulders and back.

Wayne said, "Come on, work."

Janice worked him. Janice dug in. Janice unknotted kinks.

"Something smells sweet down there."

"It smells like a felony roust, if I was inclined."

"Be nice, now. It's Christmas."

"You mean, 'It's Vegas, and the law's for sale.' "

Janice dug in. "I wouldn't be that blunt with a policeman."

Wayne leaned back. "Who's the one-star?"

"That's Brigadier General Clark D. Kinman. He has a powerful crush on yours truly."

"I noticed."

"You notice everything. And I noticed you ogle that singer."

"Did you notice her husband? The big guy?"

Janice worked his spine. "I noticed the airplane he came in, and the ankle holster he's wearing."

Wayne twitched. Janice tickled his neck.

"Did I touch a nerve there?"

Wayne coughed. "Who's the skinny guy?"

Janice laughed. "That's Mr. Chuck Rogers. He described himself as a pilot, a petroleum geologist, and a professional anti-Communist."

"You should introduce him to my father."

"I think they're fast friends already. They were discussing the Cuban cause or some such nonsense."

Wayne rolled his neck. "Who hired that combo?"

"Your father. Buddy Fritsch recommended them."

Wayne turned around. Wayne saw Lynette. Lynette saw him. She tapped the door glass. She flashed her watch. Wayne flashed ten fingers.

Janice said, "Spoilsport." Janice made claws. Janice goofed on draggy Lynette.

Wayne turned on the rail light. Janice walked downstairs. Sequins dropped behind her. The light made them glint.

The valets giggled. *Hola, señora. Gracias por la reefer.*

Wayne fucked with the light.

He swiveled it. He dipped it. He strafed the airplane. He caught a window. He saw shotguns and vests.

The hatch popped open. Pete B. jumped out. Wayne flashed him. Pete waved and winked.

Wayne fretted it. Wayne walked inside and rejoined the party. Midnite hit. Drunks waved mistletoe.

The eggnog was out. Ditto the prewar cognac. Ditto the pre-Castro cigars.

The elves were sloshed. The nymphs were bombed. The Mormons were blotto. The ice sculptures leaked. The manger scene dripped. Baby Jesus was slush. Said Savior played ashtray. His cradle held butts.

Wayne circulated. The Bondsmen packed up. Barb lugged mike stands and drums. Wayne watched her. Lynette watched him.

Wayne Senior held court. Four Mormon elders and chairs tucked in tight. Chuck Rogers sat in. Chuck balanced two bottles. Chuck sucked gin and blueberry schnapps.

Wayne Senior dropped names—Mr. Hoover said this/Dick Nixon said that. The elders laughed. Chuck shared his jugs. Wayne Senior passed him a key.

Chuck palmed it. Chuck stood up. The elders laughed. The elders shared frat-boy looks.

They stood up. They walked down the side hall. Chuck bird-dogged them. They rendezvoused. They all braced the gun-room door.

Chuck unlocked it. The elders piled in. The elders chortled and yukked. Chuck stepped in. The elders snatched his booze. Chuck shut the door fast.

Wayne watched. Wayne grabbed a stray drink. Wayne guzzled it. Vodka and fruit pulp—lipstick on the glass.

The pulp killed the burn. The lipstick tasted sweet. The rush hit him low.

He walked to the gun room. He heard yuks inside. He jerked the door. He popped it.

Movie time.

Chuck ran the projector. Film hit a pull screen. Tight on: Martin Luther King.

He's fat. He's nude. He's ecstatic. He's fucking a white woman hard.

They fucked. They fucked sans sound. They fucked missionary-style. Static hiss and film flecks. Sprocket holes and numbers—FBI code.

Covert work/surveillance film/some lens distortion.

King wore socks. The woman wore nylons. The elders yukked. The projector clicked. Film cut through a slide.

The mattress sagged—plump Reverend King—the woman more so. An ashtray bounced on the bed—butts scattered and flew.

Chuck grabbed a flashlight. Chuck centered the beam. Chuck palmed a 4-by-6 tract.

King thrashed—the camera panned—Trojan rubbers on a nightstand.

Chuck yelled—pipe down now—Chuck read from the tract. "Big Bertha said, 'Maul me, Marty! We shall overcoooooome!'"

Wayne ran up. Chuck saw him. Chuck gawked—what the—

Wayne kicked the projector. The spools flew and rolled. The film hit three walls and went dead. The elders backed up. The elders tripped and banged heads. The elders knocked the screen down.

Wayne grabbed the tract. Chuck backed off. Wayne shoved him and ran out. He cut down the side hall. He grazed the bandstand. He sideswiped some nymphs and elves.

He made the front deck. He grabbed the rail light. He honed it and flashed on the tract.

There—Wayne Senior's print style. The paper stock/the margins/the type.

Text and cartoons. Martin Luther Coon and the plump woman. Fat Jews with fangs.

Martin Luther Coon—priapic.

His dick's a branding iron. It's red hot. The head's a hammer-and-scythe.

Wayne spat on the picture. Wayne ripped it crossways. Wayne shredded it up.

21

(New Mexico, 12/24/63)

GUSTS KICKED IN. The plane dipped resultant.

The sky was black. The air was wet. Ice hit the props. Altus, Oklahoma—due east.

Chuck flew low. Chuck flew radar-proof. Chuck flew minus landing log. No airstrip. No runway. We're heading for Jack's *rural* lodge.

The cockpit was cramped. The cockpit was cold. Pete goosed the heat. He called ahead. He played tourist. He heard that Jack Z. had three guests.

Quail hunters. Praise Jesus—all men.

Chuck knew the lodge. Chuck spent time there. Chuck knew the floor plan. Jack slept in the office. Jack parked his guests close. There'd be three rooms with through doors.

Pete checked the cargo hold:

Flashlights/shotguns/magnums. Kerosene/gunnysacks. Friction tape/rubber gloves/rope. A Polaroid camera/four straitjackets/four honey jars.

It was overkill. Carlos loved wet work. Carlos thought plans up. Carlos popped his rocks secondhand.

Chuck read a hate tract. The dashboard threw light. Pete saw cartoons and FBI text. Hate and smut—a coon named Bayard Rustin—a queer cluster-fuck.

Pete laughed. Chuck said, "Why'd we go to that party? I'm not complaining, now. I met a few kindred souls."

The plane dipped. Pete bumped his head.

"I was letting someone know that I won't go away."

"You want to tell me who and why?"

Pete shook his head. The plane jumped. Pete's knees hit the dash.

Chuck said, "Mr. Tedrow's some kind of American. That's more than I can say for his son."

"Junior's a piece of work. Don't underestimate him."

Chuck popped Dramamine. "Mr. Tedrow knows all the right people. Guy B. said he put some cash into a certain operation."

Pete rubbed his neck. "There *was* no operation. Don't you read the fucking *New York Times*?"

Chuck laughed. "You mean I was dreaming then?"

"Treat it that way. You'll live longer."

"Then I must've dreamed up all those people that Carlos wants to clip."

Pete rubbed his eyes. Fuck—Headache #3,000.

"Then I'll be dreaming when we take out Jack Z., and I'll *really* be dreaming when we find old Hank and those cunts Arden and Bet—"

Pete grabbed his neck. "Nothing happened in Dallas, and nothing's happening now."

3:42 A.M.

They touched down. The ground was glass. Chuck cut the flaps and braked. They spun. They brodied on ice. They did figure eights and stalled in tall grass.

They put their vests on. They grabbed flashlights/shotguns/
magnums. They screwed on silencers.

They hiked southeast. Pete paced it out: .32 miles. Low hills.
Caves set in sheet rock. Cloud cover and a high moon.

There—the lodge—down on paved land.

Twelve rooms. A horseshoe court. Dirt-road access. No
lights. No sounds. Two jeeps upside the office.

They walked up. Chuck stood point. Pete flashed the door.
He saw a spring lock. He saw a loose knob. He saw a workable
gap.

He pulled his knife. He wedged it in. He snapped the bolt. He
walked in. The door creaked. He kept his beam low.

Three steps to the counter—hold for a ledger on a chain.

He walked up blind. Chuck's floor plan worked. He bumped
the counter. Eyes left—a side door wide open. Room #1—dark.

His eyes adjusted. He squinted. He caught gray tones in black.
He looked through room 1. He squinted. He saw the room #2
door ajar.

Ears left—snores in room 1. Ears front—snores behind the
counter.

Pete smelled paper. Pete touched the countertop. Pete
brushed the ledger. He flashed the top page. He saw three guests
logged in—housed in rooms 1/2/3.

Pete leaned on the counter. Pete pulled his piece. Pete flashed
his light and aimed at the snores. There's Jack Zangetty—face-
up on a cot—eyes shut and mouth wide for flies.

Pete aimed off the beam. Pete squeezed a shot. Jack's head
snapped. Jack's teeth exploded.

The silencer worked—sounds like a cough and a sneeze. One
more now—safekeeping.

Pete aimed off the beam. Pete squeezed a shot. Pete nailed
Jack's wig. Blood and synthetic hair/a cough and a sneeze.

Impact—the wig flew. Impact—Jack rolled off the cot.

Jack hit a bottle. The bottle fell. The bottle bumped and rolled.
Loud bumps. *Loud* noise. *Loud* rolls.

Pete killed his light. Pete ducked low. Knee cartilage
crunched. Eyes left/ears left/catch the doorway.

There now—a man laughs/a bed squeaks.

"Jack, is that a fresh jug you got?"

Light hues in the doorway—the geek's got white pajamas.

Pete flashed his light. Pete tracked up a white swath. Pete hit the man's eyes. He aimed off the beam. He squeezed a shot. He caught the 10-ring.

Blood and white blotting/a cough and a sneeze.

The man flew. The man hit the door. The man ripped the door loose. Eyes left—there's light—the #2 doorway. Ears left—there's boot thunks and zipper snags.

Pete proned out. Pete aimed. Now—watch the door.

A man opened it. Said man paused. Said man walked through room 1. Said man crouched and aimed a 30.06.

Pete aimed his piece. The man got close. A shotgun went off. Glass shattered—from the outside—pellets trashed a *side* window.

Chuck popping rounds. Chuck's special load—poison buckshot.

The man froze. Glass spritzed him. He covered his eyes. He ran blind. He bumped chairs. He coughed glass.

Pete fired. Pete missed. Chuck vaulted the window. He ran up fast. He nudged the man—BOO!—he shot the man in the back.

The man flew. Pete caught shell wads and BBs. Chuck ran south. Chuck blew out door #3.

Pete ran back. Chuck hit the lights. Light hit a man under the bed. He sobbed. His legs stuck out. He wore paisley PJs.

Chuck aimed low. Chuck blew his feet off. The man screamed. Pete shut his eyes.

The wind died. The day sparkled. The cleanup dragged.

They stole the jeeps. They drove the stiffs to the plane. They found a cave and drove the jeeps in. They fucked with some bats. They hit their horns. They evicted them. The bats bumped their windshields. They ran their wipers. They bumped the cocksuckers back.

They dumped kerosene. They torched the jeeps. The fire burned and died. The cave contained the fumes.

They walked to the plane. They wrapped the stiffs in straitjackets. They gunnysacked them. They pried their jaws out. They poured honey in. It lured hungry crabs.

Pete snapped four Polaroids—one per victim—Carlos wanted proof.

They flew low. They hit North Texas. They saw small lakes forever. They dumped three stiffs. Two splashed and sunk. One cracked hard ice.

Chuck skimmed tracts. Chuck flew low. Chuck steered with his knees.

He had a master's degree. He read comic books. He blew JFK's brains out. He lived with his parents. He stuck to his room. He built model planes and sniffed glue.

Chuck skimmed tracts. His lips moved. Pete caught the gist: The KKK klarifies a kontroversy. White men have the biggest dicks!

Pete laughed. Chuck dipped over Lake Lugert. Pete tossed Jack Z. in the drink.

22

(Las Vegas, 1/4/64)

THE SUMMIT. THE penthouse at the Dunes—one big table.

Decanters. Siphons. Candy and fruit. No cigars—Moe Dalitz was allergic.

Littell swept for bugs first. The Boys watched TV. Morning cartoons—Yogi Bear and Webster Webfoot.

The Boys took sides. Sam and Moe liked Yogi. Johnny R. liked the duck. Carlos liked Yogi's dumb pal.

Santo T. snoozed—fuck this kiddie shit.

No bugs—let's proceed.

Littell chaired the meet. The Boys dressed down—golf shirts and Bermuda shorts.

Carlos sipped brandy. "Here's the opening pitch. Hughes is non compos mental, and he thinks he's got Ward in his pocket. We sell him the hotels and make him keep our inside people. They step up the skim. He don't suspect anything, 'cause we show him some low profit figures before he buys."

Littell shook his head. "His negotiators will audit every tax return filed for every hotel, going back ten years. If you refuse to submit them, they'll try to subpoena them or bribe the right people for copies. And you can't submit doctored returns with low figures, because it will bring down your initial asking prices."

Sam said, "So?"

Littell sipped club soda. "We need the highest possible set purchase prices, with the buyout money dispersed over eighteen months. Our long-term goal is to establish the appearance of legitimately invested money, diverted into legitimate businesses and laundered within them. My plan is—"

Carlos cut in. "The plan—get to it, and lay it out in words we can understand."

Littell smiled. "We have the buyout and skim money. We purchase legitimate businesses with it. The businesses belong to recipients of pension-fund loans. They are the most specifically profitable and cosmetically noncriminal businesses that originated with loans from the 'real' books. Thus, the origin of the money is obscured. Thus, the recipients are prone to extortion and will not protest the forced buyouts. The recipients will continue to run their businesses. Our people will oversee the operations and divert the profits. We funnel the money into foreign hotel-casinos. By 'foreign' I mean Latin-American. By Latin-American I mean countries under military or strongly rightist rule. The casino profits will leave said countries untaxed. They will go into Swiss bank accounts and accrue interest. The ultimate cash withdrawals will be absolutely untraceable."

Carlos smiled. Santo clapped. Johnny said, "It's like Cuba."

Moe said, "It's ten Cubas."

Sam said, "Why stop there?"

Littell grabbed an apple. "For now, it's all long-range and theoretical. We're waiting for Mr. Hughes to dump his TWA stock and secure his seed money."

Santo said, "We're talking about years."

Sam said, "We're talking about patience."

Johnny said, "It's a virtue. I read that somewhere."

Moe said, "We watch the climate south of the border. We find ourselves a dozen Batistas."

Sam said, "Show me a spic you can't bribe."

Santo said, "All they want is a white uniform with gold epaulets."

Sam said, "They're like niggers that way."

Johnny said, "They don't tolerate Commies. You got to give them that."

Carlos grabbed some grapes. "I've got the books stashed. You have to figure that Jimmy'll fall for that jury-tampering thing."

Littell nodded. "That and his other indictments."

Sam winked. "You stole the books, Ward. Now tell us you didn't copy them over."

Johnny laughed. Moe laughed. Santo roared.

Littell smiled. "We should think about the inside people. Mr. Hughes will want to hire Mormons."

Sam cracked his knuckles. "I don't like Mormons. They hate Italians."

Carlos sipped X.O. "Do you blame them?"

Santo said, "Nevada's a Mormon state. It's like New York for the Italians."

Moe said, "You mean the Jews."

Johnny laughed. "It's a serious issue. Hughes will want to pick his own people."

Sam coughed. "We can't back down on that. We've got to keep our people inside."

Littell pared his apple. "We should find our own Mormons. I'll be talking to a man soon. He runs the Kitchen Union."

Moe said, "Wayne Tedrow Senior."

Sam said, "He hates Italians."

Moe said, "He's not wild about Jews."

Santo peeled a cigar. "To me this is bullshit. I want made guys inside."

Johnny said, "I agree."

Moe grabbed the cigar. "Are you trying to kill me?"

Carlos peeled a Mars Bar. "Let's table this for now, all right? We're talking about years down the road."

Littell said, "I agree. Mr. Hughes won't have his money for some time."

Sam peeled a banana. "It's your show, Ward. I know you got more to say."

Littell said, "Four things, actually. Two major, two minor."

Moe rolled his eyes. "So, tell us. Jesus, you have to coax this guy."

Littell smiled. "One, Jimmy knows what Jimmy knows, and Jimmy's volatile. I'm going to do my best to keep him out of jail until we've started to implement our plans for the books."

Carlos smiled. "If Jimmy knew you stole the books, he'd implement you."

Littell rubbed his eyes. "I returned them. Let's leave it at that."

Sam said, "We forgive you."

Johnny said, "You're alive, aren't you?"

Littell coughed. "Bobby Kennedy will probably resign. The new AG might have plans for Vegas, and Mr. Hoover might not be able to curtail them. I'll try to do some favors for him, learn what I can and pass it along."

Sam said, "That cocksucker Bobby."

Moe said, "The bad fucking seed."

Santo said, "That cocksucker used us. He put his faggot brother in the White House at our expense. He fucked us like the pharaohs fucked Jesus."

Johnny said, "The Romans, Santo. The pharaohs fucked Joan of Arc."

Santo said, "Fuck Bobby *and* Joan. They're both faggots."

Moe rolled his eyes. Fuck this goyishe shit.

Littell said, "Mr. Hughes hates Negroes. He wants to keep them out of his hotels, at whatever the cost. I've explained the gentlemen's agreement we've got here, but he wants more."

Santo shrugged. "Everyone hates the shines."

Sam shrugged. "Especially the civil-rights types."

Moe shrugged. "Shvartzes are shvartzes. I don't want Martin Luther King on our doorstep any more than Hughes does, but they'll get their goddamn civil rights sooner or later."

Johnny said, "It's the Reds. They agitate them and get them worked up. You can't reason with an agitated person."

Santo peeled a cigar. "They know they're not wanted. We keep the low-end spooks out and let a few uptown ones in. If King Farouk of the Congo wants to drop a hundred G's at the Sands, I say let him."

Johnny grabbed a peach. "King Farouk's a Mexican."

Santo said, "Good. If he blows all his money, we'll get him a job in the kitchen."

Sam said, "I play golf with Billy Eckstine. He's a wonderful guy."

Johnny said, "He's got white blood."

Moe said, "I play golf with Sammy Davis on a regular basis."

Carlos yawned. Carlos coughed. Carlos cued Littell.

Littell coughed. "Mr. Hughes thinks the local Negroes should be 'sedated.' It's a preposterous idea, but we may be able to turn it to our advantage."

Moe rolled his eyes. "You're the best, Ward. Nobody disputes that. But you tend to beat around the bush."

Littell crossed his legs. "Carlos has tentatively agreed that we should waive our no-narcotics rule and let Pete Bondurant sell to the Negroes here. You all know the precedent. Pete trafficked for Santo's organization in Miami from '60 to '62."

Santo shook his head. "We were funding the exiles then. That was strictly an anti-Castro thing."

Johnny shook his head. "On a one-time-only basis."

Carlos said, "I like the idea. It's a moneymaker, and Pete's a hell of a resource."

Littell said, "Let's keep him busy. We can establish a new cash source and mollify Mr. Hughes at the same time. He doesn't need to know the details. I'll call it a 'Sedation Project.' He'll like the way it sounds and be satisfied. He's like a child in some ways."

Carlos said, "It's a moneymaker. I foresee some big profits."

Sam shook his head. "I foresee ten thousand junkies turning Vegas into a shithole."

Moe shook his head. "I *live* here. I do not want to see a big fucking influx of junkie burglars, junkie heist guys, and junkie rape-os."

Santo shook his head. "Vegas is the Queen City of the West. You don't soil a place like that on purpose."

Johnny shook his head. "You've got a bunch of hopped-up niggers looking for their next fix. You're watching *The Lawrence Welk Show* and some big spook kicks the door in and steals your TV set."

Sam shook his head. "And rapes your wife while he's at it."

Santo shook his head. "You'll send tourism into the shitter."

Moe snatched Santo's cigar. "Carlos, you're outruled on this. You don't shit on your own carpet."

Carlos shrugged. Carlos turned his palms up.

Moe smiled. "You're batting five hundred, Ward. That's a hell of an average in this room. And your long-range plan is a home run."

Sam smiled. "Out of the ballpark."

Santo smiled. "Out of the fucking galaxy."

Johnny smiled. "It's Cuba all over again. With no bearded Commie faggot to fuck things up."

Littell smiled. Littell twitched. Littell almost bit his tongue.

"I want to make sure we get a unanimous license vote from the Gaming Control Board and Liquor Board. Pete tried to get a look at the LVPD intel file and got nowhere."

Santo snatched his cigar back. "We've never been able to buy off the boards. They grant their fucking licenses by whim."

Moe said, "It's the pioneer thing. You know, prejudice. We own this town, but they lump us in with the shvartzes."

Johnny said, "The files are the place to start. We've got to find the weak links and exploit them."

Sam said, "The cops guard that information. Pete B. couldn't shake it loose, so what does that tell you?"

Littell stretched. "Sam, will you have one of your people make an approach? Butch Montrose, maybe?"

Sam smiled. "For you, Ward, the moon."

Littell smiled. "I want to plant support in the state legislature. Mr. Hughes is prepared to make a series of charitable contributions and publicize them throughout Nevada, so do any of you have fav—"

Johnny cut in. "Saint Vincent de Paul."

Sam said, "The K of C."

Santo said, "Saint Francis Hospital. They cut my brother's prostrate out there."

Moe said, "The United Jewish Appeal—and fuck all you dagos."

Dracula supplied lodging—a suite at the DI. Four rooms/golf-course access/open-end lease.

His third place.

He had a place in D.C. He had a place in L.A.—two high-rise apartments. Three homes now. All ready-furnished. All depersonalized.

Littell moved in. Littell dodged golf balls. Littell tore the phones up. Littell bugswept them.

The phones were safe. He rebuilt them. He relaxed and unpacked.

Arden was in L.A. She moved toward him piecemeal. Dallas to Balboa/Balboa to L.A. Vegas scared her. The Boys partied there. She knew the Boys. She wouldn't say how.

She was his "Jane" now. She loved her new name. She loved her revised history.

He finished her transcript. She learned the details. An agent planted the goods. She told him Jane stories—straight off the cuff—she dropped details and recalled them days later.

He memorized them. He caught her subtext:

You made me. Live with your work. Don't challenge my tales. *You'll know me. I'll say who I was.*

Pete knew about Arden. Pete learned in Dallas. He trusted Pete. Pete trusted him. The Boys owned them both.

Carlos told Pete to kill Arden. Pete said, "Okay." Pete won't kill women. That's pure un-okay.

Pete killed Jack Zangetty. Pete flew to New Orleans. Pete briefed Carlos on it. Carlos loved the Polaroids. Carlos said, "Three more."

Pete drove to Dallas. Pete checked around. Pete called Carlos. Pete reported back:

Jack Ruby's nuts. He scratches. He moans. He talks to spirit husks. Hank Killiam split Dallas. Hank booked to Florida. Betty Mac split to parts unknown.

Arden? She vanished—that's all I've got. Carlos said, "Okay—for now."

The Summit succeeded. His plan wowed the Boys. They vetoed the dope plan. Pete logged a No. Pete braced Wayne Junior. Wayne Junior said No. Pete logged two Nos straight.

Doug Eversall called him—on Christmas Eve. Doug said, "I couldn't tape Bobby."

He said, "Keep your tape rig—and brace him again."

Merry Christmas. Don't fall off your high shoe. Don't drop your microphone.

He called Mr. Hoover. He said he had a Bobby source. He said he hot-wired him.

He didn't say:

I need to hear Bobby's voice.

23

(Las Vegas, 1/6/64)

THE HEAT DUCTS blew. The squadroom froze. Fucking igloo time.

Guys split en masse. Wayne worked solo. Wayne cleaned up his desk.

He sifted desk junk. He stacked the Dallas dailies first. He had some Ruby shit. He had bupkis on Moore and Durfee.

Sonny Liston sent a postcard. It rehashed their "good times." Sonny foresaw a Clay fight KO.

He cleaned up one file—the West LV whore jobs/reports and

snapshots. Colored whores/bad bruises/smeared lipstick and contusions.

He held the file. He read it. He looked for leads. Nothing popped out. The assigned cop hated Negroes. The assigned cop hated whores. The assigned cop drew dicks in their mouths.

Wayne stacked papers. Wayne cleared his desk. Wayne locked the file up. Wayne typed reports.

The squadroom froze. The ducts blew—brrr-fucking-brrr.

Wayne yawned. Wayne craved sleep. Lynette bugged him incessant. Lynette had one refrain: "What happened in Dallas?"

He dodged her. He split home early. He worked late. He logged lounge time. He nursed beers. He caught Barb B. He nursed this big crush.

He sat near the stage. Pete sat close by. They never talked. They both eyed the redhead.

Call it leverage. Call it a buffer zone—let's stay in touch.

Lynette rode him. Lynette said don't hide from me. Lynette said don't hide with Wayne Senior.

He hid there pre-Dallas. He crushed on Janice pre-Barb. Dallas changed things. He reworked his crush time now.

He watched Barb. He played chicken with Pete concurrent. Janice played supporting crush.

He dodged Wayne Senior now. Christmas tore it. The film and the hate tracts—Wayne Senior's print style.

The oldies were one thing. "Veto Tito!"/"Castrate Castro!"/"Ban the U.N.!" It was fear shit. It was Red Tides. It was no hate overt.

He saw Little Rock. Wayne Senior didn't. The Klan torched a car. The gas cap blew. It put a colored boy's eye out. Some punks raped a colored girl. They wore rubbers. They shoved them in her mouth.

Wayne yawned. Wayne pulled carbons. The fine print blurred.

Buddy Fritsch walked up. "You bored with your work?"

Wayne stretched. "Do you care if blackjack dealers have misdemeanor convictions?"

"No, but the Nevada Gaming Commission does."

Wayne yawned. "If you've got something more interesting, I'll bite."

Fritsch straddled a chair. "I want some fresh leads on the

Control Board and Liquor Board men. Everyone but the Sheriff and DA. Submit a report to me before you update your file."

Wayne said, "Why now? I update my files in the summer."

Fritsch pulled a match. His hand jumped. He missed the book. He broke the matchhead.

"Because I told you to. That's all the justifying you get."

"What kind of leads?"

"Anything derogatory. Come on, you've been there. You hold surveillance and see who gets naughty."

Wayne rocked his chair. "I'll finish my work and get on it."

"You'll get on it now."

"Why 'now'?"

Fritsch pulled a match. His hand jumped. He missed the book wide.

"Because you blew your extradition job. Because a cop went off without you and got himself killed. Because you fucked up relations between us and Dallas PD, and because I am determined to get some value out of you before you make more rank and move out of my unit."

"Value" tore it—fuck him sideways.

Wayne pulled his chair up. Wayne leaned in close. Wayne bumped Fritsch's knees hard.

"Do you think I'd kill a man for six thousand dollars and a few pats on the back? For the record, I didn't want to kill him, I couldn't have killed him, I wouldn't have killed him, and that's the best value you'll ever get out of me."

Fritsch blinked. His hands jumped. He popped big spitballs.

It played wrong. Logic 101—E follows D.

Pete wants the files. Pete knows the fail-safe procedure. One cop holds the files. Said cop probes alleged misconduct. Said cop informs the Gaming Commission.

The procedure restricts data. The procedure hinders corrupt cops. The procedure curtails corrupt PDs.

Honest cops rigged the plan—one cop/one file set. Intel cops found protégés. Intel cops passed the job on. The last intel cop died on duty. Wayne Senior pulled strings. Wayne Senior got Wayne the job.

E follows D. Pete's mobbed up. Buddy Fritsch ditto. Buddy knows the files hold *old* data. The last misconduct charge was filed in 1960.

Pete wants *new* dirt. Pete wants *hot* dirt. Pete squeezed Buddy Fritsch. Buddy's pissed at Wayne. Buddy worships Wayne Senior. Buddy knows Wayne *will* do the job.

Wayne kept his files in a bank vault. Per procedure: a safe at the main B of A.

He drove over. A clerk cracked the vault. Wayne cracked the files out. He knew the names already. He skimmed the stats and got refreshed. He wrote down addresses.

Duane Joseph Hinton. Age 46. Building contractor/Mormon. No Mob ties. Drunk/wife beater. 7/59—one accusation logged.

Hinton bribes state legislators. A snitch so states. Hinton buys them whores. Hinton gives them fight tickets. They slip him bid sheets. Thus Hinton underbids. Thus Hinton gets state building jobs.

Said tip—unverified. Case closed—9/59.

Webb Templeton Spurgeon. Age 54. Retired lawyer/Mormon. No Mob ties/no accusations logged.

Eldon Lowell Peavy. Age 46. Owner: the Monarch Cab Company/the Golden Cavern Hotel-Casino.

The Cavern drew low rollers. Monarch Cab was low-end. Cabs drove drunks to grind joints. Cabs perched at the jail. Cabs drove prostitutes. Monarch serviced West LV. Monarch drove Negroes. Monarch got cash up front.

Eldon Peavy was a fag. Eldon Peavy hired ex-cons. Eldon Peavy owned a Reno fruit bar.

Tips logged: 8/60, 9/60, 4/61, 6/61, 10/61, 1/62, 3/62, 8/62. Snitch tips—thus far unverified.

Peavy's drivers pack guns. Peavy's drivers push pills. Peavy runs male prostitutes. Peavy sells choice chicken. Peavy scouts the main-room shows. Peavy recruits dancers to fuck and suck.

They're cute. They're queer. They whore for kicks and amphetamines. They spread for male movie stars.

The last tip: logged 8/62.

Wayne worked Patrol then. Wayne made sergeant. Wayne moved to Intel: 10/8/62. The prior cop logged the tips. Said cop was bribe-proof/mean/lazy.

He crashed a market heist. He took five slugs and fed nine back. He died. He killed two wetbacks en route.

Three board men. Nine tips—unverified. Wayne checked the adjunct forms—they looked kosher.

Peavy registered his ex-cons. Peavy's tax sheets looked clean. Ditto Hinton and Spurgeon.

Wayne locked the files up. The clerk locked the vault. Wayne got some coffee. Wayne killed some time.

He dawdled. He killed more time. He drove to the station. He pulled into the lot. Buddy Fritsch pulled out. It was way weird and un-Fritsch-like.

It was 5:10. Fritsch always booked at 6:00 P.M. Fritsch booked like clockwork.

His wife divorced him—late last year. Said wife split with her dyke lover. Fritsch sulked and mooned. Fritsch grooved a cuckold routine.

He splits work at 6:00. He hits the Elks Lodge. He drinks his dinner and plays bridge.

Wayne drove past the station. Fritsch drove down 1st Street. Wayne watched him go. Fritsch turned east. The Elks Lodge was due *west*.

Wayne U-turned. Wayne laid two cars back. Fritsch hugged the curb lane. Fritsch stopped at Binion's Casino.

A man walked up. Fritsch cracked his window. The man passed an envelope. Wayne jumped lanes. Wayne nailed a view. Wayne nailed an ID:

Butch Montrose. Sam G.'s boy. One piece of shit.

24

(Las Vegas, 1/6/64)

BARB DID THE Wah-Watusi. She sang. She shimmied. She shook.

The Bondsmen played loud. Barb missed high notes. She sang for shit. She knew it. She eschewed all airs pertaining to.

The lounge was full. Barb drew men. Call them sad sacks all. Lonely geeks and retirees—plus Wayne Tedrow Junior.

Pete watched.

Barb raised her arms. Barb threw sweat. Barb showed red stubble. It jazzed him. He loved her taste there.

Barb did the Swim. The stage light burned her freckles. Pete watched Barb. Wayne Junior watched Pete. It fucked with his nerves.

His nerves were shot. The Summit came and went. The Boys said no. Ward stated his case. Carlos concurred—let's push Big "H."

They lost the referendum—down by four votes.

He saw Carlos in New Orleans. Carlos saw the Zangetty pix. Carlos said "*Bravissimo.*" They schmoozed. They schmoozed Cuba. They launched laments. The CIA shitcanned the Cuban cause. The rank & file Outfit ditto.

Pete still cared. Carlos too. The old crew found *new* work.

John Stanton was in Vietnam. The CIA was there large. Vietnam was Cuba with gooks. Laurent Guéry and Flash Elorde freelanced—right-wing muscle on call. They gigged out of Mexico City. Laurent clipped Reds in Paraguay. Flash clipped Reds in the DR.

Pete and Carlos schmoozed Tiger Kab. Good times in Miami—dope and exile recruitment. Tiger-striped cabs/black-and-gold seats/heroin and *la Causa*.

They schmoozed the hit. Carlos brought it up. Carlos schmoozed new details. Pete keyed on the pro shooter. Chuck said he was French. Carlos had *new* details.

Laurent brought him in. Laurent went Francophile. The pro had frog credentials. He was an ex-Indochine hand. He was an ex-Algerian killer.

He tried to kill Charles de Gaulle. He failed. He hated de Gaulle. He waxed homicidal. Let's kill JFK—JFK french-kissed Charlie in Paris.

Carlos waxed mad—Jack Z.'s body washed up—the Dallas paper ran news. Jack's missing guests got bupkis. Jack was dirty. Jack ran a "hideout." Jack's death vibed "gangland job."

The wash-up felt like a fuck-up. The wash-up felt like a No. Junior said "No files." The Boys said "No dope."

Carlos said, "March." You know what I want—kill the safe-house crew.

Pete drove to Dallas. Pete fake-searched for Arden. Pete searched for Betty Mac. He tapped out. That was good. He warned Betty. Betty got smart and ran.

He got a lead on Hank Killiam. Hank was now in Florida. Hank read the Dallas paper. The Jack Z. bit scared him.

Pete called Carlos. Pete reported the lead. Pete kissed some wop ass. They schmoozed. Carlos ragged on Guy B.

Guy drank too much. Guy talked too much. Guy loved his

blowhard pal Hank Hudspeth. *They* boozed too much. *They* talked too much. *They* bragged to excess.

Pete said, "I'll clip them." Carlos said, "No." Carlos changed the subject. Hey, Pete—where's that hump Maynard Moore?

Pete said a coon killed him. The DPD was pissed. The Klan kontingent issued a kontract.

Carlos laughed. Carlos howled. Carlos oozed delight.

The hit *awed* him.

They did it. They got away clean. The safe-house geeks meant shit. Carlos knew it. The hit was a kick. Let's schmooze it and relive it. Let's kill some geeks for conversation.

Pete sipped a Coke. He quit booze last week. Carlos ragged Guy. Carlos despised drunks.

Barb twirled the mike cord. Barb blew a note. Barb threw perspiration off.

Pete watched Barb. Wayne Junior watched him.

Barb gigged late. Pete went home alone.

He called room service. He stood on the terrace and dug on the Strip. He felt cold air swirl.

The phone rang. He grabbed it.

"Yeah?"

"That Pete? You know, the big guy passin' out his number on the west side?"

"Yeah, this is Pete."

"Well, that's good, 'cause I'm calling 'bout that reward."

Pete said, "I'm listening."

"You should be, 'cause Wendell Durfee's in town, and I heard he bought a gun off a craps dealer. And I also heard that Curtis and Leroy just brought in some hair-o-wine."

DOCUMENT INSERT: 1/7/64.
Covert tape-recording transcript. Recorded at
Hickory Hill, Virginia. Speaking: Doug Eversall,
Robert F. Kennedy.

(Background noise/overlapping voices)

   RFK (conversation in progress): Well, if you think
it's essen—

   DE: If you wouldn't mind, I'd (background noise/

overlapping voices) (Incidental noise. Door slam & footsteps)

RFK (conversation in progress): Have been in here. They shed all over the rugs.

DE (coughs): I've got two Airedales.

RFK: They're good dogs. They get along well with children. (Pause: 2.6 seconds) Doug, what is it? You look the way people are telling me I look.

DE: Well.

RFK: Well, what? We're here to set trial dates, remember?

DE (coughs): Well, it's about the President.

RFK: Johnson or my brother?

DE: Your brother. (Pause: 3.2 seconds) It's, well, I don't like the thing with Ruby. (Pause: 1.8 seconds) I don't want to sound out of line, but it bothers me.

RFK: You're saying? (Pause: 2.1 seconds) I know what you're saying. He's got Mob connections. Some reporters have been digging up stories.

DE (coughs): That's the main thing, yes. (Pause: DE coughs) And, well, you know, Oswald allegedly spent some time in New—

RFK: Orleans last summer, and you used to work for the State's Attorney down there.

DE: Well, that's about—

RFK: No, but thanks. (Pause: 4.0 seconds) And you're right about Ruby. He walked in there, he shot him, and he looked relieved as hell that he did it.

DE (coughs): And he's dirty.

RFK (laughs): Cough away from me. I can't afford to lose any more work days.

DE: I'm sorry I brought all this up. You don't need to be reminded.

RFK: Jesus Christ, quit apologizing every two seconds. The sooner people start treating me normally, the better off I'll be.

DE: Sir, I—

RFK: That's a good example. You didn't start calling me ''Sir'' until my brother died.

DE (coughs): I just want to help. (Pause: 2.7 seconds) It's the time-line that bothers me. The hearings, Valachi's testimony, Ruby. (Pause: 1.4 seconds) I used to prosecute homicides with multiple defendants. I learned to trust time—

RFK: I know what you're saying. (Pause: RFK coughs) Factors converge. The hearings. The raids I ordered. You know, the exile camps. The Mob was supporting the exiles, so they both had motives. (Pause: 11.2 seconds) That's what bothers me. If that's what happened, they killed Jack to get at me. (Pause: 4.8 seconds) If that . . . shit . . . they should have killed . . .

DE (coughs): Bob, I'm sorry.

RFK: Quit apologizing and coughing. I'm susceptible to colds right now.

(DE laughs.)

RFK: You're right about the time-line. It's the order of things that bothers me. (Pause: 1.9 seconds) There's another thing, too.

DE: Sir? I mean—

RFK: One of Hoffa's lawyers approached me a few days before Dallas. It was very strange.

DE: What was his name?

RFK: Littell. (Pause: 1.3 seconds) I made some inquiries. He works for Carlos Marcello. (Pause: 2.3 seconds). Don't say it. Marcello is based in New Orleans.

DE: I'd be willing to contact my sources, and—

RFK: No. It's best for the country this way. No trial, no bullshit.

DE: Well, there's the Commission.

RFK: You're being naive. Hoover and Johnson know what's best for the country, and they spell it ''Whitewash.'' (Pause: 2.6 seconds) They don't care. There's the people who care and the people who don't. They're all part of the same consensus.

DE: I care.

RFK: I know you do. Just don't labor the point. This conversation is starting to embarrass me.

DE: I'm sor—

RFK: Jesus, don't start that again.

(DE laughs.)

RFK: Will you stay on in Justice? If I resign,
I mean.

DE: It depends on the new man. (Pause: 2.2 seconds)
Are you going to?

RFK: Maybe. I'm just licking my wounds right now.
(Pause: 1.6 seconds) Johnson might put me on the
ticket. I'd take it if he asked, and some people want
me to run for Ken Keating's senate seat in New York.

DE: I'll vote for you. I've got a summer place in
Rhinebeck.

(RFK laughs.)

DE: I just wish there were something I could do.

RFK: Well, you made me feel better.

DE: I'm glad.

RFK: And you're right. Something about the time-
line feels suspicious.

DE: Yes, that's—

RFK: We can't bring my brother back, but I'll tell
you this, though. When the—(footsteps obscure
conversation)—right I'll jump on it, and devil take
the hindmost.

(Door slam & footsteps. Tape terminates here.)

25

(Los Angeles, 1/9/64)

HE BOUGHT JANE a wallet. Saks engraved it.

Soft kid. A lowercase "j.f."

Jane fanned the sleeves. "You were right. I showed them my
Alabama license, and they gave me a new one right there."

Littell smiled. Jane smiled and posed. She leaned on the window. She jutted a hip out. She blocked off the view.

Littell pulled his chair up. "We'll get you a Social Security
card. You'll have all the ID you need."

Jane smiled. "What about a master's degree? You got me the
B.A. already."

Littell crossed his legs. "You could go to UCLA and earn
one."

"How about this? I could divide my studies between L.A.,

D.C., and Vegas, just to keep up with my peripatetic lover."

Littell smiled. "Was that a jibe?"

"Just an observation."

"You're getting restless. You're overqualified for a life of leisure."

Jane pirouetted. Jane dipped low and stood on her toes. She was good. She was lithe. She'd studied somewhere.

Littell said, "Some people from the safe house have disappeared. That's good news more than bad."

Jane shrugged. Jane scissored low. Her skirt brushed the floor.

"Where did you learn that?"

Jane said, "Tulane. I audited a dance class, but you won't see it on my transcript."

Littell sat on the floor. Jane scissored up to him.

"I want to find a job. I was a good bookkeeper, even before you improved my credentials."

Littell stroked her feet. Jane wiggled her toes.

"You could find me something at Hughes Aircraft."

Littell shook his head. "Mr. Hughes is very disturbed. I'm working against him on some levels, and I want to keep you out of that side of my life."

Jane grabbed her cigarettes. "Any other ideas?"

"I could get you work with the Teamsters."

Jane shook her head. "No. That's not me."

"Why?"

She lit a cigarette. Her hand shook.

"It's just not. I'll find a job, don't worry."

Littell traced her stocking runs. "You'll do better than that. You'll excel and upstage everyone you work with."

Jane smiled. Littell pinched out her cigarette. He kissed her. He touched her hair. He saw a new gray.

Jane pulled his tie off. "Tell me about the last woman you were with."

Littell cleaned his glasses. "Her name was Helen Agee. She was a friend of my daughter's. I got in trouble with the Bureau and Helen was the first casualty."

"She left you?"

"She ran, yes."

"What kind of trouble were you in?"

"I underestimated Mr. Hoover."

"That's all you'll tell me?"

"Yes."

"What happened to Helen?"

"She's a legal-aid lawyer. The last I heard, my daughter was, too."

Jane kissed him. "We have to be who we decided to be in Dallas."

Littell said, "Yes."

Jane fell asleep. Littell feigned sleep. Littell got up slow.

He walked to his office. He set up his tape rig. He poured some coffee.

He nailed Doug Eversall. He called him yesterday. He threatened him. He crossed the line.

He said don't call Carlos. Don't tell him what Bobby said. Don't rat out Bobby.

He warned him. He said I'm working freelance. Don't fuck me or I'll retaliate. You're a drunk driver/killer. I'll expose you for that. I won't let Carlos hurt Bobby.

Bobby suspected the Boys. That meant Bobby KNEW. Bobby didn't say it flat out. Bobby didn't need to. Bobby sidestepped the pain.

Mea culpa. Cause-and-effect. *My* Mob crusade killed my brother.

Littell spooled the tape—tape copy #2.

He'd doctored a dupe. He pouched it to Mr. Hoover. He retained the small talk. He layered in static. He x'd out Bobby's Mob talk.

Littell hit Play. Bobby talked. His grief showed. His kindness showed through.

Kind Bobby—a chat with his clubfooted friend.

Bobby talked. Bobby paused. Bobby said the name "Littell."

Littell listened. Littell timed the pauses. Bobby faltered. Bobby *KNEW.* Bobby never said it.

Littell listened. Littell *lived* the pauses. The old fear came. It told him this:

You believe in him again.

DOCUMENT INSERT: 1/10/64.
Verbatim FBI telephone call transcript.
Marked: ''Recorded at the Director's Request''/
''Classified Confidential 1-A: Director's Eyes Only.''

Speaking: Director Hoover, Ward J. Littell.

JEH: Good morning, Mr. Littell.

WJL: Good morning, Sir.

JEH: Let's get to the tape. The sound quality was very poor.

WJL: Yes, Sir.

JEH: The text was unenlightening. If I wish to discuss Airedale dogs with the Dark Prince, I can dial his direct line at will.

WJL: My plant fidgeted, Sir. He moved and caused distortion.

JEH: Will you try again?

WJL: That's impossible, Sir. My plant was lucky to get one audience.

JEH: Your plant's voice was familiar. He sounded like a handicapped lawyer the Dark Prince employs.

WJL: You have a fine memory for voices, Sir.

JEH: Yes. And I have a few plants of my own.

WJL: Myself among them.

JEH: I wouldn't call you a ''plant,'' Mr. Littell. You're too gifted and diversified.

WJL: Thank you, Sir.

JEH: Do you recall our conversation of December 2nd? I said I needed a man with a ''fallen liberal'' image, and hinted that it might be you.

WJL: Yes, Sir. I recall the conversation.

JEH: I'm miffed at Martin Luther King and his egregiously unChristian Southern Christian Leadership Conference. I want to further penetrate the group, and you're the perfect ''fallen liberal'' to help me accomplish my goal.

WJL: In what way, Sir?

JEH: I already have a plant within the SCLC. He has established his ability to procure dossiers on policemen, organized-crime figures and other notables that left-wing Negroes might consider adversaries. My plan is to provide him with a dossier on you. The dossier will portray you as an ousted Bureau man with leftist tendencies, ones which you have frankly yet to outgrow.

WJL: You've piqued my interest, Sir.

JEH: Your assignment would be to appear sympathetic to the civil-rights cause, which I know will be no great stretch. You will donate numerous allotments of marked Mob money to the SCLC, in $10,000 increments, over a sustained period of time. My goal is to compromise the SCLC and render them more tractable. Your goal is to convince the SCLC that you have embezzled the money from organized-crime sources, in an effort to assuage your guilt over working for mobsters in the first place. This will also be no great stretch. I'm sure that you can tap the ambivalent aspects of your nature and front a convincing performance. I'm equally sure that you can justify the continued expense to your mobster colleagues, as a proactive means to avoid civil-rights trouble in Las Vegas, which will please them and Mr. Hughes.

WJL: It's a bold plan, Sir.

JEH: It is that.

WJL: I'd appreciate some more details.

JEH: My plant is an ex-Chicago policeman. He possesses chameleon qualities similar to yours. He's ingratiated himself with the SCLC very nicely.

WJL: His name, Sir?

JEH: Lyle Holly. His brother was with the Bureau.

WJL: Dwight Holly. He transferred out, I think.

JEH: That is correct. He's with the Federal Bureau of Narcotics in Nevada now. I think he finds the assignment enervating. A brisk dope trade would be more to his liking

WJL: And Lyle is—

JEH: Lyle is more impetuous. He drinks more than he should and comes off as a hail-fellow-well-met. The Negroes adore him. He's convinced them that he's the world's most incongruously liberal ex-cop, when in fact that prize goes to you.

WJL: You flatter me, Sir.

JEH: I do anything but.

WJL: Yes, Sir.

JEH: Holly will portray you as a Chicago law-enforcement acquaintance and present the SCLC with

documents pertaining to your Bureau expulsion. He
will point you to a Negro named Bayard Rustin. Mr.
Rustin is a close colleague of Mr. King. He is both a
Communist and a homosexual, which marks him as a rara
avis by all sane standards. I'll send you a summary on
him, and I'll have Lyle Holly call you.
    WJL: I'll wait for his call, Sir.
    JEH: Do you have other questions?
    WJL: On this topic, no. But I would like your
permission to contact Wayne Tedrow Senior, on Mr.
Hughes' behalf.
    JEH: You have it.
    WJL: Thank you, Sir.
    JEH: Good day, Mr. Littell.
    WJL: Good day, Sir.

DOCUMENT INSERT: 1/11/64.
''Subversive Persons'' summary report.
Marked: ''Chronology/Known Facts/Observations/Known
Associates/Memberships in Subversive
Organizations.'' Subject: RUSTIN, BAYARD TAYLOR
(male Negro/DOB: 3/17/12, West Chester, Pa.).
Compiled: 2/8/62.

SUBJECT RUSTIN must be viewed as a cunning subversive
with a significant history of Communist-inspired
alliances & as a pronounced security threat, due to
his alliances with perceived ''Mainstream'' Negro
demagogues, such as MARTIN LUTHER KING & A. PHILIP
RANDOLPH. SUBJECT RUSTIN'S radical Quaker background
& his parents' association with the NAACP (National
Association for the Advancement of Colored People)
point out the extent of his early radical
indoctrination. (See Addendum File #4189 on RUSTIN,
JANIFER & RUSTIN, JULIA DAVIS.)
    SUBJECT RUSTIN attended Wilberforce College (a
Negro institution) 1932-33. He refused to join the
ROTC (Reserve Officers Training Corps) and led
(abetted by numerous Communist sympathizers) a
strike to protest the allegedly poor quality of food
served to students. SUBJECT RUSTIN transferred to

Cheyney State Teachers College (Pennsylvania) early in 1934. It is believed that he communicated with numerous notable Negro subversives while at the institution. SUBJECT RUSTIN was expelled in 1936. It is widely assumed that a homosexual incident resulted in his expulsion.

SUBJECT RUSTIN moved to New York City circa 1938–39. He became a member of the so-called Negro ''Intelligentsia,'' studied the philosophy of MOHANDAS ''MAHATMA'' GANDHI & described himself as a ''Committed Trotskyite.'' SUBJECT RUSTIN (a gifted musician) fraternized with numerous white & Negro subversives, including PAUL ROBESON, who have since been identified as members of 114 certified Communist-front organizations. (See ''Known Associates,'' Addendum File #4190.)

SUBJECT RUSTIN became a member of the Young Communist League (YCL) at New York City College (NYCC) & was a frequent visitor at a Communist cell on 146th Street. He fraternized with Communist folk singers & led a YCL-inspired campaign to protest segregation in the U.S. Armed Forces. In 1941 SUBJECT RUSTIN became acquainted with Negro labor agitator A. PHILIP RANDOLPH (b. 1889) (see Randolph Files #1408, 1409, 1410). SUBJECT RUSTIN helped to organize the aborted 1941 Negro March on Washington & joined the socialist-pacifist Fellowship of Reconciliation (FOR) & the War Resisters League (WRL). During this time he became a skilled orator and disseminator of Socialist-Communist propaganda.

SUBJECT RUSTIN registered as a conscientious objector with his (Harlem, N.Y.) draft board & was ordered to appear for a physical examination on 11/13/43. SUBJECT RUSTIN sent a letter of refusal (see Addendum Carbon #19) & was apprehended on 1/12/44. He was tried & convicted of violating the Selective Serv. Act (see Addendum File #4191 for trial transcript) & sent'd to 3 yrs in the Federal Penitentiary at Ashland, Ky. SUBJECT RUSTIN led several attempts to desegregate the prison dining hall & was transferred to Lewisburg Penitentiary

(Pa). SUBJECT RUSTIN was paroled (6/46) & became a
traveling speaker for the FOR. In 1946 & '47 he
participated in numerous Communist-inspired attempts
(the ''Journey of Reconciliation'') to desegregate
interstate bus lines. In 11/47 SUBJECT RUSTIN joined
the ''Committee Against Jim Crow in Military Service
& Training'' & counseled Negro youths to avoid
military service (see Addendum File #4192 for list of
members & cross-referenced Communist front-group
memberships).

SUBJECT RUSTIN traveled extensively in India
(1948–'49), returned to the U.S. & served a 22-day
jail sentence for his subversive activities in the
''Journey of Reconciliation.'' He spent substantial
time (thruout 1950, '51, '52) in Africa & studied
insurgent & Negro nationalist movements there. On 1/
21/53, SUBJECT RUSTIN was arrested on a morals charge
in Pasadena, California (see Addendum File #4193 for
arrest rpt. & trial transcript). SUBJECT RUSTIN & 2
white youths were engaged in a homosexual tryst in a
parked car. SUBJECT RUSTIN pled guilty & served 60
days in the Los Angeles County Jail. SUBJECT RUSTIN'S
homosexuality is well known & is considered to be an
embarrassment to the alleged ''Mainstream'' Negro
''Leaders'' who utilize his skills as an organizer &
orator.

The 1/21/53 incident resulted in SUBJECT RUSTIN'S
expulsion from the FOR. SUBJECT RUSTIN moved to New
York City and cultivated friendships in the heavily
bohemian & leftist-influenced Greenwich Village
district. He rejoined the WRL & again traveled to
Africa & studied Negro nationalist movements.
SUBJECT RUSTIN returned to the U.S. & met STANLEY
LEVISON, a Communist-indoctrinated advisor to MARTIN
LUTHER KING. (See Files #5961, 5962, 5963, 5965,
5966.) LEVISON introduced SUBJECT RUSTIN to KING.
SUBJECT RUSTIN advised KING per the staging of the
Montgomery Bus Boycott of 1955–56. (See Central Index
for individual files on boycott participants.)
SUBJECT RUSTIN then became a trusted advisor to KING &
is credited with influencing KING'S Pacifist/

Socialist/Communist program of planned disruption &
social disorder. SUBJECT RUSTIN drew up a document
for the formation of the Southern Christian
Leadership Conference (SCLC) & KING adopted it at a
(1/10-11/57) church conference in Atlanta. (See
Addendum File #4194 & Electronic Surveillance File
#0809.) KING was elected leader of the SCLC on 2/14/57
& has remained in power to this (2/8/62) date.

SUBJECT RUSTIN joined the American Forum
(classified as a Communist front group in 1947) &
planned the SCLC/NAACP ''Pilgrimage of Prayer''
March on Washington (5/17/57). 30,000 people
attended, including numerous Negro celebrities (see
Surveillance Films #0704, 0705, 0706, 0708). SUBJECT
RUSTIN organized the ''Youth March for Integrated
Schools'' in 10/58. Per this march: associate A.
PHILIP RANDOLPH publicly attacked DIRECTOR HOOVER
for his comment that the march was a ''Communist-
inspired promotion.'' SUBJECT RUSTIN staged a 2nd
youth march in 4/59. (See Surveillance Films #0709,
0710, 0711.)

SUBJECT RUSTIN rejected (early 1960) an offer to
work full time for the SCLC. He has remained to this
date (2/8/62) a vociferous critic of democratic
institutions & has continued to support MARTIN LUTHER
KING and his socialist designs, serving as an advisor
& organizer of SCLC activities. SUBJECT RUSTIN is
considered the leader of the SCLC braintrust & the
mastermind behind KING'S rise to prominence as a
demagogue and fomenter of social unrest. He has
strategized & deployed white & Negro demonstrators in
the ''Sit-In'' & ''Freedom Ride'' demonstrations of
1960-'61 & has retained documented friendships with a
total of 94 members of certified Communist fronts (see
Known Associate Index #2). In conclusion, SUBJECT
RUSTIN must be classified as a Top Priority Internal
Security Risk & should be subjected to periodic
surveillance & possible mail & trash cover
operations. (Note: Addendum files, films & tapes
require Level 2 Clearance & Deputy Director Tolson's
authorization.)

26

(Las Vegas, 1/12/64)

TAILS:

Sitting tails. Moving tails. Three boring tailees. Tail work—five full days in.

Webb Spurgeon lived behind the Tropicana. Webb Spurgeon's pad brushed the golf course. Webb Spurgeon lived bland. Webb Spurgeon stayed home. Webb Spurgeon chauffeured his son.

Wayne watched his front door. Wayne fought the sitting-tail blues.

He yawned. He scratched his ass. He pissed in a milk can. The car smelled. His aim strayed. He sprayed the dash sometimes.

Spurgeon was a yawn. Duane Hinton was a snore. Eldon Peavy was a faggy snooze. The job was shit. Buddy Fritsch wanted dirt. Pete suborned him in. Fritsch met with Butch Montrose—it vibed payoff.

The job was shit. He worked it anyway. He mixed-and-matched. He juggled his tailees.

Hinton stayed home. Hinton drove to his work sites. Peavy logged time at Monarch Cab. The job was shit. Wayne worked it hard. Wayne cranked twenty hours a day.

Lynette bugged him. Lynette torqued him hard. Lynette found his Dallas paper stash. He lied. He said don't bug me. He said it's Moore and Durfee—I'm just tracking the case.

She tripped him up. She nailed his lies. She made him run. He worked his shit tail job. He gauged potential results.

Hide would-be dirt. Fuck Fritsch and Pete—file a fake report. Play ball. File the goods. Hide out at the Sultan's Lounge. Hide from your wife. Hide from Wayne Senior and his fuck film.

Wayne yawned. Wayne stretched. Wayne scratched his balls. Webb Spurgeon walked out. Webb Spurgeon locked his front door. Webb Spurgeon shagged his Olds 88.

Log it: 2:21 P.M.

Spurgeon drove south. Wayne tailed him. Spurgeon hit I-95. Wayne hit the fast lane. They both drove 50-plus.

Spurgeon signaled. His blinker blinked. He pulled off the freeway. He hit Henderson ramp #1. He drove surface streets. Wayne tailed him semi-tight.

They hit the Mormon Temple. Wayne logged the time: 2:59 P.M.

Spurgeon walked in. Wayne parked catty-corner. Time sitting-tail dragged.

Thirteen minutes. Fourteen/fifteen.

Spurgeon walked out. Wayne logged it: 3:14 P.M.

They backtracked. They hit 95 North. They jumped on two car lengths apart. Wayne hovered back. Wayne slacked his leash. Wayne tailed long-distance.

They drove back to Vegas. They stopped at Jordan High. Weird—Webb Junior went to LeConte.

Spurgeon parked. Wayne parked two slots back. Kids walked by. Spurgeon covered his face.

4:13 P.M.:

A girl walks up. Said girl looks around. Said girl gets in daddy-o's car.

Spurgeon pulled out. Wayne snapped the leash. Wayne tailed him half-tight. The girl bobbed her head down. The car swerved and weaved. The girl bobbed her head up.

She wiped her lips. She fixed her face. She teased her hair up.

They hit 95 South. They cut toward Hoover Dam. They drove through the shitkicker sticks. Traffic thinned. Wayne slacked out the leash.

Spurgeon turned left. Spurgeon hauled up a dirt road. Wayne parked by some scrub pines. Wayne grabbed his binoculars.

He tracked up. He framed shots. He caught a split-rail cabin. The car sliced into the frame. The girl got out. She was sixteen tops. She ran long on hairspray and zits.

Spurgeon got out. The girl jumped on him. They walked inside. Wayne logged the time: 5:09 P.M. Wayne logged stat rape and contributing—two Class B felonies.

Wayne watched the cabin. Wayne watched his watch. He set up his Leica. He fixed the tripod. He slapped on the zoom doohickey.

They fucked for 51 minutes. Wayne shot their exit drape. They kissed long and wet. He got their tongues in tight.

Wayne parked by Monarch Cab. Wayne logged in at 6:43.

The hut sagged. The roof drooped. Cinder blocks creaked. The lot was dusty. The fleet was old—three-tone Packards exclusive.

Wayne watched the window. Eldon Peavy ran cabs. Eldon Peavy worked a two-way box. Eldon Peavy dealt solitaire.

Drivers bopped through. Wayne made three felons—fruit rollers all. One guy beat Murder One. Said guy shivved a he-she at a drag queen ball. Said guy proved self-defense.

Cabs rolled out. The pistons knocked. The mufflers coughed. The pipes shot fumes. The Monarch logo *gleamed:*

A little man with a big crown. Red dice for teeth.

Wayne yawned. Wayne stretched. Wayne scratched his balls. He was up in North LV. The Bondsmen gigged tonite. Barb wore her blue gown most gigs.

A cab pulled out. Wayne tailed it. Rolling tails revived him. Night tails were cake. Cab tails double so—their roof lights stood out plain.

Wayne sidled close. The cab hauled out Owens. They passed the Paiute graveyard. They hit West LV.

Traffic was brisk. A car cut the cab off. Wayne swerved and hopped lanes. It was windy. It was cold. Tumbleweeds blew stray.

They passed Owens and "H." The bars rocked. The liquor stores rolled. Bottle hounds and out-the-door biz.

There—the cab's braking—upside the Cozy Nook.

The cab stopped. The cab idled. The driver tapped the horn. Wayne idled back. Wayne saw four Negroes walk out.

They saw the cab. They ran up. They flashed money. The driver dispensed packets. The Negroes paid cash. The Negroes unwrapped benny rolls.

They raised flasks. They popped pills. They did dance steps. They shucked and rehit the Nook.

The cab pulled out. Wayne tailed it. The cab hit Lake Mead and "D." There—the cab's braking—upside the Wild Goose.

A curb line stood ready—six Negroes—all with that hophead look. The cab stopped. The driver sold bennies. The Negroes shucked and rehit the Goose.

The cab pulled out. Wayne tailed it. The cab hit the Gerson Park Flats. A man got in. The cab pulled out. Wayne tailed it near-close.

There—the cab's braking—upside Jackson and "E." The driver parked. The driver got out. The driver swished into Skip's Lounge.

The driver wore rouge. The driver wore eye shadow. The

driver vibed femme fatale. The driver stayed inside. Wayne clocked his visit: 6.4 minutes flat.

The driver swished out. The driver swished and swung sacks. Said driver lugged *coin* sacks. Said driver fumbled them. Said driver tossed them in the trunk.

Call it: Backroom slots—illegal—Monarch Cab-run.

The cab pulled out. The cab hung a U-ey. Wayne tailed it close-close. There—the cab's braking—upside the Evergreen Project.

The passenger got out. The cab turned north. The headlights strafed parked cars.

There—one parked Cadillac/one white face ducked low. Fuck—it's Pete Bondurant—hunkered down low.

Wayne caught a teaser shot—that and splitsville—poof and adieu.

Wayne tailed the cab. The image stuck—Pete at the wheel. Darktown Pete—say what?—what we gots here?

The cab hauled back to Monarch. Wayne tailed it un-close. Wayne parked in his standard tail spot.

He yawned. He stretched. He pissed in his can. Time dragged. Time crawled. Time meandered.

Wayne watched the window.

Eldon Peavy shagged calls. Eldon Peavy popped pills. Eldon Peavy dealt solitaire.

Drivers clocked in. Drivers lounged. Drivers clocked out. They played cards. They rolled dice. They primped.

Time slogged. Wayne yawned. Wayne stretched. Wayne picked his nose.

A limo pulled up. Whitewalls and fender skirts/mock-leather top. Wayne clocked it: 2:03 A.M.

Peavy walked out. Peavy jumped in the limo. The limo booked south. Wayne tailed it. They hit the Strip. They stopped at the Dunes.

The limo idled doorway-close. Wayne idled three cars back. Three fags walked up. Dig their muscles and teased hair. They vibe chorus-line gash.

They scoped out the limo. They swooned and hopped in. The limo pulled out.

Wayne tailed it. They hit McCarron Field. The limo parked by the gate fence. Wayne parked four cars back.

Peavy got out. Peavy walked. Wayne had a view.

Peavy strolls. Peavy hits the main gate. A flight lands. Tourists get off.

Wayne watched. Wayne yawned. Wayne stretched. Peavy walked back. Two men walked with him. Two men walked close.

Wayne rubbed his eyes. Wayne did a double take. Fuck—it's Rock Hudson and Sal Mineo.

Peavy grins. Peavy snaps a popper. Rock and Sal snort. They grin. They giggle exultant. They get in the limo. Peavy assists them. Peavy grabs their ass cheeks and hoists.

The limo pulled out. Wayne tailed it. Wayne got tailpipe-close. A window furled down. He saw smoke. He smelled maryjane.

They hit North LV. They hit the Golden Cavern Hotel. The cuties pile out. Rock and Sal weave.

Lynette torched for Big Rock—she'd fucking shit.

Duane Hinton lived off Sahara. Wayne late-logged in: 3:07 A.M.—the late-*late* show.

He parked. He dumped his milk can. He yawned. He stretched. He scratched.

Hinton's pad was new—all prefab—one window glowed. TV test patterns—flags and geometric bands—KLXO.

Wayne watched the window. Time sluiced. Time slithered. Time slid. The pattern popped off. A room light popped on. Hinton walked outside.

Wayne clocked it: 3:41 A.M.

Hinton wore work clothes. Odds on a store run—the Food King ran all night. Hinton shagged his van. Hinton backed out. Hinton turned north.

Late tails ate shit. Wayne hated them—no traffic/no cover.

Wayne stalled. Wayne clocked off two minutes. Wayne ran up lead and leash time. 1:58, 1:59—Go—

He hit the key. He drove north. He made up time. He caught Hinton.

They passed the Food King. Wayne hovered back. Hinton cut west—Fremont to Owens.

They hit traffic. Wayne moved in close. They hit West Vegas. They hit more traffic—pimp cars and jalopies—Negro nite owls on the stroll.

Hinton stopped. There—he's braking—upside Owens and "H."

Upside Woody's Club. Famous for all-nite grease. Renowned for fried everything food.

Hinton parked. Hinton walked in. Wayne parked catty-corner. A bum walked up.

He bowed. He Watusi'd. He groomed the windshield. Wayne hit his wipers. The bum mooned him. Wino spectators cheered.

Wayne rolled down his window. P–U—the air stunk. He smelled puke. He smelled chicken grease. He rolled his window up.

Hinton walked out. Hinton held the door. Hinton squired a whore. She was dark. She was fat. She looked bombed.

They walked to the van. They got in. They drove around the corner. Wayne doused his lights. Wayne tailed them. Wayne hovered close up.

They stopped. They parked. They walked through a vacant lot. Weeds and sagebrush. Tumbleballs. A trailer on blocks.

Wayne hovered and pulled curbside. Wayne parked ten yards back. The whore unlocked the trailer. Hinton stepped in. Hinton fumbled some object.

Maybe a jug. Maybe a camera. Maybe some sex gear.

The whore stepped in. The whore shut the door. A light blipped on and blipped off.

Wayne ran his clock. Two minutes crawled. Hold for some semblance of fuck.

There—2.6 in:

The trailer rocks. The blocks sway. Both parties are fat. The trailer's thin tin.

The shakes stopped. Wayne clocked the fuck: 4.8 minutes.

The light went on. Blips blipped out a window. Blue blips—as in flashbulbs.

Wayne yawned. Wayne stretched. Wayne scratched his balls. Wayne dumped his piss cup. The trailer rocked—a minute tops—the light went off.

Hinton walked out. Hinton stumbled. Hinton fumbled some object. He cut through the lot. He got his van. He laid some good tread.

Wayne hit his lo-beams. Wayne tailed him. Wayne rubbed his eyes and yawned. The road dipped—dots hit the windshield—say what?/say what?

The car swayed. He swerved. He blew a red light. He hit his brakes. He popped the clutch and stalled the car out.

The van hit a rise. The van vamoosed. Duane Hinton—out of sight.

Wayne hit the key. Wayne punched the gas. Wayne swamped his engine too fast. He clocked two minutes. He hit the key. He kicked the gas slooooooooow.

The engine caught. He yawned and got traction. The whole world sleepytime bluuuured.

Dawn came up. Wayne got in bed dressed. Lynette stirred. Wayne played possum.

She touched him. She felt his clothes. She pulled off his gun.

"Are you having fun? Hiding out from your wife, I mean."

He yawned. He stretched. He banged the headboard.

He said, "Rock Hudson's queer."

Lynette said, "What happened in Dallas?"

He slept. He got two hours tops. He woke up woozy. Lynette was gone. Nothing happened in Dallas.

He fixed toast. He drank coffee. He went back out. He parked behind Hinton's house. He scoped the backyard.

The alley was packed—construction work next door. His shit car fit right in.

He scoped the driveway. Right there per always—Hinton's van and Deb Hinton's Impala. Clock the tail in: 9:14 A.M.

Wayne watched the house. Wayne yawned and scratched. Wayne pissed out his A.M. coffee. The workers hung drywall—six men with power tools—saws buzzed and jackhammers bit.

10:24:

Deb Hinton walks out. Deb Hinton splits. Deb's Impala knocks and pings.

12:08:

The workers break. They hit their cars. They grab lunch pails and sacks.

2:19:

Duane Hinton walks out.

He walks through the backyard. He lugs some clothes. He wore said clothes last night. He walks to the fence. He feeds the incinerator. He lights a match.

GOD FUCK JESUS CHRIST.

* * *

Wayne drove to Owens and "H." Wayne parked by Woody's Club.

He popped his trunk. He grabbed a pry bar. He circled the block—the street was dead—no wits out and about.

He walked through the lot. He knocked on the trailer. He looked around—still no wits out.

He leaned on the pry bar. He snapped the lock. He walked in. He smelled blood. He slammed the door shut.

He tapped the walls. He tripped a switch. He got overhead light.

She was dead. On the floor/stage-one rigor/maggots on call. Contusions/head wounds/shattered cheeks.

Hinton gagged her. Hinton wedged a handball in her mouth.

Ear blood. Socket blood. One eyeball gone. Buckshot on the floor. Buckshot in her blood.

Hinton wore sap gloves. The palm fabric broke. The buckshot flew.

Wayne caught his breath. Wayne tracked blood trails. Wayne read splash marks.

He slid on a rug. He stepped on the eyeball.

Eight assaults. One beating snuff.

He *heard* it. He thought it was fuck #2. It was Murder One. It vibed Manslaughter Two. Hinton was white. Hinton had pull. Hinton killed a *colored* whore.

Wayne drove back. Wayne thought it all through. The gist cohered.

The assault vics pressed charges. They said the assault man took pix. *He* saw flashbulbs pop. *He* knew the MO. He was fried to exhaustion. The gist flew by him.

He fucked up. *He* owed the whore. The cost meant shit.

Wayne parked in the alley. Wayne watched the house. Workmen yelled. Saws buzzed. Jackhammers bit.

Wayne pissed. Wayne missed his can. Wayne sprayed the seat.

Time whizzed. He watched the house. He watched the driveway. Time cranked. Dusk hit. The workmen split.

They grabbed their cars. They cut tracks. They blew horn-honk farewells. Wayne waited. Time labored and lulled.

6:19 P.M.:

The Hintons walk out. They schlep golf bags. Odds on night golf. The range down Sahara.

They take off. They take Deb's Impala. Duane's van stays put.

Wayne clocked down two minutes. Wayne got some nerve up. Wayne got out and stretched.

He walked up. He braced the fence. He vaulted it. He came down hard. He scraped his hands and brushed them off.

He ran to the porch. The door looked weak. The latch wiggled. He shook the door. He forced some slack. He snapped the latch off.

He opened the door. He hit a laundry room. Washer/dryer/ clothesline. Window light from inside—and one connecting door.

Wayne stepped inside. Wayne shut the door. Loose floor planks popped up. Wayne stubbed his feet.

He braced the inside door. He jiggled the knob. Bingo— unlocked.

He hit the kitchen. He checked his watch. *Give it twenty minutes tops.*

6:23:

The kitchen drawers—nothing hot—flatware and Green Stamps.

6:27:

The living room—nothing hot—blond wood to excess.

6:31:

The den—nothing hot—skeet guns and bookshelves.

6:34:

Hinton's office—go slow here—it's a logical spot.

File shelves/ledgers/a pegged key ring. No wall safe/one wall pic—Hinton and Lawrence Welk.

6:39:

The bedroom—nothing hot—more blond wood excess. No wall safe/no floor safe/no loose panel strips.

6:46:

The basement—go slow here—it's a logical spot.

Power tools/a workbench/*Playboy* magazines. A closet— locked up. That key ring—remember—keys on a peg.

Wayne ran upstairs. Wayne grabbed the ring. Wayne ran downstairs. Wayne jabbed keys at the lock.

6:52:

Key #9 works. The door pops. The closet unlocks.

He saw one box. That's it, no more. Let's inventory it.

Handcuffs. Handballs. Friction tape. Sap gloves. A Polaroid camera. Six rolls of film. Fourteen snapshots:

Negro whores gagged and stomped—eight certified victims plus six.

Plus:

Unused film. One roll. Twelve exposures. Twelve potential shots.

Wayne emptied the box. Wayne cleared floor space. Wayne spread the shit out. Shoot it fast. Put it back. *Display it like you found it.*

He loaded the camera. He shot twelve exposures. They developed and popped out.

Instant prints—Polaroid color.

He grouped Hinton's pix—four separate shots—he got in tight. He got the handball gags. He got the contusions. He got the smashed teeth and the blood.

27

(Las Vegas, 1/14/64)

NIGGER HEAVEN: FOUR spooks/four capsules/one spike.

They usurped the carport. They flanked an old Merc. They laid out red devils. They dumped out the goo.

They spritzed it. They cooked it. They fed the spike. They tied up. They geezed. They dipped. They nodded. They swayed.

All riiiiiiiiight.

Pete watched. Pete yawned. Pete scratched his ass. Stakeout night #6—the dawn shift—hijinx at five fucking A.M.

He parked at Truman and "J." He lounged low. He dug on the view.

That coon called and tipped him. He said Wendell be back. He said Wendell gots a gun. He said Curtis and Leroy—they baaad. They be pushin' white horse.

Check the carport. Check the Evergreen Project. Dope fiends meet there. Dice fiends too. Wendell the dice fiend soo-preem. Look for Curtis and Leroy—two fat boys—they gots big conk hairdos.

Pete popped aspirin. His headache dipped south. Six nights. Shit surveillance. Headaches and coon food. Grime on his car.

The plan:

Clip Curtis and Leroy. Appease the Boys and play civic booster. Clip Wendell Durfee. Indebt Wayne Junior thus.

You owe me, Wayne. Let's see your files.

Six nights. No luck. Six nights slumming. Six nights lounging low.

Pete watched the carport. Pete yawned. Pete stretched. Pete grew Matterhorn-size hemorrhoids.

The dope fiends swaaayed.

They fumbled Kools. They lit matches. They burned their hands. They lit filter tips.

Pete yawned. Pete dozed. Pete chained cigarettes. Whoa, what's—

Two shines cut over "J." Fat boys with big conks—big spray-can hair.

Wait—two *more* shines—full-scale shine alert.

They cut over Truman and "K." They met the conk guys. They launched some jive.

One guy schlepped a blanket. One guy schlepped dice. The dice guy schmoozed the conk guys. He called them "Leroy" and "Cur-ti."

The duos teamed up. The duos cruised the carport. The dope guys went oh shit. The conk guys evicted them. The dope guys weaved south. The conk guys threw down the blanket.

Leroy brought breakfast—T-Bird and Tokay. Cur-ti rolled. Green dice twirled. Cur-ti crapped out. Leroy rolled snake eyes.

Pete watched. The jigs whooped. The jigs shucked. The jigs stepped high.

A prowl car drove by. The cops scoped the game. The jigs paid them never-no-mind. Said prowl car split. Said cops yawned—fuck these dumb shines.

Leroy crapped out. Cur-ti exulted. The dice guys drank wine.

A new jig crossed "J." Pete made him quicksville—Wendell (NMI) Durfee.

Check his pimp threads. Check his hair net. Check that gun bulge by his balls.

Durfee joined the game. The jive multiplied. Durfee rolled. Durfee did the Wah-Watusi. Durfee slurped wine.

That prowl car reprised. That prowl car dipped by. The cops looked revitalized. Said car hovered. Said car idled. The radio squawked.

The spooks froze. The spooks went nonchalant. The cops re-revitalized. The spooks went telepathic—we sees de ofay oppressor—the spooks up and ran.

They split up. They hauled. They dispersed cluster-style. They jammed down "J" and "K."

The cops froze. The blanket guys hauled. They dumped their jugs. They moved east. They *hauled*.

The cops unfroze. The cops punched the gas. The cops laid tread and pursued. Durfee ran west. Long legs and low weight. Fat Cur-ti and Leroy pursued.

Pete punched the gas. Pete punched too hard. The pedal slipped. The engine kicked and died.

Pete got out. Pete ran. Durfee ran. Durfee outran his fat pals. The conksters waddled and huffed.

They cut down an alley—trash heaps on gravel—shacks on both sides. Durfee slid. Durfee stumbled. Durfee ripped his pants. Durfee's gun fell out.

Pete slid. Pete stumbled. Pete's belt snapped. Pete's gun fell out.

He gained ground. He stopped. He grabbed Durfee's gun. He lost ground. He gravel-slid.

A siren nudged his ass—loud and full-tilt.

Durfee hopped a fence. The conksters swung over. The prowl car swerved. It fishtailed. It brodied up. It blocked Pete off.

He dropped the gun. He raised his hands. He smiled subservient. The cops got out. The cops pulled saps. The cops raised Ithaca pumps.

They booked him—407 PC.—Clark County Sheriff's.

They dumped him in a sweat room. They cuffed him to a chair. Two dicks worked on him—phone books and verbal shit.

We traced that gun. It's hot. You're a heist man. I found the gun—fuck you.

Bullshit. Why you down here? Tell us your biz.

I crave chitlins. I crave pork rinds. I crave dark trim. Bullshit. Tell us your—

I'm a civil-rights worker. We shall over—

They swung their phone books—fat ones—L.A. directories. You're a heist man. You rob crap games. You tried to rob those coons.

You're wrong—I crave collard greens.

They whopped his ribs. They whopped his knees. They aired it out good. They torqued his cuffs two ratchets up. They let him stew.

His wrists went numb. His arms went numb. He held a class-A piss.

He ran options:

Don't call Littell. Don't call the Boys. Don't look *très* dumb. Don't call Barb—don't scare her.

His back went numb. His chest went numb. He pissed in his pants. He dug in. He dredged some juice. He snapped the cuff chain. He moved his arms and rewired his blood.

The dicks walked back in. They saw the snapped chain. One geek whistled and clapped.

Pete said, "Call Wayne Tedrow. He's on LVPD."

Wayne Junior showed up. The dicks left them alone. Wayne Junior took off his cuffs.

"They said you tried to take down a dice game."

Pete rubbed his wrists. "Do you believe that?"

Wayne Junior frowned—diva with a grievance. Wayne Junior tucked his head up his ass.

Pete stood up. Some blood rewired. His eardrums popped.

"Have they got a seventy-two-hour detention law here?"

"Yeah, release or arraign."

"I'll ride it out, then. I've been there before."

"What do you *want?* You want a favor? You want me to quit coming to your wife's shows?"

Pete jiggled his arms. Some numbness went.

"Durfee's here. He's hanging out with two guys named Curtis and Leroy. I saw them around those shacks on Truman and 'J.' "

Wayne Junior flushed—blood to his brows—blood-circuit overload.

Pete said, "Kill him. I think he came here to kill you."

28

(Washington, D.C., 1/14/64)

WHITE HOUSE PICKETS:

Civil Rights and Ban the Bomb. Young kids on the Left.

They marched. They chanted. Their shouts overlapped. It was cold. They wore overcoats. They wore Cossack hats.

Bayard Rustin was late. Littell waited. Littell sat in Lafayette Park.

Relief pickets chatted. Shop talk swirled. LBJ and Castro. The Goldwater threat.

The groups shared coffee. Lefty girls brought snacks. Littell looked around—no Bayard Rustin yet.

He knew Rustin's face. Mr. Hoover supplied pix. He met the SCLC plant. They talked last night.

Lyle Holly—ex-Chicago PD.

Lyle worked the Red Squad. Lyle studied the Left. Lyle talked Left and *thought* Right. They shared similar credentials. They shared the same disjuncture. Lyle cracked racial jokes. Lyle said he loved Dr. King.

He knew Lyle's brother. They worked the St. Louis Office—'48 to '50.

Dwight H. was Far Right. Dwight worked kovert Klan jobs. Dwight fit *right* in. The Hollys were Hoosiers. The Hollys had Klan ties. Daddy Holly was a Grand Dragon.

They were post-Klan now. They got law degrees and became cops.

Dwight was *post*-FBI. Dwight was *still* Fed. Dwight joined the Narcotics Bureau. Dwight was restless. Dwight jumped jobs. Dwight craved a bold new cop gig: Chief Investigator/U.S. Attorney's Office/Southern Nevada District.

Dwight was hard. Lyle was soft. Lyle oozed Littell-like empathy.

Lyle built the story:

Ward Littell—ex-FBI. He was dismissed. He was disgraced. He was maimed by Mr. Hoover. He's a Mob lawyer now. He's closeted Left. He's close to Mob money.

It was a sound text. Littell conceded it. Lyle laughed. Lyle said Mr. Hoover helped.

The deal was set. He had the money—Carlos and Sam donated it.

He told them straight—it's Mr. Hoover's gig—it's non-Outfit/anti-SCLC.

Carlos and Sam loved it. Lyle talked to Bayard Rustin. Lyle gushed:

Ward Littell—my old pal. Ward's kindred. Ward's got cash. Ward's pro-SCLC.

The ban-the-bomb crew walked. A YAF crew appeared. New signs: Bop the Beard and Krucify Khrushchev.

Bayard Rustin walked up.

A tall man—dressed and groomed—more gaunt than his mug shots.

He sat down. He crossed his legs. He cleared bench space.

Littell said, "How did you recognize me?"

Rustin smiled. "You were the only one not involved in the democratic process."

"Lawyers don't wave placards."

Rustin cracked his briefcase. "No, but some make donations."

Littell cracked his briefcase. "There'll be more. But I'll deny it if it ever comes to that."

Rustin took the money. "Deniability. I can appreciate it."

"You have to consider the source. The men I work for are not friends of the civil-rights movement."

"They should be. Italians have been persecuted on occasion."

"They don't see it that way."

"Perhaps that's why they're so successful in their chosen field."

"The persecuted learn to persecute. I understand the logic, but I don't accept it as wisdom."

"And you don't ascribe ruthlessness to all people of that blood?"

"No more than I ascribe stupidity to your people."

Rustin slapped his knees. "Lyle said you were quick."

"He's quick himself."

"He said you go back."

"We met at a Free-the-Rosenbergs rally. It must have been '52."

"Which side were you on?"

Littell laughed. "We were shooting surveillance film from the same building."

Rustin laughed. "I sat that one out. I was never a real Communist, despite Mr. Hoover's protestations."

Littell said, "You are by his logic. You know what that designation codifies, and how it allows him to encapsulate everything that he fears."

Rustin smiled. "Do you hate him?"

"No."

"After what he put you through?"

"I find it hard to hate people who are that true to themselves."

"Have you studied passive resistance?"

"No, but I've witnessed the futility of the alternative."

Rustin laughed. "That's an extraordinary statement for a Mafia lawyer to make."

A wind stirred. Littell shivered.

"I know something about you, Mr. Rustin. You're a gifted and compromised man. I may not have your gifts, but I suspect that I run neck-and-neck in the compromise department."

Rustin bowed. "I apologize. I try not to second-guess people's motives, but I just failed with you."

Littell shook his head. "It doesn't matter. We want the same things."

"Yes, and we both contribute in our own ways."

Littell buttoned his coat. "I admire Dr. King."

"As much as any Catholic can admire a man named Martin Luther?"

Littell laughed. "I admire Martin Luther. I made that compromise when I was more of a man of faith."

"You'll be hearing some bad things about our Martin. Mr. Hoover has been sending out missives. Martin Luther King is the devil with horns. He seduces women and employs Communists."

Littell put his gloves on. "Mr. Hoover has numerous pen pals."

"Yes. In Congress, the clergy, and the newspaper field."

"He believes, Mr. Rustin. That's how he makes them believe."

Rustin stood up. "Why now? Why did you decide to undertake such a risk at this time?"

Littell stood up. "I've been visiting Las Vegas, and I don't like the way things are run there."

Rustin smiled. "Tell those Mormons to loosen the chains."

They shook hands. Rustin walked off. Rustin whistled Chopin.

The park glowed. Mr. Hoover bestows all gifts.

29

(Las Vegas, 1/15/64)

PICTURE LOOP:

The dead whore/the eyeball/Wendell Durfee with fangs.

Pictures and flash dreams. No sleep and rolling blackouts. Two fender-benders at the wheel.

The pictures looped on. Thirty-six hours' worth. Bad rain offset them.

Wayne muscled a Monarch Cab man. Wayne stole some bennies. Wayne called Lynette's school and left a message:

Don't go home—stay with a friend—I'll call back and explain.

He ate bennies. He guzzled coffee. It juiced him. It drained him. It torqued his picture loop.

He staked out Truman and "J." He ran file checks. He glommed mug shots. He got dirt on Leroy Williams and Curtis Swasey.

Pimps. Dice fools. Twelve arrests/two convictions. Vagrants with no known address.

He stayed up—half a day/a night/a full day. He watched the carport. He watched the clubs—the Nook/Woody's/the Goose.

He watched crap games. He scoped bar-b-que lines. He saw wisps. He saw Wendell Durfee. He blinked and vaporized him.

He sat in his car. He watched the alley. It paid off two hours back.

Curtis exits a shack. The rear door flanks the alley. Curtis dumps shit in a trash can. Curtis runs straight back.

He waited. He sat in his car. He watched the alley. Dig this one hour back:

Leroy exits the shack. Leroy dumps shit in a trash can. Leroy runs straight back.

Wayne ran up then. Wayne dumped the can. Wayne saw a plastic sheet. White dust was stuck to it—white powder dregs.

He tasted it. It was Big "H."

He circled the shack. Crimped foil covered the windows. He pulled a piece up. He saw Curtis and Leroy.

That was 5:15 P.M. It was 6:19 now.

Wayne watched the shack. Wayne saw wisps and light. Light cut through rips in the foil.

The rain was bad. Fucking monsoon dimensions. Pictures looped on:

Dallas. Pete and Durfee. Pete says, "Kill him"—this sound loop two days strong.

You should have killed him *then*. He's a homing pigeon. You should have *known*.

KILL HIM. KILL HIM. KILL HIM. KILL HIM. KILL HIM.

The car sat on mud. The roof leaked. Rain seeped in. He owed Pete. Pete's call saved him. Pete's call diverted him.

Fuck Buddy Fritsch—fuck his file job—Hinton pays for the whore.

He detoured once—ten hours back. He drove by the trailer. Said trailer reeked. The whore sat and decomped.

Pictures: The blood peel/the maggots/pellets caked in blood.

Wayne watched the shack. The rain blitzed his view. Time decomped. Time redacted.

The back door opens. A man exits. He walks. He walks *this* way. He gets *close*.

Wayne watched. Wayne popped the passenger door. There— it's Leroy Williams.

He's got no hat. He's got no umbrella. He's got sodden duds.

Leroy walked by. Wayne kicked the door out. It hit Leroy flush. Leroy yelped. Leroy hit the mud. Wayne jumped on out.

Leroy stood up. Wayne pulled his piece and butt-punched him. Leroy fell and grazed the car.

Wayne kicked him in the balls. Leroy yelped. Leroy thrashed. Leroy fell down. He said mothersomething. He pulled a shiv. Wayne slammed the door on his hand.

He mashed his fingers. He pinned them. Leroy screamed and dropped the knife. Wayne popped the wind wing. Wayne reached in and popped the glove box.

He dug around. He grabbed his duct tape. He pulled up a piece. Leroy screamed. The rain ate the noise. Wayne eased off the door.

Leroy flexed his hand. Bones sheared and stuck out. Leroy screamed loud.

Wayne grabbed his conk. Wayne tape-muzzled him. Leroy squirmed. Leroy yelped. Leroy flailed his fucked hand.

Wayne taped him—three circuits—Number 2 duct. He kicked him prone. He cuffed his wrists. He threw him in the backseat.

He got in the front seat. He hit the gas. He swerved through mud and alley trash. The rain got worse. His wipers blew. He drove by feel.

He notched a mile. He saw a sign. He flashed—the auto dump—it's close—it's two clicks downwind.

He drove fifty yards. He cranked a hard right. He braked. He pulled in. He wracked the axle on the pavement.

He hit his brights. He lit the place large: Rain/epidemic rust/ a hundred dead cars.

He set the brake. He pulled Leroy up. He ripped up the tape. He ripped off skin and half his mustache.

Leroy yelped. Leroy coughed. Leroy burped bile and blood.

Wayne hit the roof light. "Wendell Durfee. Where is he?"

Leroy blinked. Leroy coughed. Wayne smelled the shit in his pants.

"Where's Wendell Durf—"

"Wendell say he got somethin' to do. He say he be back to get his stuff and leave town. Cur-ti, he say Wendell got bidness."

"What business?"

Leroy shook his head. "I don't know. Wendell's bidness is Wendell's bidness, which ain' my bidness."

Wayne leaned close. Wayne grabbed his hair. Wayne smashed his face on the door. Leroy screamed. Leroy expelled teeth. Wayne crawled over the seat.

He pinned Leroy down. He taped him full-body. He grabbed his cuff chain. He popped the door. He pulled him out. He dragged him to a Buick. He pulled his piece and shot six holes in the trunk.

He dumped Leroy in. He piled on spare tires. He slammed the trunk lid.

He was soaked. His shoes squished. His feet were somewhere else. He saw wisps. He knew they weren't real.

The rain let up. Wayne drove back. Wayne parked in the same alley spot. He got out. He circled the shack. He unpeeled a foil strip.

There's Cur-ti. He's with another guy. The guy's got Cur-ti's face. The guy's Cur-ti's brother.

Cur-ti sat on the floor. Cur-ti jived. Cur-ti crimped bindles. Cur-ti cut dope.

His brother tied off. His brother geezed. His brother untied on Cloud 9. His brother lit a Kool filter-tip.

He burned his fingers. He smiled. Cur-ti giggled. Cur-ti cut dope.

He twirled his knife. He mimed a gutting stroke. He said, "Sheeit. Like a dressed hog, man."

He twirled his knife. He mimed a shaving stroke. He said, "Wendell likes it trimmed. Cuttin' on bitches always been his MO."

He said, "His and hers, man. He lost his gun, so he gets to get in close."

Wayne HEARD it. It clicked in synaptic. Wayne SAW it— instant picture loops.

He ran. He slid. He stumbled. He fell in the mud. He got up and stumble-ran. He got in the car. He stabbed with his key. He missed the keyhole.

He got it in. He turned it. He stripped gears. The wheels spun and kicked the car free.

Lightning hit. Thunder hit. He outran the rain.

He slid through intersections. He ran yellows and reds. He banged railroad tracks. He grazed curbs. He scraped parked cars.

He got home. He brodied on the front lawn. He stumbled out and ran up. The house was dark. The door lock was cracked. His key jammed in the hole.

He kicked the door in. He looked down the hall. He saw the bedroom light. He walked up and looked in.

She was naked.

The sheets were red. She drained red. She soaked through the white.

He spread her. He cinched her. He used Wayne's neckties. He gutted her and shaved her. He trimmed off her patch.

Wayne pulled his gun. Wayne cocked it. Wayne put it in his mouth and pulled the trigger.

The hammer clicked empty. He shot his full six at the dump.

The storm passed through. It dumped power lines. Stoplights were down. People drove crazy.

Wayne drove deliberate. Wayne drove very slow.

He parked by the shack. He grabbed his shotgun. He walked up and kicked the door in.

Cur-ti was packing dope. Cur-ti's brother was watching TV.

They saw Wayne. They nodded. They grinned smack-back.

Wayne tried to talk. Wayne's tongue misfired. Cur-ti talked. Cur-ti talked hair-o-wine slow.

"Hey, man. Wendell's gone. You won't see us harboring—"

Wayne raised his shotgun. Wayne swung the butt.

He clipped Cur-ti. He knocked him down. He stepped on his chest. He grabbed six bindles. He stuffed them in his mouth.

Cur-ti gagged. Cur-ti bit plastic. Cur-ti bit at Wayne's hand. Cur-ti ate plastic and dope.

Wayne stepped on his face. The bindles snapped. His teeth snapped. His jaw snapped loose.

Cur-ti thrashed. Cur-ti's legs stiffed. Blood blew out his nose. Cur-ti spasmed and bit at Wayne's shoe.

Wayne goosed the TV. Morey Amsterdam hollered. Dick Van Dyke screamed.

The brother cried. The brother begged. The brother talked in tongues. The brother tongue-talked smacked-out on the floor.

His lips moved. His mouth moved. His lids fluttered. His eyes rolled back.

Wayne hit him.

He broke his teeth. He broke his nose. He broke the gun butt. His lips moved. His mouth moved. His eyeballs clicked up. His eyes showed pure white.

Wayne picked the TV up. Wayne dropped it on his head. The tubes burst and exploded. They burned his face up.

The power lines were rerigged. The streetlights worked fine. Wayne drove to the dump.

He pulled in. He aimed his brights. He strafed the Buick. He got out and opened the trunk.

He untaped Leroy. He said, "Where's Durfee?" Leroy said, "I don't know."

Wayne shot him—five rounds in the face—point-blank triple-aught buck.

He blew his head off. He blew up the trunk. He blew out the undercarriage. He blew the spare tires up.

He walked to his car. Smoke fizzed out the hood. He'd run it dry. The crankcase was shot.

He tossed the shotgun.

He walked home.

He sat by Lynette.

30

(Las Vegas, 1/15/64)

LITTELL SIPPED COFFEE. Wayne Senior sipped scotch.

They stood at his bar—teak and mahogany—game heads mounted above.

Wayne Senior smiled. "I'm surprised you landed in that storm."

"It was touch and go. We had a few rough moments."

"The pilot knew his business, then. He had a planeful of gamblers, who were anxious to get here and lose their money."

Littell said, "I forgot to thank you. It's late, and you saw me on very short notice."

"Mr. Hoover's name opens doors. I won't be coy about it. When Mr. Hoover says 'Jump,' I say 'How high?' "

Littell laughed. "I say the same thing."

Wayne Senior laughed. "You flew in from D.C.?"

"Yes."

"Did you see Mr. Hoover?"

"No. I saw the man he told me to see."

"Can you discuss it?"

"No."

Wayne Senior twirled a walking stick. "Mr. Hoover knows everyone. The people he knows comprise quite a loop."

"The Loop." The Dallas Office file. Maynard Moore—FBI snitch. His handler—Wayne Tedrow Senior.

Littell coughed. "Do you know Guy Banister?"

"Yes, I know Guy. How do you know him?"

"He ran the Chicago Office. I worked there from '51 to '60."

"Have you seen him more recently?"

"No."

"Oh? I thought you might have crossed paths in Texas."

Guy bragged. Guy talked too much. Guy was indiscreet.

"No, I haven't seen Guy since Chicago. We don't have much in common."

Wayne Senior arched one eyebrow—the pose meant oh-you-kid.

Littell leaned on the bar. "Your son works LVPD Intel. He's someone I'd like to know."

"I've shaped my son in more ways than he'd care to admit. He's not altogether ungrateful."

"I've heard he's a fine officer. A phrase comes to mind. 'Incorruptible by Las Vegas Police standards.' "

Wayne Senior lit a cigarette. "Mr. Hoover lets you read his files."

"On occasion."

"He permits me that pleasure, as well."

" 'Pleasure' is a good way to describe it."

Wayne Senior sipped scotch. "I arranged for my son to be sent to Dallas. You never know when you might rub shoulders with history."

Littell sipped coffee. "I'll bet you didn't tell him. A phrase comes to mind. 'Withholds sensitive data from his son.' "

"My son is uncommonly generous to unfortunate people. I've heard you used to be."

Littell coughed. "I have a major client. He wants to move his base to Las Vegas, and he's very partial to Mormons."

Wayne Senior doused his cigarette. Scotch sucked up the ash.

"I know many capable Mormons who would love to work for Mr. Hughes."

"Your son has some files that would help us."

"I won't ask him. I have a pioneer's disdain for Italians, and I'm fully aware that you have other clients beside Mr. Hughes."

Scotch and wet tobacco. Old barroom smells.

Littell moved the tumbler. "What are you saying?"

"That we all trust our own kind. That the Italians will never let Mormons run Mr. Hughes' hotels."

"We're getting ahead of ourselves. He has to purchase the properties first."

"Oh, he will. Because he wants to buy, and your other clients want to sell. I could mention the term 'conflict of interest,' but I won't."

Littell smiled. Littell raised the tumbler—touché.

"Mr. Hoover briefed you well."

"Yes. In both our best interests."

"And his own."

Wayne Senior smiled. "I discussed you with Lyle Holly as well."

"I didn't know you knew him."

"I've known his brother for years."

"I know Dwight. We worked the St. Louis Office together."

Wayne Senior nodded. "He told me. He said you were always ideologically suspect, and your current employment as a Mafia lawyer confirms it."

Littell raised the tumbler. "Touché, but I wouldn't call my employers ideological on any level."

Wayne Senior raised the tumbler. "Touché back at you."

Littell coughed. "Let's see if I can put this together. Dwight's with the Narcotics Bureau here. He used to work mail-fraud assignments for Mr. Hoover. The two of you worked together then."

"That's correct. We go back thirty-some years. His daddy was a daddy to me."

"The Grand Dragon? And a nice Mormon boy like you?"

Wayne Senior grabbed a cocktail glass. Wayne Senior built a Rob Roy.

"The Indiana Klan was never as rowdy as those boys down south. That's *too* rowdy, even for boys like Dwight and me. That's why we worked those mail-fraud assignments."

Littell said, "That's not true. Dwight did it because Mr. Hoover told him to. You did it to play G-man."

Wayne Senior stirred his drink. Littell smelled bitters and Noilly Prat. He salivated. He moved his chair back. Wayne Senior winked.

Shadows creased the bar. A woman crossed the rear deck. Proud features/black hair/gray streak.

Wayne Senior said, "I want to show you a film."

Littell stood up. Littell stretched. Wayne Senior grabbed his drink. They walked down a side hall. The scotch and bitters swirled. Littell wiped his lips.

They stopped at a storage room. Wayne Senior hit the lights. Littell saw a projector and wall screen.

Wayne Senior spooled film. Wayne Senior set the slide. Wayne Senior fed film in. Littell killed the lights. Wayne Senior hit the on switch. Words and numbers hit the screen.

Surveillance code—white-on-black. A date—8/28/63. A location—Washington, D.C.

The words dissolved. Raw footage hit. Speckled black & white film. A bedroom/Martin Luther King/a white woman.

Littell watched.

His legs dipped. He weaved hard. He grabbed at a chair. The skin tones contrasted—black-on-white—stretch marks and plaid sheets.

Littell watched the film. Wayne Senior smiled. Wayne Senior watched him.

All gifts. Mr. Hoover. A gift that he would regret.

3 1
(Las Vegas, 1/15/64)

THE COPS KICKED him loose.

They called around. They got his rep. They got *très* hip. He's mobbed up/he knows the Boys/the Boys dig on him.

Pete walked. Pete paged Barb at work. Pete said I'll be home soon.

He did forty-one hours. He ate jute balls and rice. His head hurt. His wrists hurt. He smelled like Chihuahua shit.

He cabbed to his car. He cabbed Monarch—the Browntown Express. The driver lisped. The driver wore rouge. The driver said he sold guns.

The driver dropped Pete at the carport. Pete's car was trashed/totaled/torched.

No windshield. No hubcaps. No tires. No wheels. The Cadillac Hotel—one wino booked in.

He snored. Bugs bombed him. He cradled Sterno and T-Bird. The car got a paint job—kustom nigger script:

Allah Rules/Death to Ofays/We Love Malcolm X.

Pete laughed. Pete fucking roared. He kicked the grille. He kicked the door panels. He tossed the wino his keys.

A rain hit—light and cold. Pete heard a ruckus close in. He placed it—way close—the shacks off "J" Street.

He walked over. He caught the grief.

Six prowl cars—LVPD and Sheriff's. Two Fed sleds snout-to-snout. Big voodoo upside a jig shack.

Arc lights/crime-scene rope/one ambulance. A cop-jig confluence—large.

Cops inside the crime-scene rope. Jigs outside. Jigs armed with Tokay and fried chicken.

Pete pushed up close. A cop rigged two gurneys. A cop pushed them in the shack. A cop jumped the rope. A cop briefed him. Pete eavesdropped in tight.

A kid called it in. Said kid lives next door. Said kid heard a commotion. A honky do it. Honky got a shotgun. Honky get in his car and ex-cape. Said kid enters the shack then. Said kid sees two stiffs—Curtis and Otis Swasey.

The jigs pressed up. The jigs stretched the crime-scene rope. The jigs Wah-Watusi'd. A cop placed sawhorses. A cop stretched the rope. A cop eased the jigs back.

Jigs eyeballed Pete. Jigs jostled him. White Man—bad juju. White Man—go home. White Man—he kill our kin.

Odds on: Wayne Junior. Odds on: Wendell Durfee—dead and dumped *somewhere*.

The jigs huddled. The jigs mumbled. The jigs pygmy-ized. A jig lobbed a bottle. A jig lobbed a drumstick. A jig lobbed french fries.

Four cops pulled batons. Two cops rolled out the gurneys.

There Curtis—he blue—honky beat his face. There Otis—he crisp—honky torch his face baaaaaad juju.

Pete backed off. Pete caught some elbows. Pete caught some lobbed chicken wings. Pete caught some yam pies.

He walked across "J." He mingled by a cop clique. He leaned on a prowl car. A cop sat in front. Said cop worked a hand mike. Said cop talked loud.

We got another one—shotgun DOA—a coon named Leroy Williams.

Woooooo! Blew his burrhead cleeean off! The dump guys found him inside this Buick. We got the shotgun.

Call *Leroy* Stiff #3. Wendell—where *you* at?

Pete mingled. The cops ignored him. Cops blocked traffic. Cops stood point. Cops cordoned off "J."

The rain fucking tripled. The clouds let fly. Pete grabbed a stray chicken box. Pete dumped out gizzards. Pete put it on and kept his head dry.

The jigs dispersed. The jigs booked willy-nilly. The jigs ran hellbent.

A Fed car pulled up. A big guy got out. Said guy vibed El Jefe—gray suit and gray Fed hat.

Jefe flashed a badge. Jefe got service. The point guard saluted. A baby Fed bowed. Jefe bootjacked his umbrella.

Pete circled the rope. Pete got in close. Said fuzz ignored him.

Fuck you—you're a geek—you've got a chicken-box hat.

Pete stood around. His hat leaked. Chicken grease oiled his hair. The baby Fed brown-nosed the boss Fed—yessir, Mr. Holly.

Mr. Holly was *pissed*. It's *my* case. The vics pushed narcotics. It's *my* crime scene—let's toss the shack.

Mr. Holly stayed dry. The sub-fuzz stayed wet. A sergeant walked up. Said sergeant wore squishy blues.

He talked loud. He pissed off Mr. Holly. He said it's *our* case. *We're* sealing her up. *We'll* bring in Homicide.

Mr. Holly fumed. Mr. Holly fugued out. He kicked a sawhorse. He yelped. He fucked his foot up.

A prowl car pulled up. A cop got out. He gestured wild. He talked wild. Pete heard "car at the dump." Pete heard "Tedrow."

Mr. Holly yelled. The sergeant yelled. A cop raised a bullhorn. Lock her up—let's roll code 3—the Tonopah Dump.

The fuzz dispersed.

They grabbed their cars. They peeled up "J." They fishtailed in mud. They plowed through gravel yards.

One cop stayed behind. Said cop locked the shack.

He stood by the front door. He stood in the monsoon. He smoked cigarettes. The rain doused them. He got two puffs per. He gave up. He ran to his car. He rolled the windows up.

Pete ran. The rain covered him. He kicked up mud. He ran back to the alley. He circled the shack.

No cars. No back-door guard—good. Said door was locked. The windows were tinfoil-patched.

Pete reached up. Pete tore at a foil patch. Pete de-patched a window.

He climbed up. He vaulted in. He saw chalk lines and bloodstains. He saw a burned-up TV-set.

Floor debris—chalk-circled: Bindle scraps/tube glass/fried nigger hair.

Pete tossed the shack. Pete worked *rápidamente*. He gridscoped. He saw one dresser/one toilet/no shelves.

Two mattresses. Bare walls and floors. No stash-holes inset. A window air-cooler—Frost King brand—matted screens and rusty ducts.

No cord. No plug. No intake valve. Call it dope camouflage.

Pete popped the top. Pete reached in. Pete praised Allah Himself.

White horse—all plastic-wrapped—three bonaroo bricks.

32

(Las Vegas, 1/17/64)

FIVE COPS GRILLED him.

Wayne sat. They stood. They filled the sweat room.

Buddy Fritsch and Bob Gilstrap. A Sheriff's man. A Fed named Dwight Holly. A Dallas cop named Arthur V. Brown.

The heat went off. Their breath steamed. It fogged the mirror-wall. He sat. They stood. His lawyer stood under a speaker. His lawyer stood outside.

They popped him at home—2:00 A.M.—he was still there with Lynette. Fritsch called Wayne Senior. Wayne Senior came to the jail.

Wayne blew him off. Wayne blew off his lawyer. Dwight Holly knew Wayne Senior. Dwight Holly stressed the friendship thus:

You're not your dad. You killed three men. You fucked my investigation up.

They'd braced him twice. He told the truth. He wised up and called Pete.

Pete knew the scoop. Pete knew a lawyer. His name: Ward Littell.

Wayne met with Littell. Littell quizzed him: Did they tape you? Did they transcribe?

Wayne said no. Littell advised him. Littell said he'd watch the next go. Littell said he'd veto tape and transcription.

The veto worked. The room was cherry—no tape rig/no steno.

Wayne coughed. His breath fogged out.

Fritsch said, "You got a cold? You were sure out in the rain that night."

Holly said, "He was out killing three unarmed men."

Fritsch said, "Come on. He admitted it."

The Sheriff's man coughed. "*I've* got a fucking cold. He wasn't the only one out in the rain."

Gilstrap smiled. "We've cleared up one part of your story. We know you didn't kill Lynette."

Wayne coughed. "Tell me how you know."

"Son, you don't want to know."

Holly said, "Tell him. I want to see how he reacts."

Fritsch said, "The coroner found abrasions and semen. The guy was a secretor. AB-negative blood, which is real rare. We checked Durfee's jail records. That's his blood type."

Holly smiled. "Look, he didn't even blink."

Brown said, "He's a cold one."

The Sheriff's man said, "He wasn't even crying when we found him. He was just staring at the body."

Gilstrap said, "Come on. He was in shock."

Fritsch said, "We're satisfied that Durfee killed her."

The Sheriff's man lit a cigar. "And we're satisfied that Curtis and Otis clued you in to his plan."

Holly straddled a chair. "Someone hipped you to Leroy Williams and the Swasey brothers."

Wayne coughed. "I told you. I have an informant."

"Whose name you refuse to reveal."

"Yes."

"And your intent was to find and apprehend Wendell Durfee."

"Yes."

Brown said, "You wanted to apprehend him, to make up for not doing it in Big D."

"Yes."

"Then, son, here's what bothers me. How did Durfee know that you were the officer sent down to Dallas to extradite him?"

Wayne coughed. "I told you before. I rousted him a few times when I worked Patrol. He knew my face and my name, and he saw me when we exchanged shots in Dallas."

Fritsch said, "I'll buy that."

Gilstrap said, "I will, too."

Brown said, "I won't. I think something happened between you and Durfee. Maybe in Dallas, maybe up here before they sent you down. I don't see him coming all the way up here, presumably to kill you and get his incidental jollies on your wife, unless he had a personal motive."

Tex was good. Tex was better than the Sheriff's man. Pete chased the dice men. The cops chased him. They popped Pete. They filed paper. The Sheriff's man knew shit-all about it.

Brown said, "Your business up here is your business. I wouldn't care about any of this, except for the proximity of a missing Dallas officer named Maynard D. Moore, who you reportedly did not get along with."

Wayne shrugged. "Moore was dirty. If you knew him, you

know that's true. I didn't like him, but I only had to work with him for a few days."

"You said 'knew.' You think he's dead, then?"

"That's right. Durfee or one of his asshole Klan buddies killed him."

Gilstrap said, "We've got two APBs out on Durfee. He won't get far."

Brown hovered. "You're saying Officer Moore was in the Ku Klux Klan?"

"That's right."

"I don't like the sound of that accusation. You're defaming the memory of a brother officer."

The Sheriff's man laughed. "This is hilarious. He kills three Negroes and gets on his high horse about the KKK."

Brown coughed. "DPD has been anti-Klan from the get-go."

"Bullshit. You all get your sheets cleaned at the same laundry."

"Boy, you are wearing me thin."

"Don't call me 'boy,' you redneck faggot."

Brown kicked a chair. Fritsch picked it up.

Gilstrap said, "Come on. This line of talk is getting us nowhere."

Holly rocked his chair. "Leroy Williams and the Swasey brothers were moving heroin."

Wayne said, "I know that."

"How?"

"I saw Curtis rolling bindles."

"I've had them under spot surveillance. They were pushing in Henderson and Boulder City, and they were making plans to push in West Vegas."

Wayne coughed. "They wouldn't have lasted two days. The Outfit would have clipped them."

Fritsch rolled his eyes. "He goes from the Klan to the Mob."

Gilstrap rolled his eyes. "You've got the Mob in Vegas like you've got the Klan in Dallas."

Wayne rolled *his* eyes. "Hey, Buddy, who bought you your speedboat? Hey, Bob, who got you that second mortgage?"

Fritsch kicked the wall. Gilstrap kicked a chair. Brown picked it up.

Holly said, "You're not making any friends here."

Wayne said, "I'm not trying to."

Fritsch said, "You've got the sympathy vote."

Gilstrap said, "You've got the chain of events."

The Sheriff's man coughed. "You're trying to apprehend a fugitive cop-killer. You learn that your wife may be jeopardized, so you rush home and find her dead. Your actions from that point on are entirely understandable."

Brown hitched up his pants. "It's your prior relationship with Durfee that I don't understand."

Holly said, "I concur."

Fritsch said, "Look at it our way. We're trying to give the DA a package. We don't want to see an LVPD man go down for three murders."

Gilstrap said, "Let's talk turkey. It's not like you killed three white men."

Brown cracked his knuckles. "Did you kill Maynard Moore?"

"Fuck you."

"Did Wendell Durfee take part in the killing? Is that what all this derives from?"

"Fuck you."

"Did Wendell Durfee witness the killing?"

"Fuck you."

Holly pulled his chair up. Holly bumped Wayne's chair.

"Let's discuss the condition of the shack."

Wayne shrugged. "I only saw the bindles I shoved in Curtis Swasey's mouth. I did not see any other narcotics or narcotics paraphernalia."

Holly smiled. "You anticipated the intent of my question very nicely."

Wayne coughed. "You're a narcotics agent. You want to know if I stole the large quantity of heroin that you think the victims had. You don't care about the murders or my wife."

Holly shook his head. "That's not entirely true. You know I'm friends with your father. I'm sure he cared for Lyn—"

"My father despised Lynette. He doesn't care for anyone. He only respects hard-ons like you. I'm sure he's full of warmth for your days in Indiana and your good times with Mr. Hoover."

Holly leaned in. "Don't turn me into an enemy. You're getting there already."

Wayne stood up. "Fuck you and fuck my father. If I wanted his help, I'd be out now."

Holly stood up. "I think I've got what I need."

Gilstrap shook his head. "You're playing kamikaze, son. And you're bombing your own goddamn friends."

Fritsch shook his head. "You can cross me off that list. We do our best to keep Vegas clean, while you go out and kill three niggers, which is going to bring out every civil-rights chimpanzee in captivity."

Wayne laughed. *"Vegas? Clean?"*

The cops walked out. Wayne took his pulse. It ran 180-plus.

3 3

(Las Vegas, 1/17/64)

THE ROOM WAS cold. A heat coil blew. It chilled down the jail.

Littell read his notes.

Wayne Junior was good. He diverted Sergeant Brown. He deflected his attack. Pete briefed Littell beforehand. Pete dropped a bomb: Wayne Junior knows about Dallas

Pete liked Wayne Junior. Pete mourned Lynette. Pete took the blame. Pete stopped there. Pete implied a Dallas snafu.

Littell checked his notes. The smart call: Wayne Junior killed Maynard Moore. The details played schizzy. Wendell Durfee played in somehow.

Wayne Junior had the board files. Littell needed them. Littell might need Wayne Senior. Wayne Senior called him. Wayne Senior made nice. He said I want to help my son. He said I want *him* to ask.

He informed Wayne Junior. Wayne Junior said no. He told Wayne Senior that. It angered him. That was good. He might need Wayne Senior. The "no" knocked him flat.

Wayne Junior was good. Wayne Junior pissed off Dwight Holly. Littell called Lyle Holly. They talked last night. They discussed the Bayard Rustin meet. Lyle said Dwight was mad. The killings fucked with him. Wayne Junior deep-sixed his surveillance.

He chatted Lyle up. He said, "I'm Junior's lawyer." Lyle laughed. Lyle said, "Dwight never liked you."

Littell checked his notes. The room was cold. His breath fogged and steamed. Bob Gilstrap walked in. Dwight Holly followed him. They sat down and kicked back.

Holly stretched. His coat gapped. He wore a blued .45.

"You've aged, Ward. Those scars put some years on you."

"They're hard-earned, Dwight."

"Some men learn the hard way. I hope you have."

Littell smiled. "Let's discuss Wayne Tedrow Junior."

Holly scratched his neck. "He's a punk. He's got all of his daddy's arrogance and none of his charm."

Gilstrap lit a cigarette. "They broke the mold on Senior and him. I've never been able to figure either one of them."

Holly laced his hands. "Something happened with him and Durfee. Where or when, I don't know."

Gilstrap nodded. "That likelihood is what scares me."

A vent thumped. The heat kicked on. Holly hack-coughed.

"The kid mouths off to me and passes his bug on."

Gilstrap said, "You'll survive."

Holly said, "Let's cut the shit. I'm the only one who doesn't want to bury this."

"It's not your agency he hung out to dry."

"Shit, he hung *me* out."

The room warmed up. Holly took his coat off.

"Say something, Ward. You look like the cat who ate the canary."

Littell popped his briefcase. Littell showed the Vegas *Sun*. There's a headline. It runs 40 points. There's a subhead 16:

"POLICEMAN HELD IN TRIPLE SLAYING— CIVIL-RIGHTS PROTESTS FEARED."

"NAACP: 'KILLINGS SPRINGBOARD TO EXPLICATE RACISM IN LAS VEGAS.'"

Gilstrap said, "Shit."

Holly laughed. "Big words and colored bullshit. Give them a dictionary and they think they run the world."

Littell tapped the paper. "I don't see your name, Dwight. Is that a blessing or a curse?"

Holly stood up. "I see where this is going, and if it *does* go there, I'll go to the U.S. Attorney. Civil-rights abridgement and obstruction of justice. I'll look bad, you'll look worse, the kid will do time."

A vent thumped. The heat kicked off. Holly walked out.

Gilstrap said, "The cocksucker means it."

"I don't think so. He goes back too far with Wayne Senior."

"Dwight don't go back, Dwight goes forward. Wayne Senior

could squawk and go to Mr. Hoover, who'd most likely pooh-pooh it because, according to my sources, he's got a real soft spot for Dwight."

Littell flipped the paper over. Littell squared the fold. There's the hard news and AP pix: Police dogs/angry Negroes/tear gas.

Gilstrap sighed. "Okay, I'll play."

"Does the DA want to file?"

"Nobody wants that. We're just afraid that we're too far exposed already."

"And?"

"And there's two schools of thought. Bury it and ride out all the Commie bullshit, or file and take our lumps."

Littell drummed the table. "Your department could get hurt very badly."

Gilstrap blew smoke rings. "Mr. Littell, you're leading me. You're playing me and holding back your face cards."

Littell tapped the paper. "Tell me Dallas doesn't scare you. Tell me Junior didn't fuck up there and give Durfee a motive to kill him. Tell me this won't come out in court. Tell me you're convinced that Junior didn't kill Maynard Moore. Tell me you didn't put a bounty on Durfee and pay Junior six thousand dollars to kill him. Tell me you want all this exposed and tell me Junior won't expose it just to flush his life down the toilet."

Gilstrap squeezed his ashtray. "Tell me Dallas PD will just go away."

"Tell me Junior wasn't smart enough to hide the body. Tell me the first cop who spots Durfee won't kill him and eliminate DPD's one potential witness."

Gilstrap slapped the table. "Tell me how we *do* this."

Littell tapped the paper. "I've read the accounts. There's no specified sequence of events. All you have is four killings in one evening."

"That's right."

"The evidence can be reworked to support self-defense. There may be a chance to divert demonstrations."

Gilstrap sighed. "I don't want to owe Wayne Senior."

Littell said, "You won't."

Gilstrap stuck his hand out.

He brewed a plan. He called Pete and told him. Pete said okay. Pete asked one favor.

I want to see Lynette. It's *my* fault. I fucked up in Dallas.

Buddy Fritsch had morgue shots. Littell looked at them. Durfee raped her. Durfee gutted her. Durfee shaved her.

He saw the pix. He studied them. He scared himself. He put Jane's face on Lynette's body.

He sent Pete a morgue pass. Pete said he'd talked to Wayne Junior. Wayne Junior pledged him his files.

Littell called east. Littell pulled strings. Littell buzzed Lyle Holly. He said the snuffs might hurt Dwight—so hear my plan now.

Call Bayard Rustin. Offer this advice: Do not protest the killings—call Ward Littell instead.

Rustin called him. Littell lied. Littell offered a rationale. A Negro man killed a white woman. Three more killings derived. The cop killed in self-defense. It's all certified.

Rustin *got* it—don't build hate—don't martyr an angry white cop. Vegas wasn't Birmingham. Negro junkies weren't four girls in church.

Rustin was savvy. Rustin was gracious. Littell pledged more money. Littell praised Dr. King.

He met Rustin once. He charmed and entrapped him. He *used* him forthwith.

I *believe*. I have horrible debts. I'll try to help more than I hurt.

34

(Las Vegas, 1/19/64)

HE SAW LYNETTE.

He saw the flaps. He saw the sheared ribs. He saw where the knife snapped bone. Wayne Junior didn't blame him. Wayne Junior blamed himself.

Pete stood by the freeway. Pete ate gas fumes. Pete had a replacement sled—a boss new Lin*coon*.

A prowl car pulled up. A cop got out. He fed Pete three guns. Three calibers: .38/.45/.357 mag.

Throwdown guns. Taped and initialed: L.W./O.S./C.S.

The cop knew the plan. They had two crime scenes. They had viable blood—good Red Cross stock.

The cop split. Pete drove to Henderson. Pete hit a gun shop. Pete bought ammo.

He loaded the guns. He rigged silencers. He drove back to Vegas.

Wayne Junior was out. He saw him yesterday. The DA dumped his case. They met. They talked. They hit Wayne's bank vault. Wayne dumped his board files and briefed him.

Spurgeon dug jailbait. Peavy was larcenous. Hinton whacked a nigger whore. Three board members—swing votes plus—good news for Count Drac.

Spurgeon vibed easy. Hinton vibed tough sell. Peavy vibed grief. Monarch Cab as Tiger Kab—hold that good thought.

Wayne looked frazzled. His eyes roamed. He strafed jigaboos. They ate lunch and talked.

Neutral shit—Clay versus Liston. Pete liked Liston in two. Wayne said three tops. A shine cleared their table. Wayne fucking seized up.

Pete drove to the car dump. The cop met him there. The dump was closed. The sun was up. A breeze wafted through.

They schmoozed. They jumped the crime-scene rope. Wayne's car was gone. The Buick was cut into scrap.

The cop taped a body—white tape on cement. Pete aimed the .45.

He popped six shots. He nailed a tree. He grabbed the slugs. He gauged trajectories. He dropped the slugs. He chalked them. The cop took pix.

Pete spritzed the body tape. Pete watched the blood dry. The cop took pix.

They drove to the shack. They jumped the crime-scene rope. The cop taped two bodies. The cop spritzed the tape.

Pete shot the .38. Pete popped four rounds. Pete hit the walls and dug the slugs out. The cop bagged them. The cop lab-logged them. The cop took pix.

They drove to the County Morgue. The cop greased the attendant geek. Said geek had three fish. Said fish reposed on three trays.

Leroy had no head. Leroy wore a dashiki. The cop pulled a sap. The cop broke Leroy's right hand. The cop flexed the fingers free.

Pete rolled the fingertips. Pete smudged the magnum. Pete laid two butt spreads.

Curtis was stiff. Otis was stiff. They wore Dodger T-shirts and morgue sheets.

Pete squeezed their hands. Pete broke their fingers. Pete flexed the tips. The cop rolled prints—barrel spreads—the cop rolled the .45 and .38.

The stiffs stunk of morgue rouge and sawdust. Pete coughed and sneezed.

Ward set it up. We'll meet at Wilt's Diner—it's out near Davis Dam.

They showed early. They grabbed a booth. They cleared table space and sipped coffee. Ward propped the bag up. Tabletop center—*très* hard to miss.

Dwight Holly showed. Punctual—2:00 P.M. straight.

He parked his car. He looked through the window glass. He saw them and walked straight in.

Pete made room. Holly sat beside him. Holly eyeballed the bag.

"What's that?"

Pete said, "Christmas."

Holly made the jack-off sign. Holly spread out.

He stretched. He made elbow room. He hard-nudged Pete.

He coughed. "I caught the fucking Tedrow kid's bug."

Ward smiled. "Thanks for coming out."

Holly tugged his cuff links. "Who's the big guy? The Wild Man of Borneo?"

Pete laughed. Pete slapped his knees.

Ward sipped coffee. "Have you spoken to the U.S. Attor—"

"He called me. He said Mr. Hoover told him not to file on the kid. I think Wayne Senior interceded, and I hope you didn't run me out here to gloat."

Ward tapped the bag. "Congratulations."

"For *what?* The investigation your client fucked up?"

"You must have talked to the U.S. Attorney *yesterday.*"

Holly tugged his law-school ring. "You're stringing me, Ward. You're reminding me why I never liked you."

Ward stirred his coffee. "You're the new Chief Investigator for the Southern Nevada Office. Mr. Hoover told me this morning."

Holly tugged his ring. It fell off. It hit the floor. It traveled.

Ward smiled. "We want to make friends in Nevada."

Pete smiled. "You took down Leroy Williams and the Swasey

brothers. They were out on bail when Wayne killed them.''

Ward tapped the bag. "The reports have been predated. You'll be reading about it."

Pete tapped the bag. "It's a white Christmas."

Holly grabbed the bag. Holly grabbed a steak knife. Holly stabbed one brick. Holly dipped one finger.

He licked it. He tasted it. He got the Big "H" bite.

"You convinced me. But I'm not done with the kid, and I don't care who he's got on his side."

DOCUMENT INSERT: 1/23/64.
Las Vegas Sun article.

NARCOTICS LINK TO NEGRO KILLINGS REVEALED

At a joint news conference, spokesmen for the Las Vegas Police Department and the Southern Nevada District of the U.S. Attorney's Office announced that Leroy Williams and Otis and Curtis Swasey, the three Negro men killed on the night of January 15th, had been recently arrested by agents of the Federal Bureau of Narcotics and were out on bail at the time of their deaths.

''The three men had been the focus of a long-term investigation,'' Agent Dwight C. Holly said. ''They had been selling large quantities of heroin in nearby cities and were preparing to sell it in Las Vegas. They were apprehended in the early morning hours of January 9th, and three kilos (6½ pounds) of heroin were seized at their residence in West Las Vegas. Williams and the Swasey brothers made bail on the afternoon of January 13th and returned to their residence.''

Captain Robert Gilstrap of the LVPD went on to clarify events on the night of January 15th. ''Newspaper reporters and local television commentators have assumed that the three men killed that night were killed by LVPD Sergeant Wayne Tedrow Jr. as revenge for the murder of his wife, Lynette, who was raped and killed, presumably by a male Negro named Wendell Durfee,'' he said. ''This is not the case. Durfee was a known associate of Williams and the Swasey brothers, and the brothers paid him to kill Mrs. Tedrow. What has not been revealed until now is that Mrs. Tedrow's death postdated the deaths of Williams and the Swasey brothers and that Sergeant Tedrow, as part of a combined LVPD-Narcotics Bureau operation, had Williams and the Swasey brothers under constant surveillance in an effort to insure that they did not abscond on their bail.''

''Sergeant Tedrow heard a ruckus inside their residence, late on the evening of January 15th,'' Agent Holly said. ''He investigated and was fired upon by the Swasey brothers. No shots were heard, because both men fired silencer-fitted pistols. Sergeant Tedrow managed to disable both men and killed them with makeshift weapons he found on the premises. Leroy Williams entered the residence at that time. Sergeant Tedrow chased him to an automobile dump on Tonopah Highway and exchanged gunfire with him. Williams died in the process.''

Agent Holly and Captain Gilstrap displayed photographic evidence compiled at both death scenes. Mr. Randall J. Merrins of the U.S. Attorney's Office went on to say that it had been assumed that Sergeant Tedrow was being kept in custody while possible homicide charges against him were being discussed and prepared.

''This is not the case,'' Merrins said. ''Sergeant Tedrow was held for his own safety. We were afraid of reprisals from other unknown members of the Williams-Swasey dope gang.''

Sergeant Tedrow, 29, could not be reached for comment. Mrs. Tedrow's presumed slayer, Wendell Durfee, was identified by fingerprints and other physical evidence found in the Tedrow home. Durfee is now the subject of a nationwide all-points bulletin and is also wanted by Texas authorities for the November 1963 disappearance of Dallas Police Officer Maynard D. Moore.

Agent Holly's long pursuit of the Swasey brothers and Leroy Williams was praised by Assistant U.S.

Attorney Merrins, who announced that Holly, 47, will
soon take the position of Chief Investigator for that
agency's Southern Nevada Office. Captain Gilstrap
announced that Sergeant Tedrow has been awarded the
LVPD's highest accolade, its ''Medal of Valor,'' for
''conspicuous gallantry and bravery in his
surveillance and subsequent deadly confrontation
with three armed and dangerous narcotics pushers.''

Mrs. Tedrow is survived by one sister and her
parents, Mr. and Mrs. Herbert D. Sproul, of Little
Rock, Arkansas. Her body will be shipped to Little
Rock for interment.

DOCUMENT INSERT: 1/26/64.
Las Vegas Sun article.

GRAND JURY CLEARS POLICEMAN

The standing Clark County Grand Jury today
announced that no criminal indictments will be filed
against Las Vegas Policeman Wayne Tedrow Jr. for the
deaths of three Negro dope pushers.

The Grand Jury heard six hours of testimony from
members of the Las Vegas Police Department, Clark
County Sheriff's Department and U.S. Bureau of
Narcotics. Members were in unanimous agreement that
Sergeant Tedrow's actions were warranted and
justifiable. Grand Jury foreman D. W. Kaltenborn said,
''We believe that Sergeant Tedrow acted with great
resolve and under all the due guidelines of the laws
of the State of Nevada.''

A Las Vegas Police Department spokesman attending
the grand jury proceedings said that Sergeant Tedrow
had resigned from the LVPD that morning. Sergeant
Tedrow could not be reached for comment.

DOCUMENT INSERT: 1/27/64.
Las Vegas Sun article.

NO PROTESTS, NEGRO LEADERS SAY

At a hastily arranged press conference in
Washington, D.C., a spokesman for the National
Association for the Advancement of Colored People
(NAACP) announced that that organization and several
other civil-rights groups will not protest the
January 15th killings of three Negro men by a white
policeman in Las Vegas.

Lawton J. Spofford told assembled reporters, ''Our
decision is not based upon the recent decree from the
Clark County Grand Jury, which exonerated Sergeant
Wayne Tedrow Jr. for the deaths of Leroy Williams and
Curtis and Otis Swasey. That body is a 'rubber-stamp'
implement of the Clark County political
establishment and as such has no sway with us. Our
decision is based on information we have received
from a friendly anonymous source, who told us that
Sergeant Tedrow, under great personal duress, acted
in a somewhat heedless but recognizably non-
malicious manner that did not include racist
designs.''

The NAACP, along with the Congress of Racial
Equality (CORE) and the Southern Christian
Leadership Conference (SCLC), had previously
announced their intention to stage protests in Las
Vegas, in order to ''shed light on a horribly
segregated city, where Negro citizens live in
deplorable circumstances.'' The killings, Spofford
said, ''were to have been our point of redress and
overall explication.''

Other Negro leaders present at the press conference
said that they did not rule out the possibility of
future civil-rights protests in Las Vegas. ''Where
there's smoke, there's fire,'' spokesman Welton D.
Holland of CORE said. ''We do not expect Las Vegas to
change its ways without some notable
confrontations.''

DOCUMENT INSERT: 2/6/64.
Verbatim FBI telephone call transcript.
Marked: ''Recorded at the Director's Request''/
''Classified Confidential 1-A: Director's Eyes Only.''

Speaking: Director Hoover, Ward J. Littell.

JEH: Good morning, Mr. Littell.

WJL: Good morning, Sir.

JEH: You've been meeting some charming new people and rediscovering old friends. That might be a good place to start.

WJL: ''Charming'' might describe Mr. Rustin, Sir. ''Old friend'' would never describe Dwight Holly.

JEH: I could have predicted that response. And I doubt that Lyle Holly will become your lifelong chum.

WJL: We share a wonderful friend in you, Sir.

JEH: You're feeling frisky this morning.

WJL: Yes, Sir.

JEH: Did Mr. Rustin bemoan my efforts against Mr. King and the SCLC?

WJL: He did, Sir.

JEH: And you were properly deplored?

WJL: Cosmetically, Sir, yes.

JEH: I'm sure you were entirely convincing.

WJL: I established a rapport with Mr. Rustin, Sir.

JEH: I'm sure you will sustain it.

WJL: I hope so, Sir.

JEH: Have you spoken to him again?

WJL: Lyle Holly facilitated a second conversation. I utilized Mr. Rustin to forestall some trouble in Las Vegas. It pertained to a client of mine.

JEH: I know elements of the story. We'll discuss it momentarily.

WJL: Yes, Sir.

JEH: Do you still consider it impossible to re-tape the Dark Prince?

WJL: Yes, Sir.

JEH: I would enjoy some glimpses of his private pain.

WJL: I would, too.

JEH: I doubt that. You're a voyeur, not a sadist, and I suspect that you'll never reconcile your old crush on Bobby.

WJL: Yes, Sir.

JEH: Lyndon Johnson finds him difficult to
reconcile. Many of his advisors think he should
include him on the fall ticket, but he hates the Dark
Lad too much to succumb.

WJL: I understand how he feels, Sir.

JEH: Yes, and you disapprove, in your uniquely non-
disapproving way.

WJL: I'm not that complex, Sir. Or that compromised
in my emotions.

JEH: You delight me, Mr. Littell. I will nominate
your last statement for Best Falsehood of 1964.

WJL: I'm honored, Sir.

JEH: Bobby may run for Kenneth Keating's Senate
seat in New York.

WJL: If he runs, he'll win.

JEH: Yes. He'll form a coalition of the deluded and
morally handicapped and emerge victorious.

WJL: Is he maintaining his work at Justice?

JEH: Not vigorously. He still appears to be shell-
shocked. Mr. Katzenbach and Mr. Clark are doing most
of his work. I think he'll resign, in a timely
fashion.

WJL: Is he monitoring the agents for the Warren
Commission?

JEH: I haven't discussed the investigation with
him. Of course, he receives summaries of all my field
agents' reports.

WJL: Edited summaries, Sir?

JEH: You are frisky today. Impertinent might
describe it better.

WJL: I apologize, Sir.

JEH: Don't. I'm enjoying the conversation.

WJL: Yes, Sir.

JEH: Edited summaries, yes. With all contradictory
elements deleted to conform to the thesis we first
discussed in Dallas.

WJL: I'm happy to hear that.

JEH: Your clients should be, as well.

WJL: Yes, Sir.

JEH: We can't send your plant in again. You're
certain?

WJL: Yes, Sir.

JEH: I mourn the missed opportunity. I would like
to hear a private assessment of King Jack's death.

WJL: I suspect we'll never know, Sir.

JEH: Lyndon Johnson continues to share his thoughts
with me, in his inimitably colorful manner. He has
said, quote, It all came out of that pathetic little
shithole, Cuba. Maybe it's that cocksucker with the
beard or those fucking lowlife exiles, unquote.

WJL: A lively and astute analysis.

JEH: Mr. Johnson has developed a distaste for all
things Cuban. The exile cause has succumbed to
factionalism and has scattered to the wind, which
pleases him no end.

WJL: I share his delight, Sir. I know many people
who were seduced by the cause.

JEH: Yes. Gangsters and a French-Canadian chap with
homicidal tendencies.

WJL: Yes, Sir.

JEH: Cuba appeals to hotheads and the morally
impaired. It's the cuisine and the sex. Plantains and
women who have intercourse with donkeys.

WJL: I have no fondness for the place, Sir.

JEH: Mr. Johnson has developed a fondness for
Vietnam. You should inform Mr. Hughes. Some military
contracts may be coming his way.

WJL: He'll be delighted to hear that.

JEH: You should inform him that I'll keep you
abreast of the Justice Department's plans in Las
Vegas.

WJL: I'm delighted to hear that.

JEH: On a need-to-know basis, Mr. Littell. As is
the case with all our transactions.

WJL: I understand, Sir. And I neglected to thank
you for your help in the Tedrow matter. Dwight Holly
was determined to do the boy some harm.

JEH: You deserve an accolade. You bypassed Wayne
Senior very effectively.

WJL: Thank you, Sir.

JEH: I understand that he has asked you to lunch.

WJL: Yes, Sir. We haven't scheduled yet.

JEH: He thinks you're weak. I told him that you are
a bold and occasionally reckless man who has learned
the value of restraint.

WJL: Thank you, Sir.

JEH: Dwight feels quite ambivalent. He got the job
he wanted, but he's developed quite a dislike for
Wayne Junior. My sources in the U.S. Attorney's
Office tell me that he is determined to bypass Senior
and do Junior some harm in the long run.

WJL: Despite his friendship with Senior?

JEH: Or because of it. You never know with Dwight.
He's quite the provocateur and the rogue, so I indulge
him.

WJL: Yes, Sir.

JEH: The same way I indulge you.

WJL: I caught the implication, Sir.

JEH: You dislike Dwight and Wayne Senior, so I'll
give you added cause. Their fathers belonged to the
same Klan Klavern in Indiana. That said, I should add
that it was probably more genteel than the Klan groups
currently marauding down south.

WJL: I'm sure they never lynched any Negroes.

JEH: Yes, although I'm certain they would have
enjoyed it.

WJL: Yes, Sir.

JEH: Most people have entertained the notion. You
must credit their restraint.

WJL: Yes, Sir.

JEH: You might discuss the Indiana Klan with Bayard
Rustin. I want you to make another donation.

WJL: I'll bring it up, Sir. I'm sure he'll
acknowledge it as a genteel institution.

JEH: You are assuredly frisky today.

WJL: I hope I haven't offended you, Sir.

JEH: Anything but. And I hope I haven't offended
you with Junior.

WJL: Sir?

JEH: I had to throw Dwight Holly a bone. He wanted
Junior expelled from the LVPD, so I arranged it.

WJL: I assumed that you had, Sir. The newspapers
were kind, though. They said he resigned.

JEH: Did you befriend Junior to get at his files? For Mr. Hughes' sake?

WJL: Yes, Sir.

JEH: I'm sure that Senior will enjoy Junior's expulsion. They have an odd relationship.

WJL: Yes, Sir.

JEH: Good day, Mr. Littell. I've enjoyed this conversation.

WJL: Good day, Sir.

35

(Las Vegas, 2/7/64)

THE LINCOLN GLEAMED. New paint/new chrome/new leather.

The car jazzed him. The car distracted him. He kept seeing Lynette. Flaps and sheared ribs. Durfee's knife severed bone.

Pete cruised. Pete tried gadgets. The lighter worked. The heater worked. The seats reclined.

Vegas looked good. Cool air hits mountains and sunshine. Secure-the-Vote Day—one down so far.

He muscled Webb Spurgeon. He explained stat-rape statutes. He detailed consent laws. Spurgeon gulped. Spurgeon kowtowed. Spurgeon pledged votes.

All good so far. One down—two to go.

Pete drove by Monarch Cab. Pete got electrified. Dollar signs boogied and bipped.

Cabs peeled in. Cabs peeled out. Cabs refueled. Drivers ate pills. Drivers drank lunch. Drivers palmed waistband gats.

Monarch Cab. *Maybe:* Tiger Kab redux.

A cash base. A racket hub. Bent personnel. Monarch as Tiger—hold that heady thought.

Pete cruised. Pete meandered. Pete hit West LV. Pete checked out that vacant lot.

There's the trailer. The paint's gone. The shell's cracked. The siding's all scorched.

A kid walked up. Pete jollied him. The kid sermonized.

The trailer smell bad. That be wrong. Somethin' dead be inside. This dude torch it. The stink go. He burn the stink out. No cops come. No firemen. Somethin' dead *still* be in there.

The kid buzzed off. Pete scoped the trailer. A breeze kicked up. The trailer creaked. Paint chips cracked and blew.

Pete cruised. Pete meandered. Pete drove south. Pete hit Duane Hinton's house.

He parked. He walked up. He knocked on the door. He pulled out Wayne's snapshot.

There's a fat whore bound and gagged. She's sucking a handball.

Hinton opened the door. Pete flashed the photo eye-level.

Hinton plotzed. Pete grabbed his hair. Pete raised one knee. Pete broke his nose up.

Hinton went down. Bones cracked. Cartilage blew.

Pete decreed:

Vote our way. Do not touch whores. Do not hurt whores. Do not kill whores—OR I'LL KILL YOU.

Hinton tried to talk. Hinton gagged. Hinton bit through his tongue.

36

(Little Rock, 2/8/64)

DEVOTED WIFE. SCHOOLTEACHER. Loving daughter.

The preacher ran on. The casket sat ready. Lakeside Cemetery: cheap burials and segregated plots.

The Sprouls wore black. Janice wore black. Wayne Senior wore blue. The Sprouls stood alone. Wayne stood alone. Daddy Sproul watched him.

Soldier boy. Yankee. She was seventeen. You wooed her. She killed your baby. You made her do it.

Loving spirit. Sacred child. Blessed in Christ's name.

The service was short. The casket was cheap. The plot was low-rent. The Tedrows shipped the body home. The Tedrows lost control.

Lynette despised religion. Lynette loved movie stars and John Kennedy.

A chauffeur stood around. A Negro man. Tall like Wendell Durfee.

The preacher braced Wayne pre-service. The preacher counseled him.

I feel your loss. I know your grief. I *understand*.

Wayne said it: "I'm going to kill Wendell Durfee."

God's will. The ides of fate. Snatched in her prime.

The plots adjoined Central High. He met Lynette there. Soldiers and rednecks. Negro kids scared.

The chauffeur stood around. The chauffeur filed his nails. The chauffeur wore a hair net. He had Durfee hair. He had Durfee skin. He had Durfee's lank frame.

Wayne watched him. Wayne retouched his hair. Wayne retouched his skin. Wayne made him Wendell D.

The preacher prayed. The Sprouls wept. The Tedrows stood calm. The chauffeur buffed his nails.

Wayne watched him.

He burned his face. He smashed his teeth. He fed him Big "H."

37

(Las Vegas, 2/9/64)

THE DI COUNT ROOM.

Money—coin bins and hampers stuffed. A swivel spy-camera hooked up.

Your host—Moe Dalitz.

The count men were out. The camera was off. Money sat waist-high. Littell sneezed—the fumes were bad—sting off cash dye and tin.

Moe said, "It's not that complicated. The count guys are in cahoots with the camera guys. The camera goes on the fritz, accidental on purpose, so the count guys can get the skim out and retally it. You don't need a college education."

Mesh hampers—laundry-size. Forty hampers/forty grand per.

Moe dipped in. Moe snagged ten grand—C-notes all.

"Here, for your civil-rights deal. What's their fucking motto, 'We Shall Overcome'?"

Littell grabbed the cash. Littell packed his briefcase.

"The skim interests me."

"You are not alone in that. Certain Federal agencies have been known to be curious."

"Are you looking for couriers?"

Moe said, "No. We use civilians, exclusive. Squarejohns who owe casino markers. They run the skim and pay off their debts at $7\frac{1}{2}$% of the transport."

Littell shot his cuffs. "I was thinking of Mr. Hughes' Mormons, or other trustworthy ones, at a 15% rate."

Moe shook his head. "I don't like to fuck with success, but I'll hear you out anyway."

Littell sneezed. Moe supplied a Kleenex. Littell wiped his nose.

"You're going to sell Mr. Hughes some hotels. He'll want his Mormons or *some* Mormons to run them. You'll want your men, you'll compromise, you'll want to escalate your skim operations."

Moe twirled a dime. "Don't be a cock tease. You've got this tendency to string things out."

Littell hugged his briefcase. "I want to enlist some Mormons, over time, and have them ready by the date you sell Mr. Hughes the hotels. You'd have a pool of potential inside men with skim experience."

"That's not enough inducement to pay 15%."

"At face value, no."

Moe rolled his eyes. "So, lay it out. Jesus Christ, don't make me coax you."

"All right. Mr. Hughes' people travel on Hughes Aircraft charter flights. I could hire some Mormons to work for Mr. Hughes now, and you could ship the skim bulk and avoid airport security risks."

Moe flipped the dime. Moe caught it heads-up.

"At face value, I like it. I'll talk to the other guys."

"I'd like to get started soon."

"Take a breather. Don't wear yourself out."

"I'm sure that's a good tip, but I'd—"

"Here's a better one. Bet Clay over Liston. You'll make a fucking mint."

"Is the fight fixed?"

"No, but Sonny's got some very bad habits."

Littell flew to L.A.

He flew solo. He booked a Hughes plane. The Hughes fleet moored in Burbank. Cessna Twins—six seats each—ample skim space.

The flight ran smooth. No clouds and desert sparkling up.

Moe took the bait. Moe missed the dodge. Moe thought the dodge was pro-Drac. Wrong—the dodge was pro-civil rights.

Call it:

Bagmen. Potential "casino consultants." *Hughes* men. All charter-flight cleared.

He could skim off the skim. He could feed Bayard Rustin. He could blunt Mr. Hoover's damage. Wayne Senior ran Mormon thugs. Wayne Senior knew bagmen types. *He* could coopt them.

The long-term goal: damage abatement.

Mr. Hoover filmed Dr. King. Mr. Hoover tried to entrap him. Mr. Hoover dirt-fed his "correspondents": congressmen/reporters/clergymen.

Mr. Hoover schooled them. Mr. Hoover taught them restraint. Let's collude and leak covert data. Let's leak it smart. Don't leak *strict* bug-and-tap data. Don't jeopardize bug-and-tap mounts.

Mr. Hoover held dirt. Mr. Hoover leaked dirt. Mr. Hoover caused pain. Mr. Hoover hated Dr. King. Mr. Hoover exposed his one weakness:

Sadism. *Sustained*. Inflicted over TIME.

TIME worked two ways. There was TIME to inflict harm. There was TIME to countermand the effects.

The skim plan might work. The skim plan sparked a question: Hughes money—a potential tithe source?

The plane banked. Littell pared an apple. Littell sipped coffee.

Pete had Wayne's files. Pete squeezed Spurgeon and Hinton. Spurgeon fed Pete some dirt. Key legislators and their pet charities—dirt per their philanthropy.

Pete said he bypassed Eldon Peavy. Peavy was cop-sanctioned. Peavy might balk at threats. Pete was disingenuous. Pete's threats *worked*. Pete craved Monarch Cab. Pete was gauging a takeover shot.

The plane dipped low. Burbank showed sunshine and smog.

He'd lunched with Wayne Senior. Wayne Senior praised him—you saved my son.

Junior declined Senior's help. Junior rebuffed his connections. Junior nixed good job offers. Junior nixed work in chemistry. Junior sought his own work. Junior found low-end employment.

The Wild Deuce Casino—night bouncer—6:00 to 2:00 A.M. The Deuce was rough. The Deuce welcomed Negroes. Junior welcomed pain.

Wayne Senior bought Littell's lunch. Wayne Senior made nice. Wayne Senior said ugly things.

Wayne Senior derided the civil-rights movement. Wayne Senior brought up the King film.

Littell smiled. Littell made nice. Littell thought *I will make you all pay.*

Jane said, "I got a job."

The terrace was cold. The view compensated. Littell leaned on the rail.

"Where?"

"Hertz rent-a-car. I'm doing the books for the West L.A. branches."

"Did your Tulane degree help?"

Jane smiled. "It got me the extra thousand a year I asked for."

She used hard vowels. She eschewed slurs. She dropped her southern drawl. She'd reworked her voice and diction—he just noticed it.

She said, "It feels good to rejoin the work force."

Hard *g*'s. Regionless. Pure consonants.

Littell smiled. Littell popped his briefcase. Littell pulled out six sheets.

He landed. He drove to Hughes Tool. He stopped at the bookkeeping pool and stole forms.

Invoices. Bill sheets. All standard paper.

He got in. He got out. He shaped his upcoming lie.

"Would you look at these when you get a chance? I need your advice on a few things."

Jane scanned the sheets. "They're all boilerplate. Cost-outs, overruns, that kind of thing."

Hard *b*'s and *p*'s. Lazy *o*'s deleted.

"I want to discuss embezzling techniques and how to use these forms. There's going to be a buildup in Vietnam, and Mr. Hughes will probably be awarded some contracts. He's afraid of embezzlements, and he asked me to study up."

Jane smiled. "Did you tell him your girlfriend's an embezzler?"

"No. Just that she keeps a good secret."

"God, the way that we live."

Short *a*'s and *e*'s. Crisp inflections.

Jane laughed. "Have you noticed? I gave up my accent."

* * *

Jane read in bed. Jane dozed off early. Littell played his tapes.

He got crazy. Two times of late. He ran two crazy risks.

He passed through D.C. He wired Doug Eversall. He squeezed him. He cajoled him. He paid him five G's.

Eversall taped Bobby. Two more times total—two crazy risks. Eversall balked then. Eversall cut Littell off.

That's it. Shove your threats. I refuse to hurt Bobby. You're sick. You're fucked up. Bobby's your sickness.

Littell retreated:

That's it. No more. I promise you. I'll lie to Carlos. I'll say we failed.

Eversall walked then. Eversall tripped. His high shoe buckled and slid. Littell helped him up. Eversall slapped him. Eversall spat in his face.

Littell played the 1/29 tape. Low static/spool hum.

Bobby planned trials. Eversall took notes. Bobby yawned and digressed. His potential Senate run. The VP spot. That "cornpone son-of-a-bitch Lyndon Johnson."

Bobby had a cold. Bobby waxed profane. LBJ was a "dipshit." Dick Nixon was a "numbnuts" with a "kick-me sign." Mr. Hoover was a "psycho fruitcake."

Littell pressed Rewind. The tape reversed. Littell played the 2/5 tape.

Here's Bobby—reverent now.

He toasted Jack. He quoted Housman: "To an Athlete Dying Young." Eversall sniffled. Bobby laughed—"Don't go soft on me."

A new man spoke. Static fizzed his words. Littell heard his garbled "Hoover and King."

Bobby said, "Hoover's scared. He knows King's got balls like J.C."

38

(Las Vegas, 2/10/64)

MONARCH ROCKED.

The noon rush/mucho calls/ten cabs out. The hut rocked— Eldon Peavy had guests.

Sonny Liston. Four bad-boy jigs. Conrad & the Congoites or Marvin & the Mau-Maus.

Pete watched.

He dipped his seat. He ran the heat. He did arithmetic. Peavy had twenty cabs. Peavy ran three shifts. Add airport runs and deadheads.

The hut rocked. A driver hawked fur coats. The Mau-Maus mauled them. Sonny fanned a roll. Peavy peeled bills off.

The Congoites capered. They fondled fur. They manhandled mink. They chewed up chinchilla.

Sonny looked bad. The Clay fight boded. Sonny had the odds. Sam G. demurred. Sam liked Clay. Sam said Sonny had habits.

It was cold. Brrr—Vegas winters. Pete shivered and goosed the heat.

Texas was cold. Florida ditto. He just got back from his trip. He didn't find Hank K. He didn't find Wendell Durfee. He traveled alone. He schemed a trifecta.

Plan A: Find and clip Hank. Plan B: Detain Durfee. Plan C: Bring Wayne in to kill him.

No tickee/no washee. No find/go seek.

He got back. He called Ward. He pitched him: I want to buy Monarch Cab. Ward nixed it. Ward said don't bid. Ward said don't extort ownership.

We *need* Peavy. We need his *votes*. Don't scotch his gaming-board status. Sage fucking advice—Ward Littell-style.

Pete skimmed the radio. Pete watched the hut. Peavy quaffed gin. The Mau-Maus quaffed scotch-and-milk. Sonny dumped capsules. Sonny made lines. Sonny sniffed powder up.

Peavy walked out. Sonny strolled with him. The Congoites conga'd. They slurped milk. They grew white goatees. Spooks called scotch-and-milk "pablum."

A stretch pulled up. The crew piled in. The stretch pulled out. Pete tailed it slow.

The stretch hooked west. The stretch stopped quick. There—the Honey Bunny Casino.

Peavy got out. Peavy walked in. Pete idled back. Pete scoped the window.

Peavy hit the chip cage. Peavy bought play chips. The cage man filled a sack. Peavy walked out. Peavy jumped in the stretch. The stretch pulled out fast.

Pete tailed it. It cut west. It stopped mucho quick. There—
Sugar Bear Liquor.

Five whores ran out—darkies all—prom gowns and heels.

They piled in the stretch. They huffed hard. The windows
fogged up. The stretch wiggled and bounced.

Said whores *worked*.

The axle scraped. The shocks creaked. The undercarriage
shimmied. Two hubcaps popped off and rolled.

Pete laughed. Pete fucking roared.

The whores piled out. The whores giggled and wiped their
lips. The whores waved sawbucks.

Pete flashed on the dead whore. Pete smelled the torched
trailer.

The stretch pulled out. Pete tailed it. They cut west. They hit
West Vegas. They went in *waay* deep. There—Monroe High
School.

The back gate was down. The bleachers were packed. A banner read: Welcome Champ!

Full house:

Colored kids—two hundred strong—this big schoolday
treat.

The stretch parked on the football field. Pete idled by the gate.
Pete kicked his seat back.

Sonny got out.

He weaved. He waved the chip sack. He faced the kids and
swayed blotto. The kids cheered. The kids chanted "Sonny!"
Some geek teachers watched.

The kids yelled. The kids banged their seats. The teachers
guuulped. Sonny smiled. Sonny swayed. Sonny said, "Pipe
down."

The kids cheered. Sonny swayed. Sonny yelled: "Shut up, you
punk motherfuckers!"

The kids shut up. The teachers cringed. Sonny dished
inspiration.

Study hard. Learn good. Don't rob no liquor stores. Play to
win and go to church. Use Sheik-brand rubbers. Watch me whup
Cassius Clay. Watch me kick his punk Muslim ass back to Mecca.

Sonny stopped. Sonny bowed. Sonny pulled a flask. The kids
cheered. The teachers clapped demure.

Sonny waved his sack. Sonny grabbed play chips. Sonny tossed
them wide.

The kids snatched them. The kids snared them. Kids bumped kids. Kids reached short. Kids fell on kids below.

Sonny tossed chips—big wads—dollar chips all. Kids reached high. Kids toppled. Kids engaged in fistfights.

Sonny raised his flask. Sonny waved bye-bye. Sonny jumped in the stretch.

The stretch pulled out. Pete U-turned and tailed it. Kids shrieked Champ bye-bye!

The stretch hauled. Pete hauled up close. They tore speed limits. They cut east and south. They hit downtown Vegas.

Traffic snarled. The stretch looped Fremont. The stretch braked and stopped.

There—

A parking lot. An army-navy store—Sid the Surplus Sergeant.

The crew piled out. The crew yukked and huddled. The crew piled in the backdoor. The driver waved—adios, Mau-Maus—the stretch vamoosed.

Pete parked. Pete locked his car. Pete dawdled and ambled up. Pete braced the backdoor.

He ambled in. He cut through a storeroom. He pushed through peacoats on racks. He saw crates/cartons/trench tools. He caught a cosmoline stench.

He hit a hallway. He heard sounds. He followed titters and love grunts—aaooooo!

He ambled. He tracked the noise. He crouched and crept. He saw a cracked door and peeked in.

Stag-flick time. A bedsheet screen and a projector. Lez antics—young girls entwined.

The Mau-Maus tittered. Peavy yawned. The girls ran fourteen tops. Sonny cracked a red devil. Sonny powdered a palm. Sonny sniffed the shit up.

The girls strapped on dildoes. A donkey appeared. El Burro wore *diablo* horns.

Pete walked outside. Pete found a pay phone. Pete called the Stardust book. He placed a bet—forty grand—Clay over Liston.

The Deuce rolled low—nickel slots/bingo/shots-and-beer.

The dealers wore sidearms. The bar served jar brew. The cocktail chicks whored. The Deuce pandered low. You had old-sters and wetbacks. You had more spooks than Ramar of the Jungle.

The lounge supplied a floor view. Pete lounged and sipped club soda. Pete watched the floor show.

A geez pulls his air tube. He's ninety-plus. He smokes a Camel. He hacks blood. He sucks oxygen. Two fruits lock eyes. Said fruits strut green shirts. Green shirts are fruit semaphore.

Two jigs lurk. They're snatch-and-run guys. Dig their gym shorts and sneakers. Wayne walks up. Wayne wears a belt sap. Wayne wears handcuffs.

He taps the jigs. They share a look—woe-is-fuckin'-me.

Wayne slaps them. Wayne kicks them. Wayne grabs their conk napes and shoves them. They get the picture. They evict themselves—We Shall *Not* Overcome.

Pete clapped. Pete whistled. Wayne turned and saw him. He walked up. He swiveled a chair. He nailed a floor view.

Pete said, "I didn't find him. I think he's down in Mexico."

"How hard did you look?"

"Not that hard. I was looking for a guy in Florida, mostly."

Wayne flexed his hands. Knuckle cuts oozed.

"We could teletype the *federales*. They could put out their own APB. We could pay them to hold him for me."

Pete lit a cigarette. "They'd kill him themselves. They'd lure you down there, steal your money, and kill you."

Wayne watched the floor. Pete tracked his eyes. There—one coon/one whore/unruly shit pending—

Wayne stood up. Pete grabbed his belt. Pete yanked him back down.

"Let it go. We're having a conversation."

Wayne shrugged. Wayne looked aggrieved. Wayne looked fucking deprived.

Pete glanced around. "Does your father own this place?"

"No, it's Outfit. Santo Trafficante has points."

Pete blew smoke rings. "I know Santo."

"I'm sure you do. I know who you work for, so I've put that much of Dallas together."

Pete smiled. "Nothing happened in Dallas."

A whore walked by. Wayne drifted. Wayne watched the floor. Pete grabbed his chair. Pete jerked it and centered it. Pete killed the floor view.

"Look at me when I talk to you."

Wayne made fists. His knuckles popped. His knuckles seeped.

Pete said, "Don't use your hands. Use your sap if you have to."

"Like Duane Hint—"

"Can it, all right? I've had dead women up to here."

Wayne coughed. "Durfee's good. That's the part that gets me. He's stayed ahead of everyone since Dallas."

Pete chained cigarettes. "He's not good, he's lucky. He came to Vegas like a dumb bunny, and moves like that will get him dropped."

Wayne shook his head. "He's better than that."

"No, he's not."

"He can give me up for Moore."

"Bullshit. It's his word versus yours and no body."

"He's good. That's the part . . ."

A spook walked by. Wayne eyeballed him. He saw Wayne and blinked.

Pete coughed. "Who owns Sid the Surplus Sergeant?"

Wayne said, "A clown named Eldon Peavy. He named it after some queer buddy of his who died from the syph."

Pete laughed. "He's showing smut films there. Underaged kids, the whole shot. How big a bust is that on his end?"

Wayne shrugged. "The State Code's soft on possession. He'd have to manufacture and sell the films, or coerce and suborn the kids."

Pete smiled. "Ask me why I care."

"I know why. You want to buy out Monarch and relive your fucking Miami adventures."

Pete laughed. "You've been talking to Ward Littell."

"Sure, client to lawyer. I asked him why you take so much shit from me, but he wouldn't give me an answer."

Pete cracked his knuckles. "Bet on Clay. Your boy Sonny needs more time in the gym."

Wayne flexed his hands. "There's a Sheriff's Vice guy named Farlan Moss. He investigates businessmen for people who want to take over their action. He won't fabricate, but if he gets incriminating evidence, he'll turn it over to you and let you use it any way you like. It's an old Vegas strategy."

Pete grabbed a napkin. Pete wrote it down: "Farlan Moss/ CCSD."

Wayne twirled his sap. "You've got this weird thing for me."

"I had a kid brother once. Someday I'll tell you the story."

* * *

The Bondsmen vamped. Barb grabbed the mike. She curtsied. Her gown hiked. Her nylons stretched.

Pete sat ringside. A geek had Wayne's seat. Wayne worked late now. Wayne caught Barb haphazard.

Ward said he talked to Wayne Senior. Senior ragged on Junior. Ward passed it on.

Junior was a hider. Junior was a watcher. Junior lit flames. Junior torched. Junior lived in his head.

Barb blew a kiss. Pete caught it. Pete covered his heart. He made two T's—their private signal—do "Twilight Time."

Barb caught it. Barb cued the Bondsmen. Barb kicked the tune off.

He missed her for days on. They kept diverse hours and slept diverse shifts. They stashed a cot backstage. They made love between shows.

It worked. *They* worked. It wrecked him. It *scared* him.

Barb watched the news. Barb tracked the Warren thing. Barb nursed Dallas. Barb nursed her link to Jack.

She never said it. He just *knew*. It wasn't sex. It wasn't love. "Awe" said it all. You killed him. The fix held. You killed him and walked.

He played *his* version. "Fear" said it all. You've got her. You could lose her—per Dallas.

You sweat Fear. You ooze Fear. You test the Fear logic. You know you walked because:

It was *that* big. It was *that* audacious. It was *that* wrong.

You test the logic. You fret it. You show fear. You scare people. You pass your fear on. The wrong people find you and knock.

Barb worked "Twilight Time." Barb caressed the low notes.

Wendell Durfee knocked. Lynette paid. Dead women scared him. Lynette as Barb. Lynette as "Jane."

He saw Lynette's body. He had to. The picture stuck. He conjured it. He banished it. He dreamed it and tore the sheets up.

Barb kissed off "Twilight Time." Barb did the Mashed Potato. Barb did the Swim.

The spell died. Her fast tunes deep-sixed it. A waiter schlepped a phone up.

Pete cradled it. "Yeah?"

A man said, "Carlos wants to see you."

"Where?"

"De Ridder, Louisiana."

* * *

He flew to Lake Charles. He cabbed to De Ridder. It was wet. It was hot. The heat spawned bugs.

De Ridder was Shit City. Fort Polk stood close. The town lived off Army handouts.

Chicken-fried-steak joints and rib cribs. Beer bars/tattoo parlors/nudie-mag stalls.

Carlos limo'd up. Pete met him. The local crackers watched. *Dumb* crackers—gap-mouthed bug-magnets all.

They drove east. They caught red clay and pine bluffs. They looped the Kisatchee Forest.

Pete raised a screen. Pete cut the driver off. Vents pumped cold air in. Dark tint killed the sun.

Carlos bankrolled a camp—forty Cubans total—would-be killer ops. Carlos said, "Let's see my boys." Carlos said, "Let's talk."

They drove. They talked. They passed Klan klonklaves. Carlos ragged the Klan—they hate Catholics—that means they hate *us*.

Pete nixed him—I'm Huguenot—you fucks fucked my kin.

They talked. They rehashed *la Causa*. Tiger Kab and Pigs. LBJ's big walkoff. Carlos brought a bottle. Pete brought paper cups.

Carlos said, "The Outfit's got zero affection for the Cause. Everyone thinks, 'We shot our wad, we lost the casinos, it's spilled milk under the bridge.'"

They hit a rut. Pete spilled X.O.

"Havana was beautiful. Vegas can't hold a candle."

"Littell's got a foreign-casino plan. Everyone's gaga, as well they fucking should be."

They passed Army trucks. They passed signs. Signs ragged the ACL-*Jew*.

Pete said, "The old crew was good. Laurent Guéry, Flash Elorde."

Carlos nodded. "Good narcotics men and good killers. You never doubted their sincerity."

Pete dabbed his shirt. "John Stanton was a good ops man. You had the Outfit and the Agency together."

"Yeah, like that song. 'For one brief shining moment.'"

Pete crushed his cup. "Stanton's in Indochina?"

"Don't be such a Frenchman. They call it Vietnam now."

Pete lit a cigarette. "There's a cab biz in Vegas. I could turn it into a moneymaker for us. Littell wants me to hold off, because the owner's on the license boards."

Carlos sipped X.O. "Don't work so hard to impress me. You're not Littell, but you're good."

The troops snapped to. Pete paced the line. Pete came to critique and review.

Forty Cubanos—porkers and stringbeans—jail recruits all.

Guy Banister recruited them. Guy knew a cop in John Birch. The cop fudged his jail sheets. The cop freed prospects. Said prospects were pervs. Said prospects were "musicians"—Cugie Cugat manqués.

Pete walked the line. Pete checked guns. M-1s and M-14s—dead bugs chambered in.

Barrel dust. Mildew. Moss rot.

Pete got pissed. Pete got a headache. The head geek paced the line behind him.

An Army stupe—Fort Polk trash—some kiddie kommando. He ran a Klan klique. He ran a still. He sold oat mash. He supplied alcoholic Choctaws.

The troops sucked poodle dick. The camp ditto.

Quonset huts and pup tents—fucking Boy Scout stock. A "Target Range"—scarecrows and tree stumps. An "Ammo Dump"—made from Lego logs.

The troops snapped to. The troops shot a salute. They fumbled their rifles. They fired off-sync. Eight bolts jammed up.

They made some noise. They roused some birds. Birdshit disinterred and fell.

Carlos bowed. Carlos tossed the donation bag. The head geek caught it and bowed.

"Mr. Banister and Mr. Hudspeth will be coming in soon. They're transporting some ordnance."

Carlos lit a cigar. "That my ten grand's paying for?"

"That's correct, sir. They're my chief weapons procurers."

"They're *making money* off my donations?"

"Not in the sense you imply, sir. I'm sure they're not making a personal profit."

Prime "ordnance": One picnic table/one bar-b-que pit.

The geek blew a whistle. The troops hit the range. They fired. They shot low. They missed.

Carlos shrugged. Carlos nursed a grievance. Carlos walked

off. The geek shrugged. The geek nursed hurt feelings. The geek walked off.

Pete walked. Pete checked the range. Pete checked the dump. Pete critiqued the stock.

Two machine guns—old 50s—slack triggers/loose belts. Six flamethrowers—cracked feeders/cracked pipes. Two speed-boats—pull motors —lawn-mower drive. Sixty-two revolvers—corroded and fucked.

Pete found some oil. Pete found some rags. Pete cleaned some .38s up. The sun felt good. The oil deterred mosquitoes. The "troopers" worked out.

They did push-ups. They wrecked their manicures. They huffed and puffed.

He ran *ace* troops. *He* hit Cuba. *He* scalped mucho Reds. *He* killed Fidelistos. *He* went to Pigs. *He* tried to kill Fidel. They should have won. Jack the K. fucked them. Jack paid. *He* paid. It got all shot to hell.

Pete cleaned guns. He swabbed barrels. He dipped butts. He brushed cylinders. He scoured moss rot.

An old Ford pulled in. The paint job screamed RIGHT-WING NUT!

Dig it:

Crosses. The stars & bars. Inverted swastikas.

A trailer bounced behind the Ford. Gun barrels extruded. The Ford brodied. The Ford slid. The Ford grazed the bar-b-que pit.

The Ford stalled and died. Guy B. got out. Hank Hudspeth helped him up. Guy was cardiac red. Guy survived #3. Carlos said his pump was shot.

Guy looked drunk. Guy looked frail. Guy looked diseased. Hank looked drunk. Hank looked strong. Hank looked dead mean.

Guy lugged out hot dogs. Hank dumped steaks and buns. They looked around. They saw Pete. They puckered up.

Hank whistled. Guy hit his horn. The troops shagged ass up.

Hank dumped briquettes. The head geek filled the pit. Guy gas-spritzed it. They built a fire. They torched hot dogs. The troops swamped the trailer.

They whooped. They yanked guns. They dollied them over—full-drum Thompsons/one hundred plus.

Pete grabbed one. The butt was chipped. The drum was jammed. The balance was off.

Shit knockoffs—Jap stock.

The troops stacked the Tommys. Pete ignored them. The pit whooshed. Bugs bombed the chow.

Guy walked to the limo. Carlos got out. Guy hugged him and chatted him up.

The troops lined up. Hank dispensed plates. Pete grabbed a .38. Pete dry-fired it.

Carlos walked up. Carlos said, "I hate drunks." Pete aimed at Guy. Pete dry-shot him—pop!

"I'll clip him. He knows too much."

"Maybe later. I want to see if we can whip these clowns into shape."

Pete wiped his hands. Carlos palmed the gun.

"I got a lead on Hank Killiam. He's in Pensacola."

Pete said, "I'll go tonight."

Carlos smiled. Carlos aimed at Pete. Carlos dry-shot him—pop!

"Betty McDonald's in the Dallas County Jail. She told a cop that she got warned out of town last November. I'm not saying it was *you*, but . . ."

39

(Las Vegas, 2/13/64)

THEY BLEW SKEET. They shot custom guns.

They shot off the back deck.

They shot custom clays. Janice slung them up. She sat below. She caught some rays. She wore a bikini swimsuit.

Wayne Senior scored persistent. Wayne missed fairly wide. He'd fucked up his hand. He beat up on coloreds. It fucked up his grip.

Janice popped a clay. Wayne fired. Wayne missed.

Wayne Senior reloaded. "You're not holding the stock tight enough."

Wayne flexed his hand. He'd fucked it and *re*-fucked it. It stayed fucked all the time.

"My hand's bothering me. I hurt it at work."

Wayne Senior smiled. "On Negroes or assorted riffraff?"

"You know the answer to that."

"Your employers are exploiting your reputation. That means they're exploiting you."

"Exploitation works both ways. If that sounds familiar, I got it from you."

"I'll repeat myself, then. You're overqualified for random vengeance and work as a casino bouncer."

Wayne flexed his hand. "I'm developing some new tastes. You don't know if you disapprove, or if you should take partial credit."

Wayne Senior winked. "I could help you achieve what you want, in an intelligent fashion. You'd have a good deal of latitude for individual action."

Janice moved her chair. Wayne watched her. Her top chafed. Her nipples swelled.

Wayne said, "No sale."

Wayne Senior lit a cigarette. "I've diversified. You figured that out at Christmas, and you've started coming back for visits again. You should know that I'll be doing some *very* interesting things for Mr. Hoover."

Wayne yelled, "Pull!" Janice tossed a clay. Wayne nailed it. His ears popped. His bad hand throbbed.

"I'm not going to hide under a sheet and rat off mail violators, so that you can sell more hate tracts."

"You've been talking to Ward Littell. You're in a vulnerable state, and men like Littell and Bondurant are starting to look good to you."

The sun hit the deck. Wayne squinted it off.

"They remind me of you."

"I won't take that as a compliment."

"You shouldn't."

"I'll say it once. Don't be seduced by lowlifes and thieves."

"It won't happen. I've resisted you for twenty-nine years."

Janice left for golf. Wayne Senior left for cards. Wayne stayed alone at the ranch.

He set up the gun room. He spooled the film in. He *watched*.

Said film ran high-contrast. Black and white skin/black & white stock.

King shut his eyes. King went ecstatic. King preached in Little Rock. He saw him live in '57.

The woman bit her lips. Lynette always did that. The woman had Barb-style hair.

It hurt. He watched anyway. King thrashed and threw sweat.

The film blurred—lens haze and distortion. The skin tones blurred—King went Wendell Durfee-dark.

It hurt. He watched anyway.

40

(Dallas, 2/13/64)

10:00 P.M.—lights out.

The women's tier. Twelve cells. One inmate locked up.

Pete walked in. The jailer went ssshh. A Carlos guy bribed him last night.

One cell row. One side wall. Barred-window light.

Pete walked down. His heart thumped. His arms pinged. His pulse misfired. He swilled scotch outside. The jailer supplied it. He shut down. He fueled up. He carved some will out.

He walked. He grabbed at the cell bars. He anchored himself.

There's Betty Mac.

She's on her bunk. She's smoking. She's wearing tight capris.

She saw him. She blinked. I KNOW him. He warned me last—

She screamed. He pulled her up. She bit at his nose. She stabbed him with her cigarette.

She burned his lips. She burned his nose. She burned his neck. He threw her. She hit the bars. He grabbed her neck and pinned her.

He ripped her capris. He tore a leg free. She screamed and dropped her cigarette.

He looped the leg. He looped her neck. He cinched her. He threw her up. He stretched the leg. He looped a crossbar.

She thrashed. She kicked. She swung. She clawed her neck. She broke her nails. She coughed her dentures out.

He remembered that she had a cat.

41

HE WORKED. He lived on planes. He compartmentalized.

Legal work: appeals and contracts. Money work: embezzlement and tithes.

He honed his lies. He studied Jane. He learned her lie technique. He juggled his commitments.

3/4/64: Jimmy Hoffa goes down. Chattanooga—the Test Fleet case—twelve bribe-proof jurors.

Littell filed appeals. Teamster lawyers filed writs. The Teamsters passed a resolution: We love Jimmy Hoffa. We stand behind him intact.

Jimmy got eight years Fed time. Trial #2 pends. Chicago—Pension Fund Fraud—a probable conviction.

The "real" books were safe. The Boys had them. The fund-book plan would GO.

Littell wrote briefs. Jimmy's men swooned. Littell wrote more briefs. Littell filed more writs. Littell swamped the courts.

Let's stall. Let's keep Jimmy out. Let's stall and delay—three years and up. Drac will own Vegas then. The Boys will own Drac. The fund-book plan will FLY.

He worked for Drac. He wrote stock briefs. Drac hindered him. Drac dodged subpoenas. PI Fred Otash helped.

Otash ran look-alikes—Howard Hughes clones—subpoena men served *them* thus. Otash was capable. Otash had Pete skills. Otash pulled shakedowns. Otash doped horses. Otash fixed scrapes.

Drac stuck to his coffin. Mormons tended him. Drac sucked blood. Drac ate Demerol. Drac shot codeine. Drac made phone calls. Drac wrote memos. Drac watched cartoons.

Drac called Littell frequently. Drac monologued:

Stock strategy/stock margins/the germ plague. Quell all microbes! Quell all germs! Place condoms on doorknobs!

Drac craved Las Vegas. Drac bared his fangs. Drac coveted. Drac gloated. Drac sucked blood.

He babied Drac. He coddled Drac. He bared *his* fangs. He bit Drac back.

Jane helped.

He coaxed assistance from her. He gleaned her expertise. He loved her. She loved him. He called it true. She lied to live. He lied to live. It might serve to undermine his perception.

They lived in L.A. They flew to D.C. They enjoyed work weekends. He wrote briefs. Jane wrote Hertz reports. They toured D.C. and viewed statues.

He tried to show her the Teamster building. She flushed and balked. She was *too* firm. She played him skewed. She was *mock* indifferent.

He flashed back to L.A.—one recent chat.

He said, "I can get you work with the Teamsters." She said, "No." She was intractable. She came off skewed then.

She knew the Boys. She avoided Vegas. The Boys partied there. They discussed it. Jane was oblique. Jane was *mock* indifferent.

The Teamsters scared her. He knew it. She knew he knew. She lied. She omitted. He reciprocated.

He studied Jane. He indulged conclusions. Her real name *was* Arden. She did come from Mississippi. She did go to school in De Kalb.

He was suspicious. She reciprocated.

She viewed some Hughes bill sheets. She studied them. She explained embezzlement detection. She wondered *why* he cared.

He lied. He *used* her. She helped him bilk Howard Hughes.

He stole vouchers. He forged ledgers. He retallied accounts. He rerouted payments. He billed to a dummy account.

His account—Chicago—the Mercantile Bank.

He laundered the money. He cut checks. He tithed the SCLC. Pseudonymous checks—sixty grand so far—more checks en route.

Penance payments. Damage control. Covert ops against the FBI.

He donated Mob money. Mr. Hoover kept tabs. He met Bayard Rustin. He paid him.

Mr. Hoover thought he knew Littell. Mr. Hoover misread his commitments. Mr. Hoover spent phone time with Littell. Mr. Hoover misread his loyalty.

Mr. Hoover talked to his correspondents. Mr. Hoover leaked dirt off bug placements. Mr. Hoover attacked Dr. King.

Newsmen received invective. They rephrased it. They printed it. They obscured the source.

Mr. Hoover talked. Bayard Rustin talked. Lyle Holly talked. They all talked civil rights.

LBJ pushed his big civil-rights bill. Mr. Hoover loathed it—*but:*

Age 70 bodes. Forced retirement bodes. LBJ says, "*Stay* and strut your stuff."

Mr. Hoover gives thanks. That means quid pro quo. LBJ says, "Now fight my Klan war."

Mr. Hoover agrees. Mr. Hoover complies. The New Klan is outré. Mr. Hoover knows it.

The Old Klan moved hate tracts. The Old Klan burned crosses. The Old Klan severed balls. Castration was a State crime. Mail fraud was Fed.

The Old Klan rigged postage meters. The Old Klan stole stamps. The Old Klan mailed hate tracts. They thus broke Fed laws.

Their mail content was legal. Their mail methods were fraud. The FBI fought the Old Klan. Their mandate was minutiae. Their anti-Klan credentials were soft.

The New Klan was arson. The New Klan was Murder One. The flash point was Mississippi.

Civil-rights kids converge. "Freedom Summer" descends. The Klan sits ready. New klaverns form. Cops join. Diverse klaverns bond tight.

The White Knights. The Royal Knights. Klextors/Kleagles/Kladds/Kludds/Klokards. Klonklaves and Klonvocations.

Church bombings. Mutilation deaths. Three kids in Neshoba County—missing and presumed dead.

LBJ mandates war. Two hundred agents descend. A hundred for Neshoba—three probable victims—thirty-three agents per vic.

Dr. King visits. Bayard Rustin visits. Bayard Rustin briefs Littell. He checks his atlas. De Kalb adjoins Neshoba. Jane's school is there.

Mr. Hoover was torn. The war vexed him. The war offended him. The war brought the FBI praise. Mr. Hoover took credit—reluctantly. The war disrupted him.

It was outré. It was invasive. It pissed off his klavernite plants. They infiltrated klaverns. They snitched off mail fraud. They were shrill. They were racist. They subscribed to Bureau "Guidelines":

"Acceptable Risk" and "Violence Permitted." "Deniable Actions defined."

Mr. Hoover was torn. The war ripped him up. LBJ bruised his racist aesthetic. He'd fight back. He'd fight Dr. King. He'd rack compensation up.

Mr. Hoover called him. They talked and sparred. Mr. Hoover mocked Bobby.

LBJ hated Bobby. LBJ *needed* Bobby. He might make Bobby his Veep choice. Bobby might seek that Senate seat.

He played his Bobby tapes. It was late-night communion. The tapes woke Jane up sometimes. Jane heard voices in her sleep.

He lied. He said you're not dreaming—I'm playing deposition tapes.

Mr. Hoover tracked Bobby's moves—Bobby the lame-duck AG. Bobby *should* step down. Nick Katzenbach *should* succeed.

Fed heat *might* descend then. Fed heat *might* hit Vegas. Mr. Hoover *might* warn him. The Boys *might* say yes—hire those skim men—Wayne Senior *might* provide said.

He lunched with Wayne Senior—once a month—they played at respect. Wayne Senior foresaw Drac's Vegas. Wayne Senior craved his own bite.

Let's confer. Let's place my Mormons near the Count. Let's bite ol' Drac.

Skim runs *might* work. *He* had his own skim plan. He craved yet *another* tithe source.

Money *owned* him. Money *bored* him. He had money alliances. He formed money bonds. He had one nonmoney friend.

Pete left Vegas—mid-February—Pete returned bereft.

Pete flew to Dallas. Pete flew back. Pete returned with burn scars and a cat. Littell bought the Dallas papers. Littell read back-page squibs.

There—PROSTITUTE DIES IN CUSTODY, SUICIDE RULED.

He called Carlos. He played dumb. Carlos brought it up. Carlos laughed. Carlos said she bit her tongue off.

That meant two down. That meant two at large—Hank K. and Arden-Jane.

Littell talked to Pete. They discussed the safe-house hits. They discussed Arden-Jane.

Pete said, "I won't touch her." Pete meant it. Pete looked sad and weak. He got headaches. He'd dropped weight. He worshiped his cat.

Pete wanted Monarch Cab. Pete hired a PI. The PI surveilled Eldon Peavy. Let's stay useful. Let's revive Tiger Kab. Let's help the Boys out.

Pete had money alliances. Pete formed money bonds. Pete had a new cat. Pete had a kid brother. Wayne Junior *et* Pete.

Les frères de sang. Littell, un conseiller des morts.

Everyone's scared. Everyone saw Big D.

42

(Las Vegas, 2/14/64–6/29/64)

HATE.

It moved him. It ran him. It called his shots. He stayed cool with it. He stayed justified.

He never said NIGGER. They weren't all bad. He knew it and stayed justified. He found the bad ones. They *knew* him. Wayne Junior—he *baaaaaaad*.

He worked the Deuce. He threw hurt. He spared his hands and used his sap. He never said NIGGER. He never thought NIGGER. He never condoned the concept.

He worked double shifts. He stayed double-justified. The owner had rules. The pit boss had rules. Rules ruled the Deuce high and wide.

Wayne had rules. Wayne enforced said. Do not paw women. Do not hit women. Treat whores with respect.

He enforced his rules. He bridged race lines. He enforced his Rule of Intent. He predicted rude acts. He preempted them. He employed all due force.

He tracked THEM. He trailed THEM. He prowled West LV. He looked for Wendell Durfee. It was futile. He knew it. The HATE drew him there.

He got FEAR back. Said FEAR made him *stay*.

Wayne Junior—he baaad. He kill black folk. He whip dark boodie.

The Deuce showed the Liston-Clay fight. THEY attended. THEY shucked. THEY cheered.

He perceived intent. He enforced. He preempted. Some Muslims pushed tracts. He ejected them. He abridged their civil rights.

THEY called him "Junior." It fit. It honored his HATE. It distinguished his HATE from Wayne Senior's.

Sonny Liston passed through. Sonny looked Wayne up. Sonny knew Wayne's story. Sonny said, "You did the right thing." Sonny waxed pissed. Cassius Clay kicked his ass. Fuck all that Muslim shit.

They hit the Goose. They got blitzed. They drew a crowd. Sonny said he knew umpteen niggers. Said niggers prowled Niggerland. They'd shake the nigger trees and find Wendell Durfee.

HATE:

He stole play chips. He cruised West LV. He spread said chips around. He called it tip bait. He paid THEM for help to find HIM.

THEY took the chips. THEY *used* him. THEY spit on the chips and broke them.

It was futile. He knew it.

He bought the Dallas papers. He scanned every page. He got no news on Maynard Moore. He got no news on Wendell Durfee.

He read the papers. Sergeant A. V. Brown got sometime ink. Sergeant Brown worked Homicide.

Sergeant Brown knew he killed Maynard Moore. Sergeant Brown had no proof and no body. Sergeant Brown hated him. Ditto Dwight Holly.

Holly tailed him—spot tails/odd nights. Jaunts through West LV—ten minutes per.

Show tails. Overt tails and grudge tails. Fender-to-fender.

Holly tailed him. Holly knew his Darktown biz. Holly was Fed. Holly was cosmetically pro-Negro. The snuffs fucked Holly up. The snuffs fucked Holly up with Wayne Senior.

They went back. They shared laughs in Indiana. They shared their chaste brand of HATE.

HATE lured them places. HATE lured Wayne to the ranch. He prowled the ranch cyclical. He got the urge and savored it. He picked his entry shots.

Janice leaves. Wayne Senior leaves. He watches them go and walks in. He goes to the dressing room. He smells Janice. He touches her things.

He reads Wayne Senior's files. He reads Wayne Senior's tracts.

The Papal Pipeline. Boat Tickets to the Congo—one-way passage on the Titanic.

The tracts went back to '52. The tracts "probed" Little Rock. The tracts "exposed" Emmett Till. The Little Rock kids spread gonorrhea. Emmett Till raped white girls.

It was bullshit. It was chaste and cowardly HATE.

Wayne Senior lied—"I 'diversified' last year." Bullshit—Wayne Senior pushed *long-term* hate.

HATE tracts. HATE comic boox. HATE primers. The HATE alphabet.

Wayne read Wayne Senior's mail file. Mr. Hoover wrote memorandums. Dwight Holly wrote notes. They were long-term pen pals—from 1954 up.

'54 rocked. The Supreme Court banned school segregation. The Ku Klux Klan rocked anew.

Mr. Hoover rocked. Mr. Hoover deployed Dwight Holly. Holly knew Wayne Senior. Mr. Hoover loved Wayne Senior's tracts. Mr. Hoover collected them. Mr. Hoover displayed them. Mr. Hoover rang Wayne Senior up.

They chatted. Mr. Hoover bored in:

You push hate tracts. *Someone* has to. They're harmless and fun. They appeal to the rural right. The rural right is factional. The rural right is dumb.

You have hate credentials. *You* can help me place plants. We place them in Klan groups. Dwight Holly to supervise. They snitch mail fraud. They scotch your tract rivals. They assist the FBI.

Wayne read file notes. Mr. Hoover wrote. Dwight Holly wrote. Klan klowns wrote komedy. They sucked up to Wayne Senior. They yahooed. They described their *koon*tretemps.

The mail file stopped dead—summer '63. No Fed notes/no snitch notes/no kommuniqués: *Why that? Say what?*

Wayne loved the Fed notes. The Fed-speak glowed: "Felony guidelines." "Acceptable acts to sustain informant credibility."

Wayne loved the Klan notes. The text glistened. The Klan-speak glowed.

Wayne Senior suborned rednecks. Wayne Senior koddled them. They lived on Fed money. They bought corn liquor. They pulled "minor assaults."

One note sizzled. Dwight Holly writes—10/8/57.

Holly praised Wayne Senior. Holly enthused: You toughed it out/you retained your kover.

10/6/57. Shaw, Mississippi. Six Kluxers grab a Negro. Said Kluxers employ a dull knife. They sever his balls. They feed their dogs in front of him. Wayne Senior observes.

Wayne read the note. Wayne read it fifty times. The note taught him this:

Wayne Senior fears you. Wayne Senior fears your HATE. It's unmediated. It's unexploitative. It's unrationalized.

Wayne Senior hated petty. Wayne Senior had a rationale. Wayne Senior tried to shape *his* HATE.

Wayne Senior played him a bug tape. Wayne Senior played it over drinks. The date: 5/8/64. The place: Meridian, Mississippi.

Civil-rights workers talked—four Negro males. Said Negroes defamed white girls. Said girls were "liberal cooze." Said girls were "punchboards out for black stick."

Wayne listened. Wayne replayed the tape—thirty-eight times.

Wayne Senior ran a Fed film. Wayne Senior ran it over lunch. The date: 2/19/61. The place: New York City.

A folk club/mixed dancing/dark lips and hickeys.

Wayne watched. Wayne replayed the film—forty-two times.

HATE:

He watched THEM. He found THEM. He nailed THEM in crowds. HATE moved him. HATE rejoined him with Wayne Senior.

They talked. Shit densified. Shit cohered and dispersed. Janice talked to him. Janice studied him. Janice touched him more. She dressed for him. She cut her hair. She wore a Lynette do.

Lynette lost him. She knew it. She knew Dallas cut her loose. He ran from her. He hid out. He carried sex in his head.

Janice and Barb. Snapshots from the ranch. Postcards from the lounge.

His house fucked with him. Wendell Durfee kicked the door in. Lynette died there.

He dumped the bed. He stripped the paint. He peeled the bloodstains. It wasn't enough.

He sold the house. He took a loss. He indulged a spree. He hit the Dunes and shot dice.

He won sixty grand. He rolled all night. He blew the whole stake. Moe Dalitz watched him. Moe bought him morning pancakes.

He moved to Wayne Senior's guest house. He installed a phone. He logged bullshit tips and built a tip file.

He dug his two rooms. He dug on his view. Janice strolled. Janice changed clothes. Janice chipped balls out her window.

He lived in the guest house. He played at the Sultan's Lounge. He met Pete there. They watched Barb and socialized.

Pete introduced him. He blushed. They hit the Sands. They sipped frosty mai tais. They talked. Barb got tipsy and riffed on sex extortion. Barb said, "I worked JFK."

She stopped—looks traveled—looks dispersed wiiiiiiide. Barb knew about Dallas. The looks said, "We all do."

That was March. Pete and Barb were back from Mexico. Pete and Barb were tan.

They flew to Acapulco. They flew back weird. Pete was thin. Barb was thin. Pete had lip scars. They had a cat—a stripedy tom—they loved his scraggly ass.

Wayne called Ward Littell. Wayne said, "What's up with Pete?" Wayne dropped Pete's "kid brother" line. Ward explained it all:

Pete killed his brother. Pete botched a hit. Pete killed François B. accidental. That was '49. Wayne was fifteen then. Wayne lived in Peru, Indiana.

Pete got phone calls. Pete left Vegas. Wayne met Barb for lunch. They talked. They hashed neutral topics. They eschewed Pete's work. They talked up Barb's sister in Wisconsin. They talked up her Bob's Big Boy franchise. They talked up Barb's lowlife ex.

Barb teased him. Barb saw him with Janice. He copped to his sixteen-year crush.

Pete trusted him. Pete gauged his Barb crush. Pete tagged it kid stuff. Barb was great. Barb made him laugh. Barb pulled his eyes off of THEM.

He pressed Pete—find me *real* work—Pete dodged his requests. He pressed Pete on Dallas—give me more details—Pete dodged his full press.

He said, "Why are you so fucked up and stoked on a cat?"

Pete said, "Shut up." Pete said, "Smile more and hate less."

43

(Dallas/Las Vegas/Acapulco/New Orleans/
Houston/Pensacola/Los Angeles,
2/14/64–6/29/64)

HE FOUND THE cat. He relocated him. The cat dug Vegas. The cat dug the Stardust Hotel.

The cat dug their suite. The cat dug room-service chow. Barb fucking shit. Who fucking body-snatched you?

You flew off. You flew back. You came home undone. You don't eat right. You don't sleep right. You *shudder.*

He did all that. He chain-smoked too. He gnashed his teeth. He drank himself to sleep. He reran one nightmare:

Saipan, '43. Japs. Roads rigged with slice cords. Jeeps pass by. The cords hit. Heads topple clean.

He got headaches. He popped scotch. He popped aspirin. Bedtime scared him. He read books. He watched TV. He messed with the cat. His arms pinged. He pissed more. His feet got numbed up.

He fought it. He flew to New Orleans. He rigged a slice cord. He staked Carlos out. He thought it through. He ran Yes and No lists. The Nos won in a walk.

Don't do it. The Boys would kill Barb—just for a start.

They'd kill Barb's mother. They'd kill Barb's sister. They'd kill the clan Lindscott worldwide.

He flew back to Vegas. He found a cat-sitter. Barb took a week off. They flew to Acapulco. They got a cliffside suite. They watched spics dive for tourist chump change.

He carved some nerve. He sat Barb down. He told her EVERYTHING.

François and Ruth Mildred Cressmeyer. Each and every paid hit. Betty Mac. The noose on the crossbars. Her nails at her neck.

He spilled facts. He spilled names. He spilled numbers. He spilled details. He spilled new Dallas shit. He spilled on Wendell D. and Lynette.

Barb ran.

She packed her bag. She ran from him. She moved out. He tried to stop her. She grabbed his gun. She aimed at him flush.

He backed off. She ran. He got drunk and studied the cliff. The drop ran six hundred feet.

He ran up. He swayed. He ran up ten times. He ran up sober and drunk. He punked out ten times. He dipped and caught himself. He stopped on pure lack of guts.

He scored some red devils. He slept through whole days. He dungeoned the bedroom up. He ate pills. He slept. He ate pills. He slept. He woke up and thought he was dead.

Barb was there. She said, "I'll stay." He cried and tore the bed up.

Barb shaved him. Barb fed him soup. Barb talked him off pills and cliff drops.

They flew to L.A. He saw Ward Littell. Ward knew about Betty. Carlos had bragged the job up.

They made plans. They schemed precautions. Ward was smart. Ward was good. Ward made an Arden a Jane.

Shit looked all new now. Ward said he understood. Vegas looked new—hard hues and hot weather.

He scored on the Clay fight. He cat-proofed the suite. He banked a six-digit roll. The cat dug the suite. The cat perched. The cat pounced. The cat killed wall mice.

Pete called Farlan Moss. Moss worked Sheriff's Vice. Moss entrapped fruits and whores with panache. Pete hired him. The job: Sift dirt on Monarch Cab and Eldon Peavy.

Moss said he'd do it. Moss promised full disclosure. Moss promised results.

Carlos called Pete. Carlos eschewed Betty talk. Carlos made nice.

"Pete, I hope you swing Monarch. I'd love to buy in for some points."

Pete said, "No." Betty Mac hovered. Carlos said, "Let's wait on Hank K."

Pete said, "Okay." Pete sat and waited. He shitcanned the scotch. His sleep improved. His nightmares lulled off.

He palled with Wayne. He palled with the cat. He spot-checked Monarch. He *drooled*. He called Fred Otash. He called his cop pals. They ran bulletin checks.

Wendell Durfee—where you be? Wendell be *nowhere*.

He got restless. He drove to Big D. Betty Mac hovered and laid down ghost tracks. He checked around. He checked the DPD file. He got no Durfee leads and no sightings.

Carlos called him. Carlos said, "Go. Clip Hank Killiam."

Pete drove to Houston. Pete picked up Chuck Rogers. Chuck

lived with his folks. They were dings. They wore Klan sheets to bed.

Pete and Chuck split eastward—Pensacola-bound.

They drove back roads. They dawdled. Chuck talked up Vietnam. John Stanton was there now. The CIA was in deep. Chuck knew a Saigon MP—a cat named Bob Relyea—ex-prison guard/ ex-Klan.

Chuck talked to Bob. They enjoyed shortwave chats. Bob extolled Vietnam nonstop. It was *hot*. It was groovy. It was Cuba on Meth.

Chuck talked Cuba—*Viva la Causa!*—Pete ragged the De Ridder "troops." They agreed—fuck Hank Hudspeth and Guy B. in the neck. They drank too much. They talked too much. They sold bad guns.

The South was wild—spring rains and big voodoo.

They drove through Louisiana. They bunked at exile camps. Chuck drilled the troops. Pete cleaned dirty guns.

The troops were substandard. The troops were spic trash. They split Cuba. They migrated. They scrounged right-wing welfare. They lacked balls. They lacked skills. They lacked savoir faire.

Chuck knew all the back roads. Chuck knew rib joints Dixiewide. They cut through Mississippi. They cut through Alabama. They dodged Fed cars. They hit cross burns. Chuck knew sheet boys statewide.

Nice kids—a bit dumb—a bit inbred.

They bunked at Klan kamps. They split at dawn. They passed torched churches. De-churched coons stood by.

Chuck laughed. Chuck waved. Chuck yelled, "Howdy, you-all!"

They hit Pensacola. They staked out Hank K. Hank K. stayed inside. They invaded his pad. They slit his throat. They drove his body around. They dawdled. They cruised to 3:00 A.M. They found a TV-store window.

They tossed Hank in. Hank broke the glass. Hank crashed Zeniths and RCAs.

The Pensacola *Trib*/third column/page 2: BIZARRE SUICIDE. LOCAL MAN DIVES TO DEATH.

Chuck flew to Houston. Pete drove to Vegas. Pete sloughed off Hank K. Hank was male. Hank knew the rules. Hank got no gender relief.

Pete killed time. Pete palled with the cat. Pete palled with
Wayne. They caught Barb's gigs. They sat ringside. Wayne dug
on Barb. Wayne played it straight. Wayne honored women
that way.

6/14/64: Guy Banister dies. It's heart attack #4. Chuck calls.
Chuck gloats. Chuck explicates.

Carlos said, "Kill him." Chuck employed excess digitalis.

Chuck laughed. Chuck said, "Don't be hurt. Carlos wanted
to give you a rest."

DOCUMENT INSERT: 6/30/64.
Confidential Report. From: Farlan D. Moss. Submitted
to: Pete Bondurant. Topic: ''Criminal Activities of
Eldon Lowell Peavy (White Male/46), the Monarch Cab
Business & the Golden Cavern Hotel-Casino/with Index
of Known Criminal Associates.''

Mr. Bondurant,

As promised, my report & attached rap sheet carbons
on Subject Peavy's KAs. As we discussed, please make
no copies and destroy upon reading.

OWNERSHIP & LICENSE/TAX STATUS OF
LEGITIMATELY OWNED BUSINESSES

Subject PEAVY is the sole owner of the Monarch Cab
Company (1st Clark County Licensed 9/1/55), the
Golden Cavern Hotel-Casino (Nevada Gaming Commission
licensed 6/8/57), the ''Sid the Surplus Sergeant''
Store (business license transferred to Subject PEAVY
12/16/60) & the Cockpit Cocktail Lounge in Reno
(Nevada liquor license #6044/dated 2/12/58). (Note:
Said lounge is a homosexual meeting place.) All of
Subject PEAVY's state & local operating licenses are
up-to-date & in good standing, as are his Federal,
state & county (Clark/Washoe) business taxes,
personal taxes, property taxes, workers compensation
fund taxes & his registering of ex-convicts in his
employ. Subject PEAVY (no doubt eager to guard his
reputation & retain his seats on the Nevada Gaming

Control Board & Clark County Liquor & Control Board)
is a scrupulous record keeper & observer of official
business codes.

ILLEGAL ON-SITE ACTIVITIES (PER ABOVE BUSINESSES)

Subject PEAVY's four businesses sustain criminal
enterprises & serve as gathering spots for known
criminals & homosexuals. All four are police-agency
protected, which should serve to hinder you in your
takeover strategy. The Cockpit Lounge (protected by
Washoe County Sheriff's Dept.) is a distribution
point for homosexual pornography (films &
photographs), Mexican-made fetish paraphernalia &
amyl nitrite vials pilfered from the Washoe County
Medical Center. Male prostitutes congregate on the
premises & the pay phones are used as contact points
for a ''Date-A-Boy'' service run by Cockpit
bartenders RAYMOND ''GAY RAY'' BIRNBAUM (white male/
39/see rap sheet index) & GARY DE HAVEN (white male/
28/see index). Subject PEAVY allegedly receives a
percentage of all profits accrued from felonious
enterprises conducted on the Cockpit premises.

The ''Sid the Surplus Sergeant'' Store (521 E.
Fremont) serves as a pick-up point for male
prostitutes working out of the Glo-Ann Motel (604 E.
Fremont) and as a contact point for ''Chicken Hawks''
(older or married homosexual men who prey on young
boys) attempting to instigate assignations. Losing
gamblers & male UNLV students anxious to earn money
congregate in the parking lot & sleep in their cars
there in hope of promoting ''dates.'' The store
manager, SAMMY ''SILK'' FERRER (white male/44/also a
Monarch cab driver/see rap sheet index), permits said
''dates'' to occur in back rooms on the store premises
& often surreptitiously films them thru hidden wall
peeks. FERRER compiles film footage, edits it into
pornographic ''loops'' & sells said ''loops'' out of
the Hunky Monkey Bar, a notorious establishment
catering to ''rough trade'' homosexuals. FERRER &
Subject PEAVY also screen pornographic films

(homosexual & heterosexual content) in back rooms on the premises. This is a recreational activity for Monarch Cab personnel & their favored customers. (Note: Actors ROCK HUDSON & SAL MINEO & ex-heavyweight champ SONNY LISTON are Monarch Cab/ Golden Cavern habitues & frequently view films at ''Sid the Surplus Sergeant.'')

The Monarch Cab Company & its office/dispatch hut (919 Tilden St., N. Las Vegas) is the hub of Subject PEAVY'S illegal (albeit protected) enterprises. Subject PEAVY employs 14 full & part-time drivers, 6 of whom are presumed homosexuals with no criminal records & no outstanding Nevada State traffic warrants. The other 8 (all known homosexuals) are:

The prev. ment'd SAMMY ''SILK'' FERRER; HARVEY D. BRAMS; JOHN ''CHAMP'' BEAUCHAMP; WELTON V. ANSHUTZ; SALVATORE ''SATIN SAL'' SALDONE; DARYL EHMINTINGER; NATHAN WERSHOW & DOMINIC ''DONKEY DOM'' DELLACROCIO. All 8 drivers have extensive criminal records, with offenses inc. sodomy, armed robbery, flim-flam, statutory rape, male prostitution, narcotics possession & dismissed homicide charges (see rap sheet index). DELLACROCIO, BEAUCHAMP, BRAMS & SALDONE also work out of the Golden Cavern Hotel-Casino as male prostitutes. DELLACROCIO (a part-time driver & dancer in the ''Vegas A Go-Go'' show at the New Frontier Hotel) is also a pornographic film actor. DELLACROCIO sometimes recruits other chorus dancers to work as male prostitutes.

Monarch Cab maintains & services illegally placed slot machines in numerous West Las Vegas bars. The operation is overseen by MILTON H. (HERMAN) CHARGIN (white male/53/no criminal record), a non-homosexual & former scandal magazine writer (Lowdown & Whisper magazines), a part-time Monarch Cab dispatcher & Subject PEAVY's on-site ''Executive Officer,'' i.e., the man who imposes order on Subject PEAVY's crew.

All 14 drivers sell prescription pills (Seconal, Nembutal, Tuinal, Empirin-Codeine, Dexedrine, Dexamyl, Desoxyn, Biphetamine) supplied to them by Las Vegas-based doctors. (Said doctors are paying off

gambling markers to local hotel-casinos, as part of a
reciprocal agreement between casino pit bosses &
Subject PEAVY. See Known Associates Index for list of
doctors & casino personnel.)

The drivers sell largely to Negroes in W. Las
Vegas, Mexicans & Nellis AFB enlisted men in N. Las
Vegas, lounge entertainers & Los Angeles-based
homosexual junketeers who use <u>Monarch Cab</u> limousines
for airport pick-ups & reside at the <u>Golden Cavern.</u>
Again, this operation is LVPD & CCSD-sanctioned.

<u>The Golden Cavern Hotel-Casino</u> (1289 Saturn St., N.
Las Vegas) is a 35-room/60-table establishment of the
''Grind Joint'' variety. It is properly licensed &
run & caters to ''low-roller'' tourists & gamblers.
Subject PEAVY & his on-site manager, RICHARD ''RAMROD
RICK'' RINCON (also a part-time pornographic film
actor) retain six detached bungalows as ''Party'' or
''Orgy Pads'' for visiting homosexuals, who are
supplied with male prostitutes, exotic liquors,
take-out food, room projectors, pornographic films &
the prev. ment'd illegal prescription pills, along
with amyl nitrite and marijuana. Numerous movie & TV
stars are frequent bungalow residents, inc. DANNY
KAYE, JOHNNIE RAY, LIBERACE, WALTER PIDGEON,
MONTGOMERY CLIFT, DAVE GARROWAY, BURT LANCASTER,
LEONARD BERNSTEIN, SAL MINEO, RANDOLPH SCOTT & ROCK
HUDSON. A favored male prostitute of the above is
driver/dancer/pornographic film actor DOMINIC
''DONKEY DOM'' DELLACROCIO. <u>The Golden Cavern</u> is
well-known in the homosexual underworld &
reservations are frequently secured through
''Middlemen'' who habituate local homosexual bar-
tryst spots such as the <u>Klondike, the Hunky Monkey,
the Risque Room & the Gay Caballero.</u>

PORNOGRAPHIC FILM BUSINESS OF ELDON PEAVY

Subject PEAVY has placed himself in his greatest
business-takeover jeopardy through his funding of
and participation in a pornographic film racket with
origins in Chula Vista, California (a border town) &

Tijuana, Mexico. The racket is implemented by Tijuana policemen who employ & frequently coerce underaged girls to ''act'' in them, along with male actors (of adult age) & animals used in live Tijuana stage shows. The girls are primarily runaways from California & Arizona & I have identified six of them from viewings of the films & comparisons to photographs on Missing-Persons bulletins. The girls ID'd (MARILU FAYE JEANETTE/14; DONNA RAE DARNELL/16; ROSE SHARON PAOLUCCI/14; DANA LYNN CAFFERTY/13; LUCILLE MARIE SANCHEZ/16 & WANDA CLARICE KASTELMEYER/14) appear in a total of 87 films shot in Tijuana & sold via telephone mail-order by prev. ment'd PEAVY known-associate SAMMY ''SILK'' FERRER (Note: these are the films shown at the ''Sid the Surplus Sergeant'' Store).

The films are both hetero & homosexual in content. Prev. ment'd known associate RICHARD ''RAMROD RICK'' RINCON appears in the homosexual films ''Ramrod Man,'' ''Ramrod Boy,'' ''Ramrod King,'' ''Ramrod Stud,'' ''Naughty Ramrod'' & ''Ramrod Rams It Home.'' Prev. ment'd KA DOMINIC ''DONKEY DOM'' DELLACROCIO appears in the homosexual films ''Greek Man,'' ''Back-Door Man,'' ''Hung Man,'' ''Big Dick Man,'' ''12-Inch Man,'' ''Moby Dick Man,'' ''Moby Dick's Delight,'' ''Moby Dick Misbehaves,'' ''Moby Dick's Greek Vacation'' & ''Moby Dick Meets the 69 Boys.''

The films are shot on 8-millimeter film stock & shipped to ''Sid the Surplus Sergeant'' from the main Chula Vista post office. Prev. ment'd KA SAMMY ''SILK'' FERRER receives & stores the films at his apt. (10478 Arrow Highway, Henderson) & ships them from the Henderson P.O. (See index for list of films, Chula Vista & Henderson ship dates & names & addresses of recipients.)

In conclusion, I believe that ELDON LOWELL PEAVY is indictable on a total of 43 Nevada State, California State, Arizona State & Federal charges pertaining to his suborning & exploitation of minor children, his transporting of pornographic material & his conspiring to distribute lewd & lascivious products.

(See attached mimeograph copies of applicable penal code sections & Fed. statutes.)

Again, please read & destroy.

44

(Neshoba County, 6/30/64)

THE AC DIED. Littell dipped his window.

He drove I-20. He passed Fed cars. He passed camera vans.

Klan kars tailed them. Said kars sported decals. "AYAK" meant "Are You A Klansman?" "AKIA" meant "A Klansman I Am."

He'd called Mr. Hoover. He'd mentioned his trip. Mr. Hoover approved.

"A salutary idea. You can meet with Bayard Rustin and observe 'Freedom Summer' in the flesh. I would be delighted to hear your perceptions, minus your pro-Negro views."

He brought twenty grand. Ten for Bayard Rustin/ten for some Cuban exiles. Pete scored on Clay-Liston. Pete had his own tithe.

It was hot. Bugs bombed the car. Klan kars blew by. Klan klods sneered at him. Klan kooks flipped him off.

He looked Fed. That made him a ten-ring. He brought his gun along—safety first.

Lyle Holly called him in Vegas. Lyle Holly stressed caution. Lyle Holly ragged his planned trip.

Don't do it. You look Fed. The Klan hates you. The whites hate you. The lefties hate your guts.

Littell passed Bogue Chitto Swamp. Littell saw drag-line crews. The kids were dead. Lyle said so. Mr. Hoover said some Choctaws found their car.

It vibed Klan. Mr. Hoover was pissed. We'll martyr the kids now. We'll shit on states' rights.

Littell drove I-15. Littell skimmed the radio. Nut preachers preached. It's a lie. It's a hoax. Them kids are holed up in Jew York.

He'd talked to Moe Dalitz. Moe braced all the Boys. They okayed the Hughes charter plan. That meant more money—another tithe source.

Traffic stalled. Gawkers lined the roadway. Fed cars crawled. News vans crawled. Folks rubbernecked.

State troopers and crackers. Housewives and toddlers in sheets. They flashed hand signals—kall it Klan kode—konfidential konversation.

Littell jumped lanes. Littell veered hard right. There—a cross off the road. A *used* cross—last night's business—gauze on scorched wood.

A crowd gawked the totem. Feds and Negroes. Snow-cone vendors sans sheets.

There's Bayard Rustin—spiffed in a seersucker suit.

Bayard saw him. Bayard waved. Bayard walked over. A man tossed an egg. A man tossed a snow cone. They nailed Bayard flush.

They parked. They viewed a torched church.

The church was razed. The church was molotoved. Tech crews bagged bomb debris.

Littell tithed Bayard. Bayard briefcased the money. Bayard watched the techs.

"Should I be encouraged?"

"As long as you understand that it's Lyndon Johnson's doing."

"Mr. Hoover's been talking a good game."

The sun was way high. Bayard wore egg yolk and slush.

"He wants hate and resentment sustained at what he considers the proper level, and coming down on the Klan gives him a mainstream cachet."

Bayard drummed the dashboard. "Let me ask you a question. Lyle said you have some expertise."

"All right."

"Here's the situation. Martin and Coretta enter their hotel room and want to make sure their friend Edgar hasn't gotten there first. Where do they look for bugs and what do they do when they find them?"

Littell slid his seat back. "They look for small wires with perforated metal tips extending from picture frames and lampshades. They speak innocuously until they determine that there are none, and they do not pull the ones that they find, because it would anger their friend Edgar and cause him to escalate his actions against Dr. King, who is making great strides while Edgar slowly builds a file against him, because Edgar's greatest weakness is implementing institutional sadism at a sedate pace."

Bayard smiled. "Johnson's signing the Civil Rights Bill next week. Martin's going to Washington."

Littell smiled. "That's a case in point."

"Any other advice?"

"Yes. Keep your people out of areas where the Regal and Konsolidated Knights operate. They're full of mail-fraud informants, they're almost as bad as the White Knights, and the FBI will never investigate anything that they do."

Bayard popped the passenger door. The handle burned him.

Littell said, "I'll have more money soon."

The party went late.

He stayed late. He *had* to. The town exiled him. Desk clerks sized him up. Desk clerks saw his suit and gun. Desk clerks said, "No vacancy."

The party was a wake. Guy Banister—*mort*. The camp was gulfside. The Cubans perched on four acres.

Their landlord was Klan. Maynard Moore's Klarion Koalition. They were pro-exile. They spelled "Cuba" with a K. Carlos bankrolled the site. Pete passed through last spring. Pete said the troops needed work.

Littell toured the grounds. Littell dropped off Pete's tithe. Littell chucked his coat and kicked sand.

A bunkhouse. A speedboat. A Klan/exile range. Straw-man targets with cartoon faces: LBJ/Dr. King/Fidel "Beard" Castro.

A gun hut. Stacked flamethrowers. Bazookas and BARs.

The exiles were gracious—he knew Big Pete. The Klan boys were rude—he wore a Fed suit.

The sun went down. The sand dunes launched fleas. The wet air launched mosquitoes.

Bottles traveled. Toasts went up. Klansmen rigged hibachis. They served hot dogs. They overcooked. They flamethrower-broiled.

Littell played wallflower. Guests bopped by. Littell made their reps:

Hank Hudspeth—Guy's pal—kook in mourning. Chuck Rogers clipped Guy. Guy's heart attack was assisted.

Laurent Guéry and Flash Elorde—Pete's right-wing confreres. Mercs/Dallas backup/late of Pete and Boyd's team.

Laurent was ex-CIA. Laurent clipped Patrice Lumumba. Flash clipped untold Fidelistos.

The Loop. Open secrets. Things you *just knew.*

Laurent dropped hints: *Monsieur Littell, nous savons, n'est-ce pas, ce qui s'est passé à Dallas?*

Littell smiled. Littell shrugged—*Je ne parle pas le français.* Laurent laughed. Laurent praised *"le pro shooter."*

Le pro était un français. Jean Mesplède, qui est maintenant un "merc" à Mexico City.

Littell walked off. Guéry made him nervous. Littell stopped and ate a hot dog. It was bad. It was overcooked. It was flame-thrower-broiled.

Littell played wallflower. Littell watched the party. Littell read news magazines. The Civil Rights Bill/the conventions/Bobby's shot at Veep.

The party wore on. Hank Hudspeth blew a tenor sax. The Cubans blew cherry bombs.

Pete loved *la Causa.* The Cause anchored. The Cause justified. The Cause always condoned. They shared a dilemma—penance and tithe. He knew it. Pete didn't.

Littell tried to sleep. The Cubans sang songs. Cherry bombs blew.

De Kalb adjoined Scooba. De Kalb adjoined Neshoba County.

The drive took five hours. The heat sapped his car. De Kalb fit Jane's description.

A main drag. Feed stores. Segregated shade. Whites on the sidewalk/Negroes in the street.

Littell drove through town. Negroes looked down. Whites looked straight through him.

There—the school. Jane's description etched pure.

Bungalows. Walkways. Poplar trees. Pseudo-Quonset huts.

Littell parked. Littell checked his notes. The registrar was Miss Byers—in Bungalow 1.

Littell walked. Littell followed Jane's route. The bungalow fit Jane's description.

One counter. File chutes behind it. One woman—scarves and pince-nez.

The woman saw him. The woman coughed.

"It's a hoax, you want my opinion."

Littell wiped his neck. "Pardon me?"

"Those boys in Neshoba. They're sipping cool ones in Memphis right now."

Littell smiled. "Are you Miss Byers?"

"Yes, I am. And you're an agent with the Federal Bureau of Invasion."

Littell laughed. "I need information on an old student. She would have attended classes in the late '40s."

Miss Byers smiled. "I've been here since this place was chartered in 1944, and in some ways the postwar years were the best we ever saw."

"Why was that?"

"That's because you had those rowdy GI Bill boys, and some girls just as rowdy. We had a girl who became a drug addict and two girls who became traveling prostitutes."

"This girl's name was Arden Smith or Arden Coates."

Miss Byers shook her head. "We've never had an Arden here. It's a pretty name, I would have remembered it. I've been the sole registrar of this institution, and my memory hasn't failed me yet."

Littell checked the chutes. Littell saw year-dated tabs. One chute per year/'44 up.

"Are your student files alphabetized?"

"They certainly are."

"Are student photographs included?"

"Yes, sir. Clipped to the very first page."

"Have you had teachers here named Gersh, Lane, and Harding?"

"Had and have. Teachers who come tend to stay."

"Could I look through the files?"

Miss Byers squinted. "First, you tell me that this big commotion isn't just a hoax."

Littell said, "The boys are dead. The Klan killed them."

Miss Byers blinked. Miss Byers blanched. Miss Byers pushed up the counter. Littell stepped through. Littell pulled the '44 chute.

He checked the first file. He studied the layout. He saw first-page photos and class lists. He saw last-page notes: Job referrals/placements/general postscripts.

Jane knew the school. Jane attended—or knew those who did.

Littell pulled chutes. Littell checked files. He read names. He checked photos. He worked from '44 up. No Ardens/no Jane pix/no Coateses or Smiths.

He read files. He reread files. He went back to '44. He wrote names down. He checked postgrad notes.

Miss Byers watched. Miss Byers kibitzed. Littell jotted names.

Spark points. References. Jane might mention names. Jane dropped names routinely. Jane buttressed her lies. Jane sketched vivid scenes.

Marvin Whitely/'46—a bookkeeper now. Carla Wykoff—a state auditor.

Littell pulled the '47s. Aaron/Abelfit/Aldrich/Balcher/Barrett/Bebb/Bruvick. Lowly jobs. Prosaic appointments. Construction firms/feed stores/labor stewardships.

Richard Aaron married Meg Bebb. Aldrich stayed in De Kalb. Balcher caught lupus. Barrett worked in Scooba. Bruvick moved to Kansas City. Bruvick joined the AF of L.

Littell checked files. Littell wrote names. Miss Byers kibitzed.

Bobby Cantwell got shingles. The Clunes sisters went chippy. Carl Ennis spread head lice. Gretchen Farr—Satan with bangs. A hophead and worse.

Littell stopped. His knees gave out. His pen ran dry.

Jane built whole worlds. Jane lied past their limits. Jane eclipsed him at lies.

Miss Byers said, "I still think it's a hoax."

45

(Las Vegas, 7/2/64)

BAD HEAT—pure Vegas.

Wayne cranked the AC. Wayne chilled down the room. Wayne clipped an update:

The Dallas *Morning News*—6/29—DPD CONCEDES DEATH OF MISSING POLICEMAN.

He filed the clip. He scanned his corkboard. He saw Lynette on a morgue slab. He saw a blow-up of Wendell D.'s prints.

Glossy shots all—plus some FBI pix.

The nude Dr. King. Nude and plump. Nude with a blonde in the sack.

Wayne pulled the drapes. Wayne killed the sun. Wayne killed his Janice view. Janice dressed for the heat now. Janice wore all-day bikinis.

Wayne checked his drawers. Wayne tallied weapons—throw-down shit all. Six shivs/eight pistols/one sawed-off shotgun.

He worked the Deuce. He disarmed punks. He stole their shit. He saved it to plant on Durfee. Janice loved it. Janice called it his hope chest.

He checked his tip file. He'd tallied ninety-one tips. All bull-shit/all jive.

Cars pulled up outside. Doors slammed. The carport boomed loud. Your host—Wayne Senior.

Another hate-tract "summit meet." His "biggest and best"—self-described.

Ten meets in ten days. Fund meets and "summits." Tract-distributor drives. Let's fuck civil rights. Let's laud *states'* rights. Let's push more tracts. Mr. Hoover wants speed. Mr. Hoover wants wide distribution.

Wayne Senior told Wayne that. Wayne Senior spieled EVERYTHING. Wayne Senior torqued his HATE.

He held back. *He* observed partial disclosure.

He saw Fed cars. He saw Fed surveillance. Feds perched down the road. Feds watched the meets. Feds checked license plates.

Local Feds—*non*-FBI—Dwight Holly's boys.

Wayne Senior was distracted. Wayne Senior was tract-obsessed. Wayne Senior missed the heat. Wayne Senior talked. Wayne Senior torqued Wayne. Wayne Senior worked to impress.

Wayne Senior knew Ward Littell now. Wayne Senior bragged it up: "Littell needs some help. I might be planting some of my people in the Hughes organization."

Wayne called Littell last week. Wayne warned him: Wayne Senior will fuck you—and Dwight Holly's acting up.

Wayne cleaned his knives. Wayne cleaned his guns. Wayne stacked shotgun shells. Janice walked in. Janice was pool-wet. Janice smelled like Coppertone and chlorine.

Wayne tossed her a towel. "You used to knock."

"When you were a boy, I did."

"Who's he got today?"

"The John Birch people. They want him to change the print style on the fluoridation tracts, to distinguish them from the racier stuff."

Her tan was uneven. Her swimsuit rode low. Some black hair showed.

"You're dripping all over my rug."

Janice toweled off. "Your birthday's coming up."

"I know."

"You'll be thirty."

Wayne smiled. "You want me to say, 'And you'll be forty-three in November.' You want to know if I'm keeping track of those things."

Janice dropped the towel. "Your answer satisfied me."

Wayne said, "I don't forget things. You know that."

"The things that count?"

"Things in general."

Janice scoped out the corkboard. Janice scoped M. L. King.

"He doesn't look like a Communist to me."

"I doubt if he is."

Janice smiled. "He doesn't look like Wendell Durfee, either."

Wayne flinched. Janice said, "I have to go. I've got bridge with Clark Kinman."

The Deuce was dead. Dead occupancy/dead slots/dead tables.

Wayne prowled.

He walked. He perched. He tailed Negroes. He announced his intent and deterred. They ran from him. They ignored him. They played it cooooool.

The shift dragged. *He* dragged. He sat by the teller's cage. He cranked his stool up.

A Negro walks in. He's got a brown bag. He's got a jug. He hits the slots. He drops some dimes. He hits some baaaaad luck.

Forty pulls and no payoffs—righteous baaaad luck.

The guy whips his dick out. The guy urinates. The guy sprays the dime slots. The guy sprays a dykey-ass nun.

Wayne walked over.

The guy laughs. The guy breaks his jug. Glass flies. Wine shvitzes. The nun Hail Marys.

The guy laughs. I gots me a cutter. It gots a paper-bag grip.

He lunged.

Wayne stepped back. Wayne trapped his arm. Wayne snapped his wrist. The guy puked. The guy dropped the cutter.

Wayne kicked him prone. Wayne kicked his teeth in. Wayne knee-dropped him.

46

(Las Vegas, 7/6/64)

ELDON PEAVY VIBED butch. Eldon Peavy vibed mean queen.

3:10 A.M.

The hut was dead. Peavy worked solo. Pete walked right in. Peavy hinked. Peavy reached. Peavy was *très* slow.

Pete blocked the desk. Pete yanked the drawer out. Pete grabbed the gun.

Peavy regrouped. Peavy showed savoir faire. He dipped his chair. He raised his feet. He stroked Pete's thighs.

"Tall, dark, and vicious. My type to a T."

Pete popped the clip. Pete popped the shells. They bipped and flew.

Peavy smirked. "Want to audition? Kept man or geisha boy, you call it."

Pete said, "Not tonight."

Peavy laughed. "Hey, he speaks."

The desk phone rang. Peavy ignored it. He wiggled his feet. He toe-crawled. He nuzzled Pete's thighs.

Pete lit a cigarette. " 'The film racket is implemented by Tijuana policemen, who employ and frequently coerce underaged girls.' "

Peavy wiggled his toes. "Shit, you had my hopes up. You know that song? 'Someday he'll come along, the man I love.' "

Pete turned out his pockets. Pete pulled out two hundred G's—new K-notes all.

He dropped said money. He grabbed Peavy's feet. He dropped them desk-adjacent.

"We need your Gaming and Liquor Board votes, and you get to keep a 5% interest."

Peavy pulled a comb. Peavy puffed his spitcurl.

"I know shakedowns and legal forceouts intimately, so go to the next step and say you'll blow up my cabs."

Pete shook his head. "If I go to the next step, you lose the 5%."

Peavy flipped Pete off. Pete yukked. Pete showed him three pix.

Rose Paolucci: in church. Rose Paolucci: blowing a bull mastiff. Rose Paolucci with her uncle—John Rosselli.

Peavy smirked—tee-hee-hee—Peavy focused in.

He went pale. He popped sweat. He tossed his dinner. He doused the switchboard. He soaked the phone. He grabbed the money wet.

Pete snagged the Rolodex. Pete grabbed Milt Chargin's card.

They met at Sills' Tip-Top. They talked shit. They noshed pancakes.

Milt was hip. I'm a comic. I gig local. Call me Mort Sahl unchained.

Milt knew Fred Otash. Milt knew Pete's rep. Milt dug the scandal-rag days. Milt knew Moe D. Milt knew Freddy Turentine. Freddy bugged fag pads for *Whisper*.

Pete leveled. Pete said I bought Monarch. Pete said I need your help now.

Milt was glad. Monarch was a fruit bowl. Monarch was a fruit cocktail. You need *some* fruits. The fruit biz rocks. You *don't* need a froufrou aesthetic.

Pete quizzed Milt. Milt leveled.

He eschewed the fruit scene. He eschewed the smut scene. He eschewed the froufrou aesthetic. He said he'd stay on. He made some suggestions.

Peavy owns the Cavern. That homo hut hops. Let's junket the fruits to and fro. Let's be careful. Let's be cool. Let's live with *some* froufrou aesthetics.

They talked shit. They discussed Peavy's gigs. Some to eschew/some to enhance/some to revise.

Pete quizzed Milt. Pete said strut your stuff—play Mr. Vegas insider.

"I'm on the Strip, and I want to get laid for a hundred. Where do I go?"

"Try Louis at the Flamingo. He runs a fuck pad on the premises. You get an around-the-world for a C-note."

"Suppose I want dark stuff?"

"You call Al at the chambermaids' union. It's good trim, if you don't mind shtupping in a mop closet."

"Who do I avoid?"

"Larry, at the Castaways. He runs drag queens in the guise of real women. The rule of thumb is, 'Don't trust what won't disrobe.'"

"Suppose I want a three-way with two lezzies?"

"Go to the Rugburn Room. It's a dyke den by day. Talk to

Greta, the barkeep. She'll set you up with two femmes for fifty. She'll take pictures and give you the prints and negatives for an extra twenty. You know, souvenirs."

"Sonny Tufts. What's the story on him?"

"He bites showgirls on the thighs. The girls get rabies shots when they hear he's in town."

"John Ireland?"

"Whip-out man with an eighteen-inch schlong. He goes to nudist retreats and plies his trade. He creates lots of excitement."

"Lenny Bruce?"

"Junkie and snitch for the L.A. County Sheriff's."

"Sammy Davis Jr.?"

"Switch-hitter. He digs tall blonds of both persuasions."

"Natalie Wood?"

"Lez. Currently shacked with a WAC major named Biff."

"Dick Contino?"

"Muff-diver and gamble-o-holic. In hock to the Chicago Cartel."

"The best lounge show in Vegas?"

"Barb & the Bail Bondsmen. You think I don't know which side I butter my bread on?"

"Name me one Mormon fat cat. You know, the 'Mr. Big' type."

"How about Wayne Tedrow Senior? He's a dreck merchant with oodles of gelt. His kid killed three shvoogs and walked on the beef."

"Sonny Liston?"

"Drunk, hophead, whore chaser. Pal of the aforementioned shvoog-killer Wayne Tedrow Junior. Jesus, don't get me going on Sonny."

"Bob Mitchum?"

"Grasshopper."

"Steve Cochran?"

"Rival to John Ireland's crown."

"Jayne Mansfield?"

"Shtupping the world."

"Which local cab company handles the men in the State Legislature?"

"Rapid Cab. The State guys have an account."

"What about the top guys at Nellis?"

"Ditto on Rapid. They've got some good fucking accounts."

"Are they Outfit-connected?"

"No, they're just schmucks who play by the rules."

Pete smiled. Pete bowed. Pete displayed ten grand. Milt spilled his coffee. Milt burned his hands. Milt said, "Craaaaazy."

Pete said, "That's your signing bonus. You're my new intelligence man."

DOCUMENT INSERT: 7/14/64.
Verbatim FBI telephone call transcript.
Marked: ''Recorded at the Director's Request''/
''Classified Confidential 1-A: Director's Eyes Only.''
Speaking: Director Hoover, Ward J. Littell.

  JEH: Good morning, Mr. Littell.

  WJL: Good morning, Sir.

  JEH: Describe your southern excursion. I receive updates from my field agents, but I would appreciate a contrasting perspective.

  WJL: Mr. Rustin was happy to receive my donation. He appeared to be pleased about the Civil Rights Bill and praised the Bureau's presence in Mississippi.

  JEH: Did you correct him and say ''forced presence''?

  WJL: I did, Sir. I stayed in character and credited President Johnson.

  JEH: Lyndon Johnson needs wretched people to love him. He is quite undiscerning and promiscuous in his need. He reminds me of King Jack and his lack of discernment with women.

  WJL: Yes, Sir.

  JEH: I do not share Mr. Johnson's need. I have a pet dog who fulfills my desire for unconsidered affection.

  WJL: Yes, Sir.

  JEH: Mr. Johnson and the Dark Prince are determined to make martyrs of those missing youths. The ill-revered Reverend King must feel the same way.

  WJL: I'm sure he does, Sir. I'm sure he sees the boys as Christian symbols.

  JEH: I do not. I cast the State of Mississippi in the martyr's role. Their sovereignty has been abrogated in the name of dubious ''Rights,'' and

Lyndon Johnson has made me a reluctant accomplice.

WJL: I'm sure you'll find ways to make up for it,
Sir.

JEH: I will, indeed. You will help me, and you will
perform your own acts of penance in an unfathomable
and politically suspect manner.

WJL: You know me very well, Sir.

JEH: Yes, and I can decipher your inflections and
determine when you wish to change the subject.

WJL: Yes, Sir.

JEH: I'm listening, Mr. Littell. Ask any question
or make any statement you wish.

WJL: Thank you, Sir. My first question pertains to
Lyle and Dwight Holly.

JEH: Ask your questions. I find preambles boring and
taxing.

WJL: Does Lyle share his SCLC intelligence with
Dwight?

JEH: I do not know.

WJL: Is Dwight formally investigating Wayne
Tedrow, Senior and/or Junior?

JEH: No, although I'm sure he's keeping tabs on
them in his uniquely persistent manner, an activity
which I would be loath to discourage.

WJL: I may be co-opting several of Wayne Senior's
Mormons.

JEH: Into the Hughes organization?

WJL: Yes, Sir.

JEH: Now, or in due time?

WJL: Now.

JEH: Expand your answers, Mr. Littell. I have a
lunch date for the Millennium.

WJL: The work I have in mind is potentially risky,
especially if the Justice Department should go
proactive in Las Vegas.

JEH: I do not dictate Justice Department policy.
The FBI is but one cog in a much larger system, as
Prince Bobby has pointed out to me on several
repugnant occasions.

WJL: Yes, Sir.

JEH: Tell me what you want, Mr. Littell.

WJL: I would like a provisional commitment. If the Mormons incur trouble, you could assess the situation and intercede on their behalf, or use their trouble to put Wayne Senior in your debt.

JEH: Do you want me to offer the Mormons covert protection?

WJL: No, Sir.

JEH: Will you inform Senior and the Mormons of the potential Federal risk?

WJL: The job description carries its own warning. I will not gild the lily beyond that.

JEH: And who will your co-opt strategy benefit?

WJL: Mr. Hughes and my Italian clients.

JEH: Feel free to proceed, then. And feel free to rely on my potential assistance.

WJL: Thank you, Sir.

JEH: Be sure that Mr. Hughes remains convincingly unaccountable.

WJL: Yes, Sir.

JEH: Good day, Mr. Littell.

WJL: Good day, Sir.

47

(Las Vegas, 7/14/64)

GOLF BORED HIM. Wayne Senior insisted—I'm playing the DI.

Littell stood by the drink stand. Littell dodged the heat. Vegas heat scalded. Vegas heat singed.

Some holes ran close. Littell watched the Tedrows play 8. Janice killed Wayne Senior. Janice parred and birdied. Janice drilled shots home.

She moved with grace. She flaunted her gray streak. She moved deft like Jane.

De Kalb scared him. De Kalb taught him:

You welcomed Jane's lies. *You* set up truth points within. *You* rigged the lie game. *You* have no redress.

She trashed his lie aesthetic. She trashed embellishment. She co-opted memories. She furnished her past secondhand.

She lied. She embellished. She codified. He knew her solely

through code. He couldn't brace her honestly—he'd exploited her skills. She taught him to embezzle. She helped him bilk Howard Hughes.

The Tedrows played 9. Janice birdied it. Wayne Senior shot bogey. Janice walked to 10. A caddy met her. Wayne Senior waved to Littell.

He drove his cart up. He brodied on grass. The cart awning made some nice shade.

Littell leaned in. Wayne Senior smiled.

"Do you play?"

"No. I've never enjoyed athletics."

"Golf is more of a business activity. Mr. Hughes could buy you less—"

"I want to co-opt three of your men. I can get them courier work now, and casino work when Mr. Hughes settles here."

Wayne Senior twirled his putter. " 'Courier' sounds euphemistic. Are you describing a security operation?"

"Yes, in a sense. The men would fly Hughes charters to various cities."

"Out of McCarran?"

"I was hoping to run them out of Nellis."

"For added security?"

"Yes. You have friends at Nellis, and I'd be remiss if I didn't try to arrange it."

A caddy yelled "Fore!" A ball dinged the cart.

Wayne Senior flinched. "I've got friends in food service and defense purchasing. General Kinman and I are close."

"Would you call him a colleague?"

"Colleague and conduit, yes. He's told me that Vietnam is about to get hot, and he's one who should know."

Littell smiled. "I'm impressed."

Wayne Senior twirled the putter. "You should be. There's going to be a staged naval event next month, which will help LBJ to escalate the war. Mr. Hughes should know that I know people who know things like that."

Littell said, "He'll be impressed."

"He should be."

"Have you considered my off—"

"What will the couriers be transporting?"

"I can't tell you."

"My men will tell me."

"That would be their decision."

"We're talking about accountability, then."

The awning fluttered. Littell blinked. The sun hit his eyes.

"Your men will be paid 10% of the value of each courier shipment. You can work out your cut at your discretion."

Moe agreed to 15. He could pocket and tithe 5.

Wayne Senior squeezed a golf ball. Wayne Senior chewed on a tee.

Skim.

He *knows* it. He won't *say* it. He'll stay clean. He'll risk his men instead.

Janice walked down 11. Her gray streak swirled. She dropped a ball. She set up. She winged a shot. She hit the cart clean.

Littell flinched. Janice laughed and waved.

Wayne Senior said, "I'm interested."

48

(Las Vegas, 7/15/64)

THE DEUCE WAS dead.

The dealers yawned. The barman yawned. Stray dogs meandered through. They beat the heat. They scrounged cocktail nuts. They scrounged hugs and pets.

Wayne perched by the bar. Wayne nuzzled a Lab mix. The intercom kicked: "Wayne Tedrow. See the pit boss, please."

Wayne walked over. The Lab tagged along. The pit boss yawned. The Lab pissed on a spittoon.

"You remember that colored guy? Ten, twelve days ago?"

"I remember."

"Well, you should, 'cause you broke a whole lot of bones."

Wayne flexed his hands. "It was a deterrent."

"That's your version, but the NAACP says it was an unprovoked assault, and they allegedly got two witnesses."

"You're saying it's a lawsuit."

The pit boss yawned. "I got to let you go, Wayne. They're asking twenty grand from us and the same from you, and they're hinting they might file on you for some other shit you done."

"Cover yourself. I'll take care of my end."

* * *

Wayne Senior loved it. Wayne Senior riffed:

Pay it off—don't call Littell—he's on *their* side.

The deck was hot. The air stung. Fireflies jumped.

Wayne Senior sipped rum. "You disarmed him *and* knee-dropped him. I'm curious about your justification."

"I still think like a policeman. When he broke that bottle, he signaled his intent to hurt me."

Wayne Senior smiled. "You revealed yourself with that answer."

"You're saying I still need a rationale."

"I'm saying you've revised your basis for action. You err on the aggressive side now, which you—"

"Which I rarely did as a cop."

Wayne Senior twirled his stick. "I want to pay off your suit. Will you accept the favor?"

"You can't make me hate them like you do. Will you accept that?"

Wayne Senior flicked a wall switch. Cold air hissed out.

"Am I that predictable a father?"

"In some ways."

"Can you predict my next offer?"

"Sure. It's a job offer. It relates to your quasi-legal union or one of the fourteen casinos you own in violation of Nevada Gaming Commission law."

Cold air swirled. Bugs beat their wings. Bugs evacuated.

"It sounds like you've investigated me."

"I burned my file when I left the PD."

"Your file on your *fath*—"

"You used to run card cheats out of rival casinos. A guy named Boynton and a guy named Sol Durslag, who works for the Clark County Liquor Board. You've got some Nellis guy in your pocket. You're selling pilfered food and liquor to half the hotels on the Strip."

Wayne Senior stretched. "You anticipated my offer. I need someone to run shipments to the hotels."

Wayne counted fireflies. They jumped. They lit up. They fell.

"It's 'yes' to both offers. Don't let it go to your head."

The Rugburn Room:

A hipster hive. Six tables/one stage. A beatnik gestalt.

Milt Chargin employed a duo. They were Miles Davis acolytes. They played bongos and bass sax.

Milt drew a hip crowd. Femme dykes served beer. Sonny
Liston showed and dredged some cheers up.

Sonny hugged Wayne. Sonny sat down. Sonny met Barb
and Pete. Sonny hugged them. They hugged Sonny. Sonny sized
Pete up.

They arm-wrestled. Hipsters bet. Pete won two out of three.

Milt went on. Milt did Lenny Bruce shtick. Lawrence Welk
auditions a junkie. Pat Nixon bangs Lester, the priapic shvoog.

The crowd laughed. The crowd toked maryjane. Sonny
popped dexies. Pete and Barb declined.

Wayne popped three. Wayne got a hard-on. Wayne scoped
Barb sidelong. Wayne grooved on her hair.

Milt did fresh stuff. Milt did "Fucko, the Kids' Show Clown."
Milt blew up condoms. Milt tied them off. Milt tossed them high.

The crowd went nuts.

They snared the condoms. They waved cigarettes. They
popped them—ka-pow!

Milt did Fidel Castro. Fidel hits a fag bar. Jack Kennedy walks
in. Fidel says, "Let's party, muchacho." Jack says, "I'll meet you
at the Bay of Pigs, but you've got to shtup Bobby, too."

Pete howled. Barb howled. Wayne roared.

Milt did Sonny shtick.

Sonny kidnaps Cassius Clay. Sonny dumps him in Mississippi.
The Klan holds him hostage. Martin Luther King goes down.

Marty wears whiteface. Marty digs being white. It's a bold
apostasy. Fuck this negroid shit.

Marty calls God up. God puts J.C. on. J.C.'s a swinger. He's
gigging with Judas and the Nail Drivin' Five.

Marty says to J.C., "Listen, daddy-o, I'm having a crisis of faith
here, I'm doing this revisionist number. I'm starting to think the
white man's got it dicked, he's got all the bread and the white
women and the hi-fi shit, and if you can't beat 'em, assimilate
and stop all this civil-rights shuck-and-jive."

J.C. sighs. Marty waits. Marty waits a looooong time. Marty
waits to hear his life's work affirmed.

J.C. pauses. J.C. laughs. J.C. spiels God's word on high:

NO SHIT, YOU DUMB MOTHERFUCKER!

The crowd cracked up. The room evaporated. Sonny roar-
roar-roared.

Milt did LBJ. Milt did James Dean. Jimmy, the mumble-mouthed masochist. Jimmy, the "Human Ashtray."

Milt did Jack Ruby.

Jack's in the slam. Jack's pissed off and hungry. These *farkakte goyim* jailers don't know from good nova lox. Jack needs some food gelt. Jack breaks out and flogs Israel bonds.

Wayne cracked up. The room incinerated. Pete and Barb roar-roar-roar-roared.

They shared looks. They howled. They roared more. Sonny didn't get it. Sonny dug his shtick more.

Pete took Wayne aside. Pete said, "Let's blow up some cabs."

Rapid Cab was detached. Fourteen cabs/one hut/one lot/one block between.

Pete did the grunt work. Wayne did the chemistry. They worked at Monarch. They worked *très* late.

Pete pumped gas. Pete filled fourteen bottles. Wayne mixed nitrates. Wayne mixed soap flakes. They soaked dunk cords. They soaked feeder cords. They dipped model-kit glue.

Wayne felt giddy. Barb and Dexedrine did it. Barb split from the Rugburn. Barb hugged them. Barb left her scent.

They drove to Rapid. They parked. They cut through the fence. They dollied their shit in.

Fourteen cabs—'61 Fords—snout-to-snout rows. Ground clearance and tank space.

They laid down. They placed the bombs. They looped the cords. They dumped the gas. They soaked a fourteen-car fuse.

Wayne lit the match. Pete dropped it. They ran.

The cabs exploded. Scrap metal flew. The noise hurt. Bursts overlapped.

Wayne ate smoke. Wayne ate fumes. Glass blew across the sky.

49

(Los Angeles, 7/17/64)

THEFT TOOLS—paper/pencils/pen.

Littell worked. Littell cooked Hughes Tool books. He wrote an invoice. He carbon-copied it. He revised a pay sheet.

Jane was asleep. Jane logged early bedtimes. They devised a routine. They stuck to it. They coded their needs.

Jane needed early sleep. He needed seclusion. Jane sensed his need. Jane deferred to it.

Littell switched pens. Littell blotted ink. He hit snags sometimes. He needed Jane's help. He toughed it out then. He kept Jane out. He embezzled solo.

Littell ran figures. Littell tallied accounts. Jane was edgy tonight. Their dinner was tense.

She said her job bored her. She said her co-workers vexed. He threw her a curveball—the Teamsters need help.

Jane declined. Jane declined too fast. Jane laughed too slow.

He described his trip south. He abridged the text. Jane segued and riffed on De Kalb.

Miss Gersh. Miss Lane. The boy with lupus. Miss Byers mentioned said boy. Jane omitted his name from *her* text.

He asked questions. He *played* her. He played off *his* insider's text. Jane brought up Gretchen Farr. Miss Byers brought her up. Gretchen was "Satan with bangs."

Pilfered memories. Stolen reminiscence. Borrowed anecdotes.

Littell yawned. Littell worked. Littell toughed out an invoice glitch—solo.

He played the radio. He caught the news. Pundits concur— Bobby will run in New York.

Littell rubbed his eyes. Columns blurred. Numbers wiggled.

Wayne Senior sent a list—twelve Mormon thugs—all skim candidates. Littell copied Drac. Drac read the list. Drac told *his* Mormons to pick three "casino consultants."

Littell called Drac. Littell lied:

The men will fly Hughes planes. The men will tour "various cities." They'll meet "made men." They'll "form bonds." They'll "work to procure your hotels."

Drac loved it. Drac loved intrigue. Drac said, "*We're* using *them*." Drac approved the Hughes charters. Wayne Senior cleared the Nellis takeoffs.

Skim clearance—the Air Force and the Mob.

Drac waxed deluded. Drac told his Mormons to sidestep Littell. Ward's *my* boy—*he'll* run the consultants.

Littell waxed bold. Littell ad-libbed. Littell revised his skim plan.

I'll exploit Drac's hubris. I'll write fake reports. I'll ghost-write the so-called "consultants." I'll jolly Drac—"*You're* fucking the Mob—the Mob's not fucking you."

Moe D. waxed grateful. Moe revised the skim end. Moe said, "Take 5% off the top."

Thanks, Moe. Thanks for the tithe cash. I don't have to steal it now.

Made men feed the skim. Mormons fly it. Percentages fly. Cash multiplies. His cash. The Mormons'. Wayne Senior's.

It's a ground builder. It's a pump primer. Let's ford the moat. Let's storm Drac's hotels.

Littell cooked his books. Columns wiggled. Dollar signs blurred.

50

(Las Vegas, 7/18/64–9/8/64)

RAPID CAB—*muerto.*

The torch was impromptu. The torch was unsanctioned. He informed the Boys. He informed them post-torch. He stressed his pure motive.

WE need a cab base. WE need dirt. Let's help Drac. Let's accrue dirt. Let's deploy it.

Carlos clapped. Sam G. clapped. Moe blew kiss bouquets.

Pete braced the Rapid dispatcher. Pete greased him. Pete bought his account book. Pete bought his soul. Pete hired him. Pete resigned his accounts. Pete got nine legislators. Pete got Nellis brass and fat cats galore.

Moe fixed the torch. Moe fixed it with LVPD. Arson cops took bribe cash. Arson cops framed a wino.

Moe fixed the Rapid end. Moe fixed it post-torch. Goons fucked up the owner. Goons relocated him to Dogdick, Delaware.

Pete renamed the biz. Dig it—Tiger Kab refortifies. Tiger Kab resurrects.

He sold the old Packards. He bought twenty Fords. He hired dope-addled "artist" Von Dutch.

Von Dutch ate peyote. Von Dutch painted cabs. Von Dutch laid wiiiild upholstery. He painted tiger stripes. He scrolled kustom script. He fashioned mock-tiger-tuft seats.

Pete bought four limos—high-end wheels—Lincoon Coon-tinentals. They had hi-fis and recliner seats. They were mobile fuck pads.

He consulted Milt Chargin. He steam-cleaned the hut. He dumped some fruits. He hired some straight guys. He kicked two drag queens out.

He took Milt's advice—keep Nat Wershow—Nat's smart and butch. Keep Champ Beauchamp. Keep Harvey Brams. Keep Donkey Dom—Dom's a fruit magnet—Dom draws fruit biz.

He called his Teamster contact. He signed the crew on. They got pensions. They got health plans. They paid Teamster dues.

Jimmy H. got points. Jimmy was thrilled. The fruits genu-flected and swished. They got the clap. They got the syph. The Teamsters now paid for their cures.

Pete hired two jigs—Sonny Liston boys. They were good drivers. They were semi-punch-drunk. They were good Brown-town brawn.

Biz was strong. The cash base was strong. No Monarch clients strayed.

Pete ran the hut. Pete worked three shifts. Work drove him. Work drained him. Work killed his bad thoughts.

He lived at the hut. He brought the cat in. The cat chased wall rats. He built a straight john. He kept the fruit john. The straights refused to shit with the fruits.

The straights hated the fruits. The fruits reciprocated. Pete addressed the issue. Pete stressed coexistence. Pete enforced the Law:

No bickering. No fistfights. No factional wars. No sex jive. No queer-straight flirtation.

Both factions kowtowed. Both factions obeyed.

He cut a deal with Johnny R. He got roost rights at the Dunes. He cut a deal with Sam G. He got roost rights at the Sands.

He told the crew: I WANT DIRT.

Quiz hookers. Quiz card dealers. Glom dirt. Glom dirt on celebrity tricks and gamble-o-holics. Accrue dirt. Report dirt to Milt C.

Milt was good. Milt mediated crew complaints. Milt deflected tsuris.

Milt made airport runs. Milt drove famous fruits. Milt drove state legislators. Milt drove them to fuck pads. Milt drove them to dope dens. Milt reported his dirt.

Milt dispersed tip cash. Milt greased bellhops/barkeeps/B-girls. Milt said I WANT DIRT.

Dirt meant leverage. Dirt meant status. Leverage meant juice. Juice for the Boys and Drac Hughes.

Tiger Kab: Dirt Central. The racket hub supreme.

The fruits pulled crimes. The straights pulled crimes. They achieved détente and pulled crimes together. Pete hired drivers off rap sheets. Pete hired drivers off reps. Pete hired bent guys x-clusive.

Pete consolidated. Pete worked two main gigs. Pete worked the pill and slot-machine endeavors.

He dumped the smut gig. He dumped the mule flix. He dumped the T.J. cops. He dumped the smut kids. He leaned on Eldon Peavy. He made him quit making smut.

He hired Farlan Moss. He sent him to T.J. Moss greased the spic cops. Moss shanghaied the kids. Moss sent them home *pronto más*.

Pete stole Peavy's records. Pete logged smut transactions. Pete logged DIRT.

Peavy left town. Pete lost his cab protection. Pete called Sam G. Sam Tigerized and bought points. Sam bought in for 20%.

Sam bought protection—new and improved—Sheriff's *and* LVPD. Co-op deals meant insurance. Insurance meant safety. Safety meant anesthesia.

He shut Betty out. It worked intermittent. He notched minutes and hours and sleep. He did make-work. He did real work. He stretched the time. He cultivated distraction.

He'd get frazzled. He'd get fucked up. Betty jumped him then. It scared him. It relieved him. It said THIS IS REAL.

Betty stuck with him. Dallas faded away.

The Warren thing hits. Lee O. takes the rap. Jack Ruby goes down guilty as charged. Jack stays mute. Jack gets death. Ratfuck Bobby resigns as AG.

Barb dropped the P.M. news. Wayne dropped his Dallas questions. Carlos dropped all the hit talk. Betty took a slug. Arden-Jane dodged one for now.

Jimmy took another slug—pension-fund fraud—two five-year terms concurrent. Jimmy's fucked. Jimmy knows it. Jimmy seeks solace.

His good lawyers helped. His good Teamsters helped. Likewise Ward's fund-book plan.

Tiger was solace plus. Tiger subsumed Betty—intermittent.

Tiger roared. Tiger roamed. Tiger roved West LV. That trailer was still there. That whore decomped within.

Wayne wanted work. Wayne pressed Pete. Pete always said no. Tiger Kab hired spooks. Tiger Kab drove spooks. Wayne was spook-afflicted.

Wayne worked for Wayne *père*. *Père* tied his apron strings. *Père* had big pull. *Père* foresaw that Gulf of Tonkin thing.

Wayne was wowed—dig my dad—he's a *chingón*.

Wayne Senior pressed Wayne—let's start a snitch-Klan—the Neutered Knights of Natchez or some such fucking shit.

Wayne played along. Pete said: Don't do it—Klans just ain't you.

Wayne Senior bragged to excess. Ward Littell listened. Ward knew Wayne. Ward had pull with him. Ward could cut those strings.

Wayne Senior greased the hit fund. Wayne Senior told Ward. Wayne Senior sent Wayne to Dallas.

Wayne was naive. Wayne didn't know.

Stay naive—you'll live longer. Tiger rules. Ditch the hate and I'll find you a spot. It's elite. It's effete. It helps you shut dead women out.

51

(Las Vegas, 9/10/64)

CANNED FOOD AND booze. Sauerkraut and Cointreau—all Air Force stock.

Wayne tossed crates. A swamper stacked them. They worked. They broiled. They hogged the DI dock.

Creamed corn and Smirnoff. Stuffed olives and Pernod. Cheez-Its and Old Crow.

Wayne worked fast. The swamper worked slow. The swamper yak-yakked.

"You know we lost some guys, including our steward. I heard your dad got them work with Howard Hughes. Some lawyer set it up."

Wayne tossed the last crate. The swamper caught it. The swamper peeled his roll and paid up.

He shuffled. He scratched. He played coy. He dragged out the transaction.

Wayne said, "What *is* it?"

"Well, it's sort of personal."

"I'm listening."

"Well ... you think that Durfee guy's stupid enough to come back here?"

"I don't think he's stupid at all."

Wayne drove to Nellis.

He'd scheduled two loops. A late shot for Twinkies and Jim Beam—all Flamingo stock.

Wayne yawned. Traffic was slow. The job was soporific. The job was a soggy cream puff.

He figured it out. It took him weeks. Wayne Senior *wants* you bored. Wayne Senior has *plans*.

Said plans implied:

Go to Alabama. Stress your reputation. Drop how you avenged Lynette. Start a snitch-Klan. Recruit snitches. Work for the Feds.

He told Pete about it. Pete said, "It's cowardly shit."

He hit Owens. He hit the Nellis gates. He drove straight in. Nellis was beige—beige buildings/beige barracks/beige lawns.

Big barracks. Named for Strip hotels. No goof or satire implied.

His QM contact lived off base. His QM parked on. Wayne had dupe car keys. Wayne left his coin in the car.

He passed the "Sands." He passed the "Dunes." He passed the Officers' Club. He parked. He got out. He saw the QM's Ford.

Two rows up: A '62 Vette.

Red with white side coves. Whitewalls and chrome pipes. Janice's cherried-out car.

Janice left the ranch. Janice left at noon. Janice said she was off to play golf. Boulder/thirty-six holes/Twin Palms Country Club.

Blithe Janice. Golf—shit.

Wayne unlocked the Ford. Wayne rolled down the windows. Wayne scrunched low and tucked himself in.

Cars came. Cars went. He chewed gum. He popped sweat. He stared at the Vette.

Time chugged. Time rescinded. Some instinct said *stick*.

The sun arced. The sun hit the Ford. Wayne broiled. His gum starched and dried out.

There's Janice.

She leaves the O Club. She gets in her Vette. She kicks the key and idles it.

There's Clark Kinman.

He leaves the O Club. He gets in a Dodge. He kicks the key and idles it.

Janice pulls out. Kinman pulls out behind.

Wayne pulled out. Wayne hung back. Cut the leash/cut them some slack.

Wayne hung back. Wayne read his watch dial. Wayne ticked one full minute off.

Now—

He hauled. He closed in. He caught up. Three-car caravan—eastbound—Lake Mead Boulevard.

Janice drove point. Kinman tapped his horn. Kinman goosed her pipes. They *played*. They flirted out their windows. They *goofed*.

Wayne hung back. Wayne held two car-lengths down. Wayne sidled one lane over.

They drove east. They logged eight miles. They hit a desert patch. Motel strips and beer bars. Sand and last-chance fill-ups.

Janice signaled. Janice turned right. Kinman signaled. Kinman turned right.

There—The Golden Gorge Motel.

Gold stucco. One-story/one-room row. Twelve connected rooms.

Wayne pulled right. Wayne braked. Wayne stopped. Wayne checked his rearview.

Janice parked in the motel lot. Kinman parked in close.

They got out. They embraced and kissed. They entered room #4. They bypassed the office. They had their own key.

Wayne got butterflies. Wayne locked the car and walked over.

He stood near room #4. He loitered and listened. Janice laughed. Kinman said, "Get that rascal hard."

Wayne scoped the lot. Wayne saw scrub balls and junk cars. Wayne saw Mexican brats.

Thin room walls. Voices *en español*. Bracero cribs. Crop-picker tenants.

Kinman laughed. Janice went "Oooh."

Wayne loitered. Wayne listened. Wayne lurked. Shades went up. Blinds furled. Brown faces bipped out.

He saw something:

Room #5 had no windows. The door had *two* locks.

He held it back. He bypassed Wayne Senior. He ran paper. He checked Clark County deeds. He traced the motel.

Shitfire—Wayne Senior owns it.

It's 6/3/56. Wayne Senior bids and forecloses. The motel's a bargain. The motel's a tax dodge.

Wayne stewed. Pete called the ranch and left messages. Wayne ignored them. Wayne surveilled the motel.

Early P.M. stakeouts. Room #4. Janice and one-star Clark Kinman. Two matinees/three hours per.

He parked down the road. He trained binoculars. He walked by. He listened. He heard Janice sigh.

The Golden Gorge ran twelve units. Beaners camped out in ten. Janice kept her key. It unlocked room #4.

Room #5 had two locks. Room #5 had no windows. Room #5 stayed empty.

The lot buzzed by day. Braceros mingled. Bracero kids yahooed and yelped. Braceros worked hard. Braceros crashed hard. Braceros crashed early.

He popped a burglar once—late in '60. He kept his tool kit. He kept his picklocks.

Room #5 glowed. The door was green. Green like that song:

What's that secret you're keeping?

DOCUMENT INSERT: 9/12/64.
Confidential memorandum: Howard Hughes to Ward J. Littell.

Dear Ward,

Bravo on the new casino consultants. My aides have chosen three rough and tumble, no-nonsense men from that list you submitted, and they have assured me that they are devout Mormons with germ-free blood.

Their names are Thomas D. Elwell, Lamar L. Dean and

Daryl D. Kleindienst. They have extensive union
experience in Las Vegas and, according to my aides,
will not be afraid to negotiate and ''lock horns''
with those Mafia boys that Mr. Hoover tells me you have
in your pocket. According to my aides, these men
''know the ropes.'' They did not meet with them in
person, but have corresponded with your friend Mr.
Tedrow in Las Vegas and have solicited his advice.
Mr. Tedrow is well respected in Mormon circles, they
tell me, and I confirmed that assessment with Mr. Hoover.

The new men will be traveling hither and yon to
advance our Las Vegas plans, so I'm pleased that they
are cutting down commercial airline costs by flying
Hughes charters. I've sent memos to all the charter
crews instructing them to have lots of Fritos, Pepsi-
Cola and Rocky Road ice cream on hand, because hardworking men deserve to eat well. Also, thanks for
getting charter clearance at Nellis Air Force Base,
which cuts down costs as well.

Forewarned is forearmed, Ward. You've convinced me
that our Las Vegas approach will take time, and
I think this casino consultant plan is a winner.
I look forward to receiving your first report.

All best,

H.H.

52

(Las Vegas, 9/12/64)

WAYNE SENIOR SAID, "I know what my men are transporting."

"Oh?"

"Yes, 'Oh.' They've explained the entire procedure."

They sat poolside. Janice stood close. Janice sunned and putted golf balls.

"You knew at our first meeting. It was quite evident."

"An instinct doesn't equal a certainty."

Littell raised one brow. "You're being disingenuous. You knew then, you know now, and you've known at all points in between."

Wayne Senior coughed. "Don't mimic my gestures. You don't have my flair."

Littell grabbed his prop stick. Littell twirled it. Fuck Wayne Senior sideways.

"Tell me what you want. Be direct, and feel free to use the word 'skim.' "

Wayne Senior coughed. "My men have quit the union. They refuse to pay me the percentage I requested."

Littell twirled the stick. "How much do you want?"

"I'd be satisfied with 5%."

Littell twirled the stick. Littell twirled figure-eights. Littell did all Wayne Senior's tricks.

"No."

"No?"

"No."

"Categorically?"

"Yes."

Wayne Senior smiled. "I have to assume that Mr. Hughes doesn't know what his planes are transporting."

Littell studied Janice. She flexed. She putted. She stretched.

"I would advise you not to tell him."

"Why? Because your Italian friends will hurt me?"

"Because I'll tell your son that you sent him to Dallas."

DOCUMENT INSERT: 9/12/64.
Dallas Morning News article.

REPORTER WRITING JFK BOOK; SAYS HE'LL ''BLOW
CONSPIRACY WIDE OPEN''

Dallas <u>Times-Herald</u> reporter Jim Koethe has a tale to tell, and he'll tell it to anyone who'll listen.

On Sunday evening, November 24, 1963, Koethe, along with <u>Times-Herald</u> editor Robert Cuthbert and reporter Bill Hunter of the Long Beach (California) <u>Press-Telegram</u>, visited the apartment of Jack Ruby, the convicted killer of presidential assassin Lee Harvey Oswald. The three men spent ''two or three hours'' talking to Ruby's roommate, novelty salesman George Senator. ''I can't reveal what Mr. Senator said,'' Koethe told this reporter. ''But believe you me it was an eye-opener, and it sure got me thinking about some things.''

Koethe went on to say that he's done quite a bit of digging into the assassination and is writing a book on the subject. ''It's a conspiracy, sure as shooting,'' he said. ''And my book is going to blow it wide open.''

Koethe refused to name the people he believes are responsible for the death of President John F. Kennedy and refused to reveal the basic motive and details of the conspiracy. ''You'll have to wait for the book,'' Koethe said. ''And believe me, the book will be well worth the wait.''

Koethe's friend, reporter Bill Hunter, died in April. Editor Robert Cuthbert declined to be interviewed in depth for this article. ''Jim's extracurricular activities are his business,'' Cuthbert said. ''I wish him well with his book, though, because I love a good potboiler. Personally, I think Oswald was the lone assassin, and the Warren Report sure backs me up. Still, I've got to say that Jim Koethe exemplifies the bulldog reporter, so maybe he's on to something.''

Koethe, 37, is a colorful local scribe, known for his persistence, assertive behavior and connections within the Dallas Police Department. He is reputed to be a close friend of DPD Officer Maynard D. Moore, who disappeared around the time of the assassination. Asked to comment on Officer Moore's missing status, Koethe said, ''Mum's the word. A good reporter doesn't reveal his sources and a good book writer doesn't reveal anything.''

I guess we'll have to wait for the book. In the meantime, though, interested parties will have to make do with the 16-volume Warren Report, which for this reporter stands as the authoritative final word.

53

(Las Vegas, 9/13/64)

THE CAT SNARED a rat. One chomp—adieu.

The cat prowled the hut. The cat paraded. Harvey Brams crossed himself. Donkey Dom laughed.

Milt grabbed the rat. The cat snarled. Milt dropped the rat in the shitter. The cat nuzzled Pete. The cat clawed the switchboard.

Biz was slow. The 6:00 P.M. blues descended.

Champ B. bopped through. Champ B. juked morale. Champ B. dumped some hijacked Pall Malls.

Pete bought them. Call it PR swag—potential Drac donations. *Hospital* swag—yuk-yuk—lung-ward booty.

Biz picked up. Sonny Liston called. Sonny ordered two cabs. Sonny ordered scotch and red devils.

Pete yawned. Pete stroked the cat. Wayne walked in distracted. Dom checked his basket. Dom eyeball-stroked his bulge.

Pete said, "I've been calling you."

Wayne shrugged. Wayne passed Pete a note. A news clip—two columns. A call came in. Milt plugged it. Pete steered Wayne outside.

Wayne looked frazzled. Pete sized him up. Pete stuck the clip in his pocket.

"Sol Durslag. Ring a bell?"

"Sure. He's a card cheat. He's the treasurer for the Liquor Board, and he used to work for my father."

"Did they fall out?"

"Everybody falls out with—"

"Your father owns the Land o' Gold, right? He's got covert points."

"Right. The Gold and thirteen more."

Pete lit a cigarette. "Milt's been digging up shit. He heard that Durslag's been running card counters out of the Gold. I might need his help down the line."

Wayne smiled. "My father used to run him."

"That's what Milt said."

"So you . . ."

"I want you to muscle him. Think about it. You're Wayne Senior's son, and you've got your own reputation."

Wayne said, "Is this a test?"

Pete said, "Yes."

Durslag lived on Torrey. Durslag lived middle-class. Durslag lived in the Sherlock Homes tract.

Said tract was a style clash. Mock Tudors and palm trees. Mock gables and sand lots. Mixed-message *mishegoss*.

It was dark. The house was dark. Clouds draped the moon.

Pete knocked. Pete got no answer. The garage door was up. They lounged inside.

Pete smoked. Pete got a headache. Pete popped aspirin. Wayne yawned. Wayne shadowboxed. Wayne fucked with a gooseneck lamp.

Milt dished on Sol. Milt said Sol was divorced. Good news—no women.

The wait dragged. 1:00 A.M. went south. They loitered. They stretched kinks out. They pissed the walls green.

There—

Headlights/the driveway/incoming beams.

Pete crouched. Wayne crouched. A Caddy pulled in. The beams dimmed. Sol got out. Sol sniffed—

What's that smoke sm—

He ran. Pete tripped him. Wayne threw him up on the hood. Pete grabbed the lamp. Pete whipped the neck down. Pete flashed light on Wayne.

"That's Mr. Tedrow. You used to work for his father."

Sol said, "Fuck you."

Pete flashed him. Sol blinked. Sol rolled off the hood. Wayne grabbed him. Wayne pinned him. Wayne pulled his sap out.

Pete flashed him. Wayne sapped him—tight shots—the ankles/the arms. Sol shut his eyes. Sol bit his lips. Sol squeezed up fists.

Wayne said, "Pull your crew out of the Land o' Gold."

Sol said, "Fuck you."

Wayne sapped him—tight shots—the ankles/the chest.

Sol said, "Fuck you."

Pete said, "Say yes twice. That's all we want."

Sol said, "Fuck you."

Wayne sapped him—tight shots—the ankles/the arms.

Sol said, "Fuck you."

Wayne sapped him. Pete flashed him. The bulb was bright. The bulb was hot. The bulb burned his face.

Wayne raised his sap. Wayne swung it. Pete stopped him short.

"One yes to me, one to Mr. Tedrow. Pull your crew. Do my people some liquor-board favors."

Sol said, "Fuck you."

Pete cued Wayne. Wayne sapped him—tight shots—the arms/the ribs. Sol balled up. Sol rolled. Sol clipped the hood ornament. Sol snapped a wiper blade.

Sol coughed. Sol choked. Sol said, "Fuck you, yes, okay."

Pete pulled the lamp up. The light bounced and fizzed.

"That's two 'yes's,' right?"

Sol opened his eyes. Sol had singed brows. Sol had scorched lids.

"Yeah, two. You think I want this as a steady diet?"

Pete pulled his flask—Old Crow bond—instant headache relief.

Sol grabbed it. Sol drained it. Sol coughed and flushed—Man-o-Manischewitz, that's good!

He winced. He rolled off the hood. He stood straight up. He grabbed the lamp. He bent the neck. He flashed light on Wayne.

"Your father told me some things about you, sonny boy."

Wayne said, "I'm listening."

"I could tell you some things about that sick hump."

Wayne bent the lamp down. The light bounced and fizzed.

"You can tell me. I won't hurt you."

Sol coughed. Sol hacked phlegm—thick and blood-infused.

"He said you had it bad for his wife. Like a little pervert puppy."

Wayne said, "And?"

"And you never had the gumption to act."

Pete watched Wayne. Pete watched his hands. Pete got in close.

Wayne said, "And?"

"And Daddy shouldn't preach, 'cause he's a sick hump as far as his wife is concerned."

Pete watched Wayne. Pete blocked his hands. Pete closed in close.

Wayne said, "And?"

Sol coughed. "*And* Daddy has Mommy screw these guys that

he wants to cultivate, *and* Mommy had this unauthorized thing with a colored musician named Wardell Gray, *and* Daddy beat him to death with his cane."

Wayne swayed. Sol laughed. Sol flipped his tie in his face.

"Fuck you. You're a punk. You're a hump like your daddy."

54

(Las Vegas, 9/14/64)

THE GOLDEN GORGE—11:00 P.M.

Twelve rooms. Sleepy braceros. Room #5—empty. Room #4—trysted up.

They showed at 9:00. They brought two cars. Kinman brought liquor. Janice brought the key.

Wayne watched. Wayne walked the parking lot. Wayne brought tools. Wayne brought lockpicks and a penlight.

Pervert pup. Hump like your—

The lot was dead. No loungers/no muchachos/no drunks flaked in cars. Room #5—no windows. Room #4—dark.

Wayne braced door 5. Wayne got his tools out. Wayne flashed the locks.

Eleven brown doors. One *green* door as standout. One pervert-pup joke.

Wayne worked the picks. Wayne rotated clockwise and counter. Wayne tapped both locks.

His hands jumped. He dripped sweat. He gored his thumbs. Clockwise/reverse it/go count—

The top lock snapped.

He popped one tumbler. He wiped his hands. He popped one mo—

The bottom lock snapped.

Wayne wiped his hands. Wayne leaned on the door. Wayne rode the door and stepped in.

He shut the door. He flashed the room. It was small. It smelled familiar.

Old smells—*embedded*. Wayne Senior's booze. Wayne Senior's tobacco.

Wayne flashed the floor. Wayne flashed the walls. Wayne got the gestalt.

A chair. A sideboard. One ashtray/one bottle/one glass. One mirror-peek. Room #4 access. A wall speaker/soundproof wall pads/a sound switch.

Wayne sat down. Wayne made the chair—surplus from Peru, Indiana. The peek was dark. Room #4 was dark. Wayne poured a drink.

He downed it. It singed. He rode the burn out. The peek was 3-by-3. The standard cop size—the stock mirror-mount.

Wayne hit the switch. Wayne heard Kinman moan. Wayne heard Janice moan counterpoint.

Janice moaned arch. Janice moaned smut-actress style—Stag Loop 101.

Wayne poured a drink. Wayne downed it. Wayne rode the burn out. Kinman came—ooo-ooo-ooo. Janice came concurrent. Janice came mezzo-falsetto—smut meets the Met.

Wayne heard soft talk. Wayne heard giggles. Wayne heard speaker warp. A light went on. Room #4 flared.

Janice got out of bed. Janice stood up nude. Janice walked to her side of the mirror. She lingered. She posed. She grabbed her cigarettes off a dresser.

Wayne leaned in tight. Janice blurred. Wayne leaned way back to reframe. Kinman said something. Kinman murmured sweet talk. Kinman was oblivious. Kinman knew fuck-all.

Janice rubbed her appendix scar. Janice tossed her hair.

Her breasts swayed. Her hair tousled. She raised steam. She dripped sweat. She smiled. She licked a finger. She wrote "Junior" on the mirror.

55

(Dallas, 9/21/64)

JIM KOETHE WAS queer.

He bolstered his crotch. He prowled fag bars. He brought boys home. Home was Oak Cliff—bumfuck Big D. Home was the Oak View Apartments.

Three floors. Outside walkways. All courtyard and streetside views.

Pete hogged a bus bench. Pete watched the pad. Pete carried a treat bag. 1:16 A.M.—fruit alert.

Koethe had a date. Koethe poked his dates for two hours. Pete knew Koethe. Pete knew Koethe's routine.

Wayne read the Dallas papers. Wayne passed a clip on. It pertained to Koethe's "book." It pertained to Koethe's pal Maynard Moore. Pete flew to Dallas. Pete tailed Koethe. Pete played scribe. Pete called Koethe's editor.

The guy ragged Koethe. Koethe was a jack-off. Koethe was Mr. Pipe Dream. Sure—they went to Ruby's crib. Sure—they talked to his roommate. But—the talk was all bullshit. The talk was all jive.

Conspiracy—shit. Read the Warren Report.

The guy was convincing—*but—Jim Koethe knew Maynard Moore.*

A bus pulled up—some late-night express. Pete waved it on.

He killed four days. He tailed Koethe. He grooved Koethe's routine. Koethe loved the Holiday. Koethe loved Vic's Parisian. Koethe loved Gene's Music Room. Koethe sipped sidecars. Koethe prowled the johns. Koethe buzz-bombed young flesh.

Oak Cliff was the shits. Oak Cliff was a ghost zone. Betty Mac/Ruby's pad/the Oswald-Tippit tiff.

Koethe's date walked out. Koethe's date walked bowlegged. He swished by the bench. He checked Pete out. He went uugh and swished away.

Pete put his gloves on. Pete grabbed his treat bag. Koethe lived in 306—one light extant.

Pete took the side stairs. Pete walked up slow. Pete checked the walkways. No outdoor noise/no indoor noise/no visible wits.

He walked over. He braced the door. He tapped the knob. He popped the lock-catch. He opened the door. He walked in. He saw a dark room. He caught sounds and shadows.

Shower noise—down a side hall—off a doorway. Steam and light at that spot.

Pete stood still. Pete strained his eyes. Pete got indoor sight. He saw a living room-office. He saw file drawers. He saw a kitchenette.

Down the hall: A bathroom and bedroom.

Pete dropped his treat bag. Pete crouched. Pete walked down the hall. The shower stopped. Steam whooshed out. Jim Koethe walked through it.

He wore a towel. He turned right. He walked into Pete.

They bumped. Koethe went EEK! Koethe went butch. Koethe snapped to some martial-arts pose.

His towel fell. His equipment dangled. He wore a dick extender. He wore cock rings.

Pete laughed. Pete came in low.

Koethe kicked. Koethe missed. Koethe stumbled and tripped. Pete kicked him. Pete nailed his nards good.

Koethe jackknifed. Koethe re-posed. Koethe tried some karate shit. He flailed. He threw fists. He positioned.

Pete judo-chopped him. Pete nail-raked his face.

Koethe screamed. Pete grabbed his neck. Pete held it and snapped it. Pete felt his hyoid bone shear.

Koethe gurgled. Koethe spasmed. Koethe choked on bile. Pete picked him up. Pete re-snapped his neck. Pete threw him in the shower.

He stood there. He caught his breath. He got a Godzilla-rate headache. He popped the medicine chest. He found some Bayer's. He popped half a tin.

He prowled the pad. He dumped his treat bag. He dropped treats on rugs and chairs: Dildoes/reefers/bun-boy boox/Judy Garland LPs.

His headache dimmed—Godzilla to King Kong. He found some gin. He dosed it more—King Kong to Rodan.

He searched the pad. He tossed the pad. He faked a B&E. He trashed the bedroom. He trashed the kitchen. He searched the file sleeves. He found clips. He found notes. He found a folder marked "Book."

Sixteen pages/typed text. Conspiracy—shit.

Pete skimmed the file. The story wandered. The gist cohered.

Wendell Durfee was a "dumb pimp." He was "too dumb to kill Maynard Moore." Moore had a temp job. Moore had a partner: Wayne Tedrow Junior/LVPD.

Koethe knew Sergeant A. V. Brown. Sergeant Brown said:

"There was bad blood between Moore & Junior. They got in a ruckus at the Adolphus Hotel. Moore allegedly failed to show up for a meeting with Junior. I think Junior killed him, but I've got no proof."

Koethe knew a Fed man. Koethe quoted said Fed:

"Tedrow Senior ran snitch-Klan informants. Maynard Moore reported to him, so I think it's a hell of a coincidence that

Moore and Tedrow Junior got assigned together that weekend."

Koethe riffed:

Moore knew J. D. Tippit. They were "Klanned-up." Moore knew Jack Ruby. Moore dug on the Carousel Club.

Koethe riffed *off* Ruby. Koethe quoted a "Secret Source":

"Jack brought some people by this safe house where the hit team was holed up. It might've been North Texas or Oklahoma, and it might've been some kind of motel or a hunting lodge. I think it was Jack and two women and maybe Hank Killiam. I think they saw some things they shouldn't."

Koethe riffed. Koethe listed Jack Ruby KAs. Starred names: Jack Zangetty/Betty McDonald/Hank Killiam. Koethe listed footnotes—newspaper-sourced:

Jack Zangetty disappears—Xmas '63. Jack washes out of Lake Lugert. Betty McDonald/suicide—2/13/64. Hank Killiam/suicide—3/17/64.

Jim Koethe—verbatim: "Who was the other woman at the safe house?"

Koethe riffs. Koethe thinks the "hit team" disbanded. "They had to leave Dallas. They might have crossed the Mexican border." Koethe secures a "Border-Patrol Source." Said source secures a passport-stop list.

The dates: 11/23–12/2/63.

Koethe works the list. Koethe taps "Secret Sources." Koethe runs 89 names. Koethe nails "a major suspect."

Jean Philippe Mesplède/white male/age 41. Born: Lyon, France. Ex-French Army/ex-OAS trigger.

Mesplède has "right-wing ties." Mesplède has "ties to Cuban exile groups." Mesplède's current address: 1214 Ciudad Juarez/Mexico City.

The pro shooter *was* French. Chuck Rogers said so. Chuck said he walked over the border.

Pete skimmed pages. The text decohered. Koethe's logic went south.

Let's link Oswald and Ruby. Let's link Oswald and Moore. Let's link Lady Bird Johnson. Let's link Karyn Kupcinet.

Pete skimmed pages. Shit decohered. Let's link Dorothy Kilgallen. Let's link Lenny Bruce. Let's link Mort Sahl.

Pete skimmed pages. Shit recohered—FUCK—

There's a mug shot. It's file exhibit A. It's Kansas City PD sourced—3/8/56.

It's Arden-Jane. Arden Elaine *Bruvick* then. Felony bounce—"Receipt of Stolen Goods."

One mug shot. Attached notes. "Confidential" tips:

Jack Ruby's bookkeeper splits Dallas. Her name is Arden *Smith*. She went to the safe house. She saw things she shouldn't. She split Big D. for good.

Koethe worked the name "Arden." Koethe logged tips and tapped sources. This guy knew that guy. That guy knew this. A guy glommed a mug shot. Some guys glommed some tales.

Such as:

Arden went through men. Arden had a husband. Said hubby was a Teamster. Said hubby ran the K.C. local.

Said hubby had accounting skills. Said hubby went to school in Mississippi. Said hubby was anti-Hoffa. Said hubby stole some Teamster funds.

Arden was bent. Arden trucked with whores. Arden was tight with two sisters: Pat and Pam Clunes.

The Arden notes stopped. The "Book" notes stopped. The file dead-ended. Pete felt dizzy. Pete took his pulse—1-fucking-63.

He bagged the file. He checked the drawers. He checked bookshelves and cabinets. No duplicates/no stash of loose clips.

He retossed the crib. He grid-searched it. He re-retossed it. He detossed it quick.

He trashed. He tidied. He worked fast. He worked fastidious.

He tossed the medicine chest. He restacked the shelves. He debuilt and rebuilt the toilet. He tapped the walls. He pulled up rugs. He laid them back straight. He slit-checked the chairs. He slit-checked the sofa. He slit-checked the bed.

No slits. No stash holes. No duplicates extant. No stash of loose clips.

He popped some Bayer's. He chased them with gin. He dredged up some guts. Queers overkilled queers. It was standard cop wisdom. All cops knew it.

He got a knife. He stabbed Jim Koethe ninety-four times.

South—80 miles per hour plus.

He took I-35. He cut through shit suburbs. He smelled like blood and gin. He smelled like Jim Koethe's shampoo.

He passed rest stops. He passed campgrounds. He saw kids'

swings and bar-b-que pits. A car laid back—ten car lengths—it spooked him.

He ran tail riffs. He ran no-tail riffs. 4:00 A.M.—one highway/two cars.

His headache rehit. It built and mushroomed. King Kong greets Rodan.

He saw a camp sign. He pulled down a ramp. He saw a grill pit and tables. He nosed up. He killed his lights. He worked in the dark.

He dumped Koethe's file. He filled the pit. He siphoned gas and doused it. He lit a match and got a big whooooosh.

The flames built. The flames leveled off. The heat torqued his headache. It was monster. It was Godzilla-plus. It was the Creature from the Black Lagoon.

Pete ran to his car. Pete swerved up the ramp. Pete hit the highway. Let's ditch Big D. Let's sedate forever. Let's eat secobarbital. Let's geez hair-o-wine.

That car laid back. It's a spaceship. The driver's King Kong. He's got X-ray eyes. He knows you killed Koethe and Betty.

Pete got dizzy. The windshield vaporized. It's a porthole/it's a sieve. The road dropped. It's an inkwell. It's the Black Lagoon.

The Creature bit his head. Pete puked on the wheel.

There's a ramp. It's dropping. There's a sign:

HUBBARD, TEX, POP 4001.

Japs. Slice cords. Betty Mac. Slant eyes/crossbars/capris.

It came. It went. Roads dropped. Roads resurfaced. Ink blots and lagoons.

He came. *He* went. He felt Frankensteined. Sutures and staples. Green walls and white sheets.

Behold the Body Snatchers. Behold Doc Frankenstein:

You're lucky. A man found you. It's been five days now. God must love you—you cracked up near St. Ann's.

Doc had acne scars. Doc had halitosis. Doc had a drawl.

It's been six days. We cut a fat pad from your head—it was benign. I bet you had some darn bad headaches.

Don't worry now—that man in the car called your wife.

They brought him back.

Frankenstein came. Frankenstein went. Nuns fluttered and fussed. Don't hurt me—I'm Protestant French.

Frank destapled him. Nuns shaved him. He dehazed. He saw razors and hands. He rehazed. He saw Japs and Betty.

Hands fed him soup. Hands touched his dick. Hands jabbed tubes in. The haze sputtered. Words filtered through. Decrease his dose—don't addict him.

He dehazed. He saw faces:

Student nuns—the brides of Frankenstein. A slight man—Ivy League threads—John Stanton-like. Memory Lane: Miami/ white horse/Outfit-Agency ops.

He squinted. He tried to talk. Nuns went ssshhh.

He rehazed. He dehazed. He dehazed for real. Stanton was real— dig his tan—dig his drip-dry suit.

Pete tried to talk. His throat clogged. He hocked phlegm. His dick burned. He pulled his catheter out.

Stanton smiled. Stanton pulled his chair up.

"Sleeping Beauty awakes."

Pete sat up. Pete stretched his IV taut.

"You were tailing me. You saw me go off the road."

Stanton nodded. "And I called Barb and told her you were safe, but you couldn't have visitors yet."

Pete rubbed his face. "What are you doing here?"

Stanton winked. Stanton popped his briefcase. Stanton pulled out Pete's gun.

"You rest. The doctor said we'll be able to talk tomorrow."

They grabbed a bench. They lugged it outside. Stanton wore a drip-dry. Pete wore a robe.

He felt okay. Headaches—adieu.

He called Barb yesterday. They caught eight days up. Barb was okay. Stanton prepared her. Barb held in tough.

He read the *Times-Herald*. He got the gist. The Koethe snuff came and went. DPD worked it. DPD hassled queers. DPD cut them loose. The case vibed open file. It's a queer job—fuck it.

The *Morning News* ran a piece. They ragged Koethe. They ragged his "wild talk." Koethe was a perennial crank. Koethe was a "conspiracy nut."

He burned Koethe's notes. The Arden dirt went up. He debated. He decided—don't tell Ward Littell.

It was *sketchy* dirt—fill it out first.

A nun walked by—a sweet number—Stanton studied her.

"Jackie Kennedy wore hats like that."

"She wore one to Dallas."

Stanton smiled. "You're a fast study."

"I took Latin in school. I know what 'quid pro quo' means."

The nun smiled. The nun waved and giggled. Stanton was cute. Stanton lived on salads and martinis.

"Did you hear about that reporter who got killed? I heard he was writing a book."

Pete stretched. A head stitch popped loose.

"Let's start over. You were tailing me. You saved my life. I said thank you."

Stanton stretched. His shoulder rig showed.

"We know that some Agency men were *at least* peripheral to the Kennedy thing. We're pleased with the result, we have no desire to dispute the Warren Report, but for deniability's sake, we'd like a rough sketch."

Pete stretched. A stitch popped. Pete rubbed his head. Pete said, "Cuba."

Stanton smiled. "That's not much."

"It says it all. You know who he fucked with, you know who had the money and the means. You saved my life, so I'll be generous. You've met and worked with half the personnel."

The bench was damp. The slats sustained doodles. Stanton drew stars. Stanton wrote "CUBA."

Pete rubbed his head. A stitch unraveled.

"Okay, I'll play."

Stanton drew stars. Stanton put "!" after CUBA.

"Jack broke our hearts. Now Johnson's compounding the hurt."

Pete drew "?" Stanton crossed it out.

"Johnson's quits on the Cause. He thinks it's a loser and he knows it got Jack killed. He's fucked the Agency out of our Cuban ops budget, and some colleagues of mine think it's time to circumvent his policy."

Pete drew "!" Pete drew "$." Stanton crossed his legs. His ankle rig showed.

"I want to bring you to Vietnam. I want you to move Laotian heroin back to the States. I've got a team set up in Saigon. It's all Agency and South Vietnamese Army. You can recruit your own team on both ends. Dope has financed a dozen Vietnamese coups, so let's make it work for the Cause."

Pete shut his eyes. Pete ran newsreels. The French lose Algiers. The French lose Dien Bien Phu.

Et le Cuba sera notre grande revanche.

Stanton said, "You funnel the dope to Las Vegas. I've consulted Carlos on that aspect. He thinks he can get the Outfit to rescind their no-dope rule, if you push exclusively to Negroes. We want you to set up a system, buy off the key cops and limit your street exposure to the last two links on the distribution chain. If the Vegas operation flies, we'll expand to other cities. And 65% of the profits will go to worthy exile groups."

Pete stood up. Pete swayed. Pete threw hooks and jabs and popped stitches.

A nun walked by. She saw Pete. She got spooked. She crossed herself.

C'est un fou.

C'est un diable.

C'est un monstre Protestant.

56

(Las Vegas, 9/30/64)

BREAK TIME—4:00 P.M. sharp.

He put his work down. He made coffee. He sat outside his suite. He played the news. He watched the course. Janice played most days.

She'd see him. She'd wave. She'd yell epigrams. She'd say, "You don't like my husband." She'd say, "You work too hard."

Janice played scratch golf. Janice moved lithe. She'd hit shots. Her skirts would hike. Her calves would bunch and stretch.

Littell watched 6. Littell played the news. LBJ barnstormed Virginia. Bobby barnstormed New York.

Janice played 6. Janice outdrove her friends. She saw him. She waved. She yelled.

She said, "My husband fears you." She said, "You need some rest."

Littell laughed. Littell waved. Janice aced a shot.

Jane feared Vegas. The Boys ran the town. Janice *was* Vegas direct. He enjoyed his glimpses. He took them to bed. He put Janice's body on Jane.

The news went off. Janice parred 6 and waved. Littell walked inside. Littell wrote appeal briefs.

Jimmy Hoffa was through. The Boys knew it. Carlos soldiered for Jimmy. Carlos dunned donations. Carlos built a Help Jimmy Fund. It was futile. It was hopeless. Their bribe roll had crapped out.

Littell put his brief down. Littell grabbed his bankbooks. Littell ran figures and totaled his tithes.

Glad tidings:

The bagmen aced Wayne Senior. The bagmen stole his skim fees. The bagmen were duplicitous. The bagmen were good. The bagmen were Mormon-rowdy.

He directed them. He ran the skim. He wrote fictive reports. He lied to Drac. He embezzled Drac. He sucked Drac's blood.

The bagmen bagged. The bagmen moved six hundred grand—two weeks' worth of skim. He took his 5%. He fed his Chicago account. He opened accounts in Silver Spring and D.C. He used fake ID. He laundered the cash. He tithed the SCLC.

He wrote tithe checks. Five grand per. He wrote them under pseudonyms. He print-wiped the envelopes.

Drac and the Boys meet Dr. King—We Shall Overcome.

His desk phone rang. He grabbed it.

"Yes?"

Static hiss—long distance. A garbled Pete: "Ward, it's me."

The hiss built. The line buzzed. The hiss leveled flat.

"Where are you?"

"I'm in Mexico City. I'm losing the fucking connection, and I need a favor."

"Name it."

"I need Wayne to cut the apron strings and come to work for me."

Littell said, "With pleasure."

57

(Las Vegas, 9/30/64)

JANICE FUCKED Clark Kinman. Wayne watched.

She left the lights on. She knew he was there. She rode Kinman. She showed her backside.

Wayne braced the mirror. Wayne sipped Wayne Senior's scotch. It was her sixth show. It was his sixth hide-and-see.

He surveilled the motel. Janice fucked every night. Wayne Senior caught her most times. The gigs were synced. Ditto the arrivals.

Kinman shows at 9:00. Janice shows at 9:10. Wayne Senior shows at 9:40. Kinman comes to fuck. Janice comes to act. Kinman co-stars unasked.

She fucked in the dark for Wayne Senior. She fucked in the light for Wayne.

He thought it out.

She saw him at Nellis. She *knew* him. She *knew* he'd break in. He'd log Wayne Senior's routine. He'd seize on his off nights and LOOK.

Janice bent back. Her hair flew. Wayne saw her face topsy-turvy. The speaker popped. Kinman moaned. Kinman said dumb sex things.

Janice bent up. Janice raised her hips. Wayne saw Kinman inside her.

Sol Durslag checked out. The Vegas *Sun* ran the story. May '55—Wardell Gray/tenor sax. Beaten dead/body dumped/sand dune/DOA. No suspects—case closed.

Janice bent back. Her hair dropped. Wayne saw her eyes upside down.

Kinman moaned per I'm-coming. Kinman said dumb sex things. Janice grabbed a pillow. Janice muzzled him.

His toes curled. His knees contracted. His feet clenched. Janice rolled clear and free.

Kinman dumped the pillow. Kinman smiled and scratched his balls. Kinman tapped his Saint Chris on a chain.

They talked. Their lips moved. The speaker fuzzed sighs.

Kinman kissed his Saint Chris. "I always wear this for protection. Sometimes I think you're likely to kill me."

Janice sat up. Janice faced the mirror-wall.

Kinman said, "Wayne Senior should take better care of you. Shit, I think we've gone sixteen days straight."

Janice winked. Janice said, "You're the best."

"Tell true. Is he good?"

"No, but he's got qualities."

"You mean money."

"Not exactly."

"He's got to have something, or you'd've found yourself a steady before me."

Janice winked. "I've sent out invitations, but nobody knocked on my door."

"Some boys don't know how to read signs."

"Some boys need to look first."

"Shit, if your hubby could see you now."

Janice raised her voice. Janice talked overt slow.

"I had a thing with a musician once. Wayne Senior found out."

"What did he do?"

"He killed him."

"Are you ribbing me?"

"Absolutely not."

Kinman kissed his Saint Chris. "You'll be the ruin of me. Shit, and I thought Junior was the only killer in the family."

Janice got up. Janice walked to the mirror.

She primped. She fogged the glass. She licked a finger. She drew arrows and hearts.

A dust storm kicked through. Hot winds kicked sand and sagebrush.

Wayne drove to the ranch. Wayne walked to the guest house. Wayne saw a stray car en route.

There's Ward Littell.

He ducked the wind. He blocked Wayne's door. He looked sandblown and storm-fucked.

He said, "Your father sent you to Dallas."

DOCUMENT INSERT: 10/1/64.
Covert Intelligence Dossier. From: John Stanton. To: Pete Bondurant. Marked: ''Hand-Courier Only/Destroy Upon Reading.''

P.B.,
I'm hoping this gets to you in time. It's really no more than a highlighted summary & I've edited out the extraneous details. I'm routing it through the Mexico City Station to meet that deadline you requested. Note: Data culled from Interpol files in Paris & Marseilles. Agency copy file #M-64889/Langley.

Per: MESPLEDE, JEAN PHILIPPE, W.M., 8/19/22. LKA:
1214 Ciudad Juarez, Mexico City.

1941–'45: Conflicting accts. MESPLEDE (an alleged
anti-Semite) was either a Nazi collaborator or a
member of the Armed French Resistance in Lyon.
Conflicting accts: MESPLEDE turned over Jews to the
SS/MESPLEDE assassinated Nazis at a health retreat in
the Arbois. Note: One Interpol wag concluded that he
did a little of both.

1946–'47: Whereabouts unknown.

1948–'50: Mercenary work in Paraguay. The Asuncion
Ops Station has a 41-page file. MESPLEDE infiltrated
leftist student groups at the behest of the
Paraguayan Association of Police Chiefs. MESPLEDE
(Spanish fluent) assassinated 63 suspected Communist
sympathizers per association guidelines.

1951–'55: French Army service (Indochina—now
Vietnam—& Algeria). MESPLEDE served as a
paratrooper, saw action at Dien Bien Phu & allegedly
became bitter over the French defeat & withdrawal.
Reports (unconfirmed) have him moving opium base &
hashish to his next duty station in Algiers. In
Algiers, MESPLEDE transferred to an occupation unit &
taught torture techniques to members of a mercenary
police unit employed by wealthy French colonialists.
MESPLEDE (a committed anti-Communist) allegedly
executed 44 Algerian nationalists suspected of
Communist ties & gained a reputation as a superb wet
arts specialist.

1956–'59: Whereabouts largely unknown. MESPLEDE is
believed to have traveled extensively in the U.S.
during this time. The Atlanta (Ga) PD has a 10/58 file
note on him. MESPLEDE was suspected of taking part in
the bombing of a synagogue targeted by neo-Nazis. The
New Orleans PD has a 2/9/59 file note. MESPLEDE was
suspected of 16 armed robberies in N.O., Metairie,
Baton Rouge & Shreveport. Note: unconfirmed rpts.
state that MESPLEDE traveled in Organized Crime
circles during this interval.

1960–'61: Mercenary work in the Belgian Congo.
MESPLEDE (a known associate of our KA LAURENT GUERY)

served as an enforcer for Belgian landowners & worked
with an Agency liaison in the anti-Lumumba incursion.
MESPLEDE & GUERY engineered the capture & execution
of 491 leftist rebels in Katanga Province. The
landowners gave MESPLEDE carte blanche & told him to
implement a deterrent measure to scare would-be
rebels. MESPLEDE and GUERY herded the rebels into a
gully & killed them with flamethrowers.

1962–'63: At large in France. MESPLEDE (who lost
land holdings when DeGaulle granted Algerian
independence) allegedly joined the French OAS & took
part in the 3/62 & 8/63 assassination attempts on
DeGaulle. MESPLEDE resurrected in Mexico City (9/63)
& has allegedly been in touch with our KAs GUERY &
FLASH ELORDE. MESPLEDE is known to be committed to the
anti-Castro cause & as previously stated, is
determinedly anti-Communist, Spanish fluent & has
both probable narcotics experience & military
experience in the Southeast Asian Theatre. All in
all, I think we can use him.

I'm heading back to Saigon. Pouch all future
communications through my P.O. box at Arlington.
We'll use drops & cutout couriers from here on in.
Remember: We're Stage 1 Covert, like our Tiger ops
in Miami. You know the old drill: Read, memorize &
burn.

Thumbs up on MESPLEDE, if you think he fits in. You
can recruit the rest of the team on your own autonomy.
Per MESPLEDE: Watch out. His curriculum vitae is a bit
scary.

For the Cause,

J.S.

58

(Mexico City, 10/2/64)

A MEX BROUGHT COFFEE. Said Mex kissed ass. Big teeth/big
bows/big compliance.

Pete lounged. Pete noshed rolls. Pete taped his piece under the table. The trigger sat flush. The silencer worked. The barrel faced the opposite seat.

Pete sipped coffee. Pete rubbed his head. Mexico City—*nyet*.

It's a skunk zone. It's rife with dog turds. Give me pre-Castro Havana.

He looked for Flash and Laurent. He tapped out. He dropped a note. Mesplède dropped a note back:

Let's talk—I've heard about you.

He killed time. He called Barb every day. He called the K.C. Local. He dropped names. He asked questions—per Arden Elaine Bruvick.

The gist: She was Frau Danny Bruvick. Danny ran Local 602—'53–'56. Danny stole Teamster money. Danny split. Jimmy H. decreed a hit. Danny vanished. Arden stayed in K.C.

Jimmy pulled strings. The KCPD popped Arden. Arden bailed out fast. Arden split K.C.

Pete knew a KCPD guy. Pete called him. He ran Arden's bail stats. He called Pete back.

Arden bailed out—3/10/56. The T&C Corp bailed her. Carlos M. owned T&C. T&C was his tax front.

A frayed cord. A teaser. Carlos says, "Clip Arden." His front corp bails her.

Get more. Learn more. Don't warn Littell *yet*. The cord felt thin. The cord could fray. The cord could strip.

A man walked in. He was fat. He wore glasses. His hands were smudged black. Odds on: French Para tattoos.

Para pit dogs—*très* French—fangs and parachutes.

Pete stood up. The man saw him. The man grabbed a front table.

Pete ad-libbed:

He crouched. He untaped his gun. He reholstered and walked over. He bowed to the man. They shook hands. The pit dogs had red eyes.

They sat down. Mesplède said, "You know Chuck Rogers."

"Chuck's a piece of work."

"He lives with his parents. A man more than forty years old."

He sounded *sud-Midi*. He looked *marseillais*. He dressed *très fasciste*—all-black ensemble.

Pete said, "He's a committed man."

"Yes. You can forgive his more outlandish beliefs."

"He's got a sense of humor about them."

"The Ku Klux Klan disgusts me. I enjoy Negro jazz."

"I like Cuban music."

"I like Cuban food and Cuban women."

"Fidel Castro should die."

"Yes. He is a *cochon* and a *pédé*."

"I saw Pigs. I ran troops out of the Blessington campsite."

Mesplède nodded. "Chuck told me. You shot *communistes* out an airplane window."

Pete laughed. Pete mimed gunshots. Mesplède lit a Gauloise. Mesplède offered one.

Pete lit up. Pete coughed—it was rolled muskrat shit.

"What else did Chuck tell you?"

"That you were a committed man."

"That's all?"

"He also said that you, *qu'est-ce que c'est?*, 'snipped links.' "

Pete smiled. Pete showed his pix. There's Jack Z. trussed up. There's Hank the K. dumped.

Mesplède tapped them. "Unfortunate men. They saw things they should not."

Pete coughed. Pete blew smoke rings.

Mesplède coughed. "Chuck said the blond woman killed herself in jail."

"That's right."

"You did not take her picture?"

"No."

"Then Arden is the only one left."

Pete shook his head. "She's unfindable."

"No one is that."

"She has to be."

Mesplède chained cigarettes. "I saw her once before, in New Orleans. She was with one of Carlos Marcello's men."

"She's unfindable. Leave it at that."

Mesplède shrugged. Mesplède dropped his hands. There's the click. There's the slide. There's the hammer back.

Pete smiled. Pete bowed. Pete showed his gun. Mesplède smiled. Mesplède bowed. Mesplède showed *his* gun.

Pete grabbed a napkin. Pete draped the table. Pete covered the guns.

Mesplède said, "Your note mentioned work."

Pete cracked his knuckles. "Heroin. We move it from Laos to Saigon and funnel it to the States. It's Agency-adjunct and completely unsanctioned. All the profits go to the Cause."

"Our colleagues?"

"We work under a man named John Stanton. I've run dope and exiles for him. We bring in Laurent Guéry, Flash Elorde, and an ex-cop to do the chemical work."

A whore walked by. Said whore looked down. Mesplède flashed his tattoos. He flexed his hands. The dogs snapped. The dogs grew big *chorizos*.

The whore crossed herself. The whore buzzed off—*gringos malo y feo!*

Mesplède said, "I am interested. I am devoted to the cause of a free Cuba."

"Mort à Fidel Castro. Vive l'entente franco-américaine."

Mesplède grabbed a fork. Mesplède cleaned his nails.

"Chuck described you as 'soft on women.' I will concede the unfindability of Arden if you further prove your loyalty to the Cause."

"How?"

"Hank Hudspeth has defrauded the Cause. He has sold faulty weaponry to exile groups and has diverted the good merchandise to the Klan."

Pete said, "I'll take care of it."

Mesplède flexed his hands. The dogs went priapic.

"I would appreciate a memento."

The setup worked—let's talk guns—my money/your stuff.

Pete called from Houston. Hank was eager. He said catch you a plane. I got a bunker near Polk.

Pete flew to De Ridder. Pete rented a car. Pete hit a Safeway. Pete bought a cooler. Pete bought dry ice.

He hit the local P.O. He bought a box. He air-mail-stamped it. He wrote Jean Mesplède's address on top.

He hit a gun shop. He bought a Buck knife. He hit a camera store. He bought a Polaroid. He bought some film.

He drove north. He took back roads. He cut through the Kisatchee Forest. It was hot—80 at dusk.

Hank met him. Hank was eager—I got the stuff!

The bunker was a mine shaft. Part gun hut/part igloo. Ten steps below ground.

Hank walked ahead. Hank hit the top step. Pete pulled his piece and shot him in the back.

Hank tumbled. Pete shot him again. Pete blew his ribs out.

He turned him over. He prepped his camera. He snapped a close-up. The bunker was hot—paved walls in tight.

Pete pulled his knife. Pete stretched Hank's hair. Pete cut side to side.

He notched the blade. He hit the bone. He sheared over and up. He stepped on Hank's head. He jerked hard. He pulled his scalp up.

He wiped it off. He dry-iced it. He boxed it. His hands shook—first-timer shakes—he'd scalped a hundred Reds.

He wiped his hands. He inscribed the snapshot. He wrote "Viva la Causa!" on the back.

59

(Las Vegas, 10/4/64)

JANICE WAS IN. Wayne Senior was out. Wayne paced his room. Wayne groomed and primped.

He saw Pete at Tiger. They talked an hour back. Pete worked on him. Pete hit him up.

You're a chemist. Let's go to Vietnam. *You'll* cook heroin. *We'll* work covert ops.

He said yes. It felt logical. It felt wholly right.

Wayne shaved. Wayne combed his hair. Wayne dabbed a razor cut. Ward slammed him—four nights back—Ward fucked him way up.

He tracked Ward's logic. He improvised. Wayne Senior ran snitches. Wayne Senior thus ran Maynard Moore. Thus he was in on the hit.

Ward left blank spots. Wayne improvised. Wayne Senior dumped his late snitch files. Wayne Senior ran Maynard Moore *then*.

Wayne brushed his hair. His hand jerked. He dropped the brush. It hit the floor and shattered.

Wayne walked outside. It was windy. It was hot. It was dark. There—her room/her light.

Wayne walked inside. The hi-fi was on. Cool jazz or some such shit—matched horns discordant.

He turned it off. He tracked the light. He walked over. Janice was changing clothes. Janice saw him—bam—like that.

She dropped her robe. She kicked off her golf cleats. She pulled off her bra and golf shift.

He walked up. He touched her. She pulled his shirt off. She pulled down his pants.

He grabbed her. He tried to kiss her. She slid away. She knelt down. She put his cock in her mouth.

He got hard. He leaked. He got close. He grabbed her hair and pulled her mouth away.

She stepped back. She pulled off his pants. She tripped on his shoes. She sat on the floor. She balled up a skirt. She tucked it under her.

He got down. He ratched his knees. He spread her legs. He kissed her thighs. He kissed her hair and put his tongue in.

She trembled. She made funny sounds. He tasted her. He tasted her outside. He tasted her in.

She trembled. She made scared sounds. She grabbed his hair. She hurt him. She pulled his head up.

He jammed her knees out. He spread her full. She pulled him in. She squeezed a fit. She shut her eyes.

He squeezed her brows. He forced them back open. He put his face down. He keyed on her eyes. He saw green flecks he never saw before.

They moved. They got the fit. They found the sync. They held each other's faces. They locked their eyes in.

He got close. He conjured shit up and held back. Janice buckled. Janice spasmed. Janice clamped her legs.

Wayne sweated. Wayne doused her eyes. She blinked it off. She kept her eyes locked.

A door opened. A door shut. A shadow crossed the light.

Janice buckled. Janice started to cry. Wayne got close. Wayne let go. Wayne shut his eyes.

Janice wiped off her tears. Janice kissed her fingers. Janice put them in his mouth.

They got in bed. They shut their eyes. They left the door open. They left the light on.

House sounds kicked in. Wayne heard Wayne Senior whistle. Wayne smelled Wayne Senior's smoke.

He opened his eyes. His kissed Janice. She trembled. She kept her eyes shut.

Wayne got up. Wayne got dressed. Wayne walked to the bar. Bam—there's Wayne Senior.

Wayne grabbed his stick. Wayne twirled it. Wayne did Daddy's stock tricks.

Wayne said, "You shouldn't have sent me to Dallas."

PART THREE

SUBVERSION

October 1964–July 1965

DOCUMENT INSERT: 10/16/64.
Pouch communiqué. To: Pete Bondurant. From: John
Stanton. Marked: ''Hand Pouch Deliver Only''/
''Destroy Upon Reading.''

P.B.,
Here's the summary you requested. As always, please
read and burn.

First off, there's a consensus among Agency
analysts: we're in Vietnam to stay. You know how far
the trouble goes back—with the Japanese, the Chinese
and the French. Our interest dates to '45. It was
shaped by our commitment to France and our desire to
keep Western Europe out of the Red Bloc, and was
spurred by China going Red. Vietnam is a key chunk of
real estate. We'll lose our foothold in Southeast
Asia if it goes Red. In fact, we'll risk losing the
entire region.

Much of the current situation derives from the Viet
Minh defeat of the French forces at Dien Bien Phu in
March, '54. This led to Geneva accords and the
partitioning of what is now ''North'' and ''South''
Vietnam, along the 17th parallel. The Communists
withdrew from the south and the French from the north.
A nationwide election was called for the summer of
'56.

We installed our man Ngo Dinh Diem in the south.
Diem was a Catholic who was pro-US, anti-Buddhist,
anti-French colonialist and anti-Communist. Agency
operatives rigged a referendum that allowed Diem to
succeed Premier Bao Dai. (It wasn't subtle. Our
people got Diem more votes than the actual number of
voters.)

Diem renounced the '56 Geneva Accord elections. He

said the presence of the Viet Minh insured that the elections could not be ''absolutely free.'' The election deadline approached. The U.S. backed Diem's refusal to participate. Diem initiated ''security measures'' against the Viet Minh in the south. Suspected Viet Minh or Viet Minh sympathizers were tortured and tried by local province officials appointed by Diem. This approach was successful, and Diem managed to smash 90% of the Viet Minh cells in the Mekong Delta. During this time Diem's publicists coined the pejorative term ''Vietnam Cong San'' or ''Vietnamese Communist.''

The election deadline passed. The Soviets and Red Chinese did not press for a political settlement. Early in '57, the Soviets proposed a permanent partition and a U.N. sanctioning of North and South Vietnam as separate states. The U.S. was unwilling to recognize a Communist state and rebuffed the initiative.

Diem built a base in the south. He appointed his brothers and other relatives to positions of power and in fact turned South Vietnam into a narrowly ruled, albeit stridently anti-Communist, oligarchy. Diem's brothers and relatives built up their individual fiefdoms. They were rigidly Catholic and anti-Buddhist. Diem's brother Can was a virtual warlord. His brother Ngo Dinh Nhu ran an anti-Viet Cong intelligence network with CIA funds.

Diem balked at land reforms and allied himself with wealthy landowning families in the Mekong Delta. He created the Khu Tru Mat, i.e., farm communities to buffer peasants from Viet Cong sympathizers and cells. Peasants were uprooted from their native villages and forced to build the communities without pay. Government troops often pilfered their pigs, rice and chicken.

Diem's actions created a demand for reform. Diem closed opposition newspapers, accused journalists, students and intellectuals of Communist ties and arrested them. At this time, the U.S. had a billion dollars invested in South Vietnam. Diem (dubbed ''a puppet who pulls his own strings'') knew that we needed his regime as a strategic port against the spread of Communism. He spent the bulk of his U.S.-donated money on military and police build-up, to quash Viet Cong raids below the 17th parallel and quash domestic plots against him.

In November '60, a military coup against Diem failed. Diem-loyalist troops fought the troops of South Vietnamese Army Colonel Vuong Van Dong. Diem rebuffed the coup, but his actions earned him many enemies among the Saigon and Mekong Delta elite. In the north, this internal dissent emboldened Ho Chi Minh. He embarked on a terror campaign in the south and in December '60 announced the formation of a new insurgent group: the National Liberation Movement. Ho contended that he did not violate the Geneva Accord by sending troops into the south. This was, of course, a lie. Red troops had been steadily infiltrating the south along the ''Ho Chi Minh Trail'' since '59.

Shortly after his inauguration, John Kennedy read a Pentagon analysis of the deteriorating Vietnamese situation. The analysis urged that aid to Diem be increased. Kennedy increased the number of in-country ''advisors'' to 3,000. The advisors were really military personnel, in violation of the Geneva Accord. Kennedy issued a foreign-aid order which served to increase the size of the South Vietnamese Army (the ARVN, or Army of the Republic of South Vietnam) by 20,000 men, to a total of 170,000.

Diem resented the presence of the U.S. ''advisors.'' Then large Viet Cong units began attacking ARVN posts. At that juncture, Diem told the advisors that he wanted to form a bilateral defense pact between the U.S. and South Vietnam.

Kennedy sent General Maxwell Taylor to Saigon. Taylor reported back and reconfirmed the strategic importance of a stand against the Viet Cong. He called for more advisors, along with helicopters and pilot-support for the ARVN. Taylor requested 8,000 troops. The Joint Chiefs and Secretary of Defense McNamara requested 200,000. Kennedy compromised and sent more financial aid to Diem.

Diem initiated the ''Strategic Hamlet'' program early in '62. He detained peasants in armed stockades in an effort to thwart their susceptibility to the Viet Cong. In reality, the program supplied the Viet Cong with converts. In February '62, Diem survived another coup. Two ARVN pilots attacked the presidential palace with napalm, bombs and machine-gun fire. Diem, his brother Nhu and Madame Nhu survived.

Ngo Dinh Nhu had become an embarrassment. He was an opium addict prone to bouts of paranoia. Madame Nhu had convinced Diem to sponsor edicts abolishing divorce, contraceptives, abortion, boxing matches, beauty contests and opium dens. These edicts spawned great resentment. The U.S. advisors noted a new groundswell of anger against the Diem regime.

Anti-Diem sentiment was building within the ARVN command. Diem's Can Lao (the South Vietnamese Secret Police) stepped up its arrests and torture of suspected Buddhist dissidents. Four Buddhist monks publicly incinerated themselves in protest. Madame Nhu praised the suicides and created more resentment. Kennedy and the new Vietnamese ambassador, Henry Cabot Lodge, concluded that the Diem regime was becoming an embarrassing liability, and that Ngo Dinh Nhu and Madame Nhu were the heart of the problem. Covertly, Agency operatives were told to sniff out discontent within the ARVN high command and discuss the viability of a coup.

It was determined that numerous plots already existed, in various states of readiness. Diem sensed the existing ARVN discontent and ordered a show of force against Buddhists and Buddhist sympathizers in Saigon and Hue. It was Diem's intention to turn the Buddhists against the ARVN and exploit the situation to his advantage. On 8/21/63, Diem troops attacked Buddhist temples in Saigon, Hue and other cities. Hundreds of monks and nuns were killed, injured and arrested. Riots and protests against the Diem regime followed.

The Agency learned of Diem's machinations in the ensuing weeks. Kennedy and his advisors were furious and still convinced that Ngo Dinh Nhu was the problem. Diem was instructed to get rid of Nhu. Agency operatives were told to contact potential coup leaders should he refuse, and to pledge our post-coup support.

Ambassador Lodge met with Diem. He became convinced that Diem would never drop Nhu. Lodge informed his Agency contacts. They contacted plotters within the ARVN high command. Lodge, Kennedy, McNamara and the Joint Chiefs met. They discussed the cutoff of financial aid to the Diem regime.

The cutoff was announced. The plotters proceeded. Chief among them were General Tran Van Don, General Le Van Kim and General Duong Van Minh, aka ''Big Minh.'' Agency operatives met with General Don and General Minh and promised them continued U.S. financial aid and support. Kennedy determined that his administration would remain convincingly unaccountable and that the coup would publicly present itself as an all-Vietnamese affair.

The coup was planned and postponed throughout the early fall. Kennedy's advisors included pro-coup and anti-coup factions. The anti-coup faction argued that the autonomous nature of the coup might lead to another ''Bay of Pigs fiasco.''

Internal bickering diverted the plotters. The generals argued over which position of power they would assume in post-coup Saigon. The coup was finally scheduled for 11/1/63. It was implemented that afternoon.

Madame Nhu was in the U.S. Premier Diem and Ngo Dinh Nhu hid in the basement of the presidential palace. Insurgent units captured the palace, the guard barracks and the police station. Diem and Nhu were apprehended and given ''safe passage'' in an armored personnel carrier. The carrier stopped at a railroad crossing. Diem and Nhu were shot and stabbed to death.

A 12-man ''Military Revolutionary Council'' took over and then succumbed to internal squabbles.

Concurrent with this, riots swept the south and
steady streams of Viet Cong infiltrated from the
north. ARVN troops deserted in large numbers.
Concurrent with this, Kennedy was assassinated.
Lyndon Johnson and his advisors reevaluated the
ambiguously defined Vietnamese policy of the Kennedy
administration and decided to expand our financial-
military commitment.

General Nguyen Khanh toppled the ''Military
Revolutionary Council'' on 1/28/64. (''Bloodless''
describes it best. The other generals abdicated and
returned to their military fiefdoms.) Concurrently,
the Viet Cong stepped up its southern incursion,
defeating the ARVN in several encounters and staging
a series of terrorist attacks in Saigon, including
the bombing of a movie theater, where three Americans
were killed. Throughout early '64, the Viet Cong
forces doubled to 170,000 (mostly recruited in the
south) with a commensurate improvement in their
ordnance: Red Chinese and Soviet-supplied AK-47s,
mortars and rocket launchers.

Secretary McNamara visited Vietnam in March and
toured the south in a propaganda effort to bolster
Premier Khanh. McNamara returned to Washington. He
proposed and secured President Johnson's approval of
an ''action memorandum.'' The memorandum called for
increased financial aid, to provide the ARVN with more
aircraft and other ordnance. Premier Khanh was
allowed to stage cross-border raids against
Communist strongholds in Laos and to study the
feasibility of possible incursions into Cambodia to
interdict Viet Cong supply routes. Pentagon
specialists started pinpointing North Vietnamese
targets for U.S. bombing raids.

Ambassador Lodge resigned to pursue a career in
domestic politics. President Johnson appointed
General William C. Westmoreland as Commander of the
U.S. Military Advisory Group (MACV) in Vietnam.
Westmoreland remains committed to a greatly expanded
American presence. There is now a formidable U.S.
contingent in the south, among them servicemen,

accountants, doctors, mechanics and sundry others involved in dispensing the $500,000,000 that Johnson has pledged in fiscal '64 aid. Much of the U.S. donated food, weaponry, medicine, gasoline and fertilizer has ended up on the black market. The U.S. presence in South Vietnam is rapidly becoming the foundation of the South Vietnamese economy.

Johnson has approved a covert plan called ''OPLAN 34-A,'' which calls for larger incursions north of the 17th parallel, an expanded propaganda effort and covert ops to intercept Communist ships delivering material to the Viet Cong in the south. The Gulf of Tonkin incident (8/1–8/3/64, wherein two U.S. destroyers were fired upon by Communist seacraft and returned said fire) was largely a staged and improvised event that Johnson capitalized upon to get congressional sanction for planned bombing raids. The 64 bombing sorties that followed were limited to one day, so as to not give the appearance of overreaction to the Gulf of Tonkin provocation.

As of this (10/16/64) date, there are just under 25,000 ''advisors'' in Vietnam, and the bulk of them are, in fact, combat troops. These troops are Army Special Forces, Airborne Rangers and support personnel. President Johnson has committed to a covert escalation plan which will allow him to introduce an additional 125,000 troops by next summer. Expected North Vietnamese provocations will help him push this troop commitment through Congress. The plan will allow for a large deployment of marines in the winter and spring of '65, and a large influx of army infantry in the summer. Johnson is also committed to sustained bombing raids into North Vietnam. The raids will begin in the late winter-early spring of '65. Again, Agency analysts believe that Johnson will commit to Vietnam for the long haul. The consensus is that he sees Vietnam as a way to establish his anti-Communist credentials to their fullest advantage and use them to counterbalance any political dissension he creates with his liberal domestic reforms.

This overall escalation should serve to cloak our in-country activities. Opium and its derivatives have fueled the Vietnamese economy going back to its early French-colonial days. Intelligence units of the French Army ran the opium trade and managed most of the opium dens in Saigon and Cholon from '51 to '54. The opium traffic has financed dozens of coups and coup attempts, and the late Ngo Dinh Nhu was planning to circumvent Premier Diem's anti-opium edict at the time of his death. Since the 11/1/63 coup, 1,800 opium dens have reopened in Saigon and 2,500 in the heavily Chinese enclave of Cholon (Cholon is 2.5 miles up the Ben Nghe Channel from Central Saigon). Premier Khanh has established a hands-off policy toward the dens, which will serve us well. It should be noted that Khanh is extremely malleable and beholden to our presence in South Vietnam. He loves American money and will not risk offending even adjunct Agency personnel such as our cadre. He is not a ''puppet who pulls his own strings.'' I doubt if he'll last long, and I doubt that his successor(s) will give us any trouble.

The crop source for our potential merchandise is situated in Laos, near the Vietnamese border. The fields near Ba Na Key are rich in the limestone soil component that poppy bulbs thrive on, and dozens of large-scale farms are situated there. Ba Na Key is close to the North Vietnamese border, which invalidates it for our purposes. A strip of acreage further south, near Saravan, is limestone-rich and accessible to the South Vietnamese border. Several poppy camps are situated near Saravan. They are run by Laotian ''Warlords'' who employ ''Armies'' of overseers, who work ''Cliques'' of Laotian/ Vietnamese ''Slaves,'' who harvest the bulbs. I've been grooming an English-speaking Laotian named Tran Lao Dinh, and my plan is to have you and Tran purchase or somehow co-opt the services of the Laotian warlords.

The standard procedure is to refine the poppy sap into a morphine-base that can be further refined into heroin. My goal would be to accomplish that at the farm(s) and ship the base to your chemist's lab in Saigon. We could fly it or move it by PT boat, which would require a pilot-navigator familiar with Vietnamese waterways. The standard way to move morphine-base out of Vietnam is via freighter to Europe and China. That's counterproductive in our case. We need your chemist to refine it in-country, in order to reduce the bulk size and render it easier to ship to Las Vegas. Please think of a way we can courier the finished product stateside, and limit our exposure on both ends.

Some closing thoughts.

Remember, I'm in this with six other agents, and we're Stage-1 Covert, with no Agency sanction. You'll meet the other men on a need-to-know basis. You're the operations boss and I'm the personnel runner. I know you're anxious to start funneling money to the Cause, but we're going to accrue large operating expenses in-country and out, and I want to make sure we're cash fluid first. The Agency has a front-company in Australia that will trade Vietnamese piastres for U.S. dollars, and we may be able to utilize a Swiss bank-account system for the laundering of our ultimate profits.

Let me stress this now. No morphine-base or fully refined merchandise should be allowed to slip into the hands of the U.S. military—for accountability's sake—or into the hands of ARVN personnel. Most ARVNs are highly corruptible and cannot be trusted around saleable narcotics.

I think you'll like my end of the cadre. I've co-opted an Army 1st Lt. named Preston Chaffee. He's a language whiz, Airborne-certified and an all-around good scout. He's my projected liaison to the ARVNs, the Saigon politicos and Premier Khanh.

I need to assess your projected plans and vet your chosen personnel. Can you pouch me, Vegas to Arlington?

For the Cause,

J.S.

<u>DOCUMENT INSERT</u>: 10/27/64.
Pouch communiqué. To: John Stanton. From: Pete
Bondurant. Marked: ''Hand Pouch Deliver Only''/
''Destroy Upon Reading.''

  J.S.,
  I read your summary. Vietnam sounds like my kind of
place.
  Here's my personnel:
  1 - Wayne Tedrow Jr. U.S. Army, '54-'58 (82nd
Airborne Division). Former Las Vegas policeman.
Chemistry degree/Brigham Young University/'59.
  Tedrow's solid. He's proficient with small arms &
larger weaponry. He'll do a solid job on the chemical
side. He told me he studied ''opiate balances'' &
''narcotic component theory'' in college. His plan is
to find human ''test pilots'' or ''guinea pigs'' to
test maximum dosage levels on, such as junkies or
opium addicts with opiate tolerances. That way
he can take the refining process to the final level in
Saigon & ship street-ready merchandise back to
Vegas.
  Tedrow's father is a big wheel in Nevada. Tedrow's
<u>very</u> estranged from him, but the old man has
connections at Nellis AFB that we may be able to use.
More on this later.
  2, 3 - Laurent Guery & Flash Elorde.
  You know them from our Miami days. They've been
merc'ing out of Mexico City since late '63 & they're
anxious to find a permanent duty station. They're
devoted to the Cause & will fit in on the cultivation,
enforcement & distribution ends. Both men have ties
to gulf coast-based exiles that we'll be able to
utilize.
  4 - Jean Philippe Mesplede.
  You sent me his dossier, so I won't repeat his
stats. I met him in Mexico City & liked him. He's
French-English fluent & knows some Vietnamese dialect
from his '53-'54 tour. He's got in-country narcotics
experience, along with some exile ties & is solidly
committed to the Cause.

5 – Chuck Rogers.

Another old Tiger ops grad. You know his stats: pilot, wet-arts, shortwave radio skills. Deep exile ties & connections on the southern gun circuit. A valuable all-around guy. He wants to distribute hate leaflets and broadcast short-wave tirades in-country, & I'll humor him on that until it gets out of hand.

6 – Bob Relyea.

I don't know him & I'm hiring him off Rogers' recommendation. (They've been shortwave buddies for years. Rogers vouches for him & he's already in-country.)

Relyea's a Staff Sgt. with the MP Brigade in Saigon. He was formerly a prison guard in Missouri & has strong right-wing ties in the south. He's allegedly a great sharpshooter & all-around weapons man.

Per my plan:

I want to get into Laos quick & have Tran Lao Dinh negotiate with the ''warlords'' for their poppy farms. I want to bribe the right ARVN men & other Saigon officials to procure us the right level of protection. Then I'll have Rogers fix up a small 2-engine aircraft & fly circuits from Laos to Saigon. He'll conduit the morphine-base to Tedrow's lab & double as an enforcer at the slave farm(s).

Per the stateside conduit:

I'd like to ship via Agency-courier flights to Nellis. I've got a well-placed lawyer friend who may be able to pull strings & get us clearance there. Then we'll distribute out of Tiger Kab, to (expendable) Negro pushers who'll push exclusively in West Vegas. Rogers, Guery & Elorde will funnel the final profits to exile groups on the gulf.

The team is solid. I'm confident that they'll work well together. Let's stay focused on the Cuban end of things.

Viva la Causa!

P.B.

DOCUMENT INSERT: 10/29/64.
Pouch communiqué. To: Pete Bondurant. From: John
Stanton. Marked: ''Hand Pouch Deliver Only''/
''Destroy Upon Reading.''

   P.B.,
   I like your personnel and plan, per one proviso.
   You'll need cargo-manifest cover to land at Nellis,
and it must be convincing. What do you advise?
   J.S.

DOCUMENT INSERT: 10/31/64.
Pouch communiqué. To: John Stanton. From: Pete
Bondurant. Marked: ''Hand Pouch Deliver Only''/
''Destroy Upon Reading.''

   J.S.,
   Per your last pouch:
   Howard Hughes (my old boss & my lawyer friend's
current boss) wants to curry favor with politicians &
military personnel in Nevada & already has Hughes
Aircraft-Tool Co charter clearance at Nellis. My
lawyer friend will try to convince H.H. to purchase
ARVN-surplus ordnance to donate to the Nevada
National Guard, as a PR ploy. This will expand his
ground clearance & allow us to hide our merchandise in
with the ordnance & fly it straight to Nellis & Vegas.
   What do you think?
   P.B.

DOCUMENT INSERT: 11/1/64.
Pouch communiqué. To: Pete Bondurant. From: John
Stanton. Marked: ''Hand Pouch Deliver Only''/
''Destroy Upon Reading.''

   P.B.,
   Contact your lawyer friend and try to implement
ASAP. I approve your selected personnel, and I'll
have Lt. Chaffee approach and detach Sgt. Relyea from
his regular duties. See you in Saigon: 11/3/64.
   J.S.

DOCUMENT INSERT: 11/2/64.
Verbatim FBI telephone call transcript.
Marked: ''Recorded at the Director's Request''/
''Classified Confidential 1-A: Director's Eyes Only.''
Speaking: Director Hoover, Ward J. Littell.

JEH: Good morning, Mr. Littell.

WJL: Good morning, Sir.

JEH: The election bodes. Prince Bobby's probable
victory must hearten you.

WJL: It does, Sir.

JEH: The Dark Prince has plundered New York State
with great verve. I liken it to the Visigoths storming
Rome.

WJL: It's a vivid comparison, Sir.

JEH: Lyndon Johnson was Bobby's reluctant
henchman. He told me, quote, Edgar, I hate that little
rabbit-faced cocksucker, and it galls me to hustle
him votes.

WJL: President Johnson has verve of his own.

JEH: Yes, and much of it is directed toward the
passage of dubious legislation. I view the words
''Great Society'' as fresh lyrics to ''The
Internationale.''

WJL: It's a deft analogy, Sir.

JEH: Lyndon Johnson will deplete his prestige on
the home-front and recoup it in Vietnam. History will
judge him as a tall man with big ears who needed
wretched people to love him.

WJL: Said with verve, Sir.

JEH: Lyndon Johnson appreciates the verve of one
Martin Lucifer King. I've been sending him motel-room
tapes. Lucifer performs with equal verve in bed and at
barricades.

WJL: Dr. King wears many hats, Sir.

JEH: Yes, and he also wears garishly patterned
Fruit-of-the-Loom briefs.

WJL: You're maintaining a close surveillance, Sir.

JEH: Yes, and I have Lyle Holly to direct me to
Lucifer's favored tryst-spots. I talk to Lyle on a
near-daily basis, and he tells me that Bayard Rustin

is very much taken with you and your allegedly
pilfered organized-crime donations.

WJL: Mr. Rustin finds me sincere, Sir.

JEH: Because you are.

WJL: I work at verve, Sir.

JEH: You succeed.

WJL: Thank you, Sir.

JEH: I detect a shift in tone. Do you wish to ask a
question?

WJL: Yes, Sir.

JEH: Ask, Mr. Littell. You know I find preambles
taxing.

WJL: Do you know when you'll leak word of my
donations?

JEH: When I sense that my missives on Lucifer's
Communist ties and sex life have reached their
cumulative peak.

WJL: That's a sound strategy, Sir.

JEH: It's an inspired strategy. It's inimical to
your recent gambit with Wayne Senior.

WJL: Is he peeved at me, Sir?

JEH: Yes, but he won't tell me why.

WJL: I set up a deal for him. He facilitated some
charter flights out of Nellis and wanted a higher
percentage. His Mormons have cut him out of his
existing one.

JEH: Percentage of what?

WJL: The casino skim his Mormons were moving.

JEH: I am as delighted by that bit of data as Wayne
Senior is vexed.

WJL: I'm always pleased to amuse you, Sir.

JEH: Wayne Senior has been in a thoroughly vexed
state lately. He's rebuffed all my inquiries about
his son.

WJL: I'm going to raise his percentage, Sir. That
should improve his mood.

JEH: Why? What do you need from him?

WJL: I need to expand my Nellis clearance.

JEH: To include?

WJL: Flights from Vietnam.

JEH: Data coheres in odd fashions. You're my second postcard from Vietnam this morning.

WJL: Sir?

JEH: Dwight Holly called. He told me that Wayne Tedrow Junior and Pete Bondurant were recently granted Vietnamese travel visas.

WJL: That is odd, Sir.

JEH: Yes, and you are being oddly and blithely disingenuous, so I'll change the subject. How are Count Dracula's colonization plans proceeding?

WJL: Very well, Sir. Pete Bondurant has purchased a taxi stand and is using it to accrue intelligence for Mr. Hughes. The drivers have picked up dirt on several Nevada state legislators.

JEH: It's ingenious. Cab drivers are night-riding denizens of the first order. They view wretched foibles from a gutter perspective.

WJL: I thought you'd appreciate it, Sir. And while we're on the topic of—

JEH: Don't lead me. Ask your favor while I'm still pixilated and bemused.

WJL: I'd like to initiate a standing-bug operation in Vegas. I want to bug the hotel rooms the legislators stay in most frequently. I'll bring in Fred Turentine to help me with the installation, and I'd like local agents to do the retrievals and forward copies to me.

JEH: Do it. I'll assign two agents from the Las Vegas Office.

WJL: Thank you, Sir.

JEH: Thank yourself. You charmed me out of a bad mood.

WJL: I'm glad, Sir.

JEH: What would Tedrow Junior and Le Grand Pierre be doing in Vietnam?

WJL: I couldn't begin to guess.

JEH: Good day, Mr. Littell.

WJL: Good day, Sir.

60

(Saigon, 11/3/64)

DIG IT:

Rickshaw bikes and sandbags. Gun nests and frangipani trees. Grenade nets and gooks.

Saigon at high noon—Brave New Fucking World.

It's big. It's tricultural. It's hot. It's noisy. It stinks.

The limo crawled. The limo bucked rickshaws. They bumped. They slid. They locked à la *Ben-Hur*.

White buildings. Pagodas. Propaganda signs: VIGILANCE IS FREEDOM/TREASON HAILS NORTH!

The limo crawled. The shocks creaked. The wheels slid. The cooler fan died.

Mesplède smoked. Chuck smoked. Flash smoked. The driver sold them black-market Kools. Guéry smoked a Cohiba. Chaffee smoked a Mecundo. They smoked pro-Fidel.

Wayne moaned. Wayne got green-gilled. Pete got queasy. Pete read native tongue:

A BAS LES VIET-CONG! HO CHI MINH, LE DIABLE COMMUNISTE!

Qu'est-ce que c'est, toute cette merde?

The limo crawled. They hit Tu Do Street—the Gook Sunset Strip.

Big trees and big shops. Big hotels and big traffic. Big noise *en gook*.

Pete yawned. Pete stretched. They flew nineteen hours in. Stanton set their rooms up. Hotel Catinat upcoming—sleep most ricky-tick.

The driver rode his horn. The driver clipped a rickshaw. Mesplède sniffed the air and nailed scents.

Nuoc mam—fish sauce—goat bar-b-que. Machine-gun oil/frangipani blossoms/goat shit.

Stanton said, "You'll lay up for two days, then fly to Dak Sut. You'll cross into Laos and meet Tran Lao Dinh. An ARVN rifle squad will walk point for you. Two Hueys will meet you and fly you to a dope camp near Saravan. You'll negotiate right there."

Buddhist monks jaywalked. Traffic stalled up. Pete yawned. Pete stretched. Pete elbowed more room.

Milt C. ran Tiger now. Milt ran liaison gigs. Milt ran adjunct ops:

Ward Littell to bug hotel suites. Milt to bribe hotel clerks. Milt to schmooze them. Milt to tell them: place state legislators within.

Pete's bigggg decree:

Restrict the Tiger crew. Restrict all pill ops. Rat rival pill crews. Rat said crews to Agent Dwight Holly.

Trash the Vegas pill trade. Dry up West Vegas. Deprive hopheads. Tempt taste buds. Prepare hopheads for Big "H."

Chaffee waved his ditty bag. Chaffee offered gifts. Shrunken heads—*certified*—all VC *très bien*.

Wayne tossed his out. Flash kissed his. Guéry named his "Fidel."

Pete yawned. Pete popped Dramamine. The Arden bit bugged him. It bugged him incessant. It bugged him nonstop.

He factored Carlos in. 3/56: Carlos bails Arden/Arden splits K.C.

New Orleans—'59—Mesplède sees Arden. Arden has a date. He's a Carlos man/he's a wop. 11/63: Arden visits the safe house. Carlos thus orders her clipped.

He factored Carlos in. He held back. He never told Ward. He called Fred Otash. He said call around.

Run Arden. Call your contacts. Glom me some leads. Check Arden out. Check out her ex—one Danny Bruvick.

Flash kissed his shrunken head. Flash applied some tongue. Chaffee laughed. Mesplède named his head "de Gaulle."

Chuck waved his head. Wayne grabbed it. Wayne threw it out.

Chuck said, "There's times I think we hired the wrong Tedrow."

No sleep—his head wouldn't stop.

The room was okay—*comme ci/comme ça*—likewise the Tu Do Street view.

The bed sagged. The grenade-screen creaked. The AC sputtered. Fumes cut through—*nuoc mam* sauce—*ce n'est pas bon.*

Street noise carried up. Choppers buzzed the roof.

Pete gave up. Pete oiled his piece. Pete put out his bedside pix. Barb/the cat snarling/Barb with the cat.

Stanton set up an outing—1900 hours—Saigon by night. We'll check out the natives. We'll dig the night view.

Pete sat on the terrace. Pete dug the *now* view. Pete saw ARVN cliques. Pete saw gook cops.

Chaffee called them "White Mice." Mesplède called GIs "Con Van My."

The skyline clashed—tin roofs and spires—M-60 machine guns.

He loved war zones. He saw Pearl Harbor. He saw Okinawa. He saw Saipan. He saw Pigs. He avenged Pigs. He scalped Reds *beaucoup*.

Dusk hit. The roof crews rejoiced. They arced their guns. They shot tracer rounds. They made fireworks.

The new cadre was goooood. The new cadre was #1. Cadre with a "K" now.

Stanton liked the guys. Stanton said Bob Relyea was a "Head Man." He killed VC. He chopped their heads off. He sold them to clinics.

Flash named his head "Khrushchev." Stanton named his head "Ho." Chuck named his head "JFK."

They rendezvoused. They grabbed a stretch limo.

Bob Relyea showed up. Chuck hugged him. They laughed. They shared spit. They talked Klan.

The limo sagged—nine riders plus weight.

The kadre packed sidearms. The driver packed grenades. Relyea packed a 30.06.

They swung off Tu Do. They hit side streets. The limo flew flags: The MACV/the ARVN/the skull & bones.

Rickshaws clogged traffic. The driver rode his horn. The gooks ignored it. The driver yelled, "*Di, di!*"

Mesplède popped the sunroof. Mesplède popped a clip up. The noise was bad. The shells blew down. Flash caught them hot. The gooks heard the noise. The gooks pulled over. The gooks ducked low and booked.

The driver punched it. Mesplède flexed his tattoos. Two pit bulls grew boners. Two parachutes flew.

"You must announce your intent to these people. They understand only force."

Reylea fanned playing cards—all ace-of-spades.

"They understand force and superstition. These cards, for instance. You drop one on a dead VC and scare off potential converts."

Chaffee said, "Affirmative on that. I like the Viets, but they're primitive as hell. They talk to shadows and dead chickens."

Flash chewed a shell. "Where the GIs? I only count four men so far."

Stanton said, "They tend to wear civvies. They stand out because they're white or colored, and they don't like to compound things by wearing uniforms."

Flash shrugged. *Qué pasa* "compound"?

Pete lit a cigarette. "A six-figure troop commitment by summer. That means breathing room."

Flash shrugged. *Qué pasa* "commitment"? Guery shrugged. *Qu'est-ce que c'est?*

Pete laughed. Stanton laughed. Relyea cut cards. He fanned cards. He flipped cards. He pulled cards off Wayne's shirt.

"Chuck and me got distribution plans. I been sending tracts to inmates throughout the Missouri prison system, which was my pre-U.S. Army employer. I been sending them stuck inside these Voice of America pamphlets, which means the inmates get a soft version of the truth and the real thing."

Chuck lit a cigarette. "Aerial drops are the best. You fly low and bombard the troops."

Relyea shook his head. "Negative on that. You waste good tracts on the nigger EM."

Chuck winked. "Wayne's daddy's a tract man. He throws a good party, too."

Wayne stared at Chuck. Wayne cracked his thumbs.

Chuck said, "Wayne's a Martin Luther Coon fan. He's seen all his films."

Wayne stared. Chuck stared back. The stretch swerved. Chuck blinked first. Wayne blinked last.

The stretch swayed. The driver dodged a pig. Pete looked out. Pete looked up.

He saw tracer rounds. Tracers as firefly flares.

They cruised Khanh Hoi. They scoped the clubs. They hit the Duc Quynh.

It was small. It was dark. It was French. Banquettes/mood lights/jukebox. They got a booth. They ordered wine. They ate bouillabaisse.

Wayne sulked. Pete watched him.

Ward snipped his daddy cord. Hey, Wayne, dig this: Daddy

bought you Dallas. Wayne took it hard. Wayne held his mud. Wayne waxed sullen resultant.

The food rocked—garlic and squid—chow *indigène*. Bar girls performed.

They peeled to pasties. They lip-synced tunes. They sang some Barb cover songs.

Chuck got drunk. Bob got drunk. They talked Klan shit resultant. Flash got drunk. Guéry got drunk. They talked patois.

Chaffee got drunk. Chaffee waved shrunken heads. Chaffee spooked the girls off resultant.

Stanton sipped martinis. Wayne sipped vichy. Mesplède smoked a Gauloise a minute. Pete heard bombs. Pete gauged directions.

Small bombs—two clicks over—reverb off water.

Chaffee called it—White Mice and VC. Gadfly stuff—pipe bombs *pas beaucoup*.

The club filled up. Stag GIs cruised stag nurses.

They hobnobbed. They danced. They hogged the jukebox. They played Vietrock—Ricky Nelson in gook—"Herro, Maly Roo."

Two niggers showed up. They vibed jungle stud. They vibed plantation buck.

They hit on white nurses. They sparked rapport. They sat with them. They danced with them. They danced sloooow.

Wayne seized up. Wayne watched them. Wayne gripped the table.

They danced. They did the Stroll. They did the Watusi. Wayne watched them. Chuck caught it. Chuck signaled Bob.

They watched Wayne. Pete watched Wayne. Wayne watched the niggers dance. They worked their hips. They lit cigarettes. They fed the nurses puffs.

Wayne gripped the table. Wayne tore a plank loose. The stew pot fell. Fishheads flew.

Pete said, "Let's walk."

They hit the docks. They met Stanton's ARVNs. Two *trung uys*—junior grade—first-lieutenant gooks.

The lab was close. They walked over. The ARVNs walked point. Tracers popped. Red light tinged the water.

There—

The building's white brick. It's smeared with gook graffiti.

One nightclub/one dope den/one floor per each. *Three* floors —with lab space on top.

They walked in. They scoped out the Go-Go. There's a bar. There's a bandstand. There's a shrunken-head motif.

Shrunken-head wall mounts. Shrunken-head ashtrays. Shrunken-head candlesticks.

More B-girls. More ARVNs. More GIs. More musk and more Ricky Nelson. More "Herro, Maly Roo."

They walked upstairs. The ARVNs chaperoned them. There's the dope den.

Floor pallets/wood planks recumbent/dope beds boocoo. Piss troughs and shit buckets. Four walls as fart envelopes.

O-heads boocoo. O-heads in orbit. Slants and some round-eyes. One jigaboo.

They walked through. They pallet-hopped. They dodged fumes. Pete held his nose. Scents sizzled and mixed.

Sweat/smoke/fart residue.

The ARVNs wiggled flashlights—you rook rook rook:

See the dope skin. See the dope eyes. See the Jockey shorts de rigueur.

Chaffee said, "The Americans are ex-Army. They got discharged and stuck around. The colored guy pimps slant girls out of the Go-Go."

The ARVNs flashed the spook's pallet. Said spook flew dee-luxe. Dig his silk pillow. Dig his down bed and silk sheets.

Pete sneezed. Flash coughed. Stanton squashed a turd. Chuck laughed. Guéry kicked a pallet. Guéry dislodged a gook.

Mesplède laughed. Bob laughed. Wayne watched the spook.

They walked. They hit the back door. They took side stairs up. There's the lab—dig it!

Stoves. Vats. Oil drums. Beakers/kettles/pans. Shelves. Mustard jars with taped labels.

Stanton said, "I got everything Wayne asked for."

Chaffee sneezed. "It's quality stuff. I got most of it in Hong Kong."

Coffee filters. Lime sacks. Suction pumps and extraction tubes.

Pete said, "We cook it bulk and ship it that way. Wayne and I work the in-country and Vegas ends. We follow the courier flights to Nellis and go from there."

Chuck lit a cigarette. "Ward Littell's got to get clearance, which as I understand it means he's got to brown-nose Wayne Senior."

Wayne shook his head. "He doesn't need to. There's a one-star named Kinman who can do it."

The room smelled. Caustic agents settling in. Lime dust boocoo.

Pete sneezed. "I'll call Ward and tell him."

Wayne checked the shelves. Wayne read labels:

Chloroform. Ammonia. Sulfate salts. Muriatic Acid. Hydrochloric Acid. Acetic anhydride.

He cracked jars. He smelled compounds. He touched the powder stock.

"I want to refine to the maximum viable dosage strength here. We finalize the quality here and tell the distribution guys in Vegas not to cut it any further."

Stanton smiled. "You've got your test pilots one floor down."

Chaffee smiled. "They've got opiate tolerances you can work off."

Mesplède smiled. "Inject them with a caffeine compound first. It will serve to open their capillaries and secure you a more accurate reading."

Pete cracked a window. Tracer rounds flew. Dig the streetside procession:

Slants in robes—baldies all—loud chants in sync.

Yawns went around. Looks went around. Fuck this—we're jet-fucked and fucked from no sleep.

Stanton locked the lab. Chaffee greased the ARVNs. You guard the lab/you stay all night—ten dollars U.S.

Everyone yawned. Everyone was fried. Everyone dog-yawned and stretched.

They walked downstairs. They cut through the den. They cut through the Go-Go. The Go-Go rocked anew.

More round-eyes. More GIs. Some U.S. embassy types.

The spook pimp was up. The spook pimp was de-O'd and revived.

He bossed his whores around. He made his whores strip. He made his whores hop on three tables.

They linked up. They performed table tricks. They French-kissed and went 69.

Wayne weaved. Pete steadied him. A Buddhist monk walked in.

His robe dripped. He looked stupefied. His robe reeked of gas. He bowed. He squatted. He lit a match. He gook-cooked with gas.

He whooshed. He flared. Flames hit the ceiling. The lez shows dispersed. The monk burned. The fire spread. Some clubhoppers screeched.

The barman stretched a fizz cord. The barman spritzed club soda. The barman sprayed the monk.

61

(Las Vegas, 11/4/64)

BUGWORK.

Littell twisted wires. Littell hung microphones. Fred Turentine hung feeder cords.

They laid cords. They taped wires. They perforated wall mounts. They spackled wall plates.

The Riviera—bug job #9. A big suite—three rooms in. Bugwork—Vegas-wide. Bribed access—four hotels in.

Moe Dalitz bribed managers. Milt Chargin bribed clerks. Mr. Hoover bribed the Vegas SAC. Said SAC pledged agents. Said SAC pledged speed. Said SAC pledged copied tapes.

Tapes to Mr. Hoover. Tapes to Ward Littell.

Turentine looped wires. Littell ran the TV. The news ran on. They caught LBJ's landslide. They caught Bobby's Senate sweep.

Turentine picked his nose. "I hate spackle mounts. The fucking paste stings."

LBJ praised the voters. Ken Keating conceded. Bobby hugged his kids.

"I guess I'm lucky to get the work. It's not like the scandal-rag days. Freddy Otash had me wire every fucking toilet in L.A."

Goldwater conceded. Hubert Humphrey smiled. LBJ hugged his kids.

Turentine flicked snot. "Freddy's scuffling. Pete's got him running leads on some woman. Her husband screwed Jimmy H. on a deal."

Littell killed the sound. Humphrey went mute. LBJ moved his lips.

"Who has the old scandal-rag morgue files? Would Freddy know?"

Turentine hooked wires. "You mean the *hot* dirt? The unprintable shit that never got published?"

"That's right."

"Why do you—"

"The information could help us. The rags always kept stringers in Vegas."

Turentine popped a neck zit. "If you're willing to pay, Freddy'd be willing to look."

"Call him, will you? Tell him I'll pay double his day rate and expenses."

Turentine nodded. Turentine popped a chin zit. Littell goosed the TV. LBJ praised Bobby. Bobby praised LBJ. Bobby praised the Great Society.

Littell miked a nightstand. Littell miked a couch leg. Littell miked a lamp.

Morgue dirt was old. Morgue dirt was still ripe. Morgue dirt might help Mr. Hughes. They needed dirt. Dirt incurred debt. Let's call Moe D. Let's call Milt C. Let's bug more rooms yet.

Grind joints next—bedroom mounts—Milt to retrieve. Let's bug Vegas. Let's cull dirt. Let's extort.

Littell miked a chair. Turentine flipped channels. There's Mr. Hoover in the flesh.

He said, "King." He said, "Communist sympathizer." He looked old. He looked weak.

The news ran late. Bobby's segments ran long.

Littell went "home." Littell called room service. Littell ate dinner and watched TV.

Home-*suite*-home. Room service and valets.

He missed Jane. He pressed her to come for Thanksgiving. She agreed. It scared her. The Boys owned the town.

She told lies. It disturbed him in L.A. He missed her and wanted her here.

Bobby praised LBJ. Bobby praised his programs. Bobby praised Dr. King.

He played his Bobby tapes. He played them most nights. Sometimes Jane overheard. He punted. He lied. He described depositions.

Lies:

Bayard Rustin pressed him—meet Dr. King—Bayard proposed a dinner. He declined. He *lied*. He stressed nonexistent engagements. He *lied*. He never said "distance."

Distance balanced his risk. Distance balanced his commitment. He subverted King. He aided King. He worked for a balance.

Personal moments would kill it. Affection would blitz respect. Compartments would burn. The risk would grow exponential.

Bobby promised legislation. Bobby promised hard work. Bobby did not mention organized crime. Bobby did not mention Jack.

He *knew* Bobby. Bobby *knew* the Boys killed Jack. Bobby on tape: "When the time's right I'll jump on it, and devil take the hindmost."

Don't. Please. Don't risk your safety. Don't risk yourself.

Littell flipped channels. Littell saw LBJ. Littell saw Blatz beer and Vietnam. U.S. advisors. More troops pledged. Buddhist monks on fire.

Pete called him this morning. Pete pitched a plan: Call Drac/ *work* Drac/help me work *this* new plan.

He agreed. He called Drac and snowed him. Drac agreed to Pete's "plan." Pete dropped the name Clark Kinman. Bypass Wayne Senior through him.

He called Kinman. He pitched a meet. He deciphered the gist of Pete's "plan."

Heroin/Vietnam. "Ordnance"/hidden dope/cosmetic donations.

It meant one thing. The Boys waived the no-dope rule. The Boys never told him.

Pete sounded happy. Pete came off engaged. Pete built airtight compartments. There's Betty Mac. There's heroin. There's the partition.

Littell flipped channels. Bobby waved. Bobby hugged his kids.

Kinman served drinks. Littell sipped club soda. Kinman sipped scotch himself.

"I know about you. You brought the Hughes charter deal to Wayne Senior."

The den was stuffy. The den was GI. Airplane models and airplane wall plaques.

Littell smiled. "I hope your compensation sufficed."

Kinman sipped scotch. "I'm an officer in the United States Air Force. I'm not going to tell a perfect stranger if, where, or how I was compensated, if in fact I was."

Littell twirled his coaster. "You could call Wayne Senior for a reference."

"We're not on good terms. He told me he doesn't like you, which refers you pretty good these days."

A door slammed upstairs. Music kicked on. A female voice hummed along.

Littell stirred his drink. "Do you know who I work for?"

"I was informed that it was Howard Hughes, who folks say has designs on Las Vegas. I figured he was good for the town, which is why I facilitated the charter deal."

"For which you were or were not compensated."

The music dipped. Footsteps tapped downstairs. A woman hummed along.

Kinman smiled. "I've got a friend here. That means you've got five minutes to state your case and skedaddle."

Littell toed his briefcase. "Mr. Hughes wants to donate U.S.-supplied Vietnamese Army surplus to the Air National Guard. He wants to publicize the donations and credit you with inspiring the gift. All he requires is expanded ground clearance for periodic courier flights from Saigon."

Kinman chewed ice. "With no contraband checks?"

"He would appreciate that courtesy, yes."

" 'That courtesy' will cost $5,000 per month, in cash, nonrefundable."

Littell popped his briefcase. Littell dumped forty grand. Drac gave him fifty. He kept and tithed ten.

Kinman whooped. Janice Tedrow walked in.

She limped. She swung a cane. She rubbed a scar on her lips.

62

(Dak Sut, 11/7/64)

HEAT. BUGS. BULLSHIT.

Dak Sut featured peasants. Dak Sut featured clay-mud. Dak Sut featured thirty-three huts.

ARVNs called peasants *que lam*. Chaffee called ARVNs "Marvin." Pete called them "Marv." Chuck called them "Marv." Bob Relyea called them "Sahib."

Wayne itched. Wayne slapped bugs. Wayne scoped Dak Sut. He saw pigs. He saw rice bins. He saw the Dak Poko River.

A bridge. Brown water. Thick jungle ahead.

They flew up. Three Marvs came along. Chaffee hired a Huey. The pilot slurped wine. Chuck and Bob tossed hate tracts out.

Wayne itched. Wayne slapped bugs. Wayne wore fatigues and a .45. Wayne packed a 12-gauge pump.

GI gear—kadre kustomized. Dum-dums and beehive rounds—steel darts encased.

Laos was close. The Marvs knew the way. The Marvs had *their* guide—some ex-Cong stashed in a hut.

Tran Dinh camped near Saravan. Tran Dinh had men. Tran Dinh had two Hueys prepped. They'd fly to Joe Warlord's camp. They'd "negotiate."

Wayne itched. Wayne slapped bugs. Wayne scoped Dak Sut. Peasants hovered. Mesplède dispensed Kools. Pete hit hut 16. Pete hauled the Cong out.

Chuck deshackled him. Bob rigged a collar. The Marvs leashed him up. *Nice* collar—poodle-sized and spiked.

Chuck fucked with the leash. Chuck laid some slack in. Chuck cinched the Cong up.

Wayne walked over. The Cong wore black pj's. The Cong wore torture cuts.

Chuck said, "Bow wow."

Bob sang "Walkin' the Dog."

They moved out.

They walked single-file. They crossed the Dak Poko. They hit the province hut. The Marvs greased the hut boss—five bucks U.S. The hut boss swooned.

They hit Laos. They walked foot trails. Hills and brush cover. Krazy Glue clay.

The Cong walked ahead. Chuck snapped his leash. Chuck named him "Fido." Fido tugged. Fido walked barefoot. Fido stretched his leash.

Wayne walked rear point. My craaaazy life—Army Airborne to *this*.

He killed time in Saigon. He read his chemistry texts. He hit the USO. He ordered the Vegas and Dallas papers. He moved into the lab. He stored his Durfee file.

He filed tips. He summarized tips. He ate at the Go-Go. He dug on the weird food. He offered the owner some help.

The fried monk caused damage. The fried monk burned beams. The fried monk scorched the paint job.

Wayne repainted. Wayne redrilled beams. The pimp hung around. Wayne watched him. Wayne learned his stats:

Maurice Hardell/aka Bongo/ex-QM PFC. Stockade time and a pervert DD.

He watched Bongo. He watched the kadre men. The kadre men watched him. They knew *his* stats. They dug on them. Chuck spieled them out.

He got *their* stats. Pete supplied them:

Guéry hated Reds. Mesplède hated Reds. They killed Congo rebels. They killed Algerians. Chuck hated Reds. Chuck was ex-CIA. Chuck killed Fidelistos.

Flash hated Reds. Flash killed Reds. Flash used to pimp girls in Havana. Flash split Cuba. Flash hit the U.S. Flash robbed liquor stores.

Flash knew Guéry. Flash met Pete. Flash met John Stanton. Chuck knew Bob. Bob pushed hate tracts. Bob mailed hate tracts to prisons.

Chaffee was a blueblood. Chaffee went Army. Stanton was a blue-blood. Stanton went to Yale. Stanton knew Chaffee's dad. Stanton owned United Fruit stock. The Beard kicked UF out of Cuba. The Beard fucked with their stock.

Cuba drove them. Cuba drove Pete. Cuba drove the dope plan. Cuba drove Viet ops. Something said Cuba drove Dallas.

They talked:

Guéry and Mesplède/Chuck and Pete/Flash Elorde. They spoke English. They stopped. They spoke Spanish and French. They said "Dallas" trilingual.

Dallas—a noun—a city in Texas. Dallas—the break point for *him*.

He waited since childhood. He notched a fast fuck. He dropped his Dallas punchline. He fucked Janice. He jeopardized her. They both wanted out from Wayne Senior. They fucked to burn their lives down.

He bought the Vegas papers. He checked the missing persons

logs and obits. Wayne Senior killed Wardell Gray. Wayne Senior did not kill Janice.

He cut them off. He left them. He walked. He ignored them. He thought about Bongo. He thought about Wendell D.

The kadre trudged. The trail swerved. Bush hemmed them in. Chaffee read his compass. They held northwest.

They crossed clearings. They spread out. They flanked. Wayne switched positions. Wayne took Fido's leash.

Fido walked fast—good dog—most ricky-tick.

Wayne walked fast. Fido tugged. Wayne caught up and ran abreast. Fido went darty. Wayne tracked his eyes. Fido lurched. Fido weaved.

Marv One yelled, "*Chuyen gi vay?*"

Marv Two yelled, "*Chuyen, chuyen?*"

Fido yelled, "*Khong co chuyen gi het.*"

They hit a clearing. They reflanked. Fido tugged left. Fido squatted. Fido dropped his pants.

Wayne saw a turd drop. Wayne saw a tree stump. Wayne saw an X. Fido grabbed something. Fido threw something. Something blew up.

Fuck—smoke/shrapnel/gunfire.

Chaffee caught metal scraps. Chaffee went down. Two Marvs caught it tight. An arm flew. A foot flew. Stumps spattered.

Wayne proned out. Wayne rolled. Wayne pulled his .45. Pete proned out. Chuck proned out. Marv Three fired wide.

Pete fired. Chuck fired. Fido tugged his leash. Wayne dug in. Wayne pulled the leash. Wayne reeled him in.

He's close—there's his neck/there's his eyes.

Wayne aimed. Wayne popped four shots off. Fido's teeth shattered. Fido's neck blew.

Wayne heard yells. Wayne saw three VC.

They charged. They aimed carbines. They got kadre klose. Pete stood up. Chuck stood up. Mesplède waved *come on*.

Bob stood up. Bob aimed his pump. Bob shot low. A beehive blew—darts blew—darts on fire.

The spread cohered. The spread hit. The spread severed legs. Three trunk sections detached and fell.

Pete fired. Chuck fired. Mesplède fired tight. They popped full clips—.45 ACPs—they ten-ringed head shots.

Wayne walked over. Wayne kicked a loose leg. Wayne saw a Ho Chi Minh tattoo. Wayne saw needle marks.

* * *

Pete said no burials. Chuck said no evidence. Mesplède said guts lured wild pigs.

Bob disemboweled the Marvs. Pete disemboweled Chaffee. Bob disemboweled the VC. Wayne flipped a coin. Marv Three called heads. Wayne got tails—tough luck.

He disemboweled Fido. He thought of Maynard Moore. He smelled the rest stop near Dallas.

They walked away. Chuck left hate tracts. Bob left an ace of spades.

They walked.

They lost Chaffee's compass. They tracked off the sun. Dusk hit. They tracked off starlight.

A haze hit. The stars died. The foot trail bisected. They veered instinct-right. Ursa Minor broke through. They resighted and cut back.

They walked. They used flashlights. They hit undergrowth. Thick shit—leaves and roots.

They kicked through it. A haze hit. The stars died. They cut back. They fried their flashlights. They walked in the dark.

They saw lights. Marv Three called it:

Two clicks over—village—*que lam beaucoup*. I go now. I get village help. I bring guide back.

Pete said go. Marv Three walked. They waited. Nobody talked. Nobody smoked. Wayne clocked off forty-six minutes.

Marv Three walked back. Marv Three brought Fido Two. An old guy—the papa-san type—Ho beard and tire-tread shoes.

Chuck leashed him up. Chuck named him "Rover." Chuck fed him cigarettes. Rover had good wind. Rover walked fast. Rover leaped limbs and brush piles.

They hit a clearing. They flanked wide. They aimed in a 360 arc. A flare popped at ten o'clock—pink light streaked and poofed.

They cut loose. They blew beehives. Darts disinterred.

Somebody yelled, "Friend!"

Somebody yelled, "Tran Dinh!"

Tran had a campsite. Pete called it Tran's Fontainebleau.

One acre. Weeds and mulched dirt. Bug nets and grenade nets. Brushed-steel lean-tos.

They slept hard. They slept late. Tran's men cooked brunch.

Tran scrounged off Stanton. Stanton scrounged the Army. Stanton scrounged pancake batter. Stanton scrounged pork rinds and Spam.

Tran had six slaves—all ARVN rejects. Tran vibed Baby Caesar. Tran vibed diva.

The slaves served chow. Flapjacks flambé—torched in T-bird wine.

Chuck loved it. Pete went yum-yum. Bob gagged. Mesplède gagged. Marv Three scarfed it up. Wayne took a bite. Wayne gagged. Wayne fed Tran's pet snake.

Tran spoke English. Tran spoke French. Tran ran the drill:

Two Hueys come. We go then. We co-opt poppy farms. We "negotiate."

Pete took Tran aside. Wayne watched the tête-à-tête. Wayne heard "improvisation." Pete grinned. Tran grinned. Tran went tee-hee. Wayne caught the gist—"negotiate," *shit.*

Chuck issued ammo. Chuck issued rules: We all carry birdshot—beehives verboten.

Wayne dumped his ammo. Wayne reloaded. Wayne thought it through:

Short-range loads. "Improvisation." Pete knows/Tran knows/Chuck knows. They *all* know—but *you.*

Tran gave a speech. Tran indicted the Cong. Tran indicted the French. Tran excluded Pete and Mesplède. Tran indicted Ho Chi Minh. Tran indicted Ngo Dinh Diem. Tran indicted gnarly Charlie de Gaulle.

Tran eulogized Preston Chaffee. Tran indicted the Beard. Tran extolled boss-man LBJ. Tran yelled. Tran coughed. Tran chewed an hour up and went hoarse.

Wayne heard chopper thumps. Wayne saw the Hueys.

They closed in. They hovered. They landed and perched. The doors popped. The pilot Marvs motioned them up.

Tran said a prayer. Tran issued bullet-proof vests. Wayne looked at Pete. Pete smiled and winked.

They did staggered takeoffs. Bob took Flight #1. Bob packed a 7-65 sniper-scope.

Pete clocked off ten minutes. Flight #2 readied. Tran yelled, "All aboard!"

They climbed in. Wayne grabbed a door spot. Chuck rode the

door gun. Pete got a back seat. Mesplède stuck close. Tran stuck by the Pilot Marv and Marv Three.

The Pilot Marv goosed it. The rotors whipped. They climbed. They leveled. They held.

3K level—check that green—green valleys/green hills/green brush.

Wayne looked down. Wayne saw soil rows and hollows. Wayne caught the gray tint.

Sweet soil. Good alkalines—low pH all. Poppy food. Dope slaves burn trees. Ash feeds the soil.

Calcium and potassium. High phosphate counts. Spring burns and fall plantings. Beans and corn for interim crops.

They passed Saravan. Wayne saw tin roofs and spires. Wayne saw stick figures and grids. Saravan came and went fast. The ground regreened.

Chuck got airsick. Chuck puked in a bag. Wayne looked away and looked down.

There—

Dope fields/row furrows/coolie-hat slaves.

Pete grabbed the Pilot Marv's headset. He listened. He laughed. He held three fingers up. Tran laughed. Chuck laughed. Mesplède laughed. Marv Three went bang-bang.

Wayne got the gist:

Bob's up in chopper 1. Bob's got a rifle. Bob's popping outland guards. Bob's toppled three.

The Pilot Marv banked. Wayne saw huts. Wayne saw a landing strip. He pulled his .45. He checked the clip. He jacked a round in.

The Pilot Marv leveled. The Pilot Marv rotored down.

There—

A barracks. A slave jail. A volleyball court. A welcome line—Li'l Tojo plus six. Little Laotians/fatigues and jump boots/World War II Nazi lids.

Pete laughed. Chuck pointed *way* east—check the brush/catch that glint.

Wayne looked over. Wayne caught the glint. There's Bob. There's chopper 1 perched. That glint's off a hog machine gun.

The Pilot Marv touched down. The Pilot Marv cut the props. Tojo saluted. Tojo's goons snapped to.

Tran jumped out. Pete jumped out. Chuck jumped out and tripped. The Pilot Marv jumped out. Marv Three steadied him.

Mesplède jumped out. Mesplède tripped. Wayne jumped and caught him. The ground dipped. There's seven kadre men—up against Tojo plus six.

Tran hugged Tojo. Tran played MC. Tran dropped kadre bios—all last names *di di*.

Tojo was "Dong." The Tojoettes blurred—Dinh/Minh/whoever. They all laughed. They all hugged. They all bumped sidearms and hips.

Wayne looked around. Jail slaves loitered close. They wore loincloths. They sucked pipes. It was O-head servitude.

Wayne saw Tojoette volleyball—four goons per team/a thirty-goon barracks hard right.

Wayne coughed. His vest fit tight. His breath butterflied. Tran reached in the Huey. Tran grabbed their pumps. The Tojoettes bristled uptight.

Tran passed the pumps out—all kadre/one per. Dong smiled. Dong said, "You carry guns. That all right. Guns number-one A-OK."

Tran smiled. Tran talked Viet. Dong talked Viet back. Marv Three translated—all pidgin-gook:

We get nice tour. We have lunch then. All A-OK.

Dong whistled. Dong gestured. Dong dispatched a Tojoette. He ran off. He hit the barracks. He ran back. He schlepped six M-1s.

Dong bowed. Dong issued guns—all Tojoettes/one per. Dong smiled. Dong talked Viet. Marv Three translated—all pidgin-gook:

Trust A-OK. Parity better. Lunch and peace accord.

Dong bowed. Tran bowed. Dong went you first. The kadre hiked out. The Tojoettes hiked close behind. Dong and Tran hiked back.

They cut through the dope fields—poppy stalks 4-ever—grids/rows/grid paths. Slaves raked soil. Slaves dropped seeds. Slaves trimmed stalks back.

They wore coolie hats. They wore shackles. They wore floral BVDs. They walked weird. They shuffled. Their shackles gouged bone.

It was *good* soil. It looked limestone sweet. It vibed low pH.

They hiked. The sun arced. The Tojoettes lagged behind. The Tojoettes breathed curry fumes. Wayne smelled it. Wayne gauged it—just ten feet back.

The Tojoettes had M-1s. The Tojoettes had bolt-throw rifles—one shot per throw. The Tojoettes had .38s. They were flap-holstered—slow-draw style.

Not here—not now—they won't try.

Wayne looked sideways. Pete caught it. Pete winked. Wayne read, "Your call, kid."

They had bullet-proof vests. *They* had better weapons. The Tojoettes had Nazi lids.

Wayne gulped air. Wayne stretched his vest tight. Wayne smelled fish stew.

There's the lunch hut. It's all bamboo. Four frond-and-stalk walls. Wide doorway opened up.

Wayne looked sideways. Wayne winked. Pete winked back. Wayne walked ahead. Wayne hit the hut. Wayne doorway-lounged.

The kadre caught up. Wayne bowed. Wayne went you first. The guys shook their heads. The guys aped gook manners. The guys went *you* first.

Wayne shook his head. Wayne bowed. Wayne went *you* first. The guys laughed. The guys shucked. The guys jived.

The Tojoettes caught up. The guys bowed. The guys went you first. The Tojoettes shrugged. The Tojoettes went fuck it. The Tojoettes walked straight in.

The guys blocked the door. The guys aimed. The guys jammed their backs point-blank.

Wayne shot his .45. Pete shot his pump. Bullets and bird pellets flew. The noise got four-walled—back shots/powder burns/muzzle roar.

Chuck shot. Marv Three shot—full magazines. Mesplède tripped. Mesplède shot. Rounds ricocheted.

Pete got dinged. Pete went down. Pete's vest bullet-flared. Wayne got dinged. Wayne went down. Wayne's vest popped and flamed.

Pete rolled. Wayne rolled. Dirt ate the vest flames. Recoil and reverb. Ricochets ricky-tick.

Wayne saw blood spatter. Wayne saw big stew pots. Wayne saw blood in fish stew.

He heard hog-fire—way off—Bob R. at three-o'clock high. He rolled. He pulled his vest off. He ditched his shirt.

There's Dong.

He's running. Tran's chasing him. Tran's got his hair. Tran's got him down. Tran's got a knife. Tran's waving his head.

Wayne shut his eyes. Somebody jerked him. Somebody pulled him up hard.

He opened his eyes. Pete said, "You passed."

63

(Saigon, 11/11/64)

STANTON SAID, "You fucked up."

The Go-Go was dead. That bar-b-que'd monk deterred trade.

Pete lit a cigarette. "I didn't feel like negotiating. Tran was up for it, so we ad-libbed."

"'Ad-lib' doesn't cut it. I went to Yale with Preston Chaffee's father, and now he won't be able to bury his son."

Pete blew smoke rings. "Toast a monk and ship him in a body bag. He won't know the difference."

Stanton slapped the table. Stanton kicked a chair. It roused Bongo. It roused two whores.

They twirled their stools. They looked over. They looked back.

"A fuck-up is a fuck-up and money is money, and now I'm going to have to pay some Can Lao guys to go up to Laos to guard the fields *you* stole and replace the guards *you* kill—"

Pete slapped the table. Pete kicked a chair.

"Tran had some napalm. Chuck and Bob Relyea flew over and dropped it last night. They waxed the barracks and the ops huts at both of the camps next to Dong's. They spared the refineries and the jails, so you tell me what the fucking upshot of all that is."

Stanton crossed his legs. "You're saying . . ."

"I'm saying we now own *the only three poppy farms* south of Ba Na Key. I'm saying we've got viable slaves at all three locations. I'm saying Tran knows some Chinese chemists we can bring in to work the morphine base and get it ready for Wayne. I'm saying all three camps are fucking physically connected, with forest, mountain, and river cover, and all I need from you is some warm bodies to run the slaves and work under the Laotian end of the kadre."

Stanton sighed. "Warm bodies cost money."

"The Marvins work cheap. Bob said they fucking desert a hundred a day."

"You're missing the point. Money is money, and we're stage-1 covert. I'm accountable to other Agency sources, and now I'm going to have to tell them that the cost of your escapade is coming out of the 45% profit nut that we've earmarked for the Cause."

Pete shook his head. "The Cause gets 65. You told me that."

Stanton shook his head. "There's too many hands out. The ARVN boss heard about your little adventure and upped the rent on every transport vehicle and live body he lets us have."

Pete kicked a chair. It hit the bar. It reroused the whores. They twirled their fingers. They touched their heads. They mimed he claaaazy.

Stanton smiled. "Let's hear some good news."

Pete smiled. "We took ten kilos of morphine base out of Laos. Wayne's doing tests now."

"You shouldn't have risked him on that raid. He's the only heroin chemist we've got."

"I needed to see what he had. It won't happen ag—"

"What else? Did you talk to Litt—"

"Heads up on that. Dracula gave him a hundred grand for the ordnance. It's coming in on the pouch flight at noon."

Stanton smiled. "That means . . ."

"Right, he swung Nellis. Five G's a month, cheap for what it gets us."

Stanton coughed. "Have you got a source?"

"Bob does. Some breed in Bao Loc. He's got some U.S. shit captured back from the Cong."

"Don't skimp. Let's make Hughes and the Air Force look good."

"You don't have to tell me that."

"I'm not so sure."

"*Be sure.* We're in this for the same reason."

Stanton leaned in. "We're *here* now. We're *not in Cuba*. When the buildup starts next year, we'll have a lot more cover to work in."

Pete looked around. The whores went you claaaazy.

"You're right. And I've been in worse places."

Bao Loc was north. 94 clicks. They limo'ed up.

Mesplède booked a stretch. Chuck and Flash reclined. The

pouch flight landed early. Drac delivered. Ward delivered Drac.

Old bills—C-notes—one hundred K in all.

Pete reclined. Pete dug on the countryside.

He'd called Ward. They'd talked—Saigon to Vegas. Ward ragged him. Ward ragged on narcotics.

Flash *back*—ten months—Ward *loves* dope then. Ward lauds dope at the Summit.

Dope made money. Dope pleased Drac. Dope sedated jigs.

Flash *up*—Ward is pissed—Ward has *ideals*.

Dope is bad. Dope is crass. Dope means risk. Don't disrupt my fund-book plan. Don't disrupt Drac's incursion.

Ward was Ward. Ward got pissed easy. Ward lugged a Jesus cross in his sewer.

He told Ward to visit Barb. He told Ward to watch Tiger. Check the hut/tail the cabs/vet my no-pill policy.

Pete yawned. The stretch hauled. The wheels kicked mud. Mesplède ran the radio. Chuck and Flash gawked. Dig the rivers. Dig the inlets. Dig the sampans. Dig the kute and komely gook quail.

Chuck loved Laos. Mesplède said napalm glowed. Tran said he saw a white tiger. We own it now—the Bolaven Plateau.

Three poppy farms. The Set River. Big tiger tracks.

Guéry was there now. Tran was there now. Tran ran a short-handed crew. Six goons for three camps—slaves thus on hiatus.

The slaves survived the bombing. The old goons fried. The refineries stood untorched. Tran knew potential chemists. Tran knew potential Marv guards. Tran knew geography.

Tran say you smart. You raid Bolaven. You no raid Ba Na Key. Ba Na Key north—closed to VC—tribe farms *boocoo*. Hmong tribes. Tough. No slaves there—Hmong work *en famille*. They fight. They no hide. They no run ricky-tick.

The radio blared—discordant shit—Mesplède loved nigger jazz. The highway veered. They hit Tran Phu Street. Bao Loc—2 km.

They cut right. They passed silk looms. They passed rubber farms. They crossed the Seoi Tua Ha River. They passed beggar squads.

Mesplède tossed some chump change. The beggars descended. The beggars scratched and clawed. They passed a province hut. They passed tea farms. They passed gook priests on mopeds.

There's Bob. There's the ARVN's dump.

Dig it:

ARVN guards. K-9 Korps. Gun stacks under dropcloths—open for biz.

They pulled in. They got out. Bob saw them. Bob walked a breed up.

"This is François. He's half French, and I think he likes boys, which don't discredit all the fine shit he's got for sale."

François wore pink pj's. François wore hair curlers. François wore Chanel No. 5.

Chuck vamped him. "Hey, sweetcakes, have we met before? Did you take my ticket at Grauman's Chinese?"

François said, "Fuck you. You cheap Charlie. American Punk No. 10."

Chuck howled. Flash yukked. Mesplède roared. Pete took Bob aside.

"What have we got?"

"We got .50-caliber HMGs, MMGs up the wazoo, M-132 flamethrowers with replacement parts, .45-caliber SMGs with 30-round magazines, a fucking shitload of M-14s and 34 M-79 grenade launchers."

Pete looked over. Pete saw six pallets—fat under dropcloths.

"You figure six planeloads?"

"I figure six *big* planeloads, 'cause each stack has two stacks behind it, and we got to string out the flights to keep Wayne's shit going in."

Pete lit a cigarette. "Run down the quality."

"It's just below Army standard, which is what we want, 'cause then it qualifies as surplus, which means it won't draw no suspicion when it goes through Nellis."

Pete walked over. Pete pulled dropcloths. Pete smelled cosmoline. Wood crates/nailed planks/stencil-mark designations.

Bob walked over. "It goes to Nellis, right? Some EM unload it and drive to an Agency drop."

"Right. They won't know that they're transporting covert, so we've got to hide the shit in with some stuff they won't want to pilfer."

Bob scratched his balls. "Flamethrower parts. I got to say there ain't much demand for them in Lost Wages."

Pete nodded. Pete whistled. Pete cued Mesplède. Mesplède grabbed François and bartered in.

Pete signaled—six loads/six payments.

Mesplède bartered. François bartered. Mesplède bartered back. They talked polyglot—French-Viet—diphthongs and shouts.

Pete walked up. Pete listened. He got the *bonnes affaires*. He got the *tham thams*. He got the Lyonnaise slang.

François rolled his eyes. François stamped his feet. François steamed up his pajamas. Mesplède rolled his eyes. Mesplède balled his fists. Mesplède smoked three Gauloises.

François went hoarse. Mesplède went hoarse. They coughed. They slapped backs. They bowed.

François said, "Okay, big daddy-o."

They drove back. They talked shit. They cut through Bien Hoa. The Cong hit ten days back—mortars predawn.

The stretch got close. They saw the mess. They saw flags at half-mast.

They cut back. They laughed. They slugged Bacardi. They told tales—Paraguay to Pigs—they goofed on CIA gaffes.

It's '62. Let's pluck the Beard. Let's shave him impotent. Let's dope the water. Let's spook the spics. Let's stage a visit from Christ.

They laughed. They drank. They vowed to free Cuba. They stopped and hit the Go-Go.

There's Wayne.

He's alone—per usual. He's pissed—per always. He's watching Bongo and his whores.

64

(Las Vegas, 11/22/64)

ONE YEAR.

He knew it. Jane knew it. They never *said* it.

Littell drove to Tiger Kab. Littell played the radio. Radio pundits assessed. One fool stressed Jackie. One fool stressed the kids. One fool stressed innocence lost.

Jane drove to Vegas. Jane holed up. Jane stayed in his suite. They called it "Thanksgiving." The date hit. They never factored it in.

The papers rehashed it. The TV rehashed it. It rehashed all day. He left early. Jane kissed him. Jane turned on the TV. He returned late. Jane kissed him. Jane turned off the TV.

They talked. They skirted it. They discussed prosaics. Jane was mad. He'd coaxed her to Vegas. He'd coaxed her for IT.

He said he had business. He kissed Jane and walked out. He heard Jane turn on the TV.

Littell killed the radio. Littell cruised by Tiger Kab. Littell perched across the street.

He parked. He watched the hut. He saw Barb B. There's Barb in lounge garb—heels put her over six feet.

Milt Chargin ran shtick. Barb laughed. Barb palmed a package. Barb grabbed an outgoing cab. Tiger stripes—Miami West—all roads to Cuba.

Littell watched the hut. Drivers walked through—fey minions of tolerant Pete. Pete collected strays. Pete ignored their faults. Pete courted diversion. Pete said he clocked Betty's visits. Pete said he clocked Betty gone.

Two hours tops—don't kill what you can't suppress.

Littell watched the hut. A cab pulled out. Littell tailed it. The cab drove west. Littell stuck close. They hit West LV.

The cab stopped—Monroe and "J"—two men got in. The cab pulled out. Littell stuck close. They hit Tonopah Highway.

The cab stopped. The men got out. The men hit the Moulin Rouge. The cab pulled out. Littell stuck close. They drove straight back to Tiger.

Memo to Pete: No pill sales/no inferred betrayal.

Littell yawned. Littell went queasy. He skipped his dinner. Jane cooked prime rib. She'd cooked all day. She'd watched TV concurrent.

He lied his dinner off. He walked out. He invented "business."

Littell skimmed the radio. Littell caught Jack's Greatest Hits: "Ask not" and "*Ich bin.*" The passed torch and more.

He killed the sound. He drove to the Sahara. The lounge was packed. He stood ringside. He caught Barb's closer.

Barb sang "Sugar Shack." Barb blew the crescendo. She saw him. She waved. She said, "Oops."

She was bad. She knew it. She goofed on it. She played off it. She ragged her shelf life as a chick.

Men loved her. She goofed on her height. She played off it

and went knock-kneed. She was a con. She played to the men who knew it.

The Bondsmen bowed. Barb jumped off stage. A heel jammed. She teetered. Littell caught her. He felt her pulse. He smelled her soap. He felt her perspiration.

They walked to the bar. They got a booth. Littell faced the TV.

Barb lit a cigarette. "Pete's idea, right? Look in on me."

"Partially."

"Partially, how?"

"I'm killing time. I thought I'd kill it with you."

Barb smiled. "I'm not complaining. I've got forty minutes."

The TV blipped. Jack's Greatest Hits revived. Paris with Jackie. Touch football games. Romps with his kids.

Barb looked over. Barb saw the TV. Barb looked straight back at Littell.

"You can't run from it."

Littell smiled. "Some of us try."

"Do you think about it?"

"It comes and goes."

"I'm all right until something reminds me. Then it gets scary."

Littell checked the screen. Jack and Bobby laughed. A waitress showed. Barb shooed her off.

"Pete never talks about it."

"We're useful. He knows it comes down to that."

Barb chained cigarettes. "Wayne knows. I figured it out."

"Did you brace him?"

"No, I just put it together."

Littell smiled. "He's in love with you."

Barb smiled. "In a tolerable way."

"We're useful. Tell yourself that the next time something reminds you."

Barb stubbed her cigarette. Barb burned her hand. She flinched and cradled it. She said, "Shit."

Littell checked her eyes. Littell saw pinholes—nerves off amphetamines.

Barb lit a cigarette. Littell checked the TV. Jack laughed. Jack worked That Old Jack Magic.

Barb said, "Jane knows."

Littell flinched. "You've never met her. And Pete wouldn't have—"

"He didn't. I heard you two being oblique and put it together."

Littell shook his head. "She's back at the hotel. She's teething on it right now."

"Do you talk about it?"

"We talk *around* it."

"Is she scared?"

"Yes, because she knows who did it, and there's no way she can be useful."

Barb smiled. Barb wrote "useful" in the air.

"I got a letter from Pete. He said it's going well."

"Do you know what he's doing there?"

"Yes."

"Do you approve?"

Barb shook her head. "I like the useful part, and I don't think about the other."

"Like the notion of plundering one nation in order to liberate another?"

Barb squeezed his hands. "*Stop it*. Remember what *you* do and who you're talking to."

Littell laughed. "Don't say you just want him to be happy."

Barb laughed. "To a free Cuba, then."

Janice Tedrow walked in. Littell saw her. Littell watched her. Barb watched him watch.

Janice saw him. Janice waved. Janice grabbed a side booth. She ordered a drink. She faced the TV. She watched Jack and Bobby.

Barb said, "You're blushing."

"No, I'm not. I'm fifty-one years old."

"You're *blushing*. I'm a redhead, and I know a blush when I see one."

Littell laughed. Barb pulled his sleeve up. Barb checked his watch.

"I have to go."

"I'll tell Pete you're okay."

"Tell him 'I'm useful.'"

"He knows that already."

Barb smiled. Barb walked. Barb went knock-kneed. Men stirred. Men watched her. Littell watched the TV.

There's Bobby with Jackie. There's Jack in the Senate. There's old Honey Fitz.

Littell got hungry. Littell ordered dinner—the prime rib he'd missed. The waitress was Jack-struck. The waitress perched by the TV.

Littell ate. Littell watched Janice. Janice watched the TV.

She sipped toddies. She chained cigarettes. She twirled her cane. She didn't *know*. Wayne Senior wouldn't tell her. He knew him well enough to say.

She looked over. She saw him watching. She got up. She maneuvered with her cane.

She cocked one hip. She stabbed her cane. She limped *con brio*. Littell pulled a chair out. Janice grabbed Barb's cigarettes.

"That redhead played my Christmas party last year."

"She's an entertainer, yes."

Janice lit a cigarette. "You're not sleeping with her. I could tell that."

Littell smiled. Littell twirled her cane.

Janice laughed. "Stop it. You're reminding me of someone."

Littell squeezed his napkin. "He used his stick on you."

Janice twirled her cane. "It was part of the divorce settlement. One million with no beating, two million with."

Littell sipped coffee. "You're volunteering more than I asked for."

"You hate him like I do. I thought you might like to know."

"Did he find out about General Kinman?"

Janice laughed. "Clark didn't bother him. The young man in question did."

"Was he worth it?"

"*It* was worth it. If I didn't do something drastic, I would have stayed with him forever."

Littell smiled. "I thought you had a life sentence there."

"Seventeen years was plenty. I loved his money and some of his style, but it wasn't enough anymore."

Littell spun the cane. "The young man?"

"The young man is a former client of yours, and he's currently abetting the war effort in Vietnam."

Littell dropped the cane. Janice snatched it up.

"You didn't know?"

"No."

"Are you shocked?"

"I'm hard to shock and easy to amuse sometimes."

Janice squeezed his hands. "And you've got old scars on your face that remind me of this temporary harelip of mine."

"Wayne's mentor put them there. He's my best friend now."

"He's the redhead's husband. Wayne told me."

Littell leaned back. "You're not playing golf. I've been looking for you."

"I'm retrieving my swing. I'm not going to walk eighteen holes with a cane."

"I enjoyed watching you play. I scheduled my breaks around it."

Janice smiled. "I've leased a cottage on the Sands course. Your view inspired me."

"I'm flattered. And you're right, the view makes all the difference."

Janice stood up. "It's off the first hole. The one with the blue shutters."

Littell stood up. Janice winked and walked away. She waved. She dropped her cane and left it there. She limped *molto con brio.*

He caught Barb's tenner. He stood ringside. He killed time. He ducked Jane's bedtime. He schemed up a trip.

I'll fly to L.A. You drive back. I'll meet you.

He drove home. The lights were on. Jane was still up. The TV was on. A newsman mourned Jack at great length.

Littell turned it off. "I have to fly to L.A. tomorrow. I'll be leaving early."

Jane spun her ashtray. "It's abrupt, and we're coming up on Thanksgiving."

"You should have come next week. It would have been better all around."

"You wanted me here, so I came. Now you're leaving."

Littell nodded. "I know, and I'm sorry."

"You wanted to see if I'd come. You were testing me. You broke a rule that we set for ourselves, and now I'm stuck in this suite."

Littell shook his head. "You could take a walk. You could get a golf lesson. You could read instead of watch TV for sixteen goddamn hours."

Jane threw her ashtray. It hit the TV.

"Given the date, how could you expect me to do anything else?"

"Given the date, we could have talked about it. Given the date, we could have stretched the rules. Given the date, you could have given up some of your goddamn secrets."

Jane threw a cup. It hit the TV.

"You carry a gun. You carry briefcases full of money. You fly around the country to see gangsters, you listen to tapes of Robert Kennedy when you think I'm sleeping, and *I've* got secrets?"

They slept solo.

He scooped up her butts. He packed a bag. He packed his briefcase. He packed three suits. He packed appeal briefs and money—ten grand in cash.

He made up the couch. He stretched out. He tried to sleep. He thought about Janice. He thought about Barb. He thought about Jane.

He tried to sleep. He thought about Barb. He thought about Janice.

He got up. He cleaned his gun. He read magazines. *Harper's* ran a piece—Mr. Hoover misbehaves.

He gave a speech. He fomented. He attacked Dr. King. He disrupted. He appalled. He stirred hate.

Littell turned the light off. Littell tried to sleep.

He counted sheep. He counted money. Skim cuts and embezzlements—civil-rights tithes.

He tried to sleep. He thought about Jane. He counted her lies. He lost count. He ricocheted.

Barb goes knock-kneed. Janice waves her cane. Janice smiles. Janice limps. Janice drops her cane.

He got up. He got dressed. He drove to McCarran. He saw a sign for Kool Menthol—all swimsuits and sun.

He turned around. He drove back. He drove to the Sands. He parked. He primped in his rearview mirror.

He walked by the golf course. He found the cottage and knocked. Janice opened up.

She saw him. She smiled. She plucked her curlers out.

65

(Saigon, 11/28/64)

WHITE HORSE—grad research.

Wayne mixed morph clay and ammonia. Wayne ran three hot plates. Wayne boiled three kilos. Shit filtered out.

Wayne dumped the ammonia. Wayne cleaned the beakers. Wayne dried the bricks.

Call it: Test batch #8.

He blew twenty bricks. He filtered wrong. He fucked the process. He learned. He added steps. He sluiced out organic waste.

Pete postponed the ship date. Pete let him learn.

Wayne boiled water. Wayne gauged it. Roger—182F.

He dumped it. He poured acetic anhydride. He filled three vats. He boiled it. He *got* it.

Roger—182F.

He measured base. He chopped it. He added it. He got the mix. He got the look. He got the smell—vinegar and prune.

He sniffed it. His nose burned. It looked good—good bonds—good reaction mix.

Call it batch #9—diacetyl morphine/impure.

Wayne sneezed. Wayne rubbed his eyes. Wayne scratched his nose.

He lived at the lab. He worked at the lab. He sniffed caustic agents. He built allergies. The kadre bunked away. He dodged them. He dodged Chuck and Bob.

They bugged him. They said go Klan. They said hate spooks. They said hate like we do.

His hate was his hate. They didn't KNOW.

He lived at the lab. He slept all day. He worked all night. Day noise bugged him. He heard mopeds and chants outside. He heard slogan gobbledygook.

He slept through it. He set his clock—tracer rounds at six.

Night noise unbugged him. He heard jukebox clang downstairs. He heard music up his vents.

He did dope work. He built shelves. He filed newspapers. He crossfiled his clips. The Dallas rag and Vegas rag—a week old here.

The Dallas rag flaunted the birthday. The Dallas rag flaunted old stuff. Sidebars and *more* birthdays—"unrelated" stuff.

Where's Maynard Moore? Where's that Wendell Durfee?

Wayne checked batch #9. There—the right smell/the right burn/the right mass. Precipitants—visible—nondiacetyl mass.

Wayne worked alone. Wayne worked kadre-adjunct. The kadre was in Laos. The kadre was overworked.

Their bomb raid killed camp guards. They needed new guards. Stanton told Pete to hire some Marvs. On-duty Marvs ran expensive. Tran hired deserters—Marvs *and* VC.

Forty-two guards/eighteen Marvs/twenty-four Congs.

They worked hard. They worked cheap. They shrieked their views: Ho versus Khanh/North versus South/Mao versus LBJ.

Pete got pissed. Pete chartered laws. Pete segregated guard crews. Pete pouched notes down—Saravan to Saigon—on CIA flights boocoo.

Pete praised the kadre. Pete praised Tran. Pete passed a rumor on: The Premier P.R.-prone. The Premier order "review."

Many dope dens exist now. Many GIs come here soon—troop buildup boocoo. Dope dens big. Dope dens *bad*. My den policy need review.

Stanton didn't buy it. Stanton knew said Premier. Said Premier was a puppet. Money pulled his strings. Said Premier *taxed* his dope dens boocoo.

West Vegas stood ready. Milt Chargin told Pete. Pete pouched word to Wayne. Milt ratted pill crews. Milt snitched to Dwight Holly. Holly told the apropos Feds. West LV stood dry. The funnel stood ready. Wayne pledged the goods:

Heroin—grade 4—ready by 1/9/65.

Wayne checked the clock. Wayne checked the vats. He measured sodium carbonate. He measured chloroform. He filled three tubes.

He locked the lab. He walked downstairs. The den was dark. The den was full. A Chinaman sold cubes. A Chinaman cleaned pipes. A Chinaman hosed stray turds.

Wayne blocked his nose. Wayne walked flashlight-first.

He walked bed rows. He stubbed pallets. He kicked piss bowls. O-heads stirred. O-heads cringed. O-heads kicked out.

He strafed their eyes. He strafed their arms. He strafed their needle tracks. Arm tracks/leg tracks/dick tracks/*old* tracks/*test* tracks.

The air reeked of smoke and piss. The light scattered rats.

Wayne walked. Wayne carried tape. Wayne marked eight pallet slats.

He flashed eyes. He flashed arms. He flashed a corpse. Rats had it. Rats gnawed on the crotch. Rats lapped shit water. Rats surfed the floor.

Wayne walked. Wayne checked Bongo's bed.

Bongo snored. Bongo slept with two whores. Bongo had down pillows and silk pallet slats.

Wayne flashed Bongo's eyes. Bongo slept on. Wayne made him Wendell Durfee.

It worked. It happened. It cohered. He did it—he made white horse.

He cooked all day. He filtered. He worked carbonates. He purified. He refined. He mixed charcoal and alcohol.

He hit #3—6% pure.

He walked downstairs. He selected three O-heads. He packed their pipes full. They smoked #3. They puked. They launched. They hit orbit.

He walked back up. He mixed ether. He mixed hydrochloric acid. He dissolved #3. He laced it. He mixed hydro *and* ether.

He worked all night. He waited. He watched tracer rounds. He filtered. He dried. He got precipitant flakes and got *it:*

Heroin—#4—96% pure.

He mixed sugar base. He diluted it. He cut it. He prepped eight syringes. He prepped eight swabs. He prepped eight good shots.

He yawned. He crapped out. He slept nine hours straight.

Two Marvs assisted. Two Marvs marched them in. They smelled. They outstunk his ammonia. They outfumed his carbonates.

Wayne cracked a window. Wayne measured their pupils. The Marvs jabbered in Anglo-gook:

Cleanup come—buildup come—cleanup do much good.

Wayne cooked up eight shots. Wayne fed eight spikes.

Two heads ran. Four heads grinned. Two heads pumped their veins. The Marvs grabbed the runners. The Marvs pumped their veins.

Wayne tied them off. Wayne geezed them. They seized up. They shook. Wayne flashed their eyes. Their pupils contracted. Their pupils pinned.

They nodded. They weaved. They upchucked and hurled. They doused the sink. They rubberized. They zombified.

They plopped down prone. They nodded out. The Marvs grabbed the last six. The Marvs prepped them good.

They swabbed their arms. They tied them off. They pumped out their veins. Wayne geezed them six across.

They seized up. They shook. They doused the sink. They heroinized.

The Marvs cheered. The Marvs jabbered in Anglo-gook.

Dignitaries come—that mean much money—cleanup much good.

The O-heads weaved. The O-heads bumped. The O-heads swacked and swerved. Blastoff and orbit—Big "H" *très* boocoo.

Wayne greased the Marvs. Wayne paid ten bucks U.S. The Marvs hauled the O-heads out. The lab smelled. Wayne Lysoled the sink. Wayne wiped his needles blood-free.

"If there's more of that, I'll fly."

Wayne turned around—whazzat?—Wayne dropped a needle tray.

There's Bongo. He's in bikini briefs. He's in fruit boots.

"What kind of reading can you get off little slopes like that? You need a big guy like me to gauge the fuckin' quality of your shit."

Wayne gulped a tad. Wayne checked vat dregs and spoons. Wayne saw one dose tops.

He strained it. He siphoned it. He cooked it.

Bongo said, "You always starin' at me. Then you gets to meet me formally, and you gots nothin' to say."

Wayne grabbed a tourniquet. Wayne fed a spike.

"There's this rumor goin' around that you killed these three brothers, but I don't believe it. You more the voyeur type to me."

Wayne grabbed his arms. Wayne pumped his veins. Wayne primed a fat blue.

"Cat got your tongue? You a fuckin' deaf-mute or somethin'?"

Wayne tied him off. Wayne geezed him.

Bongo seized. Bongo shook. Bongo upchucked and hurled. He doused the floor. He doused Wayne's shoes. He grinned. He weaved. He danced.

He did the Swim. He did the Wah-Watusi. He lurched. He grabbed at shelves. He stumbled out.

Wayne heard tracers. Wayne cracked his windows. There's the arc. There's the rush. There's the pink glow.

Wayne cracked the vents. Music flew up. There's "Night Train"—Sonny Liston's song.

Bongo walked back in. Bongo brought two whores. They held him. They propped him up.

He said, "Yours, baby. Around the world, free."

Wayne shook his head. One whore said, "He crazy." One whore said, "He queer."

66

(Saravan, 11/30/64)

MAIL RUN—Aéroport de Saravan.

Mail flew in. Mail hit Saigon. Mail hit Ops South. Marvs snatched kadre mail. Marvs called up the kampsite. Marvs pouched it up.

The airstrip reeked. Goats grazed adjacent. One runway/ one hut.

Pete waited. Pete jeeped in. Pete brought two guards. Pete brought an ex-Cong kontingent.

The ex-Congs mingled. The ex-Congs disdained the ex-Marvs. The ex-Marvs mingled. The ex-Marvs disdained the ex-Congs.

Pete feared riots. Pete stole their guns. Pete issued rubber-bullet pumps. Pete neutered the guards. Pete pampered the slaves. They got fresh food and water. They got fresh chains.

Tran sacked a village. Tran killed VC. Tran stole their swag. Tran got canned goods and penicillin. Tran got methamphetamine.

The slaves were soft. The slaves were weak. Harvest time was near. Pete stole their "O." Pete fed them soup. Pete fed them franks and beans.

The slaves were sick—fevers and flu—Pete fed them penicillin. The slaves lacked will. The slaves lacked oomph. Pete fed them methamphetamine.

They worked triple shifts. They soared. The fields sparkled. The bulb yield soared. Tran hired six chink chemists. Said chinks cooked M-base. The refineries soared.

Wayne worked the base. Wayne pledged white horse. Wayne's production skills soared.

The mail plane touched down. Goats scattered. The pilot tossed mail sacks. Marvs deplaned fast. Pete's Congs shagged the pouch.

They ran it over. Pete pulled the letters. Pete read them through.

Ward wrote. Ward said he checked Tiger. Ward said Tiger looked good. Nellis looked good. Kinman looked good. Kinman pledged help. Airmen to unload crates/airmen to lug crates/airmen to drive crates to the Agency drop.

Ward said he saw Barb. Barb was lonely. Barb was good.

Wayne wrote. Wayne said we're on go: 1/9/65.

Fred Otash wrote. Fred had no Arden dope. Fred had no dope on D. Bruvick. Queries out/will continue/will update as told.

Barb wrote. Barb wrote vignettes. Her thoughts jumped. Her handwriting jerked.

I'm up. I'm down. I sleep odd hours.

"Not *our* odd hours. Not where we met & made love going & coming to bed."

She saw Ward. "He's hot for Wayne's stepmom." The cat missed him. "He sleeps on your pillow now."

She hung out at Tiger. "Milt kills me. He auditions all his shticks.

"Donkey Dom drives me to work. He wonders why he can't keep boyfriends, esp. considering his 'equipment.' I said, 'Maybe it's because you're a male prostitute.'"

The cat bit a maid. The cat clawed a couch. The cat bit her drummer.

"I miss you . . . I miss you . . . I get crazy when you're gone because you're the only one who knows what I do & so I go up & down & get a little crazy pretending I'm talking to you & wondering where I'll be in 5 yrs., when my regulars trade me in for a newer model & I'm not so useful. Have you ever thought about that?"

Pete read the letter. Pete smeared the ink. He smelled Barb. He felt Barb. "Up & down" fucked him up.

The camp soared. Pete jeeped through. Pete toured.

Kall it one kamp now. Straight acres—marked by fence posts and huts.

Forested borders. Clay underbrush. Bulb rows/furrows/

walkways. Refinery huts and guard huts. Slave jails and ops huts.

Magic beasts roamed the forest. White tigers prowled boocoo.

Pete dug cats. Pete dug tigers. Pete dug nifty names. Pete kon-kokted "Tiger Kamp."

Flash sketched for kicks. Flash dug on tigers. Flash tigerized the huts. Flash painted tiger fangs and tiger stripes.

Pete cruised the walkways. Pete cruised the bulb rows. Pete watched.

Slaves raked. Slaves tilled. Slaves pulled rickshaws. Shackle lines—twelve slaves per—slaves fueled by meth.

Slaves worked. Slaves paused too long. Guards popped rubber rounds.

Laurent waved. Flash waved. Mesplède waved. Laurent urged speed—*di thi di*—Mesplède flexed his tattoos.

Pete counted stalks. Pete multiplied: bulbs per stalk/yield per bulb/sap-to-M-base. Stalks blew by. Pete blew the count. Pete mismultiplied.

He hit Ops North. The Congs took his jeep. He walked in. He saw Chuck and Bob. He saw their canned smorgasbord:

Chili and kraut. Franks and beans. Tokay/T-Bird/white port.

Chuck said, "We're losing Bob."

Pete grabbed a chair. "Why?"

"It's not like we're losing him altogether, it's more like he's relocating to help out a kindred soul."

Bob sipped T-Bird. "Chuck set me up with Wayne's daddy, unbefucking-knownst to Wayne, of course. His people offered me a chance to take over a snitch-Klan in Mississippi when the Army cuts me loose."

Chuck sipped Tokay. "The Feds are bankrolling his klavern. That means official sanction and discretionary leeway as to how much rowdy shit he can pull."

Pete cracked his knuckles. "It's bullshit. You'd give up our thing for the chance to torch a few churches?"

Chuck noshed beans. "Pete's got these gaps in his political education. He don't think much past Cuba."

Bob belched. "I like the discretionary part and the leadership part. I get to recruit my own Kluxers, pull my own shit and get me some mail-fraud indictments that can't be traced back to me."

Chuck snarfed franks. "How far can you go?"

"That's the $64,000 Question, so I gotta assume that 'discretionary' means according to the guidelines my handler sets up, along with shit he don't know about. Wayne Senior said I'm sup-posed to start with a show of force, you know, to establish my rep, which suits me just fine."

Pete lit a cigarette. "Don't let Wayne know that you're in touch with his father, and don't talk that Klan shit in front of him. He's off the deep end on niggers, and that kind of talk scares him."

Chuck laughed. "Why? He's a coon killer."

Pete laughed. "He's afraid he'll start liking your crazy shit too much."

Chuck snarfed chili. "Statements like that are politically sus-pect. I think you been spending too much time with Victor Charlie."

Rain hit. Bob shut the window.

"Here's why all this don't mean goodbye to the kadre. One, Mississippi runs down to the Gulf Coast. Two, you got lots of Cubans down there. Three, I could work liaison with Chuck, funnel our profits into guns, and shoot them down to the Gulf."

Pete said, "I like it. *If* you can get a hands-off policy going with the cops and Feds down there."

Thunder hit. Chuck cracked the window. Pete looked out. Slaves whooped. Slaves danced. Slaves did the Methedrine Mambo.

Chuck said, "This fucking 'cleanup' intrigues me. You got troops coming in, and Stanton says Khanh wants Saigon to look like Disneyland for all the fucking journalists and hotshots."

Slaves shook their chains. Slaves did the Shackle Shimmy-Shake.

Bob said, "I want to build up a roll for Mississippi. Maybe I can sell some surplus shit to the troops coming in."

Pete turned around. "No one sells to our troops. I'll kill any-one who does."

Chuck laughed. "Pete's got that World War II thing. *Semper fi*, Boss."

Bob laughed. "He *dinky dau*. He get too sentimental."

Pete pulled his piece. Pete dumped three rounds. Pete spun the chamber. Chuck laughed. Bob made the jack-off sign.

Pete aimed. Pete pulled the trigger. He shot Bob three times. The hammer clicked three times. He hit three blank chambers.

Bob screamed. Bob puked. Bob hurled franks and beans.

DOCUMENT INSERT: 11/30/64.
Verbatim FBI telephone call transcript.
Marked: ''Recorded at the Director's Request''/
''Classified Confidential 1-A: Director's Eyes Only.''
Speaking: Director Hoover, Ward J. Littell.

JEH: Good afternoon, Mr. Littell.

WJL: Good afternoon, Sir.

JEH: Let's discuss Southeast Asia.

WJL: I'm afraid I'm not informed on the topic, Sir.

JEH: I was informed that Pierre Bondurant and Wayne Tedrow Junior have gone on covert contract status with a stellar spy agency. Little birdies tell me things, and I would be remiss not to share them with you.

WJL: I was aware of that, Sir.

JEH: They are stationed in Vietnam, no less.

WJL: Yes, Sir.

JEH: Would you care to expand your answers?

WJL: I'd rather not be too specific. I think you know enough about Pete's past dealings and Wayne Junior's chemistry background to be able to extrapolate.

JEH: I am extrapolating at warp speed. I must conclude that our Italian friends have revised their fatuously conceived ''Clean-Town Policy'' in Las Vegas.

WJL: Yes, but the distribution will be rigorously localized.

JEH: I see a salutary convergence. The distribution will accommodate Count Dracula's prejudices and facilitate our Italian friends' desire to bilk him.

WJL: It's an astute observation, Sir.

JEH: Our friends must bristle at the thought of Jimmy Hoffa's forthcoming doom.

WJL: They know he's finished, Sir. They know the appeals process will terminate within two years.

JEH: The attendant irony has not escaped me. A gaudy homicide served to neutralize the Dark Prince, yet the Dark Prince toppled his bete noire in the end.

WJL: I have often considered that irony, Sir.

JEH: The Prince is now a senator-elect. Have you considered how he'll fare?

WJL: I haven't given it much thought.

JEH: A barefaced lie, Mr. Littell, and wholly unworthy of you.

WJL: I'll concede, Sir.

JEH: Do you think he will sponsor anti-organized crime legislation?

WJL: I would hope not.

JEH: Do you think he will attack organized crime from the Senate floor?

WJL: I would hope not.

JEH: Do you think he learned an enduring lesson from that gaudy homicide?

WJL: I would hope so.

JEH: I will not comment on your complex relationship with Robert F. Kennedy.

WJL: Your comments to date are most eloquent, Sir.

JEH: Let's jump from the frying pan to the fire. I'm meeting with Martin Lucifer King tomorrow.

WJL: The purpose of the meeting, Sir?

JEH: Lucifer requested it. He wants to discuss my attacks in the press. Lyle Holly has informed me that Lucifer has correctly added two and two and has determined that I've run black-bag operations against him, which must vex him as well.

WJL: How did he learn? Do you suspect a leak?

JEH: No. I publicly referred to information that Lucifer disseminated in private and betrayed bug and tap placements in that manner. Those references were, of course, deliberate.

WJL: I concluded that, Sir.

JEH: Lucifer, Rustin and the others now shut their mouths in hotel rooms. Lucifer has confined his sexual antics to beds outside my electronic range.

WJL: You're implying a larger design here, Sir.

JEH: You are correct. I am going to drastically upscale my operations against Lucifer and the SCLC. You are to stop donating organized-crime money to the organization, but to continue to meet with Bayard Rustin. You will continue to portray yourself as an

ardent supporter whose Mob pilfering source has run
dry. You will wear wires to your meetings with Rustin.
You will wheedle him into suggesting meetings. You
will exploit his homosexuality and susceptibility to
sincere and politically unstable men.

WJL: Yes, Sir.

JEH: This endeavor will be Stage-1 Covert. I have
dubbed it OPERATION BLACK RABBIT. The title bows to
the sex drive, prowess and heedlessly puerile
demeanor of our long-eared friends. You will receive
copies of most memoranda, because you are a deft
extrapolator of complex data. Code names have been
assigned to the key personnel. You will use them in
place of real names. They derive from the rabbit motif
and hint at the inherent psyches of the subjects.

WJL: You've whetted my appetite, Sir.

JEH: Martin Luther King will be RED RABBIT. Bayard
Rustin will be PINK RABBIT. Lyle Holly will be WHITE
RABBIT. You will be most appropriately known as
CRUSADER RABBIT.

WJL: It's a witty touch, Sir.

JEH: I want you to learn what King has planned in
the south. Your data will supplant Lyle Holly's. I'm
going to launch a White-Hate Cointelpro in Louisiana,
Alabama and Mississippi, and I want information to
complement that incursion.

WJL: You've targeted the Klan, Sir? For mail-fraud
indictments?

JEH: I've targeted the most violent, inept, felony-
prone and altogether outlandish Klan groups in that
three-state vector. God will punish them for
lynchings and castrations, should He lapse on the
side of compassion and find them unjustified. I will
punish them for Federal Mail Fraud.

WJL: You've divided the punishment well, Sir.

JEH: The Cointelpro will begin in June, '65. Your
old chum Wayne Senior has recruited a man to form his
own splinter Klan. The man will return from Army
service and begin his assignment in May.

WJL: Will Wayne Senior run—

JEH: Wayne Senior will be code-named FATHER RABBIT.

The Klan runner will be named WILD RABBIT. I have withdrawn the funding for all of Wayne Senior's long-standing informant Klans, with his approval. I want to consolidate my anti-Klan broadside under the banner of WILD RABBIT's stalwart group, the Regal Knights of the KKK.

WJL: The name packs a punch, Sir.

JEH: You're being egregiously flip, Mr. Littell. I know you are delighted, and I know you disapprove as well. Do not underline the latter.

WJL: I apologize, Sir.

JEH: To continue. Both operations will be run by Dwight Holly, who will be code-named BLUE RABBIT. Dwight has resigned from the U.S. Attorney's Office and has transferred back to the Bureau. I chose him because he is a brilliant operative. He is also Lyle Holly's brother, and Lyle knows the SCLC better than any white man alive.

WJL: I'm confused, Sir. I thought Dwight was estranged from Wayne Senior.

JEH: Estrangement comes and goes. Dwight and Wayne Senior have reconciled. The Negroes that Wayne Junior killed were simply a temporary roadblock. Wayne Senior is estranged from Wayne Junior now, in the manner of the patriarchy worldwide.

WJL: Will I need to deal with Wayne Sen—

JEH: Not directly. You trumped him on your courier arrangement, and he's sustained a simmering grudge.

WJL: Dwight Holly has never been a friend to me, Sir.

JEH: Dwight acknowledges your gifts, however reluctantly. You saved him face on the dead-Negro front, which indebted him to you. That said, I must observe that Dwight Chalfont Holly hates indebted-ness and was having you spot-tailed by agents of the U.S. Attorney's Office, as part of an ill-conceived plan to build a derogatory profile against you. He considered you a dangerous presence in Nevada.

WJL: Given Dwight's nature, that's a compliment.

JEH: It pained him to pull the tails. He gives up very badly. You share that trait.

WJL: Thank you, Sir.

JEH: Thank me with hard work on OPERATION BLACK RABBIT.

WJL: I will, Sir. In the meantime, would you like me to pull any of the bugs you've placed against the SCLC?

JEH: No. They might get careless and talk.

WJL: That's true, Sir.

JEH: Lucifer has been awarded the Nobel Peace Prize. It infuriates me as much as I'm sure it moves you.

WJL: I'm moved, yes.

JEH: Those three words define your value to me.

WJL: Yes, Sir.

JEH: Learn your rabbit codes.

WJL: I will, Sir.

JEH: Good afternoon, Mr. Littell.

WJL: Good afternoon, Sir.

DOCUMENT INSERT: 12/2/64.
Washington Post article.

HOOVER MEETS WITH KING; AIDES DESCRIBE ''TENSE CONFRONTATION''

Washington, D.C., December 1.

FBI Director J. Edgar Hoover and Assistant Director Cartha DeLoach today met with Dr. Martin Luther King, Jr. and his aides Ralph Abernathy and Walter Fauntroy. The meeting took place in Hoover's office at FBI Headquarters.

A range of topics were discussed, including the alleged presence of Communists and Communist sympathizers within the civil-rights movement and the FBI's handling of police brutality charges levied by Negroes and civil-rights workers in the south. King clarified recent statements he had made pertaining to the conduct of FBI agents in Mississippi and their alleged fraternizing with local law-enforcement officials. Hoover countered with a recitation of recent FBI successes in Mississippi and Alabama.

It was expected that rumors of FBI bugs and wiretaps, allegedly deployed against King and the Southern Christian Leadership Conference, would be discussed. ''This was not the case,'' Dr. Abernathy said. ''The dialogue was increasingly subsumed by Mr. Hoover's monologues against Communists and his repeated contention that 'in due time' attitudes and practices in the south would change.''

''Mr. Hoover encouraged Dr. King to 'get out the Negro vote,''' Mr. Fauntroy said. ''He did not offer a substantive pledge of support for civil-rights workers in great peril at this very moment.''

Both aides described the meeting, which lasted one hour, as ''tense.'' Following the meeting, King met with reporters and stated he believed that he and Mr. Hoover had reached ''new levels of understanding.''

Hoover declined to comment. Assistant Director DeLoach issued a press release that covered the topics discussed.

DOCUMENT INSERT: 12/11/64.
Los Angeles Times article.

KING ACCEPTS PEACE PRIZE;
EXPRESSES ''ABIDING FAITH'' IN U.S.

Oslo University. Oslo, Norway, December 10.

With Norwegian royalty and members of the Norwegian Parliament in attendance, the Reverend Martin Luther King, Jr. stepped on stage to receive the Nobel Peace Prize.

The chairman of the Norwegian Parliament introduced Dr. King as ''an undaunted champion of peace, the first person in the western world to have shown us that a struggle can be waged without violence.''

Dr. King, visibly moved by the introduction, climbed on stage to accept the award. He said that he considered it ''a profound recognition that nonviolence is the answer to the crucial political and moral question of our time, the need for man to

overcome violence and oppression without resorting
to violence and oppression.''

Speaking into glaring television lights and a sea
of rapt faces, Dr. King continued. ''I refuse to
accept the belief that man is mere flotsam and jetsam
in the river of life which surrounds him,'' he said.
''I refuse to accept the view that mankind is so
tragically bound to the starless midnight of racism
and war that the bright daylight of peace and
brotherhood can never become a reality.''

Citing the ''tortuous road which has led from
Montgomery, Alabama to Oslo,'' Dr. King said that the
Nobel Prize was really for the ''millions of Negroes
on whose behalf he stood here today.''

''Their names will never make Who's Who,'' Dr. King
said. ''Yet when the years have rolled past and when
the blazing light of truth is focused on this
marvelous age in which we live, men and women will
know and children will be taught that we have a finer
land, a better people, a more noble civilization,
because these humble children of God were willing to
suffer for righteousness' sake.''

Thunderous applause greeted Dr. King's address.
Hundreds of students, carrying torches, surrounded a
large Christmas tree and greeted Dr. King and his
entourage as they departed.

DOCUMENT INSERT: 12/16/64.
Internal memorandum. Marked: ''Stage-1 Covert''/
''Director's Eyes Only''/''Destroy After Reading.''
To: Director Hoover. From: SA Dwight Holly.

   Sir,
   Per our phone conversation:
   I agree. In light of your recent meeting with
SUBJECT KING, you should suspend all public attacks
and derogatory references to him, which should serve
to deepen the cover needed to mount the SCLC and
WHITE-HATE arms of OPERATION BLACK RABBIT. I agree
further that no memorandums should be filed by any
participant and/or circulant, that a strict

read-and-burn policy should be observed and that all telephone communiqués should be patched through Bureau scramblers.

Per said participants/targets and our stated objectives:

1 – BLUE RABBIT (the undersigned/SA D. C. Holly). To oversee and coordinate both operational arms and direct the activities of:

2 – WHITE RABBIT (Lyle D. Holly). Our plant within SCLC. Conduit for data pertaining to SCLC policy and exploitable personal data on TARGETS KING and RUSTIN.

3 – CRUSADER RABBIT (Ward J. Littell). Cosmetically vouched civil-rights sympathizer. Has donated $180,000 in cosmetically proffered organized-crime funds, allegedly pilfered from organized-crime sources. Our plant, charged to tape and extract incriminating, embarrassing and compromising data from TARGET RUSTIN.

4 – FATHER RABBIT (Wayne Tedrow Senior). Conservative pamphleteer, covert handler of FBI informants and long-term KKK mail-fraud operative. Our liaison to the WHITE-HATE arm of OPERATION BLACK RABBIT. Liaison to our newly recruited Klan runner. Charged to provide said runner with lists of his hate pamphlet subscribers, including those within the Oklahoma & Missouri state prison systems, and to aid said runner in his Klan recruiting.

5 – WILD RABBIT (U.S. Army Staff Sgt. Bob D. Relyea). Said Klan runner, currently on duty with Military Police Battalion 618 in Saigon, Vietnam, and on loan-out to (Stage-1 Covert) CIA operation in Laos. (Note: Sgt. Relyea refuses to reveal the details of his current assignment and will not divulge the names of his CIA handler or ops colleagues. I did not pursue this inquiry. Sgt. Relyea is observing Stage-1 sanctions and secrecy waivers, and this speaks well of his ability to honor such.)

Sgt. Relyea is an experienced hate pamphleteer and a former Missouri State prison guard with pre-existing segregationist contacts throughout the midwest and south. He continues to mail hate pamphlets of his own design throughout the Missouri prison system. Sgt. Relyea will be discharged from the Army 5/65 and will terminate his CIA ops at that time. We can expect him to begin work on OPERATION BLACK RABBIT in early 6/65.

Per targets RED RABBIT (Martin Luther King) and PINK RABBIT (Bayard Rustin) and our objectives.

Said objectives:

1 – To discredit RED RABBIT and PINK RABBIT and undermine their subversively socialistic designs.

2 – Via the accumulating and disseminating of incriminating and/or embarrassing data pertaining to their Communist associations, hypocritical moral behavior and sexual degeneracy.

3 – To precisely orchestrate the release of said data, in order to reveal the socialistic underpinnings of the entire civil-rights movement.

4 – To create distrust within the civil-rights movement.

5 – To engender distrust and resentment against RED RABBIT within the Negro community and undercut the recent non-Negro cache that RED RABBIT has engineered.

6 – To reveal the Socialist-Communist designs of RED RABBIT, the SCLC and the civil-rights movement and influence an effective political backlash.

7 – To assail RED RABBIT'S obviously disturbed and deteriorated psyche with an anonymous mail campaign.

8 – To implement the WHITE-HATE arm of OPERATION BLACK RABBIT concurrent with 1–7, in order to buttress the FBI's anti-Klan, anti-racist credentials and rebuff anti-FBI sentiment disseminated by civil-rights provocateurs and members of the liberal-socialist press.

In addition, I urge:

9 – SCLC MAIL COVERS. The intercepting, reading, logging and resending of all U.S. and foreign mail sent to the main and regional SCLC Offices.

10 – SCLC TRASH COVERS. The examination, logging &

evidentiary seizure of all garbage and discard material dumped in trash bins at all SCLC Offices.

11 – An anonymous letter, to be written from a Negro perspective and sent to RED RABBIT's home in Atlanta.

The letter will begin ''King, look into your heart'' and will recount what a ''grim farce'' the Nobel Peace Prize and RED RABBIT's other recent accolades are held to be within the mainstream Negro community. The letter will subtly urge RED RABBIT to commit suicide rather than risk further disfavor within the Negro community, and will include bug-tap excerpts, pertaining to RED RABBIT's promiscuity, to buttress your deliberate public statements and convince RED RABBIT that those statements are widely received and accepted by mainstream Negroes.

In closing:

Our bugs and wiretaps remain in place, although they are severely compromised. Per our last phone call, I agree with your assessment. OPERATION BLACK RABBIT must launch and sustain at Stage-1 Covert status. RED RABBIT has reached an unbearably high level of public acceptance that only our most diligent and secretive efforts will be able to dislodge.

Respectfully,

D.C.H.

DOCUMENT INSERT: 12/21/64.
Pouch communiqué. To: John Stanton. From: Pete Bondurant. Marked: ''Hand Pouch Deliver Only''/ ''Destroy Upon Reading.''

J.S.,

Wayne hit paydirt. We're on go for 1/9/65, & after final distribution, I'm predicting a net profit of $320,000. That makes the kadre's profit nut (45%) about $150,000. Right now I'm working out the details, but the plan is unchanged.

Laurent, Chuck and Flash will purchase weapons on the right-wing circuit in Texas & the south & will funnel them to exiles on the Gulf.

That's the essential plan, with one proviso.

We've both been the coastal harassment route, and running missions out of South Florida & the Gulf got us nowhere. I think our exiles should take advantage of being Cuban & should conduit the weapons to anti-Castro groups inside Cuba. I'm emphatic about this.

What do you think? Please reply ASAP.

P.B.

DOCUMENT INSERT: 12/26/64.
Pouch communiqué. To: Pete Bondurant. From John Stanton. Marked: ''Hand Pouch Deliver Only''/ ''Destroy Upon Reading.''

P.B.,

I approve the general outline of your plan and agree that our ultimate goal should be to provide on-island dissidents with the weapons our net profits secure. That said, I should again point out that you're jumping the gun on the Cuban end of things. Make no specific profit distribution plans until our in-country costs can be assessed, with all monies flagged for laundering through appropriate Agency fronts. We do not want our Cuban ''contributions'' to be traceable back to our Las Vegas business.

To close:

The Saigon cleanup will be implemented soon. A Can Lao contingent will secure the area around Khanh Hoi, but I have been assured that the lab will not be touched. Have Tedrow secure the lab and be off the premises by the A.M. of 1/8/65.

Por la Causa,

J.S.

DOCUMENT INSERT: 1/6/65.
Body-wire transcript. Marked: ''Route to: Director/ Blue Rabbit/White Rabbit/Father Rabbit/Live Tape Destroyed/Read & Burn.''

Location: Washington, D.C. (Lafayette Park). Date: 1/4/65/0842 hrs. Speaking: CRUSADER RABBIT/ PINK RABBIT.

CR (conversation in progress): What I (static/ ambient noise) read in the press. Dr. King sounded encour—

PR (laughing): With Martin, nonviolence extends to the absence of invective (pause/2.1 seconds). No, Hoover was rude and intractable. Martin said he was shaking.

CR: No progress, then?

PR: None. He did not affirm or deny the existence of the bugs and the taps. (Static/2.8 seconds.) Didn't really press it. He's so goddamn Christlike at times.

CR: Dr. King was wise not to rile him.

PR: You're right, Ward. You have a hateful lunatic in his declining years and a hugely important figure in his ascent. You have to believe that people will see through to the gist of that.

CR: Never condescend or underest (ambient noise/ 2.9 seconds) abilities.

PR: That was reinforced for Martin soon after.

CR: How—

PR (interrupting): Martin received a letter, and regretfully Coretta saw it first. It was allegedly written by a Negro man, who urged Martin to kill himself. There were (static/3.3 seconds) references, and I won't comment on their veracity, to philanderings that Martin (static/ 1.6 seconds) may or may not have committed. Coretta was (pause/0.9 seconds) well, she was devastated.

CR: Jesus Christ.

PR: That about *says* it.

(Static/ambient noise/9.3 seconds.)

PR (conversation in progress): No saint, but I never fully grasped the man's evil nature until that moment. (Pause/4.1 seconds/PR laughs) Why so glum, Ward? Really, you're looking positively spectral.

CR: I can't give you any more money, Bayard. It's getting too risky on my end. (Static/0.8 seconds) later, but not for the foreseeable future.

PR: You needn't (pause/2.2 seconds). Stop with the glum looks, child. You've done the cause a world of good, and I for one hope you'll stay in touch.

CR: I want to. You know how I feel.

PR: I do indeed. I enjoy our talks, and I rely on your perceptions of the FBI mindset.

CR: I'll continue to offer them. And I'm always passing through D.C.

PR: I'm always good for a drink or a cup of coffee.

CR (static/3.4 seconds/conversation in progress): Dr. King have planned?

PR: We've got a big push coming up in Selma, Alabama. We're making plans to reprise ''Freedom Summer'' in Mississippi, and we've targeted Eastern Louisiana in June.

CR: You've got a strong Klan presence there. The Baton Rouge Office has a substantial file.

PR: Bogalusa's a simmering hotbed of our pointy-headed friends. We're going to mount voter registration drives and vex them out of their sheets.

CR (laughing/ambient noise/20 seconds): Anticipate resistance?

PR: Yes, but Martin was encouraged by the FBI's presence in Mississippi last summer, and he's convinced that the evil Mr. Hoover will work for the safety of our people, however reluctant—

(Sustained static/tape ends here.)

DOCUMENT INSERT: 1/7/65.
Courier message: Saravan, Laos, to Saigon, South Vietnam.

To: Wayne Tedrow Junior. From: Pete Bondurant. Marked: ''Hand Pouch Deliver.''

W.T.,

Be ready to follow first shipment stateside A.M. of 1/9/65. Be off lab premises by 1/8. Urgent! Respond today!

P.B.

DOCUMENT INSERT: 1/8/65.
Courier message: Saravan, Laos, to Saigon, South Vietnam.

To: Wayne Tedrow Junior. From: Pete Bondurant.
Marked: ''Hand Pouch Deliver.''

W.T.,
Board up lab & vacate immediately! Urgent! Respond
immediately!
    P.B.

67

(Saigon, 1/9/65)

LET'S STAY. Let's get close. Let's *watch*.

The lab was secure. He pouched Chuck last night: I'll meet
Pete/Tan Son Nhut Airport/flight 29. I packed the shit. I hid
it—check the box marked "Flamethrower Parts."

Let's linger. Let's get close. Let's watch the "Cleanup."

The Can Lao hit last night. The Can Lao precleaned. They
stink-bombed the Go-Go. They ran out the patrons. They ran
out the whores. They locked up the dope den. They secured the
O-heads. Said O-heads dozed on.

Wayne checked his watch—6:14 A.M.—Wayne checked his
window.

Marvs draped flags. Marvs unfurled banners. Marvs muscled
vendors out. Marvs stole their cash. Marvs dumped their stalls.
Marvs cued hose crews up.

The crews aimed. The crews fired. Water smashed walls and
stalls. Water squashed fruit. Water launched debris and scoured
graffiti. Vendors flew—flyweights—hose confetti.

The Marvs raised banners. There's LBJ. Dig his big schnoz
and Smile of Love. There's Premier Khanh. He's got big teeth.
Dig his Big Smirk of Love.

A vendor flew. Water tossed him. Water tossed rickshaw bikes.

"You a watchin' motherfucker."

Wayne gulped a tad. Wayne turned around. Wayne saw Bongo.
In his tight fruit briefs. In his pointy fruit boots. With a chubby
whore.

"You know what I like about you? It's that 'meek-shall-
inherit-the-earth' thing. You like to watch, but you never say a
motherfuckin' word."

The whore wore skivvies. The whore wore thigh hickeys. The whore wore cigarette burns.

"You like her? I call her 'Ashtray.' You don't need to reach for one when she's around."

Wayne shut the window. Bongo hoisted his balls. Bongo pumped up his veins.

"I figured I'd trade you for a taste. I get to geez, you get to watch Ashtray french me."

Wayne smiled. Wayne gulped a tad. Wayne unlocked his closet.

He prepped water. He prepped a spike. He prepped a spoon. He prepped horse. He cooked it. He siphoned it in.

Bongo laughed. Ashtray giggled. Wayne blocked their view. He siphoned in ammonia. He siphoned in rat poison. He siphoned in strychnine.

Bongo said, "You slow, you know that?"

Wayne turned around. Bongo looped a tourniquet. Bongo tied off a vein.

Wayne saw it. Wayne tapped it. Wayne jabbed it. Wayne pushed the plunger in sloooooow.

There now—how's that?

Bongo lurched. Bongo jumped. Bongo sprayed piss and shit. Bongo fell down and spasmed and thrashed.

Wayne stepped back. Wayne watched. Ashtray stepped up close.

Bongo coughed foam. Bongo coughed blood. Bongo bit his tongue off. Wayne stepped up. Wayne stepped on his head. Wayne cracked his skull.

Ashtray held her nose. Ashtray crossed herself. Ashtray kicked Bongo in the balls. Wayne grabbed him. Wayne dragged him. Wayne dropped him down the air vent.

Ashtray said, "Bongo cheap Charlie. Bongo number ten."

Wayne saw Leroy and Cur-ti. Wayne saw Wendell Durfee.

More cleanup—his and theirs.

Wayne cleaned the lab. Wayne watched the outside show. Marvs hosed monks. Marvs hosed walls. Marvs abridged graffiti.

The vent shook. Rats bopped through. Rats found Bongo. Rats ate him.

10:05 A.M.—flight time soon.

Theeeeere—

Voices and clumps now—two clicks downstairs. There—it's coming—you knew it would.

Wayne walked down. Wayne stood on the landing. Wayne found a shadow patch.

There—ten Can Lao goons. Two five-man teams paired off. They've got flashlights and silencered magnums. They've got hoses/flamethrowers/sacks.

They dispersed. They walked the pallet rows. They shot faces in tight.

It went soft—silencers—head shots in light.

They flashed. They shot. They dumped shells and reloaded. Heads snapped inside halos. Heads cracked pallet slats.

Opium—*hush now anesthesia*—in slow and tight.

Wayne watched. Wayne saw faces alight. B-girls and Ashtray. Uncle Ho–types.

The goons finished up. The goons regrouped in the doorway. The goons stood way back.

A goon aimed a toaster. Said goon strafed low. Said goon cooked body rows tight.

Three sweeps out and back. Flame levels in tight.

The goon turned the toaster off. A goon strafed a hose. Said goon sprayed water down tight.

Flames sputtered. Bodies flared. Pallets cracked.

Wayne watched. The goons regrouped. The goons walked and dispersed.

They took their pants off. They kicked through hose water. They lugged gunnysacks. They poured out quicklime. They perfumed bodies. They flour-dipped flesh.

DOCUMENT INSERT: 2/8/65.
Internal memorandum. Topic: OPERATION BLACK RABBIT. To: DIRECTOR. From: BLUE RABBIT. Marked: ''Stage-1 Covert''/''Eyes Only''/''Read and Burn.''

Sir,
My first summary report on OBR.
1 - CRUSADER RABBIT met PINK RABBIT on two occasions in Washington, D.C. (1/6/65, 1/19/65) and forwarded his tapes to me. Per Stage-1 Covert guidelines, I personally transcribed the tapes and destroyed the live tape copies. Tape #1 and Tape #2

transcripts are included (Addendum #A) with this
memorandum. Per guidelines, please read and burn.

2 – Although there were numerous moments of poor
sound quality, I feel confident in my assessment of the
tapes. It is obvious that the effeminate and witty
PINK RABBIT is much taken with the wit, beautifully
feigned sincerity and ardently expressed ideals of
CRUSADER RABBIT. You were farsighted in your instinct
to match them up. PINK RABBIT accepted CRUSADER
RABBIT's stated withdrawal of ''pilfered''
organized-crime monies with magnanimity and both
men expressed a desire to ''keep in touch.'' That
desire, expressed on Tape #1, was confirmed by the
second meeting of PINK RABBIT and CRUSADER RABBIT,
recorded on Tape #2.

3 – CRUSADER RABBIT deftly questioned PINK RABBIT
on both tapes. (See transcripts.) To date, however,
PINK RABBIT has revealed only information already
revealed by our ''in-house'' SCLC source, WHITE
RABBIT. The broad outline includes:

3-A: Planned agitation in Selma, Alabama
(picketing, boycotts, voter-registration
drives);

3-B: A (6/65) projected school desegregation drive
in Chicago;

3-C: Early plans (but no compelling specifics)
regarding SCLC participation in a second ''Freedom
Summer'' campaign of agitation in Mississippi;

3-D: Planned agitation in and around Bogalusa,
Louisiana, to commence in 6/65.

4 – I've reviewed the recent tapes retrieved from
our remaining hotel-room bug-posts. RED RABBIT, PINK
RABBIT and other SCLC members have stayed in said
rooms on a total of 14 occasions from 1/1/65 to 2/4/
65. No salient information was gleaned. The innocuous
conversations and frequent whispers indicate that
the subjects suspected the presence of electronic
surveillance. Said bugs will remain in place.

5 - WHITE RABBIT reports that RED RABBIT, PINK
RABBIT and other SCLC members have discussed the
anonymous ''suicide letter'' sent to RED RABBIT

and concluded that it derived from an FBI source. WHITE RABBIT further reports that RED RABBIT and PINK RABBIT have verbally attacked you on numerous recent occasions, much in the manner that PINK RABBIT attacked you on Tape Transcript #1. WHITE RABBIT stated that RED RABBIT was ''very upset'' by the letter, especially the ''crippling effect'' it had on his wife.

6 – Per MAIL COVERS. To date, assigned agents have intercepted, logged and remailed numerous letters of support, along with large and small donations to the SCLC, many of them sent by notable leftist-sympathizers, members of Communist front groups and movie stars, among them Danny Kaye, Burt Lancaster, Walter Pidgeon, Burl Ives, Spencer Tracy, Rock Hudson, Natalie Wood and numerous folk singers of lesser repute. (See Addendum List #B for details. Per guidelines, please read and burn.)

7 – Per TRASH COVERS. To date, assigned agents have collected and logged large quantities of discarded left-wing periodicals and risqué magazines with photographs of nude white women, along with innocuous and non-itemized trash. (See Addendum List #C for inventory.) (Note: An Addendum List #B inventory log will soon be compiled & stored per Stage-1 Covert guidelines. It will be used to facilitate, should you so direct, an SCLC BANK ACCOUNT COVER, to determine if the above-noted contributions were banked legally, which should help us gauge the viability of an IRS cross-check of the SCLC's federal and state tax returns.)

In conclusion:

All COVERS to proceed as directed. A summary report on the WHITE-HATE arm of OPERATION BLACK RABBIT to follow.

Respectfully,
BLUE RABBIT

DOCUMENT INSERT: 2/20/65.
Internal memorandum. Topic: WHITE-HATE/OPERATION BLACK RABBIT. To: DIRECTOR. From: BLUE RABBIT.

Marked: ''Stage-1 Covert''/''Eyes Only''/''Read and Burn.''

Sir,

My first summary report on the WHITE-HATE arm of OBR.

1 – I have compiled, with the help of FATHER RABBIT's aides, a list of potentially dissident Klansmen now at loose ends since FATHER RABBIT dissolved his previously funded informant Klan groups in 12/64. (See Addendum #A for list of said Klansmen.) (Note: Per Stage-1 guidelines, please read and burn said addendum. I have retained an original copy, per guidelines.)

Also, FATHER RABBIT has supplied (see Addendum #B/ read & burn) a 14,000 name list of white male hate-pamphlet subscribers in Louisiana and Mississippi, all devotees of specific segregationist/anti-Negro tract series distributed by FATHER RABBIT's organization. A criminal records cross-check of these subscribers has yielded the names of 921 men with misdemeanor and felony arrests and memberships in extreme right-wing organizations.

2 – My plan would be to have FATHER RABBIT solicit these men by mail, under an ''anonymous patriot'' letterhead, and refer them by mail to WILD RABBIT, upon his (5/65) release from the U.S. Army. WILD RABBIT would assess the mail he has received, contact the most promising prospects and build the nucleus of his new Klan group on that basis. He will establish boundaries as to what and what not his recruits can do, and gather information on their previous hate-group associations. WILD RABBIT will also define their future informant duties.

3 – CRUSADER RABBIT and WHITE RABBIT have mentioned the proposed ''Second Freedom Summer'' agitation campaign in Mississippi and planned (6/65) agitation in and around Bogalusa, Louisiana. WILD RABBIT wants to exploit these situations, and I believe that if he delivers a properly restrained but somehow flamboyant show of force in that region at that time, he will be able to mobilize a sizable number of recruits

resultant. To further induce subservience in
his recruits, WILD RABBIT will supply them with
low-quality rifles and sidearms purchased by his
friend CHARLES ''CHUCK'' ROGERS (white male/age 43),
a covert CIA contract employee currently serving with
WILD RABBIT in Vietnam. ROGERS has extensive gun
connections among rightist Cuban exile groups in the
Gulf Coast region.

4 – WILD RABBIT has also established a ''Hate-
Leaflet Mail Ministry'' among convicts and ex-
convicts he knew while working as a Missouri state
prison guard, and plans to recruit from the ''eager
beaver'' parolees who contact him upon their release.
I believe that this is also a viable recruiting
approach.

In conclusion:

I believe that we are theoretically operational as
of this (2/20/65) date. Please respond as your
schedule allows.

Respectfully,
BLUE RABBIT

DOCUMENT INSERT: 3/1/65.
Internal memorandum. Topic: OPERATION BLACK RABBIT/
2/20/65 MEMO. To: BLUE RABBIT. From: DIRECTOR.
Marked: ''Stage-1 Covert''/''Eyes Only''/''Read and
Burn.''

BLUE RABBIT,
Consider the proposed measures described in your
2/20/65 memo approved in full. Cold funds to follow.
You may share information on a need-to-know basis
with FATHER RABBIT and WHITE RABBIT. Given his
suspect ideology, do not share any WHITE-HATE
information or in any way contact CRUSADER RABBIT,
unless so directed.

DOCUMENT INSERT: 3/8/65.
Pouch communiqué. To: John Stanton. From: Pete
Bondurant. Marked: ''Hand Pouch Deliver Only''/
''Destroy Upon Reading.''

J.S.,

We're operational on both ends now. Here's the summary you asked for.

It's all running smooth. A) – Milt Chargin greased cops working the Records Divisions of the Vegas PD & Clark County Sheriff's & got a list of all the previously busted colored junkies in West Vegas.

B) – I recruited 4 expendable colored pushers to work the bottom-rung distribution in West LV. They've got menial casino jobs & were happy to get the gigs. I gave them copies of the prev. ment'd junkie list & had them supply the junkies with free pops taken from our 1st stateside shipment of 1/9/65. The ''free samples'' got them anxious for more. I told my 4 guys to push ''free tastes'' on anybody who asked, colored only. They got a lot of takers & we got a lot of steady ''Clients'' (Milt C.'s word, not mine).

C) – I lean on the 4 guys periodically & up to now I'm convinced that they (1) haven't stolen kadre merchandise; (2) haven't sold to non-Negro clients; (3) haven't snitched off kadre or Tiger Kab personnel; (4) haven't bragged to their lowlife pals & implicated kadre or Tiger Kab personnel & will not (5) do so if they get popped, which is unlikely, because (6) Milt has greased the LVPD & Sheriff's Narco squads & has secured a hands-off policy, & if any 1 of the 4 is popped, the plan is to bail them out & clip them before they talk too much.

So, (7), everything is buffered. Tiger drivers deliver the merchandise to drop points & the pushers pick it up, distribute it & funnel the money back the same way. The drivers are all solid pros & will not talk if busted. On his one stateside run, Wayne periodically spot-tailed the pushers & determined that they weren't skimming or fucking up other ways. Wayne's got an evil reputation on the west side & it keeps the pushers on a tight leash.

D) – As you know, Wayne's made one rotation from Saigon & sent the 2nd shipment (4 lbs) stateside on 3/2/65. Rogers, Relyea, Mesplede, Guery & Elorde remain in Laos & oversee the M-base production at

Tiger Kamp (while you & the other guys who concocted this whole thing roam around S.E. Asia pulling your clandestine shit). The production level at Tiger Kamp remains high & the January-February harvest beat the chemists' estimates. Tran's methedrine ran out (mixed blessing—it killed 3 slaves) & we had a slow week (late Feb.) while the slaves smoked heavy amounts of ''O'' & rode out withdrawals. We've got to burn the fields in April to prepare the soil for the fall planting, but we've got enough back-stock of M-base to see us through to the next harvest, because the 3 refineries were overstocked when we raided & consolidated last November. So far, my rubber-bullet policy is working, because the ex-ARVNs & ex-Congs continue to feud. Mesplede is staging weekly Cong-ARVN boxing matches (slave cornermen & referees) which helps blow off steam & boosts morale.

E) – You were right about the ''cleanup.'' The Can Lao took out the den below the lab (& supposedly 600 others) but now that the initial troop arrival bullshit is over, things are back to normal. None of Chuck's Saravan-to-Saigon merchandise flights have been messed with at either end & Customs has not checked any of his cargoes. The den below the lab & the Go-Go have reopened & Wayne still tests dosage levels on the resident heads. Tran said Khanh's stopped making anti-dope statements & everyone in Saigon seems distracted by the troops coming in & the way the war is flaring up. You were right, it feels like the buildup is giving us added operational cover.

F) – The pipeline's running A-OK. So far, no Customs checks & glitches flying out of Tan Son Nhut & no trouble at Nellis. My friend Littell surveilled the 1/9/65 shipment from Nellis to the Agency drop-off point thru to the final ''donation'' point at the Nevada Guard Armory. Milt C. has been transporting the merchandise from the drop-point to Tiger Kab. It's a foolproof system & the Guard is thrilled with Mr. Hughes' ''donations.''

G) – Some unexpected expenses came up on Milt's

end, but aside from that, we're $182,000 up from our
Vegas profits on the 1/9 batch & 3/2 batch so far. I'm
ready to rotate Chuck, Laurent & Flash stateside &
have them scout exile camps, assess the troops & get
going on an arms conduit to the ones they choose. Bob
Relyea leaves the Army to work for the Feds in May, &
he'll be situated near the Gulf. He'll utilize his gun
connections & assist Chuck, Laurent & Flash in
funneling to the exiles.

That's it. I'm anxious to move on the Cuban end.
Let's put all this caution & budgetary constraint
shit aside & get going.

Viva la Causa!

P.B.

68

(Las Vegas, Los Angeles, Miami, Washington, D.C.,
Chicago, Selma, 3/21/65–6/15/65)

PENANCE. Tithe. Counterthrust.

He obeyed Mr. Hoover. He taped Bayard Rustin. He
rabbitized. He performed new betrayals—RABBIT ops—Mr.
Hoover's counter tithes.

He traveled for work. He worked for Drac and Jimmy. He
worked for Drac and the Boys. He flew D.C. to Miami. He flew
Chicago to L.A.

He cruised banks. He set up new accounts. He used fake ID.
He dumped cash. He cut checks. He tithed the SCLC.

Counter ops:

Skim fees. Embezzlement. Let's declaw BLACK RABBIT.

He drained Drac. He took small bites—little rabbit nips. It
worked. The skim plan worked. Counter cash accrued.

He worked.

He worked for Jimmy Hoffa. He filed briefs. He fought two
convictions. He dunned the Boys. He bagged two mill for
Jimmy's Hope Chest.

New hope. Nonhope. No hope. There were no bribable
jurors. There were no bribable courts.

Mr. Hoover had pull. Mr. Hoover liked Jimmy. Mr. Hoover

could help. Don't brace him or beg him. Don't incur more indebtedness—yet.

He worked for Drac. He filed briefs. He bought time. He needed twelve months—sixteen tops.

Let Drac dump his stock then. Let Drac get his stash. Let Drac inject Las Vegas.

Fred Otash worked.

Fred Otash culled. Fred Otash sifted. Fred Otash scandalized. Let's raid files. Let's find dirt. Let's utilize.

The files existed: *Confidential/Rave/Whisper/Lowdown* and *Hush-Hush*. The files existed. The files eluded. The files dirtified.

Bugs dirtified.

Littell hung Vegas bugs. Fred Turentine assisted. They bugged hotel rooms. They trapped dirt. They trapped legislators.

Three so far—three cheaters/three whorehounds/three drunks.

Feds manned the bug posts—two agents for three months. Mr. Hoover got bored. It was dirt insufficient. Call it a dirt deficit.

Mr. Hoover pulled the Feds. Fred filled in for them. Fred dirtified. Fred stored dirt. Fred aged dirt. Fred saved dirt for Pete.

Three legislators and one Pete. Compliance guaranteed. We've got the board votes. We've got YOU now. Pledge your support.

Watch us abridge antitrust laws. Watch our Vegas spree. Watch hotel profits plunge. Watch skim ops soar. Watch Littell invest skim money.

We've got the "real" books. We've got the goods. We've got the buyout stats. We co-opt businesses. We funnel cash. We build foreign casinos.

The Boys hoard. The Boys divert. The Boys avoid obstructions—*usually*.

Sam G. was obstructed now. It was recent news. Sam was in jail in Chicago. A grand jury subpoenaed him. Bobby paneled it. Bobby was AG then.

Sam refused to testify. Sam took the Fifth. The judge cited him.

Contempt of Court—Cook County Jail—for the grand-jury term. One year—jail to spring '66.

The judge ragged on Sam. The judge aped Bobby. Bobby ragged Sam in '57. Bobby was Senate counsel then. Bobby was a senator now.

He played his Bobby tapes. He toured the Senate. He prowled the gallery. He watched Bobby. He read the Senate Record. He tracked Bobby's words through.

Bobby debunks bills. Bobby lauds bills. Bobby never mentions the Boys. Bobby presses for civil rights. Bobby lauds Dr. King.

Littell taped Bayard Rustin. Bayard praised King. Littell met Bayard sans tape. Bayard waxed sad that day. Bayard showed him the letter.

"King, look into your heart."

"King, like all frauds, your end is approaching."

"You are a colossal fraud, and an evil, vicious one at that."

"King, there is only one thing left for you to do."

They met in Lafayette Park. Bayard showed him the letter. He read it. He went queasy. He walked.

He met Bayard one more time. Lafayette Park again. They talked sans tape. It sparked him. It scared him.

Tails.

Dwight Holly had him tailed. Mr. Hoover said so. *Vegas* tails— pre-RABBIT.

Holly was BLUE RABBIT. Holly ran BLACK RABBIT. Holly hated him. Spot tails meant checks. Spot tails meant notes. Spot tails meant data accrued.

He met Jane in Vegas—that one bad time—potential tails were out. He met Janice—their first time—potential tails were out.

Holly pulled the tails. Holly pulled them pre-RABBIT. Mr. Hoover said so. Holly ran RABBIT. Holly had juice. Holly could tail-reinstate.

He met Bayard. They had two meets sans tape. He ran tail checks. None were visible. None were obvious. None were probable or certified.

Bayard said, "Come to Selma. You'll see history."

He did it.

He flew down. He used fake ID. He forged a press card. He ducked the marchers. He ducked the cops. He joined a press crew.

He watched. He fretted tails. He saw Bloody Sunday.

Highway 80. The Edmund Pettus Bridge. Sheriff Clark's posse—horses and patrol cars with rebel bumper-flags.

Clark braced the marchers. Clark said disperse in two minutes. The posse charged one minute in. They charged with tear gas and billy clubs. They charged with bullwhips and barbed-wire saps.

The posse hit the marchers. The posse cut through them. The posse mowed them down. He watched. He hid behind cameras. He saw saps rip noses. He saw whips sever ears.

He hid. Meek CRUSADER RABBIT. Unworthy of brave RED and PINK.

He flew back to Vegas. He thought about tails. He thought about Mr. Hoover. Mr. Hoover pledged memos—RABBIT details—Mr. Hoover sent none.

Let's extrapolate. Let's grow some fear.

Mr. Hoover is busy. He's deep in BLACK RABBIT. BLUE RABBIT counsels him. BLUE hates CRUSADER. BLUE hoards memorandums. BLUE restricts their flow.

Or:

Mr. Hoover has plans. They're draconian. They supersede suicide letters. Why disturb CRUSADER? Why risk his specious reproach?

Don't tweak him with knowledge. Don't risk his betrayal. Don't test his silly ideals.

Or:

BLUE has a puppet—WILD RABBIT on strings—WILD RABBIT works alone. WILD runs Klansmen. WILD might run autonomous. WILD might run outright rogue.

Mr. Hoover knows it. BLUE knows it—so why tell CRUSADER that?

Need-to-know. Read-and-burn. Compartments. Sealed access. Love-and-hide.

He had Jane. Jane survived her Vegas trip. Jane never went back. They went back to their rules. They resealed their compartments. They hid in L.A.

They ignored their fight. They revived their game. He lied. She lied. They codified. Their code said we aired it. Their code said it hurt. Their code said we survived Dallas.

Jane knew he taped Bobby. Jane knew he bilked Howard Hughes. Jane knew the Boys. Jane knew the Life. Jane feared the Teamsters for real.

Compartments. Sealed access. Love-and-lie. The love worked. The lies hurt. The seal cracked.

He traveled. He sealed off Vegas. He compartmentalized. He met Barb. He joined her fan club. He sat ringside.

They were prom dates. Admiration and earnest chats. Chaste drinks and her show.

Pete rotated through—Vietnam to Vegas—they all socialized. Barb rotated with him. Her eyes went from pinholed to bright.

Pills. Her secret. Her Pete's-gone-rotation delight.

All men loved her. He told Pete. Pete said he knew that. Barb grew. Barb changed while he watched her. Barb changed her ridiculous lounge act.

She put out more knock-knees. She put out more ad-libs and goofs. I'm six feet tall. I can't sing. I know terrible things.

He loved her. He loved her more than Janice and Jane.

Janice was Vegas. Jane was L.A. He rotated through. Compartments: candor and lies/separate disclosures.

Janice spilled her secrets. Janice *never* lied. She bragged about sex. She proved her points. She flaunted her prowess.

She talked too much. She enticed men. She lived for the thrill. She thought she controlled men. Her stories disproved it. She confused prowess with heart.

She divorced Wayne Senior. She ditched his name. She went back to "Lukens." She earned her two million. She paid with cramps. She paid with a limp.

She fought back. She played golf. She broke par as a gimp. She never cried. She never whined. She never complained.

They met at her cottage. They made love. They talked.

Janice *talked*. He listened.

She fucked a Negro man. Wayne Senior found out and killed him. She fucked Clark Kinman. Wayne Senior watched. She fucked bellboys on dares and bets.

She fucked Wayne Junior. She paid.

She talked too much. She drank too much. She limped through A-club tennis. She was pure will unconsidered. She was inimical to Jane.

Janice talked. Janice digressed. Janice discussed Wayne Senior. He was bad. He was cruel. He'd do ANYTHING.

Janice talked. Janice scared him. Wayne Senior was FATHER RABBIT.

69

(Las Vegas, Miami, Port Sulphur, Saigon,
Saravan, Dac To, Dak Sut, Muang Kao,
3/21–6/15/65)

ROTATION:

East to west—V to V—Vietnam to Vegas.

He flew west—rotation 1—Barb met his plane. She sparkled. She beamed. She refuted that letter.

The letter bugged him. Jerky words and the lines "up & down." He thought about pills—lounge-popcorn uppers and reds to come down.

No/*nyet*/*nein*. *Noi* in Viet. Barb radiated. Barb fucking glowed.

They glowed three years in. They glowed with crazy shit concurrent. Barb got better. Barb got stronger. Barb got X-ray eyes.

She saw through show people. She saw through the Life. The Life was rigged. The men took the risks. The men had the fun. The men conspired. The men served causes. The women served tea.

Barb said it: "I peaked early. I extorted JFK." Barb said it: "You've got Cuba. I've got the Sultan's Lounge."

She didn't nag him. She didn't play shrew. She just said she'd changed.

They hashed it out. He sensed cabin fever. Vegas hemmed her in. He sold dope batch #1. He bought two tickets east.

They booked to Miami. They took the cat. They booked a suite at the Doral. The cat leveled it.

He clawed the drapes. He shit on chairs. He killed terrace birds. He bootjacked their room-service food.

They caught Dino. They caught Shecky Green. They got ringside seats. They slept late and made love.

They talked. He laid out Vietnam. He lied. He downplayed the killing. He downplayed the slaves.

Barb pressed him. Barb tripped him up. Barb nailed his lies. He said fuck it. He cut loose. He disclosed.

Barb said, "All that for *Cuba*?"

They got some rays. They ran into Jimmy H. They went out for stone crabs. Jimmy fumed. Jimmy fugued. Jimmy ran nonstop boo-hoo.

His legal woes. Sam G. in stir. His ripe hemorrhoids.

Pete bored in. Pete pumped him. Pete worked his mood. Pete pumped angles. Pete pumped oblique.

It's Kansas City. It's '56. Danny Bruvick fucks you.

Jimmy cut loose—six fucks!/six cocksuckers!/six Arden cunts! Jimmy dished on Arden. Jimmy tossed a bomb:

Arden Bruvick—that cunt—she was Jules Schiffrin's ex.

Pete said, "Excuse me." Pete walked to the john. Pete found a throne. Pete sat down. Pete hashed it all through.

Jules Schiffrin—Mob money man—dead in '60. The "real" fund books—Schiffrin's property. Arden Bruvick: *book*keeper.

It's '56. It's K.C. Danny Bruvick splits. Jimmy fugues out. Cops bust Arden. The T&C Corp bails her. Carlos M. owns T&C.

Cut to:

'59—New Orleans—J.P. Mesplède passes through. Mesplède sees Arden—with some Carlos goon.

Cut to:

1960—Wisconsin—Ward Littell steals the books. Schiffrin heart-attacks and drops dead.

Cut to:

Fall '63. Carlos taps Ward. Carlos says this:

You got the books. Jimmy don't know it. The Boys and I do. We know you. We *own* you. You'll sell Drac our hotels. You'll *work* the books. You'll dredge up data. You'll funnel skim through.

Cut to:

Dallas—hit time—Arden meets Ward. She works for Jack Ruby. She keeps *his* books. She's seen the safe house. She's seen the targets. She's seen the crew.

Ward falls for Arden. Carlos wants her dead. Ward makes Arden "Jane." Ward hides "Jane." Ward brews fund-book schemes.

So:

Did Carlos find Arden? Did Carlos pledge mercy? IF YOU SPY ON LITTELL? Arden was a bookkeeper. Arden knew Schiffrin. Arden *lived* with Littell.

Sound logic, but:

He saw Ward with "Jane." They were *real*. He *knew* it.

It scared him. He teethed on it. He riffed: *Real* deals with women could be undercut—and thus shot to shit.

Barb saw him pump Jimmy. Barb gauged his john run. Barb

got halfway hip. He filled her in. He abridged it. He omitted Carlos. He omitted Big D.

Barb loved it. Barb loved secrets. Barb held them tough. They discussed it. He told her—I'll probe up more stuff.

He called Fred Otash. Otash weighed in. Otash said I'm on it—don't sweat. I'll buy *more* cops. I'll put out *more* search fees. My cops will check files and call back.

They schmoozed. Otash had news. Otash said Ward hired him. Ward craved dirt. Ward bought a dirt search—let's find the old scandal-rag files.

Pete riffed on his Arden search. Pete said don't tell Ward—don't clue Ward in. Otash played ball. Otash had Arden pix already. Otash *knew* Arden was Jane.

Pete teethed on it. Pete sifted it. Pete lived with it. Pete ran rotations.

Vegas was good—100%. White horse hits. The word expands. Clients accrue: Sniffers/tasters/junkies/skin-popper geeks.

The street pushers worked. The street pushers proselytized. They wore flash threads. They drove jig rigs. They glorified "H." They glamorized it. They accessorized it. They Tupperwared it.

They cruised the projects. They drew crowds. They sniffed powdered milk and bopped strong. They debunked that addiction jive.

They wore pendants. They wore processed hair. They carried mock-gold guns. They lied. They said spooks ran the biz. They denied that the White Man existed.

Wayne tailed them. It scared them. They knew Wayne's rep. Wayne Junior be baaaaaaaaaaaad. Wayne Junior kill our kin.

Profits accrued. Milt totaled them. Milt praised the horse epidemic. It was restricted. It was contained. No whites need apply.

A dope punk moved in. Said punk brought ambition. Said punk sniffed the air. Said punk sniffed the wrong vibration:

Horse is cool—let's sell some—the Mob don't mind.

Pete dispatched his niggers. Said niggers grabbed said punk.

Santo T. had a shark named Batista. He lived in Santo's pool. He ate burgers. He ate steak. He ate pizza.

The niggers dropped the punk in the pool. Batista ate him live.

White horse stayed west. Junkies stayed home. Junkies eschewed white Vegas. Tiger Kabs prowled west. Tiger orbs glowed.

So far:

No new pushers. No pending fuzz heat. No unbribed narcs making noise.

Tiger Kab was hip. Sonny Liston tigerized. Sonny ate at the hut. Sonny drank at the hut. Sonny went on local TV.

Sonny did ads. Sonny proselytized:

"Tiger Kab packs a knockout punch." "Tiger Kab kicks Cassius Clay's patootie."

Fag drivers drove. Straight drivers drove. Pete enforced faction détente. Fag drivers sold boys. Fag celebs bought boys. Fag drivers drove fags to hotels.

Fag clerks minced. Fag clerks smirked. Fag clerks supplied rooms. Said rooms: Bugged/tapped/extortionized.

Fag drivers drove fags. Fag drivers turned tricks. Donkey Dom tricked with Sal Mineo. Donkey Dom tricked with Rock Hudson.

Sonny said it:

"Tiger prowls 24 hours! If you don't swing, don't ring!"

Tiger Kab swung in Vegas. Tiger Kamp rocked Laos hard.

Pete rotated. Pete left Vegas. Pete cut the Barb cord. Wayne rotated. Stanton worked in Saigon. Laurent and Chuck worked in Laos.

Pete detached Flash—4/65—strict orders: Hit the Gulf. Hit exile camps. Scout for good troops.

Pete detached Mesplède—4/65—strict orders: Hit the U.S. Hit the South. Scout gun dealers out.

Bob Relyea left Laos—5/65—Bob Relyea hit Mississippi. Bob was Fed now. Bob did snitch work. It was klandestine.

Chuck to follow Bob. Chuck to hit Houston. Chuck to scout guns. Chuck to scout Gulf-close—close to Mississippi. Close to Mesplède and pal Bob.

Chuck snickered to Bob. Bob snickered to Chuck. They snickered contrapuntal. They snickered through Bob's big farewell.

They implied mischief. They indulged wordplay. They inferred klownery. Birmingham, Alabama. Really BOMB-ingham. Bogalusa—tee-hee—BOMBalusa.

Bob split for Fed work. Chuck changed roommates. Chuck bunked with Laurent Guéry now. Chuck bugged him. Chuck hassled him. Chuck harangued him:

With Klan klaptrap. With klownish klaims. With klaims of krossburns to kome.

Rotations all—Dallas to Vegas—Dallas to Vietnam. Grad-school hijinx and reunions.

Chuck shot. Chuck shot from the knoll. Mesplède shot Oswald's gun. Flash and Laurent stood in Boyd's team. They got scuttled pre-hit.

Rotations—Saigon to the Gulf—the Gulf to Cuba. Flash is Cuban. Flash is dark. Flash could get in.

The plan:

Flash goes in. Flash charts resistance. Flash finds good men. Flash smuggles them out. Flash boats them in. Flash feeds Guéry and Mesplède.

They've got a shack. It's Gulf-close. They've got electrodes. They torture the men. They test their balls. They ensure their loyalty.

Rotations—Cuba to the Gulf—the Gulf to Vietnam. *Biggggggg* U.S. troop numbers.

Stanton logged said numbers. Stanton logged provocations. Stanton vibed a long war.

The Cong hits Pleiku. Eight Yankees die. LBJ reacts. Air strikes: Operation Flaming Dart.

The Cong hits Qui Nhon. Twenty-one Yankees die. LBJ reacts. More air strikes: Flaming Dart II.

U.S. troops arrive—"advisors"—two Marine battalions. More air strikes: Operation Rolling Thunder.

Two battalions arrive—logistical troops—20,000 men. They get deployed. They get dispersed. They get detached to Marv units.

Firefights. Dead Yanks. Incoming rotations. Buildups—incremental—40,000 men per.

Troops hit Saigon. Troops R&R. Troop numbers swell. Long war good. Kadre like it. Buildup most boocoo.

Wayne lived in Saigon. Wayne lived in his lab. Wayne said *his* fucking world swelled. More people. More noise. More songs up his vents. More Marvs. More O-heads. More whores.

More cover. More white horse. More money.

Stanton laundered profits. Stanton fed Pete. Pete fed Mesplède. Mesplède bought righteous *guns*.

.50-calibers/Ithacas/BARs/antitank guns.

Flash found a troop site. It was Gulf-close and gooood. It was near Port Sulphur, Louisiana. It housed sixty troopers—Cubano shitkickers all.

Mesplède dropped some guns off. The shitkickers roared. Pete rotated through. Pete dug on the troops. Pete dug their maneuvers.

The troopers were hard-ons. The troopers were *très* hard. The troopers were *très sanguinaire*.

Pete rotated. Pete hit Saigon. Pete met Stanton's CIA crew. Six men plus Stanton—all Cubafied.

They talked Cuba. They talked ops. They talked polygraph tests. They'd be mandatory and random. They'd go kadre-wide. Let's ID and whack traitors. Let's uproot thieves. Let's assure loyalty.

Stanton flew to Laos. Stanton brought his poly machine. Pete tested. Pete tested clean. Tran tested. Tran tested clean.

Stanton stayed for a visit. Stanton watched the spring burn.

Guards unshackled slaves. Slaves piled brush. Guards formed a fire brigade. They stacked the piles. They positioned them—one per stalk row.

Slaves filled drums with propane gas. Guards dipped torches. Guards whooped. Guards lit torches. Guards torched brush.

The fields burned. The sky flared. The fields burned all night. Guards cheered. Slaves cheered. Tiger Kamp cinderized.

Ash blew. Ash settled. Ash nourished kamp-wide.

Stanton loved it. Stanton stayed. Stanton stayed for the Clay-Liston fight. Chuck rigged a hookup—closed-circuit shit—a feed off MACV in Saigon.

Sonny lost. The fight vibed nonclimax. Sportswriter stupes yelled, "Fix!"

Pete laughed. Fuck it—Pete *knew:*

Sonny was old. Sonny was slow. Sonny was tigerfried.

70

(Las Vegas, Saigon, Saravan, Bao Loc,
3/21/65–6/15/65)

LET'S ESCALATE. Let's *watch*.

Khanh is in. Khanh is out. Premier Ky kreams Premier Khanh. Don't blink—koups and kreamouts kome kwick.

"Escalate"—a verb—LBJ's word: "To increase, enlarge or intensify."

The war escalated. Wayne watched.

More troops came in. More troops got pledged. Provocation meant response. More Marines came in. More Marines got pledged. More Airborne came in. More Airborne got pledged in response.

More dead:

More bomb attacks in mid-Saigon. More mid-range dead. The Brinks Hotel/the embassy—more Yankee dead.

More VC. More night patrols. More sabotage.

Pleiku—much aircraft blow—nice U.S. fleet. VC attack—most bold and sincere. VC use pole-and-satchel bombs—home-made/*très* VC. TNT/palm leaves/bamboo.

Many planes blow. *One* VC die.

Provocation meant response. Response meant bomb runs. More pilots. More troops. More artillery.

Stanton ran numbers. Provocation meets response—thus fervor meets weight. Stanton predicted two hundred K troops—in by '66.

Big numbers. Big ordnance. Big weight.

Wayne watched. Wayne dug it. Wayne missed the point. Vietnam was a shithole. The Cong couldn't lose. The Cong lived to die.

A Cong walked in the Go-Go. Said Cong wore Cong drag—black pj's deluxe. A spec-4 shot him. A chest bomb blew. Oops—Cong booby-trapped.

Six dead—all U.S.—Cong reigns six-to-one.

Stanton loved the war. Pete loved the war. Stanton and Pete loved Cuba. Cuba was a shithole. Cuba was Saigon with sand.

The kadre loved the war. The kadre kame for Kuba. Wayne came to watch.

He stayed in Saigon. He cooked dope. He watched. GIs hit the Go-Go. GIs bought whores. GIs fucked whores on floor planks. He watched.

The O-heads decomped. Quicklime ate bone. Marvs made fertilizer. Marvs sold it discount.

He watched.

The Cong burned pylons. Saigon went dark. Pilots dropped psychedelic-tint flares.

He watched. He worked. He lived in Saigon. He cabbed to Bao Loc. He bought weapons. Said weapons were dope cover. Said weapons were donation stock.

He jeeped up and back. He tailed patrols. His standard procedure was *watch*.

4/8/65—near Dinh Quan. Rice field firefight—jarheads and VC.

A road mine popped. Wayne's jeep flew. The windshield blew up. The driver ate glass. The driver died. Wayne crouched by his stiff.

Bushes—off the road. They're moving now. They're bush-wrapped VC.

They charged. The jarheads proned out. Fair fight/no cover.

Wayne rolled free. Wayne pulled his piece. Wayne shot three VC. His shots dinged. He hit tin vests—fucking trashcan lids.

The VC fired. The jarheads fired. The jarheads aimed high and low. They shot feet. They shot legs. They shot faces. They hit vest-free zones.

The VC went down. Rounds dinged off the jeep. A medic went down with one in the neck. Wayne rolled and fired free.

He hit six VC. He notched all head shots. He double-killed.

The jarheads stood up. A jarhead tripped a punji stick. Spikes slammed him—knees to nipples—punctures and rips.

Wayne rolled to the medic. Wayne grabbed his Syrettes—pure morphine cc's.

He rolled to the jarhead. He shot up the jarhead. The jarhead convulsed. The jarhead hurled chunks of his spleen.

Wayne had white horse—one spike in his pocket—one short test dose.

He found a vein. He geezed the man. The man gasped. The man smiled. The man nodded out.

Wayne timed his death. He went out in sixteen seconds. He went out wispy and numb.

Pete was World War II. Pete had a rule: Don't sell to GIs. It was naive. It negated the real rule: provocation meets response.

"Our Boys" would fight the war. "Our Boys" would look for outs. "Our Boys" would find Big "H."

Stanton had terms: "the Agency's War" and "the Personal Commitment."

He killed Bongo. He committed. He joined the war then. He squashed a bug. It felt right. It felt impersonal. He killed Bongo. He dumped Bongo. He took his own pulse. Sixty-two beats a minute—no malice/no stress.

Rats ate Bongo. Some Marvs found his bones. A rumor spread: Chemist do it—chemist kill pimp.

Whores braced Wayne. They said be our pimp—we love you. He said no. He saw that colored whore. He saw her trailer.

The rumor spread. Chuck heard it. Chuck told Bob. Bob braced him. Bob said come south and join my Klan—we'll fuck niggers up.

Wayne said no. Bob dropped hints: I work for your dad. Wayne said no. Bob laughed. Wayne said he might come to WATCH.

He watched in Saigon. He watched in Bao Loc. He watched in Vegas. He watched the pushers. He tailed the pushers. He ensured subservience.

He watched West LV. He watched the bars. He watched that trailer. Junkies used it now. Junkies geezed within. They ignored the soot. They ignored the smell. They ignored the whore's bones.

He watched West LV. He asked around. He trawled for Wendell Durfee. The locals ignored him. The locals misled him. The locals spit on his shoes.

He logged tips. He paid rewards. He logged futile data. He hit the bars. He logged fear. He brought Sonny Liston along.

Sonny quaffed J&B. Sonny popped pills. Sonny ran riffs: Wendell Durfee went Muslim—Muhammad speaks—it gots to be!

Wendell runs a mosque. Wendell knows Cassius Clay. Wendell knew the late Malcolm X.

Storm the Nigger Mosques. Climb the Nigger Grapevine. Comb the Nigger Underworld. Patch the Nigger Switchboard. Punch the Nigger Teletype—and track that nigger down!

Sonny peeled his nigger eyes. Sonny filed his nigger claws. Sonny tapped his nigger intuition. Sonny logged tips. Sonny dished out rewards. Sonny pledged results.

Pete said Durfee was dead. DPD killed him unpublicized. They killed him for Maynard Moore.

Wayne said no—you're wrong. Wayne logged tips and WATCHED.

He logged lounge time. He watched Barb. He took side seats. He looked backstage. He got candid shots.

The Bondsmen smoked weed there. Barb popped pills. Barb popped Johnnie Black. Her eyes showed it. Her pulse showed it. She cleaned up for Pete's rotations.

He watched. He saw things everywhere. He felt invisible.

He logged lounge time. He caught Barb's gigs. He saw Janice and Ward Littell. They sat close. They held hands. They brushed knees.

He saw them. They never saw him. Sonny had a theory: Only niggers see you.

7 1

(Las Vegas, 6/18/65)

JANICE HIT BALLS.

She chipped off her porch. Said porch as golf range—tee/putting strip/net.

It was hot. Janice wore a middy blouse and shorts. Littell watched her concentrate. Littell watched her hit.

Janice teed balls. Janice hit shots. Janice stretched the net. She swiveled. Her blouse gapped. Her beating scars flexed.

She said, "I saw Wayne Senior at the DI. He was making a phone call."

Littell smiled. "Why are you telling me this?"

"Because you hate him, and you're curious about the men I've slept with."

Littell sipped coffee. "I hope I haven't been prying."

"That's impossible with me. You know how I love to divulge."

"I do know. It's something that separates—"

"Me from Jane, I know."

Littell smiled. "Tell me what you heard."

Janice teed a ball. "He was in the casino, and he was using one of those courtesy phones. He didn't see me behind him."

"And?"

"And he was talking to a man named Chuck. He was talking about the bad reception from Vietnam, and he was cracking jokes about Bogalusa and 'Bombalusa.' "

Littell stirred his coffee. "That's it?"

"That and the way he was gloating, with that Indiana drawl of his."

Hold it. Stop right—

Littell stirred his coffee. Littell thought it through. Bogalusa was East Louisiana. Bogalusa was Klan kountry.

Vote drives—right now—fronted by SCLC. BLACK RABBIT on go. Wayne Senior as FATHER RABBIT.

Hold it. Stop right—

You're CRUSADER RABBIT. Bayard Rustin's PINK. You taped PINK. PINK told you about Bogalusa. You told Mr. Hoover.

Mr. Hoover knows. Mr. Hoover never calls. Mr. Hoover pledges memos. Mr. Hoover sends none.

Janice built a martini. "Is there room for two in that trance of yours, or should I leave you alone?"

Littell coughed. "Do you have any idea who Chuck is?"

"Well, I'd say he's that little man who flew a plane to Wayne Senior's Christmas party, and showed up with your caveman friend Pete."

Hold it. Stop right—

Chuck Rogers: Pilot/killer/racist nut/Dallas shooter. Vietnam and Pete's gig—covert CIA.

FATHER RABBIT runs WILD RABBIT. WILD RABBIT is Army. WILD RABBIT serves "overseas." Mr. Hoover talked rabbits. Mr. Hoover talked dates. WILD RABBIT to leave the Army—5/65. WILD RABBIT to go Klan then.

"Ward, am I going to have to do a striptease to pull you out of that trance?"

He worried it. He tested it. He dreamed RABBITS. He carried it with him. He brought it home. He slept with it.

BOMBalusa. BOMBingham: September '63. A bomb blows at 16th Street Baptist Church. Four Negro girls die.

He woke up. He made coffee. He built rationales:

Don't call Mr. Hoover. Don't raise an alarm. Don't call Pete. Don't mention Chuck. Don't breach need-to-know. Don't call Bayard. Don't probe Bogalusa. Don't sound his alarm.

Don't call BLUE RABBIT. Don't call WHITE RABBIT. Don't rouse the Holly boys. They hate Negroes. They love Mr. Hoover.

Wayne Senior's FATHER RABBIT. FATHER knows Chuck. FATHER runs WILD RABBIT. WILD RABBIT runs a klavern. The Feds fund it and impose rules:

"Operational guidelines." "Violence to sustain informant credibility." BOMBingham/BOMBalusa/BOMB—

Littell grabbed the phone. Littell called Barb. Littell ran a riff: Laos. Pete's dope clique. Is Chuck Rogers in?

Barb said, "Yes."

Littell hung up. Littell called the switchboard. Littell braced an operator: Get me U.S. Customs—the passport office—New Orleans.

The operator ran it. Littell got the number. Littell dialed direct.

A man picked up. "Customs, Agent Bryce."

"My name's Ward Littell. I'm ex-FBI, with reserve credentials. I was hoping you'd do me a favor."

"Well, sure, if I can."

Littell grabbed a pen. "I need you to check your recently collated entries for flights from Laos and Vietnam. I'm looking for commercial or military landings at Customs-manned facilities in your jurisdiction, and I need the names on the passport-check lists."

Bryce coughed. "Can you hold? I doubt if we've had more than three or four of those, tops."

Littell said, "I'll hold."

Bryce hit a button. The connection fuzzed. Static hit the line. Littell held. Littell checked his watch. Littell counted rabbits.

BLUE RABBIT/WILD RABBIT/RED RABBIT. Three minutes/forty-two sec—

Bryce picked up. "Sir? We've only got one. I—"

"Can you give—"

"One ordnance flight. Saigon to the Air National Guard facility near Houston. The crew plus one passenger, a man named Charles Rogers."

72

(Saravan, 6/19/65)

POLY TEST—pure impromptu—John Stanton dropped in.

He cleared the hut. He rolled graph sheets. He rigged the machine. He fired the needle. He fired the pulse clip. He fired the dials.

Pete rigged a chair. Laurent Guéry sat down. Stanton rigged the blood-pressure cuff.

Stanton clamped the cuff. Pete looped the chest cord. Stanton pumped the cuff. Stanton read the dial:

Normal stats—110/80.

A wind stirred. Dope seeds blew. Pete shut the window.

Stanton grabbed a chair. Stanton pulse-clipped Guéry. Pete grabbed a chair. Pete watched the needle.

Stanton said, "Do you drink water?"

Guéry said, "Yes."

The needle bumped. The needle slid. The needle flatlined. Stanton read the cuff and clip:

Okay—normal signs.

Stanton said, "Are you a citizen of the Republic of France?"

Guéry said, "Yes."

The needle bumped. The needle slid. The needle flatlined. Stanton read the cuff and clip:

Okay—normal signs.

Pete stretched. Pete yawned—fuck this pro-forma jive.

Stanton said, "Are you a committed anti-Communist?"

Guéry said, "Yes."

Flatline.

Stanton said, "Are you pro-Viet Cong?"

Guéry said, "No."

Flatline.

Stanton said, "Have you ever stolen from the kadre?"

Guéry said, "No."

The needle dipped two inches. The needle laid swerve lines. Stanton pumped the cuff. Stanton read the dial.

Not okay—140/110—*non*-normal signs.

Guéry squirmed. Pete eyeballed him. Pete read his signs: Chills/goosebumps/sweat.

Stanton said, "Have you ever stolen from kadre-adjunct personnel?"

Guéry said, "No."

The needle dipped three inches. The needle laid swerve lines.

Stanton hit the intercom switch. Stanton talked gook: "*Quon, Minh. Mau len. Di, thi, di.*"

Two gooks ran in—one Marv and one Cong doubletime. Guéry squirmed. Pete read signs: Wet hands/wet armpits/crotch leaking sweat.

Stanton nodded. The gooks flanked Guéry. The gooks pulled batons.

Stanton said, "Do you have knowledge of such thefts?"

Guéry said, "No."

The needle dipped six inches. The needle laid swerve lines.

Stanton said, "Do you have knowledge that Pete Bondurant perpetrated such thefts?"

Guéry said, "No."

Needle bump. Flatline.

Stanton said, "Do you have knowledge that Jean Philippe Mesplède perpetrated such thefts?"

Guéry said, "No."

Needle bump. Flatline.

Stanton said, "Do you have knowledge that Wayne Tedrow Junior perpetrated such thefts?"

Guéry said, "No."

Needle bump. Flatline.

Stanton said, "Do you have knowledge that Chuck Rogers perpetrated such thefts?"

Guéry said, "No."

The needle dipped eight inches. The needle laid swerve lines.

Guéry squirmed. Stanton cued the gooks. They grabbed ropes. They looped them. They tied Guéry to the chair.

Stanton pulled his piece. Stanton cocked it. Pete grabbed the field phone. Pete patched the lab.

Chuck was gone. Chuck split to Saigon. Chuck split four days back. Chuck bunked with Guéry now. Chuck hassled Guéry. Chuck drove Guéry nuts.

Pete got a dial tone. Pete got line fuzz. Pete got a click.

Wayne picked up. "Yeah?"

"It's me. Have you seen Chuck?"

"No. Was he supposed—"

"He was supposed to go through Bao Loc and Saigon and pick up some guns."

"I haven't seen him at all. He always comes by the Go-Go when he's—"

Pete hung up. Stanton cued him—go check the hooch.

Pete ran over. Pete popped the door. Pete tripped on the mat. He caught himself. He eyeball-walked. He quadrant-scanned.

Four walls/two fart sacks/two nightstands/two lockers/one shitter/one sink.

Pete dumped the nightstands. Pete combed debris. Toothpaste/rubbers/stroke books/hate tracts/*Ring* magazines.

Two passports—both Guéry's—CIA/French.

Pete dumped the lockers. Pete combed debris. Hate tracts/bug spray/beaver pix/gun oil/*Swank* magazines.

No Chuck passports. No Chuck ID.

Pete grabbed the field phone. Pete patched Saigon direct. He got Ops South. They repatched him. He got Tan Son Nhut. They repatched him. He got static. He got Customs.

He got a gook. He spoke French. The gook spoke strict Viet. The gook repatched him. He got static. He got a white man.

"Customs, Agent Lierz."

"This is Sergeant Peters, CID. I'm checking on a civilian who might've cleared Customs within the past four days."

Lierz coughed. The line coughed. Static brizzed.

"You got a name?"

"Rogers. First name Charles."

Lierz coughed. "I've got my log here. Hold on ... Rice, Ridgeway, Rippert ... yeah, Rogers. He flew out four days ago. He showed manifest docs, loaded explosive material and caught a transport to the National Guard strip in Houston, Tex—"

Pete hung up. Pete *got* it: Thefts/fake docs/explosives.

Guéry screamed. Pete heard it loud. It carried from forty yards up.

He ran back. He smelled smoke and piss. He cracked the door and *saw* it.

There's Guéry.

He's tied up. He's pantless. He's scared. Stanton's got the hot box. Stanton's got the switch. Stanton's got the clamps on his balls.

The gooks watched. The gooks smoked bootjack Kools. The gooks slurped gook wine.

Stanton said, "What did Chuck Rogers steal?"

Guéry shook his head. Stanton hit the switch. Stanton tossed volts. Guéry buckled and screamed.

Stanton said, "If the theft is kadre-adjunct and you didn't participate or report it, I'd be inclined to go easy."

Guéry shook his head. Stanton hit the switch. Stanton tossed volts. Guéry buckled and screamed.

Stanton said, "Where's Rogers now? What did he steal and who did he steal it from?"

Guéry shook his head. Stanton hit the switch. Stanton tossed volts. Guéry buckled and screamed.

Pete *got* it—for real now.

Chuck and Guéry worked Dallas. Stanton's got no clue. Guéry won't talk. Guéry won't rat Chuck for *anything*.

Stanton said, "Is Rogers in-country? Did he fly back to the States?"

Guéry shook his head. Stanton hit the switch. Stanton tossed volts. Guéry buckled and screamed.

The gooks laughed—he claaazy—he *dinky dau*.

Stanton hit the switch. Stanton tossed volts. Guéry buckled. Guéry screamed. Guéry yelled, "*Assez!*"

Stanton cued the gooks. The gooks pulled the clamps. The gooks untied Guéry. The gooks sprayed his balls with baby oil. The gooks fed him gook wine.

He slurped it. He stood up. He teetered. He fell back in his chair.

Stanton leaned in. "If I said it hurt me more than it hurt you, I'd be a fucking liar."

Pete sneezed—the hut smelled—fried ball hair and sweat.

Guéry said, "The ammo dump . . . Bao Loc . . . Chuck, *qu'est-ce que c'est*, burglarized bomb material . . . from François."

Stanton shook his head. "Did he tell you what he had in mind?"

Pete leaned in. "Chuck flew to the States. If you let me talk to him alone, I'll get the rest of it."

Stanton nodded. Stanton stood up. Stanton cued the gooks—*venez, venez*.

They walked out together. Pete grabbed the bottle. Guéry snatched it. Guéry drained it. Guéry hitched his pants up.

"I will never have children now."

"It's not like you want them."

"No. The world has become too communistic."

"I think I know why you held back."

Guéry wiped his nose. "I did not betray the kadre."

"I know you didn't."

Guéry rubbed his balls. "Chuck . . . *qu'est-ce* . . . received a letter from his parents. I think they are not sane."

Pete lit two cigarettes. Guéry snatched one.

"Chuck lives at their house. They said they found his . . . *journal*?"

"Journal, right."

"Which described our operation in Dallas ... for which ... they demanded an explanation ... which ... Chuck said he would fly home and ... *qu'est-ce* ... take care of it."

Pete kicked a doorpost. "He stole bomb ordnance for *that?*"

Guéry coughed. "No. For something else. He would not tell me."

Pete walked outside. Slaves double-timed past him. Guards popped rubber rounds.

Stanton straddled a fence rail. "How bad?"

Pete shrugged. "You tell me. Laurent said it's a family grudge, and Chuck flew out with explosives."

Stanton chewed a hangnail. "There's a courier flight leaving for Fort Sam Houston. You and Wayne go find him and kill him."

73

(Houston, 6/21/65)

GULF HEAT:

Low clouds and thick air. Air as bug propellant.

And bug catalyst. And bug haven. And bug launching pad. Bug *heat*—80 at 2:12 A.M.

The freeway was dead. Bugs bipped off the car. Pete drove. Wayne read maps.

Chez Chuck was on Driscoll. Chez Chuck was close. Chez Chuck was near Rice U.

Wayne yawned. Pete yawned. They yawned contrapuntal. They flew eighteen hours—Saigon to Houston—they plowed six time zones.

They flew transport. They sat on crates. They ate canned corn exclusive. Stanton set a car up—a '61 Ford—there at Fort Sam.

Bum wheels altogether. No muffler. No fucking Air King.

Stanton knew some of it. Pete said so. Pete said he withheld the key shit. Maybe Chuck's here. Maybe Chuck's not. Maybe Chuck's in Bogalusa.

With Bob Relyea—kadre-ex—kurrent Klan klown. Bob ran a snitch-Klan. Wayne Senior ran Bob. That meant *he* could WATCH.

They ditched the freeway. They took side streets. They ran their high beams. Houston was the shits—brick cribs and bug lights abundant.

Stanton shot them filework: stats per Chez Chuck. Chuck's dad and mom were Fred and Edwina. They had a '53 Olds.

Texas plates: DXL-841.

They hit Kirby Street. They hit Richmond. They turned hard right. There—Driscoll—1780/1800/1808.

1815 was glazed brick. No palace/no slum. Two floors and no lights extant.

Pete parked. Wayne grabbed two flashlights. They got out. They circled the house. They flashed the windows. They flashed the doors.

Bugs stirred. Owls stirred. Wasps bombed a nest.

Wayne flashed the back porch. Pete flashed a hedge. Wayne caught a glint—light on steel—Pete threw his beam down.

Wayne reached in. Wayne grabbed and pulled. Wayne sliced two fingers up.

There—

One Texas license plate—stuffed in a hedge. Bingo on DXL-841.

Pete said, "He changed plates on the Olds."

Wayne sucked his fingers. "Let's go in. We might find something."

Pete flashed the back door. Wayne walked up and looked. Okay: One lock/flat bolt/wide keyhole.

Pete cupped his light. Wayne pulled his picks and jabbed at the hole. Two missed. One hit. One slid in deep.

He twisted it. He turned it. He popped the bolt. They popped the door and walked in.

They flashed the floor. They flashed a stairwell. Wayne smelled mold. Wayne smelled baked beans.

They turned left. They hit a hall. They hit a kitchen. Wayne felt trapped heat. Moonlight sieved through venetian blinds.

Pete pulled the blinds. Wayne hit the lights. There:

Sink water—dark pink—carving knives afloat. Baked beans and fruit flies on mold. Hair in a colander. Dots on the floor. Dots by the fridge.

Pete opened it. Wayne smelled it. They *saw* it:

The severed legs. The diced hips. Mom's head in the vegetable bin.

74
(Bogalusa, 6/21/65)

PHONE WORK:

Room 6—the Glow Motel—direct calls out. Outside noise as direct counterpoint.

Shouts. Rebel yells. Nigger! Nigger! Nigger! We Shall Overcome!

We're in BOMBalusa now. We remember BOMBingham.

He slept with the riddle. He lived with it. He ran.

To: Marches and pray-ins and cross burns. To: Beatings and hecklings and shouts.

He assumed a Fed presence. He laid cover tracks. He called Carlos. He set up a meet. He flew through New Orleans.

BLUE RABBIT might be here. Add BLUE's Brother WHITE. Add Hoover confidants. Add local Feds.

He laid tracks. I was close. *It* was close. I had to see. I'm CRUSADER RABBIT. I'm a fool for civil rights.

Littell checked his phone book. Littell ran motels. He called the Texas DMV this morning. He got Chuck Rogers' stats.

Houston/Driscoll Street/one Oldsmobile. Texas plates: DXL-841.

He got the stats. He got the room. He called motels. Forty-two local—dull phone-book stats.

He played Fed. He dropped his stats. He checked registrations. He made 19 calls. He got all nos. He hit Clerk 20.

"You the second police type who called 'bout that Olds. Only this other guy didn't give me no DXL number, he said it'd have hot Texas plates."

He brainstormed the response. He ran RABBITS. FATHER RABBIT's Wayne Senior. FATHER knows Chuck. FATHER runs WILD RABBIT. WILD RABBIT's close. WILD RABBIT's Klan.

There's BLUE RABBIT. He's Fed. Who *else* wants Chuck?

He called motels. He hit 28. He got nil results. The outside noise got bad—these loud Nigger! shouts.

Littell worked. Littell called motels. Littell got nil results. Motel 29. Motel 30. Motel 31-2-3.

Motel 34: "You're the second guy askin' about that Rogers an' that car, but I ain't seen him or it."

The Moonbeam Motel/the Lark Motel/the Anchor Motel—
nil results. The Dixie/the Bayou/the Rebel's Rest:

"Office. May I help you?"

"This is Special Agent Brown, FBI."

The guy laughed. "You come to curtail these agitators?"

"No, sir. It's about something else."

"That's too bad, because—"

"I'm looking for a white man driving a 1953 Oldsmobile with
Texas license plates."

The man laughed. "Then you're one lucky member of the
Federal Bureau of Integration, 'cause he checked into room 5
yesterday."

"What? Repeat th—"

"I got it right here. Charles Jones, Houston, Texas. '53 Olds
sedan, PDL-902. By my lights, he's a mean motherhumper.
Probably gargles with antifreeze and flosses with razor
blades."

Traffic crawled. The disruption ratched it up.

Sidewalk marches. Hecklers. TV crews out. Signs and
countersigns. Shriekers with good lungs. Nonparticipants out
for yuks.

*Freedom Now!/Jim Crow Must Go!/Nigger Go Home! We shaaaall
overcome!* in re-run shouts.

Littell drove his rental car. Traffic slogged. Littell parked and
walked. Egg crews roamed. White kids chucked eggs. They
chucked at Negroes. They nailed perceived Feds.

Littell walked. Littell dodged eggs. Eggs hit marchers. Eggs hit
picket signs.

Egg crews walked. Egg trucks roamed. Egg men trucked
ammo. Eggs flew. Eggs hit doors. Eggs hit awnings and cars.

The marchers wore slickers. The slickers dripped yolk. The
slickers dripped cracked shells. Cops stood around. Cops dodged
eggs. Cops sucked Nehi and Coke.

Littell walked. Eggs creased him. Littell looked *all*-Fed.

He cut left. He walked two blocks. He passed two egg huts.
Egg crews formed. Egg crews armed. Egg trucks loaded up.

He saw it—right there—the Rebel's Rest.

One floor. Ten rooms. All street-view units. Rebel flag and
rebel sign—neon Johnny Reb.

Parking slots/outdoor walkway/the office detached.

Littell palmed a credit card. Littell cut straight over. Littell saw room 5.

He knocked. He got no answer. No car in front/no people/ no Olds 88.

He faced the street. He braced the door. He worked backwards. There now—by touch:

The jamb. The bolt. Wedge the card and slide it through fast.

He did it. The door popped. He fell backwards inside. He locked the door behind him. He hit the lights. He checked the room out.

One bed. One bathroom. One closet. One overnight bag on the floor.

He tossed the bag. He saw clothes and a razor. He saw hate tracts. He checked the closet. He checked the shelf. He saw a box of fuses—half full.

He saw a Mossberg pump. He saw a .45. He saw a .357 mag.

He grabbed the pump. He dumped the shells. He grabbed the .45. He popped the hot round. He popped the clip.

He grabbed the mag. He popped the cylinder. He dumped the shells. He pulled the rug up.

He hid the ammo. He shut the closet door. He killed the room lights. He sat down. He pulled his piece. He cocked the hammer.

He leaned on the bed. He faced the door. He counted rabbits full-out.

He dozed. He cramped up. He heard chants outside. Two words—say two blocks out.

"Freedom" and "nigger"—two words overlapped.

The sun arced—light cut through window shades—shades going black.

Littell dozed. Littell stirred. Littell heard siren bursts. Short bursts—per stalled traffic.

He got up. He walked outside. Tenants mingled. Tenants rebel-yelled.

A man laughed. A man went "Ka-pow!"

A man said, "A nigger church just went ka-blooey."

Littell ran.

He cut left. He ran two blocks. He passed the egg huts. His coat flapped. His piece showed. Some egg men perked up.

They chucked eggs. They hit him. They dosed his pants. They grazed his head.

He hit the main drag. He cut right. He pushed through pickets. He ate eggs. He ate picket signs.

He slid. He hit eggshells. He tripped. A redneck kicked him. A marcher kicked him for kicks.

Horns. Sirens. Shouts—street blockade dead ahead. Egg trucks and egg men. An ambulance stalled and bucked.

Rednecks ran over. Marchers ran over. Fat cops ran up slow. They hit the blockade. They yelled. They shoved.

The blockade held. Pushing and shoving. Horns/sirens/shouts.

Littell got up. Littell dripped eggshells. Littell ran over fast. The cops saw him. Looks traveled—check Johnny Fed.

Littell pulled his badge. Littell pulled his gun. The cops smirked. The egg men smirked. The marchers stepped back.

Louder now: Yahoos and nigger yells. Horns/sirens/shouts.

Littell grabbed an egg man. Said egg man smirked. Littell smashed his face on his truck. He hit the door. He hit the ground. His false teeth popped out and cracked.

The egg men stepped back. The cops stepped back. The cops bumped the marchers. The cops brushed picket signs.

Littell cracked the door. Littell jerked the brake. The truck rolled. The truck hit a light pole. The ambulance swerved and cut through.

Littell stepped back. Eggs hit his glasses. Tobacco juice hit his shoes.

Gutted:

Scorched timber/wet timber/wet dirt. Two dead—a boy and his dad.

The bomb hit a 4:00 P.M. service. The bomb made a floorboard blast. It reached up. Pews shattered. Wood sheared.

Littell mingled.

He saw the meat wagons. He saw the dead. He saw a boy with no toes. He saw fire trucks. He saw TV trucks. He saw some Klan youth.

They kliqued up. They klanvoked. They klowned for kamera krews.

Littell mingled.

He drew stares. He smelled like egg. He dripped shells and yolk.

Some marchers showed. Some Feds showed. The marchers consoled the victims. Folks bled and wept.

Medics hauled gurneys. Medics hauled vics. Meat wagons hauled Code 3.

Littell tailed them. Littell watched them unload. Folks limped. Folks hobbled. That boy held his toes.

The clinic was old. The clinic was unkempt. A sign read Colored Only.

Littell watched. The Feds watched Littell. Nurses pushed IV stands. A woman fell. The toe boy convulsed.

Littell drove to a liquor store. Littell bought a pint of good scotch.

75

(Bogalusa, 6/21/65)

RADIO ROCK:

Hatenanny stuff. "Who Needs Niggers?" and "Ship Those Niggers Back." Katchy. Kool kombos. Kall-ins on K-L-A-N.

Pete dipped his seat. Wayne watched the door. Door 5—the Rebel's Rest Motel.

Chuck was out. Pete was right. Chuck shagged to Bogalusa. Chuck diced his folks. Chuck stole their car. Chuck shagged his ass here.

They tossed the house. They found body parts. They found no hit notes. They drove east. They called motels. They found Chuck.

They drove fast. They drove fried. No sleep since Saigon. They stopped in Beaumont. They scored bennies. They revitalized.

Pete told Wayne the hit story. Pete spieled full disclosure.

He named names. He dropped details. He spieled perspective. He blew Wayne's mind. He framed Wayne's own Dallas tale.

Wayne talked up Wayne Senior. Wayne Senior fed the hit fund. Wayne Senior ran snitch-Klans. Wayne Senior ran Bob Relyea now.

Pete said it: Wayne Senior runs *YOU*.

Radio rock: Odis Cochran/the Coon Hunters/Rambunctious Roy.

Wayne flipped the dial. Wayne caught a newscast.

". . . leaky pipe explosion at a Negro church outside Bogalusa, which civil-rights agitators have called a 'bomb blast.' A spokesman for the Federal Bureau of Integration said that early evidence points to a faulty gas main."

Pete turned it off. "That's the Feds. They got to the radio people."

Wayne popped two bennies. "They know it's Bob."

Pete sipped RC. Bennies parched him bad.

"They've got a hunch, and they want to cover their bets. They didn't tell him to do it, they didn't want him to do it, but he figured he could get away with it, and if they made him for it, they'd let him slide and warn him not to do it again."

Wayne watched the doors. Night-lights bipped above them. Doorways glowed blue.

"You think Bob's with Chuck?"

Pete cracked his knuckles. "I hope not. I don't want to kill a Federal employee who's hooked up with your dad."

Wayne grabbed the RC. "I don't like the chronology. Chuck gets the letter, Chuck flies home and clips his parents. He's *probably* got the journal, and he *might've* told Bob about the hit."

Pete cracked his thumbs. "We'll ask him about that."

Wayne sipped RC. An Olds pulled up. Pete made the plates: PDL-902.

Chuck got out. Chuck picked his teeth and swaggered. Chuck entered room #5.

Wayne said, "He's alone."

Pete popped two bennies. Wayne grabbed their guns. Pete tapped the silencers. They pulled up their shirttails. They stuffed the guns down. They covered the grips.

They walked over. The room-row rocked—shitkicker tunes and full tenancy.

Wayne tried the door. It was locked. Pete shouldered it. The jamb cracked. The lock split. They rode the door in. There's this shit room—but where's Ch—

Chuck exits a closet. Chuck has two guns. Chuck aims and fires. Two hammers click. Chuck fucking plotzes. Chuck fucking *shits*.

Pete charged him. Pete grabbed him. Pete threw him down. Wayne shut the door. Wayne tossed his cuffs. Pete snagged them.

Chuck crawled. Chuck tried to run. Pete grabbed his hair. Pete banged his head on the floor.

Wayne cuffed him. Pete picked him up. Pete threw him into a wall. He hit hard. He made dents. He hit the floor.

Wayne knelt down. "Did you tell Bob about Dallas?"

Chuck dribbled blood. "I told your daddy you're a punk motherfucker."

"Did you and Bob bomb that church?"

Chuck dribbled bile. "Ask Daddy Rabbit. Tell him Wild Rabbit's his boy."

Pete grabbed a hot plate. Pete plugged it in. Pete sparked the coils.

Wayne said, "Where's the notes your parents found?"

Chuck pissed his pants. "Wild Rabbit says fuck you. Father Rabbit says he's your daddy."

Pete dropped the hot plate. It hit coil side down. It singed up Chuck's hair.

Chuck screeched. The coil sizzled. Chuck yelled, "All right!"

Wayne grabbed the hot plate. Wayne grabbed a pillow. Wayne fluffed out Chuck's hair.

Chuck dribbled blood. Chuck dribbled bile. Chuck rubbed his head on the floor.

"I . . . didn't . . . tell Bob. I . . . I burned them notes."

Pete cued Wayne. Wayne cranked the radio. Wayne reprised Rambunctious Roy:

". . . White Man's wise to Martin Luther Coon. Eatin' watermelon in the month of June. Big teeth chompin' sweet potato pie—"

Wayne pulled his piece. Pete pulled his piece. Chuck said, "No, *please*."

The door creaked. The jamb snapped and sheared. Ward Littell walked in.

He was egg-spattered. He was blotto. He was non compos something. He put out booze breath.

Pete said, "Fuck."

Wayne said, "Jesus Christ."

Ward turned the music off. Ward walked up to Chuck. Chuck shit his pants. Chuck dribbled teeth.

Ward said, "Wild Rabbit."

Chuck coughed. Chuck dribbled teeth.

"Wild Rabbit's got the Federal pedig—"
Ward pulled his piece. Ward shot Chuck's eyes out.

PART FOUR

COERCION

July 1965–November 1966

: 7/2/65.
Internal memorandum. To: Director. From: BLUE
RABBIT. Topic: OPERATION BLACK RABBIT. Marked:
''Stage-1 Covert''/''Eyes Only''/''Read and Burn.''

Sir,
Per the church bombing and related actions in
Bogalusa, Louisiana.

Locally assigned agents have completed their
internal investigation. They have reported to me
orally, have filed no official reports and have
confirmed the official judgment of the Bogalusa Police
Department: that the ''accidental explosion'' was
caused by a leaky pipe main. That judgment should
stand as the authoritative verdict on this matter. It
is crucial to the continued success of the WHITE-HATE
arm of OPERATION BLACK RABBIT.

I've spoken to WILD RABBIT. His denials of
complicity in the bombing were not convincing.
I warned him that church bombings were outside his
operating parameters and that no such incidents
should happen again. WILD RABBIT seemed cowed and did
not protest the reprimand. It should be noted that his
arms bore odd bruises and that in fact he seemed to
have sustained a recent beating.

WILD RABBIT refused to comment on his bruises and
overall beaten appearance. I queried him on the
possible presence of his known Vietnam associate
Charles Rogers per the time of the church incident,
and WILD RABBIT became visibly upset. It should be
noted: The dismembered bodies of Rogers' elderly
parents were found in their Houston, Texas, home on
6/23, and Rogers (who cannot be located) is the
leading suspect in this double homicide. I checked

Vietnamese-U.S. passport records for the two weeks
preceding the assumed date-of-death, learned that
Rogers flew from Saigon to Houston on 6/15 and that the
cargo on his flight included bomb material. It is my
belief that Rogers supplied the explosives for the
bombing and that WILD RABBIT assisted him in this
unsanctioned provocation.

It should also be noted that local agents spotted
CRUSADER RABBIT at the Negro hospital shortly after
the bombing. He was visibly distraught and of unkempt
appearance. I checked region-wide flight and car-
rental records and learned that CRUSADER RABBIT flew
from Las Vegas to New Orleans and drove to Bogalusa.
I consider it likely that he met his client Carlos
Marcello in New Orleans and took advantage of its
proximity to Bogalusa.

I view CRUSADER RABBIT's trip to Bogalusa as fully
in character, and it does not surprise me that he
wished to view the planned civil-rights agitation in
person. Please respond per CRUSADER RABBIT.

Respectfully,
BLUE RABBIT

DOCUMENT INSERT: 7/6/65.
Internal memorandum. To: BLUE RABBIT. From:
Director. Topic: OPERATION BLACK RABBIT. Marked:
''Stage-1 Covert''/''Eyes Only''/''Read and Burn.''

BLUE RABBIT,
Take all measures to see that the accidental
explosion verdict is sustained in the Bogalusa case.
Allow WILD RABBIT to claim credit for the ''Bombing''
and thus gain credibility for his new Klan unit.
Continue to discourage WILD RABBIT from committing
acts of violence outside his operating parameters.

I agree: CRUSADER RABBIT's presence in Bogalusa was
entirely in character, albeit marginally disturbing.
CRUSADER RABBIT is a close associate of Pete
Bondurant, who is a close associate of Charles
Rogers.

The confluence troubles me. Have Los Angeles and

Nevada-based agents tail CRUSADER RABBIT at
irregular intervals. Initiate trash and mail covers
at his Los Angeles and Las Vegas residences.

DOCUMENT INSERT: 7/8/65.
Internal memorandum. To: Director. From: BLUE
RABBIT. Topic: OPERATION BLACK RABBIT. Marked:
''Stage-1 Covert''/''Eyes Only''/''Read and Burn.''

   Sir,
   I've talked to WHITE RABBIT. He told me he'll be
taking a Las Vegas vacation soon. Should I have him
meet with CRUSADER RABBIT and judiciously assess his
state of mind?
   Respectfully,
   BLUE RABBIT

DOCUMENT INSERT: 7/10/65.
Internal memorandum. To: BLUE RABBIT. From:
Director. Topic: OPERATION BLACK RABBIT. Marked:
''Stage-1 Covert''/''Eyes Only''/''Read and Burn.''

   BLUE RABBIT,
   Yes. Have WHITE RABBIT contact CRUSADER RABBIT
during his stay in Las Vegas.

76

(Port Sulphur, 7/14/65)

PROSPECTS: Gaspar Fuentes/Miguel Díaz Arredondo. Cubano/
anti-Beard/allegedly pro-*Tigre*.

Flash boated to Cuba. Flash found them. Flash boated them
out. Flash praised their skills. Flash praised their pidgin English.
Flash praised their balls.

The venue: a cinder-block shack/10-by-10/a heat sponge.
Two electric chairs—straps and hoods—bought from Angola
Pen. A dynamo/two chair feeds/two polys.

Flash strapped Fuentes. Laurent G. strapped Arredondo.
Wayne and Mesplède watched.

Shots popped outside. Troopers hit targets. Tiger South—Kamp with a "K." Exiles in residence—sixty strong—kadre-adjunct/kadre-armed/kadre-fed.

Flash rigged the needles. Laurent pumped the cuffs. Wayne watched. Wayne drifted off.

We're in Port Sulphur. Go north a bit—you'll hit Bogalusa.

Littell shoots Chuck. Littell's drunk. Littell vows sobriety. Pete consoles him: I'll dump Chuck and brace WILD RABBIT. Wild Bob's Fed now. He's Wayne Senior's boy.

Flash ran the polys. Laurent ran the quiz: Do you drink water? Is your shirt blue? Do you hate Fidel Castro?

Needle dip—short—no lies.

Port Sulphur—stone's throw to Bogalusa.

They drove Chuck around. They found a swamp. They dumped Chuck in. Gators ate him. Wayne and Pete watched.

Wayne toured the hospital. Wayne saw the bomb damage. Wayne saw a boy minus toes.

Pictures. Add-on shots. Let's augment your Bongo pix. Let's augment Wendell D. Pictures: The icebox/Chuck's parents/those big gator teeth.

Flash ran the polys. Laurent ran the quiz: Are you a spy? Do you serve the Cuban militia?

Needle dip—short—no lies.

Wayne drifted. Wayne yawned. The stateside runs bored him. He missed Saigon. He missed the lab. He missed the war and the threat.

Are you anti-*Communisto*? Are you pro-*Tigre*? Will you serve *El Cato* supreme?

Needle dip—short—no lies.

Flash smiled. Laurent smiled. Mesplède up and cheered.

They unstrapped the prospects. They hugged them. Fuentes hugged Wayne. Fuentes oozed Brylcreem. Arredondo hugged Wayne. Arredondo oozed VO5.

Looks traveled. Hey—it's lunchtime—let's cook by electric chair.

They scrounged. They ad-libbed. Flash scrounged hot dogs. Laurent scrounged corned beef.

They packed them in. They stuffed the hoods. They pulled the switches. Sparks popped. The meat fried. The hoods dripped fat.

The meat cooked uneven. The concept rocked. The reality stunk.

Mesplède supplied mustard. Flash supplied buns.

77

(Las Vegas, 7/16/65)

CANDLES—A FULL forty-five.

Pete blew them out. One puff did it. Barb cut the cake.

"Make a wish, and don't mention Cuba."

Pete laughed. "I already did."

"So tell."

"No. You jinx it that way."

Barb cranked the AC. Barb chilled down the suite.

"Did it involve Cuba?"

"I'm not saying."

"Vietnam?"

Pete licked icing. "Vietnam's no Cuba."

Barb scratched the cat. "Tell me why. It's your birthday, so I'll indulge you."

Pete sipped coffee. "It's too big, too fucked up, and too mechanized. You've got choppers with belly lights that can flash a one-mile-square patch of jungle. You've got carpet bombing and napalm. You've got gooks with no fucking charm and a bunch of shifty little cocksuckers in black pajamas who've lived guerrilla warfare for fifty fucking years."

Barb lit a cigarette. "Cuba's got more pizzazz. It fits your imperialist aesthetic."

Pete laughed. "You've been talking to Ward."

"You mean I stole his vocabulary."

Pete cracked his knuckles. The cat humped his knees.

"Flash smuggled two guys in. They were heisting casinos and killing croupiers. In Havana, that takes balls."

"Killing unarmed men?"

Pete laughed. "Militia guys work the casinos."

Barb laughed. "Distinction noted."

Pete kissed her. "Nobody disapproves like you. It's one of the ten thousand reasons why we work."

Barb pried the cat off. Barb squeezed his knees.

"Ward said you've let me grow up."

Pete smiled. "Ward gets to you. You think you know him, then he pulls out one more stop."

"For instance?"

"He cares about people who can't do him any good, but he's not a sucker about it."

"For example?"

"He got wind of some Klan shit. He pulled a stunt that nobody else would have pulled."

Barb smiled. "Including you?"

Pete nodded. "I helped him out on the back end. I braced a kadre guy and laid down some rules."

Barb stretched. The cat clawed her skirt.

"I had lunch with Ward. He was worried. He saw Jane going through his papers."

Pete stood up. Pete spilled his coffee.

Fuck—

"The ARVN boss man's getting ready to bomb Hanoi. He's talking to his financial advisor, One Lump Sum, and his Secretary of Fruitness, Come San Chin. They're in this chink restaurant in Saigon. Come San Chin's snarfing a big bowl of cream-of-some-young-guy."

Pete yukked. Pete watched the building.

He flew to L.A. He brought Milt C. for chuckles. He shagged a rental car.

He *felt* it: Jane's bent. She's a plant. Carlos placed her with Ward.

He called Fred Otash. He quizzed him—what have *you* got? Otash spieled a tip per Danny Bruvick—Arden-Jane's ex.

Danny's a boat man. Danny's got a pseudonym. Danny runs a charter biz—"somewhere in Alabama."

Carlos lived in New Orleans. Alabama was close.

Pete watched the building. Milt picked his nose. Ward was in Chicago. Sam G. called him in. Arden-Jane was upstairs.

"The Rat Pack tours Vietnam. Frank's glomming all the slant-eyed trim. Dino's bombed out of his gourd. He's so blotto that he blunders behind the Viet Cong lines. This little slant comes up to him. Dino says, 'Take me to your leader.' The slant says, 'Ky, Mao, or Ho Chi Minh?' Dino says, 'We'll dance later. Right now, take me to your leader.' "

Pete yukked. Pete watched the building.

Milt bummed a cigarette. "Freddy T. sent me a tape. Three legislators and six hookers jungled up at the Dunes."

Pete stretched. Pete watched the building.

Milt blew smoke rings. "I'm doing some more TV ads with Sonny. 'Tiger Kab, the Vegas champ. Call now or I'll kick your patootie.' "

Pete yukked. Pete watched the building. Milt ditched his shoes. Milt aired out his feet.

"We've got some deadbeats. I do not see the wisdom of consigning white horse on credit."

"I'll take care of it."

Milt yukked. "Let's use Sonny. Dig, he loves fur coats, he's always buying them for his bitches, and Donkey Dom just clipped a fur shop in Reno. Dig, Sonny can do our collections, and we can pay him off in fur."

Pete yukked—Milt, you slay me. Pete saw Jane walk out.

The doorman smiled. The doorman shagged her car. She got in. She pulled out. She drove west.

Pete kicked the engine. Pete pulled out. Pete tailed her. They took Wilshire west. They took Bundy south. They took Pico west toward the beach.

Pete laid back. Jane jumped lanes. Jane pulled right. Jane signaled. Jane turned.

There: the B. of A.—West L.A. branch.

She pulled up. She locked the car. She walked in.

Milt scoped her. "Nice pins. I could dig her love in a semi-large way."

Pete lit a cigarette. Milt bummed one.

"So, who is she? You call me at 5:00 A.M. You say, 'Let's go to L.A.,' you don't explain yourself. I'm starting to think you just brought me along for the laughs."

Jane walked out. Jane lugged a coin sack. Jane walked to the parking-lot phone.

She dialed "0." She fed the slots. She talked. She listened. She cupped the receiver. The call dragged on. She jiggled coins. She refed the slots.

Pete watched her. Pete timed her: five minutes/six/eight.

Milt yawned. "I'm digging on the intrigue. It's not like she hasn't got a phone at her crib."

Ten minutes/twelve/fourteen.

She hung up. She walked to her car. She got in and pulled out.

Pete tailed her. They took Pico east. They drove six miles plus. They took La Brea north.

They crossed Wilshire. They crossed 3rd. They took Beverly east. They took Rossmore north.

There—she pulls left. She signals. She turns. She's upside the Algiers—a white-brick/mock-mosque motel.

She parked. She got out. She palmed a folder. The joint had big windows. Dig the see-thru surveillance.

She walked inside. She stopped a clerk. She passed him the folder.

Milt said, "I smell tsuris. Carlos has points in that joint."

Pete said, "I know."

He weighed it. He diced it. He fucking julienned it. Carlos had points. Carlos had *control* points. Carlos hired the crew.

They flew home. Milt buzzed off. Pete hit Tiger Kab. He rehearsed his shtick. He built some lies. He called PC Bell.

A clerk picked up. "Police Information. Who's requesting?"

Pete coughed. "Sergeant Peters, LAPD. I need the connect on a pay-phone call."

"Time, location, and origin number, please."

Pete grabbed a pen. "1:16 P.M. today. No origin number, but it's the pay phone outside the Bank of America at 14229 West Pico, Los Angeles."

The clerk coughed. "Please hold for that information."

Pete held. Pete watched the lot. Donkey Dom shot dice. Donkey Dom ogled boys. Donkey Dom adjusted his basket.

The line buzzed. The clerk coughed.

"That call was long-distance. The connect was a charter-boat slip in Bon Secour, Alabama."

78

(Chicago, 7/19/65)

SAM KVETCHED.

Per the jail food. Per the jail lice. Per his jail hemorrhoids.

Sam talked loud. The attorney room buzzed. The lice had feet. The lice had wings. The lice had fangs like Godzilla.

Littell stretched. His chair squeaked. The seat itched—lice like Godzilla.

Sam said, "I found a bug in my corn flakes this morning. He had a wingspan like a P-38. I attribute all this shit to the cocksucker who impaneled this cocksucking grand jury, that well-known cocksucker Robert F. Kennedy."

Littell tapped his pen. "You'll be out in ten months. The jury term expires."

Sam scratched his arms. "I'll be dead in six months. You can't go up against lice that big and survive."

Littell laughed. Sam scratched his legs.

"It's all Bobby's fault. If the cocksucker ever runs for President, he will rue the fucking day, and that is no shit, Dick Tracy."

Littell shook his head. "He'll never try to hurt you again. He has a different agenda now."

Sam scratched his neck. "Right. He's in bed with the nigger agitators, which don't mean his hard-on for us has subsided."

A bug cruised the table. Sam smashed it.

"One for the home team. Breed no more, you cocksucker."

Littell cleared his throat. "We're on schedule in Vegas. We've got the board votes and the legislators. Mr. Hughes should get his money sometime next year."

Sam scratched his feet. "Too bad Jimmy won't be around to see it."

"I may be able to keep him out until after we get in."

Sam sneezed. "So he celebrates en route to Leavenworth. We keester Howard Hughes, and Jimmy packs his pj's for the pen."

"That's about it, yes."

Sam sneezed. "I don't like that look in your eyes. It says, 'I got some momentous shit for you, even though *you* called *me* in.' "

Littell cleaned his glasses. "I've talked to the others. They have an idea that they think you should consider."

Sam rolled his eyes. "Then *tell* me. You've got this tendency to coax things and lay out these big preambles."

Littell leaned in. "They think you're through in Chicago. They think you're a sitting duck for the Feds and the State AG. They think you should move to Mexico and run your personal operations from there. They think you should start making Latin-American connections, to aid us in our foreign casino strategy, which will begin sometime after we sell Mr. Hughes the hotels."

Sam scratched his neck. Sam scratched his arms. Sam scratched his balls. A bug leaped. Sam caught it. Sam smashed it.

"Okay, I'll play. I know when over's over, and I know the future when I see it."

Littell smiled. Sam rocked his chair back.

"You still got that look. You should unload before I start itching again."

Littell squared his necktie. "I want to oversee the buyouts for the pension-book plan, assist in the foreign casino negotiations, and retire. I'm going to ask Carlos formally, but I wanted to get your blessing first."

Sam smiled. Sam stood up. Sam played street mime. He sprayed holy water. He gave Holy Communion. He ran the Stations of the Cross.

"You've got it. *If* you help us out on one last thing."

"Tell me. I'll do it."

Sam straddled his chair. "We got hurt on the '60 election. I bought Jack West Virginia and Illinois, and he sicced his cocksucking kid brother on us. Now, Johnson's okay, but he's soft on the niggers, and he might not run in '68. The thing is, we're prepared to be very generous to the right candidate, if he pardons Jimmy and helps us out on some other fronts, and we want *you* to work it out."

Littell inhaled. Littell exhaled. Littell went dead faint.

"Jesus Christ."

Sam scratched his hands. "We want Mr. Hughes to put up 25% of our contribution. We want our guy to agree to a hands-off policy on the Teamsters. We want him to slow down any Fed shit aimed at the Outfit. We want no foreign-policy grief aimed at the countries where we plant our casinos, right- or left-wing."

Littell inhaled. Littell exhaled. Littell went faint-faint.

"When?"

"The '68 primaries. Around that time. You know, the conventions."

A bug jumped. Sam caught it. Sam smashed it.

"Breed no more, you fuck."

Charts: Profit flow/overhead/debits.

Littell read charts. Littell studied charts. Littell took notes. He worked on the terrace. The view distracted him. He loved Lake Michigan.

The Drake Hotel—two-bedroom suite—on Sam Giancana.

Littell read charts. Fund-book stats jumped. Money lent/money invested/money repaid.

Business targets. Fund-financed. Potential takeover prey. Let's extort said businesses. Let's build foreign casinos. Let's buy a President. Let's shape policy. Let's reverse 1960. Let's spread our bets. Let's cover all odds. Let's subvert left-wing nations.

That was odd—the Outfit leaned right—the Outfit bribed right per said leaning.

Chicago broiled. Wind scoured the lake. Littell ditched his charts. Littell studied briefs.

Appeal briefs—let's keep Jimmy out. Stock briefs—let's get Drac in. It was shit work. It was repetitive. It was post-dead.

He got up. He stretched. He watched Lake Shore Drive. He saw car lights as streamers.

He went by his banks yesterday. He withdrew tithe money. He cut tithe checks. He mailed them. He worried a phone call.

He called Bayard Rustin. He lied off Bogalusa. He did it to protect himself. He did it to protect Pete and Wayne.

He'd read the papers. He saw the news. The church blew "accidental." No one linked Chuck. No one linked WILD RABBIT.

He called Bayard. He dittoed the news. He said a gas main blew. He cited fake sources. Bayard expressed gratitude. Bayard expressed belief. *He* lied. *He* lied deftly. *He* acted late.

The church blew. His late fees accrued—fees for *his* dead and maimed.

He saw the maimed. Some Feds saw him. Said Feds might inform Mr. Hoover. He got drunk. He killed Chuck. He got sober. He still wanted it. He still tasted it. Liquor signs glowed.

He killed Chuck. He slept twelve hours. He woke up to this: End it. Leave the Life. Cut and run when you can.

Sam said yes. Sam gave his blessing. Sam had stipulations. Carlos might say yes. Carlos might have stipulations.

Tithes/stipulations/election years.

He served Mr. Hoover. They colluded. It spawned BLACK RABBIT. It spawned WILD RABBIT. It spawned dead and maimed. He killed Chuck. Pete braced WILD RABBIT. It was catch-up penance. It was wholly insufficient.

The lake glowed. Cruise boats cruised. He saw bow lights. He saw dance bands. He saw women.

Jane was war now. Jane outflanked him. Jane *knew* him before he *knew* her. She knew he stole. She knew he bagged money. She knew he played covert tapes.

She went through his papers. He caught her at it. They retreated. They quashed talk. They quashed confrontations.

Jane had plans. He *knew* it. She might want to hurt him. She might want to use him. She might want to know him more.

It scared him. It moved him. It made him want her more.

A boat drew close. A band played. A blue dress twirled. Janice wore dresses like that.

She was still bawdy. It was still good. She still served up stories and sex.

She dished Wayne Senior. The details scared him. Wayne Senior was FATHER RABBIT. Janice dished him. Janice loathed him. Janice still felt his hold.

The boat cruised by. The blue dress vanished. Littell called the Sands. Janice was out. Littell called the DI. Littell checked his messages.

One message: Call Lyle Holly—he's at the Riv. Shit—WHITE RABBIT wants you.

Littell got the number. Littell put the call off. Littell prepped a tape. Littell grabbed a spool.

Sam scared him. Sam waxed profane. Bobby/cocksucker/rue the fucking day.

Littell prepped his tape-rig. Littell memory-laned.

Chicago, 1960—the Phantom loves Bobby. Chicago, 1965—Bobby lives on tape.

79

(Las Vegas, 7/20/65)

TIGER TEEMED.

Scribes pressed Sonny—give us quotes—rag that punk Cassius X. Sonny ignored them. Sonny quaffed Chivas. Sonny pawed mink coats.

Donkey Dom stole them. Donkey Dom sold them. Donkey Dom name-dropped. I pop fur shops/I bone Rock Hudson/I poke Sal Mineo.

His bun boy sulked. His bun boy griped hypocritical. His bun boy pimped drag queens full-time.

Wayne watched. Barb watched.

Dom shagged calls. His bun boy buzzed drivers. They juked the noon rush. Sonny bought mink mittens. Sonny bought mink jockstraps. Sonny bought mink earmuffs.

A scribe said, "Are those furs hot?"

Sonny said, "Your mama's hot. I'm your daddy."

A scribe said, "Why don't you join the civil-rights movement?"

Sonny said, "'Cause I ain't got no dog-proof ass."

The scribes yukked. Wayne yukked. Barb walked out to the lot. She popped pills. She chased them. She chugged flat 7-Up.

Wayne walked out. Wayne braced her in close.

"Pete's rotating back. You start flying the second he's gone."

Barb stepped back. "Think about what *you* do, and tell me you disapprove then."

Wayne stepped close. "Look who we sell to."

"Look at *me*. Do I look like one of the junkie whores you've created?"

"I'm looking. I'm seeing lines you didn't have a year ago."

Barb laughed. "I've earned them. I've got fifteen years in the Life."

Wayne stepped back. "You're dodging me."

"No. I'm just saying I've been around longer, and I know how things work better than you."

"Tell Pete that. He won't buy it, but tell him anyway."

Barb stepped close. "You're hooked, not me. You're hooked on the Life, and you still don't know how it works."

Wayne stepped close. They bumped knees. Wayne smelled Barb's soap.

"You're just pissed that there's no place in it for you."

Barb stepped back. "You're going to do things that you won't be able to live with."

"Maybe I have already."

"It gets worse. And you'll do worse things, just to prove you can take it."

Test run:

Four collections. Four junkie deadbeats. Sonny's collection debut.

Said junkies annexed a church basement. Said junkies had squatters' rights. Their pastor skin-popped Demerol. Said junkies geezed up in church.

Wayne drove. Sonny cleaned his nails with a switchblade. Sonny sipped scotch. West LV sizzled. Folks soaked in kiddie pools. Folks lived in air-cooled cars.

Wayne said, "I killed a colored guy in Saigon."

Sonny said, "I killed a white guy in St. Louis."

There's the church. It's dilapidated. It's sandblasted. It's neon-signed. Dig the prayer hands and crosses. Dig the Jesus rolling dice.

They parked. They walked back to the basement door. They picked the lock. They walked in.

They saw four junkies. They're crapped out on car seats—scavenged off old Cadillacs. They saw spoons and matchbooks. They saw spikes and tube ties. They saw bindles and white dregs.

There's a hi-fi. There's some LPs. It's all gospel wax.

The junkies reposed—one per seat—the land of Naugahyde Nod. They saw Sonny. They saw Wayne. They snickered. They giggled. They sighed.

Wayne said, "Go."

Sonny whistled. Sonny stomped. Sonny stormed Nauga-hyde Nod.

"You motherfuckers have got ten seconds to quit fucking with this house of worship and pay up what you owe."

One junkie giggled. One junkie scratched. One junkie chuckled. One junkie yawned.

Wayne turned on the hi-fi. Wayne flipped a disc. Wayne laid the needle down. It was loud shit. It was ecstatic—Crawdaddy's Christian Chorale.

Wayne said, "Go."

Sonny kicked the car seats. Sonny dumped the junkies. Sonny threw the junkies down. They squirmed. They squealed. They evacuated Naugahyde Nod.

Sonny kicked them. Sonny picked them up. Sonny dropped them. Sonny grabbed the car seats. Sonny aimed. Sonny dropped them on their heads.

They squealed. They screeched. They howled and bled.

Sonny slapped them. Sonny picked their pockets. Sonny tossed pocket trash. One guy turned his pockets out. One guy ran pleas.

Sonny picked him up. Sonny dropped him. Sonny kicked him. Sonny bent down. Sonny caught his pleas.

Sonny stood up. Sonny smiled. Sonny signaled Wayne. Crawdaddy crescendoed. Wayne pulled the plug and walked up.

Sonny smiled. "As of spring, Wendell Durfee was running a string of wetback whores in Bakersfield, California."

80

(Bon Secour, 7/22/65)

BOATS:

Charter jobs. Teak hulls and big motors. Forty slips/thirty bare/thirty boats out.

Pete strolled dockside. Pete scoped slip 19. There's the *Ebbtide*. It runs fifty feet. Dig those high gunwales.

Nice shit. Mounted poles and cargo space. Spiffy brass fittings.

A guy worked on deck. He was mid-size. He ran mid-forties. He had a bum leg. He had a bad limp.

It was hot. The air dripped. Clouds densified. Mobile Bay—Shitsville—bait shacks and congestion.

Pete strolled deckside. Pete scoped slip 19.

He traced Jane's call. He flew in. He ran checks. "Dave Burgess" owned the *Ebbtide*. "Dave Burgess" chartered out. "Dave Burgess" knew guys in New Orleans. Add 2 and 2. Add D.B. "Dave Burgess" was Danny Bruvick.

The T&C Corp owned the *Ebbtide*. Carlos owned T&C. Carlos *was* New Orleans.

He bribed a cop. He checked phone sheets. He ran phone checks. "Burgess" was good. "Burgess" used pay phones—right off the dock.

"Burgess" called Carlos. "Burgess" called Carlos frequent. "Burgess" called Carlos four times last month.

Pete walked slip 19. "Burgess" scrubbed fishhooks. Pete stepped on deck. "Burgess" looked up.

He tweaked a bit. He perked a bit. His antennae twitched.

That speargun—*watch*.

"Burgess" reached for it. "Burgess" grabbed. "Burgess" nailed the grip. Pete aimed. Pete kicked out. Pete nailed the grip.

The speargun skittered. "Burgess" said, "Shit."

Pete walked up. Pete grabbed the speargun. Pete popped the spear out to sea.

"Burgess" said, "Fuck."

Pete pulled his shirt up. Pete showed his piece.

"You're thinking 'Jimmy Hoffa sent this guy,' and you're wrong."

"Burgess" sucked a thumbnail. "Burgess" flexed his hand. Pete checked the boat out. The boat enticed. The boat seduced.

Nice: Steel hull/grappling posts/fittings. *Nice:* Hardwood from the Philippines.

"Burgess" flexed his wrist. "She's an old rum-runner. She's got all the—"

Pete pulled his shirt up. Pete showed his piece. Pete pointed below-deck. "Burgess" stood up. "Burgess" sighed. "Burgess" squared his bum leg and limped.

He wore shorts. Dig his scars. Dig his bullet-pocked knee.

He crossed the deck. He passed the wheelhouse. He took back stairs down. Pete tailed him. Pete scoped details.

Two wheel stands/control posts/full instruments. Teak walls/hall space/rear cabins. Rear engines/rear storage/rear cargo traps.

Pete walked ahead. Pete saw an office: two chairs/one desk/one booze shelf.

He pulled "Burgess" in. He grabbed a chair. He pushed "Burgess" down. He tucked "Burgess" in. He poured a libation.

The boat swayed. Pete sloshed Cutty. "Burgess" grabbed it. "Burgess" drained it. "Burgess" liquor-flushed.

Pete poured a refill. Pete poured big. "Burgess" refueled. "Burgess" sucked Cutty up.

Pete cocked his piece. "You're Danny Bruvick. I'm Pete Bondurant, and we've got some friends in common."

Bruvick burped. Bruvick flushed. Bruvick vibed lush.

Pete twirled his piece. "I want the whole story of you, 'Arden,' and Carlos Marcello. I want to know why Arden is shacked up with Ward Littell."

Bruvick eyed the bottle. Pete poured him a pop. Bruvick refueled. The boat dipped. Bruvick doused his lap.

"You shouldn't let me drink too much. I might get courageous."

Pete shook his head. Pete pulled his silencer. Pete tapped his piece. Bruvick gulped. Bruvick pulled beads out. Bruvick rosaried.

Pete shot the Cutty. Pete shot the Gilbey's. Pete shot the Jack D. Bottles spritzed. Teakwood cracked. Soft-points tore holes.

The room shook—sonic booms—the boat aftershocked.

Bruvick spazzed out. Bruvick squeezed his beads. Bruvick grabbed his ears.

Pete pulled his hands down. "Start with Arden. Give me her real name and lay out some perspective."

Bruvick sneezed. Gunpowder tickled noses. Gun cordite stung.

"Her real name's Arden Breen. Her old man was a labor agitator. You know, a Commie type."

Pete cracked his knuckles. "Keep going."

Bruvick tossed his hair. Glass shards flew.

"Her mother died. She got rheumatic fever. The old man raised Arden. He was a drunk and a whore chaser. He had a different name for every day of the week, and he raised Arden in whorehouses and union halls, meaning *bad* union halls, meaning the old man talked Red, but cut management deals every chance he got, which was—"

"Arden. Get back to her."

Bruvick rubbed his knees. "She quit school early, but she always had a head for figures. She met these two whores who went to the bookkeeping school I went to in Mississippi and picked up some skills from them. She kept some whorehouse and union hall books, you know, gigs her old man got her. She'd work these classier houses and spy on the johns. She'd pump them for stock tips and shit like that. She was good at anything involving numbers and ledgers. You know, money calculations."

Pete cracked his thumbs. "Get to it. You're working up to something."

Bruvick rubbed his bad knee. Scar tissue pulsed.

"She started working in some classier houses. She met this money guy Jules Schiffrin. He was tied in with—"

"I know who he was."

"Okay, so she started tricking with him regular. He *kept* her, you know, and she met lots of people in the Life, and she helped him with these so-called 'real' pension-fund books that he was working on."

Pete cracked his wrists. "Keep going."

Bruvick rubbed his knee. "Her old man got killed in '52. He screwed Jimmy H. on a management deal, so Jimmy had him clipped. Arden didn't care. She hated the old man for his god-damn hypocrisy and the shitty way he raised her."

The boat pitched. Pete grabbed the desk.

"Arden and Schiffrin. Spill on that."

"Spill *what?* She learned what she could from him and broke it off."

"And?"

"And she started hooking freelance, and got a thing going with Carlos. I met her in '55. We had mutual friends in those whores who went to school with me. I was working the K.C. local. We got married and cooked up some plans."

"Like 'Let's embezzle Jimmy.' "

Bruvick lit a cigarette. "I admit it wasn't the smartest—"

"You got caught. Jimmy put a contract out."

"Right. Some guys cornered me and shot me. I got away, but I almost lost my leg, and the fucking contract's still out."

Pete lit a cigarette. "Jimmy had the K.C. cops run Arden in. Carlos bailed her out and hid you. He didn't fuck with Jimmy's contract, because he wanted a wedge on you."

Bruvick nodded. Bruvick scoped the booze shelf.

"You're a hump. You wasted my liquor."

Pete smiled. Pete aimed. Pete cocked his piece. Pete shot Bruvick's chair.

The legs sheared. The chair crashed. Wood shattered. Bruvick tumbled. Bruvick yelped. Bruvick rosaried.

Pete blew smoke rings. "Carlos set up your charter business. What happened to Arden then?"

The boat pitched. Bruvick dropped his beads.

"She didn't trust Carlos. She didn't want to owe him, so she split to Europe. We worked out a pay-phone thing and kept in touch that way."

Pete coughed. "She came back to the States. She couldn't give up the Life."

"Right. She landed in Dallas. She got in trouble there, like late in '63. She wouldn't say what happened."

Pete flicked his cigarette. Pete nailed Bruvick flush.

"Come on, Danny. Don't make me get ugly."

Bruvick stood up. His knee went. He stumbled. He braced the wall. He slid back and sat.

He rubbed his knee. He snuffed Pete's cigarette.

"That's straight. She wouldn't tell me what happened. All I know is she hooked up with Littell, then around that time Carlos found her. He said we'd both be safe if she watchdogged Littell, but he still refused to square us with Jimmy."

Solid. Confirmed. Two-front blackmail. Jimmy's contract/ the safe-house snafu. Arden—that first name unique.

Carlos *knows* Arden. Carlos makes her *name*. Carlos distrusts Littell. Carlos finds Arden. Carlos plants Arden. Arden spies on Littell.

It vibed solid—90%—it vibed incomplete.

Pete said, "I don't want Littell to get hurt."

Bruvick stood up. His bad knee held.

"I don't think Arden does, either. She's playing out some weird thing with him."

He called Carlos. He got Frau M. He left a message:

I braced D.B.—Danny the boat man—tell Carlos that. Tell him I'll be by. Say I'd love to chat.

He drove to New Orleans. He stopped in libraries. He studied books en route.

Boats:

Galleys/bridges/radar/trawl decks/scuppers/masts.

He studied the nomenclature. He studied engine stats. He studied maps. Pine Island/Cape Sabel/Key West. Pit stops— Cuba due south.

He detoured. He cruised by Port Sulphur. He saw Tiger Kamp South. He saw the troops. He saw Flash and Laurent. He met Fuentes and Arredondo. They talked night raids. They talked scalp runs. They talked insurgency.

Wayne was in Saigon—one fast rotation—one scheduled run back. Wayne loves to WATCH. Wayne wants to GO. Wayne wants to SEE Cuba up close.

Flash had a plan. I'll do a speedboat run. I'll drop Fuentes and Arredondo. Fast—off the north shore—Varcadero Beach.

They reinfiltrate. They build drop zones. They recruit internal. They speedboat back. They funnel arms. They bounce off the Keys. They pull a boat hitch. They lug guns. They fly fast and low. They shuttle. They duck radar—six runs a week.

Pete said no. Pete said why: It's high mileage/it wastes two men/it's low capacity.

Flash said, "*Que?*"

Laurent said, "*Quoi?*"

Fuentes said, "*Que pasa?*"

Pete talked hold nets. Pete talked gunwales. Pete talked fuel efficiency.

Pete talked *boats*.

Carlos said, "Sure, she's my watchdog. Tell me Ward don't play angles, then tell me I don't need one."

Galatoire's was dead. They hogged a prime table. Carlos dipped his cigar. Mecundo meets anisette.

"Ward's fund-book thing is a fucking extravaganza, and Arden is a brilliant fucking bookkeeper. I'm protecting my franchise, and Ward gets some good cooze in the process."

Pete lit a cigarette. "He's in love with her. I don't want him to get hurt."

Carlos winked. "I don't want *you* to get hurt. We go back like Ward and me go back. Some guys would have been miffed at what you did to Danny B., but I am not one of them."

Pete smiled. "I copped to it, didn't I? I called you."

"That is correct. You did the wrong thing and covered your bets."

"I just don't want—"

"He won't be. They're good for each other. I know Arden, and Arden knows she can't shit me. Arden tells me Ward's not scheming against me, so I believe her. I've always had this feeling that Ward was skimming Howard Hughes, but Arden says it's not so, so I believe her."

Pete burped. Pete undid his belt—rich Creole food.

"Give me the warning. Let's get it over with."

Carlos burped. Carlos undid his belt—rich Creole food.

"Don't tell Ward about this. Don't make me peeved at you."

"*This*"—still solid—still incomplete.

A waiter cruised by. Pete nixed a comped brandy.

Carlos belched. "What's this about 'ideas'?"

Pete cleared some plates. Pete laid his map out. Pete swamped the table.

"Speedboat runs waste man-hours. You can't move ordnance in bulk. I want to refit and camouflage Bruvick's boat and run it out of Bon Secour. I want to move guns in quantity and pull terror missions."

Carlos checked the map. Carlos lit his cigar. Carlos burned a big hole in Cuba.

81

(Las Vegas, 8/7/65)

LYLE HOLLY: Dwight Holly built small. BLUE to WHITE RABBIT. A Hoosier/a loudmouth/a fraud.

They met at the DI. They sat in the lounge. Lyle was blunt. Lyle was coarse. Lyle was buzzed at noon.

Lyle said, "I think I'm schizophrenic. I work for the SCLC, I work for Mr. Hoover. I'm on Black Rabbit one minute, voting-rights drives the next. Dwight says I'm psychically unhinged."

Littell sipped coffee. Littell smelled Lyle's scotch.

"Did Mr. Hoover send you in to spy on me?"

Lyle slapped his knees. "Dwight suggested it. He knew I was coming to Vegas, so what the hell."

"Is there anything you'd like me to reveal?"

"Shit, no. I'll tell Dwight that the Ward I saw is the same Ward I allegedly knew back in Chicago, except now he's just as schizo as I am, and for all the same reasons."

Littell laughed. Sammy Davis Jr. walked by. Lyle stared at him.

"Look at that. He's ugly, he's got one eye, and he's colored *and* Jewish. I heard he gets lots of white pussy."

Littell smiled. Lyle waved to Sammy. Sammy waved back.

Lyle sipped Johnnie Red. "Marty gives this speech in New York. He's got a captive audience of liberal Jews with deep pockets. He starts attacking the Vietnam War and pissing all the hebes off with words like 'genocide.' He's going outside his civil-rights bailiwick and biting the hand that feeds him."

Pete was in Laos. Wayne was in Saigon. The war hid them there. He called Carlos. Carlos talked up Pete. Carlos said they'd just schemed plans for Cuba.

Littell said let me retire. Carlos said okay. Carlos dittoed Sam's consent. Carlos talked up the '68 election.

Lyle sipped scotch. Peter Lawford walked by. Lyle stared at him.

"He used to pimp for Jack Kennedy. That makes us comrades-in-arms. I get Marty all his white snatch, and sometimes I dig up young meat for Bayard Rustin. Mr. Hoover's got a photo of Bayard with a dick in his mouth. He made a dupe for President Johnson."

Littell smiled. Lyle hailed a waitress. Lyle shagged a quick refill.

"Dwight said they blew that church up with C-4 explosive. Bayard told me it really *was* a leaky gas main, which makes me think *you* told him."

Littell sipped coffee. "I told him, yes."

Lyle sipped scotch. "Crusader Rabbit's a white man. I'll tell Dwight that."

Littell smiled. Lyle grinned. Lyle pulled out a checkbook.

"I feel lucky. You think you can cash a check into play chips for me?"

"How much?"

"Two grand."

Littell smiled. "Put my initials and 'suite 108' on the check. Tell the cashier I'm a permanent resident."

Lyle smiled. Lyle wrote the check. Lyle got up and walked—half-steady.

Littell watched.

Lyle weaved. Lyle slurped scotch. Lyle trekked the casino. Lyle braced the teller's cage. Lyle passed the check. Lyle got his chips.

Littell watched. Littell let some thoughts stir—CRUSADER RABBIT/White Man/gas main.

Lyle braced a roulette stand. Lyle stacked his chips. Red chips—hundreds—two G's. The wheelman bowed. The wheelman twirled. The wheel spun. The wheel stopped. The wheelman raked chips.

Lyle slapped his forehead. Lyle moved his lips. Littell watched. Littell read his lips. Lyle said, "Oh, shit."

Schizo/comrades/young meat.

Lyle might keep *private* files. Said files might indict. Said files might indict BLACK RABBIT.

Lyle looked around. Lyle saw Littell. Lyle waved his checkbook. Littell waved and nodded.

Lyle walked to the cage. Lyle grabbed the grate. Lyle wrote a check. Lyle fumbled chips.

Their waitress walked by. Littell stopped her.

"My friend's on the floor. Bring him a triple Johnnie Walker."

She nodded. She smiled. Littell gave her ten bucks. She

walked to the bar. She poured the drink. She trekked the floor. She hit the roulette stands. She saw Lyle and fueled him.

Lyle guzzled scotch. Lyle stacked his chips. Red chips—hundreds—big stacks.

The wheelman bowed. The wheelman twirled. The wheel spun. The wheel stopped. The wheelman raked chips.

Lyle slapped his forehead. Lyle moved his lips. Littell watched. Littell read his lips. Lyle said, "Oh, shit."

Littell walked over. Littell passed the waitress. Littell slid her ten bucks. She nodded. She *got it*. She smirked.

Lyle walked up. Lyle killed his drink. Lyle chewed the ice.

"I'm down, but I'm not licked, and I've got resources."

"You were always resourceful, Lyle."

Lyle laughed. Lyle swayed half-blotto. Lyle burped.

"You're patronizing me. It's that saintly quality that Dwight hates about you."

Littell laughed. "I'm no saint."

"No, you're not. Martin Luther Coon's the only saint I know, and I've got some hair-curling shit on him."

The waitress swooped by. Lyle grabbed his refill.

"Hair-curling. Or hair-*kinking*, in his case."

Work him—slow now—ease in.

"You mean Mr. Hoover has shit."

Lyle swirled scotch. "He's got his, I've got mine. I've got a big stash at my place in L.A. Mine's better, 'cause I've got daily access to Saintly Marty himself."

Tweak him—slow now—ease in.

"Nobody has better intelligence than Mr. Hoover."

"Shit, I do. I'm saving it for my next contract powwow. I tell my handler, 'You want the goods, you raise my pay—no tickee, no washee.' "

Sammy Davis walked by. Lyle bumped into him. Sammy swerved. Sammy goofed—cat, you are blitzed!

Lyle swerved. Lyle slugged scotch. Lyle pinched a zit on his chin.

"White chicks dig him. He must be hung."

Fumes glowed. Mash and smoke—86 proof. Littell salivated. Littell stepped away.

Lyle pulled two checkbooks—both embossed—"L.H." and "SCLC." He kissed them. He slung them. He drew them quick-draw style. He twirled them and aimed.

"I've got a lucky feeling, which means I just might have to float a loan from the civil-rights movement."

Littell smiled. Lyle weaved. Lyle settled. Lyle walked off blitzed.

Littell watched.

Lyle braced the cage. Lyle showed a checkbook—blue for SCLC. Lyle wrote a check. Lyle kissed said check. Lyle fumbled chips.

Reds—ten stacks—five G's.

Slow now—ease in—this is for real.

Littell walked to the phone stand. Littell grabbed a booth. He picked up. The line clicked active. He got service quick.

"Desert Inn. How may I help you?"

"It's Littell, suite 108. I need an outside line to Washington, D.C."

"The number, please."

"EX4-2881."

"Please hold. I'll connect you."

The line buzzed—long-distance coming—static popped and clicked. Littell looked around. Littell saw Lyle. Lyle's at a crap table. Lyle's stacking chips.

The shooter rolls. Lyle slaps his forehead. Lyle says, "Oh, shit."

Static clicked. The call clicked in. Mr. Hoover said, "Yes?"

Littell said, "It's me."

"Yes? And the purpose of this unsolicited contact?"

"White Rabbit suggested a meeting. He arrived at the Desert Inn drunk. He's running up a casino debt with SCLC money."

The line fuzzed. Littell cleared the cord. Littell slapped the receiver. There's Lyle. Lyle's at the cage. Lyle's ecstatic. Lyle's got more chips.

Reds—high stacks—maybe ten G's.

The line fuzzed. The line popped. The line cleared.

Mr. Hoover said, "Cut off his credit and get him out of Las Vegas immediately."

The line fuzzed. The call faded. Littell heard hang-up clicks. There's Lyle. Lyle's at a crap table. Lyle's in a crowd. Lyle's stacking chips.

Sammy Davis bows. Sammy Davis prays. Sammy Davis rolls the dice. The crowd cheers. Lyle cheers. Sammy Davis genuflects.

Littell walked over. Littell pushed his way in.

Lyle crowded Sammy. Lyle played Sammy's foil. Sammy goofed on the white freak. He winked at a blonde. He flicked lice off his coat. He went ick.

Red chips down—pass-line bets—all Lyle's money. Good money—Lyle's up twenty G's.

Sammy gets the dice. Sammy holds them out. Lyle blows wet kisses. Sammy goofs on Lyle—he's a Rat Pack reject—the crowd genuflects.

Sammy rolls. Sammy hits 7. Lyle hits forty G's. The crowd cheers. Lyle hugs Sammy. Sammy grabs the dice.

Lyle blows on them. Lyle drools on them. Lyle genuflects. Sammy pulls a handkerchief. Sammy makes entertainment. Sammy wipes said dice.

Sammy rolls. Sammy hits 7. Lyle hits eighty G's. The crowd cheers. Lyle hugs Sammy. Lyle snuffs his cigarette.

Sammy grabs the dice. Lyle shoves up close. Sammy steps way back. The blonde horns in. Sammy grabs her. Sammy rubs the dice on her dress.

The crowd laughs. Lyle says something. Littell caught "coon" or "kike."

Sammy rolls. Sammy makes 9. Sammy craps dead out. Sammy shrugs—life's a crapshoot, baby. The crowd claps and laughs.

The dealer raked in—all Lyle's chips—big ten grand stacks.

Lyle killed his drink. Lyle dropped his glass. Lyle sucked cracked ice. The crowd dispersed. Sammy walked. The blonde chased his back.

Lyle walked. Lyle staggered. Lyle lurched. Lyle navigated. Lyle tried handholds. Lyle grabbed at slot-machine racks.

He lurched. He made the cage. Littell cut in sidelong. Littell mimed *cut him off*. Lyle bumped the window. The cashier shook his head. Lyle kicked a slot machine rack.

Littell grabbed him. Littell steered him. Littell walked him half-slack. Lyle went limp. Lyle tried to talk. Lyle blathered mumbo-jumbo.

They crossed the floor. They got outside. They made the parking lot. Hot skies—blowtorch time—dry Vegas heat.

Lyle passed out. Littell hauled him—dead weight.

He picked his coat pockets. He checked his billfold. He got his address and car stats: Merc coupe/'61/CAL-HH-492.

Littell looked around. Littell saw the car. Littell lugged Lyle

Holly slack. Lyle was small—one-forty tops—slack weight but light.

He made the car. He rolled down the windows. He rolled Lyle in and made him comfy. He pushed the seat back.

L.A.—five hours tops.

Lyle would sleep in his car. Lyle would rouse. Lyle would rouse in the DI lot. Lyle gambled compulsive. Lyle knew the drill:

First they vet you. Then you lose. Then they check your money.

Lyle lost his own coin. Lyle lost the SCLC's. The DI calls fast. The SCLC stops payment. Lyle lives in D.C. Lyle lives in L.A. Casino collectors move. Said collectors hit L.A. first.

Said collectors break laws routinely. Said collectors seize assets. Said collectors kick ass.

Littell drove. His car overheated. Littell drove I-10 west.

He gauged time. He knew booze regimens. He knew pass-outs and wake-ups. He knew pass-out stats.

Three hours—four tops. Lyle wakes up/Where am I?/Oh fuck.

The desert torched. Heat rays jumped. The heat gauge swerved. Littell made Baker. The heat ebbed. Littell made San Berdoo.

He made Redlands. He made Pomona. He made L.A. He drove one-handed. He read street maps. He logged a route.

Lyle lived on North Ivar. It was downscale Hollywood—a cul-de-sac chute.

He ditched the freeway. He took side streets. He looped through Hollywood. There—North Ivar/2200.

Small houses. Sun-scorched awnings. Drab pastel paint. 7:10/summer dusk/quiet.

A cul-de-sac. An end-of-block barrier: a fence and a cliff.

Littell cruised slow. Littell read curb plates. Littell read numbers. Lyle's house—there:

2209. Brown lawn. Peach paint weather-stripped.

He parked two doors down. He got out and popped his trunk. He grabbed a crowbar. He walked up. He looked around. He saw no eyeball wits.

Hardwood door/strong jambs/good fittings.

He worked the crowbar. He tapped the jamb. He leaned hard. He made slack. He wedged his blade in.

He pushed. He shoved. He applied. Wood cracked. Wood splintered. Wood sheared.

He regripped. He rewedged. He snapped the bolt. He popped the door. He stepped inside and shut himself in.

He brushed the walls. He tripped switches. He got lights.

WHITE RABBIT's den:

Dusty and musty. Beaten-down bachelorized.

Living room. Kitchen. Side doors. Gag wall prints—dogs at card games and dogs in black tie. Faux-leather couches. Faux-leather ottomans. Faux-leather chairs.

Littell prowled. Littell checked the kitchen. Littell checked the bedroom and den.

Old fixtures. Cold cuts and liquor. Ratty drawers and cupboards. Undusted shelves.

More prints—dogs at stag nights and dogs ogling chicks.

One desk. One file drawer. Please: No wall panels or safes.

Now: *Trash it first.*

Littell put gloves on. Littell grid-worked. Littell trashed systematic.

He dumped drawers. He scattered clothes. He stripped the bed. He found a German Luger. He found Nazi flags. He found Nazi hats. He bagged them in a pillowcase. They played burglar swag.

He found a Nazi dagger. He found Krugerrands. He found a Jap knife. He bagged them in a loose sheet. They played burglar swag.

He popped the fridge. He dumped the cold cuts. He dumped the booze. He swung the crowbar. He ripped up the couches. He sliced up the chairs.

He dumped the kitchen cabinet. He found a Mauser pistol. He found a Nazi knife. He bagged them in a paper bag. They played burglar swag.

He swung the crowbar. He ripped up floorboards. He tore up wall beams.

Now: the desk and file drawer.

He walked back. He tried them. They were unlocked.

He went through them. He bagged bills. He bagged letters. There: one file extant.

It was folder-sealed. It was doodled up. Lyle drew Nazi maidens and shivs.

It was marked. It was circled: "Marty."

* * *

He drove south. He got out of Hollywood. He found a trash bin. He dumped Lyle's swag.

Don't go home—Jane's there—find a motel.

He cruised south. He found a place on Pico. He booked a one-night room. He locked himself in. He skimmed Lyle's bills. He read Lyle's letters.

Bland: Phone bills/gas bills/second-mortgage strife. Flyers from gun shows/notes from ex-wives.

Slow now—here's "Marty."

He opened the folder. He saw typed notes—sixteen pages single-spaced.

He skimmed through. He got the gist. Dr. King plans. Dr. King plots. Dr. King *schemes*.

The intro—WHITE RABBIT verbatim:

"The following points detail MLK's overall designs between now (3/8/65) and the '68 Pres'l election. MLK has discussed the following topics in high-level SCLC staff meetings, has forbidden staff members to announce them publicly or discuss them outside staff meetings and has rebuffed all criticism that points out one obvious fact: The breadth of his socialistic agenda will divert his energies, deplete SCLC resources and undermine the credibility of the civil-rights movement. It will enrage the American status quo, perhaps cost him congressional and presidential support and will earn him the enmity of his 'limousine liberal' supporters. The true danger of his plans is that they may well serve to fuel and unite a coalition of hard-core Communists, Communist sympathizers, far-left intellectuals, disaffected college students and Negroes susceptible to inflammatory rhetoric and prone to violent action."

MLK on Vietnam:

"Genocide cloaked as anti-Communist consent. An evil war of attrition."

MLK plans speeches. MLK plans boycotts. MLK plans dissent.

MLK on slums:

"The economic perpetuation of Negro poverty. The bedrock of de facto segregation. 20th-century slavery, euphemized by politicians of all stripes and creeds. A cancerous social reality and a condition which mandates a massive redistribution of assets and wealth."

MLK plans speeches. MLK plans boycotts. MLK plans rent strikes.

MLK on poverty:

"The Negro will not be truly free until his God-given rights to coexist with whites are supplanted by economic entitlements which make him the financial equal of whites."

MLK plans speeches. MLK plans dissent. "Poor People's Unions." "Poor People's Marches." Poor people hooked on dissent.

MLK on inclusion:

"We can only topple the apple cart of the American power structure and commandeer and equitably redistribute its resources through the creation of a new consensus, a new coalition of the disenfranchised, which will not tolerate men living in luxury while other men live in wretchedness and filth."

MLK plans speeches. MLK plans workshops. MLK plans dissent.

Summits. Workshops. Brain pools. Coalitions. War protesters. Pacifists. Leftist pamphleteers. Vote drives. Reapportionment. Resultant mainstream clout.

WHITE RABBIT cited concepts. WHITE RABBIT ran timetables. WHITE RABBIT quoted dates.

MLK prophesied. MLK decried Vietnam:

"It will escalate into the most murderous misadventure of the American 20th century. It will divide, rip asunder and produce skeptics and people of conscience in epic numbers. They will form the nucleus of the consensus that will burn America as we know it to the ground."

Timetables. Fund drives. Operating costs assessed. Vote potentials. District boundaries. Registration stats. Tallies. Figures. Prognostications.

It's huge. It's grand. It's magnificent. It's insane. It's megalomaniacal.

Littell rubbed his eyes. Littell fought double-vision. Littell dribbled sweat.

Sweet and blessed Christ—

Mr. Hoover would cringe. Mr. Hoover would gasp. Mr. Hoover would FIGHT.

Littell cranked a window. Littell looked out. Littell saw freeway ramps. The cars looked new. The taillights streamed. The signposts blurred bright.

He lit a match. He burned the file. He flushed the ashes down the sink. He prayed for Martin Luther King.

His words stuck.

He savored them. He replayed them. He said them in Dr. King's voice.

He surveilled Lyle's house. He parked adjacent. No Merc extant/no collectors/no movement. Say Lyle dozed late—give him time—time the collectors' approach.

North Ivar was dead. Windows glowed black & white. The glass bounced TV shadows. He shut his eyes. He dipped his seat. He waited. He yawned. He stretched.

Headlights—

They passed his car. They swiveled. They strafed Lyle's house. There—the blue Merc.

Lyle parked in his driveway. Lyle got out and walked up. Lyle saw the door crashed and trashed.

He ran inside. He hit lights. He screeched.

Littell shut his eyes.

He heard crash sounds. He heard toss sounds. He heard oh no yells. He opened his eyes. He checked his watch. He timed Lyle *seeing* things.

More toss sounds. More crash sounds—no yells or screams.

Lyle ran out. Littell clocked it: 3.6 minutes.

Lyle stumbled. Lyle looked woozy. Lyle looked unkempt. Lyle got in his car. Lyle pulled out. Lyle hit reverse and floored it.

He gunned it. He smoked tread. He smashed the barrier fence. The car flew. The car upended and flipped.

Littell heard the crash. Littell heard the tank blow. Littell saw the flames.

DOCUMENT INSERT: 8/11/65.
Internal telephone call transcript. (OPERATION BLACK RABBIT addendum.) Marked: ''Recorded at the Director's Request''/''Classified Confidential 1-A''/ ''Director's Eyes Only.'' Speaking: Director, BLUE RABBIT.

DIR: Good morning.
BR: Good morning, Sir.

DIR: I was saddened by the news on your brother. You have my condolences.

BR: Thank you, Sir.

DIR: He was a valued colleague. That makes the circumstances surrounding his death all the more troubling.

BR: I won't apologize for him, Sir. He indulged occasional binges and behaved accordingly.

DIR: The suicide aspect troubles me. A neighbor saw him back his car off that hillside, which confirmed the LAPD's findings and the coroner's verdict.

BR: He was impetuous, Sir. He'd been married four times.

DIR: Yes, in the manner of one Mickey Rooney.

BR: Sir, did you—

DIR: I've reviewed the LAPD's paperwork and I've spoken to the Las Vegas SAC. WHITE RABBIT's house had been thoroughly ransacked. A neighbor told officers that WHITE RABBIT's souvenir gun collection had been stolen, along with the contents of his desk and file cabinets. Agents questioned the collection crew at the Desert Inn. A man admitted that he broke into WHITE RABBIT's house, two days after the suicide, and that it had already been ransacked, which is undisputedly a lie. The LAPD officers who responded to the suicide call said that they found the door open and that they viewed the ransacked state of the living room.

BR: It fits, Sir. My brother had run up casino debts before, although never to such a large amount.

DIR: Did WHITE RABBIT keep a private file on the dealings of the SCLC?

BR: I don't know, Sir. He adhered to a need-to-know policy with me on most security matters.

DIR: CRUSADER RABBIT's proximity to the incident bothers me.

BR: It bothers me as well, Sir.

DIR: Was he being spot-tailed during the time preceding WHITE RABBIT's binge?

BR: No, Sir. We had already set WHITE RABBIT up to meet him, and I didn't want complications. Nevada agents had been rotating on and off of him, though.

DIR: CRUSADER RABBIT keeps popping up. He hops from catastrophe to catastrophe with rabbitlike aplomb.

BR: Yes, Sir.

DIR: He appears in Bogalusa. Voila, WILD RABBIT's friend Charles Rogers disappears. He appears in Las Vegas. Voila, he views the prelude to WHITE RABBIT's suicide.

BR: You know my distaste for CRUSADER RABBIT, Sir. That said, I should add that he did call and warn you.

DIR: Yes, and I spoke to him yesterday. He told me that he helped WHITE RABBIT outside, and that WHITE RABBIT simply passed out in his car. His story sounded plausible, and the assigned agents have not been able to crack it. They tell me that he did terminate WHITE RABBIT's casino credit, which further buttresses his credibility.

BR: He may have somehow capitalized on the incident, Sir. I seriously doubt that he provoked it.

DIR: I'm keeping an open mind for the moment. CRUSADER RABBIT is capable of outlandish provocations.

BR: Yes, Sir.

DIR: To digress. Tell me how WILD RABBIT is behaving.

BR: He's doing well, Sir. He's building up his Klan unit nicely, chiefly on the basis of FATHER RABBIT's recruitments. He's debriefed a number of recruits with mail-fraud information on rival klaverns and paramilitary groups. The Bogalusa incident appears to have chastened him, and he seems to be adhering to his operational parameters.

DIR: WILD RABBIT is an obstreperous bunny who has endured very obvious reprimands.

BR: That's my assessment, Sir. But I don't know who the reprimander is, and the Rogers angle eludes me.

DIR: The chain of events is seductive. Rogers kills his parents and disappears. A Negro church explodes 800 miles east.

BR: I only like riddles I can solve, Sir.

DIR: I had the Houston SAC run a passport check.

Pete Bondurant and Wayne Tedrow Junior arrived in
Houston shortly after Rogers. I think they killed
him, but their motive flummoxes me.

BR: Again, Sir. CRUSADER RABBIT and his proximity.

DIR: Yes, an additional vexation.

BR: Sir, do you—

DIR: RED RABBIT will seek to attend WHITE RABBIT's
funeral. Will you allow it?

BR: Yes, Sir.

DIR: May I ask why?

BR: My reason may sound flip, Sir.

DIR: Indulge yourself. Walk on the wild side.

BR: My brother enjoyed RED RABBIT, Sir. He knew him
for what he was and liked him anyway. He can come and
give a big oration and repeat his ''I Have a Dream''
speech for all I care. Lyle only made 46, so I'm prone
to humor his memory.

DIR: The fraternal bond deconstructed. Bravo,
Dwight.

BR: Thank you, Sir.

DIR: Has it occurred to you that CRUSADER and WHITE
RABBIT share certain characteristics and a common
moral void?

BR: It has, Sir.

DIR: Is your hatred for RED RABBIT escalating?

BR: It is, Sir. It was my hope that we could
escalate BLACK RABBIT and recoup our loss.

DIR: In due time. For now I want to wait and assess
an adjunct plan.

BR: Covert ops?

DIR: No, a formal shakedown.

BR: Run by field agents?

DIR: No, run by one Pierre Bondurant, known in
unpolite circles as ''Mr. Extortion'' and ''The
Shakedown King.''

BR: He's a rough piece of work.

DIR: He's close to CRUSADER RABBIT. We might learn
a few things.

BR: Yes, Sir.

DIR: Good day, Dwight. And, again, my condolences.

BR: Good day, Sir.

82
(New Hebron, 8/12/65)

NIGGER.

He never thought it. He never said it. It was ugly. It was stupid. It made you THEM.

Wayne took back roads. Wayne saw shit shacks and crop rows. Wayne saw THEM.

They tilled dirt. They hauled brush. They dished slop. Wayne watched. Wayne made them Bongo. Wayne made them Wendell D.

Wicked Wendell—last seen in Bakersfield—redneck California. Work first/Bakersfield *soon*/New Hebron now.

New Hebron was redneck. New Hebron was small. New Hebron was *très* Mississippi. Bob Relyea gigged there. Bob ran Wild Rabbit's hutch. Bob ran his Klan kompound.

Bob had kadre guns. Wayne had kadre money. Kall it: Kadre meets Klan.

Wayne drove slow. Wayne watched THEM. He felt bifurcated. He felt travel-fucked.

He'd rotated west. He split Saigon. He had three weeks in. He cooked horse. He packaged horse. He followed horse west.

Pete was in Laos. Ditto Mesplède. Mesplède just rotated in. They ran Tiger Kamp. They ran slaves. They cooked base.

Pete got antsy there. Pete got bored. Pete bought a bomb raid. Pete bought some Marv pilots. Said pilots napalmed Ba Na Key.

They deforested. They depilatoried. They defoliated. They torched a dope camp. They torched a dope field. They spared the camp lab. They cued in Tran Lao Dinh. Tran sacked the lab. Tran stole M-base and equipment. Tran fed it to Tiger Kamp.

Laurent was in Bon Secour, Alabama. Ditto Flash E. Pete nailed a boat there. Flash knew boats. Laurent knew carpentry.

One charter boat—one overhaul—one war boat boocoo.

Pete's plan: You view the guns. You pay Bob. You route said guns—New Hebron to Tiger South. *You* drive to Bon Secour then. *You* play backup. *You* jam this clown Danny Bruvick.

Loops. Rotations. Travel fucks.

Flash was travel-fucked. Flash looped through Cuba. Flash dipped in via speedboat. Flash dropped Fuentes and Arredondo. They stayed there. Flash looped on back. Flash looped to Bon Secour.

Soon:

Arms run #1. The *Ebbtide* revamped—the new *Tiger Klaw* boocoo.

Wayne cut east. Wayne hit dirt roads. Wayne saw paper mills and compost burning. Wayne saw Bob's "farm."

One shack—Bob's "Führer Barn." One gun range adjacent. Klan klowns kluster. Klan klowns klique. Klan klowns klip targets.

Wayne pulled in. Wayne parked. Wayne smelled cordite and horse shit. Wayne walked in the barn. Cold air hit him—the "Führer Igloo."

He shut the door. He laughed. He sneezed.

Rebel-flag drapes. Rebel-flag rugs. Rebel-flag furniture. Tracts on a table—Wayne Senior's script—"Red Racemixers"/ "Spook *Coon*fidential."

Ammo on a couch/sheets on a table/hoods on a stool. Dry-cleaned and folded. All cellophaned.

Wayne laughed. Wayne sneezed. The door popped open. Bob Rabbit walked in. Bob wore fatigues. Bob wore jump boots. Bob detached his Klan hood.

Wayne laughed. Bob shut the door. Bob refroze the igloo.

"It ain't *GQ*, but it works."

Wayne tapped his pockets. "I brought the money."

"Your daddy says hi. He always asks about you."

"Let's see the guns."

"Let's jaw first. 'Hey, Bob, how's the hammer hangin'?' 'Long and strong, Wayne, how about you?' "

Wayne smiled. Pete whomped on Bob. Pete boxed his rabbit ears. Pete avenged Ward Littell.

"Let's see the guns."

Bob packed his nose. Bob jammed in Red Man snuff.

"The niggers are rioting in L.A. I told my boys, 'It'd take some napalm and two hundred Wayne Juniors to stop that thing.' "

Wayne sneezed—cold air and snuff.

"Cut the shit and show me the guns."

"Let's jaw first. We discuss the nigger problem, and I show you my correspondence file from the Missouri State Pen."

Wayne said, "You're wearing me thin."

Bob rubbed his nose. "I got letters from Jimmy Ray and Loyal G. Binns. They're both good haters and pliable as shit. I think they'll join up when they get—"

Wayne walked. Wayne bumped Bob deliberate. Wayne walked to the kitchen.

A TV was on. Negroes cavorted. Negroes threw rocks. Negroes stole liquor. The sound was off. Said Negroes yelled. Their teeth glowed bright.

Bob walked in. Bob bumped Wayne deliberate. Bob popped an unplugged meat freezer.

Guns: M-14s/pumps/bazookas.

Bob pinched a nostril. Bob blew excess snuff.

"I got all the requisite ammo and eight M-132 Zippos out at the range. Some guys heisted a National Guard post in Arkansas. My contact knows them, so we got first dibs. I figure you got plenty of shit for Tiger South and your Cuban run."

"How much?"

"Thirty-five, which is a yard-sale fucking price, if you want my opinion."

Wayne grabbed a pump. Wayne checked the slide. Burn marks/no maker code.

"It's been dipped. There's no serial numbers."

"They're all that way. The guys didn't want the shit to be traced back to the heist."

Wayne grabbed an M-14. Wayne grabbed a bazooka.

"It's good ordnance. It looks too good to be Guard issue."

"Don't complain. We got a fucking bargain."

Wayne grabbed an M-14. Wayne checked the barrel lug.

"Pete wanted the serial numbers to show. It's a terror tactic. If the stuff gets captured, the Castro guys will know it's U.S. donation stock."

Bob shrugged. "It's not like you got it at Sears, with the fucking price tag attached and the lifetime warranty."

Wayne peeled K-notes—all krisp and klean/all logged and laundered.

Bob laughed. "You don't try to break one of those at your local Tastee Freez."

Wayne tapped the TV. Wayne got some sound. Guns popped. Sirens hummed. Negroes frolicked.

Boat work:

Laurent rigged the gun nests. Flash scraped the hull. They lugged tools. They dropped tools. They dripped sweat.

They devolved the *Ebbtide*. They refaced the *Ebbtide*. They re-Cubafied.

They draped nets. They smeared sails. They scraped teakwood. They camouflaged. They built a mock-Cuban boat.

Flash gripped a sander. Flash scuffed the bridge. Flash scraped mahogany. Danny Bruvick watched. Danny Bruvick moaned. Danny Bruvick sipped Cutty Sark.

Wayne watched. Wayne prickled. Wayne yawned. He drove sixteen hours. He loop-the-looped. He scoured ol' Dixie.

He split New Hebron. He popped bennies. He drove to Port Sulphur. He hit Tiger South. He dropped the guns. He drove to Bon Secour.

Flash had orders—direct from Pete.

Pete don't trust Danny. Danny's got this ex. She's shacked with Ward Littell. We brace Danny—me and Laurent—*Jefe* Carlos too. We read Danny Tiger Law. You kowtow to Tiger Kode. You kart us to Kuba.

Danny's a punk. Danny's a souse. Danny might call his ex and boo-hoo. Your job—don't let him.

Dusk hit. Flash rigged work lights. Laurent Cubafied. Wayne sipped beer. Wayne studied maps.

Sexy Cuba and Bakersfield—bumfuck California.

Boat work:

Laurent climbed masts. Laurent stitched sails. Flash tuned the engines. Danny Bruvick watched. Danny Bruvick watched blotto.

Wayne walked to slip 18. Wayne watched long-distance. Flash had new orders—direct from Pete.

The ex is named Arden. Danny's pussy-whipped. Danny might call her and sing the blues. Your job—don't let him. It pertains to Carlos—some weird gig—thus mum's the word.

Flash hauled fuel cans. Laurent soldered drums. Wayne watched. Bennies parched him dry. Wayne sipped apple juice.

A stretch pulled up and idled. A chauffeur popped the back door. Carlos got out. He's the stock *padrone*. He's got the stock sharkskin suit.

He walked slip 19. Laurent snapped to attention. Bruvick rosaried. Flash snapped to. Carlos bowed. Carlos hugged Laurent.

Bruvick snapped to. Carlos ignored him. Carlos walked below

deck. Flash walked down. Laurent walked down. Bruvick limped down slow.

The boat pitched and settled. Wayne heard screams.

He found a slip light. He read his maps. The boat pitched. He heard thumps. He heard whimper-screams.

Flash walked up. Laurent walked up. Carlos swaggered à la Il Duce. They walked down slip 19. They wiped their hands on paper towels. They bagged the stretch limo.

The limo pulled out. Wayne watched the boat. Wayne checked his watch and ticked seconds.

There—

Bruvick comes topside. Bruvick limps. Bruvick deboats. He counts change. He hits the dock. He hits the pay phones.

Wayne ran over. Bruvick saw him. Bruvick said, "Fuck."

Wayne saw the hurt:

Loose teeth and fat ears. Puffed lips and abrasions.

Bon voyage.

They fueled up. They stocked transfer guns. They stocked their personal shit: Browning pumps and Berettas. Scalp knives and suppressors. One Zippo choked for big flames.

Tiger Klaw—kool kamouflaged. Guns port. Guns starboard. Six gunwale slits. Tommys below-deck—hooked to swivel tricks.

They shoved off—6:00 A.M.—south by southeast. Bruvick navigated. Laurent read maps. Flash read comic books. Wayne read street maps. Wayne studied Bakersfield. Truck farms and wetbacks. Stoop crops and Wendell Durfee.

They bucked waves. They made time. It was hot. They got spray wet. They caught glare off the sea.

They wore Coppertone. The boat pitched. They ate Dramamine. Bruvick got the sweats and shakes—forced sobriety.

Flash hid his booze. Flash said Pete loathed Bruvick. Flash said it was private shit—per Ward Littell.

Flash read compass stats. Flash read maps. Flash ran the script:

We rendezvous offshore—near Varcadero Beach. We meet our men. We grapple boats. They get the guns. We get carte blanche. We're upside the beach. We're close to a Militia post—one barracks with Beards.

Flash was happy. Flash was homicidal. Flash waxed cautionary. Flash said:

Watch for boat robbers—they kill fishermen—they got little skiffs. They steal fish. They steal boats. They sport Fidel beards.

Laurent was happy. Laurent was homicidal. Laurent pumiced his scalp knife.

Dusk hit. They made Snipe Key. They refueled. They ran their sails. They recamouflaged.

Bruvick begged for booze. Flash shackled him up. They walked off-boat. They found a crab shack. They ate crab claws and Dexedrine.

Wayne got buzzed. Flash went pop-eyed. Laurent ratched his teeth. They brought Bruvick dinner. They deshackled him. They brought him one *cerveza*. Bruvick siphoned it.

They shoved off. They ran south-southeast. They plowed currents. The boat pitched. Clouds hid the moon.

Bruvick steered. Bruvick sweated. Bruvick rosaried. Flash fucked with him. Flash issued threats. Flash mocked his rosaries.

They applied lampblack. Their hands jumped—wiiild Dexedrine. They went blackface. Laurent was tall. Laurent looked like Wendell Durfee.

Flash ran compass stats. They hit Cuban waters.

Wayne walked the bow. Wayne caught spray. Wayne ran his Bausch & Lombs. Waves jumped. Fish jumped. A flare popped and streaked. Wayne saw *the* boat. Wayne saw a boat in retreat.

Due right—four hundred yards—speck in retreat.

Flash popped a flare. The sky whooshed. Bruvick cut the boat near. There: *Their* boat/the meet.

The boats bumped. Flash tossed a grappling hook. Flash hooked a deck ledge clean. Wayne saw Fuentes and Arredondo.

They tossed their hooks. They jumped bows. They flew. Laurent grabbed them. They dogpiled. They rolled.

Wayne said, "The other boat? *La boata? Qué és esto?*"

Fuentes stood up. "Militia. They … *qué es* … checked us out?"

Arredondo stood up. "*Los putos de Fidel.* They smell our fish."

Wayne smelled fish. Wayne scoped the boat. Wayne saw their camouflage: Fish poles/fish guts/fish heads.

Flash ran up. Flash hugged the guys. Flash went effusive. Spanish flowed—"*chinga*" for "fuck." "*Puta roja*" for "whore red."

Wayne lugged weapons—plastic-wrapped/tape-sealed/heavy.

He double-timed. He hit the cargo holds. He ran the galley

steps. He funneled. He made eight trips. He ran the swamp line.

He tossed. Flash tossed. Fuentes caught. Arredondo caught and stacked. Little guys—strong—good catchers.

Bruvick watched. Bruvick scratched a neck rash. Bruvick rosaried. Fuentes degrappled. Fuentes waved. Arredondo shoved their boat off.

Laurent grabbed Bruvick. Flash mummyized. He cuffed him. He taped him. He made him King Tut. He taped his mouth. He taped his legs. He mast-pole mummified.

Laurent rigged a raft. Wayne dropped anchor. Flash said, "Let's kill Communists."

They took Berettas. They took knives. They took Browning pumps. They took a plastic-wrapped Zippo. They took a raft. They oared in. They surfed swells and ate grit.

Two miles of black sea. Three miles to beach lights. There now: One barracks and one sentry hut.

Off the beach. Off loose sand. Off dirt access ruts.

They flanked. They oared left. Breakers slammed them. Wayne and Flash puked.

They cut through it. A current hit. They pulled left. They scraped sand. They capsized. They rolled.

They dragged the raft up to high sand. They scoped out the hut. Twelve-by-twelve/four men in it/forty yards up.

Beside it: The barracks/one doorway/one floor.

They shared binoculars. They honed the lens. They nailed snapshots. One open door. Two bed-rows. 2:00 A.M./thirty men/bunks and bug nets.

Flash hand-talked. Flash said hut first. We go with silencer pops.

They checked their Berettas. They unwrapped the Zip. They bug-crawled three abreast. Laurent lugged the Zip.

Wayne wheezed. Wayne ate sand. Wayne jittered. They got close—six yards out—Wayne saw whole faces.

The Militia guys sat. The Militia guys smoked. Wayne saw four carbines stacked.

Flash lip-synced numbers—shoot prone on three.

One—they aimed prone. Two—they triggered up. They fired on three—synced silencer plops.

They hit strong. They hit main mass. They hit heads and

chests. They double-tapped. They aimed up. They shot fast. They hit groins. They hit backs. They hit necks.

Two fucks fell. Two chairs toppled. Two fucks scree-screeched. Two mouths gapped. Two mouths flapped sound-less—wave-noise suppressed.

Flash rolled up. Flash got close. Flash shot main mass. The bodies jerked. The bodies sponged lead.

Flash signaled. The barracks—NOW.

Laurent lit the Zippo. The cherry top flared. They crawled up. They got close. There's the target. There's the door.

Laurent stood up. Laurent braced the doorway. Laurent Zippo-ized. He strafed the beds. He strafed the bug nets. He strafed *putos Red*.

Commies burned. Commies screamed. Commies rolled out of fart-sacks. Commies tangled up bug nets and ran.

Laurent burned bed sheets. Laurent burned walls. Laurent burned men in skivvies and pajamas. Commies ran. Commies fell. Commies crashed windows out.

The barracks burned. Commies ran—Reds on fire.

They ran out the back door. They ran to the beach. They fell in the sand. They ran and hit water.

Waves doused them. Waves deflamed them. Waves sucked them in. Waves boiled. The barracks burned. Ammo ignited.

Laurent chased fireballs. Laurent strafed wet sand. Laurent cooked salt water.

Flash walked to the hut. Flash dragged two dead men out. Flash dumped them and pissed on their heads.

Wayne walked up. Wayne got stage fright. Do it. Show them. Show *Pete*.

He pulled his knife. He picked a scalp. He dug the blade in.

Bakersfield—travel-fucked. Dusty streets/dusty skies/dusty air. The San Joaquin Valley—wall-to-wall dust—farm dirt and glare.

He was travel-fucked. He jumped Cuba to Snipe Key. He jumped Snipe Key to Bon Secour. He jumped Bon Secour to New Orleans. He took three flights west. He got bad sleep. He went off Dexedrine.

He called Saigon. Mesplède patched him to Pete. He praised the run. He praised the guns. He ragged Bob's number-dips.

Pete was pissed. Pete ragged Bob. *Stamp* the numbers—*scare* the Beard—flaunt U.S. Code.

Wayne called Barb. It was tense. Tense off that fight. Barb had news. Barb had a pending gig—adjunct-USO.

We're doing Saigon. We're doing Da Nang. Please lure Pete to the show. He said sure. He said I'll be back. He said I'll be travel-fucked.

Wayne cruised Bakersfield. Wayne read his maps. He flew in. He glommed a rental car. He cruised straight back out.

Mextown ran east. The truck farms ran east. You had beer bars/trailers/motels. You had dust. You had dust bugs. You had Mex cribs galore.

He hit the bars. He sipped beer. He coaxed information. Barmen talked. Barmen travelogued.

Wetback whores? *Shit.* Wetbacks *are* whores.

They jump borders. They steal jobs. They work cheap. They over-breed. They live to fuck. They whelp like chihuahuas. They pick crops. They get paid—they fuck *real* whores then. Wetback pimps pimp wetback whores—the payday proliFUCKation.

They swarm motels. They production-fuck. They proli-FUCKate. Check the Sun-Glo. Check the Vista—check the whole scene. Payday's tomorrow—the wets proFUCKate— you'll dig the scene.

Wayne dropped the name "Wendell Durfee." Wayne dredged up some shrugs.

Who's that? Some jigaboo?

That's right—he's colored. He's quite loud and tall.

Sheeeit—

Wetbacks hate jigs. Crop men hate jigs. That jig better haul.

Payday:

Wayne cruised truck farms. Wayne loitered. Wayne watched.

Wets pick cabbage. Wets yank weeds. Wets fill garbage drums. Sirens blow. The wets yell. The wets drop hoes and run.

They hit pay trucks. They line up. They shag cash and run— families/*hombres*/*muchachos*.

Some clique up. Some walk off. Some liiiiiinger. *Hombres todos*—men with shit-eater grins.

Trucks pull up. *Hombres* greet *hombres. Hombres* dispense: Jar brew/rubbers/French ticklers/T-Bird/white port/nude Polaroids. Beaver pix of Mexi-whores—let's proFUCKate.

Wayne walked over. *Hombres* cringed. Wayne vibed *Migra* fuzz. Wayne mollified. Wayne spoke pidgin-Mex. Wayne coaxed info.

Dig:

The truck men pimped. They signed johns up early—supply meets demand. Go to the Sun-Glo and Vista. See the Fuckathon.

Wets scoped the beaver pix. Wets signed up. Wayne flashed Wendell Durfee pix and got nada. Shit—we ain't seen him/we don't know him/we hate *negritos*.

Wayne split. Wayne braced more truck pimps. Wayne got more nada. He regrouped. He read his maps. He crossed the tracks and cruised Darktown. *De facto* segregation—wets north/coloreds south.

He yawned. He fought sleep-fuckification. He slept too long last night. He slept fourteen hours. He logged some bad dreams.

Barb rags him—don't pop pills—he rags Barb back. Don't you do it—you'll age bad—I love you.

Bongo co-starred. Bongo convulsed. Bongo snitched Wendell Durfee. Wendell's in Cuba. He's got the cold six thousand. He's got a Castro beard.

Wayne cruised Darktown. Wayne hit pool halls. Wayne hit lounge spots. He vibed cop. He vibed grief. He wore his gun out.

Cops saw him. Cops waved. Cops vibed brother cop. He braced coloreds. He flashed his Wendell pix. He got huh?s. He got indignation.

You dig Watts? It could happen *here*. It could happen NOW.

He worked through it. He worked all day. He wore Darktown out. Nobody knew Wicked Wendell. Nobody knew jackshit.

Dusk hit. He drove to the Sun-Glo. He caught the Fuckathon.

Ten rooms/ten whores/ten parking-lot lines. Wets twenty-deep and pimps with stopwatches—you fuck off *my* clock.

Snack stands—all jerry-rigged/all run by *mamacitas*. They served beans. They served *cerveza*. They served *carnitas*.

It was hot. Fried pork spattered. Jalopy pipes popped.

Doors opened. Doors shut. Wayne got snapshots: Nude girls and wide-leg poses. Soiled sheets trashed up.

The lines moved fast—six minutes per fuck. Cops stood around. Pimps greased them—a dollar a fuck.

The cops ate *carnitas*. The cops worked the line. The cops sold bootjack penicillin. Wayne stood in line. Wayne drew stares. Wayne showed *his* snapshots.

Que? No se. Negrito muy feo.

Wayne braced a mama-san. Wayne waved fifty bucks. He pidgin-talked. He told her—beer on the house.

She smiled. She shagged Lucky Lagers. She served the wets. She served the pimps. She served the cops.

She praised Wayne—*gringo muy bueno.*

Wayne got applause. Wets pumped his hands. Pimps waved sombreros. He re-showed his pix. They went around. They toured all the fuckistos. The pix circuited. The pix got pawed. The pix came back.

A cop nudged Wayne. "I ran that smoke out of town three months ago. He was trying to pimp white girls, which didn't sit right with me."

Wayne goosebumped. The cop tapped his teeth.

"I heard he was tight with a smoke named King Arthur. I think he owns a queer bar in Fresno."

The Playpen Lounge was a storefront. The Playpen Lounge sat off skid row.

Wayne drove to Fresno. Wayne polled street creeps. Wayne found it. The creeps spieled lore—the Pen's a pus-pit—all fear the King!

He's this mean swish. He's Haiti-bred. He's pure calypso. He sports a crown. He's a he-she. He's a hermaphrodite.

Wayne walked in. The decor clashed—Camelot meets Liberace.

Velvet walls. Purple drapes. Nail-studded armor. A bar and wall booths—pink Naugahyde.

A jukebox cranked. Mel Tormé crooned. The natives stirred. Wayne drew looks. Wayne drew ooh-la-las.

Colored trade—queens and jockers.

There's the King. He's got a booth. He's got his crown. He's got the pedigree: Knife scars/mashed ears/pipe-wound regalia.

Wayne walked over. Wayne sat down. King Arthur sipped a frappé.

"You're too haughty to be Fresno PD, and you're too butch to be anything but a cop."

The jukebox vibrated. Wayne reached back. Wayne grabbed and yanked the cord.

"My money. Your information."

The King tapped his crown. It was kid-pageant issue—rhinestones on tin.

"I just consulted my thinking cap. It said, 'Policemen demand, they don't pay.'"

The King lisped. The King trilled. The King sashayed. Two fags swished by. One tittered. One waved.

Wayne said, "I *was* a cop."

"Oh, pshaw, you silly savage. You didn't have to say that."

Wayne pulled out his money. Wayne fanned his money. Wayne flashed a table lamp down.

"Wendell Durfee. I heard you know him."

The King tapped his crown. "I'm getting a vision ... yes ... there it is ... you're that Vegas cop who lost his poor wife to Wendell."

The jukebox popped. Kay Starr popped on. Wayne reached back and popped the cord. A fag grabbed his hand. A fag scratched his palm. A fag giggled lewd.

Wayne pulled his arm back. The fags giggled. The fags withdrew. They swished off. They vamped Wayne. They blew kisses.

Wayne wiped his hand. The King laughed. The King went oh, pshaw.

"I had a brief encounter with Wendell, several months ago. I bought a string of girls from him."

"And?"

"And the Bakersfield fuzz discouraged me from procuring in their jurisdiction."

"And?"

"And Wendell was looking for a *nom de pimp* with irresistible panache. I suggested the name Cassius Cool, which he adopted."

Wayne tapped the money. "Keep going. I know there's more."

The King tapped his crown. "I'm getting a vision ... yes ... you killed three unarmed Negro men in Las Vegas ... and ... yes ... Wendell made your wife climax before he killed her."

Wayne pulled his piece. Wayne raised it. Wayne cocked it. Wayne heard echoes. Wayne heard hammers click.

He looked around. He checked the bar. He saw fags. He saw guns. He saw suicide.

He holstered up. The King grabbed his money.

"Wendell enticed some crackers into a rigged dice game and was firmly advised to leave Bakersfield. I heard he lit out for L.A."

Wayne looked around. Wayne saw fags with guns. Wayne saw mean faces.

The King laughed. "Grow up, child. You can't kill *all* the niggers."

83
(Saigon, 8/20/65)

PETE SAID, "Wayne took some scalps."

Cocktail hour. Drinks at the Catinat. Grenade nets and gook brass galore.

Stanton snarfed pâté. "Cuban or Negro American?"

Pete smiled. "He's back. I'll tell him you asked."

"Tell him I was pleased to learn that he's diversified."

The bar was packed. MACV guys hobnobbed. Trilingual talk flowed.

Pete lit a cigarette. "The Relyea thing pissed me off. I want to move recognizable U.S.-sourced guns."

Stanton smeared toast. "You've made that clear. That said, I should state that Bob's done a bang-up job so far."

"He has, but he's deep off in all that Klan shit, which could draw heat any fucking second. You want my opinion? We should rotate Laurent back to Laos to work Tiger Kamp, and keep Mesplède in the States permanently to shag guns. He's got good connections, he's willing, and he's fucking capable."

Stanton shook his head. "One, Bob's got better connections, and he's got enough FBI cover to divert any trouble he might create. Two, you brought that Bruvick guy in, which lit a fire under Carlos, who is now all aflutter for the Cause, in a way he hasn't been since '62. He's *active* now, he's the *only* committed Outfit man, and I'm sure he's got gun sources. Three, Laurent's tight with Carlos, which is why I want him full-time stateside, instead of Mesplède. He's the best man to work with Carlos and funnel our weaponry."

Pete rolled his eyes. "Carlos is a *Mob* executive. The only gun contacts he's got are other exile groups with shit ordnance of their own. He won't be able to shag stuff as good as that Relyea batch, and how many fucking armory heists can we count on?"

A siren blew. The room froze. The gook brass drew guns. The siren died. The all-clear blew. The gook brass stashed their guns.

Stanton sipped wine. "We're covered as is. You and Wayne

rotate, because you're the A-level personnel and you know the in-country and Vegas ends of the business. When Wayne's caught up at the lab, he's free to work Vegas and the funnel, and you—"

"John, Jesus Christ, will you—"

"No, let me finish. We lost Chuck, *c'est la guerre*, but Tran and Mesplède are more than enough to run Tiger Kamp. We keep Mesplède in-country, and we leave Flash and Laurent in Port Sulphur and Bon Secour. In other words, we're *covered*, and I don't want you second-guessing a perfectly operational system."

The siren blew. The all-clear blew. The AC died. A waiter cracked doors. A waiter cracked windows. A waiter rigged bomb nets.

Pete checked his watch. "I'm meeting Wayne. He's got a lead on some donation shit in Da Nang."

Hot air settled in. Waiters pulled fan cords.

"How many scalps did he take?"

"Four."

"Do you think he enjoyed it?"

Pete smiled. "With Wayne you never know."

Stanton smiled. "Will you allow me some sort of concession before you go?"

Pete stood up. The ceiling loomed. Pete dodged fan blades.

"Your shit's operational. It's just not as passionate as my shit."

They flew up. MACV ran Hueys—milk flights from Tan Son Nhut.

They sat on the back slats. Some admin pogues flew along. Dig it—let's catch this show in Da Nang.

Wayne yawned. Wayne just rotated in. Wayne was travel-fucked.

The flight overbooked. The kiddie brass partied. They made noise. They matched coins. They twirled their .45s.

The rotors whipped. The doors shook. The radio screeched. Pete and Wayne huddled. Pete and Wayne talked loud.

Agreed: Bob Relyea bites. Agreed: He's Wayne Senior's punk rabbit. Agreed: He shags good guns. Agreed: D. Bruvick's sly and yellow.

Carlos warned Bruvick. Carlos said don't call Arden—don't rat our Cuban runs. Bruvick fudged and tried to call. Wayne interdicted.

Agreed: Let's oust him. Agreed: Let's find a new boat man.

They agreed. Pete hedged somewhat. Pete said Carlos wants Bruvick. Bruvick's his inside man. Carlos distrusts everyone. Carlos plants informants.

Ergo: Bruvick makes Cuban runs. Bruvick calls Carlos. Bruvick informs on *us*.

Wayne *got* it. Wayne digressed. Bruvick's ex Arden—now with Ward Littell. She's a spy. She watches Ward. She reports to Carlos.

Right—you got it—and that's *all* you get.

Wayne said okay. Pete riffed on Carlos—the Graduate Course.

He runs people. He eats people. He's tight with John Stanton. He's greedy. He'll press John—feed me dope points. John will bow. *We'll* bow too. We owe Carlos that. Carlos braced the other Boys. They waived Outfit laws. They let us white-dust West Vegas.

Agreed: We owe Big Carlos. Agreed: We owe Blueblood John.

The flight bumped. The gun doors shook. The pogues ate Dramamine.

Agreed: Tiger ops—overhead stratospheric—the lab/Tiger Kamp/Tiger South. Bribes to ARVNs/bribes to Can Lao boss-man "Mr. Kao"/bribes to Tran Lao Dinh.

Transport bribes. Nellis AFB bribes. Cop bribes: Sheriff's and LVPD. Ops costs: in-country and out. Ops costs trans-continental.

We ship white horse—big poundage—we dust West LV. Profits soar. Jigs love white horse. Profits dip non sequitur. Because of the fucking Watts Riot—live on fucking TV.

Jigs see the riot. Jigs exult. Monkey see/monkey do. They roam West LV. They chuck some spears. They burn some shacks. We suspend kadre business. We retrieve Tiger Kabs. Cops quell the riot. Jigs go to jail. Profits de-escalate.

Agreed: Biz is down now—we're in bear-market turf. Agreed: We'll expand—and we'll re-escalate. We'll hire more pushers—expendable jigs—we'll bull-market reintegrate.

The Huey cruised low. They saw firefights. They saw villages sacked. Wayne talked expansion—let's *re*-dust West Vegas. Let's *pre*-dust black L.A.

Pete laughed—the Boys won't vouch it—you fucking *know* that.

Know *shit*. Durfee might be there. I fucking know *that*.

Da Nang: Hot sun and hot sea winds. Spritzy sea spray.

Their gun contact no-showed. Pete got pissed. Wayne pitched diversion: Let's hit that USO show.

They rickshawed in. Their coolie pulled weight. Their coolie ran chop-chop. They raced some shavetails. Said shavetails were bombed. The rickshaw race rocked.

Pete ate Dramamine. Wayne ate salt pills. They hit access roads. They hit the naval base. They hit the bleacher setup.

The coolies saw it. The coolies braked hard. Four wheels brodied. Four wheels slid and locked.

Dead heat.

Pete laughed. Wayne laughed. The shavetails went green and up-chucked.

The show was free. A crowd filed in. Pete and Wayne lined up. It was hot-plate hot.

The stage was ground-level. The bleachers ran sixty rows up. Onstage: Hip Herbie & Ho—low-rent topical yuks.

Ho was a puppet. Hip Herbie held him. Hip Herbie held a hand mike. Hip Herbie ventriloquized. Hip Herbie moved his lips. Hip Herbie vibed hophead or souse.

They found seats. They got cramped arm- and legroom. They sat ten bleacher rows up.

Stage speakers tossed sound. Ho tossed a tantrum: "GIs scare me! Me most scared! You kill Cong ricky-tick!"

It was hot. The sun torched down. Pete got queased up. The crowd yukked halfhearted. Ho wore red devil horns. Ho wore red diapers.

Hip Herbie said, "What have you got against Uncle Sam, anyway?"

Ho said, "I come to U.S.! They no let me in Disneyland!"

The crowd yukked distracted. Ho blathered: "I get revenge! I plant land mines! I kill Donald Duck!"

The crowd yukked nonplussed. A stage geek signaled Hip Herbie—wrap this shit up.

Ho raged: "Me try sit-ins! Me try pray-ins! Me shoot Donald Duck!"

The stage geek cued a sound geek. A sax vamped low. Hip Herbie got the bum's rush.

He bowed. Ho leaked sawdust. A curtain dropped. The

crowd clapped lackluster—fuck that puppet and lush.

The sax scaled up sequential. The curtain rose. Pete saw loooooong legs furl up.

No. It can't be. Please, yes. Slow now, in sync: The curtain and sax—both scaling up.

There—not no, it's yes.

Pete saw her legs. Pete saw *her*. Pete caught her kiss standing up. Wayne smiled. The Bondsmen clicked in. Barb launched Viet rock.

Whistles/wolf calls/cheers—

Barb danced. Barb shimmied. Barb kicked a shoe off. The shoe sailed high. Guys grabbed and reached. Pete reached higher up.

It's close. It's—

His chest popped. His wind died. His left arm blew up.

It's close. It's high-heeled and spangled. It's green and—

His left arm died. His left wrist torqued. His left hand blew up.

He grabbed right. He caught the shoe. He kissed it. He fell down. He squeezed the shoe. Barb blurred white white.

84

(Washington, D.C., 9/4/65)

RIOT. REVOLT. INSURRECTION.

NBC ran replays. TV pundits assessed.

Littell watched.

Negroes threw Molotovs. Negroes threw bricks. Negroes sacked liquor stores. Chief Parker blamed hoodlums. Bobby urged reforms. Dr. King urged dissent.

Dr. King digressed. Dr. King stressed other riots. Dr. King stressed Vegas West.

Replays: Negroes throw Molotovs/Negroes throw bricks/Negroes sack liquor stores.

Littell watched replays. Littell replayed vintage Drac:

"We've got to sedate those animals, Ward. We don't want them *that* agitated *that* close to my hotels."

Don't say it: "Pete's selling sedation, sir, but it doesn't appear to be working right now."

Ditto Pete. Barb called him last week. Barb said Pete had a

heart attack. It was bad. Pete was stable now. The old Pete was fucked. Barb came on strong. Barb begged him:

Pull strings. Brace Carlos. Make Pete retire. Bring him home. Make him stay. Do this for me.

Littell said he'd try. Littell called Da Nang. Littell talked to Pete. Pete was hoarse. Pete was tired. Pete sounded weak.

Littell called Carlos. Carlos said it's up to Pete.

Littell killed the TV. Littell eyed his news pic. He'd clipped it. He'd saved it. He'd laminated it.

The Washington *Post:* "KING ATTENDS AIDE'S FUNERAL." Aide Lyle Holly—dead per suicide—FBI plant WHITE RABBIT.

King's RED RABBIT. Bayard Rustin's PINK. Brother Dwight Holly's BLUE. They all stand close. RED and PINK mourn. BLUE RABBIT smirks.

He clipped the shot. He studied it. He built some rage. He watched riot footage. He watched replays. He built more rage.

He traveled for work. He left Vegas. He drove to L.A. He saw a tail. He ignored it. He built more rage.

He knew:

Mr. Hoover doubts you. BLUE RABBIT doubts you. Said doubts plague BLACK RABBIT. WHITE RABBIT dies. You view the prelude. You spark apprehension. Mr. Hoover calls. You dissemble. He probes.

Call it a spot tail. You've seen none since. Logic meets rage.

You *were* spot-tailed pre-BLACK RABBIT. Mr. Hoover told you. Mr. Hoover pulled said tails. Mr. Hoover reinstated them—post-Lyle suicide.

Ergo:

He did not suspect you *then*. He does suspect you *now*.

He worked. He traveled—Vegas to L.A. He saw no tails en route. He saw Janice in Vegas. He saw Jane in L.A. He saw no tails at either venue.

Jane scared him. Jane *knew* him. Mr. Hoover knew about Jane. Agents planted her fake transcript. Agents gave her Tulane.

He checked for tails. He checked daily. He saw none. He replayed riot footage. He replayed Dr. King's words. He replayed Lyle's file near-verbatim.

He built a plan. He decreed escalation. He flew to D.C. He did some Teamster work. He stopped by the SCLC. He logged no tails en route.

He talked to Bayard Rustin. Bayard took a call. He excused himself. He found Lyle's old cubbyhole. He worked fast. He deployed his briefcase. He went through boxed items. He stole Lyle's typewriter. He stole Lyle's memo stack.

The office mourned Lyle. They didn't know Lyle was WHITE RABBIT.

Lyle gambled. Lyle stiffed you. You lost no respect. Lyle betrayed you. Lyle died. Now Lyle resurrects and repents.

Littell made coffee. Littell studied Lyle's memos. Littell traced the name Lyle D. Holly.

He practiced. He got it. He prepped Lyle's portable. He rolled in an envelope. He typed all caps:

"TO BE SENT IN THE CASE OF MY DEATH."

He unrolled the envelope. He rolled in a carbon sheet and paper. He squared off the SCLC letterhead.

Lyle Holly confessed.

To booze binges. To gambling. To passing bad checks. To betrayal—FBI-funded—at J. Edgar Hoover's behest.

Count 1: Mr. Hoover is crazy. He hates Dr. King. I joined his hate campaign.

Count 2: I joined the SCLC. I hoodwinked Dr. King. I hoodwinked key staff.

Count 3: I rose within the movement. I wrote policy briefs. I logged secrets shared.

Count 4: I leaked secret data. I supplied the Feds. I said tap here. I said bug there.

Addendum 1: A tap and bug list. *Certified* taps and bugs—known to Littell. Said bugs and taps—*likely* known to Lyle Holly.

Count 5: I logged Dr. King's indiscretions. I told Mr. Hoover. He penned a "suicide note." It was mailed to Dr. King. It urged him to take his own life.

Count 6: Mr. Hoover's hate grows. Mr. Hoover's hate deepens. Mr. Hoover's campaign will ascend.

Littell stopped. Littell thought it all through. Littell reassessed.

No—don't snitch BLACK RABBIT. Don't snitch BLUE RABBIT. Don't snitch WILD RABBIT's snitch-Klan. Don't exceed credibility. Don't indict yourself. Don't reveal what Lyle might not know.

Count 7: I have done great harm. I despair for Dr. King. I indulge thoughts of *my* suicide. This letter remains sealed. Staff members will find it. They will send it if I die.

Littell unrolled the document. Littell signed it Lyle D. Holly.

He rolled in an envelope. He typed an address: Chairman/ House Judiciary Committee. He rolled out the envelope. He rolled in an envelope. He typed an address: Senator Robert F. Kennedy/Senate Office Building.

It was risky. Bobby ran Justice—'61–'64. Bobby ran Mr. Hoover. Mr. Hoover ran autonomous. Mr. Hoover ran his hate campaign under Bobby's flag. Bobby might thus feel guilty. Bobby might thus feel shame.

Trust Bobby. Trust the risk. Hit the SCLC. Drop the letters. Get the meter stamp.

Wait—then read the papers. Wait—then watch TV.

Bobby might report the leak. You could contact him. *You* could resurrect anonymously.

85

(Da Nang, 9/10/65)

SICKBAY—pills/drips/IVs. Pete's world now—Pete the Zonked and Weak.

Wayne pulled a chair up. Pete laid in bed. Barb fluffed his pillow.

"I talked to Ward. He said he's dying to test his pull with the gaming boards. He thinks he can get you a license for a grind joint."

Pete yawned. Pete rolled his eyes. That meant Fuck You.

A nurse walked in. She took Pete's pulse. She checked Pete's eyes. She ran Pete's blood pressure. She logged it in.

Wayne checked the board. Wayne saw normal stats. The nurse split. Barb fluffed Pete's pillow.

"We could run the place together. Ward says it's a revolutionary concept. You with a legitimate source of income."

Pete yawned. Pete rolled his eyes. That meant Fuck You. His weight was down. His skin was slack. His bones jutted out.

He fell off that bleacher. Wayne caught him. Pete gripped Barb's shoe. Barb jumped off the stage. A guy caught her. Two medics showed.

One guy resuscitated. One guy grabbed at the shoe. Pete kicked him. Pete bit him. Pete kept the shoe.

Barb said, "I quit smoking. If you can't do it, I can't either."

She looked frazzled. She looked fried. She looked fragged. Call it a pill run—grief-justified.

Pete said, "I want a cheeseburger and a carton of Camels."

His voice held—good timbre/good wind.

Wayne laughed. Barb kissed Pete. Pete goosed her and went goo-goo eyed. She blew kisses. She walked out. She pulled the door shut.

Wayne straddled his chair. "Ward will make you buy a place. For Barb's sake, if nothing else."

Pete yawned. "She can run it. I'm too busy as it is."

Wayne smiled. "You're dying to talk business. If that's the case, I'm listening."

Pete cranked the bed up. "You're running things until I get out of here. That means in-country and stateside."

"All right."

"We've got a backlog of shit at the lab, so we're freed up there. I want Mesplède and Tran to run Tiger Kamp. I want you, Laurent, and Flash to handle the conduit and oversee the Cuban runs, and I want you to back Milt up at Tiger Kab."

Wayne nodded. Wayne leaned on the bedrail.

Pete said, "I got a pouch from Bob. He's got two truckloads of bazookas and high explosives pilfered out of Fort Polk. It's a big haul, and it might take two boat runs. You take care of the Cuban transport, but in that case and in all future fucking cases, don't go near the weaponry transactions and let Laurent and Flash drive the shit from New Hebron to Bon Secour. Bob's got FBI cover, so I want him to stand as our most expendable guy. Laurent and Flash drive the guns, so they're less expendable than Bob and a shitload more expendable than you. *You* stay safe, and *you* watch Danny Bruvick, who I do not trust worth a fucking shit."

Wayne clapped. "Your wind is back."

Pete checked the stat board. "Not bad. I'll be out of here soon."

Wayne stretched. "I talked to Tran. He said some slaves escaped with some M-base. They're ex-VC, and Tran thinks they hooked up with some VC guys running a lab near Ba Na Key. He thinks they plan to cook up some shit and distribute it to our troops in the south, to demoralize them."

Pete kicked the bedpost. The stat board fell.

"Have Mesplède interrogate the rest of the slaves. We might learn something that way."

Wayne stood up. "Get some rest, boss. You look tired."

Pete smiled. Pete grabbed Wayne's chair. Pete snapped the back slats.

Wayne clapped.

Pete said, "Rest, shit."

Barb danced. Barb obliged horny sailors. They swarmed her. They cut in. They swarmed three per song.

Canned songs/all staples/service club stock. "Sugar Shack"/ surf shit/the Watusi.

Wayne watched. Barb's hair bounced. Wayne saw new grays in the red. "Surf City" tapped out. Sailors clapped. Barb walked on back.

Wayne pulled her chair out. She sat down. She lit a match.

"I want a cigarette."

Wayne plucked those new grays. Barb made an uggh face. Wayne sheared a few reds.

"You'll get over it."

Barb lit the grays. They poofed and burned up.

"I should go home. If I stay, I'll start seeing things I don't like."

"Like our business?"

"Like the boy three wards down with no arms. Like the boy who got lost and got napalmed by his own guys."

Wayne shrugged. "It goes with the job."

"Tell Pete that. Tell him, 'The next one might kill you, if the war doesn't get you first.' "

Wayne plucked a gray. "Come on. He's better than that."

Barb lit a match. Barb lit the hair. Barb watched it burn.

"Get him out. You and Ward know the guys who can make it happen."

"They won't go for it. Pete's in hock, and you know why."

"Dallas?"

"That and the fact that he's too good to let go."

A sailor bopped by. Barb signed his napkin. Barb signed his jumper sleeve.

She lit a match. "I miss the cat. Vietnam gets me mushy for Vegas."

Wayne checked her hair. Perfect—all red now.

"You'll be home in three days."

"I'll kiss the ground, believe me."

"Come on. It's not that bad."

Barb snuffed the match. "I saw a boy who lost his equipment. He was joking with a nurse about the Army buying him a new one. The second she walked out, he started to cry."

Wayne shrugged. Barb tossed the match. It hit him. It stung. Barb walked. Sailors watched her. Barb walked to the john.

"Sugar Shack" kicked on. Time warp—that song on Jack Ruby's jukebox.

Barb walked out. A sailor braced her. He was colored. He was tall. He looked like Wendell D.

Barb danced with him. They danced semi-slow. They shared some contact.

Wayne watched.

They danced nice. They danced hip. They danced by the table. Barb was loose. Barb was cool. Barb wore white dust on her nose.

DOCUMENT INSERT: 9/16/65.
Verbatim FBI telephone call transcript. (OPERATION BLACK RABBIT Addendum.) Marked: ''Recorded at the Director's Request''/''Classified Confidential 1-A: Director's Eyes Only.'' Speaking: Director, BLUE RABBIT.

DIR: Good morning.

BR: Good morning, Sir.

DIR: Let's discuss WILD RABBIT's work in Mississippi. The oxymoronic phrase ''Redneck Intelligence Network'' comes to mind.

BR: WILD RABBIT has been doing well, Sir. Our stipends have allowed him to recruit and secure intelligence, and FATHER RABBIT has supplied him with funds as well. He told me that he's donating a portion of his hate-tract profits to WILD RABBIT's incursion.

DIR: And the well-funded WILD RABBIT is achieving results?

BR: He is, Sir. His Regal Knights have been infiltrating other hate groups and supplying WILD RABBIT with information. I think we'll have some mail-fraud indictments before too long.

DIR: FATHER RABBIT's donations are in part self-serving. He aids WILD RABBIT's cause and depletes the resources of his hate-tract rivals.

BR: Yes, Sir.

DIR: Is WILD RABBIT remaining tractable?

BR: He is, although I've learned that he's running weaponry to Pete Bondurant's narcotics cadre. As I understand it, he secures the weapons from armory heists and army base pilfering, which is odd, because I haven't been able to find any recently filed reports on such incidents, anywhere in the south.

DIR: Yes, odd does describe it. That said, do you think WILD RABBIT will retain an acceptable level of deniability pertaining to his gun-running activities?

BR: I do, Sir. But should I tell him to stop?

DIR: No. I like his connection to Bondurant. Remember, we'll be approaching Le Grand Pierre when we move BLACK RABBIT into the shakedown phase.

BR: I heard that he had a heart attack last month.

DIR: A pity. And the prognosis?

BR: I think it's guardedly positive, Sir.

DIR: Good. We'll let him recover and then add some stress to his overtaxed arteries.

BR: Yes, Sir.

DIR: Let's discuss CRUSADER RABBIT. Have you accrued any substantive data?

BR: Yes and no, Sir. We've gotten nothing off the spot tails and the trash and mail covers, and I'm convinced that he's too technically skilled to bug and tap. He's retained his friendship with PINK RABBIT and visits him in D.C., which is hardly incriminating, since you urged him to do so.

DIR: Your tone betrays you. You're tantalizing me. Shall I hazard a guess?

BR: Please do, Sir.

DIR: Your revelations pertain to CRUSADER's women.

BR: That's correct, Sir.

DIR: Expand your answers, please. I have a lunch date in the year 2000.

BR: CRUSADER has been seeing Janice Lukens, FATHER
RABBIT's ex-wife, in Las—

DIR: We know that. Pray continue.

BR: He lives with a woman in Los Angeles. Her
alleged name is Jane Fentress.

DR: ''Alleged'' is correct. I helped to establish
her identity two years ago. A New Orleans agent
planted her college transcript.

BR: There's much more to her, Sir. I think she could
serve as our wedge if we need to disrupt CRUSADER.

DIR: Expand your thoughts. The millennium bodes.

BR: I had her spot-tailed. My man took a set of
prints off a glass she left at a restaurant. We ran
them and got her real name, Arden Louise Breen,
B-R-E-E-N, married name Bruvick, B-R-U-V-I-C-K.

DIR: Continue.

BR: Her father was a left-wing unionist. The
Teamsters killed him in '52, and it's still a St.
Louis PD unsolved. Allegedly, the woman held no
grudge against the Teamsters, allegedly because her
father forced her to become a call-house prostitute.
She absconded on a KCPD receiving stolen goods
warrant in '56, at the same time her husband embezzled
some money from a Kansas City Teamster local and
disappeared.

DIR: Continue.

BR: Here's the ripe part. Carlos Marcello's front
corporation bailed her out on the Kansas City bounce.
She disappeared then, she's got a bookkeeping
background, and she's rumored to have had a long-term
affair with that old Mob hand Jules Schiffrin.

DIR: Boffo news, Dwight. Well worth your vexing
preambles.

BR: Thank you, Sir.

DIR: I think your tale boils down to one salient
truth. Carlos Marcello does not trust CRUSADER
RABBIT.

BR: I came to that conclusion, Sir.

DIR: Pull the tails, along with the trash and mail
covers. If we need to get at CRUSADER, we'll go
through the woman.

```
BR: Yes, Sir.
DIR: Good day, Dwight.
BR: Good day, Sir.
```

86

(Saravan, 9/22/65)

TORTURE:

Six slaves strapped down. Six Cong-symps wired. Six hot seats/six juice buttons/six testicle feeds.

Mesplède worked the juice box. Mesplède ran the juice. Mesplède asked the questions. Mesplède talked franglogook.

Pete watched. Pete chewed Nicorette gum. It was wet and hot—rainstorm boocoo. The hut sponged heat. The hut stored heat. The hut was a hot-plate boocoo.

Mesplède talked gook. Mesplède talked threat. Mesplède talked fast. His words slurred—gobblede*GOOK*.

Pete knew the gist. Pete wrote the script. Pete read six faces.

Slaves escape. All pro-Cong. Who let them? I no know!—all six say it— I know no who!

It droned on—you tell me!—no no! Pete watched. Pete chewed gum. Pete read eyes.

Mesplède lit a Gauloise. Pete cued him. Mesplède hit the buttons. Juice floooowed.

Testicle ticklers—black box to balls—nonlethal volts. Gooks tingle. Gooks absorb. Gooks yell boocoo.

Mesplède cut the juice. Mesplède pidgin-gooked: Congs run! Steal M-base! Tell what you know!

The gooks buzzed. The gooks squirmed. The gooks afterglowed. Talk now! You tell me! Tell what you know! Six gooks jabbered—this gook ensemble—we no know who!

One gook squeals. One gook yips. One gook salivates. Loincloths to ankles/grounded gonads/feed plugs to feet. One gook squirms. One gook prays. One gook urinates.

Pete cued Mesplède. Mesplède hit the buttons. Juice floooowed.

The gooks buckle. The gooks absorb. The gooks gyrate. The gooks scream. The gooks thrash and pop veins.

Pete cogitated. Pete chewed gum. Pete brainstormed eyes shut.

Tran tells Wayne—slaves escape—steal M-base boocoo. They cook it. They dump it. Fuck up our GIs boocoo.

But:

You don't dump Big "H." You *sell* it.

And:

Wayne rotates home. Wayne's lab is empty. Rival dope cooks could sneak in. Said cooks could utilize. Said cooks could appropriate.

Surveille the lab—do it soon—before *you* rotate.

Mesplède coughed. "Has that chewing gum put you in a trance, Pierre?"

Pete opened his eyes. "One of them has to know something. Ask them *why* the guys ran, and turn up the juice if they shit you."

Mesplède smiled. Mesplède coughed. Mesplède pidgin-gooked. He talked fast. He blurred inflections. He fastballed his words.

Gooks listen. Good absorb. Gooks say: No No No No—

Mesplède hit the buttons. Juice flowed. *Near*-lethal volts. The gooks screamed. Their nuts flushed. Their nuts swelled.

Mesplède cuts the juice. Gooks absorb pain. Gook 5 talks ricky-tick. Mesplède smiles. Mesplède absorbs. Mesplède translates.

"He said he woke up and saw Tran pull them out of the hut. Tran . . . *qu'est-ce* . . . forced them to run, and he heard shots a few minutes later."

Pete spit his gum out. "Cut them loose. Give them some extra beans for dinner."

Mesplède said, "I appreciate compassion."

The hills hurt.

He breathed hard. He walked slow. He trailed back. Mesplède walked fast. Two guards flanked him.

They cut through camp. They pushed through brush. They dodged biter snakes. The rain held. Brush slapped them. Pete gobbled breath.

He took pills. They thinned his blood. They scrubbed his veins. They sapped him. They fucked him up. They held him back.

He ran. He caught up. He gobbled breath.

They kicked through mud. The mud had weight. The weight

hurt his chest. They walked two miles. They hit downslopes. His chest weight slacked off.

Pete heard grunts and oinks. Pete saw a mud pit. Pete smelled human decomp. Pete saw wild pigs root.

There:

Said mud pit. A buffet. Said pigs and boned flesh.

Pete jumped in. The pigs scattered. The mud was deep. The mud had weight. Pete bobbed for flesh.

He rooted. He flailed. He found an arm. He found a leg. He found a head. He shook off mud. He pulled off skin. He peeled off scalp flaps.

He saw a hole. It was bullet-sized. He gripped the jaws. He cracked the skull back.

Good breath. Good strength. Good outpatient stats.

A bullet dropped. Pete caught it. It was butterflied and smashed. It was a soft-point magnum. It was Tran Lao Dinh's brand.

Tran tried charm. Tran tried shit. Tran tried shuck-and-jive. Mesplède hooked him up. Mesplède hooked dual clamps—gonads and head.

The rain held. Monsoon stats—mud 4-ever.

Pete chewed gum. Pete cracked the door. Pete stirred outside air.

"Your shit's not working. Give up the details and tell us who you're in with, and I'll see what John Stanton says."

Tran said, "You know me, boss. I no work with Victor Charles."

Pete hit the switch. Juice flowed. Tran buckled. Tran clenched.

The clamps sparked. His hair sparked. His nuts spasmed. He bit his lips. He bit his tongue. He cracked his false teeth.

Pete said, "That demoralize-the-GIs story you told Wayne was bullshit. Admit it and go from there."

Tran licked his lips. "Victor Charles, boss. You don't underestimate."

Pete hit the switch. Juice flowed. Tran buckled. Tran clenched.

His bladder blew. The clamps sparked. His head twitched. His dentures flew.

Mesplède said, "*Il est plus que dinky dau, it est carrément fou.*"

Pete kicked the dentures. They hit the doorway and popped out. They hit the mud monsoon. Tran flashed his gums. Pete saw old scars—Cong torture tattoos.

"I'll double up next time. You don't want that. You won't—"

"Okay okay okay. I kill slaves and sell base to ARVN."

Pete spit his gum out. "That's a start."

Tran worked his chair back. Tran flipped Pete off—*le bird boocoo*.

"You French fuck number ten. You *carrément fou*."

Pete popped more gum. "You're in with somebody. Tell me who."

Tran flipped Pete off. The wop stiff-arm—*il bah-fungoo*.

"Fuck the frogs. You number ten. You run at Dien Bien Phu."

Pete worked his gum. "Tell me who's running you. We'll have a drink and discuss it."

Tran wiggled. Tran worked his chair back. Tran flipped Pete off—up and rotated—you twirl boocoo.

"You French *cochon*. You fuck fat men."

Pete worked his gum. Pete blew a bubble. It popped ka-poo. "Who's running you? You're not in this all by yourself."

Tran worked his chair back. Tran spread his legs. Tran humped his hips boocoo.

"I run your wife. I eat red pussy 'cause you homo—"

Pete hit the switch. Pete *locked* the switch. Tran buckled. Tran humped his hips. Tran worked his chair back boocoo.

He slid it. He squared it. He made the doorway. Mesplède jumped. Pete tripped.

Tran flipped them off. Tran dumped his chair. Tran went BONZAI! He hit the rain. He hit the mud. He electrified.

87

(Los Angeles, 9/28/65)

MORMONS:

Mormon lawyers. Mormon aides. Mormon worker drones. Drac's Mormons—Latter-day Saints.

It was their summit. It was their turf. It was their hotel call. They stormed the Statler. They booked a suite. They brought their own refreshments. Their names blurred. Littell called them all "sir."

He was distracted. Fred O. just called him. Fred O. found the scandal-rag files. They're yours for ten G's. I want them/I'll meet you/they're mine.

The summit kicked off. Six Mormons hogged one table. A Mormon prepped a tape rig. A Mormon looped a tape in. A Mormon pressed Play.

Drac speaks:

"Good morning, gentlemen. I trust that you have clean air in your conference room, along with appropriate snacks such as Fritos corn chips and Slim Jim beef jerky. As you know, the purpose of this meeting is to establish ballpark price estimates for the hotel-casinos I wish to purchase, and to devise strategies to circumvent recent so-called civil-rights laws, which are in fact civil-wrongs laws, which will prove detrimental to the American free-enterprise system. It is my intention to cunningly and willfully abrogate these laws, retain segregated work crews and discourage Negroes from habituating my casinos, with exceptions to be made for stellar Negroes such as Wilma Rudolph, the so-called fastest woman alive, and the multi-talented Sammy Davis Jr. Before I turn the meeting over to my Las Vegas point man, Ward J. Littell, I should inform you that I have been studying the tax code for the state of California and have determined that it is in fact unconstitutional. It is my intention to avoid paying California state income tax for the upcoming fiscal year of 1966. I may decide to remain mobile until the time that I establish permanent residence in Las Vegas. I may travel by train, avoid undue stays in all fifty states and thus avoid paying state income tax in toto."

The off switch clicked. The tape died. The Mormons stirred. The Mormons checked the credenza.

Salty Fritos. Congealed cheez dip. Tasty Slim Jims.

Littell coughed. Littell dispensed graph sheets. Price projections/per twelve hotels. Gaming projections/per twelve casinos.

Doctored paper. Revised and cooked. Your chef—Moe Dalitz.

The Mormons read. The Mormons skimmed columns. The Mormons cleared their throats. The Mormons took notes.

A Mormon coughed. "The purchase prices are high by 20%."

Moe set the prices. Carlos consulted. Santo T. helped.

Littell coughed. "I think the prices are reasonable."

A Mormon said, "We'll need tax returns. We'll need to calibrate off reported profits, not estimates."

A Mormon said, "That part doesn't bother me. We're dealing with organized-crime proprietors, to one degree or another. You have to believe that they report low."

A Mormon said, "We can subpoena their tax returns from the IRS. That way they can't submit fakes."

Wrong. Mr. Hoover will act. Mr. Hoover will quash selectively. Mr. Hoover will pick what you see.

No oldies. No pre-64s. *Good* '64s/the Boys report high/the Boys bait-and-switch.

A Mormon said, "Mr. Hughes is adamant on the Negro issue."

A Mormon said, "Wayne Senior can help us out there. He segregates his work crews, and he knows his way around those new laws."

Littell stabbed his pencil. Littell hit his notepad. Littell broke the tip.

"Your suggestion offends me. It's unsavory and altogether repugnant."

The Mormons stared at him. Littell stared straight back.

Fred Otash was big. Fred Otash was gruff. Fred Otash was Lebanese. He lived in restaurants. He loved Dino's Lodge and the Luau. Clients found him there.

He doped race horses. He fixed fights. He brokered abortions. He traced fugitives. He pulled shakedowns. He sold smut pix. He knew things. He found things out. He charged high fees.

Littell hit the Luau. Otash was splitsville. Littell hit Dino's. Littell hit paydirt—there's Freddy O. in his booth.

He's in nubby silk shorts. He's in a hula shirt. He's got a tan. He's spearing calamari. He's skimming racing forms. He's sipping cold chablis.

Littell walked over. Littell sat down. Littell dropped the cash on the table.

Otash kicked a lettuce box. "It's all there. I photocopied the choice stuff, in case you were wondering."

"I thought you might."

"I found a snapshot of Rock Hudson browning a Filipino jockey. I sent a dupe to Mr. Hoover."

"That was thoughtful."

Otash laughed. "You're droll, Ward, but you're not my cup of tea. I've never understood your allure to Pete B."

Littell smiled. "Try shared history."

Otash poked a squid. "Like Dallas '63?"

"Does the whole world know?"

"Just some guys who don't care."

Littell kicked the box. "I should go."

"Go, then. And beware the ides of fucking September."

"Would you care to explain?"

"You'll see soon enough."

Jane was out. Littell lugged the box in. Littell checked the papers first. Three subscribed dailies: L.A. *Times*/New York *Times*/Washington *Post*.

He skimmed the front sections. He skimmed the B-sheets. No word—nineteen days in.

The letters went out—mea culpa/Lyle Holly—postmarked SCLC. One to the House Committee/one to Bobby.

Littell skimmed the C-sheets. Littell skimmed the D. Nothing—no word yet.

He dumped the papers. He cleared some desk space. He dumped the lettuce box.

Files and carbon sheets. Photos and tip sheets. Unpublished smears—full pieces. The gamut—*Confidential* to *Whisper/Lowdown* to *Hush-Hush*.

He stacked piles. He skimmed sheets. He read fast. He rolled in dirt.

Dipsomania. Nymphomania. Kleptomania. Pedophilia. Coprophilia. Scopophilia. Flagellation. Masturbation. Miscegenation.

Lenny Bruce rats Sammy Davis. Sammy swings bilateral/Sammy sniffs cocaine. Danny Thomas hits sepia sinspots. Bob Mitchum dips his dick in Dilaudid and fucks all nite.

Sonny Liston killed a white man. Bing Crosby knocked up Dinah Shore. Dinah got twin Binglets scraped at a clap clinic in Cleveland. Lassie has K-9 psychosis. Lassie bites kids at Lick Pier.

Paydirt: Two casino front men/one date-a-boy.

They rendezvous at the Rugburn Room. They trick at the Dunes. They party with peyote and poppers. The front men work the date-a-boy. He sustains damage and hemorrhages. The front men check the register. The front men look for doctors. The front men hit suite 302.

The doc's a drunk. The doc's a hophead. The doc's got King Kong on his back. The doc soaks his tools in vodka. The doc operates. The date-a-boy dies. The doc dips back to Des Moines. A desk clerk calls *Confidential*.

One hit. One bite for Drac. One blackmail wedge.

Littell clipped pages. Littell scanned carbons. Littell skimmed tip sheets. Payoffs/bribes/slush funds/dope cures/nut bins/car wrecks.

Johnnie Ray. Sal Mineo. Ad*lay* Stevenson. Toilet stalls/glory holes/gonorr—

No. Wait. Ides of Sept—

Hush-Hush-10/57/unpublished. The title: RED LINK TO RACKETS.

Arden Breen Bruvick. Her Commie dad—killed in '52. "Who Iced Daddy Breen? Temperamental Teamsters? Arden or Hubby Dan?"

Arden's a party girl. Arden's a call girl. Arden fled grief in K.C. Dan B.'s a lamster. He's on the run. He split K.C.

Arden's a femme fatale. Arden has Mob ties. Arden knows "Shifty" Jules Schiffrin.

A clipped photo/a caption/a date:

8/12/54—RED PARTY GIRL PARTIES WITH RANDY RACKETEER.

There's Arden. She's young. She's dancing with Carlos Marcello.

Littell trembled. Littell got the shakes. Littell got instant DTs.

He palsied. His hands jerked. He ripped the photo. He dropped the tip sheets.

He *saw* things:

Cords stuck to walls. Cords stuck to lamps. Cords off the TV.

He *heard* things:

Tap sounds. Phone buzz. Line clicks.

His chair slid. He fell. He saw wall cords. He saw bug mounts. He saw wisps. He got up. He stumbled. He braced the walls. He saw shapes. He saw flecks. He saw wisps.

88

(Las Vegas, 9/28/65)

THE CAT ABUSED him. He loved it. He lived for his shit.

The cat clawed his pants. The cat snagged his socks. The cat dropped turds on his shirts. He loved it. Shit on me now. I live for your shit.

The AC dipped. Pete slapped the wall unit. The cat clawed his shirt.

Biz was slow. The P.M. lull dragged. Pete shagged calls. His drivers smoked outside.

New rules: The Tiger Kab Manifesto.

Don't smoke near me. Don't eat near me. Don't snarf fat-rich food. Don't tempt me with taste treats—let me get back.

I've got more wind now. I've got more spunk. I've got more pizzazz. I dumped the pills. They fucked with me. I let the cat do that.

Don't smoke. Don't eat bad food—the docs said that.

Okay—I'll play.

Don't worry. Don't work hard. Don't pull rotations—fuck you on *that*.

Tran iced himself. He worried it. He worked it. He hired some Marvs. They surveilled the lab. They reported:

Some Can Lao snuck in. They let chemists in. Said chemists brought M-base boocoo. Said chemists cooked white horse. Said chemists used Wayne's shit.

Pete braced Stanton. Stanton was sheepish. Stanton said: "I was going to tell you—*after* you got well."

Pete said TELL ME NOW. Stanton said the new regime's tough. You know that. No fuck with Can Lao cat Mr. Kao. He's tough. He's greedy. He's savvy. He's cooking "H" in our lab—on Wayne's rotations. He's shipping "H" to China. He's routing "H" west. He's got a French clientele.

Pete blew up. Pete kicked walls. Pete strained arteries. Stanton smiled. Stanton jollied him. Stanton popped a ledger book.

Said book held figures. Said figures said: Mr. Kao *bought* his lab time. Mr. Kao paid big coin. The kadre made money.

Stanton reasoned. Stanton explicated. Stanton mollified. He said Kao's pro-U.S. and pro-kadre. He said Kao won't sell dope to GIs.

Pete reasoned. Stanton reasoned. They rehashed Tran's suicide.

Tran killed the slaves. Tran stole the M-base. Mr. Kao bought Tran's base ricky-tick. Tran fears Kao. Tran won't snitch Kao. Tran electrifies.

Stanton said he'd brace Kao. Stanton said he'd say this: We're your friends. Don't use us. Don't fuck us. Don't sell dope to GIs.

Pete was relieved. Pete rotated west. Pete relieved his arteries. Wayne was stateside now. Wayne was in Bon Secour. Wayne dipped south per gun-run rotations.

Pete called him. Pete spilled on Tran. Pete spilled on Can Lao Kao.

Wayne went nuts. Wayne loved his lab/Wayne loved his dope/ Wayne loved his chemistry. Pete calmed him down. Pete yelled and cursed. Pete strained his arteries.

Donkey Dom swished in. The cat hissed. The cat hated fags. The cat hated wops.

Dom hissed back. Pete laughed. The phone rang.

Pete picked up. "Tiger."

"It's Otash. I'm in L.A., and I don't need a cab."

Pete stroked the cat. "What is it? Did you find anything?"

"Yeah, I did. The trouble is, I won't fuck one client in favor of another, which means I found those files for Littell, which contained some racy shit on his girlfriend and Carlos M., so I'm telling *you*, because you're paying me for some version of the same—"

Pete hung up. Pete plugged the switchboard. Pete dialed Bon Secour direct. He got dial tones. He got rings. Ward *knows* now. Ward will—

"Charthouse Motel."

"Wayne Tedrow. He's in room—"

Dial tones/clicks/rings—

Wayne picked up. "Yeah?"

"It's me. I want—"

"Jesus, calm down. You'll have another—"

"Lock up Bruvick. Make him call Ward at 10:00 P.M. L.A. time."

Wayne said, "What *is* this?"

Pete said, "I'm not sure."

89

(Los Angeles, 9/28/65)

TRASHED: the living room/the bedrooms/the kitchen.

He saw wisps. He saw cords.

They weren't there. He trashed the phones. He looked for taps. They weren't there. He trashed the TV. He looked for bugs. They weren't there.

He trashed his study. He trashed Jane's den. They were cord and bug-free. He walked to a liquor store. He bought Chivas Regal. He walked it on back.

He opened it. He smelled it. He dumped it out.

He rebuilt the phones. He reread the story. Arden Breen Bruvick/Carlos and Jane.

He clipped the piece. He cropped the pic. He taped them inside the front door. He taped them at Jane's eye-level.

Jane was late. Jane was due—Arden Breen Bruvick Smith Coates.

Littell grabbed a chair. Littell sat outside. The terrace view enticed. West L.A./count the lights/gauge that long drop.

There's the key. It's her. It's Arden Breen Bruv—

The lock clicked. The door slammed. There's the pause. There's the gasp.

She dropped her keys. She scraped a match. She's scheming. She's lighting up. She needs hand props.

Littell heard her foot scuffs. High heels tapped hardwood. Littell smelled her smoke.

There—she's behind you.

"It's not what you're thinking. There's an explanation for all of it."

His neck went warm. He felt her breath. He stared at the lights. He hid from her face.

"Carlos protected you before Dallas. I protected you after. You went back to Carlos and started spying on me."

Jane traced his shoulders. Jane traced his neck. She probed. She worked his kinks. Geisha/spy/whore.

"Carlos found me *after* Dallas He knew I had to be the Arden at the safe house. He lied to Pete and pretended that he didn't know who I was."

She probed. She worked his neck. Call girl/liar/whore.

"Carlos was hiding my husband. He said he'd hand us up to Jimmy Hoffa if I didn't report back on you. I'd had a thing with Jules Schiffrin, and Carlos told me about your Teamster-book plan."

Her hands *worked*. Her voice *worked*. Concubine/whore.

"But I loved you, and I loved our life, and I loved what you'd done for me."

She traced his neck. She kissed his neck. Mob slattern/whore.

"Yes, I went through your things. But I didn't tell Carlos that you were stealing from Howard Hughes, or that you were sending money to the SCLC, or that you sleep with Janice Tedrow when you're not sleeping with me, or that you hoard these pathetic mementos of Robert Kennedy."

Littell rubbed his eyes. Streetlights blurred. Littell gauged the drop.

"You've got a file. You're too good not to have one."

Jane dropped her hands. Jane went through her purse. Jane dropped a key in his lap.

"The Encino B. of A. You can have it. That's how much it means to me now."

Littell squeezed the key. Jane kissed his neck.

"I loved my father. That rumor that I hated him was nonsense. Danny and I didn't kill him. Jimmy Hoffa did."

Littell rubbed his eyes. Jane leaned in. Jane rubbed her tears on his neck.

"This all goes back to Jimmy and the Outfit. I was going to complete my commitment to Carlos and go to the FBI. I was going to give them everything I had on every Outfit man I knew, and try to cut a deal to save you."

Littell rubbed his eyes. Littell rubbed his neck. Traitor/spy/whore.

He stood up. He turned around. He *saw* Jane. He made fists. Her eyes were wet. Her cheeks were wet. She'd trashed her makeup.

The phone rang. He stared at Jane. Jane stared hard back. The phone rang. He stared. He saw:

New gray hairs. New face lines. Neck veins on a roar.

The phone rang. He stared. He saw: One hip cocked/those cheekbones/her pulse on a roar.

The phone rang. Jane broke the stare. Jane walked and got it. She said, "Hello." She trembled—pulse on a roar.

He followed her. He stared at her. He saw her neck veins and cheek veins. He saw her pulse on a roar.

She turned away. She cupped the receiver. He walked around her. He grabbed the hall phone.

He heard a man. He heard "run." He heard "blown with Littell." He heard the man falter. He heard Jane get strong.

She said, "Run." She said, "Hush now." She said, "Carlos *will* care."

She hung up. The line-click boomed. Littell dropped his phone.

He walked over. He saw her eyes start to dry. He saw her pulse ebb off that roar.

"Were we ever real?"

"I think we loved risk more than we ever loved each other."

"You were always an Arden. You were never really a Jane."

DOCUMENT INSERT: 10/2/65.
Atlanta Constitution headline:
FBI RAIDS MISSISSIPPI HATE-MAIL RING

DOCUMENT INSERT: 10/11/65.
Miami Herald subhead:
GRAND JURY INDICTS KLAN LEADERS FOR MAIL-FRAUD
AND INTERSTATE COMMERCE VIOLATIONS

DOCUMENT INSERT: 10/20/65.
Jackson Sentinel headline and subhead:
NEO-NAZI LEADERS INDICTED
MEMBERS BLAST ''FBI POGROM''

DOCUMENT INSERT: 10/26/65.
Mobile Daily Journal headline and subhead:
MYSTERY AT BON SECOUR
POPULAR CHARTER SKIPPER AND BOAT DISAPPEAR

DOCUMENT INSERT: 10/31/65.
San Francisco Chronicle headline and subhead:
VIETNAMESE TROOP COUNT AT 240,000
KING CALLS FOR PROTESTS TO INFLUENCE NEGOTIATED
SETTLEMENT

DOCUMENT INSERT: 11/4/65.
Mobile Daily Journal headline and subhead:
BON SECOUR SKIPPER'S BOAT FOUND IN FLORIDA KEYS
MYSTERY DEEPENS: SKIPPER NOT ON BOARD

DOCUMENT INSERT: 11/8/65.
Los Angeles Times subhead:
RFK SAYS NO PREZ'L BID IN '68

DOCUMENT INSERT: 11/18/65.
Chicago Tribune headline and subhead:
U.S. ATTORNEY CITES ''BRILLIANT WORK'' IN FBI HATE WAR
RECORD NUMBER OF MAIL-FRAUD INDICTMENTS

DOCUMENT INSERT: 11/20/65.
Milwaukee Sentinel headline:
KING ANNOUNCES ''ANTI-SLUM CAMPAIGN'' IN CHICAGO

DOCUMENT INSERT: 11/26/65.
Washington Post headline and subhead:
HOOVER ATTACKS KING AT AMERICAN LEGION RALLY
CALLS CIVIL-RIGHTS LEADER ''DEMAGOGUE''

DOCUMENT INSERT: 11/30/65.
Washington Post headline and subhead:
CRITICS DENOUNCE HOOVER ATTACK
ANTI-KING STATEMENTS CALLED ''SHRILL'' AND ''HYSTERICAL''

DOCUMENT INSERT: 12/5/65.
Seattle Post-Intelligencer headline and subhead:
HOUSE COMMITTEE INVESTIGATING ''ILLEGAL'' BUGS AND WIRETAPS
CIVIL-RIGHTS LEADERS CALL ''FOUL''

DOCUMENT INSERT: 12/14/65.
Los Angeles Herald-Express headline and subhead:
HOWARD HUGHES AND TWA:
BILLIONAIRE RECLUSE AGREES TO DIVEST STOCK

DOCUMENT INSERT: 12/15/65.
Denver Post-Dispatch subhead:
HOFFA CONVICTION APPEALS FILED WITH SUPREME COURT

DOCUMENT INSERT: 12/18/65.
Chicago Sun-Times subhead:
KING REVEALS DETAILS OF ''ANTI-SLUM CAMPAIGN''

DOCUMENT INSERT: 12/20/65.
New York Times subhead:
''CITIZENS FOR RFK'' GROUP ANNOUNCES EXPLORATION
OF '68 CANDIDACY

DOCUMENT INSERT: 12/21/65.
Chicago Tribune headline and subhead:
GIANCANA STILL IN JAIL
REFUSES TO TESTIFY BEFORE GRAND JURY

DOCUMENT INSERT: 1/8/66.
Washington Post subhead:
JUDICIARY COMMITTEE TELLS HOOVER: REMOVE ALL BUGS
AND WIRETAPS NOT VETTED BY AG

DOCUMENT INSERT: 1/14/66.
Mobile Daily Journal headline and subhead:
MYSTERY CONTINUES:
WHERE IS POPULAR BON SECOUR SKIPPER?

DOCUMENT INSERT: 1/18/66.
Mobile Daily Journal headline and subhead:
MYSTERY DEEPENS:
DOES SKIPPER'S DISAPPEARANCE LINK TO '56 CHARGES
AND LONG-MISSING WIFE?

DOCUMENT INSERT: 1/19/66.
Atlanta Constitution headline:
MAIL FRAUD INDICTMENTS CONTINUE

DOCUMENT INSERT: 1/26/66.
Chicago Tribune headline and subhead:
BOLD WORDS FROM REV. KING:
''THE PRIMARY OBJECTIVE OF THE CHICAGO FREEDOM
MOVEMENT WILL BE TO BRING ABOUT THE UNCONDITIONAL
SURRENDER OF FORCES DEDICATED TO THE CREATION AND
MAINTENANCE OF SLUMS''

DOCUMENT INSERT: 1/31/66.
Denver Post-Dispatch headline and subhead:
JURY-TAMPERING CONVICTION UPHELD
HOFFA FACES JAIL TIME

DOCUMENT INSERT: 2/8/66.
Los Angeles Herald-Express headline and subhead:
FOES DENOUNCE HOOVER
FBI BOSS CATCHES HEAT FOR ATTACKS ON KING

DOCUMENT INSERT: 2/20/66.
Miami Herald subhead:
RFK STUMPS FOR NEGOTIATED VIET SETTLEMENT
ECHOES DR. KING'S PLEAS

DOCUMENT INSERT: 3/3/66.
Los Angeles Times headline and subhead:
HUGHES DIVESTS TWA STOCK
6.5 MILLION SHARES NET $546,000,000

DOCUMENT INSERT: 3/29/66.
Internal memorandum. To: BLUE RABBIT. From:
Director. Topic: OPERATION BLACK RABBIT.
Marked: ''Stage-1 Covert''/''Eyes Only''/''Read
and Burn.''

   BLUE RABBIT,
   Pull all SCLC bugs and wiretaps immediately.
Implement at Stage-1 Priority. It is imperative that
this be accomplished before the Judiciary Committee
begins a formal inquiry.
   Initiate the first stage of OPERATION BLACK RABBIT/
ADJUNCT. Pick a target and assess the health of P.
Bondurant, henceforth to be known as BIG RABBIT.

90

(Vietnam, Laos, Los Angeles, Las Vegas, Bon Secour,
Bay St. Louis, Cuban Waters, 4/1/66–10/30/66)

GHOSTS: Arden-Jane and Danny Bruvick.
   Wayne watchdogged Danny. Danny called Arden-Jane.

Arden-Jane left Ward Littell. Wayne stuck with Danny. Wayne wet-nursed Danny. Wayne worked to save Ward Littell.

Pete said guard Danny. Pete said release him. Pete said cut him two days' slack. Call Carlos then. Say Danny booked. Cite parts unknown.

He did it. He stayed with Danny. Danny boozed. Danny reminisced.

Danny loves Arden. Arden loves Ward. Arden loves Danny half-baked. Arden works for Carlos. Arden spies on Ward. Part-time spy/full-time lover/long-distance wife.

Wayne *got* it:

Danny was weak. Arden was strong. Arden hooked him on the Life. It all pertained to Teamster shit—embezzlement and flight.

Wayne waited. Danny waited. Arden came by. She chain-smoked. She den-mothered. She fussed.

She knew it was over. She said it: "I'm tired of running—and Ward knows that."

Wayne left the boat. Danny cast sail. Wayne killed two days. Wayne called Carlos up.

He said Danny split. He said Danny took *Tiger Klaw.* Coward Danny—scared of scalp runs/scared for his life.

Carlos yelled. Carlos fumed. Carlos made vicious threats. Wayne tracked newspapers. Wayne logged updates.

Tiger Klaw drifts. *Tiger Klaw* runs aground. Danny and Jane are nowhere. Carlos stays mum. Carlos stays clueless. Carlos does not brace Pete. Carlos does not brace Wayne.

Pete clued Ward to Arden. Pete bucked Carlos. Arden ran to Danny. They ran to their death. They held in strong. They did not rat Pete and Wayne. Pete and Wayne would have heard otherwise.

Pete loves Ward. Ward loves Jane the ghost. Pete knows they're dead. Pete never says it. Dead women fuck him up.

Pete loves Barb. Pete rotates home. Pete stays off rotation. Barb lured him home. Ward licensed him in.

Pete bought the Golden Cavern. Pete bought his own hotel-casino. Eldon Peavy had syph. Eldon Peavy sold cheap. Eldon Peavy dumped his fruit bowl.

The Cavern welcomed fruits. The Cavern housed fruits. The Cavern rejoined Tiger Kab. Fruit drivers drove fruit tenants. Fred T. bugged the rooms. Fruit moths were drawn to the flame.

Dirt accrued: Fruit dirt/hip dirt/pol dirt/fruit celebs/fruit hipsters/fruit politicos.

Pete installed "Swinger Suites." Fred bugged the walls. Pete drew non-fruit biz. State legislators/junket groups/Shriners on toots.

Pete accrued dirt. Pete accrued straight dirt and fruit dirt. The word spread—the Cavern's hip—dig the straight-fruit détente.

Biz boomed. Pete stored dirt and made money. Pete reprised health-wise. Pete looked good now. Pete restored his bad pump.

He stopped smoking. He dumped weight. He chewed gum incessant. He worked incessant. He ran the dope biz. He ran Tiger Kab. He ran the Cavern. He refurbished the lounge. He shot Barb a permanent gig.

Milt C. gigged with her. Milt did topical shtick. Milt had a puppet. Said puppet was a hairy ape. Milt called him Junkie Monkey. Junkie Monkey ragged celebs. Junkie Monkey ragged fruits. Junkie Monkey perved on Barb B.

Barb drew biz. Milt drew biz. Pete made *more* money.

Sonny Liston loved the Cavern. Sonny moved in. Sonny hid from his wife and helped Pete.

Sonny roamed the casino. Sonny made dope collections. Sonny muscled deadbeats. Wayne ran with Sonny. *They* made dope collections. Their reps drew heat.

Their reps clashed. They were salt-and-pepper. They were black-black and white-white. They prowled West LV. They talked Wendell Durfee. Sonny ran riffs. Sonny ran theories. Sonny dug that nom de pimp:

Cassius Cool—the ex-Wendell Durfee. I calls him Cassius X.

Wayne rotated. Wayne ran Saigon to Vegas. Wayne ran due west.

He cruised L.A. He stalked Wendell Durfee. He prowled Watts. He drew hate vibes. Call them riot aftershocks.

He hit pimp bars. He polled pimps. He polled whores. He got zero results. He palmed cops. He bought jail checks. He logged rumors. He got zero results. He prowled south. He tooled main drags. He watched faces. He got zero results.

He braced street creeps. He passed out cards. He logged jive. He got pushed. He got shoved. He got spit on. L.A. was L.A. He had no rep.

He rotated east. He rotated south. He did kadre biz. He cooked dope in Saigon. He ran dope in Vegas. He ran guns through Mississippi.

Profits were up. Kadre kosts accrued konkurrent. Guns moved south. They lost *Tiger Klaw*. They lost Skipper Bruvick. They bought a new boat. They armored it. They bought a new skipper. Dick Wenzel—seaborne merc—tight with Laurent Guéry.

Tiger Klaw II. Out of Bay St. Louis, Mississippi.

Wenzel made Cuban runs. Wenzel brought Laurent. Wenzel brought Flash and Wayne. Wenzel was good. Wenzel was bold. Wenzel had boulder-size balls.

The runs went goooood. No glitches/no bullshit/no surprise attacks. They probed the coast. They grappled up. They met Fuentes and Arredondo.

They dispensed weaponry. They fed insurgents. The funnel moved inland. The coast fed the hills. The kadre fed fuel to *la Causa*.

The kadre was kautious. Pete said trust no one. Pete decreed poly tests. Laurent ran said tests. Laurent ran the Port Sulphur hot seats. Wayne tested clean. Flash tested clean. Ditto Fuentes and Arredondo.

The Cuban runs worked. Mucho runs with no glitches and shit. Bob worked. Laurent worked. They shagged guns. They hid their sources. They said they hit the Minutemen. They said they hit John Birch. They said they tapped Army QMs.

Bob played it close. Bob cited need-to-know laws and source restrictions. Bob shagged good guns. Bob made concessions.

His sources feared tracebacks. His sources dipped their guns. His sources burned serial numbers. Pete hated it. Pete craved confiscation. Let's tell the Beard that it's *us*.

Bob shagged *good* guns. Bob shagged *dipped* guns. Pete went along with it.

The funnel ran to Cuba. The funnel ran back. The funnel ran information. Fuentes reported. Arredondo assisted.

Dig it: Skirmishes/village raids/running fire. Varaguay/Las Tunas/Puerto Guinico. Insurgents hit. Insurgents kill. Insurgents die. Insurgents find replacements.

Good, but:

No major battles *yet*. No major progress discernible. No kadre guns thus decisive.

Wayne loved the Cuba runs. Wayne ate Dexedrine. Wayne notched seven run-notches. Dick Wenzel played skipper. Pete made two runs. Flash and Laurent made seven.

They got close. They dropped guns off. They shot inland.

They torched huts. They scalped Fidelistos. They saved the scalps. They dry-cured them. They burned on their initials. They tallied them. They nailed them up. They served as boat decorations.

Wayne had sixteen scalps. Flash had twelve scalps. Laurent and Pete had nine each. Pete craved more. Pete craved escalation.

The war escalated. Their crops escalated. White horse escalated konkurrent. Mesplède ran Tiger Kamp solo. Mesplède brought in reinforcements.

Chuck was dead. Tran was dead. Pete was stateside. Laurent was stateside. Flash was stateside. Wayne was on rotation. Mesplède needed help. Mesplède bought more Marvs. Mesplède bought some Can Lao goons. They backstopped him. They ran the slaves. They surveilled the chemists.

Wayne knew the Tran story. Pete told him late. Pete said it's all kool. Mr. Kao's boys *rent* the lab. They work there on *your* rotations. It's kosher. Goons guard *your* lab. Said goons pay tribute to Stanton.

The war escalated. Big troop stats swelled through '66. Kao escalated. Kao pushed horse in France. Kao pushed horse in Saigon.

To slants only. No round-eyes. No GI biz.

Kao formed a dope squad. It was all Can Lao and all klandestine. They swarmed Saigon. They trashed "O" dens. They made them horse pads.

They ran said pads. They sold horse. They kept said pads klean. They scrubbed floors and swabbed spikes.

Kao had his fiefdom. Kao had export and Saigon. The kadre had Vegas.

They shared lab space. They shared vats. They shared guinea pigs. Junkies swarmed the Go-Go. Junkies geezed upstairs. Kao's chemists *used* them. They brewed new formulas. They tested dosages. They notched fatalities.

Wayne rotated east. Wayne saw the war grow. Wayne saw horse grow konkurrent. Wayne rotated west. Wayne saw the war grow—every night on TV.

Barb saw the war. Barb loathed the war. Barb watched the war on TV. There's Barb. She's in Da Nang. She scores this white powder.

She toured Da Nang. She saw the maimed. She saw Pete fucked up. She dug pills. She craved more. She found it. She found horse. She sniffed horse. She disproved Pete's assertion: *We* control horse/*we* contain horse/all whites verboten.

Barb flew home. Barb brought hospital snapshots. Barb watched the war on TV.

She had Pete full-time. She loved it. Pete loves the war. Barb hates the war. Barb sparks *their* war for real.

She ragged the war. She talked antiwar shit. She rode horseback.

She took tastes. It went up her nose. It went there under Pete's eyes. She scored horse. She disproved Pete. She disproved containment.

Small tastes. No arc up to skin pops. No mainline spikes.

Wayne knew she did it. Pete didn't. Wayne looked at her closer. Wayne loved her long-distance. Wayne lived to WATCH.

He watched in Vegas. He watched in L.A. He watched in Vietnam. The war escalated. The war was the Life uncontained.

Pete was wrong. We couldn't win. We couldn't force containment. Pete was wrong. White horse would reign. White horse would smash containment. Barb proved him wrong. GIs would follow her. White horse would reign uncontained.

Wayne watched the war. Wayne read body counts. Wayne prowled dope galleries. Wayne logged rumors.

More troops were pledged. That meant more bomb runs. That meant more ground expansion.

Mr. Kao expanded. Mr. Kao bombed Ba Na Key. Dope fields burned. Mr. Kao's Laotian rivals de-expanded.

Stanton said Kao's kool. Kao won't fuck us. We're localized. We're self-contained. We're fine in West Vegas.

Wayne and Pete knew otherwise. Wayne and Pete knew this:

We're *too* localized/we're *too* contained/we're hamstrung in West Vegas.

Wayne pressed Pete. Wayne pressed the case. Let's press Stanton. Let's press Carlos. Let's tell them this: Let's push white horse in L.A.

Pete said, "Don't shuck me." Pete said, "It's about Wendell Durfee." Pete knew him. Pete knew his shit. Pete knew his dreams.

Bongo/King Arthur/Cassius Cool/black faces/white backdrops/white sheets. Cur-ti and Leroy. Otis Swasey. The dead whore/her trailer/the ball in her teeth.

The dreams reran. The dreams dredged Wayne Senior. It was

dream clockwork. Dream and wake. Father Rabbit's there on your pillow.

The dreams recycled. The dreams reran. The dreams ran in rotation.

Rotate east—see Bongo—you killed him there. Rotate west—see black faces—you found them there. Rotate south—see new faces—they lynch that type there.

White sheets. Klan sheets. Bob Relyea—Wild Rabbit.

Bob tweaked him. Bob told him: Your daddy loves you. He misses you. He told me so. He digs on you. He's Daddy Rabbit. He's hip. He's cool. He funds my Klan. We fight mail fraud. We help Mr. Hoover.

We hate smart. We contain. We consolidate. We fuck the bad haters. We spread the good hate.

Dreams. Reruns. Rotations.

Sleep on planes—crash time zones—see faces. Hate smart. Consolidate. Hail Father Rabbit!

The dreams reran. The concept held. The gist accrued: He needs you. He sees you. He *wants* you.

91

(Las Vegas, Bay St. Louis, Cuban Waters, 4/1/66–10/30/66)

WARS:

The real war. The TV war. Barb's running fire.

They watch the news. He comments. He says we'll win. Barb says we shouldn't. Barb says we can't and we won't.

He says I've *been* there. He says I *know. She* says *I've* been there. She says *I* know. They escalate. They debate control. They debate containment. TV wars—parlor shit—sniper attacks.

It raged. It escalated. It stopped. Barb nuked him. Barb won.

She said, "Nobody's controlling the war, and *you* don't control the dope traffic, because *I* met a doctor in Da Nang, and *he* sends *me* little tastes, and I boot them when I get bored to death or afraid that you'll fall off a fucking boat in the fucking Cuban sea."

He flipped out. He threw shit. He taxed out his heart. He tossed chairs. He broke windows. He chucked the TV out. One hoist—two hundred pounds airborne. One badass heart-patient trick.

The TV flew. The TV dropped fourteen stories. The TV dive-bombed a blue Ford.

He raged. His veins throbbed. His pump swelled. He crashed. He dive-bombed the couch. Barb talked up a truce.

I'm no junkie. I sniff it. I taste it. I never shoot up. I hate your work. I hate the war—it covers you.

He tried to fight. He gobbled air. His pump puttered and slogged. Barb held his hands. Barb held the cat. Barb talked *très* slow.

I hate your work. I hate the Life. I hate Vegas now. We'll ride it out. We'll survive it. We'll win.

They made up. He got calm. He got some back-end wind. They made love. They wrecked the couch. The cat refereed.

Shit got said. Shit got aired. Shit went unsaid. No vows of abstinence/no vows to stop/no vows to change.

Truce.

They split the Stardust. They moved into the Cavern. They bought a new TV. Barb watched the war. Barb sulked and judged. He worked the biz. He ran dope. He ran guns.

Barb worked the Cavern. Barb wore go-go gowns. Barb showed off skin-plus. Dig it: No pinholes/no bruises/no tracks.

Truce.

They lived. They made love. He traveled. Barb flew then. He knew it. Barb flew White Powder Air.

They lived the truce. He nailed the Shit Clause:

Barb was right—the war was fucked—we couldn't win. Barb was right—they had big love—they'd stick and win. Barb was wrong—white horse had teeth—white horse bit to win.

White flag/ceasefire/truce.

He conceded points. He owed Barb. He brought her to Dallas. The truce held. The clause held. The ink ran.

You've got Barb. Jane is dead. Ward knows it. Ward said it once. Ward said Jane left me. Ward stopped short then.

Ward knew Jane's backstory. That scandal file told him. Ward could fill in the rest. Arden runs to Danny. They set sail. Gulf waters entice. They're tapped and tired—long years of flight.

Ward lost a woman. Carlos lost a boat. Carlos lost a spy. Carlos lost Danny. Carlos *killed* Danny. Carlos dropped *la Causa* flat.

The new boat bored him. The boat runs bored him. It was gadfly shit. The runs bored Pete. The runs vexed Pete. The runs stressed his pump.

Coast prowls and gun transfers—too easy. Raft runs and scalp hunts—light counts.

It's 1/66. Pete gets frustrated. Pete sends Flash in. Flash is Cuban. Flash is dark. Flash fits right in.

Flash tours Cuba. Flash meets Fuentes and Arredondo. They hit the hills. They tour kampsites. They see kadre gun-stocks.

Big kampsites. Big personnel. Big inventories stocked.

They lead a raid. They run sixty men. They blitz a Militia camp. They flank in. They lob shells. They pop bazookas. They run in under cover. They flank wide. They throw Zippo flames.

They killed eighty men. They lost three men. They shaved beards boocoo. Pete loved it. Pete revived behind it. Pete dropped pump weight boocoo.

Weight was weight. Shit was shit. Work was work. The docs said don't smoke. He did it. The docs said eat light. He did it. The docs said work light. He said Fuck You.

He worked the dope biz. He worked Tiger Kab. He worked the Cavern. The Cavern pandered. The Cavern rocked.

Hipsters loved it. Hipsters dug Milt C. and Junkie Monkey. Horn dogs loved it. Horn dogs drooled for Barb B. Sonny Liston loved it. Fruits loved it. Fruits swished in and Liberace'd.

Wayne Senior came by. Wayne Senior waxed nice. Need some help? Call if so—I know grind-joint casinos. Pete waxed nice. Pete said sure—I'll do that.

Wayne Senior came back. Wayne Senior lost money. Wayne Senior talked.

Life's cruel. Life's odd. Ward Littell's with my ex. How's my son? I know he's tough now. I know he works for you.

Pete waxed nice. Pete waxed bland. Pete waxed noncommittal. Wayne Senior talked. Wayne Senior talked truce. Wayne Senior said I miss my son—I know he's been wiiiiiiild places.

Wayne Senior waxed anxious. The word was out—Drac's on his way. Drac the bloodsucker. Drac the Mob puppet. Drac the greedy centipede.

The prelude ran long. Pete worked it for three years. Pete notched some gooood benefits.

You're forty-six years old. You're a killer. You're a frog arriviste. You're rich. You're worth two million legit.

Pas mal, mais je m'en fous.

Preludes and fringe benefits. Money and debits. Barb and white horse. Barb and ennui. Barb and Vietnam.

They played a game. He got her nude. He got in tight. He checked her arms. He checked her veins. He checked her toes. He tickled her all over. He checked for needle tracks.

None.

It's contained. I control it. I taste little drops.

He checked her ankles. He tickled her. He traced her veins. She touched him. She pulled him in.

The game helped. The game hurt. The game took him back: It's hot. His heart rips. He leaps for her shoe.

92

(Los Angeles, Las Vegas, Washington, D.C., Boston, New Orleans, Chicago, Mexico City, 4/1/66–10/30/66)

MOURNER. LOVER BEREFT.

She died. She left a file. She left a legacy. He tracked her southbound. He ran logic.

Logic:

Otash sees the scandal files. Otash spots Carlos and Jane. Otash calls Pete. Pete doubts Jane. Pete's doubts pre-exist. Jane runs. Jane finds Danny Bruvick.

He called airlines. He checked flights. He found the name Arden Breen. She flew to Mobile, Alabama. She flew to Bon Secour.

Logic:

Pete had Gulf ties. Pete ran guns. Pete gigged from Bon Secour. Pete interceded. Pete bucked Carlos. Pete made Jane run.

Carlos found Danny. Carlos found him with Jane.

That was theory logic. It was buttressed by facts. It was shaped by news clips.

She was dead. He mourned her. He worked with Carlos. They both kept mute. Carlos said nothing. Pete stayed mute. They both misread it. They both called it this way: Ward doesn't know what we know.

I know. I did the logic. I dream the gist.

Carlos kills flamboyant. His teams pack power tools. Carlos kills slow.

Chainsaws/shears/drills. Lathe chisels and fungo bats.

He dreamed it. He heard it. He saw it. He slept with it. He lived it. He didn't drink. He didn't seek numbness. He didn't anesthetize. He worked. He maneuvered. He hidey-hole stashed.

He hit the bank. He grabbed Jane's file. He studied it: six folders/typed notes/comprehensive.

Jane *knew* him. The file *nailed* him.

She predicted his embezzlements. She tracked his travels. She surmised his bank accounts. She critiqued his technique. She guessed at amounts. She assumed his guilt tithes.

She prowled his papers. She linked facts. She extrapolated lucidly. She prowled his trash. She studied said trash. She corroborated spectacularly.

She nailed his target businesses. She estimated profits. She ballparked skim flow. She predicted overhead. She guessed launder fees. She calibrated foreign currencies.

He devised the fund-book plan. *She* ran up to speed.

She tracked his travels. She tallied phone calls. She tracked his lies and omissions.

She nailed it:

The Hughes incursion. The full trust breach. The Boys sell Drac Las Vegas.

Casino profits/cash-flow charts/skim currency/front men/hidden points/rigged prices.

She took common knowledge—Hughes wants Las Vegas—she tracked back inductively.

The text jumped. The file nailed Jules Schiffrin. Jane knew Jules. Jules revealed things unwittingly. Jane extrapolated. Jane thus ascribed:

Jules builds the pension fund. Jules builds dummy books. Jules builds the "real" book scam.

Details. Facts. Guesses. Assertions. Astonishing—all *new* text—things *he* didn't know.

The text jumped. The file nailed Jimmy Hoffa.

Jimmy killed Arden's father. Eyewits spieled facts off-the-cuff. Jimmy cut management deals. Jimmy ordered beatings. Jimmy ordered hits.

Jane was smart. Jane *allegedly* hated her father. Jane lied. Jane drew heat off Jimmy. The file was Jane's revenge: long-standing/long-planned.

The text jumped. The file nailed the Boys.

Carlos/Sam G./John Rosselli/Santo/Moe Dalitz/hoods in K.C.

Details. Facts. Rumors. Assertions.

Per: Hits/botched hits/extortion. Judges bought/juries bought/cops purchased wide. Rackets developed/rackets ditched/rackets reborn and revised.

Astonishing. Incendiary. Densely inclusive.

Jane builds a testament. Jane grows weary then. Jane gets tweaked and runs.

Jane holds the file. Jane forfeits it. Jane pays off her Dallas debt. Jane pays him for two years as "Jane."

Her testament. *His* now. *His* safeguard. Tell Carlos. Tell *all* the Boys:

I've served you. I'm tired. Please let *me* run.

He picked a bank in Westwood. He rented a stash vault. He stashed the file. He mourned Jane.

He dreamed. He saw icepicks and drills deployed. He prayed. He tallied his dead from Big D on up.

He stole. He bilked Howard Hughes. He tithed the SCLC. He mourned. His grief transmogrified. His hurt grew into HATE.

Carlos killed Jane. His hate bypassed him. His hate bypassed all the Boys. His hate dispersed and coalesced. His hate found Mr. Hoover.

He *watched* him.

Mr. Hoover spoke in D.C. Mr. Hoover wooed the American Legion. He watched. He stood at the back of the hall.

The hall roared. Mr. Hoover sailed clichés. Mr. Hoover attacked Dr. King. Mr. Hoover looked old. Mr. Hoover looked frail. Mr. Hoover spewed HATE.

Littell watched.

Mr. Hoover ceded irony. Mr. Hoover ceded taste. Mr. Hoover relinquished control. Mr. Hoover spewed HATE. It was unassailable/unvanquishable/unmediated.

Littell gauged it.

Mr. Hoover was old. The world outgrew him. He outlived his reign of control. *His* hate dispersed. *His* hate coalesced. *His* hate found Dr. King.

Littell gauged *his own* hate.

He lived by hubris. He overcommitted. He outflanked *his* sphere of control. His hate dispersed. His hate condensed. His hate scattergunned. He outgrew his world. He retained his ideals. He outgrew his love of intrigue. His hate dispersed and coalesced. His hate found John Edgar Hoover.

He acted on it. He acted passively. Wait. Do nothing yet. Let Mr. Hoover HATE.

Let the world rock. Let Dr. King meld with Bobby. They have bold designs. They despise the war. They may collaborate.

Dr. King planned revolt. Lyle Holly detailed it. Littell destroyed Lyle's notes. Let Dr. King live the notes. Let Dr. King act *non*passively.

Peace broadsides. Voter drives. Antislum campaigns. Revolt in its early stages—planned through '68.

Wait. Do nothing yourself. Let Mr. Hoover HATE.

His hate burns. His hate shows. His hate discredits him. Dr. King plans. Dr. King schemes. Dr. King's status grows.

Don't push *too* hard. Don't push *too* fast. Don't strain credibility. Let the world rock at its own pace. Let some things go.

LBJ fights his foreign war. Mr. Hoover approves. LBJ pushes civil rights. Mr. Hoover fumes silently. Mr. Hoover spews hate.

LBJ might assess him. Edgar—you're moribund. You've got to go.

The war will extend. The war will divide. The war might derail LBJ. Bobby might run in '68. Dr. King might downscale his agenda. Bobby might endorse it.

He watched Bobby. He read the Senate Record. He tallied Bobby's votes. Bobby was smart. Bobby never said "The Boys." Bobby hated circumspectly.

Hate strong. Hate brave. Don't hate like Mr. Hoover.

Mr. Hoover called him. The phone rang in mid-July. Mr. Hoover stirred some fear.

The spot tails were gone. He *knew* it. He was safe per Chuck Rogers. He was safe per Lyle H.

Still—Mr. Hoover stirred fear.

He was brusque. He was rude. Howard Hughes and Las Vegas—update me on that.

Littell said Drac's crazy. Drac fears state taxes. Drac's booked a whole railroad train. Drac trained to Boston. Drac brought his Mormons. Drac booked a floor at the Ritz.

Drac wants hotels. I've braced the *registered* owners. It's pro forma. The Boys have the points. The Boys will rig the fees.

Mr. Hoover laughed. Mr. Hoover schemed. Mr. Hoover promised a no–skim–bust policy. Let's not stir enmity. Why stir publicity? Why sully the Count and his kingdom?

Littell digressed. Littell said Drac has a plan. He'll hit Vegas in late November.

The red tape will clear. He'll have his cash. He'll storm the DI then. He's booked a floor. He'll bring his slaves. They'll bring his blood and dope.

Mr. Hoover laughed. Mr. Hoover probed:

I pulled some bugs. I pulled some taps. A House Committee made me. I got a tip: Lyle Holly braced Bobby. Lyle sent him a posthumous "confession."

Littell feigned shock: Not Lyle H.! Not our WHITE RABBIT!

Mr. Hoover probed. Mr. Hoover ranted. Mr. Hoover steamed. He disdained WHITE and CRUSADER. He dissected their "twin moral voids." He blasphemed WHITE the betrayer.

Littell assessed the rant. Littell concluded: He doesn't suspect me/he buys the "confession"/he buys the "betrayal" that way.

Mr. Hoover digressed. Mr. Hoover attacked Dr. King. His HATE showed. His HATE beamed. His HATE crescendoed.

Littell said let me help. You know I have documents. They detail my "Mob donations."

Mr. Hoover said no. Mr. Hoover said it's too little. Mr. Hoover said it's much too late.

Littell heard hate. Littell heard resolve. Littell knew this: He's got new plans. He'll escalate.

Mr. Hoover signed off. Mr. Hoover omitted:

Mail-fraud news. News per one arm of BLACK RABBIT. A big success/gloat-worthy. A telling omission.

Littell translated said omission. Littell knew this:

He's got new plans. He'll escalate.

Wait. Do nothing. Let his hate show. Let his hate self-indict.

The Boys had plans. It's time for relocation—Sam G. leaves custody.

Littell drove him home. Sam packed his bags. They flew to Mexico City. Sam bought knick-knacks. Sam bought a house. Sam discussed his schemes.

We buy the '68 election. We throw it to *our* candidate. He takes our cash. He bows. He obeys. He pardons Jimmy Hoffa. He lets us expand. He ignores our colonizations.

We move south. We colonize. We plant our casinos. Let us thrive—don't fuck with said colonies—right- *or* left-wing.

Memo: *We* buy the candidate. *We* buy the bulk of him. Drac supplies 25%. We collude. Drac gets perks—time will determine which or what.

Jimmy's through. He's dead on appeals. He'll be jailed next spring. Let him stew. Buy a candidate. Elect him.

Said candidate waits. Said candidate pardons Jimmy. We get one pardon. We get one colony policy—per nations right- *or* left-wing.

Cuba was left-wing. They couldn't plant casinos there. Their plant targets were all *right*-wing. Think back. Go back three years—fall '63.

The hit plan's on. The Boys are mad. The Boys want their Cuban casinos. They tried to kill Castro. They indulged covert ops. They failed.

Sam enlists Santo. Santo lures Johnny Rosselli. They brace the Beard. They make nice—*please* return our casinos. The Beard says no. They clip Jack. The world rocks and sways.

Then to now—plans crass and audacious.

Like the war—Big Pete's preferred misalliance.

He met Barb for lunch. They met once a week. They discussed it. Barb hated the war. Barb felt new love for Bobby. Barb assailed Pete.

Barb talked political. Barb talked lounge gossip and segued. Barb said "exploitation." Barb said "mass murder" and "genocide."

Barb was moody. Barb took pills. Barb anesthetized. They discussed Pete's business. They discussed Pete's compartments.

Barb temporized. Barb straddled fences. Barb compartmentalized: I love Pete/I hate Pete's business/I hate Pete's war.

He loved her. Wayne loved her. She knew it. All men loved her. He told her. She knew it.

She said I like it. She said I hate it. She said I outgrew it late.

She knew Jane left him. She didn't know details. She teased him per Janice. He told her flat-out. He played it blunt—Janice was diversion.

Janice was sex. Janice was style. Janice was will bravura.

Wayne Senior beat her. Janice still limped. Janice still got cramps. Janice still shot scratch golf. Janice still played A-club tennis.

She charged the net. She limped. She cramped. She slammed shots. She made points. She won by attrition.

She rebuffed Mormon goons. Said goons were putting feelers out. Wayne Senior misses Wayne Junior.

She replied one way. Her words were Get Fucked. It was her one response verbatim.

He liked her. He loved Barb. He loved Jane.

Barb got dreamy looks. She hid from Pete then. He envied her looks. He envied her sedation.

DOCUMENT INSERT: 10/30/66.
Internal memorandum. Topic: OPERATION BLACK RABBIT.
To: BLUE RABBIT. From: Director. Marked: ''Stage-1
Covert''/''Eyes Only''/''Read and Burn.''

BLUE RABBIT,
I have been digesting my July phone call to
CRUSADER RABBIT for some time. I could not read his
response to my mention of WHITE RABBIT's alleged
confession, and perceived his mental state to be
problematic.

WHITE RABBIT was, of course, your brother. I have
given your repeated assertions that his confession
was fabricated considerable thought. You have stated
that CRUSADER RABBIT is the only one in our purview
capable of such a fabrication, and I cannot in any way
dispute that assessment.

CRUSADER RABBIT troubles me. As you have noted, his
paramour, Arden Breen/Jane Fentress, disappeared
last October and has presumably been killed by
members of organized crime. I suspect that her
absence and assuredly grisly fate have contributed
to CRUSADER RABBIT's funk. You have often
characterized CRUSADER RABBIT as a ''wimp,'' but
I would add that his propensity for kamikaze action
marks him as the world's most dangerous wimp.

All told, I think we should reinstate our spot-
surveillance of CRUSADER RABBIT and reinstate our
Trash and Mail Covers. These actions will supplant
our decision to exclude him from all aspects of
OPERATION BLACK RABBIT.

Per the ''Shakedown'' adjunct:
I veto your recommendation that we target RED RABBIT.
RED RABBIT will simply be too wary of entrapment.

The target will be PINK RABBIT. His heedless

pursuit of homosexual encounters marks him as more
suitable and vulnerable.

BIG RABBIT seems to have recovered from his heart
attack. Contact him by 12/1/66.

DOCUMENT INSERT: 11/2/66.
Miami Herald headline:
KING DECRIES ''IMPERIALISTIC'' WAR IN VIETNAM

DOCUMENT INSERT: 11/4/66.
Denver Post-Dispatch headline and subhead:
HOFFA WITH MARCH PRISON DATE
APPEAL LAWYERS GLUM

DOCUMENT INSERT: 11/12/66.
Atlanta Constitution subhead:
WAR A ''MORAL OUTRAGE,'' KING DECLARES IN SPEECH

DOCUMENT INSERT: 11/16/66.
Los Angeles Examiner subhead:
NO '68 PREZ'L PLANS, RFK TELLS PRESS

DOCUMENT INSERT: 11/17/66.
San Francisco Chronicle subhead:
''DRAFT KENNEDY'' MOVEMENT GROWING DESPITE
SENATOR'S STATED RELUCTANCE

DOCUMENT INSERT: 11/18/66.
Chicago Sun-Times headline and subhead:
KING SPEAKS TO DRAFT RESISTANCE WORKSHOP
HOOVER CALLS CIVIL-RIGHTS LEADER ''COMMUNIST
PAWN''

DOCUMENT INSERT: 11/23/66.
Washington Post subhead:
BACKLASH ON HOOVER FOR ANTI-KING REMARKS

DOCUMENT INSERT: 11/24/66.
Boston Globe subhead:
HOWARD HUGHES' BIZARRE CROSS-COUNTRY TRAIN RIDE

DOCUMENT INSERT: 11/25/66.
Las Vegas Sun headline and subhead:
HUGHES TRAIN EN ROUTE
WHAT DOES BILLIONAIRE RECLUSE BODE FOR LAS VEGAS?

PART FIVE

INCURSION

(November 27, 1966–March 18, 1968)

93

(Las Vegas, 11/27/66)

HE'S COMING.

He's Mr. Big. He's Howard Hughes. He's the Count of Las Vegas.

Littell watched.

He joined newsmen. He joined camera crews. He joined Joe Vegas. Word leaked. The Count's coming. The train station—11:00 P.M.

He's coming. Check track 14. Behold the Drac Express.

The platform rocked. Newsmen cliqued up. Grips wheeled arc lights. Camera guys lugged film.

Littell watched.

He'd braced Drac's Mormons. They talked renovation. They said they'd hit the DI. They said they'd Draculized. They germ-proofed the penthouse. They lugged freezers in. They stocked snacks and treats.

Snow cones/pizza/candy bars. Demerol/codeine/Dilaudid.

They said we launch soon. We negotiate and bargain. We *buy* the DI. The Boys said *we* launch soon. *We* bargain and set the price.

It's large. Drac will balk. Drac will pout. Drac will pay. Drac will stump for a Mormon hegemony. Drac will shout: Mormons must run my casino!

The Boys will renavigate. The Boys will plot. The Boys will decree: Littell must brace Wayne Tedrow Senior.

They'll talk. *They'll* bargain. Small talk will run cruel. Wayne Senior will tweak him on Janice.

The platform shook. The rails shook. A train whistle blew.

He's coming.

A cop van pulled up. Cops got out. Cops hauled equipment. A cop pushed a gurney. A cop wheeled a tent. A cop slung oxygen cans.

Cops shoved newsmen. Cops shoved citizens. Cops pulled cameras back. Newsmen pushed. Newsmen jockeyed. Newsmen shoved back.

Train lights coming—that whistle full blast.

Littell stood tiptoed. A kid jostled him. Littell stepped back. Littell got perspective.

Sparks flew. The train braked. The train stopped and sat. The crowd shoved. Flashbulbs popped. The crowd scattered.

They hit the train. They cupped their eyes. They peeped window slats. Doors cranked open—up and back—the crowd tailed the cop with the gurney.

Littell laughed. Littell knew Drac strategy. Littell knew diversions.

Look:

There's gurney 2. There's tent 2. They're *all* the way back.

Mormons stepped out. Mormons signaled. Mormons dropped a ramp. Mormons formed a cordon. Mormons pushed a wheelchair. Mormons wheeled Drac.

He's tall. He's thin. He's wearing a Kleenex-box hat.

94

(Las Vegas, 11/27/66)

HE'S COMING.

He's off the train. He's in the car. He's got this dumb hat.

Wayne walked the Dl. The floor buzzed electric. Ghouls circulated. Wayne logged rumors.

He's overdue. He's due soon. He's due *now*. He's got plane-crash scars. He's got skin disease. He's got neck bolts like Frankenstein.

Ghouls positioned. Ghouls vultured. Ghouls swarmed the casino. Ghouls stood on chairs. Ghouls slung cameras. Ghouls perched with autograph books.

Ghouls swarmed outside. Wayne saw Barb there. Glass walls provided views. Barb saw Wayne. Barb waved. Wayne waved back.

Ghouls prowled. Hotel fuzz prowled. Somebody yelled, "Limos!" Somebody yelled, "*Him!*"

Ghouls whooped. Ghouls dispersed. Ghouls ran outside.

Wayne checked the glass walls. Wayne caught a view.

He saw cops. He saw limos. He saw a mock Howard Hughes. He made him. He *popped* him—back in '62.

He hosted a kid's show. He flashed his dick. He groped prepubescents. Cops called him "Chester the Molester."

Ghouls jumped him. Chester posed for pix magnanimous. Chester signed autographs. A limo eased by. A window went down. Wayne caught a blip: White hair/dead eyes/dumb hat.

Somebody yelled, "He's a fake!" The ghouls up and ran. The ghouls chased the limo.

Barb walked inside. Wayne saw her. Wayne detoured up.

"Aren't you working tonight?"

Barb laughed. "I could ask you the same thing."

Wayne smiled. "I was thinking of Pete and Ward, and how this whole thing started."

Barb yawned. "Tell me over coffee, all right?"

A ghoul ran by. They dodged him. They walked to the bar. They grabbed seats and faced the casino.

A waitress showed. Barb cued her. She brought coffee fast. The floor was slow. Chester shot craps. Ghouls meandered through.

Barb sipped coffee. "It's been months, and I still want a cigarette."

"Not like Pete does."

Chester rolled. Chester crapped out. Chester blew money.

Barb watched him. "There's these secrets that people know."

"Not *everyone*."

Barb unrolled her napkin. Barb twirled her spoon.

"To start, there's a certain city in Texas. Then there's the plans the Outfit has for Mr. Hughes."

Wayne smiled. "Tell me some secrets I don't know."

"For instance?"

"Come on. Pete has half the rooms in Vegas bugged."

Barb twirled her knife. "All right. Donkey Dom's shacked at the Cavern. He's four nights in with Sal Mineo, and they haven't left the suite. Bellboys are bringing them poppers and K-Y. Pete's wondering how long it can last."

Wayne laughed. Wayne checked the floor. Chester rolled. Chester made his point. Chester made money.

Barb smiled. Barb walked. Barb hit the john. Ghouls swarmed Chester. Chester-Hughes magnetized.

Chester sponged love. Chester bowed magnanimous. Chester posed for pix.

Barb walked back. Barb walked unsteady. She sat down. Her lids dipped. Her eyes went smack-back.

She smiled. She twirled her knife. Wayne slapped her. She gripped the knife. She stabbed down. She missed Wayne's hands.

Wayne slapped her. Barb stabbed down. The blade hit the table. It stuck. It twanged. The knife held.

Barb touched her cheek. Barb rubbed her eyes. Barb shot some tears.

Wayne grabbed her hands. Wayne bent her arms. Wayne jerked her head low.

"You're strung out. You're sticking shit up your nose and fucking over Pete every time you do it. You think you're high and mighty because you hate the war and Pete's business, but it's just a bullshit excuse, because you're a no-talent lounge chick with a dope habit and limited fucking—"

Barb jerked her hands. Barb grabbed the knife. Wayne slapped her. She dropped the knife. She rubbed her cheek. She wiped her eyes.

Wayne touched her hair. "I love you. I'm not going to let you fuck yourself over without a fight."

Barb stood up. Barb wiped her eyes. Barb walked off smack-back unsteady.

Floorshow:

Chester performed. Crowds cliqued up—all drunks and geeks. Chester posed. Chester huckstered Las Vegas. Chester ran airplane crash riffs.

Newsmen bopped by. Newsmen yukked. Fuck you—you're that kids-show freak.

Wayne watched. Wayne scoped the floor.

He sipped bourbon. He sulked. He sniffed Barb's napkin. He smelled her hand cream. He smelled her bath oil.

Chester signed autographs. Chester riffed on Jane Russell's breasts. Chester eyed little kids.

Wayne sipped bourbon. His thoughts raced. He saw Janice walk by. She still limped. She still strutted. Her gray streak still glowed.

She walked the floor. She fed baby slots. She blew money. She nailed a jackpot. She scooped coins. She tithed a slot-machine bum.

The bum groveled. The bum gave thanks. The bum wore mismatched shoes. The bum braced a baby slot. The bum yanked the arm. The bum blew his dole.

He shrugged. He regrouped. He panhandled. He hit up Chester. Chester said, "Fuck you."

Janice limped. Janice strolled. Janice left Wayne's view. She's out the back door now—dig that golf-course view.

She's heading to Ward's suite. It's a late-night rendezvous.

Wayne sniffed the napkin. Wayne smelled Barb. Wayne got a Janice jolt. His thoughts raced. He vibed rendezvous.

He drove straight out. The road dipped. He drove eighty-proof. He walked straight in. He grabbed a jug off the bar. He walked straight through.

There's the deck. There's Wayne Senior. He's close to old now. He's sixty-plus. He's old as brand-new.

He's got the same grin. He's got the same chair. He's got the same view.

"You drink from the bottle now. Two years away gets me that."

Wayne grabbed a footstool. "You make it sound like it's the only thing I've learned."

"Not hardly. I get reports, so I know there's more."

Wayne smiled. "You've been putting out feelers."

"You've been rejecting them."

"I guess the time wasn't right."

Wayne Senior smiled. "Howard Hughes and my son the same evening. Be still, my heart."

The stool sat low. Wayne looked straight up.

"Don't labor it. It's just a coincidence."

"No, it's a confluence. Bondurant precipitates Hughes. Hughes means that Ward Littell will be begging favors soon."

Wayne heard gunshots due north. Call it cop familiar. Broke gambler blows town. Broke gambler unwinds.

"Ward doesn't beg. You should know that."

"You're leading me, son. You're trying to get me to praise your ex-lawyer."

Wayne shook his head. "I'm just trying to steer the conversation."

Wayne Senior toed the footstool. Wayne Senior toed Wayne's knee.

"Shitfire. What's a father-son reunion without a few blunt questions?"

Wayne stood up. Wayne stretched. Wayne kicked the stool.

"How's the hate business?"

"Shitfire. You're more of a hater than I ever was."

"Come on, answer the question."

"All right. I've relinquished my hate-tract business, in order to serve the cause of changing times at a higher level."

Wayne smiled. "I see Mr. Hoover's hand."

"You see twenty-twenty, which tells me the years have not dulled your—"

"Come on, *tell* me."

Wayne Senior twirled his cane. "I've been working with your old chums Bob Relyea and Dwight Holly. We've derailed some of the most outlandish overhaters in the whole of Dixie."

Wayne slugged bourbon. Wayne sucked dregs. Wayne killed the jug.

"Keep going. I like the 'overhaters' part."

Wayne Senior smiled. "You should. There's hating smart and hating dumb, and you've never learned the difference."

Wayne smiled. "Maybe I've been waiting for you to explain it."

Wayne Senior lit a cigarette—gold-filigreed.

"I fully believe that coloreds should be allowed to vote and have equal rights, which will serve to increase their collective intelligence and inure them to demagogues like Martin Luther King and Robert Kennedy. Your pharmaceutical endeavor gives them the sedation that most of them want and insulates them from the fatuous rhetoric of our era. My policemen friends tell me that colored crime in white Las Vegas has not increased appreciably since your operation began, and your operation serves to isolate coloreds on their side of town, where they would much rather be anyway."

Wayne stretched. Wayne looked north. Wayne checked the Strip view.

Wayne Senior blew smoke rings. "You're looking pensive. I was gearing up for a smart answer."

"I'm all out."

"I got you at the right time, then."

"In a sense, yeah."

"Tell me about Vietnam."

Wayne shrugged. "It's futile bullshit."

"Yes, but you love it."

Wayne grabbed the cane. Wayne twirled it. Wayne did dips. Wayne did spins. Wayne did curlicues.

Wayne Senior snatched it. "Look at me, son. Look at me while I say this one thing."

Look: you've got *his* face. Look: you've got *his* eyes.

Wayne Senior dropped the cane. Wayne Senior grabbed his hands. Wayne Senior squeezed them way tight.

"I'm sorry for Dallas, son. It's the one thing in this life I am truly sorry for."

Look—he *means* it—those eyes getting wet.

Wayne smiled. "There's times when I think I was born there."

"Are you grateful?"

Wayne torqued his hands free. Wayne shook some blood in. Wayne cracked his thumbs.

"Don't press me. Don't make me regret coming out."

Wayne Senior stubbed his cigarette. The ashtray jumped. His hand shook.

"Have you killed Wendell Durfee?"

"I haven't found him."

"Do you know—"

"I think he's in L.A."

"I know some LAPD men. They could issue a covert APB."

Wayne shook his head. "This is mine. Don't press me."

Gunshots popped—ten o'clock/northwest.

Wayne said, "I'm sorry for Janice."

Wayne Senior laughed. Wayne Senior howled. Wayne Senior roared shitfire.

"My son fucks my wife and tells me he's sorry. Excuse me for laughing and saying I don't care, but I always loved him more."

Look—wet eyes and laugh lines—he *means* it.

A breeze stirred. Cold air whipped. Wayne prickled.

Wayne Senior coughed. "Will you entertain an offer?"

"I'll listen."

"Dwight Holly's going to be running some very sophisticated civil-rights ops. You'd be a perfect backup man."

Wayne smiled. "Dwight hates me. You know that."

"Dwight's a smart hater. He knows how you hate, and I'm sure he knows how useful you could be."

Wayne cracked his thumbs. "I only hate the bad ones. I'm not some Klan fuck who gets his rocks off bombing churches."

Wayne Senior stood up. "You could run high-level ops. You know how the world works and how to keep things stable. You could get all this risky business out of your system, hitch your star to the right people and do some very exciting things."

Wayne shut his eyes. Wayne ran signs: *Hate/Love/Work*.

"You're waxing pensive, son. You've got your daddy's nose for opportunity."

Wayne said, "Don't press me. You'll fuck it all up."

95

(Las Vegas, 11/28/66)

THE CAT PROWLED. The bed was his turf.

He clawed the headboard. He clawed the sheets. He clawed Pete's pillow. Pete woke up. Pete kissed Barb. Pete saw this big bruise.

He sacked out early. Barb sacked out late. He missed her coming in.

He touched her hair. He kissed the bruise. The doorbell rang—Barb slept through it.

Shit—7:40 A.M.

Pete got up. Pete put a robe on. Pete walked out and popped the door. Shit—it's Fred Turentine.

Frizzy-haired Freddy—fucked-up and frazzled. In *his* robe. In fuzzy slippers. In fucking shock.

With a tape rig. With a tape. With the jit-jit-jit-jitters.

Pete pulled him inside. Pete grabbed his gear. Pete shut the door. Fred got his sea legs. Fred quashed his shit-shakes and jitters.

"I was at the listening post. I was running last night's tapes off the swinger suites. I heard this grief with Dom and Sal Mineo."

Hold on. What's—

Pete cleared chair space. Pete laid the gear out. Pete plugged the rig in. Pete looped the tape.

He hit the volume. He hit Play. He heard static hiss. He heard timed beeps—no voice to activate.

There—Sal's voice/the on-click/we activate.

"Dom . . . hey . . . you hump, that's my wall—"

Dom: ". . . not what you . . . just looking . . . that phone numb—"

Sal: "You hump. You fucking sissy cocksucker."

Dom: "*You're* the cocksucker. You suck my big *braciol'* every chance you get, you fucking has-been cock—"

Crash sounds/breath sounds/clatters. Kitchen noise/drawer noise/glass shatters.

Clatters. *Knife* pings. "Sal no no no." Yelps/gurgles/choked breath.

Silence. Timed beeps. Static. Sobs. Drag sounds. Clatters.

Sal: "Please please please. God please please please."

Sobs. Heaves. Breath and prayers—this papal shit: "O my God I am heartily sorry for having offended Thee. I detest all my sins because I dread the loss of—"

Pete got prickles. His balls contracted. His neck hair stood up. He hit Stop. He grabbed his pass keys. He grabbed his piece.

He walked outside. He checked the lot. He scoped the bungalow suites. 8:00 A.M./cars parked/all quiet.

Sal flew to Vegas. Dom drove to their tryst. Dom always drove to his shack jobs.

Dom's T-Bird: Gone.

Pete walked over. Easy now—there's the fuck pad. Easy now—jiggle the door.

He did it. The lock held stiff. He pulled his keys. He unlocked the door. He walked in. He saw:

Pink carpets—deep shag—blood-spritzed. Pizza boxes. Beer cans. Pizza crusts on plates. Dumped chairs. Dumped tables. White walls with red marks scrubbed pink.

Pete shut the door. Pete hit the kitchen. Pete checked the sink.

Ajax. Sponge. Clogged drain meat. *Organ* meat—hair-clotted—wop skintone meat.

Queers killed butch. Queers killed operatic. Queers killed *buon gusto*.

Pete checked the bathroom.

No shower curtain/knives in the toilet/knives in the sink. Floor dots—loose bristles—bath mats scrubbed pink.

A thumbprint on a wall. Print-points still visible. Print whorls scrubbed red into pink.

Pete walked the suite. Pete nailed the damage. Pete got the

gist. Pete locked up. Pete walked back. Pete unlocked his suite.

There's Fred T.

He's slugging Jack Daniel's. He's noshing corn chips. He's fine now. He's *de*shocked. He's blitzed.

Fred laughed. Fred dribbled Black Jack. Fred spewed corn chips.

"I see potential in this. Sal's an Academy Award nominee."

Pete pulled drawers. Pete grabbed his Polaroid. Pete snatched film and loaded it in.

Fred said, "I hope he saved Dom's pecker. I could use a transplant."

Barb was up. Pete heard her. Pete heard her fluff sheets.

Fred said, "I never liked Dom. He had the arrogance that always complements a big dick."

Pete grabbed him. Pete pinned his wrists.

"Talk to Barb. Keep her here while I take some pictures."

"Pete . . . Jesus . . . come on . . . I'm on your side."

Pete torqued his wrists. "Keep your mouth shut while I work this. I don't want any shit coming back to the Cavern."

"Pete, Pete, Pete. You know me. You know I am the Pharaoh's own fucking sphinx."

Pete let him go. Pete walked out. Pete jogged through the lot. Pete rehit the suite.

He unlocked it. He stepped in. He shot pix. Polaroids—twelve color prints.

He got the thumbprint. He got the bloodstains. He got the meat. He got the pink rugs. He got the knives. He got the spritz.

Pete shot twelve photos. The camera developed them. The camera made sounds. The camera cranked wet prints.

He grid-searched. He reloaded. He shot more pix:

Dom's thumb—drain-trapped—stuck between grates. A dildo/a hash pipe/hash dregs.

He dried the prints. He spread them out on a sofa. He grabbed the phone. He dialed L.A. direct.

Three rings—be *there*—

"This is Otash."

"It's Pete, Freddy."

Otash laughed. "I thought you were pissed at me. The Littell thing, remember?"

Pete coughed. His chest bipped. His pulse raced.

"I'm the forgiving type."

Otash yukked. "You're a lying frog fuck, but I'll let it go for old times' sake."

Pete coughed. His chest bipped. His pulse raced.

"Do you know Sal Mineo?"

"Yeah, I know Sal. I pulled him out of some grief with some high-school quiff."

"He's in the shit again. It's a two-man job, and I'll explain when I see you."

Otash whistled. "He's in Vegas?"

"I think he's driving back to L.A."

"Money?"

"We'll muscle him and work something out."

"When?"

"I'll catch a noon flight."

"My office, then. And bring some coin in case Sal craps out."

Pete hung up. The door jiggled. Lock tumblers clicked. Barb walked in. Pete said, "Shit."

Barb looked around. Barb saw things. Barb caught the drift. She toed a rug stain. She bent down. She pinched fiber tufts. She sniffed her fingers. She made a face. She said, "Shit."

Pete watched her. Barb rubbed her cheek. She looked around. She saw the wall stains. She saw the pix.

She studied them. She eyeball-cruised all twenty-four. She looked at Pete.

"Sal or Dom? Fred wouldn't say."

Pete stood up. His pulse raced. He grabbed a chair. He steadied in. He checked out Barb's cheek.

"What happened to your face?"

Barb winced. "Wayne did a good job of getting my attention."

Pete gripped the chair. Pete dug his hands in. Pete ripped fabric free.

Barb said, "I asked for it. I've asked for it from you, but Wayne cares about me in a different way, and he sees things you don't."

Pete threw the chair. It hit a wall. It gouged pink bloodstains.

"You're mine. Nobody's got the right to care for you, and nobody's seen things in you that I didn't see first."

Barb looked at Pete. Barb scoped the wall stains behind him. Barb closed her eyes. Barb ran. Barb ran straight past Pete.

Otash said, "Dom's in the trunk. I'll lay you six to one."

Car surveillance—Fred O.'s car—the seats pushed way back. Fred O.'s farts and Fred O.'s cologne.

They lounged. They scoped Dom's T-Bird. They scoped Sal's apartment house.

Pete said, "You're on. I say he dumped him in the desert."

Otash lit a cigarette. Smoke billowed. Pete caught the backdraft.

Barb ran. He let her. She'd run straight back. Wayne hit her. Wayne loved her. Wayne's fucking cork snapped. Wayne loved weird. Wayne was fucked up. Wayne was woman-fucked. Wayne gets muscled soon. Wayne gets lectured soon. Wayne's cork gets desnapped.

Pete yawned. Pete stretched. Pete craved Fred O.'s cigarettes.

He scrubbed the suite. He wiped the walls. He burned the rugs. He called Dom's bun boy. He played dumb. He said where's Dom at? The geek said, "Huh?" The geek didn't know. The geek knew shit from Shinola.

He talked to his bellboys. They never saw Sal. Dom signed all the room-service chits. Dom booked the suite. That was good. That played their way.

Otash said, "Sal's on the skids. What kind of movie star lives in a fucking apartment?"

Pete scoped the street. We're in West Hollywood—the fucking Swish Alps.

"You mean what kind of coin can he have?"

Otash picked his nose. "Yeah, after he spends it all on fruit hustlers and dope."

Pete cracked his knuckles. "He's got a gold Rolex."

"That'll do for a start."

The sky went dark. Rain hit. Otash rolled his window up.

"You want to hear my one concern? That he's out spilling his guts to some faggot priest or the queens at the Gold Cup."

Pete cracked his thumbs. "He's out drinking. I'll give you that."

"Dom's in the trunk. I can smell his rancid ass from here."

"The desert. A hundred says so."

"You're on."

Pete peeled off a C-note. A car pulled up. Pete made the paint job—Sal's '64 Ford.

Sal parked. Sal got out. Sal walked inside. Pete cued Otash—we roll on ten.

They ticked down. They ticked slow. They hit ten. They got out. They hauled. They ran up. They made the front door. They made the main hallway.

There's Sal. He's at *his* door. He's got his mail. He's got his key.

He saw them. He dropped his mail. He fumbled his key. They ran up. Pete frisked him. Otash grabbed his key.

He popped the door. He shoved Sal in. Pete grabbed a chair. Pete shoved Sal down. Otash pried his watch off.

"This and half your pay for your next picture. Cheap for what it gets you."

Brash Sal: "This is a gag, right? The Friars Club sent you."

Pete said, "You know what it is."

Bold Sal: "Yeah. It's a fraternity stunt. You and Freddy joined Chi Alpha Omega."

Otash buffed the Rolex. "Think back, *paisan*. You'll put it together."

Wise Sal: "I get it. I split the Cavern and didn't pay the bill. You're the collection agency."

Otash said, "The Cavern. That's a start."

Cool Sal: "I get it now. I made a bit of a mess. You want a damage deposit."

Pete said, "He's getting warm."

Otash said, "He'll be hot in two seconds."

Calm Sal: "You guys make a good team. The beefcake Abbott and Costello."

Pete sighed. "The time is upon us."

Otash sighed. "Yeah, just when I started digging on the repartee."

Smart Sal: "That's a big word, Freddy. You must have learned it in goon school."

Pete said, "The trunk or the desert?"

Otash said, "We've got a bet. I say he's outside right now."

Pete said, "The desert, right? You pulled off outside Vegas."

Otash said, "There's always Griffith Park. You've got all those hills and caves."

Pete said, "I saw one of Dom's movies. That thing had to be a yard long."

Brave Sal: "Hills, yards, shit. You're talking Sanskrit."

Pete hummed "The Man I Love." Otash flopped a limp wrist.

Sharp Sal: "I didn't think you guys were that way. Jesus, that's a revelation."

Pete sighed. Otash sighed. Pete picked Sal up. Pete slapped him. Pete dropped him.

Sal spit a tooth out. Said tooth hit Pete's coat. Otash slapped Sal. Otash wore signet rings. Otash laid cuts.

Sal wiped his face. Sal blew his nose. Sal made a mess.

Pete said, "This can all go away. I work the Vegas end, Freddy watchdogs you here. I don't want bad publicity at the Cavern, you don't want a manslaughter bounce."

Sal wiped his nose. Otash supplied a hankie. Pete pulled his photos. Pete tossed them. Pete hit Sal's lap.

Dig that disarray. Dig that drain hair. Dig that blood. Dig that severed thumb.

Sal dabbed his cuts. Sal checked the pix. Sal went gray-green.

"You know, I really liked him. He was bad, but he had this sweet side."

Otash rubbed his knuckles. Otash wiped his rings.

"Us or the fuzz?"

Sal said, "You."

Otash said, "Where is he?"

Sal said, "In the trunk."

Otash drew a dollar sign. Pete paid off—the trunk/six to one.

He flew home. The ride bumped. He worried Barb and Wayne.

Barb sniffed white horse. Wayne knew it. Wayne grieved. Wayne loves Barb. Wayne eschews women. Wayne's a watcher. Wayne's a martyr. Wayne's woman-fucked.

Warn Wayne. Tell Barb soft: *I know you—just me*.

The plane landed. Vegas glowed radioactive. Pete cabbed to the Cavern. Pete unlocked the suite.

The cat jumped him. He picked him up. He kissed him. He saw the note.

It's flat on the wall. It's taped high. It's his eye-level.

Pete,
 I'm leaving you for a while to sort some things out.
I'm not hiding; I'll be staying at my sister's house in
Sparta. I need to get away from Vegas and figure out a
way to be with you as long as you're doing the things that
you do. You're not the only one who knows me, but
you're the only one I love.

                                        Barb

Pete tore the note up. Pete kicked walls and shelves. Pete hugged the cat. Pete let the cat claw his shirt.

96

(Las Vegas, 11/29/66)

MOE DALITZ SAID, "Look."

Littell checked the window. Littell saw nuts below. Ten floors down. Nuts with cameras. Nuts with kids in tow.

Moe said, "They think Hughes sleeps in a coffin. They figure he'll wake up at dusk and sign autographs in his cape."

Littell laughed. Littell went ssshhh. Hush now—biz-in-progress.

Ten yards up. Two tables—Mormons meet front men.

Moe grinned. "It's my fucking hotel and my fucking king-size conference room. I'm supposed to whisper in my own joint?"

A Mormon glanced over. Moe smiled and waved.

"Goyishe shitheels. Mormons are roughly synonymous with the Ku Klux Klan."

Littell smiled. Littell steered Moe. They walked ten yards. They bypassed three tables.

"Would you like an update?"

Moe rolled his eyes. "Tell me. Use words of one syllable only."

"Short and sweet, then. I think we'll get our price. They're discussing undistributed profits tax now."

Moe smiled. Moe steered Littell. They walked ten yards. They bypassed three tables.

"I know you don't like him, but that well-known goyishe shit-heel Wayne Tedrow Senior is essential to our plans. We need his union, and we need to keep his ex-buddies and Mormons in general running skim on those charter flights. Now, we've got the papers and TV bribed to do this 'Hughes is cleaning out Mob influence in Vegas' number, which makes me think we should recruit some *more* clean Mormon skim guys, because Hughes will insist on hiring Mormons to work the key fucking managerial positions, and I do not want any old-line skim people hanging around looking conspicuous when we can have some well-scrubbed shitheel Mormons, *especially* since the skim ante is about to go way up."

Littell brainstormed. Littell checked the window. He saw nut swarms. He saw newsmen. He saw clowns with snack carts.

"The publicity heat will be going up, too."

Moe lit a cigarette. Moe popped digitalis.

"Tell me what you're thinking. Go to two syllables if you have to."

Littell brainstormed—one quick brain draft. Propose it/ convince Moe/refine the draft. Gift Mr. Hoover/earn a gift reciprocal/earn back to BLACK RABBIT.

Moe rolled his eyes. "A trance you're in. Like the Vegas sun finally got to your head."

Littell coughed. "Are you still buffered from your old-line skim people?"

"The ones we replaced? The ones we shitcanned for the Mormons?"

"Right."

Moe rolled his eyes. "We always buffer. It's how we survive."

Littell smiled. "Let's give some of them up to the Feds, as soon as Mr. Hughes takes over a few hotels. It will buttress our publicity campaign, it will make Mr. Hoover happy, it will tie the Feds here up in litigation."

Moe dropped his cigarette. Moe singed deep-pile carpet. Moe toed the butt flat.

"I like it. I like all deals that fuck disenfranchised personnel."

"I'll call Mr. Hoover."

"You do that. You say hi and give him our best regards, in your best lawyer way."

Voices boomed eight tables up—tax rates/tax incentives. Moe smiled. Moe steered Littell. They walked eight yards. They bypassed two tables.

"I know you been through this with Carlos and Sam, but I want you to hear it from my perspective, which is we do not want a fucking repeat of the 1960 election. We want to back a strong guy who'll come down hard on all this agitation and civil unrest and stand firm in Vietnam, as well as leave us the fuck alone. Now, per the aforementioned goyishe shitheel Wayne Tedrow Senior, let me say this. We've heard that he's no longer schlepping hate pamphlets, that he's cleaned up the seedier aspects of his act, and that him and his Mormons are getting tight with that well-known political retread Richard M. Nixon, who has always hated the Reds a good deal more than he's hated the so-called Mafia. We want you to talk to Wayne Senior and get an indication as to whether Nixon will run, and if he says yes, you know what we want and what we're willing to pay."

Voices boomed ten tables up—tax nuts/tax credits.

Littell coughed. "I'll call him when I get a—"

"You call him in the vicinity of the next five minutes. You meet him and lay it out. You get him to plant the seed with the Nixon people, and you tell him *you'll* be the guy to sit down with Nixon, if and when that shifty cocksucker runs."

Littell said, "Jesus Christ."

Moe said, "Your goyishe savior. A presidential cat in his own right."

Voices boomed ten tables up—Negro hygiene/Negro sedation.

The T-Bird—hole 10.

Play crawled. Duffers hacked. Oldsters bumped carts. Littell sipped club soda. Littell watched hole 9.

Women dumped shots. Women blew putts. Women sprayed sand. Ball beaters all—no Janice types.

He called Wayne Senior. He made the meet. He called Mr. Hoover. He got an aide. He promised news. He promised hard data. Mr. Hoover was out. The aide said he'd find him. The aide called back. The aide said:

Mr. Hoover's busy. Talk to SA Dwight Holly—he's in Vegas now.

Littell agreed. Littell assessed.

Mr. Hoover loves Dwight. Dwight's *his* assessor. Dwight will see you and assess. Work Dwight/work said assessment/work back to BLACK RABBIT.

A breeze strafed through. Golfers blew shots. Putts blew way wide. Littell brainstormed. Littell watched hole 9.

Work Wayne Senior. Glean data. His union broke laws. His union ignored civil-rights codes. Glean said data. Leak it to Bobby. Maybe now/maybe later/maybe '68.

He'd be free. He'd be "retired." Bobby might run for Prez. Funnel the leaks/buffer the leaks/cloak the source disclosure.

Littell watched hole 9. Wayne Senior played up.

He dumped his approach. He hit the trap. He chipped out wide. He three-putted. He laughed. He left his golf pals.

He walked over brisk. Littell arranged a lawn chair.

"Hello, Ward."

"Mr. Tedrow."

Wayne Senior leaned on the chair. "Things run dense with you. Every word has its meaning."

"I'll state my case briefly. I'll have you back on the tee in five minutes."

Wayne Senior smirked. Wayne Senior grinned aw-shucks.

"I thought we might work at a thaw. We could commiserate over a certain woman and go from there."

Littell shook his head. "I don't kiss and tell."

"That's a shame, because Janice certainly does."

A ball shanked close. Wayne Senior ducked.

Littell said, "My people will be needing some men to work at Mr. Hughes' hotels, along with some new couriers. I'd like to go through your union files and look for prospects."

Wayne Senior twirled his putter. "*I'll* pick the men. The last time we did business, my men quit the union and I lost my percentage."

Littell smiled. "I reinstated it."

"You reinstated it reluctantly, and you're the last man on God's green earth that I'd let in my files. Dwight Holly thinks you're a bad man to trust with information, and I would guess that Mr. Hoover concurs."

Littell cleaned his glasses. Wayne Senior blurred.

"I was told that you've become friends with Richard Nixon."

"Dick and I are getting close, yes."

"Do you think he'll run in '68?"

"I'm sure he will. He'd prefer to run against Johnson or Humphrey, but he'll buck the younger Kennedy if he has to."

Littell smiled. "He'll lose."

Wayne Senior smiled. "He'll *win*. Bobby isn't Jack by a long shot."

A ball rolled up. Littell grabbed it.

"If Mr. Nixon runs, I'll ask you to arrange a meeting with me. I'll state my clients' requests, gauge his response, and take it from there. If Mr. Nixon agrees to honor the requests, he'll be compensated."

Wayne Senior said, "How much?"

Littell said, "Twenty-five million."

97

(New Hebron, 11/30/66)

KLANTICS:

Klan klowns hauled guns. Klan klowns oiled guns. Klan klowns klipped koupons.

They sat around. They worked inside. They ducked a hailstorm outside. The Führer Bunker—ripe with farts and gun residue.

Wayne lounged. Bob Relyea dipped numbers. Bob Relyea bitched.

"My fucking contacts are getting lazy. They want to burn the serial codes as part of the deal, that's fine with me, even though Pete don't like it. But doing the job myself is another fucking thing."

Wayne watched. Wayne yawned. Bob dabbed M-14s. Bob dabbed pumps. Bob dabbed bazookas. He wore rubber gloves. He swiped a brush. He smeared caustic goo.

Wayne watched. The goo ate numbers—three-zero codes.

Bob said, "My contacts boosted some Army trucks near Memphis. There's this little town called White Haven, where all the caucasoids moved to to get away from the spooks. Half the town's Army EM."

Wayne sneezed. The caustics stung. Wayne lounged and drifted. Wayne Senior/job deals/"Hate Smart."

Bob said, "What do you call a monkey sitting in a tree with three niggers? You call him the Branch Manager."

The Klan klods howled. Bob booted snuff. Bob dipped M-14s. Pete kalled the kompound. Pete found Wayne an hour back. Pete reworked Wayne's rotation.

Don't surveille the gun run. Don't boat to Cuba. Fly to Vegas/meet Sonny/muscle a deadbeat.

Bob packed guns. Flash was due—kadre on kall. The karavan—New Hebron to Bay St. Louis.

Wayne stood up. Wayne toured the hate hut. Dig the wall-mounted shivs. Dig the Rebel drapes. Dig the wall photos: George Wallace/Ross Barnett/Orval Faubus.

Dig the group shots. There's the Regal Knights. There's a jail pic—three cons in the "Thunderbolt Legion."

Said cons wore jail garb. Said cons grinned. Said cons signed their names: Claude Dineen/Loyal Binns/Jimmy E. Ray.

Bob said, "Hey, Wayne. You ever talk to your daddy?"

He drove north. He flew Memphis to Vegas. He thought about Janice. He thought about Barb. He thought about Wayne Senior.

Janice aged strong. Good genes and will meet carnal desires. Barb aged fast. Bad habits and will meet fucked-up desires. Wayne Senior looked old. Wayne Senior looked good. Wayne Senior had hate-smart desires.

Janice limped. She'd fuck harder now. She'd outgun her handicap. She'd compensate.

The plane touched down. Wayne got off bleary—1:10 A.M.

He walked down the ramp. He trailed some nuns. He dodged skycaps with dollies.

There's Pete. He's by the gate. He's perched by some bag carts. He's *smoking*.

Wayne hitched up his garment bag. Wayne walked over bleary.

"Put that fucking cigarette—"

Pete pushed a bag cart. It hit Wayne's knees. It capsized him. It knocked him flat. Pete ran over. Pete stepped on his chest.

"Here's the warning. I don't care what you feel for Barb or what you think she's doing to herself. Hit her again and I'll kill you."

Wayne saw starbursts. Wayne saw sky. Wayne saw Pete's shoe. He sucked air. He ate jet fumes. He got breath.

"I was telling her something you won't, and I fucking did it to help you."

Pete flicked his cigarette. Pete burned Wayne's neck. Pete dropped a note on his chest.

"Take care of it. You and Sonny. Barb's gone, so we'll pretend this never happened."

A nun walked by. Said nun shot a look—you pagans stop that!

Pete walked off. Wayne sat up. Wayne got more breath. Two punks strolled by. They saw Wayne recumbent. They giggled it up.

Wayne stood up. Wayne dodged skycaps and bag carts. Wayne hit a phone booth.

He dropped coins. He dialed. He got a buzz tone. He got three rings. He got *Him*.

"Who's calling at this ungodly hour?"

Wayne said, "I want that job."

98

(Las Vegas, 12/1/66)

ONSTAGE: Milt C. and Junkie Monkey.

Milt said, "What's all this tsuris with Howard Hughes?"

Junkie Monkey said, "I heard he's a swish. He moved in to get next to Liberace."

The crowd yocked. The crowd roared.

Milt said, "Come on. I heard he was shtupping Ava Gardner."

Junkie Monkey said, "*I'm* shtupping Ava. She traded up from Sammy Davis. Sammy's on the golf course. This square comes up to him and says, 'What's your handicap?' Sammy says, 'I'm a one-eyed shvartze Jew. Nobody will sell me a house in a nice neighborhood. I'm trying to effect a peace accord between Israel and the Congo. I've got no place to hang my Sy Devore beanie.'"

The crowd yocked. Milt moved his lips. Milt puppet-talked bad. Pete watched. Pete smoked. Pete mourned Barb.

She was three days gone. She didn't call. She didn't write. *He* didn't call. *He* didn't write. He braced Wayne instead.

It was bullshit. Wayne was right. He knew it. Barb split. He exploited it. He indulged. He smoked. He ate burgers. He worked the Fuck-It Diet. He boozed. He caught Milt. He caught Barb's crew. The Bondsmen sans Barb—Shit City.

The lounge was packed. Young stuff mostly. Milt drew hip kids.

Junkie Monkey said, "Frank Sinatra saved my life. His goons were stomping me in the Sands parking lot. Frank said, 'That's enough, boys.'"

The crowd yocked. Pete smoked. A geek tapped his arm. Pete turned around. Pete saw Dwight Holly.

They hit Pete's office. They stood by the wet bar. They crowded each other. They stood in tight.

Pete said, "It's been a while."

"Yeah, as in '64. Your boy Wayne killed three shines."

Pete lit a cigarette. "And you made out."

Dwight shrugged. "Wayne fucked me up, but you and Littell set it straight. Now, ask me if I came to say thanks."

Pete poured a scotch. "You were in town, so you thought you'd drop by."

"Not quite. I'm in town to see Littell, which I'd prefer you keep to yourself."

Pete sipped scotch. Dwight tapped his chest.

"How's your ticker?"

"It's fine."

"You shouldn't be smoking."

"You shouldn't be jerking my chain."

Dwight laughed. Dwight poured a scotch.

"How'd you like to help me entrap a Commie sympathizer?"

"You and Mr. Hoover?"

"I won't say yes or no to that. Silence implies consent, so draw your own conclusions."

Pete said, "Lay it out. The money first."

Dwight swirled scotch. "Twenty grand for you. Ten each for your bait, your backup, and your bug man."

Pete laughed. "Ward's a good bug man."

"Ward's a prince of a bug man, but I'd prefer Freddy Turentine, and I'd prefer that Ward be kept in the dark about this."

Pete grabbed an ashtray. Pete stubbed his cigarette.

"Give me one good reason why I should fuck Ward over to help you."

Dwight undid his necktie. "One, all this shit is tangential to Ward. Two, it's a high-line gig that you won't be able to resist. Three, you're in the Life for life, you'll fuck up sooner or later, and Mr. Hoover will intercede for you, no questions asked."

Pete sipped scotch. Pete rolled his neck. Pete tapped his head on the wall.

"Who?"

"Bayard Rustin, male Negro, age fifty-four. Civil-rights agitator with a yen for young white boys. He's horny, he's impetuous, he's as Red as they get."

Pete tapped his head. "When?"

"Next month, in L.A. There's an SCLC fund-raiser at the Beverly Hilton."

"That's cutting it close."

Dwight shrugged. "The bait's the only holdup. Do you think you—"

"I've got the bait. He's young, he's queer, he's attractive. He's got some potential cop shit hanging over him, which—"

"Which Mr. Hoover will frost out, no questions asked."

Pete tapped his head. Pete tapped it hard. Pete sparked a headache.

"I want Fred Otash on backup."

"Agreed."

"Plus Freddy Turentine and ten grand for expenses."

"Agreed."

Pete's stomach growled. The scotch fucked with it. Pete thought Cheeseburger.

Dwight smiled. "You bit fast. I thought I'd have to work you."

"My wife left me. I've got time to kill."

Otash said, "Sal scores tonight. I'll lay you six to one."

Car surveillance—Fred O.'s car—the seats pushed way back. Fred O.'s farts and Fred O.'s cologne.

They watched the street. They watched Sal's car. They watched the Klondike Bar. Pete lit a cigarette. Pete had gas. Pete snarfed two cheeseburgers late.

"Of course he'll score. He's a half-assed movie star."

He flew straight out. He called Otash. He briefed him. They checked Sal's pad. Sal was gone. They checked Sal's known haunts: The 4-Star/the Rumpus Room/Biff's Bayou.

Shit—no Sal car/no Sal.

They checked the Gold Cup. They checked Arthur J's. They checked the Klondike—8th and LaBrea.

Tilt—

Pete said, "You're sure he won't rabbit?"

"On *Dom?* Sure I'm sure."

"Tell me why."

"Because I'm his new daddy. Because I'm the guy he has coffee with every morning. Because I'm the guy who dumped Dom and his fucking car down a lime pit in the fucking Angeles Forest."

Pete chained cigarettes. "The Vegas end's good. No cops so far."

"Dom was a fly-by-night. You think his pimp boyfriend will file a missing-persons report?"

Sal walked out. Sal had a date. Sal hung on some hunky young quiff.

Otash hit the horn. Pete hit the lights. Sal blinked. Sal saw the car. Sal stalled the quiff and walked over.

Pete rolled his window down. Sal leaned on the ledge.

"Shit. It's a life sentence with you guys."

Pete flashed a snapshot reminder. Streetlight hit Donkey Dom's thumb. Sal blinked. Sal gulped. Sal vibed sick.

Pete said, "You like dark stuff, right? You get the urge once in a while."

Sal weaved a hand—dark meat/*comme ci comme ça*.

Otash said, "We're fixing you up."

Pete said, "He's a nice guy. You'll thank us."

Otash said, "He's cute. He looks like Billy Eckstine."

Pete said, "He's a Communist."

99

(Las Vegas, 12/2/66)

TOUR TIME:

The DI sub-penthouse. Big Drac's sub-lair. Littell as tour guide. Dwight Holly as tourist.

Look:

There's the blood pumps. There's the drips. There's the freezers. There's the candy. There's the pizza. There's the ice cream. There's the codeine. There's the meth. There's the Dilaudid.

Dwight loves it. Dwight yuks. Dwight offends Mormons. Said Mormons scowl at said Fed.

Big Drac's incursion—now one week in.

The legislature waives anti-trust laws. The legislature delivers—go, Drac!

Buy the DI. Buy the Frontier. Buy the Sands. Buy big! Buy *laissez-faire!* Buy the Castaways. Gorge yourself. Buy the Silver Slipper.

Littell cracked windows. Dwight looked out. Dwight saw nuts with signs: "We love H.H.!"/"Wave to us!"/"Hughes in '68!"

Dwight laughed. Dwight tapped his watch—real business now.

They walked. They trekked hallways. They bagged a storeroom. File boxes hemmed them in.

Littell pulled his list out. Moe prepped it last night.

"Skim couriers. Easy litigations by any and all standards."

Dwight faked a yawn. "Expendable, buffered, non-Mormon couriers that divert heat from Dracula and ingratiate you with Mr. Hoover."

Littell bowed. "I won't dispute it."

"Why should you? You know we're grateful, and you know we'll prosecute."

Littell creased the list. Dwight grabbed it. Dwight dropped it in his briefcase.

"I figured you'd try to softsoap me about Lyle. The 'you lost a brother, I lost a friend' routine."

Littell coughed. "It was fifteen months ago. I didn't think it was fresh on your mind."

Dwight squared his necktie. "Lyle was doubling. He leaked some anti-Bureau shit to the House Judiciary Committee and Bobby Kennedy. Mr. Hoover had to pull a few bugs."

Littell went slack-jawed. I don't believe it! Littell made big eyes.

Dwight said, "Lyle, the closet liberal. It took some getting used to."

"I could have helped you."

Dwight laughed. "Yeah, you wrote the book."

"Not completely. You know I'd rather scheme against liberals than be one."

Dwight shook his head. "You *are* one. It's this fucked-up Catholic thing you've got going. You love high-level ops, you love the great unwashed, you're like the fucking Pope ashamed that his church makes money."

Littell roared—Blue Rabbit—*mon Dieu!*

"You flatter me, Dwight. I'm not that complex."

"Yeah, you are. It's why Mr. Hoover enjoys you. You're Bayard Rustin to his Marty King."

Littell smiled. "Bayard has his own ambiguities."

"Bayard's a piece of work. I ran surveillance on him in '60. He poured Pepsi-Cola on his Cheerios."

Littell smiled. "He's King's voice of reason. King's been pushing on too broad a front, and Bayard's been trying to restrain him."

Dwight shrugged. "King's a bullet. It's his time, and he knows it. Mr. Hoover's getting old, and he's letting his hatred show in the worst possible ways. King orates and pulls his Mahatma Gandhi shit, and Mr. Hoover plays in. He's afraid that King will team up with Bobby the K., which as fears go has its merits."

Blue Rabbit shows insight. Blue Rabbit shows balls. Blue Rabbit doubts Mr. Hoover.

"Is there anything I can do?"

Dwight tugged his necktie. "On the King front, zero. Mr. Hoover thinks you were too close to Lyle's death and that Bogalusa bombing."

Littell shrugged—*moi?*—how *could* he.

Dwight smirked. "You want back in. You got cut out of BLACK RABBIT, and it's galling you."

Littell smirked. "I'm wondering why Mr. Hoover had you pick up the list, when I could have airtelled it."

"No, you're not. You know he sent me to gauge your line of shit and decode your dissembling."

Littell sighed—how *passé*—you *know* me.

"I miss the game. Tell him that for a fucked-up liberal, I'm on his side."

Dwight winked. "I was talking to him this morning. I proposed a job for you, pending my assessment."

"Which is?"

"That you're a fucked-up liberal who disapproves of bugs and wiretaps, but loves to install them anyway. That you wouldn't mind bugging sixteen Mob joints for us, just so you can stay in the game."

Littell tingled. "Quid pro quo?"

"Sure. You plant the wires. You get out. We don't tell you where the listening posts are. You deny Bureau complicity if you get caught, and you win points with Mr. Hoover."

Littell said, "I'll do it."

The door blew open. Smells blew in: burnt pizza/spilled blood/ice cream.

DOCUMENT INSERT: 12/3/66.
Verbatim FBI telephone call transcript. (OPERATION BLACK RABBIT Addendum.) Marked: ''Recorded at the Director's Request''/''Classified Confidential 1-A: Director's Eyes Only.'' Speaking: Director, BLUE RABBIT.

DIR: Good morning.

BR: Good morning, Sir.

DIR: Start with Le Grand Pierre, henceforth to be known as BIG RABBIT.

BR: He's in, Sir. Along with Fred Otash and Freddy Turentine.

DIR: Has he recruited his bait?

BR: He has, Sir. He'll be using a homosexual actor named Sal Mineo.

DIR: I'm delighted. Young Mineo was boffo in *Exodus* and *The Gene Krupa Story*.

BR: He's a talented youth, Sir.

DIR: He is talented and given to Greek profligacy. He has indulged numerous liaisons with male movie stars, among them James Dean, the ''Human Ashtray.''

BR: BIG RABBIT has chosen well, Sir.

DIR: To continue.

BR: BIG RABBIT has a wedge on Mineo, which he declines to reveal. He wants him protected if he's arrested by an outside agency. I think BIG RABBIT is buying himself protection, too.

DIR: He's buying, we're selling. I would be delighted to protect BIG RABBIT and young Mineo.

BR: I gave BIG RABBIT a fact sheet for Mineo to memorize. We want him to be able to convince PINK RABBIT that he's a civil-rights zealot.

DIR: That will be no great stretch. Actors are morally decentered and psychically unhinged. They cling to their scripts of the moment with great verve. It fills their voids of emptiness and allots them the will to exist.

BR: Yes, Sir.

DIR: To continue. Describe your meeting with CRUSADER RABBIT.

BR: To start, I'll finally have to concede that he's just as gifted as you've always contended. That said, I don't know how trustworthy he is, or isn't, for that matter. He seemed sincerely shocked when I mentioned my brother's alleged leaks to Bobby Kennedy and the Judiciary Committee, but he may have calculated his response in advance.

DIR: Do you remain convinced that your brother did not write that ''Confession''?

BR: More than ever, Sir. Although now I'm starting to think that it was not CRUSADER RABBIT. I think there's a fair chance that it could have been someone within the SCLC, who had a private investigator or someone of that ilk sweep and find the bugs and taps, and then decide to capitalize on my brother's death and send in the ''Confession.''

DIR: I will concede the possibility.

BR: I think your basic assessment of CRUSADER RABBIT is valid, Sir. He lives for intrigue, he'll betray his moral convictions for the chance to do high-level ops, and he's trustworthy and exploitable within a limited sphere.

DIR: Did you offer him the chance to install the bugs?

BR: I did, Sir. He accepted immediately.

DIR: I thought he would.

BR: I'm glad you approved my proposal, Sir. Public opinion has turned against electronic surveillance, and we need organized-crime wires in place.

DIR: I would amend your statement. We need covertly planted, deniable bugs monitored by handpicked agents in place.

BR: Yes, Sir.

DIR: How did you describe the assignment?

BR: I said sixteen cities, Stage-2 Covert. I mentioned Mike Lyman's Restaurant in Los Angeles, Lombardo's in San Francisco, the Grapevine Tavern in St. Louis, and a few others.

DIR: Did you mention the stately El Encanto Hotel in Santa Barbara?

BR: I did, Sir.

DIR: How did CRUSADER react?

BR: He didn't. He obviously has no idea that Bobby Kennedy keeps a suite there.

DIR: The attendant irony delights me. CRUSADER RABBIT bugs Prince Bobby's hotel digs. He's convinced the suite belongs to a prince of organized crime.

BR: It's a pisser, Sir.

DIR: CRUSADER RABBIT is an entrenched Bobbyphile. You're sure that he has no knowledge of Bobby's suite?

BR: I'm certain, Sir. I've got the manager in my pocket. He told me that Bobby's policy is never to reveal that he stays there. He'll let CRUSADER in to do his work, and he'll make sure that Bobby's personal belongings are temporarily removed.

DIR: Salutary.

BR: Thank you, Sir.

DIR: We need access to Bobby. I'm convinced that he'll form an unholy alliance with RED RABBIT.

BR: We're covered on the Bobby front, Sir.

DIR: As we'll be on PINK front, assuming that young Mineo is convincingly fetching.

BR: He will be, Sir. We hired queer to entrap queer, which should pay off in the end.

DIR: I want a duplicate copy of the film. Have it processed the morning after the fund-raiser.

BR: Yes, Sir.

DIR: Make two copies. I'll give Lyndon Johnson one for his birthday.

BR: Yes, Sir.

DIR: Good day, Dwight. Go with God.

BR: Good day, Sir.

100

(Las Vegas, 12/5/66)

WAYNE PICKED THE lock.

He worked two picks. He tweaked the bolt. He jiggled hard right. Deadbeat patrol/room 6/Desert Dawn Motel.

Sonny said, "Motherfucker's got two last names. Sirhan Sirhan."

The door popped. They stepped inside. Wayne toed the door shut. Check the four-wall dump-site.

Soiled bed. No rugs. Horse-race posters/jockey silks/racing forms stacked.

Sonny said, "Motherfucker's a track nut."

The room smelled. Scents mingled. Spilled vodka and stale chink. Stale cheese spread and cigarettes.

Wayne checked the dresser. Wayne pulled drawers. Wayne sifted junk. Acne swabs/booze empties/cigarette butts.

Sonny said, "Motherfucker's a pack rat."

Wayne pulled drawers. Wayne perused. Wayne sifted junk. Racing forms and tip logs. Scratch sheets and hate tracts.

Cheap-paper tracts. Non-Wayne Senior stock. Text and cartoons—anti-Jew stuff.

Dollar-sign skullcaps. Bloody prayer shawls. Fangs dripping pus. "The Zionist Pig Order"/"The Vampire Jew"/"The Jewish Cancer Machine." Jews with claw hands. Jews with pig feet. Jews with scimitar dicks.

Wayne skimmed text. Said text waxed repetitious. The Jews fucked the Arabs. The Arabs vowed payback.

Sonny said, "Motherfucker don't like the hebes."

The text rambled. Typos reigned. Longhand margin notes crawled. "Kill Kill Kill!"/"Death to Israel!"/"Zionist Pig-Suckers Must Die!"

Sonny said, "Motherfucker's got a grievance."

Wayne dropped the tracts. Wayne shut the drawers. Wayne kicked a chair back.

"We'll give him two hours. He owes Pete a grand and change."

Sonny chewed a toothpick. "Barb split on Pete. Frankly, I seen it coming."

"Maybe I got to her."

"Maybe Pete's evil ways did. Maybe she said, 'Quit selling hair-o-wine to Sonny's fellow niggers or I'll leave your white ass, you honky motherfucker.'"

Wayne laughed. "Let's call her and ask."

"*You* call. You the motherfucker who's in love with her and too mother-fucking scared to say boo."

Wayne laughed. Wayne chewed his nails. Wayne tore a nail back.

The Pete thing hurt. Pete bruised his balls. Pete trimmed his balls back. He was wrong. Pete was right. He knew it.

He called Wayne Senior. They talked. Wayne Senior pledged Work. "Good work"/"in time"/"soon." He might take it. He might not. He owed Pete rotations: Saigon/Mississippi/the funnel.

Sonny said, "Let's go to L.A. We'll find Wendell Durfee and shoot his black ass."

Wayne laughed. Wayne chewed his nails. Wayne tore hang-nails back. Sonny said, "Let's kill some street nigger and say it's Wendell. It'll put the fucking quietus on all that shit you carrying around."

Wayne smiled. The door jiggled—whazzat?

The door stuck. The door popped. A doofus walked in. A young guy/all swarthy/thick rat's-nest hair.

He saw them. He trembled. He crap-your-pants cringed.

Sonny said, "Ahab the A-rab. Where's your camel, motherfucker?"

Wayne shut the door. "You owe the Golden Cavern eleven-sixty. Fork up or Brother Liston will hurt you."

The doofus cringed. *Don't hurt me.* His shirttail hiked up. Wayne saw a belt piece. Wayne snatched it fast. Wayne dumped the clip.

Sonny said, "How come you got two last names?"

Sirhan gestured. His hands moved mile-a-minute. He made geek semaphore.

"Forgive me . . . I take falls . . . race horses . . . many headaches . . . I forget I lose money if I don't take medicine."

Sonny said, "I don't like you. You starting to look like Cassius Clay."

Sirhan spieled some Arab shit. Sirhan spieled singsong. Sonny threw a left. Sonny hit the wall. Sonny tore plaster.

Wayne twirled the gun. "Brother Liston knocked out Floyd Patterson and Cleveland 'Big Cat' Williams."

Sonny threw a right. Sonny hit the wall. Sonny tore plaster. Sirhan moaned. Sirhan exhorted Allah. Sirhan dumped his pockets fast.

Booty: ChapStick/pen/car keys. C-notes/fives/dimes.

Wayne grabbed the money. Sonny said, "What you got against the kikes?"

Wayne hit the Cavern. Wayne unlocked his room. Wayne saw a letter on the dresser.

He opened the envelope. He smelled Barb straight off.

Wayne,
I'm sorry for that night & I hope it didn't cause any

trouble between you & Pete. I told him you were
justified, but he didn't get it. I should have told him that
I tried to stab you, which might have told him how far
down I'd sunk & how much sense you made.

I'm a coward for not writing directly to Pete, but I'm
going to invite him to Sparta for Christmas, to see if we
can work things out. I hate his business & I hate his war
& I'd be an even bigger coward if I didn't say so.

I miss Pete, I miss the cat & I miss you. I'm working at
my sister's Bob's Big Boy & avoiding the bad habits
I picked up in Vegas. I'm starting to wonder what a 35-
year-old ex-shakedown girl-lounge bunny does with the
rest of her life.

Barb

Wayne reread the letter. Wayne caught subscents. There's the
Ponds and lavender soap. He kissed the letter. He locked up his
room. He walked to the lounge.

There's Pete.

He's drinking. He's smoking. The cat's on his lap. He's watching the Bondsmen—Barb's combo sans Barb.

Wayne shagged a waiter. Wayne passed him the letter. Wayne
tipped him five bucks. Wayne pointed to Pete. The guy
understood.

The guy walked over. The guy dropped the letter. Pete tore
at the envelope.

He read the letter. He wiped his eyes. The cat clawed his
shirt.

DOCUMENT INSERT: 12/6/66.
Las Vegas Sun headline and subhead:
HOWARD HUGHES IN VEGAS!
EXCLUSIVE PIX OF HERMIT'S LAIR!

DOCUMENT INSERT: 12/7/66.
Las Vegas Sun headline and subhead:
NO CLUES IN DISAPPEARANCE OF DANCER-CAB DRIVER
FRIENDS APPEAL TO POTENTIAL WITNESSES

DOCUMENT INSERT: 12/8/66.
Las Vegas Sun headline and subhead:
HUGHES SPOKESMAN SAYS:

BILLIONAIRE HERMIT TO ''NURTURE''—NOT
''MONOPOLIZE'' HOTEL SCENE

DOCUMENT INSERT: 12/10/66.
Las Vegas Sun headline and subhead:
FBI ARRESTS SKIM BAGMEN
HUGHES SPOKESMAN PRAISES DIRECTOR HOOVER

DOCUMENT INSERT: 12/11/66.
Chicago Tribune headline and subhead:
MORE MAIL-FRAUD RAIDS IN SOUTH
22 INDICTMENTS PENDING

DOCUMENT INSERT: 12/14/66.
Chicago Sun-Times headline and subhead:
KING ATTACKS FBI'S SOUTHERN MANDATE
''KLAN TERROR—NOT MALL-FRAUD—SHOULD BE PRIORITY''

DOCUMENT INSERT: 12/15/66.
Los Angeles Times subhead:
KING INDICTS ''GENOCIDAL'' WAR IN VIETNAM

DOCUMENT INSERT: 12/18/66.
Denver Post-Dispatch subhead:
RFK DENIES RUMORS OF PREZ'L BID

DOCUMENT INSERT: 12/20/66.
Boston Globe headline:
NIXON NON-COMMITTAL ON '68 WHITE HOUSE PLANS

DOCUMENT INSERT: 12/21/66.
Washington Post headline and subhead:
SCATHING INDICTMENT:
FOREIGN JOURNALISTS ATTACK LBJ FOR CIVIL-RIGHTS-
VIETNAM ''DICHOTOMY''

DOCUMENT INSERT: 12/22/66.
San Francisco Chronicle headline and subhead:
HOOVER ATTACKS KING IN CONGRESSIONAL RECORD
CALLS CIVIL-RIGHTS LEADER ''DANGEROUS TYRANT''

DOCUMENT INSERT: 12/23/66.
Las Vegas Sun headline and subhead:
HUGHES NEGOTIATORS SWARM STRIP
HOTEL PURCHASES LOOM

DOCUMENT INSERT: 12/26/66.
Washington Post headline and subhead:
DOMESTIC STUDY GROUP VOICES OPINION:
J. EDGAR HOOVER ''OUTMODED''

DOCUMENT INSERT: 1/2/67.
Los Angeles Examiner subhead:
CIVIL-RIGHTS FUND-RAISER TO DRAW STELLAR CROWD

DOCUMENT INSERT: 1/3/67.
Dallas Morning News headline:
JACK RUBY—DEAD OF CANCER

1 0 1

(Beverly Hills, 1/3/67)

SIGNS:

Mau-Mau shit. Peace doves. Nigger hands clasped.

Said signs blitzed walls. Said walls ran high. The ballroom soared up. Said ballroom welcomed oreos—race-mixer deelites.

There's celebs and pols. There's spook matrons. There's Marty the K. There's Burl Ives. There's Banana Boat Belafonte.

Pete watched. Pete smoked. His tux fit tight. Otash watched. Otash smoked. His tux fit right.

Ballroom accoutrements—dais and lectern. Ballroom seats and ballroom fare. Steam trays leaking steam—chicken à la coon deelite.

Cops mingled. Their cheap suits stood out. Waiters roamed. Waiters schlepped trays. Waiters flogged deelites.

Pete worked the Fuck-It Diet. Pete noshed meatballs. Pete noshed pâté. Pete noshed pygmy deelites.

There's Mayor Sam Yorty. There's Governor Pat Brown. There's Bayard Rustin—he's tall and thin—dig that tartan tux. There's Sal Mineo—he's hovering—dig that swish lollapalooza.

There's Rita Hayworth. Who let *her* in? She vibes dipsomaniac.

Otash said, "Has it occurred to you that we stand out here?"

Pete lit a cigarette. "Once or twice."

"Rita looks soused. I had a two-second thing with her, about ten years ago. Redheads tend to age bad, Barb excepted."

Pete watched Rita. Rita saw Otash. Rita went ugh and stepped back.

He flew to Sparta. He spent Christmas. He shacked up with his wife. They made love. They fought. Barb ragged his "war enterprise."

Barb quit sniffing "H." Barb quit popping pills. Barb glowed non-Rita-like. Barb goosed his pulse. Barb wrung him out. Barb told him straight: I hate dope. I hate lounge work. I hate Vegas. I won't back down. I won't go back.

He regrouped. He compromised. He punted. He said I'll work in Milwaukee. I'll push white horse there. We'll live in Sparta full-time.

Barb howled. Barb said never.

They talked. They fought. They made love. He regrouped. He repunted. He recompromised. He said I'll split Vietnam. I'll dump Tiger Kamp on John Stanton. John to run it/Wayne to rotate/Mesplède to assist.

Barb tweaked him. Barb said you *love* Wayne. Barb said he hit me. Okay—he *knows* you—you win.

They talked truce. They notched points. They nailed details. He said I'll stay in Vegas. I'll run Tiger Kab and the Cavern. I won't touch the dope. I'll just surveille shipments in.

I have to—the heat's up—Drac brought publicity. I'll work in Vegas and rotate to you in Sparta.

Barb bought the plan. Said plan stressed Vietnam. Said plan stressed his exclusion.

They made love. They sealed the pact. They fucking snow-mobiled. Fucking Sparta, Wisconsin—Lutherans and trees.

Pete scoped the ballroom. Pete watched the floor. Sal M. looked over. Sal M. looked away.

Dom's bun boy filed missing-persons. LVPD worked the case. It got some ink. Cops checked out the Cavern. Pete bribed them. They dumped the case resultant.

Otash watchdogged Sal. Sal learned his script. It was simple shit: I just *loooove* civil rights! Otash worked with Dwight Holly. They redid Sal's pad. They ripped out a closet. They hung 1-way glass and rigged a camera. Said camera faced Sal's bed.

Fred T. assisted. Fred T. bugged lamps. Fred T. bugged walls. Fred T. bugged mattress springs.

Pete scoped the ballroom. Pete watched the floor. Celebs hob-nobbed. Celebs sucked up to King.

Otash said, "You see the paper? Jack Ruby died."

"I saw it."

"You guys went back. Sam G.'s dropped a few hints."

Sal looked over. Pete cued him—*go in strong now.*

Sal shagged a waiter. Sal cadged a drink. Sal chugalugged. Sal flushed bright. Sal mingled. Sal walked.

Fruit Alert—Bayard Rustin—fruit fly at ten o'clock high. Bayard's got backscratchers—Burl Ives plus two—Sal's moving in tight.

Sal sees Bayard. Bayard sees Sal. Two smiles and wet lips aflutter. Strings swell. "Strangers in the Night." "Some Enchanted Evening."

Burl's pissed. Who's *this* punk? *I'm* old-line Left. Sal said hi. Sal drifted off. Bayard eye-tracked his ass.

Otash said, "Contact."

A bell rang. It's chow time. Hold for pygmy banquet fare.

Cliques dispersed. The guests hit the tables. Sal eye-tracked Bayard. Sal sat nearby.

Bayard saw him. Bayard wrote a napkin note. Pat Brown passed it down. Sal read it. Sal blushed. Sal passed a note back.

Pete said, "Liftoff."

They killed time.

They walked next door. They hit Trader Vic's. They quaffed mai-tais. They noshed rumaki sticks.

Cops passed through. Cops dished updates.

Dinner's done. King's talking. King's dripping foam at the mouth. He's Red. He's a puppet. I know it. The peaceniks love him. It burns me. My son's in Vietnam.

A TV kicked on. The barman flipped channels. The barman shut off the sound. There's war news on three channels. There's choppers and tanks. There's Commie King on two more.

Pete checked his watch. It was 10:16. Hold for fruit flies on high. Otash wolfed a puu-puu platter. His cummerbund swelled.

10:28:

Sal walks in. Sal sits down. Sal ignores them.

10:29:

Bayard walks in. Bayard sits down. Bayard greets Sal: Child, how *are* you! I'm *such* a fan!

Otash got up. Pete got up. Pete grabbed a shrimp spear for the road.

* * *

Setup:

They hit Sal's pad. They aired out the closet. They prepped the camera. They loaded film. They waited. They sat still.

The closet was hot. They popped sweat. They stripped to socks and shorts.

They sat still. They killed the lights. Their watch dials ran fluorescent.

11:18. 11:29. 11:42.

Poof—doorway light. Off the bedroom—stage right.

Pete squared the camera. Otash rolled film. More light/bedroom fixtures/beams overhead.

Sal walked in. Bayard squeezed in tight. They laughed. They touched. They brushed hips. Bayard kissed Sal. Otash went ugh. Sal kissed Bayard back.

Pete squared the camera. Pete nailed the bed. Pete got Ground Zero in mid-shot.

Sal said, "Martin gives a good speech, but you're handsom—"

Sal stopped. Sal stopped what the—

His voice fluttered. His voice echo-chambered. His voice woofered. His voice tweetered. His voice bounced high and wide.

FUCK—

Overfeed. Overamp. Microph—

Bayard tweaked. Bayard hinked. Bayard looked around fast. Bayard yodeled. Bayard yelled, "Hell-o!" Bayard got echoes back.

Sal grabbed his neck. Sal blitzed a kiss. Sal squeezed his ass. Bayard shoved him. Sal hit the bed. A mattress-mike snapped.

It hit the floor. It bounced. It rolled. It stopped.

Pete said, "Shit."

Otash said, "Fuck."

Bayard yelled—"Hell-o, J. Edgar!"—Bayard got echoes back.

Sal grabbed a pillow. Sal hid his face. Sal nellied out. Sal kicked his legs nonstop.

Bayard looked around. Bayard saw the mirror. Bayard ran up.

He hit the glass.

He gouged his hands.

He tore his hands up.

102

(Silver Spring, 1/6/67)

BANK WORK:

The B. of A. South of D.C. Tithe tunnel 3.

Littell wrote a deposit slip. Littell wrote a withdrawal slip. Littell scrawled an envelope.

Seven grand—one Drac-pilfered deposit. Five grand—one tithe withdrawn. A donation from "Richard D. Wilkins"—tithe pseudonym 3.

Littell got in line. Littell saw a teller. Littell showed his slips and bankbook. The teller smiled. The teller ran his paperwork. The teller metered his check.

He checked his book balance. He creased the check. He sealed the envelope. He walked outside. He dodged snowdrifts. He found a mail chute.

He dropped the letter. He checked for tails. Standard procedure now.

Negative. No tails extant. He *knew* it.

He stood outside. It felt good. The cold air revived him. He was tired. He'd been running—all-Bureau ops.

He toured sixteen cities. He did sixteen bug jobs. He bugged sixteen Mob meeting spots. He worked solo. Fred T. was booked. Fred T. had work with Fred O. He had off-time himself. It was Drac-approved. Drac's Mormons filled his spot.

Said Mormons haggled in Vegas. They said sell us the DI. They said sell us more hotels.

He flew loops. He did bug jobs. He called Moe D. Moe was jazzed. Moe said we'll bilk Drac—I *know* it.

He flew circuits. Chicago/K.C./Milwaukee. St. Louis/Santa Barbara/L.A. He nursed plans. He hit L.A. He acted.

He went through Jane's file. He sifted dirt. He culled dirt on second-line hoods—all East Coast men.

It was prime Arden data. It detailed hijacks and Mob hits. It was non-tangential. It was non-fund-book-related. It was not related to: Carlos/Sam G./John Rosselli/Santo/Jimmy/et al.

He typed out the facts. He wrote succinct. He print-wiped the paper. He flew back out. He traveled. He bugged more meet spots. He hit Frisco/Phoenix/Philly. He hit D.C. and New York.

He stayed in Manhattan. He booked a hotel room. He used a

pseudonym. He altered his appearance. He cosmeticized.

He bought a beard. It was dark blond and gray. It was superb quality. It covered his scars. It reshaped his face. It aged him ten years.

He met Bobby once. He met Bobby three days pre-Dallas. Bobby would remember him. Bobby knew his look.

He bought work clothes. He bought contact lenses. He surveilled Bobby's billet: The UN Towers/old brick/off 1st Avenue.

He braced the doorman. The doorman knew Bobby. The doorman said Bobby rotates. Bobby runs south to D.C. Bobby runs back to New York.

Littell watched. Littell waited. Bobby showed two days in. Bobby brought a young aide north.

A thin boy. Dark hair and glasses. Said boy looked bright. Said boy adored Bobby. Said boy's adulation glowed.

They walked the East Side. Constituents waved. The boy rebuffed hecklers and creeps. Littell tailed them. Littell got close. Littell heard Bobby speak.

The boy had a car. Littell got the plate stats. Littell ran them through the DMV. He got Paul Michael Horvitz/age 23/address in D.C.

Littell called Horvitz. Littell dropped hints. Littell said he had information. Horvitz bit. They arranged a meet—on for tonight in D.C.

Tellers walked out. A guard locked the bank. Snow fell. It felt cold. It warmed him.

He prepped. He worked up mannerisms. He culled a new wardrobe. He dredged up a drawl.

One tweed suit. One soft chambray shirt. Beard/lisp/fey posture.

He showed early. He named the spot: Eddie Chang's Kowloon. The lighting was murky. Said lighting would camouflage.

He got a booth. He sprawled invertebrate. He ordered tea. He watched the door. He checked his watch.

There's Paul.

It's 8:01. He's punctual. He's youthful and sincere. Littell geared up—be aged/be fey.

Paul glanced around. Paul saw couples. Paul saw one solo act. He walked back. He sat down. Littell poured him tea straight off.

"Thanks for coming on such short notice."

"Well, your call intrigued me."

"I was hoping it would. Young men like you get all sorts of dubious overtures, but this is certainly not one of them."

Paul dumped his overcoat. Paul untied his scarf.

"Senator Kennedy gets the overtures, not me."

Littell smiled. "That's not what I meant, son."

"I got your meaning, but I chose to ignore it."

Littell sprawled. Littell drummed the table.

"You look like Andrew Goodman, that poor boy who died in Mississippi."

"I knew Andy at the COFO School. I almost went down myself."

"I'm glad you didn't."

"Are you from there?"

"I'm from De Kalb. It's a smidge between Scooba and Electric Mills."

Paul sipped tea. "You're some sort of lobbyist, right? You knew you couldn't get to the senator, so you thought you'd find yourself an ambitious young aide."

Littell bowed—courtly/*très* South.

"I know that ambitious young men will risk looking foolish and go out on a snowy night on the off-chance that something is real."

Paul smiled. "And you're 'real.'"

"My documents are wholly real, and one thorough reading will convince you and Senator Kennedy of their authenticity."

Paul lit a cigarette. "And yours?"

"I claim no authenticity, and would prefer that my documents speak for themselves."

"And your documents pertain to?"

"My documents pertain to misdeeds perpetrated by members of organized crime. I will supplant the initial batch with subsequent parcels and deliver them to you in discreet bunches, so that you and/or Senator Kennedy can investigate the allegations at your leisure and your discretion. My only requirement is that there be no public disclosure pertaining to any information I give you until late 1968 or early 1969."

Paul twirled his ashtray. "Do you think Senator Kennedy will be President or President-elect then?"

Littell smiled. "From your mouth to God's ears, although I was thinking more of where I'll be then."

Wall vents popped. The heat came on. Littell broke a sweat.

"Do you think he'll run?"

Paul said, "I don't know."

"Does he remain committed to the fight against organized crime?"

"Yes. It's very much on his mind, but he feels uncomfortable going public with it."

Littell popped sweat. His tweeds broiled. His faux beard slipped. He splayed his hands. He cupped his chin. It played effete. It stopped the slip.

"You can depend on my loyalty, but I would prefer to remain anonymous in all our transactions."

Paul stuck his hand out. Littell passed the notes.

DOCUMENT INSERT: 1/8/67.
Verbatim FBI telephone call transcript (OPERATION
BLACK RABBIT Addendum.) Marked: ''Recorded at the
Director's Request''/''Classified Confidential 1-A:
Director's Eyes Only.'' Speaking: Director, BLUE
RABBIT.

     DIR: Good afternoon.
     BR: Good afternoon, Sir.
     DIR: I read your memo. You attribute the failure of
a Stage-2 operation to faulty condensor plugs.
     BR: It was a technical failure, Sir. I would not
blame Fred Otash or BIG RABBIT.
     DIR: The blameworthy one is thus Fred Turentine,
the reptilian ''Bug Man to the Stars,'' a lowly minion
of Otash and BIG RABBIT.
     BR: Yes, Sir.
     DIR: I gain no succor from foisting blame on a hired
hand. I gain only dyspeptic fury.
     BR: Yes, Sir.
     DIR: Give me some good news to allay my agitation.
     BR: Otash was very good on the post-op. He leaned on
Mineo and warned him to keep quiet. I would strongly
suggest that PINK RABBIT will not risk personal
ridicule or bad publicity for the SCLC by going public
with word on the shakedown.

DIR: I was looking forward to the film. Bayard and
Sal, O bird thou never wert.

BR: Yes, Sir.

DIR: Let's discuss CRUSADER RABBIT.

BR: He did a superb job on the installations, Sir.

DIR: Did you have him spot-tailed?

BR: On three occasions, Sir. He's tail-savvy, but
my men managed to sustain surveillance.

DIR: Expand your answers. I have a lunch date in the
year 2010.

BR: CRUSADER RABBIT was not spotted doing anything
remotely suspicious.

DIR: Besides installing illegal bug-mounts at our
behest.

BR: Including Bobby Kennedy's place in Santa
Barbara, Sir.

DIR: Thrillingly ironic. CRUSADER bugs his savior
and my bete noire. Unwitting complicity of a high
order.

BR: Yes, Sir.

DIR: How long will it take to recruit men to man the
listening posts?

BR: A while, Sir. We've got sixteen locations.

DIR: To continue. Update me on WILD RABBIT.

BR: He's doing well, Sir. You've seen the results.
We keep getting mail-fraud indict—

DIR: I know what we keep getting. I know that we do
not come close to getting anything remotely
resembling satisfaction in the matter of one Martin
Luther King, aka RED RABBIT, aka the Minstrel
Antichrist. Our attempts to dislodge him and subsume
his prestige have consumed tens of thousands of man-
hours and have garnered nil results. He has turned us
into dung beetles and rare, indigenous African birds
who peck through elephant shit, and I am woefully sick
and tired of waiting for him to discredit himself.

BR: Yes, Sir.

DIR: You're a rock, Dwight. I can always count on
you to say ''Yes, Sir.''

BR: I would like to seek more radical means to
nullify RED RABBIT. Do I have your permission to bring

in a trusted friend and explore the possibilities?

    DIR: Yes.

    BR: Thank you, Sir.

    DIR: Good day, Dwight.

    BR: Good day, Sir.

DOCUMENT INSERT: 1/14/67.
Telephone call transcript. Taped by: BLUE RABBIT.
Marked: ``FBI-Scrambled''/``Stage-1 Covert''/
``Destroy Without Reading in the Event of My Death.''
Speaking: BLUE RABBIT, FATHER RABBIT.

    BR: Senior, how are you? How's the connection?

    FR: I'm hearing some clicks.

    BR: That's my scrambler. The beeps mean we're tap-proof.

    FR: We should be talking in person.

    BR: I'm down in Mississippi. I can't get away.

    FR: You're sure it's—

    BR: It's fine. Jesus, don't go cuntish on me.

    FR: I won't. It's just that—

    BR: It's just that you think he's got superhuman powers, and he doesn't. He can't read minds and he can't tap scrambled frequencies.

    FR: Well, still . . .

    BR: Still, shit. He's not God, so quit acting like he is.

    FR: He's something similar.

    BR: I'll buy that.

    FR: Did he—

    BR: He said yes.

    FR: Do you think he knows what we're planning?

    BR: No, but he'll be glad to see it happen, and if he thinks it's us, he'll make sure the investigation obfuscates.

    FR: That's good news.

    BR: No shit, Sherlock.

    FR: People hate him. King, I mean.

    BR: Those that don't love him, yeah.

    FR: What about the bug—

    BR: We're A-OK on that front. I talked him into

letting me wire sixteen spots. He'll read the
transcripts, hear the hate building and get his rocks
off.

FR: There's a scapegoat aspect here.

BR: That is correct. Guinea hoods hate coloreds and
civil-rights fucks, and they love to talk about it.
Hoover hears the hate, the whole thing starts feeling
inevitable, pow, then it happens. The whole Mob-hate
thing serves to muddy the waters and gets him thinking
that it's too big to mess with.

FR: Like Jack Kennedy.

BR: Exactly. It's coming, it's inevitable, it's
accomplished and it's good for business. The nation
mourns and hates the clown we give them.

FR: You know the metaphysic.

BR: We all went to school on Jack.

FR: How long will it take to get the bugs in place?

BR: About six weeks. You want the punch line? I had
Ward Littell do the mounts.

FR: Dwight, Jesus.

BR: I had my reasons. One, he's the best bug man
around. Two, we may need him somewhere down the line.
Three, I needed to throw him a bone to keep him in the
game.

FR: Shitfire. Any game with Littell in it is a game
to fix from the get-go.

BR: I threw Hoover a bone. He hates Bobby K. almost
as much as he hates King, and he shares all his dirt
with LBJ. I had Littell bug one of Bobby's hotel
suites.

FR: I'm getting chills, Dwight. You keep dropping
the ''Mister'' off ''Hoover.''

BR: Because I trust scrambler technology.

FR: It's more than that.

BR: Okay, it's because he's slipping. Why mince
words? King's the one guy he wanted to break the most,
and King's the one guy he can't break. Here's another
punch line for you. Lyle liked King. He worked against
him and admired him anyway, and I'm starting to feel
the same way. That grandiose cocksucker is a jigaboo
for the ages.

FR: I've heard everything now.

BR: No, you haven't. Try this. Hoover's a hophead.

FR: Dwight, come—

BR: That Dr. Feelgood guy flies down from New York every day, on the Bureau's time-card. He gives Hoover a pop of liquid methamphetamine mixed with B-complex vitamins and male hormones. The old boy fades about 1:00 P.M. and perks up like a dog in heat around 2:00.

FR: Jesus.

BR: He's not God or Jesus. He's slipping, but he's still good. We've got to be careful around him.

FR: We need to start thinking about a fall guy.

BR: I want to bring in Fred Otash and Bob Relyea to help us look. I've gotten tight with Otash, he's solid, and he's got juice on the coast. Bob's your rabbit, so you know the score there. That hump knows every expendable race-baiter in the south.

FR: I've got an idea. It might help to facilitate things.

BR: I'm listening.

FR: We should do some hate-mail intercepts on King and the SCLC, to see if we can find a guy who's sent them letters. I know the Bureau's doing mail covers, so I think we should bring in a man to go through the covered mail, photograph it and return it to the covering agent, on the sly.

BR: It's a good idea, if we can find a man we can trust.

FR: My son.

BR: Shit. Don't give me that.

FR: I'm serious.

BR: I thought you and the kid were estranged. He was moving dope with Pete Bondurant, and you two were on the outs.

FR: We've reconciled.

BR: Shit.

FR: You know how he hates coloreds. He'd be perfect for the job.

BR: Shit. He's too volatile. You recall that little run-in I had with him?

FR: He's changed, Dwight. He's a brilliant kid, and he'd be perfect for the job.

BR: I'll buy brilliant. I bought him his first chemistry set in 1944.

FR: I remember. You said he'd figure out how to split the atom.

BR: You've reconciled, you trust him, I concede he'd be good. That said, we don't want him to know what we're building up to.

FR: We'll muddy things. We'll have him cull mail on King, plus one liberal and one conservative politician. He'll think I'm just building my intelligence base.

BR: Shit.

FR: He'll be good. He's the right man for—

BR: I want a wedge. I'll bring him in, as long as we've got something on him. I know he's your son, but I'm still going to insist.

FR: Let's see if we can hand him Wendell Durfee. He's allegedly in L.A., which means I could put my LAPD contacts on him covert. You know what Wayne will do if he finds him.

BR: Yeah. And I could make like I still hate him and squeeze him with that.

FR: It might work. Shitfire, it will work.

BR: Durfee's a long shot. He might take time and we might tap out on him.

FR: I know.

BR: We need to bring in our mail guy within the next six weeks.

FR: I'll bring Wayne in. We'll work on Durfee in the meantime.

BR: That fucks up the wedge aspect.

FR: Not in the long run.

BR: What are you saying?

FR: We don't need a wedge for his mail work. We've got to have one in place when I tell him he'll be there for D-Day.

BR: Jesus Christ.

FR: My son doesn't know it, but he's been waiting his whole life for this.

BR: In your words, ''Shitfire.''

FR: That about says it.

BR: I've got to go. I want to get some coffee and think this all through.

FR: It's going to happen.

BR: You're damn fucking right it is.

DOCUMENT INSERT: 1/26/67.
Las Vegas Sun headline:
HUGHES-DESERT INN NEGOTIATIONS CONTINUE

DOCUMENT INSERT: 2/4/67.
Denver Post-Dispatch subhead:
FEDERAL INDICTMENTS ON CASINO SKIM-COURIERS

DOCUMENT INSERT: 2/14/67.
Las Vegas Sun headline and subhead:
WHERE'S DOM DELLACROCIO?
VEGAS POLICE BAFFLED

DOCUMENT INSERT: 2/22/67.
Chicago Tribune subhead:
KING PREDICTS ''VIOLENT SUMMER'' IF NEGROES DO NOT GET ''FULL JUSTICE''

DOCUMENT INSERT: 3/6/67.
Denver Post-Dispatch subhead:
SKIM COURIERS PLEAD GUILTY

DOCUMENT INSERT: 3/6/67.
Las Vegas Sun subhead:
HUGHES SPOKESMEN CITE SKIM PLEAS AND PLEDGE TO WORK FOR ''CLEAN LAS VEGAS''

DOCUMENT INSERT: 3/7/67.
Los Angeles Times headline and subhead:
HOFFA ENTERS PRISON
58-MONTH SENTENCE LOOMS

DOCUMENT INSERT: 3/27/67.
Las Vegas Sun headline:
HUGHES-DESERT INN DEAL FINALIZED

DOCUMENT INSERT: 4/2/67.
San Francisco Chronicle subhead:
KING ATTACKS ''RACIST'' WAR IN VIETNAM

DOCUMENT INSERT: 4/4/67.
Bug-extract transcript. Marked: ''Confidential''/
''Stage-1 Covert''/''Eyes Only'': Director, SA D. C.
Holly.
    Location: Office/Mike Lyman's Restaurant/Los
Angeles/listening-post-accessed. Speaking:
Unidentified Males #1 & #2, presumed organized-crime
associates. (Conversation 2.6 minutes in progress.)

    UM #1: . . . under Truman and Ike you had order. You
had Hoover, who bore us no ill fucking will. Fucking
Bobby and Jack changed all that.
    UM #2: LBJ's got schizophilia. He don't take no
shit from the Reds in Vietnam, but he sucks up to that
King like he's his long lost soul brother. The policy
guys back east see this correlation. King comes to
Harlem, gives these speeches and gets all the
pygmies hopped up. They quit playing the numbers,
our policy banks take it in the shorts, and the
fucking pygmies get agitated and start feeling their
oats.
    UM #1: I see the correlation. They quit betting
policy, their minds wander. They start thinking about
Communism and raping white women.
    UM #2: King likes white women. I heard he's a pig
for it.
    UM #1: All the niggers want it. It's the fruit of
the forbidden fucking tree.
    (Non-applicable conversation follows.)

DOCUMENT INSERT: 4/12/67.
Bug-extract transcript. Marked: ''Confidential''/
''Stage-1 Covert''/''Eyes Only'': Director, SA D. C.
Holly.
    Location: Rec room/St. Agnes Social Club/
Philadelphia/ listening-post-accessed. Speaking:
Steven ''Steve the Skeev'' DeSantis & Ralph Michael
Lauria, organized-crime associates. (Conversation
9.3 minutes in progress.)

    SDS: . . . Ralphie, Ralphie, Ralphie, you can't talk

to them. You can't reason with them like they're
regular people.

RML: This is not news to me. I have been a landlord
for many fucking years.

SDS: You're a slumlord, Ralphie. Do not try to shit
a well-known shitter like me.

RML: You're talking like that nigger fuck King,
which is just the point I wanted to make. I run to my
buildings on the first, the welfare checks are out and
it's payday for the few shvoogies who work. Now, one
old nigger lady shows me Time Magazine with King on
the cover and says, ''I don't gots to pay no rent
'cause the Reverend Dr. Martin Luther King Junior
says you a slumlord who is exploiting me.'' This fuck
two doors down demands his civil rights, which he
fucking describes as ''I don't have to pay no rent
until all my peoples is free.''

SDS: They're way out of line. As a fucking race,
I mean.

RML: That King's got them hopped up. You got a whole
race of overstimulated people.

SDS: Someone should clip that hump King. They
should slip him a poison watermelon.

RML: We should join the Ku Klux Klan.

SDS: You're too fat to wear a sheet.

RML: Fuck you. I'll join anyway.

SDS: Forget it. They don't take Italians.

RML: Why? We're white.

(Non-applicable conversation follows.)

<u>DOCUMENT INSERT</u>: 4/21/67.
Listening-post report. Marked: ''Confidential''/
''Stage-1 Covert''/''Eyes Only'': Director, SA D. C.
Holly.

Location: Suite 301/El Encanto Hotel/Santa
Barbara/listening-post-accessed.

Sirs,

During the 1st monitoring period (4/2/67–4/20/67),
Subject RFK was not in residence at the target
location. Subject RFK rents the suite on a yearly

basis & it remains empty during his absences. The
(voice-activated) mounts have thus far picked up only
the non-applicable conversations of El Encanto
caretakers & other employees. Per orders, the
listening post will continue to be manned full-time.
   Respectfully,
   SA C. W. Brundage

DOCUMENT INSERT: 5/9/67.
Bug-extract transcript. Marked: ''Confidential''/
''Stage-1 Covert''/''Eyes Only'': Director, SA D. C.
Holly.
   Location: Card room/Grapevine Tavern/St. Louis/
listening-post-accessed. Speaking: Unidentified
males #1 & #2, presumed organized-crime associates.
(Conversation 1.9 minutes in progress.)

   UM #1: . . . Klan's willing to stand up and be
counted, which means you've got to call them our shock
troops.
   UM #2: I'm for segregation, don't get me wrong.
   UM #1: St. Louis is a good example. One, it's
hillbilly. Two, it's got lots of Catholics. I ain't
ashamed to say I'm a hillbilly, you're sure as hell an
Italian and a Catholic, we work together good 'cause
you so-called Mafia guys are white men who worship
Jesus just like me, which means we hate alike, too, so
you got to concede that the Klan's got some answers,
and if they put their anti-Catholic shit aside you'd
be the first to make some big donations.
   UM #2: That is true. I sub-contract to you because
you okies, no offense, think and hate like we do.
   UM #1: If Nigger King walked in here right now, I'd
kill him.
   UM #2: I'd fight you for the right. King and Bobby
Kennedy, those are the shitbirds I hate. Bobby fucked
and fucked and fucked and fucked and fucked and fucked
the Outfit until we had no place left to bleed. King's
doing the same thing right now. He'll fuck this
country in the keester and fuck us and fuck us and
fuck us and fuck and fuck us and fuck us while the

other boogies overbreed and turn this country into a welfare-state shithole.

UM #1: I'm 3rd-generation Klan. There, I said it, and you ain't shocked. You may take your orders from Rome, but I don't care. You're a white man, just like me.

UM #2: Fuck you. I take my orders from a fat dago with a pinkie ring.

(Non-applicable conversation follows.)

DOCUMENT INSERT: 5/28/67.
Bug-extract transcript. Marked: ''Confidential''/ ''Stage-1 Covert''/''Eyes Only'': Director, SA D. C. Holly.

Location: Card room/Grapevine Tavern/St. Louis/ listening-post-accessed. Speaking: Norbert Donald Kling & Rowland Mark DeJohn, paroled felons (Armed Robbery/Bunco/GTA) & presumed organized-crime associates. (Conversation 3.9 minutes in progress.)

NDK: . . . like a kitty, I mean.

RMDJ: I get it. Guys pitch in, you watch the kitty grow.

NDK: We don't pitch in. Guys with real coin do, until you got a big enough pot to attract a guy who can do it.

RMDJ: Right. It's a bounty. The word goes out that it's there, you do the job, you prove you did it, you collect.

NDK: Right. You attract a pro, and he gets away with it. It's not like Oswald, you know, with Kennedy.

RMDJ: Oswald was a Commie and a psycho. He wanted to get caught.

NDK: Right. And people loved Kennedy.

RMDJ: Well, some people. Personally, I hated the son-of-a-bitch.

NDK: You know what I'm saying. With King you got a nigger that everyone hates. The only white people who don't hate him are some Jews and pinkos, but every other white person knows that integration will put this country in the toilet, so you get rid of Public

Nuisance Number One and nip that eventuality in the
bud.

 RMDJ: He's dead, the country rejoices.

 NDK: You put the word out. That's the thing.

 RMDJ: Yeah, the bounty.

 NDK: We ain't got the scratch, but there's guys
around here who do.

 RMDJ: He's begging for it.

 NDK: That's the part I like. You beg for it, you get
it. (Non-applicable conversation follows.)

DOCUMENT INSERT: 6/14/67.
Hate-mail extract. Compiled by: FATHER RABBIT.
Sealed and marked: ''Destroy Without Reading in the
Event of My Death.''

 Mail sender: Anonymous. Postmark: Pasadena,
California. Recipient: Senator Robert F. Kennedy.
From page 1 (of 19):

 DEAR SENATOR KENNEDY,

 I KNOW THAT YOU & THE ZIONIST WORLDWIDE PIG ORDER
HAVE PUT THE PUS IN THE JEWISH CANCER MACHINE AND GAVE
ME HEADACHES, NOT FALLS FROM HORSES AS DR'S BELIEVE.
YOU SAY THAT ALLAH DRIVES AN IMPALA BUT I KNOW THAT
THE JEWISH CONTROL APPARATUS CONTROLS AUTOMOBILE
PRODUCTION IN DETROIT AND BEVERLY HILLS. YOU ARE A PUS
PUPPET IN THE CONTROL OF THE JEWISH VAMPIRE AND MUST
STOP EMITTING HEADACHES IN THE NAME OF THE CHIEF RABBI
OF LODZ AND MIAMI BEACH AND THE PROTOCOLS OF THE
LEARNED ELDERS OF ZION.

DOCUMENT INSERT: 7/5/67.
Hate-mail extract. Compiled by: FATHER RABBIT.
Sealed and marked: ''Destroy Without Reading in the
Event of My Death.''

 Mail sender: Anonymous. Postmark: St. Louis,
Missouri. Recipient: Dr. M. L. King. From page 1 (of
1):

 Dear Nigger,

 You better fear the ides of July and June;

There's going to be a bounty on you, Coon;
You're a traitor and a Commie and an evil ape;
All you do is lie, steal and rape;
But the White Man's wise to your evil ways;
The bounty means you'd better pray and count your
    days;
You can't dodge bullets like Superman;
You can't run away from the White Man's Plan;
When you get this letter you better hide;
Because you can't escape the White Man's
    fearless tide.

Signed,
U.W.M.A. (United White Men of America)

DOCUMENT INSERT: 7/21/67.
Hate-mail extract. Compiled by: FATHER RABBIT.
Sealed and marked: ''Destroy Without Reading in the
Event of My Death.''
    Mail sender: Anonymous. Postmark: Pasadena,
California. Recipient: Senator Robert F. Kennedy.
From page 2 (of 16):

    [And] YOU HAVE BETRAYED THE ARAB PEOPLE AND STOLEN
OUR LAND OF MILK AND HONEY TO MILK PUS FROM THE
WORLDWIDE ZIONIST PIG ORDER AND THE JEWISH CANCER
MACHINE. BAYER ASPIRIN AND BUFFERIN AND ST. JUDE'S
HOSPITAL CANNOT STOP MY HEADACHES FROM THE PUS
INFLICTED BY THE JEWISH VAMPIRE AND CANNOT HEAR ME SAY
RFK MUST DIE RFK MUST DIE RFK MUST DIE RFK MUST DIE RFK
MUST DIE RFK MUST DIE RFK MUST DIE RFK MUST DIE!!!!!!!

DOCUMENT INSERT: 7/23/67.
Boston Globe headline and subhead:
RIOTS SWEEP CITY
ARSON, LOOTING, REIGN

DOCUMENT INSERT: 7/29/67.
Detroit Free Press headline and subhead:
RIOTS ROCK DETROIT
DEATHS AND DAMAGE MOUNT

DOCUMENT INSERT: 7/30/67.
Boston Globe headline and subhead:
KING TO PRESS:
RIOTS ''MANIFESTATIONS OF WHITE RACISM''

DOCUMENT INSERT: 8/2/67.
Washington Post subhead:
RIOT DAMAGE MOUNTS; POLICE CALL DISTRICT ''COMBAT
ZONE''

DOCUMENT INSERT: 8/5/67.
Los Angeles Times headline and subhead:
KING ON RIOTS:
''THE FRUIT OF WHITE INJUSTICE''

DOCUMENT INSERT: 8/6/67.
Telephone call transcript. Taped by: BLUE RABBIT.
Marked: ''FBI-Scrambled''/''Stage-1 Covert''/
''Destroy Without Reading in the Event of My Death.''
Speaking: BLUE RABBIT, FATHER RABBIT.

   BR: Senior, hi.
   FR: How are you, Dwight? It's been a while.
   BR: Don't mind the clicks. My scrambler's on the
fritz.
   FR: I don't mind. I'd rather talk than mess with
pouches.
   BR: Have you been watching the news? The natives
are restless.
   FR: King predicted it.
   BR: No, he promised it, and now he's gloating.
   FR: He's making enemies. There's times I think we
might not get there first.
   BR: There's times I agree. The Outfit hates him, and
every cracker in captivity has got his tits in a
twist. You should hear my listening-post tapes.
   FR: Shitfire, I'd like to.
   BR: There's a joint in St. Louis. A dump called the
Grapevine. Outfit guys and sub-lease hoods frequent
it. They've been talking up a fifty-grand bounty. It's
starting to feel like a giant wet dream out there in
the spiritus mundi.

FR: You slay me. ''Wet Dream'' and ''Spiritus Mundi'' in the same sentence.

BR: I'm a chameleon. I'm like Ward Littell that way. I alter my vocabulary to suit the company I'm with.

FR: At least you know it. I can't say Littell's that much in control of his effects.

BR: He is and he isn't.

FR: For instance?

BR: For instance, he watches for tails everywhere he goes. Mr. Hoover's been running spots on him off and on for years, and he knows it. He catches 90% and misses 10. He's probably got just enough hubris to think he's batting a hundred.

FR: Hubris. I like it.

BR: You should. I picked it up at Yale Law.

FR: Boola, boola.

BR: Tell me about the intercepts. By my lights, your son should be twelve weeks in.

FR: More like eight. You know how he travels for Bondurant. It took him months to set up his system.

BR: Tell me about it.

FR: He rented a place in D.C. He's pulling mail off King, Barry Goldwater, and Bobby Kennedy. The Bureau's running normal intercepts, and all their mail comes addressed to the SCLC headquarters and the Senate Office Building. There's a four-agent team running a mail drop at 16th and ''D.'' The night shift goes home at 11:00, so Wayne lets himself in at 1:00, pulls the mail, copies it and returns it at 5:00. He shuttles down from New York when he rotates in from Saigon.

BR: How does he get in?

FR: He made a mold of the door lock and had duplicate keys made.

BR: And he picks up at irregular intervals?

FR: Right. All synced to his rotations. He print-dusts the mail he picks up, since those hate-mail guys never put their return addresses on the envel—

BR: It's redundant. The mail teams dust the incomings. Everything's been wiped by the time he sees it.

FR: Shitfire. My boy's a chemist. He sprays the
pages with some goop called ninhydrin and brings up
partial prints all the time. He said he's working out
his technique, and one of these days he'll be able to
bring up completes.

BR: Okay. He's good. You've convinced me.

FR: And he's careful.

BR: He'd better be. We do not want it known that
outside eyes saw that mail.

FR: I told you. He's care—

BR: What about prospects?

FR: None so far. All he's got are a bunch of
lunatics who sound like they're one step ahead of the
net.

BR: Bob's got a prospect. We might not need Wayne's
help on that end.

FR: Bob should have told me. Shitfire, I'm his
runner.

BR: You're his Daddy Rabbit. There's things he
won't tell you for just that reason.

FR: All right. You tell me.

BR: The guy escaped from the Missouri State Pen in
April. Bob knew him when he worked as a guard there.
They were jangled up in Bob's right-wing foolishness.

FR: That's all you've got?

BR: Bob's pouching me a memo. I'll forward it to
you.

FR: Shit, Dwight. You know I've got a veto on this.

BR: Yeah, you do, and we won't use the guy unless we
both agree that he's perfect.

FR: Come on. You owe me more—

BR: He's on the lam. He was afraid to stay at Bob's
compound, so he split to Canada. Bob's got a line on
him. If we agree that he's the guy, I'll send Fred
Otash up to work him.

FR: Hands-on? I thought we'd bring in some cutouts.

BR: I made Freddy lose 60 pounds. He was tall and
heavy, now he's tall and thin.

FR: He looks different.

BR: Completely. He's Lebanese, he speaks Spanish,
we can pass him off as some kind of beaner. Bob said

the prospect is malleable. Freddy eats up that kind of
guy.

FR: You like the guy.

BR: He's a strong prospect. Read the memo and let me
know what you think.

FR: Shit. This is taking time.

BR: All good things do.

FR: Someone might beat us to it.

BR: If they do, they do.

FR: What's Mr. Hoover been—

BR: He's afraid that Marty and Bobby will team up.
It's all he talks about. BLACK RABBIT's been up in the
air since the shakedown flopped. Hoover knows I'm
''exploring more radical means,'' but he hasn't asked
me a single question about it since I made the
proposal.

FR: That means he knows what you're planning.

BR: Maybe, maybe not. Second-guessing the old poof
gets us nowhere.

FR: Dwight, Jesus.

BR: Come on. Remember what I told you? He can't read
minds and he can't patch scrambled calls.

FR: Still.

BR: What about Durfee? Have your LAPD guys turned
up anything?

FR: Nothing. They've got covert bulletins out, but
they haven't got a single goddamn bite.

BR: First we've got to find him. Then we've got to rig
it so Wayne doesn't know that we're handing him up.

FR: That's easy. We stiff a call through Sonny
Liston, who's allegedly got people out looking for
Durfee, not that that impresses—

BR: I want that wedge. I'm not bringing Wayne any
closer without one.

FR: I owe him Durfee. I have a debt to repay to him,
and Durfee will settle it.

BR: I'll put my sources on him. Between yours and
mine, we might hit.

FR: Let's try. I owe Wayne that.

BR: I'm glad I never had any kids. They end up
killing unarmed Negroes and pushing heroin.

FR: The Gospel According to Dwight Chalfont Holly.

BR: Enough. Let's discuss ops money.

FR: I'm in for two hundred cold. You know that.

BR: Otash wants fifty cold.

FR: I'm sure he's worth it.

BR: Bob's putting in a hundred.

FR: Shitfire. He hasn't got that kind of money.

BR: Are you sitting down?

FR: Yes. Why—

BR: I was down in New Hebron. I saw Bob dipping the numbers off some flamethrowers he was getting ready to route to the Gulf. They had triple-zero prefixes, which I just happened to know designates CIA-disbursement lots. I asked Bob about it. He lied, which was the wrong thing to do under the circumstances.

FR: You're talking Swahili, Dwight. I've got no idea where this is going.

BR: I leaned on Bob. He gave it up.

FR: Gave what up?

BR: His Cuban gun-running gig is nothing but a shuck. Carlos Marcello and that CIA guy John Stanton cooked it up. The guns have been going to Castro sources inside Cuba, with Marcello's best wishes. The Outfit's been sucking up to Castro, so he'll help them implement some plan they've got to plant casinos in Latin American countries. Castro's got juice with leftist insurgents in the countries the Outfit's looking at, and he's sending them the guns that Bob and the other guys smuggle in. That way, if the lefties implement takeovers in their countries, they'll let the Outfit in. If they don't take over, the Outfit will grease the right-wing guys still in power.

FR: I'm seeing visions, Dwight. I'm seeing all the Latter-day Saints.

BR: It gets better.

FR: It couldn't. And you don't need to warn me not to tell Wayne, because we both know this would drive the boy insane.

BR: The Outfit's covered on both ends. Castro's sacrificed X-number of Militia troops to the venture,

because Bondurant, Wayne and their guys have been
boating in and taking scalps with impunity. Castro's
making money, it's worth a few Soldiers of the
Revolution in the long run, it all goes to fuel the
Commie agenda in Latin America.

FR: Dwight, I'm flabber—

BR: Stanton and the other CIA guys involved have
been kicking back Bondurant's dope profits to an
Agency source. He's been supplying Bob with CIA
disbursement weaponry, which fucking Bob has been
passing off as ordnance stolen from armory heists and
Army pilferings. Stanton and Marcello have diverted
millions in profit overflow, and they've paid Bob and
these guys Laurent Guery and Flash Elorde percentage
cuts to work the scam from the beginning. Only
Bondurant, your son, and some guy named Mesplede
think the whole thing is for real. They're the stupes
and the true believers.

FR: My lord. All the Saints and the Angel Moroni.

BR: Bob's socked away a hundred cold. He'll kick it
into our operation, if we let him shoot or play backup to our fall guy.

FR: I wouldn't deny him. Not after a story like
that.

BR: He's in, then. He kept all that covert for
years, so I think we can trust him.

FR: We've got to keep this quiet. If Bondurant or my
son find out, it all hits the—

BR: I've got Bob's balls. He won't talk to anyone
else.

FR: Dwight, I should . . .

BR: Yeah, go. Have a drink and talk to your saints.

FR: Visions, Dwight. I mean it.

BR: I almost went into civil law. Can you believe
it?

DOCUMENT INSERT: 8/12/67.
Pouch communiqué. To: FATHER RABBIT. From: BLUE
RABBIT. Marked: ''Eyes Only''/''Read and Burn.''

FATHER,

Here's Bob's memo. His facts & observations are based on his personal relationship with the PROSPECT & on files he stole from the Missouri State Prison System. I cleaned up his grammar & spelling & included some perceptions. READ, BURN & pouch me your response.

The PROSPECT:

Ray, James Earl/white male/5'10"/160/DOB 3-16-28/ Alton, Illinois/1 of 10 children.

PROSPECT grew up in rural Illinois & Missouri. Father was career petty larcenist. PROSPECT first arrested (1942) at age 14 (theft). Became frequenter of traveling carnivals & houses of prostitution. Became friendly with older man (German immigrant) who was pro-Hitler & member of German-American Bund. PROSPECT began to develop anti-Negro attitude at this time.

PROSPECT enlisted in U.S. Army (2/19/46) & requested Germany as duty station. Attended basic training at Camp Crowder, Missouri & assigned (as truck driver) to Q.M. Corps in occupied Germany (7/46). Later assigned as driver to MP battalion in Bremerhaven. Trafficked in black market cigarettes, frequented prostitutes & was treated for syphilis & gonorrhea. Began drinking heavily & taking Benzedrine. Transferred to Infantry Battalion, Frankfurt (4/48) & requested immediate discharge.

Request was denied. PROSPECT charged with being drunk in quarters (10/48) & held in post stockade. PROSPECT escaped, was recaptured & sentenced to 3 months hard labor. Returned to the U.S. (12/48) & given ''general discharge.'' Spent time at family's home in Alton, Illinois. Hitchhiked to Los Angeles (9/49), arrested for burglary (12/9/49), sentenced to 8 months county jail time, released early for good behavior (3/50).

PROSPECT traveled east. Arrested for vagrancy (Marion, Iowa, 4/18/50), released 5/8/50. Arrested for vagrancy (Alton, Ill., 7/26/51), released 9/51. Arrested for armed robbery (taxicab hijack, Chicago, 5/6/52, shot while attempting escape).

PROSPECT received two-year sentence. Served time at Joliet & Pontiac facilities. Established reputation as prison ''Loner'' & habitual user of home-brew alcohol & amphetamines. Paroled 3/12/54.

PROSPECT arrested for burglary (Alton, Ill., 8/28/54). Bailed out & absconded before trial date. Traveled east with criminal companion & shared political views (e.g., all Negroes were inferior & should be killed). Arrested (robbery of post office, Kellerville, Ill.) 3/55. Sentenced to 36 mos. Federal prison. Received at Leavenworth Penitentiary, 7/7/55. Paroled 5/58.

PROSPECT's parole jurisdiction transferred to St. Louis (family members lived there). In 7 & 8/59, PROSPECT & 2 accomplices went on supermarket robbery spree (St. Louis & Alton, Ill.). PROSPECT arrested 10/10/59. Attempted jail escape 12/15/59. Sentenced to 20 yrs. Missouri State Penitentiary. Received at Jefferson City Facility, 3/17/60.

Jeff City reputedly the toughest & most harshly run prison in the U.S. White & Negro inmates largely segregated. White inmates mostly of ''Hillbilly'' lineage & vocal per their hatred of Negroes. Facility had informal chapters of KKK, National States Rights Party, National Renaissance Party & Thunderbolt Legion.

PROSPECT worked in dry cleaning plant & unsuccessfully attempted escape in 10/61. PROSPECT bootlegged prison bakery goods & amphetamines, habitually injected amphetamines & frequently indulged anti-Negro tirades when ''high.'' PROSPECT also sold & rented contraband pornographic magazines & joined informal meetings of extreme right-wing groups (attended by both convicts & guards) & often discussed his desire to ''kill niggers'' & ''Martin Luther Coon.''

PROSPECT also discussed desire to move to segregated African countries, become a ''Merc'' & ''kill niggers.'' BR contends that PROSPECT was especially vituperative, even by white convict standards.

PROSPECT openly fantasized that a ''White Businessman's Association'' had a $100,000 bounty out on King. This is enticing when considering recent ''bounty-talk'' picked up via bug at Grapevine Tavern in St. Louis. BR contends that ''Bounty'' concept strongly plays into PROSPECT's ''get-rich-quick mentality.''

PROSPECT denied parole in '64. Attempted escape 3/11/66. Escaped 4/23/67 (hiding in an outbound bread truck).

PROSPECT stated to BR:

That he walked hill roads to Kansas City, did ''odd jobs & built up a stake,'' bussed to Chicago & got dishwasher's job at restaurant in Winnetka. PROSPECT visited family members & childhood haunts in Alton, Quincy & East St. Louis & determined that no intensive manhunt was being conducted. PROSPECT robbed liquor store in East St. Louis (6/29/67) & stole $4,100.

PROSPECT traveled south & spent week at BR's compound (7/5-7/12/67). Grocery store near New Hebron robbed (7/8/67). BR believes PROSPECT was perpetrator. PROSPECT & BR discussed ''politics'' & PROSPECT apparently was not afraid that BR would report his fugitive status. PROSPECT ''kept to himself,'' drank & took amphetamines, ignored BR's Klansmen, talked to BR exclusively & frequently stated his desire to ''kill niggers,'' ''collect nigger bounties,'' ''hire on as a merc & kill niggers in the Nigger Congo'' & ''live in a white man's paradise like Rhodesia.''

PROSPECT left compound (7/13/67), told BR he was driving to Canada & would call & reestablish contact. PROSPECT called 7/17/67 & gave BR phone # in Montreal.

Summation:

BR characterizes the PROSPECT as moody, acquiescent, limitedly self-sufficient and cunning, socially clumsy, easily led by stronger personalities and easily manipulated on the level of his political beliefs. His frequently stated desire to ''kill niggers'' and his ''bounty'' fixation are encouraging and serve to underline the possibility that he may require minimal sheep-dipping. The PROSPECT may be willing to shoot himself and we may be able to manipulate him into and/or control the context he shoots in.

I think he's the one. Let me know if you agree.

To digress:

I had a long conversation with Mr. Hoover yesterday. I expressed concern about the degree to which his anti-King incursions had already become public knowledge. I mentioned his statements about King, the SCLC's bug and wiretap accusations and reports on the letter which was sent to King and urged him to commit suicide, which has been detailed in several left-wing periodicals. I told him that to further protect the WHITE-HATE and anti-King arms of OPERATION BLACK RABBIT and any escalations that might arise from them, a cosmeticized, largely downscaled anti-King file should be created and stored in the FBI Archives, where it would remain and stand ready for scrutiny in the event of congressional subpoena or subpoena for civil lawsuit.

Mr. Hoover understood that this mock-file would serve to obfuscate the rowdier aspects of OBR, protect Bureau prestige and buttress the validity of his earlier, less vindictive digs at King and the SCLC. He charged me to create file entries, combine them with file entries pertaining to events within public knowledge and whip them into an overall package.

I will undertake and accomplish this over the next several months. This mock-file will, of course, serve to obfuscate our independent escalations. I'm code-naming the file OPERATION ZORRO, a reference to the fictional do-gooder with the black mask.

I'm open to suggestions per the mock-file entries. Let me know if you have any. I would strongly advise you to burn all your OPERATION BLACK RABBIT memoranda at this time, along with this memo.

DOCUMENT INSERT: 8/14/67.
Pouch communiqué. To: BLUE RABBIT. From: FATHER
RABBIT. Marked: ''Eyes Only''/''Read and Burn.''

   BLUE,
   Per PROSPECT: I enthusiastically endorse. Has he
contacted BR from his Montreal location? If so, have
Otash establish contact.
   Per OPERATION ZORRO: I endorse the concept and laud
your farsightedness. I'll burn my BLACK RABBIT
paperwork.
   I'm assuming there's no word on Wendell Durfee. Can
you have your people step up their search?

DOCUMENT INSERT: 8/16/67.
Pouch communiqué. To: FATHER RABBIT. From: BLUE
RABBIT. Marked: ''EYES ONLY''/''READ AND BURN.''

   FATHER,
   The PROSPECT contacted BR. Otash contacted the
PROSPECT in Montreal & advises: He will sever contact
until he successfully suborns or recruits.
   Per Wendell Durfee: My people are still looking.
They've brought in three more men.
   READ THIS & BURN.

DOCUMENT INSERT: 8/22/67.
Bug-extract transcript. Marked: ''Confidential''/
''Stage-1 Covert''/''Eyes Only'': Director, SA D. C.
Holly.
   Location: Card room/Fritzie's Heidelberg
Restaurant/Milwaukee/listening-post-accessed.
Speaking: Unidentified males #1, #2 & #3, presumed
organized-crime associates. (Conversation 5.6
minutes in progress.)

   UM #1: (And) he will rue the day he comes here and
agitates, because the day he marches in the Saint-
Whoever Parade is the day all the white folks put
their goddamn internecine and intramural differences
aside and unite.

UM #2: They think they're white. That's what kills me.

UM #3: I saw a nigger march in the St. Patrick's Parade. He had this sign that said, ''Kiss Me, I'm Irish.''

UM #2: King puts them up to it. They get a toe in our world, then a foot, then an ankle.

UM #1: It's their peckers I'm worried about. Most of them bucks got ones the size of a bratwurst.

UM #2: I was talking to Phil. You know him? ''Phil the Pill.'' He runs semis out of St. Louis.

UM #3: I know him. Phil the Pill. He eats co-pilots like they're popcorn.

UM #2: Phil says there's a contract out. You know, a bounty. Like Steve McQueen in ''Wanted Dead or Alive.''

UM #1: I heard that story. You clip that nigger, you make 50 grand. It's a story I don't believe for one second.

UM #3: That's right. Some cracker clips King, he comes to the Grapevine and says, ''Pay me.'' Everybody says, ''Why? It was just a fucking rumor, and the nigger's dead, anyway.''

(Non-applicable conversation follows.)

DOCUMENT INSERT: 9/1/67.
Listening-post report. Marked: ''Confidential''/ ''Stage-1 Covert''/''Eyes Only'': Director, SA D. C. Holly.

Location: Suite 301/El Encanto Hotel/Santa Barbara/listening-post-accessed.

Sirs,
As per the last 9 monitoring periods (4/2/67 to date), Subject RFK was not in residence at the target location. Subject RFK rents the suite on a yearly basis & it remains empty during his absences. The (voice-activated) mounts have thus far picked up only the non-applicable conversations of El Encanto caretakers & other employees. Per orders, the listening post will continue to be manned full-time.

Respectfully,
SA C.W. Brundage

DOCUMENT INSERT: 9/9/67.
Bug-extract transcript. Marked: ''Confidential''/
''Stage-1 Covert''/''Eyes Only'': Director, SA D. C.
Holly.

Location: Banquet room/Sal's Trattoria
Restaurant/New York City/listening-post-accessed.
Speaking: Robert ''Fat Bob'' Paolucci & Carmine
Paolucci, organized-crime associates. (Conversation
31.8 minutes in progress.)

RP: You are seeing the fall of civilization as we
know it.

CP: It's just a phase. It's like the Twist and the
Hula Hoop. Right now, the shvoogs want their civil
rights, so they burn a few buildings and make some
woop-dee-doo. You want to stop all this riot
bullshit? Give every shvoog in the country an air-
conditioner and some Thunderbird Wine and let them
ride out the heat in style.

RP: It's more than the heat that gets them
agitated. It's that King and his soul brother Bobby
Kennedy. They get them seeing things that ain't
there. They give them an excuse that they can pin
their shitty fucking lives on, like ''the white man
fucked you, so what's his is yours.'' You get ten
million fucking people thinking like that, and maybe
one in ten acts, so you got a million angry niggers
out for white scalps like fucking Cochise and
Pocahontas.

CP: Yeah. I see what you mean.

RP: Someone should clip King and Bobby. You would
save a million white lives, minimum.

CP: I dig you. You save lives in the long run.

RP: You clip those cocksuckers. You do it and save
the world as we know it.

(Non-applicable conversation follows.)

DOCUMENT INSERT: 9/16/67.
Bug-extract transcript. Marked: ''Confidential''/
''Stage-1 Covert''/''Eyes Only'': Director, SA D. C.
Holly.
   Location: Card room/Grapevine Tavern/St. Louis/
listening-post-accessed. Speaking: Unidentified
Males #1 & #2, presumed organized-crime associates.
(Conversation 17.4 minutes in progress).

   UM #1: He saw it. My brother, I mean. He's in the
National Guard.
   UM #2: But that's Detroit. You got a higher ratio of
spooks to whites there.
   UM #1: Don't tell me it can't happen and won't
happen everywhere else. Don't tell me it won't happen,
because it will. You trace everywhere Martin Luther
Coon goes and you see pins in the map that mark dead
white people.
   UM #2: That's true. You got Watts, you got Detroit,
you got D.C. You got riots in our nation's capital.
   UM #1: You also got the bounty. I realize that it's
something like half real—
   UM #2: Yeah, at best, because—
   UM #1: Because it don't matter as long as Joe
Patriot thinks it's real and does the job.
   UM #2: Pow. He does the job. That's the goddamn
thing.
   UM #1: You got to believe there's more bounties out
there. Myth or not, it just takes one guy to believe.
   UM #2: Coon's a dead man. It's—what's that word?
   UM #1: Inevitable?
   UM #2: Yeah, right.
   UM #1: We outnumber the niggers. Like 20 to 1.
That's why I think it'll happen.
   (Non-applicable conversation follows.)

DOCUMENT INSERT: 9/21/67.
Las Vegas Sun headline and subhead:
HUGHES BUYS SANDS
PAYS $23,000,000 FOR HOTEL-CASINO

DOCUMENT INSERT: 9/23/67.
Las Vegas Sun headline and subhead:
HUGHES ON ROLL
BILLIONAIRE RECLUSE EYES CASTAWAYS AND FRONTIER

DOCUMENT INSERT: 9/26/67.
Las Vegas Sun headline and subhead:
LAS VEGANS PRAISE HUGHES:
HE'S KING O' THE STRIP!

DOCUMENT INSERT: 9/28/67.
Los Angeles Examiner subhead:
KING ESCALATES ATTACKS ON ''IMPERIALIST'' WAR

DOCUMENT INSERT: 9/30/67.
St. Louis Globe-Democrat subhead:
RFK ECHOES KING: DECRIES WAR IN SPEECH

DOCUMENT INSERT: 10/1/67.
San Francisco Chronicle subhead:
RFK MUM ON PREZ'L PLANS

DOCUMENT INSERT: 10/2/67.
Los Angeles Times headline and subhead:
NIXON TO PRESS:
KEEPING '68 OPTIONS OPEN

DOCUMENT INSERT: 10/3/67.
Washington Star subhead:
SOURCES CITE LBJ'S ''CONSTERNATION'': PREZ
PUZZLED OVER KING'S BROADSIDES AGAINST WAR

DOCUMENT INSERT: 10/4/67.
FBI field report. Marked: ''Confidential''/''Eyes
Only'': Director, SA D. C. Holly.

    Sirs,
    Per spot-tail Subject Ward J. Littell.
    Subject Littell continues to divide his work time
between Los Angeles, Las Vegas, and Washington, D.C.
He is currently working on the Las Vegas end of
negotiations for the purchase of the Castaways Hotel
and on the Washington end of conferences pertaining
to appeals on the behalf of Teamster President James

R. Hoffa. Subject Littell also continues to be
intimately involved with Janice Tedrow Lukens. I have
concluded, along with the other assigned agents, that
Subject Littell assumes the presence of sporadically
initiated tails and thus drives different workday
routes in order to thwart them. That said, I should
also state that Subject Littell has not been seen
engaging in any sort of activity that might be deemed
suspicious.

Spot-tails to be continued on the ordered basis.
Respectfully,
SA T. V. Houghton

DOCUMENT INSERT: 10/9/67.
Hate-mail extract. Compiled by: FATHER RABBIT.
Sealed and marked: ''Destroy Without Reading in the
Event of My Death.''

Mail sender: Anonymous. Postmark: St. Louis,
Missouri. Recipient: Dr. M. L. King. From page 1 (of
1):

Here's another ditty for you, Coon;
The Bounty Man's going to get your black ass
    soon;
Fear the NSRP, John Birch and the Klan;
Fear the wrath of the righteous All-White Man;
Better get your shroud and wait for Judgment Day;
The White Man says you've outlived your stay;
Grab your pickaninnies, your wine and your dope;
Grab your watermelons and don't you mope;
Better head for Africa lickety-split;
The White Man's going to tar your hide in shit;
When that happens all the white folks will go
    hooray!
And say we killed that nigger who outlived his
    stay!

DOCUMENT INSERT: 10/30/67.
Hate-mail extract. Compiled by: FATHER RABBIT.
Sealed and marked: ''Destroy Without Reading in the
Event of My Death.''

Mail sender: Anonymous. Postmark. Pasadena,
California. Recipient: Senator Robert F. Kennedy.
From page 8 (of 8):

THE WORLDWIDE JEWISH PIG ORDER HAS CHRISTENED YOU
WITH THE BLESSING OF THE RAPIST POPE AND THE LEARNED
ELDERS OF ZION WHO HAVE CAST A SPELL OF PUS OVER THE
CHILDREN WHO DARED TO FIGHT THE JEW INFIDEL IN THE
NAME OF THE ARAB DIASPORA. YOUR UGLY MOTHER KNOWS YOU
ARE THE SPAWN OF THE HEBREW COCKSEED AND THE RABID
GOAT. THE JEWISH CANCER MACHINE FEARS THE HEADACHE
DOCTOR. HE SMOKES MARLBORO CIGARETTES NOT GEFILTE
FISH. HE SAYS RFK MUST DIE! RFK MUST DIE! RFK MUST
DIE! RFK MUST DIE!!!!!!

103

(Las Vegas, Los Angeles, Washington, D.C., New Orleans, Mexico City, 11/4/67–12/3/67)

DOMINOES: the DI/the Sands/the Castaways. On tap: The
Frontier.

Ten pins: Non-Mormon skim men snitched to the Feds. Old
skim hands in custody.

Littell planned. Littell sowed. The Boys reaped. Bribes/PR/
extortion. Blackmail/philanthropy.

It took four years. Drac owns Las Vegas now. It's Drac's kingdom complete.

Three units down. More up. Eight pending. Drac buys Vegas.
Drac owns Vegas—cosmetically.

The Boys exult. The Boys praise Littell. The Boys co-opt
Wayne Senior. Wayne Senior deploys. Wayne Senior recruits:

Mormons for the DI. Mormons for the Castaways. Mormons
for the Sands. Mormon floor men/Hughes-vetted/legit. Mormon *skim* men/*non*-vetted/*non*-legit.

More hotels on tap. More Mormon hires pending. Drac gets
the inked deeds. Drac gets the glory. The Boys get the money.

Littell braced the Boys. The Boys agreed: Let's suspend the
skim. Let Drac move in. Let the ink dry. Let the shouts subside.

Skim then. Rig the vacuums. Put the hose to Drac.

Littell said we're ready. I've pegged sixty-one businesses. They're pension-fund-indebted. They're subornable. They're cake. We revive the skim. We suborn said businesses. We divert profits and plant foreign casinos.

It looked good on paper. It *was* good for him. It upped his retirement stakes.

Retire me. I'm stretched thin. I'm *scared*. Drac scared him. Drac talked PR. Drac talked financial disclosure.

I'll buff my image. I'll audit my books. I'll publish clean stats. *Don't* do it. *I've* pilfered. Don't disclose *my* tithe stats.

Retire me. I'm stretched thin. My love life's a mess. I dream about Jane. I make love to Janice.

Janice found work. Janice bought a golf shop. She sold golfwear at the Sands Hotel. She built a rep.

She did trick shots at her indoor range. She built a rep. She ragged herself like Barb did. She built a rep. She performed. She drew customers. She made money.

She still limped. She still cramped. She still spasmed up. She drank less now. She downed less. She tattled less. She laid off the Tedrows. She'd outgrown their spell.

He slept with Janice. Jane shared the bed. Jane bludgeoned/ Jane shotgunned/Jane bled.

Retire me. I'm stretched thin. It hurts to sleep. My hate life's a mess.

He worked with Wayne Senior. They haggled business points. Wayne Senior talked Image.

Shitfire—looks *count*. Screw hate tracts—*I* know Dick Nixon.

Wayne Senior talked Image. Wayne Senior talked change. Wayne Senior did not talk BLACK RABBIT. Wayne Senior performed. Wayne Senior delivered.

He saw Nixon. He passed the word. He said Dick *will* run. He said Dick wants that sitdown. He said Dick wants your cash.

Littell called Drac. Drac agreed. Drac said he'd pay that percentage. Littell called the Boys. The Boys whooped and crowed.

Dick likes money. Dick will grant "favors." Wayne Senior says so. He'll run. He'll gain ground. He'll win primaries. He'll get the nomination. He'll meet with Littell.

Retire me. I'm stretched thin. I hate Wayne Senior. I hate Tricky Dick. I love Bobby. I love Bobby's kid.

He passed through D.C. He met Paul Horvitz. He culled

Jane's file. He retyped her notes. He snitched second-line mob-sters to Bobby.

He met Paul four times. He delivered four parcels. Paul was wowed. Paul cited Bobby. Bobby was very impressed. They held the data. They verified facts. They withheld disclosure.

Paul said our deal holds. We'll hold your dirt—until late '68. Paul said Bobby might run. LBJ might retire. Let's await '68.

He met Paul. He played southern poof. He deployed a fake beard and drawl. They talked politics. He weaved lies. He described his life in Mississippi.

School in De Kalb. Liberal values. Southern gentility. The Klan drove him out. He moved north. Displaced aristocracy.

Paul heard his tales. Paul endured dinner dates. He's lonely. He's old. He loves Bobby.

Retire me. I'm stretched thin. I indulge fantasies.

He traveled. He worked. He tithed the SCLC. He ran tail checks. He caught tails. He diversionaried.

He calculated. He tail-scanned. He nailed the rotation: Spot tails/one day on/nine days off. He confirmed the nine to one ratio. He tail-checked accordingly.

Paranoia: valid and justified. Nine days free. One day restricted. Act accordingly.

Mr. Hoover never called. Ditto BLUE RABBIT. He did the bug jobs. Agents directed him. BLUE RABBIT disappeared. He got no pouches. He got no attaboys. He got no thank-yous. He got no welcome back. He got no tix to BLACK RABBIT.

It scared him. It said they've upscaled BLACK RABBIT. It said they're doing bad things.

He met Bayard Rustin once a month. They had lunch in D.C. Bayard said he almost got blackmailed—child, what a scene!

Bayard ran it down. Bayard described mirrors and mike plants. Bayard described a fruit squeeze. It felt like Freddy Otash. It could be Pete B.

Pete was bereft then. Barb had left him. Pete sulked accord-ingly. Littell tracked the date Bayard gave him. Littell tracked probability.

He was bugging Mob spots then. He braced Freddy T. Freddy declined work. Freddy *had* work. Freddy said Fred O. gigs me.

Don't ask Pete. He might say yes. He might say I pulled that queer squeeze.

Retire me. I'm stretched thin. My friends frighten me.

He met Bayard. Bayard talked. Bayard said Martin scares me. He's making plans. They're his boldest yet. He'll make more enemies.

Rent strikes/boycotts/poor people's unions/poor people's marches/poor people's heresies.

Littell heard it. Littell remembered—it's Lyle Holly's prophecy.

Bayard was scared. Martin was crazed. Martin breathed enmity. His plans would shock. His plans would divide. His plans would stir enmity. His plans would trash his triumphs. His plans would spark backlash. His plans would build heresy.

Littell *saw* it:

It's Martin Luther/1532. It's Europe aflame. There's the Pope. He's Mr. Hoover. His old world's aflame.

Retire me. I want to watch. I want to watch passively.

Jimmy Hoffa's in jail. I'll file his appeals. Retire me. I travel to excess. I country-hop. Please retire me.

He flew south. He hit Mexico City. He made four trips and met with Sam G. They talked colonization. Sam talked travel spree.

Sam toured Central America. Sam toured the Caribbean. Sam brought interpreters and money. Sam talked to dictators. Sam talked to puppet thugs. Sam talked to rebel fiends.

Sam did gruntwork. Sam did groundwork. Sam laid seeds. Sam said I love your cause. I support it and pledge fraternity. Here's some money. There'll be more. You'll hear from me.

Sam spread seed money. Sam seeded all ideologies. Plant seeds—sow revolt and repression—casino ideology.

Retire me. I get airsick. Casino smoke sickens me. Retire Pete. He's tired too. His work sickens me. I disapprove—I've got no right—it's hypocrisy.

Pete sold dope. Pete ran his cab stand. Pete ran his hotel-casino. Pete had Cuba. Pete had Vietnam. Pete had two-front lunacy. Pete missed Vietnam. Pete missed Barb more. Barb made him stay home. Pete curtailed his lunacy.

Pete stayed home. Pete travel-spreed. Pete went to Barb's turf. Pete went to smalltown Wisconsin.

Pete called him. Barb called him. He got two versions. Vegas to Sparta—Pete leaves expectant—Pete returns whipped.

Pete worked his scams. Pete praised the war. Pete indulged habits. Barb slung hash. Barb reviled the war. Barb eschewed habits.

Love as stasis. Two takes. His-and-hers.

Retire Pete. Upgrade Wayne—*le fils de* Pete.

Pete had nightmares. Pete described them. Betty Mac/the crossbars/the noose. Pete had real pictures. *He* didn't. That made it worse.

There's Jane Fentress—Arden Breen/Bruvick/Smith/Coates. She's dead by knife/dead by cudgel/dead by steel sap.

The pictures varied. One soundtrack held in. Mr. Hoover's letter—addressed to Dr. King.

"What a grim farce." "One way out." "A liability."

Retire me. I'll try to live idle. I might not succeed.

104

(Vietnam, Las Vegas, Los Angeles, Bay St. Louis,
Cuban Waters, 11/4/67–12/3/67)

MORE:

Troop infusions. Troop movements. Troops dead.

More:

Bomb raids. Ground raids. Resistance.

Resistance in-country. Resistance at home. Resistance worldwide. The war was MORE. The biz was LESS. Wayne knew it.

Less:

Territory. Profit growth. Potential.

The kadre shared lab space. The Can Lao co-opted. Why do it? The Can Lao shipped to Europe. The kadre shipped to Vegas. Note the dichotomy.

The kadre did good biz. The Can Lao did great biz. Note the discrepancy. The war defined MORE. The biz defined LESS. Note the inconsistency.

Their turf was restricted. West Vegas was sapped. They had no growth room. Pete pouched Stanton. Pete pouched once a month. Pete said let us GROW.

Out of Vegas. Into L.A. Into Frisco.

We've got Tiger Kamp. We've got poppy slaves. We've got dope fields boocoo. We can GROW. We can earn MORE. The Cause will GROW.

Stanton said no. Stanton insisted. Wayne read his tone. Said tone was hinky. Said tone was quasi-weird. Pete wants MORE. Stanton wants LESS. Note the entropy.

Wayne wanted MORE. Wayne rotated east. Wayne saw more incessant. More troops smoking weed. More troops popping pills. More troops scared incessant.

Big "H" killed fear. They'd find it. Wayne knew.

The war thrilled him. The war rocked. The war grew. The "Cause" bored him. The "Cause" vexed. The "Cause" entropied.

Log it: Cuban runs/forty-plus/no at-sea resistance. It was boring now. It was impotent. It was quasi-weird.

The Cause was flypaper. Pete was a fly. Pete was stuck on 1960. Laurent was a fly. Flash was a fly. They buzzed Cuba persistent.

They talked stale shit. They talked coups and Reds. They talked domino jive. Bob talked stale shit. Bob talked race and Reds. Bob talked domino jive.

Bob vibed hinky. Bob vibed it weeks running. Bob vibed quasi-weird. Bob vibed anxious. Bob vibed scared. Bob vibed jazzed.

Bob vibed stuck. Cuba is flypaper. Cuba is quicksand. Cuba is glue.

Vegas is quicksand. Barb knows it. Barb extricates. Pete knows it. Pete stays.

Pete hit Wayne. Wayne took it. Pete apologized. Pete was frayed. Barb was in exile. The biz was exiled.

Pete wants MORE. Pete's frustrated. Stanton's entrenched. Pete's stuck. Pete's impeded. Pete's fuse might fry.

Pete and Barb cut a truce. Said truce was a travel ban— Vietnam *nyet*. Pete was stuck. Pete was truce-restricted. Pete talked truce overrides.

I'll fly to Saigon. I'll brace Stanton. I'll demand MORE.

And Stanton will wink. And Stanton will smile. And Stanton will mollify.

The war was MORE. The biz was LESS. Wayne Senior was MORE plus. They were equals now. Friends of sorts. Friends with non–Pete dimensions.

Pete seeks MORE. Pete seeks more dope turf and money. Wayne Senior seeks MORE. Wayne Senior dumps his hate biz. Wayne Senior disdains more money. Pete finds frustration. Wayne Senior finds Dick Nixon.

Pete hobnobs with pushers. Pete schleps cab calls. Pete walks flypaper. Wayne Senior plays golf. Wayne Senior shoots skeet. Wayne Senior drinks with Dick Nixon.

He worked for them. They were inimical types. They ran real to putative father. He loved both their women. He lived sans women. Wendell D. and Lynette made that fly. He head-tripped women. He head-tripped Barb mostly. He head-tripped Barb until then.

He hit her. She grabbed a knife. She ran from him and Pete. She grabbed the war. She sifted shit through.

Pete. Pete's gigs. The Life.

She kicked dope. She kicked the Life. She ran smug now. She jumped off flypaper. Her shit cohered. She lost her allure. He loved her more. He liked her less. His torch fizzled.

He head-tripped Janice. It ran twenty years now. He fucked her for payback on Dallas. He extricated. She paid.

She still limped. She still cramped. Her breath still spasmed. He saw her in Vegas. He saw her with Ward and solo. She saw him watching sometimes. She always smiled. She always waved. She always blew kisses.

It took him back. Old glimpses in windows. Peeks through cracked doors.

She was forty-six now. He was thirty-three. Her hips cocked funny. She had limp side-effects. He wondered how far her legs spread.

Relight the torch. Dig the glow. Groove on the cause-and-effect. She's real again. She's in your head—because you're back with Wayne Senior.

Grunt work. Hate-mail duty. Let's study hate. Let's see how it works. Let's see what it says.

Wayne Senior said I'm storing intelligence. I'm skimming data off the FBI. I'm polling resentment. I'm taking its pulse. It's academic for now.

Wayne Senior spoke lofty. Wayne Senior spoke abstract. Wayne Senior spoke with forked tongue.

Wayne knew:

He's teaching you. Read the hate. Don't hate fatuously.

He rotated. He ran Saigon to D.C. He pulled intercepts. He did sneak-ins. He bagged mail. He mimeographed. He print-dusted. He got zero. He ran ninhydrin tests. He got loop whirls and partials. He learned the Hate Alphabet.

He did re-sneaks. He replaced the mail. He savored the Hate Alphabet.

A for Anger. F for Fear. I for Idiocy. D for Dumb. R for Ridiculous. J for Justification.

Coloreds mock order. Coloreds foist chaos. Coloreds breed lunacy. The haters knew it. Wayne Senior knew it. *He* knew it. The haters lived to hate. That was wrong. *That* was lunacy. The haters lived disordered lives. The haters thrived on chaos. The haters mimed the hatees.

S for Stupid. R for Resentful. W for Weak.

He learned his lessons. He took Wayne Senior's Hate Course. He searched for Wendell Durfee.

He rotated south. He made Cuban runs. He rotated west to L.A. He prowled Compton. He prowled Willowbrook. He prowled Watts.

He watched Negroes. Negroes watched him. He stayed cool. He stayed calm. He knew his ABCs. Wendell was nowhere. Wendell, where you be? I hate you. I'll kill you. Hate won't hinder me.

Hate smart—like Wayne Senior. P for Poised. B for Brave. C for Collected.

He did intercepts. He culled hate. He caught lunacy.

Weird:

He muscled a deadbeat. It was late '66. The clown was named Sirhan Sirhan. Sirhan had hate tracts. RFK got some hate notes. They were margin scrawled the same way.

All cap letters/headaches and pus/"Jewish Cancer Machine." Sirhan drools. Sirhan hates stupid. Sirhan foists lunacy.

Don't do it. It's counterproductive. It's dumb. It's insanity.

Hate smart. Like Wayne Senior. Like me.

105

(Las Vegas, Sparta, Bay St. Louis, Cuban Waters, 11/4/67–12/3/67)

YOU'RE HOMELESS.

You're a Vegas transient. You're embargoed at home. You're a fucking refugee.

It's jail. It's Skid Row. It mocks rotation. It's Splitsville. It's mock-divorce. It's past separation.

Barb split. Pete traveled—all-love rotations. Pete flew back alone—non-love rotations. The trips trashed him. The trips taught him. The trips made him see: You hate Vegas now. Without Barb it's shit. You're Joe Vegas Refugee.

He had the trifecta. It was all Vegas-bred—Tiger/the dope biz/the Cavern. He couldn't split. The Boys held his lease. It was sealed and marked "Dallas."

He loved the trifecta. He hated the venue. They all intertwined.

Stateless.

He met Barb. She slung plates. No high heels/no spangles. Her sister worked her. Her sister lubed her—goooood profit perks. Barb B.—ex-lounge queen. Waitress/restaurateur.

He couldn't have her. He couldn't have her on his terms. He couldn't have her at *his* location.

He hubbed in Vegas. He flew to Mississippi. He hated it. Dumb crackers and dumb niggers. Bugs and sand fleas.

He made boat runs. He got seasick. His pulse raced. He snarfed Dramamine. The runs bored him. Stealth and scalps and nothing more. No good resistance.

He was a transient. He was travel-screwed. He was a rotation refugee.

You want things. You can't have things. You can't give things up. You've got habits. You don't need them. You can't give them up.

Cigarettes. Pizza pie and pecan pie. Stiff drinks and steak.

He hid his habits in Sparta. Barb never saw. He flew out. He de-purified. He binged on rotations.

Transient. Glutton. Exile. Exiled on boat runs/exiled down south/exiled in Vegas.

Drac's town now—Drac's town cosmetic.

He knew Drac. They went back. They met in '53. He worked for Drac. He scored Drac dope. He scored Drac his women. Drac was a glutton then. Drac was a glutton still.

He cruised the DI. He bribed a Mormon for a look-see. He bought a looooong look.

Drac dozed. Drac wore drip cords. Drac got a transfusion. Mormon blood/hormone-laced/pure. Drac was gaunt. Drac was svelte. Drac was chic. Drac wore a Kotex-box hat and Kleenex-box slippers.

Drac was on dope. Barb was off dope. Pete pushed dope

non-boocoo. Pete was hamstrung. Pete was profit-screwed. Pete was a dope refugee.

He begged Stanton. He said *let me expand.* Stanton always refused. He pouched Stanton. He pleaded and begged. Stanton always refused. Stanton always cited Carlos. Stanton always cited the Boys.

They don't want it. Live with it. It stands as their call. He lived with it. He hated it. He felt refugized.

He got ideas.

I'll fly to Saigon. I'll brace Stanton. I'll break the truce. I'll tell Barb to stamp my visa. I'll make her unleash my gonads.

I'll tell Stanton to expand the biz or shove it up your ass. Stanton would shit. Carlos would shit. The Boys *might* temporize.

It might work. It might shake them. It might serve to de-refugize. He needed it. He needed something. He needed MORE.

He got bored. He got crazed. He fretted shit.

Like: Cuba—*mucho* boat runs—no at-sea resistance.

Like: Bob Relyea—nervous and hi-amped.

He's talking trash. He's saying our work's dead. He's saying I've got work transcendent.

He went by Bob's kompound. He saw Bob with guns. He saw Bob burn three-zero codes.

Huh? What? Don't grab at straws. Don't be this skittish refugee.

He got bored. He got crazed. His pulse skipped.

DOCUMENT INSERT: 12/3/67.
Bug-extract transcript. Marked: ''Confidential''/
''Stage-1 Covert''/''Eyes Only'': Director, SA D. C.
Holly.
    Location: Card room/Grapevine Tavern/St. Louis/
listening-post-accessed. Speaking: Norbert Donald
Kling & Rowland Mark DeJohn, paroled felons (Armed
Robbery/Bunco/GTA) & presumed organized-crime
associates. (Conversation 14.1 minutes in progress.)

    NDK: And people hear, you know. Word goes out.
    RMDJ: It's like the name of this place. The
Grapevine.
    NDK: Yeah. The grape for the ape.

RMDJ: Guys come through, they hear, they start thinking.

NDK: They think, shit, 50 G's for a good deed, and it don't go unrewarded.

RMDJ: You do it down south, no jury would convict you.

NDK: You're right. It's like those guys in Mississippi. They wax those civil rights humps and walk scot-free.

NDK: You know who I saw here? Like in May?

RMDJ: Who?

NDK: Jimmy Ray. I bought goofballs off him in Jeff City.

RMDJ: I heard he broke out.

NDK: He did. He breaks out, then he's disappointed that there's no big manhunt.

RMDJ: That's Jimmy in a nutshell. Hey, world, notice me.

NDK: He hates niggers. You got to give him that.

RMDJ: He was tight with the guards. At Jeff City, I mean. I never liked that about him.

NDK: The guards were klanned-up. That was the attraction to Jimmy.

RMDJ: That one guard was a pisser. Remember him? Bob Relyea.

NDK: Bob the Brain. Jimmy called him that.

RMDJ: I heard he's klanned-up down south now.

NDK: Klanned-up and a snitch is what I heard. As in, he works for the Feds.

RMDJ: That could be. Remember, he left Jeff and joined the Army.

NDK: Jimmy said he might go see him.

RMDJ: Jimmy's a talker. He always talked about a whole lot of things.

NDK: He heard about the bounty. He nearly bust a gut talking about that.

RMDJ: Talk's talk. Jimmy said he fucked Marilyn Monroe, which don't mean he really did it.

(Non-applicable conversation follows.)

<u>DOCUMENT INSERT</u>: 12/3/67.
Bug-extract transcript. Marked: ''Confidential''/
''Stage-1 Covert''/''Eyes Only'': Director, SA D. C.
Holly.
    Location: Office/Mike Lyman's Restaurant/Los
Angeles/listening-post-accessed. Speaking:
Unidentified Males #1 & #2, presumed organized-crime
associates. (Conversation 1.9 minutes in progress.)

    UM #1: . . . you've heard the stories, right?
    UM #2: Just glimmers. Carlos knows they're on the
boat, so he sends some guys to the Keys.
    UM #1: Not just any guys. He sends Chuck the Vice
and Nardy Scavone.
    UM #2: Oh, Jesus.
    UM #1: You have to assume that he wanted to prolong
things. It is well known that Chuck and Nardy work
slow.
    UM #2: I have heard the stories, believe me.
    UM #1: Here's the good part. You'll like it.
    UM #2: So tell me. Don't be a fucking cock-tease.
    UM #1: Okay, they spot the boat. It's docked some-
place quiet. They sneak up quiet and climb on board.
    UM #2: Come on, don't string it—
    UM #1: Arden and Danny see them coming. Danny
starts bawling and saying rosaries. Arden's got a
gun. She shoots Danny in the back of the head to put
him out of his misery. She aims at fucking Chuck and
Nardy, but the fucking gun jams.
    UM #2: Fuck, that is rich. That is just—
    UM #1: Chuck and Nardy grab her and tie her down.
Carlos wants to know why they rabbited and did someone
tip them off. Chuck's got his vice in a toolbox. He
puts Arden's head in. He leans on the handle, but
Arden won't give it up.
    UM #2: Jesus.
    UM #1: He cracked all her teeth and broke her jaw.
She still wouldn't talk.
    UM #2: Jesus.
    UM #1: She bit her tongue off. She couldn't talk if
she wanted to, so Nardy capped her.

UM #2: Jesus.

(Non-applicable conversation follows).

DOCUMENT INSERT: 12/3/67.
Pouch communiqué. To: Dwight Holly. From: Fred Otash.
Marked: ''Confidential''/''Eyes Only''/''Read & Burn
Immediately.''

DH,

Here's the summary on my dealings with the PROSPECT
to date, including my reasoning on why I think we
should use him. I hate writing things down, so READ &
BURN IMMEDIATELY.

1 – Contact with PROSPECT established 8/16/67, at
bar (''Acapulco'') downstairs from PROSPECT's
residence (''Har-K Apts'') in Montreal. PROSPECT was
using alias ''Eric Starvo Galt.'' I utilized my fake
appearance & Latin accent & used the alias ''Raul
Acias.''

2 – At Acapulco I sold PROSPECT amphetamine
capsules & posed as smuggler with segregationist
leanings. PROSPECT & I met at Acapulco & Neptune
Tavern over next several nights & discussed politics.
PROSPECT admitted 2 recent robberies in states (East
St. Louis, Ill. & New Hebron, Miss.) but did not
mention his 4/23/67 prison escape. PROSPECT stated
that he also robbed a prostitute & pimp at a ''fuck
pad'' in Montreal shortly after his arrival. He got
$1,700 but was spending $ fast & would ''soon be
broke.''

3 – PROSPECT discussed his need to secure ID which
would allow him to get a Canadian passport & thus
travel to other countries. I told him I had
connections & would help him. I lent him small amounts
of money, supplied him with amphetamines & discussed
politics with him. He frequently mentioned his hatred
of M. L. King & desire to ''kill niggers in
Rhodesia.'' I stalled him per the ID papers &
continued to lend him $. PROSPECT became nervous &
stated his desire to return to the states, go to
Alabama & ''Maybe go to work for Governor Wallace.''

I saw that he was determined to go & improvised a
plan.

4 – I told him I had some narcotics for him to drive
across the border & would pay him $1,200. He agreed to
do the job. I filled a briefcase with sand, locked it &
gave it to him, then met him on the American side.
This was a test to see if he would steal the briefcase
or would prove to be as compliant as I thought he
would be.

5 – He passed the test & made 2 other ''narcotics
runs'' for me. I saw that he was determined to drive
to Alabama & told him I would get him his ID, a new car
& more $, because I had more ''jobs'' for him to do.
PROSPECT stated that he wanted to spend time in
Birmingham, because of its history of ''nigger
bombings.'' I gave him $2,000 & told him to wait for a
letter at Birmingham General Delivery. I also gave
him a phone-drop # to call me at in New Orleans.

6 – This was the risk part of the operation, because
there was a chance the PROSPECT would ditch out on me.
If he didn't, it would confirm his pliable nature &
suitable nature for our job.

7 – PROSPECT called phone-drop on 8/25 & gave his
address as ''Economy Grill & Rooms'' in Birmingham.
I mailed him $600 & a small supply of biphetamine
capsules, flew to Birmingham & surveilled him from
discreet distances. PROSPECT visited the National
States Rights Party HQ, purchased right-wing leaflets
& bumper stickers & holed up in his room. I called him
(allegedly long-distance) & agreed to give him $2,000
(advance against future jobs) so he could buy a new
car. I wired the $ to him & surveilled his purchase of
a 1966 Mustang.

8 – PROSPECT secured an Alabama driver's license
(9/6/67) under name ''Eric Starvo Galt'' & registered
the '66 Mustang. I met PROSPECT in Birmingham, drank &
talked politics with him & told him to buy some camera
equipment to sell in Mexico. PROSPECT purchased
$2,000 worth of equipment, which I told him to ''sit
on.''

9 – PROSPECT remained in Birmingham, took a

locksmith's course & dance lessons & surreptitiously
filmed women from his rooming-house window. I remained
in Birmingham & took pains never to be seen with him.
My plan was to situate PROSPECT in various places &
give him orders that would sound ridiculous should he
be captured & interrogated after our operation.
PROSPECT's need for $ & amphetamines kept him
beholden to me.

10 — I wrote PROSPECT on 10/6/67 & told him to meet
me in Nuevo Laredo, Mexico with the camera equipment.
PROSPECT agreed to meet me after he ''fenced the
goods.'' Again, I promised to secure him valid ID
papers & added that I could get him a Canadian
passport. PROSPECT met me in Nuevo Laredo with $ from
the equipment he fenced, at a loss. I told him I was
not mad & had more ''narcotics runs'' for him.
PROSPECT was mad that I had not yet secured papers for
him, but agreed to stay in Mexico & wait for my calls.

11 — PROSPECT traveled throughout Mexico by car &
called me at phone-drop in New Orleans. I forwarded
sums of $ to him at American Express offices & paid
him for 4 ''narcotics runs'' from McAllen to Juarez.
I met with PROSPECT 4 times from 10/22/67 to 11/9/67 &
drew him out on political issues. PROSPECT described
a ''Bounty'' offered thru the Grapevine Bar in St.
Louis ($50,000 to kill MLK), which sounded like a
fantasy but indicated that he might be willing to step
up for D-Day, which would upgrade his role in our
plan. PROSPECT was drinking heavily, taking
amphetamines & smoking marijuana in Mexico & while
there got into altercations with prostitutes & pimps.
PROSPECT drove to Los Angeles (without calling me) &
called with address on 11/21/67. He stated he wants
more work from me, is taking self-hypnosis & self-
improvement courses & is visiting ''segregationist
bookstores.'' He urged me to get him his passport
papers as an ''advance against future jobs.''

12 — PROSPECT remains in L.A. I'm L.A.-based, so
I'll be able to surveil him. PROSPECT remains pliable
& I'm convinced he'll work for us. Have we got a date &
or location yet?

I'll pouch again when required. Again, READ & BURN.
F.O.

DOCUMENT INSERT: 12/4/67.
Pouch communiqué. To: Fred Otash. From: Dwight Holly.
Marked: ''Confidential''/''Eyes Only''/''Read &
Burn.''

F.O.,
No date or location yet. Continue with PROSPECT.
Will try to secure RED RABBIT's travel plans.
READ THIS & BURN.
D.C.H.

DOCUMENT INSERT: 12/4/67.
Atlanta Constitution headline and subhead:
KING ANNOUNCES ''POOR PEOPLE'S MARCH'' ON WASHINGTON
PLEDGES TO WORK FOR ''REDISTRIBUTION OF WEALTH''

DOCUMENT INSERT: 12/5/67.
Cleveland Plain Dealer headline and subhead:
KING ON SPRING MARCH:
''TIME TO CONFRONT POWER STRUCTURE MASSIVELY''

DOCUMENT INSERT: 12/6/67.
Verbatim FBI telephone call transcript. Marked:
''Recorded at the Director's Request'' /''Classified
Confidential 1-A: Director's Eyes Only.'' Speaking:
Director Hoover, President Lyndon B. Johnson.

LBJ: Is that you, Edgar?
JEH: It's me, Mr. President.
LBJ: That goddamn march. It's all over the news.
JEH: I've read the announcements. They've fulfilled
my very worst fears and apprehensions.
LBJ: That son-of-a-bitch is bringing an army to
protest me, after all I've done for the Negro people.
JEH: The march will unleash a bloodbath.
LBJ: I asked him to call it off, but the son-of-a-
bitch refused. He's killing my chance to get
reelected. He's in cahoots with that spoon-fed
cocksucker, Bobby Kennedy.

JEH: I will let you in on a little-known fact, Mr. President. Bobby allowed me to tap and bug King himself, back in '63. He has forgotten his initial misgivings in his rush to embrace that Communist.

LBJ: The cocksucker wants my job. King's creating the fucking dissent that will get it for him.

JEH: I'm putting 44 agents on King. They will disseminate derogatory data nationwide. I will do everything in my power to subvert this march.

LBJ: Edgar, was there ever a better friend to the Negro people than me?

JEH: No, Mr. President.

LBJ: Edgar, has my legislation improved the lot of the Negro people?

JEH: Yes, Mr. President.

LBJ: Edgar, have I been a friend to Martin Luther King?

JEH: Yes, Mr. President.

LBJ: Then why is that cocksucker trying to cornhole me when I've bent over backwards to befriend him?

JEH: I don't know, Mr. President.

LBJ: He's a worse bane to my fucking existence than this fucking war I'm fucking knee-deep in.

JEH: I'm going to plant a Negro in the SCLC. He used to work as my chauffeur.

LBJ: Tell him to chauffeur King off a cliff.

JEH: I understand your frustration, Sir.

LBJ: I'm getting fucked from two flanks. I'm fighting a two-front war against a King and a fucking Kennedy.

JEH: Yes, Mr. President.

LBJ: You're a good man, Edgar.

JEH: Thank you, Mr. President.

LBJ: Do what you can on this, all right?

JEH: I will, Sir.

LBJ: Goodbye, Edgar.

JEH: Goodbye, Mr. President.

DOCUMENT INSERT: 12/7/67.
Los Angeles Examiner subhead:
BUSINESS COMMUNITY ATTACKS KING FOR ''POOR PEOPLE'S MARCH''

DOCUMENT INSERT: 12/9/67.
Dallas Morning News subhead:
SPRING MARCH ON WASHINGTON ''SOCIALISTIC,''
BUSINESS LEADERS CHARGE

DOCUMENT INSERT: 12/17/67.
Chicago Tribune headline and subhead:
NIXON IN '68?
EX-VEEP TO ANNOUNCE CANDIDACY?

DOCUMENT INSERT: 12/17/67.
Miami Herald headline and subhead:
CLERGYMEN ON WASHINGTON MARCH:
''A CALL TO ANARCHY AND RIOTS''

DOCUMENT INSERT: 12/18/67.
Chicago Sun-Times subhead:
RFK PRAISES WASHINGTON MARCH
MUM ON WHITE HOUSE PLANS

DOCUMENT INSERT: 12/18/67.
Denver Post-Dispatch headline and subhead:
WILL HE OR WON'T HE?
PUNDITS ASSESS LBJ'S REELECTION PLANS

DOCUMENT INSERT: 12/20/67.
Boston Globe subhead:
KING CALLS FOR WAR PROTESTERS TO EMBRACE POOR
PEOPLE'S MARCH

DOCUMENT INSERT: 12/21/67.
Sacramento Bee subhead:
EXPECT NIXON TO RUN, GOP INSIDERS SAY

DOCUMENT INSERT: 12/22/67.
Los Angeles Times subhead:
RFK, HUMPHREY PLAYING COY?
AWAITING LBJ'S DECISION?

DOCUMENT INSERT: 12/23/67.
Kansas City Star subhead:
ROTARY PRESIDENT CALLS KING MARCH ''COMMUNIST
INSPIRED''

DOCUMENT INSERT: 12/28/67.
Las Vegas Sun headline and subhead:
FRONTIER HOTEL FALLS TO HUGHES
BILLIONAIRE'S VEGAS ROLL CONTINUES!

DOCUMENT INSERT: 1/4/68.
Verbatim FBI telephone call transcript. (OPERATION
BLACK RABBIT Addendum.) Marked: ''Recorded at the
Director's Request''/''Classified Confidential 1-A:
Director's Eyes Only.'' Speaking: Director, BLUE
RABBIT.

DIR: Good morning.

BR: Good morning, Sir.

DIR: RED RABBIT is misbehaving. He's being a very
bad bunny.

BR: I've been reading the newspapers, Sir. I think
he's stepped over the line.

DIR: He has, but not to the extent where he'll
discredit himself finitely. He is immune to that form
of censure. He is riding a wave of unjustified
discontent that is bigger than any of us.

BR: Yes, Sir.

DIR: Lyndon Johnson is furious. He despises himself
for the way he's coddled RED RABBIT. He knows that
this wave of silly discord is partially of his
manufacture.

BR: Yes, Sir.

DIR: I've planted a Negro within the SCLC. My
former chauffeur, no less.

BR: Yes, Sir.

DIR: He's a sensible Negro. He despises Communists
more than the white power structure.

BR: Yes, Sir.

DIR: He tells me the SCLC is in a state of great
disarray. They are attempting to recruit an army of
the wretched to compete with Hannibal's hordes.

BR: Yes, Sir.

DIR: They will storm our nation's capital. They
will urinate and fornicate with abandon.

BR: Yes, Sir.

DIR: This display of pique will be a catastrophic disaster. It will encourage the unruly and criminally prone and give them an unprecedented license. The ramifications will be severe and nihilistically defined.

BR: Yes, Sir.

DIR: I am at my wits' end, Dwight. I do not know what more I can do.

BR: There's a counter-consensus brewing, Sir. I know you've been reading the bug transcripts.

DIR: I would define that consensus as too localized, too little, and too late.

BR: Some men are offering a bounty.

DIR: I would not be overly perturbed to see it happen.

BR: The concept is very much out there.

DIR: I would not like to be stuck with the task of investigating such an incident. I would be inclined to work for brevity and do what was best to put it behind us.

BR: Yes, Sir.

DIR: Unreasonable actions and unjustified rage serve to spark reasoned and measured responses.

BR: Yes, Sir.

DIR: I take comfort in that.

BR: I'm glad to hear it, Sir.

DIR: Is there anything I can do for you, Dwight?

BR: Yes, Sir. Could you speak to your contact and pouch me RED RABBIT's itinerary for the next several months?

DIR: Yes.

BR: Thank you, Sir.

DIR: Good day, Dwight.

BR: Good day, Sir.

DOCUMENT INSERT: 1/8/68.
Pouch communiqué. To: Fred Otash. From: Dwight Holly. Marked: ''Confidential''/''Eyes Only''/''Read & Burn Immediately.''

F.O.,
On go. Send update on PROSPECT. RED RABBIT's travel plans to follow.

READ & BURN.
D.C.H.

DOCUMENT INSERT: 1/18/68.
Pouch communiqué. To: Dwight Holly. From: Fred Otash.
Marked: ''Confidential''/''Eyes Only''/ ''Read & Burn
Immediately.''

D.H.,
Per PROSPECT's activities from 12/3/67 to present
date.

1 – I met with PROSPECT 6 times. I continued to give
him $ as advances ''against future jobs.'' We
discussed politics & PROSPECT frequently mentioned
Geo. Wallace's presidential campaign, ''niggers'' &
''the bounty on Martin Luther Coon.'' PROSPECT
continued to press me for travel papers & as
previously I stalled him. PROSPECT divided his time
between his apt (1535 N. Serrano, Hollywood), the
Sultan's Room at the St. Francis Hotel-Apts
(Hollywood Blvd) & the Rabbit's Foot Club
(appropriate!!!!) also on Hollywood Blvd. PROSPECT
continued to discuss his plans to travel to Rhodesia &
on 3 occasions said he might ''kill Coon, collect the
bounty & seek political asylum in Rhodesia.''

2 – PROSPECT became involved with woman at Sultan's
Room, who talked him into driving her brother to New
Orleans to ''pick up her friend's kids.'' PROSPECT
told me about this & asked for travel $. I gave him
$1,000 & told him I would meet him in N.O. PROSPECT &
woman's brother drove to N.O. (12/15/67), arrived on
12/17 & stayed at the Provincial Motel. I met PROSPECT
3 times, gave him $ & promised future jobs. PROSPECT
remained in N.O. & frequented pornographic
bookstores. PROSPECT, woman's brother & 2 8-yr-old
girls left N.O. on 12/19 & arrived in L.A. on 12/21.

3 – PROSPECT settled into L.A. routine. I spot-
tailed him on 6 occasions & met with him on 6 more.
PROSPECT visited pornographic bookstores, took
hypnosis courses & told me he intended to hypnotize
women into acting in porno films that he would direct.

PROSPECT frequented the Sultan's Room & the Rabbit's Foot Club, drank habitually & habitually used amphetamines. He frequently discussed the ''bounty'' & his plans to ''escape'' to Rhodesia. During this period PROSPECT visited the office of the L.A. Free Press & placed a classified ad seeking women for oral sex. PROSPECT also purchased liquid methamphetamine at the Castle Argyle Apts (Franklin & Argyle). He routinely stays up for 2 & 3 days at a time & I have noticed recent needle tracks on his arms.

4 – PROSPECT stated (4 occasions) that his intentions are to stay in L.A. & ''do jobs'' for me, join a swinger's club & figure out a way to ''get the bounty & shag to Rhodesia.'' I've started talking about the bounty & ways to get at MLK & PROSPECT has not noticed any shift in my tone or personality, because (a) he's seriously disturbed & extremely self-obsessed; (b) he's beholden to me for $ & narcotics; (c) he's strung out & impaired by his liquor & drug use.

5 – I think I can keep him in L.A. until our go-date & then get him to the spot to either participate or work the fall-back slot. We need his prints on a rifle & some other things, which should be easy to do.

6 – He's the guy. I'm sure of it. We're buffered on him (nobody will ever believe his ''Raul'' stories) & we'll never let him get into custody anyway.

READ THIS AND BURN. Pouch me if you need further updates.

F.O.

DOCUMENT INSERT: 1/21/68.
Boston Globe subhead:
MARINES IN LIFE-OR-DEATH SIEGE AT KHE SANH

DOCUMENT INSERT: 1/24/68.
New York Times headline and subhead:
TET OFFENSIVE SHOCKS U.S. FORCES
LARGEST BATTLES OF WAR RAGE

DOCUMENT INSERT: 1/26/68.
Atlanta Constitution headline:
KHE SANH—THE BLOODY SIEGE CONTINUES

DOCUMENT INSERT: 1/27/68.
Los Angeles Examiner subhead:
MASSIVE VIET BATTLES SPARK U.S. PROTESTS

DOCUMENT INSERT: 1/30/68.
Chicago Sun-Times headline and subhead:
KING CITES TET HOLOCAUST
CALLS FOR UNCONDITIONAL U.S. TROOP WITHDRAWAL

DOCUMENT INSERT: 2/2/68.
Los Angeles Times headline and subhead:
NIXON ANNOUNCES PREZ'L CANDIDACY
PLEDGES TO WORK FOR ''HARDWORKING, FORGOTTEN MAJORITY''

DOCUMENT INSERT: 2/6/68.
Sacramento Bee subhead:
KING IN MOBILIZING EFFORT FOR POOR PEOPLE'S MARCH

DOCUMENT INSERT: 2/8/68.
Houston Chronicle headline and subhead:
RFK IN HEATED ATTACK ON WAR
CALLS FOR NEGOTIATED SETTLEMENT

DOCUMENT INSERT: 2/10/68.
Cleveland Plain Dealer subhead:
HOOVER WARNS OF BLOODSHED IF MARCH PERMITTED

DOCUMENT INSERT: 2/18/68.
Miami Herald headline and subhead:
HUGE NIXON CROWDS IN NEW HAMPSHIRE
EX-VEEP ASSUMES FRONT-RUNNER STATUS

DOCUMENT INSERT: 3/2/68.
Boston Globe headline and subhead:
U.S. CASUALTY RATE MOUNTS IN VIETNAM
KING BLASTS ''FUTILE'' CONFLICT

DOCUMENT INSERT: 3/11/68.
Tampa Tribune headline and subhead:
WILL HE OR WON'T HE?
RFK ISN'T SAYING

DOCUMENT INSERT: 3/13/68.
Bug-extract transcript. Marked: ''Confidential''/
''Stage-1 Covert''/''Eyes Only'': Director, SA D. C.
Holly.

   Location: Office/Mike Lyman's Restaurant/Los
Angeles/listening-post-accessed. Speaking: Charles
''Chuck the Vice'' Aiuppa & Bernard ''Nardy''
Scavone, organized-crime associates. (Conversation
6.8 minutes in progress.)

   CA: It's what you call a coalition. Bobby's the
president, but he needs the head ape to mobilize all
the little apes and put him in power.
   BS: Do the arithmetic, Chuck. They don't have the
votes.
   CA: Then you add the Jews, the college kids, the
comsymps and the welfare creeps. It gets to be a very
tight race with those forces in play.
   BS: Bobby scares me. That I will readily admit.
   CA: Bobby needs the head ape to create the unrest.
Then he comes in and promises all the fucked-up people
the moon.
   BS: Bobby would fuck us, Chuck. He'd fuck us like he
fucked us when he was AG and Jack was the prez.
   CA: Bobby's only happy when he's got some made
guy's dick in the vice.
   BS: Watch it, Chuck. You say ''vice,'' you give me
these urges.
   CA: Control yourself. There'll be more. Uncle
Carlos has always got work.
   BS: I'd like to put the head ape and Bobby in the
vice. One squeeze and arrivederci.
   (Non-applicable conversation follows.)

DOCUMENT INSERT: 3/14/68.
Bug-extract transcript. Marked: ''Confidential''/
''Stage-1 Covert''/''Eyes Only'': Director, SA D. C.
Holly.

   Location: Card room/Grapevine Tavern/St. Louis/
listening-post-accessed. Speaking: Norbert Donald
Kling & Rowland Mark DeJohn, paroled felons (Armed

Robbery/Bunco/GTA) & presumed organized-crime
associates. (Conversation 0.9 minutes in
progress.)

    NDK: This is rich. I grab the pay phone this morning
and who do I get?
    RMDJ: Jill St. John?
    NDK: No.
    RMDJ: What's her name? That cooze with the go-go
boots.
    NDK: No.
    RMDJ: Norb, shit—
    NDK: It's Jimmy Ray. He starts talking shit and
says he joined a French cult in L.A. He dives muff and
gets sucked off all day, and he needs money to support
all his slaves, and did I know if there was a time
limit on the bounty, 'cause he's got his hands full
with his slaves right now and he don't know when he
can get free.
    RMDJ: That is hilarious. Jimmy's got his hands
full, all right.
    NDK: One hand, at least. At Jeff City he'd geez meth
and jack off for two days at a pop. He'd read these
fucking pussy books and orbit. He said the fucking
pictures were talking to him.
    RMDJ: Jimmy's got delusions of grandeur.
    NDK: Yeah, but he hates niggers.
    (Non-applicable conversation follows.)

DOCUMENT INSERT: 3/15/68.
Bug-extract transcript. Marked: ''Confidential''/
''Stage-1 Covert''/''Eyes Only'': Director, SA D. C.
Holly.
    Location: Suite 301/El Encanto Hotel/Santa
Barbara/listening-post-accessed. Speaking: Senator
Robert F. Kennedy, Paul Horvitz (senate staff mbr.),
Unidentified Male #1. (Conversation 3.9 minutes in
progress.)

    RFK: . . . simple and matter-of-fact. That's the way
my brother announced. (Pause/3.4 seconds.) Paul, you

time the statement. Read it aloud, but don't try to imitate me.

(Laughter/2.4 seconds.)

PH: About the position paper. Do we publish—

UM #1: You want the abbreviated version, right? The long form's too dense, and the press guys will have to cut too much.

RFK: Condense it and let me read the final draft. And be damn sure there's nothing in there about organized crime.

PH: Sir, I think that's a mistake. It undercuts your credentials as Attorney General.

UM #1: Bob, shit. You know you'll go after those guys ag—

RFK: I intend to, but I don't intend to broadcast it.

UM #1: Shit, Bob. Good foes make for good campaigns. The war and Johnson are one thing, but—

PH: The Mob's dead as a campaign issue, but—

RFK: I'll do what I do, when I do it, but I'm not going to broadcast my intentions. Think ''social justice,'' ''end the war'' and ''unite the country'' and forget about the goddamn Mafia.

PH: Sir, do you think—

RFK: That's enough. I've got enough on my mind without worrying about those sons-of-bitches.

(Non-applicable conversation follows.)

DOCUMENT INSERT: 3/16/68.
Bug-extract transcript. Marked: ''Confidential''/ ''Stage-1 Covert''/''Eyes Only'': Director, SA D. C. Holly.

Location: Suite 301/El Encanto Hotel/Santa Barbara/listening-post-accessed. Speaking: Senator Robert F. Kennedy, Paul Horvitz (senate staff mbr.), Unidentified Male #1. (Conversation 7.4 minutes in progress.)

RFK: . . . a litigator I had at Justice. He was there for most of my moves against Carlos Marcello.

UM #1: Uncle Carlos. You deported him.

RFK: I dumped his fat ass in Central America.

PH: You're tipsy, Senator. You rarely say ''ass'' when you're sober.

RFK: I'm getting tipsy now because I won't be able to get tipsy until November. (Laughter/6.8 seconds.)

RFK: I'm starting to feel like a fighter before he goes into training. I'm dumping all the stuff I won't be able to talk about during the campaign.

PH: That litigator. What ab—

RFK: We were talking about the Outfit. I told him that one day I'd get my second shot, and devil take the hindmost.

PH: Is that from Shakespeare?

RFK: It's from me. It means I'm going to make those sons-of-whores pay.

(Non-applicable conversation follows).

DOCUMENT INSERT: 3/17/68.
Verbatim FBI telephone call transcript. (OPERATION BLACK RABBIT ADDENDUM.) Marked: ''Recorded at the Director's Request''/''Classified Confidential 1-A: Director's Eyes Only.'' Speaking: Director, BLUE RABBIT.

DIR: Good afternoon.

BR: Good afternoon, Sir.

DIR: You pulled me out of a meeting. I assume you have news of some import.

BR: We hit on CRUSADER RABBIT. One of my men tailed him to a bank in Silver Spring, Maryland. He has a dummy account there. I got a bank writ and checked his transaction record.

DIR: Continue.

BR: The account was opened under a pseudonym. CRUSADER uses it for one purpose, to send checks to the SCLC. I cross-checked our bank-account covers on the SCLC and determined that checks from four other accounts, in different cities and states, have been regularly sent in. They go back to '64 and they all bear CRUSADER's handwriting. He's got a different alias for each account, and he's donated close to a half million dollars total.

DIR: I am astounded.

BR: Yes, Sir.

DIR: He's embezzled the money or stolen it from some convenient source. His salaries would not sustain that degree of largesse.

BR: Yes, Sir.

DIR: He's indulging the Catholic concept of penance. He's atoning for the sins he's committed under my flag.

BR: It gets worse, Sir.

DIR: Tell me how. Fulfill my worst fears and most justified suspicions.

BR: An agent spot-tailed him in D.C. two days ago. He was heavily disguised and almost unrecognizable. He met a Kennedy staffer named Paul Horvitz at a restaurant and spent two hours with him.

DIR: More atonement. A roundelay that will not go unpunished.

BR: What do you want me—

DIR: Let CRUSADER continue to atone for his sins. Send copies of the March 15th and March 16th El Encanto bug tapes to Carlos Marcello, Sam Giancana, Moe Dalitz, Santo Trafficante and every other Mob patriarch in the United States. They should know that Prince Bobby has long-range plans for them.

BR: It's a bold and inspired gambit, Sir.

DIR: Good day, Dwight. Go with God and other felicitous sources.

BR: Good day, Sir.

DOCUMENT INSERT: 3/18/68.

New York Times headline:

RFK ANNOUNCES BID FOR DEMOCRATIC PRESIDENTIAL NOMINATION

PART SIX

INTERDICTION

March 19, 1968–June 9, 1968

106

(Saigon, 3/19/68)

YOU'RE BACK.

It's vivid. It's vicious. It's Vietnam.

See the troop swarms. See the displaced slopes. See said gooks talking Tet. See the boarded temples. See the truck convoys. See the antiaircraft guns.

You're back. Dig it. Saigon '68.

The cab crawled. Trucks hemmed it in. Gun trucks/food trucks/troop trucks. Tailpipe fumes windshield-high. Fume grit in your eyes.

Pete watched. Pete smoked. Pete chewed Tums.

He breached the truce. He flew overnight—Frisco/Tan Son Nhut. He lured Barb to Frisco. He pitched it as romance. He cloaked his truce override.

She nailed him. She said you're going back—I know it. He copped out. He said let me go. He said let me brace Stanton.

She said no. He said yes. It went waaaay bad. They yelled. They threw shit. They gouged walls. They scared the desk clerks. They scared the bellboys. They scared the hotel staff.

Barb split to Sparta. He roamed San Francisco. The hills bonked his heart. He drove to the airport. He sat in the bar. He saw some Carlos cats: Chuck "the Vice" Aiuppa and Nardy Scavone.

They hailed him. They bought him drinks. They got tanked and bragged. They said they clipped Danny Bruvick. It was a twosky. They clipped Danny's ex Arden-Jane. They supplied details. They supplied sound effects.

Pete walked out. Pete caught his plane. Pete ate Nembutal. He slept. The plane pitched. He saw vices snap heads.

The cab crawled. The driver grazed monks. The driver monologued: Tet kill many. Tet fuck things up. Tet kill GIs.

Victor Charles naughty! Victor Charles evil! Victor Charles *baaad!*

The cab pitched. The cab lurched. Pete gagged on truck fumes. Pete's knees bumped his head.

There's the Go-Go. It's still gook graffitied. You're back. It's still ARVN-guarded. There's two Marvs door-posted. You're back.

Pete grabbed his duffel. Pete grabbed Wayne's satchel—beakers and test tubes prewrapped. Drop them off/check the lab/hit Hotel Catinat.

The driver braked. Pete got out and stretched. The Marvs snapped to. Said Marvs knew Pete—*le frog grand et fou.*

They saluted. Pete walked in the Go-Go. Pete smelled white horse residue. Piss and sweat/stale excrement/cooked dope residue.

The niteclub was *mort*. The niteclub was a dope den. It was ground-floor Hades. It was the river Styx boocoo.

Slopes on pallets. Tube tourniquets. Lighters. Cooking spoons. Dope balloons. Spikes. Fifty junkies/fifty dope beds/fifty launch pads.

Slopes cooked horse. Slopes tied off. Slopes geezed. Slopes swooned. Slopes grinned wide. Slopes sighed.

Pete walked through it. Marvs and Can Laos sold balloons. Marvs and Can Laos sold spikes. Pete walked upstairs—dig it—there's the river Styx revived.

More slopes on pallets. More tube ties. More needles. More toe-crack injections. More arm and leg pops.

Pete walked upstairs. Pete hit the lab door. Pete saw a Can Lao cat. He saw Pete. He knew Pete—*le frog fou.*

Pete dropped the satchel. Pete talked Anglo-gook:

"Equipment. From Wayne Tedrow. I leave with you."

The Can Lao smiled. The Can Lao bowed. The Can Lao reached and grabbed.

Pete said, "Open up. I check lab now."

The Can Lao bristled. The Can Lao blocked the door. The Can Lao pulled a belt piece. The Can Lao snapped the slide.

The door popped open. A gook stepped out. Pete caught a view: trays/sorting chutes/bindles prepacked.

The gook bristled. The gook slammed the door. The gook blocked Pete's view. The gook braced the Can Lao. They jabbered *en gook*. They eyed *le frog fou*.

Pete got goosebumps. Pete hinked out. Pete hinked out boocoo.

They sold balloons downstairs. They packaged two ways upstairs. They sold bindle pops too. That implied wiiiiide distribution. That implied upscale use.

The gook walked downstairs. The gook walked fast. The gook slung a duffel bag. The Can Lao re-bristled. Pete bowed and smiled. Pete pidgin-gooked:

"Is alright. You good man. I go now."

The Can Lao smiled. The Can Lao de-bristled. Pete waved bye-bye.

He walked downstairs. He held his nose. He grazed pallets and squashed turds. He walked outside. He looked around. He saw the gook.

He's on the street. He's walking south. He's got that duffel bag.

Pete tailed him.

The gook walked the dock. The gook cut inland. The gook walked Dal To Street. It was hot. The street teemed. It's a slopehead ant farm run amok.

Pete stood out. Pete duck-walked low. Pete shaved half his height. The gook walked fast. The gook plowed monks. Pete huffed keeping up.

The gook cut east. The gook bopped down Tam Long. The gook swung down a warehouse block. The sidewalk narrowed. Foot traffic thinned. Pete saw Can Laos straight up.

Can Lao classics—goons in civvies—perched outside a warehouse. Cabs out front—good numbers—cabs perched down the block.

The gook stopped. A Can Lao checked his duffel. A Can Lao got the door. The gook walked in the warehouse. A Can Lao slammed the door. A Can Lao double-locked.

Six buildings down. Side alleys between each one. One connecting alley in back.

Pete walked.

He cut sideways. He hit the back alley. He cut down six buildings. He walked half a block.

Six warehouses/all glazed cement/all three-story jobs.

He cut back streetside. He saw first-floor windows. He heard the Can Laos out front. The windows were covered/mesh over glass/burglar-proof stuff.

Pete checked a window. Pete saw light through glass.

He took a breath. He grabbed the mesh. He pulled it back. He made a space. He made a fist. He punched the glass out.

He saw pallets. He saw tourniquets. He saw white arms tied up. He saw GIs buy bindles. He saw GIs cook horse. He saw GIs shoot up.

He slept bad. He slept weird. Jet lag plus Nembutal. He dreamed bad. He saw vices and crossbars. He saw white kids geezing up.

He woke up. He got some focus. He de-raged. He called John Stanton. He said I'm fried. I can't see straight. Let's meet tomorrow night. Stanton laughed. Stanton said why not?

Pete sedated. Pete reslept. Pete roused and jumped up. Dream shots reran wide awake—all broken-glass shots.

That boy with the tattoos. That boy with the gone eyes. That boy with the spike in his shvantz.

Pete hired a cab. Pete hunkered low. Pete ran tail ops. Cab stakeout by Hotel Montrachet—John Stanton's billet-drop.

He got more focus. The sleep helped. He totaled it all up. One GI dope den/*one at least*—kadre kode breach.

Don't sell to GIs. It's sacrilege. Sell and die hard. Stanton knew it. Stanton cosigned it. Stanton said Mr. Kao agreed. Ditto all the Can Lao.

Stanton assured Pete. Stanton assuaged Pete. Stanton puffed and mollified.

Mr. Kao ran dope Saigon-wide. Mr. Kao ran the Can Lao. Stanton knew Kao. Stanton quoted Kao: Me no push to GIs!

He had that much. That to start. "That" could go wide.

It was hot. The cab broiled. A dash fan swirled. It stirred hot air. It stirred gas fumes. It stirred tailpipe farts.

The Montrachet boomed. The MACV brass loved it. Dig the bay windows with grenade nets.

Pete watched the door. The driver ran the radio. The driver played Viet rock. The Bleatles and the Bleach Boys—all gook redubbed.

9:46 A.M. 10:02, 10:08. Fuck, this could go on—

There's Stanton.

He's walking out. He's got a briefcase. He shags a cab quick. Pete nudged his driver—tail that cab quick.

Stanton's cab pulled out. Pete's cab pulled up. A cab pulled between them. Cabs boxed them in. Cab traffic stalled and sat.

Traffic moved. They got free. They drove south. They drove slow. They snail-trailed.

The driver was good. The driver stayed close. The driver laid back discreet. They drove south. They hit Tam Long Street. They hit that warehouse block.

Stanton's cab braked. Stanton's cab stopped at *the* warehouse. Two Can Laos walked straight up.

They saw Stanton. They heel-clicked. They passed an envelope. Pete watched. Pete's cab hovered back.

Stanton's cab gunned it. Stanton's cab hauled south. Pete's cab pulled out and tailed back. A truck cut between them. Stanton's cab cut west. Pete's cab blew a red light.

Stanton's cab stopped. It's halfway down a side street. It's an all-warehouse block.

A short street/six warehouses/good warehouse block.

All Can Lao–guarded. Cabs perched curbside. Cabs perched down the block.

Pete watched. His cab idled. His cab hovered back.

The Can Laos ran up. The Can Laos swarmed Stanton's cab. The Can Laos dropped envelopes. A warehouse door popped. Four GIs walked out. Four GIs weaved on white horse.

Stanton's cab U-turned. Stanton's cab passed Pete's cab. Pete hunkered waaay low. Stanton's cab turned east. Pete's cab tailed it. Pete's cab tailed discreet.

Traffic slogged. Snail trail. Fucking turtle speed. Pete prickled. Pete chain-smoked. Pete chewed Tums.

They hit Tu Do Street. Stanton's cab stopped.

Pete knew the spot. One TV supply store/one CIA front. One door guard/one jarhead PFC/carbine at high port.

Stanton got out. Stanton grabbed his briefcase. Stanton walked in. Pete grabbed his binoculars. Pete framed the door.

The cab idled. His view bounced. His view settled flat. He checked the window. He saw drapes. They blocked his view.

He caught the jarhead. He got him in close. He got his carbine. He got the barrel. He got a stamped code.

He resighted. He got in *close*-close. Weird—a three-zero code—per Bob Relyea's stock.

The driver cut his engine. Pete timed Stanton's trip. Ten minutes/twelve/fourt—

There:

Stanton walks out. Stanton shags his cab. Stanton takes off.

Pete nudged the driver—you stay here now. Pete walked to the shop. The jarhead saw him. The jarhead snapped to.

Pete smiled. "It's all right, son. I'm Agency, and all I need are directions."

The kid unsnapped. "Uh . . . yessir."

"I'm new here. Can you point me to the Hotel Catinat?"

"Uh . . . yessir. It's straight left down Tu Do."

Pete smiled. "Thanks. And by the way, that code stamp on your rifle intrigues me. I'm ex-Corps myself, and I've never seen that designation."

The kid smiled. "It's an exclusive CIA allotment designation, sir. You'll never see it on regular military ordnance."

Pete got pinpricks. Pete got goosebumps. Pete got this cold flush.

He held it close. He held it calm. He didn't blow up. He hit the Catinat. He chained coffee and cigarettes. He racked logic up.

Call it:

The three-zero code/strict CIA/*non*-military.

Bob Relyea lied. Bob Relyea konned the kadre. John Stanton helped him. Bob's gun heists and "pilferings": bullshit.

Call it:

Stanton got the guns. Per some kickback scheme. His CIA pals helped. They took dope profits. They fake-purchased guns. They laundered dope cash. They paid a CIA source. Said source supplied guns. Stanton and *who else* made money?

Stanton and Bob. Carlos logically. Trace it back. Track the time line. Trust the time line logically.

Stanton knows Mr. Kao. Mr. Kao pushes white horse. Mr. Kao shares kadre lab space. Kao runs dope camps. Kao ships to Europe. Kao exports there exclusively. Kao runs Saigon dope pads. Kao excludes GIs. Kao pushes to gooks exclusively.

Bullshit.

Kao and Stanton were jungled up. They ran Saigon dope properties. Said properties serviced gooks. Said properties serviced GIs.

Warehouse dope pads/seven minimum/kadre kode breach. Death sentence/no recourse/kadre kode breach.

Backtrack:

It's 9/65. Kao starts selling dope. Kao tells Stanton this: Me bossman. I run Can Lao. We share lab space. I no hook GIs.

Stanton kowtowed. Kao *bought* lab space. Stanton told Pete. Stanton showed Pete a ledger for proof.

Stanton lubed Pete. Stanton supplied facts and figures. Stanton supplied phony proof.

Backtrack:

Tran Lao Dinh kills dope slaves. Tran Lao Dinh steals M-base. Tran Lao Dinh resists torture. Pete fries his gonads. J. P. Mesplède assists.

Tran said I steal dope. I sell to Marvs then. That all I do. Pete persisted—give me more details—Mesplède shot Tran some juice.

Tran ad-libbed then. Tran dumped his hot seat. Tran electrified.

Pete talked to Stanton. Pete told Tran's story. Pete logicked it through:

Tran stole the base. Tran sold it to Kao. Tran did not snitch Kao. Stanton bought Pete's logic. Stanton praised Pete's logic. Stanton signed Pete's logic through.

Make the jump:

Tran worked for *Stanton*. Tran roamed Tiger Kamp. Tran was *Stanton's* pet gook. Tran steals base on Stanton's orders. Tran supplies Kao. Tran fears *Stanton*. Tran won't snitch *him*. Tran fries with glee.

Kall it kold—Stanton and Kao are kolleagues. It goes back to '65. Kadre kode breach/death decree/retroactive.

Jump two:

Pete rotates. Wayne rotates. Pete moves stateside. Laurent's there. Ditto Flash. They funnel stateside. Stanton stays in-country. Ditto Mesplède. Tiger Kamp runs low-supervised. The war escalates. More troops pass through. The kadre hits Saigon half-assed.

Shit percolates. It's outside their view. It's covert supervised. Thus Stanton-vetted dope pads sell dope to GIs.

Two years in? Maybe one. Maybe Tet-time stuff.

Bogus gun sales. GI dope sales—kadre kode breach. Stanton's nailed. Bob's nailed—kadre kode breach. Who else made money? Who else gets breached?

Pete chained cigarettes. Pete sweated gobs. Pete mainlined caffeine. He brainstormed in bed. He sopped up his clothes. He soaked up the sheets.

His logic felt strong. His logic felt big. His logic felt incomplete. His pulse raced. His chest pinged. He got bips to his feet.

Stanton said, "You look tired."

Drinks at the Montrachet. Code 3 Tet Alert. More door guards. More bomb nets. More fear.

"Travel fucks with me. You know that."

"Unnecessary travel, too."

Pete seized up. Pete juked his performance. Get mad/stay mad/reveal shit.

"What are you saying?"

"I'm saying I've got eyes. You flew over to convince me to expand the business, but I'm going to say no and go you one better. I'm glad you're here, because I owe it to you to tell you to your face."

Pete flushed. Pete felt it—blood to the face.

"I'm listening."

"I'm disbanding the operation. The whole funnel. Tiger Kamp through to Bay St. Louis."

Pete flushed. Pete felt it—cardiac hues.

"Why? Give me one good fucking reason."

Stanton stabbed his swizzle stick. A piece broke off and flew.

"One, the Hughes thing has brought too much attention on Vegas, and Carlos and the Boys want to reinstate the no-dope rule. Two, the war's out of control, and it's become too unpopular at home. There's too many journalists and TV people incountry who'd love to nail some rogue CIA men for doing what we do. Three, our on-island dissidents are getting nowhere, Castro's in to stay, and my Agency colleagues all agree that it's time to pull the plug."

Pete flushed. Pete felt it—deep purple hues. *Be shocked/be pissed/be irate.*

"Four years, John. Four years and all that work for *this?*"

Stanton sipped his martini. "It's over, Pete. Sometimes the ones who care the most are the ones least able to admit it."

Pete gripped his glass. Pete snapped the rim. Ice chips spritzed and spewed. He grabbed a napkin. He blotted blood. He stanched cut residue.

Stanton leaned in. "I cut Mesplède loose. I'm selling Tiger Kamp to Mr. Kao, and I'm leaving for the States tomorrow. I'm going to disband the Mississippi end of the team and make one last Cuban run to pacify Fuentes and Arredondo."

Pete squeezed his napkin. Scotch burned the cuts. Glass shards worked through.

Stanton said, "We did what we could for the Cause. There's some consolation there."

Cab stakeout 2. 6:00 A.M./the Montrachet cab line/heat and cab fumes.

Pete hunkered low. Pete watched the door. Pete ran logic through: Stanton's disbanding/Stanton's regrouping/Stanton's kutting kadre kosts and konnektions.

Pete yawned. Pete got zero sleep. Pete prowled bars past 2:00. Pete found Mesplède. He was pissed and drunk. He was fried on his frog ass boocoo.

Stanton sacked him. Mesplède raged—*le cochon/le putain du monde.*

Pete gauged Mesplède. Mesplède gauged sincere. Mesplède gauged non-Stantonite. Pete rigged a test. Pete rigged a tour.

They drove by the dope cribs. They saw cabs pull up. They saw GIs walk out. They saw GIs bop zombified.

Mesplède was shocked. Mesplède vibed *très* sincere and *très* horrified. *On va tuer le cochon. Le cochon va mourir.*

Pete said yes. Pete amended. Pete said Die Tough.

It was hot. It was A.M.-sticky. The dash fan puffed. Pete hunkered low. Pete watched the door. Pete chewed Tums.

6:18. 6:22. 6:29. Fuck, this could go on—

There's Stanton.

With a suitcase. Errands first? *Then* the airport?

Stanton got a cab. The cab pulled out. The cab pulled out slow. Pete nudged his driver—tail that cab fast.

The driver gunned it. A cab cut him off. The driver swung around fast. Tu Do was busy. Gun trucks goosed traffic chop-chop.

Stanton's cab cut south. Pete's cab bird-dogged it. Pete's cab stuck two car lengths back. A rickshaw cut in. A coolie lugged cargo—tail cover boocoo.

Traffic slowed. They drove south. They bopped toward the docks.

Pete's cab goosed the rickshaw. The driver rode his horn. The coolie flipped him off. Pete sighted in. Pete watched Stanton's cab antenna. It wiggles/it weaves/it tracks good.

They hit the docks. Pete saw warehouse blocks. Pete saw looooong buildings laid out. Stanton's cab braked. Stanton's cab stopped. Stanton got out.

The rickshaw passed him. Pete's cab passed him. Pete ducked and looked back. Stanton grabbed his suitcase. Stanton walked. Stanton unlocked a warehouse.

He did it mock-cool. He looked around. He stepped in. He pulled the door shut.

Stanton's cab waited. Pete's cab U-turned. Pete's cab parked down the block. Pete swiveled the fan. Pete ate hot air and watched.

Time the visit. Do it now. Run your time clock.

Pete checked his watch dial. The second hand swept. Six minutes/nine/eleven.

Stanton walked out. Stanton still had his suitcase. Stanton locked the door up.

He shagged his cab. He stretched and yawned. The cab took off northbound—toward Tan Son Nhut.

Pete paid his driver. Pete got out and walked. The cab peeled off.

The warehouse stretched. It ran two football fields plus. One story/one steel door. Side walkways adjacent. Mesh-covered windows inset.

Pete pushed the buzzer. Chimes ricocheted. No footsteps/no voices/no peephole slid back. Two walkways. Side windows. No witnesses out.

Pete cut south. Pete hit the near walkway. Pete took his coat off.

He found a window. He flexed his hands. He peeled the mesh back. His bad hand tore. Glass specks got reimbedded.

He made a fist. He wrapped it up. He made a coat-fabric glove. He punched out the window. Glass blew inward.

He hauled himself up. He squeezed through the frame space. He rolled to the floor. His hand throbbed. He squeezed blood out. He patted the wall. He caught a switch. Lights went on— two football fields plus.

He saw a space. He saw a floor. He saw *merchandise*. He saw swag. He saw rows and rows. He saw piles and piles.

He walked. He touched. He looked. He counted. He inventoried. He saw:

Sixty boxes stuffed with watches—pure gold waist-high.

Mink coats dumped like trash—forty-three piles hip-high. Six hundred Jap motorcycles—laid side to side. Antique furniture—twenty-three rows stretched wide.

New cars—parked side by side. Thirty-eight rows/twenty-two cars per/stretched out lengthwise.

Bentleys. Porsches. Aston-Martin DB-5s. Volvos/Jaguars/Mercedes.

Pete walked the rows. Pete ID'd booty. Pete saw export tags attached. Point of shipment: Saigon. Point of entry: U.S.

Kall it easy. Kall it kold. Kall it dead:

Swag. Black-market-purchased. Non-U.S.-derived. Swag from Europe/Great Britain/the East.

Stanton ran the gig. His CIA pals helped. They boot-jacked kadre money. They laundered it. They glommed luxury shit.

Stanton's disbanding. They ship the goods now. They ship duty-free. The Boys help them. Carlos walks point. They resell near-retail. Carlos takes points. Carlos pays the Stanton guys. Cold millions accrue.

The dope plan. The funnel. Cash for the Cause. Wrong—the Cause was THIS.

Pete walked the warehouse. Pete kicked tires. Pete smelled leather seats. Pete flicked antennas. Pete buffed rosewood. Pete fondled mink.

THIS.

He tracked logic. He looked for loopholes. He got none.

And:

Stanton stopped here. Stanton lugged in his suitcase.

Why?

He dropped something off. He picked something up.

Which?

Pete walked the walls. Pete tapped the walls. Pete tapped whole cement. No wall panels or hidey holes—shit.

Pete checked the floor. Pete looked for chipped paint. Pete looked for off-color streaks. Pete got whole cement/solid/no streaks.

Pete checked the ceiling. It was solid cement. No patches/no caulking/no streaks.

No bathroom. No storerooms. No closets. Four walls/one looooong strrrretch/two football fields plus.

Something was *somewhere*. Something was *here*.

Cars/minks/watches. Motorcycles/antiques. It's a day's work. It's needle meets haystack. It's do it anyway.

He walked the rows. He plowed watch piles. He dug through mink. He grabbed. He touched. He fished.

Forty-three piles/sixty boxes—shit.

He walked the rows. He popped antique drawers. He rifled and dipped.

Twenty-three rows—shit.

His stomach growled. Hours flew. No food and no fucking sleep.

He checked the motorcycles. He opened saddle bags. He popped gas caps and peeked.

Six hundred bikes—shit.

He checked the cars. He checked row by row. He checked twenty-two times thirty-eight.

He popped hoods. He popped glove compartments. He popped trunks. He checked under rugs. He checked engine mounts. He checked under seats.

Porsches first. Bentleys next—shit.

The space went dark. He worked by touch. Volvos/Jaguars/DB-5s. He got the feel. He worked fast—Braille by necessity.

Five models down. One left: Mercedes.

He hit the top row. He braced the first car. He snapped the hood. He touched the valve covers. He touched the air cleaner. He brushed a cylinder ledge.

Wait—feel the bump—Braille by necess—

He felt the bump. He felt tape. He pulled. Something tore loose. Said something was textured and flat.

Rectangular. Paged. A long book.

He grabbed it. He reached up and popped a wind wing. He tapped the key and headlights. Good kraut autowerk—fog lights beamed out.

He got down. He turned pages. He read by fog light. One cross-columned listing ledger—names/money/dates.

Key dates. Back to late '64. The kadre ops inception.

Names:

Chuck Rogers. Tran Lao Dinh. Bob Relyea. Laurent Guéry. Flash Elorde. Fuentes/Wenzel/Arredondo.

Payouts/monthly stipends/covert. Odd spic names/cross-columned/starred with "CM"s.

Kall it: CM for Cuban Militia. Cuban passage paid in full.

Pete scanned columns. Pete scanned dates. Pete scanned names. Names stated/names absent/names unindicted: His name/Wayne's/Mesplède's.

Money paid out. Loyalty purchased. Kadre kode breach.

Guéry and Stanton ran poly tests. They were all *lies*. Flash snuck into Cuba. It was a *lie*. Cuban dissension—one sustained *lie*. Safe runs to Cuba—one prepaid *lie*. Cuban Militia sold out as fodder—part of the *lie*. Guns sent to Cuba—funneled to where?—key to the *lie*.

Cars.

Watches.

Furs.

Jap motorcycles.

Faggot antiques.

Years gone. One heart attack. THIS.

Pete dropped the ledger. Pete flipped the car key. Pete killed the fog lights.

The dark felt right. The dark scared him. IT WAS ALL A BIG FUCKING LIE.

DOCUMENT INSERT: 3/25/68.
Telephone call transcript. Taped by: BLUE RABBIT.
Marked: ''FBI-Scrambled''/''Stage-1 Covert''/
''Destroy Without Reading in the Event of My Death.''
Speaking: BLUE RABBIT, FATHER RABBIT.

BR: It's me, Senior. You hear those clicks?

FR: I know. Scrambler technology.

BR: Are you ready for some good news?

FR: If it relates to D-day, I am.

BR: It's connected. That's for damn sure.

FR: Have we got a date? Have we got a loc—

BR: My men found Wendell Durfee.

FR: Oh, sweet Jesus.

BR: He's in L.A. He's got a room on skid row.

FR: I hear the saints, Dwight. They're singing hymns all for me.

BR: My men make him for some rape-snuffs. You think he developed a taste with Lynette?

FR: How could he? She always struck me as frigid.

BR: RED RABBIT's on the move. I'm looking at D-day for sometime next month.

FR: Shitfire. Let's bring Wayne in, then.

BR: My guys have got Durfee staked out. I'll wait a few days, then have some jig stiff a call through Sonny Liston.

FR: Hymns, Dwight. I mean it. And all in stereo.

BR: You think Wayne's ready for this?

FR: I know he is.

BR: I'll patch you when I've got more news.

FR: Make it good news.

BR: We're close, Senior. I've got this feeling.

FR: From your mouth to God's ears.

107

(Mexico City, 3/26/68)

SHOW-AND-TELL:

Sam G.'s villa/the rumpus room/drinks with umbrellas.

A valet toiled. Said valet dished hors d'oeuvres. Said valet built gin slings.

Littell ran charts. Littell ran easel graphs. Sam watched. Moe watched. Carlos twirled his umbrella. Santo and Johnny yawned.

Littell jabbed a pointer. "We're getting our prices. Mr. Hughes should have all his hotels by the end of the year."

Sam yawned. Moe stretched. Carlos ate quesadillas.

Littell said, "There's a garbage-hauling business in Reno that I think we should take over first. It's nonunion, which helps. All told, we're on schedule in every area except one."

Moe laughed. "That is vintage Ward. Lay out this big preamble and stop short of the point."

Sam said, "Ward's a cock tease."

Santo said, "Ward dropped out of the seminary. They teach you to string things out there."

Littell smiled. "Mr. Hughes is insisting that we enforce a 'Negro sedation policy' at his hotels. He knows that it's unrealistic, but he's dug in."

Moe said, "The shvartzes need sedation. They're creating too much social unrest."

Sam said, "You don't rape and pillage when you're sedated."

Carlos said, "The sedation concept is stale bread. We're closing down Pete's business."

Littell coughed. "Why? I thought Pete's thing was solvent."

Sam looked at Carlos. Carlos shook his head.

"Solvent is as solvent does. It got us what we wanted, so we're cutting it loose."

Looks passed: Johnny to Santo/Santo to Sam.

Sam coughed. "We're covered in Costa Rica, Nicaragua, Panama, and the D.R. These guys I greased did not need a road map."

Santo coughed. "The U.S. dollar is the international language. You say 'casino gambling' and it paints a big picture."

Johnny coughed. "The U.S. dollar buys influence on both sides of the political line."

Santo coughed. "We've got our bearded pal to thank for that."

Moe looked at Santo. Sam looked at Santo. Santo went oops. The Boys regrouped. The Boys sipped drinks. The Boys snagged hors d'oeuvres.

Littell flipped graph sheets. Littell gauged the gaffe.

They screwed Pete. They screwed Pete per his Cuban deal—*somehow*. Guns to *Castro? Not* rightists? *Perhaps*. They greased leftists—said "Influence"—Pete's usefulness lapsed. *Maybe/somehow/perhaps.*

I won't tell Pete/they know it/they trust me/they own me.

Sam coughed. Sam cued the valet. Said valet split *rápidamente.*

Carlos said, "We're still waiting to see if LBJ runs again, but we're 99% committed to Nixon."

Santo said, "Nixon's the one."

Sam said, "LBJ can't change Justice Department policy like a new man can."

Johnny said, "Humphrey's too soft on the spooks. I can't see him or LBJ granting that pardon to Jimmy."

Santo said, "Nixon's the guy. He's a shoo-in for the nomination."

Carlos said, "You sit down with him in late June, Ward. Then you can retire."

Santo smiled. "I know someone else who's going to retire."

Sam smiled. "Yeah, per that little box of goodies we got in the mail."

Looks passed: Carlos to Santo/Moe D. to Sam. Santo flushed. Sam went oops.

The plane soared. Air Mexico—Vegas nonstop.

The summit soared. The Boys vouched his plans—no rebuttals/no controversy. The Boys made gaffes. They were niggling for him. They were troubling for Pete.

They dropped the dope biz. That implied trouble. That implied a pissed Pete. No more Cuban runs or Viet ops—*probably*.

The plane banked. Littell saw clouds. White puffs laced with grimey debris.

He called Janice. They talked last night. She was scared. Her cramps were worse. She saw a doctor. He ran some tests.

He cited trauma. It went long untreated. It was Wayne Senior's work. It masked her symptoms. It masked internal damage. It was cancer *possibly*.

She talked scared. She talked strong. She ran litanies: I'm young/it's not *that*/it can't *be*. He calmed her down. He said goodnight. He prayed for her. He said rosaries.

The plane leveled off. Littell shut his eyes. Littell saw Bobby.

Bobby announced. Bobby met the press nine days ago. Bobby said I want it. Bobby voiced policy.

Let's end the war. Let's work for peace. Let's end poverty. Domestic reforms. Peace accords. No *stated* Mob policy.

Prudent Bobby. Sage Bobby. Sound policy.

Barb called him last week. She saw Bobby announce on TV. They talked. They got misty on Bobby.

Barb met Bobby once. It was spring '62. Peter Lawford threw a party. Barb talked to Bobby. Barb liked Bobby then. Barb loved Bobby now. Pete deployed Shakedown Barb. Barb slept with JFK.

Barb laughed. Barb praised Bobby. Barb said he'd kick Dick Nixon's ass. Barb predicted a victory.

A stew walked by. Said stew pushed a snack cart. Littell grabbed a club soda. Littell grabbed the L.A. *Times*.

He creased it out. He saw war headlines. He flipped the fold. Columns jumped. He saw "Poor People's March"/"planning stages"/"momentum." He flipped to page 2. He saw Bobby.

There's Bobby caught candid. He's standing by a putting

green. He's near some bungalows. The backdrop's lush. The backdrop's familiar.

Littell squinted. Wait now, what's—

He saw the pathway. He saw the door. He saw the "301." It's the bungalow. It's the "Mob meet spot." It's his gig for Dwight Holly.

Littell dropped the paper. Thoughts jumped and garbled. The Boys/that gaffe/"box of goodies."

108

(Los Angeles, 3/30/68)

DEATH KIT:

Four hypos/full loads/premixed: Big "H" and Novocain anesthetic.

One .44 mag. One silencer. One roll of duct tape. One paper-bag carryall. One pack of moist towelettes.

We're here. We're at 5th and Stanford. It's Skid Row. It's Bum Hell.

Wayne lounged. Wayne watched the hotel. Wayne jiggled his sack. He stood outside a blood bank. Bums hobnobbed. Nurses culled donors up.

He's there. He's in the Hiltz Hotel. He's in room 402. It's four floors up.

Wayne watched the front door. Wayne savored. Wayne stalled.

He'd rotated south. He hit Bob's kompound. He found it cleaned out. It vibed raid. It vibed heedless. It vibed state cops. Bob had friends. Bob was Fed-vouched. It vibed *dumb* state cops.

Wayne flew to Vegas then. Wayne checked the Cavern. Wayne picked messages up:

Call Pete. He's in Sparta. Call Sonny.

He called Pete. He got no answer. He called Sonny. Sonny was jazzed. Sonny said, "This nigger called me." Sonny cited said nigger source.

Bam:

Sonny's guy saw Wendell. Wendell was nom-de-plumed. Wendell's now Abdallah X.

It was warm. It was eighty at noon. Skid Row was crammed up. Winos/amputees on skateboards/he-shes rouged up.

They jostled Wayne. Wayne felt zero. Wayne felt ate up. His skin buzzed. He rode eggshells. His bloodstream froze up.

He walked over.

He walked through the front door. He passed bums in the lobby. He passed a TV cranked up.

'68 Novas! Buy now! *Se habla español* at Giant Felix Chevrolet!

A wino convulsed. Wayne dodged his legs. Wayne took side stairs up. He lost his feet. He lost *his* legs. He fought gravity.

He hit the fourth floor landing. He saw the hallway. He saw wood doors inset.

He passed 400. He passed 401. He hit 402. He touched the knob. He turned it. The door popped.

He's right there. He's backlit. You've got window light. There's Wendell in a straight-back chair. There's Wendell with a short-dog.

Wayne stepped inside. Wayne shut the door. Wayne almost threw up. Wendell saw him. Wendell squinted. Wendell grinned all fucked up.

Wayne stood there.

Wendell said, "You looks familiar."

Wayne stood there.

Wendell said, "Give me a hint."

Wayne said, "Dallas." Wayne almost threw up.

Wendell slurped wine. Wendell looked bad. Wendell wore injection welts. Wendell wore needle tracks.

"That's a good hint. Makes me think you a certain husband with a grievance. I've fucking widowered more than a few of them, so that narrows it down somewhat."

Wayne scoped the room. Wayne saw empty short-dogs. Wayne smelled wine upchucked.

Wendell said, "That was some weekend. Remember? The President got shot."

Wayne moved. Wayne took two steps. Wayne kicked out and up. He hit the chair. He hit the jug. He knocked Wendell flat.

Wendell puked wine and bile. Wayne stepped on his neck. Wayne fullweight-pinned him. Wayne dug through his sack.

He grabbed a hypo. Wendell thrashed. He shot his neck up. Wendell de-thrashed. Wendell soared. Wendell went smack-back.

Wayne dropped the hypo. Wayne grabbed a hypo. Wayne shot

his hands up. Wendell shuddered. Wendell resoared. Wendell went more smack-back.

Wayne dropped the hypo. Wayne grabbed a hypo. Wayne shot his hips up. Wendell grinned. Wendell soar-soared. Wendell went waaay smack-back.

Wayne dropped the hypo. Wayne grabbed a hypo. Wayne shot his knees up. Wendell grinned. Wendell sooooored. Wendell smaaacked out and up.

Wayne dropped the hypo. Wayne grabbed the tape. Wayne pulled a strip up. He taped Wendell's mouth. He rolled three loops dense. He cinched Wendell's neck up.

He dropped the tape. He grabbed the mag. He cocked it back. He fixed the silencer. He bent low. Wendell's eyes rolled back.

Wayne grabbed his right hand. Wayne shot off his fingers. Wayne shot off his thumb. Wendell squirmed. Big "H" constrained him. His eyes rolled *waaaay* back.

Wayne dumped the shells. Wayne reloaded. Wayne cocked his piece back. He grabbed Wendell's left hand. He shot off his fingers. He shot off his thumb.

Wendell squirmed. Big "H" constrained him. His eyes rolled *mooooore* back.

Wayne dumped the shells. Wayne reloaded. Wayne cocked his piece back. Wendell puked. Bile blew out his nostrils. Wendell shit in his pants.

Wayne leaned down. Wayne aimed tight. Wayne shot his legs off at the knees. Blood spritzed. Bone chips flew. Wayne grabbed the towelettes.

Wendell's stumps twitched. Wayne grabbed a chair. Wayne watched him bleed to death.

The flight ran late. He flew numb. He dozed L.A. to Vegas. He smelled things that weren't there.

Cordite and blood. Cheap wine. Burned silencer threads.

The plane landed. He got off. He smelled things that weren't there.

Burned bone and vomit. Scented towelettes.

He walked through McCarran. He found a phone. He got an operator. She patched Sparta direct.

He heard eight rings. He got no answer. No Barb and Pete there.

He walked outside. He veered toward the cab line. Two men

walked up. They flanked him. They braced him. They slammed a two-cop press.

It's Dwight Holly. It's a swarthy guy. It's that guy Fred Otash.

Shakedown Fred—skinny now—this cadaver.

They grabbed him. They led him. He felt limp. He felt numb. He saw two cars double-parked. He saw a Fed sedan. He saw Wayne Senior's Cadillac.

They stopped between cars. They patted him down. They let him go slack. He stumbled. He almost fell. He smelled Wendell dead.

Holly said, "Durfee wasn't for free."

Otash said, "We stiffed that tipoff through Sonny."

Holly said, "I've got a print transparency on you. If you say no, I'll have a guy roll it around Durfee's room."

Wayne looked at them. Wayne *saw* them. Wayne got *IT*. Wayne Senior/his hate talk/the hate-mail intercepts.

Wayne said, "Who?"

Holly said, "Martin Luther King."

109

(Sparta, 3/31/68)

TV NEWS—breaking:

LBJ's out. The war fucked him up. He won't seek Term Two. It's Humphrey v. Bobby. The race looks tight.

Barb watched the news. Pete watched Barb. Barb dug on the Bobby aspects. The house was cold. Barb's sister was cheap. Barb's sister skimped on the heat.

He flew Saigon to Sparta. Barb welcomed him reluctant. Barb ragged him incessant. Barb ragged his travel-ban breach.

Barb flipped channels. Barb caught war news. Barb caught some Memphis strike.

Trash workers. A support march. One riot so far. Sixty injured/looter damage/one nigger kid dead. Crazy King's there. Crazy King's *between* riots. One "Poor People's" riot on tap.

Barb watched the news. Pete watched Barb. Barb watched the news rapt. Pete popped gum. Pete obeyed Barb's rule—don't smoke inside.

He chewed gum. He chewed double sticks. He fretted shit.

He called Bob's kompound. He got a weird tone. It vibed disconnect. He called the Cavern. He left Wayne a message. Wayne never called back. He punked out. He stalled his speech. He set his flight back.

Barb flipped channels. Barb caught Bobby. Barb caught Crazy King. Pete stood up. Pete blocked the screen. Pete turned off the set.

Barb said, "Shit."

Pete popped his gum. "Hear me out on some things. You'll like part of it."

Barb smiled. "You're getting ready to snow me. I can tell."

"Here's the good part. The Boys want to scuttle the biz, the funnel, and the whole operation. I'm going along with it."

Barb shook her head. "If that was most of it, you'd be smiling."

"You're right. There's mo—"

"I know there's more, I know it's bad, so tell me."

Pete gulped. Pete swallowed. Pete choked his gum back.

"Part of it went bad. I've got to pick Wayne up in Vegas and make one more Cuban run. I need you to hole up somewhere until it's over and I cut some kind of deal with the Outfit."

Barb said, "No."

Boom—case closed—like that.

Pete gulped. "I'll dump Tiger Kab and the Cavern then. We'll go someplace else."

Barb said, "No."

No drumroll—no pause—no inflection.

Pete gulped. "I can finesse it. There's some risk, sure, but I wouldn't do it if I didn't think the Boys would buy my explanation."

Barb said, "No."

No fanfare—all deadpan—no shit.

Pete gulped. Pete coughed his gum up.

"If I don't pay this off, the word will go out. The wrong guys will think, 'He knew the story and let it all go.' They'll start thinking I'm weak, which will cause us trouble somewhere down the line."

Barb said, "No. Whatever *it* is is bullshit, and you know it."

No recourse—I *know* you—that's that. No tears yet—tears pending— eyes wet.

Pete said, "I'll be back when it's over."

* * *

Charter flight: La Crosse to Vegas. Junket geeks/smoky cabin/ cramped seats.

The geeks were insurance men. The geeks were Shriners and Moose. They drank. They swapped hats. They cracked jokes.

Pete tried to sleep. Pete fucked with IT.

He'd called Stanton. He called loooong distance. He called Saigon to Bay St. Louis. He brought up the Cuban run. He said I want to go. Please let me say adios.

Stanton said yes.

He mopped up in Saigon. He laid cover tracks. He bought weapons. He fixed the warehouse window. He worked on the QT. He installed new glass/new mesh. He called Mesplède. He said *I'll* handle it. He said *I'll* breach the breach.

He bought three guns: one Walther and two Berettas. He bought three silencers. He bought three inside-the-pants rigs.

Booty. Swag. Cars/furs/watches/antiques. THE BIG FUCKING LIE revealed.

The flight bumped. They ran low-pressure sweeps. The junket geeks pawed the stews. The junket geeks laughed. The junket geeks preached.

Pro-war stuff. All clichés. We can't pull out. We'll forfeit Asia. We can't look weak.

Pete shut his eyes. Pete *heard* the geeks. Pete *saw* home movie flicks.

There's Betty Mac. It's visit twelve million. There's Chuck the Vice Freak. There's Barb. She says, "No"—eyes working on tears.

We stand firm. We bong the Cong. We never surrender. We stomp the peace freaks.

It droned on. It went stereophonic. He tried to sleep. He failed. He fought this exhaustion. He got this idea:

Fuck it all. Fuck it now. Forfeit the kadre kode breach.

The plane touched down. Pete got off. Pete walked to Air Midwest.

He bought a ticket. He splurged. He booked first-class to Milwaukee/connector to Sparta/two flights one-way.

He had a layover. He had four hours to kill.

He walked to the gate lounge. He schlepped his gun bag. He

sprawled across four seats. He fell. It was soft and dark. He had newspapers as sheets.

He opened his eyes. He saw ceiling lights. He saw Ward Littell. Ward had his ticket. Ward flicked the edge.

"You were going back. Barb will like that."

Pete sat up. His newspaper sheets fell.

"Jesus, you scared me."

Ward cleaned his glasses. "Barb called. She said you were going south on some insane errand, and could I stop it."

Pete yawned. "And?"

"And I put a few things together and called Carlos."

Pete lit a cigarette. It was 6:10 now. His flight left at 7:00.

"Don't stop there. I want to see where this is going."

Ward coughed. "Part of it is from Carlos, part of it I put together my—"

"Jesus, just tell—"

"Carlos is cutting off your business. It was part of a ruse to get weapons to Castro, so that he could funnel them to rebels in Central America. It all played into my foreign-casino plan, and I never knew anything about it."

Fill-in/paint-by-number/link-the-dots diverse. Stanton and Carlos/the fake funnel/the BIG LIE complete.

"It was a shuck, Ward. The whole thing."

"I know."

"Bob Relyea. What about—"

"He dropped his Klan gig and went off on another operation. Wayne's working with him, and Carlos said that's all he knows."

Pete grabbed the ticket. Ward grabbed it back.

"You flew to Saigon. You put some things together. I'm going off what you told Barb."

Pete grabbed his bag. The guns rubbed and scraped.

"You're leading me. You talked to Barb, you talked to Carlos, you found me. Let's start there."

Ward squared his glasses. "Carlos learned that Stanton, Guéry, and Elorde have been skimming off his portion of the profits. He actually *wants* you to take them and their Cuban contacts out. He said if you do that and another 'small favor,' he'll retire you."

A speaker popped. Flight 49—nonstop to Milwaukee.

"Do you think he means it?"

"Yes. They want to clean this thing up and move on."

Pete checked the gate. The flight crew stood there. Baggage carts rolled.

"Call Barb. Tell her I almost came home."

Ward nodded. Ward crumpled the ticket.

"There's one more thing."

"What's that?"

"Carlos wants you to scalp them."

110

(Memphis, 4/3/68)

RABBITS:

WILD RABBIT. RED RABBIT. DEAD RABBIT soon.

Wayne pulled curbside. Wayne parked. Wayne watched the New Rebel Motel.

The Mustang pulled up. Fred O. walked over. The shooter got out. There's skinny Fred O. He's starved to look different. There's skinny Jim Ray. He's starved off crystal meth.

They laughed. They huddled. Fred O. passed the box. It was long and bulky. It contained a 30.06.

Hi-end scope. Geared for soft-point bullets. Contact spread/blunt impact/bad for ballistic IDs.

Jimmy had his rifle. Bob had the same one. Fred O. had rifle 3. It was one-shot test-fired. It was print-smeared by Jimmy.

D-day was tomorrow. Jimmy might shoot. Jimmy might punk out. Bob *will* shoot instead.

Fred O. ran Jimmy. Fred O. said he'd shoot. Fred O. was sure.

The Plan:

There's a rooming house. It's a wino pad. It's across from the Lorraine Motel. King's at the Lorraine. He's in room 306. It's off a balcony. There's a wino pad vacancy. Fred O. made sure. Fred O. held said flop for a week.

He "checked in." He stayed away. He'll "check out" tomorrow. Jimmy will check in. He'll get that room. It's near a bathroom perch-site.

He might shoot. He might punk out. Thus Bob shoots instead.

There's a brush patch by the wino pad. It supplies cover. It supplies trajectory. The wino pad runs back to Main Street. The Lorraine's on Mulberry.

Jimmy shoots. Jimmy exits—way *off* Mulberry. He wipes his rifle. He drops the rifle. He drops it in a doorway.

Fred O. lurks near. Fred O. grabs the rifle. Fred O. drops rifle 3. It's print-smeared. It's smeared by Jimmy. It's smeared by transparency.

Jimmy splits. Jimmy drives to the safe house. Wayne's waiting there. It's a cheap apartment. It's furnished.

With booze empties/dope baggies/needles. With white powder/dope fits/crystal meth.

With a suicide note—forged by Fred Otash.

I flew on meth. I killed Nigger King. I'm scared now. I escaped Jeff City. I refuse to go back. I'm a hero. I'm a martyr. Hey, World, take that.

Wayne waits. Wayne geezes Jimmy up. Wayne shoots Jimmy then. Jimmy dies on a speed rush.

Panic. Suicide. Your stock "lone assassin"—gone on crystal meth.

Wayne watched the New Rebel. Fred O. stood outside. Jimmy walked in. Fred O. looked over. Fred O. saw Wayne and winked.

Wayne winked back. Wayne shoved off. Wayne drove to the Lorraine Motel.

He parked close in. He checked the lot. He checked the balcony. He checked the wino pad. He checked the brush patch. He checked the street.

The patch was thick. It flanked a cement wall. A passageway led to Main Street. They perch in the patch. They shoot or don't shoot. They walk to Main Street.

Wayne watched the motel. Negro men hobnobbed. They stood on that balcony.

No cops attendant. Dwight Holly confirmed said. Dwight Holly tapped cop frequencies. Memphis was uptight. They had riots and marches. They had cops alert on Code 3. More shit was planned. One more march boded. It was set for April 5th.

He'd be dead. Memphis would burn. Wayne *knew* it. Jimmy would shoot. Fred O. said so. Fred *knew* it.

Fred O. ran Jimmy. Jimmy ran L.A. to Memphis. Jimmy made stops in between. Jimmy was wacked. Jimmy took hypnosis courses. Jimmy went to bartender's school. Jimmy shot meth.

Jimmy bought skin mags. Jimmy jacked off and read porno books.

Jimmy joined the Friends of Rhodesia. Jimmy placed swinger ads. Jimmy got rhinoplasty. Jimmy stalked Dr. King in L.A. Jimmy stalked March 16/17.

Fred O. surveilled him. Fred O. *knew then:* He'll shoot proactively. Fred O. recruited him *proactive.* Fred O. was cloaked as "Raul."

Fred had King's travel plans. Dwight Holly pouched them. They came from an FBI source.

King went to Selma. He arrived on 3/22. Fred O. and Jim Ray were there. The conditions were sub-par. Fred O. stalled D-day.

King stayed in Selma. Jimmy drove to Atlanta. He knew King lived there. King foxed him. King flew to Jew York. King had business there.

Dwight got a tip. His Fed source pouched it. RED RABBIT to Memphis. Arrival 3/28. There's a garbage strike there.

Dwight recruited Wayne on 3/30. "Raul" goosed Jimmy Ray. Cash perks and meth—Memphis dead-ahead.

It was NOW. Fred said so. Fred knew it. Jimmy was strung out. Jimmy craved the "Bounty." Jimmy craved this mock Holy Grail.

Wayne watched the balcony. Wayne saw activity.

Dwight ran death-threat checks. The Memphis Feds supplied facts. King logged eighty-one death threats. Klan threats mostly.

King blew them off. King shined them on. King scorned security.

Wayne watched the balcony. Wayne saw Dr. King. They went back. They intertwined. They had symmetry.

He went to Little Rock. He enforced integration. He saw King there. He saw that fuck film. It was FBI-shot. He saw King there. He killed three coloreds. King indicted Las Vegas. King almost went there. He killed Bongo in Saigon. King hated his war. He killed Wendell Durfee. Wayne Senior found Durfee. King served his vengeance cause.

Wayne Senior knew:

You *want it.* I *made* you. It's *yours.*

He killed Durfee. Dwight suborned him. He joined Wayne Senior's cause. It's Wayne Senior's Hate School. It's the postgrad course. Coloreds foist chaos. Coloreds breed discord. Coloreds spawn doss.

Wayne Senior said you learned. Wayne Senior said you paid. Wayne Senior said you earned this shot.

Wayne Senior bragged:

Ward Littell's retiring. Mormon heavies love me. *I'll* get his Hughes spot. It's certain. I know. I was told.

Carlos Marcello called me. We talked. We discussed Littell's retirement. We discussed general business. We discussed the Hughes spot. Carlos said this:

Littell worked for Hughes *and* me. *You* take that full spot. Littell suborns Nixon. Littell retires then. *You* go from there. *You* work with Nixon. *You* secure our requests. *You* insure our warranty.

Wayne Senior said this:

My son the chemist. You know him. *I* know he's outgrown Pete B.

Carlos said this:

We'll find a spot. We'll bring Wayne in. It's adios to Pete B.

Wayne watched the balcony. Wayne saw King laugh. Wayne saw King slap his knees.

I hate smart. I've killed five. You can't outhate me.

I I I

(Bay St. Louis, 4/3/68)

CASTOFF—9:16 P.M. Light wind. Course south-southeast.

The last gun run. The kadre kurtain kall.

Pete walked the deck. His pants fit tight. He wore three guns in. He wore his shirt out. His gut bulged. The silencers chafed.

He flew in. They held castoff. He flew in late. He looked for Wayne in Vegas. He tapped out. Carlos called him.

Carlos was Carlos. Fuck the Big Lie. Carlos was brusque:

"You found some things out. So what? You were never dumb, Pete."

"Bob's off somewhere. He's working with Wayne. He don't get hurt like the rest."

"Don't act aggrieved. Bring me some scalps. Remember, you owe me for Dallas."

The boat pitched. The boat dipped. The boat leveled. Pete walked the deck. Pete thought it through. Pete fought butterflies.

They're below deck. Get them alone/get them together. Hit the arms locker. Get a shotgun. Choke a tight spread.

Pilot the boat. You know how to. Head for Cuban seas. Lure Fuentes on. Lure Arredondo. Kill them/scalp them/dump them. Scalp and dump the rest.

Six snuffs. Butch haircuts. Scalped per kadre kode breach.

The boat ran smooth. Automatic pilot. Glassy Gulf seas.

Pete climbed the bridge. Pete read dials. Pete ran instrument checks. It's OK. You know how. You'll do it.

He walked below. He got flutters—biiiig butterflies. The main cabin stood full: Stanton/Guéry/Elorde/Dick Wenzel.

Pete jittered. Pete twitched. Pete bumped his head on a beam.

Stanton said, "They don't build these boats for giants."

Guéry said, "Which is my problem, too."

Flash said, "I do not have that problem."

Wenzel said, "You're a shrimp, but you're dangerous."

They laughed. Pete laughed. Pete went lightheaded.

Four men/no sidearms/good. All relaxed/sipping scotch/good.

Note this oversight. Note this fuck-up and glitch:

You *could* have brought Seconal. You *could* have spiked the scotch. You *could* have killed them asleep.

Stanton said, "We'll refuel at Snipe Key."

Wenzel said, "They're meeting us eighty knots out. It's the only way to rendezvous before dawn."

Pete coughed. "It's my fault. I was late."

Flash shook his head. "The last time. We no go without you."

Guéry shook his head. "You were always the one with the . . . *qu'est-ce que* . . . 'greatest commitment.' "

Wenzel slugged scotch. "I'll miss the runs. I hate the Reds as much as the next white man."

Flash smiled. "I am not white."

Wenzel smiled. "In your heart you are."

Pete faked a yawn. His chest pinged. His pulse raced.

"I'm tired. I'm going to lie down for a bit."

The guys smiled. The guys nodded. The guys grinned and stretched. Pete walked back. Pete shut the door. Pete ran a cabin check:

Four units/low bulkheads/four sleeping sacks. Please get drunk. Please crap out. Please crap out in shifts.

He opened the cargo hold. The boat rolled. The boat rolled *très* light. It rolled too drifty—sans-gun-ballast light.

He popped the storage door. He looked in. He hit the light. Bam:

Empty/*no* guns/*no* ordnance packed tight.

He got butterflies. Huge now. Sized like King Kong.

No guns. *No gun run.* Loose ends scheduled up. *They* kill *you.* They dump *you.* They kill Fuentes and Arredondo.

The boat pitched. Pete dug his legs in. Pete popped the shotgun rack. He got moths—big fuckers—way up in his chest.

He pulled shotguns. He worked slides. He popped the shells chambered in. Butterfingers: four shotguns/shells popping/no hands to catch said.

Shells dropping. Shells spinning. Shells hitting the floor deck. Shells skitting and rolling free.

He grabbed them. He stuffed his pants. He stuffed his teeth. He fumbled the shotguns. He refilled the rack. He heard the cargo door creak.

He turned around. He saw Wenzel. He looked dumb. He looked *caught.* He had shells in his teeth.

Wenzel shut the door. Wenzel stepped close. Wenzel made fists.

"What the fuck are—"

Pete looked around. Pete saw the flare gun. It's close. It's on a wall hook.

He spit the shells out. He stepped back. He grabbed it and aimed. He pulled the trigger. The flare ignited. The flare hit Wenzel's face. Wenzel screeched. His hair burned. He batted his face.

The flare dropped. It burned Wenzel's clothes. It shot flames chest to feet.

Pete stepped in. Pete grabbed Wenzel's neck. Pete snuffed hair flames. He snapped left. He burned his hands. He snapped right.

Wenzel convulsed. Wenzel went limp. Wenzel's eyebrows shot flames. Pete threw him down. Pete ripped his shirt off. Pete snuffed the flames

The flare fizzled out. The door stayed shut. *Contained* stink and flames.

Pete flexed his hand. Burn blisters popped. Pete anchored his legs.

Now.

They'll miss him. They'll need him. They'll yell. The boat's rolling. It's on auto pilot. Wenzel stays on call.

Now.

Pete clenched up. Pete listened—ear to the door.

Nothing.

He pulled his Walther. He cocked it. He opened the door. One walkway/four cabins/two per side wall.

Ten yards up: the main cabin/set perpendicular/with the door shut.

Pete inched up. Pete took baby steps—slow. He hit cabin 1. He looked in. He braced the door.

Nobody.

Pete inched up. Pete took baby steps—slow. He hit cabin 2. He looked in. He braced the door.

Nobody.

Pete inched up. Pete took baby steps—slow. He hit cabin 3. He looked in. He braced the door.

There's Flash. He's sacked out asleep.

Pete walked up. Pete aimed close. Muzzle to hairline/silencer tight. He shot once. His piece went pffft. Brains doused the bed.

Pete walked out. Pete took baby steps—slow. He hit cabin 4. He looked in. He braced the door.

Nobody.

Pete inched up. Pete ate jumbo moths and butterflies. Pete popped the main cabin door.

Nobody—all hands on deck. *Slow now*—with a deeeeeep breath.

He did it. He walked topside. He took baby steps. He got fifty-foot butterflies. His breath tugged. His hands shook. His sphincter blew. He smelled his shit. He smelled his sweat. He smelled cooked silencer threads.

Baby steps—three more now. Make the deck/watch your feet.

He pulled one Beretta. He cocked it. He climbed two guns out. His breath tugged. Baby steps slow and—

He hit the deck. His breath stopped. His left arm ripped. Pain shot heart to arm—fucked arteries.

He gulped air. He sucked spray. He fell to his knees. He dropped his left-hand gun. It clattered on teak.

He made noise. Somebody yelled. Noise boomed behind him.

Stanton.

Stanton yelled, "Dick!" Stanton yelled, "Pete!"

Down the deck. Forty feet. The aft rotor-seats.

Pete pitched forward. His left arm blew. The deck cracked his teeth. He rolled over. He gulped breath. He spit out cracked teeth.

He heard Guéry—aft and left—"I don't see him."

He heard Stanton—back-stairs aft—"I think he got Dick."

He heard slides click. He heard hammers cock. He heard rounds snap in. His left arm exploded. His left arm died. His left arm flopped free.

He sucked air. He sucked hard. It hurt bad. It burned bad. He lodged some breath free.

He crawled.

One-handed. One-armed. At one-arm speed. He brushed a rope stack. It was cover. Thick ropes stacked deep.

He heard foot scuffs. They scuffed mid-deck left. He saw pantlegs and feet.

Guéry—fast-walking—*his* way.

His breath crimped. He saw starbursts. He saw twelve legs and feet. He aimed off the ropes. He aimed low. He fired.

He popped six shots fast. He got six muzzle bursts. Double vision/tracer zips/spider legs and feet.

Guéry screamed. Guéry dropped. Guéry grabbed his feet. Guéry fired way high. Shots ripped a mast sheet.

Pete sucked air. Pete *got* air. Pete got a bead. He aimed head high. He pulled slooow.

The slide jammed. Muzzle light dispersed. He saw Guéry with stump feet.

He heard foot scuffs. They scuffed way aft. They scuffed the back stairs clear. He pulled gun 3. His pump lurched. He dropped it.

Guéry fired. Shots hit the ropes. Shots ricocheted.

Pete rolled free. Pete crawled. Pete crawled with one arm and two feet. Guéry saw him. Guéry stretched prone. Guéry fired.

Tracers—loud and close in. Over his head. Scraping the gunwales. Ripping through teak. Six shots/seven/full clip.

Guéry dropped the gun. Pete got close. Pete one-arm leaped.

He bared his teeth. He bit down. He got Guéry's cheek. He raked his fingers up and out. He gouged an eye free.

Guéry screamed. Guéry swung a fist. Guéry hit bared teeth. Pete bit down. Pete snapped bone. Pete made his good hand a V.

Guéry screeched. It was high-decibel. It was half whine/half screech.

Pete drove his hand up. Pete ripped throat tissue. Pete smashed neck bones. Pete drove up to bridgework and teeth.

Guéry spasmed. Pete yanked his arm out. Pete made a hole elbow-deep. Guéry spasmed. Pete rolled back. Pete dug in and shoved with his feet.

He kicked Guéry. He kicked hard right. He kicked him off the deck. He kicked him into the sea.

He heard a splash. He heard a scream. He sucked breath. He *got* breath. He crawled free.

He crawled. He crawled one-armed. Noise cut through deck teak.

It's Stanton. He's below deck. That's steel gnashing steel. He's in the cargo hold. He's loading shotguns. Steel's jamming on steel.

Pete sucked air. Pete rolled up. Pete made his knees. His bladder blew. His breath stopped. He sucked air in deep.

He walked. He staggered. He threw lopsided weight. He made the back steps. He smashed at the door. He threw lopsided weight.

Zero—*weak* weight—no give.

He kicked the door. He shoved the door. He threw lopsided weight.

Zero—*weak* weight—no give.

Barricade/smashproof/blocked stairs below.

Pete kneeled down. Pete laid down lopsided. Pete got echoes off the deckwood. Pete heard steel gnash steel.

It's about three feet over. It's about ten feet up. The deck's scuffed there. It's threadbare. It's breakable teak.

Pete hauled his weight up. Pete heaved for breath. Pete made his knees.

He crawled. He knee-walked. He hit the anchor hub. He stood up. He invoked Barb. He did a dead squat. He threw his right arm out. He wrapped the anchor stem. He jerked and stood up.

His breath exploded. His breath held. His left arm burned up.

He stumbled. He weaved four feet starboard. He reared up to six-five plus. He let the anchor drop.

It cracked the deck. It shattered loud. It snapped threadbare teak. It fell below. It dropped straight down. It smashed John Stanton flush.

112

(Memphis, 4/4/68)

COUNTDOWN:

It's 5:59. We're heading for checkmate—pawn to RED KING. We're close. King's outside. King's on the balcony.

He's by the railing. He's with a Negro man. Negro men mill below. King's talking to them. It's jovial. Cars sit below.

Jimmy's in the wino pad. Fred O. said so. Jimmy *will* shoot. Fred O. said so. Jimmy *will* split. I'll drop gun 3. Fred O. said so.

Wayne watched the balcony. Brush covered him. Bob Relyea ditto. Bugs crawled. Ants swarmed. Pollen spritzed.

Bob held gun 2. It was aimed up and out. It was eye-sighted in. Wayne held binoculars. Wayne zeroed in tight.

He held on King. He got King's eyes. He got King's skin.

Bob said, "He ain't walking downstairs. If Jimmy don't shoot inside a minute, I do."

Code Red/all systems clear/all systems GO. No security extant/no cops visible/Feds and Fed cars ditto. Their car was parked on Main Street. Fred O.'s car ditto.

Bob shoots or Jimmy shoots. Jimmy runs then. They run faster. They run zippo. They run through the same passageway. They're younger and swift. They cut through the wino-pad wings.

They bag their car. They split. Jimmy bags his car. Jimmy splits. Fred O. drops gun 3 in a doorway—upside Canipe Novelty.

Wayne hits the safe house. Jimmy shows up. Jimmy suicides.

Countdown—6:00 P.M. sharp—pawn to RED KING.

Wayne honed his binoculars. Wayne got King's eyes. Wayne got King's skin.

"I'm on him. If Jimmy misses or wounds, I'll tap you."

"I want him to punk out. You know that."

"Otash says he's solid."

"He's a fruitcake. Always has been."

Wayne watched King. Wayne ran outtakes. Wayne saw that fuck film. The mattress jiggles. King's flab rolls. That ashtray drops.

Wayne tingled. Bob tingled. Wayne saw his veins pop. They heard a shot slam. They saw red blood on black skin. They heard concurrent pop.

Wayne saw the impact. Wayne saw the neck spray. Wayne saw King drop.

The safe house:

A two-room apartment. Bargain-basement furnished. Three miles off South Main.

Wayne dropped Bob off. Wayne went there. Wayne sat. Fucking Jimmy schizzed out. Fucking Jimmy no-showed.

Fred O. said go there. Fred O. said meet my friend. He's got the bounty. He's got your visa. He's got your Rhodesian passport.

Wayne sat. Wayne waited. Wayne shagged walkie-talkie reports. Fred O. buzzed. Fred O. talked. Fred O. culled juicy cop talk.

He dropped the gun. He did it unseen. Jimmy bagged his sled and took off. The cops showed. The cops found the gun. The cops checked it out.

They talked to folks. They got descriptions. They put broadcasts out. Look for a white man. He's got a white Mustang.

Wrong. Jimmy's 'Stang was yellow.

Fred O. buzzed. Fred O. fretted. He's gone. He smelled shit. He shut "Raul" off. The cops have the plant gun. The Feds will take over. The Feds will obfuscate.

Soft-point bullets. Hard to ID. Ballistic holocaust. It's a 30.06. It's the murder weapon. We know that's a fact.

Trust Mr. Hoover. He'll extrapolate. Big Dwight says so. Wayne agreed. Wayne said we're covered. We *both* say so.

Bob was crushed. Bob didn't shoot. Bob the Klansman bereft. Bob laughed and hailed a cab. Bob booked for West Memphis, Arkansas.

Wayne sat. Wayne waited. Wayne gave Jimmy up.

He burned the suicide note. He flushed the crystal meth. He smashed the hypodermic. He put gloves on. He wiped the pad. He played the radio.

He heard eulogies. He caught breaking news. He heard Negroes-in-the-street bereft. Riots in progress/nationwide chaos/arson and sack.

Wayne popped a window. Wayne heard sirens. Wayne saw flames sweep and crack.

Wayne thought *I Did That.*

113

(Washington, D.C., 4/6/68)

UPDATES—live on TV.

Littell watched NBC. Littell caught riots and mourning. Littell watched all-day TV.

Riot dead: four in Baltimore/nine in D.C.

Riots: L.A./Detroit/St. Louis. Chicago/New York. Outrage/chain reaction/big damage stats.

Littell cracked a window. Littell smelled smoke. Littell heard bullets smack.

A newsman pitched a D.C. update. This just teletyped:

Negroes see a white man. Negroes swamp his car. Negroes kill said white man. Other Negroes watch.

Littell watched TV. Littell kept a vigil. It ran forty-eight hours plus.

He flew to D.C. He did Teamster work. He got the news. He holed up in his apartment. He lived by his TV.

He mourned. He watched TV. He ran scenarios: Mr. Hoover/ Dwight Holly/BLACK RABBIT.

The Rustin shakedown. Attendant frustration. The Poor People's March provokes. Time lines/event chains/conclusions pro and con. The FBI investigates/cover-up pro and con/empirical lessons from Dallas.

He holed up. He wept some. He wondered:

The El Encanto bug. The Boys' "goody box." Bobby's bugged suite. Access to Bobby's campaign.

He ran scenarios. He connected them—King to Bobby. He watched TV. He debunked scenarios—King to Bobby. He stayed inside. He stayed safe. He called Janice.

She got the word. She learned eight days ago. The doctors said it's cancer.

It's in your stomach. It's spreading slow. It's in your spleen. Your cramps masked the symptoms. Your cramps cost you time. Your cramps skewed early detection.

You might live. You might die. Let us operate. Janice said maybe. Janice said let me think.

He told her:

You love the DI. Move in with me. Relax and play the golf course.

Janice did it. Janice moved in. They talked. Janice blasted Wayne Senior.

Janice wept some. Janice said he talked in his sleep. He asked what he said. She said you reach out for "Bobby" and "Jane."

She said no more. She zipped her lips and played coy. He consoled her. He convinced her—let them operate.

Janice showed courage. Janice said yes. Janice faced the knife next week.

Sick list:

Janice was gravely ill. Pete almost died. Heart attack/on his boat run/well out at sea.

Pete killed four men. Pete dumped the bodies. Pete turned the boat back. Pete radioed Bay St. Louis. Pete said call my friend in D.C.

Littell got the message. Littell called Carlos. Carlos pledged a cleanup crew. Pete got the boat in. Pete got lucky. No one saw *five* men embark.

The cleanup men got on. The cleanup men cleaned up. The doctors got Pete. The doctors operated. The doctors patched his heart.

Coronary thrombosis. Mid-range this time. You were lucky.

Pete rested. Littell called him. Pete said he got four. Pete said he missed the last two.

Littell called Carlos. Littell relayed the message. Carlos said fuck it. Carlos reprieved the last two.

Pete called Littell back. Pete asked favors. Don't tell Barb. Don't scare her. Let me get my shit back. Call Milt Chargin. Say I'm okay. Have him mind the cat.

Littell agreed. Littell called Pete. Littell called one hour back. A nurse came on. She said Pete checked out—"Against doctor's advice."

Pete had a visitor. Said visitor spooked him. It was "Carlos Somebody." It was four hours back.

Littell flipped channels. Littell saw Bobby. Bobby was solemn. Bobby condemned racial hate. Bobby mourned Dr. King.

The scenarios kicked in: bug jobs pro and con/collusion widespread. It got bad. It got wild. It got *real*.

Littell grabbed his Rolodex. Littell found Paul Horvitz.

He made the meet. Paul said he'd risk it. See you at 6:00 P.M.— Eddie Chang's Kowloon.

Littell weighed *his* risk.

The hotel bug. Potential upshots exponential. Risk it. Tell Paul. Have him warn Bobby.

Littell dressed up. Littell wore his beard and tweeds. Littell walked out.

He walked. He broke curfew laws. He heard sirens. He saw D.C. locked down tight. He saw flames two miles over. He heard klaxons overlap.

He walked fast. He broiled in tweed. A breeze blew soot flakes. A car eased by. A Negro yelled. He heard race obscenities.

A Negro hurled a beer can. A Negro dumped an ashtray. Cigarette butts breezed.

Littell hit Conn. Ave. Water mains erupted. Firemen lugged hoses. Cops stood by fire trucks.

The Kowloon was open. Eddie Chang was feisty. Eddie Chang fed local cops.

Littell walked in. Littell grabbed the back booth. The barman turned the TV up.

Live local feed. Negroes with gas cans. Cars belly-up.

Three men watched. They were bluff-hearty types. They had hardhats and beer guts.

One man said, "Goddamn animals."

One man said, "We gave them their civil rights."

One man said, "And look what we got."

Littell sprawled. Littell went invertebrate. Littell culled Deep South anecdotes.

Paul Horvitz walked in.

He saw Littell. He brushed his pants off. He walked over. He shook his coat sleeves. Ash dropped and whirled.

He dug his feet in. He spanned the booth. He gripped two hat posts.

"An FBI man talked to Senator Kennedy, an hour ago. He showed him a photograph of a man who looked very much like you, without your beard. He said your name was Ward Littell, and he called you a 'provocateur.' The senator heard that name and saw that picture and almost freaked out."

Littell stood up. His knees shook. He banged the tabletop. He tried to talk. He went cottonmouthed. He st-st-st-stuttered.

Paul grabbed his coat. Paul pulled him close. Paul tore his beard off. Paul slapped him. Paul shoved him. Paul knocked his glasses off.

Littell fell back. Littell dumped the table. Paul fast-walked out.

The hardhats twirled their stools. The hardhats looked over. The hardhats flashed shit-eating grins.

One man flashed a Fed badge.

One man said, "Hi, Ward."

One man said, "Mr. Hoover knows all."

114

(Los Angeles, 4/8/68)

SOME CRAZY A-RAB. Two names the same.

Wayne brought him up. Wayne said he muscled him. The A-rab stiffed the Cavern. The A-rab packed hate tracts. The A-rab packed a piece.

Wayne got his hate-mail gig. Wayne pulled hate letters. Guess what? The A-rab sent Bobby K. notes.

Craaaazy shit. "Jew Pigs"/"RFK Must Die."

Pete drove freeways. Pete looped L.A. Pete drove old-man slow.

He felt weak. He felt sapped. He felt drained. He took midget steps now. His breath sputtered. He carried a cane. He measured his steps. He got minor satisfaction. He got more wind each day.

You're young. You're strong. The docs said so. The next one kills you. The surgeon said so.

They split your chest. They cleared your tubes. They stitched and stapled you. You checked out. You bought surgical clippers. You de-stitched yourself slow. You used scotch for disinfectant. You used scotch for anesthetic. You used scotch for the pain.

Pete drove freeways. Pete looped downtown L.A. Pete drove old-man slow.

Carlos bopped to his bedside. Carlos said the boat job—bravo. Carlos mentioned the "small favor." I know you know about it. I know Ward told you.

Pete said sure. You get a favor. I get retirement.

Carlos said go to L.A. Find Fred Otash a stooge.

Carlos said I like Fred. Wayne Senior referred him. I like Wayne Senior too. He's classy. He'll get Ward's job. Ward retires soon.

Pete left the hospital. Pete flew to L.A. Pete saw Fred O. Fred O. was skinny. Fred O. said why.

He ran a stiff. He ran him for eight months. He ran the King fall guy.

Bob Relyea worked the gig. Dwight Holly played ramrod. Wayne Senior ran ops. Wayne Junior was sequestered now. Wayne Junior worked backup.

He killed Wendell Durfee. The LAPD caught it. They had questions still. The snuff vibed revenge/the vic killed your wife/we'd like to talk to you.

Pete weighed the details. Pete gauged Fred O. Pete tore the "small favor" up.

Oh shit. The Boys need a stooge. It's a Bobby hit.

Fred O. confirmed it. Fred O. named no names. Fred O. confirmed implicit. Pete recalled the A-rab. Fred O. was Lebanese. Call it synergy.

Pete dished on the A-rab. Pete dished partial stats. Fred O. fucking drooled. Pete flew to Vegas. Pete kissed the cat hello and goodbye. Pete tossed Wayne's Cavern room.

He found his hate-mail copies. He went through them. He found the A-rab's notes.

RFK MUST DIE! RFK MUST DIE! RFK MUST DIE!

He called Sonny Liston. He said where'd you brace that A-rab? Sonny said the Desert Dawn Motel. He hit the Desert Dawn. He bribed the desk clerk. He checked registration stats.

Bam: Sirhan B. Sirhan/Pasadena, California.

He flew back to L.A. He called the DMV. He got Sirhan's full stats. He called Fred O. He said sit tight. He said I'll stake him out.

Carlos called last night. Carlos waxed sly. You figured it out. Fred O. said so. You know, I'm not surprised.

Carlos waxed assertive then. Carlos said this:

Ward's soft on Bobby. You know Ward. He's liberal martyr Littell. Sever contact for now. Ward's smart. Ward smells things. Conniver Littell.

Pete said sure. I'll do it. You know I want out.

Carlos laughed. Pete saw Big D. Jack's head goes ka-blooey. Jackie dives for scraps.

Chez Sirhan: A small crib/old wood-frame/near Muir High School. Car Sirhan: A jig rig/spinners and skirts/a coon maroon Ford.

Pete pulled up. Pete parked. Pete waited. Pete chewed Nicorette gum.

He thought about Barb. He ran the radio. He got some Barb tunes. He got the news—dig it—King Killer at Large!

He thought about Wayne. Wayne the spook assassin. Jigs from Wendell Durfee on up. He ran instincts. He laid bets. Wayne Senior sandbagged Wayne. Wayne Senior recruited him. It was fucked-up daddy stuff.

He ran the dial. He got more King. He got Bobby campaign stuff.

Sirhan walked out.

He darted. He walked funny. He smoked. He skimmed a racing form. He sideswiped a tree. He face-plowed a hedge.

Two kids walked by. They ogled Sirhan—dig on *that* freak!

Sirhan walked funny. Sirhan looked funny. Sirhan had wild hair and big teeth. Sirhan dropped his cigarette. Sirhan lit a cigarette. Sirhan flashed yellow teeth.

Sirhan got in his car. Sirhan U-turned. Sirhan drove southeast.

Pete tailed him. Sirhan was a track nut. Odds on Santa Anita. Odds on the spring meet.

Sirhan drove funny. Sirhan waved his hands. Sirhan straddled lanes. Pete tailed him close. Fuck the laws of tail work. Sirhan was stone nuts.

They drove southeast. They hit Arcadia. They hit the track lot. Sirhan brodied. Sirhan parked erratic. Pete parked close up.

Sirhan got out. Sirhan pulled a pint of vodka. Sirhan took little pops. Pete got out. Pete tailed him. Pete dogged him cane-first.

Sirhan walked funny. Sirhan walked fast. Pete walked heart-attack slow.

Sirhan hit the turnstiles. Sirhan dropped change. Sirhan said, "Bleacher seat." Pete bought a cheap seat. Pete huffed for breath. Pete tailed Sirhan sloooooooooooow.

Sirhan pushed through people. Sirhan pushed funny. Sirhan used darty elbows. People gawked—check that clown/what a freak!

Sirhan stopped. Sirhan pulled out his scratch sheet. Sirhan cognified.

He studied the sheet. He picked his nose. He flicked snot. He licked a pencil. He circled nags. He jabbed at his ears. He dug earwax. He sniffed it. He flicked it off.

He walked. Pete cane-walked slow. Sirhan pulled a wad of dollar bills. Sirhan hit the two-dollar window.

He bet six races. He bet all longshots—two dollars per. He talked funny. He talked stilted. He talked fast.

The cage man passed him tickets. Sirhan walked. Pete tailed him slow. Sirhan walked fast. Sirhan pulled his jug every six steps.

He took a pop. He took six steps. He imbibed again. Pete counted steps. Pete tailed him. Pete yukked.

They hit the bleachers. Sirhan studied faces. Sirhan studied faces slooooow. He stared. His eyes darted. His eyes flared and flashed.

Pete *got* it:

He's looking for demons. He's scouting for Jews.

Sirhan stood still. Sirhan stared. Sirhan saw big beaks. Sirhan smelled Jew.

Sirhan walked. Sirhan grabbed a seat. Sirhan perched by some groovy girls. The girls checked him out. The girls went ugh. The girls went P-U.

Pete took a seat. Pete sat one bleacher up. Pete checked the view: the paddock/the track/the nags at the gate.

The bell rang. The nags tore ass. Sirhan went nuts.

He yelled. He shrieked go go go. His shirttail hiked up. Pete saw a bullet pouch. Pete saw a .38 snub.

Sirhan slurped vodka. Sirhan yelled in Arabic. Sirhan beat his chest to a pulp. The girls moved. The nags crossed the finish line. Sirhan tore a bet-stub up.

Sirhan sulked. Sirhan paced. Sirhan kicked paper cups. He studied his scratch sheet. He picked his nose. He flicked hunks of snot.

Some guys sat down—jarheads in dress blues. Sirhan slid close. Sirhan talked shit. Sirhan offered his jug.

The jarheads imbibed. Pete listened. Pete heard:

"The Jews steal our pussy."

"Robert Kennedy pays them."

"That is no shit I tell you."

The jarheads yukked. The jarheads goofed on the spastic. Sirhan got pissed and reached for his jug. The jarheads tossed it over his head. The jarheads goofed double-hard.

They stood up. They stretched tall. They tossed the jug high. Sirhan was short. They were tall. They made Sirhan leap.

Keep away—*Semper Fi*—three-handed.

They tossed the jug. Sirhan leaped. Sirhan lunged and jumped. Keep away/hot potato/three hands.

The jug traveled. The jug flew shell-game fast. The jug fell and broke. The jarheads laughed. Sirhan laughed—à la Daffy Duck.

An onlooker laughed. He was fat and frizzy-haired. Dig his beanie and mezuzah.

Sirhan called him a "pussylicker."

Sirhan called him a "vampire Jew."

Pete watched the races. Pete watched The Sirhan Sirhan Show.

Sirhan noshed candy bars. Sirhan picked his teeth. Sirhan lost bets. Sirhan sulked. Sirhan picked his toes. Sirhan hassled blond girls. Sirhan dug earwax. Sirhan talked shit.

Jews. RFK. The pus puppets of Zion. The Arab revolt.

Sirhan trawled for Jews. Sirhan scratched his balls. Sirhan aired his feet. Sirhan walked to the paddock. Pete tailed him close. Sirhan hassled jockeys.

I was jockey once. I was hot walker. I hate Zionist pigs. The jockeys razzed him—fuck you, Fritz—you're a *camel* jockey.

Sirhan walked to the bar. Pete tailed him. Sirhan drank vodka shooters with candy-bar chasers. Sirhan chomped ice cubes.

Sirhan trawled for Jews. Sirhan fixed on big schnozzolas. Sirhan jumped stools. Sirhan walked to the john. Pete tailed him. Sirhan trawled urinals.

Sirhan bagged a toilet stall. Pete loitered close. Sirhan shit long and loud. Sirhan walked out. Pete walked in. Pete saw toilet scrawls:

Pigs of Zion!

Blood Licker Jews!

RFK Must Die!

Pete called Fred O. Pete said, "He looks good." Pete drove downtown. Pete hit the Hall of Justice. Pete hit the state horse race board.

He flashed a Rice Krispies badge. He conned a clerk. He cadged an employee file check.

The clerk showed him a file bank. He saw six drawers alphabetic. The clerk yawned. The clerk split. The clerk took a java break.

He pulled the S drawer. He finger-walked. He found "Sirhan, Sirhan B." He skimmed two pages. He got:

Sirhan *was* a hot walker. Sirhan fell off horses. Sirhan bonked his head repeatedly. Sirhan drank too much. Sirhan gambled too much. Sirhan defamed Jews.

He found a memo. The board sent Sirhan to a shrink. A pork dodger/Dr. G. N. Blumenfeld/out in West L.A.

Pete laughed. Pete walked. Pete found a pay phone. He called Fred O. He said, "He looks great."

He tired fast. He tired hard. It killed him. The *day* fucking killed him. Cane tails at age forty-seven.

He hit his motel. He took his pills. He snarfed his blood-thinning drops. He chewed Nicorette gum. He ate his rabbit-food dinner.

He was shot. He was dead whipped. He tried to sleep. His circuits disconnected. Recent shit recohered.

Barb/the boat/the Big Lie. Wayne/the King hit/Bobby.

Barb made sense. Nothing else. Barb dug on Bobby. Barb would mourn Bobby. Barb might link him to the hit. She might do a "Not Again" number. She might freak and split. She might leave him for Bobby *and* Jack.

It scared him. Nothing else did. No outrage or fugue for *la Causa*. No fear outside that.

My shit's too exhausting. I'm dispersed and dead whipped. I'm shot.

He checked the Yellow Pages. He got the shrink's address. He slept.

He got six hours. He revived. He went out sans cane. G. N. Blumenfeld/office on Pico/out in West L.A.

2:30 A.M.—sleepytime L.A.

He drove out. He parked curbside. He checked the building: Stucco/one-story/six doors in a row.

He grabbed his penlight. He grabbed a pocket knife. He grabbed his Diners Club card. He got out. He tilt-walked. Where's my fucking cane?

He made the door. He flashed the lock. He tapped the key-hole. Go—the knife blade/the card/one sharp twist.

He got leverage. He applied force. The door popped.

He tilt-walked inside. He caught his breath. He pulled the door shut. He flashed the waiting room. He saw clown prints. He saw one desk and one couch.

He flashed a side door. He saw a caduceus. He saw G. N. BLUMENFELD. He walked over. He braced off the walls. His breath snagged and huffed.

He tried the door. It was unlocked. There's the shrink chair. There's the file bank. There's the shrink couch.

His breath jerked. He got dizzy. He stretched out on the couch. He laughed—I'm Sirhan Sirhan—RFK watch out!

He got his breath. He stowed the yuks. His pulse leveled out. He flashed the file bank: A to L/M to S/T to Z.

He got up. He pulled drawer handles. The file drawers slid out. M to S—be there, you fuck.

He pulled drawer 2. He finger-walked. He found him: one folder/two pages/three-visit summary.

He flashed the pages. Quotes leaped:

"Memory loss." "Fugue states." "Disoriented condition."

"Overdependence on supportive male figures."

Boffo quotes. Fred O. would swoon. Hello, you camel jockey!

DOCUMENT INSERT: 4/11/68.
Atlanta Constitution headline and subhead:
SEARCH FOR KING ASSASSIN BROADENS
FBI IN MASSIVE HUNT

DOCUMENT INSERT: 4/12/68.
Houston Chronicle headline and subhead:
LAUNDRY-MARK CLUE ID'S ASSASSINATION SUSPECT
SEARCH WIDENS IN LOS ANGELES

DOCUMENT INSERT: 4/14/68.
Miami Herald subhead:
RIOT DAMAGE ASSESSED IN WAKE OF KING
ASSASSINATION

DOCUMENT INSERT: 4/15/68.
Portland Oregonian headline and subhead:
ASSASSIN'S CAR FOUND IN ATLANTA
SEARCH FOR SUSPECT GALT BROADENS

DOCUMENT INSERT: 4/19/68.
Dallas Morning News subhead:
HUNT FOR KING ASSASSIN ''#1 PRIORITY,'' HOOVER
SAYS

DOCUMENT INSERT: 4/20/68.
New York Daily News headline and subhead:
FINGERPRINT CHECK YIELDS PAYDIRT!
''GALT'' REVEALED AS PRISON ESCAPEE!

DOCUMENT INSERT: 4/22/68.
Chicago Sun-Times headline and subhead:
RFK IN HUGE INDIANA PRIMARY PUSH
CITES LEGACY OF DR. KING

DOCUMENT INSERT: 4/23/68.
Los Angeles Examiner subhead:
SKID ROW MURDER VICTIM DURFEE REVEALED AS LONG-
SOUGHT RAPIST-KILLER

DOCUMENT INSERT: 5/7/68.
New York Times headline:
RFK WINS INDIANA PRIMARY

DOCUMENT INSERT: 5/10/68.
San Francisco Chronicle headline:
RFK WINS NEBRASKA PRIMARY

DOCUMENT INSERT: 5/14/68.
Los Angeles Examiner subhead:
SEARCH FOR KING ASSASSIN SHIFTS TO CANADA

DOCUMENT INSERT: 5/15/68.
Phoenix Sun subhead:
RFK IN OREGON-CALIFORNIA CAMPAIGN PUSH

DOCUMENT INSERT: 5/16/68.
Chicago Tribune subhead:
HOOVER SAYS KING ASSASSINATION ''NOT A
CONSPIRACY''

DOCUMENT INSERT: 5/22/68.
Washington Post headline and subhead:
LOW TURNOUT FOR POOR PEOPLE'S MARCH
KING'S DEATH CITED AS REASON

DOCUMENT INSERT: 5/26/68.
Cleveland Plain Dealer subhead:
HUNT FOR SUSPECT RAY WIDENS

DOCUMENT INSERT: 5/26/68.
New York Daily News subhead:
RAY DESCRIBED AS ''AMPHETAMINE ADDICT-LONER''
WITH BENT FOR ''GIRLIE'' MAGAZINES

DOCUMENT INSERT: 5/27/68.
Los Angeles Examiner subhead:
FRIENDS CITE RAY'S RACE-HATE HISTORY

DOCUMENT INSERT: 5/28/68.
Los Angeles Examiner subhead:
NO LEADS IN HUNT FOR SKID-ROW KILLER
LAPD LINKS VICTIM TO RECENT RAPE-MURDERS OF THREE
WOMEN

DOCUMENT INSERT: 5/28/68.
Portland Oregonian headline and subhead:
RFK LOSES OREGON PRIMARY
MOVES CAMPAIGN TO CRUCIAL CALIFORNIA TEST

DOCUMENT INSERT: 5/29/68.
Los Angeles Times subhead:
HUGE CROWDS AS RFK STORMS STATE

DOCUMENT INSERT: 5/30/68.
Los Angeles Times subhead:
RECORD CROWDS CHEER RFK'S PLEDGE TO END WAR

DOCUMENT INSERT: 6/1/68.
San Francisco Chronicle subhead:
RFK SETS BREAKNECK PACE IN CALIFORNIA CAMPAIGN

115

(Lake Tahoe, 6/2/68)

THE HOLE-UP:

Wayne Senior's cabin/four rooms/secluded. Up mountain roads. Wide views and trout streams.

Home for now. Home since Memphis.

He had a scrambler phone. He had a food stash. He had a TV. He had shit to sort out. He had time to think.

Let's wait. The Feds will get Jimmy Ray. LAPD will give up on Durfee.

Bob Relyea had his hole-up. Bob had some shack near Phoenix. Wayne got better lodging. Wayne made phone calls. Wayne watched TV.

The Feds traced Ray to England. The search tapped out there. They'll get him. They'll kill him or bust him. He'll give up "Raul." They'll say you're crazy. They'll say there is no "Raul."

The TV spieled news. Wayne Senior called daily. Wayne Senior spieled gossip.

I work with Carlos now. Carlos said he got some tapes. Mr. Hoover sent them. The tapes scared him. Bobby K.'s out to fuck us. Let's clip him fast.

Wayne Senior tattled. *See what I know?* Wayne Senior bragged.

Fred O.'s gigging it. He runs the new shooter. Pete B. runs backup. Wayne Senior gloated. *I'm an insider.* Wayne Senior bragged.

Pete killed some kadre men. Pete klipped loose ends at sea. Carlos told me that. Wayne Senior tattled. *Your daddy hears things.* Wayne Senior bragged.

The kadre biz was a shuck. The Boys fucked the Cause. Carlos told me that. Wayne hashed it out. Wayne came to this: I just don't care.

He watched TV. He caught the war. He caught politics. Wayne Senior puffed. Bobby's a dead man. I'll set Nixon up with the Boys.

Wayne hashed it out. It felt felicitous. Wayne grooved the details. Wayne foresaw the balance.

King's dead. Bobby soon. Shit will peak and resettle. The Poor People's March tanked. The riots upstaged it. Fools popped their rocks and resettled. Chaos is taxing. Fools tire quick. King's death let them roar and resettle. Bobby will go. Dick Nixon will reign. The country will roar and resettle.

The fix will work. Peace will reign. His type will run things. He saw it. He felt it. He *knew.*

And:

You'll step up. You'll get *your* piece. You *know* it. You're making calls. You're listening. You're *thinking.*

He called Wayne Senior. He let him talk. He let him tattle and puff.

Wayne Senior said this:

Littell will retire. I'll get his job. I'll span Howard Hughes and the Boys. Dick Nixon and *me.* Dick and the Boys—shitfire.

Wayne listened. Wayne prompted. Wayne dropped soft tell-me-mores.

Wayne Senior said:

I ran Maynard Moore. He was my snitch. I bankrolled most of Dallas. I sent you there. I got you close. I bought you history. You killed Moore—*didn't you?*—you *lived* history.

Wayne dodged the probe. Wayne rethought Dallas. Moore and the bankroll were old news. The hot news was contempt and hubris.

Dallas derailed your life. Dallas killed your wife. Dallas almost killed you. Wendell D. was there. You weekended with him. Cut to your last rendezvous.

Wayne Senior found Durfee. Dwight Holly helped. They found him and staked him for you. Durfee killed three more women. He killed them during that interval—before your last rendezvous.

Wayne Senior gloated. *Hear this now.* Wayne Senior bragged. Pete killed the kadre men. Carlos vouched the job. Carlos said Pete could "retire." Carlos lied to Pete. Carlos told Wayne Senior why.

Pete was impetuous. Pete was erratic. Pete had ideals. Pete and Barb go. Pete and Barb go after Bobby. Carlos has a guy. His name's Chuck the Vice. Chuck kills shitfire. Carlos will call Chuck *après* Bobby.

Hubris. Miscalculation. Pure contempt for YOU.

He had time. He had the phone. He had scrambled frequencies. He called out. He didn't call Barb. He didn't call Pete.

He called Janice. He listened. She talked.

She had cancer. They cut some out. Most of it spread. She had six months tops. She blamed herself. Her cramps hid the symptoms. Said cramps were Wayne Senior–derived.

She hid the prognosis. She never told Ward. She moved into his suite. She still loved the golf course. She still hit shag balls.

She was fading. Ward never sensed it. Ward was soooo Ward. Ward talked in his sleep now. Ward invoked "Bobby" and "Jane."

Ward studied ledger books. There were two separate sets. Ward had them hidey-hole stashed. Ward was secretive. Ward was heedless. She found the stash.

Teamster books. Figures and code names. One set. Anti-Mob books. Typed pages with hand scrawls. One set.

Feminine scrawl. Probably scrawled up by "Jane."

Ward mimeo'd the Jane sheets. Ward wrote cover notes. Ward filled envelopes. Ward was secretive. Ward was heedless. She watched him. She peeked and saw.

She did the pencil trick. She traced a scratch-pad sheet. She bagged a cover note verbatim. Ward wrote to "Paul Horvitz." He was on Bobby's staff. Ward pleaded. Ward groveled. Ward pressed. Ward said here's more dirt. Ward said I'm not a spy. Ward said *please don't hate me*.

It was pathetic. Janice said so.

He called her again. She disdained cancer talk. She talked about Ward.

He's guilt-wracked. He's paranoid. He's confused. He's talking crazy. He says the Feds are on me. He says the Boys might be out for Bobby.

He plays Bobby tapes. He plays them late at night. He thinks I'm asleep. He sleeps fitful. He prays for Bobby. He prays for Martin Luther King. He split ten days ago. He hasn't called. I think he wigged out.

I miss him. I might burn his stash pile. It might drive some sense home. It might wake him up.

Wayne said don't do it. Janice laughed. Janice said it was just talk. Wayne proposed a date. He said I'll pass through Vegas soon. We'll meet at Ward's suite.

Janice said yes.

He wanted her. Dying or not. He knew it. Janice got him thinking. *Everything* did.

He got an urge. It was time-travel stuff. It reached back fourteen years. He called his mother in Peru, Indiana.

The call shocked her. He let her calm down. They broke some ice. They bridged some pauses. They talked. He lied his life off. She said all good things.

You were a tender child. You loved animals. You set trapped coyotes free. You were a brilliant child. You learned complex math. You excelled at chemistry. You carried no hate. You played with colored children. You loved righteously.

I was pregnant once. It was '32—two years before you. Wayne Senior had a dream. He saw the baby as a girl. He wanted a boy.

He beat my stomach in. He used brass knuckles. The baby died. Wayne Senior was right. It was a girl. The doctor told me.

Wayne said goodbye then. His mother said God bless.

Wayne thought it through. Wayne called Janice. Wayne set up their date.

116

(Long Beach, 6/3/68)

BOBBY! BOBBY! BOBBY!

The crowd chanted it. The crowd went nuts. Speak Bobby speak!

Bobby climbed a flatbed truck. Bobby grabbed a microphone. Bobby rolled up his sleeves.

The Southglen Mall. Three thousand fans—Speak Bobby Speak! Parking-lot frenzy. Kids on daddies' shoulders. Sound speakers on stilts.

The fans loved Bobby. The fans fucked up their vocal cords. The fans fucking shrieked. Watch Bobby smile! Watch Bobby toss his hair! Hear Bobby speak!

Pete watched. Likewise Fred O.

They watched Bobby. They watched his bodyguards. They watched the cop crew. The numbers were low. Bobby loved contact. Bobby shined on security.

Fred watched cops move. Fred watched cops scan. Fred watched cops flank. Fred nailed details. Fred memorized.

Fred met Sirhan. They "met" at the track. They "met" six weeks back. Fred staged a play for Sirhan. Fred beat up a Jew.

He was a big man. He had a big beak. He wore a big beanie. He was a *very* big Jew.

Fred kicked his ass. Sirhan watched. Sirhan dug the show. Fred dished rapport—I'm Bill Habib—I'm Arab too.

Courtship/subornment/recruitment/sheep dip.

Fred palled with Sirhan. Fred bought him booze. Fred ragged the Jews. They met every day. They worked up a mojo. They ragged Bobby K. They met semi-private. Fred stayed skinny. Fred stayed camouflaged.

Fred tweaked Sirhan. Fred studied Sirhan. Fred learned:

How far to push him. How much booze to pour him. How much hate to stoke. How to get him talking. How to get him fuming: Kill RFK!

How to get him blackout drunk. How to get him fucked-up

blotto. How to push him to memory loss. How to get him stalking rallies. How to get him talking death. How to get him talking fate. How to get him target shooting out in the hills—blasting at mock-Bobby K.'s.

Fred gauged Sirhan. Fred said:

He's drinking hard. He's drinking every night. He's drinking with and without me. He's hitting rallies. He's rally-hopping countywide. He always packs his piece. I've tailed him. I've seen it. I *know.*

He hates Bobby. His logic's warped. It's misdirected and rationalized. He hates the Jews. He hates Israel. He hates Zionist Bobby. He hates Bobby because Bobby's a fucking *Kennedy.*

He's primed now. He's ready now. He's psycho. He's blackout-prone. He's booze-atrophied.

Fred picked the spot. Fred told Sirhan. Fred made Sirhan drink. Sirhan *picked* the spot. Sirhan picked it two bottles later. Sirhan usurped the idea. Sirhan thinks it's *his* idea. It's his booze epiphany.

Tomorrow night. The Ambassador Hotel. Bobby's victory gala. Bobby to shout victory.

Bobby will be fried. Bobby will be torched and zorched—cumulatively. The kitchen's the way out. It's short and fast—serendipity. Sirhan's there. Sirhan's primed—tenaciously.

Fred knew the kitchen. Fred checked it out. Fred pumped rent-a-cops. Said cops pledged this:

Tight spaces/armed guards/tight security. That meant potential combustion/potential confusion. That meant potential insanity.

Fred's suggested drama/Fred's *predicted* lunacy:

Men draw their guns. Men shoot Sirhan. Shots bounce and hit Bobby K. Fred said he *will* shoot. Fred knew the nut turf. Fred-"Raul" ran James Earl Ray.

Pete looked around. The crowd yelled. The crowd went nuts. The crowd out-yelled Bobby.

The speakers backfired. Reverb blew wide. Bobby spoke basso-falsetto. Pete heard platitudes. Pete heard "end the war." Pete heard "King's legacy."

Barb dug Bobby. Barb dug his antiwar shit. He hadn't called her. She hadn't called him. She never wrote. No contact since Sparta. No contact post-boat trip. No contact post-coronary.

The crowd yelled. Pete looked around. Pete saw a pay phone.

It was streetside. It was away from the noise. It was away from Bobby.

He pushed over. People stepped aside. People saw his cane. He made the booth. He caught his breath. He fed quarters in.

He got an operator. She patched the Cavern. He got the switchboard. He shagged his messages.

No message from Barb. One message from Wayne: Call me/ Lake Tahoe/*urgent*/this number direct.

Pete dropped quarters. Pete got an operator. She patched Tahoe direct. Pete heard two rings. Pete heard Wayne:

"Hello?"

"It's me. Where the hell have—"

"Littell's on to the hit. Grab him and bring him here. And tell Barb go someplace safe."

117

(San Diego, 6/3/68)

BOBBY SOARED.

He jabbed the air. He tossed his hair. He praised Dr. King. He co-opted him. He out-orated him. He made his praise sing.

It all worked. It all sang—the sunburn/the bray/the rolled sleeves.

The crowd soared. The crowd roared. The crowd cheered in sync. Two thousand people/crowd ropes up/parking-lot streams.

Littell watched. Littell willed Bobby: *Please look at me.*

See me. Don't fear me. I won't hurt you again. I'm a pilgrim. I fear *for* you. My fear's justified.

Bobby stood on a flatbed. The tailgate shook and dipped. Aides stood below him. Aides steadied him.

Look over. Look down. See me.

His fear boiled over. It popped two weeks back. His fear stretched and peaked. He linked fear dots. He plumbed fear lines. He read fear hieroglyphs.

The news pic/the El Encanto/suite 301. The Sam line: "Box of goodies." The Carlos line: Pete's "small favor." Fear connections/hieroglyphs/puzzle chips.

It got bad. It ate him up. It ruined his sleep. He split Vegas. He flew to D.C. He called Paul Horvitz.

Paul hung up. He called Mr. Hoover. He called Dwight Holly. They hung up. He drove to the Bureau. Door guards ejected him.

He flew to Oregon. He approached campaign staffers. Staff guards restrained him. He saw his name on a list—all "Known Enemies."

He told the guards I *sense* things. He said *please* talk to me. They said no. They manhandled him. They ejected him.

Chips dovetailed. He sensed things. Mr. Hoover *knows*—just like he knew about Jack.

He flew to Santa Barbara. He got a hotel room. He staked out the El Encanto. He watched 301. He followed wires. He found the listening post.

Suite 208/fifty yards up/manned twenty-four hours per day.

He staked it out. He wore disguises. He worked six days and nights. He waited. The post stayed manned—all day/all night.

He went schizzy. He gave up sleep—six days/six nights. He lost weight. He saw goblins. Spots torqued his eyes.

It rained on day 7. One agent stayed on-post.

Luck:

Said agent goes off-post. Said agent visits suite 63. Said agent has a prostitute.

Littell hit 208. Littell picked the door lock. Littell locked himself in. Littell tossed the post.

He found a transcript log. He found a routing log. He found transcripts stacked. He skimmed back through mid-March. He saw:

March 15/16. Two three-way talks transcribed. Bobby plus Paul Horvitz. One man un-ID'd. Bobby's voluble. Bobby's effusive. Bobby talks anti-Mob.

He skimmed the routing log. He hit 3/20. He saw tape copies routed. The tapes for March 15/16. Said tapes routed to the Boys.

To Carlos. To Moe D. To John Rosselli. To Santo and Sam G.

That was this morning. That was twelve hours back.

He tracked Bobby's schedule. He drove south. He hit San Diego. He called the Bureau office. The ASAC hung up. He called SDPD. He told his story. A sergeant blew up.

The sergeant yelled at him. The sergeant said, "You're on a list." The sergeant hung up.

He drove to the rally. He got there early. He saw sound men set up. He braced them. He braced staffers. He got the bum's rush. He left. He came back. The crowd ate him up.

Littell watched Bobby. Littell waved his hands. *Look at me please.* Bobby soared. Bobby waved. Bobby loved up the crowd. Bobby spread contact thin.

Littell waved his hands. Something jabbed him—a needle/a pin/a stick. He went woozy—BOOM like that—he saw Fred Otash thiiiiiinnn.

118

(Las Vegas, 6/4/68)

WILD JANICE—frail now.

More gray hair. More black eclipsed. More lines and hollows.

Wayne walked in. Janice shut the door. Wayne embraced her. He felt ribs. He felt hollows. He felt her curves slack.

Janice stepped back. Wayne took her hands.

"You look pretty good, considering."

"I wasn't going to put on all that powder. I'm not dead yet."

"Don't talk like that."

"Let me indulge myself. You're my first date since Ward deserted me."

Wayne smiled. "You were my first date, ever."

Janice smiled. "Are you talking about the Peru Cotillion of 1949 or the one time we did it?"

Wayne squeezed her hands. "We never got a second shot."

Janice laughed. "You weren't looking for one. It was just your way to cut loose of your father."

"I regret that. That part of it, I mean."

"You mean it was good, but you regret the timing and your motive."

"I regret what it cost you."

Janice squeezed his hands. "You're leading up to something."

Wayne blushed. Shit—you *still* do that.

"I was hoping there'd be one more time."

"You can't mean it. With me like *this?*"

"You never get things right the first time."

It went soft. It went slow. It went like he wanted. It went like he planned.

Her body showed the hurt. Sharp bones over skin. Gray tones

over white. Her breath tasted bitter. He liked her old taste—
Salem Menthols and gin.

They rolled. Her bones scraped him. They touched and kissed
long. Her breasts fell. He liked it. Her breasts used to stand.

She still had strength. She pushed him. She clutched and
grabbed. They rolled. He tasted her. She tasted him.

She tasted sick. It stunned him. The taste settled in. He
tasted her inside. He kissed her new scars. Her breath fluttered
thin.

He got her close. She pulled back. She guided him in. He
reached over. He turned on the bed lamp. The beam settled in.

It caught her face. It bounced off her gray hair. It caught her
eyes flush.

They moved together. They got close and held. They locked
their eyes up. They moved. They peaked close together. They
let their eyes shut.

Janice played the radio. KVGS—all lounge stuff.

They hit some Barb songs. They laughed and rolled. They
kicked the sheets up. Wayne dimmed the volume. The Bondsmen purred. Barb sang "Twilight Time."

Janice said, "You love her. Ward told me."

"I outgrew her. She grew up and messed with my crush."

Barb segued upbeat—"Chanson d'Amour." Janice dimmed
the volume. Barb blew a high note. The Bondsmen cued her
back up.

"I ran into her, about two years ago. We had a few drinks and
discussed certain men."

Wayne smiled. "I wish I could have been there."

"You were."

"That's all you're saying?"

Janice zipped her lips. "Yes."

Barb segued dreamy—Jimmy Rogers' "Secretly."

Janice said, "I love that song. It reminds me of the man I was
with then."

"Was it my father?"

"No."

"Did he find out?"

"Yes."

"What did he do?"

Janice touched his lips. "Be still. I want to listen."

Barb sang. Her voice held. She segued. She went upbeat. Reverb killed the mood.

Wayne killed the volume. Wayne rolled close to Janice. He kissed her. He touched her hair. He got her eyes close up.

"If I told you I could help you settle the one score that counts, would you want to do it?"

Janice said, "Yes."

She slept.

She ate pain pills. She drifted off. Wayne fluffed her hair on a pillow. Wayne pulled a quilt over her.

He checked his watch. It was 6:10 P.M.

He walked to his car. He grabbed two laundry bags. He grabbed a scratch pad and pen. He walked back. He bolted the door. He walked the living room. He pat-checked the walls. He patted and touched.

No hollow thunks/no wall seams/no panels.

He walked the bedroom. He worked around Janice. He patted and touched. No hollow thunks/no wall seams/no panels.

He walked Littell's study. He slid out a cabinet. He saw a wall seam. He found a catch and flipped it. A panel slid back.

He saw shelves. He saw a .38 snubnose. He saw ledgers stacked.

He opened the blue ones. He saw Teamster nomenclature. He opened the brown ones. He saw typed notes and hand scrawl. He skimmed the text.

Arden-Jane indicts Teamsters. Arden-Jane indicts mobsters. Arden-Jane culls anti-Mob facts.

Book 2—page 84:

Arden-Jane rats "Chuck the Vice" Aiuppa. Arden-Jane rats Carlos M. She heard a rumor. She confirmed it. She transcribed.

March '59. Outside New Orleans. Carlos gives "Chuck the Vice" work. A "cajun fuck" fucked Carlos. Carlos says clip him.

"Chuck the Vice" obeys. "Chuck the Vice" kills said fuck. "Chuck the Vice" buries him.

Across from Boo's Hot-Links—six miles from Fort Polk. Look there—you'll find the bones.

Wayne pulled page 84. Wayne grabbed his scratch pad. Wayne wrote a note:

Mr. Marcello,

My father bought Arden Breen–Jane Fentress's file from her before she left Ward Littell. Ward has no idea that such a file exists.

My father plans to extort you with information contained in the file. Can we discuss this? I'll call you within 24 hours.

Wayne Tedrow Jr.

Wayne checked Littell's desk. Wayne found an envelope. Wayne dropped the page and note in.

He sealed the envelope. He addressed it: Carlos Marcello/ Tropicana Hotel/Las Vegas.

He grabbed the ledger books. He filled a laundry bag. He walked out. He killed the bedroom lights. He kissed Janice.

He touched her hair. He said, "I love you."

119

(Lake Tahoe, 6/4/68)

NEWS FLASH! It's over! Bobby K. wins!

The TV ran figures. Percentage points and precincts. It's Bobby decisive. It's Bobby's big win.

Pete watched. Ward watched near-comatose. Ward watched shell-shocked.

They got Wayne's tip. They jumped him. They spiked him with Seconal. Pete drove him up. They hid in Wayne Senior's lodge.

Wayne was in Vegas. Fred O. was in L.A. Fred O. was priming Sirhan.

Ward slept crypt-style. Ward slept sixteen hours. Ward slept cuffed to a bed. He woke up. He saw Pete. He *knew*. He refused to talk. He said zero words. Pete knew he'd want to *see*.

Pete cooked pancakes. Ward ate zero. Pete ran the TV. They waited. Ward watched election news. Pete twirled his cane.

He'd called Barb. She said Fuck You. I won't run. I won't hide.

Pete babied Ward. Pete said talk to me please. Ward shut his eyes. Ward shook his head. Ward cupped his ears.

News flash! The Ambassador live! Bobby proclaims victory!

A camera cut to close-up. Bobby's all tousle-haired. Bobby's grinning all teeth.

The phone rang. Pete grabbed it.

"Yeah?"

Wayne said, "It's me."

Pete watched the TV. The picture skipped and settled. His pulse skipped. Bobbyphiles cheered Bobby.

"Where are—"

"I just talked to Carlos. He had plans for you and Barb, but I talked him out of it. You're free to do whatever you want, and Ward is retired as of now."

"Jesus Chr—"

"Dallas and up, partner. I pay my debts."

The picture skipped and settled. Pete put the phone down. Pete felt his pulse skip.

Bobby splits the podium. Bobby waves. Bobby steps away. The camera pans a doorway—Bobby adieu—the camera cuts back.

The camera pans Bobbyphiles. A mike gets the gunshots. A mike gets the screams.

Oh God—

Oh no.

No not *that*—

Senator Kennedy has been—

Pete hit the remote control. The TV bipped off.

Ward cupped his ears. Ward shut his eyes. Ward fucking screamed.

120

(Lake Tahoe, 6/9/68)

RERUNS:

The eulogies. The High Mass. The funeral scenes. Wakes plural—King and Bobby.

He watched. He watched all day and night. He watched four days on.

Reruns:

The kitchen chaos. The cops with Sirhan. The Feds with

James Earl Ray. Caught in London. "I'm a patsy." A familiar theme.

He watched TV. He watched four days on. It would end soon. The news would shift. The news would move on.

Littell flipped channels. Littell saw L.A. and Memphis.

He was hungry. His food was gone. Pete stocked for two days. Pete left four days back. Pete cut the phone lines free.

Pete said walk to Tahoe. It's six miles tops. Catch a Vegas train.

Pete was disingenuous. Pete knew he wouldn't. Pete knew he'd stay. Pete caught the drift. Pete left his gun behind. Pete told him straight:

They killed King too. You should know that. I owe you.

Littell said goodbye. One word and no more. Pete squeezed his hands. Pete walked away.

Littell flipped channels. Littell caught The Triad: Jack/King/Bobby. Three funeral shots. Three artful cuts. Three widows framed.

I killed them. It's my fault. Their blood's on me.

He waited. He watched the screen. Let's try for all three. He flipped channels. He got one and two. He lucked on all three.

There—old footage. It's pre-'63.

They're in the White House. Jack's at his desk. King's standing with Bobby. The image held. One picture/all three.

Littell grabbed the gun. Littell ate the barrel. The muzzle roar shut off all three.

121

(Sparta, 6/9/68)

THE CAT HISSED. The cat snarled. The cat paced his cage.

The cab hit ruts. Pete bounced. His knees bumped the cage. Sparta in bloom. Mosquitoes meet Lutherans and trees.

He flew unannounced. He brought truce papers. He brought seller's deeds. He sold the Cavern. He took a loss. He sold Tiger Kab to Milt C.

The cat hissed. Pete scratched his ears. The cab cut due east.

His wind was back. He ditched his cane. He still tired easy. He was fried/fragged/*frappéed*. He was frazzled and free.

He tried for regret. He fretted the bad shit on Ward. He ran

his fears for Wayne T. Nothing jelled persistent. You're fried/
fragged/*frappéed*. You're frazzled and free.

The cat snarled. The cab cut south. The driver read address
plates. The driver pulled over. The cab grazed the curb.

Pete got out. Pete saw Barb. She's pruning fucking trees. She
heard the cab. She looked over. She saw Pete.

Pete took one step. Barb took two steps. Pete jumped and took
three.

122

(Las Vegas, 6/9/68)

HE'S HOME.

The lights are on. The shades are up. One window's cracked
free.

Wayne parked. Wayne walked up. Wayne opened the door
and walked in.

He's upside the bar. It's ritualized. He's got his nightcap. He's
got his stick.

Wayne walked over. Wayne Senior smiled. Wayne Senior
twirled his stick.

"I knew you'd be by."

"What made you think that?"

"Certain allegedly unrelated events of the past few months and
how they relate to this burgeoning partnership of ours."

Wayne grabbed the stick. Wayne twirled it. Wayne did a few
tricks.

"That's a good place to start."

Wayne Senior winked. "I'm sitting down with Dick Nixon
next week."

Wayne winked. "No, I am."

Wayne Senior laughed—faux rube/yuk-yuk.

"You'll meet Dick in good time. I'll get you a box seat at the
inauguration."

Wayne twirled the stick. "I've spoken to Carlos and Mr.
Hughes' people. We've come to some agreements, and I'm
assuming Ward Littell's position."

Wayne Senior twitched. Wayne Senior smiled in slow-
motion. Wayne Senior built a slow-motion drink.

One hand's clenched. It's on the bar rail. One hand's pure free. Their eyes met. Their eyes held. Their eyes locked shitfire.

Wayne pulled his cuffs. Wayne freed a ratchet. Wayne snared one wrist. The cuff snapped on. Wayne Senior jerked back. Wayne jerked him back in.

Wayne flicked the spare cuff. Wayne freed the ratchet. Wayne cuffed the bar rail crisp.

Good cuffs/LVPD/Smith & Wesson.

Wayne Senior jerked. The cuff chain held. The bar rail squeaked. Wayne pulled a knife. Wayne flicked the blade. Wayne cut the bar phone cord.

Wayne Senior jerked the chain. Wayne Senior dumped his stool. Wayne Senior spilled his drink.

Wayne twirled the stick. "I reconverted. Mr. Hughes was pleased to know that I'm a Mormon."

Wayne Senior jerked. The ratchets scraped. The bar rail held strong. The chain links went *screeee*.

Wayne walked out. Wayne stood by his car. The Strip lights twinkled waaay off. Wayne saw incoming beams.

The car pulled up. The car stopped. Janice got out. Janice weaved and anchored her feet.

She twirled a golf club. Some kind of iron. Big head and fat grips.

She walked past Wayne. She looked at him. He smelled her cancer breath. She walked inside. She let the door swing.

Wayne stood tiptoed. Wayne made a picture frame. Wayne got a full window view. The club head arced. His father screamed. Blood sprayed the panes.